ISBN: 978-0-6481931-5-9

THE HIDDEN WIZARD

THE COMPLETE SERIES

VAUGHAN W. SMITH

FAIR FOLIO

POOL OF KNOWLEDGE

BOOK ONE OF THE HIDDEN WIZARD

VAUGHAN W. SMITH

For Hugo

PROLOGUE

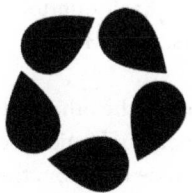

Granthion awoke with a start. His heart was pumping, and he knew that something was very wrong. He rose from his bed, cursing the aches and pains he felt in his lower back. He could overcome many things, but not age.

After a moment, he identified the feeling. It was danger, which could only mean one thing. He retrieved the sapphire ring from his bedside table and slipped it onto his finger. He chanted a few words under his breath, concentrating on visualising his target: the matching ring.

He cleared his mind and let the spell do its work. He started to see images, and with an icy rush found himself looking into a room. He saw his son, surrounded by dark shapes. He strained to look further, to see more details but he could not. The tightness in his chest and physical reaction were now confirmed in his vision. His son had been taken and was in terrible danger.

"Fool," Granthion said, including both his son and himself in the comment. His own pride and arrogance had driven his son away. But also, it was his son's foolishness and lack of care that had landed him in this predicament. The trouble was, there was no time to save him. Granthion ran his hands through his white hair, trying to think of a solution. If he didn't act fast, his son would cease to be his son. They would transform him into something else, something similar but not the same. The essence would be there, but people were never the same after the turning. He could not allow that to happen.

There were many spells at his disposal, but his mind kept going back to one. One he was saving for his final hurrah, his final gift to the world. But it came at a cost, and there was no going back.

No matter how he approached the problem, this was the only solution. It was his life's work, but it looked like fate was forcing his hand ahead of schedule.

"Oh well, now is as good a time as ever," he said. But before he left, there were preparations to be made. Granthion shuffled over to his desk and retrieved paper and a quill. He wrote swiftly but legibly, two letters. One addressed to his new successor and one to his son. After he was done, he donned his travelling robe, packed a satchel with two crystal orbs and took one last look around the room. It was his home, and he would never see it again. Relics from his many journeys littered the room: magical artifacts, books, treasures, and keepsakes. Each one told a different story. But now he had to leave, and forge one last tale. He left the room and closed the door behind him.

The tower was still and quiet, as the other elder wizards were all asleep. But he didn't want to take any chances and quickly cast an invisibility spell with a secret inverted hook that would hide him from the other wizards. He would now be completely invisible and not even a trace of magic would be detectable by standard methods. He crossed the large chamber and headed towards the stairs. He never enjoyed them, they were entirely too small, and he always felt unsteady on the long walk down. But this time they were like friends, speeding him on his way. He had a new purpose, and it would be fulfilled soon.

Once he had descended from the tower he looked out across the courtyard. It was empty as expected, but he could still see images of many of his triumphs and those of his students played out before him in his mind's eye.

"Nostalgic old fool," he told himself and kept walking. He headed straight for the stables, to retrieve his trusty horse, Whitemane. They had been on many journeys together, and it was fitting that they would go on one last quest. As he entered the stables Whitemane was awake and waiting, quietly.

"You always seem to know something before I do," Granthion muttered to the horse. He led Whitemane out and prepared him for travel. Granthion walked out the main gates beside Whitemane and looked back at the Wizard Academy. His legacy.

"May you stand the test of time, and solve that which I could not," Granthion said, then mounted Whitemane and rode off into the forest.

Once he was out of sight of the academy, Granthion let the invisibility spell lapse, now that the immediate danger of being spotted by other wizards was over. Next, he needed to travel somewhere elevated to perform the spell. He knew of a smaller mountain nearby, more of a lofty hill if he were honest. But time was against him, so he decided that it would have to do. It was also centrally located within the country of Avaria, and he knew that his son was also somewhere in the vicinity. But he could not track him further.

Whitemane ran with incredible speed as if he understood the urgency. Granthion was glad; he didn't want to push the horse too hard. There were other means of speeding this up, but he needed to preserve his strength. He would need every ounce for the spell.

He thought over his plan as he rode. By casting the spell from a height and drawing the right kind of power he could cover the entire country of Avaria. Not knowing where to target the spell wouldn't be a problem, and he would help many other people at the same time. But the cost was so great. Doing the spell would take everything he had, and most likely his life. That was the price for him doing it this way. But it would save his son and countless others.

There would be repercussions of course, not just for him. Doing this would create an imbalance in the world. If he succeeded, then Avaria would be the only country free of the Blight: something that would cause conflict and jealousy.

Not my problem now, Granthion thought. He had spent a lifetime carrying all the problems of the world on his shoulders. Today would be the last day for that.

He looked up as they were emerging from the forest. He saw the mountain peak in the distance. It didn't look that big from where he was, but he knew it would be enough.

I must make it in time.

He felt Whitemane increase his speed in response and patted his old friend in thanks. The morning sun was starting to emerge, as Granthion arrived at the mountain path. He dismounted from Whitemane and stroked the horse on his head.

"You have done well, my friend, thank you," Granthion said. Whitemane neighed in response and waited patiently. Granthion gave him one last pat on the white mane that had earned him that name and continued on foot.

The path was rough and steep, it was not meant for a lot of traffic; especially not an old man like himself. He imagined all the ways he could cheat his way up but restrained himself. It kept his mind busy, but he couldn't waste the energy. Physical exertion was one thing, but exertion of his Spark was another. He had to save up every last scrap that he had to pull this off.

Slowly, he trudged up the mountain leaning heavily on his staff. It felt like every two steps he took, he would slide back one, but he persevered. He had an important task, one that he could not fail to do. He took a moment to examine his thoughts and feelings. It wasn't out of love that he was doing this, but regret. Regret in the way he and his son had fallen out, regret at what could have been.

I set him on this path. I must set him on a new one.

He pushed harder, winding higher. Finally, he saw signs that he was reaching the top, and made one last effort to make it. As he rounded the last wind of the path he emerged at the top of the mountain. The peak was flat and cleared. There were only a few rocks strewn about.

"This will do," Granthion said, surveying the view and what he could see. The sun had risen now, and filled the sky with amazing orange colours.

The start of a new day, and a new beginning, he thought. He slowly walked over to the middle of the mountaintop and set down his satchel and staff. He retrieved the two crystal orbs. One was snow white, the other jet black: two components of the spell, two aspects. The white one was the source of the cleansing spirit, the black one the conduit and connection to the Blight. By using the two in tandem, he could accomplish the impossible. He could cleanse the taint of the Blight. But the cost was high; his life force was the currency. It was an imperfect and incomplete spell, but it should work.

Granthion took a deep breath and pictured his son.

"I love you, and I'm sorry," he said. He held the orbs in his hands, the black one in his left and the white one in his right. He prepared his mind and started to visualise the spell.

He pictured the country of Avaria, and a white silky net covering it. All those within the net would be affected. Next, he supplied his own Spark, powering up the white orb. He funnelled more and more into it and created a link between himself and the orb. Only the smallest amount remained in his body.

He sent out his purified Spark, resulting in columns of white light streaking down from the sky, each one targeting a person in the country. The light touched each person, and if they were not tainted by the blight, it dissipated immediately. But those who were couldn't shake the strange column of light that hovered over their heads.

With this done, he started the final push. By using the black orb, he drew out the Blight from each person, through the orb and into himself. Each time another person was drained of the Blight, he saw a quick flash of their face and soul. Tirelessly he continued, hoping to see the face of his son. When he least expected, it came and went, like all the rest. A feeling of peace washed over Granthion.

It came in two parts. Firstly, he was relieved that he had found and saved his son. The other more pragmatic part was that it had worked; this whole effort was not for nothing. Hopefully, he had acted before the full transition had completed. As grand a gesture as it was, this act wasn't the proper solution he had been working towards. But he was glad that at least his final act would be a successful one.

However, he didn't stop there; it was too risky, and he had a job to finish. He continued pushing until he had touched every person tainted by the Blight. Then he switched the link between him and the orbs, trapping the entirety of the Blight within himself. He felt the taint, corruption, and filth like black sludge on his soul. A monumental amount that no single person should ever have to endure. He understood what those afflicted must have felt, and the effect it had on them. It was terrible, and left unchecked it would turn him into something else entirely.

With the spell in full effect and the taint of a nation within him, he did the only thing left to do. He used the small amount of his Spark left within to call down one more ray of light from the sky. But this one was not to heal, it was to destroy.

He felt the white-hot heat searing him, and with it peace. As he was burned away, so was the sludgy taint from his soul. His final gift was to himself, a fitting end to an incredible life.

1

A WIZARD ARRIVES

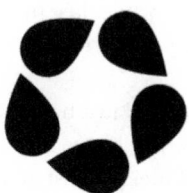

Vincent unlocked the workshop and ushered his son inside. The lanky young man hurried in, used to the routine. Vincent opened the doors all the way and let the light flood in.

He looked around, making sure everything was as it should be. The workbenches were clear, the anvil was clear, and the forge was ready. There was a clean version of the workshop smell filling his lungs.

Good, Vincent thought.

"Alrion, how does the workshop look?"

"Everything is fine. What did you expect?" Alrion didn't hide the annoyance creeping into his voice.

"It's a good habit to always assess the situation. Otherwise, you can get yourself into trouble." Vincent walked around the room, passing his eyes and hands over each of the workbenches.

"Well, a locked building is usually a safe bet." Alrion stood rooted to the spot, watching his father's routine.

"You can't always be so sure," Vincent said, with a chuckle. He had seen many strange occurrences over the years, some random accidents, some not so random. He finished his inspection after giving everything a proper look over. He was not usually so careful, but he had a strange feeling.

"It's going to be an interesting day," Vincent said.

"If you say so." Alrion looked bored already. That wasn't a good sign for the beginning of the day. Vincent decided to spice things up a little.

"Let's try and finish all the outstanding orders." Vincent watched his son's reaction closely.

"I don't think we can." Alrion looked unsure of his answer, however.

"Well, let's try." Vincent walked over to the wall and grabbed some charcoal. He wrote up all the orders for the day. There were simple knives, tools, horseshoes, and other assorted implements to be done.

"Looks doable," Vincent said, stepping back. Alrion didn't comment.

"So, do you think you can go buy me the required materials to knock these off?" Vincent watched his apprentice with interest. Alrion looked up at the board and ran his hands through his dark hair.

"Not sure."

"C'mon son, you've done this a while. Just think carefully and break it down." Vincent wanted to break through, he knew Alrion was capable. The lad just needed the right push.

"No, you've done this for a while. I just help out. You never actually let me do the work. I'm a grown man now, you know. Everyone else in the village is actually doing something with their life, not just acting as a hands-off apprentice." Alrion paused, looking a little surprised himself at the outburst. Vincent shook his head slowly.

"Well, I do admit I've been a little strict in my teaching. But there's a good reason why you haven't been doing the bulk of the work. You're just not interested in being a blacksmith. You've no focus and no desire."

"Then why keep me here? Why keep going through the motions?" Alrion looked ready to just walk out. His eyes were daring Vincent to give him a reason. But Vincent wasn't going to let his son off the hook that easily.

"I don't know exactly what the world has in store for you. I had hoped that you would follow in my footsteps. But I do know that I can teach you all you need to know through blacksmithing. It was my lifeline when I was drifting around, looking for a purpose. And also, how I met your mother." Vincent walked over to Alrion and had to crane his neck a little. He still found it difficult looking up at his taller son.

Why are kids always bigger than you?

"Seriously? I can learn all I need to know in the world from blacksmithing?" Alrion said. Vincent smiled. He had his son's curiosity aroused now.

"Sure you can. To be a successful blacksmith you need three things: the knowledge of how to work the metal, an iron will to bend it to your purpose, and a passionate heart to bring out the best in it. Those three things are the building blocks for success in any field."

"Sure, maybe." Alrion turned back to look at the list of jobs. Vincent watched carefully, curious to see how his son responded.

"Sorry, I don't know what you need," Alrion finally said. Vincent's hopes sank. Something was still missing, he hadn't quite gotten through to Alrion.

"You do, but you don't trust yourself. Fair enough, it's probably my fault. It's often easier to learn through doing. I'll write you up a list," Vincent said.

He scribbled the list on a piece of leather and handed it to Alrion. He delighted in watching his son's face as he read through, the realisation coming together that whatever he had been thinking was not far off what Vincent had written down.

"Show off," Alrion muttered, then left the room. Vincent smiled as he watched his son leave.

Some things get through, as much as he doesn't like to admit it, Vincent thought.

Alrion walked quickly through the town. He was annoyed by the way his father handled things, especially when his father was right. He couldn't fault the man's approach too, which made it all the more irritating. But it still didn't help his frustration at being stuck in the same loop. He needed to move on to something else. But for now, he would complete his errands.

The first stop was the tanner. He knew intimately where the shop was, but his nose could have guided him blindfolded. The smell was strong, even from this distance. He expected to see Bruce, the tanner when he arrived. But instead, he saw Gavin. The blonde-haired apprentice was lounging around.

"Hey, Gavin," Alrion said. Gavin looked up and smiled.

"Hey, Alrion, you running errands?"

"Yes, we're doing a big push today. Are you minding the shop?" Alrion kept looking around, but saw no sign of Bruce.

"Actually, my old man is out today so I'm running the show."

"That's great." Alrion tried to hide his annoyance. Either he did a good job at masking it or his friend didn't notice.

"What do you need?"

"Just these," Alrion said, handing the list to Gavin. The young tanner glanced over the list.

"Yeah, that's no problem, I have everything here. Although you just made more work for me. If I fulfil this whole order, I'll have to push hard to finish it." Gavin was frowning.

"Oh well," Alrion said, not worried about Gavin having to do actual work. At least it seemed like meaningful work, rather than buying materials. He watched Gavin go and collect and trim all the hides he needed and let his eyes wander over the rest of the town. It seemed so slow and sleepy, that he couldn't imagine what would keep him here.

"Hey, are you coming out stargazing tonight?" Gavin called out as he worked.

"Maybe. What's the plan?" Alrion had forgotten all about it. Suddenly his day didn't seem so bad after all. There was nothing more freeing than seeing the clear night sky full of stars. They offered more than Hamley ever would to Alrion.

"We're going to Pyrin's Peak and we have a good group going. Looks to be pretty clear, no clouds at all."

"Sure, why not?"

"Great. Meet us at the town gates after dinner and we'll hike over."

Soon Gavin returned with a pile of hides, all perfectly cured and ready for use. He dumped the pile in Alrion's arms.

"This should do it," Gavin said, taking enjoyment in Alrion's awkward handling of the hides. He was trying to carry them all without dropping them.

"Thanks. My father will come around later and pay."

"No problem, we know where you live," Gavin said with a laugh and Alrion quickly joined him. He left a bit happier than he had arrived and rushed back to the workshop, so he could drop off the hides. Alrion peeked inside and saw his father staring into space.

There he is, off in his own world again, he thought. But he didn't disturb his father and went off to find the carpenter.

Allan the carpenter was inside his own workshop. Alrion could tell that from the consistent sawing noises he heard as he approached. He walked in and watched Allan work, knowing that he wouldn't be heard until there was a natural break. Allan had several large logs lined up on his workbench, and he was methodically cutting them down into more standard sizes that he could use.

"Hi," Alrion said when Allan had finished sawing one of the logs. The older man turned to see who had addressed him.

"Oh, Alrion, how are you doing?" Allan beamed a full smile as he always did.

"I'm fine."

"Good to hear. Say, I still need an apprentice. I know you've been helping your dad, but would you be interested in trying your hand here?" It wasn't the first time Allan had asked, but there was a real earnestness to the man that made Alrion almost consider it.

"Sorry, it's not for me."

"No problem. You know me, I have to ask. Would you believe I had to ask my wife out eight times before she said yes?"

"Yes, actually I would." He really could picture Allan going back again and again with that enormous smile until she finally relented.

"Ha-ha yes she's a tough customer. But it was well worth the effort. So, what brings you in today?"

"I need a few materials, so we can complete our current orders." Alrion showed Allan the list. The carpenter nodded his head slightly as he read each item.

"Hmm, that's fairly easy. Most of it I can give you straight away. I'll need to make a few cuts first." Allan moved with purpose through the workshop, picking up planks that seemed to be placed at random. After he had a small pile assembled on one of the workbenches he set about cutting some logs to fulfil some of the other sizes that Alrion had requested.

As Allan was working, Alrion could see what his dad meant about passion. There couldn't be anything less exciting than cutting logs to a specific size. Yet Allan was some forty years into it, and cutting away with the enthusiasm of an apprentice. Alrion hoped that one day he would find himself a similar role, something to hold his passion and excitement the same way.

"There we go, all done. You need a hand hauling this back?" Allan said. He looked eager to help.

"No, it's not far I'll be fine. Thanks again." Alrion didn't want to take advantage of the man's good nature.

"No problem, I'll sort the details out with your father. Don't forget my offer."

"I won't," Alrion said, meaning that he wouldn't forget but also wouldn't take the man up on it. He struggled with all the planks, but didn't want to go back and ask for help after he had already refused it. He kept going despite almost losing his grip multiple times, dropping them in a loud heap at the entrance of his father's workshop. Vincent ran out immediately.

"What's all this? Is there a battle out here?" he said before looking over the pile of lumber and hides.

"Job's done." Alrion gestured at the rather messy piles.

"I can see that, maybe a little more care next time. Help me bring them in, and try not to drop anything." Vincent sighed and started collecting materials. They carefully brought everything inside and stacked them up according to Vincent's instructions. Alrion let out a sigh of frustration.

"There's a method to this. I've set up a workflow to quickly churn through all the jobs to be done. You'll be impressed," Vincent said. Alrion looked over the stacked benches and just felt tired.

"I'll be the judge of that," he said.

"And now we start," Vincent said with a big smile. Alrion just looked at him.

"You having fun yet?" Vincent asked, reaching for the first piece of iron.

~

Falric pulled his brown cloak tighter around him as he approached the outskirts of the town. It was a very small town, more like a village.

This has to be it, he thought, although it did seem odd. He hadn't expected to arrive at such a place. But he had done several magical pulses and the location had been confirmed every time without fail.

His cloak was too warm for the conditions, but it was more to avoid any unwanted attention. Now he just looked like a normal traveller. It was very important that he pass through the town unnoticed until he had completed his task. A small sign on the side of the path announced the town of Hamley.

I'm about to put Hamley on the map, Falric thought with a chuckle. Well, his actions here would do so, but it would take a while for the world to take notice. Such was the fate of wizards.

The town looked to be well-maintained and bustling, although from the clothing of those he saw that they were not rich. The houses had well-thatched roofs that showed signs of proper care. The people he saw looked happy and content, but busy.

A nice place to grow up I think.

Perhaps the perfect environment. There weren't many places like this left in the world. He let his horse determine the pace, only gently guiding him in the right direction. He received a few looks, but nobody paid him much attention. An old man in a dusty cloak riding a horse didn't look that out of place after all.

He passed several workshops, men and women alike working hard. There was a tanner, a blacksmith, and a carpenter servicing the town. Probably more trades as well, but those were the most obvious. He thought back to his task, a strange one. He had enjoyed the trip over, a good distraction from his otherwise administrative duties. Heading up the Wizard Academy was a busy job, and not as exciting as many would think. He enjoyed it but longed for trips such as this. Precious opportunities to explore the world.

He gently pulled on the reins, bringing his horse to a stop. It was a normal looking house, white with a red door. He dismounted and hitched his horse to a wooden post out the front. He stepped up to the front door and knocked soundly twice. At first, nothing happened. He focused more and could hear movement and footsteps within the house. Finally, the door opened, and a young woman with bronze skin and long bright blonde hair opened the door.

"Hello. Can I help you?" the woman said. She was dressed as the other villagers, in simple clothes, but Falric noticed something else about her. She seemed much more refined and was looking at him critically, trying to size him up.

"I very much hope so. My name is Falric, may I come inside?"

"You're not from around here. Care to explain why you are here?" The woman was polite but firm.

"Well, I had hoped to broach the topic inside, but why not. I am the head of the Wizard Academy, and I am here to locate the grandson of the great wizard Granthion. I know that he lives here," Falric said. He took amusement from the stunned look on the woman's face and hoped that she wouldn't leave him outside.

2

FAMILY HISTORY

Alrion moved the last knife into its proper place on the workbench and took a step back. They had completed all the work and placed each of the items together with the name of the requester.

"This was a good day's work. I think we're ahead," Vincent said.

"Yes, you did well."

"We did well. You played your part, son." Vincent clapped Alrion on the back.

"Thanks." Alrion had to admit that it was satisfying seeing all the raw materials converted into useful items for their customers. From experience in his home, he knew that the items lasted well. His father built things properly and they could be used for years with only minimal maintenance. While he didn't make particularly exciting things, they were definitely built to last.

"Well, let's head home then. I've worked up a fair appetite, how about you?" Vincent said.

"I'm starving." Alrion thought that perhaps his stomach was trying to gnaw its way out and find someone else to properly feed it.

"That's the reward for a good day's work. And your mother's cooking is also its own reward. Step outside and I'll lock up the shop," Vincent said. Alrion left and turned back to watch his father. Vincent was initially just staring at Alrion, and then nodded to himself and resumed closing the workshop.

I wonder what he's thinking.

The two of them set off to walk home. The town wasn't particularly large, so after a few minutes they had already arrived. No conversation was required.

After a long day working together they usually had nothing else to say. Vincent stopped suddenly and pointed to the horse tied up outside the house.

"You expecting visitors?" he said to Alrion.

"No." Alrion was surprised. Their friends and neighbours all lived close and didn't need to ride over.

"Maybe your mother is," Vincent said. But his tone of voice suggested he wasn't confident. The two of them walked up to the door, Vincent entering first and Alrion rushed in just behind him.

Alrion saw his mother sitting in the lounge, an old man in robes sitting across from her. On the wooden table between them was a pot of tea and two cups.

"Welcome home, dear," Celes said to Vincent. Her voice sounded strange. Alrion darted his eyes between his two parents, trying to figure out what was going on.

Something is wrong, I've never heard her call my father dear.

"Thank you, my dear wife. Who may I ask is our guest today?"

"I thought you might be able to answer that," Celes said. The old man rose quickly and approached them.

"Hello, sorry to impose. My name is Falric," he said looking at Vincent and Alrion. A look of recognition passed over his face.

"Ah, now the mystery is solved. Good to see you again, Andar," Falric said. Alrion was shocked and could see the surprise in his mother's face as well.

"I'm afraid you are mistaken. The name is Vincent."

"Really? My facts are correct, but perhaps more has happened that I am not aware of." Falric had a cautious look on his face, but still seemed quite confident.

"Who is Andar?" Celes asked, her voice rising in pitch. Alrion didn't know where to look, but settled his gaze on Falric.

"Andar ... sorry Vincent here, is the son of Granthion. That means you must be his grandson," Falric said, nodding at Alrion.

"Who is Granthion?" Alrion asked finally. There was something going on here, and he seemed to know the least about it.

"Why Granthion was the saviour of Avaria, and the great wizard who founded the Wizard Academy," Falric said.

"Let's all just sit down," Vincent said. He gave Alrion a look that made him swallow what he was about to say next and sit down on the couches provided. Celes was similarly quiet.

"I see I have caused a bit of a commotion. I'm very sorry about that. I should start again from the beginning. I am the head of the Wizard Academy, and I came here to find the grandson of our founding wizard, Granthion. I recognise Vincent here from when he was younger. And you, young man, have your grandfather's look about you. There's no mistaking it."

"My name is Alrion. I've never heard about my grandfather." Alrion looked at his father, who avoided eye contact.

"Oh, well I'm surprised your father never mentioned him. He's the most famous wizard that ever lived. He died over twenty years ago, sacrificing himself to cleanse our country of Avaria from the Blight."

"Wow, I had no idea. This is all so strange. Why are you looking for me?" Alrion felt like something was off. His stomach churned away.

"It will become much stranger soon, I'm sure. But I came here to find you because you must be tested and trained to be a wizard."

"I see," Vincent said. Alrion felt something shift. That nervous energy became a mix of curiosity and fear.

"Because my grandfather was a wizard?" he said.

"Of course. Magic is accessible by all, in various strengths and means. But the talent of a true wizard is passed through the family," Falric said.

"Shouldn't that make my father a wizard too?" Alrion looked over but again, his father avoided eye contact.

"It should," Falric said, looking at Vincent.

"Sometimes it skips a generation," Vincent said, offering no additional details. Celes gave him a questioning look.

"Well regardless, Granthion left specific instructions to search for his successor when the time was right. And here I am."

"How did you find me?" Alrion said.

"Magic. With the right spell and the right focus, you can find just about anything."

"I still don't understand, though. My grandfather was a famous wizard but until now nobody has ever talked about it. It doesn't make sense." Alrion just wanted some sort of explanation.

"It doesn't make sense, does it?" Celes said, giving Vincent a pointed look. Alrion felt better that his mother also seemed to be in the dark. It wasn't just something kept from him.

"Well, that's a fair question. To put it simply, having such a famous father is the kind of thing that follows you around and gives people the wrong impression. So, I changed my name and left it behind me. There was nothing good to come of it for me."

"But you don't deny your son the opportunity?" Falric said.

"If he's got the gift and he has the desire he can be a wizard. If it is his true calling I won't stop him." Vincent had a resigned reluctance to his voice. Alrion had never heard him sound so defeated.

"I can't believe you are the son of Granthion," Celes said, looking at Vincent with new eyes.

"I am, but that doesn't change anything," Vincent said.

"Yes, it does, a wizard has come for my son." Celes was raising her voice again.

"Are you saying that he cannot go?" Vincent said. Celes looked at him, exasperated.

"No, I just need time to adjust to this. If he does go, you must join him and make sure he is safe."

"Sure, I can accompany him. It might even be fun," Vincent said. Celes did not look impressed.

"Falric, can you tell me more about wizards and my grandfather?" Alrion said. He needed to know more about what they were talking about. Nobody in the village discussed wizards at all. Only in stories were they referenced, and rarely.

"Certainly. Wizards have been around for a while. They are the masters of magic and can do wondrous things. But for the longest time, it was a master to apprentice relationship. The skill of a wizard was very much dependent on the quality of his master. It developed a strong bond between the two wizards, but kept out other wizards and bred secrecy and competition. There were some other drawbacks too, but they were the key ones," Falric said.

"What was the answer?"

"Your grandfather realised that there was a better way to do things. A way to share the knowledge evenly to make every wizard better, and at the same time have stronger bonds with his fellow wizards. He conceived of an academy where all wizards could go to train, and absorb the knowledge from other skilled wizards."

"That sounds pretty good." Alrion liked the idea of such a place. It just seemed more open and exciting than the constraints of Hamley.

"Yes, it's a fantastic thing. Knowledge is such a key component of being a wizard; it's largely what sets us apart from others. Building a place to gather and distribute knowledge to all wizards was a fantastic idea. And now the academy is thriving and becoming bigger and bigger." Falric's excitement was obvious. He gestured with his hands to show the growth of the academy. Alrion saw in him the same passion that his father had invested in blacksmithing. Maybe this would be the answer he was looking for. But there was more to it than that. This was a whole side of his family that had never existed until now.

"What was my grandfather like?" he said.

"He was a kind soul, but a little abrasive at times. He was very abrupt and to the point. He didn't tolerate silliness at all. But he was fascinated with the world, and even without his final gift he contributed more to wizards than any other."

"You mean when he sacrificed himself?"

"Yes. He devised a means of cleansing the Blight from people. And he used it to great effect to save Avaria. Our peace and prosperity are largely due to him.

But I believe he was working on something bigger, a way to cleanse the Blight for good," Falric said.

"So, are we in agreement then, that Alrion will undergo wizard training at the academy and see if it is the life for him?" Vincent said, standing quickly.

"Yes, provided you accompany him," Celes said.

"Yes, I want to try it out. This could be what I've been looking for," Alrion said. It was an unbelievable opportunity. And he could always return here and help his father if it didn't work out. That wasn't going anywhere.

"I'm not particularly comfortable with going to the academy. But I won't deny him the opportunity," Vincent said.

"There is still a matter to discuss before we proceed. The test," Falric said.

"The test?" Alrion said. The nervousness came back.

"Yes, it's a simple matter that won't take long. As I discussed, many people can use magic to some degree, but wizards have a special talent. We have a test that proves whether you have the gift, even if it is untrained. Given your lineage I don't foresee any problems, however, you must pass to undergo the training," Falric said.

"What does this test consist of?" Alrion was fine with the idea of being a wizard, as a new concept. But this whole idea of a test made it more of a reality, one he wasn't quite ready for.

"That I will explain in due course. Is there somewhere safe to perform the test?" Falric looked at Vincent.

"Let's use the workshop," Vincent said after a short pause.

"Very good. If you don't mind, I'd like to administer the test straight away." Falric rose and stretched his legs.

"Fine by me, let's head over now," Vincent said.

"I have to see this so I'm coming as well," Celes said. Alrion looked at them both. He was trying to hide his concern, but he wasn't sure he was doing it well. He wasn't ready for a test. Not when they just announced he was a wizard.

"Don't worry, lad, you'll do fine," Falric said. Vincent strode towards the door, opened it, and waited for the rest to leave. Alrion was last.

3

THE TEST

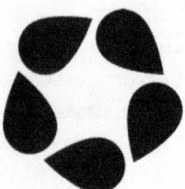

They walked in silence to Vincent's workshop. Alrion's steps were heavy and slow. He wanted more time.

He looked over at his mother and she also seemed nervous. She kept stealing looks at Vincent, trying to find an opportunity to talk. However, his father just walked on, his posture stiff and unnatural. Falric looked like he was somewhere else, his mind processing something.

This is really happening.

"We're here, let me open up," Vincent said. He unlocked the front door and swung it open, disappearing inside soon after. Again, Alrion waited and was the last to enter the workshop. He could see everyone congregated around a few lit lamps in the middle of the room.

"This should be fine," Falric said, looking around.

"Good. How is this going to work?" Vincent said.

"There's nothing to it. I'll explain as we go." Falric walked over to the nearest workbench. He reached into his bag and removed an ornate gilded lamp with a gold base and glass sides.

"This here is a magical artifact. It operates like a lamp; however, instead of being lit by oil, it is lit by the Spark of a wizard. If you have the gift, it will light without any additional spells required." Falric placed a hand on the lamp and it instantly ignited, a controlled flame dancing inside.

"Wow!" Alrion was amazed. Seeing that flame suddenly appear was magical.

"Pretty nice, isn't it?" Falric looked to be enjoying himself.

"Dad you should try it too," Alrion said.

"No thanks, this is for you," Vincent crossed his arms and took a step back. Falric extinguished the flame and looked over at Alrion.

"Care to give it a try?"

Alrion looked around the room. He shuffled his feet on the floor, hesitating. Finally, he crept closer to the lamp.

"What do I need to do?"

"Just place both hands on the lamp, close your eyes and think about it lighting up," Falric said.

"And that will work? Is that a spell?"

"No, it's just a useful way of focusing yourself to make the test work better. This is a spell," Falric said, and he made a flame appear above his open hand flickering in the slight breeze. Alrion rushed over and looked at it, curiosity overtaking him.

"Does it burn?" Alrion was tempted to wave his hand through it.

"It sure does. But let's not get too distracted. You will learn this as part of your training." Falric let the flame wink out and he pointed to the lamp.

Alrion nodded and headed back to it. He inspected it closely, procrastinating. He didn't feel magical, surely that was something you could tell. He was going to look quite foolish when he failed this test.

"It's just as simple as holding it?" he said.

"Absolutely," Falric said.

"OK, I'll try." Alrion placed his hands on the lamp gingerly, like he was afraid to hold onto it.

"A firmer grip will work better," Falric said, seeing the hesitation. Alrion held on a little tighter but was still tentative. He looked over at his parents. His mother was holding his father's hand, and squeezing it hard. He gave her a reassuring look, then returned his gaze to Alrion.

There's no other way, I just have to try.

Alrion closed his eyes, trying to think about a spark or flame lighting up the lamp. He felt so awkward with this wizard and his parents staring at him while he held a magic lamp. What if this was all some kind of prank?

Here goes, he thought, focusing his attention more. But his mind wandered. He wondered what might happen, and if this thing really was magical. He got angry about how he had been put on the spot since he knew nothing about magic or wizards. He felt a sudden intense heat within him, then realised it was real. He opened his eyes and saw a giant flame leaping out of the lamp. He removed his hands immediately, panic rising within him. The extent of the flame, and the wild manner in which it had risen scared him. He had done almost nothing, and yet the flame was colossal.

"I need some air," Alrion said, and ran for the door. It was like the flame he had created had sucked all the air out of the room, and he just needed to breathe again.

~

"There's no debate about that result." Vincent peered at the black scorch mark on the ceiling.

"That was a success," Falric said.

"Go after him," Celes said. Vincent nodded and left the room.

He stepped into the cool night air and looked around for Alrion. He saw his son striding down the street, towards the town exit. Vincent upped his pace and followed close behind. He needed to catch up with his son and calm him down.

Alrion was slowing, and Vincent slowed too. Soon they were walking together.

"Hey, slow down a minute," Vincent said. He put a hand on his son's shoulder.

"Sorry, I just had to get out of there. I couldn't breathe." Alrion finally stopped and turned to face Vincent.

"That's fine, tell me what happened."

"Well, I just felt awkward and on the spot. And I got angry and annoyed at you all. And I felt the heat of my anger and saw the flame. I don't know how else to say this, but it scared me." Alrion looked down at the ground. He seemed ashamed of himself.

"Because it was so strange?" Vincent needed to understand what was behind this sudden panic.

"Yes, and because it came from me. I know that. It was uncontrolled and unexpected. Even if that lamp was magic, it came from me."

"Well, there's nothing wrong with that. It means you have a powerful gift, and you need to learn to control it."

"What if I can't?" Alrion had a desperate look about him. Vincent sighed. This wasn't what he had wanted, but this wizard business was really happening. He had to support his son in it.

"Well, think about it. Clearly, this is something you were born with. Have you ever mysteriously burned any houses down?"

"No." Alrion looked more hopeful. Vincent could see him coming around.

"Well, there you have it. You were doing just fine up until now, and from now on, you will be safe. Falric is an old hand; he will teach you how to control your gift."

"You're right. But what about you? Why didn't you go through this?" Alrion looked at him for an answer, but Vincent just turned away.

"Let's walk back to the house," he said. He started walking and Alrion followed. After a minute or two, Vincent spoke up again.

"Like I said before, I didn't have what it takes to be a wizard. My father was one and it consumed his life, so there was a bit of friction there. He wanted me by his side regardless. I left to live my own life."

"Why me then?" Alrion stopped and looked into Vincent's eyes.

"Who knows? The world works in mysterious ways. But you clearly have his gift, so it's up to you to nurture it."

"What do wizards do anyway?" Alrion started walking again and Vincent breathed a sigh of relief.

"Well, Falric will be the best person to tell you. But, I can imagine that you will travel the world and help people. When you're not working on becoming a better wizard, that is. I don't think it's the type of thing you master overnight."

"I think you're right," Alrion said. They were back in front of their house.

"Come with me, I have something for you." Vincent entered the house and walked straight to his bedroom. He rummaged through his wardrobe and removed a dusty wooden box. Instead of a normal lock it had a strange mechanism. Vincent pressed special parts of the box and it opened. He withdrew a soft blue pouch, closed the box, and put it back where he found it.

"Here, this was given to me by my father. Now I'm giving it to you." Vincent handed Alrion the pouch. Alrion opened it and removed a silver ring with a blue stone set in the middle. The ring was on a silver chain.

"What is this?" His eyes were bright with curiosity. Vincent chuckled.

"It's a magical ring. He told me it would keep me from harm. I'm not sure how it works, but here I am. So maybe it will be of use to you."

"Thanks, I'll keep it with me." Alrion returned the ring to the pouch and put it in his pocket.

"You know it's funny, after all this time I never lost it. It always showed up when I felt like I needed it. Anyway, take good care of it and keep it with you always."

"Why didn't you ever mention all this before?"

"I wanted you to have a normal upbringing. This magic stuff is about as far from normal as you can get. I didn't even know if you would have the gift. So, I did the best job I could raising you, without all that hanging over your head. You always felt that you were meant for more than blacksmithing, and I guess this is it."

"I guess so."

"Think about me for a moment, I'm about to lose my best apprentice!" Vincent hoped he could lighten the mood.

"I'm your only apprentice," Alrion said, but he did crack half a smile.

"I think I hear your mother, let's go take a look." Vincent walked back to the living room. Falric and Celes had just arrived.

"So, you'll set off tomorrow?" Celes said. Vincent looked over at Falric.

"Yes, tomorrow is best. You will need to make a few preparations before you leave," Falric said.

"True, and the workshop will have to remain closed while I'm away." Vincent started thinking through what he needed to do.

"Well, in that case, we should celebrate. A farewell feast for my wizard son," Celes said smiling at Alrion. He returned a cautious smile.

"Don't worry, you'll become accustomed to the title soon. You will feel it in your very being," Falric said.

"If you say so." Alrion shrugged his shoulders.

Vincent disappeared to help Celes in the kitchen with the final preparations for their meal. Alrion began to realise that it would be his last meal at home for a long time.

Saul drank deeply, like he was dying of thirst. He didn't even taste the ale. He slammed the tankard down, drops of ale flying out and spilling onto the tiny, grimy table.

Never again! he thought. Images of the hideous creatures came unbidden to his mind, their screams and ferocity. He needed to distract himself. Thrusting his trembling hand into his satchel, he found and removed the sack of coins. He only dared peek inside. The glint of gold was enough of a reminder, and he hastily stashed the sack. The inn wasn't particularly safe, and even worse if you invited trouble.

Dingiest place in Altarbright, just how I like it. But he pushed the thought away. It was time to start a new chapter. He had enough gold now to start afresh. Live out his life somewhere else in peace. No more smuggling. And as far away from the Blight as possible. The memories started flooding back again.

I never should have taken that job, he thought. But maybe the gold was enough. He heard footsteps and looked up. A hooded man sat down gracefully, occupying the chair opposite. He rested his arms on the table, like he had been invited.

"Saul, I knew I could find you here. How are you?" the man said. Saul didn't recognise the voice. In the low light he couldn't see the man's face under the hood.

"I don't think we've met. Who are you?" Saul tried to hide his fear, but his voice was thin and weedy. He gulped down more ale.

"You can call me Dale. I was your most recent employer." Dale pointed to the satchel, and Saul reflexively covered it with his hand.

"I see. What can I do for you, Dale?"

"I'm in need of your services again."

"Why?" Saul swallowed hard, his throat sticking.

"The last job was just a test. I needed to make sure that everything went according to plan. This time, it will be a lot bigger. It's the real deal."

"I'm not sure," Saul stammered.

Why is this man so intimidating? Just stand up to him. The job was done, now you are done.

"I'm done with that. Sorry." Saul managed to sound more confident. Dale shook his head.

"Saul, Saul. Why would you say that?"

"I never signed up for that." Saul forced the images away.

"Oh, but I took care of everything. Everyone played their part, correct? Nobody challenged you on the way through?" Dale had a dangerous tinge to his voice. Saul swigged more ale.

"No, of course not. But, those creatures ..."

"You mean the Blighters?" Dale said. Saul shrunk away, and looked around.

"Don't worry, nobody will overhear us. You had a problem with the Blighters?" Dale talked even louder.

"Sshh. Yes, alright the Blighters. Horrible creatures. And I saw what they did to a man. I want no part of it." Saul looked around, nobody seemed to have noticed their conversation.

"I thought you were the best." Dale sounded disappointed.

"I am. Or I was. That wasn't part of the deal."

"We were upfront about the cargo. You saw it yourself before you left."

"Well it was too late then, wasn't it? Look, I won't say nothing. I'm done. Find someone else." Saul tried to lift his satchel, but Dale's hand came down quickly and held his arm.

"I'm afraid that's the wrong answer. Such a pity, you would have been more useful had you the stomach for it." Dale reached out with his other hand. As it passed through the light Saul saw a long black nail, dripping with a thick black substance.

"Welcome to the fold," Dale said and jabbed Saul's chest.

FINAL PREPARATIONS

"How far will we be travelling?" Alrion said to Falric.

"Not too far, only a couple of days' ride. The majority of it is on established roads, so it's fairly quick with horses and quite safe. Have you travelled much?"

"Not really, no." Alrion couldn't believe how little he had travelled now that he thought about it. Life had so easily revolved around their little town.

"Well, I think you'll enjoy the trip. Being a wizard will eventually require a lot of travel, once you have trained. Wizards are an important part of society."

"I didn't even know about them!"

"No offence intended, but a small place like this has little use for a wizard. We are generally more involved in cities and countries. There is a lot we can do, and a lot that people require us to do."

"I suppose I'll understand that later."

"Of course, don't worry. You will learn these things gradually. There are many mysteries to being a wizard, but I'll try and keep your training as straightforward as possible. There are enough things we don't understand without adding to that list." Falric started to speak again but suddenly stopped.

"Now, what do we have here?" he said, eyeing the food that Vincent was carrying.

"This is lemon potatoes with assorted vegetables. My wife is about to bring in her famous roast chicken," Vincent said with pride while laying down some dishes.

"We don't get that at the Wizard Academy. Looks great," Falric said.

"It's not that famous," Alrion said.

"Trust me, lad, you'll be missing this." Falric looked to be mentally devouring the food. Alrion couldn't understand the extreme reaction. Celes walked in with the roast chicken platter, placing it at the centre of the table. She put generous servings on everyone's plate.

"I feel like I should say a few words," Vincent said. He paused before continuing.

"It's been a pleasure bringing you up, Alrion, and now you are about to take your first big steps into the world beyond. There are many things that you have not learned by being here, in this village with us. However, I think that what you have learned, are the tools to becoming a great man. The path of a wizard will be a challenging one, but know that we will always support you. Always remember that you have a home here."

"Thanks, Dad," Alrion said. He had never heard his father talk like that before. He had always been kind and supportive, but this seemed different.

"He spoke for both of us, but let me add one thing. You be careful out there, Alrion. Not just of the dangers of the world but watch out for women. They'll see how good you are and will be on the attack. Remember that if you get serious with a woman you need to bring her back here to meet us," Celes said. She had a serious look on her face.

"Mum, that's just embarrassing." Alrion turned away.

"It had to be said," Celes said with a devious smile.

"Let's dig in." Vincent started to eat, and everyone else joined in.

After they ate, they returned to the living room and the couches there. Alrion continued through the room, leaving the house. Vincent followed him out. He found his son staring off towards the town gates.

"Is something up? Do you have somewhere to be?" Vincent said. Alrion was lost in thought. He wondered where his friends were right now.

"No, it's nothing. Let's go back inside," Alrion said. Vincent nodded and gave Alrion an affectionate squeeze on the shoulder. They headed back in together.

"Amazing meal Celes, I'll be dreaming about those potatoes," Falric said.

"Thanks, you are too kind." Celes beamed with the praise.

"I need to come up with a spell for that."

"I don't think there's enough magic in the world to recreate that," Vincent said.

"Do you want to stay here tonight?" Celes said to Falric.

"No, I'll go sleep in the workshop actually, if you don't mind. I have a few preparations to make myself."

"Are you sure? It'll probably be uncomfortable and cold," Celes said.

"Cold? Did you forget who you were talking to?" Falric said.

"Just don't burn the place down," Vincent said.

"I'll do my best. Would you mind accompanying me, Vincent?" Falric said, rising from his chair.

"Sure, let's go," Vincent said, and the two left the house together.

* * *

"What kind of preparations are we talking here?" Vincent asked once they were alone.

"Nothing too special, just a few things I need to go over myself. I want to see if the road ahead is clear and try to communicate with the Wizard Academy. They need to know we are on our way," Falric said.

"Sure."

"You do remember me, don't you?" Falric looked at Vincent.

"Yes, you were my father's star pupil. You've aged somewhat, though."

"Good. At least you've kept some of your faculties, if not your name."

"It was important to get a new start. You can't imagine how hard things were after that happened."

"You should have come to us. We could have helped you."

"No, you couldn't have. Here we are," Vincent said, unlocking the workshop once more.

"Thank you. I will come around in the morning, then we can set off."

"Good night. See you tomorrow," Vincent said, leaving Falric to enter the workshop.

* * *

The next morning Alrion woke up early. He hadn't slept well, his mind churning about becoming a wizard. He had so many questions, but he couldn't even articulate half of them. There were just too many unknowns. Nevertheless, he was excited to be leaving the village. It was like a huge weight had fallen from his shoulders, and the possibilities seemed endless.

He felt a little bad for how ungrateful he had seemed for his upbringing and his dad's insistence on being a blacksmith apprentice. But now he was truly discovering what he should be doing.

Alrion packed some clothes, then went to check on his father. Vincent was sipping coffee in the living room, a bulging pack sitting next to his chair. Propped up next to the pack was a sword with an ornate scabbard.

"I see you've packed already. What's that sword?" Alrion said.

"It's a relic from another life," Vincent said.

"Do you even know how to use it? I know you refuse to make weapons, so it's strange to see you with one." Alrion couldn't reconcile his father with having a sword. It seemed so foreign.

"I have made swords before, a long time ago. I may be a bit rusty using one again, but I can certainly handle myself. It's just a simple precaution. Are you packed?"

"Almost. I just need to check a few things."

"Don't worry; you won't even know half of what you really need until you need it. Just make sure you have clothes." Vincent grinned at Alrion.

"I don't remember the last time I saw you this excited," Alrion said.

"It's an adventure, even if it's a small one. We should celebrate things like this. It's a break from routine, and we're going out into the unknown."

"Well, when you put it like that, it's pretty exciting even for you."

"It's not every day you accompany your son to begin his wizard training."

"True. It's not every day you set out to train as a wizard either."

"See, something to be celebrated," Vincent said.

"How long will you be away?" Celes said as she entered the room.

"Probably a week," Vincent said.

"That doesn't sound too bad. How long until Alrion comes back?"

"No idea, that's one for Falric." Vincent shrugged his shoulders.

"I heard my name," Falric said from the front door.

"Come in!" Vincent called out. Falric opened the door and walked in. He was dressed the same as the night before.

"Celes was just asking how long Alrion will be at the academy before he can come home."

"To visit? Or for good?" Falric said.

"Both," Celes said.

"He really shouldn't visit for at least six months. That gives us time to get some traction and build in some good safeguards once he starts learning more."

"And then?" Celes said.

"Well, truthfully if his training goes well he should never return here to live. Once he becomes a wizard, he belongs to the world, and not one place. Of course, he can and should visit you when he can, but his duty will be elsewhere: either at the Wizard Academy, in a royal court, or on an expedition. I'm afraid your son's days in Hamley are numbered," Falric said. Celes nodded. She looked over at Alrion.

"This really is goodbye then. Should he go say goodbye to his friends?"

"I would advise against it," Falric said.

"Why?" Alrion said. He didn't have that many, but they deserved to know he was leaving.

"How will you explain it? They either won't understand or won't believe you. Of course, I won't stop you, but I think it's easier to just leave, and explain when you return."

"I'll think about it," Alrion said. But he suspected Falric was right about this.

"Whatever you decide, we will tell people you left to study," Vincent said.

"That is an excellent idea," Falric said.

"Are you ready?" Vincent said to Falric.

"A wizard is always ready. Occasionally they need more preparation, though."

"Are you fully prepared then?" Celes said with a laugh.

"Just about, but I do seem to be lacking some quality food, though." Falric licked his lips and looked at Celes.

"Don't worry, I'm sending some with the boys. Come over to the kitchen and take a look," Celes said. Falric rubbed his hands with glee and followed her.

"I'll bring horses and meet you outside," Vincent said. Alrion nodded and watched his father leave. A few minutes later he saw Falric return from the kitchen. But his face was white, and he looked unsettled.

"What happened in there? Did you get the food?" Alrion said.

"Oh yes, of course. Nothing important. Your mother just ... err ... shared her concerns about our trip." Falric chuckled, but it didn't have the same energy to it. Alrion wondered what could have spooked the wizard so badly.

"Excited?" he said to Alrion.

"Yes, but I'm also a bit unsure what to think," Alrion said.

"I know the feeling. It'll be a true adventure, though, you can count on that."

"I don't doubt that. Compared to Hamley, anything is an adventure. We are almost ready, I'm just waiting for my father to return with some horses," Alrion said. Celes distributed the last of the food she had prepared. Alrion watched her closely, and she stole a pointed look at Falric. The wizard pretended not to see and Celes looked satisfied. Then they all left the room to wait outside. It didn't take long to see Vincent leading two black horses over.

"Saddle up," Vincent said, handing the reins of one of the horses to Alrion.

"You can't leave without saying goodbye to your mother," Celes said. Alrion hugged her and gave her a kiss goodbye. Then he threw his bag over the back of the horse and climbed up into the saddle. Vincent and Falric followed suit.

"This is it. Are you ready?" Falric said.

"I'm ready," Alrion said with more conviction than he felt.

"I expect a full report when you get there, write me a letter," Celes said.

"Can't you just ask Dad?"

"No, it's not the same."

"Alright, I'll do it."

"You two keep him out of trouble," Celes said looking at Vincent and Falric.

"Sure thing boss," Vincent said grinning at her. Falric turned his horse around and they started to ride off. Alrion looked back at his mother one last time. But that was it. He didn't look around as they left the village, instead he just stared ahead. Once they were clear of the village, he finally turned back and had one last look.

I don't know when I'll be back, or who I'll be when I do return. Goodbye Hamley.

He watched the village go about its business and realised that apart from his mother he probably wouldn't be missed. His destiny lay elsewhere. Turning his horse, he raced to catch up with his father and Falric.

5

WIZARD PRINCIPLES

There was little conversation at the beginning. Alrion did not know why, but he was preoccupied with checking out the landscape. It was ground he was familiar with, and he could identify every farmhouse and building that they passed. He didn't know what he was looking for at all. After riding for over an hour they passed a point at which he finally understood. He had been waiting to pass from the area he knew into unknown terrain.

The transition was so subtle and fast that he did not notice it at first. However, once he did, he sat up straighter in the saddle, looking more intently at the surroundings.

"You're in unfamiliar territory now," Vincent said, confirming Alrion's reaction.

"The adventure is finally starting. It's exciting."

"It should be, there's a whole wide world out there for you," Falric said. He gently pulled on the reins, nudging his horse closer to Alrion.

"Now that we have some riding ahead of us, is there anything you want to ask me about?" Falric said.

"Too many things. But, I was wondering if you could explain magic a bit more. I don't understand it at all." Alrion shuffled his position so he could more easily ride and pay attention to Falric as well.

"Of course. The first thing that people usually don't understand is that magic is not just for wizards. Wizards are just the most well-known and complete practitioners. I'll explain that point in a minute. But it should be made clear to you that your mother could use magic with a little instruction."

"Really?"

"Absolutely. There are forces in this world which anyone who has the knowledge of how to do so can summon and use. Of course, the effect is generally quite tame because you are leaning heavily on the natural order of things and not supplying any force of your own. But there you go, that's a common misconception."

"You just need a recipe then?" Alrion tried not to sound sceptical, but it just seemed too simple.

"We do like to call them spells, but yes. With the proper instructions available, if you follow them to the letter you can achieve many things. However, this kind of knowledge is not widely available and usually guarded quite stringently because anybody can use it. It is something that Granthion started to combat with the Wizard Academy."

"And that was so wizards could collect and share these spells?"

"Exactly. This leads me to describe the first pillar of magic: Knowledge. With the right knowledge, you can cast spells with nothing else. Or, you can enhance or unlock capabilities unavailable to other people. Knowledge is something very important for wizards, as we need to be able to access and use all types of magic."

"I understand that. Is that what I'll be focusing on at the Wizard Academy?"

"Mostly, yes. There will be many types of training, but one key thing that sets wizards apart is knowledge. We will be transferring as much as possible to you. That is something you can learn most effectively at the academy."

"What about other ways of using magic? Are there ways that do not require knowledge?"

"Well, yes and no. Let's just say that knowledge is a pervasive element that usually helps. However, to answer your question, yes, the other two pillars of magic do not necessarily need knowledge. The next one is Will. By force of Will, you can perform feats thought impossible. There are monks who train exclusively in the development of the Will. They can command their bodies and the world around them to behave in different ways. You could argue that there is an element of knowledge and training to this, but there have been examples of those who discovered these abilities with no prior knowledge or instruction."

"That sounds interesting, but I can't picture it. What are some examples?" Alrion nudged his horse closer to Falric's.

"They can move objects with thought alone, and break things with their body that should be too strong. They hone the strength of their will to challenge the laws of nature."

"Wow, that's pretty cool," Alrion said.

"It is indeed and has earned them fame as a result. Nevertheless, they must undergo very strict training and mental conditioning to get to that point. It is not an easy undertaking."

"Is it easier for a wizard?" Alrion had to admit he liked the idea of moving things with his mind, or breaking the unbreakable.

"It is if they have progressed enough in the other two pillars of magic to support the Will. But, fundamentally, there are no shortcuts. The wizard should have the capacity to do more, but not skip over the development required."

"Could I just go lock myself in a cave and eventually emerge with the ability to move things with my mind?"

"Not exactly, but theoretically yes. The potential is there if you can develop yourself in the right manner. Which would be incredibly difficult without proper instruction."

"Wouldn't it be easier to use spells?"

"It's all about having the right tool for the right occasion. The most potent magic combines all three pillars."

"What's the third one?"

"Spark. This is the one that we already tested." Falric pointed at Alrion's chest. "Spark is the only thing that a wizard cannot learn or train in from nothing. You either have it when you are born, or you do not."

"Could you have tested me years ago?"

"Yes, and you would have most likely passed. However, it is better to train wizards later when they are stronger physically and mentally. It is a hard path, but very rewarding."

"What does the Spark do?"

"The Spark is like the fuel that lights the fire. Which is part of the reason the test has been designed that way. It's an easy way to explain the importance of Spark, and why it is key to being a wizard. Spark is innate magic, but you need Knowledge and Will to use it effectively. You could recite a spell to create a tiny flame, but your Spark will fuel that flame into something else entirely."

"That's why I scorched the ceiling." Alrion had not forgotten the wild nature of that flame. It still made him nervous, the fact that he could do so much from nothing.

"Exactly. Your Spark can amplify many different spells; some require your Spark as a key ingredient. Therefore, only those with the Spark can truly call themselves wizards. Since you cannot have mastery over magic without having all three." Falric finished his explanation and waited for questions. Alrion nodded along and focused more on the ride. He needed to think through everything that he had just learned.

"Let's break for lunch over there, it looks like a nice shady spot," Vincent said, pointing ahead.

"Good idea," Falric said. The three of them pushed forward and tied their horses to a giant tree to one side of the road. Vincent directed them to a nice grassy area under the shade of the tree, and they sat down to eat some of the food provided by Celes.

After Alrion ate, he spoke up.

"Falric, how did you become a wizard?"

"Your grandfather found me. He was searching for new initiates to build the Wizard Academy. He travelled the entire world, seeking out any who were willing and able to be trained." Falric had a faraway look and a smile on his face.

"What were you doing before that?"

"I was studying to be a scholar. Destined for a life with my head in books, researching and writing papers. The funny thing is, that's how it ended up anyway. Only the books were mostly spellbooks and my writing was reports and letters."

"That sounds different to the wizard's life you explained."

"It is unusual. Before Granthion, it would have been unheard of. It was one of the sacrifices required to make his vision of the Wizard Academy a reality. The life of adventure was not for me, as it turned out." Falric sighed.

"We're happy to have provided you the opportunity for a mini adventure, right, Alrion?" Vincent said, winking at Alrion.

"And you can thank us by providing a quick magic demonstration." Alrion made a flourish with his hands and laughed.

"Of what? I'm not a performer you know," Falric said, chuckling.

"Just show me the three pillars of magic in action." Alrion leaned forward, eager to watch.

"Alright. Let me think for a moment," Falric said, closing his eyes.

"I have just the thing. Let us walk slightly further from the road, just in case." Falric jumped up and set off. Alrion followed quickly behind, while Vincent was in no rush at all. Falric stopped within a minute and looked around.

"This will do just fine," he said. Alrion watched with burning curiosity.

"First, I'm going to start with a very useful spell. This one draws out water from the atmosphere." Falric held out his hand and a small pool of water formed in his palm.

"Wow!" Alrion couldn't say anything else. He was transfixed by the sudden appearance of the water.

"Next, I will use my will to work with the water," Falric said. The water started to move, drawing up, twirling into the shape of a sphere, and hovering gently above Falric's hand.

"Hang on, what you just did there isn't magic?"

"Technically no, I imposed my Will onto the water. The right shaped container would cause it to have this shape, why can't I compel it to do so as well?" Falric said. Alrion didn't have a reply.

"Next, we can spice it up a little bit," Falric said. The sphere of water grew in size and started to crystallise. With a snap, the process was completed, and a ball of ice fell back into his hand. He threw it over to Alrion.

"It's cold." Alrion laughed as he caught it.

"Exactly. I used my Spark to draw more water and cooled it past its freezing point. And now you are holding it."

"Wow. I see what you mean. Wouldn't it be a good idea to teach people that water spell? So that they can find water when they need it?" Alrion said.

"Unfortunately, the volume is far too small with the base version of the spell. There are much better ways of gathering water, so it's not really worth it. But, for a wizard, it is incredibly useful. You just need the right training and experience."

"You'll have to teach me how to do this." Alrion kept staring at the ball of ice, turning it over in his hands.

"All in good time, that, and much more."

"Nice trick," Vincent said as they were walking back to the horses. Alrion threw the ball of ice at his back and Vincent quickly turned and caught it. He removed a flask of water from his saddlebag and crushed some of the ice into it.

"Thanks," Vincent said, enjoying a swig of the colder water. Alrion laughed.

"That was a lot of magic just to cool your drink," Falric said with a chuckle. With the demonstration over, they packed up and resumed their ride.

For a time, Alrion saw nothing much to look at on the ride. The scenery was empty woodland to either side of the path, with the occasional track peeling off.

"Those tracks probably lead to homes," Vincent commented when Alrion was staring at one of them. Farms started appearing once more and signs of civilisation were apparent. Other paths forked off the main road, wooden sign-posts naming them. Alrion recognised none of the names.

"Not far now," Vincent said.

"To where?" Alrion said.

"Carford. The biggest town around here, and a bit of a trading hub. I think you'll like it," Vincent said. Alrion reserved judgement but was curious to see it. Finally, he started to see buildings looming in the distance. In front of them were large stone walls. They didn't go around the whole town, but blocked off each side of the road a good distance and converged in a peak over the main entry. He couldn't see much past them but noticed a large flow of people, horses, and wagons going in and out of the entry.

"What do you think, Son?" Vincent said.

"Big," Alrion said. He'd never seen anything like it. His eyes widened as he tried to take it all in.

"Bigger, but this is still small. Just you wait until you see somewhere like Brangtur, now that's big."

"I guess this is big enough for now," Alrion said with a laugh. He looked at the people flooding the road and noticed that they seemed less carefree and happy than those from his village. A bit more stressed, and more purposeful.

There were large guards, clad in chain mail and shiny metal helmets standing at each end of the entry scowling at the people coming in. They had swords at their hips but otherwise didn't seem too threatening. Alrion wondered how active they actually were.

As their horses stepped through the gates Alrion felt a wave of wonder pass over him as he took in the sights of Carford. It was a fitting beginning to his adventure.

6

A CHANCE ENCOUNTER

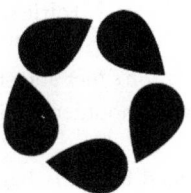

After the entry, the road opened out into a giant square. There were stalls around the edge of the square, and streets going off in four different directions. There were even a few brass statues littered about.

"Who are they?" Alrion said, pointing at the statues.

"Famous warriors from the past. Ones that either governed the town or rescued them from sieges or raids. They are immortalised in brass to commemorate their contribution," Falric said. Vincent nodded along at the information.

"Are there any statues of wizards?" Alrion didn't see any.

"Unfortunately, not, wizards don't inspire the same kind of following and support. I think it has to do with what we do. People can understand a man who fights for his people. They find it hard to understand the intricacies of what a wizard does. It isn't always clear what we actually achieve." Falric shook his head slowly. "I think many wizards would not achieve any recognition at all in their lifetime, only future generations would be able to look back and join the dots."

"So, it's a fairly thankless pursuit then?"

"On a grand scale, yes, but don't worry there will be plenty of opportunities for you to make a difference for people and they will know it. Think of your grandfather, he certainly made a big difference on the world stage," Falric said, looking at Vincent.

"I can confirm that people knew about him," Vincent said, without adding anything else. As they rode through the square, Alrion looked around at the buildings. They were all bigger than those at Hamley, and many had multiple stories. They were all made out of stone and looked solid and imposing.

"How did they build all this?" Alrion said, half talking to himself.

"Over a very long time," Falric said.

"I can imagine." Alrion pushed on straight ahead, passing through the square. Many smaller buildings started to line the streets, most of them looking like houses. They approached a corner and noticed a huge and striking building sitting there. It had a grand entrance, stables off to the side and a giant shield-shaped sign hanging from the roof.

"We are here," Falric said. Alrion read the sign.

"*The Sundered Shield*?"

"Yes, that's it, there's a great story to this place. I'll tell you once we are inside. Vincent, can you take care of the horses?" Falric said.

"Sure." Vincent dismounted and retrieved his bag. Once Alrion was ready Vincent threw his own bag at his son's feet and started gathering up the horses. Falric dismounted with grace and shouldered his bag, walking into the establishment.

Alrion bent down and grabbed both the bags, quickly straightening as he balanced the weight. As he rose he bumped into something, and stepped back in surprise. There was an olive-skinned woman walking past. Her short blonde hair and plain clothing surprised him.

"Sorry," she said, and kept walking. Alrion watched her go, fascinated. There was something different about her. It wasn't just the way she had dressed, but something about her mannerisms. She soon disappeared into the crowd and he turned back to enter the inn.

The interior of *The Sundered Shield* was dark, even though a few lamps were strung from the ceiling. There were so many long wooden tables Alrion had trouble seeing the floor and where he could walk. He saw that Falric was up at the bar talking to one of the women working there. Alrion joined him.

"If not three rooms, surely we could get two?"

"We're almost full, we could do two rooms if one of you is willing to pay for a prestige room." The woman spoke the words like that was a goodbye.

"I'll get that. What's the difference?" Falric said without hesitation. The woman looked confused.

"Nicer furnishings, private water jug and so forth."

"Sold," Falric said, dropping a small pile of gold coins into her hands. The woman counted them carefully and deposited them behind the bar.

"Excellent. Your assistant can come with me and drop off your bags," she said. Alrion wanted to say something but Falric waved him off and handed Alrion his bag as well.

With a sigh, Alrion followed the woman up the stairs. She was dressed in a blue and white dress, and it swished left and right as she ascended. She moved swiftly, her curly brown hair bouncing along as she walked. At the end of the hallway, they stopped and she unlocked the door.

"This is the prestige suite," she said. Alrion stepped inside and placed Falric's bag on the bed. It looked nice but didn't seem that special. Once he left the room, she locked the door and gave him the key.

"Next stop is your room," she said. They returned to the other end of the hallway and she stopped outside a dingy looking door, covered with scuffmarks.

"This is your room," she said as she unlocked the door. Alrion could see how cramped it was, with two tiny beds taking up most of the room. He placed the bags inside and stepped out again.

"Here's your key," the woman said, and handed it to Alrion. He locked the door and headed downstairs. He saw his father sitting with Falric in the corner of the room and walked straight over.

"We all settled in?" Falric said.

"Yes, and here's your key." Alrion threw it over. Falric almost dropped it, but kept a hold of it and tucked it into his robes somewhere. Vincent looked at Alrion with disapproval.

"You just keep our key, take a seat," he said, shuffling over. Alrion sat down next to him.

"So how far are we?" Alrion said.

"From the academy? Not far we will get there tomorrow," Falric said.

"That's not too bad." Alrion thought he could get used to this adventuring business. It seemed pretty good so far.

"Not at all. Although I think your father will be disappointed by how short his trip will be," Falric said. Vincent shrugged.

"I'd like to know more about being a wizard. And you were also going to tell me about this place," Alrion said.

"Ah yes, *The Sundered Shield*. As it so happens I can do both at the same time. I was involved in the story that gave this inn its name."

"I didn't know that," Vincent said.

"There's a lot you don't know about me," Falric said, a crafty smile on his face.

"This particular town was originally a smaller village, like your home. One day a group of mercenaries and bandits camped nearby. They were passing through and needed supplies so they performed a few raids on the local villages. Nobody put up much resistance, so the hardened warriors decided to settle in for a longer stay, which was the start of it all." Falric paused to take a swig of the ale in front of him.

"Right, so after a few of these raids, there was a man called Ryder who took issue with the bandits. He was just a local farmer but was sick of dealing with them. But, what could he do? He was just one man. So, he decided to do what one man could do: steal from them. He snuck out to their camp at night, after they had all passed out from drink. While they were asleep he took as much food as he could lay his hands on, and rose away with the food and the leader's horse."

"I bet they weren't impressed," Alrion said.

"Not at all. The townsfolk were divided. Some praised his action, some criti-cised him for making trouble. They decided to eat all the food and set the horse loose so there was no evidence. The bandits came back the next day, demanding answers. But the town denied everything, and they left."

"He got away with it?" Alrion said. It sounded too easy.

"Well, not quite. You see Ryder felt bolder after his success, and went back again. He crept back to their camp, made sure they were asleep, and started to steal more food. This time the bandit leader was lying in wait and caught Ryder red-handed. Ryder fled, but it was no use. The bandit leader had recognised him. Fearing reprisals, the farmer came to the Wizard Academy and begged for help."

"So, you met him there? Ryder?"

"Yes, I did. He made a convincing case, but we didn't want to get involved. That would just direct the ire of the bandits to the academy, and we didn't want that. Besides, I believe the role of a wizard should be less direct. There can be a truly incredible power imbalance, and the more we stay out of things the better," Falric said.

"He just left then?"

"Not before he stole a shield from our inventory. It was a curious piece that looked completely generic. But, it had a special power. I let him take it of course, curious as to what he would do. I followed him back to see what would happen next."

"You let him steal from you?" Vincent said, surprised.

"It was all very controlled; I could have stopped him at any time. He returned to the village with the shield, and told them all, that he had found a magic shield and they would now be safe. I still, to this day, wonder if he really believed that without even seeing it in action. However, the bandits were waiting in ambush; his town had sold him out. When they attacked, Ryder held up the shield, and it deflected every attack. He managed to push them back, the bandits mystified as to why all their attacks were powerless."

"It actually worked? He got away with it again?" Alrion said. This Ryder seemed to have incredible luck.

"Not quite. After they retreated, the town had a big celebration. Ryder as the hero drank a little too much, and fell into a deep sleep. While he slept, the leader of the bandit group snuck into the town and swapped the shield with an identical one that was not in any way magical. A significant downside to that particular shield."

"Because it could be so easily misplaced or changed. Were you aware of the swap?" Alrion said.

"Of course, I could tell. However, I didn't act, I just observed. The next day the bandit leader returned and said that if Ryder defeated him in single combat, they would leave the town alone forever. Ryder immediately accepted, thinking that his shield would keep him from harm. So, with the townsfolk and the bandits watching on, the bandit leader and Ryder faced off in a sword fight." Falric paused for dramatic effect. Alrion made a gesture to Falric to keep going, he needed to hear what was next.

"The leader wielded two swords, and Ryder used a sword and shield. They traded blows, and the shield held up, but something was amiss. The perfect deflection abilities of the old shield were not there, and the shield started to show damage. Ryder, to his credit continued fighting, even though it was obvious to everyone that his shield was weakening."

"And what happened?"

"Well, seeing his victory was nigh, the leader surged with a final assault, both his blades whirring at great speed as he attacked Ryder. The plucky farmer parried what he could, but kept using his shield to protect himself. His battle prowess could not match the bandit leader. Finally, the shield split in two and dropped to the ground. The bandit leader had his sword at Ryder's throat and demanded that he surrender."

"So, that's where you stepped in?" Alrion was trying to figure out what role Falric had played in this.

"Not quite. Ryder refused to surrender and rolled away. He grabbed one half of the shield and kept fighting, with a ferocity and energy that was unmatched. The leader was suddenly on the back foot. But he counter-attacked and went for broke, trying to finish Ryder once and for all." Falric again paused for drama. Alrion let go a sigh of frustration and then Falric continued again.

"It all came down to one final swing. The bandit leader had attacked high and was following up with a piercing thrust. Ryder had parried the first attack with his blade, but the shield was too small to protect him. Therefore, instead of trying to block the attack, he used the sharp jagged edge of the broken shield to attack the bandit leader. Both men took critical wounds, and neither could continue the fight."

"What did that mean for the town?"

"The bandit leader retreated and left the town alone. Ryder recovered, but could not return to a life of farming. He took to hanging around this very inn, and soon people would come from all over the area to hear his story. To capitalise on this, the owner renamed it *The Sundered Shield*, to commemorate Ryder's actions and to profit on his popularity. With the town safe from bandit attacks, and now on the map for the heroic actions of Ryder, it quickly grew in popularity and prosperity." Falric finished with a flourish and sat back in his chair.

"Hang on, there's no mention of wizards in that story at all. Apart from what you have mentioned to us," Alrion said.

"Exactly. So, you see, I knew that direct involvement would change the struggle, and maybe even escalate it. But by letting Ryder take responsibility, and a relatively risk-free item from our stores, I let the story play out to a complete and proper resolution," Falric said.

"But he profited by stealing from you? What kind of message is that?" Alrion liked the story, but didn't see the point of it. Not from a wizard's perspective anyway.

"It shows that he was prepared to do what was necessary. It also shows that his actions cost him dearly, but he still managed to win a victory for his town."

"Whatever happened to the magic shield?"

"Well, I visited the bandit camp and retrieved it without them noticing," Falric said with a grin.

"Sounds like wizards do a lot of nothing," Alrion said. Vincent grunted in agreement.

"Sometimes, yes. However, one thing you will learn is that every action has consequences, even inaction. And acting only when required will have a greater impact." Falric let his gaze linger on Alrion, and then turned his attention to Vincent.

"That's enough stories for the evening, let's get some food, then turn in," Vincent said. Alrion's stomach rumbled in agreement, and he looked forward to what was on offer.

After the meal, they all walked upstairs to retire for the evening. Alrion showed Falric to his room, and the wizard was satisfied with it. Vincent was less than impressed with their room, but at the same time, he seemed to be expecting it. Alrion lay down to sleep and dreamed about being a wizard and hurling fireballs everywhere.

When he awoke, he was alone. His father had packed up and left the room.

I don't know how he's always up so early, Alrion thought, as he started to prepare himself. He reached into his pocket to look at his ring again, only the pouch wasn't there. After a few seconds of panic, he tried his other pocket, then went through the rest of his clothes looking for it. There was no ring.

He thought back to all the things he had done since they left Hamley. The whole time it had only been the three of them, and neither his father nor Falric would have taken it. Then he had a flash of insight. When he was outside the inn, he had bumped into that young woman. She must have taken it, there was no other explanation.

But how is that possible?

He realised that perhaps he had a great deal to learn about the world, and chalked it up to experience. However, he couldn't admit to his father that he had lost such a precious heirloom so soon, so decided to keep the incident to himself. He justified it to himself by thinking back to the words his father had spoken about the ring: 'After all this time I never lost it. It always showed up when I felt like I needed it.'

7

THE WOODED PATH

Alrion descended the stairs and couldn't see his father or Falric. He handed the room key back to the woman behind the bar, then left the inn. He could see Falric standing outside, waiting.

"Good morning," Falric said.

"Good morning. We're leaving immediately?" Alrion said.

"Yes, the sooner the better. We can stop a little later and have something to eat. Your father is readying the horses." Falric pointed to the stables.

"That's fine," Alrion said. He looked around to see if he could see the girl who had stolen his ring but didn't recognise any of the people nearby. It was foolish to think she would still be here; she was probably long gone. When his father emerged, Alrion slung his bag onto the back of the horse, then mounted it.

"How are you feeling? Have you ridden this much before?" Vincent said.

"Not too bad. I don't think I have ridden this much, but I doubt it will get much worse." Alrion was a bit stiff and sore, but it didn't bother him.

"I think that's fair. We should arrive by evening, right, Falric?" Vincent said.

"Correct."

"Then let's head out." Vincent took the lead, guiding his horse back towards the main gate. Alrion followed but continued to peer into the crowd. He knew it was fruitless, but he had to look for the thief. If there was a chance he could recover the ring, he had to take it.

As they passed through the main gate, Alrion finally accepted that the ring was gone. He would keep that information to himself for a while, and tell his father later. After they left Carford, they backtracked a little, before taking another direction back at an earlier fork in the road.

"Any other towns on our route?" Alrion said.

"No, that was it. We will stay on this path initially, then cut through the forest. That will be a good place to stop and eat," Falric said. Alrion nodded and watched the countryside pass by.

The land still looked familiar, even if he hadn't travelled this far before. The grass was a lush green, and there were many trees around. The occasional dirt roads branched off the main one, with signposts directing people to homesteads or smaller tracks.

After an hour or two Falric slowed his horse and Alrion and Vincent followed suit.

"This path here to the left, leads to the Wizard Academy," Falric said, pointing it out. Alrion noticed a wooden sign next to the path.

"Needle Forest," Alrion said, reading the sign.

"That's the one. We need to pass through there to get to the academy."

"Why not have a sign for the academy?" Alrion said.

"It's better this way. The people who need to find us can do so anyway." Falric immediately set off once more. Alrion followed, and Vincent lingered, taking up the rear position.

They had to ride down the new path in single file, as it was quite narrow. The trees were incredibly tall and had long fine bristles on them. There was a fresh woody smell that filled Alrion's lungs and instilled a sense of calm.

"I can see why it is called Needle Forest." Alrion grabbed the bristles on a nearby tree and broke some off into his hand so he could take a better look at them.

"Not very imaginative, but quite apt." Falric had his eyes focused on the road ahead. Alrion continued to look around. The trees in their size and numbers were imposing and menacing. Like they didn't want him to be there. He shuddered instinctively.

"Let's stop over here." Falric turned off the path abruptly. He pushed between two trees and Alrion followed closely behind. It seemed like a poor decision at first, but they quickly emerged into a small clearing.

"I love this spot, I always stop here," Falric said. Alrion could see why. It was covered and secluded. You would never know to look for it. Yet the grass was short and looked soft. They tied up the horses and sat down to eat.

"What do you know of the Blight?" Falric asked Alrion.

"Not much really. People talk about it in hushed tones, but nobody seems to be able to talk from experience," Alrion said.

"That's a good thing. It is best to avoid experience of the Blight if possible. Although as a wizard you will have to confront it at some time or another."

"Why is that?"

"From a practical perspective, the Blight is everywhere. You have been lucky enough to grow up in the country of Avaria. Due to the sacrifice of your grandfather, this country is free from the Blight. Strong border controls at key locations do help keep it in check as well."

"It's a problem elsewhere?"

"Yes, a big problem. Every person deals with the Blight in different ways."

"But what is it?" Alrion had trouble imagining what it was.

"That's a good question. The Blight is an infection, a disease as the name implies. But, it's more than that. It has a life of its own, and it connects all those infected. The Blight cannot create creatures, but it twists creatures to its purpose."

"Can it be destroyed?"

"Wizards can cleanse the blight, as your grandfather demonstrated. But so far only he has been able to do so. Our current options are either to destroy the infected, contain them, or keep them away."

"That doesn't sound good. Weren't the infected originally people?"

"Yes, they were, so as you can imagine it's a huge problem. One that you must learn to deal with as a wizard. You will initially be sheltered as you start to learn at the academy. But eventually, you will join the world. And the Blight is a part of the world."

"How long has it been around?"

"The stories vary. Some say it has always been around. But regardless of the origins, it is well catalogued when it became a problem. Over fifty years ago, the Blight became a major problem and swept across the world incredibly quickly. We were not equipped to deal with it. It took many hard lessons to get to the point we are at today." Falric sighed and his facial expression was bleak. Alrion didn't have any follow-up questions, he just pondered what had been said. It was an explanation, but he didn't feel like he truly understood.

"That look on your face, I have seen it before from others when hearing about the Blight. Trust me, once you encounter it, you will understand." Falric turned his gaze toward Vincent.

"I would normally say I hope you don't encounter it, but it seems like you will have no choice," Vincent said.

"So, you've dealt with it?" Alrion was curious. His father never spoke of his life before Hamley. And if he had experience about the Blight, it had to have been earlier.

"Yes, quite a bit. I travelled a lot before I met your mother and we settled here. Avaria is a precious gift. Unfortunately, when you venture forth to other countries, you will see something a lot grimmer. It is the state of the world right now, and hopefully one day we can end the Blight for good," Vincent said.

"It was your grandfather's wish to end the Blight. I don't believe that his cleansing of Avaria was the final piece in his plan, just the beginning. However, the fact that he already achieved so much means that it is possible for us. We just need to find the right way." Falric had a hopeful look again.

"That makes sense. If it's so bad, and it's a more recent thing, then maybe it's not as hard as you think?" Alrion said. Falric and Vincent laughed.

"Maybe not, we'll see," Falric said.

Alrion however, had another question.

"What happens when we get to the academy?" he said.

"You and your father will be welcomed, then there are some formalities to go through before you can start your training," Falric said.

"What kind of formalities?" Alrion had already had the surprise test. He wondered what else was in store for him.

"There is an induction ceremony. You will be introduced as a new student to the rest of your peers at the academy. Then you will take part in the ceremony and receive a gift given to all the wizards."

"But what does that actually mean?"

"It means that there are a few secrets that are yet to be revealed," Falric said, a crafty smile on his face.

"Get used to this." Vincent pointed at Falric.

"Mystery and secrecy are important tools in a wizard's kit," Falric said.

"Can't you at least give him a little more detail?" Vincent said.

"Honestly, there is some value in it being a surprise. I have sat through countless induction ceremonies, and still find them interesting and moving. So, I'm very hesitant to say more."

"Has there always been an induction?" Alrion said.

"Yes, there has. When your grandfather established the academy, he was adamant that all initiates must take part in the ceremony. He designed it himself. It's a unifying moment that gives all wizards a shared history, and a greater connection to each other."

"Sorry son, but I think that's all you are going to get," Vincent said.

"It just sounds like that is the way it is."

"Well put. Should we get going then?" Falric said.

"Sure, let's pack up." Vincent stood and started packing their bags. They each carefully guided the horses out of the clearing and onto the main path once more.

Alrion looked around the forest as they progressed, and noticed there didn't seem to be a lot of wildlife.

"Is there something wrong with this forest?" he said.

"Why do you ask?" Falric said.

"I don't see any animals."

"That's a good observation. Mostly smaller animals live here, and they are nocturnal. It is very quiet during the day."

"Is there a reason for that?"

"I'm not entirely sure; I've never looked into it. The academy has always been nearby, but I didn't think that this forest had any significance," Falric said.

"I guess it's just different to what I'm used to." Alrion kept looking around in vain. The lack of animals was really obvious once he had spotted it.

"You have good instincts, Son, there's definitely something different about this forest. There must be a history," Vincent said.

"Tell you what; I'll have someone look into it later. Even if for educational purposes, it would be worthwhile understanding more of the history surrounding this place," Falric said. They continued in silence, as if in keeping with the wishes of the forest. Falric looked like he was about to announce something but stopped. Alrion soon found out why.

The trees began to thin, and the path snaked around a bend. As they followed it, Falric slowed down and let Alrion and Vincent ride ahead.

"Wow," Alrion said as he caught the first few glimpses of their destination. At the edge of the forest stood a massive structure, a cross between a manor house and a castle. Its walls were made of stone, with large windows wrapping around the building. Rising behind the main building was a tall tower also made of stone.

"Welcome to your new home," Falric said, gesturing at the academy with a sweeping arm movement.

8

A WIZARD'S WELCOME

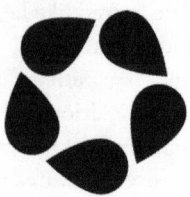

Alrion took it all in as they rode closer. The sun was setting behind the academy, an orange and pink glow illuminating it. He was impressed; he had never seen anything like it.

"How many wizards live here?"

"It varies; we have had up to one hundred. Around fifty are here at the moment," Falric said.

"Why so few?"

"Various reasons. Some move away for long periods, some leave the academy never to return. Some are lost." Falric's voice dropped a little and he looked away.

"I see."

"But they are a good group. You will meet them all tomorrow." Falric's tone changed back to normal.

"What's the plan?" Vincent said.

"We shall get you settled inside tonight, and tomorrow the ceremony will be performed. You can stay as long as you like, and return home when you are ready."

"Sure. I think I'll stay for a few days to make sure Alrion is comfortable."

"Of course. We always have room for Granthion's family," Falric said. As they neared the front gate, a robed man was waiting for them. He seemed a bit shorter with a stocky frame. The hood of the robe was pushed back so you could easily see his thick black hair.

"Hello, Falric, welcome home," the man said. He opened his hands in a welcoming gesture.

"Hello, Branthor, thank you. It is good to be home." Falric dismounted and Alrion and Vincent followed his lead.

"Were you successful? I see you have guests." Branthor studied them closely, and Alrion felt uncomfortable.

"Yes, I was. This is Vincent, and his son Alrion. Alrion will be inducted tomorrow morning."

"Alrion. A good name. Nice to meet you, I am Branthor, and I am Falric's right-hand wizard. I knew your grandfather, and I am honoured to make your acquaintance." Branthor bowed then offered his hand.

"Thank you, nice to meet you too." Alrion shook Branthor's hand and was surprised at how firm the grip was.

"I didn't know Granthion had any surviving family until recently. Vincent, was it?"

"Yes. I kept out of my father's business and also out of his shadow."

"Yes, quite a big shadow, and a big legacy. We have high hopes for Alrion." Branthor gave Vincent a hard stare.

"So do I." Vincent returned the stare.

"Let's all get inside before it turns dark," Falric said. Branthor walked ahead, and the rest followed, leading their horses on foot. As they neared the main building, two young men ran out to attend to them.

"Please take your bags, and leave the horses. We will bring them through to the stables," the shorter of the two men said.

"Are you wizards too?" Alrion said.

"No, we are apprentices." The man sounded proud. Alrion was surprised.

"And they have you doing errands?"

"Everyone must pitch in here. It's a part of the training," the taller of the two apprentices said. They offered no further explanation and quickly took off with the horses.

Looks like becoming a wizard won't get me out of errands, Alrion thought. He was a bit disappointed, but realised that was silly. He had to change his expectations. Of course there would be hard work becoming a wizard too.

"This way." Branthor pointed ahead and led them inside. They found themselves in a reception area. An open door to their right revealed a giant hall. Along each wall were wooden benches with a lectern at the end of the hall.

"That is where the wizards meet to discuss the matters of the world," Branthor explained. Alrion peered into the room but said nothing. Branthor continued walking and they all followed. They ended up in a hallway, with doors on either side.

"These doors lead to the rooms, we will take you to yours." Branthor opened one of the doors on the left and stepped inside. Another corridor was within, with many doors visible. Branthor opened the first door and stood to the side. Falric stood next to Branthor and waved Alrion in. Vincent and Alrion walked over and looked inside. The room was incredibly plain, with two single beds, a chest of drawers, and bedside tables.

"Is this for us?" Vincent said.

"Yes, we live simply here. Branthor will arrange for some dinner for you both. Have a restful night and we will see you tomorrow," Falric said.

"Goodnight, and thanks," Alrion said. Falric left and after he had disappeared into the main hallway, Branthor spoke.

"As Falric mentioned I'll arrange for dinner to be brought here. Unfortunately, you cannot dine with the other wizards until you have been inducted."

"No problem." Alrion liked the idea of not meeting everyone just yet.

"If you need anything, go down to the room at the end of this corridor. There will be someone there who can help. Goodnight," Branthor said.

"Goodnight." Alrion watched the wizard leave. Vincent stepped inside the room and looked around. Alrion took one look at the hallway and stepped in also.

"At least we're not eating on our laps." Vincent pointed to a tiny table with two chairs in the corner behind the door.

"Yes, I guess so. This is it then?" Alrion said.

"This is it. How do you feel?"

"I'm not sure. Nervous."

"It'll go well, and don't forget I'm here too." Vincent threw his bag down on the far bed. Alrion moved to close the door but stopped. He saw a face just outside the half-closed door.

"Hello, could you open the door for me?" a voice said. Alrion opened the door and saw a bald young man outside balancing a tray of food in each hand. Alrion stepped out of the way and the man put the trays down on the little table, visibly relaxing after he was done.

"Are you an apprentice?" Alrion said, looking at the young man. He had a simple robe, but no adornments on it.

"Yes."

"How long have you been here?"

"A few years. My name is Eric."

"Nice to meet you, Eric. I'm Alrion, and that's my dad Vincent."

"Nice to meet you both. Are you here to study?" Eric looked at Alrion.

"Yes, my induction ceremony is tomorrow." Alrion noticed that Eric's eyes widened at the news.

"That's exciting. Well, I'll see you tomorrow then."

"Can you tell me about it?"

"No, we're not allowed to say anything. It's not bad, though, so don't worry. Goodnight." Eric left immediately.

"Isn't he a bit young to have no hair?" Alrion said.

"Maybe he cut it himself," Vincent said.

"Maybe he had a magical accident."

"Ha-ha you could be right," Vincent said, sitting down in front of one of the trays, eyeing off the food. It was a thin chicken soup and a piece of brown bread.

"It's simple but it's food," he said. He waited for Alrion to sit down, then started eating.

"Do you really think I should be doing this?" Alrion was looking at his food but not eating.

"It's your choice. You haven't really taken to blacksmithing, so maybe this is why." Vincent took a big bite out of a piece of bread.

"But you don't seem to like wizards at all. I can see that." Alrion watched his father put his food down and look him in the eye.

"I'm a little cautious with them, I agree. Hopefully, your experience will be more positive."

"What do you mean? Wasn't your dad a wizard?"

"Yes, he was, and he pulled off a lot of amazing feats, but we didn't see eye to eye on many things. And he put his duties as a wizard ahead of everything else. He wanted that life for me too, but it didn't fit. So, that caused some friction between us." A look of sadness passed over Vincent's face, but it was gone in a flash.

"But he's just one person."

"Yes, but this whole system was set up by him. I admit that I'm a bit sceptical, but I am working on having an open mind." Vincent helped himself to another spoonful of food. Alrion wasn't finished with the conversation though.

"It's our legacy, we should take it seriously. I still can't believe you never told me."

"It was for your own good."

"Would you have brought me here?" Alrion blurted out. But as soon as he said it he wanted to know the answer. His father sighed and put down his spoon.

"Maybe, maybe not. Although I was curious to see if you would show any signs of magic. Falric came and put that mystery to rest."

"I see," Alrion said. He wasn't convinced that his father would have brought him unless there was some sort of incident that required it. His father seemed to be wrestling with something, and spoke up again.

"You know, I should be clearer. I absolutely would have brought you here had you shown any signs. In fact, I think eventually I would have brought you anyway just to make sure you weren't supposed to be a wizard. Because I owe it to my father. He sacrificed so much, for me and for the rest of the people of Avaria. As much as I spent my life avoiding wizards, I can't ignore what he did." Vincent paused, watching Alrion's reaction. Alrion tried to speak but his father started again.

"I just want you to think of it this way. There's magic in our family. But, you always have a choice. You can decide that you don't want this, and we can leave and that is the end of it. There's no danger for you if you choose not to pursue being a wizard. As much as you may not believe it, I'm not advocating a choice either way. It is important to me that you understand that it's not a requirement thrust upon you. The choice is, and always will be, yours."

"Thanks for being open about this. But, I know that I need to continue. I can't make any other choice until I know more. It does feel right, though," Alrion said.

"I'm glad you feel that way. Always trust your instincts. I never felt like I was allowed a choice. It was a large part of our falling out." Vincent paused. It looked like he was going to talk again, but he just stared into his meal. Alrion started eating finally and Vincent dove back in. They finished their food and pushed the plates to the far corner of the table.

"I think it's time to turn in," Vincent said.

"Sure."

"Goodnight, Son." Vincent walked over and gave Alrion a big hug. He couldn't remember the last time his father had just done that out of the blue. Vincent then dropped unceremoniously into his bed.

"Goodnight, Dad," Alrion said. He kicked off his boots and settled into the small wooden bed. The mattress wasn't as uncomfortable as it looked, but he had trouble sleeping.

He kept playing the events of the last few days over in his mind and imagining what would happen at the ceremony. He drifted in and out of a light sleep, but didn't feel like he was even sleeping. He just couldn't switch his mind off. He tried to reason with himself, explaining that he needed the rest and it was a big day coming up, but it was hopeless.

Eventually, he did feel sleep taking effect, and felt relaxed that finally he would enjoy a proper rest. He started to dream, and in his dream, the door was knocked three times. He ignored it. The door was knocked three more times, then finally it opened. A shape appeared in the doorway and spoke.

"It is time," the voice said. Something about the voice seemed real, so Alrion struggled to open his eyes. The door to their room was open, and there was a person standing there. As his eyes opened more, he peered closer and recognised the person. It was Eric.

"Eric? What time is it?"

"It is time," Eric said, in the same monotone manner. Alrion sat up in the bed and turned to look over at his father. Vincent was sitting quietly in the bed, watching but not speaking. He nodded at Alrion. Trying to shake the cobwebs from his mind, Alrion stood and stepped towards Eric.

"In that case, let's not keep them waiting," Alrion said, sounding much more confident than he felt. Eric turned and started to walk away and Alrion followed close behind. He heard his father close the door behind them but didn't look back.

9

THE WHITE FLAME

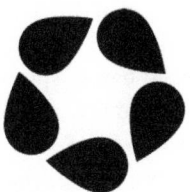

They didn't walk far, and at the end of the corridor, they stepped through a door that led to another, narrower corridor.

This place is like a maze.

He emerged into a simple room, with a table, two meals, and two chairs. Eric pointed at the table.

"The ceremony draws on your strength. Savour your last meal as a normal man." Eric left the room and closed the door behind him.

"That sounded very formal," Alrion said.

"It must be part of the ceremony," Vincent said.

"Well I am hungry, and I don't know what to expect. We should eat." Alrion sat down and started eating. The food was simple and consisted of bread, cheese, and milk.

"It looks like it is a formal ritual. That's a good thing. Just follow their instructions and you will do fine," Vincent said.

"That sounds almost positive. Not trying to talk me out of it?"

"I never was, just because I have some history doesn't mean you should be held back. Try to enjoy it," Vincent said. He even cracked a smile.

"You must have slept much better than I did." Alrion returned the smile. He appreciated his father's support, even though he still didn't fully understand why his father was so touchy about wizards.

"I did, it's a skill you learn as you age," Vincent said. Before he could say more, there was a knock at the door. Alrion opened the door and saw Eric standing there once more.

"You must be clad in the garments of your calling. Take this and wear it proudly." Eric said, handing over a bundle of white cloth. Alrion accepted it and opened it up with care. He was holding a snow-white hooded robe, trimmed in navy blue around the hood. Alrion put the robe on over his clothes and drew the hood down. He looked at Eric for confirmation.

"Come now, your brothers await," Eric said. Alrion nodded and stepped out of the room. Vincent followed closely behind. They retraced their steps through the narrow corridors until they reached the main connecting room. This time they continued, finally reaching a pair of double doors. Alrion could see light coming from behind them. Eric pushed open the doors and stepped through. Alrion and Vincent followed.

They stood outside, the sun rising in the distance. Surrounding them was a paved square courtyard, with robed figures spread around the perimeter. In the middle of the square, two figures stood in front of a tall tower.

"The applicant must step towards his destiny." Eric pointed to the middle of the courtyard. Alrion stepped forward and Vincent began to follow. Eric and another wizard stepped in front of Vincent. Alrion stopped suddenly and turned to see what had happened.

"Only the applicant can enter, observers must stay back," Eric said. Vincent nodded and retreated, watching with interest. Alrion watched his father step back, and then looked around at the wizards; they all had their head and hoods down.

Alrion continued to the middle of the courtyard. He saw Falric and Branthor standing there. They were both wearing white robes but had different coloured bands around the hood. Alrion pressed on, hoping that a slow and steady walk would calm his nerves. Even though it seemed like the wizards were not watching, he felt countless eyes following his progress. As he arrived, he saw Falric raise his head and address him.

"State your name, wizard-to-be."

"Alrion."

"Do you swear to combat the forces of darkness and bring light and illumination to the world?"

"I swear."

"We symbolise this struggle, between light and darkness by bestowing each wizard a crystal of their own. A pure white crystal that contains a vein of darkness. Select yours." Falric held up a spherical translucent bowl, full of crystal shards.

Each was about the size of his thumb. Alrion picked one up to get a better look at it. It was roughly a diamond shape and had a black streak through the middle. He turned the crystal around, trying to see how it had gotten there. He looked over to see if he should select another, but the bowl was gone.

"You have selected your crystal. Keep it with you always."

"I will."

"Now, you must activate your crystal. Show your peers the spark of magic within you," Falric said. Alrion didn't know what to do. He looked at Falric, then at Branthor. Neither gave him any direction, they just waited. Alrion looked again at the crystal. It had to be similar to how they had tested him with the lamp. If he could activate that, surely he could do this. If only he could remember how he did it.

Alrion turned the crystal over in his hands, studying it. However, he knew that looking at it would do nothing, he would need to exert some sort of force upon it. He closed his hands around it, feeling the texture of the crystal; holding the crystal within his hands. It seemed so small that way. He closed his eyes and concentrated. He felt the heartbeat within his hands. Only it was not. It was different.

Alrion isolated the feeling. It was as if the crystal itself was beating, to a different rhythm than his heartbeat. He visualised the crystal, trying to understand how it could beat. It was a hard surface, it didn't make sense. Then he had a sudden realisation. It was the black streak within the crystal, not the crystal. That streak was beating, as much as it seemed impossible. He could sense the life force within the crystal, the other alien thing inside. It could only be one thing, the Blight.

An irrational fear took over Alrion. How could he be holding something with the Blight within it? He had to protect himself, but he couldn't let go of the crystal. Something else was happening. It was reacting to him. He had to get away; he had to stop it somehow. Then he felt a surge within him, a cool heat that burned hotter and hotter until he could feel the fire on his face. He could sense a bright light, even with his eyes closed.

Confused, he opened his eyes to see what was going on. A white flame engulfed his hands, burning, yet not burning. He opened his hands to see the crystal. It was burning white, the black streak within dancing in time with the licking flames.

Burn away.

The flames contracted within the crystal, then shot out from the top, a thin pillar of white light that arced up to the sky, then vanished.

Alrion looked back at the crystal in disbelief. It looked the same as before, the black streak within it appeared undisturbed.

Was that a dream? What happened, he thought. He looked to Falric for reassurance. Falric had a strange look on his face, and so did Branthor.

"The crystal." Falric extended his hand. Alrion gave it to him. Falric removed an amulet and silver chain from his robes and enclosed the crystal within. He handed the amulet back to Alrion.

"Wear it with pride."

"I will."

"The ceremony is concluded. You are welcomed here, Wizard Alrion," Falric said, his voice projected so it echoed around the courtyard. The pronouncement shook everyone out of their stunned silence, and cheers rose out around the courtyard.

"Come with us," Falric said, and headed towards the tower. Alrion followed closely behind. He needed to find out what had just happened.

My father.

Alrion turned to see what had happened to his father. At first, he could not spot him, but then as the crowds started to disperse, Vincent pushed his way through, running towards Alrion.

I bet he didn't expect that, Alrion thought.

10

DESTINY

Falric and Branthor walked ahead, and Alrion rushed forward until he was right on their heels. They entered the tower together and started to ascend the stairs.

Something doesn't feel right. That can't have been normal, Alrion thought. However, he had no point of reference. As they walked, he heard hurried steps behind. He looked back and saw his father rushing up the stairs.

"Quite a spectacle, I'd like to be part of this next discussion," Vincent said.

"That is quite alright, and expected," Falric said from ahead. Alrion waited for his father to join him, then resumed walking.

"You did great, let's find out what that was all about," Vincent whispered. Alrion nodded and kept walking. Within a few minutes, they emerged into a large circular room.

The centre of the room held only a desk and a few chairs; however, the perimeter was full of artifacts of different kinds. Falric sat down behind the desk and Branthor retrieved a few chairs from around the room and placed them around the desk.

"Please sit." Falric gestured at the chairs.

"What just happened?" Vincent said.

"The ceremony. However, it was a variation not seen before." Falric let his gaze rest on Alrion.

"What do you mean?" Alrion said.

"The ceremony is a rite of passage for our wizards. It is a way of binding them together and reminding them of their shared purpose to combat evil and in particular the Blight. However, as it was designed by your grandfather, it also serves a second purpose."

"A second purpose?" Alrion looked at his father. Vincent shrugged.

"Yes. It is also a test. A test to see whether the wizard can overcome the Blight, transform it if you will. To date, only Granthion has been able to do so. In fact, when he established the wizard school, he didn't tell anyone about the secondary purpose of the ceremony. Since nobody activated it, he didn't have to. But he wrote me a letter explaining what needed to be done and how to recognise the person who passed the test."

"Did he hand you the letter himself?" Vincent said.

"The note was waiting for me after he had left to perform the cleansing spell, so I didn't know about this aspect of the ceremony until afterward. In it, he explained his actions. But it was only one of two notes. Did you read the one addressed to you?" Falric said, looking at Vincent. Alrion looked over in surprise.

"Yes, I did." Vincent was intently focused on Falric.

"I wasn't able to read it, so I don't know what it said. Was any of this explained?"

"No."

"Perhaps yours was of a more personal nature. In my letter, he explained his actions and his plan for the future. The plan to end the Blight."

"What has that got to do with the ceremony? How was it a test?" Alrion said.

"The crystals used in the ceremony were all created by Granthion. They were by-products of his research into containing the Blight. That black streak within is the Blight." Falric pointed to the amulet that Alrion was now wearing. Alrion glanced down at it again.

"How is the test supposed to work?" he said.

"The normal result is a black flame. It is a reaction between the Blight, the crystal, and the spark of the wizard. It is a symbol to remember that wizards must ever be vigilant for the Blight, and the darkness within. The black flame is something that is remembered vividly by every wizard," Falric said.

"What does the white flame mean?"

"It means that your spark can convert and cleanse the Blight. We have not yet seen a person achieve that feat since Granthion," Falric said. Alrion pulled out the amulet and studied the crystal.

"The black streak is still there." Alrion was surprised at the obvious disappointment in his voice.

"Correct, but that is because you didn't cleanse the crystal of the Blight. You created a reaction where your spark altered the flame from black to white. This is very significant."

"So, I'm special?"

"Yes, you are special and you, therefore, have a special mission. To end the

Blight for good," Falric said. Alrion didn't respond immediately, letting the thought sink in.

"It's up to me to end the Blight?"

"Yes, and only you can do so."

"You're sure that nobody else can do it?" Alrion couldn't understand. He was untrained, he was not who they were looking for.

"Nobody that we've identified. Perhaps there is another, but in all the years I have been head of the academy, we have not seen one. You are our best, and so far, only hope."

"How do you even know that? Are there instructions?" Alrion said. Falric laughed.

"That's a good question. Actually, the instructions and information we have are minimal. Granthion explained briefly the spell that he was about to undertake, and that it wasn't the ideal solution. And that the answers to fixing it would be available elsewhere."

"What was wrong with his solution? If it wasn't perfect, why did he do it?" Alrion's mind was racing away. This was all too much.

"I can answer part of that. The rest would come from your father." Falric pointed at Vincent. Vincent recoiled like Falric had fired something at him.

"Dad, what's your part in this?" Alrion knew something was going on. Maybe he would finally find out what had happened between his father and grandfather.

"The day that your grandfather performed the ritual, I was captured. Held by a group of people infected by the Blight, who wanted to infect me too. I'm not sure exactly what their plan was, but I guess I was targeted because I was Granthion's son. They could get to him through me." Vincent looked away, shame on his face.

"The ritual performed by Granthion, whilst imperfect, was an incredible feat. He connected to every single Blight infected soul within the country of Avaria, drew the Blight into himself, then destroyed the Blight within him. It saved the lives of many, and prevented harm for many more," Falric said.

"And he did it to save you?" Alrion said to Vincent. He was struggling to believe what he had just heard.

"Yes. He succeeded, and I escaped unharmed."

"No. That can't be." Alrion started to understand. His father felt responsible for Granthion's death. For robbing the world of their greatest wizard.

"It's a fact not known by the general population," Falric said.

"I had no idea that Granthion was capable of that, and had plans for a better spell," Branthor said, speaking up for the first time.

"I was also in the dark until Granthion's disappearance. He did like to keep his secrets," Falric said.

"But keeping this knowledge hidden for all this time?" Branthor said. Alrion was surprised by the harshness in Branthor's tone.

"It was Granthion's wishes. He wanted his vision to be kept a secret until the right person was unveiled."

"If that spell was so effective, why can't it be used again? What's wrong with it?" Alrion said.

"I don't have an exact answer for that. My guess is that the amount of power required to target the entire world with such a spell is impossible. There would have to be another way. But for whatever reason, Granthion didn't know the way, or could not document what he had discovered," Falric said.

"What am I supposed to do, then?" Alrion couldn't see the way forward. It was all just a mess. It was one thing to throw this responsibility onto him. It was another to do so without any form of guidance or support. He shook his head.

"He did leave us with something to follow up. The Pool of Knowledge."

"The Pool of Knowledge?" Alrion's curiosity was roused.

"It is a sacred place hidden within Avaria. It is said that all knowledge is preserved there. The answers you need to complete your quest must be there."

"I'm the only one who can cleanse the Blight, but we don't know how. If I go to this Pool of Knowledge, then I'll know what to do next?"

"That's right. It may seem like an odd request, but I believe it to be the best course of action. Armed with the knowledge of what the spell requires, we can better plan our next steps."

"What warrants all this secrecy?"

"We have to trust in Granthion's approach. He must have had a good reason for having this requirement." Falric kept a calm and confident tone. It helped reassure Alrion a little.

"Have you been there?"

"No. It is a sacred place that few know of, and even fewer are allowed access. However, I do know its location."

"I'm a bit overwhelmed, to be honest. So much has just happened. First, I'm a wizard, and now I'm some special wizard who can end the Blight? It's a lot to take in." Alrion could have said much more, but held his tongue.

"Don't worry Son, we'll do this together," Vincent said. Alrion looked over at his father with surprise.

"You'll go with me?"

"Of course. You have lived a sheltered life, because of me. But I have travelled the world. I can help guide you through the dangers out there, and keep you safe."

"I will go also," Falric said. This time Branthor looked over at Falric with surprise.

"But Falric, you are needed here," he said.

"You are perfectly capable of looking after the academy. What Alrion needs is teaching in the ways of being a wizard if he is to succeed."

"Which is why he should stay here. Train with his peers then set out when he is more capable," Branthor said.

"This is an incredible opportunity; we can't just sit on it. We don't even know what is required. What if we wait around for years before setting off, and discover that we could have been preparing all along? No, this is too important. We must set out at once," Falric said.

"If that is so, I can accompany them. Your place is here at the academy!" Branthor raised his voice. But the look on Falric's face caused him to lose some of his boldness.

"My place has been here my entire life, to serve the cause of my teacher. Now there is an opportunity to continue his work, and you want me to stay here idle? No. I have earned this right and I will exercise it." Falric looked like he was daring Branthor to challenge him.

"By your command." Branthor turned to look away.

"It will be one of my last. I will arrange a proclamation today that you are the new leader of the academy."

"Won't that just be a temporary arrangement? Why go to all the trouble?"

"Let's just see. Maybe you'll do such a great job, I'll come back as a trusted advisor."

"Of course, I would be honoured," Branthor said. Alrion thought Branthor would be more pleased with such an honour.

"I knew you would be." Falric turned to address Vincent and Alrion once more.

"Take some time to wander around and think everything through. I'll send someone to find you and we can finalise our preparations."

"Sure." Alrion felt like he was in a daze.

"Thanks. Let's go." Vincent led Alrion over to the stairs. They slowly descended, not uttering a single word. As they emerged outside there were still some wizards in the courtyard. They stared at Alrion as he emerged.

"Awkward," Alrion said as he walked.

"They don't understand, this has never happened before. But don't worry about them; it looks like we won't be staying here."

"Why me?" Alrion looked to his father.

"That's the eternal question," Vincent said with a laugh. Alrion wasn't amused.

"You can't be flippant about this. Seriously, why?"

"It's fate, or destiny, or just bad luck. Alternatively, good luck. Depends on how you look at it." Vincent looked like he was enjoying himself.

"How come you're so happy all of a sudden?"

"I'm not. But this is so much more than what I expected to happen. I wanted nothing more to do with wizards, and now you're their last hope to fulfil my father's work. At some point you just need to give up, and laugh about it. Either that or cry."

"I shouldn't have complained about being bored at home." Alrion sighed.

"That's the problem with wishes; sometimes you get what you wished for."

"I still don't get it. How can you be so cheery and upbeat? This is crazy!"

"This is an opportunity. One that nobody else has. You owe it to yourself to go after it. We don't know what is involved. Maybe you'll get to the Pool of Knowledge and find out you just need to read books for a few years. We just don't know. But I bet if you look inside, and really think about it, you'll realise that, underneath this annoyance and complaining, you're excited by the possibilities." Vincent gave Alrion a knowing look. Alrion thought about what his father said and let out a deep sigh.

"You're right. Of course, you're right. But I need time," he said.

"There will be plenty of that. But you need to take that first step."

"It feels like the first step is taking me," Alrion said. He snuck a tiny smile onto his face, which Vincent picked up on.

"That's the spirit. Own the unknown. Maybe when you return here you'll get a different look from these guys."

"I hope so. I just feel like even more of an outsider."

"Your grandfather started this place. You couldn't be any less of an outsider."

"Tell that to them. The whole feeling is noticeably different since the initiation."

"Don't worry about them. Let's just go for a walk," Vincent said. Alrion nodded and they set off.

They walked around the perimeter of the courtyard and watched the remaining wizards filter back indoors.

"You've already seen the tower, let's check out indoors," Vincent said.

"Have you been here before?" Alrion said.

"No, this place was established later. Your grandfather and I and the first founding wizards lived somewhere else. When we parted ways, he came here to found the academy, and I travelled."

"Will you ever talk about him? I mean properly."

"One day. However, all you need to know is that he was a great wizard, and did a lot for many people. You have a lot to live up to in that regard."

"Sure beats being a blacksmith." Alrion pushed ahead.

After wandering through the main building, they found themselves back at the entry.

"Let's take a seat," Vincent said and settled down on a leather couch. Alrion sat down next to him.

"So, what now?" he said.

"I think they'll come and find us before long," Vincent said. As if on cue, a wizard walked in and addressed them both.

"Please come with me, your equipment needs to be provisioned," the wizard said.

"Now this should be fun." Vincent winked at Alrion.

11

ADVENTURE

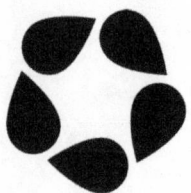

Vincent and Alrion followed the young wizard out of the main building, across the courtyard and into a smaller building that they had not spotted before. It was made of stone with a heavy steel door.

"This is our store." The wizard placed his hand on the door and unlocked it. He pulled the door open and walked inside. After he stepped in, he held his hand up and lit a lamp. As the light danced around the room, Alrion started to see what it contained.

There were shelves all around the walls, containing objects of different types and sizes. There were racks of equipment in the middle of the room. Alrion spotted robes, bags, staves, shoes, and other clothing.

"You are well stocked here," Vincent said.

"Of course, a wizard must be prepared," their guide said. He walked down the aisles, collecting things in a bundle before returning to present them to Alrion.

"Here are your things. Treat them well, and they will serve you for a long time," he said.

"Do I get anything?" Vincent said.

"You will both be given ample provisions from the kitchen store," the wizard said.

"That's a no, Dad," Alrion said.

"There is one more thing, follow me, young wizard." The guide beckoned to Alrion. Alrion handed his bundle to his father and followed the wizard. They walked to the end of the room, where there was a small doorway otherwise not visible.

"Go through and select one item. Do not show anyone," he said. Alrion turned to ask a question, but the man had left. He shrugged and decided to walk through the door.

The room was pitch black, and he couldn't see a thing. He felt around with his hand, wondering what was there. It seemed to be a collection of objects on shelves, but he couldn't tell what they were. They all had a cold, metallic feeling to them. As he brushed his hand across them, he felt a sudden surge of warmth and jumped.

He returned his hand to confirm it. One of the objects was warm to the touch, so he decided to grab it and stash it in his pocket. Then he left the room. He saw his father standing near the entrance, and no sign of the wizard except the light he had left anchored to the wall.

"All done?" Vincent said.

"I think so," Alrion said. Vincent handed back the bundle of clothing.

"Good, let's head back to the main building and get some food." Vincent stepped outside.

"Aren't you going to ask me what I found back there?"

"Not my business."

"Fair enough." Alrion was a bit surprised, but they did say not to show anyone.

"Looks like you have a full outfit there." Vincent gestured at the bundle of clothes Alrion was holding as they crossed the courtyard.

"I hope they fit," Alrion said. Vincent laughed.

"You have a lot to learn about magic, my boy."

"Now that you put it that way, it seems like they really should fit."

"You would hope so. After you." Vincent held the door open for Alrion. They walked through the hallway of the main building and returned to the room they had stayed in overnight. Alrion had a better look at the things he had been given.

"This looks like a robe." He put it on and was surprised at how comfortable it was.

"Definitely. And feel the material too. It's quite hardy, for travelling."

"Shoes, a walking stick. Why a walking stick?"

"They can be quite useful especially on uneven terrain, but I bet there's another reason for having it. Ask Falric about it," Vincent said.

"This bag looks useful; I can hang it over my shoulder. These things are all geared for walking I think."

"There are many places a horse cannot go, so that seems like a good idea. Let me know when you're ready and we can finalise our preparations." Vincent lay back on his bed and closed his eyes.

"I think I'm done," Alrion said, as he finished buckling his new shoes on. They were surprisingly comfortable, given how sturdy they looked. He looked at himself in the mirror. Despite the plain nature of everything he was wearing, he felt like a wizard.

"You look the part." Vincent stood and nodded with approval.

"They don't seem particularly fashionable, but are comfortable," Alrion said.

"Comfort is the much better of the two possibilities. Wear them in good health."

"Thanks. I guess we go see about provisions then," Alrion said. Vincent opened the door and they walked through the hallway in an attempt to locate the kitchen. They followed the sound and smells of food, and found themselves in front of a petite young woman with a rolling pin across her folded arms.

"Hello, we were just looking for the kitchen," Vincent said.

"You the travellers? This way," the woman said in a gruff voice. Vincent and Alrion looked at each other in surprise at the tone of her voice, then followed her through a door into a storeroom.

"You looked like you were guarding something," Vincent said.

"I was. You have no idea how many wizards get it in their heads to go steal some food from the kitchen. It's like some sort of ritual or initiation or something, and they don't even eat the food. It ends up being buried or exploded or something else," the woman said.

"Boys will be boys," Vincent said.

"Some of these boys are old enough to be grandparents," the woman said.

"Not surprised at all. I'm Vincent, and this is Alrion. Nice to meet you."

"Pamela. Nice to meet you too." Pamela kept on rummaging around. She started collecting food, her long red hair swishing around as she moved.

"Since you are going on a trip, I'll give you some of this flatbread. It lasts a while and is sufficient by itself at a pinch. Here, try some." Pamela handed them both a sample.

"Wow, that's delicious," Vincent said.

"I could eat that for days," Alrion said.

"Be careful what you wish for." Pamela laughed, the movement rippling through her chest.

"Sounds like you have a story about that," Vincent said.

"Yeah, it's a good one. I'll tell you when you come back. Maybe you'll have a story of your own." Pamela continued collecting other food and handed them each a sack full to the brim.

"There's a week's worth there. All I was instructed to provide. Either it's a short trip or you will have opportunities to restock yourself. But make it last," she said.

"We'll be careful," Vincent said.

"Travel safe, I'm going back to my guard post."

"Aren't you a cook?" Alrion said.

"First and foremost, but you need ingredients to cook with, so back I go," Pamela said.

"Good luck." Vincent waved goodbye. Pamela waved her rolling pin at them and marched off like she was on a mission.

"I like her," Alrion said.

"Yeah, she seems like a good sort. But regardless, always be nice to the help. The cooks, the stable boy, the assistants. Not only is it the right thing to do, you'll find yourself having allies in useful places."

"That sounds like good advice. I'll do it." Alrion guessed there were some interesting stories behind the advice, but didn't ask. Vincent looked around a bit more.

"I think you'll like it here," he said.

"If I ever make it back." Alrion hadn't even had time to unpack, and he was off again.

"Don't worry about that, you'll be back. It's just a matter of when."

"You're probably right. What do we do now?" Alrion said.

"We have equipment and food, and our horses are in the stables. I just need to do one more thing before we go." Vincent left Alrion in the hallway and walked off with purpose. He returned a few minutes later with a piece of paper and a pen.

"I need to let your mother know that I won't be back so soon. But I won't include all the details, she may worry," Vincent said while writing.

"She would definitely worry. Any reasonable person would," Alrion said.

"Then let's not cause your mother any undue distress. There, that should do it." Vincent folded the letter in half.

"I think you're saving yourself distress." Alrion was half-joking. His father laughed.

"You know her too well. Let's go see what Falric is up to."

They walked back to the central hallway of the main building, and seeing nobody around continued to the back door. They emerged into the courtyard, surprised by what they saw.

Just as in the morning, the courtyard was full of wizards. Like earlier, they had arranged themselves around the perimeter of the courtyard. In the centre, they saw Falric and Branthor with their heads bowed. Vincent and Alrion found a spot amongst the wizards and waited to see what would happen.

"Today is an auspicious day. Our newest member, Alrion, has passed his initiation and revealed his true identity. He is a bringer of light, one that can turn back the darkness of the Blight," Falric said, his voice somehow amplified so that it rang through the courtyard. He paused. There was a quiet murmur throughout the wizards, which quickly died down.

"I have been waiting for this day, since I took over from our founding father, Granthion. Now I have an opportunity to take on his legacy and complete the work that he began. I will be leaving you, and travelling with Alrion to train him and assist with his journey," Falric said. There was louder murmuring and discussion amongst the wizards, but within a minute, it quieted down once more.

"I don't know when I will return, but I know that I cannot provide the same support for this beloved academy as I have before. Therefore, I am passing on leadership to my dear and trusted friend, Branthor." Falric gestured to Branthor, who bowed.

"This must be a big moment. There's only been one other handover of leadership, and that was when your grandfather died," Vincent said to Alrion.

"As a symbol of the transition, I am handing over the Crystal Staff to Branthor. May you lead the academy to an era of even greater prosperity," Falric said. He knelt in front of Branthor and held up the staff. It was a dark brown wood, with a cloudy crystal ball set in the top. Branthor accepted the staff and held it aloft. A pulse of light radiated out from the staff, covering the entire courtyard for a second, before disappearing completely. A cheer rose up amongst the wizards.

"They're gone," Alrion said.

"Theatrics! Let's go up to the tower," Vincent said. Alrion nodded and they walked across the courtyard as the wizards dispersed.

"This is really happening then," Alrion said.

"It certainly is," Vincent said. As they reached the bottom of the tower, they saw Falric step out of the stairwell.

"How was that?" Falric said.

"Impressive," Alrion said. He looked over at his father who said nothing.

"You have to give these occasions the proper ceremony. Otherwise, their significance can be lost. Branthor is only the third person to lead the academy, which is a major event. If we can establish something now, then future generations can carry on and keep the ceremony alive."

"I understand that this is a big ask of you, to walk away from your life's work. I appreciate your help," Alrion said.

"Thank you. But it's also a good excuse to let go. It's time for some new blood, and Branthor has shadowed me long enough. Let's get a move on before we get noticed." Falric started walking away and Vincent and Alrion followed closely behind.

They headed straight to the stables. A young wizard was waiting there with the horses. Vincent approached the young wizard first.

"Excuse me; I need to send this letter to my wife. I've addressed it appropriately. Can you see that it gets delivered?" Vincent offered the letter. The wizard looked over at Falric.

"It's fine, send a rider to hand deliver it," he said.

"As you wish, we will take care of it," the wizard said. Vincent mounted up, and Alrion and Falric followed. They secured their bags and rode out to the main gate.

"I shall return, with more stories and more knowledge," Falric said, looking back at the academy.

"Do you always say that?" Vincent said.

"Always. It has become a mantra of mine. Always bring something back, to share with the wizards. Not that I leave the academy as much these days." Falric shook his head slightly.

"That's nice. I shall return, with more stories and knowledge," Alrion said.

"I'll see to it," Falric said. Vincent grunted and started to ride. Alrion looked back and thought about how he was leaving before he had even settled in.

"When will I have a new place to call home?" he wondered as he turned his horse and began to ride.

12

PASSAGE TO THE MOUNTAIN

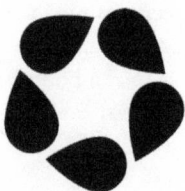

They started slowly, leaving the academy at a stately pace, but gradually increased their speed as they traversed the woods and reached bigger and bigger roads. Once they were back on the main road, Vincent nudged his horse closer to Falric.

"Where are we heading?" he said.

"To the Pool of Knowledge, of course," Falric said.

"I got that bit. But where is it?"

"I have been charged with keeping the location secret." Falric tilted his head down and looked at Vincent with a serious gaze.

"Can you at least tell me what area we are heading to?"

"A place near Mirror Lake."

"I see." Vincent paused and looked thoughtful, "So then, we will want to be heading to Altarbright?"

"Yes. But that's all you will get out of me."

"That's fine. In fact, I even know a shortcut."

"I'm all ears, although in my experience you never save time with a shortcut." Falric grinned at Alrion.

"It's certainly a concern. But this one is on the way, so it's low risk."

"What are you proposing?"

"We use the tunnel underneath the Thundering Mountain." Vincent carefully watched Falric's reaction.

Falric doesn't seem happy with that suggestion, Alrion thought.

"Hmm. I have heard of it, but a long time ago. Is it still in use?" Falric's voice had a doubtful tilt to it.

"I'm not sure, it's been a while. But it cuts days off the journey if it works."

"I will defer to your judgement in this case. As you said, it is on the way, so we can investigate and make a call." Falric still didn't look confident.

"Excellent," Vincent said. Alrion waited for a moment to ensure the conversation was concluded.

"Falric, I have something I wanted to ask. Why is it that all wizards are male?"

"Excellent question. One that I often wonder myself. The truth is we don't know exactly. But I can explain the main reason. Do you remember the pillars of magic that I mentioned before?"

"Yes. Knowledge, Will, and Spark." Alrion recounted them without hesitation.

"Excellent. Well, you no doubt remember, that which sets the wizard apart in the true mastery of magic is the Spark. However, women do not have it."

"Women don't have the Spark?"

"No. I don't understand the reasoning or detail behind it. But without the Spark, they cannot be wizards." Falric shrugged.

"But they can still use magic?"

"Of course, like any other, if they lean on the other pillars of Knowledge and Will they can do many things. But they cannot be a wizard."

"Seems odd."

"Certainly. There is still a lot we don't understand. I hope that answers your question."

"It does, well at face value." Alrion was beginning to realise that there were a lot of unanswered questions.

"Good. With a healthy curiosity, I expect you will do quite well as a wizard. It is only in more recent times with the establishment of the academy that we have built up a good body of knowledge about magic." Falric was lost in thought and shook his head. "In the past, the knowledge and practices were quite dispersed. There were fine wizards, but they kept many secrets to themselves, and only had one or two apprentices, who didn't even learn everything their masters knew. So much was lost." Falric sighed.

"Your grandfather had the foresight and desire to do better than that."

Alrion took in the information with interest. There was certainly a lot more that he needed to learn about magic. As they rode further along the road, they approached another wooded area.

"If I remember correctly, this forest is the best place to stop for the night, even though it is a little early," Vincent said.

"Correct. I believe the vegetation becomes quite sparse if we push on much further, and the area is very open and exposed. Stopping early suits me actually. I'd like to work on something with Alrion," Falric said.

"I'll keep my eyes out for a spot then." Vincent brought his horse to a slow clip, then stopped. To the side of the path nestled a small clearing, sheltered by a nearby hill.

Vincent busied himself getting the horses settled and comfortable, and setting up camp. Falric and Alrion walked deeper into the forest. Falric spotted a chunky log and sat down, asking Alrion to join him.

"This is as good a spot as any. Normally you would be learning a few books worth of theory and demonstration, but I think we need to start with something useful. Today we are going to work on your first spell," Falric said.

"Sounds great." Alrion ignored the uneasiness in his stomach and focused on the excitement.

"I like your enthusiasm. What we are starting with is by no means the simplest, but it has so many applications and is a good representation of the basics of magic."

"What is it? A fireball?"

"Not quite. I may be accelerating things somewhat, but I'm not looking to invite disaster! No, Alrion, we will be starting with a push spell."

"Push? Like pushing things around?" Alrion made a pushing motion with his hand.

"Exactly. This spell draws on all three pillars of magic. However, interestingly enough, it can be performed with only one given the right amount of training. Care to guess which?"

"Hmm, I'll say Spark."

"Interesting answer, but incorrect. It is actually Will."

"Will?"

"Yes, there are people who with the force of their Will alone can push objects around."

"Wouldn't they also need Knowledge?"

"No, although it is a useful component. There are accounts of people who moved things purely with the power of their Will and no knowledge that it was even possible." Falric smiled.

"That's crazy." Alrion shook his head slowly. There really was another world out there that he had no idea about.

"It sounds a bit crazy, doesn't it? However, the reality is that many things in our world are there to be manipulated in interesting ways, even if you don't realise it. Do you see why we harp on about knowledge so much?"

"Yes. The more you know about what's possible, the more you can do."

"Exactly. Part of the lesson here has already begun. I have told you that it is possible, and that you can do it without being a wizard, and without even knowing that it can be done. That is the most basic level of knowledge."

"Alright." Alrion nodded along. However, he was doubtful that he would be able to do this.

"There is a lot more that I can tell you, and we'll get to that, but let's move on.

The main component to this is your Will. You need to focus the strength of your mind and resolve to overcome the laws of nature. You can compel an object to move. We won't get into the nitty-gritty details of how it actually moves."

"What are we using? What am I moving?"

"Let's start simple." Falric hunted around and placed a small stone on the edge of a nearby tree branch. It was a low hanging branch, around Alrion's head height while seated.

"You are going to push that stone off that branch. I've placed it within an easy gaze, so you can easily focus on it."

"Sure." Alrion started sizing up the task.

"What you will need to do in your mind is to will that stone to move just enough that it topples off the branch."

"I'm not sure that I know how to will things to move," Alrion said. Falric laughed.

"It takes practice. To start with, you need to think about it moving. But not the passive, intellectual type of thinking. A more direct thought. Like you are imposing your Will upon the rock."

"Should I try?"

"A little bit, just practice thinking about it," Falric said. Alrion turned back to face the stone and stared at it. He thought about the stone moving, and how he could push it. He visualised it falling. He continued the effort for a good thirty seconds.

"OK, that's a good start. Take a break," Falric said. Alrion sat back and visibly relaxed.

"Now that's just the mental part, which is absolutely necessary. The next component to help us out is to draw on your Spark."

"How do I do that?"

"This is a little more abstract. Your Spark is what you drew on when you lit the lamp and caused the light show at the academy. It is your source of power. To be philosophical, the Spark ignites your Will. If your Will is a wind of change, then your Spark ignites it into a rolling flame. It feeds on, and amplifies, whatever you apply it to." Falric waved his hands in a dramatic flourish.

"I see, so it's in a way a source of fuel."

"That's a good way of looking at it. Maybe your Will isn't targeted well or imposing enough to move that rock. But if you draw upon your Spark, you can compensate and send that rock away." Falric mimicked the stone flying off the tree branch. Alrion nodded.

"I get it. However, I just don't understand how you draw upon it. I didn't do anything those other two times."

"Each person is unique, and the exact trigger to draw upon their Spark is also different, but the mechanism is always the same. You must see the internal power that is within you, and draw it out. Open it up, or even let it loose, but you must be careful because without the right safeguards unforeseen things can occur." Falric gave Alrion a knowing look, and he picked up on it.

"Like burning the roof of my dad's workshop?"

"Exactly. So, let's give it a try again. Start as before with your thoughts, and once you feel like you are ready, see if you can draw upon your Spark to amplify the effect," Falric said. Alrion looked back at the stone and started up again.

He thought about the stone, and the force required to move it. He thought about how the stone was just teetering on the branch, and that it just needed a nudge to get it moving. He intensified his concentration and focused on the thought. He pushed everything else away. It was as if he was floating above the stone, leaning against it with all his might. It started to move, and rock back and forth in its position. As if it was under a force but resisting. Alrion kept up his focus but he needed something more, it wasn't moving.

He looked inside himself, and his focus dropped a little. He got annoyed that such a tiny stone on such a thin branch could be so solid. He felt the frustration that it wouldn't move. That his Will wasn't strong enough, and he felt a heat within him, a fire burning hotter and hotter. He opened the door to that place, and the fire leaped out and consumed him. The stone stopped rocking and flew at great speed into a nearby tree with a gigantic 'thunk' and the resulting disturbance echoed through the forest like a shockwave.

Alrion stood up swiftly, a stunned look on his face. He walked over and inspected the stone. It was embedded in the tree trunk; scorch marks around it showed the size of the impact.

"Take it," Falric said. Alrion removed the stone and held it in his hand. It was a little warm to the touch.

"I did that?" Alrion looked at the stone and then back at the branch.

"You sure did. You used your Spark, didn't you?" Falric had a knowing smile.

"Yes, I could feel it coming through, but it was wild and uncontrolled. I think my anger and frustration fuelled it."

"That's very honest of you, and perceptive. Yes, it is quite common for those kinds of feelings to draw upon your Spark. But as you grow, you will get better at harnessing it at will."

"That sounds better. It was so strange, though, like the stone was waiting for that extra push."

"I have a small confession to make." Falric had a guilty smile, and he beamed it at Alrion.

"What?"

"I was holding the stone there, so it didn't fall off by itself."

"What!"

"And I wanted to give you a reason to dig deeper."

"Unbelievable!" Alrion swore under his breath, "Why didn't you pick a bigger rock then?"

"Because I needed you to believe that it was an achievable task. The stone sure looked precarious the way it was balancing on that branch didn't it?" Falric chuckled with warmth and looked directly at Alrion. The young wizard went quiet, thinking it over.

"I see why you did that. Pretty clever." Alrion sighed. He had been played with, but Falric had come through.

"Well, I've done this a few times you know," Falric said with a confident smile. Alrion heard footsteps and turned to face them.

"What's all this racket?" Vincent said.

"Alrion used a spell to send a stone flying into that tree." Falric pointed and Vincent walked over immediately. He stopped and assessed the mark.

"This looks pretty nasty. Alrion, you did this?"

"Surprisingly, yes."

"Well, maybe you'll be protecting me pretty soon."

"That's the plan," Falric said. Alrion had a smile creep onto his face.

"It's a fantastic first effort, but there's much more to be learned," Falric said.

"I know. I don't think I could do that on the spot if I had to," Alrion said.

"That's quite alright, it will come with time." Falric walked over and slapped Alrion on the back.

"Food is ready if you've worked up an appetite," Vincent said.

"Definitely." Alrion rubbed his back and stretched his legs.

"That's enough for now, let's go eat," Falric said. They walked back to their camp and ate a simple meal of bread and cheese.

"So how was your first lesson?" Falric said once the food was finished.

"Unexpected, but I'm excited to learn more. The possibilities seem endless." Alrion felt energised, once he was over the initial shock of it all.

"That's the right attitude but remember that you must use caution and care. From now on, you have incredible potential and power, but that also means that you must act with responsibility. The consequences are significant."

"I understand," Alrion said. After more general conversation, they turned in for the night. Alrion had trouble sleeping. The world of magic had taken his mind by storm, and his mind was racing with ideas.

The next morning, they had a quick snack and packed up. The horses were keen to get moving, so Vincent suggested they make a start sooner rather than later. Within an hour of riding, they passed through the end of the forest and re-joined the main road.

"So where to next?" Alrion said.

"Wait just a moment," Vincent said. Alrion was curious but played along. The road was still flanked by tall trees, but they were riding into a flatter, clearer area. Once they emerged from the trees, a completely different landscape awaited them.

"They call that the Thundering Mountain," Vincent said. Far in the distance, they could see a large mountain rising above the landscape. It was tall and imposing, and clouds surrounded its peak.

"Is the weather always that bad? It's like the clouds are anchored to that spot." Alrion said.

"Yes, that's how it was named. There are rumours and legends as to what is on the peak that is attracting all those clouds and storms. But nobody knows," Falric said.

"Could just be a freak weather formation," Vincent said.

"Either way, that's pretty impressive." Alrion couldn't take his eyes off it.

"It's where we will be heading today. Hopefully, it won't take too long, I'd like to investigate the tunnel below it before it gets too late." Vincent kicked his horse back into a faster gallop, and the others followed suit.

I've never seen anything that big. It's massive, Alrion thought as they rode. It felt like for the first time, the adventure was starting to feel real. He had goosebumps on his arms at the thought of exploring the mountain. He cautiously looked at both his father and Falric. Neither seemed to have noticed his excitement. They were focused on other things.

13

A DISTURBANCE

The lushness of the forest they had recently left faded gradually. At first, Alrion didn't really notice any change, but after a time he realised that something had changed. After a more focused look at the countryside, he concluded that the vegetation was dead or dying.

"This area looks different, less alive."

"You have good instincts. I've noticed as well. Not as many signs of wildlife either," Vincent said.

"I haven't been through here for a long time, how about you?" Falric asked.

"No. There should be a town up ahead before the mountain, though. A good community there of hardworking people. I'm a good friend with the blacksmith there. A man called Malcolm."

"I'll be interested in talking with him, to see if he has any information about what's been happening in this area. It's probably nothing, but it just seems so different." Falric had a worried look on his face. Vincent grunted his agreement. Alrion was pleased that he had picked up on something of note.

Every time he looked up at the mountain, it seemed to be the same distance away. But when he took the time to really look at it, and compare to other landmarks, he could tell that they were getting closer. With the comments made by Falric and his father, the mystery surrounding the mountain was even deeper now.

As noon approached, they started to see signs of the town ahead. There were a few abandoned carts on the side of the road and weathered signposts.

"These seem to have been here for a while," Vincent said.

"Agreed," Falric said. They rode on. Houses and other buildings were visible in the distance.

"Usually there would be a bit of traffic on the road at this time," Vincent said, mostly to himself. They continued. Alrion could feel the difference, between this place and his hometown. The feeling of life was not present, but he told himself that he was getting ahead of things, that he knew his own home so well that it skewed his expectations. Once they were closer to entering the town, Falric finally spoke.

"I think it's deserted."

"Are you sure?" Vincent seemed anxious.

"I can't sense any people within. It's also uncommonly quiet." Falric closed his eyes and concentrated

"Too quiet." Vincent swept his gaze back and forth. Alrion didn't say a word but just listened carefully. It was true that the normal sounds you expect; of work being done, of people and animals were missing. It just sounded empty.

They slowed the horses, making the final approach at a gentle clip. Their reduced speed increased the tension for Alrion. He didn't know what was going to happen next. As they passed through the town gates they got a better look at the buildings and the main street. Alrion read the sign.

"Welcome to Hopetarn," he said. There were no signs of life or recent habitation whatsoever.

"Certainly looks empty," Vincent said.

"There's an inn." Alrion pointed it out. A sign for *The Titanic Tankard* gently swung in the wind, squeaking as it went.

"If there's life, it'll be with the booze," Falric said with a chuckle.

"Truer words were never spoken." Vincent spurred his horse forward, heading directly for the inn.

"Let's just tie the horses out front." He stopped and dismounted, leading by example. Once the horses were secured Vincent stepped up to the entrance.

"Let's see what's in store for us." He pushed the main door open and entered the building. Falric and Alrion kept close behind. It was dark inside, the stench of rotting food hitting Alrion's nose before he could become accustomed to the low light.

"Something's off," Vincent said.

"Here." Falric raised his hand. An orb of light materialised above it and slowly floated up until it reached the ceiling.

"More warning next time," Vincent said as he shielded himself from the bright light. Alrion shied back too, surprised by the sudden brightness. Once his eyes had adjusted, he got a good look at the room. There were rows of wooden tables and benches and a bar up one end. Food was left on most tables, which was probably the source of the smell. Vincent walked over to the bar to inspect it. He turned one of the taps behind the bar and beer flowed out.

"Interesting," he said.

"Looks like they left in a hurry. Or had no form of transportation," Falric said.

"Why do you say that?" Alrion was curious how he had come to such a precise conclusion.

"The food mess. That shows that they didn't intend on coming back. Or couldn't think about that. Leaving kegs full of beer, now that's an unusual situation. I would expect either the people leaving or any people attacking the place to take it with them." Falric looked to Vincent.

"I agree, nothing raises morale like a drink or two. It was obviously considered unnecessary in the rush," he said. Alrion maintained a blank stare.

"You never liked the taste, so you wouldn't understand." Vincent laughed.

"Alrion and I will look around here if you want to take upstairs." Falric gestured to the staircase.

"Sure." Vincent strode forward with confidence, but kept his hand on the hilt of his sword.

"What are we looking for?" Alrion said.

"Anything of note. We want to work out why the people left."

"Why is it important? Maybe they just wanted to move on."

"This used to be a prosperous town with a long history. People wouldn't leave without a good reason, and nobody has come back. That's what it looks like. Let's see what we can find."

"You think there's some potential danger around here and it forced them to leave."

"Exactly. This kind of evacuation shouldn't be happening around here. Avaria is a very safe place. See what you can turn up." Falric started by looking behind the bar. Alrion wandered the room. He turned over some chairs that had been knocked over and inspected the food that was left. But he didn't find any personal belongings.

"I don't really see anything," Alrion said after a few minutes.

"Nothing special behind the bar either. We'll see what your father says."

"Not much to report." Vincent descended the staircase.

"Abandoned at seemingly short notice?" Falric said.

"That's my assessment. Did you find anything here?"

"Just something for the road." Falric held up a metal flask and wiggled it.

"At least we can leave with something. I'd like to get out of here immediately, the stench is terrible." Vincent headed directly for the door and Alrion followed without argument.

"Any ideas on what happened?" Falric said once he was outside.

"Not really, but I want to check out the blacksmith."

"Sure, lead the way," Falric said. Vincent started untying the horses.

"Did you know him well?" Alrion said as they walked with the horses.

"The blacksmith? I used to, but we lost touch a while ago."

"What was he like?"

"An orderly man. Had everything in the right place, and a good system for running his shop. I definitely learned some things from his approach." A smile crept to Vincent's face as he looked in the distance, like he was remembering something.

"What do you think we will find at his shop?"

"Well, I don't know yet. But I understood him well, so whatever condition the shop is in should be very telling," Vincent said. No more was said until they arrived at the blacksmith workshop. It had no name, just a sign with an anvil on it. Vincent tied up the horses and was the first to enter the shop.

It looked like a scene frozen in time. A piece of iron sat idly on the table, with a hammer next to it. Other items were out, but most were tucked neatly away.

"He was making a sword." Vincent walked through, letting his hand linger on some surfaces or tools as he went, "Look at this. I told you he was organised. Only the parts he needed were out, everything else is packed away."

"Well, there's definitely a pattern. People left suddenly. How long ago do you think?" Falric said.

"Judging by the rust, and the decay we spotted at the tavern I'd say recently. Days or a week at most," Vincent said.

"That seems plausible. However, there's no evidence of what made them leave. I didn't notice any signs of attack," Falric said.

"Attack by what?" Alrion said. His heart started to race, and he looked at Falric.

"Could be any number of things. Perhaps even Blighters," the master wizard said.

"Let's not get ahead of ourselves. Why don't we rest here and eat, then we can move on and leave this ghost town behind us," Vincent said.

"Sure," Falric said.

"C'mon, Alrion." Vincent walked outside, holding the door open. Alrion helped him bring in some food, and move some stools so they could all sit around one of the workbenches.

"I can't believe I'm already back in a blacksmith workshop," Alrion said, trying to lighten the mood.

"You can't escape your destiny." Vincent chuckled.

"So it would seem. What do we do next?" Alrion said.

"Before we move on, I want you to practice your push spell again," Falric said.

"Sure. What do I push?" Alrion looked around the room for another object of similar size to the stone he had moved.

"Let's be careful, after what you did to that tree," Vincent said. Falric laughed.

"How about we use that." Falric walked over and opened the heavy wooden door. He left it at just the right spot that it caught on the floor and held itself open.

"This should be simple. Just close the door."

"It looks a lot heavier than the stone," Alrion said.

"Doesn't matter, you'll be fine. Just remember the process. Feel the thought in your mind, apply it to the door, and amplify it if required," Falric said. Alrion nodded and closed his eyes.

"Eyes open. You need to see your target," Falric said. Alrion opened them and stared at the door. It seemed harder to focus his mind with all the distraction of what he could see. But he managed to push his thoughts aside and focus on the door. He imagined the force building up, ready to slam the door shut. He imagined the door slamming in his mind; saw the splinters of wood flying out with the force. Then he applied that thought to the door. He could feel its resistance.

He wondered if Falric was playing games with him again, keeping the door in place. He got annoyed at the possibility that Falric was interfering.

He can't just leave things alone.

Alrion drew upon his annoyance and fanned the flame. He drew out a heat from within and forced it against the door, propping up his will and mental image. The door wobbled slightly then slammed shut, splinters of wood spraying out from the impact. Just as he had imagined.

"How strange," Alrion said.

"In what way?" Falric said.

"I imagined what it would look like when the door slammed, and it looked exactly the same when it happened."

"Of course, you imposed your Will on the door."

"Really?"

"Yes. Well, it's a bit of give and take. You understood the possible reaction from slamming the door, then you made it happen."

"But that literally?"

"They don't call it magic for no reason," Falric said.

"Nice job." Vincent walked over to the door and yanked it open, "That was shut pretty tight."

"Of course," Alrion said, delighted.

"Very good progress. You have the basics there, now we need to work on your control and speed. Eventually, a push will be as effortless as the thought required to dream it up."

"That sounds crazy, the potential. How do you just not push everything constantly?" Alrion said.

"The novelty does wear off, but there is also a price for everything and a balance. Every action has a reaction and consequences. This you will learn," Falric said.

"Alright." Alrion started looking around at the room for other things that he could push.

"Don't even think about it," Vincent said, catching Alrion's intention. Alrion shrugged and stood up.

"Let's head off then. I'm still keen to investigate the mountain," Vincent said.

"Even after what we observed here?" Falric said.

"More so. I'm concerned about what has happened, and also quite motivated to avoid the forest if at all possible." Vincent's face was grim.

He seems quite concerned. About a forest?

"Well it isn't far, and we can be safe about it. Let's head to the mountain and see if your shortcut is available," Falric said.

"Fingers crossed." Vincent stepped outside and started moving quickly.

They rode through the town with speed. Now that they were used to it, the eerie quiet was less disconcerting, but still as unexplainable. Alrion found the experience quite strange. A town full of all the things he expected, except any signs of life. Soon they had reached the town limits and joined another main road. Alrion looked up and the mountain loomed larger still.

They rode on in silence, like they were infected with the empty quiet of the town. It felt strange to speak, so Alrion didn't try and break the peace. They passed a less populated area, with evidence of the occasional farm, but it was a lot of nothing. Just a road. Every time he looked up the mountain looked different. It confused him at first, then he had a realisation.

I'm too close, I can't even take in the whole size of it.

"We're almost there." Vincent finally broke the silence.

"What should we expect?" Alrion said.

"The gate to the passage should be open, and there should be two guards posted outside," Vincent said.

"And if there isn't?"

"Then something has changed." Vincent had a grim look on his face.

Maybe the emptiness of Hopetarn has changed his expectations.

"And that's when we become awfully suspicious," Falric said.

"It's hard to see from here, but those are the gates." Vincent pointed to something in the distance. Alrion couldn't really make it out. As they travelled, he looked repeatedly and started to see the distinction.

"They look closed," Alrion said.

"Not a good start," Falric said.

"We'll see." Vincent's voice was tight, and he nudged his horse to pick up speed. The light was starting to fade and soon he was riding hard to reach the gate. As soon as he arrived he tied his horse to a nearby post and started investigating. Alrion and Falric caught up and waited on horseback. The gates were massive, the frames built from giant steel bars. They were easily big enough for five men to enter at once.

"What's your assessment?" Falric said.

"The gate is closed, but not locked." Vincent demonstrated by pushing on the door. It started to open, but all that was inside was darkness.

"Doesn't look good." Alrion surprised himself with those words. They had leapt unbidden to his mouth.

"Agreed. Are we sure about this?" Falric looked at Vincent with uncertainty.

"We have to try. The alternative is much longer and more dangerous," Vincent said.

"As you wish. Keep your wits about you." Falric dismounted and directed Alrion to do the same.

What are we getting ourselves into? Alrion thought with a sigh.

14

INSIDE THE MOUNTAIN

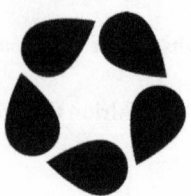

Vincent leaned heavily on the doors and they slowly swung completely open. The light from outside did little to penetrate the darkness.

"The horses will be spooked," he said.

"I'll provide light." Falric conjured up a ball of light and held it in front of him, "Follow me."

Alrion looked around at the passage. It was carved into the stone, with strong square lines.

"I think there are torches along the wall." He pointed them out.

"Well spotted, let's try this." Falric walked over to one of the torches, and his ball of light morphed into a dancing flame. He lit the torch and it illuminated the area.

"Not bad," Vincent said.

"Just the one?" Alrion said. Falric looked at Vincent, then Alrion, then waved his arm dramatically. The flame from the lit torch leapt to the nearest torch, lighting it as well. With another wave of his arm, it set off again, the flame rippling along all the torches lighting them as far as they could see.

"Much more convenient. So dramatic, though." Vincent sighed.

"I think he meant to say that was amazing," Alrion said. Falric smiled at him.

"Thank you. Let's just say it was a combination of showing you what's possible, making our lives a bit easier, and squeezing in a bit of fun too. That's allowed, right?"

"Fine by me," Alrion said.

"Now that we can see, I'll take the lead. Alrion you take care of the horses." Vincent rushed forward without waiting for a response. Alrion took all the reins for the horses and started slowly from the rear. Falric kept up pace with Vincent, staying only a few steps behind.

With the improved lighting, Alrion could see the detail on the walls. They were actually quite sparse, the same strong but basic construction as used on the door.

"What did they use this path for?"

"Mostly trade, but also normal travellers. It was the preferred route to get to Altarbright, but it doesn't appear to be in use right now. And I'm not sure how long it has been left," Vincent said.

"Does that make it safer?" Alrion said.

"Potentially." Vincent sounded unconvinced, but didn't offer any other details.

There's something he's not saying but I won't push the issue, Alrion thought and decided to keep his eyes open. The path was sloping down gently, the walls the same stark blandness.

"It was so different before. You didn't notice how plain the whole thing was, because of all the life that was flowing through," Vincent said.

"I was just thinking that there's no decoration at all."

"Exactly. Probably more due to the utility of the path than anything else. I think it was used as soon as it was completed."

"Are there any kinds of animals that live underground that we may find?"

"Generally, yes, but I'd be surprised if we did," Vincent said. Falric stopped walking and within seconds Vincent stopped too.

"What is it?" he said to the wizard.

"I feel like something is off. Just a feeling, though, it's not based on anything," Falric said.

"Firm enough to turn back?" Vincent glanced back at the way they had come.

"Not sure, we have come a fair way already. We should continue. Turning back is always an option if things change," Falric said.

"Sure, let's just take care." Vincent resumed his position out front and looked even more alert. As they progressed, he pointed out odd pieces of furniture, sometimes a table, or a wooden chair, strewn about.

"They had vendors with sales tables here to tempt the passing traffic," Vincent said.

"Again, deserted," Alrion said.

"Certainly a theme, my guess is that we will discover something here," Falric said. Vincent pushed on, staying a few lengths in front of them. Falric seemed intent on figuring out whatever in the distance had made him unsettled. Alrion himself couldn't pay much attention, he was lagging behind, struggling to handle the three horses.

"Now we're getting somewhere." Vincent stopped next to a structure built into the tunnel, with a large gate and a small building to the side. Alrion looked up to properly take it in. It looked like a checkpoint or outpost of some kind.

"Is this empty too?" he said.

"I'd say so, but there should be some books here or logs or something. This was a checkpoint with more security. I think at one stage they even charged a toll here." Vincent entered the structure and began looking around. Falric paused and started peering into the darkness ahead of them, focused on something.

"What is it?" Alrion asked. He could sense that Falric was concerned. Alrion also felt a sense of unease that he couldn't place. Falric didn't respond, but closed his eyes and put his head down. He seemed to be concentrating intensely.

"Vincent, come back and protect the horses," Falric shouted. Vincent immediately ran out of the building, confusion on his face, but after a brief pause, he continued over to stand by Alrion.

"What's the problem?" he said.

"Blighters." Falric stepped forward.

Vincent drew his sword and moved behind the horses, protecting them from the rear.

"Stay in the middle and try and keep them from bolting," he said to Alrion.

"Sure." Alrion wanted to ask more but sensed the urgency of the situation.

"Time for some fireworks." Falric conjured a ball of fire in his hands. The dancing flames lit the path ahead even more, and Alrion at last understood what was coming. He saw a horde of ashen-skinned people, hunched over, and running on all their limbs. He couldn't make out their faces but heard their grunts and cries. Once they closed in, Falric let loose.

A wave of fire cascaded out from his hands, sweeping over the first row of Blighters. They screamed in pain and fell down. Alrion had to fight the urge to block his ears. He turned back to look behind him and saw his father swinging his sword.

Vincent cut with finesse and efficiency, each strike moving into the next. He was dispatching the Blighters in one or two attacks, making a concerted effort to keep them from advancing.

"Tell Falric we need a plan. We don't know how many there are, and I can't see an end to them. We can't keep fighting them on both sides," Vincent said.

"Got it." Alrion carefully walked the horses over a bit further and called out to Falric.

"What do we do? We need a way to fight them smarter, their numbers are too great!"

"Use your head," Falric said, focusing on his fire waves. Alrion looked at the environment trying to come up with a plan. He noticed a support beam for the checkpoint building that looked unsteady. Maybe if he could dislodge it, that would cause a diversion or at least reduce the space the Blighters had to attack.

It's my only option, I have to try.

He kept his eye on the beam and started to focus. All he had to do was push it enough to move or break it, and the weight of the structure would do the rest. He focused his will, as before, but trying to ignore the chaos around him. He got annoyed at how slow he was, right when the situation was urgent. And found a way to draw upon his inner power. As he was about to release it, something jumped into his peripheral vision.

"Incoming!" Falric shouted. A burned but not beaten Blighter was heading right for Alrion. He froze. *What am I supposed to do?*

"PUSH!" Falric yelled out. Alrion didn't even think, he just acted. He pushed the Blighter with all the force he had been accumulating. Unlike before, it happened immediately. The Blighter flew back with incredible speed, a stunned look on its face. But there was a problem. It was heading right for Falric.

"Look out!" Alrion yelled. Falric turned in time to see what was happening and managed to push the Blighter enough to alter its trajectory. It slammed into the building next to the checkpoint.

Great, I saved myself but ruined the opportunity and put Falric in danger.

Falric had exposed himself by pushing away the Blighter thrown at him. Another blighter took advantage and tried to bite him. The master wizard frantically threw a fireball at close range, charring the Blighter instantly and sending the body flying. But the power with which he unleashed the fireball did not stop at one Blighter.

It blossomed out, killing the rest within range and consuming the checkpoint and nearby building. It could not withstand the resultant force and heat and started to collapse.

"Get back!" Falric cried out and he turned to run. Alrion could say nothing, but turned and tried to get the horses moving once more. They were frozen still with fear, and took a lot of encouragement. Vincent increased the intensity of his attacks in an effort to push the Blighters back. The checkpoint building slammed to the ground with a great crash, blocking the path and any Blighters behind.

"That's one problem solved," Falric said. As he finished speaking a rumbling sound echoed above them.

"That could be another one," Alrion said. Falric stepped past the young wizard and stood next to Vincent, shooting streaks of fiery death at the Blighters in the rows behind. With the two of them working tirelessly, they pushed their way forward, the Blighters unable to stand up to the combined onslaught.

We might just survive this, if the tunnel doesn't collapse on us first.

Alrion followed as close as he could. He watched on in awe, seeing a side of his father that he never expected. Vincent had always been a peaceful man, working hard at the forge and supporting his family. Alrion had no idea that he was so proficient with a sword and so fearless.

Falric, too, was impressive. The Blighters pushed on and on, but the two men slashed and blasted them down as soon as they emerged.

"Where are they all coming from?" Vincent said. Alrion had no idea. On their way in they had passed no other tunnels or structures that could hold anything. He concentrated on keeping the horses under control and looked forward and back to gauge the potential dangers from the Blighters and the stability of the tunnel.

Suddenly, the stream of Blighters ended. Vincent and Falric stopped and waited. There was quiet. No more snarling or yelling. But they couldn't escape the mess of bodies and the smell of burned flesh.

"I think the path is clear, let's leave," Vincent said. Alrion nodded.

I need to get out of here as soon as possible.

He followed along as best he could, assisting the horses through.

They trudged back, away from the battle scene and back to the entrance. Alrion could smell the fresher air and knew they were close. With each step, he relaxed a bit more and could feel the horses relax too. He pushed harder and harder for the exit, feeling so enclosed by the tunnel and the battle they had just experienced.

"And here we are," Vincent said. The giant doors were wide open.

"Wait," Vincent said before anyone could move. Alrion stopped, holding the horses still. Vincent knelt to the ground and looked carefully.

"I think there are tracks. Can you do something with those Falric?"

"With magic? Not really. I'm afraid old-fashioned tracking is the way to go here."

"Hold up and let me see if I can follow them," Vincent said. Alrion kept the horses inside the tunnel and Falric stood by his side. They watched Vincent work. He stalked along, keeping a close eye on the ground and kneeling down on occasion to have a closer look. Soon he had disappeared around a corner.

"Sorry about back there," Alrion said.

"For what?" Falric gave the young wizard a questioning look.

"I almost hit you." Alrion felt so embarrassed, but Falric's face relaxed.

"Never mind that, the important thing is that we are all safe."

"But still ..."

"Listen carefully. You are still new at this, but you reacted well and protected yourself. That is the most important thing. You must never let yourself be infected by the Blight," Falric said. Alrion was about to respond but saw his father returning.

"Do you want the good news or the bad news?" Vincent said.

"Let's have some good news," Falric said.

"I was able to follow the tracks well enough to see where they came from. The sheer volume of Blighters made it relatively easy, even for a novice such as me."

"Great, so what's the bad news?"

"The tracks lead into the forest."

"Oh, I see," Falric said.

"What's the significance of that?" Alrion said.

"Now that the tunnel is closed, the forest is our only option. Even without the threat of Blighters, your father wanted to avoid it. And if the Blighters came from there, we could be in for far more trouble." Falric cradled his chin with his thumb and index finger and looked off into the distance.

"Which forest? You've mentioned it a few times," Alrion said

"The Whispering Forest." Falric's concern was clearly evident.

They left the tunnel and Alrion looked back.

Why did you have to screw up and cause all these problems?

He looked at both his father and Falric and could feel the tension. They also looked a bit shaken by the attack, and Alrion could tell that something was very wrong about the forest they were about to enter. There had to be a reason that his father was so adamant that they try the tunnel first.

"You'll have to tell me about this forest." Alrion mounted up and prepared to ride.

15

A NEW PATH

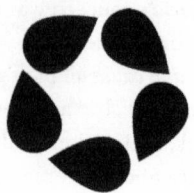

"The Whispering Forest is called that, because of what you hear within," Falric said as they rode.

"Whispering?" Alrion said.

"Exactly. It's probably something to do with the trees and the wind patterns, but the whispering sound is unmistakable. Of course, many believe that the forest is haunted and steer clear. The fact that there are many recorded cases of people disappearing within the forest keeps these beliefs going."

"Haunted? By ghosts?" Alrion wasn't sure he believed in that. The Blighters were one thing, but ghosts were something else.

"That's what the stories say. Visibility is also very poor, there seems to be a mist that hangs over the place. It would be a place ripe for theft or kidnapping, but most people avoid it."

"Maybe not as many avoid it now since the tunnel under the mountain was abandoned," Alrion said.

"You're probably right about that. I guess we shall see who we encounter," Vincent said, joining the conversation.

"Speaking of that, maybe you can tell me more about those creatures we fought. Blighters?" Alrion said. Falric nodded and prepared to explain.

"A Blighter is a person, or was a person, that has been tainted by the Blight. But more than tainted, transformed. Your grandfather studied them closely, and could not ascertain if the person still existed within. Their skin is darker, a greyish hue, and they stoop and often travel on hands and feet. As you saw."

"Why do they act like that?" Alrion said.

"It's a good question. The best theory is that the Blight changes them somehow, to a more animalistic state. They don't appear to have any leaders among them but do travel in packs. We believe there's some sort of shared consciousness or communication going on."

"What do they do? What's their goal?"

"I'm not sure they have one. If they do, it's to attack people. They can infect you with the Blight, which as I mentioned is something you absolutely must avoid as a wizard."

"Is it worse for wizards?" Alrion couldn't imagine what would be worse than transforming into a Blighter.

"The Blight reacts differently to a wizard. It corrupts their Spark. As you know, the Spark is the inner power of a wizard that makes them unique. Imagine instead of that fire you have within you, it was a lump of tar, which pulsed with a power that sickened you," Falric said.

"That's horrible."

"Yes. It would affect you in many different ways, the most obvious being that you would be unable to use your Spark in the normal way. The wizards that tried, well each spell they cast became corrupted. Usually, in ways they did not anticipate. And it hastened their transformation." Falric grew very quiet.

"You sold me on not getting infected." Alrion felt a cold shiver run down his spine.

"Good. You must avoid that at all costs. The fact that we were attacked by such a large contingent of them is concerning. Was it pure chance that they were here, or are we being targeted?" Falric said.

"A good question. We need to know," Vincent said.

"I'll think about it. However, I fear there's too little information right now to know for sure. The evacuation of Hopetarn and that mass of Blighters are likely related." Falric seemed lost in his thoughts. Alrion looked up and could see the edge of the forest.

A milky haze hung over and permeated the entire place. The trees were impossibly tall and quite narrow but extremely numerous. Their only way in was a dirt path through the middle, wide enough for single file.

"How did they even make a path through there?" Alrion asked.

"Not sure. Maybe nobody ever did?" Falric said.

"The forest is not enchanted, it didn't make the path itself," Vincent said.

"You never know." Falric shrugged.

"You of all people should know," Vincent said to Falric.

"I think you'll find, that the more you learn about the world we live in, the more you realise that there's so much we don't know or understand," Falric said.

"That is a typical wizard answer." Vincent pointed at Falric with his thumb.

"He's right about that. But for the wrong reason," Falric said. Alrion left it at that.

"We'll be in the forest soon, you can draw your own conclusions as to if it is haunted or otherwise," Vincent said.

The entrance to the forest snuck up on them, the mist making the distances harder to judge. Before they knew it, they were surrounded by giant trees. Vincent brought his horse to a halt and the other two followed. They sat in silence for a minute.

This must be for my benefit, Alrion thought. He listened out and concentrated on the sounds of the forest. He could hear the wind swirling through the trees and the sounds of wood moving. He couldn't hear much in the way of animals, though, it was quiet.

"Alllllllllllllrionnnnnnnnnnn," the faintest of whispers said. Alrion jumped with surprise, almost falling out of the saddle.

"Did you hear that?" he said.

"Hear what? The trees?" Vincent said.

"They whispered my name."

"Don't be silly, you're imagining that," Vincent said. Falric gave Alrion a curious look.

"I think the jury is out. Let's get a move on and see if you continue to hear it," he said.

"Sure." Alrion didn't trust his voice enough to say more. He was spooked. It was one thing to hear the strange whispers; it was another to hear his name.

Is it just my mind playing tricks on me?

They set off once more, slowly progressing through the forest. The heavy mist reduced visibility, so they took their time navigating the slim path. Vincent was in front, Alrion in the middle and Falric to the rear.

"I feel like I shouldn't be talking here. It's like we are interrupting something," Alrion said.

"Everyone reports feeling uneasy in here. Like they are trespassing. There's a reason I don't slam the door shut on all those theories of haunting. Too much is unexplainable," Falric said.

"Is this feeling the mist? My clothes are sticking to me, but it's so cold." Alrion tried loosening his shirt.

"That's the mist. It keeps the moisture level very high here. Not good for campfires," Vincent said.

"Good point," Alrion said.

"There's a whole host of reasons why people avoid this place. However, we don't have many options. The mountain path is blocked now, and if we went around the forest, it would take days and days. It's not worth it," Vincent said.

"How long will this take?"

"We will have to camp overnight, but we can make it out tomorrow easily."

"That doesn't sound too bad."

"It shouldn't be. Hang on." Vincent slowed his horse and peered into the distance.

"Do you see something up ahead?" Falric said.

"I think so; I can make out a few shapes. Do you think there are people here?"

"There might be. Why don't you investigate, and we will stay further behind?" Falric said.

Vincent set off again, and Alrion waited before continuing.

I hope it's fellow travellers and not more Blighters, Alrion thought. He had seen enough for one day.

~

Vincent waved at them to stop, and dismounted. He slapped his horse and sent it back towards Alrion. Then Vincent proceeded alone and on foot into the mist. He walked with care, each step placed as softly as possible. He was not a hunter or a woodsman, but he could be quiet when he needed to be.

It was hard to make out the shapes ahead, but it looked like two people. Two would be manageable if it turned out they were hostile. As he crept closer, he could start to hear voices.

"This mist is terrible, I can't see anything," a man said.

"Well I told you this would happen, you shouldn't complain," an older man said.

"We had no choice."

"Stop grumbling about it then."

"I'll complain as much as I want," the first voice responded, but was quiet after.

They don't sound particularly dangerous, Vincent thought and continued his approach. As he closed in, he was still at a loss as to who they were. The outlines of the shapes improved, and he could see they were on foot without horses, but no details were clear. He had to make a decision, to slow down progress and try to avoid them, or confront them and travel together.

I'll confront them, and decide based on their reaction. I won't be able to determine much of anything without being right next to them.

Their pace was slow, so he increased his speed and called out once he was almost upon them.

"Hello, friends!" Vincent said. They stopped immediately and turned around.

"Is someone there?" one of the men said.

"Yes, hold still and I'll come closer. Damn this mist," Vincent said.

"You can say that again," the voice said. Vincent continued to approach and finally got a good look at the pair. They were two men, one older and one much younger. They wore simple travelling clothes with no jewellery and sturdy boots.

"I'm Vincent, nice to meet you," he said, holding his hand out to the older man first.

"Fitzgerald, nice to meet you."

"Grant, also nice to meet you," the younger man said.

"What brings you to this awful place?" Vincent said.

"We are merchants. We'll sell anything really. But profits aren't as good, so we're looking to see if we can get new lines from further abroad." Fitzgerald gestured into the distance.

"Heading to Altarbright then?"

"You know it, that's the place to be. You heading there also?" Fitzgerald was studying Vincent carefully.

"Yes. We're so close, yet so far." Vincent threw up his hands, referencing the mist.

"Tell me about it. I've had it up to here with this mist and the strange whispers," Grant said.

"Yeah, I'll be happy to be out of here. You two travel safe," Vincent said.

"Hang on, aren't we going the same way? Why don't you join us? At least we could camp together," Fitzgerald said.

"That sounds reasonable. I came ahead to investigate who was here. Since you two seem like stand-up fellows I'll report back to the others."

"How many others?" Fitzgerald spoke quickly, and a panicked look flashed across his face.

"Just two more. My son and father. Don't go anywhere."

"I feel like we've been doing that all day," Grant muttered. Vincent waved and turned to walk back the way he had come.

Something is up with these two, but I can't put my finger on it.

16

COMPANIONS

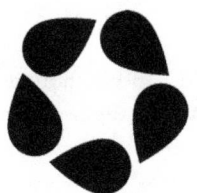

Vincent stepped out of the mist and saw Falric and Alrion staring out at him.

"That took a while," Alrion said.

"I was careful, but I spoke to them," he said.

"Who are they?" Falric said.

"They said they are travellers, going to Altarbright to find new goods to trade with."

"It seems plausible, but why come through here?" Falric said

"Exactly. However, like us, they could be trying to save time. There are not a lot of options."

"What's your gut feeling?" Falric said.

"There's something not quite right but I can't place it. I'm not worried about them, though, they don't seem dangerous," Vincent said.

"I trust your assessment. So, what's the plan?"

"They suggested we camp together. It's not a bad idea, and it would raise suspicion if we said no."

"Why do we care if they are suspicious?" Alrion said.

"If they are a danger, it's better we play along and assess. Disappearing on them may cause them to behave differently and come after us," Falric said.

"Isn't that better than us being right with them?" Alrion's stomach started churning with the thought of another intense encounter.

"Keep your friends close, and your enemies closer," Falric said.

I don't like this.

"I agree. With the narrowness of the path, it would be very hard to pass them and impossible to do so without being noticed. If there is something up, I think we can deal with them easily," Vincent said.

"After seeing you with a sword back there, I'm confident of that," Falric said.

An adventure was supposed to be more fun than wading through hordes of feral creatures and camping with strangers who might want to kill you.

"We'll move ahead then. Don't say anything about your true purpose or mission. I said you were my son and father, so play along with that." Vincent looked at Alrion and then at Falric.

"Sure," Alrion said. He could do this. He wouldn't be the one to hold them back.

"I can play along," Falric said. Vincent mounted his horse and pushed ahead. It didn't take them long to catch up to the two figures on the path.

"Ho, Vincent!" Grant called out.

"I'm here. Proper introductions when we stop for the night," Vincent said.

"Sure thing." Grant started walking again, with Fitzgerald just behind. Vincent had to slow his horse to match their pace.

"No more lessons in the forest, not until we are alone again," Falric said to Alrion.

"I understand." It made sense to be cautious with these strangers, even if his father did not consider them dangerous. Progress was slow, and Alrion found the forest even more intimidating now that they were deep inside it.

I wish I could just spur the horse on and rush out of here.

The swaying of the trees and the whispering sounds were almost hypnotic. Alrion strained to hear the whispering properly, to discern if there were actual words, but unlike earlier, he couldn't quite hear.

Did I imagine the whole thing?

Their pace slowed even more, and Alrion looked around wondering why. However, he saw that the path had opened out into a natural clearing.

"This looks like the camp spot," Vincent said.

"It is the only place so far that has been wider than that narrow path," Falric said.

"The layout of this forest certainly is strange. Bring the horses over here." Vincent pointed and then dismounted. They tied up their horses securely to a tree at the edge of the clearing and grabbed their bags.

"I'll introduce you." Vincent walked over to the two other men, who were busy laying out their own things.

"Looks like a good camp spot," he said.

"Aye, I've been on the lookout all day," Fitzgerald said.

"I'm travelling with my family. This is Falric and this is Alrion."

"Nice to meet you both. I'm Fitzgerald and that's Grant."

"Likewise," Falric said. Alrion nodded but didn't speak up.

"I don't know about you all, but trekking through this forest has worked up my appetite," Grant said.

"I think it's safe to say that we are all starving," Vincent said. Grant laughed and reached into his pack for some food.

"What I wouldn't give for a nice warm cup of tea right now." Grant continued munching on some bread.

"Good luck lighting a fire here. The air feels so damp, I think it would actually be impossible," Vincent said. Falric said nothing.

"Yeah. Water, water everywhere but no way to heat it," Grant said.

"Vincent told us that you were merchants," Falric said.

"That's right. We'll sell anything of value. Used to be raw materials for building. We would link up the quarries and builders or deal with carpenters and tanners and so on. Do the deals that the individual craftsmen wouldn't bother with. But times are changing, and there's not as much construction going on. I blame the peace we have had." Fitzgerald spat out something into the tree line and wiped his face with the back of his hand.

"That's an interesting take on it," Vincent said.

"Yeah, he's right, though. There was a lot of rebuilding to be done due to the Blight. Then there were all the people who flocked here when they heard that Avaria was safe and untainted. But those who could afford to move have done so, and those that can't are stuck," Grant said.

"What are you after now?" Vincent said.

"We don't know. Well, we know we are after a solid earner, but we don't know what it will be." Fitzgerald shrugged.

"I have no idea what we will find. But Altarbright seems to be a good trading hub because of the lake, so maybe we will get some goods from outside Avaria?" Grant looked over at his companion for confirmation.

"Maybe, fingers crossed," Fitzgerald said.

"You've never been to Altarbright?" Vincent said. His eyes darted between the two men, watching their faces.

"No, never needed to venture that far. Have you?" The older man seemed to be challenging Vincent.

"A long time ago, I probably wouldn't recognise the place now." Vincent laughed, but it sounded forced to Alrion.

"Yeah, times change. So, what's your business there, if you don't mind me asking?" Fitzgerald said. Vincent paused for a moment and then replied.

"Nothing as serious as your trip. Wanted to show my son some more of the country before he ends up settling down. It's good to broaden your mind some."

"Great idea, travel is a fantastic way of learning more about the world. But I must ask, why did you come to this awful place?" Grant said.

"Why did you?" Vincent said. Grant licked his lips before he responded.

"We couldn't afford the detour, such a long walk otherwise."

"Same deal." Vincent kept his gaze squarely on Grant. The merchant adjusted his position on the ground.

"I see. Do you believe any of the stories about this place?"

"That it's haunted?"

"Yeah. Every person you talk to has a different theory about why it is so creepy," Grant said.

"I don't believe in that stuff. It's just stories," Vincent said.

"You are probably correct. But I still wonder." Fitzgerald looked over at Falric.

"I must agree that it seems very unlikely that anything untoward is happening in the forest. It is just a process that we don't know or understand that is causing these effects," Falric said.

"I'm starved." Vincent cut off the conversation and rummaged through his pack. He passed bread and cheese to Falric and Alrion who devoured it with gusto. Vincent continue to study their new companions while he ate.

He seems quite suspicious of those two. I can see why, there's something not quite right about them. Alrion noticed his father exchanging a grim look with Falric. They both seemed to be in agreement about the strangers.

"I think it's time to turn in," Vincent said. As they started to prepare for sleep, Fitzgerald approached them.

"Look, I've been polite, but I have to ask. What are wizards doing here?" he said. Vincent whirled around quickly and looked at him with caution.

"What are you talking about?"

"I haven't travelled that widely, but I know a wizard when I see one. Those robes are so distinctive. They may be simple and not flashy, but there's nothing else like them. I'm right, even if you don't admit it," he said. Vincent looked conflicted and didn't reply immediately.

How do we deal with this? Alrion thought.

"How would you know what a wizard looks like?" Falric said, a playful tone to his voice.

"We had some visit the town, so I know."

"Which town?" Falric said.

"You wouldn't have heard of it."

"If I'm a wizard, then wouldn't you expect me to have heard of it? If wizards have visited there?" Falric was giving Fitzgerald an icy stare that was at odds with the friendly tone of his voice.

"No, actually. They stayed and didn't return." Fitzgerald stammered and looked down before meeting Falric's gaze again.

"We found these cloaks abandoned in a town we passed through. If you say they are wizard cloaks, then I guess we should be more careful. Thanks for your concern," Vincent said. Fitzgerald looked at him, then over at Falric. He looked like he was evaluating his next move.

"Well glad I could be of help and apologies for any misunderstanding. I think it is time for us to retire, so have a good night and we shall see you in the morning." Fitzgerald turned and walked back to the other end of the clearing, helping Grant get their bedrolls laid out. Vincent turned and approached Falric and Alrion.

"This just gets weirder and weirder. There's something going on. Falric and I will take turns keeping watch tonight. I don't trust them."

"I agree. They are nervous about something, and I did notice them staring at our robes the whole time. They are only distinctive to those who know what to look for. I'm not buying the fact that they had some wizards visit a town he didn't want to name," Falric said.

"What about me?" Alrion said.

"You sleep," Vincent said.

"How can I sleep knowing you're watching those guys to see if they try and pull something?"

"You will. We have a long trip ahead of us, so the more you can rest the better. We'll wake you up if anything starts happening, don't worry about that." Vincent put a hand on Alrion's shoulder.

"At least one of us should get a proper sleep, and as the man learning the most right now it should be you. Your time will come, mark my words," Falric said.

"Sure." Alrion didn't want to make a big deal.

I know I can pull my weight. But they seem really uneasy about this. I'll just have to try and sleep.

They started their preparations for sleep. Falric and Alrion tried to get some rest, while Vincent sat up pretending to read.

~

"Falric, you awake?" Vincent said. Alrion awoke immediately and sat up. He hadn't managed to get into a deep sleep.

"Almost. I'm trying to work out what disturbed my sleep. Be quiet for a moment," he said. Vincent turned back to look at the travellers. They still appeared to be in their beds. Falric had sat bolt upright. His eyes were fixated on the distance.

"This is not good. Wake Alrion and get ready to leave," Falric said.

"I'm already awake. What is it?" Alrion said.

"Trouble. Get ready," Vincent said. Alrion started to stand but sank back down. Something was bugging him. He listened carefully to the sounds of the forest. They were the same as before, the wind and the swaying of the trees. And the strange whispering sound, that was almost inaudible, running beneath the rest of the sounds like an undercurrent.

"Runnnnn AAAAAlrion," the forest whispered and Alrion felt a chill run down his spine. Before he could speak he heard a new sound. Something was rushing in their direction. He looked up and saw a giant flame in the shape of a man hurtling towards them. Vincent grabbed Alrion and hurled him out of the way. They both fell to the ground and heard the flame pass over their heads. A gigantic explosion blasted behind them, and the smell of smoke filled the air.

"I thought you said it was impossible to start a fire in here," Alrion said.

"Looks like I was wrong." Vincent drew his sword.

17

UNDER FIRE

Vincent stepped forward and looked out into the darkness.

"It must be a wizard. Falric are you there?"

"I'm here. It is a wizard, which is surprising," Falric said.

"Aren't all the wizards with you?"

"No, not all wizards. Be careful," Falric said. Vincent gave Alrion a hand up. The young wizard brushed himself off and strained to see what had attacked them. The smoke and mist were hampering visibility. He saw a shape in the distance, walking closer. He couldn't make out who it was.

"It's the wizard," Falric said.

"We don't know what he can do, so just duck and run if you have to," Vincent said. Alrion nodded.

"Don't act rashly, this is extremely dangerous," Falric said. The figure stopped and observed them. Falric held his hands up, and a gust of wind flew out and dispersed the mist and smoke nearby. They finally got a good look at who had attacked them.

He was average height, wearing a full black hooded robe. His face was hidden from view. In his right hand, he held a jet-black staff with a dark crystal orb at the top.

"Who are you?" Falric called out.

"You don't need my name, and I don't need yours. You are well known to me Falric," a voice said. It was somehow amplified and boomed around the clearing.

"What do you want?" Falric said. The man started to speak but stopped himself. Instead, he just laughed. Falric looked at Vincent.

"What's the plan?" Vincent said.

"We should counter-attack from different directions at the same time. He will have difficulty tracking us both," Falric said.

"Just give me the signal." Vincent dropped into a ready stance and started circling around. The hooded wizard stopped laughing and looked at them. He raised his staff and brought it down upon the ground. The earth beneath his staff rose up, a wave of rock and stone lurching from the ground and barrelling towards them.

"Get down!" Falric shouted, and he threw his hands up in response. The rolling wall of earth slowed as it approached them and paused in mid-air.

"Move!" Falric cried out. Vincent dragged Alrion away and Falric dived to the opposite side. Falric managed to hold onto his spell just long enough for them to get clear of the main thrust. The ground suddenly fell everywhere all at once and Alrion felt like he was being buried alive.

After a few moments, Alrion realised he was holding his breath. He breathed in and got air, which surprised him. He struggled up and found that only a light layer of rock and soil had settled over him. His father was more covered, so Alrion dragged him out. Vincent coughed and sat up, looking over at Falric.

"Don't worry, I'm alright." Falric dusted himself off.

"That was insane." Alrion looked around. The clearing was like a war zone.

"Horses are gone," Vincent said, looking out.

"So are our travelling companions. Do you think they were buried?" Alrion said.

"Not a chance," Falric said.

"I think this was a setup. They were waiting for us, then the wizard came. They knew what to look for." Vincent shook his head and retrieved his sword, sheathing it.

"That sounds fair. What can you tell us about that wizard?" Alrion said.

"I don't know who he is. From his dress and manner, you would think he was touched by the Blight. Yet I didn't notice the taint in his Spark."

"Then where did he come from?" Alrion said.

"I'm not sure. But he was clearly after us, and almost succeeded," Falric said.

"Do you think you can find him again? Or be more prepared next time?" Vincent said.

"We'll have to be more cautious. But no, I don't have a way of tracking him. Until we find out more, or manage to capture his staff, we won't have a way of locating him." Falric sighed. "Battle and tracking are not my specialty I'm afraid."

"What did you mean about his Spark?" Alrion said.

"Remember how I mentioned that when you are tainted by the Blight it taints your Spark as well? Other wizards can sense that taint when you use your Spark. It has a strange resonance to it, which you will understand when you notice it. I assumed that due to the attack by the Blighters, the dark dress and dark crystal on his staff that he was tainted. But his magic had none of the tell-tale signs," Falric said.

"Perhaps you were wrong, and he is just a rogue wizard?" Vincent said.

"Possibly. But it's too coincidental that we were forced out of the tunnel by Blighters and into the forest where he was waiting."

"True, it does seem like we are being tracked," Vincent said.

"How are they doing that?" Alrion said.

"I'm not sure, but I'll think about it. But one thing I know for certain, we need to modify our appearance. No matter how they tracked us to this forest, they were able to confirm our presence by our clothing. We need to be more careful. Perhaps what your grandfather said in his letter is to be taken more literally," Falric said.

"What did he say?" Alrion said.

Finally, he's mentioning something specific about my grandfather.

"In his letter to me, he referred to the Hidden Wizard as being the one to destroy the Blight. I thought he was being metaphorical, or referring to the fact that you had been hidden in your upbringing. But perhaps he also meant it more literally. That you need to be hidden to achieve your mission."

"You could definitely interpret it like that. I just don't know," Alrion said.

"Either way, it's good advice. Is there a way we can disguise ourselves with magic?" Vincent said.

"Not a good way, and it will be difficult to hide that from other wizards. These particular cloaks are also protected from altering. We will just need to do it the old-fashioned way and get some new clothing from the next place we visit."

"Fine. Let's see what we can salvage and get out of this damned forest." Vincent waved his arms in frustration. Alrion understood the feeling. It had been such a frustrating leg of their journey. The slow approach, and the creepy trees and whispers. The additional slowdown of the travellers, the ambush, and the loss of their horses just added to it.

What a terrible day. I'll be glad to put it behind me.

"I can't wait to be out of here," Alrion said.

"Truer words were never spoken," Falric said. They picked through the debris in the clearing, claiming whatever food and supplies they could find. Alrion dug through his pockets, to see if he had left anything. But he found something he wasn't expecting. He removed it from his pocket and looked at it.

It was a book or journal. Small in size, with a blue leather cover, and blank pages inside. He didn't remember it at all.

"What do you have there?" Falric said.

"I'm not sure, I don't remember where I found it, or how it came into my possession."

"I recognise that. You would have taken it from the supply building," Falric said. Alrion thought back and a realisation dawned on him.

The magical artifact! I never even looked at it.

"You're right. The memory is coming back now, why was that room in the dark?"

"Your grandfather believed that magical artifacts were not as simple as they looked. That they could influence who used them and when. So, he bought into the idea completely and instituted a system whereby each new wizard selects his own artifact to take with him. The idea behind the dark room was to increase the chances of the wizard selecting the right artifact, by senses other than sight."

"Really? That's interesting. I do remember this one feeling different to the rest, it was warm to the touch."

"It must have been reacting to your Spark. That's a good sign."

"What is it?"

"That will be revealed in time. It looks like a magical notebook to me." Falric had a wry smile.

"Did you see that?" Vincent pointed at Falric.

"Yes, I believe you would call that a textbook wizard answer," Alrion said.

"Good, you're learning," Vincent said. Alrion couldn't help cracking a smile himself. It was nice to break the tension of what had just happened.

"Well, I think we should get a move on. The sooner we leave this place the better," Falric said.

"Do you think he will come back?" Alrion said.

"The wizard? I doubt it. I feel like this was a show of power, and a test of sorts."

"Some test. I don't want to see the final exam," Vincent muttered.

"I must clarify that we don't do tests like that at the academy," Falric said as they walked.

"I had assumed not, but I'm glad you clarified that." Alrion could still feel the adrenalin pumping through him, although he tried to relax as they walked.

I can't believe I was useless again. I can't seem to do anything right.

He had screwed up back in the mountain path and was rescued in the forest. Rationally he knew that everything was fine and that he had survived. But he just felt like he wasn't useful at all.

I'm going to have to fix that.

It was still quite dark as they set out, being so early in the morning. It made the walk seem longer than it was. The trees continued their relentless rhythmic swaying, and the just-inaudible whispers persisted. Thankfully, though, they didn't seem to address Alrion any longer.

I wonder if that wizard was playing tricks on me, Alrion thought. But a worse thing than that came to mind.

If that's true, then the wizard already knows who I am.

He couldn't explain why that was so chilling, but Alrion got the shivers at the idea. He shoved the thought away and focused again on walking. Hours passed, without any breaks.

"We can't afford to waste any more time in the forest," Vincent explained. Falric was in agreement and Alrion could see why. He told his stomach to be quiet and kept walking. Finally, he saw a change in the mist. For so long it had hung before them, obscuring the path. But now it seemed to be thinning.

"Are we almost out?" Alrion said.

"I think so. Did you notice the mist?" Vincent said.

"Yes, that was it. Although I'm not sure when it changed."

"Not that long ago, it was a fairly quick transition. What do you say Falric?"

"We should be out within minutes if it's like this," Falric said.

"Good." Vincent increased his walking pace. Alrion matched it, keen to see the sun again. It hadn't even been that long, but he had never been in such a strange place before either. Each step granted him additional strength and optimism, and he could see further and further ahead. Finally, he could see a space outside the forest and almost ran towards it.

"This is it," Vincent said as they emerged from the path.

They stepped onto a dusty track, in a deserted area. There were patches of brush and shrubs but no structures or any trees. The vast openness seemed like an incredible contrast after the narrow paths and constricting nature of the forest.

"I feel like I can breathe again," Alrion said.

"It's no wonder people avoid going through that, but we made good time. All things considered," Vincent said.

"Very good time, but too eventful for my liking," Falric said.

"No arguments about that. I'm all for less excitement," Vincent said, and Alrion nodded too.

"How far to the next town? That's where we are going right?" he said.

"It's pretty close, maybe an hour or two? I think we should push through and stop there. It's called Altarbright," Vincent said.

"That's an interesting name, why is it called that?" Alrion said.

"I'll let the good wizard fill you in." Vincent deferred to Falric, who seemed excited at the opportunity. He drew himself up and began his explanation.

"It's actually a very simple name. Before this town became such an important trading hub, it was a sacred place where an ancient people worshipped a goddess in the lake. They created a large altar to worship her, and it was made from a bright gold that was polished daily to maintain its shine. On a still day, you could see the reflection of the altar in the water, and the people believed it was the goddess giving her approval," Falric said.

"Is it still there? The altar?" Alrion said.

"No, it was stolen many years ago. A giant gold altar is just too tempting for thieves. But the name stuck, so we still call it Altarbright."

"That's a shame." Alrion sighed deeply.

A giant gold altar is just the kind of thing I hoped to see.

"Yes, it is. But you can see where it used to stand."

"So, it's a big town?" Alrion said.

"Yes, very big. Avaria has grown from strength to strength. As much as those two back in the forest were hiding something, they were right about what happened when Granthion cleansed the Blight from here. Trade from other countries exploded and Altarbright was the prime spot to conduct trade. The lake is a natural border to some of our neighbours," Falric said.

"Are we crossing the lake?" Alrion perked up again.

"Yes."

"Are we leaving Avaria?" Vincent said.

"No, but we can use the lake as a shortcut." Falric revealed no more. As they walked on Alrion started to see signs of something in the distance. They came upon a crossroads and noticed that many people were streaming in towards the town in the distance, but from other directions.

"I guess nobody comes the way we did," Alrion said.

"For good reason." Vincent laughed. Alrion looked over at the others on the road ahead. There were some people walking, others on horses, and some driving coaches or wagons, multiple horses pulling them along.

"Are they all merchants?" he said.

"Not all but many. Some are just travellers, others are people looking for a better life in a bigger town," Falric said.

"Why would life be better here?"

"A lot of money flows through Altarbright. That means opportunities to make a living, both honestly and not," Vincent said.

I wonder if that thief will be there, Alrion thought, remembering how his ring had been stolen at Carford.

"Wow, this is incredible. I can barely recognise the place," Vincent said. Alrion looked up and was impressed. Huge stone gates rose up before them, with a wall going all the way around the perimeter. Alrion could see lots of large buildings, with a few incredibly tall towers further back.

"Are they wizard towers?"

"No, I believe they are for the officials that overlook the port," Falric said.

"Now this is going to be an adventure," Vincent said, taking in the town.

I couldn't agree more, thought Alrion, excited at the possibilities.

18

REGROUPING

Entering Altarbright reminded Alrion of Carford, only everything was twice as big. The road was twice as wide, the gates twice as tall and twice as many people flowed through. There were a large number of guards milling around, and even guard posts at each end of the gate. People were being let through, but larger vehicles were being stopped for inspections.

"Why are they stopping them?" Alrion said as a nearby wagon was halted.

"They are looking for smuggled goods I suspect." Vincent watched the guard interrogate the travellers and examine the wagon before continuing, "As this is a key entry point into Avaria they are very wary of what comes in and out. This looks much stricter, though."

"Since Avaria has been free of the Blight, officials have been trying to keep it that way," Falric said.

"It can't be that free of the Blight, considering what we ran into yesterday," Alrion said.

"And that's an important lesson," Falric said. Alrion mulled it over as they continued into the town. Unlike the main street that dominated the other places they had visited, Altarbright was a sprawling place with dozens of streets. Even his father was wide-eyed, trying to take in the enormity of it.

"I can see the looks on your faces. You can tell the town is bursting at the seams." Falric chuckled. Once they reached the first crossroad, Vincent stopped.

"The first thing we should do is resupply," he said.

"Agreed," Falric said. "I know a good place."

"Lead the way." Vincent stepped back and gave the wizard a fake bow. Falric nodded graciously and took the lead. He turned left and the other two followed close behind. They walked along another busy street, then turned abruptly into an alley.

"I don't like the look of this," Vincent said.

"You're not supposed to," Falric said. Vincent said no more and put his hand on his sword hilt. Halfway down the alley, they stopped before a door and Falric knocked three times. The door opened, and he stepped through. Vincent ushered Alrion through and entered last.

The interior of the building was quite spacious. They were in a shop of some kind, which was stocked with just about everything and anything. There were racks of clothes, supplies, equipment, and herbs.

"Who runs this place?" Vincent said.

"It's a store run by the wizards. Seeing as how Altarbright is such a hub, there's value in us having a presence here." Falric walked down one of the aisles, running his hand over the goods.

"I see, looks well-stocked."

"We take pride in it. Although I admit it is somewhat easier to do here considering the amount of trade goods that flow through this town." Falric stopped his walk and started to look around in earnest.

"Is there anyone else here?" Alrion said as he wandered.

"No, there's nobody tending the place right now. From time to time wizards get an assignment here, but generally, it is maintained on an as-needed basis by those who use it." Falric picked up a leather-bound book and leafed through it.

"Nobody has been here for a few months." He put the book back down.

"Don't suppose you got horses back here?" Vincent said.

"No, I'm afraid we don't. But we should be fine from here on. I wouldn't want to take them on the boat anyway."

"Fair enough." Vincent started browsing the available clothing. "Is this all normal stuff?"

"Yes, none of it is magical. We need to blend in sometimes," Falric said.

"Now seems like a good time."

"That's the idea."

"Pick yourself something from here," Vincent said to Alrion. The young wizard looked through the rack and selected a green cloak with a hood. It was quite plain, save for a jewelled brooch, and stretched down past his hips when he tried it on.

"The fit looks alright, and you can pull over the hood as required." Vincent checked Alrion's shoulders and pulled the hood over.

"How do I look?" Alrion said.

"Like a young merchant, with something to hide." Falric pushed the hood back, "Now, I think that's appropriate. You next."

Vincent grabbed something similar, in a dark-navy colour. Falric found a plain light-brown cloak that he could wear.

"Isn't that too close to your robe?" Vincent said.

"Not at all. Trust me, an old man like myself is more likely to insulate himself from the cold wind," Falric said. Vincent laughed.

"I'll see what supplies I can rustle up." He walked through the room and disappeared into the back area.

"So, we leave our robes here?" Alrion said.

"Yes, someone will either use them or return them to the academy." Falric returned his robe to one of the racks. Alrion took a closer look and noticed that it was different to his own. It was white inside and had a variety of colours along the trim.

"Is this special?" he asked Falric.

"Yes, only the head wizard wears that one." Falric reached out and straightened up the robe on the rack. His hand trembled slightly.

"Don't you feel odd taking it off?"

"Yes, but wearing it this far was an indulgence. I should have removed it back at the academy."

"I see. It's a new time for us all."

"It sure is." Falric noticed Vincent waiting. "Are we ready?"

"Yes, let's head out." Vincent handed out a leather pack to both Alrion and Falric. "There are a few essentials within to keep us going."

Alrion rummaged through and found some food and some blankets. He closed the pack back up, slung it over his shoulder and left the room.

"Where to next?" he said.

"We need to go to the docks and book passage on a boat," Falric said.

"Sure." Alrion followed along. They returned to the main road from the alley and followed the flow of people towards the docks.

"Do you mind if I wander around and meet you there? It looks like if I just follow this group I can find my way," Alrion said as they walked. Falric looked at Vincent.

"I suppose so. There's not much of interest there for you anyway. If you lose your way, return to the wizard store."

"Yes, good idea. Knock three times and the door will respond to you," Falric said.

"Don't get into any trouble, we've had enough already." Vincent gave Alrion a stern look.

"Promise. I just want an opportunity to explore a bit while we are here."

"You have one hour," Vincent said.

"Done," Alrion said. He diverted to turn right at the next crossroads.

"I wonder what got into him?" Falric said.

Alrion didn't hear his father's response, he was already walking fast in a different direction. He had flirted with the idea of exploring the town, but it had suddenly become an urgent idea once he had spotted her.

He tried to blend into the crowd as he walked, to not let her catch on. He had recognised the woman instantly, even though he hadn't seen her since Carford.

Let's see what you have to say for yourself, Alrion thought as he closed in. She was wearing the same clothes and appeared to be walking casually down the road in no hurry. Not once did she look back, so Alrion felt like he could get closer. As he started to approach her, she darted into a side street.

Alrion quickly ran after her. He couldn't see her once he turned the corner, but there were multiple cross alleys, so he kept running until he could look to see where she went. Once he reached the first set, he slowed and whirled around to look at the other directions. But he felt a presence behind him.

"Hello again," she said. Alrion turned fully to face her.

"That was my line."

"Why? Because you thought you had snuck up on me?" She gave him a dismissive laugh. Alrion's cheeks started reddening.

"I did."

"No, I let you see me and you followed me here." She gestured at the dark street they were in. "If I was up to no good, you would be in real trouble. Consider this a free lesson."

"What about stealing? Doesn't that count as up to no good?"

"No, that's just a habit. And pretty fun. But I'm glad I did it because once I saw what it was, you piqued my interest." She winked at him.

"What do you mean?"

"Well, you were carrying a magic ring. Then looking closer at you, I started to see an interesting picture emerging. An old wizard, a young man presumably also a wizard, and a strange man accompanying them both. Probably a mercenary."

"You think you know a lot."

"I do know a lot, Alrion." She stretched his name out and laughed as she watched his reaction. "Don't act so surprised that I knew your name, I've been paying attention."

"What's your name then?" Alrion struggled to get things back on even terms, but clearly this woman was a step ahead of him.

At least I can learn her name. If she'll even tell the truth.

"Lara."

"Well, Lara, if you have been paying attention then maybe you would have noticed that the strange man accompanying us is my father, and he's also a blacksmith, not a mercenary."

"So cute of you to provide me with all that information, but I don't buy that. I've never seen a blacksmith with such slim arms. They are usually thick as tree trunks." Lara demonstrated with her hands.

"I don't even know why we are arguing about this. What are you after?"

"I'm just after something interesting to do. And following your little group has been just the distraction I was looking for. My you've had some adventures already."

"You've been following us? The whole time?"

I can't believe it. What would make someone do that? And how could we not have noticed?

"Of course! How else did you think I made it here, just as you arrived?" Lara looked to be enjoying Alrion's reaction.

"I still don't get it. Do you want to rob us again? Following us to look for a bigger score?" Alrion said, the frustration showing in his voice.

"I thieve, but I'm not a thief. There's a difference. There's not a lot of value in things, but once you realise they can be taken so effortlessly you get a different perspective. Experiences are worth something, and following you all has been quite the experience already." Lara looked quite satisfied. It just infuriated Alrion more.

"Fine, why don't you hand over my ring then if you don't see the value in it?"

"Oh, but you clearly do, so I'll hold onto it for now. I'm glad we could have this chat, Alrion, but we both need to be places." Lara didn't wait for a response, but spun around and sprinted away.

"Wait!" Alrion called out, but she paid no attention. He saw an old crate against the alley wall and lashed out at it. Without really thinking he shoved the crate with extreme force, hurtling it on a collision course with Lara.

She turned in response to the sound, and once she noticed the crate she bent down, vaulted off the ground and landed on it as it travelled, riding it for a few seconds before jumping off and continuing on her way. She turned and gave Alrion a little wave before she disappeared around the corner.

She's gone.

He didn't try to follow but instead inspected his hands, as if expecting to see something on them.

What just happened there? How did I lash out so quickly? And what if I'd hurt her or someone else?

He had just been given a lesson on the value of control. Nothing serious had come of it, but he had thrown that crate with great speed and little thought. He was a little scared of what he was capable of, even after such little training.

"Maybe because of such little training," Alrion said to himself. Yes, he had to watch himself and judge his reactions. He had the power to harm already, and without a doubt, his power would grow and grow. He walked away, trying to find his way back to the main streets. It wouldn't look good if he couldn't find his father and Falric at the docks.

He took a few wrong turns but found his way back to the main road that he recognised eventually. Following it returned him to where they originally parted ways. From there it was easy enough to let the crowds lead him to the docks.

Alrion didn't look at too much as he went, he was trying to solve the puzzle around Lara.

Who is she?

She was always dressed in plain clothes, which were not feminine at all. She was clearly an adept thief, as she had stolen his ring without any trouble at all. He panicked as he felt through his pockets again. But nothing else was missing.

That's a relief. How embarrassing would it be to lose something again, he thought. If what she said was true, she had been following them since that first encounter. He didn't exactly trust her, but there had to be some truth to what she was saying. They were both here, and she knew his name. She was up to something. He started to wonder if she was somehow connected to the mysterious wizard in black who had attacked them.

"Now there's a man deep in thought," Vincent said. Alrion looked up and noticed that he had arrived at the docks. Vincent and Falric were standing by the side of the road, waiting.

"Oh, I'm here already," Alrion said.

"Here already? You almost made us start looking." Vincent glared at Alrion.

"Well, I lost my way, but here I am."

"We've booked passage on a ferry that leaves soon. It will be travelling overnight to our destination," Falric said.

"Where are we going?"

"We'll fill you in somewhere more private," Vincent said.

"Sure."

"Let's get settled in." Falric gestured to a vessel ahead. At the end of the dock was a huge wooden boat, with a large cabin area and massive deck. There were people already stepping onto the boat, and many crowding around up top.

"We're not riding outside, are we?" Alrion said.

"No, we paid for a cabin," Falric said.

"That's a relief, thanks for that."

"It's not for you, it's for me. You'll understand when you get to my age," Falric said. Vincent laughed but Alrion didn't get it. He looked up at the ferry.

"Does it have a name?"

"Sure does, look there on the side." Vincent pointed it out.

"*The Glider*. Sounds promising. I've never been on the water before."

"First trip of many. Let's go," Falric said. Vincent went first and showed their tickets to the deckhand. Falric and Alrion followed. As they boarded, Alrion felt the ferry move gently beneath their feet. The first time the ground underneath him had been so unsteady. It was a strange feeling, as it completely mirrored how he felt. After his encounter with Lara, he felt like he was no longer grounded, and that everything could shift again in an instant.

19

BOATING ACCIDENT

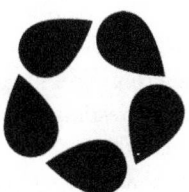

They pushed through the growing crowds and entered the main cabin of the ferry. In front of them was a well-worn stairwell. They walked down the stairs carefully, emerging into a long corridor at the bottom. There were rooms along the corridor, each one marked with a number.

"We are room number four," the wizard said. It was the second door on the right. Vincent entered first and Falric and Alrion followed.

"Wow, this is tiny," Alrion said. The room had a set of two wooden bunk beds against one wall, another tiny wooden bed on the floor, and a small window at the end of the room.

"Space is at a premium, you probably don't want to know how much this room cost us," Vincent said.

"You two can take the bunks, I'll take the floor," Falric said.

"Sure. Top or bottom, Alrion?" Vincent gestured to the bunk beds.

"I'll take the top." Alrion threw his bag up there.

"Why don't you two investigate the ship, I'll mind our things." Falric lay back on his bed and made himself comfortable.

"Don't get too relaxed there," Vincent said with a chuckle and held the door open for Alrion. They left the room, and returned to the stairs, walking all the way back up to the deck.

"Why are we going overnight?" Alrion said.

"They only do two runs a day, one first thing in the morning and one in the early evening. The reason for that is this ferry has a few possible stops, but the end point is a long trip. It's a ten- to twelve-hour trip."

"All on the same lake?"

"Yes, it's a huge one. That's why the ferry takes the long way around, it's a horrendously long trip either way, so they have more stops to service more passengers."

"Makes sense. Where are all these people going?" Alrion pointed at the surging crowds on the deck of the ferry.

"I'd say they are going all the way. To Dendra."

"Dendra?"

"Yes, it's our closest ally country and main trading partner."

"Another country. That's pretty cool."

"Yes, there's a whole world out there. Avaria is just a small part of it."

"Do you think I'll see it all?"

"Definitely. I'm not sure where this trip will take us, but as a wizard, you will travel the world and meet a lot of interesting people."

"Did you travel a lot with grandfather?"

"No, not much at all. I think that it was too dangerous to take me. So, he alternated between staying with me, and leaving me behind. He was also establishing the academy."

"Oh, so you travelled later?"

"Yes, by myself. I roamed a lot after he passed," Vincent said. Alrion didn't know what to say. He was interested in learning more about his father's travels, but noticed that it was an awkward topic. So, he let it go. As he was thinking about what to say next he heard a giant horn sounding.

"What's that?"

"That's the signal. We're off," Vincent said. They pushed through the crowd until they could get closer to the edge of the ferry. Alrion could feel the movement and also see their passage through the water.

"Hang on, what's moving the boat?"

"They have an engine room at the bottom," Vincent said.

"Engine? How does that work?"

"Not sure. It's a closely guarded secret. I suspect there's some magic involved. Probably a wizard set it up, and there are some specially trained people who keep it running."

"Wow."

"It's pretty remarkable. Although the last time I rode it was before you were born, and they had the option for passengers to be backup rowers." Vincent chuckled.

"That wouldn't be fun." Alrion couldn't imagine how much effort would be required to row a boat of this size.

"It was a risk some took, as it greatly reduced the ticket price. But I don't think it is an option anymore. The progress that has been made in the last twenty years or so has been tremendous. It's pretty exciting."

"Sure is. I'll have to find out how this ferry works."

"You'll find out in time, I have no doubt about that," Vincent said. They watched the town of Altarbright slowly fade from view, as they went deeper and deeper into the dark night.

"Not much left to see here, let's head below," Vincent said. Alrion followed, and they descended the stairs to return to their cabin. Falric was lying in his bed, soundly asleep.

"Now there's a reliable security guard," Vincent said.

"I heard that," Falric remarked, keeping his eyes closed.

"At least he noticed us come in," Alrion said, playing along. Falric snorted.

"Hey, Falric, my father said that this ferry runs on magical engines. Do you know how they work?"

"I do indeed."

"You'll have to explain later. But I was thinking, if they're magical and wizards were involved setting them up, then why did you say that the cabin was so expensive? Wouldn't there be a wizard rate?" Alrion said. Falric opened his eyes and sat up.

"You're a quick one. They don't need us anymore. They have their own specialists who maintain the engines, so we don't get preferential treatment. I could have twisted their arm, but we want to go unnoticed, so I just paid."

"Oh, I see."

Another situation where being a wizard doesn't make a difference.

"The world owes us a lot, but they don't sit around being respectful. They move on, so we have to keep earning their trust and respect. Some places are easier than others," Falric said.

"I thought that it was obvious that wizards would be well-respected and listened to. I guess that's not the case."

"No, it is not. Your grandfather earned us a place of favour for sure, but I have not been able to maintain our standing I'm afraid. The world is moving on, and taking our contributions for granted." Falric sighed.

"Maybe I can change that."

"I am hoping so," Falric said with a smile. "How're things up top?"

"Absolutely bursting at the seams, makes this room seem spacious," Vincent said.

"Well, at least we got our money's worth. We are the first stop. It's a little town called Paperton."

"I don't know it." Vincent had a puzzled expression on his face.

At least we're both new to this area, I'm sick of being the only one who doesn't know anything.

"Good. I hope those who are after us don't know it either. We should eat and have an early night. They will be dropping us off at some ungodly hour in the morning." Falric shook his head.

"Sounds like fun," Alrion said. "I take it we won't be able to look at any more spells."

"Not tonight, but soon. We can't have you being a one-trick pony," Falric said. Vincent laughed and grabbed his bag. Alrion did the same and they ate a simple meal.

Alrion clambered up onto the top bunk and lay still listening to the sounds. A lot of murmuring filtered down from the deck above him, but things were fairly quiet down below. He heard a faint hum coming from somewhere and decided it had to be something to do with the engine driving the ferry. The rippling of the water as they pushed through was consistent and calming. Despite his excitement and the earliness of the night, he found sleep was not far away.

Alrion awoke, unsure of the reason. He tried to shake the fog from his head and looked around the room, letting his eyes adjust to the dark. Falric was not in his bed. He clambered down from the bunk and looked for his father. He, too, was gone. Alrion ran across the room but stopped before leaving. He thought he had heard something. He listened carefully, and a terrifying sound echoed through the ferry. Screaming.

Alrion burst through the door and scrambled up the staircase.

Something is going on, and I bet we're involved. I have to see what I can do.

It was no coincidence that he had been left alone in what could be classed as relative safety. But he couldn't sit around waiting for whatever it was to be over, he had to investigate.

He confirmed his suspicions as soon as he reached the deck. The space in front of him was completely bare. He looked over and saw throngs of people around the edge of the boat. But the centre of the main deck was cleared. Only as he looked closer did he notice some bodies on the ground. He searched the crowds and saw Falric and his father at the edge of the group of people. Everyone was focused on a single man, stumbling through the empty space on the deck. He was the one screaming.

Alrion couldn't see what was happening clearly, so carefully made his way over to join his father.

"What's going on?"

"We are under attack. It's a Shade." Vincent's voice was tight and he didn't even look at Alrion.

"A Shade?"

"Yes, it's a rare and terrible creature of the Blight. It is perfectly black and blends in perfectly with darkness. It is practically invisible at night."

"So, it's there somewhere?" Alrion started looking for it.

Great, so we find some invisible death monster while we're on a boat.

"Yes, it's holding that poor man who is screaming," Falric said.

"What do we do?"

"We have to kill it or drive it away. Chances are that it is here for us," Falric said.

"How do we kill it? I won't be able to sleep until I know this thing isn't waiting to sneak up on us," Vincent said.

"Only magic can kill it. Directly or indirectly. Well-made equipment can damage it, but it must be magically enhanced to deliver a killing blow. You have to remove or destroy the heart."

"It's got a heart?" Alrion said.

"It was originally a person. Just one that was twisted by the Blight. Their heart absorbs the essence of the Blight and becomes a black stone. As long as it remains intact, the Shade will reform overnight. No matter what damage you do to the rest of the Shade."

"Sounds fun," Vincent said.

"What do I do?" Alrion asked.

"You stay back and let us handle this. No debate."

"Got it," Alrion said. He knew the tone of his father's voice, the one when he was laying down the law. Vincent didn't use it often, but he would not back down once he did. Alrion could sense the terror in the crowd, and the tension felt by Falric and his father. So, he decided to stay out of the way. For now.

"Is there a way you can make it visible?" Vincent said.

"It's difficult out here in the open. I know of a way that will definitely work, but it's a last resort."

"Alright, keep that in your pocket then. I'll try and bait it, and you do your thing," Vincent said. He drew his sword and stepped out from the crowd. Falric followed closely behind.

"Why does it still have that man?" Vincent asked as they crept forward.

"Not sure, I think they use the screams of the victim to terrify and distract," Falric said.

"Lovely." Vincent crept forward. The screaming man turned towards him. The poor man screamed even louder for help.

"I guess that means we've been spotted," Vincent said. Falric didn't reply. Vincent took care in stepping forward. Alrion edged closer too, trying to get a better look. He noticed that something was poking through the man's stomach.

"I think I can see where it's holding him," Vincent said. Alrion held his tongue, he didn't want them to know how close he was.

"Good, but I'm not sure how much we can do for him," Falric said. Vincent stepped closer again.

"He wants your boy!" the man squealed before screaming in pain once again. Vincent reacted swiftly, swinging his sword towards the man. Whatever was holding him disengaged and let the man fall to the ground.

"Take him away from here," Vincent yelled to a person nearby, who just stared at him in horror.

"Now we can't see it," Vincent said. He swung his sword out and it collided with something and was pushed back.

"It's here. Not sure how I'm going to fight blind!"

"Give me a minute," Falric said. Vincent walked in a circle, running through a sword style that sliced the air in front of him.

It's hanging back, but where, Alrion thought.

"You need to draw it in," Falric said. Vincent stopped moving and closed his eyes. He looked like he was trying another way to discover the Shade.

It's hopeless. There's too much noise here, and I can't see anything. He needs help.

"C'mon Shade, show me your worst!" Vincent called out. He flinched with what had to be a stabbing pain and reflexively grabbed with his left hand. He was holding onto something.

"To my left, I've got a hold on it!" Vincent yelled. Falric opened his hand and small fingers of flame shot out, arcing through the air. They hit the Shade and started to burn. Vincent waited a moment and then swung his sword at the burning shape. He connected with something, and it pulled away from him sharply.

I can see it now. The fire is illuminating it.

"That worked." Vincent maintained a defensive stance.

"Yes, but it's quite risky. They burn incredibly easily and with great intensity. Not only is it a danger to everyone here, but it doesn't actually damage the Shade at all," Falric said.

Alrion realised the danger of what Falric had said as he watched the Shade transform into the burning silhouette of a man. The flames leaped onto the deck, causing it to catch fire as well.

"This has to end fast." Vincent charged forward.

He has to hurry. The ferry will burn up. What can I do?

Vincent stepped forward and swung at one of the Shade's arms. He connected and hit some resistance, but managed to continue his momentum and slice through.

Vincent tried to reel in his attack and redirect it as the Shade reached for him with its other arm. This time it didn't try and pierce him, but instead smashed him in the same place with what felt like an open palm. Vincent fell down, the wind knocked out of him. He dropped his sword and swore with pain.

The Shade moved forward to attack again.

Now's my chance! Alrion tried not to think too much, and remembered how he had instinctively thrown force at Lara. But it wasn't coming easily. He couldn't waste any more time, his father was struggling to stand up.

Stay away from him! Like that, the spell flowed through him. The Shade was shoved back, and it almost lost its footing. The flames continued to burn as if nothing had happened. The creature cocked its head, staring in Alrion's direction.

"What are you doing?" Vincent yelled at Alrion. He managed to prop himself up, but looked unsteady. Alrion could see the anger in his father's eyes. And also fear.

"Get up, and get back to it. They're adept at fighting magic, so additional attacks will be less effective," Falric said. Vincent bent down and retrieved his sword.

"At least that worked." He pointed at the severed arm, still burning on the deck. "Can you put it out?"

"I have an idea," Falric said. The flames slowly dissipated from the burning limb, and started collecting in the palm of his hand. He compacted them into a ball and hurled it at the Shade. It didn't even try to dodge the attack and was knocked back again. The flames already on it flared up briefly then went back to their prior state.

"Tough bugger," Vincent said.

"You have to go for the heart, or this will drag on forever!" Falric threw another wave of force at the Shade, unsteadying it. But it seemed to be less effective than Alrion's attack.

It's already adapting to our spells. I'll wait in the wings for now.

"Go for the heart? Easier said than done," Vincent muttered. He dashed in again, aiming a slashing strike at the Shade's other arm. But the Shade had anticipated this and jumped back at the same time. As Vincent's strike fell short, the Shade reached out and grabbed the blade, tipping Vincent off-balance.

Stumbling, Vincent managed to pull out a knife from his belt and hurl it at the Shade's chest. The creature was caught by surprise and had no counter. The blade embedded itself in the Shade's chest. Right where its heart should be. The Shade stopped moving and tried to reach the blade with its arm.

I can't believe he did it. But it's not dead yet. It mustn't have pierced through. Maybe I can help it along?

"Falric!" Vincent yelled. Falric responded by throwing a wave of force at the knife, embedding it to the hilt. The Shade stumbled back a few steps. Vincent dropped his sword and ran towards it. It was trying to reach the blade and pull it out.

Vincent reached out with his right hand and pushed forcefully against the tip of the blade handle, tumbling over in the effort. The knife drove in slightly more and the Shade fell backward. It toppled towards the edge of the ferry, boosted by an extra force wave from Falric. The Shade clawed at the ground, trying to stop itself.

"Just die, you monster!" Alrion yelled. Without thinking he unleashed a powerful wave of force. The Shade's tenuous hold failed, and it disappeared over the edge and into the water with a sizzling hiss.

20

UNCHARTED TERRAIN

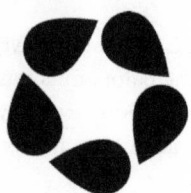

V incent stood up and surveyed the damage. He traced his hand over a giant scorch mark in the deck where the Shade had tried to hang on, and it continued over the edge of the ferry. Flames licked the deck and other areas, flowing through the gaps in the flooring caused by the Shade.

"Do you think it's dead now?" Vincent peered over the edge of the ferry.

"Depends if you destroyed the heart. I don't suppose that was a magic blade?" Falric said.

"I think it might have been. I bought it from Brangtur."

"The city of blacksmiths? There are those there that know the secrets of magical metalworking, so there's a chance. If you bought wisely, that is."

"So, it might be dead?" Alrion said.

"Might be, can't say for sure. We are safe for now. But the ferry has sustained serious damage." Falric walked around, extinguishing flames where he could.

"I can't believe the Shade did so much damage. Some of these areas look like molten metal burned through." Vincent stepped around them.

"The unique makeup of the Shade burns so much hotter, that's why I was hesitant to light it up. Battling creatures of the Blight is not my specialty. But we achieved our aim," Falric said. Alrion joined his father, and examined the wreckage caused by the Shade. He too looked over the edge, trying to see if the Shade was anywhere. Vincent yanked him back from the edge.

"You've done enough for one night. How about you explain what it is you think you were doing?" Vincent's voice was loud and angry.

"I'd also like an explanation before I turf the lot of you into the drink," a male voice said behind them.

"The captain, I presume?" Falric said.

"Yes. Start talking."

"We encountered a Shade, a rather vile and dangerous creature of the Blight. You should be thankful that we dispatched it." Falric adjusted his posture and stood up straighter.

"Oh, I should be thanking you for destroying half of my deck? I can't continue with this kind of damage, not without going ashore and assessing." The captain didn't seem like he was responding to Falric's attempt at authority. Alrion stifled a chuckle.

"You can thank us that you are still alive, and this ferry is not completely and utterly destroyed." Vincent turned his back on the captain and walked off. Alrion turned back to the water, staring out in search for the Shade.

It was here for me, no question. I'm out of my depth, Alrion thought. He looked over at his father, a newfound admiration building. He crossed the deck to talk to him.

"I'm sorry, but I couldn't idly stand by. Don't be too angry."

"I worry about you. And you made yourself known to the Shade. But, you did well. We should include you more in the future, so your involvement can be more planned. And you cannot scare me so badly. Deal?" Vincent held out his hand. Alrion shook it, and his father brought him in close and slapped him on the back.

"We should make ourselves scarce before the captain gets too many ideas," Vincent said.

How did you do that? I've never seen that side of you before," Alrion said.

"I've had some training, a long time ago. But you'll be surprised by the things you are capable of once you have a child of your own," Vincent said with a grim smile on his face.

Alrion headed downstairs to collect their things. The captain had decided to land at the nearest safe place on the shore and assess the boat for repairs during the day. Their group wanted to be ready to leave as soon as possible.

Just what was that? Alrion kept thinking over and over. It was different than the other encounters he had seen. As strange as they were, they made sense. People reduced to animals by the Blight and behaving as such. A wizard gone rogue, attacking them. Not your everyday occurrence, but they made sense in a way. But the Shade was something else entirely. He needed to know more about them.

I'll ask Falric when I get the chance. We might not be so lucky next time.

The ferry travelled much slower, as it diverted course. Alrion struggled up the steps with all the bags, and unceremoniously dumped them on the ground once he reached his father. Vincent gave Alrion a sideways glance, and picked up Falric's bag, handing it over to the wizard. He left his on the ground, but shifted its position with his boot. Alrion looked out over the water.

"I can't tell if we're moving."

"We're definitely moving, but it's a painful crawl. They don't travel this way often; the water is shallower and probably has more dangers," Vincent said.

"Another setback. I fear that we haven't managed to shake our pursuit at all." Falric furrowed his brow.

"Yes, clearly we are still being followed. Although it would have been easy to guess our intentions by following our route. Hopefully, now that we're stranded, we will get a chance to pass by unnoticed." Vincent looked over at Falric.

"Perhaps, that depends on where we end up," Falric said.

"How will we move on?" Alrion said.

"We will find the nearest town, then resupply and hopefully find some horses. I'd hate to have to walk the rest of the way." Falric looked pained just thinking about it.

"I guess we are taking the scenic route then," Alrion said. Vincent laughed.

"You could say that. I'm glad you can have a joke after the night we just had," he said.

"Just being philosophical."

"Good. Some perspective is always useful," Falric said. The sun was beginning to rise, and they caught their first glimpses of the shoreline. Ahead they could see a place to land. A section covered by small stones, which gently sloped up to grassy terrain.

"Could be worse," Vincent said. They watched in silence as the ferry closed the gap, and the crew steered it onto the shore. Vincent looked over at the side of the ferry and pointed out the damage.

"Now that's worse than I realised. That Shade sure tore the ferry up."

"I hope we've seen the last of that creature," Falric said.

"You need to explain Shades more, in case we come across them again," Alrion said.

"Of course. I will brief you on our way to the nearest town. To be honest I didn't expect to come across one on this journey, they are quite rare." Falric shook his head slowly and sighed. "There's been a lot of things I didn't expect, or was prepared for. But don't worry, I won't hold anything back."

"Thanks. That's all I can ask for."

"Be careful what you wish for," Vincent said. Alrion didn't reply. The crew steadied the ferry and adjusted the landing gear so that the passengers could walk down to the shore. Alrion stayed close to his father, and they inched along amongst the throng of people pushing and shoving to get off.

As they stepped onto dry land, the groups of people started to thin out. Some hung close to the boat, hovering around the captain and asking questions. Others started hiking off immediately. Vincent took the lead and walked with confidence, leading them through the throngs and further inland.

"This is a stroke of luck." Vincent pointed to a dirt track ahead.

It's barely there, and doesn't look heavily used, Alrion thought. He looked at his father and was about to speak, when Vincent interrupted.

"Look, I know it doesn't seem like much, but right now all we need is a route back to civilisation. And this is our ticket." Vincent looked behind them. "Others have figured this out too, let's get a move on." Without waiting for a response Vincent pressed ahead. Falric sighed and started to walk again. He appeared to be having a little difficulty. Alrion kept pace with Falric, not wanting the older wizard to strain unnecessarily.

"I appreciate you staying with me, lad. My joints aren't what they used to be. You wanted to hear about Shades didn't you?"

"Yes. Ideally before we encounter another one." Alrion laughed, trying to make a joke out of it. But there was an awkward tension hanging in the air.

Falric doesn't know when we will have another attack.

"As you were saying, now is a good time to begin. Shades are strange creatures, only really spotted in more recent times. I think the first reported and verified occurrence was around thirty years ago."

"What are they? I mean really."

"Shades are people, or at least were. As I mentioned before their bodies are different. They are stronger, more resilient, and retain more of their normal form. If you think of Blighters as being stage one of contamination, then Shades are stage two."

"More like stage ten," Vincent muttered.

"Well in terms of development and challenge, yes, it is a big step up. But I don't think there are any other stages between Blighters and Shades."

"Can Blighters become Shades?"

"No, but that was a logical conclusion to make. The answer is in something else. There are those called Tainted Ones, which we need to discuss."

"Tainted Ones?"

I've never heard of those either.

"Yes. Imagine a Blighter, except that they retain their mental faculties and can pass themselves off as a normal person. In most ways actually, they are still a person."

"They look and act like a person? What's different?"

"They have been tainted by the Blight but did not convert to the animalistic form that you have seen in the Blighters. In rare cases they can still infect others. But they have all the intelligence and cunning of a man, perhaps even more so."

"They still just sound like a normal person. Or at least a bad one."

"More or less. But there's one more thing that is crucial to understand. They are also connected to the Blight," Falric said. Alrion stopped walking instantly. Something about the statement seemed important.

"Connected to the Blight? What do you mean by that?"

"We believe that all creatures that are tainted by the Blight share a common communication method. It might be a shared mind or shared thoughts, but they can somehow communicate through their shared link to the Blight." Falric seemed to be distracted and looked up. Vincent was joining them. He motioned to Alrion to continue with his question.

"So, they can coordinate?" Alrion said.

"Exactly. And that's where Tainted Ones come into their own. As they have access to a normal mind, they can control and manipulate Blighters. The number and success do vary depending on the Tainted Ones doing the controlling," Falric said. Alrion let the idea work its way through. He spoke up again after he had time to process it.

"You think one of these Tainted Ones sent those Blighters after us in the mountain."

"Exactly."

"And those travellers we met in the forest might have been Tainted?"

"I think it is quite likely. They aren't common here in Avaria, but there's nothing stopping them from coming here."

"But that wizard wasn't a Tainted One?"

"No, I don't think so." Falric leaned against a nearby tree and waited. Alrion let the ideas sink in and settle.

I'm still missing something.

"What's this got to do with Shades?" he said.

"I wanted to take the opportunity to be as forthcoming as possible, now that we need to be completely vigilant for creatures of the Blight." Falric adjusted his position and let out a tired sigh. "But the connection is this: Tainted Ones can also become Shades. I don't know the exact process. It could be they are sought out and transformed by other Shades, or it could be they take on too much of the Blight. But we know of at least one Shade that used to be a Tainted One."

"Do the Shades remain intelligent?"

"Yes, very much so. But their bodies are changed significantly. They not only look perfectly black, they are transformed. Their body changes from flesh to something else. Strong like stone, but still soft. As I mentioned before their hearts crystallise and can regenerate their new body. It makes them incredibly difficult to kill."

"Do they communicate too?"

"They must do, but I haven't heard of any speaking with a person. Our theory is that they are so connected with the Blight that they can only communicate with other creatures of the Blight. Namely Tainted Ones and Blighters." Falric looked to Vincent, as if to invite him to comment. But Vincent remained silent.

I think I'm starting to understand this. But I wish I had been introduced to this sooner. It would have been much less of a shock than just encountering that Shade. I'll just confirm I have it right.

"If I'm understanding this correctly, then Blighters and Tainted Ones are two sides of the same stage of Blight taint. But the Shades are the next level."

"Exactly. Once set upon something, Shades are relentless. I hope we managed to kill the one that attacked us last night. But if we did not, at least we have severely damaged it and slowed it down."

"I hope it's gone for good. I don't want to face that thing again," Vincent said.

"I need to accept the fact that it's probably still after me but will be delayed. And that someone put it onto our path," Alrion said.

"I believe so. It could be the travellers we met, it could be the wizard that attacked us. It could even be someone else we have not yet encountered." Falric had an apologetic look on his face.

"But you don't know. That doesn't make me feel better," Alrion said.

"It's the truth. We know enough to take steps in our defence," Falric said.

"He's right, Son. We have to keep adjusting what we are doing and keep an eye out. The more we change our pattern, the more we can stay one step ahead."

"We're shipwrecked and on foot."

They clearly have the upper hand.

"But we are alive," Falric said.

"What do they want with me? I can't do anything yet?" Alrion's frustration was starting to come through.

I've done everything asked of me. I've played along. But disaster after disaster keeps happening. And there's no guarantee that I can even do anything remarkable.

"They must be fearful of what you may do, or what you might learn. It's a good sign that we are on the right path. I wish it were less dangerous, but at least we are following the right path." Falric gave Alrion a warm smile.

"I guess so," Alrion said.

That Shade terrified me. It was so different and alien. And looked relentless. Something about its inability to communicate made it even more terrifying. Like there was a force of evil on my trail. I'm not ready for this.

Alrion decided to not let himself dwell on it. He started to walk again and his father nodded, pushing ahead once more. Alrion took a greater look at the terrain they were walking through. It was lightly wooded, with a clear path to follow. As they had progressed, the path had improved.

"Strange area. Why is it deserted but also has a good path?" Alrion said.

"I would say people come down to the lake from a town nearby, but don't necessarily inhabit this area," Vincent said.

"That sounds reasonable," Alrion said. "Is Avaria a big country? In the grand scheme of things?"

"Avaria? No, it is quite a small place. But it rose in power and popularity after the cleansing of the Blight," Falric said.

"Did what my grandfather do prevent the Blight from existing here?"

"No, there's actually no protection here at all. It was all one event, a single cleanse. However, as a consequence of that, any Blighters or exposed Tainted Ones were dealt with swiftly and harshly. They stick out more, and people are more inclined to be proactive in removing them. So, it's a safer place overall."

"How bad is the Blight elsewhere?"

If what I've experienced is a safe place, I hate to think what the rest of the world are going through.

"There are some places where there are more people affected by the Blight than those not. Some even think that's because the origin of the Blight is nearby. But it varies. I must admit I haven't travelled a lot lately, so I'm not sure. Vincent, you haven't travelled in years, have you?"

"I haven't been outside Avaria since before Alrion was born."

"Yes, so we are as curious as you. But don't worry, we won't need to leave Avaria to complete your tasks. The Pool of Knowledge is hidden within its borders." Falric winked.

"Good. Are we close?" Alrion asked.

"Closer. I apologise but I want to keep our final destination under wraps a little longer. We've had a dark trail nipping at our heels all along, I won't feel safe sharing details like that until we can figure out how they are tracking us." Falric looked weary.

"As much as it frustrates me, I concur," Vincent said.

"As long as we're getting closer," Alrion said.

"Well, we're getting closer to something. I'd say that's a town ahead," Falric said. Alrion could see houses in the distance, puffs of smoke rising from their chimneys.

"That's a relief, I had wondered how long we were going to be wandering," Vincent said.

"You were wondering? I would have relished twice a walk at your age." Falric scoffed at Vincent.

"Next, you'll be telling us how in your day you had to drag yourself out of the womb and fix yourself a meal," Vincent said. Alrion laughed.

"No respect," Falric muttered, but the grin on his face was unmistakable.

21

THE BRIGHT CARAVAN

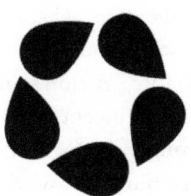

There was no sign proclaiming the name of the town, or any formal entrance. They just ended up within the town. Alrion looked around as they walked, spotting a tanner, blacksmith, and a healer.

"Falric, do local healers use magic?"

"Some do, although many do not."

"Is healing magic hard?"

"It can be, but the basics are not too bad. And incredibly useful. Are you interested in learning some?" Falric's eyes lit up.

"Yes, at least that's something I can work on outside of being attacked."

"Good point. If our trip continues the way it has been, we are going to rack up some injuries. I'll teach you a spell soon."

"Thanks." Alrion hadn't even considered the possibility before now, but seeing the healer's house, with its mystic symbols scrawled all over the walls had inspired him.

"I'm going to find out some information." Vincent pointed out a boy who was wandering through the town and intercepted him.

"Excuse me, can you please tell me where we are?"

"You don't know? This is Bowlern." The boy seemed less than impressed at Vincent's lack of knowledge.

"Bowlern? Don't know it. Our ferry landed nearby so we weren't planning on visiting."

"Wow, that's exciting. Nothing much happens here, it's pretty boring mostly."

"Is there a general store or somewhere we can buy things?"

"Yeah, but there's not much there." The boy looked down for a moment, but then perked up. "Actually, you're much better off checking out the caravan."

"The caravan?"

"The Bright Caravan is in town. They have heaps of cool things, and since they travel around a lot they can probably help you more." The boy's eyes were alight with excitement.

"Thanks, kid," Vincent said.

"You're welcome, I hope it helps." The boy ran off.

"I've got a good feeling about this," Falric said.

"A caravan?" Vincent said.

"We can find out what route they use, get some supplies, and ask them about the area more. It could be very useful."

"I don't think I've seen one before," Alrion said.

"You'll know it when you see it," Vincent said.

They continued walking through the town, Alrion keeping his eyes open. He had heard of caravans mentioned but never witnessed one. He wondered how it would help.

As they neared what looked like the edge of town, he saw a row of brightly coloured wagons arranged in a semi-circle. There were streams of people, and lots of horses either wandering or tied up. Everyone appeared to be moving constantly, and the noise of conversations, banging, and general business filled the air.

"Wow," Alrion said. They were right, he did know it when he saw it. The people looked like a different sort, but he couldn't quite pinpoint why. But they were so strange when compared to the other townsfolk they had seen on their trip.

"This could be good," Alrion said.

"I hope so, we could use a break," Vincent said.

They made their way through the campsite, heading for the Bright Caravan. A lead wagon with 'Bright Caravan' painted on it occupied the entire space, the letters a garish yellow on a light blue background.

"Let's talk to their leader." Falric directed them to a man with a large decorative hat sitting near the lead wagon. He was surrounded by other people who were asking him questions.

"I'd say that's our man," Vincent said.

"He certainly stands out," Alrion said. As they approached the man the small crowd around him spread out and turned to face them.

"How may we help you fine folks? My name is Farver and the Bright Caravan is at your service." Farver tipped his hat, then replaced it on his head with a flourish. His voice had richness to it and energy that seemed out of place.

He looks a lot older than he sounds, Alrion thought.

"Farver, nice to meet you. I'm Falric, and this is Vincent and Alrion." Falric gestured to his companions. The movement looked positively spartan in comparison to what Farver had just done. "We just arrived here, and are looking to move on to Paperton. I was wondering if we could buy some supplies from you, or get some advice on the best way to go."

"Ah, Paperton. We don't trade there anymore, we're too big now and access is tricky. But we pass close by on our way. It's actually quite easy, there's a main road that will take you most of the way there."

"That's great. Do you have any horses you could part with?" Vincent said.

"No, I'm afraid we don't. But we can help you with some supplies."

"That'll do. Where do I go?"

"The rear wagon holds all our supplies." Farver looked Vincent up and down. "Are you good with that sword?"

"Good enough to be still walking and talking."

"We really can't spare the horses, but maybe you could travel with us until we are close to Paperton. It's slow going, but it would beat travelling on foot. You don't have any faster options."

"And in return?"

"In return, you help us out if we run into any difficulties. Saves you walking, and you can help yourself to supplies and food. I'll feel more comfortable, and maybe you won't even be needed."

"That's a pretty good offer." Vincent looked over at Falric.

"Are you expecting difficulties?" Falric said.

"No, it's a safe run and we are big enough to deter most would-be bandits. But I've heard some rumours flying around and thought it would make sense to travel together," Farver said.

"Sure, just give us a moment to discuss," Vincent said.

"By all means, but we will be packing up and leaving soon so we can make it to a good campsite this evening. If we don't see you, we will assume you are staying here."

"We'll let you know either way. I'll be back soon." Vincent walked away with Falric and Alrion close behind.

"What's wrong? Don't you trust this guy?" Alrion said.

"He's probably alright, but you never know. I'm more concerned for them, though."

"You think we will make them a target?" Falric said.

"Exactly. We have been attacked at just about every step since we left the academy. If it happens again while we are with them, there might be casualties. That would be on us."

"It's a concern for sure. But surely by being with them, we could be more invisible? The three of us walking alone will stick out. By going with the caravan, we might blend in and destroy the trail," Falric said.

"True. It's a risk either way." Vincent looked quite conflicted. He didn't seem particularly happy about either option.

I know that look. I've seen it before when he's been in the workshop and trying to choose between two awful choices.

"I'll leave it up to you to decide," Falric said.

Exactly what my father wouldn't want.

Alrion could see Vincent running through the scenarios in his mind. After a minute of deliberation, the blacksmith spoke up.

"Let's do it. The benefit outweighs the risks, and if they run into any trouble unrelated to us, we can sort that too."

"And if trouble does come looking for us, we can divert them away," Falric said.

"Agreed. Let's head back and let him know. Are you fine with this Alrion?"

They asked my opinion. Wow.

"It's what I would have chosen. We have the opportunity to help them and it may help us too." Alrion beamed at the sense of being included, finally.

"Great." Vincent started back towards the caravan. As before, the crowd around Farver parted when they were close.

"I see you approaching again, am I right that you're on-board?" Farver said.

"Yes, we're in. Thanks for the opportunity," Vincent said. Farver made a quick hand signal and a young boy ran off towards the rear of the caravan.

"He will let them know you are joining us. Head down and ask for anything you need urgently. There'll be another opportunity later today when we stop to make camp."

"How long until we make it to Paperton?" Alrion said.

"I expect we will part ways around midday tomorrow. It shouldn't take you more than a few hours to complete your journey from that point."

"Thanks again, we will see you later," Falric said.

"My pleasure. Donna will sort you out," Farver said. The three of them stepped away and watched him swamped by people once more.

"Busy guy," Alrion said.

"Yes, but very clever. He sized us up and determined we were not a risk, and could be useful to him. But he also offered a mutually beneficial proposition. He's a smooth operator." Vincent sounded quite impressed but wore a frown.

"Isn't that good?" Alrion was confused.

"Oh yes, it's good. It means that he has been doing this a while and knows how to work with people. He's quite alert, so let's assume that there will be trouble and have our guard up. I don't take him to be the type to worry unnecessarily."

And there it is. Trouble ahead.

"I agree," Falric said. They continued over to the rear wagon in the caravan and saw a tall, thin woman with short brown hair and glasses on. She was on the move constantly, packing things away, and rearranging storage in the wagon.

"You must be Donna?" Falric said.

"That's me. You must be the new folks. Anything, in particular, you need before we head off?"

"Something to snack on?" Alrion said. He couldn't ignore his stomach any longer.

"Not much here, it's all been packed away. I can find you something, though. Anything else?"

"No, I think we're fine. We may need some bedding later," Vincent said.

"We will handle that later tonight. Take this." Donna shoved a parcel at Alrion, then returned to rearranging things.

"Thanks, see you later," Alrion said.

"Bye," Donna said without turning around. She started muttering to herself and increased the pace at which she was working.

"What did you score?" Falric said.

"I think these are biscuits?" Alrion opened the packet and inspected the hard, round objects.

"You enjoy those. I have some stale bread for later," Vincent said with a chuckle.

"Sure, I'll take my chances with their food," Alrion said.

"Suit yourself," Vincent said. "Let's make ourselves useful."

"Sure." Together father and son helped pack up the caravan. Donna was quick to give them jobs once she saw them helping. Falric sat off to the side, supervising and chiming in with clever quips when he saw an opportunity.

"Bend with your knees!" Falric cried.

"He's enjoying himself too much," Vincent said. Alrion flashed him back a smile.

"Well you two, thanks for your help. You did more than my so-called helpers." Donna sighed.

"Since we're coming along, we thought it was worth giving you a hand," Vincent said.

"It made a difference. And now you can help me in another way. The three of you can ride in our wagon, and my helpers can walk alongside. That'll teach them to let guests outwork them."

"It's a tough job, but someone has to do it. You name it, we're your men," Falric said.

"Typical that he's all hands on deck when it comes to sitting around," Vincent said.

"Of course. Efficient use of resources. I have years of experience sitting down. I've been training all my life for this." Falric grinned at Donna.

"I'm all about efficiency. Now off you go, before you hold us up." Donna pointed to the rear of the wagon and the three of them headed over. They found a small space at the end, where they could sit on crates and barrels and enjoy the fresh air.

"This was a good idea." Vincent leaned back and looked relaxed for the first time in a long time.

"Agreed. If we can't get horses, then traveling with the caravan will do nicely. This trip has been a lot more eventful than I had expected. The sooner we reach Paperton the better," Falric said.

"Is that the last place we will be going?"

"No, but our way will be simpler once we get there."

"Still cryptic," Vincent said.

"I don't want to disappoint." Falric waved his hand in a mystical way. Alrion laughed. The conversation died down and he watched the countryside as they went.

The progress of the caravan was very slow, it was easy enough for the lazy workers to walk alongside the wagons. But they travelled consistently and without breaks.

"We are making good time. All things considered," Falric said. Vincent nodded.

"Looks like we won't be stopping for lunch." He pointed at the men walking alongside and saw that they were eating as they walked.

"I guess it would be too much effort to stop and restart this big a group," Alrion said.

"Exactly. And if they are wary of trouble, the more time they are in motion the better. There's probably some food here, let's check," Vincent said. He rummaged through the boxes and brought out some more biscuits, only these were plainer and more bread-like.

"These should do the job." Vincent handed them out but didn't start eating. Alrion bit into one and was surprised by the flavour. They were crispy, salted, and felt substantial.

"Pretty good," Alrion said. Vincent took a bite and seemed satisfied.

"Don't eat too many. You'll get too thirsty."

"Got it."

"This is nice and peaceful. Let's hope the rest of the journey is as uneventful," Falric said, and Vincent and Alrion murmured agreement.

The afternoon progressed steadily. Alrion could tell that they seemed to be climbing slowly, the ground rising in elevation.

"We're going up," he said.

"That's probably why they aren't going to Paperton. It's down by the water, and hard to access with this number of wagons," Falric said. Alrion was about to respond when he noticed the wagon jolt. It rapidly slowed, then stopped.

"Must be trouble, let me investigate." Vincent jumped out immediately and ran towards the front of the caravan.

"Let us also exit, I have a bad feeling," Falric said.

22

DIVIDED

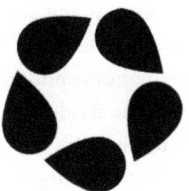

A lrion looked ahead and could see the whole caravan had stopped and there was a huddle of people next to the front wagon. He watched his father step into the huddle and converse with them.

"Definitely looks like something is happening," Alrion said.

"Let me see," Falric said. He closed his eyes and concentrated. His eyes opened, and he started walking away.

"I need to warn them."

"What is it?"

"Blighters," Falric whispered and Alrion took off after him. As they neared the huddle it opened as if welcoming them in.

"We've had a sighting," Vincent said.

"Blighters," Falric said.

"So, let's take that as confirmed. Do we know where they are coming from?"

"Not sure, we may even be surrounded."

"I have an idea. But you're not going to like it."

"No, if it's what I think it is." Falric shook his head furiously.

"I'm going to move forward, see if I can lure them away. The caravan is a sitting duck, and will be hard to defend."

"By yourself? That is suicide," Farver said. The people surrounding him murmured their agreement.

"It's a calculated risk. Not all will follow, but it will split them up and I can probably track where they are coming from. If there's a Tainted One directing them I can take him out and scatter the rest." Vincent sounded resolute.

"Then I can defend the caravan from any stragglers," Falric commented.

"Is this really a good idea?" Alrion said.

My father can handle himself, but this is something else. It doesn't feel right.

"It's the best we have. There's no time. If we get separated I will move on to Brangtur. That should confuse them. I will wait for you there," Vincent said.

"Sure. But we will be seeing you soon," Falric said.

"Take care of the old man." Vincent gave Alrion an affectionate pat on the shoulder.

"Dad, are you sure about this?"

"Don't worry about me, I can handle myself. Got a horse I can use?"

"Yes, take mine. She's black with a white stripe up around the front wagon. With luck, you will bring her back," Farver said.

"Done." Vincent ran towards the horse and jumped up into the saddle. After steadying himself he rode off along the road.

"Be safe," Alrion said, mostly to himself.

I know I'll see you again. But it doesn't feel like it will be soon.

Falric drew Farver aside.

"I am no tactician, but make sure you evenly spread your people out. The more we spread out the Blighters, the better. They will get more confused and be easier targets. Give me a horse and I will ride up and down the length of the caravan, taking them down as I can."

"Who are you?" Farver said.

"I'm a wizard. Battle is not my forte, but I can be useful. Very useful."

"Whatever you need. This caravan isn't just our livelihoods, it is also our home. Take Master Falric here to our fastest horse," Farver said.

"I'm coming too," Alrion said.

"Good, I need your help. Help me spot targets, and pay attention. It's going to get chaotic."

"Absolutely." Alrion felt the nerves come back, and his stomach churning. But inside the maelstrom was a tiny piece of calm.

This is what you should be doing. Just trust it.

"Incoming!" a voice yelled from the rear of the caravan. Falric was in the middle of mounting up when he stopped.

"Actually, you take the reins, so I can concentrate on the fight."

"No problem." Alrion mounted up and leaned forward, giving Falric room to sit behind him.

"Go!" Falric said. Alrion kicked the horse into action and headed towards the commotion. As they thundered along the caravan, he saw a pack of Blighters converging on the rear wagon.

"Ride past them in an arc," Falric said. Alrion spurred the horse on, heading directly at them and when close, steering the horse away. As they rode alongside the Blighters, a stream of fire flew out from Falric's hands and consumed them. Alrion continued the arc and turned the horse around.

"Good. Let's go back and look for more," Falric said. Alrion could see that the Blighters had either been killed outright or were being finished off by caravan folk. They returned to the main wagons and saw several Blighters splitting up and going after individual people.

"Slow down, I need more finesse here," Falric said. Alrion did as instructed, keeping a safe distance but riding closer to the Blighters. Falric pointed at one and a thin spear of fire shot out and pierced a Blighter through the eye. He dropped to the ground instantly.

"Wow, that's precise," Alrion said.

"Yes, but it takes a lot of concentration. Let's get the rest."

"On my way." Alrion picked up the pace and headed to the next Blighters. This time he slowed between two of them, and Falric let loose two more spears of fire. They continued in this fashion until they had reached the head of the caravan.

"There's a few here," Alrion commented.

"You aren't joking," Falric said. There must have been fifty Blighters streaming towards the caravan, a lone figure in the distance behind them.

"Who is that?"

"It's not the wizard; I'd say it is a Tainted One directing this lot. I want you to ride through the pack, so we can go after him," Falric said.

"I hope you know what you're doing." Alrion spurred the horse on.

"I'm going to have some fun with this," Falric said. Alrion wondered what he was talking about but soon saw. A giant bird comprised of flame hovered above them, swooped over their heads, and rushed ahead. The flame bird attacked the group of Blighters head on, the intense heat incinerating all it touched and blazing a path through them.

Alrion rode hot on its trail, making the most of the impact. As they rode through Falric fanned flames on either side, torching those that were still alive but confused by the attack.

One of them stumbled towards the horse, despite the burning flames. Alrion had no time to think. He summoned his power, channelling it into a forceful push knocking the Blighter far away. It didn't get up again.

"Good instincts. Leave the rest of the stragglers and let's go for the leader," Falric said. Alrion's face lit up with the thrill of battle and his successful contribution and urged the horse on, towards the lone man standing at the back.

The man was just standing there, motionless.

"Something's not right," Alrion said.

"Slow down and approach at a walk," Falric said. Alrion dropped his speed and the horse trotted towards the man, who remained motionless. Alrion could sense that Falric was up to something. He kept his eyes on the man and saw a cage built of fire assemble itself around the enemy.

"That should hold him, let's go have a chat," Falric said. Alrion looked back to see how the caravan was faring.

"Don't worry about them, they can finish up."

"Why did he let us capture him without a fight?" Alrion said.

"I'm not completely sure. However, I suspect it has to do with their communication link. I can imagine it would be disruptive having large numbers of Blighters in pain and dying all at once."

"Interesting." Alrion tucked that thought away for later. He dismounted and helped Falric down. Up close, the Tainted One looked normal. He had short dark hair, green eyes, and was looking down at the ground.

"Who sent you?" Falric said. The man looked up, not really seeing them. It was as if he was gazing past them.

"Who sent you?"

"The reclaimer."

"The reclaimer? Who is that?"

"He is the one that reclaims the world for us. For those touched by the Blight. He gives us a future."

"Does he have a name?"

"He is the reclaimer." The man had a fanatical look to his features.

"Is he a wizard?" Alrion said. The question seemed to jolt the man out of his trance-like state.

"What's it to you?"

"You attacked us. Why?" Alrion said.

"It's all part of his plan."

"Tell me more of this plan," Falric said.

"That's not part of the plan." The man reached into his boot and retrieved a small vial of liquid, downing it in one gulp.

"You have triumphed here, but you will not win," the man said, then collapsed to the ground. Falric released the fire cage and walked up to inspect him.

"He's dead. It must have been poison."

"That's crazy," Alrion said.

"Perhaps, perhaps not. However, there is a serious plot here that we cannot ignore. I am continually surprised by their ability to track us."

"What about my father? The fight is done now."

"Yes, the immediate danger is over, but I doubt he will return. He has good instincts, I think he will try and lure them away from us." Falric seemed quite clear on that.

There's something too neat about all this.

"You planned this? All along?"

"No, but we considered it if we were attacked again. He convinced me that it was a good idea. Don't worry about him, he can take care of himself. You and I also have an important job to do."

"I know."

"Let us return, and talk to Farver. He will want an update." Falric walked back to the horse. The two of them rode back to the caravan, Alrion trying not to look at the damage and devastation.

"Is that it?" Farver said as they approached.

"Yes, their leader is dead. Our friend is out looking for any others," Falric said.

"What were they after? I have not heard of such attacks."

"I'm not sure, but perhaps they were after us," Falric said. Farver's attitude changed completely. He regarded Falric with caution.

"Really?"

"It's our best theory. I am a wizard after all. We appreciate your help and hospitality, but we cannot endanger you any further."

I can see the relief on Farver's face.

"I appreciate your honesty and your gesture. Given what has happened, I think I would be forced to ask you to leave otherwise."

"No problem here. We will gather a few things and be on our way."

"Please take the horse as a token of friendship. It will speed you on your way."

"And if trouble follows us, it will be further from you."

"Indeed, it serves us both." Farver smiled.

"Thank you, and good luck," Falric said. Farver bowed.

"I'll fetch some supplies." Alrion darted off to the rear wagon.

"That was quite a fight," Donna said.

"It was quite intense. Is everyone alright?"

"I think so, apart from a few scares and some damage, I think we came out unscathed. Thanks to your help."

"Thanks. If you don't mind, I will grab a few things before we leave."

"You're leaving?" Donna gave him a sidelong glance.

"We are travelling with a wizard. We may be drawing their attention." Alrion braced himself for the response, but Donna seemed unfazed.

"Oh, I see. Well, take what you need and good luck."

"Thanks, Donna. Safe travels." Alrion quickly grabbed some blankets and food and stuffed them into his bag and ran off.

The sooner we leave the better. This is way too awkward. And I don't feel comfortable that we've put these people in danger.

"All set?" Falric said.

"Yes."

"Off we go."

"Sure." Alrion looked back and reflected on the situation.

The Bright Caravan is not as bright now, but it will endure. He nudged the horse forward and they galloped away.

Their progress on the horse was much faster than the caravan was travelling. Despite some initial discomfort they settled into the ride. Alrion was running through their last encounter with the Blighters over and over in his mind. He spoke at last.

"Falric, I have a question about magic."

"Go ahead."

"How come you seem to use a lot of fire magic? Is that on purpose, or is that just a coincidence?" Alrion ducked to avoid a low hanging tree branch and steered the horse towards the middle of the path.

"Good question. The simple answer is that everyone has different affinities with the various elements. A talent if you will. It just so happens that I have a talent with fire. It comes more naturally, so I end up using it more. That reinforces my comfort and ability with fire. It is generally a self-supporting cycle."

"Everyone has their own specialty?"

"More or less. Everyone will have an element that they lean towards, that is easier and generally more powerful for them." Falric leaned to the side, and a thin column of fire burst from his hand. It incinerated another branch that was looming from the other side of the path. The branch crumbled into ash, and started to fill the air. That reminded Alrion of something.

"Do you think the wizard that attacked us is fire-based as well?" he said.

"You really have been thinking about this. I'm not sure; I don't know enough to say. Maybe, but maybe not."

"I guess we will find out. I just thought it might be a way to narrow down who it is. Is there a way to test for an affinity?"

"We generally don't, it just comes out as part of the training. It is worth recognising and remembering. Knowledge about yourself is just as important as knowledge about magic and others."

"Makes sense to me." Alrion nodded along.

I wonder what I have? Maybe it is fire because I created such a big flame in that initial test.

"If you're wondering about your own affinity, then we shall have to wait and find out. Although if you're anything like your grandfather, it won't be so readily apparent."

"What do you mean?"

"He used all elements interchangeably without any sign of preference. Either he had no preference, or he masked it well."

"Interesting." The more he found out about his grandfather, the more amazing he seemed to be.

No pressure there.

"Yes, it made him a more rounded wizard. A very talented and dangerous man when he wanted to be."

"I guess I'll see how I go. Is all magic associated with an element?"

"Most, but there's no hard and fast rule on it." Falric leaned out again, unleashing a wave of force to push away some rubble that Alrion hadn't spotted. The horse startled a bit, but recovered quickly.

He's more aware than me and I'm steering us. Not a good look.

"How about healing magic?" Alrion said.

"Water."

"I can see how that would work."

"Yes, we will get to that tonight. Once we reach the campsite that the caravan was aiming for," Falric said. Alrion was satisfied with that response and kept riding.

After all that's happening, a healing spell would be nice. A chance to repair and not just destroy.

A NEW SKILL

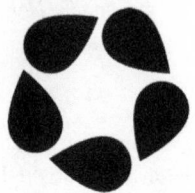

The terrain was sparse now, with grass, shrubs, and only the occasional tree. They were slowly ascending as they went, climbing what seemed like a small hill.

"We must be close now," Alrion said.

"Yes, not far to go. At the top of this hill should be a nice flat site. It's the most popular campsite in this area. Well, it used to be, a long time ago," Falric said. Alrion kept his eyes on the horizon, trying to spot their destination.

The countryside rolled on, and he lapsed back into just enjoying the ride and keeping his eyes on the dirt road. Finally, they crested a particularly steep section and emerged onto what had to be the campsite. To the side of the road was a large dirt area, with a big pit dug in the middle.

"That's where they light their fire," Falric said. Alrion rode on past it, observing the ground.

"Just stop somewhere at the end over there." Falric pointed. Alrion looked where Falric had suggested and picked a grass covered spot. He jumped down and held the horse steady while Falric dismounted. Then he led the horse to a nearby tree and tied it up.

"This will do nicely. It will be dark soon, and this is a good place to rest." Falric eased himself down onto the ground, sitting on his robe.

"What about the caravan?" Alrion said.

"They will have to make do I'm afraid, they won't make it here in time. It's for the best, though, if anything comes for us they won't be involved."

"True. I hope my father is alright."

I wonder where he is now. Maybe he's close we weren't delayed that long.

"He is, don't you worry. After we complete our task, we will go to Brangtur and meet up with him. The journey will do you good."

"Is it far?"

"Yes, quite a distance, and he's got a good head start on us. But that just means we have some time to advance your training."

"Speaking of which?"

"Yes, after dinner we shall go over a healing spell."

"Great." Alrion laid out their food and they ate in silence. Alrion was thinking about the battle they had just survived, and his small victory.

I'm not quite pulling my weight yet, but I'm contributing. It feels good. It feels different to being a blacksmith. It's less forced and the potential is huge.

Falric had done an amazing job with the Blighters and he wasn't even considered a battle-hardened wizard. There was a lot of room for Alrion to improve there. He could already tell there would be many battles in his future. It was hard for him to stop going over how he had screwed up in the tunnel beneath the Thundering Mountain.

Just get over it and focus on the path ahead. You can't go back and do better.

"We were going to discuss the healing spell," Falric said. "A very useful spell, with near infinite uses. It is water-based, which will help in your understanding of it. However, there is one thing that I must state at the beginning."

"Yes?" Alrion was fully alert.

"It is largely ineffective on yourself."

"I can't heal myself?" Alrion's heart sank.

But I was going to keep myself alive with this!

"Not effectively, no."

"Why not?"

"How should I explain this? The Spark is a special energy created by your body. You cannot use it to rebuild your own body. Does that make sense?" Falric was giving Alrion that same 'I'm sorry we just don't know but you'll learn to accept it' look that he had done a few times now.

"Sort of but what's the reason?"

"Your grandfather would have a good philosophical response to that, but I can't give you the technical explanation, I just understand it as fact. It's one of the basic laws of magic."

"That seems like quite a flaw," Alrion said, the disappointment clear in his voice.

"You could look at it that way or you could think about it this way. It works more effectively on other people. So, it is best used to support companions who are assisting you." Falric pointed to himself and smiled.

"I'll be able to heal you?"

"Not just me, anybody. But think of two wizards healing each other, sounds more useful now, doesn't it?"

"Yes, I suppose."

"Remember to think about what utility it can provide, and what that means for you. I think it's clear that you should not travel alone. And the healing spell is a good incentive for others to travel with you."

"That's a good way to think about it."

I did want another way of contributing, so it still does that.

"Of course. So, should we continue?" Falric said.

"Yes."

"Good. Another thing to mention, which you may have already guessed from the restrictions I explained, is that this spell absolutely requires the Spark to function. It cannot work otherwise."

"That makes sense, from what you said."

"It does, and will make more sense once you have tried it. The best explanation for the spell is like this. You know how with the push spell, you visualised the force it took to move an object?" Falric mimicked a push motion.

"Yes."

"This spell also includes a visualisation, but an entirely different one. Hand me that spoon." Falric pointed at a spoon that Alrion had used to eat some soup with. Falric wiped the spoon on his cloak and showed it to Alrion.

"Now it's not exactly polished, but what can you see?"

"I can see myself in the reflection. It's a bit warped though."

"No surprises there. Now I add a bit of water, what can you see now?" Falric said. Alrion stared intently at the water.

"Move the spoon around, and see what happens to the water," Falric said. Alrion did as instructed, slowly moving the spoon, and observing the water.

"Well depending on the position of the water, I can see myself."

"Great. I would have preferred to discuss this in another location, like say the Great Mirror Lake but I think you can understand it. But the key to this visualisation is your reflection in the water."

"Sure." Alrion wasn't quite sure where Falric was going with this. But his explanation of the push spell had been quite effective.

"You have some scepticism, which is good. Allow me to explain further. What I need you to do here is picture yourself reflected in the water. The way you are now, without injury. And what the spell does, is use the water as a medium in which to return your body to the state it is in now," Falric said. Alrion took a minute to absorb the information.

"That's crazy."

"Maybe a little, but your body is more water than anything else. Does it still sound so crazy?"

"Yes," Alrion said emphatically. Falric laughed.

"I can't argue the point; it's a little out there but you'll come around to my line of thinking. Anyway, the water component of this spell is both a medium and a visualisation aid, but the Spark is what makes the spell work. So, take any thoughts of crazy and get rid of them."

"I'm sorry, I'll try and focus more."

"Good. Don't worry, everyone goes through this. However, this is not an easy spell, and you wanted to learn. It's a vital lesson, for my health as well as yours."

"Yeah, I can see why it might be useful being able to heal you," Alrion said.

"Yes, like I said its uses are infinite. Now, let's try something." Falric sidled closer to Alrion.

"Take a good look at my hand," Falric said. After he had Alrion's attention, he continued.

"Make a mental picture of how my hand looks. All the lines, the spots, the roughness in parts. Is it firm in your mind? Good. Because now I'm going to do this." Falric took a knife and cut across his palm. A red line instantly appeared, and blood began to ooze out immediately.

"What!" Alrion called out.

"That really stings. Please heal my hand if you don't mind."

"How do I do it?" Alrion started to panic.

This is too intense.

"Find your Spark. Instead of letting the fire of it take over, think about the cool clarity of the water. Imagine a sheet of water hovering over my hand, and its reflection showing my healed hand and guiding my hand back to that state." Falric was quite calm in his explanation, even though the blood continued to flow. Alrion closed his eyes and listened to Falric's words.

He had trouble reaching his Spark, but his frustration quickly jumped up and helped him locate it. He wrestled with it, trying not to channel it the same way as he had before. He knew instinctively that an explosive burst could be quite catastrophic.

"Careful, my hand is starting to heat up."

"Sorry." Alrion continued his concentration. He used Falric's words to construct a visualisation, to see a circular sheet of water reflecting a healed hand, and a stream of mist flowing down to repair the hand, guiding it into the new state. In his mind, the hand was slowly repairing itself. He could see the cut closing, the skin knitting together to repair the slice. Once he was finished, he could see in his mind a perfectly formed hand, untouched.

Alrion opened his eyes and looked for real. Falric's hand looked different but there was a mess of blood on it.

"What happened?" Alrion said.

"Don't worry, it just wasn't as picture-perfect as your visualisation. But it's fine," Falric said. He took some water and slowly poured it over his hand. The blood washed away, and the hand looked completely healed.

"Wow! I did it! I don't believe it."

It's a miracle. I healed his hand. That's not possible.

"You sure did, you have good instincts. Looks and feels fine."

"But why did it look so bloody?"

"Well just because you healed me, doesn't mean that it wasn't a bit of a process. With time and skill, you can make it a cleaner fix. But it was nothing a bit of water couldn't clear away."

"I get it. But, wow, I can't believe I healed you." Alrion grabbed Falric's hand and examined it up close.

"Yes, I am also a little surprised." Falric took his hand back.

"Really? You cut yourself unsure if I could heal you?"

"Of course, it's the best way to learn. Besides, if it really bugged me I could stick a bandage on. It's minor enough."

"Ha-ha alright," Alrion said. He was beaming from the success of the spell.

"You have done well, and this is actually an important milestone. However, before we move on, let's quickly reflect on this spell. It is powered by Spark, but requires a precise visualisation."

"You need the proper knowledge to do it."

"Exactly, you're catching on. If I had just told you to heal my hand, who knows what would have happened," Falric said. He laughed, a mixture of mirth and horror at the thought.

"That could be messy. But all is well."

"Indeed. The reason why this is an important milestone is that you have successfully used visualisation to focus your Spark in a different and unusual way. This means that with practice and preparation, your ability to cast many and varied spells can be expanded."

"Great! I'm sorry for being sceptical. Twice now you have taught me new spells, in a very effective way."

"Don't worry, it's completely normal. And we are skipping through this process rather quickly."

"Now I can learn more spells." Alrion felt like he had caught the bug. He needed more spells to cast.

"You can even learn some by yourself. Let me fetch something." Falric rummaged through his bags and removed an old book with a navy-blue cover, but without a title.

"Here, take this." Falric handed the book to Alrion. Alrion felt the weight of it and the age.

"What is this?"

"That is my spellbook. There is a wealth of knowledge contained within that tome. All kinds of wonderful spells, with notes about how to cast them, and which pillar of magic is key."

"This is incredible." Alrion leafed through it. "Hang on; there are so many blank pages."

"Yes, well you see it is a magic spellbook. You infuse the spellbook with the new spells, and it understands what they are. And it will only show you those that are within your means."

"Have you cast every spell in here?"

"Yes, I built that spellbook myself. Your grandfather had his own, with pages even I could not read," Falric said, chuckling to himself.

"Thanks. Can you really give this to me? Isn't it too much?" Alrion started to hand it back. Falric refused to take it.

"Not really, all the knowledge is up here now." Falric tapped his head, "and it's good for you to discover some things on your own."

"I really appreciate it; I will take good care of it."

"Good, that is all I ask."

"One other question, about the healing spell."

"Sure, what is it?"

"Can it heal anything?"

"Just about. There are a few odd cases, but it is quite versatile."

"What about the Blight?" Alrion said. Falric smiled.

"I was wondering if you were going to ask about that. No, the Blight is a different thing altogether. I don't know the spell your grandfather used, but it was not a healing spell. Not at all."

"Oh, OK. I was just curious."

Did you really think it was going to be that easy?

"It was a good question, and many have pondered why. Why is the Blight not treatable as a wound or illness? Food for thought. However, let's not get too bogged down in those things. I think we have had a pretty big day, and I'm keen to turn in."

"I'm a bit tired," Alrion said, not realising it until Falric brought it up.

"That's also due to the healing. It is quite Spark intensive, so keep that in mind."

"Will do."

There's a lot of things I need to keep in mind.

"Now help me clear up here," Falric said. Alrion helped him put everything away and they readied themselves for sleep.

"It's a clear night. So lovely to sleep under the stars," Falric said.

"I agree. I used to do this often, back in Hamley." Alrion sighed. "I was supposed to go the day you arrived but never did. And I never spoke to my friends about leaving."

"They will understand. It's a different life you need to live now, and your quest is more urgent than we initially thought. Cherish the quiet life you had there, and perhaps one day you'll achieve it once again."

"Are you speaking from experience?"

"This is more excitement than I've ever had. I was destined to live as an administrator. When I was a young boy, I was growing up in Paperton. Bound to be a scholar, until your grandfather found me. And yet I ended up behind a desk anyway!"

"I guess we never know what's in store for us." Alrion looked at the stars. They appeared different tonight. A little brighter.

"We never do and it's a privilege for us to have this quest. We have the chance to make a difference in the lives of many people. However, enough philosophy, this old wizard is tired. Goodnight, Alrion."

"Goodnight," Alrion said but he could already hear Falric snoring.

How did he fall asleep so fast? Alrion wondered. It had to be something about being old. Alrion couldn't sleep easily, despite his tiredness. He thought about the fight they recently were in, the Blighters and the Tainted One. Then about his father.

I hope you are alright. Why couldn't you meet us at Paperton? Alrion thought. Surely, a diversion wouldn't require such a long journey. Well, he would get to the bottom of it but first they had to get to Paperton and wherever the next destination was. As he fell asleep, Alrion imagined what it would be like to be a fully trained wizard, fearless and with spells at his fingertips.

24

FIRE AND EARTH

Alrion woke, a feeling of dread filling him. Something was not right. He sat up swiftly and turned his head, looking for Falric. He wasn't there, and it looked like he had just upped and left.

"Not good," Alrion said to himself. He rose and tried to shake the sleepiness from his head. He sensed something happening in the distance, so took off at a run.

He heard sounds, which helped him pinpoint what was happening. He couldn't describe what they were exactly, but it sounded like the earth was cracking. Alrion reached the road, but the sound was coming from further away. He kept running, trying to track the noise, and figure out what was going on.

I hope it's not more Blighters. This wasn't supposed to happen, Alrion thought. He increased his speed and searched the horizon for anything of note. He started to notice disturbances in the terrain. Land turned over, soil everywhere. Scorch marks on trees and the grass.

This is some kind of battle. Maybe it's the wizard?

He pushed on, the urgency of the situation raised in his mind. If there was a fight, he had to help somehow. He couldn't do much, but he could do something. The noises got louder and louder. It wasn't just that he was closing in, but the fight was escalating. He pushed through a small bunch of trees, sure that whatever he was after was on the other side.

As Alrion emerged from between the trees he stopped dead still. The ground was torn up, big mounds of earth missing. Large rock formations littered the space, and a few small fires burned. But what took Alrion's breath away was the view of the two wizards locked in battle. Falric, and the wizard in black.

A ring of flame surrounded Falric. He was shooting a wave of fire from his hand at the black wizard, but the black wizard had protection from a wall of earth and was hurling lances of stone at Falric. Alrion realised that what he was sensing was the magic being wielded by these wizards. It was their Spark, raging in conflict. He looked between the two, unsure of how to help. Now that he was here, he didn't know whether to go to Falric's aid or try and attack the enemy wizard.

I'll try a push attack. Maybe I can destabilise the wizard and give Falric an opening.

He was just preparing when he saw Falric's face. Falric had spotted him, and a sudden look of anger surged across it. Alrion was surprised and shocked. Falric shook his head, then turned his attention back to the black wizard.

What does that mean? What should I do? Alrion thought. The black wizard caught his attention. All his stone lances had been melted and turned away by Falric's fire. He was trying a new approach.

The ground started to crack and split apart, and Falric lost his footing temporarily as the dirt beneath him rose up in a jagged chunk. However, he wasn't just being raised, a whole section of the cliff was being pushed towards the edge. In concert, a rolling wave of earth was coming in to block any possible escape.

Falric could sense what was happening, and started to react. However, he stopped all of a sudden. His gaze met Alrion, and he closed his eyes. Falric and the mound of earth he was standing on toppled over the cliff. The wave of earth crashed over the top. And then all of a sudden, the seismic activity ceased, and the black-garbed wizard walked over to inspect his handiwork.

I'm next, Alrion thought, and he ducked back behind the trees he had just emerged from. He continued to peer through to see what the wizard was doing. He seemed to be watching carefully for any signs of Falric. After he was satisfied, the black wizard looked over at where Alrion was hiding. Alrion froze with fear, unable to act.

I can't fight that, he thought. The black wizard's gaze remained fixed on Alrion's location for a moment, then continued. The wizard relaxed and started walking away, back toward the road. Alrion ducked down and crept away in the opposite direction, trying to stay hidden. Once he had reached the last piece of cover, he stayed in the brush waiting.

After he thought it was safe, he emerged to inspect the scene of the battle. There were huge tracts of earth missing or displaced, some appearing molten and still glowing. He avoided those and carefully stepped over to the edge. Below were the lake and the shore, but there was a huge mess of earth and rocks now on the ground. A colossal chunk of the cliff was missing and dispersed down below.

Falric is down there somewhere. But there's no way he survived.

But he couldn't abandon his friend and mentor. So, he found a way to clamber down the broken cliff, the destruction forging a path for him. He picked up some cuts and bruises on the way, but he arrived at the bottom on unsteady feet. The extent of the damage was even worse up close. He couldn't believe how much rubble was here.

Better get started.

He wasn't sure where to look, so started moving larger stones that looked like they could roll. It was slow progress and felt reassuring but when he stepped back to survey his progress, it looked like he had achieved nothing.

"Falric!" he called out. His desperation had increased, and time was against him. There was little chance that the wizard would come back. He listened closely for any signs of a response. Nothing.

I've got to do something, Alrion thought. His frustration was rising. He couldn't help Falric in his time of need. He felt useless.

"Damn it!" Alrion cried out, kicking out at rocks. He latched onto the feelings of doubt, frustration, and helplessness and tried to use them. He felt his Spark and amplified it. Then he pictured in his mind, all the earth and the rocks and the dirt flying away and revealing Falric. He focused all his might and once he had reached his limit let it all out in an explosive push.

It was cathartic and freeing. And destructive. He couldn't see anything due to all the dust in the air. He closed his eyes and waited for it all to settle. His senses were heightened by his tension and the magic he had just unleashed, and he could feel the dust falling to the ground. His breathing slowed, and panic took over.

What if the wizard sensed the magic and returned looking for Falric? Alrion thought. He felt a pit in his stomach, knowing that he would be powerless in that situation. As visibility returned to the area, he surveyed what he had done. Damaged and scattered rocks covered the whole area. But all he had done was remove a layer or two of rubble. There were still plenty of rocks covering the ground.

How could there be so much? Alrion wondered as he walked around. He prodded rocks here and there, hoping that he would find a giant nook with Falric lying safely within, but he found nothing.

"No!" Alrion called out, softer this time. Despair was rising within him as he realised that Falric was gone. Even if he had survived the fall and the rockslide, he was too weak to free himself and Alrion had been unable to excavate the rocks either. He could do nothing more. Alrion slammed his arm against a nearby pile of rocks, briefly enjoying the release but not relishing the pain. He looked around once more and felt only one thing: alone.

Alrion walked along the shore, looking for a way to return to their camp without having to climb up the rocks. He was also secretly hoping that he would spot something on his way but once he passed the impact site, nothing else suggested that anyone was there. With each step away, his heart felt heavier as he walked away from his mentor. He remembered his fear of the black wizard returning, but in that moment, he didn't care.

How can I be the chosen one, when I can't even help one person? There's no way I can reach the Pool of Knowledge by myself.

He kept walking, unsure of what to do next but knowing he should at least collect their things. He arrived back at the camp, expecting to see it ransacked and destroyed but it was exactly as he had left it. Alrion carefully examined Falric's belongings, trying to find any clues as to how things had happened. His bag was undisturbed, and his bed had been slept in.

It just looks like he awoke and went straight to confront the black wizard.

He rifled through Falric's things, looking for anything that might be of use. There was a notebook and some clothes, but nothing of note.

He already gave me the spellbook, Alrion thought. That would have been the most valuable thing. Alrion packed up Falric's things and left the bag on the ground. Then he did the same for his own belongings. Soon he was staring at an empty campsite, with two bags and a horse tied up. He mounted the horse with both the bags and started to ride away.

He took the long path around, returning to the shore where Falric had fallen. He dismounted and walked on foot to the middle of the destruction. He dug out a few rocks and placed Falric's bag into the nook.

"Farewell my friend, you deserved better. I am sorry I couldn't be more help. I feel responsible for the whole thing. You were only here to protect me, but you shouldn't have lost your life." Alrion choked back the tears. "I'm not worth it, no matter what that trial said. I can't go on, I can't complete our quest. But I'll return your spellbook to the academy so that your knowledge will not be lost." Despite his best efforts, a tear dripped onto the bag, and he quickly covered it with more stones.

This is not right. Why did this happen? Alrion thought as he walked away. He mounted the horse and turned away, wanting to put the whole thing behind him as fast as possible. He took his time returning to the road, not wishing to injure the horse, then kicked the horse into a gallop.

Let's go home, he thought. It would mean dealing with the issue of his father having gone ahead, but he would understand.

I'll send a letter when I get to a proper town.

It would still be an adventure getting home, but he just had to retrace his steps. With care, he could do it; it would just take time. He barely even took in the scenery, instead focusing on what he would need to return. He almost didn't notice the lone figure standing on the road ahead. When he did he stopped abruptly, almost falling off the horse. He couldn't see who it was, the shape of the person concealed by a cloak.

Alrion's first thought was that the black wizard had indeed found him but after the initial shock, he saw that it wasn't the case. The figure was too short and didn't have the same aura of dread and despair. No, this was someone else. But it was too coincidental that they were just standing there, looking at him. Waiting.

I guess I don't really have a choice. That's the way home, and that person is in the way. I'll have to go and see who they are.

He nudged the horse forward, and slowly approached the mysterious figure.

At least since I'm mounted I can make a hasty escape if required. He knew that trouble was up, one way or another.

25

THE RETURN

"Hello there, stranger," a female voice said. At first, Alrion didn't recognise it but knew it was familiar. He squinted at the figure, trying to discern more detail about who it was.

"Don't tell me you forgot about me already?" the voice continued, tinged with disappointment.

"Show your face," Alrion said. The figure drew back her hood.

"Lara, wasn't it? I don't really have the patience for your games today." Alrion glared at her. She seemed a little startled by the depth of his anger.

Of all the times to show up!

"Not even to get your ring back?" Her voice lost some of its playfulness.

"Sorry, too late. Don't care."

"That's a big change of heart. Where are your friends?" Lara looked around, concern starting to show on her face.

"One is dead, the other has gone ahead." Alrion was too weary to sugarcoat his response. He sagged down in the saddle a little.

"I didn't expect that ..." Lara said.

"Neither did I."

"So, where are you heading now?"

"Home. If you feel like following me again, I can guarantee that it will be a boring trip, so you shouldn't bother." Alrion nudged the horse forward. It took a few tentative steps.

"You don't have the look of someone who completed his quest." Lara challenged him with her eyes. He stopped the horse again.

"My quest? What would you know anyway?"

"I've been watching and following. I know your group was up to something. Something important. But it looks like you are giving up." She jabbed an accusing finger at him.

"Not that it's any of your business, but you're right. But I don't care for your judgement. You are just a petty thief." Alrion nudged his horse forward again.

I can't deal with this right now. I just have to get away.

"I am neither of those things." Lara tossed something at Alrion hard. He caught it against his chest and looked closely. It was the pouch containing his ring, the one given to him by his father.

"This doesn't change anything. Just leave me alone." Alrion pocketed the ring and directed the horse to the side to navigate around her. Lara stepped in front of the horse.

"That was a sign of good faith. Just talk to me about this." She paused to watch his reaction, and then continued, "You may think of me as a nobody, but I've followed your trail since Carford and I've seen some crazy things on the way. The more I think about it, the more I realise that something important is happening and I want to get involved. So just talk to me."

Alrion looked and listened. The edge from her voice was completely gone. It was flat and direct.

Maybe she is telling the truth? He thought. He wanted to just storm off, but there was something oddly sincere about what she had said. He searched her face for a reason to ride away. He didn't see one, and let out a deep sigh.

"There's a campsite not far from here. Let's go there."

"Are you going to make me walk?"

"Fine." Alrion shuffled forward on the horse and gave her a spot to jump on. She clambered up with ease and held onto him.

"Don't fall off." Alrion turned the horse around, riding back to the campsite. He didn't really want to return, but it was the only sensible place to go and it wasn't far. Lara didn't even try to say anything, which was fine by him. It would be hard enough talking to her as it was, so any break in the conversation was good.

When they arrived back at the campsite, Alrion immediately looked over at where he had spent the night. He could see the impression where Falric had slept. He held back a tear, it was still all so raw. He mechanically dismounted and pulled out a blanket from his pack, and laid it out on the ground. Lara sat down, and he sat next to her.

"So, what are we talking about?"

"What happened here?" Lara said. She sat quietly, waiting for him.

"We stayed here overnight. I awoke early, noticing something was wrong. I found my friend Falric battling an evil wizard." Alrion looked at Lara, but she remained silent, waiting for him to continue.

"I was frozen, unsure of what to do. Falric noticed me and waved me away, so

I hid. Within minutes it was over, and he was buried under the rubble of the collapsed hillside."

"I'm so sorry. He looked like a genuinely nice person. Is that wizard still around?"

"No, I think he has left now."

"Is that the same one that has been following you the whole time?"

"How do you know about that?" Alrion couldn't hide the suspicion in his voice.

"Like I said, I've been following along, and you have left a massive trail behind you. So much destruction."

"It's not my fault, and that's why we split up. To try and confuse them and stop the pursuit." Alrion threw up his hands in frustration. This talk wasn't helping.

"What are they after?"

"I don't know. Either me, or what I am after."

"Which is?" Lara leaned in closer.

"I don't know if I can trust you."

"Why not?" She leaned in closer again, staring into his eyes. There was an intensity there that surprised him.

"Like you said, you have been here all along. You could be part of their plan, and giving me the ring is a ruse to gain my trust!" Alrion let loose. Lara flinched a little, but maintained her gaze.

"Don't hold back there. Look, I don't know what else I can do to convince you, but let me say this. You're alone, and you're abandoning your quest, whatever it is. Do you really think it's acceptable to do that and make your friend's sacrifice meaningless?"

"What do you mean my friend's sacrifice?"

"From what you said it is clear that Falric ended the fight before you could intervene. He did that to protect you from the other wizard."

"It does seem like that," Alrion said, looking down at the ground. He felt worse.

Why is she doing this?

"I've been drifting for a long time. Floating from town to town, taking what I needed to survive, doing odd jobs. Not classy stuff. I didn't know what I was seeking all that time. More running than seeking to be honest. But now I know. It's a purpose. I've been adrift with no purpose." Lara looked resolute. Like she had finally decided.

"And now?" Alrion was curious to hear what she had to say.

"And now I've seen that you are on an important mission and you need my help. I want to help."

"Why do I need your help?"

"No offense, but you're greener than the grass. You've no experience of the world, and despite what you have been doing on this trip you're still new. I have many useful skills, I've been just about everywhere, and I can spot danger coming. I've got great instincts," Lara said. He didn't respond immediately.

"What do you get out of it?"

"I get to do something meaningful. I am tired of wandering aimlessly."

Maybe this is a real offer. Can I really say no to that, and turn my back on everything?

"Where do we go from here? If I agree that is."

"You tell me what we're doing, and we turn around and we hit the trail again. You set the rules of engagement." Lara stood. Alrion joined her.

"I'm tired, and I've been through hell this last day. You're right, in that I was giving up. I feel helpless and alone and like a failure. What's to stop us failing at the next trial anyway?" he said.

"I tailed you here, without being spotted by your pursuers, across several forms of transport and without any of you spotting me except when I baited you. Don't underestimate what I can do," Lara said.

Alrion considered her words and paced around the campground. He was unsure. Her help seemed too convenient and unexplainable but since he was about to abandon his task anyway, what did he have to lose? If they failed together, that was her fate for joining him.

If I try again and fail, it's no worse than abandoning. It's better, because at least I tried. I can't turn my back on Falric, and everything he believed in.

"I'll tell you a bit more. And if you still want to come, I'll take your help. There will be some rules."

"Of course."

"I'll explain later, as required but I guess this is key. As you originally guessed, my friend Falric was a wizard. In fact, he was head of the Wizard Academy. He was also the successor to the wizard Granthion, who cleansed Avaria of the Blight." Alrion watched her reaction, and was secretly pleased that her eyes widened.

"I've heard of Granthion, that's amazing."

"It was an incredible feat. Here's where it gets crazier. I am Granthion's grandson, and Falric was convinced that I have the ability to cleanse the world of the Blight."

"What?" Lara practically shouted. Alrion let out a tiny laugh.

"Yes, that's right. I know it sounds ridiculous."

"For a wizard like Falric to believe it, it must be true." Lara recovered from the shock and looked even more intense than before.

Just who is she?

"And that's why we were on this journey. There is a place not far from here, called the Pool of Knowledge."

"I've heard of it." Lara didn't sound like she was bluffing.

"What?"

"I have an interest in hidden things and places, especially incredibly valuable ones. Don't look so surprised." Lara seemed annoyed.

"I guess in your line of work, it wouldn't be too strange. Anyway, my task is to visit the Pool of Knowledge and see if I can learn the spell required to cleanse the Blight."

"We have to get there!" Lara started heading for the horse.

"We? You're still up for this? Knowing that there's an evil wizard and potentially every creature afflicted with the Blight out to get us?" Alrion watched Lara stop and turn around to face him.

"Of course. I have a stake in this. Not only do I believe in fate, and that I found you for a reason, but also, I have a personal connection. The Blight took my brother. It tore our family apart, and I would not want that to happen to anyone else. If I can help, if I can make the difference to remove the Blight from the world, I will do it. A hundred times over." The fire in her eyes was unmistakable, and undeniable.

"I'm sorry to hear about that. Until recently I never had to deal with the Blight."

"It's fine, but don't you ever try and abandon this quest again. If you do I will hunt you down." Lara let slip a tiny smile.

"Deal. However, don't steal anything else from me, or I'll hunt you down myself. And while I may not be as tricky as you, I'm learning a lot of tricks of my own."

I don't understand this. But it seems right somehow.

"Deal. So, what's the plan?"

"We need to get to Paperton. That's my next lead, as far as I know there will be people there who can direct me further."

"Paperton is not far. In fact, it is the only place of note around here. I'm sorry to say this, but that wizard after you is probably headed there."

"Then I guess we need to hurry along. But there's one thing I need to do before we leave here."

"What's that?" Lara had been returning to the horse but turned back again.

"I need a new spell, something with a bit more firepower."

"Such as?"

"Fire. I was being pretty literal." Alrion chuckled.

"Oh, right. How do you learn those?"

"I have a book, given to me by Falric. Fire was his specialty, so it seems fitting to learn the basics next. I want to have something else up my sleeve before my next encounter. I've seen firsthand how useful it is in dealing with the creatures of the Blight."

"Can I see?" Lara said.

"Sure, this is it." Alrion pulled out the spellbook. As he leafed through it, he gave Lara occasional sidelong glances.

"Look, I promised I wouldn't steal anything else from you. Not that I would try anyway, all the pages are blank."

"Ha, to you maybe. To a wizard, they are full of instructions, diagrams, and other useful information. Falric said that the spellbook was somehow protected magically."

"That's good to know."

"You know not all magic requires a wizard, but that's a talk for another day. This looks promising, basic fire conjuring." Alrion went quiet and studied the pages carefully, leafing back and forth in the same section. Lara watched him with curiosity.

"I've never seen magic up close."

"It won't be that spectacular. Let me concentrate." Alrion closed his eyes and ran through the spell in his head. It was simple really, there was a visualisation aspect, but it seemed easy. His Spark could easily start a fire, he had even done it before any training as part of his initial test.

He rotated his hand so that his palm faced up, then concentrated on his Spark. He channelled his frustration and anger at his powerlessness, drawing upon his Spark and expanding it. Then he channelled it into his hand, imagining a flame appearing above his hand, extending upwards. He could feel the heat and hear the whoosh as it flared up.

"Wow!" Lara called out and jumped backward. Alrion opened his eyes and saw a flame dancing above his hand. It was alternating between being small and contained, and rising like a giant pillar.

"It's harder than it looks," he said apologetically, and focused on it more. He took the huge surge of Spark within him and put it in a box, then visualised it to be the lamp that he had originally used when Falric came to test him. The flame started to take shape and looked like it was contained within a lamp.

"It's actually working," Alrion said, some surprised joy sneaking into his voice.

"It sure is!" Lara was transfixed by the dancing flame, her eyes following its motion.

"I think I'll quit while I'm ahead," Alrion said, as he felt his focus dropping a little. He mentally extinguished the flame and it puffed out in an instant. He examined his hand carefully, expecting to see some signs of the fire.

"Hand survived?" Lara said.

"Yes, it looks fine. Just a little warm." Alrion turned it over and felt it with his other hand. "I feel better."

"Better because you learned another spell?"

"Partly. Better because I released some of my frustration into the fire."

"Sounds good to me. And you avoided burning down this entire area."

"Yeah, that's also a plus." Alrion managed a small chuckle.

"Are we good to go?" Lara looked quite impatient.

"Yes. We really should leave. How long to Paperton?"

"Riding we should be there today, provided there are no more adventures." Lara climbed up onto the horse, leaving a space at the front for Alrion.

"I can't promise anything, but I think there's been enough excitement for today." Alrion checked to make sure everything he needed was packed and looked over the campsite one more time.

"It feels better leaving this time. More hopeful, less depressing." Alrion untied the horse.

"Good. You can do this."

"Thanks. I appreciate the help, I know I've been cautious and not trusting, but sorry in advance I will continue to be. Just realise that it's not because I'm ungrateful." Alrion clambered onto the horse, and steadied himself. He grasped the reins. Before he could direct the horse, he felt Lara holding onto him. It felt completely natural.

"Don't worry, I understand. You'll see, your trust today is well-founded."

"I take it we follow the road?"

"Yes, I'll show you the path when we need to divert to Paperton."

"Let's go then." Alrion wheeled the horse around and started their journey. The wounds were still raw, but he left some of the pain behind him.

26

THE PAPER GATEKEEPERS

The ride went smoothly, and they progressed swiftly along the main road. Alrion explained more to Lara as they went, including some basic information and filling in some of the gaps.

"You've come a long way. I probably haven't given you enough credit," she said.

"Not really."

"I apologise, but now's the time to prove it. We are almost there." Lara pointed into the distance. Alrion could see Paperton now, nestled down in a valley next to the lake. It was a sprawling collection of stone buildings with tiled roofs.

"Doesn't look very organised," he said.

"That is the town of scholars. It looks perfectly appropriate. Like stacks of paper left haphazardly around the place." Lara laughed.

"When you put it that way it does seem about right. You've been here before?"

"A while ago, but only as a visitor. I can direct you to their main hall, from what you said we should start there."

"Sounds good to me. Here we go." Alrion began the descent. As they traversed the winding path down to Paperton Alrion understood why the caravan did not take the route anymore. At times the path was relatively narrow, and the turns were tight. It would take the caravan a very long time to navigate that path, with no guarantee that they would be able to complete the journey.

"What can you tell me about them? The scholars?" he said.

"Not much, but they are sticklers for rules and regulations. They have laws and by-laws and statutes and all other kinds of things that must be followed. They do not believe in just figuring it out. You may have some difficulty getting their help."

"Thanks for the tip. I'd rather know before going in there, so I can try and start on the right foot." Alrion pulled the reins harshly, avoiding a nasty tumble. Lara didn't say anything, but did grip his shoulder so hard he felt her nails dig in.

Almost killing myself by falling off a horse wouldn't be the best introduction

"They sure do love their paperwork there." Lara picked up the conversation without much of a pause, "But you definitely need their help, from what Falric mentioned to you only they will know how to get to the Pool of Knowledge."

"Imagine that. What we need is kept safe by paper-pushers and not guards."

"A refreshing change."

"Definitely." Alrion could see more of the town now. It had a quaint quality to it, like it was a small village that had grown organically. It didn't have the harshness of some of the larger towns he had seen.

"Keep along here, there is a large hall at the end of this road," Lara said as they entered the town. Alrion couldn't see what she was referring to, due to the winding of the road but he followed the route, taking in the odd architecture as he went. Unlike other places, there weren't many people on the street.

"Where is everyone?"

"Not sure, maybe there's something on?"

"I hope we're not too late," Alrion said. If the black wizard knew about Paperton he could already be here.

Just focus on the task here. You can worry about him later.

A few turns later and Alrion finally spotted what Lara had been talking about. A giant stone hall sat above the rest of the town at the end of the road. It had a large black and white clock mounted at the top, and multiple stone columns framing the entrance.

"That must be it."

"That's it. It's the heart of their town, and also the brains." Lara laughed. Alrion smiled.

That was a terrible joke.

"Into the scholar's den," he muttered as they pushed forward. He noticed several horses tied up out the front, so he slowed and dismounted. After Lara bounded off, he tied up their horse and started to ascend the steps to the front door. He could hear the sound of talking from inside.

"Try and keep quiet so we can figure out what is going on," Lara said.

"Sure." Alrion slowed his walk and looked for people who might challenge him but there was nobody around. He reached the main doors, which were closed. With care, he pushed against one door.

It's not locked!

He continued to open the door and slipped inside, holding it for Lara to join him.

Alrion found himself inside a massive hall. The main floor was full of people, with a stage and a lectern at the end housing several others. He looked up and could see gallery after gallery of people in attendance as well.

"The whole town must be here," Alrion whispered.

"Must be. Let's keep it quiet," Lara said and Alrion nodded. He moved closer and lurked behind the back row of people.

"That concludes item eighty-seven of the agenda. Seal the room for the last agenda item," a strong male voice called out from the front. Two imposing men stepped forward towards the doors and stopped.

"Who are you?" the first man said.

What do I say? They'll probably realise I'm a stranger. I better just be straight with them.

"I'm Alrion, a visitor."

"This is a private meeting, get out." The man reached out to assist them leaving.

"I'm sorry but I really must see your leader. It's an urgent matter." Alrion stood his ground. Lara stood with him.

"You may file a meeting request tomorrow, and it will be processed in due course. But you must leave now." The man sighed wearily and pointed to the door.

"He's a wizard, very important business. Can't we file the paperwork later?" Lara said.

"Wizards have no special permissions, they must also follow the same rules and regulations as the rest of us," the second man said.

"You don't understand, this is an emergency. Now is the time to raise this, and I think with everyone here the perfect chance to brief everybody at once," Alrion said.

"No. Please leave before we are forced to escort you out. With force." The first man took a step forward.

"Why are we delayed in securing the room?" the man at the front called out.

"Out of my way," Alrion said, his frustration building. He threw his hand out in front of him, mentally attaching a push to it. Not a normal push but a spear-like column that forged ahead. It parted the mob, clearing a path ahead of him.

Each displaced scholar gasped and turned with surprise. Alrion capitalised on their confusion and walked along the newly made path, using the distraction to progress. Lara followed closely behind, smirking at any of the scholars that looked over at her.

The scholars stood back in silence, surprised by the intrusion. Alrion walked all the way up to the front. His burst of frustration had made him act tough, but it was running thin now. He had realised what he had just done, and was alternating between feeling embarrassed and trying to stoke the fires of frustration and urgency and stay on the offensive. He looked up at the speaker standing at the lectern. The man was old and wrinkled, with a long grey beard. He regarded Alrion with disdain.

"Are you the leader?"

"No, you impudent whelp, I am the Speaker. What gives you the right to barge in here?"

"My name is Alrion and I have a very urgent need. I don't have the luxury of waiting for the paperwork to be completed. I must speak with your leader about the Pool of Knowledge." Alrion was surprised that his voice sounded more confident than he felt.

"You are wasting our time with such fairy tales," the Speaker said.

"No fairy tale at all. I was brought here by the wizard Falric who not only confirmed that it exists but also that Paperton was the place to gain access." Alrion had fudged the facts a little, but he needed to confirm that the scholars could actually help him.

"Falric. Yes, we know him. Perhaps he can clear up this confusion?" The Speaker looked behind Alrion. Lara smiled back at him.

"Unfortunately, he was killed this morning by an evil wizard. One who is on his way here. That's why I am in your hall without my mentor, and also why this matter is so urgent," Alrion said. A gasp went up among those on the stage.

"A major loss, if that is true. However, how are we to know that you are who you say you are, and Falric is indeed lost to us? How do we know you are not the one that killed him?" the Speaker said. Alrion paused for a moment. He had to rein in his annoyance and think of a solution.

"Show them the spellbook," Lara whispered to him. Alrion nodded and rummaged through his bag.

"Look at this, it is Falric's spellbook!" Alrion said. He handed it to the Speaker.

"Looks legitimate, but the pages are all blank."

"It is protected by magic, but surely a scholar such as yourself can read some of the pages."

"I can indeed, I was testing you. I can see his mark on the book. It would be hard to come into possession of this without him desiring it. But are you even a wizard?"

"Yes. I am a wizard." Alrion decided to demonstrate, and at the same time do a little tribute to Falric. He closed his eyes and focused again on his Spark, fanning the flames, and increasing the intensity. He channelled it into a flame and tried this time to give the flame some shape. More than the simple flare he had done earlier.

"What?" the Speaker called out.

"I like what you did there," Lara said, enjoying the reaction. Alrion opened his eyes to see how his spell had turned out. Shock and surprise were on the Speaker's face. The whole group on the stage were on their feet, backing away. It was even better than Alrion had hoped.

A flame extended from his upturned palm, but it didn't just go straight up. It bent and split into many smaller and connected flames, depicting the outline of a book with the letter 'F' in the middle of the cover. It filled the air above the stage, the heat threatening to set the stage alight.

"That's quite enough," the Speaker said, and Alrion let the flame dissipate.

"Are you satisfied?" Alrion said.

"While your demonstration was acceptable, we need to confer before we come to you with a decision."

"How long will this take?"

"As long as it needs to take," the Speaker said. Alrion felt Lara leaning in close.

"Great that you got this far, I don't think you can push your luck much further. Be gracious," she whispered.

"That's all I can ask. I shall wait for your response. But please do be mindful of the urgency here. A deadly wizard is after the Pool of Knowledge, and we need to be ready for that."

"Don't worry; there are those who have been prepared for such things. Please wait in the guest rooms until you have an answer. We will return the spellbook to you at the same time," the Speaker said.

"Thank you." Alrion turned to leave. He tried to ignore all the strange looks and keep his composure as he walked through the crowd.

I can't believe I did that, he thought. Nevertheless, he pushed the thought away. He couldn't afford to undermine himself with doubt. There would be plenty of time for that later if he so wished.

A short man pushed through all the people and stopped in front of Alrion.

"Alrion, my name is Caleb. I have been tasked with directing you to your accommodation."

"Caleb? Thanks. This is Lara."

"Nice to meet you, Caleb. Are you a scholar too?" Lara said.

"Of course, but a junior one. That was quite a display back there."

"It had to be. I hope this process doesn't take too long," Alrion said.

"I think they like you, they never agree to convene on such short notice."

"Wow, I'd hate to see what happens if they don't like you." Alrion laughed.

"It's always according to the letter of our law, but if you really ticked off the wrong person you could be waiting months for the most basic decision to be taken." Caleb had a serious look on his face.

He's not joking around.

"Sounds pretty awful," Lara said.

"It probably sounds worse than it is. I don't think they would force outsiders to wait for months. That's saved for internal squabbles. Let's just get ourselves out of the hall," Caleb said.

Within a few minutes, they were outside, even with the commotion and the curious scholars trying to stop them with questions.

"Now we can breathe. What an exciting time!" Caleb said.

"You think this is exciting? It gets better, or worse depending on your perspective," Alrion said.

"Surely better, a little excitement could never hurt. Paperton is quiet, with good reason. It was explicitly designed to be so. It's conducive to research and learning."

"Makes sense to me. Do you get a chance to travel?"

"Yes, but only once you are formally admitted into the Fellowship."

"I hope you get there soon. I too lived a fairly sheltered life, but since I set foot outside my home it's been quite an adventure." Alrion was already starting to feel a kinship with this Caleb. They had a lot in common.

"Much appreciated, I look forward to the opportunity. Here we are." Caleb stopped in front of a small house. It was a simple structure, painted all in white with a bright blue door. Caleb unlocked the door and walked inside. Alrion and Lara followed.

The house was tiny but functional. Alrion saw a sitting room with a couch and two chairs, a basic kitchen and larder, and a bedroom.

"I hope we won't need to stay that long." Alrion put his bag down, and Lara did the same.

"Hopefully not, but the place is kitted out for longer stays just in case," Caleb said.

"How long do you think I'll have to wait?"

"A few hours at the earliest, it's quite a strange request."

"Can you tell me anything about the Pool of Knowledge?"

"Not much, it's a well-kept secret. The less that people know, the better. We wouldn't even acknowledge its existence for most visitors."

"Sure, but can you tell me anything?"

"Just generally available information. Access is restricted, nobody gets to go there. Which is why it is incredible they are even deliberating about your request. I don't know exactly why it is so restricted, but I get the impression that it is about protecting the pool from the wrong people." Caleb looked uncomfortable talking about it.

"That's pretty vague. Why not just tell us something interesting, even if it is just a rumour?" Lara said.

"Fine, that's a fair point. And maybe you'll get to see it anyway. They say it is an actual pool, and the knowledge of the world is contained there. You can see why they would want to protect that. Knowledge is power after all," Caleb said.

"That's exactly why I need to be there. Also, why the black wizard wants access too. Knowledge is a key pillar of magic. In most cases, you can't cast the spell if you don't know it is possible." Alrion saw Caleb nodding along.

I don't think I'm telling him anything he doesn't already know.

"Very interesting. I'm sorry I can't be of more help, but I don't know enough. I will suggest though that you rest. We don't know how long they will be deliberating. They will send for you when there is a decision," Caleb said.

"Thanks for your help. Will they be sending you?"

"Not sure, but likely."

"Then I hope I see you soon," Alrion said.

"Me too." Caleb waved and left the tiny house.

"He's right, you know," Lara said, after the door closed.

"About what?"

"Resting. It has been a long day, and you don't know how long the wait will be. But when they say yes, you need to be ready."

"I agree in theory, but resting now will be hard. I'll try." Alrion headed off for the bedroom. He knew he couldn't sleep immediately, so he decided to try and mentally rehearse some of his spells. He didn't have his spellbook or the time to try and learn something new, but he knew that he would need as much magic as he could muster for whatever lay ahead.

27

THE ABANDONED GATE

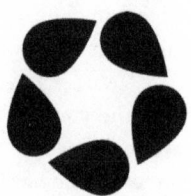

Alrion awoke to the sound of a bell and sat upright. He hadn't even remembered falling asleep. He dashed out of the bedroom.

"Talk about a rude awakening," Lara said. She was lying on the couch, and let out a little yawn. Alrion could see it was still dark outside. He walked straight to the front door and opened it. Caleb was standing outside, holding a torch and a handheld brass bell.

"Alrion, the hall has completed their deliberation. You have been summoned to receive their judgement."

"Thank you, I will come immediately," Alrion said. Lara jumped up and joined him.

"Any indication of what the decision is?" Alrion asked.

"I am acting in the official capacity of the Notifier. I cannot engage in discourse."

"Fine." Alrion didn't really expect an answer but was desperate to find out. He had no idea how long he had slept, and he felt like he was already behind. They walked swiftly back to the hall. Caleb opened the main doors and held them open. After Alrion and Lara walked through, he closed the doors behind them and stood guard.

Alrion heard the doors locking behind him.

"They mean business," Lara said.

"They sure do, I just hope it's good for us," Alrion said, his doubt growing. The hall was empty save for the men collected on the stage. Alrion walked through the echoing empty hall with as much courage as he could gather, but he felt like with each step the giant space was mocking his approach. Such a huge and old structure seemed to impose itself unfairly upon him. The Speaker was standing at the lectern. As Alrion approached he spoke up.

"Alrion, the student of Falric, stop right there and await your judgement!" Alrion stopped, confusion and fear foremost in his thoughts. He waited for the Speaker to continue.

"We have deliberated over your case, your history, and your actions before us. We must say that we are concerned by your brash behaviour and the ignorance you have shown in your plea," he said before pausing.

I don't like where this is heading.

"We have balanced that against the great need you have explained to us, and the passing of the great wizard Falric, one of our own. Would that he was here today, we would feel a lot more comfortable," the Speaker said, again pausing.

"They're not comfortable, do you think this means they're considering it?" Alrion whispered to Lara.

"Sounds like it to me, but you never know with these types," she said.

"As we are just the initial gatekeepers, we have decided to allow your request. Your merit will be judged by others more worthy. Approach, so that you may be admitted." The Speaker beckoned for Alrion to come closer. The young wizard took a moment to process what was said.

"Go, don't let them second-guess themselves," Lara hissed at him. Alrion stepped forward and continued walking towards the stage. It sounded like they had grudgingly agreed to his request, but there was another barrier to get past. Whatever the circumstances it didn't matter, it was progress. Alrion ascended the stairs onto the stage and approached the Speaker.

"These are strange times Alrion, and we must act in kind. At the rear of the stage is a doorway, which will lead you to a secret passage. That passage will take you to the Ancient Gates. There you will be tested, by the wisest and strongest among us. If they consider you worthy, they will grant you access."

"Thank you, for your help. Is this the only way to access the Pool?"

"Yes, there is no other way. Therefore, this other wizard you mentioned has not come, or we would know about it. We will prevent him if he is as you have described."

"Be careful, he is incredibly powerful. What test awaits me further in?"

"We cannot comment on that. It is for you to discover." A smile crept over the Speaker's face, but disappeared quickly.

That's something Falric would say.

"Can I have my spellbook back?"

"Yes, but not until you return. You may take nothing with you, save the clothes on your back. And she must wait here." The Speaker pointed at Lara.

"No problem, I can't help you in there anyway. Take care, Alrion." Lara gave him a reassuring smile, and he couldn't help smiling back.

"I guess I should go then. Who knows how much time I have?" Alrion nodded at the Speaker, then turned to walk across the stage. The group of scholars stood and stepped to the side, the path between their chairs leading to a darkened area. Alrion walked through as confidently as possible, trying not to think of all the eyes watching and scrutinising his every step. As he passed them, he could see more detail in the distance. It was a simple wooden door, reinforced with steel bars and a steel handle. He reached out and grabbed the handle, pulling the door open.

A cold breeze reached him, and he could feel moisture in the air. Ahead was a dark tunnel, hewn out of the rock. There were lit torches at intervals along the tunnel.

"Here I go." Alrion stepped inside and let the door close behind him. The sound of the door locking had finality to it. As if the way back was now sealed. He could only go forward. Alrion walked down the hallway, wondering what test awaited him. It sounded like there were some special elders that he needed to confront next.

As if the scholars I just dealt with weren't enough of a pain, he thought. However, if any of the stories Caleb had told him was true, then it made sense. All the knowledge in the world would be a huge gift for any person, as well as an incredible responsibility. One that needs guarding and using sparingly.

I don't think I'm worthy, not yet. But it's my quest, and I must continue.

The secret behind his grandfather's spell would be here, and the knowledge needed to make it work for good. Maybe he could teach others instead, maybe he would just be a conduit for that knowledge. But he wouldn't know what lay ahead until he completed this task.

Alrion progressed down the path and started to see what was at the end. It widened out into a larger room, cut out of the rock. Torches circled the room and highlighted a giant circular stone door. On either side of the door were two stone thrones, roughly cut with sharp angles on a raised platform. But the thrones were empty. A set of stone steps led up to the platform.

There's nobody here, Alrion thought as he stepped into the room. He had expected somebody to confront him, and the presence of the two thrones suggested it would be two people but there was no sign of a living soul. He noticed carvings on the door, so he approached to investigate.

One way or another, I need to get this door open, he thought but he had a bad feeling in the pit of his stomach. Something was not right. The door was not supposed to be abandoned. Especially since they knew he was coming.

"Just focus on the task," Alrion whispered. He ascended the stone steps carefully, focusing on reaching the top. As he climbed the last stair, he walked over to the thrones and looked at them. One had three wavy lines carved into the right armrest. The other had a star carved into the left armrest.

I wonder what they are for? Do they mean something?

The thrones were otherwise unmarked. He stepped forward and took in the big circular door. There were pictures carved into it that depicted people, and books, and a pool.

It must be related to the story of this place. Or part of a riddle, Alrion thought. He noticed some writing carved into the base of the door and bent down to examine it.

The provider of all things gives access to those who are worthy.

"This is a riddle," Alrion said quietly. He examined the pictures up close, trying to discern their meaning. He pressed carefully over different shapes and symbols on the door, to see if anything happened. The stone door remained silent and unresponsive.

I don't think there's a secret handle, it must be something else, Alrion thought. At the very centre of the door, he saw that the stone looked slightly different. He ran his hand over it and noticed something. The surface and colour of the stone changed slightly when he touched it. However, within a second, it had reverted back.

"This section responds to touch, that has to be significant," Alrion said as he stepped back and regarded the whole door. No other areas looked the same.

The area that responds to touch must be the place for my answer. But what is the answer and how do I represent it?

He decided to tackle the riddle first. It referenced a test of worth, and the prize at the other end was access to the Pool of Knowledge. By Alrion's reckoning, it had to be a test of knowledge or application of knowledge. A student who was worthy would be granted access to more knowledge. He decided to look again at the pictures on the door.

The first depicted a man lying in a house with the sunlight streaming in. The second showed him working and planting crops. The third depicted him returning home with the sun setting and stars visible. The stars made him think of the carving in the throne, so he went back and had another look at it.

"Stars provide light at night and so does the sun during the day," Alrion said aloud. He looked at the other throne.

"I don't know what these wavy lines mean, they could be the sun's rays but maybe that is already covered? What else could it be?" Alrion said under his breath as he walked back to the stone door and examined the pictures once more.

The man is growing crops under the sun, the heat from the sun helping them to grow. Maybe that's it?

He tried drawing the wavy lines with his hand on the stone centre. Nothing happened. Alrion thought over the riddle some more. It had to be something else. The constant in all the images were the man and the sun.

Well if you think about it, the sun seems to be giving him something in every picture. In the first, it wakes him up. In the second, it helps him to grow food. And in the last one it helps him return home to rest, the stars taking over, Alrion thought, pointing at the sun in each picture. That was the common element and tied in with the riddle.

"Worth a try," Alrion said and reached out. He placed his hand onto the centre of the door and traced a circle shape. He heard a clank and stepped back. The massive circular door moved forward, then started to roll to the right exposing another corridor behind. Before Alrion could see what lay beyond, he was assaulted by a strange smell.

What is that?

He stepped forward and looked around. Something was there on the ground, but he couldn't quite make it out. He focused and drew forth his Spark, igniting a small flame above his upturned palm. With the additional light, he could see what it was. Two bodies.

These must be the guardians, Alrion thought. They were wearing dark-blue robes and looked quite old. After examining them, he could see what the cause of death was. Thick stone rods pierced them. Alrion stumbled back as the realisation dawned upon him.

The black wizard must have done this. He used a lot of earth magic against Falric. That means he's already here and has been for a while.

Alrion wasn't prepared for this, even though he thought he was. The Pool of Knowledge was there beyond the darkness, but the black wizard was probably also there. The one who had killed Falric.

Alrion turned back, considering a retreat. It was tantalising and seductive, but it didn't solve his problem, and he ran the risk that the Pool would be destroyed. He didn't take that wizard for the sharing type.

"You can do this," Alrion told himself as he carefully stepped around the dead bodies. However, as much as he tried, he didn't really believe it. Not yet.

28

THE SPARK IGNITES

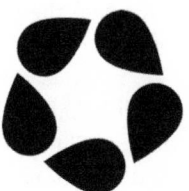

Alrion walked steadily down the pitch-black tunnel, his tiny flame only lighting the area in front of him. His mind played tricks on him, projecting dread shapes from the blackness. However, he forged on, determined to reach his goal. The sound of his steps was small and insignificant as they echoed around the tunnel. He could smell something else as he got further and further from the slain gatekeepers. He couldn't quite place it, but it was like damp.

I'm looking for a pool, that would make sense, he thought, happy to have something other than the menacing dark to focus on. He started to see something in the distance and tried to make it out as he walked.

It was a light-blue glow coming from up ahead. An unnatural glow that suggested it was magical. Feeling bolder, Alrion upped the pace. Perhaps there was a chance he could access the Pool safely. The tunnel narrowed, then started widening rapidly. He was about to reach his destination.

The tunnel ended in another cavernous room. In the centre of the room, he saw what looked like a naturally created stone formation. The blue glow was from the liquid within. It seemed to swirl around slowly, without any reason for it but another detail grabbed Alrion's complete attention.

A man stood in front of the Pool, with his head bowed and his back to Alrion.

"So, you're here at last," the man said. Alrion stopped. He knew it was the black wizard, and that things would finally come to a head. There was no avoiding it. So many thoughts ran through his head.

What do I say?

"You were waiting for me?" Alrion stepped closer trying to get a better look.

"Yes. I knew that you would show yourself eventually. And I wanted to thank you." The wizard turned around, keeping his face hidden.

"Thank me? For what?"

"If it wasn't for you, I would never have known that this place existed," the wizard said. Alrion was confused.

How have I helped him?

"Reveal yourself then." Alrion could see the wizard thinking it over.

"I suppose it is only fair, for you to see who killed your mentor and will be killing you next." The wizard pushed back the black hood and showed his face. He had a cruel smile which looked scary with the blue light from the pool dancing over it.

"Branthor!" Alrion called out in disbelief. It didn't make sense. Falric's right-hand man, and most trusted wizard. It did explain how the black wizard had been tracking them and knew their destination.

"Why? How could you do this?"

"There are many reasons, but it comes down to the fact that I am sick of being treated like a second-class citizen. Just because I am not of your blood-line." Branthor spoke the words with real venom, his mouth curled into a sneer.

"What do you mean?"

"This here, this Pool is a revelation. The knowledge of the world, and in particular the knowledge of Granthion. All of it is available to me now. I can set things right, do what must be done."

"I don't understand. Why is this so important to you?"

What happened to him?

"Your grandfather performed the cleansing ritual twenty years ago. Nobody knew it was even possible; he kept that nugget to himself. He didn't share any of his knowledge. But his process was imperfect." Branthor stepped forward and showed his forearm. "See this mark?"

"What of it?" Alrion noticed the curved black line.

"Those who are tainted by the Blight are all marked in a similar way."

"You're tainted?"

This doesn't make sense. Falric said that he wasn't, that he would have sensed the change to his Spark.

"Yes, and no. I was in fact. But your grandfather's spell cleansed me, or so it would seem. I can use my Spark without fear of corruption and my mind is my own. But, it's not that simple." Branthor said. He started approaching Alrion, very slowly.

"My connection to the Blight remains. I can feel the others and if I concentrate, I can communicate with them. I am straddling worlds, the light, and the dark. I cannot lose myself to the darkness, but I cannot escape it. I am cursed because of the spell used by your grandfather!" Branthor's voice was rising in anger and intensity with every word.

"What do you intend to do? Aside from killing everyone in your way?"

"I'm going to take the knowledge from here, and I'm going to create a new breed of man. Tied to, but free from the Blight. And we will rule this world like no other has before."

"That's crazy. You want to make others like yourself?" Alrion instinctively took a step back.

I don't like where this conversation is going. He's out of his mind.

"Of course. The Blight has strength to it. The kinship and shared communication creates a powerful force. United in purpose. Foot soldiers, commanders, and specialists all working in perfect unity. We can take this curse and turn it to our advantage. Until now, I had no hope. I could not unlock the secrets of the Blight, of how to alter or reverse the process. But now, I have all I need." Branthor clenched his hand into a fist.

"Why kill me then?"

"Because I won't let the knowledge leave this place. Once you are dealt with, I will destroy the Pool and kill all who have access. The secrets that were once denied to me will be denied to all but those I choose. It's time for me to be in the inner circle, not left to suffer in ignorance."

"This isn't the only way, we can work together to cure you."

"It is far too late for that. I will not waste the knowledge here on such a petty plan. No, I will do far more. I will place my stamp on the world!" Branthor waved his hand and a wall of stone rose behind Alrion, blocking the tunnel behind him. Blocking his only way out.

There goes my chance at escaping. And he can't be reasoned with.

"As my way of saying thanks, I will let you die in honour. Fight me, and perish in battle," Branthor said.

"You killed Falric. You killed or injured countless others. You would kill me and start up your crazy quest for revenge on my family and the world. I will not let that happen!" Alrion said. His anger, and hurt, and loss fanned the flames of his Spark. He could feel the heat rising through him. Building and gathering. He poured more of himself into it, feeding the flames, adding fuel to the fire. Then something happened.

His Spark blew up, surging, and building with a life of its own. As if it were feeding and sustaining itself.

"Impressive, you have managed to ignite your Spark. But it won't be enough little wizard." Branthor raised a spear of earth from the ground and flung it at Alrion. Purely on instinct, he unleashed a force spell to deflect the spear. Even with all his strength behind it, he only just managed to move it far enough so that it thudded right next to him.

"Nice start, but you can't keep this up." Branthor started raising chunks of earth from the ground, moulding them into giant stones.

He's not going to let up. He's going to keep going until I'm dead.

Alrion combined the fire and push spells, sending out a rolling wave of fire at Branthor. It twirled and writhed as it flew, as if it had a life of its own. Branthor countered by dropping some of the stones down and forming them into a quick wall to shield himself.

At least he can be hurt, he's defending himself, Alrion thought. He had no idea how to fight a wizard, so that was reassuring that Branthor deemed his attacks dangerous enough to defend against. But it's all he had. While Branthor was distracted, Alrion picked up the stone spear next to him and readied it. He ran a few steps to the side and aimed it around Branthor's wall.

As he threw it, he put all his power into a force spell behind it. The column of stone flew through the air, spiralling as it went. Branthor noticed it, closed his eyes, and held out a hand. The stone spear slowed, then disintegrated.

"Earth is my strong suit. You can't hurt me with it," Branthor said, chuckling.

"If you're so good with it, why did you attack us with fire back in the Whispering Forest?" Alrion said.

Maybe I can buy myself some time to come up with a better attack. He's quite confident.

"Hah, that was just fun and games. The fire did its job of confusing Falric, and I didn't intend to kill you then. I just wanted to keep you running. Worked perfectly." Branthor changed his stance and put his hand on the ground.

A wave of rock rose up from the ground, undulating towards Alrion. He ran to the side as fast as he could, trying to get away. The rock wave was so fast and wide that he wasn't going to make it. Alrion closed his eyes and tried to push himself aside with magic. It didn't work well, but he got enough of a result to narrowly escape.

"You have good reactions. You are definitely talented. Such a shame. Perhaps I should rethink my approach. Do you wish to join me?" Branthor said. Alrion paused, catching his breath. He wanted Branthor to think that he was giving the option real consideration.

"No, I'm not going to betray everyone like you did. I want to improve the world, not make it suffer."

"Very well, I had to ask. It would have been nice to have a talented protégé like yourself. Oh well, there are plenty more where you came from. A whole academy in fact." Branthor focused again, causing rocks from the ceiling to start falling down above Alrion.

Not good, Alrion thought as he tried to avoid the falling debris. But try as he might, he got nicked and slammed by smaller rocks.

"I can do this all day. What's your next move?" Branthor said. He was clearly enjoying himself. Alrion was so busy scrambling to avoid being crushed and buried, he couldn't think of what to do next.

All or nothing.

Alrion weaved through the falling stones, changing his direction to head straight at Branthor.

I just need one good hit.

He noticed the rocks thinning out, as he got closer to Branthor.

"Rushing to your death? I appreciate the sentiment," Branthor said, mocking Alrion. As the young wizard closed in he accumulated as much heat and power in his hand as possible, pouring in everything he had.

One shot, he thought. Suddenly he released it all. An explosion of flame erupted from his hand, giving Branthor almost no time to react. But the wizard had expected it, and a rock formation rose to block the flame. The shield of earth didn't stay still, it continued moving forward. Alrion's flame melted through half of it but enough remained of the moving earthen barrier that he was smashed back into the rubble. Alrion lay still, the wind knocked out of him.

"It's been fun, Alrion, but you are no match for me. Perhaps one day, but not today."

"It's not over," Alrion said, coughing. Everything hurt, but he hadn't given up.

"It is now." Branthor closed his fist. The rock around Alrion solidified into spikes and plunged into him. He felt a sharp pain, then blackness.

29

ONE STRIKE

Alrion regained consciousness and tried to move. When he couldn't, he remembered what had happened.

"I'm surprised that you're still alive, but keep doing that and you'll end it faster," Branthor said. He was standing over Alrion, a wicked smile on his face.

"What now?" Alrion said, struggling to get the words out.

"I guess I have a decision to make. I can kill you immediately, let you bleed out, or I can hope you last long enough to infect you with the Blight."

"What?"

"Yes, you heard me right. I can call a creature here to turn you. It's not ideal, but it would make you easier to control and I could always restore you later once I have the capability. Decisions, decisions." Branthor turned and started pacing.

"Where are you going?"

"To drink from the Pool. Now that you and Falric are out of the picture, it is safe to do so. I wasn't able to get much information from those so-called guardians. I'm not entirely sure how it works." Branthor continued to the Pool at a leisurely pace.

This is an opportunity.

Maybe there was a way he could free himself while Branthor was occupied. He started to probe his restraints to determine how he was held and what damage had been done.

"Can you believe it is actually a pool? These stories are never so literal, it is refreshing," Branthor said. "Still with me? Don't worry, I can see that you are." Alrion decided not to respond and save his energy.

He discovered at least two stone spikes that had pierced through him and were restricting his movement. There were likely more. He felt weak and knew that he was in serious trouble. Branthor may not have killed him outright, but he had badly wounded him.

"What do you think the protocol is here? Do I just stick my head inside? Is there a special cup to use?" Branthor said as he inspected the Pool closely. He didn't wait for Alrion to respond.

"You're being awfully quiet back there, I had best drink immediately. Perhaps my newfound knowledge will give me some great ideas about what to do with you."

"You could heal me," Alrion said, his voice a little stronger than he expected.

"Don't be silly, why would I do that? If I turned you, the Blight would save you. Besides, healing just isn't my strong point. Never really saw the point." Branthor turned back and bent over the Pool.

"No point in delaying further, I hope it tastes good." He knelt down and cupped his hands, filling them with water from the Pool. He drank the water swiftly, wiping his face afterwards. While he was distracted, Alrion tried weakening the spikes so that he could detach them from the ground and hopefully remove them. He could get to one with his hands, but the others would require magic which would potentially tip off Branthor.

"Doesn't taste like anything, so that's a good sign. I'm probably not poisoned. Did they tell you how long it takes to work?" Branthor said, walking back to Alrion.

"I know nothing."

"Truer words than you realise. I've come to a decision."

"What's that?" Alrion gently probed with a force spell, feeling where the stone spikes had impaled him. He didn't realise he could morph a push spell this way. He wasn't sure how much Branthor could detect, but if he was careful and used minimal Spark perhaps he could get by unnoticed.

"You shouldn't be wasted; you would be a good addition to the cause. It's not ideal, but I think you should be infected. All you need to do is stay alive long enough for the process to happen."

"I'd rather die."

"Empty words. You can't do anything. And I doubt you have the strength of Will to do so anyway."

"How long do I have?" Alrion said.

I need to buy some time, keep him occupied.

"Not long, probably an hour or so. It looks like I was tidy with my attack, I don't think I hit any vital organs. You should be happy."

"Happy that you've pinned me down and want to infect me with the Blight?"

"Exactly. It's a privilege, you just don't know it yet. Now then, how do I access this new knowledge?" Branthor said.

"Maybe you are not worthy." Alrion coughed, pain wracking his chest.

"If anybody here is not worthy, it is you. You are a simple fledgling, just following orders. It's a miracle you made it this far. If I had wanted to destroy you earlier, I had ample opportunity. Yes, you are not worthy. But in time, you will prove useful." Branthor continued pacing around the room.

Alrion felt himself weakening by the second. Even if Branthor was right and his wounds were not immediately fatal, in his weakened state he would not be able to resist when they infected him, and all would be for nothing. He couldn't let Branthor win. He had to find a way.

Suddenly, he had an idea. One last roll of the dice. One gamble for it all. He smiled and forced a laugh, the pain in his chest worth it.

"What are you laughing about?" Branthor looked at Alrion with suspicion and started to walk back.

"You don't even know how to activate the knowledge you have acquired. It's actually hilarious. It doesn't matter if I die here today, you will not succeed. You have failed all by yourself," Alrion said.

"You ignorant little ant. How dare you act all high and mighty? You're on the brink of death, and I could kill you at any time. Time is what I have, time is what you lack. Even if it takes me years to obtain the knowledge I require, that is fine. You will be powerless to stop me. In fact, you will be helping me very soon." Branthor's flare of anger simmered down into malice, a wicked smile mocking Alrion.

Alrion tried to respond but instead coughed harshly.

Maybe it's too late, he thought. Regardless, it was now or never. He forced out a harsh whisper that was inaudible.

"What was that? Having trouble talking back? Let me hear your clever retort," Branthor said. He approached Alrion and leaned closer.

"C'mon, let's hear it." Branthor pointed to his ear. Alrion grabbed his entire Spark as if he was wielding an iron fist. He wrenched it all out and threw it in a single surge. Everything he had, in one attack but focused on the stone spears and spikes impaling him. He forced every single one out of his body, and into Branthor's chest.

The speed and force of the attack surprised Branthor, and he was so close he couldn't react in time. Alrion almost passed out from the pain, but he had the presence of mind to clutch at his own chest, trying to stem the blood flow.

Branthor stumbled backward, a stunned look on his face.

"How?" he said, muttering the word just loud enough for Alrion to hear.

"I got lucky." Alrion reached for his Spark, and found a small pocket available. His head was spinning, and the pain was threatening to make him faint, but he focused just enough to start a healing spell.

"You fool, that will never work. You can't heal yourself," Branthor said.

"I don't need it to work, I just need it to hold me together a little longer,"

Alrion said. He didn't have much Spark left but used what he could. He remembered Falric's lecture about the healing spell. About how it relied on the Spark, so it wasn't effective on your own body but he didn't care.

Alrion focused his Will on making it work better, on his own body responding to the treatment. He drew on whatever power he had within to somehow hold himself together. He refused to die here, or wait for infection by the Blight. He would complete his mission, and live to fight on.

"You'll never make it out of here," Branthor said as he fell to the ground.

"That's my line," Alrion said. Branthor was breathing with difficulty.

"I can survive this, just you wait."

"Not going to, I'm going to leave while I can." Alrion dragged himself up to a seated position. He felt over his chest and found that the wounds had sealed up somewhat.

At least my guts won't be falling out, he thought. He steeled himself and forced himself up into a crouch. A sharp pain went right through him, but he managed to stay in the position. He leaned against some nearby fallen rocks and lifted himself to a semi-upright stance.

"Don't think that you've won," Branthor said.

"Save your energy," Alrion said, and started to head towards the Pool of Knowledge. Its glow was calling him. But he took his time. Each foot placed in front of the other, methodically and with care. Any loss of concentration would cause him to fall over, and he wasn't sure if he could get up again. When he hadn't heard any more taunting from Branthor, he paused and looked over.

Branthor was quiet, his eyes were closed but his chest still moved up and down, although in a slow and laboured way.

He's not my problem, Alrion thought and continued on. Gradually he continued, at a crawling pace.

"Almost there, hold it together," he told himself. One more step. Then one more. Then he arrived. The Pool glowed, its mystical blue water looking every bit as magical as he assumed it was.

I just need a sip, at least for now. Let's not overdo things.

He bent down slowly, making sure he was stable. He reached out with his right hand and steadied himself with his left. As he touched the water, his strength failed him, and he toppled into the Pool headfirst.

30

BAPTISM

Alrion awoke with a gasp. His body was cold, too cold. Everything hurt, and he struggled to move. He realised that he was immersed in the Pool of Knowledge.

I could have drowned.

He had fallen in a lucky way, with his body leaning against the contours of the bottom of the pool and his head out of the water. He managed to shuffle backward so that he was sitting more upright in the water.

I hope I haven't ruined it, he thought. He forced his right arm to move and cupped some water within it, after a few attempts. He managed to gulp the water down and did it a second time for good measure.

Since I'm here, I'd better make this work.

The fluids seemed to revive him a little, so he decided to make the best of it and get moving. In one big movement, he stood up and tumbled out of the Pool. He landed on the ground with a *thud* and regretted it instantly.

At least I won't drown.

With some care, he got back onto his feet and started walking away.

How long was I out? He wondered. The room he was in looked the same, there were no signs of the passage of time. Branthor was still there, but Alrion couldn't see if he was still breathing.

"Not your problem, just keep moving," Alrion told himself. He turned to face the exit. The blockage that Branthor had created had been damaged during the fight but was still mostly intact. Alrion paused and looked around. He selected an area that looked promising and staggered over. There were multiple holes and large cracks all concentrated in this one place.

Don't fail me now, he thought, searching for his Spark. He could sense some there, but grabbing at it was like water slipping through his fingers. With enough persistence, he did manage to gather some Spark and placed his hand on the middle of the weakest area. He unleashed his entire Spark into an explosion of force, rocking the stone wall.

Sections of the wall collapsed, and large cracks formed throughout the rest. The impact was much greater than he expected.

I better not get buried alive in here with Branthor, he thought, watching the wall crack, and contort. The motion finally died down, and he eased himself through a large hole.

"That wasn't so bad," he said and started walking away. A loud crash startled him, and he turned back. The rest of the wall collapsed in waves, showering where he had been standing in rubble. Alrion gulped hard and decided not to think too much about it. He looked ahead.

The tunnel was pitch black, but Alrion was unable to cast any magic. He found the tunnel wall and used it to guide him along. The intense darkness and his slow progress made him lose all sense of time. He knew he had to hurry, in case the reinforcements that Branthor had requested arrived but he also knew that if he rushed, he would fall, and his luck wouldn't extend enough to let him get up again.

After a long, painful slog, he reached the door. It had sealed behind him. He felt a mixture of relief and annoyance.

Well, maybe it opens the same way on this side, Alrion thought. He felt his way along the stone door until he noticed the change in texture in the centre. He was careful not to move too far over, in case he stumbled over the bodies of the guardians. He drew a circle with his hand and stepped back. Nothing happened.

"Work, damn you!" Alrion cried out, and smashed the door with his palm. A loud *thunk* rang out and the door started to move. Alrion staggered back to avoid it and leaned on the tunnel wall. A crack of light, then a flood washed over his eyes. The dimly lit entrance hall was a bright beacon of hope. Once his eye adjusted, he stepped out cautiously and leaned on one of the stone thrones. He edged around it and let himself sink into it. He was too quick to do so and felt the pain as his body hit the stone, but it was a relief to sit down.

Maybe I shouldn't have done this, I won't want to get up, Alrion thought but then he pictured a horde of Blighters or worse streaming down the tunnel and he stood up again. He had to keep moving.

He felt somewhat renewed by the better-lit entrance and the fact that he was close to civilisation again. He just had to struggle on. Step after agonising step. He was so deathly tired.

I could just sink down over there, close my eyes and rest.

The cold stone looked so inviting but he knew if he did so he would never wake. And while there was some comfort in that in his weary state, he didn't want it. So, he pushed on, ignoring the cries of his body.

He finally reached the wooden door that led to the main hall and he rejoiced. He pulled the door open with such force that he almost lost balance and fell through the doorway, but he caught himself and only fell to one knee. He looked up, expecting an audience, but the room was empty. The Speaker and the council had all left.

Great, Alrion thought. His trek was not over. He picked himself up and continued walking. Across the stage, down the steps, and through the hall. His lonely trek felt like the entire length of his journey up until this point but all he could do was move forward, so he did. One step at a time. He reached the giant doors at the end of the hall, which were also deserted. Alrion sighed, and pushed on them, gaining access to the outside.

It was still dark out, and the streets were still. He remembered the way back to his lodging and praised the fact that it was close. He considered calling out but didn't think he had the voice to do it. He kept walking, pausing to lean on buildings and fences as required.

"Just keep going, you made it this far," he told himself. "You can't waste the knowledge that you have gained." Alrion spotted the small house and felt a wave of relief. It wasn't far now. His body started to fail on him, sensing that his destination was nearby.

"Hold on," he whispered. The last dozen steps were almost impossible. He took them one at a time, resting between each one. When he finally reached the door, he reached out to knock and fell against it with a crash.

Alrion sat upright. He had blacked out, and not really dreamed.

How long has it been? He thought. He looked around and noticed that he was in a bed. Lara and Caleb were sitting next to him and looked up with concern.

"What happened?"

"You collapsed outside, I brought you in, and Caleb came looking for you a bit later. You're barely alive, so don't push your luck," Lara said.

"You must search the Pool; the black wizard is there."

"We already did. There's nobody else there in the areas we can access, apart from the bodies of the two guardians," Caleb said, his features downcast.

"Is he alive? That seems impossible."

"There was also a fairly significant cave-in. It will take a long time to properly excavate," Caleb said. Alrion slumped back down in the bed, his body reminding him of his many injuries.

"What happened in there?" Lara said.

"The wizard was waiting for me. Turns out, I knew him. It was Branthor, the new head of the Wizard Academy."

"Why would such a distinguished wizard act like that?" Lara looked shocked.

"Apparently, he was infected by the Blight many years ago, and was cleansed by my grandfather's spell. However, the effect wasn't complete. He was still connected to the Blight. Once he realised that the Pool of Knowledge existed and contained the knowledge of my grandfather, he wanted it for himself. He has crazy plans to make more like him." Alrion still couldn't believe what he was saying.

"That's insane," Lara said.

"Did he drink from the Pool?" Caleb said.

"Yes, he did."

"If there's a chance he is alive as you suspect, that is not good. The Pool does not discriminate and provides the same benefit to all who drink from it." Caleb looked quite concerned.

"What do you mean? And I thought you didn't know much about it?"

Something's not adding up here.

"I'm afraid I wasn't entirely honest with you. Yes, I am a junior scholar but that is because I am training to become a guardian of the Pool. The two you discovered were my mentors. They were great men, and powerful in their own right." Caleb sighed again, and his shoulders slumped.

"What? Why didn't you tell me more?" Alrion tempered his anger out of concern for Caleb.

"It was part of a test. They sent me in to report my evaluation of you as part of the decision. It wouldn't be a fair test if you thought I had valuable information."

I went in there blind!

"I'm not particularly happy about this, but can you at least answer some questions now?"

"Of course."

"How does the Pool work? What does it do? I can't seem to tell any difference, and neither could Branthor."

"The Pool of Knowledge is not just a source of knowledge. It works both ways. By drinking the waters, you drink from its knowledge. However, you also contribute your knowledge. Did Branthor drink before you did?"

"Yes, he did."

"That's good; you may ascertain key knowledge that he had." Caleb stroked his chin, deep in thought.

"That could be useful. How does it work, though?"

"There are safeguards in place. Can you imagine the enormity of that reservoir? All the knowledge compiled from years of scholars and other learned people?" Caleb's eyes were alight with excitement. "Your mind must take in and absorb all that information."

"So, when do I get it?"

"You have it already, but there's a catch. You are not in control of the delivery of the knowledge. It will be fed to you as you need it, as your mind processes it as necessary."

"It's some sort of subconscious control?"

"Essentially. The most common mechanism is through dreams, but sometimes people can access knowledge they never knew they had as if it were their own. It's a strange and inconsistent process."

"Sounds like it. At least, though, I got everything. So, from what you mentioned, I now have all of my grandfather's knowledge." Alrion watched Caleb's response carefully.

"Yes. All that he knew, amongst many other things, are now within your mind. But that's the problem; you can't pick out the things you want on demand."

"I just have to trust my mind to process it?"

This could be a problem.

"Yes. Few are selected to partake and feedback knowledge to the Pool. Branthor killed the only two here that had drunk from the Pool. Precious little is written down about the exact ways of best accessing the information. I will be their successor, in time. There is more preparation for me to do."

"You aren't ready yet?" Alrion sank back down into the bed. He had succeeded, but there were so many more problems to resolve.

"No, I need to expand my knowledge and also practice techniques to more easily access what I require. Had you more time, we could have better prepared you. But now it is done."

"It is, and that is reassuring. How many other people have this knowledge?"

"I will have to consult the records, but outsiders have not accessed the Pool for many years. It is possible that only you and Branthor have it right now."

"I guess we will find out soon enough. My head is killing me, is that normal?"

"Yes, although I am surprised you have noticed based on the other injuries you sustained." Caleb grinned at Alrion.

"I definitely got lucky." Alrion cracked a smile too.

"You sure did. Speaking of which, you should rest some more," Lara said. "It will take a long time to recover, and from what Caleb said I think it will take even longer since you are also incorporating the knowledge from the Pool."

"I think you're right. Thank you both, I really needed your help I would not have survived otherwise."

"That's what we are here for." Lara picked up his pillow and fluffed it. Alrion laughed and even Caleb chuckled.

"Take care," Caleb said and left the room. Lara winked and then left also. But Alrion noticed her looking back at him before he collapsed back into sleep.

Lara left the small building and walked along the main road of Paperton. She took a thin path hemmed in by trees and bushes and ended up down near the lake, in a secluded spot free from passers-by. She looked around for the man she was supposed to meet, but could not see him.

"How is he?" a male voice said from behind her. Lara spun quickly to confront him. It was a man dressed in a nondescript brown robe and he had his face hidden by the hood.

"He's alive, but barely. He had an encounter with another wizard, called Branthor. It's a miracle he survived."

"Did he access the Pool?" The man's voice was insistent and had hints of desperation.

"Yes." Lara watched the man's reaction. He seemed to relax a little.

"Good. Stay with him, keep him safe."

"He won't need my protection soon."

Hopefully I can get this guy off my back. Then I don't have to hide anything from Alrion anymore.

"Wrong. He has gained knowledge and is increasing his power. But he is naive, and needs someone to watch his back while he learns more of the world." The man stopped talking and waited patiently. For her answer.

"Why do you need me?"

"Because you are the best person to accompany him and allow him to grow. Have you changed your mind?" Lara paused before replying. "No."

"Good. Remember that I know who you really are. Until next time." The mysterious man disappeared in front of Lara's eyes. She looked at where he had been, but couldn't see a trace.

"Wish I could do that," she whispered and left to return to Alrion's side.

31

IN DREAMS

Alrion dreamed. At first, it was just so many flashing images, he couldn't make sense of them. There was a vague awareness in his mind that this was to be expected, and not to worry, so he didn't pay them much attention.

The swirling images slowed down and he became immersed within them. He could see an old man standing in front of him. The man sat at a wooden desk and wrote in a book. It looked similar to Falric's spellbook but much older and more ornate. Alrion walked up and looked over the man's shoulder. The man was writing a new entry.

Cleansing the Blight

Alrion found that particular entry very interesting. He continued to hover, watching the man write.

This must be my grandfather, Alrion thought but he didn't look at the man, instead, he focused on the spellbook. He could see the words as the man wrote them on the page, but as they were being written they turned invisible.

Why? Alrion wondered, but he also knew why at the same time. The spell was beyond him, so he couldn't read it. Much like with Falric's spellbook. Knowing that he couldn't understand it, he walked around to get a better look at the man. Alrion had expected an old man, but he looked to be middle-aged.

"If this is my grandfather, why is he so young?" Alrion thought but the more he looked, the more he knew it was his grandfather. The wizard known as

Granthion. The family resemblance was there, he could see his father within the man's face.

Granthion continued writing for what seemed like a long time. Then he finished and closed the book. He stood up and looked directly at Alrion.

"This is for you," he said and passed the spellbook over. Alrion was shocked, but he accepted the book.

"Please tell me how it works," Alrion said.

"You already know, you have the knowledge."

"But how do I access it?" Alrion needed answers.

"You must be worthy of the spell, then you will know it."

"That's fine, but I need help. I have nobody to guide me," Alrion said. Granthion looked thoughtful, then took a few steps, staring into the distance.

"Very well." He waved his arm. A door with a silver shimmering outline appeared in front of them. Granthion gestured at it. Alrion stepped forward and opened the door. Within he could see the Pool of Knowledge.

"I've already done this." Alrion looked back at Granthion. The wizard pointed at the doorway again. Alrion turned, trying to see what was important about the image but it had changed.

Instead, he saw another room carved into the rock. Spread throughout the room were four old men. They were bald and wearing strange robes and long yellow scarves. Emblazoned on the scarves was a symbol Alrion didn't recognise. It looked like a mountain and a sun with additional markings.

The four men were seated on the ground and concentrating. In the middle of them was another doorway glowing white, but Alrion could not see inside it.

"What is this?" he asked, turning back to Granthion, but the wizard was gone. Alrion quickly looked over at the doorway again, but it was disappearing and the scenery around him was fading away. Everything turned white and Alrion started falling.

He awoke with a jerk, pain rocking his body.

Back to reality.

"You OK there?" Lara said.

"Yes, I think so." Alrion checked his body. Everything was as before.

Definitely a dream.

"You look like you saw a ghost."

"Maybe I did." Alrion chuckled. He had to make the best of the situation.

"That's going to require an explanation."

"I'm also interested if you don't mind." Caleb stepped into the room.

"You were also here?" Alrion said.

"I was checking in on you. You've been out for a while. Although I must admit, I wanted to observe the process since I haven't seen anyone react to the Pool of Knowledge. It's an educational experience."

"I definitely agree with you there." Alrion collected his thoughts. "I had a strange dream, with all these images swirling around. I think it was a way of incorporating the knowledge, because I couldn't read any of it. But then it got really strange."

"How so?" Caleb asked.

"I saw my grandfather writing out a spell, only I couldn't read it. When I questioned him about it, instead of explaining he showed me some visions. One of the Pool of Knowledge, and one of something else."

"Clearly your grandfather has passed on and isn't visiting you in your dreams," Lara said.

"That sounds more plausible," Alrion said.

"It could be a way to help you focus. You are seeking something to do with him correct?" Caleb said.

"Yes, I am."

"It would make sense if your mind was using him to call attention to whatever it showed you next," Caleb said.

"If you saw a vision of the Pool of Knowledge, and then something else. Well, to me that sounds to me like you just got a vision of our next destination. What did it look like?" Lara said.

"It didn't make any sense. A few old men, wearing strange clothes and some sort of doorway between them." Alrion struggled to recall all the details. Like a dream, some of it was fading.

"It will probably make more sense in time. Does it always work like this?" Lara said to Caleb.

"As far as I know. It's a protection mechanism, and designed to allow gradual integration of knowledge."

"Well, it's a start. Hang on a minute, you said our next destination?" Alrion looked at Lara.

"Yes, have you forgotten already? I signed up for this, not just the first step. But the whole thing. Besides, you need my help. You almost died without me at your side." Lara smiled. Alrion laughed.

She's right.

"If having you around can prevent this terrible pain I'm experiencing, I'm all for it."

"Great. You tagging along too, Caleb?" Lara said. Alrion wasn't sure if she was serious or not.

"Unfortunately, no. I am not the adventuring type, and I need to prepare to take over the role of guardian of the Pool. There is much I must learn. But perhaps I can be of use to you again in the future, once I am more acquainted with how it works." Caleb bowed.

"We mustn't forget that you have a place here and an important duty." Alrion held out his hand and Caleb shook it firmly. Alrion grimaced and almost managed to disguise the pain.

"Thanks for understanding. This is goodbye, for now, I will be shutting myself away for a while to complete my accelerated training. I have to do it in complete seclusion and secrecy. All the best for your recovery, I hope we meet again soon." Caleb bowed again.

"Thanks for your help, I hope everything goes well. I'm sure I'll need your help in the future if all I have to go on is these cryptic images." Alrion waved goodbye and watched Caleb leave.

"He's a particularly good man, I doubt any of the other scholars would have taken such an interest in you. He cares," Lara said.

"I think you're right. I hope he does well, and finds a way to protect himself and the Pool. I think basing their main defence around secrecy didn't quite hit the mark." Alrion thought back to how easily Branthor had infiltrated the Pool.

"But this place has been hidden for many years. It took a surprising betrayal to unveil it."

"It did," Alrion said.

What happened to Branthor? I wonder.

"You have to be at peace with what happened. You could do nothing more, or nothing less. He may be alive, or he may be dead. We don't know."

"And that's what's killing me. If he's alive with the knowledge of the Pool, then it is only a matter of time before he puts his plan into action. And it will probably involve coming after me and everyone with me." Alrion's hand hurt, and he looked down. He had clenched it into a fist. With an effort he forced it to relax.

"Then you had better sort yourself out, so next time he doesn't actually kill you, or those with you. Just in case." Lara winked at him.

"Sometimes I wonder how I ended up here, and with you no less. I never really thanked you. You convinced me not to give up, you helped me navigate the hall of scholars, and you've been watching my back while I have been helpless. I can't thank you enough, but I will try and make our adventures memorable enough to help pay you back," Alrion said.

"Don't get all mushy on me. I did what needed to be done, and I take satisfaction that you gave that Branthor a real surprise. You sort out the Blight and we will be even."

"Quite a tall order, don't you think? We won't be even until then?"

"Nope. You're stuck with me until then," Lara said, laughing.

"So be it, I guess I'll just have to make the most of it." Alrion tried to stifle another laugh but failed. His ribs complained.

"You may as well. Also, Caleb brought back Falric's spellbook. I put it with the rest of your things. They are all in the corner there." Lara pointed to a bulging pack in the room.

"Thanks."

"You should take a look when you can, just to make sure it is all there. Maybe something else will trigger that jumble of knowledge you have up there. I'm going to go stretch my legs, back soon," Lara said.

"Sure, take care," Alrion said.

Strange girl, he thought after she had left. However, she had done a lot for him already, so she had earned his trust. The impossible goal before him seemed that little bit more achievable. He sat up straighter, testing his body. Once he was moving a little, the pain wasn't as bad.

I should at least do something, he thought and decided to look through his things. What Lara had said made sense, and since he was resting up for a while, anything that kept his mind ticking over was useful.

Alrion struggled to swing his legs off the bed so that he was seated on the edge. Then he shuffled himself over, not trusting his legs with his weight just yet. With the right amount of leaning and good luck, he managed to grasp the leather pack with his left hand and drag it over onto the bed. The contents started to spill out, but he was happy with the result. He tucked himself back into bed and started to leaf through them.

He noticed the spellbook first and flipped through it. There were a few extra pages that he didn't remember from before, so that was useful. It made him think back to something Branthor had said.

I ignited my Spark. Falric never mentioned that. I wonder if it's like a tap that I have turned on now, he thought. Even through his pain and discomfort, he could feel it there, weak but accessible. It wasn't like when he first started, having to work it up. It flowed freely, and he could more easily access it. He was tempted to try it but restrained himself.

I'll ask another wizard when I can.

Alrion returned to the spellbook but it couldn't hold his interest. He looked through his other things. It was all there. His ring, which he had retrieved from Lara. Some clothes and equipment, but his food was gone.

It probably wasn't fit for consumption now, he thought with a chuckle. Finally, he found the notebook that he had taken from the academy.

"This old thing. Falric never explained what it was for," Alrion said. He opened the book to the first page. However, this time it wasn't blank. There were words on the page.

Well done, you have completed the first trial all by yourself. However, don't rest too long, there is much more to do. Whatever happens, you must remember this: you are never alone.

Alrion stared in disbelief on the page. Something was strange about the message. The tone of the speaker seemed familiar. When he examined the page closely, it wasn't written in ink. It was as if the message was etched into the page itself. Like it had always been there.

Who are you? Alrion thought, feeling the letters with his fingers. Another mystery to solve. He put the notebook aside and closed his eyes.

Rest faster. You have to keep moving.

"Am I interrupting something?" Lara said. Alrion opened his eyes. He hadn't meant to fall asleep again, but he felt better for it.

"No, I'll fill you in later. But I've made a decision." Alrion sat up, with slightly less pain this time.

"What's that?"

"As soon as I am fit, we will set out for Brangtur."

"What's there?" Lara gave him a curious look.

"My father. And with any luck by the time we get there, I'll know where my next trial is."

"Trial?"

"Yes, it's clear that there's no easy solution for this. I'll have to earn my chance to cleanse the Blight but I'm going to do it. Nothing will stand in my way." Alrion was surprised at the words coming out of his mouth. But the more he probed his feelings, the truer they were.

"With my help, that's a given," Lara said, and walked over to sit beside him. And for the first time, Alrion truly believed it was possible.

VAULT OF
SILENCE

BOOK TWO OF THE HIDDEN WIZARD

VAUGHAN W. SMITH

For Elli

1

A NEW FIRE

Lara crept up to the edge of the hill and peered over. She could see a large mass of Blighters, all of them hunched over and roaming in no discernible pattern. The terrain was a mix between rocky and sandy, with very little vegetation. She shielded her eyes from the harsh sun as she scanned the entire scene. Her nose wrinkling as she caught the putrid smell coming off them.

"It's as you expected, we have a whole barrel of them down there," she said.

"Blighters?" Alrion said.

"Looks like it. But there are others too. I think we should go around them." Lara swept her head over to take in the view and plot a course around the mob.

"Aren't we close to Brangtur?" Alrion gestured into the distance to emphasise his point.

"Yes, really close. If we avoided them it may take another day to do so safely."

"I don't want to waste the time, and we've dealt with Blighters before. This can be a fun romp." The young wizard had a mad grin on his face, which made Lara annoyed.

"Fun? There's an awful lot of them. I really think stealth is the preferred approach." It didn't make any sense to willingly take on such a force. Not when it could be avoided.

"Not this time. I want to make a statement. I need them to know I'm not the same person they encountered before," Alrion said.

Lara looked at him and sighed. He had certainly awakened to his power following his near-death confrontation with Branthor. But she wasn't sure this new Alrion was necessarily better equipped. Not yet. "So just because you defeated a wizard you think you're the king of wizards now?"

"Not yet. I still need you to watch my back," he said as he pushed off and starting jogging down the other side of the hill. "It's not as bad as you said," Alrion shouted as he descended.

Lara could see him working himself up. How much did he really want this, and how much was he just playing the part?

"Time to announce ourselves," Alrion said gleefully. He created a giant ball of flame and kept it right in front of him.

Lara staggered back for safety. "You better know what you're doing," she said, shielding her face with her arm. But instead of just throwing it, Alrion gave it a great push. The giant sphere of flame tumbled down the hill towards the seething mass of Blighters. Within seconds there were cries of concern and surprise.

The Blighters started to move away, but there were huge clumps that had nowhere to go and were pummelled by the rolling flame. The smelled of charred Blighter smelt even worse than Lara had expected.

"You better keep them contained if you want this to work!" she shouted over the carnage.

Alrion nodded and brought up a tall wall of fire from the left, boxing in the Blighters. The ones nearest the wall couldn't stop in time and were caught by the flame. Alrion launched another ball of fire into the air, and had it hover over the middle of the pack.

"You're just showing off now," Lara said. Now the flames were further away, she could stand beside him.

"Not really, I'm just letting loose. It feels good." Alrion concentrated and the ball of fire split into many smaller parts, showering fire over the Blighters. "That should be enough to scatter them," he said.

The Blighters were running in all directions, the scene was total chaos. But there was a change, and they began to reform.

"There's something organising them. Leaders?" Lara said.

"There must be. I'll have to take them out," Alrion said.

Lara could see the determination on his face. She had to dissuade him from taking this too far. "You know I would like nothing more, but is it really worth it? It's one thing raining fire on them from here, but that's a huge pack. You would have to go amongst them to identify and eliminate their leaders. It's too risky," she said.

"Don't be so shy, we'll be fine." Alrion's face lit up with what Lara could only define as intense hatred. It seemed at odds with his light banter.

"If you insist," Lara said. There would be no way to turn him away now. The two of them descended the hill and Alrion raised another wall of fire.

"Is there any limit to how much of that you can do?" she said. It did seem like a ridiculous amount of magic.

"Yes, but I haven't found it yet. Don't worry there's a fair bit left in reserve."

"In that case, you better box them in on three sides. We can funnel them into a smaller space to make it easier."

"Done," Alrion said with a smile, raising the third wall of fire. Lara watched him work, and noticed a steady stream of sweat beading around his hairline. The fire was too far away, was the sweat from something else?

She watched the Blighters react, and the more they were confined and the fewer the number, the more controlled they appeared to be. Many streamed forward away from the fire, but most stayed within the walls of fire, just far enough away to be safe.

"I don't like this. It's as if they're inviting you in," Lara said.

"I wouldn't want to keep them waiting." Alrion threw out a wave of fire to burn those that had advanced.

Lara dashed ahead and dealt killing blows to those still standing.

They waited for a moment, to see what was next.

"No more are coming over. We can still walk away," Lara said.

"This is interesting, I haven't seen this level of control yet."

"Let's save that for the post-battle discussion. Keep your wits about you. This could be a trap." Lara knew to trust her instincts, and something within that swirling dust bowl was making her unusually uncomfortable.

"If it's a trap I will destroy it." Alrion clenched his fist as if to demonstrate.

"Less talking, more doing." Lara didn't want this to drag on too long. Alrion already looked weakened, despite his previous comments. The wizard nodded and started walking towards the smaller, but still significant mass of Blighters.

"Call out any you think are leaders. Better yet, take them out," he said.

"I'll do what I can," Lara said, scanning them. She had a few potential targets picked out, but wanted to watch their behaviour first. To give themselves an opening Alrion sent out a force wave that knocked over the first few rows of Blighters. He followed it with streams of fire that dispersed those standing behind.

"There." Lara pointed at a heavyset man with dark features surrounded by Blighters. Alrion sent a spear of fire over. A Blighter tried to block it, but it pierced through and burned its target.

"Nice one," Lara said. There was a chance that this would work. Provided that Alrion kept his head and stuck to the plan. The Blighters rearranged themselves, and all those Lara considered to be leaders moved further back, surrounding themselves with Blighters.

"They're on to our plan and have protected themselves. At least we can confirm who the leaders are," she said.

"Then let's finish this quickly. Follow closely behind me." Alrion ran forward, throwing out waves of force to clear the path in front of him.

Lara kept pace, throwing daggers at key targets as they went. The leaders amongst the Blighters appeared alarmed, as they had nowhere to escape to. Then, they all closed their eyes and looked downward. Alrion continued forward, but Lara felt that something was off and she slowed down. Looking around she could see the Blighters rearranging again. They were making space. "They're up to something. I don't like this. Pull back," she said.

"It won't matter soon enough." Alrion paused briefly to concentrate and created a ring of fire above the leaders.

"They're going to surround us. Be quick before it's too late!" Lara shouted.

"This is over," Alrion said. The ring of fire descended swiftly, capturing all the leaders. Then the ring slowly constricted, pushing the trapped leaders into the middle and catching them in the fire.

"All done," Alrion said. "Now they're broken."

"I'm not so sure about that." Lara could see that the Blighters weren't fleeing. They cried out in anguish and lost control. She didn't hesitate. She threw daggers and followed up to cut down those that had managed to get closer. Alrion just stood and stared.

"Snap out of it!" Lara shouted.

Alrion blasted two back. They knocked over the Blighters behind them and he ignited the whole group at once.

"I'll make a path out." Alrion threw out a wave of fire that swept along the ground in continuous motion. "This way!" he shouted over the roar and followed his wave of flame.

Lara cut down a Blighter and turned to run alongside. They trailed behind the wave of fire, pushing aside any Blighters that managed to come close. The fire died out and they continued running, leaving chaos and confusion in their wake.

Lara took the lead and headed for a neighbouring hill, hoping to drop down the other side and out of sight. Alrion was looking back, trying to gauge if they were being followed.

"Eyes in front!" Lara shouted. There was a group of five Blighters blocking their path. Alrion turned quickly and threw out another ball of fire. But it was weak and slow, only catching one of them. He stopped in his tracks, surprised.

Lara bounded ahead, aiming straight for the leader. The Blighters swarmed to attack her at once. She grabbed one and bounced off its shoulder, flipping over the Blighter and into a tight roll on the ground. She rose and dispatched the leader from behind. The Blighters had ignored her however, and were now after Alrion. His hand was covered in flame, and he used it to attack one and push it into the rest. While they were off balance, Lara swooped in and put them all down with accurate strikes from her twin daggers.

Alrion took a few steps away from the fight, and staggered. He dropped to his knees and took in some deep breaths.

"We barely made it. And you look half-dead. More than you bargained for huh?" Lara could feel the dryness in her throat and her limbs crying out. She could only imagine what Alrion was feeling.

"You could say that. I've never pushed that hard." Alrion was bent over, drawing shallow breaths.

"Was it worth it?"

"We're still alive, and well, they're defeated and broken," Alrion said, looking over at the survivors. They had finally broken rank and were fleeing in groups of ones and twos.

"True, we got the result. Bit too close for my liking. And not worth it."

"Would any fight in the open be to your liking?"

"Probably not, you know I prefer to operate in the shadows. But a little planning to stack the odds in our favour never hurts. You should remember that."

"The odds are already stacked in our favour, but I'll consider your idea of planning," Alrion said, throwing her a smile. Despite her reservations, she couldn't help but get caught up in his smile. But she had to make sure he understood the seriousness of what had just happened.

"Is that the first time you have run out of power?"

"Yes."

"Something to keep in mind. Especially if we keep getting into these kinds of situations."

"Yeah, I know, I'm on it." Alrion put his hand on her shoulder. She wasn't sure if that was supposed to be reassuring, but it was.

"Good, let's leave this mess behind us." She waited for him to take his hand back then stretched.

"You have to admit you were impressed though," Alrion said, giving Lara a cheeky grin.

"Yes, I was impressed. But no more ridiculous stunts. I'd rather we didn't die."

"I'll try," Alrion said and started to walk away. Lara jogged after him and they cut downhill and across the plain they were on to get back to the main road. Alrion started to see buildings rising in the distance.

"Is that it?"

"Yes, that's Brangtur." Just the sight of it, brought back the strong scents of sweat, steel and hides for her.

"Have you been here before?"

"Not for a long time. But I'm sure it is the same. Did your father say where to meet him?"

"No, but he's a blacksmith. It should be easy," Alrion said.

Lara laughed and smacked Alrion on the back.

"What's so funny?" he said.

"This is the city of blacksmiths. It will be like finding a needle in a haystack."

"We'll figure something out," Alrion said.

She could see the embarrassment on his face and decided not to take the joke too far. After a few moments, she changed the topic.

"I have another question. You know how you showed me that notebook a few weeks ago?" Lara said.

"The one with the strange message in it?"

"Yes, that one. Now that you've had a chance to think about it, do you have an idea of who left that message? It has to be a wizard, right?"

"It has to be, I can't think of another way. Nobody else has had proper access to it. And I even tried writing in it. I couldn't leave a reply message."

"So, who do you think it is?"

"I have a theory, but it's a bit crazy."

"Let me hear it. Can't be crazier than what we just did." Lara wanted him to open up a bit, to see if this had anything to do with his reckless behaviour.

"What if my mentor Falric survived? Maybe he's trying to contact me from afar. He knows about the notebook, he saw it before."

"That does sound possible, since he's a wizard, knows about it and wants to help you. But aren't you sure he died?" Lara could see a possible connection to Alrion's new attitude. He was still obsessed about Falric's death. And by his own admission he had been unable to do anything. Was he trying to overcompensate?

"I was sure, but who knows. He was a master of magic. Anyway, like I said it was a crazy theory. It seems better than the alternative."

The alternative that he actually died and you need to deal with that, she thought.

"Which is?" Lara said.

"That some wizard I have never met is following my progress. That just creeps me out," Alrion said.

Lara didn't reply, looking out into the distance. That did seem like the scarier alternative. "Take a look now," she said.

They could see the city better now, giant stone walls topped with immense bronze domes. The walls seemed to be decorated with intricate metalwork with huge metal doors hanging off the main gate.

"Wow," Alrion said, taking it all in.

"I forgot how big it all is. Makes sense for a city of blacksmiths no?"

"Definitely. Although I'm surprised the whole walls aren't made of metal." Alrion had a thoughtful look on his face.

"Good point, we'll have to find out why. Maybe they ran out?" Lara said.

Alrion laughed. "I could imagine my father designing such a city. Although I doubt he would have gone for the entirely metal design. He always harps on about harmony between different materials."

"He's been to Brangtur before, right?"

"I'm sure of it. He's such a passionate blacksmith that this seems like the perfect place for him. Why did he ever leave?"

"You'll have to ask him," Lara said. But she knew that finding a blacksmith in Brangtur would be difficult. For now, there was no need to burden Alrion with those details. She looked over at him and saw the bravado of the fight wearing off. It was being replaced by the look of a boy eager to see his father.

"What is it?" Alrion said, turning back to her.

He must have noticed her staring. "Oh nothing, just taking in the scenery. Let's get a move on," Lara said, picking up the pace.

2

BRANGTUR

T he giant gates towered over them as they walked into the city. Streams of people were travelling in both directions. Alrion could smell the smoke and steel being worked. It was strange, smelling it outside of the workshop.

"It feels like a blacksmith workshop, and we are outdoors," he said.

"Not surprised that you get that impression. There's a lot of workshops here. They can make some seriously massive things."

"Do you know where the main workshops are?"

"I think they are this way. I'm sure you can follow the sounds and smells though," Lara said.

"You're probably right," Alrion said. They continued along the dusty path and turned right down a major road.

"The people seem busy, but happy," Alrion said as he took in the surroundings.

"I agree. I guess it's a safe and prosperous city," Lara said.

"Prosperous? What have you stolen from here?" Alrion was instantly suspicious.

"A good thief never tells. Besides, I don't steal from everywhere," Lara said, giving him an innocent smile.

"I'm not convinced. It's alright, you don't have to spill all your secrets just yet," Alrion said.

Lara was right about the sound of the metalworking though. He could hear the hammering getting louder as they progressed.

The houses were all simply made, in the same style as the city gates. Basic stone shapes, with ornamental metal trimmings. Alrion spotted the odd shop on the way, selling a variety of tools and household items.

"No weapons," he said with a surprised look. It seemed to him like an oversight in a city of blacksmiths.

"Weapons are a smaller market here. Tightly controlled."

"Makes sense, there are so many blacksmiths you could turn over a vast number," Alrion said.

Lara could see him thinking through the problem. He was more like his father than he would admit. "Yes, but I don't think that's all there is to it. I get the sense that they prefer not to make them."

"My father definitely prefers not to. He doesn't want to be known as making tools of war, or being responsible for that. He has always been happy making simple things to help people in their day to day. I didn't think others shared that view." Alrion paused and took a closer look at their surroundings. "I think we've started to stumble across the workshops. Keep an eye out for my father. You remember what he looks like right?"

"Of course. I don't forget a face," Lara said. They slowed their pace, and scanned the faces of the working blacksmiths. They were all shapes and sizes, but the common features being the sweating brows and the arms the width of tree trunks.

"No sign yet," Alrion said.

"I think we are running out of workshops," Lara said, pointing ahead. There was another gate coming up. The doors were open, but there was a sign above the top. It was a sword and shield embossed into metal.

"Looks like the weapons section. Let's take a look," Alrion said.

Lara nodded and followed closely. Stepping through the gate felt like a totally different place. There were still workshops, but there was an air of seriousness and reservation. The blacksmiths Alrion could see had an extra determination and responsibility about them.

"Who are they?" Alrion said, pointing to a stranger. He was a tall man in a red coat wandering through the area.

"No idea, but he looks like an inspector to me," Lara said.

"You're probably right," Alrion said.

"Alrion!" Vincent shouted. He put down his hammer and rushed over, grabbing Alrion in his arms. "You made it. I was so worried."

"Yeah we did. Glad I found you here," Alrion said, relieved and happy to see his father again. He even forgot Lara was there and felt safe and at home once again. Then he noticed her watching them and stiffened up. Vincent released his son and stepped back.

"Where's Falric? And who is this lovely young woman?" he said.

"This is Lara, she's helping out. It's a long story." Alrion choked on his words and stared at the floor.

"Nice to meet you Lara. And Falric?"

"He...is gone. Killed by the enemy wizard that was chasing us," Alrion said in almost a whisper. It was so hard to say the words out loud again. The sense of loss came back completely.

"No... I can't believe it. Let's walk somewhere private so you can fill me in." Vincent guided them in silence down a side street and they emerged in a tiny park. Just a small patch of grass, a single leafy tree, and a large wooden bench seat. "Let's sit here. Please tell everything," Vincent said.

Alrion took a deep breath and launched into a long discussion of everything that had happened since they parted. Vincent did not interrupt once, he just sat quietly and absorbed the information. "So that brings us here," Alrion said, gesturing at his surroundings.

"The enemy wizard was Branthor, and he may still be alive?" Vincent said.

"Yes, we don't know for sure. And there's one other thing. It's about Falric," Alrion said, reaching for his bag. He pulled out the magic notebook.

"Look at this," Alrion said.

Vincent reached out and opened the book. He read the note.

"Who wrote that?" he asked.

"I don't know. It must be a wizard, I couldn't find any other way of writing in it. But the only wizard that it could be is Falric. Nobody else other than Branthor knows about my quest, or about this notebook. Maybe wizards are tougher than we thought?" Alrion was holding on to the hope. He desperately wanted his father to buy into the theory.

"Possibly. Losing Falric is unbelievable, and a huge loss. It's worth considering that he might be out there somewhere. Let's put that aside for a moment. Against all odds, you reached the Pool of Knowledge and you found me. What's next?"

"I'm not sure. The knowledge from the Pool comes in drips here and there, in dreams or integrated into my day to day activities. I can't draw on it like a reference book. But I did have a dream, and my grandfather was in it."

"Really?" Vincent sat up straight and his eyes lit up.

"Yes. I don't think it was a message or anything like that. But I think it was a way of showing me what I needed to do next."

"What was it?"

"I was shown a room, which was guarded by four strangely dressed bald men. They had flowing robes and a special sigil on their clothing."

"Sounds like monks, the way you described them. There are a few different orders of monks throughout the world, we would need to locate the exact ones." Vincent started pacing.

"That's a start. I am sure if I saw the sigil again I would recognise it."

"I will ask around, maybe someone here knows something about them. But before that, I have something to show you," Vincent said and took off. Alrion and Lara jumped up to follow closely behind.

Vincent didn't say anything, he just moved with passion and speed. Alrion struggled to keep up.

What is my father up to? he thought.

"Your father is so energised by something. This is exciting," Lara said.

"He's a blacksmith, it can't be that exciting," Alrion said.

Lara laughed. As they rounded the corner they saw Vincent enter a workshop.

"See. Just blacksmith stuff," Alrion said.

"Just get in there and we will find out," Lara said. The two of them entered the workshop and were assaulted with an array of smells, tinged with the smell of sweat.

"I don't know how you can work in here." Lara was covering her nose and looking around.

"I try not to. There he is," Alrion said, pointing to the far corner. Vincent was standing next to a forge and had something on the anvil. As Alrion walked through the workshop he saw a variety of weapons being forged.

"Look at this!" Vincent said as they approached.

Alrion looked down and saw a blade sitting on the anvil. It required a bit more working to be complete, but it was stunning. The metal had a soft white glow to it, and the surface was perfect. "This looks pretty amazing. I thought you didn't make weapons?"

"It has been a while, but the guys here have been helping me. But that's not the best bit, touch the blade. It's not hot right now," Vincent said. Alrion reached out and dragged his fingers across the metal.

"What is that? It feels like it is vibrating," Alrion said.

"Runesteel. It can cut through anything, and never dulls. I thought the art of making it was long lost, but it seems not. Pretty amazing, isn't it?"

"Don't you need magic to make this?"

"Yes, but you don't need the wizard to make it on the spot. If you had some previously enhanced metal lying around then it wouldn't be so hard, would it?" Vincent said. He was grinning from ear to ear.

"What's this for?" Lara said, speaking up for the first time.

"Did Alrion tell you about how we had a nasty encounter with a Shade?" Vincent said.

"In passing," Lara said.

"Well, it was a rather inconvenient place to encounter one, on the deck of a ship. And as you may be aware, even though we had a wizard with us, Shades are highly magic resistant. It kept me up at night, knowing that potentially the Shade was still out there somewhere."

"This will help?"

"Yes. Their skins are incredibly hard to pierce, but magically enhanced weapons do work. All we had last time was a dagger, and I'm not confident that we finished the job. But with this, and its twin, I think we will be better equipped." Vincent made a thrusting motion with the blade.

"Twin?" Alrion said.

"I'm making two. One for you, and one for me. You need to learn how to defend yourself without magic." Vincent put the blade back down.

"Maybe you can make me one of these? A bit smaller though, I prefer a dagger," Lara said, illustrating the preferred length with her hands.

"I hadn't expected to, but since you're with us you need to be able to defend yourself. It may take a while. I'll have to finish the others first, and source some more Runesteel. But leave it with me."

"Great, I think that would be incredibly handy." Lara reached out and felt the blade herself.

"It will be. So Alrion, what do you think?"

"It looks impressive, I just hope I can learn to use it effectively. I thought you hated making weapons?" he said. Vincent looked away for a moment before answering.

"In principle, yes I do. But there are times when it is necessary. I am happy to do so when I know that what I create will stay in good hands and be of use to my family. I still wouldn't make weapons for anyone I didn't trust."

"You trust me already?" Lara said, a teasing tone to her voice.

"If Alrion trusts you, then I trust you. Until you give me a reason not to." Vincent gave Lara a questioning look, but she held his gaze.

"Is the metal heavier or lighter than usual?" Alrion said, changing the topic.

"The Runesteel? It's lighter, one of the many benefits. Feel for yourself." Alrion picked up the blade and felt it. It was much lighter than he was used to working with. He handed it to Lara and she pretended to struggle with the weight, dropping to her knees. Vincent laughed and she handed it back.

Alrion tried not to laugh, but he did show a grin. "Alright you sold me. When will it be ready?" he said.

"A day or two perhaps, but we will see how I go. I'm not in a rush right now, and you don't seem to have a destination just yet."

"That's true, we need to find out where the monks are from." Alrion had no idea where to even start with that.

"I'm sure a few days to rest before heading out again will be of help. In fact, why don't I shout you both to a meal and free drinks to welcome you to Brangtur?"

"What's the catch? We never went out at home, and you always cautioned me on drinking anything remotely alcoholic," Alrion said.

"No catch, let's just have a moment to relax. We're reunited again. And we need to honour our fallen friend."

"That's true. I haven't done enough." Alrion looked away, as if trying to locate the humble grave he had constructed for Falric.

"We've all been through a lot, and I fear this is only the beginning. Let's take a moment," Vincent said.

"Don't look a gift horse in the mouth Alrion," Lara said.

"Alright you convinced me. Let's go," Alrion said.

"Right behind you. Lara, would you mind staying back a second so I can ask you something?" Vincent said.

"Sure. Meet you out front," Lara shouted to Alrion.

Vincent watched Alrion leave then stepped closer to Lara.

"I appreciate the help you have given my son. However, I need to understand how you so quickly got caught up in this."

"I noticed the three of you back at Carford, and I knew there was something unusual going on. So, I lifted a ring from Alrion, and noticed that it was magical. I tracked you all since then, curious about what you were up to. Every adventure you had further confirmed to me that you were doing something monumental!"

"You followed us the entire way?" Vincent said. He couldn't disguise the surprise in his voice.

"Of course, it was easy. All I had to was keep hidden, you burnt a huge trail across the country."

"We did encounter a few situations."

"Exactly, so I kept track of you."

"What changed? What made you a helper instead of a watcher?" Vincent regarded her closely, interested in her answer.

"I noticed that Alrion was in trouble. So, I offered to help," Lara said. Vincent walked closer, until he was inches away from Lara's face.

"I know that you are caught up in this, and you want to keep going. And I don't need to know all your reasons. But I do know that you didn't just decide to help out. What happened?" Vincent said, in a low and steady voice that didn't accept excuses. She appeared shaken by the change in his tone and approach.

Hopefully with a direct approach I can surprise her into telling me the truth, Vincent thought.

"He doesn't know. This mysterious wizard found me. He had tracked me using the ring that I stole from Alrion. He forced me to give it back, and to keep following."

"Who was it?"

"I don't know, he somehow hidden his face so that it is always in the shadows."

"How did he force you to help Alrion?"

"He had a way of getting into my mind. He didn't force me, but it was like he knew what to say. I can't explain it," Lara said. Vincent could see the truth on her face, her confusion and worry. She wasn't faking it.

"I see. Alrion knows nothing of this?"

"No."

"That's fine, better that way. I believe your story, but this other wizard concerns me. It is troubling that the wizard only appeared around the time of Falric's death."

"I couldn't say if it was before or after his death. I only met up with Alrion afterward."

"Hey, you two, come see this," Alrion shouted.

"Keep this from Alrion, let's go." Vincent directed Lara to leave and followed her out. Alrion was standing just outside the door. Once he saw them he pointed to a man across the street. He was sitting on a bench reading a book.

"Who is that?" Lara said.

"I have no idea, but can you see that strange scarf he has wrapped around himself?"

"That's a monk's scarf," Vincent said.

"And from here it looks exactly like what the monks wore in my dream," Alrion said.

"He doesn't look like a monk to me, but let's go see what he has to say for himself," Lara said. Before Alrion or Vincent could reply she started walking off.

3

TRACKING THE SCARF

Lara stopped right in front of the man, looking him over without pretending to hide what she was doing. The man didn't react, his head focused on his book.

"Excuse me," Lara said. He didn't immediately react, but after a moment placed a small ribbon in the book and closed it. He looked up at her.

"Yes, can I help you?" he said. A puzzled look crossed his face when Vincent and Alrion also joined Lara.

"My name is Lara. And you are?"

"Brett," the man said. He looked them all over, a confused expression on his face.

"That scarf is quite impressive. Where did you get it?" Lara said.

"Oh this? It's nice, isn't it? Unfortunately, it is not for sale."

"That's fine, I just would love to know where you got it?" Lara said in her sweetest voice. Alrion had to stifle a laugh and she quickly jerked her head around to silence him with a blistering look.

"I'm afraid you really can't get one, so I don't see how that would help."

"Please, humour me. I absolutely must know." Lara thought back to all the women she knew who were fashion obsessed, and tried to channel that.

"Very well, if it means you will leave me to my book?" Brett said, his increasing annoyance clear in his voice.

"Of course."

"Last night I was enjoying a quiet drink in my favoured inn. It's called The Amber Anvil. I was just about to leave for the night, when a strange man burst in. He was clad in what looked like rags, his hair was strangely cut, and he had a wild look about him. But he had on this amazing scarf which had somehow survived whatever he had been through."

"So, a strange man came in wearing it. How did you get it?" Lara said. Alrion and Vincent stayed quiet, eager to hear what Brett had to say.

"Other than acknowledging his strange manner and dress, I returned to my book and my drink. A few minutes later I could smell something strange. I turned to notice that the man was hovering behind me. When I questioned him about what he wanted, he didn't say anything. He just stared at my drink."

"That is very odd." Lara said.

"It is indeed. He finally spoke, and said that he was in dire need of a drink, and asked if I could buy him a bottle to tide him over. I of course declined, which made him quite act quite erratic. I suspected that he was already drunk, and was perhaps fearing the prospect of sobering up." Lara was getting impatient with the way this guy was dragging out the story.

"You traded him for the scarf?" Lara said. For a man annoyed about being interrupted, he sure was taking his time with the story. Maybe he was punishing them.

"Please let me finish. At first, he challenged me to a drinking contest, with me supplying the bottle. I politely declined once again. But he was determined. So that's when he offered me the trade."

"You bought him a bottle and he gave you the scarf?"

"Not at first. He seemed quite reluctant to hand it over. But I was adamant that it was the only thing he had of value. He did finally relent, and I think he buried himself in the bottle even faster to forget about what he had lost."

"Great story, thanks for sharing. Where is this inn exactly?" Alrion said.

"It's on the other end of town. In the Vine district." Brett gestured off into the distance.

"Thank you, Brett, I apologise for taking you away from your book," Lara said.

"Well I did find it entertaining to share that particular story. Good luck with your search. I doubt that man has another scarf though."

"Don't you worry, I'll find out where I can get myself one," Lara said, winking at Brett. Brett immediately re-opened his book, and resumed where he was reading. Lara stepped away and Alrion and Vincent followed.

"Do you think that man he described is one of the monks?" Alrion said.

"Definitely. But clearly something has happened, it sounds like he has been through demanding times. You said that the monks in your dream were bald? From the way Brett described his hair it could have regrown in a strange way," Vincent said.

"I agree. If we find this monk we can find out where he is from. This is a huge break," Lara said. Luck was definitely with them. Finding Vincent and now the lead they needed. But things weren't always so smooth in her experience. She was waiting for the catch.

"Good. I needed one of those. Do you know where that inn is?" Alrion said.

"I don't know that one in particular, but all the inns are together. Follow me." Vincent took off with a confident stride through the district, leading them back to the area where they had entered the city.

"Has it changed much? The city?" Alrion asked his father as they walked.

"Not that much, I am a little surprised. The people are changing, and there are newer areas that are more developed. But the core is the same. I think this is what happens when you build things to last."

"I can definitely imagine this place never changing. It feels like it has always been this way." Lara noticed that the pace of the people seemed as slow as she remembered, even though it was now much more crowded. It seemed like the city had its own special pace that everyone could feel and maintain.

"So, are you a bit of a drinker yourself?" Lara said, looking at Vincent.

"In my younger days, perhaps. But not now. I think it's the kind of thing most men grow out of."

"What about him?" Lara said pointing at Alrion.

"I can't say, I haven't seen him in action. But I've heard a few stories," Vincent said, chuckling to himself.

"Honestly, I don't really get into it that much. But I've had a few experiences, like everyone has. What about you?" Alrion said.

"Nope, don't touch the stuff. Hate the taste. I can't understand how you could drink that." Lara shuddered at the memory.

"Neither can we," Vincent said, laughing out loud. Alrion kept looking around as they walked, taking in the changes in scenery.

He really hasn't been anywhere at all, Lara thought, observing him.

They had entered what looked like a market district. There were lots of stalls in the street, as well as a huge variety of shops. As expected the wares were mostly things made by blacksmiths.

"I still don't see any weapons," Alrion said.

"Yes, there are special outlets that deal in weapons. Either that or you commission them directly from the blacksmith," Vincent said.

"The swords that you are making, would they sell for a lot?"

"Priceless."

"You can't say that. Give me a number." Lara knew that when it came to priceless artefacts, there was always a number.

"Let's just say, that people would offer me enough money to buy a house here and never work another day in my life, spending my evenings in the inn and my days doing whatever I pleased," Vincent said.

Lara whistled with admiration. "That's quite a lot. It may not be enough for my tastes though. A start, perhaps," she said.

"Don't get any ideas," Vincent said, looking directly at Lara.

She laughed. "A girl can dream."

"I think we're in the right area now," Alrion said. They had crossed into another district with a wider street and lots of large inns. Each sign was bigger than the last, trying to grab the attention of passers-by. "What was the name again? The Amber Anvil?" he said.

"That's right. Haven't heard of it, but we shouldn't have too much trouble," Vincent said.

They continued at a slow pace examining the signs as they went.

"The Sloshed Shield, The Hammered Hammer. Wow these aren't very imaginative." Lara had never really thought about the names before, but now they really stood out.

"That's a fair call. But they're effective. Blacksmiths are a folk that like things to be straightforward," Vincent said.

"Surely the owners of these places could try a bit harder though?"

"Maybe, but I'm sure it works well," Vincent said. Alrion stopped abruptly.

"Is that it?" Alrion pointed at a smaller building on the corner of a block. It had a vaulted ceiling and a lot more wooden features than the surrounding buildings. It looked a lot more like a traditional inn.

"That's definitely it," Lara said.

"I'll be interested to see this monk," Vincent said.

The three of them headed directly for the inn. Judging from the exterior and the look of Brett, Alrion guessed this place had targeted a higher class of clientele. No wonder the dishevelled monk had seemed so out of place.

Lara's nose wrinkled at the familiar wave of beer smell as she stepped inside. The decor was well-maintained wood, with attractive lamps used to brighten the otherwise poorly lit interior. Since it was daytime the place was relatively empty.

"Let's head straight to the bartender," she said. She took the lead and didn't wait for Alrion and Vincent.

"Excuse me good man, I was hoping you could help me out," Lara said. The portly man with thinning hair looked up at her with a puzzled expression.

"That's not how people usually order a drink. What can I get you?"

"Some information. We are looking for a strange man you had in last night. Odd hairstyle, dressed in rags but had a beautifully crafted scarf with him," Lara said.

"Oh him? He's been around these last few weeks. Does the rounds, going from inn to inn. He bothers the customers, trying to get free drinks. However, he's been getting less and less luck. Last night he had to trade that fancy scarf of his, and you could tell he was upset."

"If he's such a nuisance why tolerate him?" Alrion said.

"Oh, one of my friends tried. He runs The Plastered Plate and wanted to teach the stranger a lesson. Had one of his bouncers try and run the stranger out. But this monk, he knew how to fight. Even while drunk he made short work of the bouncer and didn't even spill his drink."

"Wow, that's not something you see every day," Alrion said.

"Yeah, he's a nuisance but less trouble than he would be if we interfered with him. So, we just try and let him run free. He will probably get bored of this area and move on, so we're just waiting him out." The bartender shrugged and resumed cleaning a glass. Lara's stomach churned when he spat on the glass to shift a particularly stubborn speck.

"Does he come in here at a particular time?" Vincent said.

"Nah, I don't see him every day. He spreads himself evenly over all the inns here. Since he was here last night, I wouldn't expect to see him back right away. If you're looking for him specifically, it won't be hard but you'll need to do the rounds," the barkeeper said.

"Thanks so much for your help, much appreciated," Lara said.

"If you can get him to leave you'll be forever in my debt," the barkeeper said, his frustration quite obvious.

"We'll see what we can do," Lara said with a wink and turned to leave. All three of them left the inn, and reconvened outside.

"Looks like we need to make ourselves acquainted with the local night life," Lara said.

"Not me, I need to get back to the workshop so I can finish off these swords. Let me know how you go," Vincent said.

"If you insist. Have fun," Lara said.

"Where should we meet you?" Alrion said.

"Back at the workshop. I'll work until you come get me, then I'll take you back to where I am staying."

"Alright, we'll see you there."

"Good luck," Vincent said, and waved as he left.

"Now the real fun begins," Lara said.

"I'm not sure I can handle any more drinking related blacksmith puns," Alrion said.

"Nonsense, you'll love it. We just need to forge ahead." Lara saw Alrion's face break out into a smile.

"Fine, I'll give you that. Let's go," he said. The grin was still firmly planted on him.

~

Ten inns later, Alrion eased himself down onto a wooden bench on the street.

"Is there anywhere we haven't tried?" he said, weariness in his voice.

"You just have no staying power. There's probably a few left. But the good news is that none of them have seen him tonight, so we're almost there." Lara knew this monk would be out there, it was just a matter of elimination.

"I sure hope so, they are all beginning to be a blur."

"Just a few more, then we can regroup and figure out what to do next."

"You're right, I just need a minute," Alrion yawned, stretched out on the seat, and relaxed.

"Are you ready yet?" Lara said after exactly one minute.

"Yeah, bring it on," Alrion said. "Let's try this place."

"The Lucky Lance? Maybe it'll be lucky for us too," Lara said. There was a good chance that this was the place they would find the link to Alrion's dream. The strange, wild, drunken monk.

Lara stepped into an explosion of light and sound. There were musicians playing a loud catchy tune, on a variety of stringed instruments. People were dancing between tables, and there was double the number of lamps as any other place they had visited.

"Quite a spirited place," she said, dodging some slightly drunk dancers.

"Knowing our luck, he will be hidden in the crowd here," Alrion said.

Lara took the lead and slowly navigated through the packed crowds, avoiding wayward dance moves and swaying drunks. "What do you think about him?" she said, pointing to the corner of the room. There was a man sitting by himself, nursing a glass of beer. His hair looked like it had been roughly cut by a child, and his clothes were so worn and dirty that you could no longer tell what the original colour was.

"Has to be him, but we would never have known he was a monk without the connection to the scarf," Alrion said.

"True, it was a lucky break. Maybe our luck will continue, let's see what he has to say for himself."

"I'm all ears," Alrion said. They changed direction, winding their way through the people and tables until they were standing right in front of the monk. It appeared as if he hadn't seen them, but he spoke up before they could address him. "What do you want? Go away," he said.

"My name is Lara and this is Alrion. What's your name?"

"Why should I tell you?"

"We're looking for a monk, and you fit the description."

"I used to be a monk, so you're half right."

"Then we need your help." Lara decided she would appeal to his charitable side first. He was, after all, originally a monk.

"And I need another drink, something better than this swill," the monk said, swirling around the dark liquid in his glass.

"We only have a few questions, maybe we can arrange some sort of trade," Lara said. The monk stopped staring into his glass and looked up.

"A trade? Hmm no, that won't do. A contest. Now's that a better way to do things," he said.

"A contest?" Alrion said.

"Yes, bring back a bottle of their best stuff. If you can best me in a drinking contest then I'll spill my life story."

"I don't..." Alrion said, but Lara put a hand on his arm.

"You're on," Lara said and immediately walked over towards the bar.

AN UNUSUAL CHALLENGE

Alrion looked uncomfortable. Lara could understand why. Clearly the monk was a seasoned drinker, and would be hard to match, let alone overcome in a drinking contest. She half ran the final stretch back to make sure she missed nothing.

"Are you sure that's necessary. I'm sure there are other ways we can figure this out," Alrion said.

"No, it's all I want right now. You can't convince me any other way," the monk said. He held his glass with both hands, and carefully sipped it, a disgusted look briefly passing over his face.

"One bottle of their finest liquor," Lara said, placing a brown bottle down on the table, with two short glasses. The third glass she kept hidden in her tunic. The monk reached out for the bottle immediately, and Lara quickly withdrew it.

"I just want to test it," the monk said. Lara uncapped the bottle, and waved it near his face so he could get a whiff of its contents.

"Is that acceptable?" she said. Alrion could smell the alcohol quite well from where he was standing.

"Yes, that is acceptable. You, are my opponent," the monk said, pointing at Alrion.

"I'll go for it, but he might win you know?" Alrion whispered to Lara.

"Don't worry, I'll cheat," Lara whispered back. Alrion nodded slowly.

"What are the rules then?" Alrion said.

"Very simple. I pour both glasses, we drink at the same time. If I am unable to pour the next round, you win. If you are unable to drink the next round, I win."

"Is this bottle even enough for you to lose?" Alrion said.

"Yes, it's strong enough. And we won't waste time. A quick game is a good game." The monk rearranged himself on the seat, and looked like he was ready.

"You're going to have to do the first few on your own," Lara whispered to Alrion as the monk poured the first round of drinks.

"I suppose since we are drinking together I should share my name. I'm Certan, nice to meet you both." He did a mini bow then picked up one of the glasses. "Cheers," Certan said, and held out his glass. Alrion raised his, and they clinked. Before Alrion could react Certan had thrown down his drink and placed the empty glass back down on the table. "Quickly lad, we don't have all day," Certan said.

Alrion raised the glass to his lips and drank it swiftly. Lara watched him choke it down, and struggle to prevent it coming up again. He used his palm to hit his chest a few times. "That's strong stuff," Alrion said, his voice hoarse and croaky.

"Only the best. That'll put some extra hair on your chest," Certan said.

"Really? That's horrible."

"I never really thought about it that way. Good thing it doesn't then eh?" Certan said, pouring another round. "Ready?"

Alrion looked apprehensive, but he reached for the glass.

"Just hang in there, we can't afford to lose this. I can assist soon," Lara whispered to Alrion. He nodded.

"Bottoms up," Certan shouted as he chugged his drink, almost as fast as the first time. Alrion handled the cup more carefully the second time. The reaction on his face was almost as bad as the first time.

"Trying to minimise the burn? Good idea, but it won't work," Certan said.

He's not going to last long at this rate. I have to intervene.

"Next time, you two should coordinate your drinking. It's fairer," she said.

"I agree. You have to match me," Certan said to Alrion.

"Sure." Alrion didn't look sure at all, but Lara had a plan for that.

Certan raised his glass and Alrion did the same, so they were touching. "Now!" Certan shouted. In unison, they tipped back their glasses.

Before Alrion could drink his, Lara quickly swapped the glass for her spare so that Alrion drank an empty one. He slammed it back down convincingly at the same time as Certan, while Lara tipped the contents of the full glass onto the sawdust covered floor behind her back ready to switch again on the next round.

"Now that's a nice burn," Alrion said.

"That's the spirit." Certan hadn't seemed to notice any foul play.

Lara gave Alrion a reassuring look while Certan was busy refilling the glasses.

"Round four!" he said.

Alrion readied himself, and as before prepared to actually drink. But as before, Lara swiftly swapped the glass out and Alrion continued his pretence. "Ooh I think it's starting to hit me," Alrion said.

"You just don't have my stamina. It takes a lot of training," Certan said, laughing.

"I think I've been training the wrong things then," Alrion said with a chuckle. A few more rounds progressed the same way, each time Certan slowing down just a little bit more.

The swap is getting easier and easier. We can win this.

"I must admit, you are doing better than I expected," Certan said.

"I am a bit younger, I have that advantage," Alrion said.

"He's just playing it down because he doesn't want to admit his history of drinking. Shame on you Alrion. You can never tell, can you?" Lara said to Certan.

"True, the young ones always find their way to the drink. Well nice chat, let's keep going. Round ten!" Certan said.

Alrion and Lara continued their deception.

"How long is this going to take?" Lara wondered.

"Round fourteen!" Certan said, but before he could lift his glass to pour again he slumped over in his seat.

"I think that makes you the winner Alrion," Lara said.

"I think it does. What's my prize?"

"You get to carry this drunk across the entire city," Lara said, pointing at Certan. There was no way he could walk. And the way he was staring into space, it seemed unlikely that he would be able to answer any questions.

"Come with us, we'll take you somewhere more comfortable to talk," Alrion said. Certan nodded his head and waved, but didn't utter anything other than some vague drool ridden nonsense.

"I think that's a yes. Let's go," Lara said. Alrion leaned in and dragged Certan to his feet. Alrion put one arm around him, and made some odd movements with Certan's body jerking around.

"Need a hand there?" Lara said pointing to Certan.

"No, I'm fine. Just fine tuning some magical assistance," Alrion said.

"You may want to make some more adjustments," Lara said, pointing.

The way that Certan was propped up on the other side looked completely unnatural.

"Oh yes, you're right I'll have some unwanted attention soon," Alrion said.

Lara rolled her eyes and came around to the other side to help. She assumed the right position as if she were helping. Alrion seemed to understand her plan, and Lara didn't have to hold any of the monk's weight.

They emerged from the inn into the cool air and Certan cheered.

"At least he's happy," Alrion said.

"You two are good folk," Certan said or at least that was what the slurring noise sounded like.

"Thanks for that. Are you curious where we are headed?" Lara said.

"Nope, doesn't matter as long as it is warm and I'll have something to drink." Certan threw back an imaginary shot.

"It's warm, and you'll have plenty of water," Alrion said.

"You did win, fair and square," Certan said. However, the way he emphasised the words fair and square suggested that he wasn't entirely convinced.

"You made the rules, not us," Lara said.

"Yes, I did. But I didn't say you could break them!"

"Don't be a sore loser," Lara said.

"Ho hum," Certan said, staring off into space. Lara looked up and they were still only halfway through the entertainment district.

"This is going to take a while," she said.

"I hope he actually has some useful information for us to make this whole effort worthwhile," Alrion said.

Lara could see from his face how uncomfortable he was. She almost felt bad for not helping to hold Certan's weight. But Alrion had magic, he could handle it.

They received more strange and judgemental looks in the market district.

"I feel like everyone is watching us, but at the same time isn't looking," Alrion said.

"Yeah, they are noticing us but are too polite to stare. I don't think this is a particularly new sight at all. So, they see us, try not to look then dismiss us."

"If that's the case, we should carry drunk people around more often," Alrion said.

Lara laughed a little. "It's a bit of a drag though," she said and Alrion joined her in laughing. Certan started laughing too, which was infectious.

"Does he even know why we are laughing?" Alrion said.

"I don't think he even cares," Lara said.

They continued this strange routine, with Certan becoming less and less coherent and Alrion looking more and more strained. But they finally made their way through to the working district and the entrance to the workshop where Vincent was toiling away.

"Hello there, I see you have a guest," Vincent said.

"They beat me fair and square," Certan said, piping up out of nowhere. Again, he emphasised the words fair and square.

"Good to see you are so gracious in defeat. Let's get him back to my quarters. I'll take over here," Vincent said, walking over and talking the load off Lara. Alrion shifted his stance and looked relieved.

"This is definitely the monk we need to talk to," Alrion said.

"He's not like any monk I've ever met," Vincent said.

"Most monks would not accompany you in this fashion," Certan said.

"Why is that?" Alrion said.

"They would have dismissed your pathetic attempts at cheating and stormed off. But me, I'm much more generous." Certan gestured with his arms wide, no doubt trying to show the extent of his generosity.

"I think most monks wouldn't engage in drinking contests. Not that I hold that against you," Lara said.

"You got me!" Certan said, mumbling the words. Vincent laughed, shaking his head. They hauled the man the rest of the way in silence.

"This is it," Vincent said.

They were standing in front of a small square building. It was the same style as the rest, rough but well cut stone, with a range of metal adornments on the doors, windows, and trims.

"This is your place?" Lara said.

"It's not mine exactly, but working blacksmiths that are qualified are given quarters to inhabit. These are for our use," Vincent said.

Lara opened the door, and Vincent and Alrion shuffled inside, trying not to knock Certan against any walls or doorways. The interior was sparsely decorated, but there was an old couch in a living room so they carefully set Certan down there.

"I appreciate the assistance," Certan said, in a drunken drawl.

"Let me whip up something to help," Vincent said, disappearing into another room.

"I don't blame you for what you did. Clearly this man here cannot match me in drinking. And I went along with it, because that was some good stuff. Thanks for playing along," Certan said slowly and carefully. Lara was about to reply when he slid to the side and started snoring.

"Well I guess you weren't fast enough with your switching," Alrion said.

"I guess not. But you know, I think the fact that he noticed even after drinking that much means that he's very skilled. Under that strange behaviour and clothing, he's the real deal," Lara said.

"I hope so, I need a good lead. I'd prefer it if my dream had contained some sort of map and directions, but it did not. I've not had any noteworthy dreams since."

"He's asleep already? Let him doze for a while. We can get more out of him when he sobers up," Vincent was holding a glass with a dark liquid in it.

"What's that?" Alrion asked.

"A special concoction to help sober him up and wake him up. But I'll save it for the morning. Let's all get some rest."

"Sounds good to me," Alrion said.

Vincent showed them to the additional areas he had prepared, with a separate mattress to sleep on. Lara watched Alrion fall asleep almost instantly, and she made herself comfortable.

Lara had the strange feeling that she was being watched, and she sat up instantly. It was the break of dawn, with a dim light filtering into the room. She could see a shape sitting in front of her, legs crossed. As her eyes adjusted she could see it was Certan, sipping the drink that Vincent had prepared the night before.

"This is good stuff, I'll have to get the recipe. As for last night, I must applaud your ingenuity and quick reflexes. You would have completely fooled anyone else." Certan held up his glass in a mock toast.

"Thanks for letting me get away with it."

"Are you ready for a story?" Certan said. There was a fire and intensity to his eyes that Lara had not noticed before.

"Glad to finally meet you. I think we're all ready for that story, and it better be a good one."

5

THE FALLEN MONK

Alrion awoke to the sound of voices. He rose quickly and investigated. Lara and Certan were sitting opposite each other.

"I see you are awake and enjoying my father's vile drink. Story time?" he asked.

"Yes," Certan said before taking another sip.

"I'll go get my father," Alrion wandered through the small dwelling into the main bedroom. His father was fast asleep. Alrion shook him gently.

"Yes?" Vincent said, drawing the word out.

"He's awake and sober. I figured you would want to hear what he has to say."

"Of course," Vincent said, scrambling out of bed.

"Plus, you'll be pleased to know that he likes your strange drink."

"He likes it? Everyone hates it. That's half the point of it," Vincent said.

Alrion left his father to wake himself up and returned to Certan. Lara and Certan had rearranged their seating to accommodate more people comfortably. "My father will be here in a moment, but you can begin. So, your name is Certan. What else should we know?"

"Yes, that is my name. As you guessed I was part of a highly secretive and skilled order of monks. They call themselves the Unbroken Wall."

"I've never heard of them," Vincent said as he entered the room. He found a few pillows to sit down on, and made himself comfortable.

"That's the idea. They are based out of a temple hidden in the middle of the desert. Hard to find, and away from any trade routes. You have to know the way there or else you'll die wandering."

"Lucky we have you then," Lara said.

"Do not get ahead of yourself, let me continue. This order of monks is incredibly old, and there are four masters at any one time. The eldest of the masters is hundreds of years old," Certan said.

"How is that possible?" Alrion said.

"By the nature of their study and skill. Their speciality is the study and application of the will. With it, many things can be altered, many so-called rules broken. They are able to push the boundaries of time and space, and the limits of the human body."

"As strange as that sounds, it is starting to make sense to me," Alrion said.

"I've never heard someone respond like that, very interesting." Certan tilted his head slightly and studied Alrion as if he was a puzzle to solve.

"What's an example of what they can do?" Lara said.

"They can break steel or stone with any part of their body. They can avoid attacks that no other can even detect. They can move with speed and strength that is impossible. They can even move things with their mind," Certan said.

"Sign me up," Lara said.

"They do take women, but it requires dedication and years of training. I doubt you have the determination to do it," Certan said.

"I liked him more when he was drunk," Lara said.

"They sound like a formidable force, and well-trained and disciplined. What happened to you?" Vincent said. Certan visibly stiffened, taken aback by the comment.

"I don't mean to offend, I'm sorry," Vincent said quickly.

"No, I am not offended by your question, it is quite valid. I was thinking on my failure, and my situation. I will explain." Certan stood up and paced around the room a little, looking out into the distance. Then he resumed his seated position. "Unlike many of the monks, I was not inducted as a child. I was a teenager, living out on the fringes of the desert. It was a small town, kept alive by the travellers who needed to cross the desert and could afford to pay for our overpriced supplies. We were not greedy, but the number of travellers was so low, we had to extract as much as we could from them to survive."

"You learned to live with very little?" Vincent said.

"Yes, it was a simple life. Looking back, you don't realise how special it is. Happiness without wealth feels hard at the time, but is infinitely easier. There is a lightness to it. As long as you can find a way to keep going, there are no particularly hard burdens. Your life and daily responsibilities consume your mind, keeping you safe."

"Sounds like good preparation for joining an order of monks," Alrion said.

"It was, in a fashion. But as a teenager, I acted as most do. I rebelled against the conditions we lived in. I found some like-minded friends and we started to roam further and further from our home. We found new people to trade with, stumbled across things left by desperate travellers and felt like we had additional freedom and wealth. We shared only amongst ourselves and became wealthy, in comparison to those around us."

"So, what happened?" Lara said.

"We became greedy. We heard that a caravan had lost a wheel and a huge amount of valuables were abandoned in the desert. We were the only ones with the strength, knowledge, and resources to salvage it. Even though it was further than we had ever roamed before, we didn't even think twice. The lure of the prize was too great."

"What was so alluring about it?"

"It would have been enough for us to leave and build a life somewhere else. When you are young, the urge to wander is so strong. You will do anything to follow it. But as you can guess, things did not go so well. We found the caravan. Of course, it was further than we had planned for, and laden with even more goods that we expected. We argued about what to do. One of us wanted to drag it closer, and bring about another group to collect it all. One wanted to try to fix the caravan and ride it home. I wanted us to take a few valuables and go home, just enough to get us on our way."

"Who won?" Vincent said.

"Not me. My friends decided to take our supplies, and set off to find a way to fix the caravan. My theory is that they thought I would wait until they returned and be forced to help them. But I was impatient and took off in another direction, hoping to go home. Unfortunately, it was the wrong direction and I got lost in the middle of the desert. Alone, hungry and parched. I collapsed, and considered myself done for."

"How did you get out of that?" Alrion said, captivated by the story. He needed to hear more.

"One of the monks found me. They took me in, and offered me a chance to join them. I had nothing more to do, my friends had abandoned me and it was a chance to join something incredible. I really enjoyed my time there." Certan's tone of voice changed and he started to look downwards.

"But something happened?" Vincent said.

"Yes, it was one of the final trials. They have a room there, it is called the Room of Desire. And it is filled with all the things that a young man desires, but does not need. Gold, wine, beer, treasures, you name it. As part of the trial they take you in there, and show you that it exists. They make you sample the wine, select a piece of gold and a treasure. Then they lead you out, not locking the door or saying anything else."

"Did you know it was a trial?" Alrion said.

"They didn't explain it as such, but I suspected something was up. However, once that wine passed my lips, I was obsessed. I couldn't stop thinking about it. The thoughts drove me mad. So, one night, I snuck back into the room and helped myself. The flood gates were open, and I didn't care who knew." Certan closed his eyes, a pained look crossing his features. It looked like he was reliving the moment.

"Presumably you were caught?" Lara said.

"Yes, immediately. It's like they knew. They weren't mean about it, they just said that everyone responds differently to the trial, and that I could not stay. I packed my things and left. Luckily, I knew how to navigate the desert by that point, so I could safely rejoin society."

"What did you do?" Alrion said.

"I wandered from here to there. I took odd jobs as a mercenary, labourer, whatever was available. When I wasn't working, I availed myself of local entertainments. Establishments like the one where you found me. It's a strange spiral down that I found myself in. I started to avoid the paying jobs, to deny myself access to the coin that would immediately go back into more drinks. But that just led to other behaviour, like trading away the scarf which was my last tie to the monks."

"Are you happy with your current lifestyle?" Vincent said.

"No, I'm not. But I don't see a way out. I am trapped in a downwards spiral that only ends in one way." Certan didn't shy away from it.

"Help us. This is your chance to turn things around. Please, I need to ask you a very important question," Alrion said.

Certan did not respond. After a long pause, he opened his eyes. "I don't think I have another chance, but I am a man of my word and will help you. What do you need to know?"

"I had a dream, and in it I saw four monks, dressed in garments with the same symbol that was on your scarf. They were sitting outside a doorway, to a pure white room. I need to go there, and undertake whatever trial that is. Does that make any sense?" Alrion said. Certan closed his eyes again. He looked asleep. After a few minutes, he opened his eyes once more and addressed Alrion.

"I know of what you speak. I have meditated to recall as much detail as possible. The room you speak of is called the Vault of Silence. It is the final trial a monk undergoes. Very few make it that far, and very few succeed. Yet we are all told about it, early on in our training. I am not sure why, but that's no matter now. It is all about the mastery of the will. If you can pass that trial, you have achieved the pinnacle of monkhood," Certan said.

"I have to pass that trial. What else can you tell me about it?"

"Unfortunately, I don't know the specific details. I just know that the four elder monks administer the test. It requires you to enter the room. I've only heard of one monk taking the test in all the time I have been there."

"What happened?" Lara said.

"We never saw him again. I guess he failed? I can't say for sure."

"That's reassuring," Alrion said.

"I am just telling you what I know. Without being aware of your background,

I think you will find it very challenging. You do not have the proper training to succeed." Certan's face was emotionless.

Alrion could tell the monk was not trying to belittle him. Even still, he couldn't accept that statement. "I have to pass, so I will find a way," Alrion said.

"I can see the fire within your eyes. You have the passion, and the embers of a strong will. Perhaps that will be enough." Certan stood up and paced around the room. "I will draw you a map, so you can find your way through the desert. Then our business is concluded."

"That would be very helpful," Vincent said.

"Why not come with us? You can show us the way yourself, and you can resume your training," Alrion said.

"No, I cannot go back. It's not possible."

"Did they even say that? Or are you just being stubborn and embarrassed?" Alrion said. Certan stopped his pacing. Alrion could see that he was getting through to the monk.

"I am not sure. I will think on it. That is the best answer I can give you right now," he said.

"Thanks," Alrion said. It was a start, he could work on it. After hearing the story, he couldn't imagine undertaking the journey without Certan.

"You know, it'll be fun. We can all go, it will be an adventure," Lara said.

"Not on my watch," a voice said from the doorway. They all turned to look at their visitor. It was a woman dressed in leather travelling clothes, with tall boots and a short jacket thrown over her shoulders.

"Celes?" Vincent said, shock in his voice.

"You thought I would just wait at home after hearing what you were up to? Lucky I did turn up. You look like you are about to let my son run off with this young delinquent and this fallen monk," Celes said. Certan looked away, embarrassment on his face.

"Delinquent? I am no such thing," Lara said. Alrion could see her face flare up in anger.

"Mum, what is going on?" Alrion had never seen this side of her. She was always strong and loving and fair. But here she seemed different. He had never seen her dressed like this before. There was now an edge to her strength, and a confidence in her stance that suggested a whole other part to her story that he never knew about. He didn't know whether to be relieved or scared.

6

AN UNEXPECTED REUNION

Celes strode around the room, looking them all up and down.

"I see no need to change my initial assessment. Are things so dire?"

"Honey, calm down. There's a lot to discuss," Vincent said.

"You bet there is. You told me you were taking him to study at the Academy. Then I get a letter saying that you're on this huge quest and you'll write again from Brangtur? Not good enough."

"Sorry, we couldn't exactly turn around," Vincent said.

"So, where's that troublemaking wizard anyway? I want to give Falric a piece of my mind. I warned him quite clearly." Celes had a look in her eye that caused even Alrion to shrink back.

"He's no longer with us," Vincent said.

Celes stopped, and her mood changed completely. She stopped pacing around and her expression visibly softened. "I'm sorry, I had no idea. What kind of mess is this?" she said.

"Take a seat, we will talk you through it," Vincent said.

Certan rose and started to leave the room.

"Stay and listen, please. You're a part of this now," Alrion said. Certan hesitated, then returned.

"What I will say, must not leave this room," Vincent started to tell the story, and let Alrion take over in the parts where they were separated.

⁓

Celes showed no reaction until the story was finished. "I am sorry for my outburst," she said. Immediately she rose and walked over to Alrion, giving him a huge hug. He returned it, happy to have his mother back. His eyes teared up a bit, and he turned away to hide them. Celes returned to where she was sitting.

"Don't worry about any of that, I am happy to accept the blame. I should have explained more," Vincent said.

"What now?" Alrion said.

"I can't stop what is already in motion. But I can influence what happens next. I'll even support this quest you are on. But before we can leave, you two need to pass a test." Celes pointed at Certan and Lara.

"What kind of test?" Lara said.

"For you, it's simple. You will accompany Alrion and me on a little recovery mission. Vincent knows what it is," Celes said, looking at Vincent and smiling. Vincent laughed after a moment of recognition but didn't say anything. Celes turned to Certan next.

"For you, it's even easier. Go retrieve your scarf and return to us dressed as a person who has pride in his appearance. That will signify to me that are you ready," Celes said.

"I haven't even agreed to go anywhere, why would I undertake your test?" Certan said.

"Because you have nothing to lose, and everything to gain. I only just met you, but I can tell that a life of wandering is not fulfilling. You have made a mistake, now go rectify it," Celes said. Certan looked at her with a strange expression, like he was trying to puzzle out the meaning of her words. He looked away, deep in thought.

"I accept," he said and left the room without looking back.

"Wow, that was quick," Alrion said.

"He would have agreed eventually, I just sped up the process," Celes said.

"That's one problem solved. Maybe you can now explain our part of the test?" Lara said.

"It is better to show you. Let's go." Celes left the room and waited for them at the front door. Alrion gave his father a confused look, but followed along. Lara was quicker to move, and sidled up to Celes. Alrion couldn't make out what they were saying. But it looked like the two women were challenging each other.

"I feel like I don't know who mum is," Alrion said.

"Don't worry, she's the same. It's just a side of her that she hasn't needed for a long time. You'll be fine," Vincent said.

Alrion was not completely satisfied with the answer, but rushed to join Lara and his mother at the front door.

"We are off to the Market District," Celes said, and opened the door. She walked out onto the street with confidence, as if she knew the place well.

"How did you find us?" Lara said.

"Easy. Vincent and I stayed here many years ago, before we had Alrion." For a brief moment Celes let a smile dart across her face. But a serious gaze soon replaced it.

"Oh, that's interesting. You have a history here."

"We do, which will be explained soon," Celes said. A strong silence hung over them as they walked. Alrion looked at his mother with a confused expression. The strong, nurturing figure he had always known didn't quite fit with the person he was observing. There was a piece missing, which was driving him crazy.

I hope this makes sense soon.

He could see Lara trying to puzzle it out as well, with furtive sidelong glances.

The Market District was teeming with people, much more so than the night before. The stalls were packed full of interesting trinkets, and the cries of sellers competing for attention made it quite noisy. There were even food vendors set up, peddling fruit or cooked meat on sticks. They wove their way through the crowd and bustle and headed to a far corner of the district. As they progressed the crowds thinned out, until there were only a few passing people.

"Where are we going?" Alrion said.

"Wilhelm's Fine Wares," Celes said. Sure enough, they stopped in front of a large building that looked like it was a mansion. Anywhere else he would have assumed that a person of immense importance resided there.

"Does someone live here?"

"Yes, the owner lives here and also operates the front as a gallery and show-room." Celes walked up to the burly guard outside the front door and held up her hands. The guard patted her down and ushered her through.

"What's this?" Alrion said.

"Weapon and tool checks," the guard said. His voice was as rough as his face.

"They want to make sure we aren't going to steal anything," Celes said.

"Sure, nothing to hide here." Alrion raised his arms and had the same check done. Lara stepped up next.

The guard checked her the same way, then stopped suddenly. "What's this?" he said.

"Sorry, I forgot about those. I wasn't expecting to come here," Lara said innocently. She retrieved a stack of daggers from the small of her back.

"I'll hold them until you are done shopping," the guard said with a healthy measure of sarcasm.

"Thanks." Lara joined the others inside the building.

Alrion was shocked at the room on display. There were polished marble floors and cabinets full of jewels, treasures, and fine cloths. One table had rings, another amulets and earrings. In the middle of the whole collection was a stone pedestal. On it was a red velvet cushion with a clear dome over it. Inside was most incredible jewel Alrion had ever seen. "What is that?" he whispered to Celes.

"That's the Pure Diamond. It is the biggest diamond in the world, and said to have been created with magic. There's even talk that it glows blue when encountering those tainted with the Blight."

"Wow, that's incredible," Alrion turned to look at Lara to see her reaction. Her eyes were darting around the room, taking it all in.

"A girl after my own heart," Celes said softly. Alrion walked closer to take a closer look. He was immediately stopped by a thin man dressed all in black. Alrion hadn't even seen him.

"Excuse me," Alrion said.

"No closer. You cannot approach the diamond without prior approval," the man said. Alrion examined the man's face. It was hard and emotionless, with piercing blue eyes.

"Sure, I just thought it looked incredible," Alrion said. The man nodded and waved him away. Alrion diverted his attention to inspecting the table of rings. However, he also watched his mother and Lara wander through the room. It looked like they were just browsing, but he sensed a different intent and purpose from them. It was so methodical.

Thick as thieves, Alrion thought. Then he had a sudden epiphany. There was a reason his mother seemed so different and was instantly so critical of Lara. Maybe his mother used to be a thief too. He wanted to blurt it out, then realised that it wasn't wise given their current situation. But the more he thought about it, the more he was convinced.

"I can see that look on your face, save it for later," Celes said to him. Alrion nodded and found some more jewellery to examine. He didn't know much about it, but everything looked expensive and well-made. He could tell the craftsmanship was incredible.

"Thanks for your time," Celes said to nobody in particular and headed for the door. Lara was close behind her, and Alrion rushed to join them. They left the premises, Lara collected her daggers with a smile and a wink and the three of them walked off in silence. After they were almost out of the Market District, Celes led them into a quiet alley and stopped.

"I can tell you have questions," Celes said.

"More like statements. You want us to steal that jewel. And you're also a thief. And maybe you tried to steal it when you were here before," Alrion said quickly.

"That's actually quite correct. When I met your father, I was a thief. This jewel was my target. And we failed to steal it, and had to leave the city."

"We? He was in on it?"

"Of course. Who do you think crafted the keys for me?" Celes said with a sly smile. Alrion couldn't believe it. His father had always been so straight and by the letter of the law.

"Seems like a lot of security," Lara said.

"I didn't notice much. One guard out front and a man inside?" Alrion said.

"There's many more hidden around the place. And magical traps I'm guessing," Celes said.

"So, what's the plan?" Alrion said.

"I'm still working through it. But we will go tonight."

"Sounds good to me. This will be a real thrill. I'm excited," Lara said. Celes gave her a questioning look but didn't say anything.

"I'm going to investigate the area a little more, but we will draw too much attention as a group. You two go back to the house," Celes said.

"Sure, let's go," Alrion said to Lara.

"You don't want any help?" Lara said.

"No, I've got this. I need to see how much things have changed," Celes said.

"Understood, we'll see you later," Lara said. The two of them walked out of the laneway, leaving Celes alone.

"I can't believe it, she's a thief. I never knew," Alrion said once they were a safe distance away.

"I must admit, I had my suspicions when she showed up," Lara said.

"How could you tell?"

"The way she was dressed initially. Normal looking clothing, but it is light, protective, and quiet. She had lots of pockets for stashing tools, and she was very particular about assessing the situation."

"What's so unusual about being careful?"

"It was the type of careful. When you're ... retrieving something, you don't want any surprises. You must be able to predict everything that will happen, and plan ahead. You also have to be very adaptable and change things on the fly as required."

"So how many so-called retrieval jobs have you done?"

"More than I care to remember. But only a few really memorable ones."

"Have you ever been caught?"

"Once or twice when I was starting out. But I didn't know what I was doing, and it was small stakes. That doesn't happen later on. Not if you're careful and learn from your mistakes."

"So, what does happen?"

"You have an escape plan, and you abandon the job. If you get away, you can retry another day. You never stick around, that's suicide."

"I'll remember that," Alrion said.

"Yeah, if things go wrong on the job, you need to cut and run. It's not worth it."

"Got it. Have you had a job like they did with this one? Where you had to abandon?"

"Yes. Just the one."

"What happened?"

"I don't really want to talk about it. Another time." Lara avoided eye contact and started focusing on something in the distance. Alrion took her cue and stopped asking questions.

Once they arrived back at the house, Alrion looked for his father but couldn't find him.

"He'll be working on those swords," Lara said.

"Good point. So how do I prepare for one of these jobs?" Alrion said.

"In a day? No chance you'll be prepared. But I'll teach you one thing.

"What's that?"

"How to walk quietly." Lara walked across the room soundlessly, doing a pirouette at the other end.

"Now you're just showing off," Alrion said, impressed but laughing.

"Why not? Don't worry you'll be dancing along in silence in no time." Lara stepped back to Alrion then started demonstrating her footwork.

"Take a normal step," she said. Alrion did as instructed, his boot making a resounding thud.

"I think you overdid it, but that's fine. Now what you need to do is imagine that you are spreading out your entire weight over the entire surface of your foot. And gently rolling your weight as you step." Lara demonstrated in slow motion.

Alrion tried it, and stepped very quietly. He looked up at her in shock.

"If you go slow enough it's easy. The trick is doing it at pace."

Lara darted into the next room and even though Alrion was watching and listening closely he could barely hear her footsteps.

Shouldn't be too hard.

He started walking softly as Lara had demonstrated, and quickly sped up. For a moment, he was swift and silent, and feeling like a gliding shadow. However, he started to lose his balance and came to a sudden stop with a loud stamping of his feet.

"That's going to get us into trouble. What's the saying? You need learn to walk before you can run?" Lara said. Her eyes sparkled with amusement and she laughed heartily at Alrion.

"Hey, I'm a wizard, I don't have to obey the normal rules," Alrion said, joining her in the laughter.

"Just practice a bit more so we can rely on you tonight," Lara said.

"Of course. I was just thinking though, maybe there's a way I can do it with magic." Alrion ran to get his spell book and look through it.

Lara watched him go and just shook her head gently.

7

A TEST

C ertan left the house in a hurry. Partly because he had a purpose, partly because he had to get out of there. His crazy wild ride had crashed and burned in style.

I can't believe what I have gotten myself into, he thought. Less than a day ago, he was living his practically unconscious life of oblivion. He had hit rock bottom, giving away the last precious memento of his time with the monks. The fact that he regarded the monks as another people also saddened him.

"This is your second chance," a voice inside him said. It was right. For some time, he didn't believe that he deserved it. But these people thought so, and they needed his help. So, he had to earn their trust.

Certan started to head to the Entertainment District, but then quickly changed his mind. Even if he could find the man who now had his scarf, he had nothing to bargain with. And he certainly looked like a mess. Certan glanced at a nearby puddle and saw his reflection. He had tried to ignore it, but he forced himself to look properly. He had been living hard, and it had taken its toll.

"Enough is enough," he said. He changed course and headed for the Black-smith district. With any luck, he could pick up some work as a labourer or assistant. The Blacksmith District was alive with action, the clanging could be easily heard as he approached.

"It's a numbers game," Certan said to himself. As he entered he wandered up to the first workshop.

"We don't have any handouts, move on," a bearded man said as Certan approached.

"I'm just looking for an honest day's work," Certan said.

"Keep looking," the man said and turned his back.

"Thanks," Certan said, not even sarcastically. If he wanted to succeed he needed to return to the self that he was with the monks. In control and humble, throwing his ego to the winds. He continued to the next workshop. This time he at least managed to make eye contact with someone and speak first.

"Hello, I am looking for some work. Do you need a strong pair of hands?" Certan said.

"I'm sorry, we're fine right now. I appreciate the offer though. My brother works in the last workshop. Right before the restricted weapon section, why don't you give him a try?" the blacksmith said.

"I will do, thanks for the tip." Certan bowed and continued walking.

He ignored the rest of the workshops, and continued to the next set of gates. The workshop he was after was quite obvious, it was humongous and was the only one right next to the gates. Before he could approach though, he saw a commotion up ahead.

"Stop! Thief!" a male voiced shouted. Certan could see one of the local guards chasing after a young man. The youth was carrying a bag full of something and brandishing a sword. Without thinking twice, Certan moved into the youth's path to intercept him. The youth swung his sword, hoping to scare Certan away. But Certan didn't flinch, he dodged the attack and grabbed the young man's arm and nimbly threw him to the ground. The young thief was quick, and darted back to his feet, but Certan was standing in front of him.

"Move it or I'll cut you down," the youth said.

"You cannot. Accept that you have been caught," Certan said. The youth lashed out at Certan's legs with the sword. Certan saw the attack just in time to dodge, and kicked the sword so hard it clattered against a nearby building. The guard in pursuit finally caught up to them, panting with the exertion.

"Thanks for your help, citizen. We aren't equipped for foot chases and he had a head start."

"Happy to help out since I was here anyway," Certan said. The guard looked him over, a confused expression on his face.

"Are you some kind of monk? Or just homeless?"

"Probably both are accurate. I have been wandering for a time. I'm looking for some work now though."

"I have something for you. My friend runs security for a place in the Market District. They are always looking for more help, and you're quite capable. Here take this," the guard said, handing Certan a coin.

"I cannot accept this," Certan said.

"Just take it, I get a commission for anyone I send over anyway. Get yourself cleaned up and some better clothes. They will provide you everything else you need. Report to the Wondrous Wall Inn and tell them that Sean sent you for a job," Sean said.

"Thank you for your help, I really appreciate it."

"Don't mention it, you've helped me out and I get paid if they hire you so it's a win for me either way. What's your name by the way?"

"Certan."

"Well Certan, you take care of yourself. See you around."

"Thanks, Sean." Certan bowed and turned back the way he had come.

This is the break I needed. The money I earn from this job can buy back my scarf and I'll be back on the path. The right path, Certan thought. Things had turned the corner.

Lara heard a noise and walked over to investigate. She saw Vincent arriving back at the house. He looked exhausted after a long day.

"What's all this?" he said.

"I'm trying to teach Alrion how not to be a lumbering beast," Lara said.

"That may take a while," Vincent said.

"I would agree, but you might be surprised," Alrion seemed to be taking the gentle ribbing in good spirits.

"I must admit, he's at least trying," Lara said.

"Good to hear. Where's your mother?" Vincent said.

"She's doing some investigating," Alrion said.

"Casing the place for guards, traps and entry points more specifically," Lara said.

"She must be pretty serious about this heist. I wonder why, after all this time," Vincent said.

"Is it really true that the two of you tried to steal this jewel back in the day?" Alrion said.

"It's all true. It's the main reason why we left Brangtur. It was only a matter of time before they figured out who it was. We were so close. I didn't realise she was still thinking about it, all these years later. But that's a story for another time," Vincent said.

"How are the swords going?" Alrion said.

"Very well. I should be able to finish them tomorrow, if everything goes to plan. I'm pretty excited. They have surpassed all my expectations."

"And my dagger?" Lara said.

"I think I can get there, but only if I can finish the others first."

"Just don't forget. You know he's going to need someone watching his back," Lara said pointing at Alrion.

"Oh, I know, don't you worry. Let me prepare something to eat, you two keep training." Vincent left them and entered the kitchen. Lara could hear a lot of banging pots and pans around. He eventually emerged with dinner, as promised. It smelled better than it looked.

After they all finished up a simple meal of meat, bread, and potatoes Celes entered the house.

"I've done as much as I can do. We are definitely going in tonight," she said.

"Hungry? We saved you some," Vincent said, pointing to a plate of food.

"Starving. You haven't cooked for me for a while," Celes said with delight.

"Trying to win my way back into the good books," Vincent said, giving her a cheeky grin. Celes gave him a wry smile.

"Keep trying, but good start," she said.

"And we've been busy too. I've taught Alrion how to not barge around like a drunken bull." Lara gave Alrion an approving look and he smiled back.

"Good, that will come in handy. This is going to be a tough one. But we are in luck. They seem to be understaffed. A lot fewer guards than my previous attempt. Maybe there's a lot less interest in the diamond," Celes said.

"So, we can actually pull this off?" Alrion said.

"Of course, one way or another. Where's the monk?" she said looking around.

"Not sure, I haven't seen him today," Alrion said.

"He will return, when he's ready," Vincent said.

"He'd better do it soon. Since we are taking this jewel, we need to be leaving town as soon as possible," Celes said.

"I'm sure he will be here," Alrion said.

"If you say so. Now, everyone make your final preparations. We should leave as soon as possible. It's going to be a long night," Celes said. Alrion adjusted his clothing to have a cloak with a hood covering his face. Lara did the same, but also had to select which tools she would be taking, expertly stashing them away.

"Don't wait up," Celes said to Vincent, giving him a quick kiss.

"You know I will. Take care," he said to all of them. Alrion and Lara said their farewells and followed Celes out into the cold night air.

"Shouldn't we be discussing the plan?" Alrion said.

"No, we are keeping this simple. Do as I say exactly and everything will go smoothly," Celes said.

"She's right," Lara said.

"Alright, I can do that." Alrion let Lara and his mother take the lead, and fell in behind them. Celes directed them back to the Market District.

"How do you feel?" Nervous?" Lara said.

"No. Well, maybe a little. But just because I have no experience as a thief. My magic is a little..."

"Over the top?"

"That's fair. Which will be quite helpful if we get caught."

"Which we won't. Right Celes?"

"Right. Just so long as you follow my instructions." Celes didn't bother turning to face them, her eyes were locked into gazing into the distance.

Lara was excited. She hadn't been on a heist for a long time, especially one with another thief. It had been a long string of solo efforts. She realised how much she had missed it. The joint excitement of sharing the risk and reward with others.

I'll have to convince Alrion to do more of these, she thought. That would be fun.

"Keep up," Celes said, increasing her speed. Lara understood the approach. It would take them a long time to enter the building quietly and unseen, so the sooner they reached their destination the better.

She spent some time studying Celes as they went. There was an ease to the way she moved, which obviously came from a lot of experience. But Lara sensed something else. A nervous energy too.

This has to be huge for her. She's going back for this diamond, so many years later. And with her son in tow too. I better do well in this trial.

"We're here," Celes said and stopped. They were in a dark alley in the middle of the Market District. Alrion and Lara paused and looked around.

"There," Celes said pointing to a grate for drainage. Alrion knelt down and lifted it, carefully dragged it away.

"I hate this part of stealing stuff," Lara said as she peered into the hole.

"It's the best way in, and nobody wants to guard it," Celes said.

"Is this ladies first?" Alrion said.

"No, this is the exception," Celes said and Alrion prepared to climb down. Lara went next. They were in a completely dark tunnel.

"Seems deserted. Is it safe to light our path?" Alrion said.

"Yes," Celes said. Alrion lit the way with a small flame dancing above his palm. As the flickering light bounced around the tunnel they could see what it really was.

"This doesn't look like any ordinary tunnel." Lara subconsciously checked her tools.

"No, this is actually a secret exit. It's the escape tunnel for the mansion we are entering."

"Won't they be expecting that?" Alrion said.

"No, there's only one key. Or so Wilhelm thinks." Celes pulled a tiny intricate key from her pocket.

"How did you get that?" Lara said.

"Vincent made it for me many years ago. But I never used it."

"And you kept it all this time?" Alrion said.

"It was a keepsake from the old days. But now, it's an opportunity. Let's keep moving," Celes said. Alrion walked ahead, lighting the way. The tunnel was old, and grimy. As they walked it became less damp and smelled different. The pungent odour was replaced by something different. Alrion moved his hand slightly as they walked, to better illuminate the area. Lara used that opportunity to study the walls, but didn't see anything of note. The tunnel just kept going and going. Finally, she saw something different in the distance.

"I think we're coming up to something," Lara said. As they approached she could see it more clearly. A massive iron door. Incredibly thick with lots of rein-forcement. The lock was a large square protrusion with a tiny keyhole.

"Just as I would expect," Celes said.

"There's no breaking through that. Lucky there's a keyhole on the outside," Lara said.

"Turns out that while Wilhelm's definitely paranoid, he's not an idiot. Here goes," Celes said, walking forward and inserting the key into the lock. She turned the key slowly, a bead of sweat appearing on her brow.

It seems to be moving, Lara thought, observing Celes. Then she heard a loud click.

8

DIAMONDS ARE FOREVER

Celes stepped back and pushed the door hard. At first it didn't give, but then began to give way. It creaked like it had never been opened, and revealed a store room of sorts.

"It looks like we are in. Extinguish the light please," Celes said. Alrion let the flame disappear and waited for additional instructions.

"Where to?" Lara said.

"Alrion, stay in this room and guard our exit. Lara and I will retrieve the diamond and meet you back here," Celes said.

"Sure, take care," Alrion said. Celes went ahead, noting the state of the room as they passed through. Just crates and other storage, and it didn't look used recently.

"We won't keep you waiting too long," Lara said and she followed Celes through the room.

Celes kept up a quick pace, but maintained her stealthy movement. She had never been in this part of the mansion, so she was using her intuition to guide her. Once they left the storeroom she paused and felt for the direction of the wind. There was a slight draft coming from the right, so she decided to start there. Lara stayed close behind and didn't say anything.

What a relief she's a professional. This will make things simpler, Celes thought. At the end of the corridor they came to a stone staircase.

"Half a flight of stairs at a time, wait for my signal before following," Celes whispered. Lara nodded, her eyes clear and focused. Celes lightly dashed up the stairs, pausing at the turn and scanning ahead. When it was clear she signalled

Lara, and continued. They continued this ritual a few times until Celes noticed that they were emerging into a habited area.

Kitchen. Another area she wasn't particularly familiar with, but she knew it was located near the rear of the mansion. She crept carefully to the nearest corridor and peered through. Again, she had the choice of left or right.

"Left," she whispered to Lara. It was a pure gut decision, but she didn't have time for any other. The corridor was well-lit, so Celes moved with caution. She expected quite a few guards but wasn't sure where they would be posted. It seemed unlikely to have them congregated around the kitchen, but she wouldn't put it past Wilhelm. He was incredibly protective and could easily have randomly reallocated patrols.

Celes passed a doorway and stopped. She stepped back and looked again. She recognised it.

"This way," she said to Lara. The two of them entered the room. It was a connecting room, filled with coats and boots.

"Utility room for the guards. We're going to come across some soon," Celes whispered.

"I'm ready," Lara said.

"No kills."

"Of course."

"Good, now keep close." Celes crept through the room, noting the changes that had happened. But the ugly painting of Wilhelm's father preparing for a hunt was still there. She would never forget it.

Celes finally spotted a guard. He was tall and thin, lounging against the wall. She almost didn't spot him, his dark black clothing blending into the shadows. Celes tapped Lara and pointed at the guard then at a doorway behind him. Lara understood and stood at the ready. Celes crept into the hallway and dashed past where the guard was posted. If her memory was right, she would be able to weave through another room and take him by surprise.

The first room had an open door, so she snuck in. It was a dining room.

Was this here before? It had been a long time, but she didn't recognise it. But she pressed on anyway. She stepped around chairs left out, and cursed at one that she almost tripped over. But she kept her composure and could see the silhouette of the guard from the light of a faraway torch. She retrieved a dagger from her belt, and readied it. Her heart beat faster and faster. Her instincts were still good, but it had been a long time.

Gradually she crept forward, readying her weapon. She wouldn't need to inflict any damage, just take the guard by surprise then tie him up in the dining room. That would be enough. She practised the manoeuvre in her mind then reached out to put the dagger up against his throat.

But the guard seemed to anticipate her movement. He moved towards her and grabbed the dagger before she could alter her stance. She grabbed another and tried again, but he saw that coming and held her other hand. There they stood, face to face, hands interlocked.

"The monk?" Celes said in disbelief. What was he doing there?

"Celes?" Certan said. He was in shock. He didn't even notice Lara behind him, kicking his legs out from under him.

"Wait!" Celes whispered with force, before Lara could land a knockout blow. Lara paused, confused. Celes pointed to the dining room and dragged Certan over with her.

"What's going on?" Lara said.

"This is the monk."

"Certan?" Lara said.

"Yes. I got a job, I didn't expect this. It was part of my plan to start on a new path."

"Yes, yes very good. Just stay here and come with us when we leave. How many other guards are there?" Celes said.

"At least five. But I'm new so that won't tell me anything. That's why I'm here, away from the valuables," he said.

"Fine. Just act normal and don't leave this spot," Celes said.

"As you wish," Certan said, and walked back to where he was previously posted.

"There's always something," Celes whispered to Lara.

"Always," Lara whispered back. Celes pointed to a far doorway and made her way over. Lara followed close behind.

Celes noticed two other guards as they wound through the main floor but decided to avoid them. Running into Certan had been a sign, she had decided. And they didn't have time to disable all the guards. If only they could avoid detection on their way in, they could manage anything on the way out.

The entry to the main hall was visible, but Celes paused before rushing over. She didn't want to trip over any traps or security. Her quick look around during the day had only spotted guards, not anything special. But she knew how tricky Wilhelm was, there was bound to be something.

"Stay close," she whispered to Lara and began her approach. Creeping softly along and sticking to the shadows, she made good progress. She could see a guard walking around the main hall, and timed herself so that she would arrive at the entry while he was on the other end of the room. She entered the main hall and swiftly ducked down to hide behind a table. Lara joined her immediately.

"So far so good, but I've got a feeling there's going to be some traps. Tread carefully," Celes said.

"Got it," Lara said. Celes snuck over to the end of the table and peered around the corner. The guard was just passing and wouldn't see her. She darted out and took cover behind another table, leaving space for Lara to join her.

Before making another move she scanned the room again. She could not see any other guards.

That's odd, I was sure he would keep more here, Celes thought. But she didn't share that with Lara, there was no need to worry her unnecessarily. Satisfied that there were no obvious threats, Celes waited for the guard and used his patrol route to move closer. They repeated this two more times to be almost within reach of the Pure Diamond.

"I'll get the diamond, if something happens you leave and take Certan and Alrion with you," Celes said.

"Are you sure?"

"Yes, I can handle this. And if for some reason I can't, for me it's only a delay. You cannot afford a delay."

"If you insist," Lara said.

"Good. Here goes," Celes said and made her move. She crouch ran with steps as light as a feather, ducking under the rope and appearing right next to the Pure Diamond. She remained low to the ground though, in case she had to hide quickly. Celes slowly rose and examined the glass housing.

Doesn't appear to be any traps. That is a concern, but I can't back out now.

With her left hand, she gently lifted the glass housing, and with her right she reached for the diamond. She grabbed it without incident and replaced the glass housing. *Done.*

"Once a thief, always a thief." A man's voice rang out from the gallery above. Lamps were quickly lit around the room, illuminating it within seconds.

Celes stood, not trying to hide herself. "Stay down," she whispered to Lara and deliberately dropped the diamond.

"Don't think you can try anything. And that's just a dummy. Well, a beautiful dummy. Good enough to fool you and everyone else." Wilhelm showed off another diamond in his hand, then tucked it back into his coat. He started to descend from the gallery. He was flanked by at least twenty guards.

"What game are you playing?" Celes said, acting confident. She wasn't sure how she had been tricked so easily.

"I never forget a face. Especially one that got away. I did never find out your real name though. Which is a shame. But I guess you can tell me now, Shadow Fox," Wilhelm said. Lara drew in a startled breath.

"So, you're still obsessed after all these years," Celes said.

"I could say the same to you."

"What tipped you off?" Celes said. She was pretty sure she knew, but wanted to give him a moment to gloat. That may provide her an opportunity.

"I saw you here today. You were discreet and fast, but I remembered you. Even after all these years. And I knew that you would be impatient, so I just had to wait. I'm not even sure how you made it in, but it doesn't matter. All I had to do was wait for you to take the bait. And here you are." Wilhelm was standing right in front of her now. He looked about the same. He was a gnarly old man before, and he still was now. He just looked like he had shrunk a little and walked with more difficulty.

"For now." She would find an opening, some way or other.

"Oh, you aren't getting away this time. No, all exits are sealed and you are surrounded. There's no way to get out," Wilhelm said.

Celes looked around, sizing up the guards. They didn't look that tough, and only a few had crossbows. There was always a chance. But before she could put a plan into action, she saw some movement out of the corner of her eye.

Lara darted from nowhere and had a knife to Wilhelm's throat. "We'll be leaving thanks. Call off your dogs," Lara said.

Wilhelm was visibly shaken, but recovered quickly. "Why would I do that?"

"Because I could kill you if I sneezed, and it's awfully dusty in here," Lara said.

"I guess that is a risk, but if anything happens to me, you're as good as dead. I'm your only hope."

"You're right about that. But you're going to help me whether you like it or not." Lara threw a glass vial on the ground with her free hand and it shattered instantly. Smoke started to spew from the ground and Lara shoved Wilhelm into it.

"Get them!" he shouted, choking on the smoke.

"Follow me," Celes said, heading for the nearest exit from the hall. She kept low, trying to break line of sight. The diversion with the smoke worked well, splitting up the guards nicely. There were two posted at each door, but they didn't see Celes coming. By the time they noticed, the first guard was already on the floor and the second was taken down by Lara as he tried to attack Celes.

"Just run!" Celes shouted once they were through the door. They retraced their steps, not worrying about being silent anymore. Speed was of the essence. They initially had no problems, the guards rushing around not aware of their presence or too slow to react. But there were three guards waiting where they had left Certan.

"Doesn't look good," Celes said. However, she noticed another guard walking up to them. He glided between them, quickly knocking all three down.

"Nice!" Lara said. Certan waved at them, and disappeared into the nearby dining room. Celes and Lara rushed to join him.

"I'm not sure where your exit is, but we should have a relatively clear run," he said. True to his word, they didn't see anyone else.

Alrion was waiting for them at the exit.

"What's going on? I heard a commotion," Alrion said.

"Complications. Don't worry, let's just head out," Celes said.

"Certan?" Alrion said as he noticed the monk.

"Plenty of time for explanations later," he said.

"Sure, well nothing happened here let's go." Alrion led the way out into the tunnel.

"Can you see that light in the distance?" Alrion said.

"Yes, what do you think it is?" Celes said.

"Not sure, but there's no way that is coming in from the street." Alrion created a miniature ball of fire and threw it along the tunnel.

Celes watched its progress, and heard a cry of pain.

"We're not alone," Lara said.

"Slow down, let's not rush in," Celes said. The group slowed their advance, and continued at a more measured pace. As they closed the distance, it became obvious what the light was. There was a force of twenty armed guards standing in formation at the end of the tunnel and blocking the exit.

"Those are city guards," Celes said.

"Waiting for us," Alrion said.

"That Wilhelm, he was well-prepared," Celes said.

"Not prepared enough. Otherwise they would have known that such a small force is not going to cut it. It's a shame I couldn't use your stealth lessons Lara, but this will be more fun. Leave it to me," Alrion said with a smile.

Who is this young man, and what did he do with my son? Celes thought. At least she had an opportunity to see for herself just what he could do.

9

SETTING OUT

A lrion took two steps forward. He had an idea he wanted to try. Clearing his throat, he weaved a wave of force in front of him, but instead of sending it out he let it hover and vibrate. Then he spoke into it.

"Leave now and you will not be harmed," Alrion said. His voice sounded lower than in pitch than normal and boomed around the tunnel.

"How did you do that?" Lara said.

"I just had an idea, and it worked," Alrion whispered back at her. The soldiers looked a little rattled, but had not moved.

"As you wish!" Alrion shouted, then let the spell dissipate. It had worked surprisingly well. He wasn't sure if he had melded ideas he already had, or drawn upon some knowledge hidden in his mind. But it didn't matter.

Alrion started walking forward with purpose, preparing his next move. He could see the soldiers take a defensive stance. Alrion drew upon his spark and ignited flames above his hands. Then he combined them with a wave of force. Rolling spirals of flame tumbled along the ground, arcing up before they hit the soldiers. They dove to the ground, narrowly avoiding the flames. Alrion kept walking. He threw another wave of force, this time adding no fire. The dust swirled around as it travelled along the ground, but this one didn't suddenly jump up. It stayed low and knocked around all the soldiers who had ducked the previous attack.

"They have a wizard!" one of the soldiers said.

Another replied "We're sitting ducks in here."

Alrion noticed that they had retreated a few metres. A bit further and he would have access to the ladder. He drew upon his spark one more time, concentrating on the ground in front of the soldiers. A low wall of flame rose up, stopping at chest height. The front row of soldiers scrambled back. Alrion advanced, and moved the wall of fire forward as well. The soldiers continued to retreat.

"Just a little bit further." Alrion pushed the wall forward, the soldiers bunching up as they ran out of the tunnel.

"That should do," Alrion said, maintaining the wall of fire in its current location.

"And that will work. Nice work!" Lara said, noticing that the path to the tunnel stairs was now clear.

"Let's be quick, I can't do this all day and I don't want them to try anything," Alrion said.

"Agreed. Time to leave," Celes said. Alrion continued his steady pace while he concentrated on the spell. The rest ran ahead, climbing out of the tunnel.

"You won't get away with this. We know who you are!" one of the soldiers shouted. But Alrion didn't take any notice. Once the rest were out he climbed out himself.

"Is the spell still active?" Celes said.

"Yes, what's our next move?" Alrion said.

"Just hold it long enough for us to block this exit. That will buy us enough time," she said. Lara noticed a nearby box full of scrapped metal items.

"Help me with this," she said to Certan. The two of them dragged the box over the top of the tunnel exit.

"That should do," Celes said. Alrion let the spell go and they ran from the alley as quickly as possible. Once they re-joined the market streets Celes slowed and the rest matched her pace.

"Quickly and quietly, let's get back to the house," she said. Alrion looked back, but couldn't see any pursuers. He was happy at what he had done. The spells had taken more Spark that he had expected, but it all worked out fine. And he didn't need to let on just how much power he had expended. Each step away helped him relax a bit more, but he couldn't calm down until they reached the safety of the house.

Celes was inside first, with Certan ushering the others in ahead of himself. They found Vincent standing inside, arms crossed.

"How'd you go?" he said. He didn't seem impressed, as if he knew something had gone wrong.

"We had a small hiccup. Wilhelm was waiting for us. But we escaped, due to some ingenuity from Lara and some pyrotechnics from Alrion," Celes said.

"Sounds like a disaster," Vincent said.

"Well, a partial disaster. But we all made it out, and Lara and Certan passed the test," Celes said.

"I may have gotten a job and cleaned up, but I have not retrieved my scarf," Certan said.

"That is not an issue. You can get another, if the monks find you worthy," Vincent said.

"This is true, I agree with your plan. I will join you," Certan said, bowing to Vincent.

"It wasn't a total loss," Lara said, retrieving something from her jacket. It was a massive, pristine diamond.

"Is that the replica?" Celes said.

"No, it's the real deal. I swapped them in the confusion. Wilhelm won't realise until it is too late," Lara said.

"Give me that," Celes said, snatching it from Lara's hands. She looked it over carefully.

"You really did it. I underestimated you," Celes said. Alrion could see the begrudging look of admiration on his mother's face.

"Mission accomplished then," Lara said with a laugh. "Although on a more serious note it was my honour to accompany the fabled Shadow Fox."

"Thankfully we kept my record intact." Celes handed the diamond to Vincent. "Incorporate this into Alrion's sword. He will need it the most,"

"Good idea, I could lodge it into the pommel without too much effort. And it won't draw attention that way, people will just think it is an ornament," Vincent said, turning it over.

"Does that stone really work? Will it react to the Blight?" Alrion said.

"I'm sure you will have a chance to test it soon enough," Vincent said, putting the stone away.

"Those soldiers said they knew who you were," Lara said to Celes.

"They know my alias, not who I am. As long as we leave soon, there won't be a problem," Celes said.

"They will eventually track us here if we stay. But I agree we should be safe to sleep here tonight," Vincent said.

"Then let's make our preparations. Do they have rules against using the forges at night?" Celes said.

"No, I'll get to work," Vincent said with a sigh. He walked over to the door and disappeared into the night.

"The rest of you, get some rest. We leave tomorrow," Celes said.

"You're coming too?" Alrion said.

"Of course, I'm wanted remember?" Celes said. Alrion just shook his head.

"Who is she?" he wondered to himself.

~

The next morning Alrion awoke to find everyone else ready and waiting.

"Sorry, were you all waiting for me?" Alrion said.

"Yes, but don't feel bad. A wizard needs rest to replenish his energy," Vincent said.

"How would you know that?"

"I may not be one, but I was the son of one. Now go ready yourself, we need to leave as soon as possible," Vincent said. Alrion gathered his things, and did a final check of the house. He noticed something sitting on a table near the front door and walked closer. "That's for you," Vincent said, pride in his voice.

Alrion saw that it was a sword in a leather scabbard with an ornate leather strap. The diamond was expertly attached to the pommel of the sword, and looked like it was always meant to be there. Alrion slowly drew the sword out, the pale metal gently shining in the sunlight. He touched the edge and instantly recoiled his finger. "That's sharp," Alrion said.

"What did you expect?" Vincent said, chuckling. Alrion shook his hand, feeling foolish.

"It looks great. How did you finish it in time?" he said, returning the sword.

"Finish them in time." Vincent turned to show Alrion the sword strapped to his back. "I have a matching one, although with no giant diamond. I was a lot closer to completing them than I was letting on. I had originally wanted to take more time with the finishing. But I'm happy with the result," he said.

"What about me?" Lara said, sticking her empty hands out in front of her.

"I didn't forget. Lucky for you there was some leftover metal. Use it wisely." Vincent tossed over a dagger within a plain leather scabbard.

Lara pulled the dagger out and examined the edge. "Looks really sharp. Is this the real deal?"

"Of course. You'll be able to take down a Shade with that," Vincent said.

"Good, that makes a girl feel more comfortable."

"Glad I could help."

"I just have to say, this is a crazy gift," Lara said.

"I know. Forget about that and just use it well. You've proved yourself."

"If we're all ready, we need to leave immediately." Celes tapped her foot impatiently.

"After you," Vincent said and Celes stepped through the front door without hesitation. The rest followed close behind. Alrion paused to look back at the house. It already had a lot of memories for him, let alone his parents. He decided to return here one day, when things were simpler.

They walked with purpose towards the main gates.

"Can't we pass through the city and exit from the other end?" Alrion said.

"Yes, but it's a smaller gate and it will be closely watched by the guards. This one may be as well, but we have a better chance of slipping through," Vincent said.

"I hadn't thought of that." Alrion felt a little silly for even asking.

"I was thinking we head straight to Vainbly," Celes said.

"Excellent idea," Vincent said.

"Is it close?" Alrion said.

"Yes, we can get there on foot within a few hours, then plan our next move. Hopefully there's also horses available to speed up our journey."

"It's a long walk, I wouldn't recommend it," Certan said. Alrion gave him a smile. As they approached the main gates, Alrion could see that the guard had been doubled. People were being stopped too and interrogated.

"Follow my lead." Celes quickly grabbed Lara and shoved her a few steps ahead. "Stop! Thief!" she shouted, pointing at Lara.

The young thief was initially stunned, then quickly cottoned on. She took off, swiftly weaving into the crowd. The ruse worked, the patrolling guards quickly set off after Lara.

"Don't worry they won't catch her," Celes said to Alrion. After a quick look around, she started walking forward once more. Alrion tried to keep an eye out for Lara, to see how she fared. His mother was completely right.

The guards were hampered by their armour and the crowds. Lara was nimble and crafty, changing direction and weaving through gaps in the crowd that were impossible for them to follow. But she didn't speed too far ahead, always pausing just enough for the guards to feel as if they were gaining.

"She's something else," Alrion said under his breath.

"Take care of that one," Vincent said, slapping his son on the shoulder. Alrion didn't realise his father had heard his comment, and decided to focus on Lara's progress rather than continue that potentially awkward conversation.

Lara laughed as she ran, it was good fun. She hadn't been chased like this in a while, in an open street during the middle of the day. As she glanced back she could see her group advancing carefully through the crowd, not garnering a second glance from any of the guards.

Too easy. She looked ahead, to plan out her escape from the city. She spotted a group of guards blocking the path. They must have heard the commotion and formed a mini blockade.

"No time to think, just react," Lara told herself. She spied one of the city banners hanging from the gates and instantly decided to go for it. Adjusting her direction, she instead headed for the walls of the gates. There were studs in the wall that were quite large, so she grabbed the first one within reach and started clambering up. The guards started to catch up as she ascended, and she could hear their shouts from below. Lara paused long enough to look back down and smirk at them, and decided that she was out of harm's way. Now she just had to exit.

After a quick tug of the banner, she observed its strength and how it hung. It wasn't ideal, but she had no time.

"Here we go," she whispered, steadying herself then leaping forward. She grabbed the cloth banner, using it to slow her descent. The force of her fall caused the banner to start detaching from the wall, and this gave her a nice arc through the air. Just before the banner was about to fall completely she let go, and toppled straight into one of the guards.

Before they could react, she scrambled to her feet and darted away and into the crowd of onlookers beyond the city walls. The guard line crumbled and they took off after her, two of them staying behind and watching the pursuit.

Now that she was beyond the walls, Lara increased her speed. There was less reason to keep them close, as her party would also be out soon. She needed to finish this chase, so she could disappear and rejoin the gang.

One guard was particularly swift, and Lara noticed that he had ditched some of his armour to run faster. She wasn't worried about being caught, but if he was fit he could keep within range for a long distance, which would be a problem. So, she slowed a little and dropped a few glass balls onto the ground. The guard didn't notice, and when he stepped on one completely lost his balance and toppled over.

Lara laughed and increased her speed. She had to disappear quickly to make the most of the opening.

10

IN THE SHADE OF A BLAZE

S treams of travellers looked on in amusement as Lara ducked and weaved through them. She stayed low and fast, looking for a way to escape from the road and into cover. There was a small bunch of trees to her left but she ignored them. It was too obvious. She needed something a bit better.

A partially-covered wagon caught her eye and Lara headed straight for it. It was being pulled by a horse with a weary man urging the plodding horse onwards. Lara stayed low to avoid the man's line of sight and quietly vaulted into the wagon, ducking under the cloth covering. An overpowering smell of animal hides assaulted her nose, but it was worth it.

She heard the rhythmic clank of the guard's remaining armour as he ran past, he didn't even pause for a moment.

"Gotcha!" Lara whispered, a big smile on her face. As he ran in the wrong direction she was slowly being taken back to the rest of the group. She waited a few minutes for safety, then peeked out of the wagon. There was no sign of the pursuing guard. Lara leapt out of the wagon and joined the stream of travellers, trying to blend in. She spotted Alrion in the distance, and slowly worked her way through to join him.

"Nice moves," Alrion said.

"They never had a chance." Lara flashed Alrion her biggest smile.

"We can take this path, it diverts around the city and passes through a few farming communities," Vincent said, and the rest followed his lead.

"You did well. Nice improvisation too," Celes said to Lara once they were off the main road.

"Thanks, although you didn't give me much warning."

"You didn't need it, and the stunned look on your face was perfect!"

"I think you enjoyed that way too much," Lara said and Celes could not contain her laughter.

"It was certainly entertaining, but we've lost time. Let's push on. No breaks until we reach Vainbly," Vincent said.

Nobody said another word.

Lara kept an eye on the countryside, interested in the new environment. She had never travelled this way before. She mostly kept to the bigger cities, and the ways to get in and out unseen. They passed through several small farming communities. Each one was a small cluster of farms and houses, with vast tracts between them. But the road persisted.

"This road seems out of place in such a quiet and rural place," Alrion said.

"They still need to access the cities, and sell their goods. In fact, my first commission as a blacksmith was for farms just like these," Vincent said.

"Really? What was it?"

"Horseshoes. Quite tricky actually. But it brings back fond memories."

"It must have been a fun time," Alrion said. Vincent didn't comment further and Alrion returned to gazing at the landscape. Lara did the same.

Vainbly came up sooner than she expected. In between some snacks, the rolling countryside looked so similar that she was almost entranced by the trip. The town was rather unassuming, with a small river running out in front. They crossed a petite stone bridge to enter the town.

"There should be a decent inn here, although it's been a while I have no idea if it's still open," Vincent said.

"What was it called again? The Frisky Farmer?" Celes said.

"Something like that."

"Looks like it's still here," Lara said, pointing to a distant building. Right in the centre of the town was a large structure with a peaked roof and large wooden doors. A simple sign hung above the entrance.

"Let's get inside and have a decent meal," Vincent said.

Lara glanced around as they walked through Vainbly. It looked like a fairly quiet town, without much going on. But she could see the evidence of trade from Brangtur. There was a bustle and clinking of coins that betrayed the simple setting.

The smell of ale smacked them in the face as they entered the inn. The hall was full of patrons, each with a beer or two.

"Looks like the whole town is here," Lara said.

"Are you alright?" she said to Certan. He nodded without replying, but he was visibly affected. Once she had mentioned it the others seemed to cotton on as well.

"I'm sorry, you just sobered up and the first place we took you was an inn. Do you want us to go somewhere else?" Alrion said.

"Thank you for your concern. It's more of a physical reaction right now, which I can manage. Despite the unpleasantness, I'm finding value in it as a type of penance." Certan looked uncomfortable but resolute.

"Wow that's harsh," Lara said.

"I'll enquire about rooms, try and find a table," Vincent said.

Lara disappeared into the crowd, reappearing at a far corner of the hall and waving.

Celes spotted the wave and directed the rest over. They managed to squeeze onto a tiny table, knocking elbows. "It'll be a brawl just trying to eat anything," Celes said.

"If this lot can handle it, we should be able to," Lara said gesturing at the crowd. They were predominantly men and of large builds.

"Must all be labourers from the area," Alrion said.

"Or travellers? I'd say this is the first stop out of Brangtur for many, depending on your destination. Do you think they will look for us here?" Certan said.

"They may do, but I doubt the guard has the resources to venture outside the city. As long as we don't hang around longer than a night I don't see any danger," Celes said.

"There'll be danger, regardless," Certan said looking around the room. He seemed quite distracted. A slim woman deftly weaved through the tables and dropped down an armful of ales. To her credit very little sloshed out and onto the table.

"We didn't order these," Celes said.

"The man up there did. This is the only drink we have available. Food is on its way, but there's a delay in the kitchen," the dark-haired woman said. Before there could be any further questioning she disappeared into the crowd. Celes looked over and saw Vincent waving at her in the distance.

"Fine," she muttered and pulled one of the ales closer. Alrion followed suit, and Certan who found a spot on the ceiling to examine in detail instead.

"Don't worry, I'm with you," Lara said, pushing aside the ale.

"We have rooms for the night, and dinner as well. Lucky that we found a table, this is the busiest time of the day. It should be much quieter in the evening," Vincent said, squeezing in next to his wife. She passed over his ale and he drank deep.

"Sounds good to me. What do you we in the meantime?" Alrion said.

"We need to source some horses. Any volunteers?"

"I'll do it," Lara said.

"Great. Celes and I will scout around the town, and make sure there's no unwanted attention from Brangtur. Alrion, did you want to come with us?" Vincent said.

"No, I think I'll do some training. I have a few things to look into as well," he said. Lara saw the excited glimmer in his eye.

He's up to something, I wonder what.

"How about you hang around here too Certan, although our rooms may be more comfortable," Vincent said.

"I will remain to assist Alrion." Certan paused just long enough to give direct eye contact to Vincent then turned his attention elsewhere.

After a brief meal of meat and potatoes, the group went their separate ways. Alrion and Certan walked upstairs to find the rooms. Certan settled into a corner and meditated, while Alrion retrieved his spell book.

He leafed through the pages quickly, hoping to not find his recently discovered spell for amplifying his voice. His excitement grew as he reached the end of the book and didn't find it. He combed through once more, paying special attention to the pages that might contain a mention of it. But there was not a single reference to be found.

According to what Falric said, I should be able to read the spells that I am capable of using. And if I used it, and it's not in the book, that means either I created it or I just know it now.

It seemed unlikely that he had created such an obvious spell. Which meant he had probably absorbed it from the Pool of Knowledge. He was buzzing with excitement.

"I wonder what else I can do," Alrion whispered. He leafed through the spell book again, but this time with a different purpose. Instead of a specific spell, he wanted information on how to increase his strength and capacity.

"The knowledge I have gained must work in a similar way to the books. The more capable I am, the more spells I can unlock for my use. I just need to keep pushing my strength and try new spells," Alrion said quietly to himself. It was important to find a focus for himself. His current goal was so far away, some strange test in a distant land. On the way, he had to improve his skill. His encounter with Branthor was a lucky escape. Next time he didn't want to rely on luck. He looked over at Certan, but the monk didn't react.

He must be busy, I'll push on, Alrion thought.

After an afternoon consulting the book, Alrion didn't have many more answers. But he had consolidated some of his learning, and was excited about his new focus. His plan now meant finding opportunities to use his magic as much as possible.

"You're still up here?" Lara said as she entered the room. Alrion put away the book.

"Yes, is it late?"

"Yes, the sun has already set. We are about to have dinner. Come down," Lara said. Alrion was confused, he hadn't noticed it getting dark. He looked again, and saw that he had cast a light spell and hovered a sphere of light above his shoulder. Unlike his previous attempts, this one didn't emit any heat. Just light. He waved it away and rushed off to join Lara.

"Certan, come down when you're ready, you need to eat some at some stage," Alrion shouted.

"You're just in time," Vincent said as Alrion arrived downstairs.

"Of..." Alrion began to say, but was cut off by a loud groan. He spun quickly and noticed the main doors of the inn slowly bending over. Suddenly they splintered into large chunks, and a massive shape occupied the doorway. Alrion knew what it was instantly. He looked over at his father.

"Yes, I know what it is. Lara, can you fetch the swords?" Vincent said calmly, without taking his eyes off the creature.

"Is that a Shade?" Lara said.

"Yes," Vincent said.

"On my way." Lara turned and sprinted off.

"My body is my weapon. I will engage the creature while you wait for yours," Certan said, rising gracefully from his seat. There was an intensity to the look in his eyes.

The Shade stepped forward, and grabbed a nearby patron who hadn't had time to flee. The rest had retreated to the bar and hidden behind it. The poor man screamed in terror. But Certan did not hesitate. He dashed ahead, engaging the Shade head on. The Shade threw the limp body it was holding at Certan, who adjusted his stance to duck underneath. He didn't just dodge though, he caught the body and carefully set it down on the ground behind him. The Shade was enraged, lashing out at Certan. He blocked the attack with his arms, and slid under to continue his approach. The Shade moved to strike him again, but Certan was too fast. He landed a strong blow to the creature's side, knocking it back.

"It's tough," Certan said.

"Incredibly tough. It's why we need these," Vincent said.

Lara had returned with the two blades. The diamond on the end of Alrion's sword glowed furiously.

"I'd say it works," Alrion said, accepting the sword from Lara and looking it over. Then he set it aside. Before his father could say anything, Alrion launched into an attack. Last time he had been on the sidelines, but this time he could prove how much he had grown since then. He led with a wave of force, which rocked the Shade slightly.

"Be careful, it looks like the same one. It remembers our last fight," Vincent shouted. Alrion heard, but did not respond. He was completely focused.

Fire didn't do much, but maybe it was the intensity. I'll overload it.

He drew on his spark and started building for a fire based attack. But this time, rather than just let it loose, he tried compacting it. He launched a miniature ball of flame. It was so hot that it started to ignite the air that it passed through. The Shade didn't even try to block the attack, which hit right in the middle of the chest.

"Damn I missed," Alrion whispered. Before he could initiate another attack, he saw that his previous one was behaving strangely. Rather than just exploding on the surface of the Shade's skin, it was still continuing.

"It's burning right through," Vincent said.

The Shade seemed to notice too, trying to shake off the ball of intense heat that was slowly passing through its body. But once it realised that the attack was not fatal, it stopped and focused its attention back on Alrion.

I have to get the upper hand, so we can finish it.

His force attacks had been quite powerful, but hadn't done that much to the creature. He decided that he could overcome that with sheer quantity. He concentrated and drew up several strands of force.

Alrion unleashed them in a barrage, trying to hit the same target area with each strike. He could see the attacks landing, each one having a minimal effect on the Shade. But it did seem like something was happening. Lara noticed the attack, and pulled out her new dagger.

"This will do the trick," she said and hurled the dagger at the Shade. Despite the movement of the Shade and the multiple attacks from Alrion, the dagger flew true and pierced the Shade in the chest, right where the heart was. The monster staggered back, not expecting the attack and furiously grasping for the dagger. However, Certan was faster, darting in amongst the confusion and striking the dagger with his open palm, forcing it in up to the hilt.

The Shade stumbled back and fell against the bar. As it came to rest, it's skin started to change undoing its transformation. The black surface was crumbling away, revealing pale skin underneath. Alrion looked on in wonder.

Lara retrieved her dagger, wiped it quickly and stashed it away.

"Never forget that this was once a person, even if they are beyond help now," Vincent said, walking closer and sheathing his sword.

"I don't want to alarm anyone, but I think we have a bigger problem here," Celes said pointing at the bar. Alrion's concentrated flame ball had passed through the body of the Shade and was about to hit the kegs behind the bar.

11

ALTERNATE PATHS

"**E**veryone out!" Vincent shouted, pointing at the door, and making his way there. The group scrambled out as fast as possible.

"I can probably stop it," Alrion said.

"No time, and too risky," Vincent said, grabbing Alrion's arm. A whoosh sound and a forceful shockwave buffeted them and as they looked back at the inn, they could see it was being consumed with flames.

I wonder, Alrion thought. He watched the flames with interest. If he could create flames, and issue them from himself, maybe he could bring them back.

"Let's try this," Alrion whispered. He reached out with his hand, trying a reverse of his previous spell. It was a twist on the fireballs. Instead, he was drawing the flame back to him, trying to build it into another ball. He visualised the ball of flame hovering above his hand, and containing all the flames and fire that had overtaken the inn. He could feel the heat and the power concentrated in a single spot.

Alrion opened his eyes and looked. The spell had worked.

"What are you planning to do with that?" Vincent said, looking over at Alrion. There was a curious concern in his features.

"Extinguish it," Alrion said, but what he really wanted to try, was to integrate the flames and the power. What if the Spark was more than just a concept? Maybe it was more literal than that. He tried feeding the flames into himself, trying to absorb their essence. He could feel himself heating up and the fireball shrinking.

"Stop it, that's not safe. Dump it," Vincent shouted. Alrion couldn't understand the concern, then looked at where Vincent was pointing. His arm was glowing bright red and looked wrong. Alrion panicked and looked around, finding a patch of dirt next to the inn. He funnelled all the flames into it without any finesse. The ball of flame streamed over and collected within the dirt, extinguishing but not without displacing quite a bit of dirt. Alrion sank down to his knees.

"What were you thinking?" Vincent said. Alrion looked around and the whole group were looking at him with concern.

"That's my line. Do you have an answer?" Celes said.

"I was just trying something out. I saved the inn, didn't I?" Alrion said.

"This isn't a game, you shouldn't take risks like that," Celes said.

"Your mother is right. The situation was contained, you didn't need to do more," Vincent said.

"Yes I did. I have to grow and learn an incredible amount in a short time, and there's nobody around to teach me. So, I will take every opportunity to do that," Alrion said.

Vincent sighed and walked into the inn. Celes followed after him. Lara walked over to Alrion.

"See I'm right, you should listen to me more and not take as many risks," she said, hoping to get a smile from Alrion. When she didn't she tried a different angle. "They're just worried, don't take it to heart."

"I know, but there's this incredible pressure on me and I have to do it. I can't let everyone down." Alrion felt older, like the weight of the world was on his shoulders.

"You have help, so don't forget that," Certan said.

"Yeah, look at the monk. He did the killing blow on that Shade. Now that's a team effort," Lara said.

"Well, you're right about that. Let's take a closer look at it," Alrion said.

Lara helped him up and they walked over to look at the body of the former Shade. "At least it works. But look here, mine isn't the only wound in the heart," Lara said.

"We encountered a Shade earlier, and it took a dagger in the heart and was knocked overboard. This must be the same one. I wonder how it tracked us here," Alrion said.

"Overboard?"

"Yes, we fought it on the ferry," Alrion said.

"Wow." Lara wiped the dagger she had pulled out earlier on her clothing and hid it once more.

Certan was kneeling over the body. "I haven't seen one of these up close. It looks like the body has completely reverted to a normal state. What a strange process," he said.

"I don't understand it myself, but this is what happens to people who have an advanced taint from the Blight," Alrion said.

"We've worn out our welcome," Vincent said, tossing a bag at Alrion.

"Time to leave, we will camp outside the town. At least we have horses now," Celes said joining them.

"It looks like the same Shade that attacked us on the ferry," Alrion said to his father as they walked over to the stables.

"I know, I recognised it instantly."

"How?" Alrion couldn't contain his surprise. Since when was his father an expert on Shades?

"I've seen a few in my day, they tend to closely resemble the person they originally were. It's there plain as day if you look closely."

"I'll remember for next time."

"I'd like to say there won't be a next time, but that would be a lie. We need to divert from the main path. I'm not sure what tipped them off, but they tracked us too easily. I'll think it over tonight," Vincent said.

They entered the stables, and only the horses greeted them.

"Where is everyone?" Lara said.

"Evacuated. They don't feel safe now. I can't blame them," Vincent said.

"I know the feeling," Lara said. The group saddled up and rode out of town. Alrion could sense eyes watching them, and hoped it was just scared townsfolk and not more creatures of the Blight.

After a short ride, they took a minor dirt track and left the main road.

"Can you give me a light?" Vincent asked and Alrion paused for a moment. After a minute a small orb of light danced above Vincent's shoulder.

"Thanks," Vincent said, and continued riding.

"I wouldn't have tried that if he hadn't asked, good to know," Alrion said to himself. The group rode in silence until they came to a small clearing.

"We will set up camp here. Alrion, help me with the horses," Vincent said.

Alrion nodded and helped guide the horses to a nearby spot and tie them up. He was about to head back, when he noticed his father's eyes looking directly at him.

"What happened back there?" Vincent said.

"What do you mean?"

"Is something happening with you. I've never seen you act so recklessly. Your mother is worried." Vincent looked worried too, although he didn't mention it.

"I almost died when I fought Branthor. It was only through luck and sheer determination that I caught him off-guard. But I can't let that happen again. There's too much at stake. And..."

"And?"

"There seems to be stuff spilling over from when I drank from the Pool. Knowledge of spells, intuition on how to combine things. I can't discern what is something that should work, and what is some crazy idea of mine. Or even things that should work but I can't do yet," Alrion said.

Vincent looked at him thoughtfully. "I hadn't thought of that, I guess I need to find out more about how this all works. You're right though, you don't have the luxury of time to slowly learn all you need. Just make sure you rely on the rest of us to help. It's not a criticism of you, it's just a safety net."

"Alright, I agree. I'll let everyone help and try not to do too many crazy things." Alrion wasn't sure how long that would last.

"Good, I feel better now."

"I thought it was mum that was the worrier?" Alrion knew his father had been worried too.

"It is," Vincent said and walked back to the camp.

Vincent and Certan took turns taking watch, but the night passed without incident. The next morning, they snacked on some bread and Vincent addressed the group.

"I've been doing some thinking, and I have a plan for how we move forward."

"We're all ears," Lara said.

"We need to split up. I'm confident that you and Certan can support Alrion. Celes and I will go a different route."

"Why?" Alrion said.

"We know we are being tracked, so it's better to split up and divert their attention. Celes and I can go back to the main road and continue on to Plynth. It's a massive town, and we can do some digging into who and what are following. With any luck, we will draw them in," Vincent said, tossing a lump of hard bread into the dying embers of the fire.

"So where do we go?" Alrion said.

"There is another path, and a longer route. You can follow it and stay off the beaten track. It will cost you time, but it will be safer and you will have the necessary seclusion to work on your spells," Vincent said.

"We'll be crossing the river?" Certan said.

"Yes, exactly."

"It's a well-known detour, but the best plan given the circumstances. Where will we meet you?" Certan said.

"You can find us at Plynth. By the time you arrive, we would ideally have taken care of our pursuers. Then we will set off together for the desert. If we miss there, we can agree to meet at the desert entry. We will find you," Vincent said.

"That would work," Certan said.

"There's a single desert entry? Won't that be obvious?"

"There are many, but only one that will take us where we need to go. And it is not well-known. I have discussed this with your father," Certan said.

"If you say so. When do we part ways?" Alrion said.

"As soon as we pack up," Vincent said.

Alrion nodded, a bit surprised even though he understood the reasoning.

They packed up in silence, Alrion double checking he had everything with particular care. Once he was prepared he walked over to the horses. Vincent was standing there talking to Celes. "Well, you two make sure you take care of yourselves," Alrion said as he approached.

"Will do boss," Vincent said, winking.

"You'll do well," Celes said, giving Alrion a hug.

"Isn't this fun? All of us on an adventure together," she said, gesturing at the group.

"It would be more fun without a Shade crashing the party," Vincent said.

"He doesn't mean that," Celes said, speaking behind her hand, and pretending to whisper.

"How will we find you in Plynth?" Alrion said.

"Don't worry, we will find you," Celes said.

"Alright, I guess this is it then. See you soon," Alrion said, giving them a wave. He mounted his horse and rode back towards the camp. As he turned he saw his parents mounting up and preparing to ride in the opposite direction. Impulsively he drew on his Spark and prepared a spell. He shot a flash of fire through the air, arcing high over the trees and vanishing into the distance in the direction that Vincent and Celes would be heading.

"We've got our marching orders," Vincent said to Celes with a chuckle, and the two of them started to ride away.

"Are we doing the right thing?" Celes said.

"Of course. He needs room to grow, and we can help from afar." Vincent needed to be strong, to make sure his wife didn't worry.

"As long as you're convinced. It's hard for me to let go."

"I know," Vincent said, giving Celes a kiss.

"Let's get moving, the faster we get there, the more we can do," Vincent said.

"I'll race you," Celes said, spurring her horse on and laughing.

Alrion saw his parents disappear into the distance and turned back to face Lara and Certan.

"Should we head out?" Certan said.

"Definitely. Are you familiar with the route?" Alrion said.

"Yes, I have travelled through here before. We should hurry to try and cross the bridge as soon as possible. Once we cross over the river, it will be harder to track us."

"Let's go then," Alrion said, letting Certan take the lead. Lara rode alongside him, but looking straight ahead. Alrion thought about his companions. With Certan's skill, strength and familiarity of the territory and Lara's instincts and adaptability he had nothing to worry about. Together they had taken down the Shade that had eluded them with Falric's aid.

"Why am I so worried then?" Alrion asked himself as they rode. He couldn't shake the feeling that they were not out of the woods yet.

12
_____

THE QUIET ROAD

The way back was quick and simple, and Alrion didn't spot a single
person. They were able to move onto the secondary path without fear
of being watched.

"So now this is uncharted territory," Alrion said, half to himself.

"For you, perhaps. But we are far from safe. This is still a well-travelled alternate route. Many do not continue the way we are going, so the further we travel the safer it will be. But I again suggest we make haste," Certan said.

"Agreed. While we're riding though I had a question," Alrion said.

"Yes, please ask." Certan slowed so that they were closer together.

"It's for both of you. Until recently I had never encountered the Blight. Blighters and Shades are new to me. But what about you? I feel like I've been quite sheltered," Alrion said.

"You have been, but don't feel dismayed. It's a good problem to have. I am lucky in that my exposure has been quite limited. The areas where I have lived, and especially with the monks, have been unpopular places for creatures of the Blight. There are few people, or much food or water," Certan said.

"Do they still function like a person?" Alrion said.

"In terms of having to eat and drink, yes. But their minds are warped. They also seem to have some sort of communal connection. You don't see them attempting speech much, yet they seem to be able to coordinate."

"What about you Lara?" Alrion said.

"My whole life, they have been present. I hate them with a passion. But I've enjoyed the relative safety of Avaria these last few years. I think they've only recently infiltrated this place in any numbers, and I'm sorry to say that's largely because of you." Lara pointed directly at Alrion.

"Sorry," Alrion said.

"Don't be sorry, they fear what can destroy them."

"Exactly. You have the knowledge now, deep within you. You must unlock it and set things right," Certan said.

"You make it sound so easy," Alrion said, trying to lighten the mood. He did get a laugh from them both. He kept an eye on the scenery as they went by, and it looked like another relatively deserted area. Alrion looked for signs of people passing through, and didn't see any. The path seemed undisturbed and they didn't see anyone in either direction.

"I thought you said that this was a well-known route, albeit longer and more secluded," Alrion said to Certan.

"It is."

"Then why is it so quiet? There's no sign of any activity," Alrion said.

"That's a good point. I admit I haven't travelled through here recently. Perhaps things have changed. Are you familiar Lara?"

"No, I haven't been this way," Lara said. Alrion spotted a clearing coming up off the right of the path and diverted his horse.

"Come here for a moment," Alrion said. The others followed, Lara giving Certan a confused look. Certan didn't have an explanation. "Shouldn't there be signs of people camping here?" Alrion said.

"It's not that far from Brangtur, maybe it's not a popular spot," Lara said.

"Not that far? Anyway, since we are here I need a break. And I want to try something." Alrion dismounted and tied up his horse to a tree. Certan and Lara followed. "So, we lucked out a bit last time, but then I did almost burn down an inn. If we encounter another Shade, what's the plan?" Alrion said.

"My attacks seem mostly ineffective, I think their skin is too protected," Certan said.

"Do you have attacks that penetrate? I think that underneath, they are still vulnerable. And their heart seems to be the weak spot," Alrion said.

"I do have something, but it requires focus and attention. Hard to use in the middle of a fight," Certan said.

"But what if we bought you time?" Lara said.

"Possibly, I need to be in close proximity too." Certan had a thoughtful expression on his face.

"That's fine. I don't currently have an effective way of defeating them with my magic, I can only assist. Lara and I have the right weapons to pierce the Shade's skin, but the amount of force required is quite substantial and it's not always reliable. So maybe we can try your attack next?" Alrion said.

"It's worth a try. What are you proposing?"

"See that tree over there? It looks pretty sturdy. Let's try a coordinated attack.

Lara and I will provide an initial attack to distract and wear it down, and you can come in with the big finish."

"Sure. I'll signal when I am ready." Certan sat on the ground, legs crossed and began to meditate.

"Do what you do, pretend it's a Shade," Alrion said to Lara.

"After you," Lara said. Alrion stepped to the side and began to prepare a barrage of spells. His best success was the force based waves, and he decided to try a variation of that. We wove a pattern of intertwined waves, all hitting the similar zone but at various times and from different directions and angles. He kept the intensity a little lower, just in case the tree wasn't as sturdy as it looked.

Once Lara could see the tree begin to be hammered by invisible force, she started running in an arc towards it. She opened with an array of tiny daggers hurled with precision. Thud, thud, thud, thud, they impacted with the tree in a neat line. Alrion adjusted his spells to avoid the areas where the daggers were implanted. He glanced over at Certan and saw no change.

Lara darted back and began another run, approaching from another direction. She produced more daggers and they hit one by one neatly underneath the first row. Alrion watched her through the last one and tried to catch it with a wave of force and push it even harder. The dagger wobbled slightly but stayed on track, only this time disappearing completely into the tree trunk.

"Ready," Certan said. Lara tossed a small vial at the tree and it smashed against the trunk letting out a cloud of smoke. Certan stood and ran towards the tree, keeping his right hand above his hip. Once he reached the tree he raised his hand and held it just above the surface of the trunk. He unleashed all the internal force he had accumulated all at once.

Alrion heard the almost deafening blast and ceased his attacks. Certan remained in place, sinking to a crouched position. Lara stood down, returning to Alrion's side. Once the smoke cleared Lara gasped.

"Wow!" she whispered.

"That's quite effective," Alrion said. Only the stump of the tree could be seen. And what was remaining looked to have been cleanly sliced in an arc. There were tiny fragments of splintered wood floating through the air.

"Perhaps I overdid it, but we needed to be sure." Certan stood with difficult and walked over to join Alrion.

"I feel bad for that tree," Alrion said.

"It was a necessary act, so that more good can be done. The tree knows that," Certan said.

"If you say so. How long does it take you to recover from that?" Lara said.

"Completely? A day. I can be effective again within a few minutes, but any additional attacks will be less powerful."

"So just don't miss then," Lara said.

"Of course," Certan said.

"I'm happy with this. If for some reason the Shade survives that attack, we should be able to disable it or finish it off. I liked the smoke screen, nice touch," Alrion said.

"Well, he did say he had to be very close. That's a vulnerable place to be, so why not mask his approach as much as possible?" Lara said.

"I hope you have more of those, quite useful," Certan said.

"I do, I can make them. The ingredients are a little hard to get a hold of, but I have my sources." Lara tapped her nose and looked around innocently.

"I bet you do," Alrion said, laughing. They took a short meal break before heading out once more. As they rode, Alrion steered his horse over to join Certan.

"I was curious about the power you have. Where is it from?" Alrion said.

"It the power of the body. You all have it, but do not use it. It takes both physical and mental training to master it," Certan said.

"So, there's no reason I couldn't do that?" Alrion said.

"Theoretically, but I am not one of the four masters so I don't know all the secrets. I suspect however that your other power would make this task difficult, as you would need to essentially not use it at all."

"That makes sense. So, anybody could do that with the right training?"

"Or the right situation. Not as effectively or as controlled. There is a story shared with us, about a young mother whose son has been trapped under a fallen tree. There is nobody to help, and there are wolves circling in. What does she do?"

"Destroy the tree. Or prop it up with something else and get the boy out," Lara said.

"Impossible without the right tools or training. And there is no time for planning and execution. So, what she does is lift the tree and push it aside, then carry her son home. But how does she do it?"

"I don't know," Alrion said.

"Because her need is so strong, her body can perform the impossible. She does not know how it was done, and could not do it again when asked. But because it is her only choice, she can do it. So, it is with this. We train our bodies and acquire the knowledge of how they work, but we unlock the power with our minds. We use our wills," Certan said.

"You use your will to unlock the power in your body and direct it as you see fit?" Alrion said.

"Exactly. Only the four masters have ascended to the heights of control and passed the final test. It is known as the Vault of Silence."

"Vault of Silence, you mentioned it before. Is that what I described in my dream?"

"I believe so. If they allow you to undertake that test, then you can achieve the same mastery perhaps. But I do not know all the details. That is one reason it is known as such," Certan said.

"The silence part is also keeping the trial secret, huh?" Lara said.

"Exactly. I believe that the information shared about it is only to give the monks something to strive for."

"Sounds daunting," Alrion said.

"It should be. Much of what we do is masked in secrecy, and I am not sure how far down the path I was. But I don't think I was anywhere near ready for that trial." Certan had a downcast look again.

"And you just obliterated that tree with the instruction from your mind. That paints quite a picture," Alrion said. Those words hung in silence, and Alrion let his horse fall back in pace to be beside Lara.

"You'll be fine, don't forget you have us," she said.

"I won't. It's just such a huge mountain to climb. Anyway, that's a future problem. Let's just enjoy the ride," Alrion said.

The road started to incline upwards, slowly but surely. As they continued they started to see glimpses of the river. It was larger than Alrion expected, and seemed to move with speed.

"The bridge is up ahead," Certan said. As Alrion caught up he finally saw it. Built with wood, the bridge was not as impressive as Alrion expected. The main surface was a plain walkway. But it looked sturdy and was secured on each end by large columns and decorative elements. What really caught his attention however, was a single shape in the distance. It looked like a man, standing in the middle of the bridge.

"We have company," Lara said.

"Who is it?" Alrion said.

"I don't mean to alarm anyone, but I think it's a case of what, not who," Lara said.

"A Shade?"

"Likely," Certan said.

"See what your sword says," Lara said. Alrion pulled out his sword and examined the stone on the pommel. It was a light glow, but matched the colour exactly from when they last encountered a Shade.

"So, it is," Alrion said, tensing up without even realising. He dismounted and tied up his horse, signalling to the others to do the same.

13

AN OLD FRIEND

They approached the Shade carefully on foot, watching its movements.

"I don't like this. It's just waiting for us," Lara said.

"Something definitely seems different," Certan said.

"You're probably right, but we need to take the advantage. We are prepared, let's see if we can take it down before anything bad happens," Alrion said.

"Did you want to take the bridge out?" Lara said.

"No, I don't want to be looking over my shoulder for this thing. We finish it now." Alrion needed to do this right. He couldn't stand having another Shade hunting him down. For his peace of mind, he had to see it destroyed.

"Fine by me. I will wait on the edge of the bridge and begin my preparation. Be careful of the tight quarters." Certan knelt down before the bridge and started to meditate.

"It's still just standing there," Lara said.

"I know. But let's open the attack, we don't want Certan charging in without cover," Alrion said.

Lara nodded and pulled out a handful of daggers.

"Go!" Alrion whispered and started preparing his spells. As Lara threw her first salvo of daggers, Alrion hurled his force spells, focusing on the legs. He wanted to make the Shade unsteady on the bridge. Lara's daggers bounced harmlessly off the Shade, and it remained motionless. Alrion's spells also had no effect.

"My throwing daggers didn't work, I'll need some assistance," Lara said.

"Sure." Alrion couldn't understand why his other attacks had just failed to do anything, but he didn't have time to ponder it over. He instead changed his focus to supercharging the speed of Lara's daggers. They flew faster and harder directly at the Shade, who was still motionless.

Three daggers dug into the Shade's torso with the additional force provided by Alrion, but again the Shade didn't react.

"I don't like this," Lara said.

"I know. But Certan will be ready soon," Alrion said.

"Here we go again," Lara said, and prepared another round of daggers. Alrion prepared his spells and watched them fly, throwing twice as much force behind them. He was finding it easier to spot and catch the daggers with his force waves. The Shade made no attempt to dodge, and the daggers made a neat row just below the first three.

"Ready," Certan said, and Lara stepped forward to lob a crystal vial through the air. It smashed right before the Shade, throwing up a smokescreen. Certan rose swiftly and moved with incredible speed, as if he was flying along the ground. He disappeared into the smoke and Alrion heard the impact of Certan's attack.

"It connected!" Lara said.

"Definitely. I hope that did it." Alrion found the smoke screen a hindrance, unsure of what happened. He started to walk closer, and Lara joined him. As the smoke cleared they saw Certan kneeling before the Shade. It had been knocked back but otherwise appeared unharmed.

"What? That can't be," Lara said.

"I felt something strange happen. I can't describe it though," Alrion said. Suddenly the Shade reached out and grabbed Certan, drawing him close. Certan cried out in pain as the Shade spun him around and seemed to dig its fingers in.

"We. Meet. Again," Certan shouted, in harsh and disjointed words.

"What are you saying?" Alrion continued approaching his friend.

"You. Left. Me. For. Dead," Certan said.

Alrion stopped dead in his tracks.

"What is it?" Lara said.

"No. It can't be!" Alrion said.

"Yes! This. Is. What. Happens. When. You. Turn. A. Wizard. Further," Certan said.

"What is he talking about?" Lara said. Alrion looked closer at the face of the Shade, and saw the confirmation he was after.

"This Shade is Branthor. He's become something else. I don't know how, but he survived and he's morphed into some sort of monster. That's why none of our attacks worked on him," Alrion said.

"No!" Lara said, shocked.

"I. Did. Not. Expect. This. It. Is. New. But. I. Will. Conquer. This. Form,"

Certan said. The pauses in-between words had reduced, but it seemed hard for
him to communicate.

"What do we do? We need to rescue Certan," Lara said.

"Let's see if we can just release him first, then together we can come up with
something. I get the feeling that it's not completely in control, so we may have an
opportunity," Alrion said.

"How do we do that?"

"Let's just grab him, I'll use my sword to sever the hand holding Certan back,"
Alrion said.

"Good, I'll come with you, I'll try and distract it," Lara said. The two of them
carefully advanced, step by step. There was no further communication from the
Shade via Certan.

"What do you want?" Alrion said.

"You. Know. You. Can. Still. Join. Me," Certan said.

"Why would he join a freak like you? You're an absolute monster. All you
deserve is a sword through your heart!" Lara said to Branthor, lacing the words
with as much spite and disdain as she could muster. Certan and Branthor
pivoted to look at Lara. Branthor's face still seemed straight and emotionless, but
Lara thought she could see the anger within it.

Alrion took the opportunity to draw his sword and empower his swing with
additional speed and force. Before Branthor could react, Alrion sliced through
the Shade's hand, freeing Certan. Lara reached out and grabbed Certan, dragging him away.

Branthor let out an unearthly scream, that seemed to come from the depths
of the ground. Alrion helped Lara drag Certan back to safety. He looked back as
they ran, and Branthor was motionless but still screaming.

Then there was silence. Lara and Certan collapsed just past the bridge, and
Alrion stopped to look back. There was no movement. Then Branthor rose. He
lashed out with his arms, the bridge starting to disintegrate around him. Branthor reached out but there was nothing to hold on to and he fell into the river.

Alrion leaned over, trying to see where Branthor had ended up, but there
was no sign of the Shade. The river carried on, as if nothing had happened.

"Thank you for the rescue." Certan seemed to have recovered his senses.

"Are you alright?" Alrion said.

"I believe so. I felt like a puppet at the hands of a child." Certan had a
distasteful look on his face. "He does not seem in full control of his new form."

"I can believe that. But he seems almost indestructible," Lara said.

"He might be. My spells had no effect. Whatever he is, he is more than a
normal Shade. And what he just did then, I don't think that was a physical
attack. I think he accessed some of his Spark," Alrion said.

"An almost invulnerable monster with magical powers, now that's a disaster!"
Lara said.

"He may never regain control, we don't know," Certan said.

"Regardless, we need to be ready next time we encounter him. We can't always rely on him destroying a bridge and floating away," Alrion said.

"How do you think he found us?" Lara said.

"It has to be deduction. He sent the Shade to confront us at Vainbly, and came here himself. It is the main alternate route, isn't it?" Lara said.

"That would mean he either knows where we are headed, is coordinating his attacks or maybe even both," Alrion said.

"He drank from the Pool of Knowledge too, didn't he?" Lara said.

"Yes, even before I did."

"Then he may have all the same information. Maybe he also had the vision about the monks?"

"If he did, we are in grave danger. We must get there before he has a chance," Certan said.

"Was it absolutely critical that we cross the bridge?" Alrion said, looking out. The bridge was completely destroyed, with only remnants hanging from either side.

"It's ideal. Let's find a way down and see if there's another way to cross." Certan stood up by himself, and tested his legs.

"Everything ok there?" Lara said.

"Yes, I'll be fine. Need to stick to normal activity levels for the next day though," Certan said.

"I can't promise anything," Alrion said, trying to make a joke out of it. Certan looked at him and didn't react.

"Let's try over here," Lara said, pointing at a mostly overgrown track. She took the lead and the others followed.

"There's no way we can get the horses down there," Alrion said.

"We'll have to leave them. I'll just untie them so they can go forage," Lara said. As she darted off Alrion inspected the track from closer. It appeared to be an old path, that was overgrown and worn down by the elements and time.

"Looks like it hadn't been used in a long time," Certan said.

"No need with the bridge," Lara said, returning.

"I'll miss those horses, we made great time," Alrion said, looking back, trying to catch a glimpse of them.

"They will survive. To be honest, I am more comfortable on my own feet. Others will be along and find them soon enough," Certan said, starting on the path and stepping over a slippery stone. The group had to walk slowly and carefully, as the path was quite steep and the growth had to be continually pushed back just to make progress. Alrion almost tripped and lost his balance several times, but he held on and hoped that his friends didn't notice.

After an hour, they had managed to find their way down to the bank of the river.

"It looks quite swift, but I can't offer much wisdom here. I grew up in and around the desert," Certan said.

"I'll take this one, don't worry." Lara started to wade into the river, one step at a time. After a few steps, she wobbled then quickly regained her balance. Heading straight back she kicked her legs out to try and shake off some of the excess water.

"What do you think?" Alrion said.

"Too dangerous to cross safely, although we could manage it. But I had a better idea." Lara had a wicked smile which was slowly breaking out.

"Why does that make me nervous?" Alrion said.

"No reason. You're the one that takes all the foolish risks around here," Lara said looking around.

"She's right you know," Certan said.

"Fine. What is it?" Alrion said.

"Why fight the river, when we can use it to our advantage. Go with the flow as it were," Lara said.

"If you're thinking what I think you are, Certan is going to be more nervous than with the horses," Alrion said.

14

GOING WITH THE FLOW

Lara inspected some of the plants by the shore. She selected a few samples, and sliced the long tendrils with her dagger.

"This will work for a short-term solution," she said.

"We're going to a build a boat of some kind?" Alrion said.

"More like a raft. There's plenty of trees around, and you and Certan are handy at knocking them around."

"For now, he can do the knocking," Certan said. The monk didn't even look up when speaking, he was so focused on his recovery.

"I'm on it," Alrion said.

Lara watched him concentrate, a comical expression on his face. She suppressed a laugh, and watched carefully. After a pause, she heard a noise nearby and watched a branch fall to the ground. Alrion ran over and inspected the fallen limb, unbridled glee in his steps. Lara joined him and looked for herself. The cut was precise and perfect.

"You could be in for a new career as a carpenter," she said.

"I don't think my father would approve."

"I guess he would rather you be a blacksmith?"

"With the right care and focus, I could probably work the metal with spells instead. But I think the time for that has passed." Alrion broke eye contact with her.

"You never know," Lara said, trying to keep things light. Under her direction Alrion cut down the nearest trees, and cut the trunk and branches to her specifi-cations. Lara prepared the ropes by binding together the strands from the plants.

Certan joined them at this point and lashed the logs together, under Lara's watchful eye. It took longer that she had expected, but Lara stepped back and saw what looked like a serviceable raft.

"Not my finest work, but it should float," she said.

"Are you sure?" Certan said.

"Of course, let's go test it." Lara identified an appropriate spot on the bank and pointed it out. The three of them pushed it into the water, and Lara waded in further. While Certan and Alrion steadied it, she climbed on.

"Watch this." Lara jumped up and down on the raft. It rocked a little, and took on some water, but kept its buoyancy.

"I'm satisfied, please don't do that again," Certan said. Alrion couldn't help laughing. He climbed on next and helped Certan onboard.

"Can you shove us off?" Lara said to Alrion. He held on tightly to the raft and leaned into it. The raft lurched away, almost flipping over. But Certan and Lara were able to scramble and balance it out, then the raft was caught in the river's flow.

"And now we wait," Lara said, sitting back, and looking very satisfied with herself. The countryside was going past at a reasonable rate.

"I must say I'm impressed. We seem to be going quite quickly. Is this a more direct route?" Alrion said.

"I believe so, what do you think Certan?" Lara said.

"Probably. The benefit is also that we will continue overnight. Perhaps we should take turns sleeping?" he said.

"Definitely. This isn't exactly the safest vessel," Lara said with a laugh.

"Have you given her a name, Captain?" Alrion said.

"Her?" Lara said.

"I thought all ships had female names."

"Only in the books. But for you, sure. Let's name her Lady Grace after her poise and elegance," Lara said. Alrion burst out laughing again. Even Certan cracked a smile.

"Is that an aspirational name?" Alrion said.

"No, she is exceptionally graceful already. Look at how she navigates these dark and stormy waters," Lara said with a straight face.

"Can't argue with that. And you even got Certan to smile. He's not been this jovial since we first met him."

"It was fuelled by alcohol then, as you know," Certan said.

"How do you feel now?" Lara said.

"Not quite myself yet. I feel as if life has been muted. Before I was in a haze of loud sounds, bright colours, and ridiculous antics. Now that they have been stripped away, things seem duller than they should. I know it's just perception, but it may take time to readjust."

"How long did you live like that?" Alrion said.

"It must have been a few years. I am amazed that I didn't completely lose my skills and conditioning. I can't explain it."

"And that all stemmed from one event?"

"Yes, sadly. It was like the flood gates opened and I was swept away. I relinquished control, so I could pretend I had no responsibility over my actions. But that is not true, I was just hiding away."

"Do you miss it?"

"The mind and the body still ache for it. I find myself thirsty despite having drunk lots of water. It might be a while before that passes. But it wasn't real. It was a long dream with no substance, and I don't want to lose myself like that again." Certan looked out over the river, not really focusing on anything in particular.

"We'll help you with that, and I'll continue trying to get you to crack a smile," Lara said.

"Sounds fine to me," Certan said.

"Good, good," Alrion said, watching the terrain fly past. They rode the river in silence for a time, each lost in their own thoughts. Certan broke the silence abruptly.

"I've been watching our progress, and I had a good idea," he said.

"What is it?" Alrion said.

"It would help to provide you with some training in times like this, so that you might be better prepared for your trial."

"What did you have in mind?"

"I must admit I know little of magic. But there is a certain visualisation and mental focus, right?"

"Yes. When I prepare a force spell, I am visualising what will happen, applying my will, then fuelling the spell with my internal force or Spark."

"Good. Then we can do an exercise to help you train your will." Certan peeled off a sliver of wood from their raft and tossed it onto the river. It landed on the water, but instead of bobbing along the surface, it rose up and floated just above the water.

"That's odd," Lara said. Whatever it was looked like magic to her.

"Yes, and it's not hovering in place. Somehow, it's still moving with the water just floating at a fixed height above. Are you doing that with your mind?" Alrion said.

"Yes. Now you try," Certan said. Alrion looked at the sliver of wood, then worked on peeling off another one. He tossed it off the raft, and it bobbed on the water as expected.

"Try harder," Certan said. Alrion went silent. Lara watched him with interest. The young wizard's eyes squinted increasingly. Eventually the tiny piece of wood lifted up and floated alongside Certan's piece and Alrion let out a loud breath.

"There!" Alrion said.

"It's not the same," Lara said. Alrion's sliver of wood seemed motionless, yet Certan's seemed to go with the flow of the river.

"You have achieved an appropriate result, but not mastered the process. Keep trying," Certan said. Alrion kept it up, and soon sweat dripped down his face. While he was still trying Certan spoke up again.

"Lara, why don't you try it," he said.

"Me?"

"Of course. It's using your mind, there's no magic involved. Alrion has an advantage in that he has been practising the visualisation more, but otherwise there's no difference," Certan said.

"Watch out, I'm going to beat you." Lara prepared a sliver of wood of her own and threw it next to the two others. It plopped into the water and floated along.

"Not like that you won't," Alrion said.

Lara scowled at him, and returned to her concentration. She knew how to focus herself, surely this piece of wood wouldn't mind falling in line. Little by little it began to rock from side to side, then floated slowly up to match Alrion's piece.

"See!" Lara said.

"Well done. I'm still winning though," Certan said. Neither Lara nor Alrion could seem to make their piece move the same way as Certan's.

The competition continued in the same fashion for a while without any change. Alrion and Lara seemed to be quite tired from the effort, but Certan was relaxed and confident.

"I think it's time to mix things up," he said. He leaned over and whispered something into Lara's ear.

"Really?" Lara said with interest, and refocused on her tiny wood shaving. She tried harder and harder, then just sat back. Her piece of wood was moving in concert with Certan's.

"Looks like I did it. How's things over there Alrion?" Lara said. Alrion's piece was the same, but looked stilted and forced in comparison to the other two.

"That's not fair, you told her the trick," Alrion said.

"No, I gave her a hint. But you need to discover it for yourself," Certan said. Alrion just huffed at them both and went back to his concentration. After some intense focus his piece of wood moved more, mimicking the flow of the water.

"Nice try, but you're faking it. It's unrealistic," Certan said. Alrion gritted his teeth and kept trying to work even harder. Finally, something snapped. He relaxed and sat back, losing the intense look on his face as if he had given up. But now his piece was in sync with the other two.

"I don't understand," Alrion said.

"Give it a minute," Certan said. Alrion look thoughtful.

I hope he gets it.

"Hang on. I'm not controlling the piece of wood, but I am maintaining the belief that it must float above the water," Alrion said.

"Exactly. Beliefs are powerful things. See the difference between forcefully propping up the wood shaving, and changing your belief to alter its behaviour?" Certan said.

"Wow. So how much can you do with this?" Alrion said.

"Everything. You are only limited by the strength of your will. Some things will be harder to alter than others, and knowledge of the way the world functions does make things easier," Certan said.

"So, anyone could do this. Why aren't they?" Lara said.

"Firstly, they don't believe it is possible. Very few would accidentally find a way to do this. Secondly, a strong will is required. The two of you have already gone through many trials, so you are better qualified to do it," Certan said.

"Incredible. I am starting to understand how you can do what you do," Alrion said.

"Excellent. This class is over. But let's see how long we can keep our tiny wood shavings floating," Certan said, grinning at them.

"You're on," Lara said.

"I'll win this, you just watch," Alrion said.

"You know, you're a pretty good teacher," Lara said to Certan. She was impressed at the ease with which he had gotten them to succeed.

"Thank you, I hadn't considered that."

"You're probably not as far behind in your monk training as you think," Alrion said.

"Perhaps, but it may be for nothing. They may not accept me back."

"If they're as wise as you say, they definitely will," Alrion said.

"Shush, I need to concentrate," Lara said. The competition wasn't over after all, and she had to win.

"Fair enough," Alrion said.

Hours later, Certan let his wood shaving gently drop to the surface of the water.

"You could have kept that up all day," Lara said, accusing Certan.

"Of course."

"Did you really think you would beat him?" Alrion said.

"Well, I beat you," Lara said. Alrion didn't reply.

"I think we may be nearing our destination," Certan said. In the distance they could see walls, indicating a city of some kind.

"I wonder if we will find my parents there," Alrion said.

"Of course." Lara scanned the distance, as if she were able to see them. She had a bad feeling, as though there were more troubles ahead. But she kept that to herself.

15

INVESTIGATION

Vincent urged the horse to go faster. Now they were on the open road, he wanted to travel as quickly as possible. Celes did the same, pulling even with him.

"This reminds me of the old days," she said, a glint of mischief in her eyes.

"It sure does. We were so carefree back then," Vincent said, his voice taking a heavier tone.

"Yes, well these are serious times I admit. But I know I'm ready for another adventure. Aren't you?"

"Yes and no. I've been dreading this."

"Because you knew that Alrion may be a wizard?"

"Yes, and I knew that it would not be an easy life, given what my father accomplished."

"He will rise to it, he already has. You've taught him well," Celes said, reaching out to place a hand on Vincent's shoulder.

"We both have. Now we just need to support him." Vincent placed his hand over his wife's.

"And we are. What do you expect us to find out there?" Celes said, taking her hand back.

"We have been tracked the whole way. The only explanation is that Branthor built a network of followers. Regardless of whether Branthor is alive or not, we still have to deal with that. I don't believe that Shade attack was random."

"I think you're right. Just as well you have the world's best thief with you," Celes said.

"World's best? I'd like to see the finalists for that prize lined up. That would be a sight," Vincent said.

"Yes, maybe even some contenders that we don't know about."

"I would hope so, the world has changed a lot in the last twenty years or so that we've been hidden away," Vincent said.

The extent of the changes was evident, even in the empty stretch of road they were riding down.

"So how do we pinpoint these followers? Any tricks we can use?" Celes said.

"I don't know of any ways to detect Tainted Ones, other than that diamond we gave to Alrion. I think we will need to be observant and do an investigation. Who would you start with?"

"Guards and officials," Celes said.

"Why?"

"If you want to track people and have access to information, that's the best way. I'd say if we can find Tainted Ones in official posts, they will be connected to Branthor."

"Sounds reasonable to me. I'll be the muscle, and you can be the brains," Vincent said.

"So, the usual," Celes said with a smirk. Vincent shook his head gently and laughed.

"The usual then," Vincent said.

The city gates of Plynth loomed large, yet appeared unchanged. The black metal gate was as imposing as ever, and the stone walls looked just as ancient as Vincent remembered.

"Are there more guard towers now?" Vincent said.

"I think so. Lots more guards too," Celes said, looking around.

"Seems like a lot more security overall," Vincent said.

"Definitely. Take a look at her," Celes said, directing Vincent to a guard. The woman was referring to a drawing and questioning a young couple trying to enter the city.

"They're looking for someone," Vincent said.

"Exactly. Why don't you hang back and I'll investigate?" Celes said. She threw her reins at Vincent and hopped off the horse. Within moments she had disappeared into the crowd.

"There she goes," Vincent said to himself. After a moment, he stopped trying to look for her, and shuffled off the main road with the two horses.

Celes felt a thrill from the intrigue and curiosity of the situation. She had to get a look at whoever they were after, and needed to do so without revealing herself in a crowded thoroughfare.

Good exercise as a refresher.

As she approached the guard, Celes tried to blend in with some other travellers. She continued walking, and leaned in to try and catch some of the conversation.

"You aren't listening to me. You are a young couple and look almost exactly like the ones I have here," the female guard said.

"It's a passing resemblance at best. What does that have to do this us?" the young man said. He was quite agitated and trying to contain himself but slowly failing.

"I can't let you in, it's too much of a risk. What I can do though is take you into a holding area, where you can be interviewed by someone else. If that passes, we will let you in," the guard said.

"Just do it, we need to enter the city and they will discover soon enough that we aren't who they are looking for," the young woman said to her companion.

"Fine, but I think this is ridiculous," the man said, trying to get the last word in. The female guard nodded.

"Yes, I appreciate your frustration. This way please," she said, leading them into a side passage off the main gate. As she rolled up the drawing Celes managed to get a quick glance at it. Then she reversed direction and made her way back to Vincent.

"So?" he said.

"Not good. They're holding that young couple for a further interview because of their likeness to a drawing."

"And the drawing looks like?"

"Alrion and Lara." She could see Vincent's expression drop.

"I had feared that."

"Yes, it's not subtle at all." Celes was worried by the brashness of their actions. How far had they infiltrated?

"Do you think that guard is in on it?"

"Probably not. But I would suggest that whoever comes to interview the couple will be," Celes said.

"Sounds logical. I guess we need to infiltrate that guard post then," Vincent said.

"Exactly, and you're going to help."

"Of course, and I'm sure you have a plan already." Vincent had a weariness to his voice.

"Yes, I do. Let's head over to the armourer that makes the guard uniforms. You can find that out, right?" Celes said.

"I'm sure I can. Let's get to it," Vincent said. Celes winked at Vincent then expertly leapt back into the saddle. "I don't know how you can still do that," he said, chuckling.

"I'm allowed to have a few secrets of my own," Celes said.

"Fair enough. I won't ask." Together they rode through the gates, avoiding any unwanted attention.

"At least they're not looking for us," Celes said.

"Yet."

"Yet?"

"After whatever you are going to pull off today, they most certainly are going to," Vincent said.

"Not necessarily," Celes said, her voice trailing off. But they both knew that there was little chance that their investigation would go unnoticed.

Vincent introduced himself to the first blacksmith that they encountered, and steered the conversation around to who did the guard uniforms.

"Oh, that's most likely John down the hill. Why?" the blacksmith said.

"Well I'm looking for work, and I'm over making household implements. I'd like to do something more interesting," Vincent said.

"After a few of those, I doubt you'd find it interesting. But fair enough. I could use an extra hand, let me know if you're interested. Or maybe see me after you get bored," the blacksmith said.

"Definitely. Thanks for the help." Vincent left the workshop and met Celes back on the street.

"You found it alright?" she said.

"Yes, it should be just down this hill. Man named John."

"See! I told you."

"You did indeed. What's the plan?"

"You just distract the blacksmith and I'll take care of the rest," Celes said.

"As you wish." Vincent was curious to see what she would do. The guard armour was not fully plated, but it would be heavy and noisy.

There was only one blacksmith at the bottom of the hill, and Vincent approached him directly.

"John, is it?" Vincent said.

"Yes, who is asking?"

"My name is Will. I'm interested in some blacksmithing work, and I heard that you work on the guard uniforms."

"That's right. Why are you interested in that?" John said. He was looking at Vincent with suspicion.

"I've been working in a small town so long, there's only so many knives, and horse shoes and other boring items that I can make. I thought the work you do might have a bit more sophistication to it," Vincent said.

"You're right about one thing, it is more sophisticated. But it's still boring. Just a different kind," John said.

"A change is as good as a journey, so they say," Vincent said.

"All the same, I don't think I can afford to bring on more help, not with what they pay for these," John said.

"Do you mind if I work with you for free then? I could learn some new skills, you could get some free labour and we can both profit before I move on," Vincent could see John's mind ticking over, considering the pros and cons.

"I could use the help. But you should understand that I have an exclusive contract for these, it will do you no good trying to set up shop here," John said.

"I wouldn't dream of it. I can see you are busy today, could I get a quick tour then we start proper tomorrow?" Vincent said.

"I will need to structure my day differently, so that works for me. Come this way." John waved at Vincent and disappeared further into the workshop.

Celes observed the conversation and smiled.

Thanks for the help my dear husband. Once the two men had disappeared she snuck into the workshop looking for a suitable uniform. She spotted one that looked like it had just been completed.

No, too obvious. She continued the search, locating a temporary store nearby.

"This will work," Celes said to herself. Not everything was there, but the main elements were. It wouldn't too difficult to complete the look herself. Once she had extracted the chest pieces and helmet, she paused to listen out. She could hear voices in the distance, but wasn't sure if they were coming closer.

"It's a noisy place, I'll just get going," she told herself. She found a bundle of leather and wrapped up the pieces within it, and left the shop as quickly as she could. Once she was out the door she slowed her pace to look less suspicious, then found a quiet alley nearby to rest.

After a few minutes, she heard footsteps and readied herself.

"It's just me," Vincent said as he turned the corner. He saw Celes ready to pounce. She visibly relaxed and stepped aside to show off her prize.

"Nice work. Clearly, I bought you enough time," Vincent said.

"It was a charming gesture, but you didn't need to."

"Are you going to try this on now?"

"Yes, if you'll assist," she said. Vincent looked out for passers-by, and helped Celes into the outfit.

"You'll need a white tunic to match," he said.

"I know, I spotted a stall not far from here. Would you mind?"

"No, I'll be right back," Vincent quickly left and returned shortly, showing Celes the clothing.

"Approved," she said, and they adjusted her outfit to allow her to put it on.

"How do I look?" Celes said.

"Like an unusually attractive guard," Vincent said.

"Right answer."

"Just try not and get it too dirty, you need to return it tonight," Vincent said.

"Why?"

"I'm going to work there for a few days."

"Whatever for?"

"I could learn a thing or two from John, and it gives us a reason to be here. I thought it would help us blend in." Celes had to admit that he made sense.

"That would be useful, I guess I'll have to be extra careful then," she said, winking at Vincent.

"What's the plan?" he said. She leaned in close and whispered to him for a full minute.

"I stand around and bail you out if you need help?" Vincent said.

"Exactly," she said and waved goodbye.

"Good luck," Vincent said, and watched her leave.

Celes walked down the street with confidence. She had to assume the role of the guard perfectly. The guards belonged here, and were respected and obeyed. So, she acted like she owned the place.

She strode into the guard block without even pausing. As another guard passed by Celes nodded her head, and the guard did the same.

"Now to find that interview room," Celes said to herself. The building was one long corridor, with many rooms off either side.

This must be built alongside the city walls. She noticed that one door in the distance had a guard posted outside. That was promising. Celes walked up to the door and addressed the guard.

"Is this the couple that are awaiting questioning?" she said.

"Yes. Are you the examiner?" the guard said.

"No, I'm here to relieve you as the examiner has been delayed," Celes said.

"Oh, that's unusual. Are you sure?"

"Yes, they aren't sure how long it will take and you're needed back on patrol," Celes said.

"Great, thanks for letting me know," the guard said and left the post.

This is too easy, Celes thought. She opened the door and stepped inside. The young couple were seated at a table, but the rest of the room was empty. They looked up at her expectantly.

"Sorry, I am not your examiner. Just checking in on you. One should be on the way soon," Celes said.

"Fine," the man said, and did not engage in any further questions. Celes stepped back outside and stood just as the previous guard had. Now it was time to wait.

After an hour or two, and many guards passing back and forth, she noticed someone different walking down the corridor. It was a male guard, but he was wearing a black cloak with white trim.

He looks different, I must keep an eye on him. The guard walked briskly, then stopped suddenly in front of the door.

"The couple awaiting questioning are inside?" the guard said. His speech was precise and calculated.

"Yes," Celes said, thinking it best to be as brief as possible.

"You are dismissed," the guard said, waving her away.

"Yes sir," she said, and turned to leave. After she had taken a few steps she heard the door open and close. She didn't have a good feeling about him, and the sound of the lock clanking shut was chilling to her ears.

Celes wasn't sure what to do. She had identified the examiner, but was fearful for the couple. It wasn't based on anything, but she just didn't feel right. So, she decided to circle around and find another way to access that room.

Turning around, Celes walked past the room and listened out. She didn't hear anything. Continuing on, she located the next door and entered it. It was another holding cell, but was empty. It looked identical to the one she had already seen.

"That's a start," Celes said to herself. She examined the room to look for any strange designs or flaws in the construction that would allow her to access or hear from the adjoining room. The stone was solid, and ceiling was well-constructed. But she did notice a smaller stone slightly out of place near the floor. She carefully lowered herself to the ground, and manipulated the stone with her hand. Very slowly it moved. With some persistence, she was able to remove it.

There was a gap behind the stone, and another stone on the other side for the adjoining room. She wouldn't be able to budge the other stone, but she hoped that it might be able to be moved. She reached into the hole, but couldn't touch the other stone. She used a dagger instead, levering it just enough to dislodge it. This created a passage for the air to travel between the rooms. Now she just had to try and listen in.

"I can see immediately that the two of you are not who we are looking for," a male voice said. Celes assumed that it was the examiner.

"Good. Can we go?" the young man said.

"Not quite yet. There seems to be a complication," the examiner said.

"What's going on? We have been completely cooperative through all this," the young woman said.

"You've been caught up in something by mistake. But unfortunately, that means that you need to be dealt with. Perhaps after I deal with the person listening in on this conversation," the examiner said. Celes heard footsteps approaching her.

16

DARK TIDINGS

C eles knew that somehow, she had been detected. She pushed up quickly and considered her options. She couldn't wait for him to find her, she had to be aggressive and take him off guard. She wouldn't have the element of surprise, but he might not expect her to be so bold.

She headed for the door immediately and looked out into the corridor. There was nobody.

"This is it," Celes told herself, and ran over to the holding cell next to her. She tried to minimise the noise, but she maintained her speed. The examiner seemed confident, she had to try and exploit that. As she reached the door she heard a scream from within. Celes burst through and assessed the situation.

The examiner was holding the young woman hostage with a knife to her throat.

"Well hello, lovely of you to join us," he said to Celes.

"This is against regulation, why are you doing this?" Celes said.

"What would you know of regulations, you're not a real guard," he said.

"Who are you really?" Celes countered.

"I'm the one asking the questions here, you're not really in a place to be making demands," the examiner said. He pointed to an empty chair.

"Take a seat," he said. Celes considered the request, then complied.

I need to keep him thinking he is in control. Then I can use an opening.

"You look somehow familiar, but I can't pick it," the examiner said.

"We've never met before, I wouldn't forget that face," Celes said. The examiner's features were not extraordinary, but he had a deep black scar on his forehead.

"You mean this? It's a souvenir from my encounter with some rather nasty Blighters. Such bothersome creatures, but useful with the right motivation and stimulation," he said.

"You're tainted then. You admit it?"

"Yes, there's no harm in doing that. None of you will leave this room alive," the examiner said. The young man started to yell in protest but an icy look from the examiner silenced him.

"What do I call you?" Celes said.

"You can call me Brine. Not that it matters really." He dismissed her with his eyes, looking elsewhere.

"Brine, interesting name. So, have you been tainted long?" Celes said.

"I said I was doing the interrogation here," Brine said, tightening his grip on the young woman. She whimpered as the knife edged closer.

"Ask away," Celes said. There was not yet an opening that was safe.

"Let's begin with your name. What is it?"

"Celes."

"Good, that wasn't hard, was it? Why were you spying on this couple?" Brine said. Celes decided that she would answer truthfully, it would help her later when the tables were turned and she was trying to get information from him.

"I noticed that they were stopped for looking like people I know. I wanted to see who was asking. Now my fears are confirmed."

"Oh, this is interesting. I want to hear more." Brine half turned to face her.

"I can't concentrate properly seeing that woman so distressed," Celes said, trying her luck.

"Naughty, naughty. Trying to convince me to let her go when you drop the juicy information? So amateur. But you know what, I'll let you have this one." Brine withdrew the knife from the young woman and shoved her into the corner violently. Her husband ran over and comforted her. "You two stay there for now, if you become a distraction I'll deal with you permanently." He turned his attention back to Celes. "So, can you talk now?"

"Yes, I can. I have a question though, what makes you so confident? You're just a man who is tainted. You don't have any special powers," she said.

"Maybe I do, maybe I don't. But I suggest you answer my questions and this will go smoother for everyone. You don't want to make me angry," Brine twirled the knife in his hand to ensure his words had the correct impact.

"I'd need to see the sketch again, but it looked like my son." Celes watched Brine's reaction carefully.

His eyes lit up in interest. "Take as close a look as you want," he said. He removed a rolled-up parchment from his cloak and threw it at her. Celes unrolled it and studied the picture. It was a very good sketch, of Alrion and Lara. Celes adjusted her seated position, and loosened one of the knives strapped to her foot.

"There's no doubt about it. That's my son. Why are you looking for him?" Celes said.

"Never you mind, the important thing is, where is he?" Brine said. He started to walk over, licking his lips. It was like he could taste the information, and he wanted more. Celes saw the opportunity and took it. She used her leg to fling the loosened knife at Brine's leg.

"What?" he cried at is it made impact, and Celes used the opportunity to jump up onto the table and vault off it, launching herself at Brine. He didn't notice in time, and all he could do was throw up his hands. They landed on the ground, Celes with a knife at Brine's throat, and Brine using all his strength to hold it at bay.

"I can do this all day, and time is not on your side," Brine said.

"Why is that?"

"I have reinforcements coming. Reinforcements of the Blighter variety."

"If you do that you'll blow your cover." Celes knew she had to dissuade him from doing that. If it were at all possible.

"Not if there's no witnesses. It'll be so tragic," Brine said.

Celes banged her right boot on the ground and a small blade popped out. She used that to kick Brine's left leg. He cried out in pain, and Celes used that moment to overpower him and flip him over. In seconds, he was face down on the floor with his arms pinned behind him.

"You can't possibly escape," Brine said.

"Watch me." Celes pushed harder and Brine stopped struggling. She quickly extracted a short rope and bound his hands.

"Are you alright? Run for it," Celes said to the young couple. They looked bewildered, but Celes's speech seemed to snap them out of it. The young man helped his wife up and they ran to the door.

"They're coming," Brine said, in a sing-song way.

"Get up," Celes said, kicking Brine in the small of the back and dragging him up. He complied and stood shakily.

"This leg injury is going to slow me down," he said.

"You'll live. We're leaving." Celes shoved him closer to the door but kept a knife pressed at his back.

"On the double," Brine said, mocking her. They entered the corridor and Celes could hear commotion from one end.

"I told you they're coming," Brine said.

"This way," Celes said, pushing her prisoner in the opposite direction. He began walking and Celes stayed close behind. She could hear the noises of conflict getting louder and louder.

"Would you mind if I had a rest?" Brine said. He was practically laughing, and was struggling to contain himself.

"Yes, keep moving." Celes really hoped that there was an exit at the end of the corridor, she hadn't scouted that far ahead.

"They're inside! To arms!" a male voice shouted. Celes didn't even turn around, she just pressed on and forced Brine to increase his pace. She could see the sweat forming on his dark locks, either walking with that injury or something else was causing his quite a bit of exertion. As they reached the door at the end of the corridor, Celes pushed Brine to the side and kicked the door open. The last rays of daylight peeked in, and Celes felt relief.

There was a small training area before them, and a path.

"Keep moving," Celes said, pushing Brine out the door. They shuffled slowly through the yard, Celes looking back to see if they had company. Nothing yet. As they reached the path, she could see that it led to a main street. "Almost there," she said. Just then she heard another scream, and watched a hapless guard be overwhelmed by Blighters. He fell to their attacks and they started to pour out from the compound. Celes pressed on even faster, Brine almost fell instantly due to the shove.

"Oh, who might you be?" Brine said. He stopped completely, looking at a man on the path. The man stepped forward and punched Brine in the face. He fell in a heap instantly.

"I wanted to do that for a while, but I don't have the strength to carry him," Celes said.

"Happy to assist. I think we better make a move." Vincent reached down and picked up Brine, slinging him over his shoulder.

"I don't know how you made it here but I don't care. Can you move with him?" Celes said.

"Fast enough. Do you think they can track us?" he said.

"No idea, let's just get some distance between us." Celes put her knife away and started to run.

Vincent did his best to keep up, and they pushed for the main street. The Blighters seemed distracted, and weren't sure where to go.

Celes and Vincent ducked off the main street and took any available lanes. After ten solid minutes, they slowed and took a breath.

"Any sign of them?" Vincent said.

"I don't think so." Celes glanced around, but the streets looked empty. She let some of the tension go.

"Good, let's take it a bit easier from here."

"Where will we go?"

"John gave me keys to a place we can stay. Let's start there," Vincent said.

"Great, take us away." Celes looked back once more, but couldn't see or hear any Blighters.

"They seemed to lose the trail when you knocked him out," Celes said.

"I doubt it's a coincidence. He's tainted, right?"

"Yes, he admitted it, even seemed proud of the fact."

"Crazy. Well let's get him back so we can ask him more. However, we need to be comfortable with the possibility that he can call more of them upon us." Vincent upped his speed and caught up with Celes.

They arrived at the tiny house within minutes. It was surrounded by what looked like an abandoned workshop.

"This it is. He runs a few jobs through here when he needs extra hands, and they stay here. It should work well," Vincent said.

"At least we will have some privacy," Celes said. They entered the house and Celes located a chair. Vincent plonked Brine down, then bound his feet to the chair.

"That should hold him, let's wake him up," Vincent said.

"Not just yet, let me find something." Celes rifled through her things and found a small vial. She showed it to Vincent.

"What is that?" he said.

"It's a serum that should keep him talking. Hopefully it still works. I used to use them all the time to ease key information out of people," Celes said.

"I thought you just got them drunk."

"This works better and, sometimes they work well together. Let's see what he has to say," Celes said. Vincent shook Brine a little until the man began to show signs of consciousness.

"Where am I?" Brine asked. Once his vision improved he saw Celes and Vincent standing in front of him.

"Right, I was knocked out. Nice punch there," Brine said, nodding at Vincent.

"We have some questions. Drink this." Celes shoved the vial into Brine's mouth and he swallowed it without question.

"You probably didn't need that, but it doesn't hurt. Does it?" Brine said.

"No, you won't feel anything," Celes said.

"Good. My mind feels very fuzzy though. What did you want to know anyway?"

"Why are you after this couple," Celes said, showing Brine the drawing he had tossed to her earlier. Vincent sneaked a peek at it too, and noticed the perfect likeness for Alrion and Lara.

"Just following orders. They're to be found," Brine said.

"Whose orders?" Vincent said.

"Wraith." Brine squirmed after he said it, as if he were trying to retract the words.

"Never heard of him," Vincent said.

"He's a new player, at least in this form." Brine seemed surprised that he had said that. "Looks like your vile concoction is working."

"Good. Why does Wraith want these two?" Celes said.

"He didn't say, but then again I never asked. I guess they are a problem for him?" Brine said.

"How do you communicate with him? Do you meet somewhere?" Vincent said.

"Oh, I met him once, not that I had to really. I think he wanted to impress us, so he made an appearance. No, we talk up here," Brine said, tapping his head.

"You can communicate via thoughts?" Vincent said, surprised.

"You don't know anything, do you? How do you think I called all those Blighters before? We're all linked. Everything you have told me about yourselves, I have passed on," Brine said, quite pleased with himself.

"To who?" Celes said.

"Everyone who is tapped in. All those who are tainted can access the channel. It's like a river of consciousness that we all share. The more powerful can broadcast their message and rise above other chatter," Brine said.

"I see," Vincent said, starting to pace around the room.

"Tell me more about Wraith. What does he look like?" Celes said.

"Like a Shade," Brine said.

"A Shade? He's a Shade?" Vincent said.

"Yes, believe it or not. He's a strange one. But he is mighty powerful so we listen, yes we do."

"Did he have a name before he was turned?" Vincent said.

"Yes," Brine said. He seemed to be holding back.

"What is it?" Celes said. Brine started to twitch, like something was affecting him. He started to have trouble breathing.

"What is it?" Vincent said, grabbing Brine by the coat.

"B...Branthor," Brine said, before collapsing down in the chair. Vincent stepped back, surprised at the response. He noticed that Brine didn't seem to be breathing, so leaned in close to examine him closer.

"He's dead. I don't believe it," Vincent said.

"How?" Celes felt panicked.

"Not sure, maybe it was this psychic link they seem to have. If that's the case, it means Branthor is on to us."

"It means he always has been."

"What about Alrion? Before that we must think. It's not safe here."

"I'll go on the lookout. If they try and enter tonight I'll find them."

"Good. Why don't you change out of the guard uniform before you go? I'll take care of that and figure out what to do with Brine," Vincent said.

Their day had taken a vastly darker turn.

17

DENIED ENTRY

L ara skilfully guided her companions in steering their makeshift raft towards a safe landing spot. There was a low embankment with a lot of mud, perfect for a solid dock.

"Lean more this side, paddle faster," she shouted. Alrion and Certan did their best, still somewhat confused by her angry and rapid instructions.

"Easy, easy, there," Lara said. The raft shuddered with a quick contact with the bank, but stopped completely.

"Not bad for her maiden voyage," Lara said.

"I'd go again," Alrion said.

"It was definitely a learning experience," Certan said. Lara wasn't sure if Certan was too keen on their little river excursion. But he had been a good sport. And they had made good time.

"Do you think we can reach the city gates before nightfall?" Alrion said.

"Plynth isn't that far, we should be able to. But I'm not an expert on this area, it depends on how close we landed," Lara said.

"Either way, I don't think such a thing as nightfall will be able to stop us," Certan said, looking at Lara.

"You're right, I can get us in anywhere, anytime. Provided we can find our way back onto the main path," she said, picking her way between trees and large shrubs. They were in a heavily wooded area, with no sign of any trails or paths.

After an hour of uncertain heading, they found what looked like a minor path.

"This has got to be it, let's follow it," Lara said.

"Fine by me, it's the only thing even slightly resembling a path around here," Alrion said. Certan didn't comment, just followed quietly.

"Everything alright back there?" Lara said.

"Of course, don't mind my quietness. I'm not usually that talkative anyway. It comes in fits and spurts," Certan said.

"You make talking sound like a disease," Alrion said.

"That's probably quite a good comparison. It is quite infectious, and some people are terrible carriers," Certan said. Lara laughed.

"I like your brand of humour Certan. It's a little strange, but always surprising," she said.

"I've never heard it described as such, so thank you," Certan said, performing a small bow.

"That may be the road we are looking for," Alrion said, pointing out a much wider track that was connected up ahead.

"Looks about right, let's follow it." Lara led the group there, keeping a little ahead to spot any potential dangers. When she was satisfied, she slowed down and waved the others on. They followed along and joined the main road. "Signs of life, we must be close now." Lara pointed at a few travellers in the distance.

"I have a good feeling," Alrion said.

Lara couldn't agree, something still felt off to her. It was probably just the encounter with Branthor, but her gut wouldn't let her relax.

The city gates loomed large in the distance, and Lara could see a crowd of people milling in front of them. Something was definitely off.

"Looks busy, but at least we made it in time," Alrion said.

"Something doesn't look right. I can't put my finger on it yet, but I don't think that's normal," Lara said. Alrion gave her a puzzled look but didn't question it.

As they approached they heard commotion and yelling.

"I told you something was up," Lara said. There were signs of a recent battle at the gates, with the guards bloodied and weary. They had formed a line blocking entry to the gates, and they were actively pushing people back.

"Let us in!" An older man was pleading with them.

"No entry, the gates are closed," the guard said. His tone suggested that he was sick of repeating it.

"Certan, why don't you go ask them what the problem is? Alrion will hang back and observe, and I'll tail you to see for myself," Lara said.

"Certainly," he said, and started to make this way through the crowd. He was insistent yet polite, and made consistent progress through the large throng of people. Certan stopped in front of a relatively energetic and talkative guard at the end of the formation

"Excuse me, can you please explain what all the commotion is about?" he said.

"I'm sorry but there's just been a Blighter attack. It occurred after we detained a suspicious couple, so for security reasons we are letting nobody else in. I am sorry, try again tomorrow," the guard said.

"Of course, safety is the primary concern. Although I do fear for my own safety being trapped outside. Should I be on the lookout for anyone in particular?" Certan said.

"I can't comment on specifics, but we have a drawing here," the guard said, removing a parchment, and handing it to Certan. He examined it carefully and returned it.

"And these two tried to gain entry?"

"Yes, well two people matching that description. If you spot them I advise you to keep your distance and come alert the guard of their location. They may still be at large."

"Good advice. Thank you for your assistance," Certan said, bowing.

"You're welcome, thank you for your understanding. Take care, I am sure the situation will be improved tomorrow," the guard said. Certan returned to the others as quickly as he could navigate through the impatient mob.

"Blighter attack is why they closed the gates and are keeping people out," Certan said as he joined his companions.

"That makes sense. Not good for us," Lara said.

"It gets worse. They detained a couple that look exactly like you two. They even showed me the drawing they are using for the comparison. Even if they open the gates tomorrow you can't enter. They're looking for you," Certan said.

"That, I did not expect. You contained your reaction well," Lara said.

"What! That's ridiculous. How many guards are there? Could we just storm in?" Alrion said.

"Calm down, it must be some sort of misunderstanding," Lara said.

"They think we are tainted or something. We've done nothing wrong. I can't believe it," Alrion said.

"It could be a coincidence that there was a Blighter attack, or it could be related. Either way, there's no way the two of you are passing through the gates anytime soon," Certan said.

"Maybe I can destroy part of the wall," Alrion said.

"A man with only a hammer sees everything as nails," Lara said.

"I think it would work. What do you suggest?" Alrion said.

"Certan or I should sneak in or climb the wall. We will find your parents and figure out what's going on. Then we can decide whether to pass through the city or go around it," Lara said.

"That is a good plan. I agree," Certan said.

"Sure, but it's not as fun as my idea. Magic makes everything better," Alrion threw a mock fireball at the walls.

"There'll be plenty of opportunity for that, I have no doubt. But let's start with a stealthy approach. Do you think you are best suited to infiltrate?" Certan said to Lara.

"Yes, leave this one with me. Let's find a place to camp, and once we are settled I'll come back. I'll have a better chance once the crowd disperse and the guard relaxes a little," Lara said.

"Let's go." Alrion made a start and the others followed close behind.

"What's the big rush?" Lara said to Alrion.

"It's just so frustrating. We're hitting problem after problem, it's like we are always one step behind. I'm working so hard on improving my magic, but it's not helping," Alrion said.

"There will come a time when we may need to rely on it. However, growing in strength and experience is more than just increasing your power. Most of us can achieve quite a bit without a touch of magic," Certan said.

"That makes sense. It's like there's something inside that I just need to unleash," Alrion said.

"Unfortunately, your mentor Falric is not here, I am sure he would know what to say. Maybe there's a way you can deal with that without blowing things up," Lara said.

"You're right. I'll consult my book and think it through, do some exercises. It will keep my occupied while we wait," Alrion said. They continued walking and found a nice clearing a little off the main tracks.

Certan and Alrion settled in and Lara prepared to leave. "Keep an eye on him and make sure he doesn't do anything stupid," Lara whispered to Certan.

"Of course, we'll be fine."

"Don't do anything I wouldn't do. Wish me luck," Lara said loud enough for Alrion to hear.

"Good luck," Certan said.

"Don't get caught," Alrion said.

"I'll do my best," Lara said with a wink, and dashed off into the cover of the nearby trees.

Lara took her time weaving back through the woods. She didn't want to return too quickly, and also wished to avoid being spotted by anyone. If the guard had showed the drawing to Certan, there could be others on the lookout for her and she didn't want to bring unwanted attention. Once she returned to the city gates, she noticed that the crowd had mostly dispersed. The gates were firmly closed, and there were two guards posted in a guard station above the walls.

I can't waltz in the front door, I'll need to find another way in. Without going too close, she started to skirt around the walls and see if there were any additional entrances.

As she progressed she didn't find any, but she did notice that there were no more guard towers.

"They don't expect to encounter anyone outside the main gate, I wonder if there's a way to climb the walls," Lara said to herself. Since it was quiet she approached the walls and looked at them closely. There were quite a few cracks, metallic supports, and other decorations on the wall to act as climbing aids. Of course, if she fell there was no safety net, but with the help of her dagger it would be possible.

"Only one way to find out. This better not end horribly," Lara whispered. She scrambled up the wall, using a large crack as her initial hand-hold. Next, she swung herself up to another crack, using her dagger to wedge in and hold her weight. It was a little unsteady, but worked.

Only a million manoeuvres left, Lara thought, staring up.

"Maybe I should have let Alrion blast a hole through here," she said as shuffled up to metal bar she could hang from. Her fingers started to slip, so she furiously kicked around to find a better foothold, and once she did, moved to another handhold. Sweat started to pour down her face.

Looking down, then regretting it, Lara realised that she was halfway up the wall.

May as well keep going. After some mental preparation, she began again. There was a relatively sizeable chunk of wall missing halfway up the remaining distance. If she could get there, then she would be able to rest a bit before completing the climb. Feeling a second wave of energy coming on, Lara pushed forward with confidence, spotting the best hand holds as quickly as she needed them.

With a concerted effort, she was poised to leap into the safe nook, but her feet slipped. Lashing out frantically with her dagger, she pierced the wall enough to slow her descent, find another handhold and propelling herself into the space.

"That was not very ladylike," she said, laughing quietly. Her adrenalin was pumping as she considered what could have happened. After taking a minute to calm down, she took more care approaching the last leg of the climb.

With great relief, she toppled over the top of the wall. Recognising it as a battlement, she quickly scanned both directions to see if there were any guards patrolling. She noticed a torch in the distance to her left, and started to crouch run in the opposite direction.

"Great another torch," she whispered. There was nowhere to run. She crept over to look at the way down inside the walls. There were a few houses and some trees nearby, but nothing to climb down easily.

That tree isn't so far away, she thought as she heard footsteps converging from both directions. Not wanting a confrontation, she leapt out into the darkness, aiming for a relatively thick tree branch. She landed on it, but couldn't maintain her balance, and stumbled further into the tree. Her hand couldn't seem to grasp any of the branches and she braced herself for a rough landing.

Suddenly she stopped. One arm had somehow snagged something, and she was hanging in mid-air. It was hard to see what was below her, but it looked like grass.

"Please don't break anything," she told herself as she let go of the branch.

18

A NEW LEAD

A s she saw the ground approaching Lara put her arms out and tried to go into a roll. She had partial success, but didn't land straight and tumbled out of control thumping into another tree trunk. Everything was dead quiet.

I'm alive, but how noisy was that? she thought. The eerie calm continued, raising the tension. She heard voices conversing above her, but couldn't hear what they were saying.

"I hope those guards didn't notice," she wondered. When nothing happened, she slowly tested all her limbs. Everything seemed to work. Taking care, she stood up a bit shakily, but as she walked everything seemed to improve.

"Let's not do that again," Lara said to herself. She tried to appear like she belonged, as she stumbled around looking for a main road.

"It would help if it wasn't so damn dark," she whispered. But the darkness was also useful, since it kept her hidden. She crept past the nearest houses and found her way to some signs of life.

"Now, assuming Vincent and Celes are here, where would they be?" Lara mused. She decided to try and head to the most populated area of the city. That would be a good place to start. It just depended on whether the couple wanted to be found or not.

Lara didn't notice many people on the streets, which made sense if there had been a Blighter attack recently. That made her job a little easier, although she could stand out a little because of it. The buildings became bigger and bigger and Lara realised she had reached the main hub.

She had been here before, and as she stopped to look the place became more familiar. Her unorthodox entry and the dark had confused her a bit. Deciding to take a methodical approach, she walked over to the main gates to start her search. The buildings in the area were devoted to the guards, and it looked like they had borne the brunt of the Blighter attack.

What drove them here all of a sudden? Not a good sign. Moving on she came to a crossroads. To her left she could continue on to the trade and commercial district, or she could go right and enter the worker's area.

Vincent likes to associate with other blacksmiths, but I doubt he'll be able to stay there. I'll try the local inns, Lara thought. She headed left and followed the lights and signs of life.

The bleak, quiet streets she had encountered quickly melted away. It seemed like the people who weren't hiding indoors were out celebrating. As Lara walked past, she decided to try the quietest inn. There was no way that Vincent and Celes would be joining the celebrations.

After scouting a few locations Lara settled on 'The Jocular Javelin-Thrower'. The crowd wasn't bursting out onto the street, and the noise level seemed lower. She stepped in and looked around.

The clientele was a lot less jocular than whoever the inn was named after, with minimal conversation. Most were just nursing their drinks in silence. However, Lara did spot some friendly faces in the corner. She made a beeline for them.

"Bit of a depressing place, isn't it?" Lara said.

"Lara! Great to see you!" Vincent said, jumping out of his chair to envelop Lara in a big hug. "Where's Alrion?" he said, instantly suspicious.

"Camping outside with Certan. I had to climb the bloody wall to get in." Lara made a show of dusting off her clothes.

"Yes, I'm not surprised. It's been a bit of an adventure here. Take a seat, we have some information to share with you," Celes said.

"I'm sure you do, but you won't believe what happened to us," Lara said as she sat down. Vincent and Celes sat quietly, waiting to hear.

"We ran into Branthor. He's become a Shade!" Lara said. She looked at Vincent and Celes's reactions, and was confused.

"You don't seem surprised about that?" Lara said.

"The Shade part is interesting, but otherwise it confirms what we just heard. Branthor is calling himself Wraith and running quite a network of Tainted ones," Celes said.

"Figures, we have this absolutely crazy encounter and you have uncovered the same information."

"Tell us what happened," Vincent said.

"We went the alternate route, and nothing interesting happened. We saw this figure on the bridge, and it looked like a Shade. We attacked it with everything we had, and nothing seemed to really damage it."

"That's unusual. How did you get away?"

"It grabbed Certan and used him to talk to us. It seemed distracted, or unable to fully control its new form. But you know what worked on it? That sword you made. We managed to sever the hand holding Branthor, and it raged, destroying the bridge, and disappearing," Lara said.

"Good to know we have a weapon against it. We've had some similar excitement here, finding a Tainted One deep in Branthor's network. He summoned the Blighters to attack us. We think that perhaps as he was talking to us he was killed via his mental link," Vincent said.

"How is that even possible?" Lara said. She felt a chill go down her spine.

"I am not sure, but clearly there is a lot we don't know about how they operate. Let's get you some food and drink and talk this all through," Vincent said.

Lara relaxed a little, and settled back into the chair.

Hours later, they had shared all the details of their exploits.

"So where to from here," Celes said.

"I think we should continue our investigation, and let Alrion continue to the desert," Vincent said.

"So, we're the diversion?" Celes said.

"Yes. I don't like what happened here, but at least that army of Blighters was not directed at Alrion."

"It may help, keeping us a smaller group. We have Certan to guide us there," Lara said.

"Yes, he's all you need. Hopefully with this information you can dodge Wraith and his attackers more easily," Vincent said.

"Wraith?" Lara said.

"I don't think it is worth calling him Branthor anymore. He has become something else. May as well use his new name."

"Wraith it is. I guess I'll return to Alrion tonight and we can leave tomorrow, avoiding the city."

"That's best, they'll still be looking for you. Perhaps even more keenly since they have associated the Blighter attack with your presence," Celes said.

"More forest. Yay," Lara said.

"It'll be worth it. One more thing," Vincent said, leaning in closer.

"Yes?"

"Take care in the desert. It's a bleak place, so I hear. We may try and join you later if possible," Vincent said.

Lara said her goodbyes and left the inn. She felt re-energised by the familiar company, food, and the news. There wasn't much for her to go on, but she still felt like it was a success. She had found Alrion's parents, shared the situation and learnt some key information that may help them travel more safely.

Lara walked back the way she came, wondering if she should try and sneak out via the main gate or try her climbing trick again.

"I really don't want to scale that wall, once is enough," she said to herself, looking over at the looming structure. As she went to turn she almost walked into a man standing right in front of her.

"Sorry," she said, before looking more closely. He was tall and in a dark cloak, his face hidden.

"Not a problem, I did in fact step in front of you," the man said. He was in no hurry to move either.

"It's you! What's going on?" Lara said.

"Come this way so we can talk more," the man said. Lara followed along, puzzled at why this mysterious wizard was contacting her again.

"How are you?" he said.

"Fine. We've had a few adventures, but nothing we couldn't handle."

"Good. Things are going to become more difficult soon. You won't be able to hide your journey to the desert," the wizard said. Lara stopped in her tracks.

"How do you know about that?"

"It doesn't matter, let's just say I am invested in your journey. You're going to need help. Alrion needs more training," the wizard said. He stopped off the main path, under a tree.

"Give this to the monk, he will understand it," he said, handing Lara a slip of paper. She unfolded it and read the contents.

"What is this?" she said.

"Directions to a wizard who lives in the desert. You must make sure that Alrion meets him. He is called the Desert Wizard for good reason."

"He's going to wonder where I got this information," Lara said.

"You'll figure something out. What's important is that you find him and that he trains Alrion."

Lara thought that was a good plan. But she didn't trust this mysterious wizard. "I can do that. How is it that you can just tell me what to do?" she said.

"Because I am asking things you already want to do."

"That doesn't make any sense."

"It will, in time. I won't hold you up any longer, good luck," the wizard said.

"How will I contact you if I need help?"

"Alrion knows how."

"But he doesn't know about you?"

"He will discover the way. Don't worry that about that. Just don't lose that note, it's critical," the wizard said. He gave Lara a short wave and vanished.

"Gone again. How do I keep getting caught up in these things?" Lara wondered. She pocketed the note and thought about how to get out.

"Not climbing that wall again," she told herself and headed for the main gate.

She noticed that there was only a light presence guarding the gate.

Not trying to keep people from going out. It would be easy to sneak past, but the gate itself would be an issue. However, she did notice something peculiar. She crept closer, avoiding the guards, and sticking to the darkness. Once she reached the gate she took a closer look.

"This is useful," she whispered. There was a square cut into the side of the gate. It looked like it opened. She carefully pushed it, to see what it did. The square pushed forward, revealing a small opening in the door.

Probably used for accepting things through the door, or negotiating. I wonder if I could fit, Lara thought. There was only one way to find out. She glanced back and saw that the guards were continuing their patrol, not particularly paying attention to the gate.

"Here goes." Lara grasped onto the gate frame with both her hands and thrust her head through the square gap. With a little finessing, she was able to get her shoulders through then she fell out onto the other side. A quick movement as she landed helped soften the blow, and she stood up quickly. There were no signs of movement on the other side of the gate.

That was a lot easier. She dusted herself off and walked off into the night, slowly increasing her pace. The crowds had subsided, but she could see small fires in the distance, where some were camping overnight.

All they had to do was climb the wall, she thought with a laugh. Quickly weaving through the woods, she found Certan and Alrion seated comfortably leaning against some trees. Alrion had hung a magical light sphere from one of the hanging branches, which illuminated the area nicely.

"You look like you've had a bit of an adventure," Alrion said, looking up from the books he was reading.

"Don't get me started. Next time I consider climbing a city wall, just stop me please," Lara said.

"That's quite an impressive feat. How you did get down?" Certan said.

"With great difficulty and luck. I'll fill you in on all the details but there's two important things. First, there was a Blighter attack in the city. It was due to a Tainted One. He was looking for Alrion and me," Lara said.

"That's not a good sign. What's the other thing? Did you find my parents?" Alrion said.

"Yes, they told me all about the man they discovered. We think the Tainted share some sort of mental link and coordinate their movements that way," Lara said.

"That may explain a lot." Alrion looked deep in thought.

"We need to better understand our enemy," Certan said.

"We have news too," Alrion said.

"What's that?" Lara said with concern. Nothing should have happened while she was away.

"I found another message in this notebook. Take a look." Alrion handed it to Lara to review.

Find Ashra in the desert, he will advise you further.

"Who is Ashra?" Lara said. She had a sinking feeling in her stomach that she knew what the answer would be.

"I have heard that name before, he's a wizard. Hates visitors, which is why he lives in the desert," Certan said.

"Interesting. Do you know how to find him?" Lara said.

"No, he doesn't like to be found."

"It's a lead right, we will figure it out," Alrion said.

"I wasn't sure what to make of this, but I think it will help." Lara retrieved the slip of paper the mysterious wizard had given her and handed it to Alrion.

"Where did you get this?" Alrion said.

"Some raving drunk was going on about a wizard in the desert. I thought it would be a good lead, so I stole these directions," she said.

"This is awfully coincidental, you finding this and me seeing this message. What did that man look like?" Alrion was looking at Lara with a questioning gaze.

"Unremarkable. Maybe he got it from someone else? He had nothing else of interest to say or on him," Lara said. Alrion turned the paper over and handed it to Certan.

"I can follow these directions. It would make sense to head there before the temple. It's more or less on the way. Additional training sounds quite important to me," Certan said.

"Then I guess we see where they lead. But I don't like this. I feel like we're being led by the nose and I don't know by who," Alrion said.

"Wow, I thought you would be happy with this. It's another wizard. Isn't that good?" Lara said.

"Sorry, it's not your fault. Why don't you tell us more about what my parents said? There could be something in there that is crucial," Alrion said.

Lara was happy to do so. She didn't want him thinking too much on how she could have happened upon that information just as the mysterious message was left. At least now she knew for sure who was leaving the notes in Alrion's book. But she still didn't know his identity.

Next time, I'll find a way.

19

ENTER THE DESERT

The next morning Alrion rose early. He didn't sleep well and was anxious to get a move on.

"I just have to see if there's anything to this wizard. Or if it's a trap, I want it over with," Alrion said.

"We can rush to get started, but we mustn't rush the journey. The desert is a hard place to traverse. I know the way, but we must take care. If we are attacked while we are weakened it will be disastrous," Certan said.

"Are there many tainted in the desert?" Lara said.

"It depends where you go. Usually not, as it is not a good environment for them to survive. I saw more than I expected on this journey, so we should be prepared for anything," Certan said.

"We won't be able to go through the city, so we may lose some time. Does it matter which way we enter?" Lara said.

"It does, but all our current options are equivalent in utility and danger. This detour won't have much impact. But I do agree we should start now," Certan said. Alrion did a final check, and they left their makeshift camp site.

"Do we need to stock up on water?" Alrion said as they walked.

"No, provided we take a small amount with us. The wizard will have a source," Certan said.

"That's if we find him. You said he doesn't like visitors," Lara said.

"We will find a way, it's too important," Alrion said.

"Exactly. Besides, you have me. I can survive in the desert, and so you will too," Certan said. They spotted a small fast flowing river on their walk and stopped to fill a flask each. Certan paused, looking over his flask. He swapped it with another then filled it to the brim.

"What was that about?" Alrion said. Certan retrieved the flask he had hidden away.

"For a long time this flask here meant something different. It was my supply of alcohol and everything that went with that. But now it is something else, something better," he said.

"Are you using it?" Lara said.

"No. It's my penance, a reminder of my excesses." Certan's voice had a pang of regret.

"A reminder of how strong you are," Alrion said.

"Thank you, I will remember that." Certan put the flask away and started off once more.

They took a meandering route, avoiding the city, and using the best paths available. This took longer than they had initially wanted. Slowly Alrion saw the terrain transform. The colours of the grass and plants slowly changed, from a bright green to a washed out green and yellow. The grass become thinner and shorter and the trees were also reduced in height.

"You can see the availability of water decreasing," Certan said, pointing out the surroundings.

"I was just thinking the same thing," Alrion said.

"Are we close?" Lara said.

"Yes, we are, we have come further than I had expected. We will stop soon," Certan said.

"Stop?" I don't see the desert? How far is it?" Lara said.

"Not much further, it's a little deceptive. However, from here on it is best to travel at night. We need to rest soon, so we can make proper progress when it is cooler," Certan said.

"You're the expert," Alrion said, slapping Certan on the back.

"Trust me, it's better this way," Certan said. Alrion was trying to imagine the intensity of the heat, but struggled.

"I trust you. It's probably going to be one of those things that needs to be experienced to be explained," Alrion said.

"I can explain, but you won't know. Not really," Certan said.

"Night works for me," Lara said.

"We already knew that," Alrion said. Certan let out a small chuckle.

"Let's make camp up there, it looks relatively sheltered and quiet," he said. They put down their equipment and tried to make the area comfortable for sleeping. Alrion had difficulty getting to sleep, as it was only the afternoon. But sleep eventually found him when he least expected.

A firm hand woke him from sleep and Alrion noticed Certan standing over him.

"It's time, great," Alrion said with a start, jumping up. Certan and Lara were ready to go.

"I see you took the time to get yourselves sorted before waking me," he said.

"You need your beauty sleep," Lara said. Certan had a grin on his face.

"Sure, sure. I'll just need a minute," Alrion took his time preparing, not wanting to miss anything.

"Let's go," Certan said, heading out. Lara and Alrion followed close.

"How dark will it get?" Alrion said.

"Travelling by moonlight is possible, depending on its size. However, we may need additional light," Certan said.

"Just let me know," Alrion said.

"I will, although I suspect you won't need my prompting. We will be entering the desert shortly," Certan said, pointing at a spot in the distance. It was harder to see, but the grasses seemed to almost completely withered out.

"There's still some grass, or maybe shrubs," Lara said.

"Yes, that's normal. Not every part is completely sandy, although the overall effect is the same," Certan said. They walked on in silence, taking in the new environment. The ground was shifting more under their feet, gradually become less solid. Certan walked with purpose, but still regularly paused to get his bearings.

"I thought you were the desert master, we seem to be stopping a lot," Lara said.

"Realising the folly in having contempt for the desert is usually the last lesson one learns," Certan said and Lara laughed. Alrion stumbled on a small mound that he didn't spot and paused to create a ball of light. He visualised it attaching to an invisible string and floating above them. As he walked he looked at it, and monitored its progress, pleased that it seemed to be behaving as he expected.

"The light is a big help, it's not usually practical to have one," Certan said.

"Happy to help, and it'll stop me tripping as well," Alrion said.

"How can you make sense of these directions?" Lara said.

"They rely on markers and waypoints that only those familiar with the desert would understand. Whoever wrote these knows the place well. Many people would be unable to use these references to find the way," Certan said.

"Good thing we have you. I've been thinking and I want your opinion. Do you think this is a setup?" Alrion said.

"Do you mean are we walking into a trap?" Certan said.

"Yes exactly. We recently learned that Wraith as he calls himself now can communicate and coordinate a network of tainted. What if this lead is just to direct us how he wants?"

"This lead was definitely not from a tainted person," Lara said.

"Maybe not directly, but maybe it was planted with that person?" Alrion said. Lara felt confident that he was wrong, but was unable to prove it.

"I just don't see it," Lara said.

"Regardless, we can prepare ourselves and look out for signs. It would be very hard to hide that kind of presence in the desert," Certan said.

"Fair enough. Let's remain cautious," Alrion wasn't convinced that they would really find a wizard out here. Part of him was also anxious that maybe they would. How would a wizard react to him? Especially one that hates company.

The walk dragged on, but Certan kept a strong pace that made Alrion feel like they were at least getting somewhere. But he had no idea of the distances required, so just followed along. He played over scenarios in his head, for how he would deal with Blighters, another Shade or even a hostile wizard. The last one was the most worrying. He still felt like he lucked out when taking on Branthor, and wasn't confident he could handle himself with an experienced wizard.

This is all crazy. I shouldn't have to be worrying about wizards. The creatures of the Blight are supposed to be the enemy, Alrion thought.

Certan paused, reviewing the directions again. He held them up to Alrion's magical light.

"We are up to the last step. This is unusual. I was sure that nothing lay down this way, but perhaps that is why the instructions are correct," he said.

"If I wanted to be left alone, I would live in a desert in a place where locals thought nothing existed," Lara said.

"I still keep thinking what kind of person would do this? Can we even expect help?" Alrion said.

"We shall remain cautious, but there's no need to worry. All types live in the desert, let us give this wizard the benefit of the doubt," Certan said.

"You're right. This wizard is going to help, one way or another," Alrion said.

"I'll make sure of that," Lara said, flashing a smile at Alrion. The party turned off and took a right into an even more sparse area of the desert. There were no signs of passage, and nothing to mark the way. Yet Certan kept walking with confidence. Slowly but surely, they started going through their water supply. The journey became increasingly difficult, as there were no markers to show how they were progressing and they could see the sun beginning to rise in the distance.

"I hope we get there soon, otherwise we may be stranded in the sun," Lara said.

"We have ways of dealing with that, but yes let's hope we find him soon," Certan said. They trudged on, but soon they saw what looked like a small building in the distance.

"Finally!" Alrion said.

"It exists. The desert is so tricky, I'm relieved that we made it," Certan said.

"I thought you were more confident than that," Lara said.

"I was confident that we were following the directions properly, and that we were reaching the proper landmarks. However, this wizard is like a myth of the desert. There are many tales of him, but nobody you meet has actually seen him," Certan said.

"Don't speak too soon, we may be in the same boat. Does that hut look a little deserted to you?" Lara said. As they approached they could see inside the hut. It was tiny and sparse, with a mattress, some blankets and a table being the only pieces of furniture. A thin layer of dust covered everything, suggesting that the place had been vacant for some time.

Certan ran his hand along the surfaces, and examined the quantity of dust.

"This is not unusual for the desert. It could be that someone has just been away for a matter of days. We should not give up hope," he said.

"Any clues here?" Alrion gently probed the mattress to see if it hid anything, and looked over the table.

"I don't see anything to suggest that a wizard lives here. But maybe that's the point? He doesn't like to be visited after all," Lara said.

"What's that over there?" Alrion pointed at the lone window in the hut and what was visible in the distance. It looked like a tree.

"An oasis? That would explain why he chose this location and why he may not need to spend as much time here," Certan said.

"Oasis? Those are real?" Lara said.

"Yes, but they were quite rare and well-guarded secrets. There are very easily overwhelmed if overused," he said.

"I could use a drink, and maybe we will find the wizard there," Alrion said.

"It's worth a look," Lara said.

"Of course, but let us approach with caution. There could be traps." Certan led the way, stepping cautiously across the desert sand. Lara and Alrion followed close behind, looking around for signs of danger.

"Something seems off, but I cannot describe what it is. Stay alert," Certan said.

"I'm ready," Alrion said.

Lara removed her dagger from her jacket and twirled it in her hand. As they advanced they could see the tree was next to a small pond that was encircled by small green tufts of grass and shrubs. "Signs of life, that's promising," she said.

"We shall see." Certan walked closer and the other two kept pace. As they were about to reach the tree it started to shimmer. And once they stepped closer still, the tree vanished. Instead they were confronted with a stone wall.

"A mirage? Classic," Lara said.

"I suspected something was off. I didn't sense the amount of life that I expected from an oasis," Certan said.

"There's something to be said for an appreciation of the classics. How did you find this place?" a male voice said from behind them.

Alrion spun quickly to see who it was.

20

AN IMPORTANT LEAD

V incent escorted Lara out of the inn, and made sure she was safe before returning inside. He navigated through the crowd and sat back down next to his wife.

"Things are escalating a lot faster than you expected," Celes said.

"I know. We have underestimated what we are up against. I did not think that Alrion would be intercepted like that," Vincent said.

"Hopefully after Lara tells them of Wraith's network, they can be more careful. At least they are near the desert now."

"Yes, it will be easier to hide in the desert and less chance of running into Tainted. I don't think they like it in there."

"Fingers crossed. So, what do we do now? Investigate here more or try and meet up with them?" Celes said.

"We're definitely on their radar, after that attack and the death of the Tainted guard. We would lead them straight to Alrion wouldn't we?"

"I think so. My gut tells me there's more here. I doubt that Wraith's network would end with one guard. Let's dig around here more, and see what we can find. Worst case scenario all we do is act as a distraction which still helps them."

"Sounds good to me." Vincent looked quite satisfied.

"You're just glad you get to do more blacksmithing. Do you miss it that much?" Celes said, making a face at him.

"No, but it does help me focus. I feel like we have been caught off guard, so I'm glad to slow down a little and feel our way forward rather than acting rashly. Banging a few things with a hammer is just a bonus," Vincent said.

"Let's head back then. It is safe to return, right?"

"Yes, there's nothing there," Vincent said.

"Good I would find it hard to sleep otherwise," Celes said and stood up quickly from the chair. Vincent walked ahead and they left the inn together.

The next morning Vincent went to find John, and made sure the blacksmith was distracted while Celes returned the armour she had borrowed.

"Why don't you start over there, I've got some pieces that need finishing. Here's a sample of how they should look." John handed Vincent a metallic cylinder that looked like it fit around the arm.

"Sure, I can follow that."

"Come grab me if you're unsure, we'll move on to the tricky stuff later," John said. Vincent walked over and placed the finished piece next to the pile of half-finished ones.

"I was pretty sneaky, wasn't I?" Celes whispered.

"You were, don't blow it now," Vincent said.

"I'll be around here and there, have fun," Celes said and quickly crept away. Vincent got to work on the first piece. He could see that it was a simple job and wouldn't require any input from John. He decided to lose himself in the work for a while.

After a few hours, he heard some commotion and walked over to investigate.

"I know for sure that you're selling pieces on the side. Don't even try and deny it," a female voice said.

"As I have said before, I don't do that. I value this contract, and I have no idea what you are talking about." John looked quite frustrated. As Vincent approached he could see a female guard standing over the blacksmith.

"We had a female impersonating a guard wearing a full uniform. We have checked and this is the only place it could have come from," the female guard said.

"I'll check again, but everything is here." John walked off.

"Yes?" the guard said looking at Vincent.

"I just heard an argument and came over. I'll leave you to it," Vincent said.

The guard instantly dismissed him with her eyes and returned to glaring at John.

Vincent walked back to his work area and looked around. "Where is she when you need her," he said, muttering to himself.

"Right here," Celes said.

"Good. Do you hear the argument over there?" Vincent said.

"Yes, hard not to."

"Do you think it is suspicious?"

"Definitely. Only the man we captured knew I was there. This guard must be Tainted as well."

"You're welcome," Vincent said and returned to his work.

"That's right, you go back to the blacksmithing and I'll follow her," Celes said.

"Sounds good to me," Vincent said grinning. Celes crept away and found a good vantage point to watch the guard.

John returned and repeated his story. The female guard spat in disgust and stormed off.

~

"Here we go," Celes said to herself. She started walking, keeping a safe distance between herself and the guard.

"Now where is she off to," Celes wondered. The guard had turned to the right, veering away from the guard building. Celes upped her speed, rushing to the corner so that she would not lose her lead. Once she reached the corner she peeked around it. The guard was looking back to see if she was being followed, but Celes managed to quickly hide herself.

Just as well I was cautious, Celes thought. A few seconds later she ducked her head out and saw the guard turning another corner. Celes quietly dashed down the street, slowing as she reached the corner and followed the same process. As before the guard was carefully looking behind.

"The cat and mouse game continues," Celes whispered. After rounding the next corner there was a long straight road. The guard walked quickly, not looking back. Celes made sure that she walked near other people, or buildings so that she could hide herself if required. But the guard seemed to have decided that nobody was following and just charged ahead.

Celes noticed a building at the end of the street. It had a high pointed roof, with lavish stonework on the walls and a series of steps leading into the entrance.

"That looks quite formal, this is interesting," Celes said to herself. There was a steady stream of people filing in and out of the building, so Celes upped her pace and entered alongside another group. Inside she found a large open room, with benches all around the sides. It looked like there were public officials working there, making notes, and having conversations. She looked around the room, trying to spot the guard. It was almost too late, but she noticed the guard turning into a room at the end. Celes quickly crossed the space and glanced up at the sign.

Council chambers, this just gets even more interesting. She stepped inside, and looked around. There was no sign of the guard, but a door slammed in the distance. Celes approached the source of the sound.

At the end of the hall there were two doors, one on the left and one on the right.

Which one? she wondered as she crept down the hall. It wasn't obvious as she progressed, but she did hear voices coming from one of the rooms.

This must be it. Celes checked the other door, and it opened. Nobody was inside.

"That was lucky," she whispered. But she wouldn't be able to repeat her trick of listening in, because the rooms were on opposite sides of the corridor. She looked up at the ceiling and didn't notice any obvious places to climb up.

I just have to risk it, she thought and returned to the hall. She left the door open for the empty room and sidled up to the other door to listen closely. As she pressed closer she could make out the voices more distinctly.

"So, you have no leads at all then," a male voice said.

"I'm sorry councillor. We have exhausted all the avenues. It's not apparent how the intruder got access to a uniform," the female guard said.

"Unacceptable! Wraith will not tolerate this kind of failure. We need to deal with this quickly. Do you understand why we are meeting in person?" the councillor said.

"Yes, because we don't want to broadcast the fact that we have nothing yet."

"Exactly. Questions are being asked, we need something immediately. What's the best lead?"

"I've cross-examined all the guards. Everything was accounted for and verified. It can't be a guard. It has to be the blacksmith."

"But he's adamant about not creating more uniforms? Do you believe him?"

"Yes, I do. But maybe someone accessed his stocks. It's the only explanation available," the guard said.

"Go back there, and be friendlier this time. Try and find out how someone could have gained access. Maybe ask about unfamiliar faces showing up. We need to really work this, you don't want to see what happens to people who fail," the councillor said.

"I understand, I'll go back to the blacksmith with a new approach," the guard said. Celes quickly backed away from the door and returned to the other room. She closed the door as quietly as possible and waited to hear what was happening next.

A minute passed by slowly, and another. But soon she heard the sound of the other door opening and footsteps proceeding down the corridor. Once she decided that it was relatively safe she slowly opened the door enough to catch a glimpse of the person leaving. It was the guard, as expected.

The councillor must still be inside, Celes thought. But she didn't have a name or a face to identify him. She had to decide when to confront him.

I can't do it here, it's too public. I'll have to tail him and find an opportunity. She wanted to go warn Vincent that there would be additional questioning, but this lead was too important She had to follow the trail further.

He'll be fine, I'll check in later, she decided and waited for the councillor to make a move.

Within a few minutes, she heard footsteps and a door slamming. She listened to the steps retreating down the hall then snuck a peek. There was a balding man in a long black robe about to exit the hallway. She quickly retreated back into the room in case he looked back, then entered the hallway.

He had already left, so she made her way down the corridor as quickly as possible. She took care leaving the council chambers to make sure she was not watched. It looked safe so she quickly mingled with a group wandering through the hallway.

Searching the crowd, she spotted the councillor nearing the exit. She sped up, ducking in-between people, and trying not to draw too much attention.

I'm just someone late for an appointment, Celes thought. She had to make sure she caught up with the councillor once he left the building to keep on his trail. As Celes left the building she slowed then stopped. People were walking in all directions, some of them wearing the same black robe. Again and again she looked everywhere trying to find the balding man. Finally, she saw him turn into a side street and rushed to catch up.

I'm probably going too fast, she thought but it didn't matter. It was fine for people to notice her, it was so important to find this councillor. He was clearly high up in the group of Tainted and would have valuable information. Celes reached the street he had entered and stopped to assess. She was just in time to watch him enter a house at the end of the street.

Hopefully that's where he lives. She walked with more care down the street, trying to fit in. She looked over the houses, and noticed that they were all quite large and had gardens. It was clearly a special street reserved for people of importance who also had strong finances. As she arrived at the house she noticed that it had a large iron gate in front. The gate wasn't locked but it looked quite noisy. Celes walked up and down and found a smaller section that could be climbed.

I wonder how many of these I have climbed in my life, she thought with a laugh. In seconds, she was up and over, landing softly on her feet. She rocked a little, and regained her balance.

"Not as easy as it once was," Celes said to herself. But she had entered the property without alerting anyone. Rather than entering through the front door, she walked down the side of the house and looked for a servant's entrance. About halfway down she spotted a plain door and tried the handle. It was unlocked.

"Here we go," Celes whispered and entered the house. She could hear people milling about, and the sound of clanking pots and pans. Avoiding the kitchen, she headed towards what she thought looked like more formal spaces. She passed through two sitting rooms and spotted a library at the end of the house. She couldn't hear anything but decided to investigate anyway. In her experience, rich people liked to pretend the help didn't exist, and libraries were set up for that quite nicely.

She padded quietly down the hall, using the long rug to hide her footsteps. She kept her eyes and ears open, but couldn't notice any signs of life. But her instincts told her this was the right place, so she persisted. She couldn't move on until she had eliminated it as an option.

As she reached the doorway she noticed that a large reading chair had been moved and there was a man sitting there looking out at her.

"Please, come in," he said.

Not again. I must be getting sloppy. Twice now she had been caught snooping by Tainted.

"Did you prepare me a chair?" she said, acting like she expected it.

"Sorry no, I had no time to arrange for additional furnishings. You'll have to remain standing where I can see you," he said. There was a hint of venom to his polite talk.

"What would you like to discuss?" Celes said, giving him a chance to open the conversation. He gave her a positively evil grin.

21

THE MIRAGE

The man before them was dressed in light sand-coloured robes. His hair was a mixture of black and grey, and was tied back but uncut. He had a wild beard and fierce green eyes.

"The desert wizard himself," Certan said.

"You have me at a loss. Yes, I am Ashra. Who are you? And I must repeat my question: how did you find this place?"

"We had directions. I'm Alrion and I am a wizard," Alrion said.

"I can see that. Very few people know how to get here. I'll need to find out more about those directions. But for now, why are you here?" Ashra said.

"We're heading to the desert temple, so that I can undertake the trial of the monks. I was hoping to get your help," Alrion said.

"Desert temple eh? I take it he's one of the monks. Looks a bit out of sorts though," Ashra said, pointing at Certan.

"Hello my name is Certan. I am accompanying Alrion to assist with his quest and will rejoin the monks," Certan said.

"Then who are you?" Ashra said to Lara.

"The name's Lara. I am a specialist in the art of acquiring hard to get things. I am also assisting with Alrion's quest," Lara said.

"A wizard, a thief and a monk. What an odd bunch. So, tell me, what is this quest you are all talking about?"

"I will cleanse the Blight from the world," Alrion said simply. Ashra was silent for a moment, then burst out laughing.

"Oh, that's cute. Cleanse the Blight from the world. You would sooner cleanse the air from it than accomplish that," Ashra said.

"My grandfather cleansed Avaria, I can recreate his spell. A key part of what I need is at the temple and guarded by the monks," Alrion said.

Ashra abruptly stopped laughing and started stroking his beard. "Granthion, yes I remember him. No doubt you want to master the power of Will, that's what the monks are known for. It would take great Will indeed to cleanse the Blight. Come back to the hut and tell me more about your journey so far and I will decide whether I can help you," Ashra said. He started walking off without waiting for an answer. Alrion looked at Certan and Lara for input.

"We've nothing to lose, let's see what he thinks," Lara said.

"Agreed. He seems to know about the monks, he may even be able to give us additional insights or advice in addition to any wizard training," Certan said.

"I hope he's not completely crazy," Alrion said and started walking. As they entered the hut they could see three glasses filled with water and a clear jug nearby also full.

"Drink your fill and tell me a story," Ashra said. He settled into some cushions in the corner. Alrion had to look again to trust his eyes. The hut seemed a lot nicer and much more furnished than when they had passed through.

"Just a parlour trick to confuse any that may stumble through here. Please sit," Ashra said. Alrion found somewhere to sit, and began to talk.

A few hours later, the three companions had shared their story. Ashra had been quiet and not asked anything.

"That's it?" he said.

"Yes," Alrion said.

"You're incredibly lucky, you should have died several times already," Ashra said.

"You're probably right," Alrion said.

"No, I'm definitely right. It's not just luck, there's something else at play here." Alrion didn't like the implication.

"What do you mean?" Alrion said.

"You have the mark of a wizard on you. Is Falric the only one you travelled with?"

"Yes."

"There was nobody else?" Ashra said. He stared intensely at Alrion.

"Just one thing," Alrion said reluctantly. He retrieved his notebook from his pack and showed it to Ashra.

"Ah, now this is interesting. It's a wizard communicator. You can share messages anywhere across the world. Where did you get this?"

"I found it in the wizard academy. As part of my initiation I was directed to select a relic at random from their store. This was it," Alrion said.

"And Falric knew about it?"

"Yes."

"When did you receive the first message?"

"After I visited the Pool of Knowledge. After Falric died. "

"Are you sure that Falric died? He was more of a thinker than a fighter. He would know how to use these quite effectively, and he might just continue to assist you with this," Ashra said.

"I have wondered, but I couldn't find any sign of him. But I can't help thinking that if these messages were from him, he would tell me," Alrion said.

"Perhaps, let's leave that as something to puzzle out later. But I definitely believe that a wizard is monitoring your progress. How did you get the directions to come here?" Ashra said.

"I found them," Lara said.

"Found them? Where?"

"Somebody was boasting that they had insider knowledge on the desert, and could find a wizard. I pickpocketed him," Lara said.

"No, that doesn't make sense. Show me the directions," Ashra said. Certan stood up and handed over the slip of paper.

"These are too specific meaning the person who wrote it must have knowledge of this place. Very few do, and they would not commit it to paper unless absolutely necessary. Something is wrong," Ashra said.

"Well that's what happened," Lara said, with an annoyed and defensive tone.

"If you insist, but I must wonder. Who really gave you these directions," Ashra said. He paused and stared off into the distance.

"Well, either way we made it here. Are you going to help us? We answered all your questions and told you everything," Alrion said.

"Maybe. I need to see something first," Ashra said.

"What?"

"I need to see you in action. Beat me in a fight and I'll consider helping you."

"Seriously? If I can beat you in a fight I probably don't need your help," Alrion said.

"Your journey of learning is never ended. I don't care if you drank from the Pool of Knowledge. There is always more to learn from others. There's a free lesson. But my requirement stands. You will get nothing from me until you beat me," Ashra said.

"If that's how it is, I'll just be leaving," Alrion said, standing up quickly. He had pinned so many hopes on finding this wizard, despite not really looking forward to it. But the wizard had just cast doubt on them all, and refused to help. He wasn't going to waste his time any further.

"By all means, show yourself out," Ashra said. Alrion stormed out of the hut and started walking. Lara and Certan quickly caught up to him.

"You're being impulsive, we need his help. You almost died fighting Branthor the first time. We couldn't really manage him the second time. What's your plan?" Lara said.

"She's right, Ashra must know a lot of useful information. Maybe there's strategies or special applications of your magic that will be key to our success," Certan said.

"He's just an arrogant loner who wants to show off. I don't have time for that. The sooner we get to the next trial, the sooner I'll learn something useful." Alrion increased his speed.

"We need to regroup, we cannot progress without proper water supplies and it's unwise to travel in the heat of the day," Certan said.

"I've left now, I don't want to go crawling back," Alrion said.

"We've come a long way, but we can't throw it all away now. Swallow your pride and don't risk our lives because of your childishness!" Lara shouted. She stopped walking. Certan stopped beside her.

Alrion stopped and looked back at them. He then looked ahead. Something was off. Alrion walked slowly forward. "Unbelievable," Alrion stopped and turned back to his friends. "Look at this wall. Does it look familiar?" Alrion said.

"That's the same wall that we came across at the mirage," Certan said.

"He's messing with us still," Alrion said.

"I'm impressed," Certan said.

"Clearly he doesn't want to let you go yet. At least talk to him again." Lara had calmed down and looked Alrion in the eyes.

He could see the concern on her face. "Looks like I don't have a choice," Alrion said, and turned to head back. The other two followed close.

Certan marvelled at the illusion as they walked.

Ashra was seated casually on a pillow, and he appeared surprised that they had returned.

"Welcome back," he said.

"Nice trick," Alrion said.

"It's not a trick. How do you think I've lived here all these years?"

"So, I figured you weren't finished. What else was there to discuss?"

"I know I'm a little unorthodox, and you do seem a bit unsettled by my approach. But this is a necessary step. I must test you in the heat of battle, and you must hold nothing back. Can you do that?"

"I can. I just don't understand why," Alrion said.

"It's not a big thing, you won't be hurt. Is there something else troubling you?" Ashra said. He stared at Alrion, which made him feel as if the eccentric wizard could hear all his thoughts. Alrion felt a cold shiver run down his spine.

"I'm just a little nervous about my power. It's a little wild, and I've had very little training." Alrion found that very hard to admit.

"Don't you worry, that's what I would expect. Do you see an academy around here?" Ashra said, gesturing at the barren desert.

"No."

"Exactly. Here's an additional piece of information that may interest you. I have been in the Vault of Silence," Ashra said. Alrion was dumbstruck.

"How interesting. I was not aware of anyone doing that," Certan said.

"It's not something the monks advertise, perhaps contrary to what you have been told. But that's all I can say," Ashra said.

"You win. Let's get this over with," Alrion said.

"Excellent, follow me please," Ashra said. He jumped up from his seated position with startling agility and left the hut.

"Come everyone," Ashra said, and continued walking. They walked past where the mirage was, and continued down a tight winding path between sand dunes. There were rocky formations holding the sand at bay.

Just as the sun was getting to Alrion, Ashra stopped suddenly. There was a fork in the path. There was a branch off to the left.

"Your friends should go left, it will lead to a vantage point up on the ridge. We will continue down," he said.

"We'll be watching," Lara said to Alrion, and started off. Certan slapped Alrion on the shoulders and followed close by. Once they had left Ashra spoke again.

"I have been where you are now. I have seen the academy and what it can offer, and it's a fantastic environment. But I wrestled with my power the same way you are now. With persistence, and experimentation and seeking whatever knowledge I could find," he said. He poked Alrion in the head. "I don't know how that works up there, but I can sense your apprehension. You have started to do things that you are not aware of, correct?" Ashra said.

"That's right," Alrion said.

"Don't worry, your mind will protect you. You have to quiet it, and let it do its work. Where we are going is a safe place and protected. Don't worry about me or the environment. You must treat this like you are in a life or death battle. Otherwise I cannot help you," Ashra said.

"If you insist," Alrion said, and followed Ashra down into the natural arena. He wasn't sure if he was more nervous, or more excited. But despite his reluctance he knew Ashra was right. He needed to test himself before his next battle.

22

AN OFFER

Alrion stood still, watching his opponent. Ashra stood with a relaxed stance at the opposite end of the natural arena. A gust of wind pushed sand and dust along the hard ground.

"Whenever you are ready," Ashra said loudly. Alrion heard the man, but wasn't sure how to start. He thought back to how they had launched their assault of the shade version of Branthor, and how ineffective it had been.

"Forget about that, just let go," he told himself. Shuffling his feet, he adjusted his stance and started to gather his Spark. It was time to begin.

Alrion began by throwing some ripples of force at Ashra, hoping to unsettle him or at least make him do some defence. Ashra must have seen them coming, because a wall of earth rose before him and easily absorbed the attack.

Earth too, how interesting. Branthor had been strong with that, and it had proven hard to deal with.

How about this then? Alrion thought, preparing a fire spell. He focused an intense beam of fire and force and projected it at the wall of earth.

There's no way it will withstand this, Alrion thought. He was curious how the other wizard would counter it. He didn't have to wait long for the answer.

As the fire began to hit the earth wall, it became wet. There seemed to be water seeping out of the wall, deflecting the heat, and turning it into steam.

How? Alrion wondered, confused by what he was seeing. He let the spell go and the area around Ashra was now covered in a haze of steam.

As Alrion was readying another spell the ground beneath him parted, causing him to stumble. As he looked down he saw a jet of water spray up. He had no time to dodge it and the force of the spray knocked him over. Alrion scrambled to his feet and watched the ground for more attacks. There was nothing else yet.

I have to do more, Alrion thought. He paused for a moment, then stoked his Spark once more. He channelled it into a huge wall of fire, completely separating both halves of the arena.

"That should buy me some time," he thought, and started to move slowly to avoid being a sitting target. As he moved he had an idea of how to attack. First, he created a large ball of fire and threw it into the air, holding it high above the wall of flame.

"Show yourself, or are you scared of my next attack?" Alrion shouted. He could see Ashra's silhouette standing on the other side of the wall of fire. Then it began to move. Alrion stared in disbelief, Ashra was walking through the wall of fire. When he emerged Alrion let out a surprised gasp.

The figure before him was no longer Ashra. It looked like a Shade. The figure shrugged off the flames that had come from the firewall and focused its gaze on Alrion.

"This is not possible," Alrion said to himself.

In a panic Alrion increased the intensity of the wall of fire, then flung down the fireball at the Shade. The fireball flew fast, but stopped suddenly as if it were being held by another force.

"Now you go down," Alrion whispered to himself. He concentrated all the flames, heat, and power of the wall of fire into a wave that was half as high but twice as powerful and sent it forward. He saw his fireball deflected aside, but his wave of fire continued unrestricted.

This may actually work, he thought, ready to disperse the flames once they started to get too close to him. However, the flames passed through the shade and did no discernible damage. As Alrion prepared to extinguish the flames, a huge shift in the ground occurred. A large amount of earth rose up towards him. It was a dome of reinforced sand that not only smothered the flame, but quickly enclosed Alrion within.

Alrion furiously threw waves of force at the sand structure, trying to break a hole in it. But the sand absorbed each attack and stayed resilient.

This is not happening.

"You have lost," Ashra's voice said from outside the dome.

"No!" Alrion shouted. He channelled everything he had into one last attack. He poured his fear, frustration and embarrassment and the rest of his Spark into a modified wave of force. It started as a white hot glowing orb above him, and it expanded out quickly. It shimmered and exploded outwards, obliterating the sand prison and everything in the area. Alrion fell to the ground, exhausted. As the dust settled he looked around him at what had just happened.

A spherical shape was neatly cut out of sides of the arena and the surface was now perfectly flat like it has been swept and polished. On one ridge Alrion could see Ashra standing tall, and Lara and Certan were crouched behind him.

What did I do? Alrion rose to his feet, and stumbled, so he dropped back to the ground and sat down, waiting for his friends to return.

Lara and Certan had concerned looks of their faces. Ashra had a blank look, that was undecipherable.

"You are not ready," he said to Alrion.

"I know."

"I don't think you do. Where did you learn how to craft a lightbomb?"

"I don't know, it must have come from the Pool." Alrion shrugged, it was as good a guess as any.

"Partial knowledge is incredibly dangerous. You very nearly killed your friends. Such a spell is not taught lightly, and much caution is used in its practice and application. You don't even know what you did do you?"

"I know enough to recreate it, but you're right. It was all instinctive."

"You have good survival instincts, that attack would certainly have destroyed your enemy or forced him to retreat. But the cost is too great. If I were not here to shield your friends, they would be gone," Ashra said. Alrion let that sink in.

"I'm sorry. But what are you?" Alrion said.

"I'm a wizard. What did you expect?"

"But the Shade?"

"An illusion to test you. It caused quite a stir I can see. I was actually up on the ridge with your friends for the majority of the battle. My instincts are pretty good too," Ashra said.

"He was commenting on what was happening, which helped us follow along. Lucky he was there to protect us. What about next time?" Lara said.

"I am really sorry. Maybe I can work on controlling this spell better for next time," Alrion said.

"You will not!" Ashra shouted.

"Why?"

"It's too dangerous, it cannot be easily controlled. You should forget that you even know it."

"What do I do then? I have no effective spells against Wraith, the creature that Branthor has become." Alrion felt incredibly frustrated.

"I will train you and show you how to harness the power of earth and water. You have too few tools at your disposal."

"You will then?"

"Yes, on one condition."

"Which is?"

"You never use a spell you don't understand when there is the potential for friendly casualties. I never quite understood what the legends of the Pool of Knowledge were about, but now I know for sure. You have everything ever used and recorded stuffed into that mind of yours. Anything could come out. You cannot let yourself lose control. The risk is very high. This is why I will train you. It would be incredibly irresponsible otherwise. Who knows what you could do," Ashra said.

"I accept your condition. But first I have a question."

"Yes?"

"How did you do water spells? And how useful will they be in the desert?" Alrion said. Ashra laughed and even Certan chuckled.

"There is much water in the desert. Some in the air, but most of it is deep underground. You just need to know how to harvest it. I imagine the desert wizard is quite adept at that," Certan said.

"You are quite correct. It's also a rather important ingredient in my illusion spells."

"Illusion spells require water?"

"Of course. Once I explain it will make perfect sense. But for now, let's return to the hut and rest," Ashra said. He leaned down and offered a hand to Alrion. The young wizard accepted it and rose again to his feet, a bit more steadily this time.

"Do you need assistance?" Certan said.

"No, I'm alright now. Each step I regain some strength," Alrion said.

"Very well, we are here to help," Certan said. They walked together, following Ashra back to the hut.

The hut was cool and comfortable compared to the intensity of the heat outside.

"How long have you lived here?" Alrion said.

"Many years. I don't fit in well with society. Your grandfather approached me back in the day and offered me a place in the academy. But I declined, and stayed here, living out my days in peace. Refining my spells and helping the odd traveller. Secretly of course," Ashra said.

"The stories are true!" Certan said.

"Yes, well some of them at least."

"What stories?" Lara said.

"Tales of travellers who are lost, thirsty and unable to move. They find themselves in a mysterious oasis and a voice tells them to refresh and guides them on the path out. They've even given a name to the voice."

"Which is?" Lara said.

"Caretaker of the desert."

"That's you? The man who doesn't like people?" Alrion said.

"I didn't say I helped everyone. Just the ones I come across that I can't avoid helping. It gives me a way to practice my craft," Ashra said.

"On your own terms," Alrion said.

"Exactly. I don't want every man and his dog wandering out here and forming an orderly line at my front door. It's more fun this way."

"When does training start?"

"Tomorrow. I know you are in a rush, but you need to recover today so we can do it properly."

"That's fine, I understand. Maybe you can at least explain a bit about the illusion spells then?"

"I may as well, and it may benefit your friends to know a little about it too. Have you ever seen a rainbow?" Ashra said.

"Yes."

"They're created by the light passing through water and splitting into distinct colours. Building upon this basic principle, you can make the light do whatever you want. With a few tricks to complete the illusion you can fool people into believing that your image is real."

"Wow, I hadn't thought of it that way."

"Knowledge is so important, as you are discovering. It is the gateway to the formerly impossible," Ashra said, giving them a wry smile.

"Sounds like something I could use," Lara said.

"I'm sure you could. Unfortunately, there's very little that can be accomplished by knowledge and will. You need the power of Spark to fuel these spells. But knowing the principles may help you to see through the illusions of others, and understand the limitations of what Alrion will be able to do," Ashra said.

"True, but I'm definitely disappointed," Lara said.

"Sorry, that's just how it is. The wizards get the interesting toys," Ashra said.

"Why don't you come with us? You can train me on the way and escort us to the desert temple," Alrion said.

"Absolutely not," Ashra said without hesitation.

"Why not?"

"This is my home here, and I feel a responsibility for aiding in your training. But I will not be pulled into your quest. It is yours alone. Besides, as I mentioned before I think there is already a wizard following your progress."

"I can't convince you?"

"No. This is the way it must be. If you want more help figure out who that wizard is that's already involved," Ashra said. He gave Alrion a cryptic smile.

"You've figured something out, haven't you?" Alrion said.

"Maybe, maybe not. But all of you should rest and prepare. Tomorrow we begin," Ashra said. He gestured at the room, pointing out food, water, and cushions. Then he walked out of the hut.

"Such a strange man," Certan said.

"But he will help, in some way. That's what counts." Alrion pondered what kind of training he would receive. From early impressions, it would be quite different to what he received from Falric.

23

IMPENDING DANGER

Vincent put down his tools and wiped the sweat from his brow. John was sure working him hard.

I guess he's trying to get back into the good graces for the guards. They seemed pretty persistent with their questioning before. Thinking back, he realised that he hadn't seen Celes for a while either.

It's not like her to dally. Maybe she actually found something? Vincent mused. He wandered around to see what John was working on.

"Hello there Vincent, how are you going today?" he said.

"Great. I finished up those pieces you asked for." Vincent pointed over at his completed work.

"Really? You're pretty fast, I must admit I wasn't sure what to expect."

"I have a lot of experience, just not in these. It's been a good exercise," Vincent said.

"You've done way more than I thought. I'll have to give you some gold to compensate you."

"Don't be silly, you're letting me stay that's payment enough. Earlier, was everything alright? What ended up happening with that guard?"

"Oh, I really don't know what their problem is. Everything here is business as usual. I didn't like their tone either." John seemed quite hurt by the accusatory manner of the conversation.

"Yeah, they didn't seem particularly friendly, lots of accusations being thrown around. Are they always like that?"

"No, not generally. Now they aren't the friendliest folk, but generally politer and by the book. Something must have really stirred them up." John heard footsteps nearby and turned to look at who was approaching. "Speaking of which," he said and stepped forward.

Vincent looked over and noticed a female guard approaching.

"Hello again blacksmith, how are you?" she said. She flashed a smile that Vincent was certain was purely false.

"Same as before, busy. To what do I owe this pleasure?" John said.

"I realised I was a little harsh earlier, and wanted to come apologise. You have been a trusted partner to the guard for a long time, and I didn't give you due respect. To explain my actions a little more, I would just like to add that we're under a lot of pressure. It doesn't excuse my actions, but I hope it provides some context," she said. John looked to be swayed by her words, but Vincent was more sceptical.

"That's good of you, not enough folks take responsibility for their actions these days," John said.

"Absolutely. I don't think I was properly introduced to your colleague before," the guard said.

"Vincent, nice to meet you," Vincent said, offering his hand. The guard took off her gauntlet and shook his hand. Her grip was firm, a little too firm. Vincent was used to strong shakes, and with his strength could crush a hand if he wanted. But he was surprised.

"Tanya, nice to meet you also. You are new here?" she said.

"Yes, he joined recently, helping me get through the additional work. He's been a big help," John said.

"Been in town long?" Tanya said.

"Not that long. Looking to pick up some new skills and work on some more interesting pieces. I've done enough horse shoes for a lifetime," Vincent said chuckling. Tanya smiled but continued her questioning.

"Of course. Have you seen anything suspicious around? Maybe you've left things where they shouldn't have been?" she said.

"Can't say I have, it's been quiet here. John, have you seen anything left where it shouldn't be?" Vincent said.

"No, everything's been where it should. I even double checked today just to make sure," he said.

"Of course. I just need to make sure I leave no stone unturned, this is quite a high-pressure environment right now," Tanya said. John nodded sympathetically.

"Tell me about it. I've got huge orders to fulfil, and no time to do it. The work is detail orientated so it's incredibly time consuming," he said.

"I understand. Please think about it and let me know if you hear anything. You can come to the guard station and ask for Glinda," Glinda said.

"Will do. Thank you for coming back, I really value a good working relationship with the guards," John said.

"And we value your work too. Good day," Glinda said and left.

"What did you make of that?" Vincent said.

"She's had to change her tune, probably due to someone higher up getting annoyed. She was almost convincing, but you could see through it all."

"I agree completely. She clearly could care less about you but had to come back and be politer. One to watch out for."

"Wise words. You had enough for the day?"

"Yes, if you don't mind I'd like some time to explore the city and rest." Vincent scanned the background and took note of the direction in which Glinda had left.

"Not a problem, you've done a day's work anyway. Let me get you a few gold to enjoy yourself." John reached for his pouch.

"No, I insist. If you're really adamant at the end we can figure something out. But for now, I'm happy with the experience. It's invaluable," Vincent said.

"As you wish. Have a good rest, see you tomorrow," John said.

"Thanks, you too," Vincent said and returned to his work area. He put everything away and changed clothes.

If I rush I can catch up to her, Vincent thought. He was worried about not seeing Celes again, and decided that Glinda was his best avenue. He jogged along the street, trying to catch sight of the guard again. She wasn't headed towards the guard station, but in the opposite direction. He considered trying to follow her, but decided that it wasn't the best idea. Being direct would suit him better.

Once he was within range he shouted.

"Glinda, have you a moment!" Vincent said. The female guard stopped and turned around. She had an annoyed look on her face, but forced it away when she saw Vincent.

"Yes, of course," she said.

"Great, I was thinking about what you said and thought of something that may help. I did see a woman around the other night. I didn't think anything of it, but since I saw her more than once I remembered her face. It could be nothing but..."

"That is a fantastic lead. Let me think for a moment." Glinda seemed to stare off into space for a while. Suddenly she refocused on Vincent. "Would you be able to recognise her if you saw her?" she said.

"Absolutely."

"Come with me then, we could definitely use your help," Glinda said.

"Happy to help," Vincent said with a smile. The guard walked off with purpose, and Vincent followed close behind.

"Do you have this woman in custody?" Vincent said.

"No, but we have a suspicious woman that is our main suspect. You could provide the additional verification we require," Glinda said.

This is not good. What is Celes mixed up in? It could be a coincidence, but it really seemed like they had Celes and wanted to confirm she was the one they were after.

That strange pause and look from the guard, maybe that's what they look like when they communicate, Vincent thought. It was a good theory, and they suspected the guard was Tainted. Now he just had to think about what to do if his suspicions were right. He was definitely walking into a dangerous situation.

He mused over that scenario as they walked. Vincent noticed a disruption up head. There was a shape moving fast through the crowd of people. From the reactions of the people shifting and complaining it was coming towards them. Suddenly a shape broke out from the crowd and leapt at Glinda.

It was a tiny girl with short brown hair. She tackled Glinda and the guard caught the girl and swung her into a more comfortable position.

"Baby girl, I'm working right now. Where's the rest of your friends?"

"Over there with the teacher. They're talking about the trees, it's so boring!"

"If you pay attention you may learn something interesting. I have to escort this gentleman somewhere, so please rejoin your friends and I will see you after work!"

"Sorry," Vincent said, shrugging his shoulders, and apologising to the young girl. She responded by playfully poking her tongue out at him.

"Alright, I guess I can do that. See you later!" the girl said, jumped back to the ground and tore off with fantastic speed back through the crowds.

"She's quite energetic, that's good. Such a nice age," Vincent said.

"Thanks. I take it you have kids?" Glinda said.

"Just the one. But he's older now, doing his own thing. No more running hugs," Vincent said with a chuckle.

"Yeah those can't last, can they?" Glinda said. Her tone of voice had changed, and she was silent for the rest of the walk.

Maybe we've all misjudged her? What would an ordinary person do when put in an extraordinary situation? What if she had to play along to keep your daughter safe?

"He's with me," Glinda said, and Vincent broke out of his inner thought. They were in front of a manor house with a large gate and guards.

This looks like trouble. He started to focus on the job ahead.

Glinda led him down a side passage and into the house. Vincent could tell the house was home to a very important person. It was richly furnished and had extremely elaborate floorings and paintings.

I hope she's here.

"In here please," Glinda didn't even look at Vincent while she opened the door. He stepped inside and saw it was a drab grey room with no furnishings. He could see Celes sitting in the corner. He rushed over immediately.

"Did they hurt you?" he said.

"No, I'm fine. I refused to talk so they threw me in here. I think they were planning something else, but they suddenly changed their minds."

"Good. When you didn't return, I told the guard that I saw a woman sneaking around so that they would bring me in. It worked," Vincent said softly.

"I see you recognise her, perhaps even know her?" a sarcastic voice said from the doorway. Vincent looked up and saw a well-dressed man in ornate robes addressing them. Glinda had retreated into the corridor and had turned to leave.

"And who might you be?" Vincent said.

"None of your concern," he said.

"He's a councillor," Celes said.

"Corrupt official? That's a bit of a cliché, isn't it? Couldn't help yourself?" Vincent said. The councillor pursed his lips but suppressed an outburst.

"I'm quite pleased. We have the spy and her accomplice in our custody. Wraith will give a lot to have his hands on you," the councillor said with a dark laugh. He continued to smirk then slammed the door. Vincent stood up and examined the room. It looked solid and the door was heavy and metal. There was a keyhole though.

"Do you think you could pick this?" he said to Celes.

"Probably. But I don't want to try just yet, we haven't gotten the information we need."

"That councillor runs the show around here?"

"Looks like it. That guard reported in to him, she's a piece of work, isn't she?"

"I had thought that too, but we ran into her daughter on the way here. It showed another side of her. Maybe she's just caught up in this?"

"But she's Tainted, I know that for sure." Celes looked adamant and quite irate.

"Yes, but do you think that's by choice? Especially with a daughter to look after," Vincent said.

Celes started to speak, but stopped. She looked thoughtful. "I hadn't considered that. You could be right," she said.

"I think I am, at least on this. Do you have a plan?"

"Yes. Let's appear like we can't escape, and see what they have in store for us. They appear quite confident, they didn't take anything from me," Celes said.

"Sure, we can give them a hard time if they are asking for it. I just hope we get something out of this."

"Did you have anything better to do?" Celes said with a laugh.

"I don't suppose that I do. At least we're here together." Vincent was all jokes and comfort, but he didn't feel right. These people were more dangerous than they appeared. But for now, he would wait, and see what opportunities were presented.

24

SAND AND WATER

Alrion followed Ashra out into the oasis.

"As you know, this is all an illusion. I'll demonstrate," Ashra said. He snapped his fingers and the lush scenery disappeared and was replaced by the desert, some rubble, and a stone wall.

"It's still amazing to see," Alrion said.

"Yes, it's a neat trick. But very difficult to do. We're not going start with that, and we may not even get there. But at least I will help you understand the principles at work and how to get started with manipulating water. The first thing we need to do, is to tap into your senses," Ashra said. He said down on the ground and directed Alrion to join him.

"It's really hot," he said.

"It is, but it's not dangerous. Your reaction to the heat can be managed, it's just another sense. Something that will come easier once you complete the Vault of Silence." Ashra paused for dramatic effect.

"Can you tell me more about that?"

"No. Concentrate on what we are here to do. Place your hand on the ground like this," Ashra said, demonstrating by placing his own palm on the ground.

"Done."

"Now there is a large reservoir of water below us, but it's deep. You need to visualise a drop of water falling from your palm, through the earth and rejoining the water below. Imagine that single drop rippling through the calm surface of the water, and sounding like the toll of a high-pitched bell," Ashra said. Alrion concentrated hard but struggled to do so. The only water he could imagine leaving his palm was his sweat from the extreme heat.

"I can see that you are struggling. I'll help a little," Ashra said. He snapped his fingers again and a large tree put them in shade. Alrion felt cooler and more focused immediately.

He focused again, visualising the droplet of water passing through the layers of earth and dripping into a large reservoir. He could hear the bell-like chime of the water echoing in the space and his mind filled with the awareness of the body of water.

"Yes! That's it. Draw it up into your palm!" Ashra said.

Alrion didn't know how to do that, but he could imagine it. He pictured himself scooping a handful of water and saw it materialise in his hand. "Wow! My hand is wet," Alrion said with surprise. He lifted his hand and saw the water below it sink back into the ground. He felt the wetness of his hand, and was amazed. "But how? Can anyone do that?" he said.

"No, you need Spark for that. But the heavy lifting is done by your mind and visualisation. How are you feeling?" Ashra said.

"Refreshed, which makes me wonder where this shelter came from," Alrion said, looking around.

"It's all in your mind," Ashra said, snapping his fingers. The shade and shelter vanished and the sun was beating down on Alrion again.

"Do you believe that I can create shelter and destroy it with merely a thought?"

"No." Alrion could almost believe it though. But he would have felt silly to admit that.

"Then how did I do it?"

"An illusion?"

"Precisely. But how did you feel when I did it?"

"I felt like I was cooler, sheltered and I could focus better," Alrion said.

"Exactly! And yet the same amount of sun was hitting you, and the ground was just as hot. But your perception changed. So, you felt more comfortable. Let that sink in," Ashra said. He stood up and paced around the area. Alrion was amazed by the revelation.

"Seems like there's a lot you can do with illusions," Alrion said.

"There certainly is. But they are very difficult. We'll only be able to lay down the groundwork before you leave."

"Why?"

"I can't keep you long, a day or two at most. And we also need to work on other things. For now, I want you to fill this bowl," Ashra said. He retrieved a plain circular bowl and placed it down in front of Alrion.

"Fill it with water?"

"Yes, you can draw it, so let's gather it," Ashra said.

"Sure, let's give this a go." Alrion concentrated once more and began the visualisation.

Hours passed and Alrion had finally filled the bowl.

"I feel like I have sweated enough to fill it twice over," he said.

"You also lost some to the heat of the desert," Ashra said.

"That makes me feel a bit better."

"Good. You did well, now drink it and let's move on." Ashra pointed at the water.

"Drink it? Isn't that a waste?"

"Do you see any other water around here? We can't have you fainting on me," Ashra said, laughing. Alrion drank the water, and it seemed particularly refreshing.

"You can work on that more as you travel, but water is an essential element in many different spells. Next, we will work on earth manipulation. You need to understand how to use it, and how to counter it," Ashra said. He walked away and made a motion with his hands like he was pulling up the earth. A small mound of dirt piled up in front of him.

"This should be easier for you. It's developing an affinity with the earth, then using force to manipulate it. You seem to be pretty good at using force through the air, this is just a different application," Ashra said.

"Sounds sensible," Alrion said.

"It is. Try it now. Focus yourself and gather up a pile of dirt like mine," Ashra said. Alrion looked at the ground and gathered his Spark, fuelling the fire within. He sent his force at the ground and imagined drawing out the earth into a mound. However, the opposite happened. He managed to fling the dust everywhere. He could hear Ashra laughing amidst it.

"That's an effective escape tool, but not quite what we were after. Pull, not push," he said.

"That's what I was trying to do," Alrion said. Annoyed with himself.

"You need to think about what you are doing, and not just assume that a simple change in your thinking will alter the result," Ashra said patiently. Alrion thought over what the older wizard had said, and decided to try again. He broke down his actions into smaller steps. It was working. He could sense that the process was working differently, and slowly but surely, he created a small dust pile.

"That's better. See what I mean?" Ashra said.

"Yes, there are fundamental steps that are different that I didn't alter the first time."

"Yes. Your instincts are good, but you can't shortcut everything. But you see this pile, it's not useful. It has no strength of structure," Ashra said, kicking his pile of dirt. It dispersed without effort. He focused again and created a small wall of the same height.

"Come and examine this," he said. Alrion walked over and felt the wall with his hand.

"It's solid," he said.

"Good. And what else?"

"It's not as dry, is there water within it?"

"Good. The sand and dirt here is so dry it is harder to maintain forms with it. A bit of water to bind it works wonders. Now you try to build a wall," he said. Alrion looked unsure, but looked back down at the ground and started to concentrate.

He started to assemble the pile of dirt, and placed his hand on it to assist with drawing the water. And it worked, but not the way he had hoped. The water pooled into the middle of the pile, muddying it, and not assisting with any structural integrity.

"That's quite a common problem," Ashra said.

"How do I fix it?" Alrion said.

"Less water and more distributed. You need to find a way to draw the water with more finesse. A pool of it doesn't help, as you can see."

"Is there a trick to it?"

"Of course, but it's something you need to puzzle out," Ashra said. He disassembled his wall and created himself a chair to sit in. He sat back, crossed his legs, and watched Alrion work.

Show-off! Alrion thought. He had to figure out how to make the wall work. He could see how useful the technique was. "I need to first figure out how to draw less water," Alrion said to himself. He started by practising variations of how he drew the water, but instead of the water forming into a greater body, he imagined thin wispy strands of it travelling through the air. He used the strands to define blocks and bind them together. It started working. His pile of dust and sand started to form into something with more structure, even though it wasn't particularly neat.

"That's the way," Ashra said. Once Alrion had finished, the desert wizard stood up and walked over. He kicked the wall and it practically disintegrated.

"Needs a bit more strength," he said with a chuckle.

"Just a tiny bit," Alrion said, sharing a smile.

"You've done well, let's rest for a while," Ashra said, heading back to his little hut. Alrion followed closely, pausing to look back at the remnants of his small wall.

They found Lara and Certan lounging in the hut, avoiding the heat.

"Aren't you hungry? We ate hours ago," Lara said as they approached. Alrion hadn't even realised how much time had passed.

"No, although I can definitely eat now. Too much concentration required," Alrion said, flopping down onto one of the cushions.

"How's he doing?" Certan said to Ashra.

"Fairly well, I don't have a comparison because I don't teach others. But I think he's getting the principles which is the most important part. We will practise more today on what we have learned, and try a few new things tomorrow," Ashra said.

"How long will it take?" Alrion said.

"Years, but you get two days with me. You'll be leaving tomorrow evening."

"How is that going to be enough?"

"Time is against you. Your enemy has been one step ahead the entire time, and knows everything you do since he has also drunk from the Pool of Knowledge. Have you considered that?" Ashra said. Alrion felt defensive immediately.

"Sure, but I still need to prepare. He's practically invincible!"

"There is always a way. All I can do is help you start down the path. You must follow it yourself. Be prepared for anything is my best advice," he said. Alrion ate quickly, and took the opportunity to rest out of the heat. Just as he became comfortable Ashra abruptly stood up.

"Time to get back to work, you have rested enough," he said.

"Have fun!" Lara said.

"You too, I hope I don't miss anything," Alrion said, trying to make a joke.

"We shall keep a detailed log," Certan said, getting in on the joke. Alrion shook his head at the lameness of the reply and followed Ashra back to where they had been training.

The hours passed quickly once more, and Alrion refined his ability to draw water and form the earth into a simple wall. He felt pleased by that, but wasn't sure if it would be effective for anything useful.

"That's enough for today, let's join the others," Ashra said. Together they walked back to the hut and found Lara and Certan in the same spots. It looked like they hadn't moved at all.

"Having a nice time?" Alrion said.

"It's not too bad, I could get used to this. I'd get bored though I think," Lara said.

"Some additional time to rest and recover is quite important. I would advise it for you, if we had the capacity to spare it," Certan said.

"Someday perhaps. I've been meaning to ask, where do you get this food from?" Alrion pointed at the various breads and biscuits and other food that was available.

"I do leave the hut occasionally you know, but I do also have to provide for myself quite a bit," Ashra said. He walked over to a corner of the hut and lifted the dirty brown rug there. Underneath was a trap door.

"This is interesting," Lara said jumping up immediately. Ashra opened the trap door and revealed a ladder going down into the ground. He started to descend and the others followed close.

Alrion found himself in a giant cavern. There were stores of food on shelves carved into the walls, benches, and other furnishing. Two fire pits were in the middle of the room.

"This is your kitchen then," Certan said.

"That's it. I use a few shortcuts, but otherwise it keeps me busy. I usually sleep down here as well when it gets particularly cold."

"This is incredible!" Lara said walking around the room.

"Thank you, I appreciate that. This is my home, so I need a few things. I can't live off the wind and sand you know," Ashra said. Certan laughed.

"Alrion, recover as best you can, we have an early start tomorrow," Ashra said, starting to prepare a meal for dinner.

Alrion awoke suddenly to Ashra's face in close proximity.

"Time to start, we eat later," Ashra said. Alrion rose quietly and they left Certan and Lara asleep. A short walk later they were back to the training area.

"First thing today, I want you to build a curved wall. Same principles as yesterday, but more complexity in the construction," Ashra said. He demonstrated by building a wall that curved slightly towards him.

"You used something similar to enclose me in the fight," Alrion said.

"Exactly. That's the end-game for a technique such as this. It can be used for many different things. Enclosing an enemy, shielding a target, hiding things, or protecting them from harm. I don't expect you to master it now, but I want you to understand the principles," Ashra said. Alrion could see the benefits, and threw himself into the practice. His few two attempts were barely curved at all. When Ashra chided him for being too cautious, Alrion changed his approach and made a wall that couldn't stand at all. But the extreme curvature did teach him something about the technique. He ended up with something similar to what Ashra had built eventually.

"I think you're beginning to understand. Still lacking strength," Ashra commented, collapsing the wall with his palm without exerting any effort.

"What can I do to improve that?" Alrion said.

"More compacting of the sand, injecting more Spark into the binding process. It takes a bit of experimentation to understand how it works." Ashra did another quick demonstration.

"I see," Alrion said, preparing to try again.

"Leave that for now, I have one other things you must learn. Wait here a moment," Ashra said. He walked off back to the hut and returned soon after. He was holding a large red cushion. The colour was a little faded, but it was still a bright red.

"You're going to make this cushion blue," Ashra said.

"Really?"

"Yes. Observe," Ashra said. He waved his hand over the cushion and it looked a vibrant blue colour.

"Wow, that was quick!"

"Come over here," Ashra said. Alrion walked around and Ashra directed him to look at the cushion from behind.

"It's red," Alrion said.

"Yes, it is. The first rule of an illusion is that you need to understand how it will be viewed," Ashra said.

"Is it possible to completely cover something?" Alrion said.

"Yes, but it requires you to consider all the angles and prepare appropriately. The spell becomes much more complex. It's a trade-off between the quality of the illusion and the effort of creating and maintaining it."

"So, you can't just create it and leave it?"

"You can, there are ways. But it lacks the nuance that your mind brings to it. Suitable for things that would not get close scrutiny, but the effect eventually fades. For now though, let's just focus on something that you must create yourself," Ashra said.

"How do I do it?"

"You draw water, like we have practised. But you imagine it as a light spray intersecting with the air and the light, bending the rays. Then you inject your vision into the water, and create the illusion."

"Sounds tricky," Alrion said, doubt entering his voice.

"It is, but it's incredibly useful. Just try to make this cushion green," Ashra said.

"I'll do it!" Alrion reminded himself that he had come a long way, and already learned some new skills. This was just another one. He concentrated and found the underground water reservoir, drawing the water once more. He tried to disperse it and use it as a fine blanket in front of the cushion.

"It looks like you're wetting it, finer again and not so close," Ashra said. Alrion doubled his efforts, and kept trying. He kept the vision in his head completely clear, the cushion was not blue it was green.

"You're getting it, keep going," Ashra said. He could see that the pillow was starting to appear green in places, where Alrion had been successful. As he watched the cushion slowly alternated between the two colours in constantly changing patches. Then all of a sudden it locked in, and the cushion was green.

"That's it, now just open your eyes," Ashra said. Alrion opened his eyes and saw that the cushion was still blue.

"Come around here and look," Ashra said. Alrion walked slowly, trying to maintain his focus. As he took the last step he cautiously looked over at the cushion.

"It's green!" Alrion shouted in excitement. In that instant, the illusion dropped and the cushion was blue once more.

"Well done. Now you just need to practise some more. By the end of the day I need you to be able to make this cushion appear any colour I specify from any direction," Ashra said. Alrion felt exhausted already from the effort. It wasn't just a case of drawing on his Spark, the focus and concentration required were huge.

"I just didn't expect it to be so tiring," he said.

"That's why Will is such a key component of magic. The more you train and enhance it, the less effort it takes to create and maintain all these spells that require your mind's focus. Raw power is not always the answer, as you are no doubt finding out," Ashra said. Alrion nodded with understanding. He had discovered vast tracts of power, but Ashra had easily beaten him. Defeated by the desert wizard's superior Will and training. Alrion had to improve in all areas if he was going to succeed.

"Almost there," Alrion whispered to himself, then threw everything back into his training.

BUNKERING DOWN

Alrion stumbled twice while walking back to the hut. Extreme exhaustion was making every step a challenge.

At least the heat is dropping, he thought. The relative cool of the hut was incredibly soothing, and he quickly dropped down onto one of the pillows.

"Tough day?" Lara said. Alrion just nodded.

"He did well, but you'll need to let him rest a few hours before you leave," Ashra said.

"What did you learn today?" Certan said.

"Basic illusions. I can make that cushion appear a different colour," Alrion said, pointing at a cushion at random.

"Can you show me?" Lara said. Alrion just groaned.

"He's a little tired, I'm sure he will perk up and give a demonstration later," Ashra said.

"You seem fine," Lara said.

"I have a little more practise. Alrion has been doing this the hard way. The burden of that extreme focus has worn him out. I'm sure Certan understands what I mean." Ashra gave Certan a knowing look.

"Yes, until you achieve competency then mastery, exerting the Will is very draining. We had a little exercise demonstrating that a few days ago," Certan said.

"And I was the winner!" Lara said.

"That doesn't surprise me," Ashra said with a laugh. He disappeared downstairs and Lara followed him.

"Don't worry it will get easier," Certan said.

"I don't doubt you, I just can't understand it right now," Alrion said.

"Yes, your mind is too tired. But you are strengthening it every day, so don't worry. Maintaining your Will is a constant effort, you cannot just achieve a milestone then ignore it."

"But you're a monk, surely you just have it now?" Alrion said.

"In some ways yes, but in others no. Let me show you something." Certan removed a small flask from his robes and handed it to Alrion. It was metallic and had the symbol of the monk order on it.

"What is this?" Alrion said.

"It was made for the monks by a craftsman who they had saved in the desert. It was originally intended for water, but it was too heavy and impractical for daily use. So, it was instead filled with a strong alcoholic spirit and kept in storage."

"And you took it? When you left?"

"Yes, I don't know why. It seemed like an even worse thing to do on top of everything else. And I drank from it nearly every day, just a drop to make sure I could keep it as long as possible. But since I met you, I stopped." A lightness broke up the sadness on Certan's face. He looked hopeful.

"You haven't drunk from it since then?"

"No, there's still some left. Every day I look at the flask, and I am tempted to drink from it. Just for a taste. But every day I stop and remind myself, that this symbol of my failure can be a sign of my success. If I can return to the monks and show that there is still alcohol left in this flask, then I can prove to them that I overcame my weakness and strengthened my Will," Certan said.

"Thanks for sharing that story. I never realised that this was still such a struggle for you." Alrion handed back the flask.

Certan carefully returned it to within his robes. "I suspect I may never be clear of it, but perhaps I can forgive myself one day and it will become easier. Ah, it looks like the food is now here." Certan rose and helped Lara and Ashra distribute the bread.

"Eat well, you will need your strength. You must leave tonight so you can make good time. Certan, are you familiar with this area at night?" Ashra said.

"Mostly, it will not be an issue," he said.

"Good, you all eat your fill I will pack you some supplies," Ashra said, and disappeared again downstairs. Alrion and the others started to get ready, and soon they were standing at the entrance to the hut, packing away the food provided by Ashra.

"You've been such an incredible help. I was a little resistant, and I'm sorry," Alrion said.

"Don't worry, we are all under our own pressures. You did well here, good luck on your journey," Ashra said.

"Are you sure I can't convince you to come with us? Just to the temple? You wouldn't need to leave the desert," Alrion said.

"Not a chance. This is your journey, and I have played my part. Everything will be fine, just remember what I have shown you. And trust your companions, they are quite resourceful."

"Alright then. Goodbye and thanks again," Alrion said.

"It was enlightening to meet the legend himself, and to confirm your existence," Certan said.

"You keep that conformation to yourself. It's too troublesome diverting large numbers of visitors," Ashra said.

"I think you'd secretly let some in, you aren't as bad as you make out," Lara said.

"I'd appreciate if you don't share those sentiments," Ashra said.

"Don't worry, we won't send anyone here," Alrion said, and waved as they set off.

"Good luck young man. You have the slimmest of chances, but maybe you will succeed," Ashra whispered, then retreated to his hut. He looked out into the desert, and felt a chill run down his spine. Something bad was coming.

Certan lead the way, making as much haste as possible. He wanted to capitalise on the available light. Alrion was a bit slow, but once they worked into a rhythm the steps flowed easier.

"What a strange man, I don't know how you could live in such a place all by yourself," Lara said.

"There must be a story behind that. Something significant changed that man," Certan said.

"I wonder why," Alrion said. From what he knew of wizards, Ashra seemed positively brilliant. He would be remarkable in any setting, but had chosen to stay in such an isolated and remote place.

"We shouldn't stop yet, but the light is fading. Can you assist?" Certan said. Alrion created three orbs of light, and placed one above his right shoulder and positioned the other two with Certan and Lara.

"A bit brighter," Lara said. Alrion increased the intensity slowly.

"That's it," Certan said. Alrion took a moment to stabilise the spell and make it easier to maintain, then continued on.

They trekked down minor paths which wouldn't be visible unless they were known. But the path ended soon, and they had to traverse up and down sand dunes.

"Is there no other way?" Alrion said, struggling to keep up. He was already tired and had to keep up the light spells as well.

"There is, but it is a much further distance and would result in more effort. This is definitely worth the additional fatigue," Certan said.

"Fine," Alrion said, and persevered. With each step, he felt like he was sliding back ever slightly, which increased the strain and the feeling that he was not progressing.

"A bit further," Certan said, then they suddenly passed over a dune and down onto a nice flat surface.

"Can you illuminate the distance?" Certan said. Alrion repositioned and repurposed Certan's light, casting rays into the distance. Before them spread an expanse of desert. There was nothing as far as they could see.

"We have arrived at the plain of despair," Certan said.

"That's a lovely name," Lara said.

"Yes, it's named because we are relatively central to the desert and there is nothing for a long way. Just flat desert. Many get stuck here and lose their sense of direction, and despair. It is the despair that kills, the feeling of helplessness. If you keep a cool head and keep travelling in a single direction you will get somewhere in time," Certan said. Alrion could believe the despair, he couldn't see anything that would serve as a landmark.

"Definitely not sure I would like to get stranded. How much further should we go tonight?" Lara said.

"As far as Alrion can make it. There's nowhere to take shelter here, and we can rest during the day if we can find somewhere suitable," Certan said.

"Shelter from what?" Alrion said.

"Dust storms. They're relatively rare, and don't last long. But you can be sure if we are caught up in the middle of nowhere we will get one. Best to move along as far as possible."

"You've convinced me, let's get moving. Can you keep up Alrion?" Lara said.

"For now, let's just get on with it." Alrion let the light dim to assist with his concentration. He had to concentrate more on walking faster and more carefully.

They continued in relative quiet for the next few hours. Alrion had no idea how long had actually elapsed, because the dark and the bare surroundings didn't offer any idea of how far they had travelled.

"How do you keep us on track?" Alrion said.

"You learn to develop a good internal compass. There are minor clues spread around, and also our footsteps are a good marker," Certan said. Alrion paused and looked back. There was definitely evidence of their passing.

"How long do they stick around?" Lara said.

"It depends on the winds. Hours probably, not more usually. There's not as much shifting around here unless there's a storm so it can be longer if the weather permits. Are you worried about us being followed?" Certan said.

"Not really, I was just curious. I like to know what kind of trail we are leaving."

"That's quite wise. It would be easy for someone to follow us right now. We would probably see evidence of their light if that were the case, but you never know," Certan said. Alrion started to imagine people tracking them through the desert then dismissed the thought. He quickened his pace to catch up to Certan. Just as he drew close, Certan abruptly stopped.

"Alrion, magnify the light again please," he said. Alrion complied, giving Certan a good view of the distance.

"Do you see that?" Certan said, pointing.

"No, what is it?" Alrion said.

"Is that a storm?" Lara said.

"Yes. Quite a big one if you can see it from this distance in the dark," Certan said.

"What do we do?" Alrion said.

"We look for shelter, we can't take any chances. I don't like the way it is moving, it seems unnatural." Certan started to look around at the area. As before, there was nothing around just the flat expanse of sand.

"I can build something," Alrion said.

"It's our only chance. I just hope you can make it strong, this is going to be a nasty storm," Certan said.

"No pressure then. I've just been training all day and walking all night," Alrion said with a sigh.

"Dig deep please. I've heard of these storms and they're awful," Lara said. Alrion tried to shake off his exhaustion and concentrate.

"It's approaching quite fast. You've probably got five minutes," Certan said.

"That will do," Alrion said, trying to sound confident. He had made a slightly curved wall, but that wasn't going to be enough. He needed to completely cover them.

"Here goes," he said to himself, and started gathering his Spark. It seemed to be in good supply, which was reassuring. It was the mental exertion and fatigue that he had to combat. He first detected a body of water nearby, then began to draw together his wall. Rather than just go with the curve, he visualised it extending further in the shape of a dome. Several times he had to stop, and reform a section because it wasn't right. But he seemed to be getting the structural integrity right.

"I don't mean to alarm you, but it's almost upon us. If we don't have a complete shield we're going to be buried alive in sand," Certan said. Alrion increased his efforts, but also increased his mistakes.

"I think you just need to finish this," Lara said. Alrion didn't look up but he heard the fear in her voice. His dome was only three-quarters completed, and they were all hunched over to stay within it.

"Get down now! Alrion do what you can to finish," Certan said. Lara lay down quickly, and Certan joined her. Alrion slowly sank down as he held his concentration. He could hear the whistling and howling of the wind, and the sand flying everywhere. It was almost upon them. He extended his dome, just as the first wave of sand hit it. He could feel the impact of the wind and sand on his creation.

"It's not going to hold, do something!" Lara said. Certan half stood up and braced the weak section with his hands. Alrion infused the sand with his Spark, trying to reinforce it. He felt the structure of the dome altering and re-forming. It was hardening in a way that he had never achieved in his practise. "Over there, is that another storm?" Lara shouted above the howling.

Sand was entering from the not-quite closed rear of the dome. Certan lay down, blocking the gap with his body and Alrion rushed to complete the dome. As he was extending it he was trying to strengthen it. He collapsed to his knees, and released the spell. The three of them sat very quietly, listening to the storm rage around them.

"I think you did it," Certain said with caution. Lara crept around the whole structure, listening carefully, and feeling it with her hands.

"I think it will hold, for now," she said, looking at Alrion with concern.

26

KEY FINDING

Keys jangled and the lock creaked and groaned. The heavy metal door slowly opened, making even more noise than anything else. Vincent looked up with interest to see who was coming in.

"Glinda, lovely to see you," he said.

"I'm here to ask more questions," she said, closing the door behind herself and making sure it locked.

"Don't trust us?" Celes said.

"Not at all. As you may be aware, you are being held here for Wraith," she said.

"Oh, he's not nearby? Where might he be?" Celes said.

"Not here. Only the councillor would know his location and plans," Glinda said. The tone of her voice was the same, but Vincent noticed something odd. She seemed to be giving them more information than was actually necessary.

"So, it may take a while for him to get here?" Vincent said.

"Not sure, probably. That's why it's worth me asking you some additional questions," Glinda said.

"I'm not sure what you would want to know," Celes said.

"We want to know where your son is. Where is Alrion?" Glinda said. Her tone was very formal and stiff.

"I don't actually know," Celes said.

"And you? What's your answer?" Glinda said to Vincent.

"Sorry, I also don't know." Vincent showed his open palms.

"Unfortunately, they are not going to accept those answers," Glinda said.

"That's a shame now isn't it. Will that look bad for you?" Vincent said. He didn't have any malice in his voice. He was more interested in getting a real response from the female guard.

"Yes, it will. They will escalate to more extreme methods of questioning," she said.

"All we know is that he was here recently, but have no idea where he is now," Vincent said, offering her something.

"He was here? Tell me more," Glinda said.

"He didn't enter the city, you had it all locked up. But he managed to get word through to us regardless," Celes said.

"I see," Glinda said, staring off into space.

"Perhaps you could satisfy a curiosity of mine. You seem to have that far-away look when you are communicating with your...colleagues. Is that something that you must concentrate to do, or do you always overhear each other?" Vincent said. His comments snapped Glinda out of her apparent daze.

"You have been somewhat accommodating so I'll answer. It is a conscious communication. You must purposefully broadcast, and the others must be listening out. But there are some who can dominate with their message regardless of the listeners," Glinda said.

"I see, like Wraith," Vincent said.

"Exactly." Glinda nodded.

"They only know what you tell them? They can't spy on you?" Vincent said.

"No."

"Good. So, if you were to help us, nobody would have to know," Vincent said. Celes looked at him and realised that Vincent had been working towards this.

"Why would I help you?" Glinda said.

"Because you have a child. You don't seem like a bad person. I don't know how you ended up in this situation, but it's not something you can easily escape. Can't we help each other?" Vincent said.

"I don't see how you could help me. I would risk everything for nothing," Glinda said.

"I'm sure there is something we can do for you right now. But what our son is doing, is cleansing the Blight from the world. You won't have to live with this forever," Vincent said.

That got Glinda's attention. "He can cure us?" That's not possible," Glinda said.

"It happened to Avaria, there's your proof that it's possible," Vincent said.

"But that was twenty years ago. And it was a spell cast by the greatest of all wizards," Glinda said.

"Yes, my father and Alrion's grandfather. If you help us, you are helping that future." Vincent could see that he had the guard's attention. He could see the struggle in her features, as much as she tried to hide them. His assessment had been correct, she wasn't willingly a part of this. But she looked afraid. He needed something to offer her right now. "I know that sounds like a long shot. But what if we took care of the councillor. He seems to run things around here. If he were gone, would you be able to disappear? Or at least fade into the background?" Vincent said.

"You don't know what you are suggesting," Glinda said.

"Yes, we do. We are offering to remove the man who is controlling this city, and freeing you up to make your own decisions," Celes said. Glinda seemed to be weakening.

"You just need to give us the opportunity and we will do the rest. We won't divulge your involvement at all, so you won't be under suspicion. Can you help us?" Vincent said. Glinda appeared conflicted. Her fear was obvious. But a look of resolve crossed her face. She had decided.

"I will help you in this. But if anything goes wrong, I will side with him. I must," Glinda said.

"Perfectly fair. Celes, do you have a plan in mind?" Vincent said.

"Yes, let me explain it to you both," she said, a smile breaking out on her face.

~

Glinda locked the door behind her and strode down the corridor. Her involvement was minimal, but she couldn't afford to make any mistakes. The trickiest part was just ahead of her.

She didn't run into anyone else in the hallways, which was a relief. She didn't know the others that well, and there was little chance that they would notice anything different. But she was glad to not have the encounters, they were a possibility for throwing her off her guard. As expected she found the councillor in his library.

"Any news?" he said, looking up from a pile of papers.

"They won't talk," she said.

"And have you tried persuading them?" he said with annoyance.

"No, I really don't have the skill for it and I thought that you would have better luck. I figured that in the meantime I could search their accommodation," she said.

"They wouldn't talk but you know where they live?" the councillor said with suspicion. He had put his papers away and was focusing entirely on her. Glinda cursed herself inwardly. She had embellished too much on the detail with real facts she had been told.

"They made a mistake, a slight one, then retracted it. But I believe I know where they have been staying and wish to investigate it as soon as possible," Glinda said.

"I see, that's wise. There may be evidence of their plans there. Go look into it, and I'll let you know if I learn anything or confirm where they have been stay-ing," the councillor said. He rose from his chair slowly.

"If only you were more resourceful, I wouldn't have to do these things myself," he said.

"My apologies, hopefully I can make up for it," Glinda said.

"Yes, let's hope so. Go on, get out my sight before I make you join me. I haven't forgotten your reluctance for proper interrogation, and may just change my mind and attempt to instruct you further," he said. Glinda bowed quickly and left immediately.

Almost there. She went directly to the side entrance of the house and left the door ajar as she left. Finally, she made her way around the perimeter to the front.

"You are relieved, I'm taking over until shift change," she told the guards.

"Really?" But there's not long left until changeover. Why?" the first guard said.

"I have to wait around anyway, figured I could cut you a break. Hurry up before I reconsider," Glinda said.

"That won't be a problem. Thanks!" the second guard said, and almost dragged his companion away. Glinda watched them leave and waited. She had to stop herself from tapping her foot. The nervous energy was almost too much.

"They better know what they are doing," she said to herself.

Vincent heard the steady footsteps outside the door, and stepped to the side, ready to strike. As the door opened, he rushed over and threw an elbow at the man entering. He saw the attack coming, but couldn't react in time and crum-pled to the ground.

"Ugly, but effective," Vincent said.

"Let's get him somewhere else," Celes said. Vincent picked up the coun-cillor and Celes helped carry him out into the hallway. One of them held the man up under each arm, and Vincent freed a hand to close the door behind them.

"She better be right about the patrols and servants, because we look mighty suspicious right now," Celes said.

"She's trustworthy. Let's just be quick," Vincent said. They slowly navigated around several corners, ending up back in a small private library. "This looks like the place," he said. They shuffled inside and dropped the councillor down into his large reading chair. "I'll watch him while you review the material there," Vincent said pointing to the pile of papers.

Celes quickly leafed through, scanning each page. "Not much of interest, it's pretty mundane. Maybe they don't put anything dangerous down on paper?" she said.

"Anything at all out of the ordinary?" Vincent said.

"They have a note about trade routes through the desert," Celes said.

"Isn't that unusual? We should ask him about that," Vincent said.

"Good idea. Give me a moment and I'll prepare the elixir." Celes retrieved a few vials from her cloak and mixed them carefully.

"Down the hatch," she said, as Vincent helped her open the councillor's mouth. He coughed suddenly and woke up, looking around the room.

"What's happening?" he said. His voice was a little slurred, and his speech slower than usual.

"You're drugged, and you're going to tell us exactly what we want to know," Celes said.

"The prisoners? How can this be?"

"You underestimated us. Don't even think about calling for help, the concoction you drank has dulled your senses," Vincent said.

"You think you're clever, but you won't get away with this," the councillor said with considerable effort.

"If you're so sure, just tell us what we want to know," Celes said. The councillor looked conflicted and confused. His confidence was still there, but he was a little unsure of himself.

"What could you possibly want to know anyway?" he said with satisfaction. Like he was both showing off and resisting at the same time.

"We want to know what Wraith is planning. He's organised you all - for what purpose?" Vincent said.

"Oh, I can't possibly tell you that. But I can share something. Something that you will find interesting," the councillor said. He had an odd grin on his face.

"Did you know that Wraith is in the desert? He's heading for an old temple to destroy it before a certain someone gets the chance to visit," he said, attempting a slow chuckle that sounded horrible.

"Wraith is in the desert? How long as he been there?" Vincent said.

"Oh, I don't know. But he's got an army with him. I sure hope your son isn't there, he'll be in for some trouble," the councillor said again. He couldn't contain his awkward laughter.

"Time to end this," Celes said. Vincent belted the councillor in the jaw and the man slumped down in his chair, unconscious.

"What do we do with him?" Celes said.

"I was going to ask you what the plan is. I think we can discredit him enough to neuter his authority." Vincent saw Celes's face light up with the possibilities.

Celes scouted ahead while Vincent half carried half dragged the councillor along. They had stripped him of all his clothes and soaked him in the expensive liquor they found in his library.

"I can't handle the stench from here, not sure how you're managing," Celes said.

"Just moving forward," Vincent said.

Celes laughed and went further ahead once more. She stepped out and made eye contact with Glinda. Glinda nodded, left the gate unattended and stepped out onto the street. "Coast is clear, let's finish this." Celes returned to help Vincent and they rushed out of the grounds as quickly as possible and eased the councillor down onto a wooden bench across from his house. "I hope this does the trick," Celes said.

"You can stick around and monitor the situation. I must go after Alrion," Vincent said.

"But that's suicide! You don't know the desert!" Celes said. Her eyes pleaded with him.

"No, it's fine. I can manage, I have the directions. Take care, I'll find our son." Vincent gave Celes a quick kiss and ran off into the street.

Celes watched him go, all the elation of their escape and victory dispersing all at once.

27

THE DESERT TEMPLE

As the storm settled in Alrion began to relax a little.

"We should take turns remaining on watch, so we can warn Alrion if there's danger of the shelter breaking," Certan said.

"That sounds wise, I'm not sure if I could sleep otherwise. I don't trust this, no offence Alrion," Lara said.

"None taken, I'm a little amazed it actually worked. How about you both sleep first, I can't sleep immediately anyway, I need to monitor this a bit more and try to relax," Alrion said.

"No problem. Make sure you wake me before you get too sleepy. Then I'll wake Lara for her shift," Certan said. Then he and Lara slowly prepared to sleep, laying out some blankets to lie on. They took additional care to not bump into any of the walls protecting them.

Alrion couldn't sleep yet, but needed something else to focus on. He decided to review his spell book, and that strange notebook he had been receiving messages in.

I wonder if it's Falric sending them? He still wasn't sure of Falric's fate, although he secretly wished the wizard had survived. Alrion still carried the guilt of not being able to help his mentor.

Next time, I won't fail. He saw the notebook first, and reached for it. Leafing through the pages, he found a new entry.

You must use time to your advantage.

"That's odd," Alrion whispered, and turned to the next page. There was no other message, just that one. Alrion had the distinct feeling that someone was watching him.

Does this wizard know that I am trapped in a storm? Maybe it's Ashra, Alrion thought. There were some aspects that made sense, but he never met Ashra until recently. The advice seemed timely, but it was too neat.

There has to be something else to this, but what? I am using my time as effectively as possible. We kept my training short so that I could make my way to the temple as soon as possible. Is there something I'm missing?

Alrion worked through all the interpretations of the message. He was still missing something, but decided to capitalise on the fact that he was stuck in a storm and reviewed his spell book.

With delight Alrion noticed that the spells he had practised with Ashra were now documented in the book. Reading about them from a different author provided an additional perspective and helped his understanding. It was as if what he read resonated strongly with him.

Somewhere in my head, I have this knowledge already. It must be the act of joining the lines from something I instinctively know, to something I actively know. It was an interesting perspective that he would have to try out on someone.

"Next time I go to Paperton I'll have a lot of questions," Alrion said to himself. But first, he had other things to focus on. He used the time to do some minor reinforcement of his walls, and rework small sections to learn some of the slightly different techniques in his spell book.

As his confidence climbed, and the protective dome retained its strength, Alrion felt sleep coming on.

It's safe now, and I have no energy left. It's time, he thought. He shuffled over and shook Certan. At the slightest touch the monk's eyes darted open and he was completely alert.

"Time for my shift? Great. Have a good rest." Certan sat up carefully and inspected the walls and listened carefully. "This will be set in for a while, but I think we are safe. Don't worry I will wake you if required," he said.

"Thanks, I'm exhausted." Alrion laid out a blanket and collapsed onto it. Sleep was close, but it was a restless sleep.

He awoke by himself, and was quite groggy and confused.

Lara and Certan were up and talking quietly.

"Welcome back. I would ask how your sleep was, but I could tell from all the tossing and turning that it wasn't great," Lara said.

"I'm not sure, maybe I was overtired. Is everything alright?" Alrion started to test the walls.

"Seems fine, storm has died down a bit. It's still too much to go out yet, but I think we are over the worst. Eat and we shall keep an ear out," Certan said. Alrion drank some water and ate some biscuits and bread. He felt a bit better than the day before, even his restless sleep had done the job.

"Have you ever experienced a storm like this?" Alrion said.

"No, nothing quite this bad. It's suspicious," Certan said.

"In what way? It's unnatural?" Lara said.

"Yes." Certan didn't elaborate but he looked concerned.

"So maybe a wizard is behind it?" Alrion said.

"I don't know what's possible, but it seems likely. We should be very careful during the rest of our journey," Certan said.

"You know, it seems like a crazy spell, but it's plausible," Alrion said after a moment of consideration.

"At least if that's the case, they don't know where we are. It's not very targeted," Lara said.

"Agreed. We just need to remain cautious and prepare ourselves," Certan said.

"Sure. I'll review my spells and do some training," Alrion went back to the spell book and tried miniature versions of his spells within the dome. By practising at a very small scale, he would not disrupt their shelter and he could focus more on how he was controlling the spells.

Hours passed, and Alrion felt in more control of his new techniques. He built a tiny dome that surrounded Certan's foot and he kicked it away.

"Aww that was cute," Lara said with a laugh. Certan was about to respond when he stopped suddenly and pressed his ear against the dome wall.

"Something has changed. I think the storm is dying down," he said. Lara and Alrion became still and tried listening as well. The howling seemed more distant, and less enthusiastic.

"I think you're right," Lara said softly.

"How long until we can emerge?" Alrion said.

"Let's wait a bit longer," Certan said. They all waited cautiously. Alrion stopped practising his spells and Lara sat still, occasionally trying to listen through the wall. After a while Certan broke the silence again.

"Can you open a tiny part of the wall? I want to test the environment outside," Certan said. Alrion concentrated, and thought about how to adjust the wall. He couldn't just attack it, he needed a way of altering the structure in just the right way.

"I need a minute to figure this out," Alrion said, and began his work. It was almost like building the shelter again, but this time looking for places that he could remove. He projected an invisible framework over it, then tried moving a section out. The wall shook, but then settled and a rectangular chunk shuffled over along the sand. Alrion was just about to cheer when a rush of sand blocked the gap he had created.

"Something must have gone wrong," Alrion said, confused. He was sure he had done it carefully.

"It wasn't your mistake, I think we are quite buried. Have you noticed the air going stale?" Certan said.

"Now that you mention it. But why now?" Lara said.

"I think it took a long time to build up, but we are quite buried. I have been monitoring it but didn't say anything in order to prevent panic. The last thing we needed was to unnecessarily waste the air," Certan said.

"What do we do?" Lara said.

"We need to take a chance that the storm has moved on. Alrion will need to clear a path for us," Certan said.

"That can be arranged. Let's pack up then give me the word," Alrion said.

The three of them took care in packing their things, working methodically.

"That looks to be it," Lara said.

"So, I just clear a path in front of us?" Alrion said.

"Correct. Just be careful of sand coming in." Certan shuffled over to behind Alrion, and Lara joined him.

Alrion considered his options. "I should clear and build at the same time, that's safer," he decided. He drew in a deep breath, then built up his Spark. He prepared a tightly compacted ball of force, and held it ready. Before he unleashed it, he prepared himself to build up some walls.

"I hope this works," he whispered and let his spell loose. The ball of force rocked ahead, displacing a huge curtain of sand. Alrion had not expected so much to come back to him. He quickly brought up a protective wall in front of them and extended the dome roof to try and prevent additional burial by the sand.

"More sand is coming in," Certan said. Alrion tried again, but altered his technique. Instead he built a moving sand wall, and advanced it ahead. The length of their dome kept extending. With a sigh, he stopped it and paused, letting the wall in front of him drop down.

"You've extended our space. What's the plan?" Lara said.

"We have to assume the sand cover is extensive. I am hoping that if I poke a hole up, if we have enough space we can reinforce an exit before we get buried for good," Alrion said,

"Worth a try, I will advise you if the situation is worsening," Certan said.

This better work. Alrion had underestimated the seriousness of their situation. He shuffled closer, and picked a spot in the ceiling. He gathered his Spark, and prepared another ball of force. But this time he packed more and more power into it, and tried to compact the energy as much as possible.

"Here goes," he whispered and put everything into the spell. There was an explosion of force above them, displacing the sand everywhere. But the intensity and power of the force pushed most of the sand out and they saw the daylight finally.

"Quick, reinforce!" Certan shouted.

Alrion created walls either side of the relatively small hole and only minimal sand dropped back in.

"We have an exit, if we can get there," Lara said, looking up at the daylight.

"Maybe I can build a ladder," Alrion said, thinking out loud. He shuffled over then examined his new reinforced vertical walls. With some experimentation, he managed to create some bricks sticking out of the wall. Lara tested on.

"It's a bit crumbly, can you do better?" she said. Alrion tried again, putting more water into the mix and compacting the sand further.

"That'll do. Keep going," Lara said. Alrion built additional blocks, and Lara kept climbing.

"Keep it up, I'm almost there," Lara said. Soon her head disappeared into the hole and she dragged herself out.

"Wow. Get up here," she said. Alrion let Certan go next, and watched carefully to ensure the makeshift ladder held. Once Certan had reached the top, he called down to Alrion.

"Can you throw the bags up?" Certan said. Alrion picked up the bags with waves of force and gently carried them up to Certan's waiting hands. Once they were taken, Alrion started climbing by himself. The rungs on his sand ladder were stronger than he had expected.

I'm getting this finally. He took care and soon his head poked out of the opening. He had to take care to ensure his sword didn't get stuck as he climbed out of the hole. He dusted himself off and took a look around. There were now sand dunes where before they were none.

"The whole landscape has changed," Alrion said.

"Yes, an unimaginable amount of sand has settled here. I have a bad feeling about this," Certan said.

"How will we navigate now?" Lara said.

"Don't worry, I can look at the position of the sun and adjust our course. Eventually we will start to see landmarks that I can use as a guide," Certan said.

"Good. Let's get started?" Alrion said.

"Certainly. This way." Certan walked off with confidence, and Alrion followed close behind.

Lara lingered, looking back at the mostly buried shelter. "Shouldn't you close that up? What if someone fell in?" she said.

"Good point, it's useful but more likely a person would fall in unexpectedly. I'll close it in." Alrion reached out and visualised the structure of the wall, as he had done previously when taking out a small piece. However, this time he started to crack and destabilise the entire wall. The sand shifted suddenly and the mini dune next to them sunk swiftly into the ground. Alrion stepped back with a start, surprised at the speed of the movement.

"Lucky you weren't standing any closer," Lara said.

"I know, I won't miscalculate that again," Alrion said.

"The sand is a dangerous and often misjudged element," Certan said, then he turned back and started walking again. Lara and Alrion rushed to catch up.

Up and down they went, navigating the new dunes. Certan only paused occasionally to check they were heading in the right direction. There seemed to be a lot of sand and dust still in the air, which helped reduce the sun's rays a little. But it was hot and slow going.

Hours later, Alrion was tired and hot. He couldn't see that they had made any progress at all. But Certan seemed confident, so he kept going. His mind started drifting off when suddenly, he ran into Certan. The monk had stopped completely.

"What is it?" Alrion said.

"That should be the temple in the distance. Take a look," Certan said. Alrion squinted and looked where the monk was pointing.

"All I can see is the haze. Is that smoke?"

"That's definitely smoke. I take it you don't have massive bonfires at the temple?" Lara said.

"Not at all. I believe the temple is under attack," Certan said. Alrion didn't know what to say. Despite everything they had done, they were too late.

28

WAVERING

C ertan started walking again, increasing his speed.

"What are we doing? What's the plan?" Alrion said.

"We must get closer and assess. Don't you agree?" Certan said.

"Sure, we don't know what we are dealing with," Alrion said, although he felt quite rattled. They had been so quick in travelling here, and only paused for a while.

"Maybe we shouldn't have stopped," Alrion said.

"We may have been caught in the storm anyway, and you wouldn't have had the required training. Besides, you needed that to take on Wraith," Lara said.

"Maybe it's not enough? My spells did nothing last time. I should have focused on learning how to use this sword, that seemed to work," Alrion said.

"Don't second guess yourself, everything you did was the best choice. You weren't going to be an effective fighter in such a brief time anyway, so it's best that you worked on being a better wizard. Don't you agree Certan?" Lara said.

"Absolutely. You need the right focus and mindset to fight effectively. Some of that you have already from your previous encounters so you are at an advantage. But the body has many secrets, which take time to master. Your sword may be an effective weapon against Wraith, but you are not ready to wield it properly. There is time for that," Certan said.

"You both make sense. I just feel a bit lost now that it seems as though he is here and ahead of us. I secretly thought that we could get there first, so I could use the second trial to be better prepared for him," Alrion said.

"You beat him once with even less training, don't let yourself get defeated already," Lara said, giving him a big smile. Alrion couldn't help but smile back. His doubts were still there, but he could push them back. For a time.

They continued on, gradually through the burning hot desert. The addition of the new dunes made the going tougher, and Alrion frequently wanted the flat wasteland back. At least it was less work. The route seemed to be slowly taking them higher and higher. Lara mentioned it first.

"We seem to be slowly ascending. Is that normal?" Lara said.

"No, this is not natural. I suspect it because we are getting closer to the source of the storm," Certan said.

"Let's say Wraith or someone near the temple created the storm?" Alrion said.

"That would be my guess," Certan said.

"Lucky we weren't any closer, we would have struggled to get out from that much sand," Lara said. Alrion stopped and looked back. When he looked for it, he could see the gentle slope of the sand all the way back. The amount of sand displaced was staggering. He thought about the power required to fuel such a storm and a chill ran down his spine.

Don't think about it, you're fine, he thought, and took some quicker steps to catch up.

"We are getting closer, I think we shall see better once we reach the top of this dune," Certan said.

"You would hope so, that thing is massive," Lara said. The incline was steeper than anything they had traversed yet, and it was obviously towering over the rest of the area.

With more measured steps, they ascended the giant dune. The sand still shifted considerably, so they had to take care with each step forward. Alrion found this section very frustrating. His footing was constantly sliding back, and he felt like he was making very little progress. But each time he paused and looked back, he could see how far they had come. Not as far as he would have liked for the effort expended but at least he could see.

"If I'm right, we should be able to see the temple once we reach the top. Very close now." Certan increased his speed, his urge to see the temple once more spurring him on. Lara also sped up, but Alrion let them go ahead. He wanted to conserve his energy.

The monk reached the top first, and crouched. He said nothing. Lara joined him shortly after and let out a quiet gasp. Alrion was intrigued by what they were seeing, and pushed on to look for himself. He crested the top of the dune and almost toppled over, the ridge was actually quite narrow. Once he steadied himself he looked out.

The desert temple was in clear view. The large blocks of stone covered in sand looked like something from a long-forgotten time. But that was not what took his breath away. The smoke was a sign of danger, as Certan had pointed out. But the horrifying thing was the black mass of seething Tainted swarming the temple and surrounding it. As far as he could see, they ground was covered with Tainted. He could pick out Blighters, Tainted Ones and even several Shades.

"This is bad," Alrion said. It was a lot more than that, but he couldn't put the words together.

"It is probably the worst-case scenario, given the circumstances," Certan said.

"We can't take that head on," Lara said.

"We can't take that period," Alrion said.

"There are ways and means. The temple is not yet overcome, so our quest is not in vain." Certan was studying the scene with a thoughtful look.

"You're just getting sentimental over returning to your home. Lara and I took on a tiny fraction of the force here, and I used the entirety of my Spark. She had to save me at the last moment," Alrion said.

"We wouldn't have to fight them all," Certan said.

"There must be another way into the temple," Lara said.

"No, stealth takes time. By the time, we enter it will be too late. The monks will be defeated, the temple will be taken and the Vault of Silence will be destroyed or locked away. This is a no-win situation," Alrion said.

"You've dealt with long-shots before and succeeded. We can't give up, not at this stage," Lara said.

"I won't allow you to falter now. We have come too far, and the monks need our help. You have an important responsibility that you cannot give up," Certan said,

"I can find Ashra, and he can teach me instead. He has passed the trial, he understands how it works and what it teaches. It won't be the same, but at least I can prepare in safety. I can't deal with this, it's too much too soon. No amount of power can overcome these odds," Alrion said. Certan stood up and walked off the dune. He stood in front of Alrion, blocking the way back.

"To retreat, you must go through me," Certan said.

"Don't make me do this. Just let me go," Alrion said.

"Don't be silly Alrion, let's just figure this out." Lara reached out for Alrion's arm, but he shook her off.

"Move, Certan," Alrion said. The monk shrugged and shook his head. Alrion sent a wave of force at the monk's feet. Certan was moved, but regained his footing and resumed his stance. Alrion threw another wave, this time at Certan's chest. The monk absorbed the force, moving slightly, but without losing his ground.

"You will need more than that," Certan said.

Alrion started to get frustrated. "Just leave me be," he said. He prepared a fire spell, and as he readied it Certan moved. He dashed with incredible speed, knocking Alrion to the side and disrupting the spell. Alrion recovered, and went

VAUGHAN W. SMITH

all out, throwing waves of force at Certan from all directions. The monk seemed to anticipate most of them, and either dodged or blocked the force with minimal impact. Alrion kept up the onslaught and prepared another spell.

Since Certan was within a smaller area, Alrion raised a large block of wet sand and formed a powerful seal around Certan's feet. As the sand solidified it contracted, binding the monk's feet tighter and tighter. Certan noticed it happening, and started to struggle with increasing force. But it was too late. Alrion managed to strengthen the block so much that the monk was completely trapped.

"So, it has come to this," Certan said. There was a sadness and regret in his voice.

"I'm sorry, but I can't do this," Alrion said. Certan nodded, and reached into his robes. He retrieved the metal flask, and held it out.

"What's what?" Lara said.

"My saving grace." Certan unscrewed the lid and held it still in front of him.

"Don't drink it, it's not worth it," Alrion said. Certan chuckled quietly.

"You misunderstand," he said. He tipped the flask over and poured it out into the sand. Quite a bit flowed out. Each drop was one that Certan had avoided drinking.

"They will never know," Certan said wistfully.

"What is he talking about? What did you make him do?" Lara said.

"He took that flask from the temple when he was banished. He swore that he would not drink from it again, no matter what happened. So that one day, he could return and show them that had regained his honour and mastered his weakness," Alrion said.

"Why Certan?" she said.

"If all hope is lost for you Alrion, then it is for me also," Certan said. Alrion was shocked. His fear at his powerlessness had not only turned him away from his quest, it had damaged his friend's chances at being accepted again by his people.

"Why would you do that?" Alrion said.

"Because you need to learn. Will is not something you use. Will is a part of how you live. Will means persevering no matter the odds. I will find a way to succeed with an empty flask, just as you will find a way to succeed now," Certan said.

"I...I don't know what to say." Alrion dispersed all the sand around Certan's feet and dropped into a crouch. He buried his head in his hands, trying to think.

"You have come a long way. You have been putting on a big front, and showing off with the use of your new-found power. But you still carry fear for your enemy. And healthy doses of self-doubt. This is normal, especially given the situation. But you mustn't give it power. Acknowledge it and move on. There is much more you must achieve," Certan said.

Alrion looked up. The monk was right about a lot of things. He had been trying to compensate with his magic, to bluff about his confidence and mastery. But it had been a front, and had crumbled spectacularly in front of overwhelming odds. Would that realisation change anything though?

"But where do we go from here? Acknowledging my fear and uncertainty is not going to make that ridiculous army go away," Alrion said.

"Who said anything about fighting them all. There is another way," Certan said.

"I'm all ears, I don't want to deal with that," Lara said, jerking her thumb over her shoulder towards the teeming mass of Tainted.

"You don't take me as the type to just saunter in the front door. Do you think the monks don't have other ways of getting around?" Certan said. A wry smile broke out on his face.

"You have a way of getting us in?" Lara said.

"Yes. Provided you have the courage to join me."

"I'll go. Maybe there's a chance," Alrion said.

"Me too. I need to see this place for myself. Maybe even liberate some treasure," Lara said with a wink.

"Follow me," Certan said, shaking off the sand around his feet and walking off with purpose.

29

ENTERING THE TEMPLE

T he trio walked with renewed hope. Certan took them along the newly formed ridge and they tried to avoid looking at the black mass of enemies. They started to approach the temple in a round-about way, avoiding danger.

"We can't do this the whole way, it will take all day," Lara said.

"I agree, just a bit further," Certan said. Lara didn't respond, and decided to see what the monk had to show them. A few minutes later he stopped quickly, and crouched down. He motioned for Lara and Alrion to do the same.

"This is as close as we can come without the need to approach directly," Certan said.

"The front door perhaps, but you said there was another way," Lara said.

"There is, but not for us. You yourself said, it will take too long to take the long way in. If I show Alrion the way, he can enter the temple from the secret passage and we can create a diversion so that he doesn't get noticed," Certan said.

"Hang on, you want us to go into that?" Lara said.

"I said we had a chance, not that it was safe," Certan said.

"Why are you smiling? This is terrible!" Lara said.

"Nothing is certain, except death. We don't know when it will come, but that it will claim us eventually. I don't want it to be today, but it wouldn't be the worst end, would it?" Certan said.

"You monks are crazy. Alrion say something," Lara said.

"I don't know the area well, and I certainly don't want to sacrifice anyone today. But Certan must know that I can't sneak in unnoticed. If there's a way for you to enable that and survive, it's not a bad idea," Alrion said.

"Lara is quite resourceful, I've noticed she has a few interesting things hidden up her sleeves. I'm not sacrificing myself just yet," Certan said.

"If you're going to do this, I'll promise that I'll make it to the trial. One way or another," Alrion said.

"I guess it's up to us then," Lara said.

"I'll leave you to ponder about our chances of survival, and I'll show Alrion where the entrance is." Certan led Alrion aside, and they crept down the ridge on the other side.

"The entrance is marked by a statue of a cat. The cat' tail is actually a lever, and if you pull it the entrance will be revealed. But you must close the entrance immediately. If the enemy notices it, the temple's defenses will be overrun in no time," Certan said.

"Understood," Alrion said.

"See that curve in the ridge down there?"

"Yes, I see it."

"Make your way down there as quietly as possible. You should be able to see the cat statue from there. Await our signal, then make a run for it. I'm not sure how much time you will have."

"I can do that. Thank you Certan, I wouldn't have made it this far without you. Now go survive so I can repay you," Alrion said.

"That's my intention."

"What's the signal?"

"I'm not sure, but knowing Lara, you will know it when you see it," Certan said.

"I'm sure you are right about that," Alrion said, and held out his hand. Certan shook it firmly then headed back. Alrion started working his way down. He wanted to get his bearings and locate the statue before he noticed the signal. It would be a disaster if he didn't get there in time.

The ridge was quite steep, and following it without going over the top was hard going. He was walking on an angle and each step threatened to have him toppling down the slope. But he persevered and made consistent progress. Soon he reached the spot that Certan had pointed out and paused for a rest.

Once he had composed himself, Alrion crept up the ridge and looked out. They were around the side of the temple, but there was still a large mass of Blighters and Tainted milling around. It seemed as though they were looking for another entry.

Not just a large mass, they're coordinating. This is bad, Alrion thought. He could see why a diversion was required. There was a decent chance that Alrion could make it to that entrance, and get inside. But there was purpose behind the enemy's actions. If they got wind of a secret entrance hidden here, and thought to investigate the statue it was only a matter of time until they managed to open it.

I won't be able to do a single thing. Certan and Lara are on their own, Alrion realised. He dismissed the thought and focused on what he could do himself.

He noticed strange movement out on the ground, and tracked it with his eyes. Something was moving really fast, but wasn't being noticed by the enemy. That is until it started attacking. It was like an invisible whirlwind of death, carving a path through the mass of Blighters. It took them seconds to figure out what was going on, and in that time at least twenty of them had fallen.

As they began to react in anger, a large explosion went off a bit further away. A wave of Blighters was sent flying, sending the whole group into disarray. The deathly blur that was Certan changed direction, moving towards the explosion. The confused and angry Blighters started to follow, the Tainted spurring them on.

Alrion watched carefully. That was definitely the signal. But there were still one or two Blighters that had not followed. He had to make a call. Should he wait more, or take them out?

I'll wait a tiny bit more, just in case. Despite the commotion and damage that Certan and Lara were causing, the few straggling Blighters were not going over. Either they were oblivious or reacting to different orders.

They're not that close to the statue, maybe I can creep past them. It was worth a try. He didn't want to draw any attention, because it would detract from what was being done by his friends.

Alrion cautiously crested the ridge and slid down the other side. He rose quickly and kept an eye on the Blighters. There were three worth worrying about, and two of them were roving around and not too close to the statue. However, there was one patrolling around that was a danger. If Alrion was careless he would get spotted for sure.

He kept low and ensured his hood was up over his face. He slowly moved along, watching all three Blighters. As he closed in on the cat statue he realised that the timing wasn't going to work. The roving Blighter would be too close, and Alrion had nowhere to hide. He had to take care of it.

Alrion altered his path, and closed in on the Blighter. He wanted to get close, to make things easier. He stalked behind it, waiting until it reached what appeared to be the limit of its patrol. Alrion carefully prepared a wave of force and directed it at the creature's neck, providing a powerful spin to quickly and efficiently break its neck. The Blighter dropped silently, and Alrion stalked back to the cat statue.

So far so good. I hope the other ones don't notice. As he neared the statue, he kept an eye on the other Blighters. They didn't seem to notice anything unusual, and in the distance Alrion could still hear the noises of fighting and explosions.

"I hope they're alright over there. Better take care of this now," he whispered.

As he examined the cat, he could see the amazing detail. It looked ancient too, but was quite well preserved considering the circumstances. He found the tail without trouble, and gave it a yank. Nothing happened.

Alrion held onto the tail and tried manipulating it in different directions. Down, side to side and diagonally had no effect. He tried lifting it up and it started to move. Throwing more effort into it he managed to force the tail up, and heard a nearby clunk. Then nothing.

Alrion's eyes darted back to the other two Blighters. It may have been his imagination but they seemed like they were heading over. They seemed to be moving with a bit more purpose than before.

"Come on statue, let's go," Alrion whispered. The Blighters were still a way off, but if they came too close he wouldn't be able to hide. Suddenly the ground beneath him shifted, and he almost toppled over. He saw steps appearing in the sand, descending into a dark passage. Alrion ran down as quickly as he could, almost slipping several times. Once he reached the bottom he created a light above his hand and looked everywhere for another lever. He found one on the wall, and yanked it as hard as possible.

Another clank, then silence.

Where are those Blighters? I hope they're not too inquisitive. He was completely exposed if they came close and noticed the stairs down. He strained his ears but couldn't hear anything. With a start, the stairs began to move. They shifted back and up, forming a neat wall where there was once an incline.

I guess that's closed. Time to investigate this passage.

Certan was beginning to get overwhelmed. Lara's explosives had helped thin out and confuse the Blighters. But the Tainted that were controlling the horde had recovered from the initial shock, and were sending wave after wave at them. He knew from counting the explosions that Lara was almost out of her bombs. He made his way closer to the latest one, hoping to find her.

Spinning and rolling he made his way through the throng like a scythe, cutting down Blighters left and right. He couldn't keep this up forever, but at least he could hold his own. He was waiting for another explosion, but it didn't come.

"Lara!" Certan shouted. He needed to have an indication of where she was, or even if she was still alive.

"Over here, bit busy!" she shouted back. Certan redirected his efforts and headed in her direction. A deadly claw strike interrupted his train of thought, almost catching him in the neck. A last-minute reaction saved him, and he took the offending Blighter down quickly.

I'm slowing, getting sloppy, Certan thought. Time was running out. He found

Lara surrounded by a wreath of Blighter corpses. She was in the centre, alternating between slicing with her dagger and throwing knives with pinpoint precision.

"Out of bombs?" Certan said as he joined her.

"Yes. How much longer do we need to do this?" she said.

"Enough time has passed. We are no use to him dead. We need to get into the temple," Certan said.

"I'm with you there. Any ideas?"

"There are columns holding up the main entrance. They may provide a narrow corridor for us to fight through, where numbers won't be as big an issue." Certan pointed in the general direction.

"If we can get there." Lara threw two knives, taking down two Blighters who had managed to get close. Another was right behind him, its eyes beaming murder and its mouth was slightly open. Lara could see the drool running down its chin and its sharp fangs.

Certan was contending with three others, and had not noticed. Lara panicked. She wasn't sure she had the right space to fend it off without taking a serious injury. As she was awaiting its move she noticed the creature slow then fall down, splitting at the middle as it fell. A blade of Runesteel emerged and Lara finally smiled.

30

THE TRIAL

A s Alrion became accustomed with the passage he increased his speed. He needed to enter the temple as quickly as possible and find the trial. There were no guarantees as to what would happen, but at least he had a chance. It didn't look like the temple was overrun yet.

He had heard nothing behind him, so it appeared as though he had entered without attracting any attention. If the Blighters discovered their fallen friend, they would not know where to look.

The passage was long and winding. Luckily there were no turns to take, so he could move fast and not worry about losing his way. But that was about to change.

The passage ended in a set of stairs. Alrion ran up as fast as he could without risking a fall. He looked up and could not see the end of the stairs. Finally, he reached the end, which was not an exit. It was a dead end. Alrion examined the walls with his light, and could see nothing of use. The ceiling at the landing was very low, so he tried pushing on that instead. It moved slightly.

Encouraged by the movement, Alrion pushed more and a piece of stone above him rotated, acting like a trap door. Alrion felt around with his hands and found something. It was a rope of some kind. He tugged at it, and a simple rope ladder fell down and landed on his head. He pushed it away, then tested it.

Feeling satisfied, Alrion climbed up and hauled himself out of the hole. He was in a tiny room with no other furnishings and only one open doorway.

"Here we are," Alrion whispered. He dusted himself off and left the room immediately. He found himself in a corridor with the option of going left or right. It was well-lit, so he let his light vanish.

This isn't good. I'll try the path on the right. He walked quickly down the corridor, hoping to establish if it was the right way. He passed several rooms that looked like they were sleeping quarters. But nobody was around.

Makes sense, everyone will be out fighting. But that didn't help him. He had no idea where the trial would be. He came to another crossroads and had another decision to make.

"Right again," he decided, and headed off. This time he emerged in a large hall. Weapons lined the walls, and there was a square marked out in the centre of the room.

"This is not it," he decided. But he did notice another doorway at the other end of the room and kept going. He pressed through and found a staircase going up.

"May as well try it," he whispered. He was trying to keep up-beat but felt so frustrated at not knowing what the Vault of Silence even looked like.

I probably should have asked Certan or Ashra more about it. They could have at least told me where to look, he thought. But nobody had expected there to be such trouble.

The staircase wound up and up and rays of daylight stole through the occasional slit. Alrion didn't bother trying to look through, he had no time. He noticed a doorway at the top bathed in light. He ran for it, and burst through.

Alrion emerged onto a rooftop of some sort. The sun blinded him for a second, and he had to adjust. There was a lone monk on the roof, firing arrows down at the horde of Tainted. His tall build gave him a good vantage over his targets. From this view, Alrion decided that things looked even worse.

"Hello!" Alrion shouted as he approached. The monk looked back in surprise, but resumed his attacks. "I need your help," Alrion said when he reached the monk.

"Whatever it is, we are in greater need. Are you a wizard?" the monk said.

"Yes, I'm here to do the trial of Will. It's vital that you take me there as soon as possible," Alrion said.

"If you don't help me, there won't be a temple left to do the trial in," the monk said. He motioned with his head and Alrion looked over to see what he meant. There were streams of Blighters climbing the walls, using the nooks and crevasses built up by the passage of time.

"If I help with this, you'll take me to the trial?" Alrion said.

"I'll escort you myself and introduce you. My name is Graem," the monk said.

"Let's work together then Graem. I am Alrion. Is there a leader here?"

"I would say so. Look over there, see that lone Tainted One?" Graem said.

"Yes, you might be right. First, we can deal with these Blighters who are advancing and see his reaction," Alrion took up a position next to Graem and started building up his Spark. He formed up many spheres and infused them with fire and hurled them down at the Blighters. There was a punch of force behind each one, so not only did the affected Blighters catch fire but they also lost their handholds and tumbled down, taking others with them.

"Where have you been? This is much faster," Graem said.

"Trying to get here. We had to bunker down during the storm." Alrion launched another volley, taking out the next row of hopeful Blighters.

"Must be the work of a wizard. Someone has to be coordinating all these Tainted and Blighters. Haven't seen anything like this in my entire life. The only edge we've had over the Tainted is that they weren't organised. This is too much." Graem launched another arrow, and took out a Blighter that had been hiding and had dodged the previous attacks.

After that attack, there seemed to be a lull.

"They're planning the next move. Look at that Tainted One," Graem said, pointing out the same one as before. He was waving his hands and seemingly talking to himself.

"I think you're right. I'm not sure how effective my spells are at this range. Hard to aim and he will probably see them coming," Alrion said.

"You ever worked with projectiles before?" Graem said.

"Yes, I've sped up daggers over short distances," Alrion said.

"Let's try that, only with an arrow. I can aim true, but I can't shoot that far either. But if I line up the shot properly and you can provide enough force and ensure it flies straight, we can nail their leader," Graem said.

"Worth a try, give me a moment." Alrion prepared a lance of air that he could catch the arrow within and propel forward.

"Are you ready? You have to act quickly, I won't be compensating for height," Graem said.

"Ready, just let me know when you're firing," Alrion said.

"Now!" Graem shouted. Alrion let loose the spell in anticipation and focused all his attention on the archer. He saw the arrow launching and caught it with his lance of air. The arrow increased in speed and hurtled towards its target. However, the aim was slightly off, and all the arrow did was graze the ear of the Tainted One.

He screamed in pain and looked over. When he noticed Alrion and Graem standing together, he paused then started running.

"Not bad for a first, if you can repeat that same level of force I can aim the next shot better. But it's going to be more difficult with a moving target." Graem already had the next arrow nocked and was aiming at the Tainted One.

"Just a moment." Alrion prepared another spell and watched Graem closely.

"Any minute now. There!" Graem said and launched his arrow. Alrion repeated his spell, but this time tried to have less impact on the arrow's path. It flew away with rapid speed, toward the target. Alrion tracked its progress, and was unsure if it would hit. But Graem had aimed true, and the arrow struck the man in the head and he dropped immediately.

"Wow, great shot," Alrion said.

"Thanks, but I had help. If you wouldn't mind assisting again," Graem said. Alrion looked back and saw another wave of Blighters preparing to climb over the temple walls. He prepared and launched another wave of fireballs, this time completely incinerating all those that had reached the top.

They waited patiently for another minute, but no more Blighters followed their fallen.

"I think we've done enough here, let's go and I'll settle my end of the bargain." Graem put his bow over his shoulder and ran towards the stairwell.

"Do you know Certan?" Alrion asked as they descended.

"Yes. Great monk with an even greater weakness. He will be missed," Graem said.

"He has returned, he guided me here and showed me the secret passage," Alrion said.

"I've never heard of anyone returning after being banished, and betraying our secrets too. I'll be glad to see him again, but I am not sure if he can rejoin us," Graem said.

"That would be a shame." Alrion knew his friend had pinned so much on being able to return to the temple. He would do all he could to help that become a reality.

As they weaved through the various passages and rooms Alrion realised that he would never have found his way in time. The temple was a maze, and he had trouble keeping track of the way they had gone.

"This place is huge," Alrion said.

"Yes, it's been extended constantly over its lifetime. It's a great deterrent for attackers. Something that will be tested today," Graem said.

"Do you know anything about the trial of Will? The Vault of Silence? Have you seen it?" Alrion said.

"I only know of its location. Unfortunately, I can offer no other help, but that's all you need." Alrion appreciated the monk's straight forward approach.

"I appreciate it, time is of the essence."

"You are welcome, you have helped us greatly already. I would be interested to hear your story at another time. It would be a curious one for sure. You would need a special reason to turn up here at such a time and still require to take the trial."

"It is an impossible quest, one that I hope to achieve regardless," Alrion said.

"Sounds like a challenge. I wish you luck, Alrion. I cannot stay, but I hope we meet again." Graem left the young wizard standing before an impressive set of doors. Unlike the rest of the temple they were made of a strange metal.

Alrion pushed them open and they floated inwards with ease.

Inside was a great chamber, which looked like it had been carved out of rock. There were four monks sitting cross-legged on the ground.

"Close the doors behind you Alrion," one of the monks said. Alrion followed the instruction immediately, then continued to approach.

"I'm sorry, this is such a rush. I need to take the trial immediately," Alrion said.

"We know who you are and why you are here," the second monk said.

"Great. How do I start it?"

"Why do you deserve to take this trial?" The third monk said.

"I need to, to fulfil my quest. I need the power of Will to succeed," Alrion said.

"All could use it, but few can use it. Why you?" the fourth monk said.

"I just told you. I need it to cast the spell. The spell to end the Blight," Alrion said.

"And why do you deserve that responsibility?" The fourth monk said.

"It was given to me," Alrion said.

"Responsibility is not given, it is taken and borne," the fourth monk said.

"I accepted this quest, and all it entailed. Yes, I have faltered on my way. But I have made it here today. Isn't that proof enough?" Alrion said.

"Why do YOU deserve it?" the fourth monk said.

"I don't have time for this. Enemies are at the gate, an army bigger than you have ever seen. Why all the questioning?" Alrion said.

"Only those who are deserving can perform the trial," the first monk said.

"Why are YOU deserving?" the fourth monk said. Alrion was getting increasingly frustrated. He didn't have time for this, Wraith and his creatures could break through at any moment. He racked his brain, for the right response. He needed a way to convince them.

Suddenly he remembered Certan's words. Yes, that was it.

"I am deserving because I have encountered many setbacks on the way here. I have been almost killed, turned away by people, and almost buried alive in the sand. But I persevered. Because Will is about persevering no matter what. Getting up and trying again. It's about knowing that eventually you will succeed," Alrion said. The monks did not respond. Minutes seemed to pass. Alrion did not try to add anything, he knew nothing else would affect them.

"You are deserving. Go forth and perform the trial. You may enter the Vault of Silence," the first monk said. He gestured with his hand and a glowing portal opened in-between the four monks. Alrion walked closer, and was amazed by what lay within.

31

THE VAULT OF SILENCE

Alrion was in a completely white room. As soon as he entered, he turned back to look at how he had entered, and the entry was gone. He was completely sealed in.

That's a little unnerving. But the wonder of the space he was in overcame that. With care, he walked around the vault, examining all the walls. They were perfectly smooth and white, built from a material he didn't recognise. There were no seams anywhere. It was as if the whole space was one surface.

The Vault of Silence. It certainly is impressive, but very minimal. There's nothing here, Alrion thought. He reached out and touched the wall. It felt cool to the touch, but was impossibly smooth. He ran his hand around the wall, feeling for any inconsistencies in it. There were none.

I suppose the trial is to find a way out. As he walked through the vault, his mind was telling him that something was wrong. He stopped, trying to puzzle it out.

"My footsteps are not making any sound," he said. But no words came out. He tried to call out. No sound was made at all.

This vault is actually silent. That seems impossible, Alrion thought. But no matter what he did, there was no sound. It was a bit overwhelming, so he sank down and sat on the floor, leaning his back against the wall.

I'm here, I can't make a sound no matter what I do and I need to get out. But it's a trial of Will, so that has to be the key. As Certan said, perseverance is vital. I'll examine every part of the Vault to see if there's any weakness or secret. He stood up and walked around the room, taking his time to feel the entire surface.

It took a long time, but he managed to complete a circuit, with only the ceiling and other high places unchecked.

I'll try a spell. He gathered his Spark and prepared a wave of force. He spread it out like a blanket and ran it across the ceiling and other areas he could not access. He didn't notice any resistance to the spell. It seemed that the surfaces were all identical and there were no imperfections or secret nooks.

"At least my magic works here," Alrion said to himself. He sat down again and thought about how to pass the trial. He had one other tool to try. He unsheathed his sword and examined the diamond. It wasn't glowing at all.

Wherever I am, is not close to the Blight monsters. That may mean something, he thought. Holding the sword, he tried several times to pierce or damage the walls. As before, there were no signs of damage.

Maybe it's a matter of breaking down the wall, without anything external. That would take willpower and persistence. I have an advantage because I'm a wizard, Alrion thought. He was happy with the plan and gathered his Spark once more. He systematically hit the entire room with waves of force, then rotated into pinpointing an exact spot. Since the vault didn't seem to take any damage, he increased the intensity slowly to a level he didn't normally try.

This is good training, if nothing else. Soon he tired though, and the room appeared perfectly untouched.

This will require further thought. But his mind was not at ease. He kept thinking back to his friends, and the assault on the temple. Time was not something he had ample supply of.

~

"Vincent! It's a relief to see you here. How did you find your way?" Certan said, as he knocked down another Blighter and stood back to back with Lara.

"You gave me directions remember? When we found out that there was going to be an attack on the temple I rushed here immediately," Vincent said.

"We'll have to hear the story later, when we're not about to get killed!" Lara said.

"I'll cover us, you two make a path through to the temple," Vincent said as he sliced through another two Blighters.

Certan took the lead, using his attacks to knock the Blighters away as far as possible, and Lara stood close behind, taking out any trying to attack from strange angles. As a unit, the three of them managed to slowly work their way to the temple entrance, and take cover between the vast columns of the entrance area and the temple walls.

"If we make it back there will the monks let us in?" Vincent said.

"They should, if we can make it safe enough to risk it," Certan said.

"That's quite an ask," Lara said, slashing at another Blighter. The reduced space meant that there was less space for the Blighters to attack them. But it also meant it was harder to strike back.

"Do you have any other interesting things to throw?" Certan said.

"Only a few, and I'm saving them for later. But I have something that should help us get inside," Lara said.

"We'll need it," Vincent said, cutting down another Blighter and kicking the lifeless body away. As they neared the main entry they saw the monks shooting arrows and throwing metal discs through a rectangular slit in the massive metal doors.

"Here's the plan. I'll create a space, you do some sort of diversion, then we'll get the monks to sneak us in," Vincent said.

"That sounds possible, but we need to tell them the plan. We may be stranded otherwise," Certan said. They fought their way closer, so that Certan could speak with the monks.

"Friends, if we can make a safe opportunity can you open the doors?" Certan said.

"The banished one returns, interesting timing," one of the monks said.

"I am here to help. Let us in so that we may recover then fight again," Certan said.

"Let them try, if they can create a gap we can manage the doors," a second monk said.

"Very well, do your best," the first monk said and ducked to let his companion fire another arrow.

"When you're ready!" Certan shouted to Vincent.

The blacksmith waved his hand to signify that he understood, then started advancing. His blade whirled with skill as he stepped forward, pressing the Blighters back with his fury. In their surprise, he managed to cut down a Tainted one and push the offensive even further.

Lara followed close behind, watching Vincent's progress. She needed to wait as long as possible, so that they would have time and space to enter the temple.

The Blighters started to rally again, the initial surprise wearing off. Vincent saw some Shades in the distance moving in, and knew that his attack was losing its effectiveness.

Lara noticed too, and lobbed a glass vial into the crowd just past Vincent. It broke and released plumes of thick black smoke.

That's the signal, Vincent thought, and quickly retreated. As he ran he heard the giant doors begin to open. Some of the Blighters were ignoring the smoke and starting to advance.

I hope this works, Vincent thought, looking back. He wouldn't have nearly as much time as he had hoped for. Certan and Lara were at the door, just inside and waving him in. A monk pointed to three Blighters running ahead of the pack, trying to intercept Vincent.

"That's not a problem." Lara snatched three metallic discs off a nearby monk and let them loose. Just as Vincent reached the doors, the three Blighters sank to the ground and the great doors closed once more.

Another monk said, "Now that you are here, you can make yourselves useful,"

"Just let me catch my breath," Vincent said with a laugh.

"We are not by any means safe, but we have earned a small breather," Certan said.

"Very small breather. I saw some Shades advancing before I came back. These doors will not hold them. We need to ensure the temple is ready to be defended.

"We are already taking care of that," one of the monks said, steel and fire in his eyes.

Alrion woke up. He looked around in amazement.

How did I fall asleep? He reviewed what he remembered happening. He had inspected the entire vault, and cast multiple spells testing the integrity of the walls. He had even tried fire spells too. Nothing had worked.

Then I was exhausted and sat down to take a break. How long as I asleep? Alrion wondered. He had no time for sleep, or resting. But something was strange indeed. If he had slept, what had happened outside? Was there a chance that his friends had defeated Wraith?

This just doesn't make sense. I have no idea how much time has passed. Wherever he was, he was completely sealed away from the outside world. There were no signs of passing time whatsoever.

No time for solving that, I'm rested so I must keep trying, Alrion decided. He stood up and did a quick lap of the room. There was nothing new.

He had tried his main spells, but he hadn't tried his new spells.

"Maybe Ashra was on to something. Maybe earth spells are effective here," Alrion said to himself. He focused his mind, trying to feel a source or water or earth nearby. But nothing resonated at all. There wasn't even any in the walls.

The walls aren't made of earth, I'm confused, Alrion thought. He had tried force, he had tried inspection and care and nothing had achieved any result.

Maybe I just need to Will a door? It was a bit of a crazy thought, but perhaps some out of the box thinking was required to escape this vault. He approached a wall, closed his eyes, and imagined a door opening in it. The door shimmered and glowed, and was big enough for him to step through.

Alrion opened his eyes and observed the wall. It was unchanged.

Maybe it's a trust exercise too? He repeated his visualisation technique and instead of opening his eyes, stepped through his newly imagined door. The wall smacked him in the face and he stumbled.

Not quite there. But at least he had a new avenue to try.

Bang. Bang. Bang. The great doors of the temple were under assault by three Shades. Nothing the monks could throw through the slits in the door had any effect of them.

"The door is lost, it's just a matter of time," Vincent said.

"Time is everything. If what you said is true and your son is in the Vault of Silence he needs as much time as possible," said Rengin, the seeming leader of the monks' defences.

"Have you undergone the trial?" Certan said.

"I cannot say," Rengin said.

"I guess we keep annoying them then," Lara said, hurling more discs through the slits in the doors. One of the Shades bent down to peer through the slit and Lara let loose another disc that hit it between the eyes.

"Oh, I think he's angry," Lara said, judging the reaction of the Shade. The blows against the door stopped.

"Maybe you convinced them to go away?" Vincent said.

"Listen carefully," Certan said. Amongst the general clamour there was the sound of heavy footsteps.

"Are they charging the door?" Lara said.

"Everyone move back, defensive positions around the entry," Rengin said. The monks all stepped back, and moved their ammunition to further back in the room. With a gigantic crash the doors bent, and one of the three Shades pushed through and emerged in the room.

"Now the real fight begins," Vincent said.

Certan and Lara moved next to him, and all three readied themselves.

32

TIME AND TIME AGAIN

A lrion bashed the wall in frustration. As always, it made no sound and had no impact ruining any possible satisfaction from the act.

This is insane. How do I get out? I don't even care about this stupid trial, I need to help my friends, Alrion thought. He had no idea what was going on outside, everyone could be dead for all he knew.

There's that one spell. The light bomb that he had been forbidden to use. There was nobody else here, and it had seemed ridiculously effective.

I've nothing to lose. Let's try it. He built up his Spark cautiously, and remembered how he had built it. He combined the light, fire, and force into the unique combination, and let it build and build. Once he had injected all of his power he let it go. He planned for it to explode once it reached the furthest wall.

As the bomb impacted, the walls began to shimmer, but instead of being destroyed they were absorbing and repelling the force.

Oh no, Alrion thought before his world was enveloped in light.

∽

"We need to keep them separated if we have any chance of doing this," Vincent said.

The three Shades were fighting together, and any time there seemed to be an opening, more Blighters flooded into the entryway.

"We will try and contain the rest, if you focus on that one." Rengin pointed at the Shade nearest the wall.

"Excellent choice, we may be able to steer him into the corner." Lara grabbed a handful of the monks' metal discs and started to advance.

"As we discussed, Lara and Certan you create the opportunity and I'll capitalise," Vincent said.

Lara dashed forward, launching more discs at the Shade. *If only Alrion were here to make them more effective,* she thought. She did miss him, and wanted him by her side. But he was the reason they were fighting, and chances were he had made it to his trial by now.

Just make it back safely, she thought and continued her assault on the Shade. The discs bounced harmlessly off, but the Shade was annoyed and focused his attention on her.

Certan dashed in, raining blows on the Shade's stomach, then disappearing. The Shade whirled quickly to counter attack, but Certan was gone. As it turned to face Lara again it noticed too late that Vincent was there, swinging his sword. The Shade moved quickly to block with its right arm, but it had made a critical mistake. The sword cut cleanly through and the severed arm dropped to the ground. The Shade howled in pain, a strangely muffled and muted sound despite the high volume.

"Nice one," Lara said as Certan and Vincent retreated.

"We weren't fast enough, so the surprise is lost. It will be more cautious now," Vincent said.

"True, we will need to be more cunning. Lara, is your blade made of the same material?"

"Yes, thanks to Vincent."

"I see where you are going with this. It won't expect her to attack up close. Let's try that," Vincent said.

This time he advanced upon the Shade, whirling his sword in large arcs, capturing its attention. After having a taste of the Runesteel, it was keen not to have another.

With the Shade occupied, Certan moved in to attack from the side. He got in several quick blows, which unsteadied the Shade. It didn't move to counter though, as it was carefully watching Vincent. The Shade wasn't going to make the same mistake twice. However, it had made another mistake, in not looking for Lara.

While the fight had carried on, Lara had crept through the other concurrent battles, and sliced the occasional Blighter in her path. But now she was positioned behind the Shade, and it had no idea of her location.

I don't think I can kill it from behind, but I can do some major damage. When she saw the Shade was completely occupied she quietly stalked behind it, leapt, and drove her dagger into the creature's neck.

The Shade lurched back in pain, grasping for the dagger. Lara pulled it out and rolled away. As the Shade lost its balance Vincent lunged forward with his sword and pierced the Shade through the heart. The strike was precise and deep, and within a second the Shade perished. It fell to the ground, lifeless.

The other two Shades recoiled in pain, and looked over. One of them became quite enraged, and grabbed a nearby monk who was momentarily distracted by the commotion. The monk cried out in pain, communicating the anguish that the Shade now felt.

"I think somehow things just got worse," Lara said.

"You could be right," Certan said. Vincent removed his sword and turned his attention onto the other Shade.

~

Alrion slowly regained consciousness. His body ached, and he had no strength. As his eyes opened fully, he sat up and examined his body. Everything was fine, he just felt incredible pain. Once he had done that initial check he looked around the room. It was exactly the same as before. Nothing had happened.

Nothing except almost killing myself. He reached for his Spark and found that it was not available. He had used up all his power.

I keep failing. Why? He lay down and looked at the ceiling, hoping for a breakthrough. What he did attain though was sleep.

Alrion awoke, not knowing how long had passed. But his back was stiff and his muscles restless.

I must have been asleep for hours. But everything is still the same, and I'm still here. What does this all mean? Alrion thought, running his hands through his hair. There was only one possible explanation. Time had to act differently within the vault. It was the only way he could think of to explain how long he had been toiling with no answer.

Shouldn't I be hungry? But he wasn't hungry, or thirsty. He was just in this place, unable to leave.

I have recovered my strength, I am going to train while I think of another way out, Alrion decided. The decision triggered a memory, of the notebook message that he had recently received.

Time is always against us. Use it to your advantage.

*I thought the message was about being stuck in the sandstorm, or my training. But maybe it's about this?*Regardless, it seemed practical. He would find a way out, but while he pondered the solution he would use the time he had available to train. If he had additional time here, he would put it to good use. He was going to emerge more capable in many ways, not just one.

~

Vincent and Certan stepped back, exhausted. They had managed to defeat another Shade, capitalising on its anger, and finding an opening. But they were quite spent. Lara looked around at the monks. Many had fallen, and many were wounded.

"This doesn't look too good," Lara said.

"No, this space is becoming too hard to defend," Vincent said.

"I was going to say the same thing, but I wanted to wait until you toppled that second beast. It's time to pull back," Rengin said.

"Something else prepared?" Vincent said.

"Of course, we're just not sitting on our hands while you take down Shades." Rengin let out a piercing whistle with his hands and the monks started to retreat. Vincent and Lara followed closely, and Certan was helping another monk get away. Once they all passed into the main passage Rengin directed them around a corner. "Now!" he shouted. Two monks hit a wall with a coordinated strike and it started to fall over, blocking the passage. "This will buy us some time, fall back," Rengin said, directing the monks to retreat even further. "This is our home and it's a maze. We can use that to our advantage."

"And the Vault of Silence?" Vincent said.

"At the heart of the temple. It's where we make our last stand."

"Let's hope it doesn't come to that," Certan said.

"You have fought with honour today, brother. I will stand for you, when this is over," Rengin said.

"That is a great honour, coming from you. I will continue to be worthy of your praise," Certan said.

"Take a position in one of these rooms. You can rest a little until they break through, then ambush them," Rengin said. The rooms he pointed to were all tiny, single occupant nooks. Vincent took the first one, Lara the second and Certan the third. The other monks distributed themselves down the passageway, similarly hidden and waiting.

A giant crash and the sounds of rubble echoed down the passageway.

"They're making progress, get ready," Rengin shouted while he was standing in the middle of the passage, monitoring the enemy's progress.

"Here they come!" he shouted. He ran down past the first set of rooms and waited. A stream of Blighters ran down the passageway, heading straight for Rengin. As soon as the first one attacked, the defenders emerged from the nooks and cut down the Blighters from the side. The whole encounter was over within seconds.

The next wave was not as hasty, and the third Shade was standing behind them.

"It's probably directing them, springing the traps. They're crafty," Lara said.

"Yes, it's a shame they're not just dumb beasts. They're certainly strong enough to qualify. At least the narrow passage here helps us with numbers. But we won't be able to flank the Shade, so we may need to retreat again," Vincent said.

"You're right. Rengin will call it, just keep up the fight," Certan said.

"I never said I was going to stop, it's just more challenging." Vincent stretched his shoulders and prepared for the next wave of Blighters.

As predicted the narrow corridor suited the defenders, and the Blighters were unable to make a dent in them. Seeing this, the Shade began to advance by itself. Two monks tried using the rooms to ambush the creature, but it knew they were coming and they didn't have enough space to manoeuvre. They were crushed quickly.

"It has the advantage here for sure," Certan said.

"Let's go back to Rengin," Vincent said.

The three of them retreated and joined the monk leader.

"Unfortunately, this isn't a simple change of tactics. Much of the ground we will retreat to is the same layout. We need to balance safety and time. If we retreat too soon, we will be defeated too quickly," Rengin said.

"I saw your monks topple a wall, isn't there a way we can make a better space?" Lara said.

"There could be something. You come with me, Certan hold here. Retreat as you need to." Rengin dashed down the passage with Lara and showed her a few spaces further down.

"I think this could work. But we would need these two walls knocked down. And these over here," Lara said.

"That can be done, I'll task some monks to assist. Hopefully we have enough time," Rengin said.

"Is it possible to have them one strike away from falling over?" Lara said.

"Should be. Why?"

"I think that could work better. Bring the monks and I'll talk you through it." Lara had a smile on her face. *This might just work*, she thought, the smile her reaction to imagining the last remaining Shade go down.

33

A LOSING BATTLE

Certan threw a punch at the Shade, then rolled away before it could retaliate.

"Fall back!" he shouted, and lead the retreat. They had held up the Shade as best as they could, but it moved forward with relentless power and they couldn't use their numbers to overwhelm it.

"Don't worry, Lara will have a good ambush cooked up," Vincent said.

"I'm not worried about that, I'm worried about them having enough time to prepare it," Certan said.

"If that's your concern perhaps I can help," Vincent said. As they turned the corner he waited instead of joining the rest. As he heard the Shade lumbering through he sliced low and fast, aiming for the feet. He managed to connect, slicing off one of the Shade's feet and causing it to tumble. Vincent hesitated, wondering if he could get in a fatal blow.

"Don't risk it, come back!" Certan shouted. His friend's advice tipped the scales in one direction and Vincent ran off to join the rest.

"That will certainly help," Rengin said.

"Should slow it down a little. How's things back there?" Vincent said.

"Almost ready. Don't lose too many up here, we will need them to spring the ambush."

"It's your command again, just give us the orders," Vincent said

"Just follow my lead. Here it comes," Rengin said. The Shade walked slower, but it seemed otherwise unfazed by the loss of a foot. It walked on the stump instead, losing a little of its balance in the process.

"Harrying strikes only, we need to annoy and slow it down," Rengin shouted.

Many of the monks used arrows or discs to pester the Shade, and it began to stop trying to block them. One monk got a little too greedy with the arrows, and the Shade suddenly closed the gap between them and grabbed the monk with its right hand. Rengin loosed his bow immediately, putting the monk out of his misery.

"Retreat!" Rengin shouted. He led the group back, into a slightly wider room with multiple rooms off it.

"You need to get him into the middle of this room," Rengin said.

"Done. Leave it to us." Vincent stood at the entry of the room, to ensure the Shade saw him. Once it arrived it charged immediately at Vincent. "Good to see I have its attention," Vincent said, stepping back, and parrying the Shade's attack. It put Vincent off balance, and he struggled to block the next attack.

Certan circled around, trying to find an opening to capitalise on the creature's compromised balance. It was wise to his tricks, whirling and stepping to keep its distance while still keeping Vincent its focus. Vincent kept retreating, leading the creature closer and closer to the middle of the room.

The Shade increased its onslaught. Vincent desperately parried attack after attack, losing ground faster than he had wanted.

"You're too close! Get away!" Lara shouted. Certan retreated instantly, but Vincent could not. If he gave the Shade any opening at all, it would have him.

"Just do it anyway!" Vincent shouted. Lara did not hesitate and gave the signal. The walls to either side of Vincent shook and started to collapse inwards. Vincent dived to the ground, trying to stay clear of the rubble. The Shade paused its attacks, and focused on batting away the debris from the collapsing wall.

Two additional walls came down behind the Shade, and as they fell monks emerged from the dust and attacked the Shade from behind. It quickly turned to face these foes, angrier than ever.

Vincent stood up, and navigated the unstable ground. He was joined by three other monks, who could now attack the Shade in greater numbers. As they started to land blows, it wheeled around and lunged at them. The monks darted back, only one of them receiving a glancing injury.

In all this commotion Lara dashed in, and dodged the monks, the crumbled walls and the Shade's flailing attack. She manoeuvred in-between it all and planted her dagger squarely in the creature's heart. It shuddered and released a muted cry. Certan stepped up and slammed the dagger with his palm, forcing it the rest of the way and killing the Shade. It toppled to the ground with a crash, surrounded by the broken walls and stones.

The victory was short-lived. As the Shade fell more waves of Blighters entered the room. They were followed by Tainted Ones, clearly giving the orders.

"It never ends," Lara said.

"It will eventually," Certan said, not elaborating. But they were all thinking the same thing. There was only one way this fight could end. They needed a miracle.

"Reinforcements coming through. Change over," Rengin shouted as he came up to the front. The injured and tired monks fell back, and others took their place on the front lines. The room was bigger and full of hazards, but it was still tighter than the entry hallway, so they had a chance at holding it.

Lara stood back, aiming for the Tainted Ones. She took down two before they caught on and stood much further back, directing the Blighters from afar.

"This might sound crazy, but if we can continue this rotation, and there's no more Shades, we can hold this," Vincent said.

"Until we have no energy left yes, but for quite a time. Let's hope there's nothing else to throw at us," Rengin said. It was clear the leader was tiring, despite not fighting as much as some others.

The strategy worked for a little while, the scores of fallen Blighters helping by providing additional barriers and hazards for the enemies to traverse. But the defenders slowed, and little by little they were whittled down.

Their front line retreated. Before long they were holding at the end of the room.

"Why don't we fall back again, use the narrow corridor?" Lara said.

"It's hard to reinforce, and we are getting closer and closer to the Vault. Any setback at all would have us practically running backwards," Rengin said.

"So, we're going to hold here as long as possible," Lara said.

"Exactly." Rengin was about to shout out again but abruptly stopped. Vincent noticed it too. The Blighters were all moving to the sides of the room, filling the space but leaving a passageway through the middle. The Tainted Ones too.

"I don't like the look of this," Vincent said.

"It's an odd arrangement." Certan leaned against a wall to catch his breath.

Stomp. Stomp. Stomp. A shape was slowly advancing from the distance. Each step was measured and powerful. Deliberate and strong. Designed to cause fear. The monks looked at each other. A mixture of curiosity and anxiety crossing their faces. Rengin was resolute, overly so. Vincent could see him putting on a brave face for the other monks. As the shape advanced, it began to take shape.

"No," Lara said softly.

"Is it him?" Vincent said, peering into the distance.

"Definitely," Certan said, clenching his fist. The shape continued to advance.

"What is it? You seem to recognise it," Rengin said.

"You'll see soon enough. It is our enemy," Lara said, spitting onto the ground. In answer to her question the creature arrived and stood in the middle of the room.

"It's a Shade?" Rengin said.

"And here we are at last. Thank you for the welcoming party," Wraith said. His voice still had the muted and shrill harshness of a Shade, but it was more controlled and understandable.

"It speaks?" What are you?" Rengin said.

"I am Wraith. I am the epitome of the power and majesty of the Blight. I have come here to destroy your pathetic little trial and claim the wizard for myself," Wraith said.

"I've never seen this before," Rengin said to Certan as quietly as possible.

"It's a wizard turned into a Shade. He's managed to overcome this form, and use it to his advantage. When we encountered him he was still wrestling with it, but he seems in control now," Certan said.

"Are you going to be smart and give in, or are you going to die horribly?" Wraith said.

"You will not reach the heart of this temple, you foul thing. We have already dealt with three of your kind," Rengin said. His monks rallied behind him.

"Don't underestimate him, we don't know how powerful he is," Lara said.

"I won't. I expect I won't survive this encounter either. I will make a stand here. Certan, stay with me and learn what you can to aid the monks. Vincent and Lara, you should retreat and prepare to fight him again. I fear you will have the best chance against this monster," Rengin said.

"Are you sure?" Certan said.

"Of course, the rest of you go now," Rengin said. Vincent and Lara turned and ran swiftly out of the room and into the dark corridor beyond.

"Leaving already? I'm glad someone has the courage to stand here. What's your answer?" Wraith said.

"You will die here!" Rengin said. Before Wraith could respond the monk charged ahead. Rengin quickly feinted an attack, then dashed behind to try an additional strike. None of the Blighters or Tainted Ones moved to protect their master.

Wraith let Rengin's attack connect. He moved slightly with the blow, but was otherwise unharmed. Rengin darted back to his waiting monks.

"Was that it?" Wraith said, mockery in his voice.

"Just an initial attack," Rengin said.

"Charming. I'll allow this for now, but I can't let it drag on. I have other business to attend to," Wraith said.

"I need to prepare something. The rest of you, attack in constant waves. Test all of his body for weak areas. But don't stand around, dodge away after each strike. Let there be no cheap deaths." Rengin sat on the floor, legs crossed and eyes closed.

The monks attacked as ordered, landing blows all over Wraith's body. Mostly he let them land, others he swatted away. But subsequent attacks to that area left no mark.

A Shade would have felt at least some impact; his form can't be that different. He must be using some sort of spell, Certan thought. He looked back at Rengin, intrigued by what the older monk was doing. It had to be something more than his own technique of gathering energy into a single strike.

"Ugh," a monk said, rolling away, nursing a broken arm. He had been a little sloppy and Wraith had punished him.

"I tire with these simple attacks. Show me something else, or I'm moving on," Wraith said.

"It is now time for you to answer for your actions," Rengin shouted. He stood but his feet were not on the ground. He was hovering.

"Watch carefully then retreat. My final act is a gift to you. A gift of time, and also a demonstration of what is possible. Farewell Certan, and good luck." Rengin gently placed his hand on Certan's shoulder.

"Thank you for your generosity and leadership," Certan said.

Rengin nodded and readied his stance. "I call this the seven strikes of salvation," Rengin said. Wraith just laughed and waited. Rengin dashed forward at incredible speed. Certan could not follow him. It was if Rengin appeared next to Wraith and delivered a stunning blow. The sound of the impact reverberated around the room. Wraith was knocked back slightly, but showed no other signs of damage. Before he could recover, Rengin appeared behind Wraith, and circled around again at great speed hitting the same spot a second time. This time Wraith lunged out with his arm, but was too slow and Rengin slipped away.

The super speed monk appeared above Wraith, and dove down, striking this time with a foot on the same spot. The impact was so great, that Wraith was forced to stumble backwards. Clearly the attacks were beginning to have an effect. Wraith created a wall of stone around himself, to prevent the next strike. But Rengin came again, and passed through the stone as if it weren't there, landing another crushing blow. Wraith dropped to one knee, then quickly stood again.

The older monk appeared back with the others, but before they could see anything he was off again. Wraith held his arms out to block the strike. Rengin, dodged under, and with two successive palm strikes hammered the same spot again.

Wraith was knocked over, skidding along the ground. He rose, and dusted himself off. There was a small crack in his skin, where Rengin had been attacking.

"That was only six. Is that all you have?" Wraith said. Rengin was frozen in the pose of his last attack. He was motionless as a statue.

"Maybe you can't move anymore? Oh well, I'll enjoy this!" Wraith said, he ran forward leading with his right arm. As he connected with Rengin's head something strange happened. An explosion of light appeared at the point of impact, knocking Wraith back to the end of the room. Rengin dropped to the ground. The monks rushed to his aid.

"Bring him with us, and let's retreat," Certan said. Rengin had bought them some time and space, but it looked like at a great cost.

34

THE CROSSROADS

A lrion let the spell dissipate and sank down with frustration. He had made the most of his confinement in the Vault, but it was time to get out. He had tried many things, none of which had worked.

He knew that spells would not be the answer, so he tried many different tricks to use his Will to alter the situation. Nothing had even looked like working.

What am I missing? This Vault doesn't seem to be a real space, everything is wrong about it. The monks must have something to do with it. Maybe they are using their Will to keep this place as is, and prevent me from leaving. That must be what is happening, Alrion thought. If that was true though, how could he counter that?

He let his mind wander, to imagine the construction of the Vault. How would he build it, if it was his own creation? He designed the entire construction in his mind, down to the smallest detail. A model so impressive that if he could just flick a switch in his mind it would become reality.

Why can't I just do that? There was no reason why not. He took his model of the Vault, and implanted it on the surroundings. There seemed to be some sort of resistance, but he ignored it. His reality was fact, and it had the construction of the room in a particular way. He felt the walls vibrating and moving, as if they were alternating between different extremes. Finally, they settled, and he knew that the Vault was as he designed.

Time for a change. He walked over to a wall, and redesigned it. He added a doorway to the outside world. The wall reshaped itself to his command. He could see out into the room. There was a great battle going on.

Time to make my grand entrance. It wasn't too early, or too late. It was the perfect timing.

~

"There's no time!" Certan said as he reached the heart of the temple. Vincent and Lara were in a defensive position in front of the four monks. Certan and the rest of the monks moved to the front of the room. They could hear Wraith stomping down the corridor towards them.

The monks bearing Rengin placed him down carefully at the rear of the room and joined their companions.

"Any weaknesses you can help us with?" Lara said.

"No, he seems almost impervious to harm. Rengin managed to create a small hole in Wraith's skin, but that was after repeated attacks of amazing power. He seems stronger than when we first encountered him. I think he is using his spells to somehow shield his body further," Certan said.

"Maybe Alrion will be able to counter. But there's still a good chance Runesteel will work," Vincent said.

"I hope so. Good luck to all." Certan turned to face the sound of Wraith entering.

"Here we are, everyone together at last. We never met officially, but I assume you are Alrion's father?" Wraith said, pointing at Vincent.

"That's correct. And you are Branthor the monster?" Vincent said.

"Actually, we did meet a long time ago. Back when you were following your father around like a puppy," Wraith said.

"I don't remember, I guess you weren't that memorable without your costume," Vincent said.

"Are you still disappointed that you couldn't cut it? Don't take that out on me. Anyway, I'm more interested in your son. Where is Alrion?" Wraith said.

"He'll be here when he's ready."

"I've come all this way, it would be rude not to wait. You can entertain me instead," Wraith said. He raised his arm and sent spirals of earth and fire at Vincent.

"Look out!" Lara shouted, pushing Vincent to the side. He rolled to the ground and held up his sword, blocking the last trail of fiery death and knocking it aside. "Certan would have a decent attack, if we can buy him some time and opportunity," Lara said.

"Seeing Rengin's attacks I am not sure how effective it will be, but it is worth a chance," Certan said.

"Very well, let's see what we can do," Vincent cautiously advanced on Wraith.

Lara let loose a series of discs which bounced harmlessly off Wraith's chest, but did get his attention.

"You can't possibly hope to hurt me, I have become something more than any other wizard," Wraith said.

"That may be, but there is nothing that Runesteel cannot cut through," Vincent said, twirling his sword with menace. Wraith watched the blade very carefully, which confirmed Vincent's suspicions. Despite his improved power and control, the blade was still effective.

Wraith raised a wall of earth right in front of Vincent, but he sliced it in half and kicked it down. A wave of force tugged at his feet and a spear of earth flew through the air, but Vincent used the momentum of force beneath him to roll to safety.

Vincent quickly rose and kept walking, closing the distance between them. Lara crept forward from another angle, waiting for an opportunity.

He doesn't know that my dagger is also Runesteel, he may give me an opening. As Wraith focused on Vincent, she stalked closer and closer.

This is it! she thought and stepped forward with a quick slice. Wraith noticed at the last moment, and moved just enough. The slice became a light graze, but it did break the skin. Wraith looked at her in horror.

"Too slow!" Vincent said as he swung his sword. Wraith managed to blast Vincent back with a wave of force, slowing his strike and increasing the gap between them.

Out of nowhere Certan appeared, and struck with his charged palm. The blow exploded with power and knocked Wraith back. He paused to examine his body. The crack created by Rengin was larger now, and appeared to be an open wound, albeit minor.

In a fury, Wraith whipped through the air with his arm. It created a diagonal wave of shearing force, striking all of his three opponents. All the surfaces that were hit suffered deep cuts, and all three limped back to a defensive position.

"That was our best shot, and he just blew us away," Lara said.

"True, I'm not sure how much more we can do," Vincent said.

"What's that?" Certan said. They looked over and saw a shimmering doorway appear at the rear of the room, in-between the four older monks. All they could see on the other side was white. A man stepped through. It was Alrion.

"Sorry to keep you waiting," he said.

"Alrion!" Vincent shouted. He staggered to his feet and ran over to his son.

"Easy there, you're hurt." Alrion accepted the hug, then guided his father to crouch down. Alrion gathered his Spark and used his healing spell, knotting the skin back together. "That's different," Alrion said, but said nothing further.

"I feel like I should be saving you, not the opposite," Vincent said.

"Sorry, this a once-off. You can save me again later," Alrion said.

"Good, that's better. Did you pass the trial?"

"Yes, otherwise I wouldn't be here. Lara and Certan come over here," Alrion said.

"You look different. Better and stronger." Lara gave him a hug too.

"Good to see you," Certan said, slapping Alrion on the back.

"Let me patch you up a bit." Alrion healed their wounds in the same way. "Anything I should know?" Alrion said.

"He's terribly strong, but the Runesteel seems to work a bit. Do you have any ideas?" Lara said.

"I think we should just leave, Rengin mentioned a secret passage in this room," Certan said.

"Find the passage, I'll deal with Wraith," Alrion stepped forward and looked at his enemy.

"Alrion, finally. We've all been waiting so long. What took you?" Wraith said.

"I was busy. I see you have been too. Do you have any humanity left?" Alrion said. Wraith just laughed.

"Maybe you have just misplaced it. Why don't you just leave?" Alrion said.

"Clearly, I can't do the trial, not with you all here and it relies on those pesky monks. But you are here, so I'll settle for that. I made you an offer before, and it's still available. If you're feeling a little shy, I'll just accept on your behalf. It's easier that way," Wraith said.

"I won't join you, there's nothing you can say to convince me."

"Who said you needed to be convinced?" Wraith said, and launched a rolling wave of earth at Alrion. The young wizard concentrated then stopped the earth in its tracks, letting it settle back down into the ground.

"Oh, learned a few new tricks? That won't be enough." Wraith let loose with a stream of fire and earth, attacking in a criss-cross pattern.

Alrion extinguished the fire and knocked the earth back down to the ground.

"My turn," Alrion sent wave after wave of force at Wraith. Nothing happened, as each one hit. Alrion did the same again, but alternated with fire. Again, Wraith let each attack hit and nothing happened.

"You thought that would work?" Wraith said. Alrion did not respond, but tried again. This time the waves of force alternated with waves of fire and earth. Like before Wraith let them crash against him. But something was different.

The ground around Wraith's feet sucked him in like quicksand. It quickly solidified, binding him in place. As he struggled to break free, Alrion fired an intensely bright white-hot rod of fire directly at Wraith's chest wound. He roared in pain and broke his feet free.

"That smarts, it really does. But it's not enough." Wraith was trying to shake off the pain, but it seemed to linger.

"Alrion we found the path. Come with us," Certan said.

"No, I have a chance. I can beat him," Alrion said.

"It's too risky. Just come with us, it'll be fine," Lara said.

"She's right Alrion. You've done enough, let's regroup and move forward," Vincent said.

"No, I'm sorry. I can't have this thing following me around forever. I need to deal with it now, so I can focus on the next trial. Just go on ahead, I'll catch up." Alrion felt his friends had not moved, so he turned to face them. "Please go, I need to do this. I promise I'll come find you," he said.

"Very well, let's go. Don't keep us waiting," Vincent said.

Alrion watched them go, then turned back to face his enemy.

"I see you are now alone. Such a pity," Wraith said.

"You sure do talk a lot," Alrion said. A grin stole across Wraith's face and suddenly hundreds of projectiles flew towards Alrion. They came from every direction and were incredibly fast. He dove for cover and built an earth shield around himself. As fast as he could reinforce it, dents embedded in the surface at an alarming rate. In seconds the whole thing would collapse. Alrion threw up more walls, opened an exit and ran. With a crash the whole thing toppled and Alrion was scrambling for breath.

"You were saying?" Wraith said.

"That you don't talk nearly enough," Alrion said, chuckling.

"I think I should be honest with you, it's only fair. You got a good attack in, I have to admire that. It's the least I expect from you. However, you can't possibly win."

"Why is that?"

"The Blight has a power all its own. I can break the rules, enhance this already strong body even further, and employ a bag of tricks so large I can't even begin to tell you all about them. No spell you throw at me will be enough."

"So, what do we do then?"

"You come with me and we leave. And I bring you into the fold. I have great plans for us," Wraith said.

"For the last time, no," Alrion said. As much as Wraith was a liar, there was probably some truth in his words. Alrion drew the Runesteel sword, and the diamond glowed bright blue.

"You're definitely a piece of work, but I can cut you down to size," Alrion said, readying himself.

35

INFECTED

Alrion knew he had neither the skill nor the strength to wield the sword properly. But he knew it was effective, so perhaps he could create an opening that anyone could exploit.

Wraith eyed the sword carefully, which told Alrion he had made the right choice. The creature must have remembered losing its hand. Alrion had one chance to make this work, so he prepared himself. Wraith wasn't ready to wait, and sent multiple waves of fire and earth before following them in himself.

"This is my shot," Alrion decided. He would not dodge the attacks, he would use them as a shield. As the attacks came in Alrion did not move, he readied his sword in a lunge position, the blade pointing out at Wraith. Alrion gathered his Spark, and deflected or destroyed all the attacks that would hit. When the last wave of earth came, and Wraith was right behind it, Alrion pierced a small hole in the wave and thrust his sword through. He let the rest of the wave hit him, committing everything to enhancing his single strike.

Wraith thought that his attack had succeeded, and was committed to grabbing Alrion. He noticed too late the sword emerging from the rock straight for his chest. All he could do was twist slightly, which was just enough.

The Runesteel sword pierced Wraith in the chest, but missed the heart. It sunk in right up to the hilt. Wraith reached out and grabbed Alrion by the neck.

"So near, yet so far," Wraith said. His second finger turned ash-black and he jabbed Alrion with it. Alrion recoiled in surprise, and fell back.

"It is done. You are mine now," Wraith said with glee, removing the sword, and tossing it aside.

"No!" Alrion cried, reaching for his neck. He could feel the wound pulsing.

"You are infected, it's only a matter of time now," Wraith said. Alrion backed away, stumbling over the littered rocks. He made it over to his sword and picked it up, rocking with the weight. "You are weak now, it is overcoming your system. I must say you seem to be handling it well, some become unconscious immediately," Wraith said. He slowly advanced towards Alrion.

"This can't be happening," Alrion said, shocked. How had he let this happen? He could have left with his friends, as they had wanted. But he had chosen to stay, and he had failed.

"Try and use your Spark, I dare you," Wraith said. Alrion reached for it, hoping to find something to throw at his enemy. But the fire was tainted. It wasn't the pure heat he was used it, there was already a smoky black mass over it. Alrion recoiled again. "Ahh that's right. By all means reach through the filth and use the Spark. You may as well speed things up, and you need to get used to it. The real magic happens when you learn to accept it," Wraith said.

"No, never. I'll die before that happens," Alrion said.

"Impossible I'm afraid. If you die it just completes the process. The Blight has you now. Welcome."

"I'll find a way, there's always a way."

"Oh, there's that ritual you are looking for, but good luck casting that while infected. Not going to work too well is it?" Wraith said. He was right, and Alrion was scared. But deep down, he knew something else. But he couldn't put his finger on it. As Wraith came closer and closer, Alrion scrambled for that thought in his brain, the one that had hope attached to it.

He put aside all the fear, and emotion and worries that coursed through him and focused on that thought. He found it and spoke it out loud.

"I have passed the trial of Will, and left the Vault of Silence. The power of will is exercised by persistence, and getting back up. This is not the end, this is another step on my journey. I will not submit to you, in life or in death," Alrion said. Wraith stopped, puzzled by the outburst. Before he could move further Alrion had already decided what to do next.

Magic was not available to him, and his strength was quickly fading. But he had the power of Will, which was not constrained by those things. He tapped into the reality around him, and remade it into his design.

The ground underneath Wraith suddenly dropped hundreds of feet, and sand filled its place. It was if it had always been so, and the change was instantaneous. Wraith was now trapped within a prison of sand.

Alrion didn't revel in the victory, he stumbled over to the back of the room. He found the secret passage and tumbled down the stairs. With great difficulty he picked himself up, and dragged himself forward, using the sword as a walking stick.

Just ... have ... to ... get ... out, Alrion thought. He pushed on for as long as he could, before collapsing on the ground.

Please, help me, he thought finally.

36

RECOVERY

Vincent started to slow down, and Certan did the same. The rest of the monks continued their escape. Lara stopped suddenly, looking at the other two.

"What is it?" she said.

"Something has happened." Certan paused and listened carefully.

"I can't explain it myself, I just felt like Alrion needed us," Vincent said.

"Let us just wait a bit, we are far enough for relative safety," Certan said. The three of them waited in silence, staring back at the darkness behind them.

The tunnel they were in was long and straight, with no indication of how far it went. As the footsteps of the monks ahead became softer and softer they were surrounded by true silence as they waited patiently under the earth.

A strange sound surrounded them. It was like an immense amount of sand just shifted incredibly quickly.

"That shouldn't be possible. We must head back." Certan looked at the tunnel ahead, and back at where they had come from.

"Go to the monks, they may need your assistance. The two of us can handle this. Just keep the door open for us at the other end," Vincent said.

"Thank you, I will accept your offer. Hurry back, I will see you soon." Certan ran off into the darkness and Vincent and Lara ran back the way they had come.

"What do you think happened?" Lara said.

"Some sort of gigantic shift happened, that's what we heard. It doesn't matter who did that, it is bad news. Certan seemed to have felt it too, and he seemed quite shaken," Vincent said.

"He was definitely spooked. But was equally worried about the other monks."

"We don't know where that shift happened. He is right to be concerned."

"I have a bad feeling about this. Let's keep quiet and see what we can find." Lara increased her pace and Vincent kept up.

The going was tough as the only guide they had was the tunnel wall. There were no lights and they weren't going to try and create any. Lara's pulse quickened as they ran, more from worry than from exertion. Alrion had seemed off, like it was his last chance to do something. She hoped he hadn't run into more trouble than he could handle.

He managed to survive last time, maybe he's fine, she thought. The start of the tunnel was approaching, and a thin light crept in from the room above. "Is someone there?" Lara said. As they continued they could see better.

"It's Alrion?" Vincent said. He fell to his knees and cradled his son in his arms.

"He's alive, but he feels cold. Help me get him up," Vincent said.

Together the two of them hauled the young wizard up onto his feet, but he couldn't stand by himself.

"He seems a bit out of it, and his forehead is burning up. This doesn't feel right," Lara said.

"Let's just get him out of here," Vincent said. Together they moved forward at a fast walk. "Alrion can you hear me?" he said. There was no response.

"He must have passed out. It's like he's sick. You don't think?" Lara said.

"We don't know, let's not jump to conclusions. Whatever has happened, he got away. Our responsibility is to ensure that he gets to safety," Vincent said.

"Of course, let's see if we can pick up the pace," Lara said. `

Alrion felt himself be picked up, but his body was so heavy. He couldn't help whoever was helping him. He had brief flashes of awareness, but it was so dark he couldn't distinguish them from when he blacked out.

There were more voices soon, some calling his name. But they seemed so distant, so far away. He didn't have the energy to respond. He could sense the concern, but he couldn't address it. All he could do was what he was already doing which was letting them take him.

He could feel the light and heat building around him, but he couldn't open his eyes. It was too difficult. The more he tried to exert himself, the more he felt the strange thumping in his heart. Better to rest, and not stir that unwelcome addition.

Finally, he was laid down, and he felt like he could finally rest. He let himself sink into the depth of sleep, and forgot all his worries. They were for another time, when he had the strength to deal with them. For a while, he was at peace.

Alrion could sense the light, and it was annoying him. He tried opening his eyes. They did as instructed, and the room slowly became visible. His surroundings were familiar. He was in Ashra's hut.

He sat up too quickly, and nursed his head.

"Alrion, you're awake. How are you?" Lara said. She was sitting by his side. The concern in her eyes was obvious.

"I've been better. What happened?"

"We found you at the entrance of the secret tunnel. And we brought you here as quickly as possible. You're safe now," Lara said. Vincent walked over and crouched by Alrion's other side.

"Welcome back to the land of the living. You did well son. Everything's alright now, although you probably need more rest before you can get back on your feet," Vincent said. Alrion nodded. He thought back to what had happened. He remembered the infection, and quickly felt around his neck. "The wound has healed, but you have been tainted," Vincent said.

"This, this isn't right," Alrion said. The memories came flooding back.

"There is a cure, you're working on it right now remember?" Ashra said from the other side of the room.

"But I can't learn the spell like this?"

"There's always a way. But in the meantime, you need to know a few things. The Blight travels different speeds in different people. Some change overnight, for others it is a gradual process. I have done what I could do to slow it down, and I feel like time is on our side. But it cannot be stopped with the tools we have at our disposal," Ashra said.

"What can I do?"

"Have you felt your Spark?" Ashra said. Alrion thought back and remembered the feeling when he tried to access it before.

"Yes, I tried immediately. Wraith was quite pleased with himself at my reaction," Alrion said.

"Then you know not to touch it. Not under any circumstances. Not only will it speed up the transformation, but it may also put the cure at risk. We don't know how it works," Ashra said.

"I understand."

"This is very important. It's not worth it, you must find another way of dealing with things," Ashra said. Alrion looked around the room.

"I have your sword, if that's what you are after," Vincent said.

"Now's as good a time as any. I'm not particularly skilled with it," Alrion said.

"We can work on that, when you get your strength back. Can you tell us what happened back there?"

"I passed the trial, and I fought Wraith. Even with my best spells and tricks all I managed to do was injure him with the sword. But my aim was off, it wasn't a fatal strike and he had the opportunity to infect me," Alrion said.

"It was an achievement for you to keep up with him in battle, he had us all beaten," Vincent said.

"From what I have been told, he is a formidable foe. An unnatural fusion of Shade and Wizard. How did you get away after he infected you?" Ashra said.

"I had only one tool left, my Will. I remade the structure of the temple, trapping him in a deep pit below the ground. I doubt it will kill him, but it was enough to escape," Alrion said.

"Remarkable that you mastered your Will so quickly," Certan said as he joined them.

"I can't really talk about that, it's called the Vault of Silence for a reason," Alrion said, forcing out a shaky laugh.

"You are talking like one of the masters already," Certan said, chuckling.

"Are you able to do the same here?" Ashra said. Vincent shot Ashra a strange look and was about to speak up, when Ashra signalled him to be quiet. Alrion focused on his will, and tried to replicate what he had done at the temple. It didn't feel the same though. He couldn't seem to tap into the fabric of reality the same way.

"No, it's different. Maybe I don't have the same strength," Alrion said.

"It's not that, although I'm sure it is a factor. I believe the temple itself is either built in a unique way, or sits upon a unique location. The temple facilitates the use of Will, and the bending of reality. It would explain why it's in the middle of the desert. That's my theory at least, and your experience cements that in my mind," Ashra said.

"So, what happened to the temple?" Alrion said.

"Scouts have suggested that all the Tainted have left. The temple is still intact, although heavily damaged. The remaining monks will be returning and building it back up," Certan said.

"Will you be joining them?" Alrion said.

"I'm sorry, but I must. With the loss of Rengin and many others, our numbers have dwindled. It is my first responsibility to help repair what was done."

"It sounds like they have accepted you back though," Alrion said with a smile.

"Yes, the flask didn't even factor in. It turns out, my behaviour is not unique. In many cases, it is expected. Thank you for convincing me to return. I would like to believe that I would have returned eventually, but how many years would have passed?"

"You are welcome, in fact I should be thanking you. With your guidance, I made it in time, and completed the Trial of Will."

"You are now my senior. I will catch up to you, and I'll find you again to help with the completion of your quest," Certan said, bowing to Alrion.

"I look forward to it. Please, don't hang around on my account, if you are needed there please go," Alrion said. Certan approached Alrion, and kissed him on the forehead.

"Where I come from, that is how we say goodbye to family that we will not see for a long time. Take care young wizard, when we meet again I will be your equal." Certan bowed again and left the hut.

"Bye, Certan, I'll always consider you my teacher," Alrion said quietly, after the monk had left.

"For now, you need to rest more. You will be safe here until you are ready to leave," Ashra said.

"I don't even know where to go next," Alrion said.

"We'll figure it out, don't worry. That's not a job for today." Lara stroked his arm softly.

"Are you hungry?" Vincent said.

"I think so?"

"Let's get you some food and rest. You need to build up your strength for our journey," Vincent said.

"If you insist," Alrion said, and rearranged himself to be in a better seated position. He had to focus on his recovery first, and worry about the next steps later. And with sleep, came dreams.

A NEW DREAM

Alrion dreamed. Again, the rush of images and scenes, a massive blur. Everything settled, and he saw his grandfather once more sitting at a desk. Alrion walked over.

"Grandfather, I need your help," Alrion said.

"I cannot help you. I am merely a guide to the knowledge within you," Granthion said.

"I am infected with the Blight. Can you show me the cure?" Alrion said.

"I already gave you the spell. You will know it when you are ready."

"How can I be ready when I am tainted?" Alrion said with frustration. Granthion thought carefully, then responded.

"How can you cure others, before you cure yourself?" he said.

"That's exactly what I am talking about!" Alrion said.

"You have the knowledge and you have the Will. What's missing?"

"Well, the third component would be Spark. But I already have that."

"No, you have only half."

"What do you mean?" Alrion said. Granthion stood up from the desk and gestured into the distance. A shimmering doorway opened and Alrion ran through without a moment's hesitation.

He was cold, really cold. Snow was falling, and covered the ground. It was so thick as he walked he seemed to be sinking into it. Alrion instinctively went to cast a fire spell, but stopped himself.

Even if this is a dream, I can't use it, he thought. He trekked forward through the snow, towards what looked like a summit. As he stepped onto it, he saw a woman with black hair and purple robes standing with her back turned to him.

"Hello!" Alrion shouted over the wind. But there was no response. She raised her hands and looked to be casting some sort of spell. Her body shimmered with magic, and within her pulsed a strange glow. Alrion walked closer fascinated. As he approached he noticed a strange heat within himself. He looked at his own body, and noticed a fierce core burning inside. If he concentrated he could also see a black tinge on the edges.

He looked again at the woman and noticed she was different. Within her was a core of pure water, still and at peace. As he stared, she suddenly turned and looked directly at Alrion. Her eyes glowed an icy blue and she reached out for him.

Alrion awoke suddenly, feeling the heat of his surroundings immediately. Part of him wished for that cool to return.

"Did you have another strange dream? You seemed unusually restless," Lara said.

"Yes, I think it's a clue for my next step or trial," Alrion said.

"Let me hear it," Ashra said, coming over and sitting down. Alrion looked around.

"Where's my father?" he said.

"He went to visit the monks to see how they were doing. I think he was restless sitting around here doing nothing. Don't worry he will return soon. What was in your dream?"

"My grandfather told me that Spark was only half of what I needed for the spell. He created a doorway that took me to a wintery place, a snowy mountain. At its peak, I found a woman who was casting some sort of spell. Only where I had a core of fire, she had one of water. And when she turned to look at me, her eyes were glowing blue," Alrion said.

"That's very interesting. I think you have your next goal," Ashra said.

"You know where this is?" Lara said.

"There are stories, but not confirmed, of a group of women. Some call them witches, others refer to them as mystics. They can cast magic of a different sort, from a different source. I had never really taken much stock in the stories, because I had no need to. But it seems plausible," Ashra said.

"Do you know any more about them? Where do they live? What can do they?" Alrion said.

"Well you already know where they live, deep in the north amongst the mountains. Although there are stories that they travel and are hidden in many places. In plain sight. In terms of what they can do, it's hard to really distinguish fairy tales from the potentially real."

"Give some examples?" Lara said.

"Healing, fortune telling, granting wishes, and mind control for example. Fairly outlandish don't you think?" Ashra said.

"That's useful, even if most of it is nonsense. It will help us find women who fit that description," Alrion said.

"Indeed, you may even find one on your way there. I think this is the right path for you, there is enormous potential. They may be able to assist you with the Blight's taint, or even show you how to harness their power," Ashra said.

"I have a goal and I have a direction. How long will it take?" Alrion said.

"You need more time to heal, because the journey is harsh. After you cross the desert, you need to travel quite a distance north. You should have horses for that. Then the trek into the mountains is not for the faint of heart."

"Have you been there?"

"No, I haven't. Perhaps if I had, I could offer you more guidance. But you will have able companions, so you will be fine. The only other issue is the Blight," Ashra said, pointing at Alrion's chest.

"What do I do about it?" Alrion said.

"Don't use your Spark for starters. Just use your Will and whatever skill you can muster up with a sword. I also recommend meditating every day. The body resists the Blight by itself, any effort to assist will buy you some more time."

"Thanks, for everything. Are you sure you won't come with us? You can see the women of the north for yourself, these mystics," Alrion said.

"No, as before. My place is here, and your quest is your own. Come visit me again, and I will hear your tales of them," Ashra said.

"As you wish, but if you change your mind..." Alrion said.

"I will not, but thank you for the offer. If you apply yourself, you can leave in a week," Ashra said.

"A week? Not sooner?"

"That's up to you. But I won't let you leave here until it is safe. I have my ways," Ashra said with a grin on his face.

"Yes, I've noticed," Alrion said, remembering the last time he had tried to leave without Ashra's blessing. The idea of meeting the women magic users, and the possibility for a new type of magic filled him with hope. But there was a nagging doubt below it all. He pushed it away, but knew it would return. For now, he just had to keep his focus on recovering his strength and beginning his journey.

EPILOGUE

Ashra waved goodbye to Alrion, Lara and Vincent and wished them well. Alrion had recovered incredibly well over the last week, although Ashra could see that the Blight was having an effect on the young wizard. He had taken Vincent aside and mentioned it specifically. Vincent would monitor the situation and keep Alrion's spirits up.

I hope he makes it, but it's such a tall order. How can he reach them in time? Ashra thought. He had seen many suffer the Blight's taint, and even the ones that resisted the most had turned in time. Alrion had a long journey ahead of him, one that would be a race against the infection.

"Better he keeps his hope up. Any dark thoughts will work against him," Ashra said to himself. It was his justification for hiding from Alrion the true timeline he was fighting against. In some cases, ignorance was definitely the better option.

The desert wizard had a restless afternoon, and evening. He tried to get into his normal routines and carry on as normal, but he couldn't settle down. The events that had just occurred were momentous.

A young wizard accessing the Pool of Knowledge, conquering the Vault of Silence, and surviving against a Shade born from a Wizard. It's unheard of. It excited him in a way that he had not been for some time. He felt a little disappointed that he hadn't taken Alrion up on his offer, although he absolutely could not tag along. Some journeys could not accept extra passengers.

As he pondered the entire situation he noticed movement out of the corner of his eye.

"Such simple tricks won't get past me," Ashra said, calling out to the intruder.

"I didn't expect so, but you can forgive my caution in coming here," a voice said from the shadows. A man emerged, wearing a dark hooded robe covering his face.

"So, you're the mysterious wizard following young Alrion around," Ashra said.

"Yes, the very same."

"I take it you don't need an update from me then," Ashra said.

"No, I do not."

"So why have you come?" Ashra said, about to say the man's name.

"Call me Aydan," the man said.

"Aydan? What's that mean? It's in the ancient language, isn't it?"

"Yes, it means The Lost One," Aydan said.

"Very well Aydan, I will keep your secret. What brings you to my humble home?"

"First, I wanted to thank you for assisting Alrion."

"Of course, but no need to thank me. I may be an outcast, but I can see what's in front of me."

"An outcast only by your own making. That was my second reason for seeing you."

"Yes? You have my attention," Ashra said.

"I want you to return to the Academy, they need a new leader. You did wonders with Alrion, think of what you can contribute to the rest!" Aydan said.

"I don't think you have the authority to make that request."

"All the same, what do you think? Can you really stay here in the desert, knowing events are happening out in the world?" Aydan said. Ashra didn't have a response ready.

"Maybe not," he said finally.

"Then consider it as a possibility."

"I will indeed. What about you?"

"That's not my place, I gave that up. Alrion is my responsibility," Aydan said.

"I thought as much, but thought it worth asking anyway. Thanks for coming to see me. I appreciate it," Ashra said.

"I know that I can trust you, and I think you are wasted here. You're not as much of a loner as you think. Why have you saved all those lost idiots over the years?" Aydan said. Before Ashra could respond Aydan turned to leave and blended into shadows.

"Such theatrics. Farewell," Ashra said, staring into the darkness.

～

Alrion walked carefully, not trusting his body. His recovery had been frustrating and slow. And he could feel the Blight within him. Ashra and Certan had provided useful advice for trying to slow its spread. But he could sense the darkness within marching on regardless.

He stopped suddenly, a curious thought entering his mind. He unstrapped his sword, and looked at it carefully. The diamond embedded in the hilt let off a faint but noticeable glow.

"Don't worry, there's still time," Vincent said.

Alrion nodded and put the sword away. At least he had a way of judging how far he had gone. He knew how bright the diamond had been when encountering Wraith.

That detestable monster. How do I defeat him now, when I have no access to my power? Alrion thought. His recent mastery of Will didn't seem like it would be enough by itself. The monks had not fared particularly well. He could almost hear Wraith laughing, in that strange and strained Shade voice.

"It's not your imagination. We are linked now," Wraith said in Alrion's mind.

The hideous laughter returned, much louder now.

SPARK OF
TRUTH

BOOK THREE OF   THE HIDDEN WIZARD

VAUGHAN W. SMITH

For Katarina

1

A NEW BATTLE

Alyx stumbled through the brush, narrowly avoiding a Blighter.

"Classy," she told herself, and leaned back against a nearby tree. The thick branches were a steadying force, although the leaves bristled in an uncomfortable way. The stench of Blighters was all around her and it caused her stomach to turn. She checked her hair, ensuring that it was still reliably tied up. With care, she looked around and noticed that the vile creatures were scattered everywhere.

Why are they in this forest? Nobody was tracking me.

By force of habit she checked for weapons. All she had was a short sword strapped to her lower back. It was useful, but it was not the sword that she had carried her entire life. Not that she ever really got much use out of it. But it was a comfort and reminder of her father, and now it was gone.

She crouched down and slowly approached the nearest Blighter. She winced as a twig snapped, but the Blighter didn't react. She pulled back her arm, tensed her muscles, and dived in with a deadly swipe. The Blighter dropped quickly and quietly, folding into the nearby bushes. Movement caught her eye, and she looked over. Another Blighter had entered the area and had witnessed her kill.

It looked at her blankly, and turned its head to go somewhere else.

It ignored me? Impossible!

Blighters acted on instinct alone. Or under the direct supervision of a powerful force. But she had already taken out the biggest threat around here.

"If they're not here for me, who is controlling them? And for what?" she said to herself. Her body ached, and her limbs felt stiff. But her curiosity was sparked. She had to investigate.

Sticking to the cover of the trees, Alyx stalked the Blighter that had ignored her. It seemed like a good plan, since it hadn't reacted to her at all. And it was more likely to lead her to whatever it was looking for. More accurately, whatever it was being targeted at.

She spotted more Blighters around, each behaving the same way. Like they were combing the forest for something important. Watching their movements, she noticed a pattern. They seemed to be converging on something.

This I have to see.

She knew she should leave this alone, and she should be recovering. She had done the impossible, and had earned a rest. She had fulfilled her life's purpose.

Weren't you supposed to just ride off into the sunset? Not find another problem to solve?

She pushed those thoughts aside and focused on the problem at hand. It was time to see what these Blighters were up to.

She tracked them with care, ignoring the complaints of her body. Light was fading, gloom rising around her and fewer shafts of sunlight pierced through the thick canopy. Everything was building towards something. But what?

She sensed something shift, and the Blighters started moving with purpose. They increased their speed and their snarls started to fill the forest.

"It's beginning," Alyx whispered, and increased her speed. She didn't worry about making noise now. She had to get to the bottom of what was happening.

Some of the Blighters were stalled, as if waiting for something. Alyx couldn't help herself, since they were easy targets. She ended each with a quick slash and kept her pace.

Never a bad time to put down some Blighters.

As she progressed, she started seeing larger and larger groups. It was unheard of for them to group up in such confined spaces, which further fuelled her curiosity. If there were any doubts left in her mind, they were completely dispelled now. She was committed to whatever this was.

A burst of sunlight startled her, as she emerged into a large clearing. There was a campsite, and in the middle, were three people. Each had weapons drawn, and they were facing off against the hordes of Blighters.

In a few seconds Alyx had appraised the group.

Fighter, thief, and civilian with a sword, she thought. They needed her help. And in return they could explain why they were such Blight magnets. Alyx stepped forward with confidence; the firm ground underfoot provided a good place to make a stand. She headed directly for the small group, pausing only to cut down Blighters in her path. There was a clear trail of bodies in her wake, and the group ahead noticed her approach.

"I don't know who you are, but thanks for the help," the fighter said.

"You stand with me, the others can support from behind," Alyx said. The fighter nodded and accepted her suggestion. A dagger whizzed past her face and embedded itself into a nearby Blighter.

"Don't mind me, just supporting from behind," the thief said, her voice dripping with sarcasm. Alyx understood the gesture and gave her a respectful nod. It was important to have them all on side. She then turned to fight.

Blighters were converging from all locations. Alyx moved next to the fighter, and readied herself.

"In case anything happens, I'm Alyx," she said as she pivoted to slash at an encroaching Blighter. Her name came out with a grunt, less eloquently than she had hoped.

"I'm Vincent. Nice to meet you." He stepped forward and tripped a Blighter, slicing through the other just behind it. Alyx finished off the Blighter that stumbled towards her and took a moment to glance at Vincent's sword.

Unbelievable. He noticed her gaze.

"Yes, it's Runesteel. You can take a better look when we aren't being killed."

"Sounds good." Alyx eyed the next group. Sweat started to drip down her face. She shouldn't be this tired, but her body was weary. She hadn't had a chance to recover from her previous fight, and had landed herself in a surprisingly large battle.

No rest for a weapon, she thought and prepared for the next assault. She pointed into the heart of the group with her weapon, and Vincent nodded. Alyx launched herself in, ignoring the strained cries of her legs as she pushed them even harder. She accepted none of the pain, focusing on the impending attack. With two quick slashes she took down a Blighter and wounded another. The thickly packed group dispersed immediately. While their attention was kept by Alyx, Vincent swept in and whirled through the rest, his sword flashing as he advanced.

Alyx stole another glance of admiration at the Runesteel sword, then retreated back with Vincent.

"Nice job up there, but they aren't slowing down," the thief said.

"That's Lara," Vincent said.

"And the master swordsman over there with the angry face is Alrion," Lara said. She smirked at him and he grunted at the comment.

"Alyx here. Do you have an escape plan? I don't like our chances if this continues."

"No. They cornered us here over several days," Lara said. She gestured at the clearing. There were Blighters surrounding the perimeter.

"Fine. We stand together for now, and if we get overwhelmed I'll create an opening for you," Alyx said. She didn't take her eyes off the approaching Blighters.

Why am I offering myself up for these people? she thought. But then she answered herself quickly.

I am a discarded weapon. I no longer have a purpose.

"I'm sorry how useless I am. Lara and I have taken on more than this just by ourselves," Alrion said. The frustration in his voice was obvious, and Alyx could sense that something must have happened to him. Clearly the sword was not his preferred weapon.

"Never mind that, focus on the task at hand," Vincent said. He pointed at the encroaching group and Alyx joined him in advancing.

Wave after wave of Blighters poured into the clearing. Each time Vincent and Alyx moved together, picking apart the Blighters with relative ease. Vincent and his Runesteel opened them up, and Alyx finished off the rest. Lara and Alrion stayed back, Lara providing some spotting and long-range assistance while Alrion just scowled. As the fight wore on he grew angrier and angrier.

Alyx could hear bits of conversation and noticed that Lara was trying to calm Alrion down. But she didn't focus on it; the battle carried her full attention. As it continued, her hair tumbled free. Her long flowing brown locks swayed just above her shoulder line. She had never fought with her hair loose, and enjoyed the carefree nature of it. Although it did restrict her head movements to ensure her vision wasn't obstructed.

Vincent was proving to be a capable fighter, as she had initially assessed. He was clearly older and not as fast as her, but he was strong and sure. His blade more than compensated for any lack in his speed and technique, and the Blighters were not enough to trouble him in capability. But the vast number and constant stream were wearing him down too.

The clearing was now full of Blighters. Every time Alyx cut one down, another was right there, ready and eager. She had never seen Blighters in this volume or with such intensity before.

"There's no end to them," she said.

"There is, but it may take a while," Vincent said. He kicked over a Blighter and slashed at another that was approaching. He looked slower. Alyx was worried. She chanced a look behind and saw that Alrion and Lara were in the thick of it too. Lara was dancing around, dodging, slashing, and harrying. Alrion was using slow and deliberate strikes to finish off any Blighters that were still standing.

Good pairing to make the most of this, but they can't continue for much longer.

She still couldn't believe what she had gotten herself into. It was time to make a difference. She remembered the path she had taken to reach them. It had been narrow, and would provide them a reprieve. If they could get there. But she would see to it.

"I'm going to advance, stick with me and let's make it through to a better place," she said. Alyx summoned the last of her reserve strength and made a final push forward. The first few Blighters were taken by surprise, falling before they could react. The next layer stepped back, unsure of what to do. Alyx dashed into the space, Vincent sticking with her. She couldn't risk turning back, to check on the others. But she knew that Lara would do the right thing.

The thief has good instincts. She's a survivor. She looks familiar somehow, Alyx thought. But she pushed the thoughts away. She had an impossible mission to complete. One she had set herself, but one she would still achieve.

Her left foot slipped and threw her balance off. But she compensated and lurched forward. She stabbed at a Blighter with her sword and grabbed another to steady herself. Before it could lunge in to bite her Vincent cut it down in a smooth motion. Working together they made slow progress, but more and more incidents threatened to end their battle prematurely.

Swaying on her feet, Alyx spun around and changed her approach. Gesturing behind her, the group readjusted their position. She had reached the edge of the clearing, and was shielding their retreat.

"There's Blighters on the path," Lara shouted.

"Less than here. And it's tighter," Alyx shouted back. She missed a Blighter, and it lunged for the advantage. Desperately she kicked it away, and managed to inflict a slight cut with her sword. Vincent finished it off, and stepped in front of her.

"You've done enough. You won't survive any longer," he said.

"It doesn't matter now. This is a fitting end for a weapon like me," Alyx said. She shoved Vincent aside, and ran into the thick of the remaining Blighters. Vincent swore, and started to follow. But he hesitated.

"Pull back," he said. Alyx smiled. At least he understood what lay ahead. Now all she had to do was make sure it was a fitting death. She ignored defence and focused all her energy on attack. The Blighters shrunk back, confused, and frightened by this new approach. Alyx let loose, years of discipline and training and focus falling away. She could be free, and let her cares go. And this horde of Blighters would be a thrilling final stand.

There were too many. Her muscles started to cramp up and freeze. Her movements became stiff and the Blighters grew bolder. They started to surge forward, tripping over each other in their eagerness. Despite her best efforts, she was starting to get nicks and scratches from their claws and rudimentary blades.

Death by a thousand cuts. How ironic.

She laughed to herself. However, she didn't notice one particular Blighter that wasn't dead. It jumped up from the ground and went in for the bite. Alyx threw her arm up at the last instant to shield her face, but couldn't stop the bite. Its fangs sank in deep and her arm felt hot and cold at the same time.

No! Not like this!

She kicked the Blighter away and threw down her weapon, hoping they would kill her outright. She closed her eyes and waited for the end. But around her she only heard death and mayhem.

Cautiously she opened her eyes and looked around. Vincent and Alrion had joined the fight, and were finishing off the final few Blighters. Lara was holding off those trying to join in from the path.

"I don't understand," she said as they approached her.

"I couldn't stand by and watch you sacrifice yourself," Alrion said. She could see a strange mix of anger and sadness in his expression. She knelt and retrieved her sword. She also used the movement to cover her arm. It didn't feel right to reveal her situation just yet.

"What do I do now?" she whispered. She had let go and accepted her fate. But now, a new path was showing itself. But how long could she last before succumbing to the infection?

2

A KINDRED SPIRIT

"I'd love to complete the introductions, but I've had enough of Blighter innards for one day," Lara said. She surveyed the area around them in disgust. What had originally been a simple camping spot was now a Blighter graveyard of horrors.

"Agreed. Do you know this forest well?" Alrion said to Alyx.

"Relatively. There's no other spot like this, but I can lead us somewhere we can stop and rest a little," she said. Lara could see the exhaustion on the warrior's face, as much as she tried to ignore it. She couldn't help wondering why this stranger had risked her life to help them.

I'll keep an eye on her. If she's hiding something, I'll find it.

She stuck close to Alyx as they picked their way through the battlefield. She looked over at Alrion and saw him lost in thought.

Something is troubling him. Something more than just his condition. I'll have to figure that out later, she thought. Another thing to take care of. Vincent seemed like the practical sort, but Lara wondered how they would fare without her. Alrion was in his own world more days than not, and this was dangerous country. Especially with the horde of Blighters they had just encountered. She hoped it wasn't a sign of things to come.

Soon the clearing was behind them, and they continued along a narrow trail. The vegetation was thick and lush, suggesting the path had not been used in a while. Alyx was out front, stepping slowly but surely. She held her sword out, but only slashed at the most troublesome plants. Lara wasn't sure if it was due to respect for nature or lack of energy. Either option seemed equally likely. She glanced over at Vincent to gauge his reaction.

He didn't seem any different, just focused on the task ahead of them. He had been checking on Alrion though. So, he must have suspected something too.

I wish I knew more about this infection. There has to be more we can do.

Although it had been progressing slowly, it weighed on her mind every day. Every night she lay awake, listening out for signs of it progressing. Nothing was obvious, but the lack of any signs was in itself troubling. Her greatest fear was that it was progressing silently, and there would be no sign of it until too late.

In time they reached a small area with thinner tree cover. There was still thick vegetation, but also places to sit. Lara threw her pack onto a nearby shrub and sank into the grass. It was hard and slightly damp but she didn't care.

The rest did the same thing. Vincent spoke up first.

"Alyx, we are in your debt. You made the difference today, and I will be forever grateful." He stood and bowed to her. Alyx waved him away.

"I accept your thanks, but it is not necessary. I followed my curiosity, and decided I could not stand aside."

"You were ready to die for us! Why?" Alrion said, full of wonder.

"I'd like to know too," Lara said. Unlike Alrion, she gave Alyx a questioning look.

"I am not afraid of death. Especially now that my life's work is done. It seemed like a fitting end, if that were the case. But, here we are. My story is not done yet," Alyx said. She lay back, using one of the bushes behind her as a makeshift pillow.

"Please, share your story. At least some of it," Vincent said.

"Very well. As you know, my name is Alyx. I was the only child to my father, and therefore the only heir to the Warden of the North."

"Your father was Fenkirk?" Lara said. She couldn't hide the surprise in her voice.

"That is correct. You may be aware, but he was slain by the Skull King when I was only eight years old." Alyx paused. Lara knew of the story, but didn't know Fenkirk had had a daughter. She looked over at Alrion and Vincent and they appeared lost.

"I don't think they are as familiar with the history around here. You may need to explain a little," Lara said.

"The Skull King was one of the Four Generals of the Blight. We can discuss them later. All you need to know, however, is that he was completely evil and his head was all black with only his skull showing. He killed my father to prove his dominance, and conquered the rest of the area without opposition," Alyx said. She spat into a nearby shrub. Lara could see the anger boiling up in Alyx. Surprisingly she noticed something similar in Alrion too.

What's happening with him?

"I had no future. No woman can become the Warden. And the title means nothing if you can't provide the people with leadership and safety. So, I took up my family sword, and swore revenge on the Skull King," Alyx said. There was a satisfied look upon her face as she spoke, and Lara thought that perhaps Alyx had succeeded.

"That's a hard life, to take on such a burden at such a young age," Vincent said.

"It's the life I chose, so it is not hard."

"Your family's sword? Wasn't it famous?" Lara said.

"Yes. Both for its size and its legacy. It is called Andrylir." Alyx looked at her hands, despondent for a moment. She quickly recovered, but not before Lara noticed.

"What does that mean?" Alrion said.

"It means 'One Strike'."

"Is there a reason for that? Is there a story around it?" Lara said.

"Yes, there is, and the legend is true. One strike from it can kill anything."

"Impossible!" Vincent said.

"Believe what you want. But I took up the giant sword of my father, and turned myself into a living weapon. I thought of nothing else, did nothing else, until I could have my revenge."

"You did it, didn't you?" Lara said. A wicked smile crept along Alyx's face.

"I did. At great cost, but I did. And now I'm here."

"Without your sword and without a purpose," Alrion said. Alyx looked like the wind had been knocked out of her. Lara turned her attention to Alrion.

That was incisive of him, she thought. Wonder and curiosity flowed through her in relation to his words.

"You have me at a loss, but I cannot deny your words. Perhaps there is another purpose for a weapon like me," she said, her voice much quieter now. The pride that had infected it before was gone.

"I also said that I would show you my sword," Vincent said. He stood slowly, taking the opportunity to stretch.

"Allow me. My father made both swords," Alrion said. Before Vincent could react, Alrion unsheathed his sword and offered it to Alyx, pommel first. She grabbed it and Alrion sat back, satisfied.

"This is a beautiful blade," Alyx said, turning it over and admiring it from many angles.

"The stone ..." Lara said, pointing. She almost thought she had imagined it. A quick glow from the diamond in the pommel of the sword. But it wasn't reflected light. There was a pale blue to the glow. She looked over at Alrion and he was looking at Alyx with interest.

"What do you mean?" Alyx said. But Vincent understood immediately. He strode over and examined the diamond while Alyx still held it.

"It's faint but unmistakeable. You were bitten," he said. Alyx shrank back.

"Who are you?" she said.

"The diamond reacts to those tainted by the Blight. If you were a Shade it would be bright blue," Alrion said as he rose. He quietly stepped over to Alyx and retrieved the blade. The stone had a distinct glow to it, stronger than before. But still relatively pale.

"You also?" Alyx said, pointing at the diamond.

"Yes. But it hasn't claimed me yet," Alrion said before returning to his previous seat. He put the sword away, and watched Alyx with a curious gaze. Lara wanted to quiz Alrion, but she decided to wait until later. For now, she had to get to the bottom of this new problem.

"When were you thinking of telling us?" Lara said. She didn't hide the anger in her voice.

"Soon. I didn't want to taint the purity of the gesture you made."

"That's why you threw your sword down," Vincent said.

"Yes, I knew it was over. I am sorry for the confusion. It seemed like a fitting end, that was all."

"It is a fitting end," Lara said.

"It might be, if it was the end. But it won't be. You're coming with us," Alrion said.

"She's infected! This isn't a game!" Lara shouted. She couldn't believe what he was saying.

"She saved us. It's the least I can do."

"No, the least we can do is not harbour a threat like her. No offence, Alyx," Lara said. She had to shut down this idea before it grew any further.

"What is she going to do? Infect me?" Alrion said, laughing. He had to be losing his mind.

"I do appreciate your kindness, but it would not be a kindness travelling with you and knowing that I will succumb to the infection and be a danger to you," Alyx said.

"Would you change your mind if I told you I am going to find a cure," Alrion said. He had a gleam in his eye and stared straight at Alyx. She sat up straighter, giving him all her attention.

"You should not toy with me like this."

"I'm not. I'm on a quest to end the Blight, and I have a lead for how to get cured. The Mystics who live up in the mountains."

"Fairy tales. You shouldn't give yourself false hope," Alyx said. She sank back into the greenery and watched the sky.

"No less of a fairy tale than the Pool of Knowledge. Which I found and drank from. Or the fact that my grandfather cured the Blight from Avaria," Alrion said.

"You did what?" Alyx rose and stood over Alrion.

"I found the Pool and drank from it. It gives me visions of what I need for my quest. It showed me to the monks of the desert, and their secret trial of the Will.

And now it is bringing me to the Mystics of the north. I know their power is crucial to cleansing the Blight. I just need to get there."

"Your story is fanciful, yet plausible. But no matter, we will never get there in time."

"How infected do I look?" Alrion said. He rose and stood close to Alyx. She looked him up and down.

"Judging from the mark a few days. But you don't seem to have some of the other signs."

"It's been a week," Alrion said quietly.

"We can't let this happen," Lara said to Vincent. She could sense the conversation turning, and didn't want it to continue.

"I'm seeing both sides here. Alyx is an incredibly effective fighter. We could use the help," Vincent said.

"And when she turns?" Lara said.

"If we don't make it in time, we can deal with her. We just dealt with a whole clearing of Blighters," Vincent said.

"I'm already infected. We just need to keep you two safe. And monitor her progress. The diamond should help," Alrion said.

"I just—" Lara said, but Alrion interrupted.

"There's something you all should know. This whole attack was my fault." Alrion paused and waited. After a few seconds he continued.

"Wraith has been taunting me ever since that day. He's inside my head, whenever he wants. I have been working at blocking him out, but it's exhausting and I'm still learning how to deal with this. The Blight is affecting me too somehow. My emotions surge more, especially what we might consider darker emotions. Like anger. And so earlier today I lost it. And look what happened!" Alrion grew very quiet. Lara tried to speak but choked up. She walked over and gave him a hug.

"Don't beat yourself up, we're here for you remember. Have you been carrying this all by yourself?" she said.

"Yes, I've been trying to be strong. And I've given Alyx a death sentence at the same time. That's why we have to bring her with us. It's her only chance. And we owe her that much."

Alyx closed her eyes and looked down. Vincent walked over to join Alrion too.

"We're with you son, and don't worry Alyx can join us if she's willing. I actually think it's her best chance too. The risk is not too great, and she will be a fine addition to our group," he said.

"I understand why you want her to come and won't stop it. I guess I'll just have to keep my eyes on you," Lara said, looking directly at Alyx. She finally understood what was going on with Alrion.

Why didn't he just say something? They were close enough for that.

"You are all assuming that I want to come," Alyx said finally.

"I know you will," Alrion said. His voice had a confidence that Lara didn't understand.

"How can you know my mind when I haven't even decided?"

"Because you haven't said no yet. And I need to cure you. You are infected because of me, so as soon as I am cured and I have the power to do so myself you will be my first case. That's why you must come."

Alyx rose stiffly from the ground. She walked over to Alrion.

"Please stand," she said. Alrion stood with a little rockiness.

"I, Alyx Vanstar, Warden of the North and Slayer of the Skull King, do hereby pledge my life into the service of Alrion." She completed the gesture by plugging her short sword into the ground in front of her.

"I accept your service. And I hereby pledge that I will cure you from this infection. Once I do so, you will be released to do whatever you wish," Alrion said. He removed her sword and handed it back to her. Alyx bowed and sat back down.

"Now that we're all friends, what's the plan?" Lara said.

"We need to brief Alyx on the way, and continue on our journey."

"Do you know your destination?" Alyx said.

"Not exactly. Just that it's north, at the snowy peaks," Alrion said.

"That helps, there is only one region that could be. But those mountains are vast and treacherous. We will need more guidance."

"It will come."

"Very well. Then I suggest we head to the nearest town and resupply ourselves. We will need much for this journey."

"Agreed. Do you have a place in mind?" Vincent said.

"I do."

"Then let's make a start. We can talk on the way, and the further we get from this mess the better," Vincent said. He started to work through their belongings. Lara approached Alrion with care, putting a hand on his shoulder. He turned to face her.

"You're not alone. Don't carry this burden by yourself," she said softly. Alrion took her hand gingerly, and warmed between his own. Then he returned her hand.

"I must. I can't taint you with it, and weigh you down. You deserve to be free," he said, sadness in his eyes. He blinked away a potential tear and turned to look for his belongings. Lara's heart cried out.

I have to find a way to help him.

3

LEFT BEHIND

Celes had been incredibly patient. She had kept a low profile, avoiding areas of Plynth that would be accessed by the network of Tainted. It was infuriating but she knew it was important. Eventually Vincent would send word and confirm that everything was all right.

Except he hadn't. It had been over a week, and she was tired of waiting.

I just need a way to find them. And I know just the place, she thought. The one place she had been avoiding, was the place she needed to go. Regardless of the outcome of the clash in the desert, she knew that the Tainted would have information and perhaps even instructions on what to do next.

I need to start with Glinda.

It made perfect sense. Glinda was either an ally, or too compromised by the help she had already given them to run to the leaders of the Tainted. If Glinda was still trusted, she might find out something useful.

She will definitely tell me something.

She checked her outfit, and left the small house with confidence. Her boots echoed noisily on the stone walkway outside. For the first time she wasn't trying to sneak around. She didn't care if she was found.

Celes started by walking around to the barracks near the town gates. She knew Glinda was a guard, so it was the most logical place to look. Acting like she belonged, Celes walked right into the building. There were a few people loitering around, and those that were paid her no attention.

"Head up, you belong here," Celes told herself. After a quick lap around the barracks she saw no sign of Glinda. She stopped beside a guard standing around near the entrance. He was staring off at something else, his mind elsewhere.

"Have you seen Glinda this morning?" Celes said. The guard was initially startled, and ran his hand through his hair.

"Oh, ahh no, I don't think so. She must be on patrol," he said. Celes thought he was very odd.

"Are you new?" she said.

"Yes, how did you know?"

"Oh, I just know most of the faces around here."

"Do you want me to pass on a message?"

"No, that's fine I'll just see her later. Thanks," Celes said. She waved at the guard and left. As helpful as it would have been to leave a message, she didn't trust that guard. And she didn't want to compromise Glinda. There was no knowing how many of the guard were Tainted.

It was a strange position to be in, relying on a Tainted guard. She would never have expected it, but Vincent had been insistent and she had come to realise that there was something different about Glinda. She was Tainted, but trying to live her own life.

Maybe there's a whole lot of people like that out there. Wanting to be different, but trapped by the infection? she thought. It was certainly a perspective she had never considered before. But then again, she had been living another life. Sheltered, and focusing on her family. Tales of the Blight had been fanciful stories to the folk of Hamley.

Celes headed back to the blacksmith shop where Vincent had been working. She found the owner working in the shop, and approached him.

"Hello, I'm sorry I forgot your name. But my husband Will was working here recently," she said.

"Oh, no problem. It's John. Is everything alright?"

"Everything is fine. He had to leave suddenly for family reasons, but I thought he would be back by now. So, I just wanted to stop by and let you know." Celes could see the real concern on the man's face slowly change into relief.

"Oh, great. I was really worried. I never really paid him, and he completed a lot of work. I felt really bad that something had happened, and I never had a chance to properly compensate him!"

"It's all fine, don't worry he was happy enough for the experience. Have you had more trouble with the guards?"

"No, they backed right off after that last incident. It's been very quiet. I managed to get my orders out and it's all been busy. I do miss having Will around though, he's fantastic. I hope everything's all right. I didn't know what to do, I didn't even know where he was staying!" John looked flustered and apologetic. Lara thought it was sweet.

"I feel bad about not coming to see you sooner. For now, assume that he won't be back for a while. I'll make sure he does see you though."

"That would be nice, I need to thank him in person, even if he won't be sticking around. You take care," John said. He waved at Celes then returned to his work.

At least that's taken care of now.

Next, she took the main path between the blacksmith and the council chambers. It was the best next step. She knew Glinda frequented that route in the past. Plus, she expected that the councilman would still be active. All they had done was embarrass him, and probably only to a limited audience.

She spotted several guards as she went, but none paid her any attention. There were market stalls up, and she could smell the spiced meats tempting her in. There were many other handmade goods as well, such as garments, wooden trinkets, and even some blacksmith toys and tools.

Celes stopped suddenly. She picked up a blacksmith puzzle and looked it over carefully. It was so similar to one that Vincent had made for her years ago.

I remember the day so vividly, she thought. It was her test, to see how good he was and how willing he was to work on other things. He had passed with flying colours. Even then she had spotted something special in him.

Just be safe. She put the puzzle back down, smiled at the vendor, and kept walking.

"You're getting too sentimental. Everything is fine," she told herself. Celes quickened her pace and soon saw the council building looming. A shiver went down her spine as she remembered her last encounter there, and what happened after.

I'll just have a quick look, she thought. After a quick glance left and right, she eased into the flow of pedestrians and entered the council building. As before the room was full of people, some bunched together in conversations, others trying to get the attention of officials. Celes wove her way through, heading directly for the passage that led to the council chambers.

It was a risk heading back there, but she needed to investigate. And she felt confident that she could leave quickly if she was spotted. With a sure step she entered the hallway and looked for people. There were some administrators walking around, but few others. Celes carefully navigated down the corridor, heading for the room at the end. Where the councillor worked.

It's safer here, it's more public, she thought, reassuring herself. As she approached she slowed down, ensuring her footsteps were quiet and wouldn't draw attention. She listened out for voices, and only heard the general murmur coming from the main hall. Most of the doors she had passed were closed, which explained the lack of noise.

She crept along, trying not to look too suspicious. The door to the councillor's chamber was half-open. When she couldn't hear anything, she flattened herself next to the wall and listened closely. Nothing.

Next, she peered through the crack in the door hinge, trying to see inside. She didn't see any evidence of people.

Seems empty, I'll take a quick peek.

She quickly entered the room and verified it was empty. Then she reached for the door.

"No, better it's untouched," she told herself. She retracted her arm and looked around the room. It was a simple arrangement, even though each piece of furniture was heavy and expensive. A large desk dominated the space, with the councillor's chair behind. It was larger, more padded, and detailed than the two visitor chairs.

Celes stepped around the ornate desk, skimming her eyes over the stacks of paper. Most were reports or letters, but all were concerned with general council matters. Nothing she could use.

To be expected. They seem to do all their communication another way, she thought. Satisfied that there was nothing useful, she approached the door and glanced out.

"Damn!" she whispered and hid behind the door. There was a guard walking down the hallway. His steps were heavy and loud, and they weren't slowing.

I'll talk my way out.

She started working on her story. The footsteps started to slow, and finally stopped. Celes could see the guard standing in the doorway.

"I know you're in there. Meet me in the laneway behind the chambers, and don't attract any attention," a female voice said. It sounded familiar, so Celes could only assume it was Glinda.

If I keep getting spotted like this, I'll have to hand in my thief card, Celes thought with a laugh. Although, to be fair, she normally operated at night. These daytime infiltrations were a new thing. She retraced her steps, walking through the corridor like she belonged there. Nobody challenged her, although most were busy or behind closed doors.

She emerged into the main room and joined the flow of people.

Well, I found Glinda. Doesn't matter how it happened. Now I can get some answers, she thought as she left the building and walked around looking for the lane access. She turned left into the first cross street, and before long found a lane that extended behind the council chambers.

It was narrow and full of rubbish. Celes could smell that before she saw it. There were plenty of places to hide, which was comforting and risky at the same time. She stepped through carefully, trying to find the guard.

"Over here," a voice said. Celes followed the voice and stepped behind a large crate full of wet paper. She saw Glinda standing there.

"Oh, good it is you. Come here often?" Celes said, gesturing at the lovely surroundings.

"No, which means we will not be spotted together. What are you doing?"

"Looking for leads. Vincent hasn't returned, and the Tainted are my best link to find him."

"There's some sort of upheaval going on. Wraith is mobilising lots of Tainted in the north. But I don't get most of the communication," Glinda said. She sounded tired.

"Is everything alright? Were there any repercussions from when we escaped?"

"Some. I was put on guard duty for the mansion. I had to stand outside for fourteen hours a day. It was my punishment."

"They didn't suspect anything?"

"If they did, they're over it now. By having me there I proved my loyalty since they were able to observe everything. Thanks for backing off."

"Of course. And the councillor?"

"He flew into a terrible rage. But he didn't really have anyone to focus it on. So, we all copped it. I think Wraith was more amused than anything else. It was just a humiliation that passed. All in all, it could have been worse," Glinda said. She had a concerned look on her face and she directed it at Celes.

"So now you're wondering why I'm showing up to cause you more trouble?"

"Exactly."

"Well, I've been hiding out and staying out of sight. But it's been over a week now and I haven't heard anything from Vincent. I was hoping you might have something you can tell me?" Celes really needed something. Glinda was her last hope. Glinda looked around the alley, and stepped in closer. She expertly avoided some trash on the ground.

"There has been some talk. The last thing you heard about was the desert attack, right?"

"Yes. And the damn councillor was so gleeful about it as well."

"I'm not sure what happened, but it didn't end as expected. There's some sort of chase on now."

"That sounds promising. Like they made it away."

"I would assume so. But I have a bad feeling. I can't explain it, but I don't think Wraith achieved nothing. I've heard him before when something completely failed, and he's ruthless. And if something went wrong and it was his fault, he still makes everyone else feel it. But I don't get the same feeling."

"You think he achieved a victory of some kind? Even if there's some sort of chase going on?"

"Yes. I know it's a little vague, but it feels like an important detail," Glinda said with care. Her eyes darted around again, and she crept closer still, leaning in. She whispered in Celes's ear.

"There's something else. They're using some sort of special Trackers. It's a type of Tainted I've never heard of before," she said. As soon as she had spoken she stepped back. Celes's eyes widened and she thought through the implications.

"I need to meet one," she finally said. Glinda nodded.

"I have someone in mind actually. But I'm warning you, he'll want some kind of deal in return for helping you."

"That's fine, I can negotiate that. It's too important to pass up," Celes said. Glinda acknowledged Celes with a slight nod and beckoned her to follow. Celes's mind was running wild with theories and plans. But she solidified it all into one thought.

I'm coming.

4

PATH OF THE SWORD

Alyx led them through the woods and back to a path of sorts. Alrion welcomed the open space. He had felt so confined, especially when the Blighters boxed them in.

It's crowded enough in my head, need a little space out here, he thought, laughing to himself. He appreciated Lara's offer of help, but he couldn't accept it. Not in its current form. He wouldn't burden her with the taunting, the feeling of being weighed down slowly. The weight of a thousand angry, mindless beings trying to pile on him. No, this was better. He just had to watch his temper.

In these times he would almost reach out to his Spark. But he shuddered at the memory of the one time he had. Even the thought of reaching through that murky filth was enough to put him off. There was no reason to keep thinking about it. But he couldn't resist, since it was off limits. He needed to occupy himself. He sped up until he was alongside Alyx.

"How did you learn to fight like that?" he said.

"Years of intense training. And focus. Why?"

"I need to learn something. I'm useless right now without my power. I can't afford to be a liability when the stakes are this high."

"It will help with your anger management too," Alyx said. She turned to look at him again, sizing him up. Alrion felt inadequate, but he didn't know why.

"That sounds like it could help. I need something to focus on, since I can't do any magic. Would you be able to train me?"

"I can. But you must follow my instructions to the letter. There's no point otherwise."

"I can do that." Alrion imagined fighting better. It seemed like a great idea to defend himself without using his power. He could see himself fighting off nearby Blighters with a sword then burning others at range seconds later. He got a little carried away with his imagination, and found himself swinging his right arm. Alyx stifled a small laugh, but Lara didn't hold back at all.

"Practicing, are we?" she joked.

"Just warming up," Alrion said, his cheeks reddening.

Why do I have to be so awkward?

It hurt more with Alyx there. She was so cool and focused and to the point, that he felt like more of a clown in comparison.

"I used to do that kind of thing. You must have inherited it," Vincent said with a chuckle. That made Alrion feel better. His father had a knack for changing the mood.

"I've never trained anyone before, but you seem keen so I'm sure it will work. We will start slow, and ramp it up. I'm afraid my body needs a proper recovery before we get too advanced," Alyx said. Alrion nodded and turned to take in the scenery. The windy road was taking them far away from the forest, and into some sparse plains.

They stopped briefly for a snack, before pushing on.

"It's so exposed here, we need to reach somewhere more sheltered to rest this evening," Alyx said.

"I couldn't agree more," Vincent said. He was looking around at their surroundings and seemed concerned. Alrion was looking forward to a rest, but not the quiet it would bring. He wasn't looking forward to fending off Wraith again. Things were easier during the day when he was occupied and had people around. But at night it was far worse. Sometimes his mind turned to thoughts of Wraith and the Blight unbidden. He found it difficult to think of anything else.

Soon they came upon some rolling hills, and Alyx led them into a dense copse of trees nestled into a hill. It made for a nice sheltered spot, with lots of space around.

"This looks great," Vincent said. He immediately started setting up camp with what they had available.

"I'm just going to do a quick scout around," Lara said. She dropped her bag and took off.

"Don't worry, it's safe here," Alyx said to Alrion.

"Have you used this spot before?"

"A long time ago during a terrible storm. Hopefully we fare better tonight." Alyx slowly seated herself against a tree. She closed her eyes and relaxed.

"How did you become so focused?"

"It's just a state of mind. With practice you can achieve it."

"You sound like the monks I met in the desert," Alrion said, laughing.

"I've heard of them. Capable warriors and strong willed. Didn't you mention some sort of trial there?"

"Yes. I can't talk about it, but it taught me a lot."

"Well, you probably have all the tools you need. It then becomes about throwing away the distractions. For me it was simple."

"Why?"

"I watched my father be murdered in front of me. It was nothing to discard everything else. Too easy, in fact," Alyx said. She stared off into the distance.

"I'm sorry, I didn't mean to bring that up," Alrion said.

"It's fine, it was a long time ago. And he has been avenged."

"What happened to your family sword?"

"Long story. Suffice to say it's gone." She drew her short sword and turned it over in her hands.

"This is not suitable for training. Not ideal for sparring due to its length, not safe enough and won't last long against your Runesteel. Let's skip to real swords. Vincent, can I borrow yours?"

"Sure," he said, handing her the scabbard. Alyx put her sword away on the grass nearby and drew the Runesteel sword.

"Let's see how this works," she said. She strode over to one of the trees nearby with purpose in her step. In one fluid motion she slashed out with her arm. The tree offered no resistance, and after a momentary delay was neatly sliced open. The cut portion tumbled down causing a loud bang.

"Well, now they know where we are!" Lara said with frustration.

"The sound will carry, but not far. Don't worry. The sword has a good balance to it, you are very skilled, Vincent."

"Thank you." Vincent gave her a short bow.

"Alrion we will train with these. You shouldn't be fast enough to injure me, but let's start slow, just in case. I'd rather not lose any limbs."

"Not until I can heal you," Alrion said, trying to make a joke. He thought he saw a partial smile from Alyx, but it was gone in an instant, so he wasn't sure.

"Ready your sword," she said. Alrion shuffled his feet and drew his sword, holding it out. His muscles were tense, awaiting his commands.

"Too stiff, and too forced. You need to be light and reactive. Tension will cause you to move slowly and make mistakes. You will drop your blade." Alyx walked over and shifted Alrion's legs, and adjusted his posture.

"Still too stiff. Imagine that you just had a long hot bath," she said. Alrion gave her a strange look.

Did she really just say that?

"You think that I don't bathe? That's quite insulting," Alyx said. Lara burst out laughing.

"It just seemed like an odd suggestion," Alrion said.

"I think it's quite accurate really. Heat is a great way to relax your muscles," Vincent said. Alrion started to speak again, but stopped himself. He tried to loosen up.

"Better, for now." Alyx walked back until she was several paces away. "Follow my movements," she said, taking him through a simple exercise. Alrion followed along, paying particular attention to allow him to copy her exactly.

~

Hours later they took a break. Alrion was bent over, drawing in deep breaths and leaning on his sword.

"You look tired now," Alyx said.

"I am."

"Good. One final movement. Do the whole sequence," she said. Alrion's arms were heavy, and his shoulders ached. Even his legs were complaining. The day's events, the walking, and now the training had worn him out. But he complied all the same.

He was too tired to worry about the finer movements, letting his sword flow the easiest way.

"Good. Again. Continue," Alyx said. Alrion gathered one final burst of energy, and rather than step away Alyx blocked it. The meeting of the swords rang out through the clearing. With a slight push she sent Alrion tumbling back, and he found himself seated on the ground.

"Now you can rest," Alyx said. She slowly walked over to Vincent to return the sword then eased herself down. Alrion watched her very carefully.

"I see you're sore and tired too!"

"Of course. After two battles, hours of walking and another training session with you. I'm only human after all."

"So you say," Alrion muttered under his breath.

"You did a lot better at the end there. What changed?" Lara said. She quickly dropped down and sat right next to him.

"I was too tired to think about what I was doing. It was part memory, part instinct."

"And that's why it looked more fluid. Don't you think Vincent?" Lara said.

"Definitely. You're making great progress. Maybe you can hang up your wizard robe," Vincent said.

"I wouldn't do that just yet," Alyx said with a smile.

"If you insist. Not that I can do anything right now," Alrion said. He had reminded himself of the infection. He felt around his neck, seeing if there was any change. But there was nothing to feel. The mark had spread, but it was only colouring. It didn't have any dimension to it.

"It seems to have stabilised, well in terms of looks," Lara said.

"I might have to start wearing a scarf."

"It won't look out of place once we get further north," Vincent said.

"True. I think I might turn in," Alrion said. He said his goodnights and found himself a comfortable nook to set up for sleep. As he lay down, he had one last thought.

I'm way too tired to care about anything right now. What a relief.

Alrion rose gingerly, feeling the stiffness and pain throughout his muscles. He hadn't felt like this since the first days of his apprenticeship as a blacksmith.

"You look a little uncomfortable," Lara said. She was perched on a rock nearby watching him.

"I haven't had a workout like that, probably ever." Alrion tried massaging his calf muscles, but they remained the same.

"It gets harder before it gets easier," Alyx said. She approached and tossed him a hunk of bread.

"Eat quickly and get packed. We need to make it to town today, and the sooner the better," she said. Before Alrion could respond she had turned and walked away.

"She looks well-rested," he said.

"I know. Maybe she's not human," Lara said, chuckling.

"Well she did kill the Skull King. That sounds like a big thing."

"Oh, it is. He was known as the face of the Blight. Apart from the obvious reasons, he just seemed to embody everything people hated about it."

"Do you think she will tell us the whole story?"

"Maybe, in time. Less chatting, more packing. You don't want her angry at your next training session," Lara said, winking at Alrion. He sighed and forced his muscles to move. The training was definitely a good thing, even if there was some discomfort. He hadn't heard or thought of Wraith yet. And with luck he wouldn't again for some time.

As usual Vincent was packed and ready, so they set off as soon as Alrion was prepared. Alyx led them with confidence through the hills, and by midday they had stopped at the top of a hill and surveyed the land beyond.

"Do you see that settlement down there?" Alyx said.

"Yes, it looks impressive," Alrion said.

"That's Rolyntide. Nice town, and there's a resident Healer. They say she's incredibly gifted."

"Have you ever used her?" Lara said.

"No, I've just passed through really. Visited the inn, resupplied myself. But it's worth us paying her a visit. Not only for some assistance, but also information."

"You think she knows something?" Vincent said.

"When you talk about Mystics, I think about Healers. There's one in every town, and some of the stories are wild and out there. I'd say this Healer knows something that will help guide us on the way north."

"Sounds plausible," Alrion said. He tried to pick out where in the town the Healer may live. But he didn't know what to look for.

"I suppose we should get going then so we are settled in before dark," Vincent said.

"Definitely. We don't want to stay out here overnight. It's too exposed, and we'll be easy targets if we're being tracked," Alyx said.

"I agree," Lara said. She turned and looked into the distance. Alrion could see the worry on her face.

"Then let's go," Alrion said. He knew that Lara was cautious, but she also had good instincts. He definitely didn't want to risk being caught out. He still wasn't confident he could assist in a fight without being a burden.

5

THE HEALER'S SECRET

T he town felt welcoming, and Alrion even thought the single guard looked friendly. He turned his disinterested gaze towards them and started to speak.

"Hello there. State your business," the guard said, a weariness and boredom to his words.

"Just passing through to visit family up north," Alyx said.

"Very well. Staying the night?"

"Yes. We'd like to visit a Healer tomorrow too before we go. You have one here?"

"We do. You'll find her in the middle of town. Not far from the inn."

"Thank you. We'll be good," Alyx said.

"I'm sure you will. I'd hate for you to make work for me," the guard said. He patted his sword and gave them a friendly grin. Alyx waved and continued along the road. Alrion nodded at the guard and kept close.

"I get the feeling that he'd actually be dangerous. He would feel so wronged by having to do something," Alrion said.

"You're right about that. It's easy to keep the peace around here. People like to keep to themselves, don't want to cause trouble. It's only really the Blight," Alyx said. She led them through the town with ease, even though the light was starting to fade.

"You have a favourite place to stay?" Lara said.

"There's only one place to stay. It's the inn we are headed to. Also, if the guard doesn't see us there tonight he will be suspicious. So just remember to be seen and not heard."

"I can do that. Do they do awful puns for the inns around here?" Lara said.

"I'm not sure what you mean. We're almost there," Alyx said. Alrion gave Lara a funny look.

I guess we'll understand when we see it.

The inn loomed large before them, and the sounds of merriment and light spilling out was alluring.

"The Tanked Tankard?" Lara said, barely able to get the words out. She looked at Alrion then at Alyx.

"Yes?" Alyx said.

"That's the worst name. It's terrible." Alrion couldn't help but laugh.

"I know. I thought we had already seen the worst in Brangtur!" Lara managed to say before bursting into laughter herself. Vincent had an amused look on his face but Alyx was just confused.

"I don't get it. It's a perfectly normal name. In my home we have a place called 'Alcoholic Ale'."

"Cultural differences I suppose," Vincent said, opening the door, and ushering everyone in.

It feels good to laugh, Alrion thought as he entered the inn. It made him forget about what was happening, if only for an instant. They walked up to the bar, and Vincent enquired about rooms. Alrion saw something out of the corner of his eye and took another look. It was an extremely polished tankard sitting on the bar. It looked too ornamental to be in everyday use. He picked it up to look it over and caught his reflection. He almost jumped, and managed to put it down with a shaky arm before dropping it completely.

"Everything alright?" Lara said. She had her arm on his shoulder and looked concerned.

"Oh, just a trick of the light. I thought I saw something," Alrion lied. Lara gave him an odd look and nodded.

I'm not sure she bought that, but I'll worry about that later.

He couldn't shake the image from his mind. He had seen his reflection, and the black mark on his neck had grown. And now it had more marks around it. But the thing that scared Alrion the most was his eyes. They looked somehow different. Like he was ill, or hadn't slept.

Both of which are accurate, he thought. But the scariest thing was the fact that his body was changing. It wasn't just a feeling, or an idea. It was really happening. And he felt an intense fear deep down in the pit of his stomach.

"What if I fail?"

"Son, snap out of it. Let's put our things upstairs," Vincent said. Alrion looked up and saw his father gesturing towards the back of the room.

"Sure, let's go." Alrion followed close behind, and made sure he didn't lose them in the crowd.

"Just don't lose it," he told himself. He managed to negotiate the boisterous crowd, dodge a man's dropped drink and ascend the stairs. The hustle and bustle of the inn soon faded away and all he could hear was the sound of footsteps on the wooden floor.

"We're in here; ladies over there. Meet downstairs in a few minutes," Vincent said. He pointed at the two rooms and entered one immediately. Alrion followed closely behind.

"Are you feeling alright?" he said.

"No. I am infected remember?" Alrion said. It came across more sharply than he had intended. But his father didn't seem to react to that.

"I know, which is why I am checking in. I need to know how far things are going."

"About this far," Alrion said. He drew his sword and looked at the diamond. The glow seemed stronger, and had more colour to it. Not the bright blue it would be eventually, but noticeable.

"Still a way to go then. Did you want to talk about Wraith?" Vincent sat down on one of the beds.

"No. It's just a problem I have to deal with. The training helps. When I'm too tired for anything else, I don't worry as much."

"I'm glad the physical activity is helping. But that's just putting off the problem. If you don't find a way to deal with this, it's only going to get worse. You can't ignore it."

"Ignoring it is all I can do. I can't give that thing any of my attention," Alrion said. He didn't even want to say its name. He considered the topic over, and noticed his father standing again.

"That's fine. But I'm here, and we can talk anytime. I'm hungry," Vincent said, walking over to the door. Alrion stayed behind to ensure his things were put away, then walked down by himself.

He's only trying to help. He couldn't understand why his father annoyed him so much.

The next morning Alrion was last to rise. He had slept terribly. His dreams were full of images of the Blight, Tainted, and other related scenes and events. He couldn't remember anything concrete, just the feeling that remained.

"Time to visit the Healer," Vincent said.

"I'm ready," Alrion said. He felt dizzy but didn't say anything, and negotiated the stairs with a little more care than normal. Alyx and Lara were waiting outside. Alrion thought he sensed a bit of tension, but everything changed once they noticed him.

"Is it far?" he said.

"No, I had a look earlier. We only need to walk past a few buildings to find the Healer," Alyx said.

"Let's see what she says. I hope there's a lead, like you suggested," Vincent said. Alyx led the way, the rest of them falling in just behind. Alrion almost tripped over a raised cobblestone.

"Still half-asleep?" Lara said.

"Something like that," Alrion said. He decided to concentrate a bit more on his steps. He managed to stay on his feet and they arrived at the Healer's residence within a few minutes.

It was a multi-storey house with a large wooden door, and potted plants everywhere. There were even vines climbing the walls in places.

"It's like a house in the forest," Lara said with wonder. Alrion couldn't have agreed more. It looked out of place in the town, even though it was big.

Alyx opened the door roughly and entered the house with Alrion and the rest following close behind. They stepped into a large foyer with only another large room and a staircase visible. The furnishings were all simple, but were well constructed and maintained. A woman sat at a table, working on some papers, and looked up at them.

"Good morning. Do you have an appointment?"

"No, but we would like to see the Healer."

"Freyda is busy right now. You will need to come back later. I'm sorry," the woman said. She tossed her hair to the side, and returned to her papers.

She doesn't look particularly sorry, Alrion thought. He stepped forward.

"Please let her know that we will be waiting here until she can see us," he said.

"I'm sorry, but that's not how we work," the woman said. Alrion grabbed a chair and sat down.

"That's fine, I'll be here when she's ready. Taking his cue, Alyx grabbed a nearby chair and did the same. Soon they were all seated, watching the woman. She watched them for a short while, then returned to her papers.

Half an hour passed that way, in complete silence. Except for the rustling of the paper as the woman worked through her stack. Nobody else entered or left the room. Finally, the woman put her papers aside and looked up.

"Now that's done, I can explain to you further about why you should leave."

"I'm listening," Alrion said.

"We don't treat Tainted here. If you would please leave that would be appreciated," the woman said. She had a matter-of-fact tone to her voice and pointed at the door.

"Why would you say that?" Alyx said. She rose and started walking over.

"Don't think you can intimidate me. I know Tainted when I see them."

"Why don't you hang back Alyx? We want the Healer to talk to us," Alrion said. He rose from the chair and walked over himself.

"Why do you think it's her?" Alyx said.

"Because she can see we are infected. A normal person wouldn't be able to tell from that distance. Isn't that right?" Alrion held a hand out, beckoning the woman to answer.

"That is correct. Being clever doesn't change my mind. I'll call the guard."

"I'd rather you didn't, Freyda. I bet you can also see that we haven't turned yet, and I'm not a normal infected. Am I?" Alrion said. He was taking a risk with this, but he had a feeling about her. She was definitely different somehow, and not just for recognising Tainted.

"It's true, you are different. Him too." Freyda pointed at Vincent.

"And her?" Alrion said, looking at Alyx.

"Just normal infected. Sorry."

"It's fine," Alyx said, unconcerned.

"Now we've established that you are a Healer, you do have some sort of special power, and you know we're not just an ordinary group. So why are you telling us to leave?" Alrion said. He wasn't going to leave without a straight answer, and he still felt like there was something they could get from this woman. Alyx had been right about the Healers.

We're so lucky we met her.

"You're trouble, too much trouble. And I don't know how long you have." Freyda looked ready to march them straight out.

"Until we turn?" Alyx said.

"That. And until they catch up to you."

"You can sense them?" Alrion said. He hadn't expected that.

"I'm not going to explain myself, but I know that there's a lot of Tainted on the way. The whole area is going crazy." Freyda sighed and sank down into her chair.

"Help us then. We'll leave town and nothing will happen. The mess will just follow us north," Alrion said.

"What do you need from me? I can't cure you."

"Information and directions. We seek the home of the Mystics."

"I don't know what you are talking about," Freyda said. Her body language became incredibly closed off and she folded her arms.

"Is that so?" Alrion said. He walked back and sidled up to Lara.

"I'm no expert, but she's lying, right?" he said.

"Absolutely. Alyx gave us a good tip here," Lara said. She glared at the warrior, but said nothing else. Alrion nodded, and walked back to Freyda.

"We know that you're lying, and I understand. We're just this big bundle of trouble just landed on your doorstep. You probably have truly sick people upstairs that you need to protect. But we're not just any group. My grandfather was Granthion, and I've been charged with taking on his life's work: to cure the Blight. But I can't do that in my current state. I need the help of the Mystics."

"Why do you talk about them like they're fact?" Freyda said. There was a curious tone to her voice.

"Because I've seen one, in a vision. A vision granted to me from the Pool of Knowledge. I know the power they have is the key to my quest. And time is against me. Please, I know you know something. Just tell us what you know, and we'll be on our way!" Alrion had nothing left to lose. If Freyda was going to keep quiet, they had to move. He couldn't lose more time. He felt drawn, and nervous. Like the Tainted were just one step behind. Looking at Freyda, he could see something changing. She had come to a decision at last.

"I can tell you something. The Mystics do exist, I have met them. I don't think they can solve your problem. It's not how they work. But I won't rob you of the opportunity to ask them yourself."

"Thank you. It means a lot to me," Alrion said. Freyda stood and walked to a cupboard at the back of the room. She opened the doors and busied herself inside looking for something.

"A-ha!" she said, and closed the doors. She returned holding a silver amulet with a pure white stone in the middle. She handed it to Alyx. Alyx held it gingerly in her hand.

"What is this?" she asked.

"It's an amulet that they gave me. It's charged with their power. It will help you in two ways," Freyda said. She pointed at Alyx's chest.

"It will slow that process down a little bit. And you need as much time as you can get," she said. Alyx gripped the amulet a little tighter.

"This is an incredible gift," Alyx said.

"You need it more than me. But you must return it."

"I swear. I will return it!" Alyx was incredibly serious and Freyda looked a little shocked at the intensity.

"There is one other way that it will help you. It is attuned to the power of the place that they reside. It will help guide you there."

"Have you been there?" Alrion said.

"No. I can't explain how it works, I just know that it does."

"Thank you. You've really helped us. I don't know what else to say," Alrion said. He looked around at the others.

"Your thanks are enough. Now leave, before you endanger others." There was no harshness to her voice now, but it was still direct.

"Sure. Let's go," Alrion said. Lara and Vincent said their goodbyes and they left the house immediately.

"We will be able to travel quite a distance before it gets mountainous. We need horses."

"Agreed. Do you have something in mind?" Vincent said.

"Yes, follow me," Alyx said. She was still gripping the amulet in her hand.

"Can I see that for a minute?" Alrion said. She stopped abruptly and handed it to him. The metal was cold but he could feel some sort of warm pulsing coming from it. He peered at the stone within then started to hand it back. He stopped and motioned to Alyx.

"Turn around," he said. He unclasped the amulet and Alyx understood. She moved her hair and Alrion carefully fastened it around her neck.

"That's better," he said. Alyx felt the amulet with her hand then started walking again. Alrion did the same with his own amulet. He had been wearing it so long it just felt like part of him. He hadn't even looked at it properly in a long time.

The black streak in the white stone around his neck looked exactly the same. But it felt different for him now, looking at it. Knowing that the tiny sliver of Blight within that stone was within him also. He felt over the surface of the stone and had a realisation.

This is the same stone as the amulet Alyx was given. What's the connection between the wizards and the Mystics? Alrion thought. It was another question for when he eventually found them.

6

AN UNUSUAL ALLY

Celes stayed close to Glinda. After leaving the alley they stuck to main streets. But Celes had to push hard not to lose the guard in the crowds. Slowly they moved through smaller streets, with fewer people and less wealth. More rubbish, smells, and homeless. Large spaces were vacant, or had temporary residents camping out.

"Where are you taking me?"

"A place nobody likes to go. Which is the perfect place for hiding."

"Hiding from normal people? Or hiding from Tainted?" The distinction was important to her. She needed to know if this man could work with her.

"Both. It's a bit complicated. We're almost there," Glinda said. She entered another seemingly empty yard. But there was a small shack at the back of the property. This one had nobody trying to camp out.

"This is suitably creepy. Even the homeless are avoiding it," Celes said.

"For good reason. Quickly now," Glinda said. She led Celes to the front door. It was old and weathered, hanging at a slight angle. Glinda pulled it roughly and disappeared inside.

"It's me," she said. Celes followed close behind and stopped suddenly. It was very dark in the shack and her eyes needed to adjust. She could make out the outlines of some simple furniture. A chair, a couch, a desk, and some sort of side table. All placed irregularly around the room. There was a figure seated on the couch.

"I know it's you. I just don't know who she is," a raspy voice said from the darkness.

"This is Celes. She needs your help."

"Celes. That name is familiar. I'm Tarren. I have an idea on what you might want from me."

"Nice to meet you. Has Glinda mentioned anything?"

"No. In fact I'm surprised that she brought someone. But she knows me, and my desires. Perhaps there is an overlap in what we want." Tarren shifted on the couch but Celes couldn't see exactly what he was doing.

"I'm looking for my son. I heard that you have specialised tracking skills and could be of assistance," she said.

Tarren laughed, a scratchy grating sound. "I am good at many things. That's why they call us Trackers. That's why I was selected in the first place. Because I knew how to follow trails and find people."

"Selected?"

"I was not born this way, nor did I succumb to an attack by a Blighter or similar. No, I was transformed into this. One of the first I believe."

"I'm sorry. I didn't know that was possible," Celes said. She was glad for the dark, they couldn't see the horrified look on her face.

"It's of benefit to you now. I can probably help you, and I have the freedom to do it. I believe they have since perfected their process."

"That sounds promising," Celes said. She wanted to remain cautious until she found out just what Tarren was after.

"Why don't you take a seat? Glinda, you can wait outside," Tarren said.

"Sure, see you soon," Glinda said, and left quickly. Celes watched her leave, not feeling confident at being left in the dark with Tarren. But this was her best lead; one she had to make the most of. She grabbed the chair and brought it a bit closer to Tarren and sat facing him.

"First, let's discuss your son. Is he infected?" Tarren said.

"Why?"

"Easier to track. Once you're infected you are connected to everyone else. It's part of how the Blight works."

"Not to my knowledge. I hope not."

"That will make it harder to find him. What else can you tell me about him?"

"He's a wizard and his name is Alrion."

"Interesting," Tarren said. "Continue."

"He's on a quest to cure the Blight. There's this wizard who was transformed into a Shade who is after him as well. I think he calls himself Wraith now."

"Oh."

"You're going to have to say something now. Clearly you know something!" Celes was trying hard to restrain herself. She could tell that something she said had triggered a connection for Tarren.

"Wraith has assembled a team of Trackers to chase down a wizard. I get the impression he is infected, but I haven't been told explicitly. It would make him easier to track. From what you've said, there's a good chance it's your son."

Tarren went quiet. There wasn't any emotion in his voice. Celes couldn't believe it. Alrion was infected? It didn't make sense. Vincent had rushed there to prevent an issue like this. If Alrion was infected where were they going and why?

"This is a lot to take in. As much as I want you to be wrong, there's too many elements that ring true. Can you track the Trackers? Can we find my son?"

"You're asking a lot. I need to actively work against Wraith. That comes with significant dangers."

"You said something there. You said work against Wraith, not work against the Blight. What's that about?" Celes rose from her chair and stared intently at Tarren.

"While there seems to be this central thread that connects us all, there are factions. And Wraith leads one of them. He didn't create me."

"I'm going to need to know more about that."

"Another time perhaps. Are you ready to hear my price?"

"Fine. What is it?"

"I want to be cured of the Blight." Tarren said the words and just let them hang without any follow up. He stood as well. Celes noticed that he was taller than her. But it was hard to make out the details in the dim light.

"It's not in my power to grant that," she said.

"I know that. But you mentioned your wizard son is on a quest to cure the Blight. You need to guarantee that he will cure me."

"If you help me find him, then I will encourage him to cure you. I can't guarantee it because I don't control him. But I'm confident he will want to help you, especially since you will be helping me. Maybe that's not what you want to hear, but I'd rather you had the truth upfront." Celes was taking a risk, but she couldn't agree to that bargain without a caveat. She couldn't sign up Alrion to something he may not be comfortable doing. Tarren appeared to be looking into the distance.

"There's more chatter. Things are happening. You have played this well. You want me to serve, then I will get my reward. Very well, I accept." Tarren stuck out an arm. Celes was a bit apprehensive about shaking it, having no idea what she was shaking. But a deal was a deal, and she had no other options. She grasped his hand and shook firmly.

"Good, you have strength. I will meet you outside in a moment." Tarren disappeared into a back room. Celes rushed outside and breathed deeply from the fresh air.

"You look a bit spooked," Glinda said.

"It's creepy in there, and his voice ... it's not reassuring. But I agreed to his terms. He will help find Alrion."

"That's good. He's not a bad guy, Celes. That's why I brought you. I figured you could help each other."

"I hope you're right."

"When I'm right, you'll be one step closer to curing us all. That day cannot come soon enough." Glinda turned and watched the door open. Celes watched too, fearful of what would emerge.

Tarren was a tall man, with black hair and a black scarf wrapping around his neck. He wore a dark brown robe, covering all his body with the hood pulled up.

"Is this acceptable?" he said. He looked suspicious but not outright concerning.

"Yes."

"Good. However, I must warn you. Once we leave the city we'll travel lighter than this. My markings will be harder to hide."

"That's fine. We will adjust, as we need to. Where should we be heading?"

"North."

"Not the desert?"

"Not anymore."

"This is where I'll leave you two. Take care and come see me when you return," Glinda said. She came in for a hug, which surprised Celes. She gave the hug and Glinda whispered in her ear.

"He has a good heart. Just try and listen."

"Thank you for introducing us. I'll come find you when I return. Take care of yourself and your daughter," Celes said. Glinda waved and walked off quickly.

"This way," Tarren said. He moved faster than Celes expected. She had to up her pace to stay with him.

"I'm not just a Tracker, which you will find out. Speed is one of my abilities. You'll probably need a horse to keep up."

"That can be arranged."

"No need to fuss. We can get one on the way."

"Are you sure? I don't want to make more trouble for you."

"I have resources at my disposal. It will only be trouble later when they figure out what I am doing," Tarren said. He didn't add any more. They progressed through the dark streets and emerged at a small inn with stables attached.

"Wait here," Tarren said. He quickly entered the stables.

What a strange man. Hopefully he's everything he says he is. I have to at least see where things progress, she thought. Tarren emerged quickly, leading a black horse.

"Here. Keep it to a trot for appearances, but you can ride faster once we are in the wilderness."

"Sure, I'll follow your lead," Celes said. She jumped onto the horse and nudged him forward. Tarren walked alongside without any effort. If anything, he was restraining himself from going faster.

They wound through many tightly packed streets, in an area of the city Celes had not really explored. Finally, they arrived at a small gate.

"Oh, I didn't know there was another gate here," Celes said.

"It's not advertised widely. It's a service entrance. More security too. But we won't be challenged on the way out," Tarren said. Celes nodded and kept pace. The gate was only wide enough to fit a standard wagon through. Two guards maintained watch. When they saw Tarren, one of them walked over to the metal winding mechanism. He grunted and puffed and slowly lifted the gate up in the air. Celes felt a little nervous with such a large weight hanging over them, but put it to one side.

They passed through the gate without incident, and Celes heard it crash back down to the ground moments later.

"We are free of the city. Soon we can start in earnest," Tarren said.

"Do you know exactly where to go?"

"Enough to chart our course. I want to keep our goal as hidden as possible. That way we can travel fast and remain safe."

"That makes sense to me," Celes said. She looked at Tarren more intently, wondering what he was thinking. He didn't seem to be completely focused on the trail in front of them. He suddenly turned and looked exactly at her.

"Everything is fine. I am monitoring communication as we go. Do not be alarmed."

"That's fine, I was just curious."

"Understandably. You will know much more by the time we are through. But for now, while we need to appear quite normal I will see what information I can glean. Later we will focus on speed."

"Thank you I appreciate that. I'll leave you to it," Celes said. She continued to take in the countryside. She didn't recognise this path, and saw a large cart coming towards them.

I wonder what's inside?

The driver of the cart didn't look at them twice; he just focused on the path ahead. Even though Tarren seemed preoccupied he moved to the side to allow the cart to pass. Celes peeked over and saw stacks of cloth and wool.

Nothing exciting.

But she was sure more illicit things had to come in this way. It was not a coincidence that Tarren was familiar with the service entrance to the city. They continued along the path joining another she was more familiar with. This too had a lot of people on it. It was a major route. She was about to mention that to Tarren but he spoke first.

"We are taking a path just ahead so we can travel faster."

"Of course," Celes said. She kept her eyes open and looked for the other path. There didn't seem to be one, and the path they were on seemed the same as it had been all those years before.

"Here," Tarren said. He veered off onto a dirt track. It was so well disguised that Celes almost missed it. She nudged her horse across and followed close.

After a few turns they appeared to be travelling parallel to the main path, but with a lot more tree and vegetation cover.

"This is a safer path. Not as well known, and not as frequently travelled. Plus, we won't be spotted from the road. I will take point and you try and keep up," Tarren said. Celes felt like scoffing at the statement but she held off. Tarren started to stretch his legs then took off like a bolt of lightning. She quickly spurred the horse into action.

I don't know how that works, but he sure is quick, she thought. It was comforting that they could make great progress. But it made her nervous thinking of what else he could do.

7

GENERALS OF THE BLIGHT

Alyx headed for the edge of town. There, they found an older man selling fruit and vegetables out of a wooden cart. He had an old brown hat tipped over his face and Lara thought he was asleep.

"Is this him?" she said.

"Yes, it is. Hey, Wilson!" she shouted.

"Not so loud, I was enjoying the warm sun. There's precious little up here at the best of times. Who is that?"

"It's Alyx. We met on the road before. I helped you out of a sticky situation."

"Oh yes. Those stinking thieves. They never knew what hit 'em," Wilson said, chuckling. He grabbed an apple and threw it to Alyx. She caught it and took a bite out.

"One of my best seasons. What do you think?"

"Delicious," she said. She tossed it over to Alrion. He took a bite and surprise overtook his features. Without saying anything he tossed it to Lara.

It's just an apple, she thought, biting into it. The juices almost dripped down her chin, and it was the perfect blend of sweet and sour.

"Fine, it's pretty good," she said.

"What brings you to my neck of the woods?" Wilson said.

"We're heading up north, and I remembered you lived around here. We're going to need some horses," Alyx said.

"I don't know about that. I've only a few left, and I don't want to part with them."

"Can you spare two at least? Or three?"

"Hmm. I suppose I could let go of two. Would you be needing them long?"

"We would ideally be bringing them back, but we'll buy them all the same. You never know what will happen on the road," Alyx said.

"I doubt you'll run into anything you can't handle. Although, you do seem to be missing that giant sword of yours."

"I do miss it."

"Now that's going to be a story and a half! Tell me when you come back this way. Young man, you push this cart. We'll head back to the farm and I'll give you a deal on two horses," Wilson said. He stood and adjusted his hat, waiting for Alrion to come over and assist with the cart.

~

Hours later Alyx had negotiated a deal and they had the two horses saddled and ready to go.

"I'll go with Alrion. You two share," Lara said.

"Fine by me. You alright with that, Alyx?" Vincent said.

"Of course. Better to distribute the weight for a long ride."

"Here we go," Alrion said. He mounted and helped Lara up.

"Have fun you lot. And bring back my horses and some good stories!" Wilson shouted after them as they left.

They rode hard until noon, maintaining a cracking pace. The countryside was becoming less dense with greenery, and the road became flatter and rougher.

"Let's dismount and give the horses a rest. We can walk them for a while," Alyx said. They dismounted, and Vincent handed out bread to snack on.

"There's something from your story I'd like to hear more about," Alrion said to Alyx. She bit a big chunk of bread and chewed it slowly before responding.

"Some things I will not discuss. But ask."

"You mentioned the four generals of the Blight. What's that all about?"

"That's actually an interesting story. Surely you know it Vincent?"

"I've heard a version, but not sure how accurate it is. You tell it."

"Very well. Many years ago, the last King of Valrytir decided he would put an end to the Blight. This was before your grandfather cured Avaria. Valrytir is a huge kingdom, renowned for its fighting prowess and advanced armour and weaponry. They have the best army, and they can usually avoid outright battle because of their reputation. The King decided to task his four greatest generals with ending the Blight." Alyx glanced over at Lara, and Lara flinched. But she didn't think anyone else noticed.

"Four generals?" Alrion said.

"Yes. Each of them, a specialist in a different way. And each one worth one hundred men in terms of skill and strength."

"Who were they? What exactly did they do?"

"Rindale was an Assassin. Expert at stealth and taking out single targets. Cathar was a skilled warrior. He was incredibly strong and wielded a great sword. He was unmatched in taking on multiple foes due to his speed and reach."

"Cathar, I think I know which one you mean," Vincent said. Alrion looked puzzled but said nothing.

"Yes, well that will be explained soon," Alyx said looking at Alrion. "The next was Darvin. He was a protector, and renowned for his skill with the sword and shield. He could weather any onslaught, and navigate situations too dangerous for anyone else. Finally, there was Fermur. He was an archer without peer, and could scout like nobody else."

"They sound like great warriors. Did they lead an army?" Alrion said. He looked like he was trying to puzzle out what had happened.

"No, they had information on a lead for what was the source of the Blight. So, the four of them went alone to assess and see what they could do. They didn't wish to lead a huge expedition without knowing what they were walking into."

"What's the next part of the story?" Lara said. She was curious to see how much Alyx knew.

"Nobody knows what they encountered. It seems likely that they found the source of the Blight, but failed. Instead of accomplishing their task they returned as changed men. Transformed and corrupted by the Blight. And they took on different names and aspects."

"What are they called now? I assume one of them was the Skull King?" Alrion said.

"Exactly. Cathar became known as the 'Face of the Blight' due to his unique transformation. But he was widely known as the Skull King and actively embraced the name. Rindale was known as the 'Hand of the Blight'. We're not sure what happened to him."

"I can answer part of that," Vincent said quietly. All eyes turned to him instantly. Lara was shocked. But Alrion spoke before she could.

"I don't understand. What did you have to do with him?"

"He was the one that captured me, and infected me with the Blight. He was targeting my father. However, since he was with me he was also healed of the Blight when Avaria was cleansed. Well, that's what I assume. I never did go and check for myself."

"That's quite interesting, I never would have suspected that," Alyx said.

"Wow, I hope your grandfather's spell worked. If it can cure the four generals of the Blight, it can cure anyone!" Lara said.

"I hope so. The fact that nobody has kept track of Rindale since then is a good sign," Vincent said. Alrion nodded, and looked to be thinking over something.

"What about the others?" he said.

"Darvin became known as the 'Heart of the Blight' and is thought to be leading them in some capacity. And finally, we have Fermur, who became the 'Legs of the Blight'. Some believe he is being used as a messenger, since he has been seen all around the country."

"How do you know all this?" Lara said.

"I spent my entire life devoted to one thing; getting revenge on the Skull King. It made sense to track those he was working with."

"There's so much more to this than I knew. How does Wraith factor in?" Alrion said.

"You've mentioned him a few times. What is he exactly?"

"He's a wizard that has drunk from the Pool of Knowledge, as I have. But he's been transformed into a Shade. But he retains his power. So, he's this impossible creature now. All the resilience and danger of a Shade, with the magical power of a wizard."

"I can see why that would be a problem," Alyx said. She looked thoughtful.

"I must say though, I'm not sure how much magic he can actually use. It did seem like he was either holding back, or there's some constraints," Alrion said.

"Hopefully we don't need to find that out," Lara said.

"Oh, we will at some stage. I need to take him out."

"One step at a time," Vincent said.

"You also seem quite knowledgeable about Valrytir. Did you live there?" Alrion said to Alyx.

"Of course. How else did you think I trained to be a living weapon?"

"Sounds like an interesting place.

"It is if you need to learn about battle. All the best smiths work there, and are constantly refining weapons of war. For warriors the training is brutal. Sparring is done with slightly muted versions of real weapons, no wooden swords allowed. Fractures, bruises, and even cuts and slashes are common, and you soon learn to avoid them."

"That sounds intense. Have either of you been there?" Alrion said. He looked at his father and Lara. Lara looked away, not wanting to respond.

"I spent some time there, many years ago. But I decided that I didn't want to create tools of war and revolve my life around that so, I ended up in Brangtur," Vincent said. He looked over at Lara.

"I lived there a long time ago, but didn't really get into all that military stuff. Not my style," she said. She hated that she couldn't really talk about it, and she didn't have the impressive battle experience that Alyx did. It seemed to be important to Alrion. She could understand that, given all they had gone through. And now his power was unavailable, he needed something else to defend himself.

"Wow. It's just me then who hasn't been?" Alrion said.

"I did give you a pretty sheltered life, sorry about that," Vincent said. He chuckled and looked a bit sheepish.

"Well, it sounds like somewhere I should visit. Especially if they know where the source of the Blight is!" Alrion said. He looked at Alyx expectantly.

"I'm not sure there's anyone alive who still knows that. But it could be an option. I must admit I never thought about that myself. Is that somewhere you need to go?"

"I really don't know. I've been relying on the information from the Pool to guide me. Maybe I need to find that place, maybe I don't. It's a bit frustrating, but I have other things to focus on first. Like finding a cure."

"I'd like you to focus on that too."

"Of course! I'm responsible for your infection, and I am taking it seriously," Alrion said.

"Very well. Let us walk a bit further and when we find a suitable spot we should settle in for the night. The horses can rest and we will leave at first light."

"I agree," Vincent said. He started actively looking around, presumably for good places to set up camp.

"Anything coming from that amulet?" Alrion said. Alyx held it up and peered at it.

"I don't see anything special. How about you?" She offered it to Alrion and he took a look as well.

"Doesn't look any different."

"Then we continue on the same way tomorrow. I'll check it periodically as we go, see if there's anything we can use."

"I'm happy with the camp," Vincent said. He had settled into a spot leaning against a nearby tree. One of the few around.

"In that case, you need to train some more. I'll just be borrowing this," Alyx said, grabbing Vincent's sword. He gave out a friendly laugh, and watched the two square off. Lara felt a bit left out, so had to find herself something to do.

"I'll just go scout a bit, see what's out there."

"Good idea, take care and don't go too far. We're not familiar with the country here," Vincent said.

"Sure." Lara looked over at Alrion but he was already engrossed in watching Alyx demonstrate a movement.

Typical. Lara took off, heading further ahead and towards the area with the most trees. She was actually curious if they were entering another area, and the way they had come had so little cover it wasn't even worth looking over. Any sign of anyone coming would be obvious a long way away.

Lara pushed forward, the smells of moisture and flowers coming on stronger as she explored. It looked like they were on the boundary of another forest. Before long she was amongst it. She didn't recognise the trees, they had a distinctive curled look to their branches and leaves. She plucked one of the leaves off and crushed it in her hand. It gave off a clean, fragrant smell.

I wonder if they use this in medicines, she thought. But her attention was quickly taken by something else.

That was definitely something.

She darted forward towards whatever she spotted, trying not to make too much noise. But she trampled fallen sticks and brushed past some thin branches, causing them to snap or bend noisily.

"Just press on," she told herself. There were definitely signs of movement ahead. Lara pushed through some underbrush, trying to anticipate the direction. She stopped and looked around. Everything was quiet around her. She peered into the distance, trying to figure out where the natural paths were. Then she saw it. It was dark and faint and far away. But a dark shape flitted through her view and deeper into the forest.

What was that? She thought. It could have been nothing. But it did worry her. *It didn't move like a Blighter. Maybe I'll just keep an eye out.*

She felt defeated and didn't want to admit that she had let something get away. It seemed fine for now, to just be more watchful.

"I'll find it again and confirm without alarming anyone," she said to herself.

8

HUNTED

Alrion awoke swiftly, forcing his eyes open. It took a moment to reorient himself. It was just before daybreak and they were camped in the forest.

It's fine, just more dreams.

But the feelings lingered. It felt so real. But he couldn't put anything specific to it. Just thoughts of darkness, fear, pain, and more.

"Right on time, let's get ready," Vincent said. He was packed and waiting.

"Do you ever sleep?" Alrion said.

"When I need to. You need less, as you get older. One of the few benefits."

"If you say so. I'll need a minute," Alrion said. He packed as quickly as possible, but his hands were unresponsive and cold. Without the sun the morning was incredibly chilly.

"Get used to that, it's only going to get worse as we travel north," Alyx said. Alrion cupped his hands and blew hot air into them.

"If I only had my Spark," he said, looking at his hands. He could generate as much heat as he wanted if that was the case.

"You'll appreciate it more after this," Vincent said. Alrion could tell his father was trying to lighten the mood a bit. But he wasn't interested. He could hear the traces of whispers in his mind. Which meant that someone was trying to communicate with him. Most likely Wraith, but he had received other messages. He looked over at Alyx and she seemed preoccupied with something. She noticed his look and spoke.

"You did better yesterday. More controlled, better instincts. But you are very inconsistent. You can be making sudden progress then become clumsy."

"Thanks," Alrion said. He knew exactly what she was talking about. It made sense too, he was still figuring out what he was supposed to do. It was a completely different set of activities to what he was used to. Everything he had done had been so slow, precise, and careful. Especially the blacksmithing.

But the sword work had the same demands of precision, with the addition of speed, balance, and agility. But he feared something else was happening. The effects of the infection. It was like his body was starting to get confused, and there was interference from within. But he didn't want to say anything yet. He would keep an eye on it. And also see how Alyx moved. Surely it would affect her too.

"How'd you sleep?" Lara said as she walked over. She was ready to go but looked tired.

"Not well. You too?"

"I was thinking about too many things."

"Same."

"You can tell me if anything else happens. I want to help," she said. Alrion could see the truth in her words. And he knew he could trust her. But something felt off. Like he couldn't share what was happening.

Maybe I don't want to burden her with this? That was probably it. He didn't want to dwell on it.

"Let's get going, I don't want to get caught here," he said. He walked over to the horse and mounted, helping Lara up. She leaned against him as they rode off, and he appreciated the closeness.

Initially the ride was difficult, navigating the poor trails and finding a way through the new forest they had discovered nearby. Alrion had to concentrate fiercely, to not be ejected from the saddle by an obstacle or on steering the horse into dangerous territory.

Chirps of birds and unknown animals rang out from the forest, and Alrion found the sounds interesting but had no attention for them. He was not just focusing on the horse, but the growing distractions within.

The whispers he had felt before were becoming louder, and occasionally a word sounded within his mind. Often, they were too soft or unintelligible. But every now and then one popped up and he was sure of what it was, but ignored it. He glanced over at Alyx and saw her deep in concentration too.

Maybe she's noticing as well?

Slowly the noise rose, but it didn't become any more understandable. It became loud and annoying, like standing in a room full of people talking but not understanding what they were saying.

Alrion maintained his composure as best he could, but he needed his attention to be on navigating the dense forest. A bump here, a nick there, and quick adjustment of the horse, all these things niggled at him. All the while the cacophony grew inside his mind.

"Just shut up!" he yelled in frustration. Everyone stopped and stared at him. He realised in that instant that he had spoken the words aloud. He noticed a sympathetic look from Alyx, but concern and surprise from Vincent.

"What's happening?" Lara said from behind. She put her hand on his shoulder. He didn't need to turn around to know she was worried.

"Sorry, there's some sort of Blight communication going on. It's so loud and intense, but just noise. I hate it and I can't get rid of it. Please tell me you have it too?" he said, looking at Alyx.

"I do. But perhaps it is louder for you. For me, it's more background noise."

"It's so frustrating. I can't concentrate on anything else. And I can't even understand what they are saying."

"Do you even want to?" Lara said.

"No. But it just makes it all the more infuriating. Have you been in a room full of people shouting in another language?"

"I have. I see what you mean," Lara said with a thoughtful look on her face.

"That does sound infuriating. Has it been happening a lot?" Vincent said.

"On and off. I can usually switch off or ignore it. But something is different. Like it's insistent. That's the only way I can describe it."

"Just do your best. I think we should keep moving," Vincent said.

"Agreed," Alyx said.

"Sure, I'll do what I can," Alrion said. At least the Blight chatter had seemed to die down after his outburst. Although he didn't want to continue that as a strategy. It didn't seem like a good idea. And he had everyone worried.

As they rode on, the distractions started again. He could hear more of the insistent whispers, and almost understood words. But there was a changing intensity to it. Like it was building up to something.

"Hunt. Trap. Go." Alrion heard these words amongst other garbled nonsense. He was sure of it. He looked over at Alyx.

"Did you hear something different?" he said.

"Yes. I heard the word 'hunt' quite clearly. What do you think?"

"I think they're coordinating something. They must be tracking us, hunting us down. I even caught the word trap as well. Is there anything about this area that is special Alyx?"

"I'm not that familiar with it. I think we will be emerging from the forest soon. That could be opportunity to spring an attack."

"Let's just take a few precautions. I suggest we dismount, walk the horses from here. When we reach what we think is an ambush spot, approach carefully on foot," Vincent said.

"You're thinking of springing the trap if there is one, and keeping the horses safe."

"Exactly. If they do this properly the horses won't be able to get us away and could be injured or worse during the fighting. So, let's be cautious."

"That sounds wise. I will be able to point out when we need to leave them," Alyx said. She seemed lost in thought.

"I hope I'm not alarming everyone for no reason, but I think it's significant," Alrion said. He didn't want to ignore a possible sign then get them into trouble later.

They dismounted carefully, and stored all their extra provisions with the horses. Travelling light now, they would be ready to fight in an instant. Alrion grabbed the handle of his sword in anticipation. He felt more comfortable with it, but knew he would still struggle in a fight.

I'll deal with that when it comes up. At least they can't infect me. Can they? He thought. He had to chuckle to himself. There had to be some benefit to being infected, surely. And if they did indeed get attacked, it was good he had some sort of warning.

"Let's tie up the horses now," Alyx said. She gestured to a small space between trees that would do. Looking ahead Alrion could see more light penetrating the trees. It had to be the way out that Alyx had spotted.

Alrion patted his horse, checked that everything was tied up correctly and stood next to his father.

"I'm ready," Alrion said. He was only half-lying.

"Good. Stay close to me. We will let Alyx take the front foot."

"I'm expendable," she said as they walked.

"I didn't mean it like that," Vincent said.

"I did," Alyx replied. She was focused on the path ahead and said nothing more. Within a few moments, she drew her sword and ran forward.

"There must be something ahead, stay calm and follow my lead," Vincent said. He drew his sword and Alrion did the same. He could see a light glow from the diamond, and it didn't seem like it was coming from him. Lara was close behind, scanning the area for any attackers.

"I'll ensure we don't get jumped from behind," she said.

"Good. Let's advance, we don't want Alyx to get overwhelmed," Vincent said. He moved forward at a steady pace and Alrion kept up.

As the forest started to drop away, the scene before them expanded into a mess. The ground was torn up and Alyx was fighting off several Blighters at once. There were more coming, but each group seemed to be paired up with a Tainted.

"They're organised!" she shouted as Vincent approached. He didn't bother replying, instead swinging his sword, and slicing through a Blighter that was trying to attack Alyx from the side.

"Thanks!" Alyx shouted, spinning to cut down another and move on to another angle. Vincent stepped up into the space where she had been, reinforcing her. Alrion hung back a few steps. A Blighter came out directly at him and he froze momentarily. He forced himself to step into one of the moves Alyx showed him and he managed to force the Blighter to stop and dodge.

Being mobile allowed Alrion the opportunity to let his muscles take over. He started to remember the feeling of the sword movement, and let it guide him. He mentally stepped back, allowing the sword form to swing and poke at the Blighter, effectively cutting it down.

I can do this.

Another two Blighters jumped in to replace the fallen one. As the first drew back its arm it fell to the ground, a dagger catching it square in the head.

"Got your back!" Lara shouted. Alrion used the opportunity to press the attack on the other one. The Blighter was distracted and didn't defend itself well, going down quickly. Sweat started to form on Alrion's brow, and he drew in some quick breaths. Looking up he could see more waves of creatures descending upon them. But they were trying to bypass Alyx.

Vincent looked around as he fought, and seemed to be coming to a similar conclusion.

"I'm going to try and draw them over here," he shouted. Vincent pushed forward into the oncoming Blighters, knocking two down but not finishing them off. He was instead carving a path forward. Alyx dropped back a little to be closer to Alrion.

"What's he doing?" Alrion said.

"Giving them an easy target. Or making them think he is trying to flee. Hopefully it works."

"I hope so too," Alrion said. Initially it did seem to make an impact. The two that his father had spared immediately rose and charged after the blacksmith. Fewer Blighters were making the effort to come over and challenge Alyx. But then Alrion noticed something odd in the movements. There was a clump of Blighters moving forward as a formation. Not only that, but they kept looking around for something.

"Look at that group. They seem to be following orders. They're not like the rest," he said. Pointing over at them, he drew Alyx and Lara's attention.

"Lara, you watch them, I'll keep my eyes on the ones closer," Alyx said.

"Sure, don't lose concentration," Lara said. Alrion trusted her with that task too. He needed to keep his focus on the enemies closest. He knew Alyx was good, but it didn't take much for one to slip through in the circumstances.

"I think I have something," Lara said. Alrion looked over at her immediately.

"At the back there's a pair together. They seem to be directing that pack of Blighters. What do you think?" she said. As Alrion turned back to look properly a dagger whizzed past his face and dropped a Blighter right in front of him.

"Got your back, but that doesn't mean you can turn away!" Lara shouted. Alrion knew she was right. He had let his attention be drawn too easily. So, between the intense encounters of the battle, he let his view wander over to the two that Lara had pointed out. One of the two seemed to be a leader of sorts, barking out orders but also pointing and surveying the fight. The one next to him seemed different. As if he was providing advice.

"Wizard," Alrion heard in his mind, amongst the blaring and confusing noise of the Blight communication. He somehow knew that the Tainted one advising the leader had uttered that word. Alrion decided in that instant that he had to move.

"Follow me!" he shouted at Alyx, and started moving. He threw his weight behind a long slice, cutting down a Blighter from behind and moved away into the space behind it. Alyx cursed and dashed over, whirling through another group with a slashing of blades.

"I hope you know what you're doing," she said, kicking another Blighter to force an opening.

"Keep going, they're following!" Lara shouted. Alrion looked up and saw the tight group of Blighters had changed direction again.

"Vincent come back and cut them off!" Alyx bellowed. She stayed one step behind Alrion, keeping the Blighters at bay. Alrion stopped; he had reached a dead end. There was no way further back, he had ventured too far from the forest entry.

"This is as far as we go," he said. He readied his sword, trying to ignore the slight trembling of his wrist.

"We've got this!" Alyx said, pushing forward once more. Alrion was amazed by her intensity, and it seemed to be working. At the same time, he could see his father working his way over. The Blighters didn't know which way to turn, and they struggled to put up much of a fight. Within minutes the fighting started to die down.

"They're sneaking away!" Lara shouted. She pointed to the odd pair of leader and advisor. They were re-entering the forest.

"Come with me. Vincent, you finish up here," Alyx said. She ran off with Lara, barely stopping, avoiding any straggling Blighters. Vincent methodically worked his way back to Alrion's side, and together they fought off the remaining Blighters. Alrion sank down to the ground, exhausted.

"Not here, let's get back to the horses," Vincent said. Alrion nodded, it was too much effort to talk. He hauled himself back up and they made their way back into the forest.

9

A NEW TYPE

Lara was light on her feet, easily getting ahead of Alyx. There was little danger now, and she wasn't concerned about the threat from the two Tainted. Especially since they were fleeing the scene.

What if one of those two spotted me before?

The thought of it made a pit in her stomach. What if her mistake had resulted in that ambush?

I have to catch them!

Lara increased her speed, almost tumbling over when her foot caught on an extended tree root. She staggered forward and regained her balance. But her knee felt the pain of the sharp movement required and she pushed the sensation away.

Where are they? She thought as she continued. She slowly let her speed drop, and instead focused on looking for where they may have gone.

"Lara, come back here!" Alyx shouted. Lara was reluctant to give up the chase, but she could sense the urgency in Alyx's voice. She jogged back, and found Alyx standing where they had left the horses. Only there were no horses.

"They're gone," Alyx said. She sheathed her short sword and looked around.

"I checked those knots, they were tied properly," Lara said. There was no sign of the ropes either.

"Then they must have come and let the horses free. There's no trace of them. Not much in the way of tracks either, it's quite a mess." Alyx bent down and examined the ground. But she just shook her head and stood. She kept her eyes on the area, but looked unimpressed.

"It must have happened earlier, they didn't have time right now. We would have heard something," Lara said.

"Right. Maybe those two did it before, to hedge their bets in case the ambush failed. They did seem familiar with the area. You tracked them pretty quickly, yet they still got away."

"They did," Lara said. She was searching for excuses, but didn't know what to say. She had failed several times now and it felt terrible. She saw Alrion and Vincent approach. Vincent had his usual demeanour, and looked fine albeit a bit tired. Alrion looked completely washed out.

"Horses are gone. Looks like they did it during the fight," Alyx said.

"They've definitely been here before. Even chasing them I lost them," Lara said.

"This is a setback. But we're all intact. Anything valuable in your bags Alrion?" Vincent said.

"I have your ring and my amulet on me. And I was wielding my sword. But the notebook was in there."

"The one with the mysterious wizard messages?" Lara said.

"That's the one. Any messages now will go to them," Alrion said. He let out a sigh and looked around the area.

"Don't worry about it, if it turns up, it turns up. We don't need those messages to move forward," Vincent said. Alrion looked up at him, his face brightening a little.

"Exactly! Everything we need is here. We'll just be slowed down a bit," Lara said. She hoped to cheer him up a bit more.

"Wilson is going to be annoyed. I'll have to explain when I get back," Alyx said.

"If they cut the horses loose, maybe they'll find their way back one way or another," Vincent said.

"Let's go with that theory. So what next?" Lara said.

"We must move forward to a safe location. It is quite a walk I think. It would be unwise to camp on the plains tonight," Alyx said.

"How's everyone doing? Just tired? No injuries?" Vincent said.

"Nothing major," Lara said.

"Nothing here. Muscles are tight though, still not rested enough," Alyx said. Alrion mumbled something but didn't clarify.

"Let's move out then. The sooner we get away from here the better," Vincent said. He shook his head once more and returned to the path.

"I'll go ahead and scout out," Lara said. Before anyone could respond she dashed forward. She just had to do something useful. She thought she could survey the scene of the battle and see if there were any Tainted that had fallen. They might hold clues as to how the ambush had worked, and any planning that had gone into it. But she couldn't shake the image of that shadow she had almost caught before.

What if they were here and I missed it? And even now I was too slow to catch them. Tainted are not stealthy or fast. What's going on here?

Lara slowed to look through the fallen bodies. They were predominantly Blighters, which she found interesting. Usually there were more Tainted to direct and control the Blighters.

Further afield she found what looked like more Tainted. She turned them over gingerly, looking for anything that might help. But she found nothing.

"Typical. But to be expected. They do seem to do a lot of communication by thought," she pondered. It was time to return to the group. They weren't far behind, and Alyx urged them all forward.

"Keep moving," Alyx said.

"Anything there?" Alrion said.

"Nothing of use. But I have an interesting theory."

"Which is?"

"There's a new type of Tainted that we haven't encountered before. One that's fast and stealthy and can even track people," Lara said. It seemed almost silly saying it out loud. But she saw nodding heads and interested looks all around.

"What's your reasoning?" Vincent said. He moved in closer and gave her his full attention.

"Well, look at how they managed to get away. But they also knew where our horses were and made sure the horses were chased away while we were busy with the fighting."

"Agreed, good point about the tactics. Some manner of stealth required there."

"How did they know where our horses were? Have they been watching us?" Alyx said.

"I think so. I saw something last night when scouting. But I couldn't make it out and it disappeared," Lara said. She couldn't keep it to herself any longer, even if it looked bad for her. She felt her cheeks colouring as she said it. Alyx looked angrier than the others and her footsteps were louder and more like stomping.

"What? You saw something and didn't say anything? We could have done more to prepare. I don't understand your silence," Alyx said.

"It was just a shadow, it could have been anyone or anything. I didn't want to alarm anyone. Obviously, I won't do that again, now that we know what we are dealing with."

"I am a bit surprised you didn't mention it," Alrion said. Lara didn't know what to say. She didn't want to try and explain it more, it would just be embarrassing. They wouldn't understand.

"I just made a mistake," she said.

"And another one letting them get away now," Alyx said.

"I think that's a little unfair. Since they got the jump on us, and as you said at least one of them seems a bit different, it makes sense that they could escape," Vincent said. He stepped forward and put a hand on both Alyx and Lara's shoulders. "We need to calm this down a bit before it escalates. The enemy is out there, and we are doing them favours by doubting each other."

"I have something important to add," Alrion said.

"Let's hear it," Vincent said. There was silence until Alrion spoke again.

"When we were trying to distract them away, and those two Tainted directed the Blighters back to me. I heard a word amongst their communication. Wizard." Alrion paused.

"You think they could pinpoint you as the wizard?" Lara said. With each word she grew more incredulous. That was a serious problem if it was true. But it did help explain some of the behaviour.

"There could be something to that." Vincent turned away, deep in thought.

"But how is that even possible? Do you think they have some way of recognising what you look like?" Alyx said.

"It felt like it was more than that. The battle was pretty chaotic, yet they knew exactly where I was. I think there's something going on. What if this theory of a new type of Tainted isn't just one who is fast and stealthy. What if they're actually a Tracker?" Alrion looked around at the group. Lara felt stunned. Of course, that had to be it.

"That would explain how they've tracked so closely behind. But that would mean we can never shake them off," Lara said.

"It's just a theory," Alrion said quickly.

"There's definitely some merit to it. But let's not jump to conclusions. There's always a way around an obstacle," Vincent said.

"Exactly. You can just kill the Trackers," Alyx said.

"Is that your solution for everything? Lara said. It was an easy comment to make, and she felt a bit bad for it. But in a way, it felt like a valid question. Alyx had devoted her entire life to killing the Skull King. And a lot of Tainted and Blighters on the way.

"I won't take offence at that, but when it comes to the Blight it's a tried and tested solution," Alyx said. She was right too. Lara decided to leave it for now.

"Lots to think about," Vincent said. He looked worried. That, Lara could easily understand.

The walk was longer and harder than Lara had expected. But she eventually figured out why. They were ever so slowly ascending. It was so slight; it was hard to notice at first. But once she figured it out she looked back and it was obvious.

"What is it?" Alrion said. He looked back too, with a puzzled look.

"We're ascending. Slowly but definitely getting higher up."

"There's a reason the north gets cold. The height is a major factor," Alyx said.

"We may need to better equip ourselves," Vincent said.

"There'll be other towns, or villages. The further we go the less built up it is. As the land gets harsher, the settlements grow smaller," Alyx said. She emphasised the word harsher when she spoke.

"Speaking of harsher, this is getting tougher by the minute and I think we're all fading. Any ideas on where to stop?" Vincent said. Alyx slowed then stopped completely. She surveyed the area. There were large rocks around, with mostly rough shrubs.

"There's a good selection of rocks over there, should provide enough shelter in case it rains," she said, pointing with her right arm. Lara's gaze followed and she saw a large cluster of rocks. The biggest ones on an incline, casting a shadow in the afternoon sun.

"Works for me, let's head over," Vincent said. He looked like he had an extra spring in his step and led the way over.

"I don't know where he gets the energy," Alrion said. He just shook his head slowly.

"It's all in your mind. You should know all about that," Vincent said.

"Well, I've been a bit preoccupied," Alrion said. For the briefest instant Lara saw a look of pain and exhaustion sweep over Alrion's face. But he hid it quickly.

It's taking a toll on him, she thought. Hopefully this journey would not drag on too long. But if the frequent battles, travel, and the Blight communication were wearing Alrion down, he was going to struggle even more if the terrain became any more demanding. Which she assumed it would.

I need to change the mood, she thought. Lara bounded ahead, pretending she had hidden reserves of energy.

"Last one there has to cook!" she shouted. Alrion came alive, and increased his pace. Alyx maintained her speed, and was the last one to arrive.

"I think letting Alyx come last may not have been the most strategic move," Alrion said with a laugh as he watched her join them.

Alyx said nothing, busying herself with building a fire. Once it was going she disappeared into the twilight, and returned with two rabbits. She prepped them, put them on the fire and used some wet leaves to create additional smoke. Lara was sceptical, but also intrigued by what she was seeing.

"Finished," Alyx announced. She handed out portions of smoked rabbit on sticks to the others and settled back near the fire. Lara bit into the meat hesitantly. But it wasn't burned, and it wasn't raw. A wonderfully subtle smoky flavour permeated the meat and she was surprised that her mouth was filling with saliva.

"Wow, this is amazing!" Alrion said, between mouthfuls. Vincent was too busy eating to add anything.

"It's surprisingly tasty," Lara said. Alyx nodded.

"When you've lived the life I have, you get plenty of practise cooking out in the wilderness. A few small things make these kinds of meals more palatable," Alyx explained. She took another bite and Lara was just impressed that Alyx had bothered to learn how to do that.

"If the food is not palatable, it's harder to eat. And often you don't know when your next meal will be so you must be prepared," Alyx said. Lara just laughed. The rest of them gave her odd looks.

"What? I thought that maybe Alyx was some sort of closet gourmet, living on the land. But then she just killed it all by being so practical," Lara said. Alrion laughed too, almost choking on his food. Lara gave him a smile.

After they had eaten Alyx rose, and walked over to Alrion.

"You did well today, but now is not the time to rest. Get up, you need to train," she said, grabbing Alrion's hand. He looked shocked, but let her help him up.

"You too," she said to Vincent. He rose slowly, a curious look on his face.

"You two will spar and I will stop you as appropriate to demonstrate a point," she said in a matter of fact way.

"I really hadn't expected this, but fine. I'll do my best," Alrion said.

"She's probably just teaching you a lesson for doubting her cooking," Lara said, poking some fun at him. Alrion gave her a quick smile before readying his sword. It had been an intense day, and she felt like she had let everyone down. But these few moments of lightness and humour at the end of the day had helped.

As much as Alyx grated on her, she could appreciate the woman and her contribution to the team. They really did feel like a team already. And that was going to be important for what was to come. It was so easy to forget in a light moment what was going on. But Alrion and Alyx were infected, and time was marching on. Far too quickly for Lara's liking.

10

RENEWED FOCUS

Alrion awoke from a dreamless sleep. He felt groggy and sore and stiff. But relieved. He hadn't been tormented overnight. It took him a moment to remember exactly where he was and what the plan was.

"You look a bit out of it," Lara said.

"I think I am. Which is great considering everything. That training session at the end of the day was way too much, but it meant that I slept well," Alrion said. He looked over at where Alyx was standing. She noticed his gaze.

"As expected. I don't know if you were too tired, but your progress seems to be slowing," Alyx said. There was no criticism in her voice, just fact. But Alrion felt it sting.

"Hey, I'm still learning," he said indignantly. His anger started to flare up, but he forced it back down with some effort.

"Just stating the facts. You need to be aware of your condition. Maybe the Blight is affecting you," Alyx said. She turned away and walked over to talk to Vincent.

"She could be right. You need to be mindful of this," Lara said. She looked worried.

"I think it's more the extreme schedule we're on. No time for rest, constantly harried by the Blight. Then weapons training on top of that. It's too much. I'm not even complaining, just saying how it is," Alrion said. He actually thought that Alyx could be on to something. He had noticed several situations where his balance was off, or his strength was not what he expected. But he wanted to set Lara at ease, and judging by her reaction he had done just enough.

"That's true, but keep an eye on it. You can't push this hard forever, not with the infection ticking along. You've been lucky so far, but luck can only get you so far," she said. Her eyes lingered on him for a moment longer, then she turned to go join Alyx and Vincent.

Alrion rose, dusted himself off and joined the others.

"We need to keep walking. From here on we'll start getting into the lower mountains. That means fewer places to stop, less shelter, and terrible paths. But there is another village we can rest at not too far away," Alyx said.

"Definitely looking forward to the rest part," Alrion said.

"You shouldn't get his hopes up like that," Lara said.

"No, it's quite protected. You can't get large numbers through there due to the paths. I'm not familiar with the terrain much further north, so it may be our last chance to just take a break before we make the final push."

"Then let's get there as soon as possible. We can't rest properly like this," Vincent said, gesturing at the rocky surroundings. Alyx nodded and started out. Alrion let them get ahead, and followed at the rear.

He started to think back to the previous encounters and his reactions. And he began to see a pattern, as much as he didn't want to. But the more he mulled it over, the more he was convinced.

All the attacks so far, they're my fault. Even if they're tracking us, I always seem to lose it before they launch their assault. There has to be something about that. Maybe I am making things easy for them?

He felt a lurching in the pit of his stomach at the realisation. The Blight was affecting him, he was sure of it. And the mental noise and communication didn't help. But he wasn't in control of himself.

How much is that my lack of discipline, and how much is it due to the infection?

It was easy to just explain it all away. But he looked back at his journey so far. Anger had been there all along.

My first attempts at drawing my Spark were fuelled by anger. How much have I been relying on it?

Alrion felt like the wind had been taken out of him. All this time, his anger had been simmering away. It was his outlet every time he felt weak, or embarrassed, or wronged. And it had felt like it had served him well at the time. Like he had been using it to his advantage. But maybe that wasn't the case.

It's been festering and I've been nurturing it. And now I'm paying the price, he thought. It rang so true that he felt despondent. How would he make a change now? When he was so far gone to this infection?

He noticed Lara looking at him and forced a smile.

"Just lost in my thoughts," he said.

"They're not tormenting you again are they?" she said. A concerned frown was on her face again.

"No, just my own thoughts. You shouldn't worry so much, it doesn't look so good on you," Alrion said. He saw anger and annoyance flash over her face, but it was quickly replaced with a smile.

"Well, you shouldn't cause me so much reason to worry then!" Lara turned away and seemed to focus on the path ahead. Alrion chuckled to himself.

Still terrible with the ladies.

But he quickly moved on to thinking about other things. And the increasing difficulty of their trek gave him something to focus on.

A few bunches of red berries were cause enough to stop for lunch, Alrion's stomach rumbling despite the number that he shoved into his mouth.

"While we are paused, I wanted to consider how we would be keeping safe today. These paths are getting narrower, and there's less space either side," Vincent said.

"We will probably need to sleep out. I'm not sure how long it will take us. But it's a risk; the terrain around here is so exposed. It's even hard to take shelter from the elements, let alone a hostile force," Alyx said.

"Do we have any idea how they are tracking us? If we could confuse that, it would buy some safety," Lara said. Vincent shook his head and Alyx had a blank look.

"We aren't exactly hiding our trail, but we're not creating one either. It could be any number of ways," she said. Alrion sighed. He didn't really want to share his recent revelation, but knew he had to. It could be crucial to their survival.

"I have an idea, well, a guess," Alrion said. "It's related to me."

"In what way?" Lara said quickly.

"I think they have a way to determine my location because I'm infected. But I get the feeling it's not incredibly accurate."

"Then how are they always so close? And setting ambushes?" Alyx said.

"I've noticed a pattern. Around each of the major attacks, I've had an outburst. Generally, anger. And the attacks have been very soon after. It's like they just needed a final confirmation before beginning." He saw some thoughtful looks, and nodding.

"Are you sure about that? You don't necessarily need to assume it's your fault," Lara said.

"That sounds like a decent theory to me. Especially since you've managed to catch some of their communication. It's you they are after," Alyx said. She stood from the rock she was leaning on and started pacing.

"We must treat it as true, until we have a better idea. Then we can take steps to help minimise our chances of being discovered. It may not make any difference though, given our location. If they've tracked us this far, it will be easy to find us," Vincent said.

"Agreed. But if they're relying on Alrion to be a beacon as means of coordination as well, we can deny them that. You mentioned monks before, didn't they help you with this?" Alyx said.

"The trial I completed, and the monk I travelled with did help me refine my Will. And the ability to focus it. But this seems different. It's not just my emotions. I mean, yes I have responsibility but it's not the same now I'm infected," Alrion said.

"In what way?" Vincent said. He approached Alrion slowly.

"I can't believe I'm actually saying this. But I feel like I'm getting clumsier somehow. That things are a little bit harder to do, or not guaranteed to happen like I expect. Maybe I'm just imagining it all," Alrion said. He felt silly for even mentioning it, but it had started to weigh on him. And he didn't know what to think.

"That's not as crazy as you may think. The Blight doesn't just attack you at one point. It takes over your whole body," Alyx said.

"How much do you know about this?" Alrion said.

"Quite a bit. I've never experienced it myself, well until now. But I've seen many turn, and I've watched some do it slowly like we are now. I made it my business to know how they tick, because it was crucial to my revenge. I had to understand how they worked, so I could ensure that I would not fail. I only had one chance," Alyx said. There was no passion in her voice, only cold fact.

"How can you detach yourself like that? Those are quite intense experiences I can imagine."

"It's a technique you should try and learn. Maybe you can keep these creatures away by not giving them any help."

"How would I learn?"

"I'll teach you what I can. It's all about separating the fuel of the emotion from the emotion itself. You can deal with the emotion rationally, but harness the fire from it any way you like."

"That sounds interesting. You must be an expert," Alrion said. The more he spoke to Alyx, the more impressed he was. She had discarded everything unnecessary to her purpose, and in the process constantly refined what she was to perfection. He had gone through no such process. He'd just been fumbling along, taking the information he could get his hands on, and trusting his instincts and the people around him. But this was too important to leave to chance.

"I am too much an expert. Let's leave it at that," Alyx said. Alrion wanted to know more, but he respected her wishes.

Maybe she can't go back?

It was sad, if true. But then, it looked like she had made peace with that choice a long time ago.

"I have a suggestion," Alyx said. She stopped walking and turned around. She had a defiant pose to her.

"Let's hear it," Vincent said.

"Up ahead I can see we have a bit more room. I suggest that we give Alrion a quick sparring session. He can improve his technique a little, and also work on getting some of this anger out. It may improve our chances for the next attack," Alyx said. She looked at them all in turn and waited for a response.

"It's worth a try I think. It may buy us more time later," Vincent said. He looked over at Lara.

"I can keep a look out and advise of anything approaching. It should be easy to spot travellers on this road."

"I'm game. We need to try something. Either I'm giving them our location or contributing nothing in these fights. This works for both," Alrion said. He was willing to try anything. And he thought that just maybe he could stay a step ahead of the infection if he kept trying to hone his skills. It was worth a shot.

Alyx pointed out the area she had mentioned. It was a rough circle of dirt to the left of the path. There were steep drops all around it.

"You may want to avoid the edges," Lara said, peering down.

"Vincent you're up again. I need to observe the fight without participating," Alyx said. Vincent nodded and drew his sword. Alrion did the same. For some reason, it felt different this time. Like a lot more was riding on it than just a normal sparring match.

Here we go.

"Alrion, go on the attack. Use the sequences we worked on," Alyx said. Alrion stepped forward, thinking of how to begin. He started the first one he had learnt, the rolling barrel. However, instead of just flowing into the next, he repeated it. This time with more speed and intensity. The change caught Vincent by surprise, but he easily defended it all.

"It's too easy for him. Are you feeling frustrated yet?" Alyx said. Alrion did in fact feel a bit frustrated. Normally he would ignore it, but he let it rise up.

"Imagine that the frustration you feel is actually fuel. It's making your muscles burn with feverish intensity. You can move even faster," Alyx said. Alrion listened carefully and tried to follow. He tried to recognise the emotion within him, and locate the intensity of the frustration. Channel it like he had done before.

He almost channelled it into his Spark, which came naturally. It was how he had originally increased his power. But he caught himself and instead did as Alyx had instructed. He imagined that it enhanced his muscles. The heat of the frustration working his muscles harder and faster. He could feel the intensity of the heat rising from them. He pushed more and more, upping the speed.

His arms moved almost automatically, seamlessly flowing into another sequence, interrupting it halfway to change into the rolling wave. With a bang their swords collided, Vincent stepping forward to halt the assault. Alrion looked up and saw sweat dripping down his father's brow. Alrion stepped back, letting go of all the tension. He felt wiped out.

"Much better. Don't you agree Vincent?" Alyx said.

"Definite improvement. I was almost overwhelmed by that slight change in intensity. It's a very powerful tool if you can harness it correctly," Vincent said. His breathing was deep as he recovered.

"And how do you feel now?" Alyx said to Alrion. He pondered that for a moment before replying.

"Better. Emptier, if that makes sense. Ready to go collapse somewhere."

"Not just yet, we have a way to go. Take a few minutes to recover, and when Lara returns we will be on our way again," Alyx said. She walked down the road to look for Lara. Alrion sheathed his sword and slump down next to a large rock. It dug into him a little but he ignored it. He needed to rest.

"ALRION." Wraith's voice thundered within his head.

And here we go, Alrion thought. But he kept his composure and prepared to listen as carefully as possible.

11

TRACKING

C eles slowed and finally dismounted. Everything hurt. She had travelled hard, but never like this. She looked over at Tarren and he looked like he could keep going. It had already been days of constant travel. Avoiding settlements and eating and drinking minimally.

"I don't know how you do it," she said.

"You don't want to know. I'd rather not," he said. Celes found a softer patch of ground near a tree and sat down. She should have stretched her legs more, but it felt nice to be sitting and not in motion.

"We're finally in a secluded place. I will rest also," Tarren said. He started to remove the bulky cloak he had been wearing.

This will be interesting.

She watched carefully, curiosity with a bit of fear mixed in. She would finally see him for what he was.

Tarren's face was relatively normal, although he had some black markings on his neck and forehead. He was skinny and wore all black clothing. From what she could see from his arms, they were covered in intricate tattoos. His pants were only knee length; his legs displayed the same pattern of tattoos.

"Interesting tattoos," she said. Tarren glanced at them and looked back at her.

"Part of the process. As far as I understand they were made with a liquid form of the Blight. The application and the design are crucial. It was an incredibly painful process."

"I can imagine. You seem quite hardy, and can travel incredibly fast for long periods. Apart from the tracking capability, what else can you do?"

"I don't want to spill all my secrets just yet." Tarren found a place to sit opposite Celes. He did look weary now that she could see him properly.

"I need an idea of what you can do. Otherwise how do we work together? What if we get attacked?"

"That's fair. I will add, that I can also meld into the shadows. Only useful at night, but it makes me just about invisible."

"That's very handy. Are there any limitations? Things I need to consider?"

"I can't hide in direct light. But where it casts a shadow I can obscure, to make myself harder to target."

"Thank you. I hope that nothing happens, but this is useful information. Since I know how you can be effective, we can play to that."

"How about you?"

"I'm good at stealth and picking locks. I also have a few potions that can be used to create opportunities."

"You're basically a thief then?"

"More or less."

"You don't see many your age. They tend to die out," Tarren said. Celes laughed.

"I am retired for a while."

"To bring up your son. And now you're out helping him?"

"That's right. You're quite perceptive," Celes said. The Tracker before her clearly had his full mental faculties. She always wondered how much people were transformed by the Blight.

"You could say I'm lucky in that way, since I've retained my memories, identity and ability to think for myself. But, that's also quite unlucky."

"Because you know what you're part of?"

"Yes. And there's no opportunity for me in normal society. I am shunned, and rightfully so." Tarren let out a sigh.

"What did you do before all this?"

"I was a thief catcher." Tarren let a tiny smile loose. Celes laughed again.

"That's too perfect. You would track down people like me?"

"Yes. I was incredibly good at it too. I could put myself in the right mindset, and used my skill to follow the trail. Or in some cases get one step ahead of the thief."

"You would make an excellent thief now!"

"That is true. I hadn't really considered it. I think somehow that's been a good thing. They would find me regardless, and then I'd be stealing for them as well."

"There's no escape at all?"

"No. Especially not with people like me out there. We are attuned to the Blight. With enough preparation and the right stimulus, we can find and track anyone infected."

"Like Alrion. My son."

"Yes. I hate to say it, but I am more and more convinced that he is the target for another group of Trackers. And he's infected too. Is there a chance that he's travelling with an infected wizard?"

"Unlikely. I mean, it's possible but it doesn't sound right."

"Then let's work on the assumption that he is until we find out more."

"Speaking of which, you haven't really told me much about where we are heading. Just that it's north." Celes stood and started stretching her legs again. They felt so stiff.

"Still north. Do you know where he might be heading?" Tarren said.

"I really have no idea. The only information I had was him needing to get to the desert. He must have a new destination that he's working towards."

"There's not much in the north lands. Fewer people, more mountains and lots of cold. Although you don't get much Blight activity up there."

"Could be something to it. If he's infected, it has to be something that he can use to get cured. Otherwise they wouldn't be tracking him so closely, would they?"

"They could wait for the transformation to take place and then move in. It would be less effort, and easier to track. That's what I would do." Tarren looked away after the comment.

"Don't worry, I'm sure you've had to do things you aren't comfortable with. There's a reason it's called the Blight, and why we're working to put a stop to it."

"Thank you for your understanding. I fear I've been a monster for so long now, I sometimes find the line blurred."

"I understand. But tell me a story about your life before. It will make me feel more comfortable."

"I like to reminisce about those times. Very well, but we should not dally telling stories. Let's take a slower pace but still progress." Tarren stretched carefully, then retrieved the heavy coat. Celes imagined him sighing as he put it back on. His disguise, hiding his real form.

He so desperately wants to be past it. I think we can work with that.

She cringed at the thought of getting on the horse again so soon, but there was nothing else to it.

Alrion needs me.

Celes gingerly mounted the horse and pretended it wasn't instantly uncomfortable.

"Story time, let me think," Tarren said. His eyes got a faraway look, but he started walking. Celes kept pace with him.

"Long ago, I was working in Altarbright. Very busy place, always something valuable being traded or transported. Lots to do for a man like myself. I was never without a job, sometimes having several on the go at once."

"How long ago was this?"

"Probably ten years ago."

"And when were you ... transformed?"

"A year ago. Recently, in the grand scheme of things."

"Very recently. Not that it's a short amount of time," Celes said. She didn't want to belittle his condition. He was certainly worried enough about it and the effect on his mind already.

"On this one particular day I was offered a job that was quite unusual. There was a rare and prized sword coming from Valrytir via the ferry. I was to catch the thief who was planning to steal it."

"You had a tip beforehand?"

"Yes. I was brought aboard the ferry not long before it was due to land, and concealed myself in the cargo. From there I kept track of all who came and went."

"Did the thief succeed?"

"Not initially. In fact, I started to believe that it was a hoax. Nobody came to check on it. I heard the ferry dock and all the passengers disembark but not a soul came to retrieve the cargo. There were other things than the sword. Which made it so strange."

"Please continue," Celes said. She adjusted her position on the saddle and nudged the horse closer to Tarren. Once she was used to his raspy voice, he was a good storyteller.

"Eventually, I decided to leave my hiding place and go find out what had happened. It didn't take long. As soon as I reached the deck I knew."

"What was it?"

"The first sign that something was not right was the location. We were not at Altarbright. We were in some sort of giant cavern. The ferry had been hijacked and brought somewhere else. Some sort of smuggler's cave no doubt."

"That's one way to steal a sword," Celes said. She was impressed by how bold it was.

"Indeed. The only other problem was that I had been betrayed. As soon as I reached the deck I was surrounded and had to surrender all my weapons."

"You were set up?"

"No, I don't think so. Not on purpose. I think that whoever was behind the scheme knew I would be planted on the ferry and therefore changed their tactics to suit. But they didn't know where I would be so they waited for me to emerge. I felt quite foolish for falling into their trap."

"How were you to know? That's not something you would normally expect."

"In hindsight yes, it was not something you could anticipate. Not without a precedent but there I was, captured and humiliated." Tarren had obvious emotion in his voice, like the feelings were still fresh.

"How'd you get out of that one?"

"Like you, I'm no stranger to locks. They locked me in a cargo storage cage and I let myself out when it was convenient. I suspected the captain was involved, but didn't know with enough certainty to take action. So I hid and watched and waited. I finally spotted the perpetrator."

"Who was it?'

"The quartermaster at the docks in Altarbright. He must have gotten wind of the sword and decided to make a play for it. I never did find out if he had prior arrangements with the smugglers."

"Corruption, it's almost always the answer," Celes said. She was a little disappointed.

"I know, it's at the heart of many things. I know I had an uphill battle trying to pin the whole thing on the quartermaster. The man who hired me would never believe it. The whole incident was completely unbelievable. So, I did the only thing possible."

"You stole the sword?"

"Of course. I had already memorised the manifest and knew where the sword was destined to go. I stole it back and rowed my way out of the cave and back to Altarbright. After quite an adventure I delivered the sword as promised, and was paid by its new owner after relaying my tale."

"We're not that different after all," Celes said. She smiled at him and tried to get a reaction. He chuckled a little, the sound horrifying to her ears. But she smiled back all the same.

There's still humanity there. How many of those who are Tainted or similar have we been tarring with the same brush as Blighters? There's way more to this than anyone understands, she thought.

"Speaking of which, what was your biggest heist?" Tarren said.

"There's been a few, but one stands out. One that spanned the beginning and end of my career. The Pure Diamond."

"I know of it. Last I checked it wasn't stolen."

"It has been now. That single gem has been so central to my life; I almost can't believe it thinking back. It's what prompted me to change my approach from small-scale thefts."

"Something I always wondered. What turns people to thieving?"

"Haven't you caught enough to figure that one out?" Celes said. Tarren shook his head slowly.

"I heard many excuses, but never a reason."

"That's fair. I never thought too much about it. But it has something to do with upsetting the order of things. And anyone can do it. There's no requirement for being born into the right family, or having wealth or privilege. Just the hunger for more, and the will to make it so."

"That does seem to be a central thread. I think that hunger is a disease for many, and they keep going after bigger and bigger targets."

"It certainly is. My obsession with the Pure Diamond introduced me to my husband, it made us flee Brangtur when we failed, and it recently led me back there. But here's the funniest part."

"Yes?" Tarren stopped walking and looked at Celes.

"In the end, I was caught. I needed help to escape, and someone else took it for me. That's life, isn't it?"

"Nothing ever goes to plan," Tarren said. He seemed lost in his thoughts, so Celes stopped talking. After a time, with there still being no settlement in sight, she had to ask him about it.

"Will we ever pass through another town?"

"Yes, soon enough. From the little that I know of the north, we can't help but pass through Rolyntide. And from there, I fear there aren't many paths to take. Good in some ways and bad in others."

"Easier to track them."

"And harder to remain hidden," Tarren said.

"We can defend ourselves, that's an acceptable risk." Celes withdrew two of her knives in a flourish.

"I don't doubt that. But, if we really get their attention we will be in considerable danger." Tarren stopped suddenly.

"What is it?" Celes said. She could sense something was wrong.

"They're preparing an attack on the wizard. It's significant. Perhaps even an ambush."

"How far?"

"I'm not sure. Too far for us. I need to be careful," he said. Tarren slowly sunk to the ground and sat cross-legged. He looked to be concentrating intensely with his eyes closed.

"Only a small Tracker presence, but they're not going to engage. There's something else. Something dark. This is not a good sign. Does he have help?"

"He does. My husband and another thief."

"That may not be enough." Tarren went quiet again. Celes felt so powerless. Her son was in danger again, and she was too far away. She had to catch up. She could help. She was about to speak to Tarren again, but his eyes suddenly opened and he looked right at her.

"We have a problem. They've detected my snooping and they're suspicious. We should prepare ourselves for the possibility of an attack."

12

A SURPRISING FOE

Alrion braced himself for another communication. But he didn't dare respond.

"Giving me the silent treatment? That is fine. It was about time you wised up," Wraith said. Alrion looked at his father.

"Find them," he whispered. Vincent seemed to understand, and took off to look for Lara and Alyx.

"You've been very helpful, aiding my Trackers. And we're not far away. That's why I'm communicating with you now. I am sending you a special gift," Wraith said. Alrion decided to respond, but without emotion. He had to see what he could do.

"Always so thoughtful," Alrion said.

"So, he speaks. I thought that perhaps you had been rendered mute from fear. Have you been enjoying the Blighters?"

"I'm a little tired of them to be honest. So dull," Alrion said. He was trying to turn the tables, to wind up Wraith rather than be the one that got angry. It did help that he felt a little calmer after his training.

"I completely agree. But that was just the warm-up. I'm sending you a taste of what's to come. I won't be there myself, but just imagine me coming soon."

"You're all talk, Wraith. For all I know you're still stuck in that pit."

"That was a clever move. But we both know you're not powerful enough to do that anywhere else. And without your Spark you're powerless. Just admit it," Wraith said. The mocking tone in his voice would normally trigger Alrion. But he had just enough control to keep his reaction down.

"I know what you're trying to do and I'm not going to bite. I'm still here, and all your attacks have failed."

"Oh, have they? I beg to differ. But all in good time. Just remember that there's nowhere you can go. Nowhere you can hide. I will be there and claim you for myself. You belong to me; it's just a matter of time. Keep struggling if you like. It'll just make your eventual failure all the more enjoyable," Wraith roared. He did seem a little annoyed. Alrion took pleasure in that.

"Just more empty words, Wraith. I'll see you when I feel it necessary. Good-bye," Alrion said. He tried blocking out any further communication. He wasn't sure if it was working, or if Wraith had just stopped talking. Vincent soon returned with Alyx and Lara.

"What's going on?" Lara said.

"Wraith was communicating with me. It seems out of the ordinary, I get the feeling that it's difficult for him to do it."

"And what did he say?" Vincent said.

"He said that he's not far behind, and he's sent me a special gift. One that's not as dull as a horde of Blighters. Make of that what you will." Alrion shrugged his shoulders.

"I don't like the sound of that. Could be a Shade?" Lara said.

"I get the impression that it's something else. Something different."

"Either way he's told you that something is coming. We should prepare for that," Vincent said. He looked at Alyx.

"I can't suggest a location specifically, although I do think we should move to a narrower section. That way we can control how we are engaged, at least in terms of numbers," Alyx said.

"But he said it wasn't as dull as a horde of Blighters. What if we get boxed in?" Lara said. Nobody had a good answer for that.

"Let's just move further down and assess places to make a stand. Clearly, we shouldn't remain here," Vincent said. Alyx started taking off and Alrion hurried to catch up.

"Do you have any ideas?" Lara said to Alrion as they walked.

"Not really. I just know that it is different. He seemed excited. That's a bad sign. I tried to antagonise him a bit, to see how he reacted. But I don't think it made much of a difference. He was too pleased with himself."

"That definitely doesn't sound good. I'll make sure we have a good place to defend ourselves," Lara said. She ran ahead to confer with Alyx and scout ahead. Alrion kept walking, lost in his thoughts.

"Alrion, prepare yourself!" Vincent shouted. Alrion was startled, and drew his sword. The rest of his group were clustered together ahead, but he couldn't see what they were talking about. He stepped forward, the nerves giving him both pause and also a manic energy.

"What is this gift from Wraith?" Alrion wondered. He stood beside his father and looked ahead. Blocking the path was what looked like a Shade. But it was completely quiet and looked asleep with its head lowered.

"Stop the games, we see you!" Alrion shouted. He didn't know what game was being played, but the tension was uncomfortable. He needed to know what he was dealing with. The creature slowly raised its head and looked at them.

"I bring the gift of fire!" it said. Its voice was reminiscent of Wraith's, with an alien, harsh tone to it. The gift was a fireball, slowly increasing in speed and size as it hurtled towards them. Alrion's first reaction was to swat it away, but Lara tackled him to the ground. He felt the searing heat passing over him and curled up into a ball. It passed and exploded against a large rock behind them, showering sparks everywhere. As he regained his senses he realised that Lara was shielding him.

"I'm sorry," he said, as she quickly rolled off and stood. Alyx and Vincent also rose from where they had sheltered and stepped in front of Alrion.

"You can't stop them right now. You have to remember that," Lara said. Alrion propped himself up with the help of his sword and looked over at their enemy. It was laughing.

"To think that you almost stood there and took the blast. You're more idiotic than I was led to believe," it said.

"Who are you?" Alrion said.

"Call me Fury. I am a former wizard and the first disciple of Wraith. I will show you the power that you will soon have when you join us!" Fury started to run forward with incredible speed. It drew back its right arm, preparing a strike. Vincent stepped forward and swung his sword, aiming at Fury's arm. The creature continued forward with the strike, knocking Vincent back.

Vincent steadied himself, keeping his eyes on the Shade. Fury examined its arm.

"No damage. Your sword won't work on me," it said. It laughed, a terrifying screaming sound coming out.

"He must be shielding himself. The sword can still work, you may need to create an opening," Alrion said. He approached Alyx and handed over his sword. The diamond glowed bright blue.

"Take this. You can do more with it than me, and your weapon has no chance of doing anything against this kind of enemy," he said. Alyx didn't argue and accepted the weapon readily. She gave her short sword to Alrion.

"I will take the lead. Vincent and Lara, you shadow me and look for opportunities. But make sure one of you can always cover Alrion. That short sword won't do much."

"Agreed. I'll follow your lead," Vincent said. Alyx started immediately, hurling herself at the Shade. It raised his arm, blasting a wave of force at her. She shielded herself with the sword, but flew back several paces. Vincent attacked from another angle with the same level of ferocity. Fury turned its attention over to him, throwing another wave of force. Vincent defended himself the same way. Lara used the opportunity to start flanking the creature.

"Don't think you can sneak up on me!" Fury roared. It spun completely and let loose a spray of fire that swept along aimed at Lara. She turned and ran, just fast enough to outpace the fire. Fury kept laughing as the flames licked just behind Lara's heels.

Alyx attacked again, a little bit faster than before. This time Vincent was beside her. Fury noticed them and stopped his attack, swinging around to take a swipe at Alyx. She slid down, maintaining her momentum, and slicing at the creature's legs. Fury quickly brought up his other arm and fired a blast of force at her, pushing her back and preventing her weapon from coming into contact.

"Got you!" Vincent shouted as his sword came down. Fury quickly grabbed the blade with his free hand, screaming in pain. The sword cut free of the creature's grasp, and Fury stumbled back. Vincent held his ground, watching the scene unfold.

Fury stared at its hand and clenched it. It composed itself then let out a furious cry.

"That stung. But nothing more than that I'm afraid. I'm just getting warmed up," it said.

"That means you can hurt it, you just need to create an opening," Alrion shouted. He wished he could help more, but he had no power to use. The best he could do was watch the creature and figure out its limitations. It was clearly the same sort of creation as Wraith himself. But even Wraith had used magic sparingly. There had to be a degree of difficulty or cost to using magic in that Shade-like form. So Alrion would watch and think. He would figure out a strategy for them to use to bring this thing down.

Lara returned to Alrion's side panting.

"That was close," she said.

"I could see that. I know it has limitations so the more we push it the better chance we have of finding a weakness. Just make sure you have enough speed to get away," he said without taking his eyes off Fury.

"I understand. See what you can figure out," Lara said. She paused for a moment, her eyes darting back and forth, before diving back into the fight.

Alyx was crouched down and watching Fury. The Shade Wizard just looked back.

"Maybe he's waiting," Vincent said quietly. He took up a position next to Alyx. Lara joined them moments later.

"I will press from the front, you two go for the flanks," Alyx said. The other two just nodded and waited.

"Come entertain me, you weaklings!" Fury shouted. It had stopped clutching its hand and was now observing them. Alyx crouched even lower and sprung forward with incredible speed. It was like she was trying to win a foot race, not enter a fight. She held the sword in front of her like a spear. Fury laughed and threw a wave of force at her. But it just seemed to wrap around her. She increased her speed, moving forward with a single-minded purpose.

Fury scrambled to counter. It brought both hands together and looked like it was concentrating intensely. Another blast of force exploded, knocking Alyx aside. Rather than go down, she rolled and continued forward like it had been nothing. Fury didn't try another spell, instead readying to strike out at her.

Interesting. It needs to concentrate properly to cast spells with anything more than just general targeting. And doesn't like to chain together too many at once. I think we can use that. He continued to watch the fight.

Vincent crossed over, approaching Fury from the opposite angle. The creature stepped aside to bring both Alyx and Vincent into its field of vision. Lara ran further, coming back in a wide arc and splitting the Shade Wizard's attention further. She threw some daggers at it. Fury glanced at them, then turned away. They bounced harmlessly off his body. The distraction however bought Alyx an extra second of approach and she changed her stance. Instead of looking to spear the creature, she instead sliced at its legs again.

However, this time Fury couldn't stop the strike. A wave of fire started to emanate from its hands. Alyx must have noticed but ignored it. She continued her swing. As she connected, a wave of fire enveloped her legs. Alyx continued the arc of the strike, slicing through then rolling to safety. She rolled around quickly, trying to put out the fire.

Lara dived in to help, moving Alyx around and extinguishing any other flames. Vincent moved to capitalise on the attack and slashed again at the creature. Fury moved just enough, and caught the attack on the shoulder. The Runesteel cut deep and Fury cried out in pain and anguish.

The simultaneous attack did the trick. They didn't even need me to point that out. I hope they can finish this, Alrion thought. He didn't like the look of what happened to Alyx. Even if she had escaped the worst, her mobility would be gone.

Fury grew quiet, and looked to be testing its limbs. Without warning, it lurched forward charging towards Alyx. She just lay there, her legs twitching. Lara crouched over her, with her Runesteel dagger at the ready.

"You'll pay for that! I won't even keep you for the Blight. DIE NOW!" the Shade Wizard cried out. His right hand was aflame and his nails were extended out like knives.

There's no way Lara can stop that. And Alyx can't stand. Alrion's blood boiled and he felt powerless. He scrambled within himself, trying to find a way to access his Spark without reaching through the dark mass of Blight. He even considered trying it anyway, knowing the consequences. But movement ahead caught his attention. It was his father.

Vincent had launched himself at Fury's back, his sword outstretched. By some miracle he seemed to reach the creature before it could hit Alyx. The

Runesteel slid effortlessly through the Shade Wizard's chest all the way to the hilt. But Fury kept moving.

Lara held her ground and moved with lightning speed. She grasped Fury's outstretched hand just enough to divert it, and with her right hand she drove her Dagger into its heart.

"Die, you abomination!" she shouted. Fury halted. It lost its momentum and started to topple.

"Move it over!" Vincent called out. He started to guide Fury over to the side and Lara aided him. With a resounding crash the creature fell to the ground just to the side of Alyx. Its protective skin started to flake away and turn to dust. Alrion ran forward to join them. He couldn't believe how close that had been. And Alyx wasn't moving.

Before he could reach her side, Vincent and Lara were standing over the weapon master with concerned looks.

"How is she?" Alrion said.

"Badly burned on her legs, but otherwise alright it seems," Vincent said.

"I've had worse," Alyx said hoarsely. But she looked to be in incredible pain.

"You did well Lara, I wasn't able to do enough to stop it," Vincent said.

"Thanks, but it was a team effort. We only managed that because Alyx slowed it down. At great cost."

"Just doing my duty," Alyx said. Lara and Vincent returned their weapons and Alrion carefully unclasped Alyx's grip and sheathed his sword. He stepped over and looked at the body of Fury. The transformation had been reversed. Now it just looked like an ordinary man.

"This could be me. This is why I must succeed. Death should not be the only release from this curse," he said. He turned and walked a few paces away, a surge of emotions within him. Alyx had almost died, they had killed a wizard, and Alrion had felt powerless throughout the whole thing.

As much as it was about him finding a cure for himself, he realised that he had a greater responsibility. It wasn't only his own fate that was doomed if he failed, it was all those who were infected. That was a heavy weight on his shoulders.

13

SLOW PROGRESS

Alrion was staring off into space, obviously affected by the battle. Lara decided to focus on practical matters.

"Can you sit up?" she said. Alyx didn't respond so Lara knelt to help prop her up. Vincent dropped down beside her, and the two of them managed to lift Alyx and rest her against a nearby rock in a seated position.

"How's that?" Lara said. Alyx paused to gather her breath, then responded.

"A bit better. I'm not sure how well I can move," she said.

"Let us worry about that," Vincent said. He looked around the area.

"He was waiting for us. Do you think there's more ahead?" Lara said.

"No, Wraith would have been here himself if they were that prepared. I think we have a window of opportunity to create some distance. But it will be hard with Alyx's injury," Vincent said. Alrion approached suddenly.

"I can heal her. My power isn't gone, it's just a bit beyond my usual reach," he said.

"No!" Vincent shouted. He cleared his throat and continued. "Sorry, but it's not negotiable. You do not use your gift while infected. I've been told too many horror stories."

"But ..."

"Not ever. We need to get to a Healer. We don't have any supplies to even treat her," Vincent said.

"I'm done, leave me here. My legs are burned and I'm infected. I don't want to be the reason your quest fails. I'm already a lost cause," Alyx said. There was silence.

"We should consider it. If they aren't after her, maybe we can send help back. We're in the middle of nowhere and will have difficulty moving forward otherwise. You can't afford to be caught," Lara said. She had had disagreements with Alyx, and disliked the often-critical nature of the weapon master. But she had come to respect her and didn't like the idea of leaving her behind. In this situation, though, it sounded like common sense. It was too risky otherwise.

"I can't leave her here. They will do worse to her if they find her, or if she's left alone she won't make it. Alyx is the reason we survived that fight. What happens next time? If I can't heal her, then we find someone who can," Alrion said. Lara was surprised by the amount of passion in his voice. It was hard to argue against him. She just didn't want to get caught again in a difficult situation. It would be worse next time with an injured companion.

"We can't lose the time debating this. Alrion, let's try and get Alyx up and assess," Vincent said. Alrion nodded and helped his father. They strained and hauled her up. They held her weight and slowly lowered her feet to the ground. Lara could see the pain on Alyx's face.

"How bad is it?" Vincent said. Alyx tried putting weight down on each foot, one at a time.

"Quite excruciating. If you're insistent on taking me, then I can deal with the pain. But all I can do is try and prevent my feet dragging. I can't walk properly. I'll just fall," Alyx said.

"We will make this right," Alrion said. He already looked tired. And who knew how much of his strength had already been sapped by the Blight.

"Give me your weapons," Lara said. She walked over and unbuckled all three swords, strapped one to her back and let the other two hang from her hips. They were heavy and a bit unwieldy, but at least Vincent and Alrion didn't have the additional weight. They shifted their holds then moved forward slowly. With great concentration Alyx managed to coordinate her feet to match their rhythm.

"Looking good." Lara wanted to encourage them, but it was way too slow. She could have crawled quicker.

"I'll be slightly ahead to spot any potential dangers or good places for breaks. Shout out if you need anything," she said. She knew she couldn't keep the same pace as them. It would frustrate her no end. At least this way she could keep occupied and help point out or avoid any obstacles.

The path narrowed, with what looked like sharp drops on each side. Due to the way it wound she had trouble seeing what lay too far ahead. It was a mix of rocks, short-cropped grass, and lots of dirt. There was a chill to the air, which felt refreshing while you moved, but would set in deep if you were still.

Lara felt the urge to push further forward to see what lay behind each bend. But she had to restrain herself. Otherwise she would bound too far ahead and be unable to hear any cries for help. So, she reined herself in, albeit with difficulty.

Her stomach rumbled but she ignored it. There were more important things to focus on. The clouds seemed closer now, and there were some strange grey puffs rising in the distance. Lara stopped quickly and looked closer.

That's not clouds. Maybe smoke?

Fighting the urge to run ahead and investigate, she turned and rushed back to find the others.

They were seated in the middle of the path. There was nothing to rest on.

"Sorry, we couldn't make it anywhere more sensible. It's been a long day already," Vincent said.

"Don't apologise, I wish I could help more. Should I swap with one of you?" Lara said.

"No, it's fine. We are in a rhythm now, and it would be good to have you fresh. Anything ahead?"

"I think I've spotted some smoke in the distance. Which could mean some sort of settlement. Maybe a village?"

"It has to be. We should press on and see if we can get there before dark," Alyx said. She grimaced and looked away. Lara looked over at Alrion.

"Is she alright?" she mouthed to him. He shook his head slowly.

"You've rested enough surely, Alrion. Don't let your father's age slow you down," Lara said. She wanted to break the mood. Alrion at least laughed.

"You're right. This ground is too cold for my liking anyway. Up we get," Alrion said. With another great effort they lifted Alyx up and started moving.

"Pick up the pace a bit?" Lara said. Alrion nodded and Vincent complied. Alyx looked pained but went along with it.

"Not far now, just keep it up," Lara said. She had no idea how far it was; the terrain being deceptive, but she knew that if they stopped again, it might be the last stop for a while.

⌒

Lara pushed forward again.

"Just one more bend," she told herself. The sight and smell of the smoke had strengthened which meant they were getting closer. She had started to wonder if perhaps the village was under attack, but dismissed the thought. That was just pessimistic thinking. It was going to be a collection of hearth fires that they could be warmed by.

Lara rounded the corner and almost cheered. Ahead there was a large wooden gate, and behind it a small village. There were several pillars of smoke rising up from houses. Some big and some small. They were roughly constructed out of stones but looked like they had been there a long time.

Finally, a place to rest.

She felt guilty because she'd had an easy time of it comparatively and still felt tired. It had been a draining day.

"Time to pass on the good news." Lara raced back to find the others. They were still mobile, which was a relief.

"Don't stop now, there's a village just beyond us," she said. She saw Alrion's shoulders instantly perk up. The weight he must've felt had been lessened.

"You heard her, let's finish strong," Alrion said. With a visible effort he shifted his hold and held Alyx even higher. She was practically being carried now. Vincent did the same and they almost doubled their speed.

"That's more like it. Don't drop her!" Lara said. This time she kept pace with them, keeping an eye on their progress and helping them maintain the pace. As they returned to where she had spotted the village she watched for Alrion's reaction.

"I've never seen a more welcoming place," he said with a laugh. Lara hoped that the village would be as welcoming as they all wanted it to be. But with a small village in a remote location, you never could tell. They had to knock on that giant door and find out. Just a few hundred more agonising steps to go.

"You can do the honours," Vincent said when they finally reached the gate. The huge wooden doors hung on titanic steel hinges. The wood was weathered by the elements and had a metallic rectangular slot in the middle of the right door. Lara walked up and rapped loudly just below the slot.

"Hello! We have an emergency and need to enter!" Lara shouted. She waited for a response.

"Hello!" she shouted again. The metallic panel slid open but Lara couldn't see anything through it.

"We aren't expecting visitors," a man said. He must have been standing near the opening.

"We didn't know we had to send word. We need immediate attention for one of our party. We must get to your Healer as soon as possible," Lara said.

"I'm sorry I can't allow that. There's been too many strange happenings lately, the gates are closed. You can make your case tomorrow when the town magistrate is accepting submissions for entry," the man said. He didn't sound particularly sorry. More annoyed that he was being disturbed.

"We have someone in dire need of attention. Your Healer will vouch for us," Lara said. She was gambling a bit, but needed something. They couldn't afford to wait outside all night.

"If you know the Healer, then what's her name?" the man said. He sounded doubly annoyed now. At least Lara was getting somewhere.

"I haven't met this Healer, but we were sent ahead by another Healer. Freyda from Rolyntide."

"Prove it."

"Well, she gave us directions. Said we could find help here on our way. How else do you think we found you?" Lara said. She was grasping at straws now, but she had little choice. Something had to work.

"There's only one main path, you would have found us anyway. I need more than that. Otherwise you can sleep out under the stars," the man said. He sounded like he was looking forward to that being the conclusion of their business. Lara looked over at the group. Alyx was struggling with something.

"Take the amulet," she said weakly. Alrion and Vincent adjusted their stance, and Lara came in close. She unclasped the amulet and dangled it into the hole in the door.

"She gave us this to help us on our way. Show that to your Healer and she will insist we come inside," Lara said. The man roughly grabbed the amulet from her hands and she heard him walk off.

"I hope this works," Alrion said.

"I think there's a good chance," Vincent said. "Alyx has good instincts."

"Well, if it doesn't I'm sure I can climb over this wall. Plynth was much higher," Lara said, chuckling. She managed to get a smile out of Alrion.

Good, he's still alright, she thought. Alyx looked terrible though. It was like she had expended all her energy and willpower getting here, and now she had nothing left. Lara felt bad for the animosity between them.

Why does she rub me the wrong way so badly?

Before she could ponder further, footsteps approached. And another sound. Metal clanking, and bars being drawn back. The doors started to lurch open with a creaking roar. A simply dressed guard stood before them. He looked less armoured than the ones they had encountered elsewhere and was suitably unimpressed at having to open the doors.

"You can enter. Take the first right and enter the house with the vines crawling the walls. That's the Healer's residence," he said.

"What about our amulet?" Lara said.

"The Healer will return it if she believes you obtained it lawfully. Otherwise I'll be around to throw you out," the guard said. It sounded like he would enjoy that, even though it would require him to do something. Lara didn't want to push their luck.

"Sounds fair, sorry for the trouble," she said. The guard shook his head and walked off.

"That was quite restrained of you," Alrion said.

"Well, we can't mess around right now. I'll make up for it later," she said. Alrion shook his head at the thought and Lara bounded ahead.

"Just a bit further," Lara said, urging them on. The main road was paved with cobblestones which were uneven and worn down. The entry to the village had a few houses and buildings packed in close, but as they turned the corner the houses started to spread out more. The Healer's house was easily spotted, as there was nothing around it. It spanned two levels and was the only one with a mess of vines wrapped around it.

I'll have to ask about that, Lara thought. It seemed at odds with the surroundings. She went ahead, and rapped smartly on the red, wooden door. After a delay she was about to knock again when she thought she heard footsteps.

"Who is it?" a female voice said from within.

"It's the travellers who brought the amulet. We have a critical injury," Lara said. The door opened immediately and a young woman peered out. She looked only slightly older than Lara and had darker skin. She looked completely out of place with the local residents and the colder climate.

"I'm Lara. Older gentleman is Vincent, the other one is Alrion, and the sickly-looking woman is called Alyx."

"Beatrix. Please come in, I see she needs immediate attention. I have a special couch set up in the room next door," Beatrix said. The Healer walked off immediately. Lara waited for Alrion and Vincent to make a start, and she stepped back to close the door behind them.

So far so good. It felt good to finally be within some enclosed walls, and not stuck out in the cold wilderness.

I'm definitely a city girl.

Now they could get Alyx some help, and prepare for the next leg of their journey.

I just hope we make it in time. He has to make it, Lara thought as she joined the others.

14

POISON

Alyx felt an initial surge of relief as she lay down on the couch. She had been tense for hours, and it was the first time she could fully relax. The feeling was enough to temporarily overpower the extreme burning sensation in her legs.

"This is quite a serious burn, and strange in its application. What did this?" Beatrix said. She looked at them with concern.

"You wouldn't believe us if we told you," Lara said.

"Try me."

"It's from a wizard that was transformed into a Shade," Alrion said. Beatrix's eyes widened.

"That's not possible," she said.

"We've seen it twice now. It's plenty possible," Vincent added. Alyx just nodded, not adding any commentary. The pain was flaring up, so she clenched her teeth and tried to ignore it.

"Wizard fire is a bit different to normal fire. More intensity and it also attacks the nerves. Let me fetch something," Beatrix said. She disappeared into another room. Alrion came over and held Alyx's hand.

"You're almost there. She is going to help you. I had no idea that this was even worse than a normal burn," he said. Alyx nodded. But she realised he probably wanted a response so she swallowed hard and prepared to speak.

"It was the right decision. I can rest now," Alyx said. She closed her eyes. Another wave of pain assaulted her and she tried to compartmentalise her mind and shut out the feeling in her legs. She heard footsteps approaching and opened her eyes.

"This will help," Beatrix said. She was holding a clear jar with white contents.

"Remove the pants," Beatrix said. Alrion looked away in embarrassment and Vincent and Lara struggled to get Alyx's pants off. Before the intense pain Alyx had to laugh to herself at Alrion's response.

He forgets that I'm not a woman, I'm a weapon.

Although, it was nice for someone to think of her as something else. Lara and Vincent were rough, but efficient. Soon the cool air was a relief to Alyx's legs. She shuddered suddenly, as she felt an icy touch. She looked over and saw Beatrix applying the cream liberally.

"So. Cold," Alyx said. It was unbelievable, almost the exact extreme to what she had been feeling.

"It's necessary. Don't worry it will settle down soon," Beatrix said. She continued to apply the cream, and Alyx finally relaxed. The burning started to subside, and her legs started to feel numb.

"That should do the trick. It's lucky you got here when you did, the damage is not as bad as it could have been," Beatrix said. She pulled a light blanket over Alyx.

"How's that?" Beatrix said.

"Better," Alyx said. The feeling of relief was incredible. She had trained herself to ignore pain, and focus herself. But the effort was incredibly taxing, and she had had to fight through it to get here. But at last she could start to relax.

"Good. It will take time for your legs to heal enough to put weight on. Why don't you all go somewhere to stay for the night?"

"Shouldn't we stay here?" Alrion said.

"And where is here?" Lara said.

"This town? Highroad. There's nothing more you can do, and I don't need more people underfoot. I prefer a quiet home. Your friend will be quite safe," Beatrix said.

"We can't thank you enough. Why did you help us?" Alrion said.

"That amulet is very special. It would not have been handed over to you otherwise. Let's talk more tomorrow," Beatrix said. She walked off to the edge of the room pointing them back to the front door.

"We will return at first light," Alrion said.

"I'll have to wake you up for that to be true," Lara said. The group had a bit of a laugh then left. Alyx heard the door close and footsteps return.

"Just me. I'll bring you some water, then you should sleep. Your body needs that more than anything else right now," Beatrix said. Alyx nodded, it was too much effort to talk again. But the Healer seemed to understand that. Alyx closed her eyes, and the padding of returning footsteps alerted her.

"Here, drink slowly," Beatrix said. Alyx forced herself to drink slowly, even though she was incredibly parched. The water was cool and delicious. She felt like she noticed a slight aftertaste though.

"Sleep well. I'll be upstairs and I'll check on you later tonight," Beatrix said. Alyx was about to nod off, but forced out a few words.

"I am in your debt," she said.

"No, you are not. You have bigger problems than worrying about repaying me. Rest, and we can talk more tomorrow," Beatrix said. Alyx couldn't keep her eyes open any longer and fell into a deep sleep.

Alyx heard footsteps padding closer to her on the soft carpet.

Oh, it's Beatrix checking on me, she thought. She listened out for any words of comfort or reassurance but Beatrix was strangely silent.

That's odd.

She was too tired to worry about small details like that. She felt a metallic cup pressed up against her lips.

Beatrix could at least warn me.

Alyx started to sip on the contents when she caught a whiff of something. She lashed out her hand and grabbed Beatrix's arm. The fluid spilled everywhere and Alyx's eyes shot open.

"D ... Darkroot," Alyx stammered and looked at Beatrix in surprise. It was dark in the room and Beatrix was strangely silent. But struggling against the firm grip that Alyx had.

"You're. Not. Going. Anywhere," Alyx said, digging her nails in harder. As her eyes adjusted to the surroundings she saw that the dark shape before her didn't look like Beatrix.

"Who are you?" Alyx said. She started to feel her stomach churn. How much of the Darkroot had she drunk? Was this an assassin? The figure continued to struggle and started to change tactics. It reached over to drag Alyx off the couch. Alyx couldn't stop it, but tried to break her fall as well as possible. The figure started kicking her, using the leverage to break her grip. Arcs of pain shot through her arm, but she dismissed it. She had dealt with worse. And this was a matter of life and death.

"This is going to hurt," she told herself, and lashed out her legs. They were not responsive, given their stiffness and burns. But they did obey, and her assailant didn't notice them coming. She managed to trip over the assassin and roll over on top of it and pinned down one of its arms.

A sliver of light through the window illuminated its face. It looked like a man, probably Tainted. He had dark hair and black clothes. His face was snarling and she noticed some black marks on his face.

"Tainted? Who sent you?" she said.

"You know the answer to that. I won't let you take me," the Tainted said. He used his free hand to pull out a dagger and swung it at Alyx. She saw it coming, threw out her hand and stopped it just in time. She was staring at the point of the blade. They struggled, the Tainted trying to drive the dagger home and Alyx trying to drive it away. Her strength was not what it used to be, and she felt a thrumming and shuddering inside her.

Cursed Blight. Or Darkroot. Or both, she thought. The Tainted smiled a cruel grin, victory on his face.

"Not today," Alyx said. She brought her leg up and kneed the Tainted in the crotch. He cried out and Alyx used the distraction to force the dagger down into the Tainted's chest.

Panting, Alyx rolled off him. She turned her head to look over, and he appeared to be dying.

That's a shame, but I couldn't take the chance.

The effort had reignited the flaming pain in her legs, and her breathing was laboured.

"Beatrix!" Alyx shouted, then blacked out.

Alyx opened her eyes again. She tried to sit up, remembering what had happened. She was restrained and she looked around frantically. Beatrix was seated on a chair next to the couch.

"What's going on?" Alyx said.

"You mustn't move. That will help the Darkroot spread," Beatrix said.

"Do you have an antidote?"

"I'm making one. But it's not perfect, and time is against us. Hopefully you didn't consume too much."

"I noticed what it was immediately," Alyx said. She started coughing. Beatrix put a reassuring hand on her shoulder.

"You did well, I'm impressed that you survived that attack. What's going on here? I've never seen Tainted so aggressively pursuing someone already infect-ed," Beatrix said. She gave Alyx a pointed look.

"We can explain later. But Alrion is the key. I don't matter, as long as he makes it," Alyx said.

"He doesn't seem to believe that, based on his behaviour before. What's so special about him?"

"That's his story to tell."

"Fair enough. You know what's going to happen to you, right?" Beatrix said.

"With the poison?"

"No, with the Blight. You don't have a lot of time. You need that amulet," Beatrix said. She pointed and Alyx realised that she was wearing it again.

"What can you tell me about it?"

"Nothing. It's a secret. Just keep it close. You're going to need all the help you can get. Have some rest. We can talk more in the morning. Unless you think there'll be another attack?"

"I doubt it. They seem to be more concerned with slowing us down."

"Very well. Sleep," Beatrix said. She placed a hand on Alyx's forehead, then walked away. Alyx watched her walk away then let herself drift off again.

Yet again I had a chance to die, but did not. What's my fate? Why am I still here? She thought as sleep took her.

❧

"What's going on?" Alrion said. The concern in his voice was obvious. Alyx awoke and looked around. Everyone seemed to be back, and Alrion was talking to Beatrix.

"There was an attacker overnight. I have kept the body in the next room. She was poisoned with Darkroot, but I'm not sure how much. I've been working on an antidote, which I can administer soon," Beatrix said. She kept her cool in the face of Alrion's emotion.

"What does it do? The Darkroot?" he said.

"It kills," Alyx said. She could feel her temperature rising, and knew that the poison was doing something.

"Slowly, so we have time. You needn't worry I haven't seen any warning signs yet," Beatrix said. She left the room and Alrion rushed over to Alyx.

"I'm so sorry. Who did this?"

"Not sure, you should go look. He looked like a Tainted, from what I saw," Alyx said. She wanted to say more but started coughing.

"It's all my fault. Ever since you've been with us you've suffered," Alrion said.

"It's not on you, it's just the journey we are on. I signed up to this you know. Let the Healer do her work," Alyx said.

"You're wearing the amulet again," Lara said.

"Yes, Beatrix said it would help. But she wouldn't say more. Incredibly frustrating," Alyx said.

"I think there's a connection between them," Lara said.

"Perhaps. The amulet did seem to be important. Why don't you take a look at the attacker and see what you can find out?" Alyx said. She needed a break from all the attention, and was curious about the man. She'd never had anyone try and assassinate her in her sleep before. And she wondered why she had been targeted.

It must be because I'm already injured.

If that was the case, then the objective was definitely to slow them down.

Going to so much effort to capture us. It must mean a great deal, Alyx thought.

But she was too tired to puzzle it out further. She heard noise from the other room.

"What is it?" she said as loudly as she could. Lara and Alrion rushed back.

"Are you sure?" Alrion said to Lara.

"No doubt about that. That's the Tainted one that escaped from the fight. The one that we thought was advising the leader."

"He's a sneaky one. Anything else unusual?" Alrion said.

"He had a strange mark on his hand."

"I'll go take a look," Vincent said. He had been sitting quietly in the corner and Alyx hadn't even noticed his presence. Beatrix entered swiftly, going directly to Alyx.

"Drink this quickly," she said. It was a white liquid in a small vial. Alyx sat up as much as possible and drank down the liquid. It was thick and milky but had no real flavour. She eased back down with a sigh.

"That's the antidote?" Alyx said.

"Close enough to one. It should purge all traces of the poison. But it will take a day or so for you to be considered safe," Beatrix said.

"I'm not comfortable with that," Alyx said.

"We can discuss it later. For now, you need to rest. I'm going to see what my father thinks about the attacker," Alrion said. He strode off into the next room.

"You know, I think they got more than they bargained for. They've thrown a monster at you, burned you, and tried to poison you. But you're still alive and kicking," Lara said.

"Still here."

"I'm glad that you are. But I'm beginning to think you can't be killed!" Lara said, a smile breaking out on her face. Alyx appreciated the attempt at humour, even though she was exhausted.

"If only to frustrate them, I will live on," Alyx said. She felt a coolness slowly washing over her. Hopefully the antidote was working. At least she felt a little better.

This better not be for nothing. I don't want to be healed just for the Blight to take me, Alyx thought. She looked over at Lara. A strange girl, but very skilled and very intelligent. She seemed familiar too. Alyx couldn't shake the thought.

I'll ask her about it later. For now, she had to sleep again. Her body needed to focus on its recovery.

15

THE TRACKER'S STAND

"There's no doubt about it now," Tarren said. He slowed down and started walking slowly.

"You mean about them tracking you?" Celes said.

"Yes. Once they had reason to suspect me, there was not much I could do. They know I'm not on this assignment, and I'm operating on my own. They will attack soon."

"How do you know?"

"Because they are collectively blocking me. They don't want me to know they're coming."

"Do we need to make a stand?" Celes didn't like where this was going. First, Tarren had detected something dark going after Alrion. And now, they were under attack too.

"That would increase our chances of survival."

"Can we make it to Rolyntide? That's the next town, right?"

"I would not advise it. We would have to push hard to make it before we were attacked, and maybe we would not make it in time. And then we would be tired and in a poor position."

"That's a good point. I also wouldn't want to endanger innocents unnecessarily."

"They will not restrain themselves for anything. You must take that into account."

"So, let's find a place we can defend. Do you know this area at all?"

"Not well. We have to assume that we can't hide. And if we stop moving they will approach with caution. The only thing we have working for us, is that they don't know how many we are."

"Really? They won't expect you to be alone?"

"No. It would be very strange for me to act independently like this without some sort of other party involved."

"I would have thought if you knew what Alrion was up to, you would seek him out anyway."

"That is true, I am certainly dissatisfied enough to do so. But they will not think that. They are suspicious and in this case, they are right."

"Alright that's settled. Let's find a place where we have a fighting chance."

"Agreed. Let us travel a little slower and look for appropriate locations." Tarren walked at a normal pace and seemed preoccupied. Celes looked at their surroundings. They were travelling alongside a small forest. That had potential as a way to thin out any attackers.

"Do you think they will attack at night?"

"They prefer to. But they will know I can see them. We can't rule out an earlier strike."

"Now's the time, if there's anything else you can tell me. Are you armed?"

"I have only a dagger with me. However, I am quite strong, so I can use my body as well."

"Then we need to get them in close. And not get surrounded. The nearby woods are a good possibility."

"I had thought that too. Let's enter here," Tarren said. He pushed through some smaller shrubs and brushed a tree branch aside. He held it back, and Celes nudged the horse carefully and passed through as well. They ended up on a partial track that led deeper into the trees.

"Somewhere along here then."

"Yes. Keep your eyes open for a suitable location." Tarren swung his head from side to side slowly. Celes did something similar, analysing the surroundings for anything that would be useful.

I wish I was better outdoors. Vincent was always the woodsman among us.

But she would make do. Alrion was counting on her.

"This could do," Tarren said. He pointed out a side track. It was rough and mostly overgrown. But it was narrow with thick tree density either side.

"Let's try it." Celes followed closely behind. It felt closed in as they navigated down the track. Which was a good thing for what they needed. Although it gave her no comfort in the moment. The horse seemed uncomfortable as well. The track ended at a small clearing with a giant rock at the end.

"It's a dead end. At least we can't get attacked from behind," Celes said. She dismounted and tied up the horse.

"And there's a little extra room here, but not too much. We could avoid being overwhelmed with any luck." Tarren paced around the area, staring out into the surroundings. He removed his cloak and draped it over the horse.

Celes did an inventory of what she had on her. Two smoke vials, one poison and a vial of exploding powder. Not too bad.

"You any good at rigging traps?" Celes said.

"I know a little, from another time. Let me take a look," Tarren said. He set off down the track once more. He returned a bit later.

"Sorry, there's not enough to work with. I only have a dagger. We just need to wait."

"That's fine, it was worth a shot." Celes paced around the area. What would Vincent do? He'd probably find a way to rig some sort of log trap. But that was only a diversion really. It wouldn't take out any of the enemy.

"Now we wait," Celes said. She hated this part. But there was nothing else she could do. Tarren sat in the middle of the clearing, deep in concentration.

Hopefully he can give us some sort of warning.

Tarren stood quickly. He started to walk forward.

"What's going on?" Celes said. Tarren was unresponsive.

"Hey! Tarren!" Celes shouted. He kept walking. She ran over and slapped him hard on the face. He shook his head and turned to look at her. The expression on his face was strange. Almost inhuman. Like he wasn't present.

"Are they here? What are you doing?" Celes said. Tarren's eyes flickered and he seemed to see her once more.

"I was too deep, trying to find them. They were inside my mind. There's Trackers here. Probably more too. Thank you for shocking me back here. We have work to do." Tarren crouched down, looking down the track. Celes heard something approaching.

"Blighters," Tarren said without emotion. As the first two came through the track, they changed from single file to side by side as they reached the clearing. Tarren sped forward at incredible speed, taking out both Blighters with his dagger in a blur. They fell and he returned to Celes.

"They're just testing us and wasting time. Stay on guard." Tarren went back to a crouch and Celes nodded. She readied herself and thought about when to use her tools.

"Don't overanalyse, you'll know," she told herself. There was more rustling ahead and she noticed what looked like more Blighters. Many more.

"More time wasting," Tarren growled. As before he dashed in, taking down the Blighters quickly. He paused to wait for the next two to come through. But they parted and a blur of black sped between them. With a loud ringing the attack was parried by Tarren, but he suffered another strike on his leg. He retreated quickly.

Celes saw the attacker now. It was another Tracker. He seemed taller than Tarren, and his skin was completely black. She wasn't sure if it was more tattoos or some other effect.

"They're crafty, I'll give them that," Celes said. Tarren nodded but kept his attention on the other Tracker. The Tracker stepped back and four more Blighters ran into the clearing.

"They're yours," Tarren said. Celes didn't waste any time, she ran over to the closest one. She feigned an attack then struck out at the one next to it. The Blighter dropped quickly, letting out a cry as it did. The other three converged on Celes. She retreated a step, then kicked her leg out. Thud, thud, thud she connected hard with a few legs. Two Blighters went down, not seeing the attack. The third dived at Celes. She fell back throwing a dagger as she fell. The Blighter landed on her, twitched then became still. Her dagger had pierced its eye.

A bit of luck to start.

Celes pulled out the dagger and shoved the Blighter off. The other two were circling around, trying to flank her. Sparing a second, she glanced over at Tarren. He had two Trackers attacking him from different angles. He was in trouble.

They don't even care about me. It's about him.

Celes knew that she had to end this quickly so she could help him. She threw a smoke vial. It shattered and a large plume rose instantly. The smoke distracted and slowed the Blighters. She waited a moment for the smoke to spread, then went after one Blighter. Before it could realise she had snuck behind it. A quick strike to the neck and it went down.

The other Blighter was still noisy, and Celes had a good idea of where it was. She ran over and tried to be quiet. It worked well enough, that the Blighter wasn't aware of her presence until too late. It shouted something, but she launched herself at it with her knees, knocking the Blighter down then finishing it on the ground.

Panting, Celes stood and surveyed the scene. The smoke was starting to clear. Tarren seemed to be on his knees. Without thinking Celes threw the vial with the exploding powder. It shattered between the two Trackers, knocking them over. The sound of the explosion was almost deafening. But Celes didn't waste any time. She rushed to the nearest Tracker and aimed for its chest. Just as she landed on it, the Tracker grabbed her hands. It was preventing the knife from piercing its chest.

It's too strong.

The Tracker gave her an evil smile and started to overpower her. Suddenly it stopped all resistance and the dagger plunged into its chest. Celes looked up and saw that Tarren was there, holding the Tracker's head in his hands.

"Nice save," Celes said. Tarren didn't even acknowledge her, he was turning to view another threat. He fell to the ground, clutching his chest. Celes stood quickly and assessed. The other Tracker had taken the opportunity to stab Tarren.

This is our last chance.

Celes could see that the Tracker thought it had won. It looked to be mocking Tarren, as he struggled to remove the dagger. She crept up, trying to remain unseen. The Tracker spun quickly as she was upon it. But she had expected that. And unlike before she didn't go for the chest. She drove her dagger through its foot. The Tracker screamed out in pain. Celes kicked it down while it was distracted. Before it could stand Tarren was on it. He had removed the dagger and forced it into the Tracker's chest. It groaned, then went limp. Tarren staggered off. Celes ran after him.

"Are there more?" she said.

"No, that was it. More than you bargained for, right?"

"Yes. But we survived." Celes checked herself but had no injuries. Tarren looked to be in worse shape.

"You're still with me. You look pretty tough, we can work through this," she said. Tarren coughed and slumped to the floor. He was clutching his chest.

"Not. Good," he said, then coughed more. Celes grabbed her dagger and cut off a section of his cloak. She knelt and applied pressure to his chest wound.

"It's no use. It was deep enough. They know what they're doing."

"I've seen normal people survive worse. Don't be a baby," Celes said. She looked around for anything else she could use.

"You're good. I almost believe you. The problem is, that even if this doesn't kill me outright, I can't walk. I'm too weak and my leg is also injured." Tarren touched his leg with his hand and winced.

"We have the horse, it's fine," Celes said. She looked over and the horse was gone.

"What?" she said, confused.

"They're crafty. Always have a strategy. Even though they perished here, they achieved their objective. I'm as good as dead and you're crippled. You can never catch up now." Tarren's eyes closed.

"Hey, open those eyes. You can't die on me now. How am I going to keep tracking them?" Celes said. Tarren let off a raspy chuckle.

"I'm busy helping you. I need to concentrate." Tarren remained still. Celes kept pressure on the wound with her elbow and cut another long strip of cloak. She then tied it around his waist, keeping the cloth pressed hard against the wound.

"And now the leg," she said. It wasn't a deep cut, but it was right across the calf muscle. And it also went straight through the middle of his tattoos.

"I'll do what I can here," she muttered. Working quickly, she bound the wound as well as possible, to keep it together and limit the blood loss. Tarren moaned and tried to sit up.

"I feel a little under the weather," he said. He smiled. Celes knew that something was wrong.

"You're smiling. What's happening?"

"I have helped you. They're at, or near, a town called Highroad. You need to get there."

"Thank you. But I would prefer a guide."

"I'm sorry Celes, but your son Alrion is infected. There's no doubt." Tarren looked genuinely upset.

"He's got good help, and I'm sure he's got a plan. I just need your help to get there faster."

"It's no use. I don't have the energy to move. Or a way to get help. So, I'm going out my own way. I sent them a message."

"What do you mean?"

"I broadcast something that your son will definitely get. I told him that you are coming. The rest is up to you now." Tarren sighed and tried to lie down. Celes dragged him across the ground so that he could lean against the giant rock. He seemed more comfortable.

"That's better."

"You seem different. Are you really dying?" Celes felt terrible. She had convinced this tortured soul to help her, and now he was losing his life and his chance at a better one.

"Yes. It's very freeing. I don't have to worry anymore. I should have done this a long time ago."

"Done what?"

"Helped someone. That's my only regret. That I let my shame prevent me from being true to myself. But you have given me an opportunity to play a part. A part in creating the cure for the Blight. Your son will succeed."

"Thank you for saying that."

"I'm not just saying that. I have seen his mind. He struggles, but he has the fire to succeed. That makes me feel better."

"What can I do for you?" Celes said. She needed to do something. To recognise what had just happened. Tarren just smiled at her.

"Go find your son. He cannot succeed alone. I'm fine here. I can finally find peace. But you must go. It is a long way to travel on foot, and I can't let this be for nothing." Tarren waved Celes off and closed his eyes.

"Thank you, Tarren. I won't forget what you've done." Celes draped the cloak over him and turned to leave.

A noble spirit can survive within a cursed shell. There is hope for us all. Even you, my son. The infection is not the end. I'm coming Alrion, just keep fighting, she thought. She had a destination, and a path to follow. Nothing would keep her from her son.

16

THE HOUSE OF HEALING

Alrion pulled a chair over so he could sit near Alyx. She seemed peaceful but was starting to stir.

"She is doing well," Beatrix said.

"Good. We're going to be staying here with her until she can be safely moved," Alrion said. He gave Lara and his father a challenging look but they said nothing. He felt reassured by that and looked back at Alyx.

Another casualty of my quest.

Another reason he had to succeed. To make all this worthwhile. Alyx opened her eyes and looked around.

"I'm still here," she said.

"Yes, you are. We are too," Alrion said.

"How long has it been?"

"Not that long. It's only just after midday."

"I see. How long do I need to stay here?" Alyx said to Beatrix.

"It depends. It might be a few days, given your previous injuries and then the Darkroot. I certainly wouldn't encourage any strenuous activity then either."

"Days?" Lara blurted out. She seemed shocked.

"I hope you understand the seriousness of her injuries," Beatrix said.

"But we don't have days," Lara said. She looked over at Vincent and he shrugged.

"It's hard to say. This assassin and the Shade Wizard both came alone. It could be that Wraith and whomever he is with are still a way behind," he said.

"That's not an assassin. It's that Tracker, and he tried his hand at poisoning.

Look at what we think he has done so far: tracked me, scattered our horses, escaped the battle, tracked us again, and poisoned Alyx," Alrion said.

"Let's assume that's correct. He's a special type of Tainted. Are you saying that's more reason for him to be working alone and in advance of other Tainted?" Lara said.

"Yes. It seems like a specialised set of skills, right? They wouldn't be able to keep up. Nor would he want them to if he needed to travel without being spotted," Alrion said.

"That does seem plausible. There's a lot of evidence to suggest a new type of Tainted. I've never heard of that before though," Vincent said.

"We never saw Shade Wizards before either. Now we've seen two!" Alrion said. He stood from the chair and paced around the room.

"Who is making these creatures?" Alyx said. Alrion stopped pacing and looked at her.

"That's the right question. Who could do that? Wraith can't do that, surely?" he said.

"I have no idea. This is way out of my experience," Lara said.

"You know, it could be one of those Generals of the Blight," Vincent said. He looked thoughtful. He walked over and sat on the far edge of Alyx's couch.

"When I encountered Rindale, many years ago, he did something unusual. He made this black tar come from his finger. And he said that he could control how the infection reacted to me. That's why he had me captured. He was able to control my conversion to Tainted," Vincent said.

"Didn't you say he was cleansed by your father's spell?" Alyx said.

"He had to have been. Maybe he's still around, maybe not. But if he could do that, maybe the others have special abilities too," Vincent said.

"What did the Skull King do that was special?" Lara said.

"He did seem to have particularly good control of Blighters and Tainted. But I think it was his extreme strength and resistance to damage. He was practically indestructible," Alyx said.

"How'd you kill him?" Lara said.

"With my family's sword. It was special," Alyx said. She stopped talking and offered no further details. After a pause, Vincent continued.

"Let's assume then that there's someone out there who can create new types of Tainted, and it's not Wraith. Maybe that same person is working with Wraith. Another Shade Wizard attacked us recently. Maybe Wraith needs to be involved though," he said.

"Which is why he can't catch up as easily? He's trying to create more like him at the same time?" Alrion said.

"It's just a theory," Vincent said. He stood and walked around the room.

"I must admit, this is a strange conversation to be witnessing," Beatrix said. Alrion felt embarrassed, he had forgotten that she was even there.

"I'm sorry, we were a bit carried away there. Given all your help, I feel like I should at least explain what we're doing. Especially since we may be placing you in danger too. Alyx, you can listen in, and hopefully you can fill in any gaps," Alrion said. Beatrix brought another chair in and joined them. Alrion looked around to ensure everyone was ready, and started from the beginning.

"That's quite a story. Thank you for sharing it with me," Beatrix said.

"Thank you for saving Alyx," Alrion said.

"Thank me when she's walking again. Although I suspect it won't be that long. There are still things that I cannot tell you, but I will say this. I don't think the Mystics can help you, not the way you think. But that should not prevent you from seeking them out."

"That's interesting," Alrion said. He stood and stretched his legs. It wasn't something that he wanted to hear. He was relying on the Mystics to cure him and Alyx. But at the same time Beatrix had not said the Mystics couldn't help him.

"Can you tell us about them?" Lara said.

"No, I cannot. I just know they exist."

"Still sounds like more stories," Alyx said.

"Stories that will save you," Alrion said.

"I don't think I have that much time. Neither do you. Be honest, Beatrix, how long until I could walk out of here and be well enough to ride a horse," Alyx said. Beatrix looked away, a concerned look on her face. She turned back to face Alyx.

"At least another day, if not more. I need to monitor your progress to give you more certainty. But definitely no sooner than that. You need time," she said. Beatrix had an apologetic look on her face.

"That's too long. Even if Wraith is delayed, and he's sending attackers ahead to slow us down, he can't be that far behind. We will be swamped. And we must be days away from the Mystics. It doesn't work," Alyx said.

"What are you suggesting?" Alrion said. He didn't like where this was going.

"I should stay here. Rest up, and slow them down when they arrive. You can go ahead, and get to the Mystics safely. It can be my final service to you." Alyx stared at Alrion. She looked a mixture of defiant but resigned to her fate. Alrion shook his head.

"I don't accept that. Not after everything we have done to get here."

"We've already been delayed getting to this point. Another day or two has to be too dangerous," Lara said. She sounded exasperated. Alrion looked to Vincent.

"We seem to be getting stuck on this again and again. Is there a point at which you would leave her behind?" he said to his son quietly. Alrion thought about it.

"No."

"You would risk everything we have done?" Vincent said.

"Yes. If I can't save her, why should I save myself?" Alrion said. He hated having to justify his actions over and over. He knew they weren't being callous, but he couldn't accept leaving her behind. He had failed Falric already. He wouldn't fail Alyx.

"We can't change your mind?" Lara said. She didn't look angry, just sad. Alrion didn't understand why.

"No, you can't. I admit, I'm a burden right now. I can't help you much with anything. Especially with these new types of attackers. But I've taken on this quest at the cost of everything else. And I have to feel like I am comfortable with every decision on the way. And I won't abandon anyone to save myself," he said. Alrion looked around at them, and waited for a response. He finally rested his gaze on Alyx. She noticed him looking at her.

"I won't bring it up again. Beatrix, how can we accelerate my healing?" Alyx said. The Healer grabbed a lock of hair and twirled it as she thought.

"I could make you a sleeping potion. That may make the difference. Your body can just focus on healing."

"Are there any dangers with that?" Alrion said.

"None, providing I get the dose right. I'll go work on it now," Beatrix said. She left the room immediately.

"So, what do we do now?" Lara said.

"We need to prepare our defences. And no more staying at the inn," Vincent said.

"Good point. We have to assume they know where we are. If that assassin was a Tracker and found us, it makes sense that he reported back with the location."

"We just don't know how far behind they are, and what's coming," Lara said.

"Is there a way we can reverse track them? Since they can track us?" Alyx said.

"That's a great idea," Lara said. She looked at Alrion for confirmation.

"Well, we aren't as concerned about hiding our location. Maybe there's a chance I can do something. From everything they have said, it sounds like the method of communication they use works both ways. But it is probably harder to broadcast than it is to receive," Alrion said. He rubbed his chin thoughtfully and pondered it further. He hadn't really considered trying to use the Blight communication to his advantage.

Wraith had been a big proponent of it, even when he was still Branthor. There was no reason Alrion couldn't try something. He sat down and concentrated. He let his mind go clear, and tried to amplify the various noises that he was so used to dampening. Slowly but surely, he could hear more come through. It seemed too garbled though.

Alrion strained harder, trying to accept and navigate through all the possible sources of communication. He remembered what he had stumbled upon before and decided to use it as focus. The word wizard.

It took a few minutes of concentration, but slowly he started to notice something. The noise started to drift away. Like it was being blocked. And he was soon listening to nothing at all.

What's going on?

He had done something, that much was clear. But he didn't know why focusing on the word wizard would have that effect. Either way, if he could keep up this type of concentration in an ongoing fashion, at least it would give him peace and quiet.

That would be worth it, he thought. And it would be a good way to practice exercising his Will. He had ignored it since his time at the temple, and that was probably a poor choice. He had so few tools at his disposal right now, but potentially Will was the strongest and least compromised.

I'll continue this approach no matter if there's results or not, he thought. Suddenly out of the silence he heard something.

Wizard. Location. Tonight.

Alrion was stunned. He regained his composure and focus and kept listening.

Four. Trackers. Party. Approved.

Alrion kept listening, trying to find out more. But there was nothing else. Before he broke the news to his companions, he tested ways to keep alert. He found that he could at a less intense level keep that kind of filter open in his mind. He might not get all, but he would get some much-deserved silence and hopefully catch other messages concerning him.

Alrion opened his eyes and looked around. Alyx was sound asleep. Lara and his father were watching him with curiosity.

"What's going on?" Lara said.

"I have news. I found a way to listen in on their communication. And it's as you suspected."

"What?" Lara said.

"There's a team of four Trackers coming tonight. We need to prepare," Alrion said. Lara looked shocked, and his father was similarly surprised. Alrion felt some of his old confidence coming back.

I've found a way to contribute again, he thought with great relief. Now he just had to figure out how to help in the coming attack.

17

A DIFFICULT CONVERSATION

L ara regained her composure quickly.

"That's disturbing to hear, but great that you found that out. We can prepare," she said.

"Alyx managed to take out one by herself, so we have a chance," Vincent said.

"Especially since we know they're coming. Do we know how the other one managed to get in?" Alrion said.

"Lara would be best placed to determine that. Why don't you two look into that, I'll find Beatrix and fill her in," Vincent said. Lara watched Vincent walk off and beckoned to Alrion.

"Let's start here. This is where Alyx was lying. The attacker approached here, and tried to poison her."

"And mostly succeeded. Then they had a confrontation," Alrion said, pointing to the carpet next to the couch.

"Exactly. So, what are the most direct ways into this room?" Lara said. She looked around. They weren't far from the front door, but she didn't expect that to be the place of entry. Someone would have likely heard that. But, it was only Alyx and Beatrix. It was worth investigating.

"Let's start with the front door and see if we can eliminate that as an entry point," Lara said. Alrion nodded and followed along. They walked swiftly to the front door and examined it.

"Looks solid," Alrion said, feeling the wood with his hands. Lara inspected the lock. It was a standard lock, and didn't look to have obvious signs of tampering.

"It's not a complex lock, but it looks normal. We will have to ask your father if he found any lock picking tools on the other attacker," Lara said.

"Good idea. You don't think there's another way to open this door quietly without damaging it?"

"Not unless they can turn their fingers into keys," Lara said with a laugh. Alrion gave her a confused look.

"I'm not suggesting that," she said.

"I don't know what is and isn't possible these days," he said. Lara could understand the sentiment.

"True, but let's assume not for the time being." Lara walked back the way they had come, and pointed out the staircase.

"The staircase is not far from the room where Alyx is staying. It could be an option."

"Doesn't Beatrix stay upstairs?" Alrion said.

"I believe so. That would only make sense if the Tracker was so focused on Alyx that it snuck past her and ignored her. It seems less likely, but not impossible." Lara personally wouldn't have risked that sort of approach herself. Not if there was a more direct way.

"Isn't that assuming the Tracker knew exactly where she was?" Alrion said.

"Yes, that's a fair point. But let's exhaust this floor first," Lara said. She pointed down the corridor and Alrion followed.

"There's two rooms here. Let's try the one on the left first," she said. Lara opened the door and stepped inside. It had a large window and was filled with shelves full of different jars. Some were full of coloured liquids, others were empty.

"There isn't much space here," Alrion said. He pointed at the large quantity of tables and boxes littered throughout the space.

"And the potential for a lot of noise if coming through here in the dark. But there is a window," Lara said. She carefully navigated the mess and stood under the window. It could be pushed open and there was no lock.

"It would be tricky, but you could open this from the outside," she said.

"So that's an option we need to consider," Alrion said.

"Yes. Let's try that other room," Lara said. She weaved back through the many tables and boxes and squeezed past Alrion to reach the corridor.

"Let's see what's in here," Lara said. She opened the door and stepped inside. The room was almost empty. She saw a small mattress in the corner and another large window. The only other thing of note was a cheap rickety table pushed against a wall.

"This has potential," Alrion said.

"I agree. Especially if this window is the same style," Lara said. She walked over and inspected it.

"Yes, it's the same. My guess is that the Tracker came in through this room."

"We'll have to ask Beatrix if this window was left open," Alrion said.

"And get her opinion on upstairs too. For now, let's return to Alyx." Lara led the way again. She found Vincent and Beatrix talking near Alyx's sleeping form.

"Here they are. I just briefed Beatrix on the attack," Vincent said.

"We think the spare room with the bed was the most likely place of entry for the Tracker that poisoned Alyx. Was the window open?" Lara said.

"Yes, it was. I couldn't remember if I had left it open or not. The room is rarely used so I often air it out. Sorry, I should have mentioned that," Beatrix said.

"That's fine, don't worry. This is your home, not a fortress. We are incredibly grateful for you extending your hospitality this far," Vincent said.

"On that point, I don't think we should reinforce the house. In fact, we should do the opposite. We should make the entries we wish to defend look inviting. And at the same time reduce the chances of collateral damage," Lara said. Vincent looked like he was thinking it over. She was pretty sure he would agree.

"Don't concern yourselves about the house. It's just a building. Your lives are more important, and we need to stop these creatures," Beatrix said.

"No, Lara is right. If we do anything to give them pause they will know we are prepared and may change their plans. This is the best course. We just need to confer on how best to proceed," Vincent said.

"What about Alyx? Should she stay asleep?" Alrion said. Lara hadn't thought of that, but it was a good point. They had to balance the rate of Alyx's recovery against what she could contribute to the fight.

"It may be too risky to let her sleep through, even though she's not going to be expected to participate," Lara said. She walked over and sat on the end of Alyx's couch. She looked across the room, seeing what entry points she could observe.

"Agreed. She needs to be alert so she can at least protect herself," Alrion said.

"Then let's wake her up next time, that makes sense. Beatrix?" Vincent said, looking at the Healer.

"In an hour or two the effects of the drink should be wearing off, that's the best time."

"Let's reconvene then," Vincent said.

"I'll sit in the spare room and see if I can figure out anything more about the attack," Alrion said. Lara watched him go and approached Vincent.

"What do you intend to do?" she said.

"Nothing too fancy, just set up a good defensive position. Although, I was thinking maybe we can get something for Alyx. Perhaps a crossbow. That could make the difference," he said.

"Great idea. She is supposed to be a weapon master after all. I'll focus on downstairs and what we can do to alter the conditions," Lara said. Vincent nodded and walked over to the front door. Lara left Alrion alone and busied herself making preparations for an attack.

Beatrix ran down the stairs sooner than Lara expected.

"What's wrong?" Lara said.

"There's a presence here already. I can sense it. In the spare room."

"Alrion is there." Lara felt her stomach lurch then ran towards the spare room. Beatrix was close behind. The door was closed, so Lara shoved it open and dashed inside. The room was the same, and the window was still closed. Alrion sat cross-legged in the middle of the room. He looked up in a daze.

"I don't get it," Lara said, looking at Beatrix.

"It's you. What are you doing?" Beatrix said to Alrion. She sounded horrified.

"I'm tuning into the Blight communication to try and get more details on their attack," Alrion said.

"Stop that immediately. It's way too dangerous!" Beatrix shouted. Alrion looked over at Lara, his face a picture of confusion.

"Do as she says. She ran all the way down here because she sensed Tainted. And it was you. Don't you think that's kind of scary?" Lara said. Alrion closed his eyes and the tension disappeared from his body. He slumped down.

"Seriously? My one way of helping out and now that's outlawed too?"

"You are hastening your infection. I don't know how to describe it, but it's like you're inviting it in. It's so much worse than before!" Beatrix said. She sounded distraught.

"Maybe we should just get it over with then," Alrion said. Lara ran over and slapped him as hard as she could.

"I think you have this covered, I'm going back upstairs," Beatrix said. She left quickly and once she was gone Lara closed the door.

"What were you thinking? Have you lost your mind?" Lara said.

"It was just a comment. I'm not serious, I'm just so sick of being afflicted and powerless," Alrion said. He was nursing his cheek with his hand.

"It's not just a comment. Saying that, and seeing what Beatrix said; it's clear that this is affecting you deeply. You've already admitted to bursts of anger, some coordination issues, and now this negative defeatist thinking. This is not you!" Lara said. The exasperation was hard to contain. Because he was amongst it he was not seeing it the same way as her.

"I'll think about it. At the least I'll stop occupying that headspace. It's probably true that immersing myself in their communication and thinking, is affecting my own thinking."

"It's doing more than that. You need to buy us time, not squander it. Especially since you insist on staying here with Alyx. You owe it to us all." Lara didn't know what to do with him. She wanted to give him sympathy and a comforting hug, but it didn't feel like what he needed.

"Look, it's hard. I'm just travelling along, hoping that we find these Mystics who can help. And I'm being hounded every step of the way, with new and difficult obstacles. And Wraith himself is on his way. I don't think I'm strong enough to escape again." Alrion's voice became much quieter. Lara knew she was finally getting to the heart of it.

"He defeated you at the peak of your power. And you are scared of facing him again when you don't even have that?"

"Of course. Wouldn't you be?"

"You're not getting another chance to face him alone. It will be different this time. You'll be different by the time you need to face him again."

"If you insist," Alrion said, grinning.

"I do insist. Now let's go see how Alyx is going," Lara said. She held out her hand and Alrion grasped it firmly, standing with her help. He staggered a bit, and she caught him in her arms.

"I knew you were falling for me," she said playfully. He turned a bit red and smiled at her. She chuckled and released him, walking out of the room. Alrion followed close behind.

They found Alyx awake with Beatrix offering another drink of some kind.

"Why am I up?" Alyx said.

"We've another attack coming tonight," Lara said, Alyx finished drinking and nodded.

"At least we know this time. What's coming?"

"Four Trackers. The same as the one that tried to poison you," Alrion said. He walked over and stood next to the couch.

"Sounds fun. I'd like to give them a piece of my mind. I am not impressed with the poisoning," Alyx said. She looked over her body, a perplexed look on her face.

"Any change?" Beatrix said.

"No, not really. Which I suppose is to be expected. But I want to be more active in this fight."

"I thought you might say that. I've a present for you," Vincent said from afar. He stepped into the room and held up a simple but effective crossbow.

"Hand it over," Alyx said. It was like a new energy had entered her. She sat up straight and started checking the weapon over immediately. The winding mechanism, the bolt placement, and strength of the structure.

"This will do fine. I hope there's something I can fire too," she said.

Vincent handed her a leather pouch full of simple bolts.

"You know how to use that right?" Alrion said.

"Of course. I told you I was a weapon master remember. It's not just an empty title. I trained in and mastered all weapons."

"Why not just focus on the sword?" Lara said.

"I had my reasons for needing a variety of weapons. But that aside, mastery of a weapon also helps understand how to counter it."

"Would you like to coat the bolts with something?" Beatrix said.

"No, it's probably better not to. Just in case there's friendly fire."

"Friendly fire? I thought you said you knew how to use that," Alrion said. He had taken a step back.

"Anything can happen in a fight, never forget that. Don't worry I'll be careful."

"Maybe I can defend a different room," Alrion said with a chuckle. Lara shook her head. At least he was cracking jokes. He seemed a bit more like his old self. But the more she watched him; she could see something under the surface. He was definitely dealing with a lot. Alyx seemed to be handling the infection better, although she was not as far along.

"Time to finish our preparations, eat, and wait for dark," Vincent said. There were no arguments and Vincent walked them through the initial plan.

All was quiet. Lara peered out the window again. The moon was high in the sky, and lit the surroundings well.

Maybe they won't come.

She had taken up a position in the spare room that they thought the first Tracker had come through. When she wasn't peering out the window, she was hidden from view. Nobody entering would spot her.

With any luck I can take one down for free, she thought. But her nerves were starting to fray. She had been waiting for what seemed like hours. On edge. As her mind started wandering again she heard a light patter on the ground. She looked around and saw nothing. She had purposefully left the door ajar and almost closed. It started to open slowly by itself.

No way. It's invisible?

There was no time to second-guess. She threw a dagger at what she thought was where the back of the Tracker had to be. It embedded into nothing, and she heard a cry of pain. The dagger was quickly dislodged, but not without some blood spilling.

Got you!

But she needed to alert the others.

"They're here. At least one is invisible!" Lara shouted. There was no more benefit to be gained by pretending they were caught unaware. If all four were invisible it would be hard to contend with them. Lara dashed out of the room trying to track the one she had injured.

Lara saw a few drops of blood in the corridor near the other spare room. She crept over and fully opened the door. The moonlight spilled into the middle of the room, illuminating one of the few places to stand in the mess. She could see the outline of the figure.

It's not perfect. Light still shows it.

The Tracker didn't seem to be fully aware of her presence, or it was preoccupied with the wound.

No time for games. Just end it and move on.

Lara placed one foot in front of the other. Desperately looking for any signs that the Tracker was aware. She imagined that it was trying to patch up the wound. Once she had closed the gap Lara dropped all pretence at stealth. She loudly crossed the remaining distance. The silhouette of the Tracker changed shape, suddenly readying itself. But Lara was upon it too quickly. Before it could do much, she had her Runesteel dagger plunged into what she thought was its chest. They both fell, Lara looking for signs of life.

Whatever effect had been hiding the Tracker was slowly reverting. It looked like a normal man. She had indeed pierced its chest, but it wasn't dead. Lara debated what to do next, but her thoughts were interrupted. She heard a scream from the other room. Lara retrieved her dagger and ran to investigate.

18

FURTHER NORTH

Alrion noticed the shape too late. As he drew his sword he felt strong hands around his throat.

I don't believe it, was his only thought. He was too surprised to think properly, and his air was steadily running out. The strength started to drain from him.

"Turn around!" Alyx shouted. Alrion understood what she meant. He dropped his sword and threw his weight around in a desperate attempt to turn. He wasn't sure it was enough but heard the crossbow bolt fire with a distinctive sound and thud into whoever was holding him. The grip relaxed and Alrion shoved it off. As he peered into the darkness to determine what it was he felt a stabbing pain in his leg.

"Argh!" Alrion screamed, the pain taking him by surprise. He scrambled around for his sword and plunged it into the shape. It stopped moving and he stumbled back trying to see how he had been wounded. He heard Lara shouting out.

"Too late for that warning," he muttered to himself. If she had found one, that meant there were two more lurking somewhere.

"Lights!" Alyx shouted. Vincent handed her his single torch.

"I'll get more," he said, and ran upstairs.

"Stay close to me, we've got a chance if we can spot them," Alyx said. Alrion shuffled closer. He could still feel something in this leg but didn't want to lose focus investigating it too much.

"Here take this," Alyx said, handing Alrion the torch. "I need my hands free. You can still swing with your other arm."

"Sure," Alrion said. He felt comforted by the heat of the torch, and swung it slowly back and forth to illuminate the room. The small hearth in the corner had long since burnt out, and only some smouldering coals remained.

We weren't prepared for this.

There had been ample light available to deal with normal attackers. They had even hoped the dimness would work in their favour, since they were ready and waiting. But it had done the opposite. Alrion spotted a blur of something out of the corner of his eye and lashed out with the sword. Nothing connected. He slowly approached the area, swinging the torch rhythmically.

I just need something to work with.

The pain ran up his leg but he ignored it. He was more concerned about not getting choked again.

"Behind you!" Alyx shouted. Alrion whirled as quickly as he could, leading with his sword and following up with the torch. He hit nothing, but did notice some movement as a shape tried to slip past him. He frantically lashed out with the torch, hoping to catch something. The flames showed the figure briefly, but weren't enough to set it alight.

Alrion tried to reorient himself so he could attack it properly, but it was too fast. A sudden noise startled him and he heard a crossbow bolt impacting the Tracker. It fell to the ground and Alrion rushed in with his torch. He watched carefully, using his torch to see better.

"It's cloaked in shadow," Alrion said. He couldn't believe it. The Tracker struggled, and looked to be reaching for something. Alrion was about to finish it with his sword but hesitated.

Maybe we can learn something.

He watched the Tracker to make sure it couldn't move significantly, then turned his attention to the stairs. His father was running down with two torches.

"There!" Alrion shouted, pointing with his torch. There was another shape creeping by the stairs, looking to pounce on Vincent. As Vincent whirled to face the threat, Lara was already there. She stabbed the Tracker with her dagger then quickly knelt to finish the job. Alrion rushed over, as fast as his leg would allow.

"Is it over?" he said.

"Lara?" Vincent said.

"That should be all four. Let's check," she said. They returned to Alyx. The one that had stabbed Alrion was still motionless on the ground.

"And one more over here," Alrion said. But as he approached something looked wrong.

"Hang on, I'm sure it was here," Alrion said. He waved the torch over, inspecting the ground. There was a crossbow bolt on the ground, it's end soaked in blood. Alrion picked up the bolt and turned it around in his hand.

"It still lives," Lara said. Alyx cursed.

"You should have finished it," Alyx said.

"I thought we could get information. It was originally a person, right?" Alrion said. He thought his instincts were right, but was starting to doubt himself.

"It was worth a try. And yes, nothing we have learned suggests that they still aren't infecting people to create these new variants of Tainted. Don't worry about it," Vincent said.

"You're injured!" Lara said, looking at Alrion.

"Yes, one of them stabbed me in the leg." Alrion sat down on a chair and properly examined his leg. The dagger was halfway up his calf muscle, and was well embedded.

"You were walking around with this?" Lara said.

"I didn't see any other choice," Alrion said.

"Oh no, I'm just impressed."

"If we're sure it's safe, I'll go fetch Beatrix. We need to treat that wound immediately. Anything else she needs to know about?" Vincent said.

"Not me," Lara said.

"Nothing here, well nothing new," Alyx said. Vincent nodded and disappeared up the stairs again.

"That crossbow sure came in handy," Alrion said.

"I knew it would. I wish we had known about their strange invisibility beforehand. I never noticed on the original attacker," Alyx said.

"Maybe because you were asleep he never activated it. It's quite unusual, it was like they were cloaked in shadows," Alrion said.

"That sounds appropriate when you think about it. But I'm amazed that it's even possible," Lara said. She brought over another chair and sat next to Alrion. When Vincent and Beatrix arrived, she moved the chair back to make space.

"Good, you're seated. This is going to hurt," Beatrix said. She had a bag of supplies, which she placed, on the floor near Alrion. She knelt and inspected the wound.

"Drink this," Beatrix said. She handed Alrion a small flask and he took a swig. It burned his throat and he started coughing.

"What is that?"

"My own concoction. It'll take the edge off."

"The edge off what?" Alrion said. He received an answer immediately. A wrenching pain went through his leg, and for an instant he couldn't handle it. The pain subsided and he opened his eyes, not realising he had closed them. Beatrix had removed the dagger and placed a cloth over the wound. She handed the dagger to Vincent who looked it over.

"Look at this," he said to Lara. She peered over his shoulder and examined it.

"Is there something on the tip? Is it poisoned?" she said.

"I don't think so. I've seen something like it before."

"What is it?"

"If I'm right, it's a liquid form of the Blight," Vincent said. That got Alrion's attention.

"What? You can get infected from a dagger?" Alrion couldn't believe it.

"I believe so. I've only seen it once. That was how they infected me. I think only the generals can do it. This doesn't bode well," Vincent said. He looked worried. Alrion could understand why. Wraith was bad enough, but to have one of those generals of the Blight involved too was terrible news.

"Seems to go with the whole idea that they're making these Trackers, right?" Alrion said. Vincent nodded.

"But why would they try and infect me again?"

"It could be that they wish to speed up the process. I wonder if it's working?" Vincent said. He looked over the dagger more.

"Is there any way of telling how much was on it?" Lara said.

"I don't think so."

"I'm just about done here," Beatrix said. She set aside her ointments and wrapped the bandage around Alrion's leg a little tighter.

"How's that feel now?"

"Much better," Alrion said. It was more of a dull pain now. He didn't want to test walking on it again just yet though.

"They've really worked you two over. Injured and infected," Lara said.

"It must be because we're the biggest threat," Alrion said, trying to keep things light. He got a small smile out of Lara and his father. Alyx didn't seem impressed.

"We need to rotate a sentry overnight in case they attack again," she said.

"I'll do it. You can all rest," Vincent said.

"No, its fine. Let me take a turn," Lara said. Vincent thought for a moment then responded.

"I'll wake you then. Thanks again for your help, Beatrix. And apologies for what we've done to your home."

"I wish I could say it's not your fault. But at least you're polite about it. Just make sure you deal with those bodies. This is my house!" Beatrix said.

"I'll take care of it. See you in the morning," Vincent said. Beatrix nodded and walked back upstairs.

"Everyone else get some sleep. You're fine with the spare room with the bed?" Vincent said to Lara.

"Not a problem."

"Good. Let's hope we can make a move sometime tomorrow," Vincent said. Alrion used some cushions to make himself comfortable on the floor. He wasn't sure if it was his imagination or not, but he was sure he could feel something new happening in his leg.

It's probably nothing, just sleep, he thought. Thankfully, sleep was not far away.

~

Alrion awoke to a ray of sunlight warming his face. He sat up quickly, unsure of the time. Looking around, he noticed that Alyx was still sleeping. The morning sun made the events of the previous night seem like a dream.

It really is a new day, he thought with relief. He stretched out and tested his leg. It felt a bit better but was definitely still sore. He didn't think walking would be a problem, but it might become an issue if they had a long trek ahead. Which he assumed they would.

"Maybe there are horses in town," he wondered. He rose slowly, and tested his weight on his injured leg. It stung, but wasn't too bad. He just had to take care. With measured steps he crossed the room and over to the spare room where Lara would be sleeping.

He opened the door slowly and looked inside. Lara was still asleep. He crept back without waking her.

I thought she was on watch?

Maybe something else had happened. He wandered into the spare room and peered inside. There were some signs of the night's activities, but nothing else new. He didn't want to venture upstairs, especially if Beatrix was still asleep, so he slowly returned to the living room and sat in a chair near Alyx.

She looked peaceful. Her strength was not so obvious when she slept. She almost looked normal.

What's normal these days?

It seemed like she'd had a hard life. He'd always thought of the stories of heroes, and their adventures and what their lives must have been like. He was sure that if he had heard a story like Alyx's it would have been glorified. And yes, she was an amazing fighter and incredibly skilled. She was a true survivor. But it didn't seem like that life had given her joy. And she'd had a hard time since joining them as well. He didn't like the thought of that.

We've just made her life worse, at the time that she had finally earned some rest.

There had to be a way to make that right again. He heard the front door open, so Alrion eased himself up and walked over to investigate. It was his father coming in.

"Good morning. How's the leg going?" he said.

"Could be worse. Not going to do well on a long hike though. Although I think Alyx is in the same situation. Any chance of horses here?"

"I've been looking into that this morning. There are some in town, but they won't part with them easily. I'm hoping that Beatrix can convince them."

"Why is that?"

"Healers seem to have some authority, or at least they seem to be a voice that is listened to. I suppose it's because they provide a lot of safety and assistance. These are dangerous parts. If there was no Healer in town, where would the people turn?" Vincent pointed back at the living room and they walked back there. They saw Beatrix hovering over Alyx.

"Everything alright?" Alrion said.

"She seems stable. I do wish we didn't have the adventures from last night, but at least she avoided additional injuries."

"Do you think there's any chance we can leave today?" Vincent said. He pulled up another chair and sat down. He looked weary. Alrion wondered if he had slept at all. He was starting to think that his father had never woken Lara.

"It all depends on Alyx. But you may have to. I hate to say this, but I think you're risking everyone's lives by staying here."

"That's completely fair. I think we need to risk it today. But to do that, we'll need horses," Vincent said to Beatrix.

"And they're not something anybody will part with lightly."

"Exactly. Do you think you could have a word?" Vincent said. Beatrix stopped to think.

"Yes. I know exactly who you are talking about. And he owes me a favour. But I won't badger him too much, I'll let him know it's for everyone's benefit."

"That would be a big help to us. And we'd also be out of your hair. No more late-night visitors," Vincent said with a smile.

"Yes, I'm afraid I'm not interested in any more of those. I'll need some time to prepare, and then I'll go see what I can organise for you. Some gold will help smooth things over."

"Take this," Vincent said. He withdrew a small sack and handed it to Beatrix. She didn't even bother opening it.

"That will do. I'll return soon with good news."

"I hope so. We really need it," Vincent said.

"Thank you, Beatrix," Alrion said. Beatrix acknowledged him and hurried upstairs.

"Do you really think she will succeed?" Alrion said.

"Absolutely. They're all better off with us gone. She can't get us out without horses. One way or another we will be off later today."

"Good. I don't want to put anyone else in danger," Alrion said. He had already endangered too many people, and been responsible for too much pain and suffering. He had to lead Wraith away from innocent people. He just needed enough time to find a cure so he could settle things once and for all. He was sick of being sick. Wraith was going to pay.

19

THE DIVISIVE MESSAGE

Vincent paced around the room. He didn't like waiting around when he could be preparing something. Alrion and Alyx were resting, and Lara looked as restless as he felt. But his hands were tied until Beatrix returned with news. He couldn't start until he knew what she had managed to bargain for.

She will definitely get horses. It's just how many.

He heard footsteps approach the front door and walked quickly across. Lara must have noticed and followed along.

Beatrix opened the door and stepped inside, making an effort to lock the door properly.

"Ahh, you're here," she said when she noticed Vincent.

"Just waiting for the good news," he said.

"I wasn't so sure, and I even struggled at the beginning of that conversation. But the more I described, the more he came around. The gold was not as big a lure as you may think. We're in quite a remote place here."

"I know, but it never hurts. When someone does come here to trade, it sure does help make the most of it," Vincent said.

"True. I've managed to secure three horses with saddlebags. You just need to go pick them up when you are ready to leave."

"Fantastic! That's plenty, we can figure that out. It might even make sense for Alyx to ride with someone anyway. She may not be strong enough to ride alone."

"That's a good idea," Lara said.

"I need some information on the terrain ahead. What will we be riding into?"

"The trails become thinner and harder to navigate. The weather will be increasingly cold until you reach the snow. You need to be prepared for that."

"Our destination is in the snow?" Vincent said. Beatrix paused before answering.

"My assumption is yes. We are well acquainted with the lands closer to home."

"You're still being evasive," Lara said.

"I cannot say more. Follow the paths, and then the amulet will show you the way."

"That's what the other Healer told us."

"I know. So, you will need lots of food supplies, as game to hunt, and foraging are slim pickings as you track north. Also, cold weather gear."

"Makes sense," Vincent said. He started making a mental checklist of the things he needed to procure.

"Why are they in such a remote location?" Lara said.

"You'll have to ask them," Beatrix said.

"They certainly don't like attention," Vincent said. He looked at Beatrix for any reaction and saw none.

"Well, thank you again for your assistance. Would it be unsafe to leave this afternoon?" Vincent said. Beatrix looked away, clearly concentrating on something else.

"I don't travel north that frequently. I believe there will be places to camp overnight, and you shouldn't be in the worst of the cold by then. I also believe that you can't leave any earlier. It's too risky, considering the injuries you have to contend with."

"And if we are gone by nightfall, then hopefully those following us will realise and leave you all alone," Lara said.

"That would be ideal. But don't think that I am making the recommendation based on that alone. Considering your need to move forward, the opportunities for staying somewhere overnight and the risk to the village, it's the best approach."

"I agree. Lara, are you interested in helping me prepare?" Vincent said.

"Why not? Nothing to do here now."

"Good. Let's go directly."

"You'll find a trading store at the edge of town. They should have everything you need," Beatrix said.

"Great, we will be back soon," Vincent said. He opened the front door, and held it open for Lara. After she stepped through he followed behind, hearing the door lock behind him.

"She doesn't feel safe," Lara said.

"Can you blame her?"

"No, it's quite a fair response. I don't feel safe."

"We'll be fine."

"You do seem to just take all this in your stride," Lara said. She slowed down and Vincent drew alongside her.

"I've had many interesting life experiences. Plus, my father was an exceptional wizard. It wasn't your usual upbringing."

"It sounds like Alrion had quite the opposite. Was that on purpose?"

"Definitely. I wanted him to have the routine, a home of his own. A place to return to. Even if he never feels the need later in life."

"I think you've done that. But don't you think he needed to be introduced to the world? Considering the legacy of your family?" Lara said. Vincent stopped walking. He was surprised to hear her go down this line of discussion. But she seemed to have his son's best interests at heart.

"Part of me was hoping he wouldn't need that. So instead I focused on an upbringing that would be a good foundation for whatever he wanted to do. He's learning about the world now, isn't he?" Vincent said.

"He sure is. He sure is," Lara said. Vincent let the comment go, not wishing to add more to that conversation. He sensed that Lara didn't want to talk about her past, since she never brought it up. He'd have to ask Alrion about it one time. Maybe she had opened up to him.

"I'd say that's the place over there," he said, pointing into the distance. There was a well-built stone building with a peaked wooden roof. Large double doors dominated the front porch, although there were some leather goods piled outside as well.

"I'm really curious what they have here," Lara said.

"It's a remote community. They probably have everything," Vincent said. He stepped up onto the porch, the wooden boards creaking as he put his weight down. He quickly glanced at the goods outside, and determined that they weren't for sale. They were more weathered and not saleable.

At least I hope they're not representative of what's inside.

He pushed on one of the great doors and it gave way easily, offering up some warmth from inside. Vincent entered eagerly, keen to escape the cold.

It's only going to get worse as we push further north, he thought. He waited for Lara to enter then closed the door. Looking around he saw a wide array of various goods. But what immediately drew his attention was the crackling fire at one end of the room. A withered old man sat there, reading a book in a comfortable cushioned chair.

"I think we will find what we need," Lara said. Vincent agreed. There were racks of coats and jackets, boots, and even ropes and saddles.

"Looks like you've got everything for an expedition," Vincent said as he approached the fire.

"Can't be too prepared in these conditions. Nor can you let someone go out there unprepared. That's akin to murder," the old man said without looking up. He carefully pulled a red ribbon to save his place in the book and put it down.

"Haven't seen you around these parts? Are you the visitors causing so much commotion?"

"We must be. I'm Vincent, it's a pleasure to meet you."

"Weyland. And the lovely lady is?"

"Lara. Nice to meet you. Great place you have here."

"Thank you. It has taken many years to build it up, but it has proven useful time and time again. I needed something to do when I was unable to keep exploring."

"Have you ventured far north?" Vincent said.

"Aye. It's a hard road if that's what you're thinking. Where are you going?"

"We're looking for the Mystics." Vincent carefully watched Weyland's reaction. The old man raised an eyebrow.

"People do from time to time. Some return, others do not. I gave up trying to dissuade folk a while back."

"Have you met them?" Lara said. Weyland was deep in thought.

"I believe one saved me, when I was younger and more foolish. There was no way I could have survived otherwise. I never did find where they live though. Very private and secretive bunch."

"But you know they exist?"

"Of course. You come to understand that some things exist without having to see them yourself. There's too many stories, too many coincidences and occurrences to believe otherwise."

"Thanks for the information," Lara said.

"You'll need cold weather gear. And lots of food and water. Fire-starting gear as well."

"What about this?" Lara pulled something off the wall. It was a long leather whip.

"That's a quality whip, but I wouldn't recommend it unless you were proficient with wielding one. From the way you are holding it, I would assume you are not," Weyland said.

"It's for a friend." Lara winked and Weyland nodded.

"Maybe you can recommend a full detail? Assume we have nothing. Well, we have three horses," Vincent said.

"I bet I know which three they are too," Weyland said, winking. "How many travelling?"

"Four."

"Alright, I'll write you a list but you can go pick it out. It's too cold for me away from the fire," Weyland said with a grin.

"Not a problem," Vincent said. Weyland hauled himself up and trotted over to a nearby desk. He wrote up a list of items and handed it to Vincent before taking his place back by the fire.

"Looks fine. How much?" Vincent said.

"No charge. But I have a request."

"Name it."

"I want you to bring something back. That will be payment enough."

"Something?"

"Anything."

"That we can do. I'll go assemble everything," Vincent said.

"Call out if you need help, I'll be here," Weyland said. Vincent nodded and walked off.

Within an hour, he and Lara had arranged a neat pile next to the door. They had clothing, a few tools, and some dried food.

"Next, we need the horses," Vincent said.

"Right. Lead the way," Lara said.

"We'll be back with the horses!" Vincent shouted. Weyland waved and returned to his book. Vincent opened the door, waited for Lara to leave, and followed close behind.

"Just up here," Vincent said. He pointed to a set of buildings at the end of the road. As they approached a man stepped out.

"Ho there! Here for the horses?" he said.

"Yes."

"They're ready to go. Come with me," the man said. He led them into the stables. Three horses were ready and saddled up. Two were brown and one was black. Vincent walked past, patting each one.

"You didn't waste any time," he said.

"I was informed that time was of the essence."

"Absolutely. Thank you for your help. Let's go Lara," Vincent said. He mounted the horse and looked around.

"Don't worry, here's a lead. They're used to working together," the man said. Vincent accepted the lead and nudged his horse forward. The other brown one followed closely. Lara wasn't far behind on the black horse.

Vincent took his time, navigating back to the street and taking care on the road. The horses seemed calm, which was reassuring. They would all be tested soon enough. They tied the horses up outside the store, and methodically packed as much as possible. Vincent donned his cold weather gear and stepped back to check it all.

"Looks good, you wear it well," Lara said.

"Thanks. I'm curious to know how much mobility we get with this."

"Enough. It would be harder without it if the cold gets much worse."

"Very true. Suit up and we can join the others," Vincent said. Lara threw on the extra layers, and helped Vincent pack the leftover gear. They took their time trotting down the street, not in a hurry. It was more important to build trust with the horses and not lose anything in the process.

Vincent tied up the horses outside Beatrix's house, and they knocked on the door.

"Who is it?"

"Vincent." The door opened promptly and Beatrix looked them over.

"You look ready. Come in."

"The real question is, are they ready?" Vincent said. He stepped inside and strode directly into the other room. He saw Alrion and Alyx seated together on the couch.

"Ready to ride?" Vincent said.

"Not sure really. But we can try," Alyx said.

"I should be fine," Alrion said. He reached out and touched his leg.

"Eat and prepare yourselves properly. You can leave anytime today that suits," Beatrix said.

"Especially the eat part. The food we are taking with us isn't exactly gourmet," Lara said. Alrion laughed.

"Sure, I'll stock up," he said, patting his belly.

Hours later they were on the horses and crossing the edge of town. A single path connected with the wilderness beyond. Vincent rode out front, Alrion and Alyx shared the black horse in the middle, and Lara rode the other brown horse bringing up the rear.

"Keep this formation, the path ahead looks narrow," Vincent said.

"Sure," Alrion said. Alyx was quiet.

"How's the ride for you two?"

"It's not too bad for me, just need to be careful with my leg. Alyx?" Alrion said.

"Not ideal, but it's manageable. It should get easier as we progress." Alyx reached down and pulled the whip out from the saddlebag. "What was the inspiration behind this?"

"I'm not sure, I just saw it and thought of you," Lara said.

"Lucky for you I am not just a weapon master in name. It won't be my preferred weapon, but you never know when you will need it. I think I'm fine to get started." Alyx looked back at Vincent.

"Good. I'll slowly increase the pace where possible. Everything fine back there Lara?"

"So far, so good," she said loudly and clearly, Vincent nodded and focused on the path ahead. He had chosen to ride up front to shield them from any obstacles or attacks. He wanted Lara's keen eyes watching the rear to see if they were being followed. They were approaching a rocky area, with the path seemingly carved between massive stones in places. The tight nature of the way forward made Vincent feel nervous. It was good that they could hold their own in tight quarters. However, he was concerned that they could easily be boxed in.

Just have to see how things go.

It was slow progress initially though. The path was strewn with smaller stones, which were enough to disrupt the horses. They had to pick a careful path through to not sustain any injuries.

At least this pace will help ease them into the ride, Vincent thought. He had no idea how far they had to travel, but he could tell it was a fair way. The fact that it was cold but not even close to snow was telling.

"Stop!" Lara yelled from behind. Vincent pulled up quickly and wheeled around. They hadn't left the village limits that long ago, and already there was trouble. It was too narrow to track all the way back past Alrion and Alyx, so he settled for coming closer.

"We have trouble. I spotted a Tracker skulking in the rocks. It must be the one that got away," Lara said.

"Is it still around?" Vincent said.

"No, it noticed me and took off. I think it just wanted to confirm our location."

"Not again! This is ridiculous we can't shake them," Alrion said. He was starting to get worked up. Vincent had to defuse the situation.

"Clearly they are resorting to more manual methods of tracking because you've been containing your anger. Well done," he said. Alrion looked up, a puzzled look on his face. Vincent looked over at Lara and caught her attention. He motioned towards Alrion with his head slightly.

"That's a good point. And I have to admit that there's only one path north. It wasn't going to be difficult to pick up the trail, as annoying as that is," Lara said.

"But that Tracker is only alive because of me. I didn't finish it off," Alrion said.

"Nothing wrong with that, son. This doesn't change our plan or our approach. We just need to be mindful that we will be followed every step of the way," Vincent said. He had hoped they were going to get a break, but it just wasn't going to happen. Suddenly Alrion clutched his head. Alyx did the same.

"What's happening?" Vincent said. He jumped off his horse and ran over. Alrion and Alyx were slumped over in the saddle. Vincent supported them both with his hands to make sure they didn't fall off.

What is this?

He had a terrible feeling. Alrion sat up again quickly, almost toppling off the horse. Vincent saw Alyx stirring and managed to switch focus to stabilising her.

"You're back with us?" Vincent said. He noticed Lara had joined him. She looked very concerned.

"I don't understand what happened exactly, but we just received a very clear message. It must have been from a Tracker." Alrion looked right at Vincent.

"What was it?"

"Celes is coming," Alrion said. Vincent was momentarily stunned. Then he started laughing.

"There's no stopping your mother is there?" he said.

"I guess not. I wonder where she is? And how did she even send that message?"

"If you think a Tracker sent it, there's your answer," Lara said.

"We can't rely on that. I need to go back and leave a message," Vincent said.

"We will wait for you," Alrion said.

"No, keep pushing. It's too risky otherwise. I'll catch up, and hopefully your mother will be not too far behind."

"I agree. Don't worry Alrion I still have this," Alyx said. She patted the crossbow hanging off the side of the saddle. "And at a pinch this lovely new gift you gave me." Alyx grabbed the whip now hanging off her belt.

"And I still have these," Lara said, twirling her daggers. Alrion sighed.

"Please hurry back," he said. He looked worried.

"Of course. You won't even know I'm gone," Vincent said. He put a hand on Alrion's shoulder and looked him in the eye.

Be safe.

Vincent carefully led the horse through and remounted once he was behind the rest. With one look back, he spurred the horse into action.

I have no idea what I'm riding into. But there's too much happening to not leave something for Celes. If she makes it this far, it will be very dangerous to continue, he thought. He admired his wife, and was constantly surprised by her. But this was a very dangerous situation to be wading into. Vincent pushed the horse to go even faster.

20

THE WAY FORWARD

Alrion watched his father ride away, fear dominating his thoughts. He hadn't realised how much he had depended on the reassurance and safety of his father's presence.

It must be because of my current condition.

It wasn't like his father was all-powerful or all-knowing. Although he did have a way of figuring things out and surviving no matter the odds.

"Let's pause when we get to a nice spot to stop. And then we will switch things up a bit," Lara said.

"Sure. Ready?" Alrion said to Alyx.

"Yes. Keep moving."

"As you command," Alrion said. He was trying to lighten the mood a bit by being flippant but his heart wasn't in it. Something about the recent communication had really thrown him. It wasn't just his father's departure.

How did it affect me so much?

The power of the Trackers was scary. The more he found out, the more elusive and surprising they were. But if his mother had discovered a way to use them, that was a bonus.

Alyx lay against his back, using him as support. He didn't think she was as good as she pretended. But he let it slide. They had to keep moving, and she was coming along. That was already decided.

His thoughts turned again to the infection within him. It seemed to be affecting his dreams more. Dark images and shapes. There was also a recurring scene. It was a plain and serviceable fireplace. A healthy and crackling fire burned brightly, sustained by thick chunky logs. But tendrils of darkness slowly crept in, looking to smother the fire. But instead of snuffing it out completely, the fire burned even fiercer. This time with a murky black flame.

He was under no illusions as to what the dream meant. Whether it was real or just his fear, it represented him being overcome and turned by the Blight. It showed his gift being turned into a tool of darkness. That was scarier than anything else. And he had now seen two examples of Shade Wizards. That is not what he wanted to be. He'd rather die than be a monster.

"Everything good up there?" Lara said. Alrion was shaken out of his thoughts. He looked around properly, realising that he hadn't even been paying attention to the surroundings. He was still on the path, but his pace had slowed considerably.

"Fine, just lost in my thoughts."

"Keep your eyes on the road, that's the priority," Lara said.

"On it," Alrion said. He wished it were that easy. His throat was throbbing, exactly where he imagined his black marks to be. He felt it with his hand, and touched the amulet he had been given at the academy.

He pulled it out from his clothing and looked at it again. It appeared unchanged, the pure white of the stone contrasting with the deep black of what was inside. The more he stared at it, the more he thought it was somehow throbbing in time with the marks on his neck.

Just your imagination.

It seemed funny though. In a way he and the amulet were the same. They both had a dark streak trying to spread. He stopped himself focusing on that and instead deliberately took in the landscape.

It was bleak and windswept. Very rocky with very little in the way of vegetation. There were some trees, but none accessible. The trees themselves seemed spindly and anaemic too, like they were on their last legs.

A bit like me.

It was hard to pinpoint but he just felt an overall sensation of unease. His infection was definitely progressing.

The path widened and they approached a broader section. Alrion slowed the horse to take a better look.

"We should pause here to take a break. There's even a few tufts of grass for the horses to nibble on," Lara said. Alrion led the horse over and dismounted carefully. He helped Alyx down then secured the horse to the lone tree nearby. Lara did the same. Alrion pulled his coat around tighter, then sat down with one of the saddlebags.

"Let's see what passes for food up here," he said. He retrieved some dried meat and some fruit and passed it around.

"Let's eat sparingly, we don't know how long we need it," Alyx said.

"Good idea. How are you feeling?" Alrion bit down on a strip of meat and it had way more flavour than he had expected. That was a relief.

"Worse. But we're making progress," she said.

"You mean in terms of getting closer to the Mystics?"

"Mainly." Alyx looked to have more to say, but ended up coughing. "Anyway, you have been neglecting your training."

"I wouldn't say that."

"Now. You and Lara. I want to see how you've progressed."

"I'm not sure we have time," Lara said.

"He won't last long enough for it to make an impact. Go get ready," Alyx said. Alrion looked over at Lara and she shrugged. He had to give Alyx the benefit of the doubt; she usually had some strategy behind whatever she asked for. Alrion stood with reluctance, and walked over to a clear space. He drew his sword and tried to ready himself. Lara stood nearby, drawing her Runesteel dagger and holding it at the ready.

"What's the plan?" Alrion said.

"Go through some forms. Lara will defend," Alyx said. Alrion looked at Lara and she nodded. He took a step forward and winced. He had forgotten about the injured leg. He pushed on, bringing his sword up into a whirling sequence. He started slow, letting his body warm up. Lara dodged and ducked mostly. However, as he was launching a big strike she timed a parry perfectly and threw him off balance. Before he could react, she kicked him in his good leg and he stumbled back.

"Good. You need to take this more seriously," Alyx said. Alrion felt annoyed. He was still injured and had been riding all morning. He didn't think it was fair to push him like this. Lara gave him an apologetic look but readied herself once more. Alrion spent a moment composing himself and launched into another attack. He decided that this time he would go straight to full intensity. They didn't have time, and he didn't have the energy for a long session.

He selected a flowing sequence that quickly alternated between low and high strikes. He hoped that he could use the extra reach to put Lara on the back foot. By intentionally keeping the first few strikes a little slower, he thought he could catch her off guard.

Lara dodged and lightly parried, keeping a defensive approach. Alrion saw his opportunity and pushed much harder. He really needed to move his feet, and struggled a little to keep the agility up. The pain in his leg flared up, which annoyed him. But he used the annoyance as fuel for his continued attack. Faster, harder he pushed. Lara became more active in her defence. She looked like she was finally being challenged.

There! Alrion thought. He swept low after forcing Lara to deflect a strike. Her position and posture were all wrong, and with only a short dagger she would struggle to parry it. As his sword swung she noticed the trajectory. Alrion knew it was too late. He turned his sword so that only the flat of the blade would make an impact.

Lara recovered into a crouch and launched herself. Just as Alrion's sword was meant to bowl her over she jumped over the blade and dived into Alrion. They tumbled down together, Alrion dropping his sword and losing all sense of what had happened. He looked up and saw Lara lying on him, her dagger at his throat.

"You're too slow. That's enough," Alyx said.

"Don't feel bad," Lara whispered, and winked at him. She lingered for a moment longer than necessary then rose. Alrion shook his head and collected himself.

"What do you think about that?" Alyx said. Alrion sat up and rested his palms on the cold ground.

"I can't beat Lara, that's for sure. My leg injury is also a problem."

"You had forgotten about it, hadn't you?"

"In the moment I did, yes."

"I know I saw that. Even when you pushed your hardest, you still weren't fast enough."

"I know," Alrion said. He didn't understand why she was labouring the point. He wiped the sweat off his brow. That had been a thorough workout, even though it was fast.

"You need to know your limitations. Even accounting for your injury, you're slowing down. You are no match for those Trackers, let alone a Shade Wizard."

"I get that. That's why you're here."

"You need to understand that you cannot fight them. You will struggle to run away from them. And you can't rely on me."

"Because of your injury?"

"Not just that. Take your right hand off the ground and hold up a few fingers," Alyx said. Alrion was puzzled but complied. He held up three fingers at waist height.

"I can't tell if that's three or four fingers," Alyx said after a pause.

"What?" Lara said.

"There's a darkness starting to cloud my vision. It's only a recent thing. But it is obscuring details right now."

"Wait a minute. The other night with the crossbow in the relatively dark room?" Alrion said.

"Yes, it was the same then. Don't worry they were big enough targets," Alyx said. Lara just laughed out loud.

"I'm sorry, but I just couldn't help myself seeing Alrion's face right then."

"This sounds really serious. I haven't encountered that side effect and I've been infected longer," Alrion said. Alyx paused and looked deep in thought.

"I think it is reacting differently, but I can't say for sure. From observing you, I think it is mostly making you appear sick and worn down. You seem clumsier and more sluggish. There seems to be a toll on your emotions as well. Steering them darker."

"And for you?"

"I feel like darkness is overtaking me. Look at the skin on my arm." Alyx rolled back the layers and showed her forearm. Alrion walked over and took a look. The skin was darker and slightly scaly.

"This reminds me of ..." Alrion started to say, but quickly stopped himself.

"Don't censor yourself, I am thinking the same thing. It is like a Shade. Perhaps that is my fate," Alyx said. Alrion didn't know what to say. It was one thing that Alyx was infected and carrying that around. And one thing that it was more rapidly affecting her. But it was another entirely that rather than be Tainted, or even a Blighter, that she might be on the path to becoming a Shade.

"I've never witnessed this transformation. I don't know what the trigger signs will be," Alyx said.

"You don't need to be so damned detached about it. This is terrible!" Alrion shouted.

"Sorry, but we need to consider the fact that in your current state I will be a danger to you both if I turn unexpectedly."

"It's much harder to contain a Shade without killing," Lara said softly.

"I've never seen it done. I don't expect you to do that. If I've turned, you must end my life. You must swear this to me," Alyx said. She stared at Alrion.

"I will not. Doing so would go against my very quest. If I can cure myself, I can cure you as well." Alrion kept his gaze level at Alyx. She looked at Lara.

"I will do what is necessary to defend us. But not before trying to restrain you," Lara said finally.

"That is sufficient. We should continue," Alyx said.

"Agreed. We need to reach our destination before anything else happens," Alrion said. He gathered his things and prepared the horse, before helping Alyx up.

"You take the lead again, I fear more from what's behind us than what is before," Lara said once she was mounted.

"Sure," Alrion said. He didn't disguise the weariness in his voice. Even nudging the horse forward was more effort than he wanted. That short stint of sparring had really shown how much weaker he was. They were going to struggle if they were attacked. And his father wasn't anywhere near.

Just keep moving forward.

There would be plenty of opportunity to fix things once they arrived. He rode for a time, focusing initially on the bleak landscape. Eventually though he decided to talk to Alyx.

"Why didn't you say anything earlier? About your condition?"

"It didn't seem worth mentioning, especially since I was burned and then poisoned. For a time there, I wondered if the Darkroot had somehow contributed. But I'm confident now that it's just the Blight, especially given how my arm is reacting."

"I'm not going to let you down," Alrion said. He clenched his jaw and urged the horse forward faster. The cold wind whipped up even faster, and it cut through all his clothing. His teeth chattered.

"We're really pushing north now," he muttered. "Is that snow in the distance?"

"Looks like it," Lara said.

"I'm the wrong person to ask," Alyx said. Her view was mostly blocked, and Alrion remembered the effect on her eyesight too.

"Just take our word for it. We can't be that far now. Explains the biting cold."

"Luckily, I have you to shield me," Alyx said. Alrion chuckled. At least he was good for something right now.

"Stop!" Alyx said, and Alrion tugged at the reins suddenly. The horse whimpered in complaint but stopped.

"What is it?"

"The amulet they gave me is reacting somehow. It's warm and glowing?" Alyx said. She removed it from her clothing and held it out. Alrion turned awkwardly to see it.

"Something is definitely happening there," he said. Lara slowly sidled up and took a look as well.

"I think that's the sign. What did she say? It would show the path?" Lara said.

"I think so. It wouldn't be the path we're on, would it?" Alrion said.

"No, that's too obvious. Every traveller would end up there. Hold my horse," Lara said. She handed the reins to Alrion and jumped down quickly. Alrion followed her with his gaze, and took in the surroundings. There was little to note, save that rock formations and small raised sections surrounded them. It didn't look like there was anything else. Lara walked over to the rocks and felt them with her hand. Holding both hands out she carefully progressed along, checking all the surfaces.

"You think there's a hidden path?" Alrion said.

"Yes. And that amulet is warning us about it," she said. "Oh, what do we have here?"

This could be the break we needed, Alrion thought.

21

HIDDEN BY SNOW

Alrion dismounted and paused to ensure Alyx was still stable on the horse. Then he walked over to see what Lara had found.

"This is quite clever," she said, standing back.

"What is it?"

"It's an optical illusion. It looks like the rock extends all the way, but there's actually a path here." Lara pointed but Alrion didn't get it. He stepped over to where she was standing.

"Oh, I see. Even from here I can't see the whole thing."

"Exactly! It's incredible."

"Do you think we can fit a horse through?" Alrion said. It was all well and good that they had found a secret path, but they would be in trouble if the horses couldn't get through.

"There's only one way to find out. I'll try it on foot," Lara said.

"What was it?" Alyx said when Alrion returned.

"It's definitely a path. You'll see it soon. But Lara is going first to make sure the horses can get through."

"Good. Isn't this a problem though? How will Vincent find it?" Alyx said. Alrion paused. That was a good question.

"We need to leave some sort of marker," he said. He thought hard about what to leave. It had to be something that his father would recognise. However, it also had to be something that would stay in place, and hopefully not be noticed by anyone else passing through.

"This is pretty important. I'm going to have to take a chance," Alrion said.

"What do you mean?"

"Well, I need to leave something valuable. The ring my father gave me. He said that it always protected him, and was of value. Even after Lara originally stole it, it still found its way back to me. I have to trust that he will find it and figure out the trick."

"As strange as that sounds, there could be something to it. It's magical, right?"

"Supposedly. Not that we know what it does."

"Do it. Just try and hide it a little though. I don't think it'll work if you leave it in the middle of the path," Alyx said.

"I agree. It's worth a try, Alrion. Now wish me luck," Lara said. She was leading her horse by the reins and she was in position.

"Good luck," Alrion said. He watched her intently. As she stepped forward she disappeared from view.

"Wow, that's pretty good," Alyx said.

"You saw that?"

"I may have reduced vision, but I'm not blind."

"True. Well, here comes the test. Let's see how the horse goes," Alrion said. The horse did seem resistant, but started to step forward. It also began to disappear until it was completely hidden from view.

"I'd say that's a success. Let me place this ring, then I'll do the same as Lara." Alrion walked over to where the secret path could be seen. He looked around at the ground, trying to find a good place to leave the ring. He spotted a cavity in one of the rocks lying around. It was shallow, but was deep enough to protect the ring. He placed it inside and stepped back.

The angle of the cavity did protect it from a casual glance. But if you looked closer it caught your attention.

That's as good as it's going to get.

He returned to his horse and began to lead it over.

"Here we go," he said.

"I'm ready," Alyx said. Alrion stepped forward carefully. He expected to feel something, but nothing happened. He continued pushing forward until the path widened a little. Looking back the path looked normal. Like it was obviously there.

"Maybe it only works in one direction," he said. Alyx turned and looked herself.

"Must do. You'd never think it, looking from here."

"And there's Lara," Alrion said, pointing. She was a bit further ahead, sitting on her horse and watching them. Alrion continued, on foot, deciding not to mount until he reached Lara. There was probably a reason she had stopped there.

"What did you think?"

"Very impressive. How's the amulet going?" Alrion said.

"It seems to have quietened down. How odd," Alyx said.

"They can explain it to us when we get there. Let's get a move on," Lara said.

"Sure." Alrion carefully jumped up onto the horse once more, and sidled up to Lara.

"Since we're on the path, I'll take the lead from now on. If we're lucky we'll lose them completely. Otherwise we should at least buy ourselves a head start."

"We could use some luck, there's been a terrible lack of it," Alrion said.

"Just make your own," Alyx said. Lara laughed and took off at a faster pace. Alrion didn't try to match it, but did try and increase his speed.

The winds were harsher in terms of both speed and chill. Alrion could see his breath, and soon there was evidence of snow. Not a lot, but enough to show that they would encounter it soon.

"What an inhospitable place. Who would live here?" Alyx said.

"It's just my luck you know? The last place I had to travel to was in the middle of the desert."

"Sounds like the people you need don't want to be found."

"Couldn't agree more. But I found the monks, and I'll find the Mystics."

"You will. I must say I am impressed, Alrion. You do yourself a disservice sometimes. How many can say they have done as much as you in such a short time and with no experience of the world at large?" Alyx said. Alrion was surprised. He hadn't expected a compliment from her. It was even more valuable, since she always seemed so driven and practical.

"Thank you. It doesn't hurt to be reminded of that sometimes. It helps me forget about the failures along the way."

"Failures are just lessons with harsher consequences."

"Interesting words," Alrion said. It sounded like something Certan would have said. He wondered what the monk would think of Alyx. Surely, they had a lot in common.

Lara had stopped ahead, so Alrion increased his speed a little to catch up.

"How's it going back there?" she said.

"Nothing much to report. How about you?"

"Weather is deteriorating. We should have a short food break and then push on. But stay closer together this time."

"Sure, sounds like a plan." Alrion dismounted and started rummaging through the saddlebag.

"Let me down, I need to stretch my legs," Alyx said. Alrion readied himself to help her down, but Alyx slid off the opposite side of the horse. She landed hard on the ground with a thud. Alrion and Lara ran over to investigate.

"What happened?" Alrion said. He helped Alyx back into a seated position on the path. She looked dazed.

"I was foolish. I thought I could get down unassisted, but I just made things worse."

"Any injuries?" Lara said.

"I think I landed on the burnt leg," Alyx said. She reached down with her hand and grimaced with pain.

"Do we have anything for pain?" Alrion said to Lara. She paused to consider before replying.

"I have something. But that's only a secondary effect. The main thing it does is dull whoever drinks it from many things. It's too potent though, there's no way she could stay on a horse if she had it."

"That's no good. Let's at least eat and figure out what to do." Alrion fetched some more dried meat and fruit, and some water. They all sat on the cold ground next to Alyx.

"Sure beats sitting on a horse, although it's definitely colder," Alrion said. He received a small chuckle from Lara and the smallest hint of amusement from Alyx.

"Good to see you acting like your old self," Lara said.

"I think I've crossed over to the other side. Things are actually so dire, I can't help but act like this."

"It still helps. Mindset is very important," Alyx said.

"The monks believe that too. Do you think you can sit on the horse?" Alrion said.

"Probably, although it may be uncomfortable."

"Good. We can keep on moving then."

"I can wait here though. Vincent can take me and you can go ahead," Alyx said. Alrion was about to speak but Lara piped up first.

"Absolutely not. We all made a decision, so the matter is closed. You can't even suggest it yourself. If I have to strap you to my back and ride like that you'll still be coming," Lara said. Alrion was surprised by the intensity in her eyes. He felt reassured by that.

"Glad I didn't have to say that. I just want to add that we sure aren't turning our back so close to our goal."

"Very well. I know what you said before. I just felt I had to offer it just in case. I cannot become a burden. Well, I believe I am, but you won't accept it as that. I will endure," Alyx said.

"Good, glad to see that you've accepted you can't change our minds. Now, with that in mind let's get going again." Alrion rose quickly, the activity waking his legs up again. It was definitely not a good idea to stop for too long in the cold. Especially if snow was ahead. Lara helped him get both himself and Alyx back on the horse and secured. Once they were satisfied that Alyx would not fall off, they set off once more.

The cold increased, and they came across the first snowfalls. At first, it was just a light dusting that didn't persist on the ground. But as they pushed on further it became heavier, and the ground itself became more blanketed. Alrion started to shiver through his layers, and wished he could use a fire spell. That would fix everything. But he accepted that he could not and pushed on.

The path started to become covered in snow, and the horses slowed down considerably. They were also slowly but surely ascending.

"This is so slow," Alrion said.

"At least we're not on foot." Lara grinned at him.

"You're right. I should be careful what I complain about."

"At least you can walk. If we were on foot, you'd be carrying me too," Alyx said.

"You've both made your point." Alrion looked around, trying to see if there were any significant landmarks. A thick blanket of white was starting to cover everything and it was hard to see into the distance.

"At least we're masked by the conditions," he said.

"Don't be so sure about that," Lara said, looking around. She looked spooked by something. "Tracker!"

Alrion wheeled the horse around quickly, looking for the danger. He couldn't see the Tracker, but didn't wait for confirmation. He quickly jumped down and drew his sword. Once he was confident he had a few more seconds to prepare, he handed the crossbow to Alyx. She accepted it quickly without words.

"Here!" Lara shouted. Alrion heard the clang of steel and ran over to help. He saw Lara defending herself from a barrage of strikes. The Tracker was wielding a short sword and pushing her backwards. Lara stumbled back a few steps and readied herself for another assault. But the Tracker used the opportunity to run. It was heading straight for Alrion.

Here we go.

He tensed himself, preparing for the fight. As the Tracker approached Alrion stepped forward and launched into a sword formation. The Tracker quickly parried two strikes and kept moving.

Alyx!

The Tracker was trying to finish the job. He turned quickly and chased the Tracker. It was almost upon Alyx. She fired the crossbow, but it only caught the Tracker in the shoulder. It slowed for a few moments before getting back into the assault. Alrion pushed forward with more urgency, using the Tracker's delay to close the gap. He swung out with his sword trying to knock it down, or at least cause it to slow down.

The Tracker didn't turn to face the attack, and didn't properly account for the strike. Alrion's sword sliced into the Tracker's leg and it toppled over. Before it could stand again Alyx had another crossbow bolt fired. It caught the Tracker in the chest.

"Not this time," Alrion said. He didn't hesitate and drove his sword through the Tracker's chest. It shuddered once then went still.

"I think that's it," Alyx said. Lara was with them within seconds.

"Is it over?" Lara said. She slowed and stood next to Alrion.

"Yes. It is done," Alrion said. He looked over the Tracker in more detail. In the daylight it looked more like a normal man. There were only subtle details betraying its transformation. Some black marks around the eyes, some strange tattoos on its arms, and the jet-black clothing.

"Why did you kill it this time?" Lara said.

"I couldn't let it get away again. It wouldn't stop otherwise."

"I didn't expect you to do that," Lara said. Alrion looked over at Alyx.

"Likewise. That was a surprise."

"Do you disagree with my decision?" Alrion said. He felt uncomfortable now. Had he gone too far?

"No. It was a sensible one. Just not one I thought you would make," Alyx said. Alrion looked back at Lara. He thought he saw a look of sadness quickly pass over her face. But she replaced it so quickly he wasn't sure.

"I'll check it for anything that might help us. Then we should get moving once more."

"Sure," Alrion said. He walked away a few paces, kicking the snow with his feet. He had a strange conflict within. He felt sickened that he'd had to essentially finish off a wounded and defenceless enemy. But the last time he had shown restraint the same creature had escaped and kept hounding them.

I don't know what to do. Do I feel bad because I didn't even hesitate? he thought. What weighed on him the most was the concern that maybe it was the infection within changing his thinking as well as his body. A thought so terrifying that he pushed it away immediately.

"I think you'll want to see this," Lara said. Alrion walked back quickly. She held a book in her hand. He snatched it quickly to confirm what it was. He opened the notebook and saw that it was exactly what he had guessed. It was the magical notebook that he had been carrying with him since the academy.

"They stole this," he said. Leafing through the messages. He didn't think any of the messages would give away too much. They were all so vague and related to his goals. But he noticed a new message.

The Mystics are not the solution. They are only the next step.

"There's a new message. Take a look," Alrion said. Lara read the message and handed it back.

"Well, they know about the Mystics now."

"They must. Also, I'm a bit worried. Does this mean they are not the solution to my infection? I don't think I, or for that matter Alyx, have enough time if that's not the case."

"I hope not. We can't read too much into it. What do you think, Alyx?"

"You cannot spend time speculating. It is good we have the notebook back, correct?"

"Yes."

"Then accept that as a good thing and let's keep moving. Do not waste the opportunity that this Tracker has given us."

"Can't argue with that. Let's go Alrion," Lara said.

"On my way," Alrion said. He mounted up and tried not to think of the Tracker lying on the snowy path. He took the lead, pushing forward as fast as he could. The message in the notebook had given him even more reason to be quick. He had to prepare himself for the fact that maybe the Mystics could not cure him. It was not an easy thought. But he tried to accept it as he pushed ahead.

"Looks like we won't have to wait long for an answer," Alrion shouted. He slowed and pulled up. Ahead he saw what looked like a settlement. The buildings were hard to make out in the conditions, but it was definitely a place. Their destination.

"Is that it?" Lara said.

"It has to be. We should hurry before we get snowed in."

"Lead the way."

"Happy to. Alyx, we'll be there soon. And one way or another they'll be able to help," Alrion said. Alyx didn't respond, which made Alrion even more worried.

You have to help us, he thought and spurred the horse on again.

22

FAST FOLLOWER

Weariness threatened to topple Celes over. She had pushed as hard as possible. But she had been on her feet the entire time. There were no horses in Rolyntide, although she did manage to confirm with the residents that Alrion had passed through there.

The trek since then had been hard and long. Her feet were screaming out, and her shins were riddled with sharp pains. But as she rounded the bend she saw the gates in the distance.

That has to be Highroad.

The gates were closed but that didn't bother her. There was always a way inside. But first you had to get there. Now she finally was.

The final approach was agonising. It was like her body had decided that since she was close to rest, it would let out all the complaining it had been keeping inside. She persevered and leaned against the giant wooden doors.

At least the weather keeps you cool.

After taking a minute, she banged on the door twice. The metal grate on the door slid open and a male voice spoke.

"State your business."

"I'm following some friends of mine that came here. I am hoping to meet them."

"What are their names?"

"Alrion and Vincent."

"They're not residents here." The grate started to close.

"I know. I know. They're travellers. Truth be told they're my son and my husband. I must find them!" Celes was desperate. She didn't have the energy to find another way into this town.

"What's your name?"

"Celes." She decided to be honest and not use a fake name.

"Fine. The Healer mentioned you." The metal grate closed swiftly and the great doors began to open. Celes saw a surly guard standing within.

"Come with me," he said.

"Thank you." Celes followed close, despite her aches and pains. Another guard began closing the gates. It looked like a small town.

Reminds me of home. But a bit more suspicious, she thought. The guard stopped abruptly outside a house.

"In here. Healer is called Beatrix and is expecting you."

"Thank you. I am in your debt," Celes said. The guard's face softened a bit.

"Well, it's fine. Just don't cause any trouble." He walked off quickly and Celes knocked on the door.

A woman opened the door slowly and cautiously.

"Who is it?" she said.

"Beatrix, isn't it? My name is Celes. I hear you are expecting me?"

"Yes, I am. Please come in." Beatrix opened the door the rest of the way and smiled. Celes rushed inside and Beatrix closed the door behind them.

"I take it you've come a long way. I can see the resemblance, by the way."

"Thank you. Yes, it's been a long slog. It would have been a lot easier back in the day. But here we are. You must be aware I'm following my family."

"Yes, I am. Vincent left a message with me to expect you."

"Great. Because the information I have only led me this far. I have no idea where they are heading and for what purpose. But first, is Alrion infected?"

"Yes, he is," Beatrix said. Celes cursed inwardly. She knew it had to be true, but hearing it confirmed was something else.

"How bad is it?"

"Well, he's infected. But he seemed well enough. For some reason it seems to be progressing slowly. There's a good chance for him, if what he believes is true."

"And that is?"

"A group called the Mystics can help cure him. They are based further north. He is pushing to reach them. Not just for his own sake, but for one of the women travelling with him."

"Lara?"

"No, not her. She's fine. Alyx."

"I don't know her," Celes said. There was obviously a lot she had missed.

"They filled me in on a lot of the story. Come in the next room and sit. I'll make some tea and we can talk over everything."

"That's a lovely idea, but I don't know if I have time." Celes felt exhausted, but knowing that she had a link to where Alrion had gone, was like she was being pulled north immediately. Beatrix looked Celes up and down.

"You're in no condition to travel immediately, and you need to know what you're walking into."

"How far ahead are they?"

"A few days. And they have horses. Resting a little won't make any difference."

"Fine, I guess I can stay a little while," Celes said. Beatrix smiled quickly and led her into the next room.

I can sit for a short while. It might be nice, Celes thought.

"That brings us to now," Beatrix said. Celes had been quiet, choosing not to interrupt too much. She just absorbed the story.

"I was attacked by two Trackers on my way here, I know how dangerous they can be."

"Why were they after you? Because you were following them?"

"No, it was the man with me. He was one of the original Trackers and was helping me. They noticed and went after him. I was just someone with him. He fought them off, but he received a mortal injury."

"I'm sorry to hear that. There's been so much life lost."

"There really has. I feel like everything is changing under us. Maybe I've been living in peace and quiet for too long. But Shade Wizards and Trackers? It was never like this."

"Things are definitely changing very rapidly. I think the Blight is coming to a head. It's no coincidence that as your son succeeds in his quest, that the enemy starts to reveal its true colours."

"How was Alrion? How was he really?" Celes needed to know. Beatrix paused and thought before she answered.

"He's had trouble dealing with the infection. Especially the loss of his magic. But he seems to be coping. But I fear it's the kind of coping that can't be maintained forever. If he keeps going like this he may snap." Beatrix looked like she was ready to say more, but she stopped.

"Thank you for being candid. Well, they're surviving. That's all I can ask. Next question. What was the message for me?"

"There wasn't much to it. Mostly Vincent wanted to ensure that you were let inside and I told you everything I knew. One thing he did mention in particular was that you should just keep pushing north; there is only really one main trail. He would find a way to alert you to the path when a deviation was required."

"That's suitably vague. I bet he doesn't know what the path looks like or how he will mark it," Celes said. She chuckled to herself. Same old Vincent.

"I do fear they are figuring things out as they go."

"Understandably. Since I'm here, do you mind if I stay a little longer?" Celes was not used to just inviting herself to stay. But she was so tired, and Beatrix had hosted her family already.

"No problem at all. I just hope you don't get attacked like they were."

"Oh no, I'm not anything for them to worry about. It's been very quiet since I've been travelling alone. Too quiet in fact. It's so nice to have company, even if for only a short time." Celes relaxed back into the couch. She could fall asleep so easily. But she couldn't. Not just yet.

"I can see you're about to crash out. Let's get some food into you and sort out a proper bed." Beatrix had an amused glint to her eye.

"I think you're right," Celes said. She could use some rest. It had been such a hard slog to get this far.

~

Celes opened her eyes and turned over. Vincent was still not there.

This better not be the new normal.

She sat up and took in a deep breath. She felt better and refreshed. Not perfect, but much better. She stood and looked out the single window. It was definitely morning, but not too late.

I can't lose any more time.

Leaving the room, she found Beatrix seated in the lounge and before her, a tray of breakfast. The smell tantalised Celes, causing her mouth to water.

"That smells amazing!"

"It's not much. But please enjoy," Beatrix said. Celes sat down and started eating.

"I can't thank you enough for what you have done for me. I promise I will find a way to repay you." Celes resumed eating. She needed to eat slower but couldn't restrain herself.

"Not required. I believe in what you are all doing. The Blight has taken so many lives, caused so much pain. I want a world without it. This small assistance is nothing compared to what we may all gain."

"While you're feeling generous, I need something else." Celes paused to drink some juice.

"I'm sorry we cannot spare any more horses." Beatrix looked apologetic.

"Oh well, I had to ask."

"But I do insist that you take some cold weather gear. You'll encounter snow further up and you aren't equipped for it."

"You're absolutely right. I do have a question though. You're a Healer, what brought you here? It's a very remote town." Celes was genuinely curious. It made sense to have a Healer here. But what would entice one to stay?

"That's a long story. Suffice to say, I once made a trip to visit the Mystics. They helped me, so I decided I would make my home here and help those who would also make the trip. Along with the rest of the town of course."

"Oh, now that's interesting. What else can you tell me about them?"

"Nothing. You must see for yourself. I can only confirm that if you persist you will find them." Beatrix looked apologetic.

"Sure. Don't worry, I'm not upset. How could I be when you've already been so helpful?"

"I'm glad. Please take your time and ready yourself. I went to the liberty of getting you some equipment early this morning. I'll bring it now," Beatrix said. She quickly left the room.

This was the break I needed. There's no horse, but I've got a second wind. I can make it now, Celes thought. When Beatrix returned she was laden with clothing and bags. Celes looked through and selected an appropriate coat, scarf, and boots. She also packed a bag to get her through the final leg of the journey.

"I think this is goodbye. I'll return soon with the rest of them. We all owe you our thanks."

"Good luck and good speed to your travels. I look forward to hearing of your adventures. Follow the path outside and you'll reach the way north." Beatrix waved and Celes left. She heard the door locking behind her.

On my way again. This time I'll finally catch up with them.

She still lamented the lack of a horse. But there was no use worrying about it. They'd given her everything else.

The walk through the town was quick, and soon she was on the trail. It didn't take long for the weather to deteriorate, and the cold chill to start piercing through her layers of clothing. The track was slowly ascending the whole time, which made things harder without seeming like it should be.

Just accept that you're climbing the whole time, she thought. She just needed to put one foot in front of the other for a while.

How will I know when to look for Vincent's marker?

Whatever he left had to be something subtle; otherwise someone else would take it. She thought over the information she had already. The Mystics were far north. Beatrix had visited them and told her that there would be snow. That was a good indicator at least. Until there were decent amounts of snowfall she just had to keep going.

"But snow may also obscure the marker. This won't be easy," Celes realised. But that was fine. She had a destination and was on the path. Alrion and Vincent were up there somewhere. Hopefully already with the Mystics.

Alrion, I'm still coming.

She hoped that he would be all right. The infection had to hold out a bit longer. Together they could figure something out. Their family had been apart for so much of this quest. Surely, they were better off together.

23

THE MYSTICAL DESTINATION

The settlement started to take the shape of buildings. And as they approached the buildings took on real forms. They were large domes of some material that Alrion couldn't figure out.

"This has to be it. Look at those buildings," he said.

"I think you're right. There can't be anything else all the way out here. And those structures certainly look different," Lara said.

"Let's speed up, we're so close."

"Hold up there. The snow is getting deeper, and the wind is picking up. Let's not stumble at the finish line." Lara gave him a serious look so Alrion took note. It wasn't just his desire to get Alyx and himself to what he hoped was safety. He was genuinely excited about discovering this place. What an incredible find. A group of magic users hidden from the world, their very existence a secret. He could learn so much.

He suddenly realised something he had lost since being infected. His sense of wonder had all but dried up. Sucked away by the vile infection coursing through him. He had been so preoccupied with it; he couldn't see beyond it. But even at the first sight of the Mystic's home, hope was rekindled. It was so reassuring.

"I have a good feeling about this," he said.

"Me too," Lara said. She nudged ahead, and Alrion let her lead.

The snow was falling and visibility was poor. They were initially shocked when they saw a figure standing in the snow before them.

"Welcome," a female voice said. Lara stopped and Alrion slowed down, stopping beside her. The woman was wearing thick blue robes with a hood. It was hard to make out any other features.

"Hello. We have come a long way to find you. We need your help," Alrion said.

"You can tell us everything inside. Follow me," the woman said. She walked effortlessly through the snow like it wasn't there at all. Alrion started to wonder what this place would really look like. He looked for gates, but saw none.

"Are there no gates here?" he said.

"No. Why would we need any? Only those who are truly determined come here."

"Fair enough." Alrion didn't understand, but it was a very remote location and hard to get to. Maybe they didn't need gates.

There was a clearly marked path now that they were entering the settlement. It consisted of carefully laid stones. The horses' hooves reached the stone through the varying layers of snow and the loud clop sound initially surprised Alrion. He looked around and saw the dome-shaped buildings in more detail. They were also built from carefully arranged stone, which he had never seen before. Each only had a single entrance. None of them seemed to have windows. He didn't want to question it though. It seemed better to just follow along quietly.

"Where are you taking us?" Alrion said.

"To a place where you can rest and recover."

"We need urgent attention first. Two of us are infected."

"You will be able to rest here. The Blight infection will struggle here, and take longer to complete," the woman said without even breaking stride. Alrion pulled up his horse instantly.

"I don't need time, I need a cure."

"We don't cure the Blight here."

"I don't accept that. I need to meet with your leader." Alrion remained still, not moving any further along. The woman finally stopped walking and turned to regard them.

"I don't think you will get what you want," she said.

"That's my problem, not yours." He was not going to be shuffled off somewhere to rest and wait for the infection to do its work. No, he was going to tackle this. There had to be a reason he had dreamed of the Mystics, and travelled so far to find them. He needed answers, not a bed. The woman continued to stare at him. Her gaze shifted over to Lara then back to him.

"Very well, as you wish. This way," she said. The woman left the path and they cut through the snow to another path. Alrion didn't notice anybody else walking around.

Must be the poor weather.

He doubted that the place was deserted. Before them rose a much larger structure. It was one giant dome with two others either side of it. Each structure had its own door, the main one with two giant wooden doors. The woman walked up and threw them open with only the slightest touch.

"Something is definitely going on here," he said to Lara.

"Agreed. But I'm going to keep quiet and observe. You take the lead, you're doing well."

"Thanks. This can't be for nothing." Alrion checked on Alyx and she seemed to be asleep. He dismounted and looked at how he was going to get Alyx down safely. Two women appeared next to him.

"We will take her to a bed. Don't worry she won't be far," one woman said. Alrion looked over to Lara and she nodded.

"Thanks," he said. He watched them carefully take Alyx away and Alrion walked into the giant dome with purpose. He wasn't going to be turned away.

It was surprisingly warm inside. There was a large fire in the centre of the room. The edges of the room were littered with torches on the walls, and lots of padded seats. Some had women sitting in them, but many of them were empty. At the end of the room, on a raised section was a crystal throne. On it sat an older woman, and before her was a small fountain filled with water.

The woman who had been leading them continued, and they followed her through the room. Alrion felt the eyes of the women on him, but he tried to ignore it. It was a disconcerting feeling though, like they were looking through him. Once they reached the foot of the throne, the young woman who had led them pushed back her hood and moved up the steps to take a position next to the older woman. Their leader presumably.

She looked old, yet still strong. She didn't carry the same frailty he normally attributed to old women. She was dressed in similar robes to the rest, but had more jewellery. There was a fire in her eyes, and something about them was familiar.

This is the woman from my dream!

Alrion realised it wasn't just a vision, it was a memory. His grandfather had known this woman, known of her powers.

"So, you have finally come to Wyr's Peak. Cutting it fine, aren't we?"

"My name is Alrion. This is Lara. And you are?"

"Jovana. I would ask you what brings you here, but I know the answer already. Therefore, I have a different question for you. Where is your father?" Jovana stared directly at Alrion. It made him a little uncomfortable. And the comment about his father threw him completely.

"He's on his way, he was delayed. That doesn't matter. I'm here and I need your help."

"That's a pity. I wonder if he did that intentionally. Come back when your father is here." Jovana turned her attention to the pool of water in the fountain before her. Alrion waited, and she said nothing further and didn't even look in his direction. He looked at Lara and she shrugged.

"I don't think you understand why I am here." Alrion was about to say more but he was cut off.

"Why are you still talking? You're dismissed. Come back when your father is here." Jovana waved him away and returned to staring into the water. Alrion didn't understand. He needed her help. His father being here was irrelevant. Any important information could be relayed later.

"You won't even let me explain my situation," he said. Jovana looked at him once more, this time giving him an icy stare that caused him to shiver.

"You are Alrion, son of Andar and grandson of Granthion. You, and one of your companions are infected. You believe that by coming here you can be cured. You have been informed that the Blight infection will travel slower here, yet you still push for this cure. We can help you, but at the proper time. Go wait and rest, and when your father is here I will see you again. Until then we have nothing to discuss and I won't even acknowledge you speaking. That is all." Jovana finished speaking and stared into the water once more. The woman standing next to her had a grin on her face.

Alrion was stunned. He hadn't expected this. First the strange refusal to help, then the way in which the woman had known all about what they were doing. He just shook his head. He looked at Lara and she seemed as confused as he was. The young woman walked down the steps and joined them.

"My name is Marla. I'm sorry about that, but I tried to warn you. She's very particular about things. Don't worry. You will get the help you need. But come with me now." Marla gestured towards the exit. Alrion appreciated the kindness after the stern talking to they had just received.

"This is not what I was expecting," he said.

"Good, then everything is as it should be," Marla said.

"You know more than you're telling us," Lara said.

"Yes, I do. But you have nothing to fear. All will make sense soon." Marla reached the exit doors, and held them open for Alrion and Lara. They stepped through and Marla continued to lead them back the way they had come.

"We're just supposed to wait around until my father arrives. What's so important about that?"

"You will see. And are you suggesting that you aren't exhausted and hungry?"

"No," Alrion said stubbornly.

"Then you need the rest anyway and you will be better prepared for when your father does arrive. Doesn't that make sense?"

"That part does. I'm sorry, but you can't understand what we've gone through to get here. And to be treated like that, it's difficult."

"Jovana is our eldest, and our leader. She is the wisest of us all, and very particular about things. But she is always right. You will see," Marla said with a smile. Alrion just shook his head again. Lara smiled.

"You are just used to getting your own way. This is a nice change," she said with a laugh.

"At least you're seeing the humour in this."

"Have you lived here your entire life?" Lara said.

"Yes. I have travelled extensively, but this has always been my home."

"Is it always this cold?" Lara pulled her coat around her tighter.

"Usually. It does vary by season, but it's always cold here. You get used to it. Here's your room," Marla said. She stopped in front of a smaller dome. She didn't walk inside. Alrion walked up to the door and pushed it open. It was a lot heavier than he'd expected, given how easily Marla had been opening them.

There's a lot of surprises here, he thought. Inside was a small fireplace at the rear and four beds. Alyx occupied one. They were low to the ground without any frames. In the middle of the room was a round table laden with food. Mostly fruit, but some bread and meat were also there.

"This looks comfortable," Lara said as she entered.

"Yes, it does. Perhaps we can rest a little," Alrion said.

"You can find me in the great hall if you need anything. But I wouldn't bother our elder until your father arrives. Don't worry, there is plenty of time," Marla said from the entry.

"But it's not just the infection. There are some who are chasing us. They may find this place."

"It is unlikely, since we are protected here. But if that is the case we will know before they arrive. You have time. Rest." Marla left and once the door closed fully the room felt much warmer and comforting.

"You know, we don't get a lot of opportunities like this. Let's just take advantage of it," Lara said. Alrion just sat down on one of the beds and started picking at the food. He was much hungrier than he had realised.

"We made it," Lara said when she had finished eating.

"We did. And Alyx too." Alrion looked over at her again. She seemed to be sleeping peacefully.

"Don't worry, everything will work out. They're mysterious and cryptic, just like everyone said they would be. And they're still helping us."

"I know. I'm grateful. But I can't rest properly until this infection is behind us. And my responsibility to Alyx. I can't move on with my quest otherwise."

"I know. But we have time now. Rest."

"I'll try," Alrion said. He was incredibly tired, and the food had done the job. But he had trouble relaxing. There was still so much to do, so much resting on his shoulders. But sleep came faster than he realised it would.

24

FAMILY REUNITED

Vincent slowed the horse down. He had been riding hard for a long time and he felt like the terrain was changing significantly. And he worried that he may have missed the path.

He had expected it to be obvious, as few would bother to travel this far. In his mind the amulet that Freyda had handed them was more of a token to make them feel more comfortable. But more and more he suspected that it was more than that. That there was something else that he was missing.

The path travelled up and up, and he didn't feel like it was the right direction. It seemed to be meandering into more rocky cliffs than a real destination. So, he turned the horse around and retraced his steps.

He worked his back to another narrow pass and paused. There was something different about this area. He remembered it from when he rode through initially, but he was too preoccupied with his speed to pay it any attention. But now, once again, he had a feeling that something was off. But he couldn't put his finger on it.

Vincent dismounted and tied the horse to a large stone nearby. If there was something here he had to take care and look properly. His feet crunched on the ground as he walked around, looking for some signs of an alternate path. Something was nagging at him, but he couldn't spot anything of note. As he turned something did finally catch his eye. A glint that didn't belong. He turned back and crouched down, carefully examining the area. There had been some snowfall recently, but he spotted the glint again. In a recess of a rock he spotted something. He reached in and plucked it out.

"My father's ring," he said quietly in astonishment. It had been placed there deliberately, a sign for him to follow.

"Well done Alrion. I feel bad that I almost missed it, but you did well to sign-post the way." Vincent cleaned off the snow and put it back where he found it.

With any luck my wife will find it too, he thought. It was worth a shot. He had no better way of alerting her, and if need be they could always retrieve the ring. He stood and examined the rock wall from another angle, and saw something odd. He placed his hand on the stone and it passed right through.

An actual hidden path. Now this is certainly mysterious. They give the wizards some competition!

After experimenting with the effect briefly, he strode back to his horse and quickly untied it. Leading it behind him, he ventured through what he thought was the new pass.

It was unnerving but soon he and the horse had passed through completely. Looking back, it was like there was no wall at all.

"Very clever. But now I need to make up for lost time." He mounted the horse swiftly and nudged a little too enthusiastically. The horse bolted forward, and Vincent scrambled to hang on.

That's the way, he thought with a chuckle. Although with the weather ahead, he expected he would need to slow down considerably.

The ride moved ahead without anything of interest, although he did spot a black hand sticking out of the snow. After investigating he realised it was a dead Tracker, and that they had managed to account for the last one that was closely tailing them.

"I should have been here," he said as he remounted the horse. But he couldn't have continued without leaving a message for Celes. She was incredibly resourceful, but needed to be updated. It was dangerous country and she would most likely be alone. He had no choice but to make arrangements.

The first view of the buildings should have filled him with wonder, but instead it just focused his thinking.

"I'm not far now. Hopefully I make it in time." He tried to spur the horse faster, but the snow was falling thicker and caused plenty of trouble. Light was fading too, so he had to balance the need for speed and the danger of rushing along in treacherous conditions and low visibility.

Finally, he saw a figure standing before him. He slowed the horse to a slow walk and approached carefully. The figure was in a robe and was waiting.

"Hello there!" Vincent shouted as he closed in. He wanted to know if the figure was friendly or another attacker.

"Welcome, Andar," the female voice said. Vincent was initially shocked but hid it quickly. He had to assume they knew all about him. It was just a shock hearing his original name used again. He would have to get used to it, since he doubted they would call him Vincent.

"My son has arrived already?" he said after he dismounted.

"Yes, he is resting. Did you want to meet the elder now or wait until morning?" The woman gave him an odd look. He knew she was waiting to see how he would respond. He knew what he should do.

"Has she met him already?"

"Yes, he insisted. She sent him away until you arrived."

"Then I'll wait. Let's do everything at once," Vincent said. In a way she had given him an out by mentioning how Alrion had been sent away. But he could guess as to why.

"I didn't get your name."

"Marla."

"Nice to meet you."

"And you too. I'll take you to where they are staying." Marla strode off confidently and Vincent rushed to keep up. Two women came to take the horse, and he handed over the reins. He looked around now at the domed buildings, marvelling at how they had been built.

Not by any means I know of.

Perhaps they were a clue as to the abilities of the Mystics. The cold was sharp and biting, and he looked forward to getting inside. It had been a long and hard ride to get here. Marla stopped in front of one of the domes and threw the doors open. She gestured inside.

Vincent entered quickly, and saw Lara jump to her feet.

"You still have great instincts. But it's just me," Vincent said. Lara ran over and hugged him.

"That's a welcome. Everything alright?"

"It's fine. Just happy to see a familiar face. And Alrion was turned away because of you."

"I heard. I also spotted the fourth Tracker on the way here. Sorry you had to deal with that."

"We survived. Alyx too." Lara looked down at her. The weapon master was sleeping soundly.

"Good. I suppose I should take a rest too."

"We will summon you in the morning," Marla said, and closed the doors.

"They sure do love their mystery and ceremony here," Vincent said.

"They do. I hope they can help. We found the missing notebook and there was another message?"

"What was it?" Vincent walked over and sat on the last bed.

"The Mystics are not the solution, just a step."

"Hmm how did Alrion take it?"

"He seemed fine generally. But a bit worried." Lara looked over at him sleeping, then sat on her bed.

"Anything worth mentioning for you?"

"No. I rode back and asked Beatrix to pass on a message to my wife and explain what we're up to. Then I came straight here."

"And you found the clue?" Lara chuckled.

"I did. Well, after I rode past it once. It was a clever idea. I left it for Celes, hopefully she finds it too."

"I'm sure she will. I hope whatever happens here, it happens quickly. Alyx's infection is quite progressed."

"That is a worry. But we're here now; there will be what we need. Looking back, I can't imagine this trip without her. She's been instrumental in our survival."

"I know. Well, you probably need to rest. All will be revealed tomorrow."

"It most certainly will," Vincent said. He doused a nearby light and prepared for sleep. He was nervous about what would happen tomorrow. He had no idea how it would go. But one thing was for certain. It would not go well for him.

Vincent awoke first. It was to be expected but still he was glad. He had time to prepare himself before Alrion woke. Lara woke next, but they didn't talk much. They waited for Alrion. When he did eventually wake he sat bolt upright.

"Where are we?" he said, looking around.

"The Mystics, remember?" Lara said. Alrion nodded, but he had already spotted his father.

"Dad! You made it."

"Of course I did. And I appreciated you leaving that ring. I had underestimated the difficulty in finding that path, and I had already missed it once. How are you feeling?"

"Not amazing, but good enough. Now that you're here we can go get some answers from the Mystics."

"Of course. Marla did mention something about summoning us, but I'm sure we can initiate something," Vincent said with a wink.

"Absolutely. I didn't trek to the end of the world to wait around for a summons." Alrion rose quickly and walked around the room. He spotted some food and started to eat. Vincent chuckled to himself and joined his son.

They all ate quickly, and prepared to leave.

"We'll be back soon with a cure, Alyx. Keep resting," Alrion said. Alyx made no response.

"She'll be fine, just needs to recover a bit more," Lara said.

"They will take good care of her. Let's go get those answers you're after," Vincent said. He felt a clenching in the pit of his stomach. But he couldn't avoid it any longer. He had to face up to it.

They walked slowly through the settlement. There were still very few people moving around. Those that were continued going about their business, completely ignoring the travellers.

"Here we are," Alrion said. They stood before the giant hall. Vincent whistled.

"Looks spectacular. I should have expected it. I'll do the honours," Vincent said. He opened the giant doors and walked inside. The room was almost full. The sides were packed with seated women in robes. A large fire burned in the centre of the room and at the very end sat an older woman in a throne, with what looked like Marla at her side.

"That's the elder, Jovana," Alrion whispered to his father.

"Thanks," Vincent said. *And here we go*, he thought. He walked through the room with fake confidence, his footsteps echoing through the eerie quiet. Alrion and Lara followed close behind, remaining quiet. As they approached the throne the older woman waved her hand and Vincent stopped. He saw her disapproving gaze and felt the full force.

"Only now, at your most desperate, have you come to me. My son," Jovana said.

"I'm sorry. You seemed more of a memory than a person I could actually visit," Vincent said. His voice was stronger than he expected. Alrion pulled him aside.

"She called you her son. She's your mother?"

"Yes, she is. My father took me away when I was very young."

"You knew this the whole time? And you said nothing?" Alrion looked angry and confused. Vincent sighed.

"I see your son is surprised also. Rightfully so. You kept this from him too?" Jovana said.

"Until recently he even hid the fact that Granthion was my grandfather," Alrion said. Jovana shook her head.

"You have disrespected and neglected your family. For what?" Jovana looked through Vincent. He didn't have a good answer.

"It was easier that way. You may not know, but I left my father. I forged my own path."

"Of course I know, you're my son. And what good did that do you? You're here with the same problem that he was faced with."

"The Blight."

"Exactly. It was his obsession, and eventually his undoing. Your sticking your head in the sand for over two decades didn't help at all did it?"

"At least my son had a normal upbringing!" Vincent felt like he was right in what he had done. Even if he had insulted his family in the process.

"A normal upbringing? He's the grandson of the greatest wizard and Mystic that ever lived. Why should he have a normal upbringing?"

"Because I never had one." The room went quiet.

"Well, because of your decision you have missed a lot. Did you know that you had a twin sister?" Jovana said. Vincent was floored.

"No," he managed to say, his voice cracking. He looked around the room.

"She's not with us anymore. She passed giving birth to her daughter, Marla." Jovana reached out and held Marla's hand. Vincent looked at her more closely. He could see a resemblance. It made sense now.

"I'm sorry, I have done you all a disservice. But it was not out of malice."

"Of course not. You're just a foolish boy. I knew that you would be in trouble with your father, but that was how it had to be. So here we are. Much too late you have arrived on my doorstep asking for help. You should have done so sooner, and all of this could have been avoided!"

"What do you mean?" Alrion said.

"You really should know better. Had you come to me earlier, you could have been trained properly."

"Trained in what?"

"The power of Soul. Our power. It runs through your veins, because you are my grandson. My son has it also, not that he ever thought to use it." Jovana had a defiant smile on her face. Vincent felt his blood run cold. He had never considered that. He always assumed that his parentage was just a fact, that it had no repercussions.

"That's not possible. Only women are Mystics," he said.

"Generally, yes. But there are exceptions. And a wizard can make a big difference."

"I am a wizard and a Mystic?" Alrion said.

"Yes. And as a Mystic, if you had come to train with us, you would already be immune to the Blight." Joana's look was half-amusement, half-concern. Alrion looked incredulous.

"I don't believe it."

"Why do you think the infection has moved so slowly?" Marla said. Alrion just stared at his hands.

This is not quite what I expected, Vincent thought. He was as blindsided as Alrion. Perhaps things could have been different. If he had embraced his family, really thought about what the benefits could be to Alrion, he could have avoided so much. He felt sick. His own selfishness in doing what he thought was right had cost them so dearly.

"You are not beyond help. You can both be trained. We should not waste time," Jovana said.

"How will training help me now? I'm so far gone. Can't you just heal me?" Alrion sounded defeated and overwhelmed.

"I can't heal you. Why do you think we never cured the Blight? Because that is not how our power works. I have done the impossible many times in my life, but that is one thing that cannot be done with Soul power alone."

"So what hope is there for me then?"

"Learn the power. Unlike your Spark, it cannot be tainted by the Blight. Unlock your full potential and you will cure yourself!" Jovana looked triumphant. Alrion looked up at her, a hopeful look on his face. But he needed encouragement.

"Alrion, we will do this together. We will set things right. Correct the course that we are on. You can cure yourself, then you can learn how to cure Alyx. He can do that right?"

"Your father found a way, and he had no Soul power. I'm sure Alrion will discover the secret. That's the whole point of your quest, isn't it?"

"Yes," Alrion said.

"And I will learn too. So that I can't be infected. Then I can protect you." Vincent was resolute. He would not fail his family again.

25

A NEW POWER

"Marla will start your training. Immediately," Jovana said. She waved them away and returned to staring into the bowl of water before her. Marla descended the steps smiling.

"There's a lot for you to learn, cousin," Marla said. Alrion blinked. Of course.

"Sure. Sorry I had no idea we were related. I had no idea of a lot of things," Alrion said. He felt completely blindsided. He had travelled all this way, not knowing the real reason. And his father had gone with him, all the while saying nothing. He couldn't believe that, after all that had happened, he still hadn't revealed this. He looked at his father as they walked through the hall. The women on chairs had been silent the entire time. Just watching proceedings.

"Mum was so angry at you when you revealed who your father was. This is just the next level," Alrion said. Vincent winced in pain.

"You're right. I'm in serious trouble when she arrives."

"Jovana would say you deserve it."

"I would agree." Vincent paused and opened the giant doors. Lara walked through first. Alrion watched her go. She had been quiet the whole time. He rushed past his father to catch up to her.

"Dad we will discuss this again later. Lara, what are you thinking?"

"I'm still trying to grasp everything. You're not just a wizard, but also a male Mystic? It's a lot to take in. They can't cure Alyx?"

"I guess not."

"What the eldest said is true. But, we can help her. We are Healers after all," Marla said. She overtook them and started to lead the way.

"Before we start, we need to see her. To explain what is going on." Alrion needed Alyx to understand the situation. He had promised to cure her, but he hadn't expected to be the one to do it himself. She had to understand that it was his top priority.

"Very well, we will stop there first. But this is not a fast process. Even though you are descended from the eldest, it will be very difficult for you. Perhaps even more so with your ... infection." Marla looked at Alrion's neck as she spoke, and he shied away. He was very self-conscious of the marks. They showed how far his infection had come. But it sounded like he could do something about it. The Soul power could keep the infection away, or even overpower it. That was something he desperately needed. The sooner he could be rid of it, the sooner he could access his Spark.

"Don't be alarmed, we already have some Mystics visiting your friend," Marla said. They had reached their dome, and Marla opened the door. She waited outside and ushered them in.

Alyx was sitting up and alert. There were two Mystics beside her, their hands glowing with a bright white light.

"What are they doing? The elder told me you can't cure the Blight," Alrion said.

"The Blight is repelled by the power of Soul, so by using it in an appropriate way it can help slow the process," Marla said. The two Mystics remained quiet.

"I think it's helping," Alyx said.

"How are you feeling?" Alrion said. He moved a little closer.

"Mostly the same, but I have a bit more energy. The final part of the journey was a bit hazy, but I see we made it. What's the plan now?"

"It's a long story, but essentially my father and I seem to possess the same power as the Mystics. The eldest, Jovana, is my grandmother."

"That seems like quite a revelation. Your father said nothing before today?"

"No." Alrion looked at his father. Vincent didn't say anything.

"Very well. How does that help us?"

"If I train in this power, I can cure myself. And then I suppose figure out how to cure others. They weren't particularly clear on that."

"That's because it's your part of the equation. Soul power will be required, but we can't cleanse the Blight in others with it. As a wizard you have that capability," Marla said patiently.

"I see. Well, there seems to be a lot more to this, but it seems clear that they should be able to hold off my infection long enough for you to cure yourself. Then you are both more effective at fighting the Blight, and you can figure out how to cure me."

"That's it."

"A better position than we were in a day ago. You'd best get started though," Alyx said. She pointed at the door.

"As you wish. Good to see you're doing relatively well. Take care," Alrion said. Vincent said his goodbyes too and they left the dome.

"Soon you're going to have to explain things more. I'm not quite satisfied," Alrion said to his father.

"That's reasonable. But there's not much else I can say. Try to imagine that you don't remember your mother, and I described her as living in a faraway place and never talked about her. Would you feel compelled to seek her out?"

"Yes. I would need to know."

"Then we are different in that respect. Let's talk about it more later." Vincent looked away, clearly uncomfortable. Alrion wanted to say more, but decided to leave it. They had something else more important to do.

The snow crunched under their boots as they made their way to another dome. This one initially looked like it was completely covered in snow. But once Alrion was closer, he saw that it was made from a lighter colour of stone.

"This one looks different," he said.

"Yes, this is the Pool of Reflection. It is instrumental to our training." Marla stopped in front of the building, next to the main door.

"That's interesting. Any connection to the Pool of Knowledge?"

"I don't think so. Come inside," Marla said. She opened the door and ushered them in.

Inside the lighting was dim, but Alrion could see the pool immediately. It was large and still, began in the centre of the room and took up half the space inside. The most interesting aspect though was the light glow that shone off the surface of the water.

"This is incredible," Lara said. She stepped forward carefully.

"Is the water the only source of light in here?" Alrion said. He couldn't spot any torches or windows anywhere.

"Yes. Below the ground is what we call the Great Source. It is a large well of water that is infused with Soul power," Marla said. She walked forward and sat cross-legged before the pool.

"Was that done by the Mystics?" Alrion said.

"No, it has always been that way. We believe that is why our home is here."

"Is that what the elder peers into as well?" Lara said.

"You are quite perceptive. Yes, every day water is drawn from here and taken there. The elder uses it for various purposes."

"Such as?" Alrion said.

"She can see a great many things in the reflection."

"Is that how she would have watched me?" Vincent said. He still looked uncomfortable.

"I suppose so. Nobody else knows how to do that, it's a skill only the elder possesses."

"Why do you call her the elder, and not grandmother? Or something similar?"

"She is the eldest first, and my grandmother second."

"Can this water give us power?" Alrion said.

"No, the water is a focus and an aid. Nobody can give you Soul power. It is within you. Much like your Spark."

"You said we could train it?"

"Yes, that's what we are here for. I will begin by explaining some of the basic concepts. Then your friend will need to return to the visitor residence. She cannot participate in the training."

"But ..."

"Don't worry, I have other things to attend to. Let's hear the overview," Lara said. Marla swivelled around so she faced them.

"I hinted at this earlier, but in many ways Soul power is the complete opposite to Spark. You use it to manipulate the world outside, but struggle to manipulate yourself."

"That's right. I learned a healing spell, and I was told that it was next to useless on myself. I needed another wizard to heal me."

"Exactly. Soul power is used to manipulate yourself, and cannot be used on others. That is why we cannot cure people of the Blight."

"There has to be exceptions though. When I was almost dead at the Pool of Knowledge, I managed to heal myself enough to not die. The wizard who attacked me couldn't believe it."

"Your Spark did not do that."

"Then what did?"

"In your time of need, you must have tapped into your Soul power. Even a trickle would have been enough to make the difference."

"I never considered that." Alrion went quiet, he was thinking over what it meant. He didn't think there were any other situations where he may have used it.

"If Soul power only affects you, how come you can heal others?" Lara said.

"Excellent question. There are two aspects to the healing. The first is that by having mastery over our own bodies, we can better diagnose and cure others."

"That makes sense. Mostly," Lara said.

"The other aspect is that we can enhance our bodies with Soul power, perhaps even to the point of saturation. Then the effect spills out and can affect others. That is what you witnessed with your friend Alyx."

"Wouldn't that be a lot less effective?" Alrion said.

"Of course. But with the proper training you can overcome that. There are also other tricks where you can help convince the body to better heal itself. We've been doing this for a long time."

"And doing it in a subtle way. Were those Healers we encountered on the way Mystics?" Vincent said.

"In this area, yes all the Healers are Mystics. Some return here regularly, others only come once to master their gift and never return."

"And they never said anything. It was all vague and supportive, but not specific," Lara said.

"Of course. Our order survives on its secrecy. Many years ago, some of us acted openly. But they were cursed as witches and hunted ruthlessly. We learned our lesson, and hide in plain sight. There is a good reason why we also learn the art of herbs and other treatments."

"She's got an answer for everything," Lara said.

"They're not answers, they're explanations. This is what we do, and why."

"Anything else I need to know?" Lara said.

"Yes. Soul power regenerates slowly over time. There are only a few ways to speed it up, and they are not particularly effective either."

"Well, I wouldn't need to use it that much, would I?" Alrion said.

"To overcome your infection, you would need to draw upon perhaps the entire amount. That is significant. I also assume curing anyone else of the Blight, should you figure out the method, would also be very taxing. You could probably only do one person at a time."

"That's worth considering," Lara said.

"Yes, although it's not that strange. I have limits to my Spark too and I have to rest to recover."

"Good. You will just need time to become accustomed to your Soul power and its reserves. Now, I believe that is enough of the introductory statements. Lara, you will need to leave now." Marla gestured to the door and Lara nodded.

"I'll keep Alyx company. You better learn fast, we need more options for when Wraith eventually knocks on the door."

"I'll do my best," Alrion said.

"Do better!" Lara said, and left. Marla waited until the door had fully closed then turned her attention back to Vincent and Alrion.

"Any other questions before we proceed?"

"How long will this take?" Alrion said.

"It will take a lifetime to master, as with anything. However, the eldest believes that since you are her descendent, you should have a large capacity. Therefore, even if you lack the skill and finesse, within days you should be able to access enough to overturn your infection."

"Good that she thinks it is possible. If we didn't have terrible things bearing down on us I would jump for joy at that suggestion. To think that I may be rid of this curse that soon is incredible. But, it may be too long."

"It's a fantastic opportunity, don't overanalyse it just yet. Let her begin, and we will get a feel for how it is progressing," Vincent said. Alrion saw the value in that, and he gave his full attention to Marla.

"Good, now we can begin." Marla quickly spun around, facing the water once more. "Sit next to me and cross your legs as I am."

"Sure," Alrion said. He sat on her left, and Vincent sat on her right. Alrion found it uncomfortable sitting with his legs crossed but ignored it.

"Now, take your right hand and hold it out with your palm facing the water." Marla demonstrated and Alrion followed along. His hand was hovering above the glowing water. He looked over and saw his father doing the same.

"Good. Now focus your attention on your hand. Can you feel a warm tingling sensation?" Marla's face was calm and she looked over at Alrion. He concentrated but didn't feel anything yet.

"I can," Vincent said.

"Good, hold that feeling. Alrion try harder," Marla said. Alrion sighed and resumed his concentration. He tried to remember the exercise he had done with Certan, maintaining his will over the floating strip of wood. There had been effortlessness to it, once he'd figured it out. This would be the same kind of thing. He slowed everything down, isolating the feeling in his arm, then his hand. He felt a cool sensation, almost slimy. He had a good idea of what that was, but pushed it away. He searched harder for what Marla had described. Focusing on his hand, letting it tell him what it was feeling above all else. He started to feel it, faint at first, but getting stronger and stronger.

"I'm getting it," Alrion said, almost in a panic. He felt he could lose it at any moment.

"Excellent. The water helps as a focus, and an amplifier. That's why we train here. Now I need you to take that feeling, and trace it all the way back to your heart."

"Easier said than done." Alrion had struggled to even get that far. And now to go even further? But it was all he could do right now, so he set his mind to it. He latched onto that feeling, and nurtured it. He coaxed it back up his arm slowly. He suspected that actually the feeling was emanating from somewhere else, that he wasn't really working it up his arm. But the idea helped him continue, so he ran with it. Bit by bit, he felt the sensation travelling up his arm. Then it started to cross over to his chest, just under his collarbone.

His thoughts immediately turned to the black marks on his neck, the source of his infection. And like that, it was as if the slimy ooze of the Blight had overwhelmed him. The warm sensation was lost immediately, and Alrion slumped down in despair. He looked over at his father, sitting calmly.

"I have done it," Vincent said quietly. Marla nodded and looked over at Alrion.

"What happened?"

"It was working, but then something happened. I'm not sure if my focus was too close to where I was infected, or it was my thinking about it. But it was all lost in an instant. It was like the Blight overtook the feeling and my concentration."

"There's something to that. Partially in your mind, but partially interference. The infection coursing through you does not want you tapping into your Soul power. It fears it. You will have difficulty learning."

"Great, just want I needed to hear!" Alrion said. He felt defeated.

"The reward is worth it. Or are you going to give up on Alyx?" Vincent said. Alrion felt a surge of anger.

"Just because it's so easy for you! Of course I won't give up." Alrion knew his father was only trying to help. And holding onto the anger wouldn't be helpful. But at the same time, he couldn't seem to let go of it just yet.

26

FALTERING

Alrion lay back down, exhausted.

"You've earned a break," Marla said. Despite the cold, Alrion oozed sweat from the sheer concentration required. It was slow and frustrating progress. His father seemed to be having an easier time of it, which just made it all harder.

"Will it at some point get easier?" Alrion said.

"It will, when you cure yourself. Until then, I doubt there will be a significant change," Marla said. Alrion looked over at his father.

"You seem to be doing better."

"Only because I don't have the handicap you do. You're working harder than both of us," Vincent said. He gave Alrion a reassuring smile. It should have worked, but it just annoyed Alrion more.

"I just wish there was a way to know it was working."

"Of course it's working. You are finding a way to work through the exercises. What else do you need?" Marla said.

"Some sort of feedback that's more tangible than this feeling I'm chasing. Being a wizard is very different. You see something happening from the very beginning."

"Again, that's because your talent lies with manipulating the world. Soul power will be less tangible, because you are just affecting yourself. And you are at the same time learning to be more sensitive to your body. It's just how it is." Marla sounded like she was sick of repeating herself. Alrion figured that she had probably never trained anyone who was infected before.

There's a first time for everything, he thought.

"I do think Alrion has a good point though. When will we know that we've reached a breakthrough?"

"You'll know it when you feel it. It's like an explosion of warmth and light and envelops your entire body. You feel calm and at peace, a tranquillity that feels like it will never end."

"That would be obvious."

"Does that mean that I would be cured?" Alrion said.

"Yes. I don't see how the Blight would be able to survive such a transformation."

"That's good to know. I'll just have to keep working at it then."

"Good. Now that you've had a short rest, we should continue. Next we will be focusing on your head." Marla stood and gestured for Alrion and Vincent to do the same.

"This time you get to cheat a little bit. We're going to dunk our heads in the water." Marla looked at them both, awaiting their response.

"Wouldn't that contaminate it?" Vincent said.

"You think this water cares about whatever's on your skin?" Marla raised one eyebrow.

"I suppose not."

"What about me? Can't I taint it somehow?" Alrion was still concerned about his infection.

"Have you been paying attention? Your infection is internal, and there's enough Soul power infused in this water to drive the Blight away. No more excuses, just follow my lead." Marla stepped up to the water. She knelt carefully, then with a swift motion dunked her head in. It was over before they realised and she quickly swept her hair back to keep the water from running into her eyes.

"Alrion next," she said. Alrion joined her, and kneeled on her left side.

Let's see what this does.

He ducked his head into the water without thinking. It felt heavy, like it could pull him in. He struggled against it, pulling his head back and gasping for air. The water streamed down his face and he wiped it away.

"Why did you keep your head in the water?" Marla said. Alrion gave her a confused look. He noticed his father was hovering over them, concern on his face.

"I didn't keep it under. My head felt heavy, like the water was pulling me in. I had to force myself back up again."

"I've never heard of that before." Marla went very quiet.

"You were under for a good thirty seconds," Vincent said. Alrion felt sick.

"It didn't feel like that long. Wow, was the water trying to drown me. Can it do that?"

"Of course not. Never mind, it's done now. Vincent your turn now," she said.

Alrion watched very closely. His father dunked his head in swiftly, and had it back out of the water instantaneously.

"That's what I expected," Marla said. Vincent swept the hair out of his face and looked at Alrion.

"We have to assume it was a weird reaction due to the Blight. Don't dwell on it too much. What do we do now?" Vincent said.

"Now we focus once more. This time we need to feel the energy within our core. Then we are going to run it up to our head. This will be tricky, but is a crucial step in both your training and preparation."

This is going to be difficult.

All the exercises that seemed to come close to his neck had either been sabotaged or a strain on him. It was no coincidence either, with that being where he had been infected.

Well, one way or another I need to get this to work. Here we go, he thought. He started to focus, capturing the feeling within his chest. The strange vibration and tingling. As he felt it he kept the sensation going. He made sure it was as strong as he could get it. Then he started to move it upwards.

It was slow to travel. He wasn't sure if that was because of the weight of it, or whether it was due to where he was moving it. But he pushed the thoughts away and kept his focus. He pushed more and more. Guiding that feeling along. It was half-pushing, half-coaxing. He couldn't describe it properly, just that it was a strange mix of actions to keep it moving along.

It began to approach his neck. There was no other way to reach his head; he had to push through it. As expected there was resistance. Like a wall, or a blockage that would not budge. He urged the feeling onwards, did everything he knew to keep it going. He tried to tear down that blockage, to will it away.

He tried and tried, and it seemed like he was slowly wearing it down. He could feel the energy within him gathering, getting ready to smash through and continue on the path he had set for it. Then suddenly he crashed. The feeling dissipated completely and he felt groggy.

Alrion was lying on the floor. He sat up slowly, and looked around. Something was wrong. He looked up at the ceiling and it was slowly oscillating. The room looked like it was threatening to spin around.

"That was not good. I feel dizzy," he said. It was scary. Like his senses were working against him.

"Your infection wound is on your neck, right?" Marla said. She was examining him closely.

"Yes, take a look."

"Hmm, this is obviously new territory for us all. It seems to be quite resistant. You may need to skip this exercise."

"Skip? What do you mean?"

"Let me explain. As I mentioned before, these exercises are a mix of training, but also preparation. You must learn how to feel the Soul power within, as well as move it around the body. But at the same time, we are unlocking your ability to use it."

"What do you mean by that?" Vincent said.

"There are multiple places in your body that are like gateways for Soul power. You need to activate those gateways to allow it to be easier to flow. It will not only amplify your total power, but also speed up the flow and transfer. The head is a very important connection to make, so that's why I asked you to dunk your head. Saturating it with water infused with Soul power helps overcome some blockages. But not all, it would seem." Marla stared at Alrion's neck. He felt really self-conscious and found himself adjusting his cloak to better hide it.

"That makes sense. But what does it mean for me?" Alrion said.

"You may need to come back to that exercise last. When the rest of your body is better prepared for the Soul power. Then you can overwhelm the Blight and cure yourself in one go."

"That's probably better than I had thought. I can just come back to it?"

"Yes. It will make the rest of your training harder, but you're already used to that right?" Marla smiled. Alrion shook his head and laughed. It was much louder and fuller than he had expected.

"Yes, nothing is ever easy. How much more are we expected to do today?"

"That's it. You should return and rest. I will brief the eldest and we will continue again tomorrow." Marla rose gracefully and tied up her wet hair.

"Should we dry this off?" Vincent said.

"No, it's better if you leave it."

"As you wish." Alrion stood and stretched a little. He felt quite stiff from all the sitting. He'd started to have a headache too.

That's the last thing I needed.

But he tried to stop the inner complaints. He followed Marla back to the entrance. She opened the door and pointed outside.

"I must remain here a bit longer before I report back. You can find your way back to your accommodation."

"Of course. Thank you for your assistance," Vincent said.

"You are welcome. You are family after all."

"So we are. Thank you and see you tomorrow," Alrion said. He followed his father out into the freezing cold. He had forgotten just how cold it was.

At first, he thought it was due to how well the building had been heated. However, he realised that it hadn't been well heated at all.

I wonder if that's a result of us training? I'll have to ask tomorrow.

They walked back to their room in silence. Alrion didn't feel like conversation, and his father seemed to understand that.

"Welcome back. How was everything?" Lara said as they entered the room. It felt a lot warmer inside.

"It was a difficult day. But we made good progress didn't we, Alrion?" Vincent said.

"I suppose so. The Blight is holding me back, but I'll find a way. I'm starving too!"

"Dig in, we can hear all about it later." Lara gestured to the food. Alrion looked over at Alyx and saw that she was asleep.

"Don't worry, she's fine. Sat up all day, but finally crashed," Lara said.

"Good." Alrion started with the food immediately. The more he ate, the more ravenous he felt.

It was deceptively hard. I hope I can do this in time, he thought. As he ate he glanced up periodically. It felt like Lara was watching him closely. But every time she appeared to be looking elsewhere.

Once Alrion finished, he shuffled over to his bed.

"Sorry, but I'm exhausted. It was a tough day, and I had a few setbacks. My dad can fill you in. But the good news is, when I do eventually have a breakthrough it will hopefully cure me of the Blight."

"Wow, that's amazing! It sounds worth the effort."

"It truly is. You rest son, I'll update Lara. You need to recover and get back to it tomorrow with your full focus."

"Thanks. Goodnight," Alrion said. He didn't even wait to hear what they said. He closed his eyes and sleep was waiting to pounce on him.

Alrion did not have a restful sleep. He kept dreaming of white orbs of light, travelling down dark hallways, being blocked by black walls. A part of him knew this was somehow related to his day, but it was only a dim awareness. Each time the orb was blocked, he felt his anger and frustration rising. Finally, there was a group of four lights all trying to go down a single corridor. But the black wall was steadfast, and oozed a black liquid. One by one it extinguished the lights. Alrion screamed in frustration.

"There you are!" Wraith said, his voice echoing and booming. Alrion found himself inside the dream corridor. He hadn't just been dreaming it, he had been present.

"What's going on?" he said.

"Oh, I was just hosting this little show for you. I see you enjoyed it!"

"These are my dreams. How can you do this?"

"With great difficulty I'm afraid. And a little outside help. But you left me no choice. You ran away to a secret place and started plotting your own cure. But now I have you."

"What do you mean? This is just a dream."

"Oh, that is true. But I know where you are. I have your location. It doesn't matter how many secret paths or tricks there are before getting to you. I know where you are, so I will find the way. You can't run any longer."

"I don't need to run. I'll face you. And I have help here." Alrion hoped Wraith fell for the bluff. He didn't feel confident in the slightest, but he had to try something.

"Your little band of Mystics? They don't scare me. In fact, I have one of them with me now. She's quite the interesting sort. We're poking and prodding her. Learning all about that special power." Wraith laughed, the sound rising in volume and echoing all around. Alrion blocked his ears trying to ignore it.

"You're lying!" Alrion said. The laughter died down.

"I'm really not. Her name is Freyda. And when I'm done with her, she won't be resistant to the Blight anymore," Wraith said. Alrion's spirit dropped. She had helped them. She had given them the amulet that had shown them the way. And Wraith had taken her and done who knows what. It was his fault.

"You've gone silent. You know I'm telling the truth. Good. It doesn't matter what you're up to over there. I know where you are, I know how to handle your Mystics, and I can create more Shade Wizards. You have no chance. So just sit tight and get ready to hand yourself over." Wraith shrieked one more terrifying laugh then went silent. Alrion looked around at the space around him. In the dream all the ways had become black and oozing. And they were closing in.

"You won't win. I'll never let you!" Alrion shouted. As the walls finally came into contact with him everything went bright white.

Alrion sat up quickly, gasping for air. He looked around the room in shock. He was in his bed. It was the visitor room. Nobody else seemed to be around.

That's odd.

He stood and paced around the room. There was food laid out. And the other beds were neatly made. He spotted a folded piece of paper on his father's bed. He opened it up and read the contents.

You look like you need the rest. Lara and Alyx have been summoned to see the eldest. I am starting the training early. Come join us when you are up.

- Dad

Alrion folded the note and replaced it. He now had an explanation for where everyone was, which was good. The details of his dream were firmly etched in his mind There was no forgetting them. He immediately started thinking of Freya, and what Wraith might be doing. His appetite quickly disappeared.

"Try not to think about that. Eat, and come up with a plan," he told himself. Walking over to the food, Alrion sat and forced himself to eat. He felt his hunger reappear as he ate, even though he wasn't enjoying the food.

Wraith knows where I am. He has more Shade Wizards, he has captured Freyda and he will probably know all he needs to know before he gets here. All because of me.

No matter how he twisted it around, it all came back to him. He had failed to deal with Wraith. He had become infected. He had led everyone to the Mystics, and in doing so put them in Wraith's path.

What if they're not?

He could leave the settlement. Let Wraith track him somewhere else. The Mystics would be spared and he could surely continue the training they had started him on.

This might be better for everyone, he thought. He didn't want anyone else to suffer for him. He started to feel his anger rise again at the thought. His failings had put him in this position, and everyone else had suffered because of it. He had an opportunity now to set things right. He could draw Wraith away from them, and spare them. At least he would do something right It was a move he could actually make by himself.

"I have to do it. They'll understand. But I have to start now. Otherwise Wraith will be too close and won't divert himself." Alrion started packing his things. He packed some food that would last well, and thought about making his bed.

No, that's too obvious. I need to buy time.

Taking one last look around the room, he cemented his decision.

"No more being a burden. I'm finally doing something." He opened the door to leave, before he lost the will to follow it through.

"Where do you think you're going?" Lara said. She was standing right outside with Alyx. Alyx looked a lot better, and Alrion was surprised to see her on her feet. He was about to explain when he felt Lara shove him back inside.

"We need to talk. Before you do something stupid," she said.

27

MEETING OF THE MINDS

"Unbelievable!" Lara said as she entered the room. The shock on Alrion's face was worth it though. She had to capitalise on that.

"We were summoned by the eldest, Jovana. I was surprised quite frankly. She didn't seem to be the sort to want anything to do with us. But she said we needed to convince you not to leave."

"I thought she was mistaken, that you would never leave us. But here we are," Alyx said. She sat down on her bed.

"Sit!" Lara said, pointing at Alrion's bed. He sat down. That was good, he was listening. She had a chance.

"So, what was going through your mind? Why were you trying to sneak off?" Lara said.

"Why would you?" Alrion started to say.

"Don't bother with that. Jovana told us she saw it happening, and here we are. Do you think we're going to believe that you packed that bag to go train?" Lara stared at Alrion with all her fury, and he seemed to resign himself.

"You would agree if you'd been through what I did last night."

"Just talk to us. What happened?" Alyx said. Alrion sighed. He looked reluctant but he started to talk.

"The training was hard. And frustrating. The Blight is holding me back. I got angry a few times, and I think it tipped off Wraith."

"What do you mean?" Lara said.

"He was in my dreams last night. He told me he knows where I am, that the Mystics wouldn't stop him. And he's bringing more Shade Wizards."

"That's not great news, but we can stop them. Look, even Alyx is on her feet!"

"I'm happy about that, but that's not all. He has Freyda!"

"The Healer? That's not good," Lara said.

"And whatever he's up to, he knows she's a Mystic. He even said that he's figuring out how to bypass her resistance to the Blight!"

"He's bluffing," Lara said. She looked at Alyx.

"Of course he is. Don't take it all to heart," Alyx said.

"He's not. I can feel it. He's not just saying that, he believes it. If he can create Shade Wizards, and Trackers, or whatever else he's been up to, then he can with enough time turn a Mystic. I can't let them suffer for my mistakes."

"Oh, now we're getting somewhere. You're going off by yourself to protect everyone else?" Lara said. Now she was beginning to understand. It was still ridiculous, but made more sense.

"It's me he's after. How many more need to suffer? If I leave now, he won't even make it to this place. He will need to track me somewhere else."

"And how will you cure yourself?"

"If I can succeed with the Mystic training, I will be cured. They've shown me most of it, I just need to continue until I get a breakthrough. It's not ideal, but at least I'll be doing something to help them." Alrion looked desperate. Lara could see that Wraith had really rattled him.

"How are you going to heal me then? He'll track you down, and you'll be alone. You'll just get captured and infected again," Alyx said.

"Didn't you swear you would cure her? Going off by yourself is just irresponsible!" Lara said. Alrion looked down. He seemed to be weakening.

"I know it's a long shot. But I can't stay here knowing what's coming."

"You are progressing in your training, your father told us all about it. Yes, there have been some setbacks. It was never going to be easy. Not with your infection. But we can all work together to take down Wraith," Lara said.

"You will be able to cure yourself and then me a lot faster if you stay. Isn't that worth the risk? Doesn't that tip the odds in our favour? You and me full strength standing together?" Alyx said. Alrion looked up at her, a new look of hope on his face. He didn't seem as defeated.

"Isn't it better to gamble on us, than to gamble on yourself alone? We're stronger together, and the Mystics are your family. They won't desert you. I doubt they would let you leave. Just save everyone the time and hassle and stay." Lara could see him coming around. He just needed another push.

"You don't even need to think about our next move. Lara and I will figure out a plan of attack. You just need to focus on working with the Mystics. Focus on the training. That's what's most important!" Alyx said. Alrion sighed one more time and closed his eyes. He sat still for a long time.

"I can't fail again. Not to him," Alrion said quietly.

"You won't. We'll be beside you," Lara said.

"Fine. I'm sorry about all this, but it felt like the right move. Maybe Wraith did all that to make me do something stupid. Anyway, I'm too scattered right now. You're right. You figure out a plan, and I'll focus on my training. Once I'm cured, I can stand on an equal footing with you both." Alrion stood tall with a new determination in his eyes.

"That works for me. Alyx?" Lara said.

"Yes, that is a good plan. Good luck with your training."

"I better get to it. See you later," Alrion said. He walked to the door, opened it quickly and strode out of the building. Lara watched and waited. After he was gone for thirty seconds she went and collapsed on her bed.

"We did it. He bought it. You can rest now," she said. Alyx slumped down onto the bed. She looked completely exhausted.

"Did they say you would improve?" Lara said.

"No. They could only keep things at bay. And the more I exert myself, the weaker their techniques get. I'll have to be careful and only do what I must to show Alrion."

"Yes, please just be comfortable now. I have to say, I only half-believed Jovana. But she was completely right. Had we been any later we would have missed him!"

"That's the proof. I'm not sure what she can see in that water of hers, but it saved us right now. It would have been catastrophic if he left now."

"Exactly. He's not ready to be alone. But it's certainly alarming that Wraith knows about this place now, and has a way to deal with or even infect the Mystics. We need to go tell Jovana about that."

"Maybe she already knows," Alyx said. She used a pillow to prop herself up a little and face Lara.

"It's definitely possible. I'll go talk to her later just in case. So, we convinced Alrion to stay the course. It took some bluffing but we did it. Now we need to come up with a plan."

"It's not like I can do anything else like this," Alyx said. She closed her eyes and lay back. Her hair spilled out of the tie she usually used. Lara could see that underneath the facade and the dress, Alyx was actually beautiful. That reminded her of how Alrion kept looking at the weapon master. Maybe he saw it also.

"I want to ask you something, before we start," Lara said. Just even broaching the topic made her uncomfortable, but she would have no better opportunity.

"Yes of course."

"I've seen how Alrion looks at you," Lara said, watching Alyx's reaction.

"Oh," Alyx said, sitting up with some effort. "He's sweet, but it doesn't mean anything."

"I'm not so sure about that," Lara said. It had been worrying her, and she was convinced it was why for the longest time she was hostile with Alyx.

"No, truly. I'm not that experienced in these matters, but I am familiar with this situation. It is not an attraction, it is equal components admiration and responsibility."

"What do you mean?"

"He was overwhelmed by my skill with weapons and my fighting style. Only because he is just a recent student of the sword, and his recent circumstances have led him to be reliant on it. Secondly, he feels responsible for my infection. So, he places the burden upon himself, which extends to anything that happens to me. To be fair, I've had a rough time since we met." Alyx didn't show any emotion. Lara understood what was said, but still wasn't convinced.

"You have feelings for him, right?" Alyx said.

"Yes," Lara said, after a long pause. Alyx nodded.

"He feels the same."

"Has he told you?"

"No, but I am confident."

"There's no way to know for sure," Lara said. She felt troubled. From the very start there had been something about him. Even that first encounter where she stole from him. She never did that anymore, not to strangers on the street. But it was an opportunity to interact with him, in some way.

"When two people are so focused on something, they don't have the time to acknowledge any feelings. As you know, I have spent my life avenging my father's death."

"Yes. I still can't believe it."

"It gets easier with time. Too easy, in fact. It will be difficult to live a different life. Anyway, there was a time when I opened my eyes to another possibility."

"What happened?"

"It was my commanding officer when I trained at Valrytir. He was kind and strong and understanding. He treated me like a human, not like the weapon I had forged myself into. Much like Alrion treats me. I did not say anything, and told myself that he felt nothing. So, we continued, like normal."

"What happened?"

"I volunteered for a scouting mission with him. He wanted to take another woman with us, a specialist archer. I convinced him otherwise, keen to have the opportunity to spend some time with him. But it was my great undoing." Alyx sighed and a tear rolled down her face.

"Why?"

"We sprung an enemy ambush meant for our main force. We retreated quickly, but there were too many. He saved my life, and we escaped. But he had been hit with two poisoned arrows. If we had taken the archer, it would have been a different story."

"He died?"

"Yes. I confessed to him before he passed, explaining my foolishness. He admitted to me he had feelings too, but thought that it was nothing as well. But in the vain hope he had let himself be talked out of taking the archer. We were both fools, but he paid the price." Alyx turned her head away and lay back down. Silence sat upon the room. Lara couldn't believe the story. She had treated Alyx like everyone else had. Assuming that she was just a soldier. But, of course, deep down she was like everyone else.

"I'm so sorry," Lara said.

"It was a long time ago. I keep it buried. I just wanted to say, the reason I shared the story was to show you that I only appreciate Alrion's attention and kindness for what it is. I seek nothing more. And as a warning for you. We come to dangerous times. If you both fail to acknowledge anything, you may make a fatal mistake. Like I did."

"I don't know what to say. But thank you."

"You are welcome. Now, perhaps some planning?"

"Yes, absolutely. I've actually been thinking for a while, there seems to be no way to defeat Wraith. But today, I had a revelation."

"What was it?"

"He's a monster in his current form. Almost indestructible and has a good selection of spells. He seems much more adept than the Shade Wizard we defeated."

"Yes, I believe the tactic we used may only create an opening for Wraith, and it would be hard to defeat him in a single strike."

"Exactly. But, what if Wraith wasn't a Shade Wizard? Then we could deal with him."

"True. But we can't change that."

"Maybe we can. What if Alrion cures him?" Lara said. It sounded crazy out loud. Healing their enemy. But it also took away his power.

"If it worked, then yes. He would be a normal wizard. We could work with that." Alyx was suddenly more alert.

"I know. But, Alrion hasn't even cured himself. Let alone someone else."

"Do you think Wraith would back off if Alrion was cured?"

"Maybe. I guess it would depend on the situation. He didn't back off at the temple with the monks."

"But that was before Alrion could cure the Blight." Alyx sat up again, energy in her features.

"Alrion curing himself could make Wraith reconsider coming here, because he's at danger of being cured. That might buy us the time we need." Lara thought there was something to that. But it didn't seem altogether right.

"There's something we are missing," Alyx said. Lara felt that too. But she couldn't put her finger on it.

"He would just wait and come back with more firepower. We would lose the advantage," Lara said.

"What advantage?"

"That we know that Alrion can learn to cure himself, and then cure others."

"True. But at least he wouldn't be able to track Alrion so easily," Alyx said. Lara nodded. That was definitely a benefit.

"That's right but he still had no trouble tracking us before Alrion was infected. I still think we need to play on this edge we have over Wraith." Lara stood and paced around. There had to be an angle they could exploit.

"I have it. But it's incredibly risky," Alyx said. Her voice sounded unsure, but her eyes shone.

"I can see that you've got something good. What is it?"

"What if Alrion only cures himself when Wraith is already here. Then Wraith has no chance to back off, then Alrion can cure him too. Then he becomes a normal wizard," Alyx said slowly. Lara thought through the suggestion. It was a good one. They could lay a trap for Wraith. They could finally go on the offensive.

"I love the idea, but it's definitely risky. We have to draw Wraith in, get Alrion to cure himself, and then have Alrion cure Wraith. There's a lot of things that could go wrong."

"There is." Alyx looked undisturbed though. She still seemed interested in the idea.

"The more I think about it, the more I think we have no other option. Alrion is sick of being chased by this monster. It's quite poetic to take its power away. I think we need to go to them with this." Lara felt like they had a unique chance. They had to try it.

"She seems like a tough one. I would get Alrion to buy into it first."

"You're right. I guess we wait until he returns this evening. Then we will know where we stand."

"Sounds good to me. I'll rest up as much as possible. You're going to need me in this fight."

"We really will," Lara said. She was concerned about the difficulty they would have laying a trap for Wraith. But she was excited by the possibility of turning the tables on him. It just felt right. They had to find a way to make it work.

28

THE STRENGTH OF SOUL

Alrion collapsed on the floor. Sweat dripped from every part of his body, and his head throbbed. His muscles ached and cried out.

"This is too hard," he groaned. He rolled onto his back and stared at the ceiling.

"You're so close. You just need to rest a little more and attack it again," Marla said. Alrion nodded weakly. He looked over at his father. He was sitting cross-legged and composed.

"Vincent, this is it. You've done the worst of it. If you can do this final ritual, you should open the door," Marla said. Vincent nodded.

"I'm ready."

"Good. What you need to do now is focus on your heart. That's the centre of everything, of your Soul power. You need to gather it then push it to all areas of your body at the same time. Every individual gate we unlocked. Touch them all at the same time. This will allow you to activate the power." Marla walked around and crouched in front of Vincent, watching him closely. Then she wandered off.

Alrion watched his father. There was an intense concentration in his face. But he seemed calm and collected. It was like he was almost resting. But his face showed the true effort of what he was doing. Alrion felt bad that he was lagging behind. He had worked hard to conquer the other areas of his body. But the final test of accessing his head with the power had proved too difficult. He would need some sort of special approach to finish it.

Suddenly Vincent flashed bright white, and he let out a cry. He blinked and looked at his hands.

"Yes! You've done it! You have enhanced your vision with Soul power. You are looking at the channels of Soul power that you have been training and working on," Marla said. Vincent turned and looked at Alrion.

"Oh my," he said.

"What is it?" Alrion said.

"I can see the Blight within you," Vincent said. He closed his eyes and opened them again.

"Back to normal?" Marla said.

"Yes. Do you always use that?" he said.

"No, it's quite taxing and as you saw shows a lot of things you don't need to normally see."

"I can believe that. It's a bit overwhelming actually."

"Good, that means it was working properly. Once you have more mastery over it, you can switch it on and off as required."

"Very handy. There's a whole world I wasn't aware of. I know, I know, I could have found out a long time ago." Vincent chuckled and looked over at Alrion.

"I'm glad you made it. Didn't take as long as I thought. It means there's still hope for me," Alrion said.

"Due in no small part to your lineage. But I must admit you have applied yourselves well," Marla said.

"Thanks," Vincent said.

"I'm just glad that there's light at the end of the tunnel, so to speak." Alrion laughed, and his father joined in. Even Marla smiled.

"It's good that you haven't lost your sense of humour. You're so close now," Vincent said.

"Your father is right. You know what to focus on now. I think you will want to meditate for a while to help build up your reserves. It will probably take everything you have to break through your infection."

"I have a question," Vincent said. He stood and stretched his muscles.

"Yes?" Marla said.

"Am I ready now? Can I just start using my new power?"

"Yes and no." Marla paused before speaking again. "Yes, you have now unlocked proper use of your Soul power. However, you expended a lot in the act of unlocking it. I would caution against using it much at the moment, give it time to replenish."

"I can handle that. How does it regenerate?"

"Naturally over time. Your body rebuilds it automatically. You can also meditate, that would help speed up the process."

"Great. Take note Alrion, I'm sure you'll want to be up and running immediately so I hope you've been paying attention."

"Can't use it immediately. Wait or meditate to hurry it up," Alrion said. He kept his eyes closed and rested on the ground.

"You don't strike me as the patient type. There's one more lesson that I think will be doubly useful for you," Marla said. Alrion opened his eyes and looked back at her.

"And that is?"

"Meditation."

"I can't argue with that. Well, I could but I don't really have the energy. You've sold me on the benefits. I think I need a minute to rest though."

"It's actually better to start immediately. Sorry," Marla said.

"I don't think she's actually sorry," Alrion said to Vincent, pretending to whisper. His father laughed.

"I'll stick around for this one too. It should be quite useful."

"Well then, sit next to me. Much of this will be familiar, but don't skip any steps. There are shortcuts," Marla said. Alrion forced himself up and he trudged over. He was physically and mentally exhausted. And he felt more and more like the Blight had a hold over him. But this was his only way to move forward, so he just found a way.

"I think you're doing quite well. But now's a good time to return to your friends and actually rest," Marla said. She stood quickly and gracefully. Alrion had more trouble.

"I think my legs fell asleep. Is that normal?"

"More normal than you may think. Don't worry."

"I was going to blame it on my more advanced age," Vincent said. He also looked a bit wobbly getting up. But Alrion didn't say anything.

"Alrion, take it easy tonight. You've done enough and forcing it won't help. Tomorrow is another day," Marla said.

"Do we have enough time?" Alrion said, looking at his father.

"We should do. This is important, don't rush it."

"Fine. I'll probably find it easy to rest, to be honest."

"Good. I'll see you back here, first thing tomorrow." Marla left the room with purpose, letting in a gust of freezing wind.

"Just in case you forgot what it's like out there. Better rug up again," Vincent said. They put on their discarded heavy layers and stepped out into the cold once more.

At first the cold was a welcome change. But soon, it wore thin and Alrion grew irritated and his muscles became stiff. At least it wasn't too far to walk. When they reached their room Alrion let his father open the door, and stumbled through it. He noticed Alyx and Lara deep in conversation. They abruptly stopped when they saw him.

"You've returned. What news do you have?" Lara said. Vincent nodded at Alrion.

"My father has unlocked the power of Soul. I am a bit further behind, due to my delightful infection."

"That's fantastic!" Alyx said.

"I'm glad how enthusiastic you are for my father, but it's not quite the outcome I wanted." Alrion was confused by her excitement.

"No, she means it's fantastic that you're not cured yet. We have a plan now," Lara said.

"I'm curious," Alrion said. He allowed himself to lie down on the bed and rest. But he remained alert.

"I came up with a way to defeat Wraith for good," Lara said.

"I'm all ears," Alrion said.

"You cure him of the Blight," Lara said. Alrion sat bolt upright. He immediately regretted it.

"What? Why would I do that?"

"Just think. He has few weaknesses, and is incredibly dangerous. But if you cured him, he would just be another wizard," Alyx said.

"And you defeated him before when he was just a wizard," Lara said. Alrion could see the logic there, but it didn't feel right.

"To be fair I got lucky back then. But you're right in that he was vulnerable. Something doesn't seem right though," Alrion said.

"I think it's a good plan. What's it got to do with Alrion not being cured yet?" Vincent said.

"Well, from what we know Wraith is quite bullish. But he's also cunning. He could have followed us faster I'm sure. But he's taken the time to slow us down. Why do you think that is?" Alyx said.

"Clearly his experiments with Shade Wizards, and now Mystics," Alrion said. He felt horrible just saying the words out loud.

"Why would he do that if he can just snatch you up quickly?" Alyx said.

"Because he knows I'll be infected eventually anyway. Or, at least he believes that," Alrion said.

"Yes, but he's also not prepared to fail again. Remember, even with the huge force he sent to the temple, you managed to clear the trial and escape," Lara said.

"Let's say I buy into your thinking that he's cautious and careful right now. What does that mean?" Alrion said.

"If you were Wraith, and you were tracking yourself via your infection. You would know if something were to happen, right?" Lara said.

"He'd probably know immediately that something was up," Alrion said.

"And he would quickly come to the conclusion that you are cured in that scenario. Correct?" Lara said. Alrion nodded. He looked over at his father who also nodded.

"What's the first thing you would do when healed?" Alyx said.

"Heal you of course."

"Which he will also detect," Lara said.

"He will figure out that I have healed myself, and one other."

"What position does that put him in? What power does he have over you in that situation?" Lara said. Alrion could see their point. If Wraith had any sort of consideration or caution, then he would stop his approach. He'd need to stack the odds in his favour again.

"He might back off and regroup. But it would get the Mystics out of the line of fire."

"For how long?" Alyx said. Alrion thought it over.

"Well, what's your proposal then? That I just not cure myself?"

"We propose that you wait until he arrives. Then heal yourself. He won't have time to prepare any counter-attacks, and then you can cure him. The tides will turn immediately. With their leader gone, the rest will either flee or be easy targets," Alyx said.

"There's just one problem with that," Alrion said. He sighed and sunk back into the bed.

"What is it?" Lara said.

"There's a delay. Alrion will expend all his Soul power cleansing himself. He needs to wait for it to replenish. It doesn't sound like a fast process," Vincent said.

"They said I can meditate, but I don't think that's going to cut it," Alrion said. He could see what they were getting at. But there was no way to make it work.

"But you don't know how long is required. You're just making assumptions," Lara said. She looked determined. Alrion just felt weary.

"You're right. We shouldn't eliminate it completely. As tiring as it sounds, I'm starting to warm to it. I can picture Wraith's face when I am healed. It will be a sight to see," Alrion said.

"We should consult with my mother. Alrion, I know you're tired. But this can't wait. We need to know if this strategy will work. Otherwise, we need to come up with something else," Vincent said. Alrion knew his father was right, but he didn't want to move. Summoning vast amounts of energy, he sat up once more, then stood. His left leg wavered a bit, but he stayed up.

"I swear the Blight is messing with me. I don't know how you're walking around, Alyx," he said. He took a few steps and felt his strength return. It wasn't much, but at least he was solid on his feet.

"Please be quick. Good luck," Lara said.

"Of course," Alrion said. He let his father open the door and he charged back into the freezing cold.

The walk over to the grand hall was agonising. Alrion just wanted to nestle into the snow and sleep. It looked positively inviting.

"Easy there," Vincent said. He gave Alrion a steadying hand.

"Sorry, that patch of snow there looks thick and soft," Alrion said, half-joking. His father chuckled.

"That particular patch does look especially warm and cosy," Vincent said.

"Sounds like you want it now. I saw it first!" Alrion said.

"Once you defeat Wraith, it's all yours," Vincent said. He paused before the great doors. "Are you ready?"

"Yes. I'll fall through if you don't open them soon." Alrion smiled and waited for his father to push back the doors. They stepped into the relative warmth and Alrion felt sleepy.

Stay with it, he thought and pinched himself. The room had emptied out once more. Only his grandmother sat at the far end of the room, peering once more into the water before her.

"Approach!" she said, her voice carrying across the empty space. Alrion walked steadily over, his father staying close and sneaking lots of worried glances.

"I won't fall over here, don't worry," Alrion whispered. But he wasn't as confident as he sounded, and it didn't look like his father bought the act. As they approached the giant throne, Alrion saw a chair had been placed before it.

"Sit, Alrion. I know you are tired," Jovana said. Alrion didn't think twice and rushed over. The comfort was initially overwhelming. He looked up at her suspiciously.

"Of course you're exhausted, you've been training all day. I can see that you have almost achieved your goal. You're very close to not disappointing me."

"Uh, thank you," Alrion said. He looked at his father.

"You are very kind. We thank you again for your understanding and help."

"You are family after all. Did you think anything else would happen?" Jovana said. There was silence.

"I see you have come to ask for help? Spit it out then," she said.

"Yes. We wanted to find out how long it would take Alrion to replenish his Soul power after curing himself. Enough to cure someone else," Vincent said.

"I've been thinking of this myself. To answer your question, several hours at least. Partially because it is his first time, and partially because he will need every fibre of his being infused with Soul power to even consider expelling the Blight from another being. No matter what wizard tricks he uses to do it," Jovana said. She gave Alrion a stern look, and he wilted. Hours were no good. Even speeding that up to an hour would be way too long.

"Thank you for your time. That tells us what we needed to know," Alrion said. He started to rise, but heard Jovana clearing her throat. He looked up at her, puzzled.

"I told you I was thinking about it already. Why haven't you asked what can be done to speed up the process?" she said.

"Well, even an hour is way too long. I just presumed," Alrion said but was cut off immediately.

"You presumed to know better than me? The greatest Mystic that has ever lived, and the one who built this place?" Jovana stood slowly, looking down on Alrion. He suddenly felt very small.

"Surely even meditation cannot make that much of a difference," Vincent said.

"Who said you could only use meditation?" Jovana said. Her voice had a dangerous edge to it. Alrion started to speak but his father silenced him with a touch.

"What else could be used?" Vincent said. Jovana started to smile.

"It seems that you can learn, eventually. You're looking at it," she said, pointing to the small stone water fountain before her.

"You've witnessed the pool in the training room. This source is purer and more potent. With the right focus and application, you could be recharged in minutes."

"How many minutes?" Alrion said.

"At best, between five to ten. Will that be fast enough?" Jovana said. Alrion looked at his father.

"There's a lot riding on it. It's up to everyone else. I think we need to let them make that decision," Alrion said.

"I think you're right," Vincent said.

"You're not going to consult me? You don't think my Mystics will be involved in holding that creature at bay while you ready yourself to cure it?" Jovana said. Alrion's jaw dropped. Vincent just laughed.

"I'm so sorry mother. Time and time again we keep underestimating you, even when you remind us. Of course, we need your blessing to even consider such a plan. To be honest, we wanted to consider it ourselves first, before even bringing it to you."

"I know that. It's your only choice, if you want to get on with your quest. That man will never stop until you take away his power."

"You'll help us?" Alrion said. Jovana looked down into the water for a long time.

"If your friends agree that it can be done, I will support you in whatever your plan requires," she said finally. There was a sadness to her face, which Alrion was surprised by. As soon as he thought to comment on it, it was gone.

"We have some planning to do. I'll advise you as soon as we have something," Vincent said.

"Go now. Time is shorter than you think," Jovana said, pointing to the door. Alrion didn't like the warning in her voice.

29

SACRED GROUND

"You must stay here, no matter what you hear," Vincent said. Alrion nodded. He was back in the grand hall. The night had passed so quickly that he felt like he had just blinked and come back.

"Wraith is close?" Alrion said.

"We believe so. Preparations are underway now. But forget about all that. You have an important job to do. Meditate and prepare, you need to be ready." Vincent held out his hand. Alrion looked at it oddly and shook it. His father's grip was strong. He saw something pass quickly over his father's eyes.

"What was that?" Alrion said.

"You're a man now, and I wanted to treat you as such. I believe in you, and I know that you can do this. We're all putting our trust in you."

"Thank you. I don't feel confident right now, but I'll pretend that I am. But I was more asking about your eyes." Alrion pointed. Vincent gave a small laugh.

"Here I am making some gesture and you're just noticing something else. I took a look at you through Soul-enhanced eyes."

"And?"

"You look a lot better. The infection is still a mess, but it seems to have mostly consolidated into the one area. It will be hard, but you will succeed. I know it."

"That's actually good to hear. You can't stay here encouraging me the whole time, I'm sure they're waiting for you."

"They are. See you soon," Vincent said. He gave a quick wave and marched out. Alrion turned to see Jovana watching him.

"Should I just sit down somewhere?"

"No. You need to practice with the source. Come up here." Jovana stood and stepped aside, making space for Alrion in front of the pool of water. He carefully walked up the steps, and stood beside her. He stared into the water. It seemed to have layers to it. The surface seemed crystal clear, but it became darker the deeper you looked.

"This is unusual. Why is the water like that?" he said.

"That's not the water, that's a feature of the fountain it sits within. It aids with seeing."

"Seeing?"

"I am all-knowing, but how do you think I am so well informed?"

"Because you can see things in the water?"

"I don't stare in here because I'm senile!" Jovana said. Alrion shrugged.

"I still don't know half of what's possible. How does the Soul power help you see things?"

"It's a special property of blending your own power with that of the Source. Imagine that the water becomes a mirror, showing you that which your eyes wish to see but cannot."

"You can see great distances?"

"Oh, and more. But we don't have the time to properly instruct you now. And in your current condition it would not work properly. For now, you need to acquaint yourself with the water." Jovana rolled the sleeves up on her robe and placed both hands above the water.

"You too," she said. Alrion did the same, placing his hands close to hers.

"Now, the first thing we will be repeating is the first exercise you were taught. Feel the sensation in your hand and run it back to your heart." She closed her eyes and concentrated.

Alrion closed his eyes, and tried to push away all his feelings. He couldn't worry about what was about to happen. He had to focus on the here and now. With some difficulty he managed to recreate the sensation in his hands and slowly moved it along his arm and to his heart. It seemed a bit easier than the first time.

"Good, you've been paying attention. Was that easier or harder?"

"Easier. Is it due to the water?"

"No, well an insignificant amount may be. It was easier because you have been training yourself and reinforcing those pathways. Now, try again, but have your hand touching the surface of the water ever so gently." Jovana demonstrated, placing one hand down carefully. She just touched the surface of the water with her hand. She closed her eyes and Alrion nodded. It was his turn.

He followed her example very carefully. The water felt cool, but at the same time had a warm tingle to it. But he didn't worry about that so much. He started to repeat the exercise, but found it very different. His hand felt like it was almost on fire, rather than the light tingling from before. Moving the feeling down his arm was different too. It felt like it was easier to get momentum, but harder to control. He gasped when it reached his heart.

"Good. Feels different, doesn't it?"

"Much stronger. Harder to control."

"Exactly. Now one final example. This time fully submerge your hand." Jovana demonstrated once more. She was less careful this time, just plunging her hand under the water. But she did only use her hand; her arm was out of the water. After she closed her eyes Alrion tried himself.

Even though he knew the water was cold, it felt hot. It was the strangest sensation. As he began the exercise once more he was so shocked he almost pulled his arm out immediately. His whole arm was aflame with the Soul power, and directing it was incredibly difficult. But he focused his mind and contained it. With great trouble and persistence, he managed to push it along into his heart. But he also felt a spark within his stomach. He fell back with the shock, pulling his arm out of the water completely.

Jovana grabbed his arm roughly, steadying him. She was a lot stronger than she looked. Alrion just stared at her in confusion.

"I must admit, you're better than I thought. But even the control you did exert was not enough. You activated two gateways at the same time!" Jovana nudged him back until he was seated in the chair. She stood in front, looking him over. He noticed the strange flash over her eyes too.

"This is good. You will be able to contain the power. So, tell me, what did you think about that?" Jovana stared at him intently, waiting for an answer. He closed his eyes and thought. It was too distracting watching her watch him.

"The more contact I have with the water, the more of the power I absorb. But it is a lot harder to control. I'll need to balance the control and the speed of absorption if I am to use it effectively," he said. He opened his eyes and saw a smile on her face.

"You're smarter than your father. That's a relief. I'd prefer it if you learned more on your own, since that's the most effective method. But I'll need to feed you a few more pointers."

"I'm ready."

"As you are probably figuring out, I'm going to ask you to repeat all your activation exercises. This will help reinforce your Soul power and give you practice with the source. When the time comes, you will flood yourself and direct it all at that infection. It will most likely be agonising, but you will defeat it." Jovana gestured for him to stand and she sat down.

"That sounds easier."

"It won't be. But it will be faster. To complete the activation, you must not use the water. It will complicate things."

"I understand."

"Good. Now, after you are cured, you will want to replenish yourself as fast as possible. Balance is the key. Directing a torrent of power will not be effective. Save that for when you are desperate. We will give you the time you need to do it properly." Jovana stopped talking and sat back in the chair. She seemed weary.

"I'm sorry for all the trouble I've caused," Alrion said. Jovana laughed. A loud cackling that rang all over the room.

"Don't be sorry, there was no other way for it to happen. It will be an honour to have you succeed in my presence. Now, go back there and continue your exercises. You need to be ready for when they come."

"I will be," Alrion said. Against all odds he had a plan and the means to succeed. He couldn't let anyone down now. For the first time in a long time, he felt like the Blight was being held back. He was in control. And he would make sure that was how things stayed.

~

Vincent left the hall quickly.

That went well. Alrion doesn't suspect just how close they are. Although surely my mother knows, he thought. He almost ran to the entrance of the Mystic settlement. Marla was standing out front but there was nobody else.

"Are we ready?" Vincent said.

"Yes. My Mystics are spreading out throughout the space. Lara will join us soon and can relay messages quickly."

"You don't have other ways?"

"We do, but it's important to keep things simple. We also don't know what the situation is with Freyda. I'd rather not risk giving too much away."

"That seems wise. Here's Lara now," Vincent said. The thief ran along the snow with ease. She pulled up quickly, then took a moment to catch her breath.

"The Mystics are in position. I just need to report in when the party starts."

"Good. Alrion is working with my mother. He will be ready."

"Do you think we will see a large number?" Marla said.

"No, I think it will be a more focused group. Shade Wizards, Wraith, and Freyda. Maybe some Trackers?" Vincent said.

"That would play to our strengths more. Provided we can be effective at negating the wizards," Marla said.

"Amplifying your speed will be key. I hope your combat training is still fresh," Vincent said.

"You'd be surprised. All of us require it frequently. We are targets, even though people don't know who we really are. Just being women is enough. We see to ourselves, and are often posted as Healers. To many we look like easy marks."

"Those that heal can also harm," Vincent said.

"Only when required. We will do what is required, don't you worry."

"I'm not, I'm just nervous with all the waiting," Vincent said.

"Oh, I love the suspense. And every moment we wait, Alrion gets more time. Maybe I'll take a nap," Lara said, laughing. Vincent appreciated the gesture, although he saw that the laughter was a bit forced. She was right though. As tense as it may be, waiting was for the best. He dug his feet in and tried to think of other things.

～

"They're here," Marla said softly. Vincent peered into the distance but couldn't see anything yet.

"Look properly," she said. He realised what she meant, and reached for his Soul power. He wondered if it would ever feel natural, but assumed it would in time. By channelling it into his eyes and focusing on the distance he could see the colours around much more vividly. The landscape was not as bleak and white as he had thought. What captured his attention however was the procession heading towards them. It was a long column, all heading in single file. He had trouble discerning what they were. All he could see were dark shapes.

"I can see them now, but not any details. Is that me, or are they just that far away?" he said.

"A bit of both. You can increase your focus and definition with practice. Right now, you are probably getting a lot of different sensations all at once. You can be more selective with what you see in time," Marla said.

"It's like I'm pouring the paint on, but you're selectively brushing in exactly what you want to see?" Vincent said. He was struggling to find a way to describe it. Marla laughed.

"Never heard it described like that, but that's fairly accurate."

"Whatever you're doing to your vision must be extremely potent, because I still can't see anything," Lara said. She started to walk off.

"Lara, trust me they're coming. Just stay close please," Vincent said. Lara slowed down and waited a few paces beyond Vincent. She was peering into the distance.

Minutes passed. Agonising minutes. Vincent looked again and again, and had trouble discerning any features on the shapes that were advancing.

"I think they're purposefully approaching slowly. Maybe they're wary of traps," he said.

"I think you're right. We know he's coming," Lara said.

"We did account for that in our planning. We had to assume that by having Freyda, he would be wise to our usual defensive mechanisms," Marla said.

"I can see now. Wraith is at the front," Vincent said. It was mixed feelings. Relief that the enemy had finally been identified and spotted. But dread at the ensuing confrontation. It had been a long and bloody fight at the temple, and most of that was before Wraith had even shown up. Now he was leading the group. He would not be sitting back.

"Makes sense. He would survive any traps, so he's going first," Lara said.

"Do you need to alert anyone about anything?" Vincent said.

"Not until he's closer," she said.

"Don't wait too long," Marla said. Vincent could hear the concern in her voice. He had to assume that she could see Wraith clearly now, and was starting to finally get an idea of what he actually was.

"Just a bit further," Lara said. She continued to stare off into the distance. Vincent was not sure what she was looking for exactly.

"That should be enough. I'll be back soon, just need to set something in motion," Lara said. She took off at great speed through the snow.

"How are you feeling?" Vincent said.

"I'm fine. Ready to rescue our sister."

"Good. Just keep a cool head. It looks like there's probably quite a few Shade Wizards there."

"I know. Don't worry about me," Marla said. But her voice was strained. Vincent didn't press the issue. He had to trust that they could protect themselves. He still didn't fully understand all they could do, although he had seen lots of potential.

"I'm here!" Wraith shouted. He was almost upon them, and his voice thundered through the space. It had to be amplified through magical means. It still carried that harsh, stinging tone. The sound brought back memories for Vincent.

I can't believe Alrion has had to deal with this, inside his head, he thought with horror. It sounded bad enough in theory, but hearing this reminder of what it would actually be like was scary. Vincent drew his sword and held it ready.

"Are you sure you want to welcome it with a weapon?" Marla said.

"Wraith won't be at ease otherwise. He will suspect something," Vincent said.

"I won't argue with that. Let's see what this thing looks like up close." Marla stayed in a neutral pose, but she looked alert and ready. Vincent peered out, trying to see Wraith's final approach.

This time, he looked different. His height, physique, and skin were all the same. But he was dressed in a black cloak. And he held a staff. It was wooden and ornamental with a jet-black orb at the top.

"Vincent! So nice to see you again. I'm touched that you chose to welcome me," Wraith said. Vincent looked past Wraith, trying to see what else he needed to deal with.

"There'll be plenty of time for introductions later. Why don't you start with the woman?" Wraith said.

"Marla, one of the Mystics. And you are?"

"Wraith. First amongst the Shade Wizards, and leader of the Blight."

"Funny that, I've never heard of you until today."

"Because I work in the shadows, your ignorance is testament to my power."

"Hardly," Vincent said. He adjusted his stance and stayed in the ready position.

"You only had half a chance with that blade last time, you have no chance this time. Where's Alrion? Hiding away?"

"He's waiting for you, and completing his preparations," Vincent said.

"Oh, that's nice. Are you going to start the fight now? Or can we start off with a civil chat?" Wraith said. He clicked his fingers and four similarly dressed figures broke out from single file and stood next to Wraith.

Shade Wizards.

He looked over at Marla and pretended like he was considering his next move. But they knew what to do. Marla nodded at him. Vincent sheathed his sword.

"I suppose we can try that first, she said it was fine. But keep your manners," Vincent said. Wraith laughed, the evil sound causing Marla to flinch.

You don't know the half of it, Vincent thought. But they had met Wraith and convinced him to waltz in like he owned the place. That was all they needed to do for now. The rest would happen soon enough.

30

FIRST STRIKE

Vincent couldn't decide whether it was better to know or not know what was coming. He was tense because he knew something would happen. But at least he had no way of tipping off Wraith accidentally. Vincent looked around as they walked, and spotted nobody.

"I expected more of a welcoming party," Wraith said.

"Why would they be here, when they could be with Alrion?" Vincent said.

"I'm the one you need to appease here. You all live by my whim alone. As soon as I decide otherwise, it's over for you." Wraith snapped his fingers to demonstrate how easy he considered it.

I can't wait for Alrion to take you down a notch.

But Vincent held his tongue. It was not the right time to antagonise Wraith. The walk was slow and considered. Vincent wanted to look back and see who else Wraith had brought. But the odd glances he had risked earlier showed only the Shade Wizards. They were flanking Wraith and trailing behind him. Vincent had to assume that Freyda was back there somewhere. But now was not the time to verify that.

A flash of light startled Vincent and he stopped suddenly. Before he could even empower his eyesight, he noticed a group of Mystics had attacked. They had come in pairs. Four groups were there now. The front Mystic in each pairing was streaking forward with a glowing hand. They had each singled out one of the Shade Wizards.

Before their enemies could react, the Mystics landed their attacks. An explosion of light enveloped each Shade Wizard and almost in unison they clutched at their chests.

That's amazing. But it's a suicide strike. Wraith won't let them get away, Vincent thought. But then he saw the purpose of the second Mystic. Before the lead Mystics had even finished moving, the rear ones were gathering their Soul power and pushing it to their legs. Their role was now clear. As the pieces connected in Vincent's mind he saw them streak away from danger, taking their partner with them.

Wraith had cottoned on, but the wave of fire he unleashed was too slow. The Mystics were all gone.

"Take advantage of my leniency, do you? What a foolish decision!" Wraith roared. He whirled around and faced Vincent.

"And now we leave," Marla said. She grabbed Vincent's hand and the two of them sped away before Vincent could say anything. The terrain flew by like a dream, and before Vincent could get his bearings he was standing in front of the great hall.

"Inside. We have no time," Marla said. Vincent opened the doors and stepped inside. He looked for Alrion and saw him at the end of the room with Jovana. The rest of the room was filled with Mystics. He spotted what he assumed were the eight that had just attacked. They were all crouched down and meditating. Marla seemed tired already. She walked past Vincent and took a position meditating as well.

"Well done," Vincent said.

"I'm quite impressed," Lara said. Vincent hadn't spotted her in the corner.

"So, we're all here then. This is the final stand?" Vincent said.

"That's the one. Once our visitors have arrived nobody is allowed to leave," Lara said.

"Sounds like quite a party," Vincent said. He understood that much of the plan. But he didn't like the thought of how it was going to work. Clearly that sneak attack had expended the full power of eight Mystics. And it wasn't likely to work again.

"It'll work. We don't have a choice," Lara said. Vincent nodded. She was right about that. But for now, his priority was Alrion. He walked up and joined his son.

~

Alrion looked up at the noise. He noticed a lot of people entering the hall. First it was a group of eight Mystics. And then his father and Marla.

Wraith must already be here. I feel like I'm ready as I'll ever be, but at the same time it doesn't seem like enough, he thought. But he felt reassured seeing his father there.

Lara entered soon after, and Vincent walked over.

"Are you ready?" Jovana said.

"Yes. I've done what I can," Alrion said.

"Good. Now you must remain calm and push through at the appropriate time. The clock starts then."

"I know," Alrion said. He was not looking forward to that. The intense pressure having to regather his power to cure Wraith. It would take a lot of restraint to focus on his task, rather than on whatever fight was there.

"I can see that you're ready. Wraith is here, and in fine form. He's already had a taste of the Mystics, and let's just say they wiped the smile off his ugly face," Vincent said. Alrion grinned.

"Good. So, he'll be here soon. I noticed that Lara is here."

"He can't be far behind. I'll give you the signal when you can complete activation."

"I'm waiting." Alrion could feel the tension in the room, and he himself couldn't sit still. He stood and tried to remain calm.

The giant doors to the hall flew off their hinges and embedded into the nearby walls. Wraith strode through the open doorway, a short procession trailing him closely.

"He certainly looks angry," Alrion said. Wraith looked the same as he remembered, but the addition of a black cloak and staff was interesting.

Maybe he has more completely mastered his transformation?

But he decided not to jump to any conclusions. For now, he just had to watch and wait.

"You ignorant insects! You dare attack me? I thought you were interested in avoiding unnecessary death and destruction. Now, you will pay!" Wraith shouted. Jovana motioned for Vincent and Alrion to stand aside. She rose to her full height slowly from the throne.

"Abominations should know their place. Show some respect before I throw you out," Jovana said. Her voice rang loud and clear throughout the hall. Wraith looked so angry that his eyes were about to pop out.

"What did you say to me?" Wraith roared.

"Come closer if you're hard of hearing." Jovana maintained her calm demeanour and poise, which seemed to annoy Wraith even more. He whirled around, looking at his retinue. After a few moments he signalled to them to hold and he walked slowly through the room. Wraith glared at the Mystics as he walked.

"That is far enough," Jovana said once Wraith had reached the midpoint of the room. "State your business."

"I'm here for Alrion. He has evaded me long enough. If you hand him over now, I will show some leniency when dealing with your Mystics."

"Alrion is my grandson. He will not be leaving with you," Jovana said.

"Start the process Alrion," Vincent whispered. Alrion nodded and closed his eyes. He started checking on each of the gateways within his body. Each one had been bolstered and filled with Soul power. All except one. But he knew what he had to do.

One by one he transferred the available Soul power to his heart. He wasn't sure how much could be contained in a single point, but nobody had cautioned him against it. He had a strange feeling of being full, and yet more and more power accumulated. He could already feel a strange resonance in his neck. Like the Blight could feel something was happening.

"What's going on over there? What's Alrion doing?" Wraith said. It sounded so distant, but Alrion could sense the fear within it. He could tell something was changing. But Alrion maintained his focus.

He took all his gathered Soul power and started to move it up, on a familiar path. At first a stroke of panic entered his mind. He remembered how hard it was to move so much energy at once. But his concerns were unfounded. It was not as bad as when he was dealing with the pool's energy. There was a weight and momentum to contend with, but the energy seemed to do a better job of staying on the path.

He pushed it along, building up pace. He could feel the inevitability of it. Such a large and dense mass of Soul power. The Blight could not stand by and resist that. Suddenly, the two forces collided within him.

As before, the Blight put up resistance. But Alrion knew it could not survive. He didn't panic, he just pushed gently. He knew it would falter, and give in to the overwhelming light. So, he kept up the pressure. And the Blight began to give way. But as it did so, the light kept going. It overran the infection and took up all the space within Alrion's body. He could feel the Blight bending, breaking, and then with one final explosion it was gone completely. Alrion experienced a moment of tranquillity, then blackness.

Alrion awoke in a haze. He was lying on the cold floor. As he dragged himself up he could hear commotion around him. Memories started to flood back.

Wraith's here. I cured myself. Didn't I?

He sat up and tested himself for any signs of the Blight. There was nothing. But he didn't feel different. The Soul power was not there. He started to panic. Something was wrong.

A warm hand settled down on his shoulder.

"You didn't finish the activation. Nothing is wrong," Jovana said. Alrion felt embarrassed first, then relieved.

"Thank you. I'm still catching up," he said. He looked at her. The stern look on her features had softened a little.

"Don't dilly dally. Time has not frozen for you." Jovana pointed at the room. Alrion looked over and saw a battle raging. That was the source of commotion.

His father was fighting side by side with Marla, and Lara was backing them up. There were other Mystics in the battle too. Wraith was largely unengaged, but observing. He seemed to be waiting for something. Alrion spotted some Trackers in the fight too.

"Don't get distracted. Finish the activation and start gathering your power," Jovana said. This time it was harsher and it shocked Alrion out of his stupor.

"Of course," he said. He remembered the exercise when his father did it. He just needed to connect all his internal gateways just once. He reached out and felt his heart point. It was weak but there.

This may be harder, because I've expended all my power.

But that was no excuse. He just had to keep at it.

"I thought you'd gone and killed yourself. But I see you didn't have the nerve!" Wraith shouted. He stepped past the fight and started walking closer.

"Keep going," Jovana said. Alrion tried to focus, but he couldn't take his eyes off Wraith.

"I did the impossible. It was a little more taxing than I expected," Alrion said. Wraith stopped walking and looked at him with a curious look. Alrion closed his eyes and made another connection.

"I thought that perhaps you had done it. My pet Mystic told me that was what you were trying to do. I told her you couldn't do it, but look at this. You proved me wrong. But I don't want you getting any ideas. Come here pet," Wraith said. He beckoned without turning around. A woman stepped out from the back of the room and slowly approached. She was too far to identify properly.

Another connection. Don't lose focus.

Alrion looked out again and recognised Freyda. She wore a cloak with the arms exposed, and long black tattoos covered much of her skin. Another pattern criss-crossed her forehead. She kept her head down a little, and shuffled along like she was broken.

"Here she comes now. She is a wielder of this Soul power you seem to be after now. But look at her. She's been infected. It doesn't protect you, it just makes us have to work a bit harder." Wraith started laughing. He forcibly pulled up Freyda's face so she could look Alrion in the eyes. He could see her fear, and realised that whatever had been done, she was still aware of it. In some fashion. Alrion closed his eyes, and forced himself to connect another gateway. He was almost there.

"Too much to look at, is it? Well, that there is your fate Alrion. No matter what tricks you think you have up your sleeve," Wraith said. Alrion ignored him, he needed to finish up. Just a bit further.

"He's not listening to me. What's he doing?" Wraith said to Freyda.

"I cannot sense that, you have blocked me," she said. Wraith smacked her over the head.

"What do you think he's doing then?"

"Activating his Soul power," she said.

"Oh, this will be good. How long does that take?"

"The sequence shouldn't take longer than a minute if uninterrupted."

"And then?"

"Then ... he can use his new power," Freyda said. She trailed off at the end. Wraith lifted her head up and stared into her face.

"I can sense you are holding back. What do you want to share with me?"

"Because he passed out, he probably expended all his stored Soul power curing himself," Freyda said.

"I don't care about that. He's a wizard, that's what he will use," Wraith said. Alrion closed his eyes; he just had to concentrate one last time.

"Go ahead, Alrion, do your thing. It won't make a difference!" Wraith said. Alrion did as instructed, making the last link. A sudden surge of power within him took his breath again. He coughed suddenly, then felt like the wind had been taken out from him. He started to fall forward but Jovana grabbed him and hauled him back.

"It's a bit disorientating with your power drained like that. Not as it is meant to be. But welcome back," she said.

"Thank you. I will never be able to thank you enough," Alrion said.

"Don't let that stop you trying. But for now, you better start with that pool," she said. Jovana gave Alrion a short shove and he rose unsteadily. He stepped over and leaned over the pool of water, hovering his right hand above it. It was easier now, to start to harness the power. And it felt great to be restored. Like he was thirsty but in a different way.

"It's like another sense. It's incredible," Alrion said. He tried diverting some to his eyes, like his father had done. The room blazed with colour, and he had to immediately close them. But he opened his eyes again carefully and started to see. Jovana had a strong core of blue, and a powerful aura. Marla was the same, but the strength seemed different.

Next, he looked over at Wraith. He was a seething mess of black and purple energy. His core was a purple flame.

Makes sense, Alrion thought. He looked over the room, trying to find Alyx. He spotted her in the corner, sitting down. She was filled with black energy, scarily so. But there seemed to be blue and white orbs of energy breaking up what he assumed to be the Blight.

You're so close, I have to cure you, he thought. But he couldn't. Not yet Not with Wraith right in front of him.

"You look like you need a minute, Alrion. I'll let the others fight for now, and then step in myself. I want you to watch me crush you again. Only this time, you won't be able to drop me into a pit of sand." Wraith started to laugh and walked back to the main fray. Freyda followed close behind. She glimpsed one soulful look back at Alrion.

She must have guessed what we are doing, but held back. Good, I just need a bit more time, he thought. Hopefully they could pull it off. He had no idea how to cure Wraith, but that was something he could ponder as he built his power. It wasn't like he could do anything else while the fighting continued.

31

ELDER INTERVENTION

Vincent placed a reassuring hand on Alrion's shoulder, then walked off. He needed to return to the fighting. After the initial excitement, the Shade Wizards had been cautious and had been keeping themselves alive. One by one the Mystics had been dangerously injured or forced to retire.

We need to press hard while Wraith is not fully engaged in the battle, Vincent thought. He headed straight over to Alyx. The weapon master was sitting at the edge of the room, watching the battle play out.

"It's time to whittle down the enemy forces," he said.

"I'm surprised you waited this long. I'm ready."

"Will you know when you've pushed too far?" Vincent looked at her again with Soul power infused eyes. The infection was rampant in her body. It was a miracle that she hadn't turned yet.

"You'll see it. Whatever they did to me to give me strength, also keeps the Blight at bay."

"Well, try not to get there. Conserve your energy. But we need you out there now." Vincent handed her Alrion's sword.

"Are you sure about this?"

"I need to know you can efficiently take out the Shade Wizards."

"Consider it done."

"Good. Let's not waste any more time then." Vincent strode off to re-engage with the enemy. He experimented with the Soul power a little. He decided to try and divert some to his legs. He was hoping it would give him better strength and mobility. But he would have to see if it worked.

Vincent tried to remain inconspicuous as he approached the fighting. If he played his cards right there would be some opening he could exploit. He heard a loud scream and quickly turned around. Alyx was charging in with two swords held out in front of her. She immediately grabbed the attention of all the Shade Wizards nearby.

That'll do nicely.

He used the distraction to slip past the front lines and flank. He could see Freyda had retreated and was surrounded by four Trackers.

"I can do this," Vincent told himself. He instantly increased his speed and dashed towards the nearest Tracker. His legs moved with uncharacteristic speed, which he wasn't used to. He almost tripped over himself after the fifth step, but managed to rein in the speed a little. The Trackers were on alert, but didn't seem to expect an attack so swiftly or for Vincent to close the distance so fast. He managed to get the jump on one, and had launched a deadly strike before the Tracker could even react. It tried to move out of the way but Vincent had anticipated the movement and had already accounted for it. He cut the Tracker down and whirled into another strike, putting the next Tracker on the back foot.

One down. Keep pushing.

Another Tracker stepped around and launched at Vincent from his blind spot. Sensing the movement Vincent swung his sword out and turned to get a better look. The Tracker dropped down into a slide, heading for Vincent's legs. Vincent pushed more Soul power into his legs and kicked out at the Tracker. He connected with its head, sending the Tracker skidding along the ground and smashing into the wall.

I could get used to this, Vincent thought. He ran over to the two remaining Trackers. One Tracker grabbed Freyda and retreated to the back of the room. Vincent decided to let that go for now, and turned his attention to the last one. It pulled out a crossbow and started firing.

"Quickly now," Vincent said to himself. He ducked low and ran as fast as he could. The Tracker lined up another shot. Vincent weaved, but the bolt caught him in the shoulder. The searing pain and force almost caused Vincent to tumble to the ground. But he pushed some Soul power to the area to support the wound and regained his balance. As the Tracker prepared another shot Vincent threw his sword. It flew straight and true, piercing the Tracker in the chest before it could get off another shot. Vincent dropped to the ground over the Tracker, retrieving his sword and taking a moment to rest.

We can't keep up this intensity.

The crossbow bolt thrummed in his shoulder and he turned his attention to removing it. He tried pulling it out, but the bolt was barbed and was catching.

Great.

He looked around and it seemed as though everyone's attention was elsewhere for the moment. He turned his focus back to the wound.

I need to try something else, he thought. He gathered the Soul power he had diverted to his shoulder and tried to imagine it healing his shoulder and forcing out the bolt. At first it was like trying to grab a handful of water. But the more he tried, the more the Soul power responded to his attempts and seemed to actually interact with the bolt.

Vincent felt an intense heat in his shoulder, and the crossbow bolt started to emerge. He grabbed the shaft to help it along, and after a few more seconds of concerted effort it came free and clattered onto the floor. There was an intense stinging pain, but it quickly subsided.

That could have gone worse. I better get back into it, he thought. He crept back around, keeping an eye on Wraith and the other combatants.

Alyx was proving a handful for them. She had already taken out one Shade Wizard, and was putting pressure on two more. If Wraith wasn't sending out the occasional fireball or stone javelin she would have taken out another. But whilst Wraith wasn't fully contributing to the fight, he wasn't sitting it out either. Lara was darting in and out, trying to bait them into attacking and providing an opening for Alyx. But they seemed to be wising up to that tactic and were more restrained.

I need to tip the balance.

There were three more Shade Wizards left. The other one was fighting off a handful of Mystics. But rather than help them, he decided to tip the scales for Alyx and Lara. After assessing the situation, Vincent charged in. But he picked a route that kept him as far away from Wraith as possible. It wasn't worth tempting fate.

The Shade Wizard turned to see who was attacking, and studied Vincent. It quickly threw out a wave of Force. Vincent tried to shield himself with his sword, but was thrown backwards. But he resumed his attack immediately. The Shade Wizard cast a wave of fire, forcing Alyx and Lara to retreat. His companion pressed the attack, a wave of rolling earth taking up the floor and threatening to throw them to the ground.

It's now or never.

Vincent gathered a large chunk of Soul power and again empowered his legs. But he held nothing back. The speed he attained was unbelievable, and he had trouble seeing what was ahead. But he readied his sword in an outstretched stance and hoped to impale the nearest Shade Wizard.

The enemy turned with a frustrated look on its face. But it seemed to be unable to comprehend Vincent's speed. It raised its hands and started to unleash a fire spell. But an attack from behind stopped the spell. The Shade Wizard slumped slightly. The delay was enough for Vincent to reach his target, and he plunged the Runesteel deep into the creature's heart. Together they fell, and Vincent scrambled to pick himself up again.

"Thanks for joining us," Lara said. She was crouched down next to him, checking to make sure the Shade Wizard was down.

"Only two left," Vincent said.

"Soon to be one," Lara said. Vincent looked over and could see she was right. Now that the Shade Wizard was more or less alone, Alyx was all over it. It was all the enemy could do to block the relentless assault. It seemed to be enhancing its arm to prevent the Runesteel from slicing through, and the benefit to Alyx was that the Shade Wizard seemed unable to find the time to bring out an offensive spell.

"Too easy," Wraith said, holding up a hand. A powerful wave of force knocked Alyx's weapons from her hands. She shouted with pain, but didn't stop. She retrieved the leather whip from her belt, and with almost no loss in momentum unfurled it and lashed out at the Shade Wizard.

It didn't expect the arc of the attack, and the whip wrapped around the Shade Wizard's leg. She yanked it closer, the creature toppling quickly and sliding along the ground desperately trying to regain control.

"Here!" Lara said, throwing her Runesteel dagger. Alyx plucked it out of the air and in a smooth motion slammed it into the Shade Wizard. It went limp and completely still on the floor. Alyx started to slump down, but caught herself. She looked exhausted.

That's too much, Vincent thought. He stood and decided to rush over and help her.

"Enough!" Wraith shouted. He generated a massive wave of force that radiated out from his body. It swept along at tremendous speed, knocking everyone back. No matter how Vincent tried to brace himself, he was suddenly on the floor.

"I didn't come all the way here to serve up my followers like this. No more stalling for time. Alrion, it is time to face me." Wraith pointed at Alrion and started advancing.

"I'm not ready yet. Curing myself drained too much of my power. I need time before we fight. That way it can be a fair fight," Alrion said.

"I don't care. Fight, don't fight. Use your Spark, don't. Either way, you're coming with me. It's over now. No more running, no more escape."

"Why are you so obsessed with me? Because I almost killed you?"

"You don't understand, do you? This isn't just about me, and it's not just about you. Yes, I'm a monster now. I can't pretend that I'm not. But there is worse than me out there. Join me now, and prevent a worse evil. If you come willingly I will stop attacking your friends." Wraith swept his staff out, gesturing at the rest of the room. Vincent's gaze followed. He could see a lot of injured, tired, and broken people. Despite their success at taking out Wraith's followers, it had been at a great cost.

Alrion closed his eyes. Vincent wondered what his son was thinking.

Surely, he won't give up now. Not when we've come so far.

Vincent noticed the last Tracker dragging Freyda closer to Wraith.

"This one knows something," the Tracker said.

"I doubt it's important," Wraith said.

"She thinks it is."

"More time wasting," Wraith said. He reached out and hauled Freyda up with one hand. She struggled weakly in his grasp.

"What is it you're hiding? Spit it out before I lose my temper."

"Soul power. It is the key to curing the Blight," Freya said. She looked terrified.

"Yes, yes I just saw him heal himself. What's so important?" Wraith shook Freyda like she was a rag doll.

"A wizard can use that power to cure others. Granthion proved that." Freyda looked like she was torn between talking, and trying to remain quiet.

"Look at what they are doing. They're stalling for time while the wizard prepares to heal you," the Tracker said. Wraith tossed Freyda to the ground. Her body hit the ground with a thud and she whimpered as she tried to sit up.

"It's starting to make sense now. Inviting me in, curing yourself with me here. Trying to buy time until you are ready. All to sneak in and take my power away. No, I won't stand for that. I've worked too hard, come too far for you to steal away my advantage now." Wraith looked livid. He started to stomp towards Alrion.

We can't let this happen. He needs more time, Vincent thought. He tried to sense his Soul power. It seemed low.

I'll just have to make do.

Speed would be his best bet now. He could surprise Wraith and get an attack in. Vincent gathered all his remaining Soul power, and as before directed it into his legs. He imagined it providing him with amazing speed. He took up an attacking stance and leapt forward.

He travelled much further than he expected with that initial surge, but managed to correct his course and not topple over. Wraith was continuing forward, not paying attention.

I have a chance.

As Vincent closed in he prepared a strike. His sword swung out, seeking its target. Wraith suddenly turned around, and caught the blade. With his other hand he drew a spear of earth from the ground and flung it at Vincent from close range. Vincent could do nothing. The spear sent him flying backwards, piercing his shoulder, and pinning him to the wall behind.

Great.

Vincent didn't have any Soul power left. And the pain was almost crippling. He saw Alyx standing, her legs wavering. Lara was by her side, helping her up.

"No," Vincent shouted. Alyx looked over at him, and shook her head. She picked up Alrion's sword and held it in both hands. Lara armed herself with the Runesteel dagger and dashed out first. Wraith waved his arm, and the ground rippled up into short pillars, blocking Lara's path. She vaulted over one and kept going. Wraith sent out waves of fire. Lara dodged between them, ignoring the intense heat.

It's not going to work.

Vincent struggled to remove the stone spear but it was tightly wedged into the wall. Lara threw some glass vials at Wraith. Two large plumes of smoke started spreading, blanketing the area. Wraith threw more waves of force, the spells dissipating the smoke and revealing Lara. She was right in front readying an attack. Wraith held up both hands.

"Die," he said. A wall of earth rose up before him, and he charged it with intense fire turning it into a wall of magma. As he was preparing to push it towards Lara, Alyx appeared behind Wraith. She had been using the attacks as a diversion to creep closer. She swung out with the Runesteel blade. It swung true and on target.

Wraith stuck out an arm and the Runesteel blade bit into it. But it didn't slice all the way through. With his other arm Wraith punched Alyx in the head and she fell to the ground in a heap. Wraith removed the sword from his arm and tossed it away.

Lara was already retreating, but Wraith saw her flee. He rotated his wall to be facing her and sent it flying at incredible speed. Lara looked back, and saw the massive wall of superheated rock heading towards her.

She can't get away, Vincent thought. He strained again at the spear holding him. It moved a little. With a blur of light, Marla streaked past and whisked Lara out of danger. They stopped next to Alrion. Marla dropped to her feet, panting. Lara looked worse for wear, but otherwise uninjured.

"No more games. It's over now," Wraith said. He dashed forward heading for Alrion.

No. Not now.

Vincent had to stop them somehow. He drew upon all his strength and surged forward, forcing himself off the stone spear and leaving it embedded in the wall. He stumbled and almost fell, the pain threatening to make him pass out.

I have to get to Alrion.

Things were not happening the right way. But Wraith was too far ahead, and too fast. He was moving with anger and determination.

"That's enough!" Jovana shouted. She stood from her throne and started walking towards Wraith.

"Sit down old woman, you'll only get yourself hurt," Wraith said, mocking her. He laughed. But Jovana wasn't backing down. She stepped between Wraith and Alrion.

"You'll have to get through me."

"As you wish." Wraith surged forward, a maniacal look on his face. Vincent moved forward as best he could, but wasn't going to catch up with them. Not before Wraith and Jovana collided. He feared the worst. Mystics weren't fighters, even though they had done admirably in the fight.

"It's time you stopped and considered your manners," Jovana said. As Wraith closed in she put her hands out in front of her and a bright light started to radiate out. Vincent was blinded; he couldn't see what was going on. He had to get closer, help out in some way. Whatever his mother was doing, it had to be some sort of last resort.

32

A TIMELY APPEARANCE

Alrion wasn't surprised when his grandmother stepped up. He had noticed her gathering Soul power as well. But he had no idea what she was thinking. She was still a complete mystery, and the extent of her power was also unknown.

The light blinded him but he could feel the surge of Soul power. It seemed so unusual feeling it from the outside. That shouldn't be possible from what he was told.

The initial flash was over, and Alrion's eyes started to recover. He could start to see what had happened. Wraith and Jovana were standing close together, just meters away from Alrion. A white dome of light surrounded them, and both were frozen in time.

"What have you done to me?" Wraith said. He was completely motionless.

"I have trapped you within my Soul power. You cannot move until I allow you to." Jovana was triumphant, but there was a weariness to her voice. Alrion couldn't even begin to comprehend what she had done. To extend her Soul power so far outside her body and do this, it was remarkable. And it was just what they needed.

Alrion looked across the room. His father was stumbling over, a major wound in his shoulder. Alyx had collapsed on the ground. Marla was off to the side, exhausted. Lara was with her, also exhausted and trying to catch her breath. The rest of the Mystics were either injured or trying to recover their power. It was a sorry sight. His grandmother had intervened just in time.

"I don't know what you're trying to achieve here. This barrier you have created will not last long," Wraith said.

"It will last long enough. Then Alrion can deal with you."

"No. I don't buy this at all. He may be able to do something, but he can't cure me. Not when he's just cured himself. I don't know exactly what he's going to try, but it's pointless."

"Then why the big rush to take me out?" Alrion said.

"I'm sick of your games. One lucky break in the temple and I've had to chase you across the world. All the while, trying to build up my forces. No more running. You will join me today, one way or another. And we will crush our enemies."

"Never. I'll stop you, as I have before. And you won't be able to hurt anyone else. You won't be able to create more monsters like yourself. Your time is over." Alrion couldn't understand Wraith's obsession with him. He clearly had worked with other wizards, although none of them seemed as powerful or as capable as Wraith. But Alrion didn't think he was that different. Not in ways that would be useful to Wraith.

"I can feel this barrier weakening already. It's just a matter of time. And you won't have enough for whatever it is you're trying. Just accept that it's going to happen." Wraith struggled more in the barrier. And Alrion could see Wraith's fingers moving a little. Time was definitely moving against them.

"Grandmother, how long do we have?" Alrion said quietly.

"Almost enough," she said. "Now's the time to speed things up."

"Sure." Alrion knew what she meant. He had to try and accelerate the absorption of the Soul power. He took his hand and slowly dipped it into the water. The rush of power was a shock, but he quickly adjusted.

Alrion focused carefully. He slowed the flow of Soul power to help direct it better. As he felt more comfortable, he relaxed his control and let it flow faster. It was an exhilarating feeling, like he was being carried down river rapids. But he also sensed the danger at the end.

"You're running out of time," Wraith said. He had some movement in his arms now.

"How did you let yourself become such an abomination?" Jovana said.

"We're all only one difficult choice away from this. I had to accept this form, or accept death."

"I know which one I would have taken," Jovana said.

"You're old, you've lived a full life. I have things yet to be achieved. I have wrongs that must be set right. I couldn't let death take me, so I did what needed to be done. And it's opened my eyes to much more. You'll all thank me when we're done here." Wraith sounded serious. But Alrion couldn't imagine a time in which he would thank that cursed man. He had been tormenting Alrion for as long as he had been a wizard. The very thought caused Alrion's blood to boil. He could feel his anger rising. It had been contained, but Wraith's presence and his insistence on being right was just too much.

I can't let him get away with this.

Alrion immediately started to consider using his Spark. If the barrier holding Wraith let spells through, he could potentially end the monster now.

"What are you doing?" Jovana said. She was giving Alrion a cold and distasteful look. His anger rose again, annoyed at her judgement. But then it suddenly dropped away. She was right. Everyone had sacrificed so much for this, and him getting angry could jeopardise it all.

"I'm sorry. He just has a way of making me so angry. I hate him," Alrion said. Wraith laughed. Jovana's eyes softened a little.

"He's not worth it. The more you become accustomed to your Soul power, the more you will understand how your emotions affect your body, and your energy. You may have used your anger as a tool in the past, but it's destructive. You need to leave it behind." Jovana went back into lecture mode. But Alrion knew she was right.

"Don't listen to that nonsense, use every tool at your disposal. You need it," Wraith said. Alrion looked at the creature. Wraith was an illustration of what could go wrong. He had taken the desperate options, he had kindled his rage. And he had been transformed into something obscene. And still didn't understand the extent of what he had done to himself, or was still finding a way to justify it.

"What made you like this? Why are you so intent on doing this at any cost?" Alrion said.

"Why do you care?" Wraith said. He looked wary.

"I don't understand why you could think this is acceptable. And you really seem to be obsessed with my family. Why?" Alrion genuinely wanted to know. He had to understand why Wraith had been so fixated on him this whole time.

"It's complicated. But I will say this. I lost my wife because of your father, and grandfather."

"How?" Vincent said. He was slowly staggering over. Wraith struggled more against the barrier. He was a bit more successful, but was still being held properly. Jovana stumbled, but managed to stand back up. Alrion could see the toll it was taking on her.

"It was my first assignment as a wizard. I was tasked with following and observing a young man who had run away. My wife was an accomplished archer and woodworker and decided to come with me." Wraith looked at Vincent with a look of intense hatred. Vincent stopped walking suddenly.

"Wait a minute," he said.

"Yes, you're getting the picture now. The young man was captured by some infected. My wife and I covered his escape by holding off a horde of Blighters and Tainted. But we were both infected in the process."

"Your wife lived then? When Granthion cured everyone?" Vincent said.

"No. She made me take her life. In order that she wouldn't get turned. It was her greatest fear, to lose control of her life. She opted to die with dignity." Wraith spoke the words with such venom Alrion could scarcely believe it. He watched his father look over in horror.

"What's going on?" Alrion said. He could see the intense toll this had taken on Wraith. But now his father was somehow involved.

"I was that young man. I ran from my father, to forge my own path. He had sent a wizard after me. Which must have been Branthor. And I assume the reason Branthor hates us so much, is because nobody told him that the Blight could be cured. So, his wife died for nothing, and Branthor was forced to live with that." Vincent's voice was quiet and almost breaking. Alrion could suddenly see what had happened. Branthor's life had been destroyed by his devotion to Granthion.

"You got it in one. Do you understand now? Or do we have to keep going over it again and again?" Wraith shouted at them. He renewed his struggling with additional purpose. Jovana collapsed down to her knees. Vincent continued staggering over, until he was next to Alrion.

"Your pain is my fault. Leave my son out of this," Vincent said.

"No. Never. I need his power. And I want you to suffer. It's the only way."

"You will never have him while I am still breathing," Vincent said.

"I'm only too happy to help you with that," Wraith roared. He lashed out with all his limbs at once, and the white barrier shattered. Sparing only a moment to ensure he was free, Wraith dashed forward aiming straight at Alrion.

Vincent held his ground, holding his sword out in front.

"I'll cut you down," Vincent said. He had a fierce determination in his eyes. Alrion had to think quickly. He wasn't ready, he could feel it. And he couldn't speed up at all. His grandmother was slowly getting up. She looked completely spent. He realised he had to do something himself. To buy them some time so he could finish things. Curing Wraith was the only way to stop him; that was certain. But Alrion realised that he couldn't keep passively waiting.

He noticed Lara by his side.

"Don't do it. Let us fight for you," she said. Alrion could see the exhaustion in her eyes. But there was still a steely glimmer of determination.

"Not at the cost of your lives. Not when I can do something."

"You must endure the pain of this fight, so that you can end it for good. Trust us." Lara had a tear in her eye and she quickly wiped it away.

"I can't lose you." Alrion reached out with his free hand and touched her cheek where the tear had fallen. Lara closed her eyes and leaned into his hand.

"You won't. Just stop him for good." She took his hand away and stood in front of him, her Runesteel dagger at the ready. With a crash Wraith and Vincent collided. Vincent swung hard and fast, but Wraith was too strong. He knocked the sword away and punished Vincent with a blow of force at close range.

Vincent flew back and crashed against the wall again. He crumpled, and stayed down.

"No!" Alrion shouted. Wraith laughed again, and resumed his approach. Lara was next. Alrion furiously tested his Soul power. It wasn't there. He knew he couldn't risk attacking without having it all there. It was too risky. He had to make sure that the cure worked. But he was out of time.

Lara moved much faster than Alrion thought possible, given her exhaustion and her previous fighting. She evaded Wraith's strikes, and managed to sneak into a good position to strike at its heart. But Wraith had seen it coming. A burst of fire from his hands made Lara duck and roll. Wraith followed up with a cascade of stone, and the rising floor pummelled Lara over and over until she settled yards away. She just lay on the ground.

"And now, it's just you. Are you going to continue to sit there and wait for your fate?" Wraith said. He had a satisfied smile on his face. Alrion was torn. He needed more time, but he wouldn't go down without a fight. He debated what to do. He needed to do something. But what?"

"You really are a monster. It's time you were put down for good!" Celes shouted. Wraith turned just in time to see a vial hurtling towards him. He shielded himself with his arm, the contact smashing the vial and unleashing an explosion of epic proportions. Alrion ducked down behind the water fountain and felt the heat wash over him.

"I'm here Alrion, as promised. Let's finish this," Celes said.

33

THE PRICE OF LIGHT

Alrion stood and surveyed the scene. His mother was standing there, readying another explosive vial. Wraith stood there looking confused but was otherwise unhurt. Nobody else seemed to be injured by the blast, but they were all already in bad shape.

"Nice trick, won't work again, so don't even bother," Wraith said. He turned to Alrion.

"No more delays. You're mine." Wraith didn't wait around, and leapt forward once more. Alrion was trapped. He couldn't leave the water fountain, and he couldn't fight back. His time was out, but he wasn't ready. It hadn't worked. He froze.

Wraith continued forward, a wicked grin on his face. He discarded his staff and reached out with his hand. Alrion knew what was coming. But he couldn't act. Wraith reached him and grabbed his shoulder. Alrion could feel the claw-like hand trying to burrow within. He could feel the injection of the Blight. A piercing scream shocked him out of his state.

Alyx was writhing around. And she started to change colour.

"Oh no," Alrion whispered. It was happening. She was finally turning. He was too late.

"Watch her transform. You will be next," Wraith said. Alrion looked on in horror. Alyx's body contorted in every direction, her skin hardening and becoming like black stone. She was turning into a Shade. One final unearthly scream and it was over. Alyx looked around in confusion then sped out of the room.

"It's quite a traumatic experience, I'm afraid to say. But you will be with her soon," Wraith said. He had an intense look of concentration on his face.

Alrion didn't know what to do. Alyx had turned, Marla and Jovana were spent. His father and Lara were knocked out or too injured. It was just him, and he was being infected again.

There has to be a way.

Then Alrion had a realisation. His body was fighting the infection. And he was still taking on Soul power from the well.

Maybe I can fight back, he thought. He reached for his Spark. It was a strange sensation now, with the Soul power in the mix. He grabbed his Spark and sent out a wave of force.

Wraith didn't expect it and was knocked back. He looked at Alrion suspiciously. Alrion inspected his wound, and it was already healing.

The Soul power, he thought. It was protecting him, and he was refilling it at a high rate. He threw out another wave of force. Wraith swatted it away with minimal effort. But Alrion noticed something strange. He enhanced his eyes with Soul power and sent another wave of force. And then a small wave of fire. Wraith was more annoyed than anything else and not hurt. But that's not what Alrion was trying to do.

His eyes confirmed what he was feeling. Each time he drew and used his Spark, Soul power mixed in at the same time. He couldn't seem to create a spell without using both.

"Soul power is the key to curing him. Mystics can't use it outside their body, well not ordinarily. But I can with my Spark. I have a chance." Alrion came up with a plan.

"I was using a light touch, like last time. But since that's not working you're going to get the full treatment," Wraith said. He held up his hand and it started to transform. His fingers turned into razor-sharp claws, and they started dripping with a thick, black substance.

"You won't resist this." Wraith laughed and started to close in.

Alrion saw the Shade Wizard approaching and he thought back to one of his earlier encounters with a Shade. How he had created a ball of fire so hot it could penetrate the skin of the Shade. With a bit of tweaking, that could do the trick.

Alrion gathered his Spark and tried to limit the amount of Soul power that went into it. As Wraith approached Alrion created a small ball of red-hot fire. He pushed it forward straight at Wraith's chest. The Shade Wizard didn't even flinch and let it hit him.

As expected the ball of fire started to penetrate through Wraith's skin. But he seemed more focused on getting his claws on Alrion.

I've got him.

Alrion could see a small trail of Soul power linking him and the ball of fire. This was his chance. He took one more influx of Soul power from the pool, then channelled everything he had into that ball of fire. Using his Spark as a conduit, the Soul power had a path to travel. And it surged along. Alrion could see it travel like a thick rope of golden fibres. The Soul power entered Wraith's body. He stopped abruptly and looked down.

"What have you done?" he said. Alrion didn't answer, but focused on the Soul power. He channelled it into the raging hot fireball, and smothered it. He converted the burning ball of fire within Wraith's body into a ball of pulsing Soul power. Slowly but surely it grew and grew. Wraith dropped to his knees and clutched at his chest. Alrion remembered the struggle he had dealt with, forcing out that one big blockage of Blight. He couldn't begin to understand what Wraith was now going through.

He probably deserves it, Alrion thought. But at the same time, he realised that there had to be a better way. He couldn't do this for everyone else.

"This is not possible!" Wraith shouted. Again, Alrion didn't respond. He just kept pouring more and more Soul power into Wraith. He had an established conduit now, and it wasn't much more difficult than moving it around within his own body. He hadn't reached his peak Soul power, but he had somehow managed to get enough into Wraith that he could keep adding to it and still keep Wraith at bay.

The Shade Wizard started to glow white. It was like the light from within was shining through his skin. The intensity increased, until Wraith was completely submerged in a cocoon of light. He screamed once more, then became quiet.

Alrion released the spell, and stopped the Soul power. His hand slipped out of the water and he slumped down to the ground. He felt so tired and drained. With great effort he dragged himself up and leaned on the fountain to look over at Wraith.

The light was subsiding now. Wraith was no more. Branthor lay naked on the ground, the black cloak acting like a blanket.

It worked.

He couldn't believe it. But there Branthor lay, living and breathing. There were no signs of the infection. Alrion used the little Soul power he had left to examine Branthor. He could not see any Blight left within the man.

"You're cured," Alrion said. Branthor opened his eyes and looked up. His face was a mixture of fear and wonder.

"I don't believe it," Branthor said. He seemed to jump a little at the sound of his voice, and he stared at his hands.

"There's not a speck of Blight left within you. I think this is the part where you say thanks?"

"I feel so displaced. My mind. They were manipulating me too. Only a little, but enough. I can't believe I didn't see it," Branthor said, muttering to himself. He looked back at Alrion.

"I am thankful. You have proven yourself to be far greater than I imagined.

But you cannot understand the gravity of what you have just done."

"What do you mean? I stopped you."

"Yes, I was a thorn in your side and fixated on you. But that's partially because they wanted it. I can see that now. I was never your greatest threat. I was standing between you and them. You're no longer safe."

"You were keeping me safe?" Alrion couldn't believe what he was hearing.

"Now that I'm out of the picture, there's nothing stopping them from coming for you."

"Who's they?"

"The generals. They're rebuilding, and now you've shown how dangerous you are. They won't rest until they have you. And now me. I can't stay here, it's too dangerous." Branthor sat up and looked around.

"You're not leaving until I'm ready for you to leave," Alrion said. He needed to know more. He also didn't trust Branthor. Who knew what he would do now?

"My Spark is intact. And I hold all the wisdom from the Pool of Knowledge. You cannot hold me here. I am sorry for what happened, it was more than I should have done. You now know why. But there was no other way. And I would still make the same choices."

"Just stay. Explain what's going on."

"No, I have no way of knowing where they are now. I have to disappear. Goodbye Alrion, we will meet again." Branthor vanished. Alrion blinked and looked around the room. He couldn't see the wizard anywhere. Alrion plunged his arm into the pool of water and siphoned off some Soul power. He enhanced his vision and got a glimpse of a shape leaving the room. But he did notice that Branthor had left behind the staff that he had been using.

He's gone, I'm in no condition to follow, Alrion thought. Branthor had sounded scared, which was not a good sign. Celes ran over and hugged Alrion. He had forgotten she was there. He welcomed the hug.

"Alrion that was incredible! I realised that I couldn't do anything to help. I felt so helpless watching."

"You intervened at the right moment. And it all worked out." Alrion heard a groan from nearby.

"I need to check on everyone now." Alrion walked over to check on Jovana.

"What did you do?" he said.

"Something foolish. But it worked, as I knew it would. Check on the others, they seem to be injured." Jovana waved him away. Alrion thought she looked in bad shape herself, but he knew that he was dismissed. First, he found his father. Vincent was against the wall in a seated position. He lifted his head slightly as Alrion and Celes approached.

"What did I miss?" he said.

"It's over now. Wraith is no more, and Branthor has escaped. I'm just checking on everyone."

"Don't worry about me, I've been worse. Your mother can help me up. Where's Lara?"

"I'll go check," Alrion said. He spotted her at the other end of the room. She was still lying down.

Oh no.

He forced himself into an awkward jog. His muscles were tired and lethargic. The broken ground was hard to traverse, and he almost fell a few times. But he arrived next to her and quickly dropped down. She was lying still on her side, but seemed to be breathing. Alrion gently turned her so she was on her back, and put his hand on the side of her face.

"Lara. Lara can you hear me?" Alrion looked over her for signs of injury. There was nothing obvious. He noticed her eyes open slowly.

"I had a bit of a nap. What's going on?" she said.

"It's over now. Are you hurt?"

"Nothing life threatening. I'm sorry I couldn't protect you."

"Shh, don't worry. It was my fault; I wasn't strong enough to protect you all. But the plan worked. I'll help you up." Alrion reached down and gently eased Lara into a seated position. She winced in pain, but her breathing slowed and she looked comfortable.

"Everything hurts," she said. Alrion nodded and helped her up again. With significant effort they were both standing, leaning on each other. They staggered along until they were closer to the throne. The ground there was undisturbed and they sat together.

"I bet you regret stealing that ring from me now," Alrion said, trying to lighten the mood.

"It was the best thing I ever stole," Lara said with a smile. A look of concern quickly passed over her face.

"Where's Alyx?" Lara said. Alrion looked away.

"What happened?"

"She turned into a Shade right as Wraith attacked me. There was nothing I could do."

"Where is she now?"

"I have no idea. She ran away. Wraith said something about the turning process being traumatic. I failed her."

"But you stopped Wraith. You cured yourself!"

"I did. But I promised I would cure her, and I failed. She's a monster now, and I don't know where she is."

"Don't worry, we'll find her together. And we'll bring her back. That's a promise." Lara leaned against him and he put his arms around her. It felt good to have her close. They had come so far together and finally defeated the man who had been hounding them the whole way. But the victory felt hollow. He couldn't enjoy it.

34

AFTERMATH

"I told you I would come," Celes said.

"I should have known you would come at the last minute. You have impeccable timing," Vincent said.

"Always. How's your injury?" Celes crouched down and examined it. She seemed concerned.

"I'll live. For now, I'm more worried about my mother."

"Then let's go to her. Although I wish I was meeting her under better circumstances." Celes helped Vincent stand, and supported him with an arm around his back.

Together they walked forward, one step at a time. Vincent could see his mother was struggling, which was alarming. In the short time he had known her she had always projected herself as strong. Showing any weakness was not a good sign.

What has she done? Vincent thought. He knelt next to her. "How are you feeling?"

"I've been better."

"I'll help you up." Vincent gently eased her up into the throne. She settled back into it with a sigh. Celes stood quietly off to the side of the throne.

"Something's not right. Do you need to use the water?" Vincent was really worried now.

"That won't help. I believe you have someone to introduce?"

"Yes. This is Celes, my wife." Vincent beckoned for Celes to come over. She walked over and crouched down to kiss Jovana's hand.

"Jovana. I'm your mother-in-law. Aren't you lucky that you haven't had to deal with me all this time?" Jovana laughed which turned into a cough.

"I would have loved for you to be in our lives. I'm truly sorry that it took so long."

"I think we are very alike, you and I. It takes a certain person to follow their family to the ends of the earth. You have a good fire, and he's needed that kind of person to challenge him. I feel comfortable that he has you looking after him."

"Thank you so much for your kind words. Don't worry, I'll keep him in line. I look forward to getting to know you better."

"You won't I'm afraid. It was lovely to meet you. Andar, make sure everyone else is fine then come back." Jovana dismissed Vincent, then closed her eyes.

"Lovely to meet you too," Celes said. She gave Vincent a questioning look. He shook his head and she started walking out.

I have a bad feeling about this.

He slowly did the rounds. Alrion and Lara were fine. Marla was just exhausted, but uninjured. The rest of the Mystics were in various states of injury, but nothing life threatening. He spotted Freyda sitting against the wall, rocking back and forth.

"Freyda. Are you alright?"

"No. Yes. They ran off when Wraith was defeated." Her voice was quiet and shaky.

"I don't know what he did to you. But Alrion can cure you and remove the Blight."

"That will be good. But he can't cure me, not truly." Freyda's voice cracked and she stared out of the open door.

"Everything will be fine, you'll see." Vincent looked around and saw no signs of any enemies. It was not worth pursuing them now. Satisfied that he had checked on everyone he returned to his mother.

She had slumped in the chair, and her breathing was now laboured.

"What's happening? Please tell me."

"I'm dying, Andar."

"How? Alrion can help you. Or Marla." Vincent was in a panic. "Alrion get over here!" he shouted. Alrion said something to Lara, and rushed back.

"It's no use. I did it to myself. I overextended myself, I burned myself out. Too much Soul power, and expending it the way I did. It's like burning the candle at both ends with two infernos." Jovana's eyes closed and she reopened them moments later.

"This can't be happening. We're finally reunited. And you saved Alrion."

"I knew this would happen, I saw it in the waters. But I went ahead anyway. It was my turn." Jovana let out a weak smile.

"What's going on?" Alrion said. He looked over Jovana. "You're hurt?"

"Dying. It was my turn to sacrifice myself. That's our lot I suppose. Your grandfather started it all."

"Why?" Alrion said. He looked distraught. Vincent put a reassuring hand on his son's shoulder.

"It was her choice. Sometimes you need to choose between two choices, neither good. But this, can't we do something?"

"No, you can't. All you can do is take the gifts you have, and use them well. You both have an important legacy to live up to. You are the descendants of the greatest wizard and greatest Mystic to ever live. You must succeed in your quest."

"I will. I promise. Can't I do something for you?" Alrion said.

"No, there's no going back. I've fulfilled my purpose, and I finally met you. As much as I wanted things to be different, there was no other way. I've had a good run. It's been a long and full life. And I didn't just drift away in my sleep. I went out with a bang." Jovana slumped down on her side, lying on the throne. After a few moments she opened her eyes again.

"Everyone must leave. I want to be alone with my son." Jovana closed her eyes again. Her chest rose and fell with difficulty. Vincent turned to Alrion.

"Please respect her wishes. Go find your mother, I'll come get you," he said. Alrion nodded.

"I'll take this, so we can study it," Alrion said, picking up Branthor's staff. Then with Lara they found Marla and escorted everyone out slowly.

"We're alone now," Vincent said. He tried to choke back the emotion, but it was rushing out.

"Good. I forgive you, Andar. And I know the burden you have been carrying. You are a foolish man, but I understand."

"I'm sorry. I've let everyone down, one way or another."

"But not him," Jovana said. Vincent was silent.

"He will understand when the time comes." Jovana gave Vincent a knowing look. Vincent didn't know how to respond.

"Come now, did you think you could hide from your mother?"

"I suppose not. You have a few tricks up your sleeve."

"More than you know. Hopefully, you'll learn a few. There's a book in my private quarters. It is a manual to the power of Soul. You and Alrion must study it carefully. Mastery will take a lifetime, but you need the knowledge to be on the path. This, you understand."

"I do. What can I do for you now?" Vincent held back his tears with great difficulty.

"Hold my hand and stay with me. It will remind me of when you were a sweet young boy. A simpler time, before all this madness." Jovana closed her eyes and Vincent held her hand. Her breathing slowed and he could see the life slowly fading from her. The tears broke free and streamed down his face. There was no more holding back. And, like that, her life drifted away.

Vincent emerged from the great hall into the blistering wind. He noticed Marla standing just outside.

"I will go to her now. You are not familiar with our customs."

"I'm sorry."

"I know. We will talk later." Marla walked back into the building with purpose. Vincent watched her leave, and had to decide where to go next.

I'll try our room. Maybe the others are there.

He trudged through the snow, putting one foot before the other. His mother's passing had hit him harder than he realised. He had spent his whole life treating her as a fact, and not a person. He thought he was immune to those feelings, due to the separation and the passing of time. But he was wrong. Being there, seeing her, even for a limited time had brought everything back. Memories of feelings from their short time together. And the selflessness of all she had done to help, to her final act of sacrifice.

Vincent stopped his train of thought. It was just going to end in more tears, and he had to be strong for Alrion. His son had just gone through so much. Every trial and injury that Alrion had to suffer was like a dagger through Vincent. He should have spared his son all this. But he could not. All he could do was support him as best as he could. But even that was not enough. At least they were together.

Vincent arrived at the small quarters they had been staying in and paused before opening the door. He sighed, then entered. He saw Alrion, Lara, and Celes inside all conversing. They stopped suddenly when they saw him.

"Is she ...?" Alrion said.

"Yes. Marla is attending to her now." Vincent sat down on one of the beds. Celes rushed over and gave him a hug.

"I'm sorry," she said.

"Thanks. I think she understood the separation we had. But it shouldn't have been that way. It's my fault."

"Don't beat yourself up. Didn't your father take you away at a young age? Your mother didn't exactly live around the corner either," Celes said.

"True, but it just doesn't feel like I did enough."

"You need to be kind to yourself," Alrion said. Vincent looked up, surprised. Alrion continued.

"I've been thinking the same way. Blaming myself for what I could have done differently. But that was just the journey that led us here. All we can do is learn to be better." Alrion paused and looked at Vincent. Vincent was stunned. He didn't expect this maturity from his son. He felt so conflicted. Incredible pride at how Alrion had grown and matured. And also, a little guilty that recent events had accelerated this growth, and perhaps he could have shielded his son better.

"It's going to be hard, but you're right. Thank you Alrion."

"I could just see you doing the same thing, and we need to snap out of it. That's how the Blight controls people. It plays on their negative emotions and keeps them from breaking free."

"Something interesting to consider. What do we do now?" Vincent said. There was silence.

"We need to honour my grandmother. Then, we need to find Alyx. I have a promise to keep," Alrion said.

"Don't forget Freyda," Vincent said. Alrion nodded.

"When we're ready for that, I'll look for Alyx. If I find her, I'll bring her to you. And you can help Freyda in the meantime," Lara said.

"That's probably for the best."

"I'll help you. I don't know who Alyx is, but I witnessed her transformation. I'll do anything I can to help," Celes said.

"So, we have a plan. There's just one thing we need to take care of now," Vincent said. He let out a deep sigh. He wasn't looking forward to this. And not just because his mother had sacrificed herself for them. He realised that he had never done this for his father. He had never held a proper memorial.

I'm sorry, he thought and left, looking for Marla.

"Thank you for your patience, please come now," Marla said. She walked serenely through the settled snow, leading them to a smaller building they had never entered before. Marla opened the heavy metal door, and held it open for Vincent. Once he was inside she went ahead.

It took a minute for Vincent's eyes to adjust, as it was a lot darker. He saw steps before them going down.

"Be careful, there's lots of steps," he said. He heard murmurs of acknowledgment behind him, and pressed on. There was the occasional torch to light the way, but it wasn't enough. He descended carefully, wondering where they were going. As he reached the bottom he let out a gasp.

Before him was a small stone structure like a tiny house, and beyond it was a vast lake. But it was no ordinary water. It shone like a star, bright and white. He could feel his skin tingling from just being near it. Surrounding the edge were all the Mystics. They stood with their heads bowed.

This is something else.

"This is the source. The most concentrated collection of Soul power in the whole world," Marla said. Vincent could believe that. It seemed so immense; he was actually scared of it. Marla must have noticed his reaction.

"Yes, it is something to be treated with care and respect. The water that you have used in your training is only a diluted feed from this source."

"Incredible," Vincent said. He couldn't believe something like this existed. No wonder his grandmother had lived here.

"We are ready now. Please take a position," Marla said. Vincent found a place to stand near the edge of the lake. Alrion and Celes stood on either side of him and Lara stood next to Alrion. Vincent noticed them holding hands.

Good.

"We gather here today, to recognise the passing of our eldest, Jovana. She was the guiding light that we have all followed, and her wisdom has kept us all safe and given us purpose. We owe everything we have to her." Marla paused before speaking.

"As is the custom, we will return her Soul to the source, so that she can continue to guide and assist us forever more." Marla walked over to the stone structure. Marla's hand glowed and she placed it on one of the walls. The structure began to glow white, and resonate with a strange sound. It was like something was building and building within.

A bright light suddenly burst from the top of the structure, then as it rose it began to bend. It rushed into the middle of the lake with immense force. A giant peak of water rose up, like a giant stone had been tossed into the lake. It gradually subsided and the waters settled down. But Vincent was sure it looked brighter than before.

He knelt, and reached down to touch the water. Marla rushed over to stop him, but he waved her off. He carefully put his hand into the water. The Soul power was intense and overwhelming. It was nothing like he had experienced before.

Farewell mother. I will strive to live up to your memory and will forever cherish the gifts you have given me, Vincent thought. He slowly removed his hand from the water.

"That was incredibly dangerous. You know now how potent the waters are," Marla said.

"I had to, to bring a piece of my mother with me," Vincent said. He rose and slowly walked out. He didn't want anyone else to see the tears.

35

GONE

Lara slowed her steps and eventually stopped.

"I think we need a break," she said. Sitting on a nearby rock Lara stretched her legs. Celes sat down next to her.

"We've been all over this mountain today. I'm not sure we will find anything," Celes said.

"We have to. Alrion really needs to set this right."

"He does seem rather attached to Alyx from what you said. Is there something going on there?"

"No." Lara almost shouted the words and reined herself in.

"I seem to have touched on something," Celes said with a smile. "Don't worry, I've seen you two together. I approve."

"This just seems awkward, discussing it with you."

"It doesn't need to be. Just promise me that you won't hurt him." Celes looked Lara directly in the eyes. Lara held her gaze.

"I promise."

"Good." Celes looked away. "You think his obsession with Alyx is just his sense of responsibility?"

"Mostly. The only reason she was infected was because she saved us. But I think it's more than that. I think he admires her, and her fighting ability. And her fierce independence. She's done amazing things all by herself. But that's all been taken away from her, because she's infected."

"That does seem like a big responsibility for him. We need to find something. I don't want to go back empty handed." Celes rose and looked around the area.

"We could try over here. It's not a proper track, but that wouldn't stop her. Especially in the state she's in." Lara pointed at what was little more than a gap between rocks. But it extended further than they could see.

"Worth a try. After you," Celes said. Lara took the initiative and pushed forward. The ground sloped up quickly, and they almost had to climb up in sections.

"I'm really not sure about this," Lara said.

"I know what you mean. But can you head back knowing you hadn't checked this?"

"Absolutely not. We have to exhaust all the possibilities."

"I thought the same."

"I just hope we find something, even if it's not her." Lara was desperate to find Alyx. Alrion seemed so lost in his thoughts. But he didn't want to talk about it.

"Ooh, look at this," Lara said. She stopped and let Celes catch up. Then she pointed at some markings just ahead.

"Looks like signs of a struggle. Look how torn up the ground is," Celes said.

"My thoughts exactly. This isn't what I would call a heavily frequented area. We could be on to something."

"I sure hope so." Celes signalled forward with her eyes and Lara pushed ahead. She took care following the trail, but also trying not to step on it or damage it in any way. The search took them around the corner and off on another small trail. It ended in a dead end. But there was something waiting for them.

"Is that a Tracker?" Lara said.

"Definitely. I wonder what happened?" Celes crept closer to inspect. Lara could tell from the way the Tracker was lying that it was dead. It was in an unnatural position.

"Look at this." Celes waved Lara over. With care Lara stepped around the body to see what Celes was pointing at.

"The neck?"

"Yes. It looks like it has been crushed. That's unusual." Celes ran her fingers over the skin.

"It's horrible. What could do this?"

"A Shade could do this." Celes looked at Lara.

"You don't think ..."

"This guy escaped. Alyx escaped. She had just been transformed, a lot was going on. Maybe she chased it down and killed it. Do you have a better explanation?"

"Not really."

"I travelled extensively with a Tracker. He was a bit different I think, but they're incredibly resourceful, tricky, and quite strong. I don't see what else could have happened." Celes stood and looked over the rest of the area.

"You're probably right. But where would Alyx go next?"

"If she hasn't come back ..." Celes trailed off and looked at Lara.

"Then she's gone away? To protect us?"

"Or for some other reason. But I think we're out of luck. And we're almost out of daylight. We need to head back."

"I wish I had more than this. Let me look around here one last time." Lara gingerly turned over the Tracker, looking for any other clues. There was nothing at all. She looked over at Celes and shook her head.

"We're done here, let's head back." Celes marched forward and Lara rushed to catch up with her.

Alrion was not in their room when they returned.

"Let's try the great hall," Lara said. Celes nodded. They walked quickly and with purpose to see if he was there.

"How do you think he will react?" Celes said.

"To the news of Alyx? I think it will rekindle his disappointment in himself. I really wanted to get him something more concrete."

"He was always terrified of failure. I think it's been holding him back for a long time. Vincent used to always say that he knew Alrion was capable of more in the workshop, but never tried."

"He's been trying pretty hard here."

"I can see that. It's hard to explain, but as a parent it's so difficult to see your child go through things like this. You want them to succeed, and learn the lesson. But you don't want them to suffer anything. So, I'm glad that he's found something to care about. But you'd never want it under these circumstances."

"I can understand that. I can't even begin to imagine that sort of responsibility." Lara shook her head.

"It grows on you," Celes said, and flashed her a smile. Lara returned the smile and stepped through the giant doorway.

She spotted Alrion instantly. He was at the back of the room, standing over the water fountain that Jovana always used. Next to him was Freyda. He looked up when they entered.

"Good timing, come over," Alrion shouted. Lara headed right over, with Celes at her side.

"I'm about to cure Freyda. I've been thinking about it a lot, and talking it through with Marla. I think I have a way that will be kinder than what Branthor went through."

"Sounds good, I hope it works well," Lara said.

"Me too," Freyda said. She still looked out of sorts.

"Before I start, do you have any good news for me?" Alrion said.

"Well, we have some news," Celes said. She looked at Lara.

"We found evidence of Alyx. Off the main trail we found the Tracker that fled. His throat had been crushed."

"And you think Alyx did that?"

"Looking at the injury, I don't think a person of average strength could have done that. It's our best explanation." Lara looked over at Celes and she nodded. Alrion looked thoughtful.

"That's good in that she seems to have retained her mind, even if only a little. Did you find anything else?"

"No, that was all. She's gone." Lara looked down.

"But we'll find a way to track her. It's important," Celes said. Lara looked over at her and nodded along.

"I know we will, I have a promise to fulfil. But first, I have to help Freyda." Alrion waved Freyda closer. She closed the distance with hesitation.

"I am so sorry for what you went through. I can never fully atone for that, but I will set things right."

"You are not accountable for the actions of a monster." Freyda's voice was quiet, yet defiant.

"I failed to stop him before, which I am responsible for. I'll have to find a way to balance that out. But at least, this is something I can do for now." Alrion put his right hand slowly into the water, so it was touching the surface. With this left hand he placed it on Freyda's chest.

"I'm amazed they managed to get the Blight to take hold. But I believe I can fix that right now." Alrion closed his eyes. His left hand glowed white, and Freyda's body seemed to respond. She gasped and almost stumbled, but she held her footing. A bright light soon surrounded her. It suddenly exploded and vanished, leaving Freyda stumbling forward. Alrion managed to catch her in time and ease her back onto the throne.

Lara couldn't believe it. He had made it look so easy.

It's really happening.

Sure, Wraith and Freyda had been special cases. But if Alrion could cure them, he could cure anyone. It was incredible. Freyda opened her eyes after a minute and looked around. Her eyes flashed quickly.

She must be using her power, Lara thought. Tears streamed down Freyda's face.

"You did it. You drove it away. I can't thank you enough." She clutched Alrion and sobbed into his chest. Alrion looked shocked, but held the woman tenderly. Freyda recovered and wiped her face.

"I'm sorry, I didn't mean to do that. I felt like my life had been taken away. It was so horrible!" Freyda visibly shuddered.

"I understand completely. And I am glad that I could help you."

"I feel renewed." Freyda stood quickly. There was a new spring and energy to her that hadn't been there just minutes ago.

This really is the stuff of miracles, Lara thought.

"What will you do now?" Alrion said.

"First, I will return home. But I'm not sure if I can stay. This whole experience, it's been like returning from the dead. I can't settle into my old life, well not straight away."

"Journey as far as you need. We will always be here to help," Marla said. Freyda bowed.

"Lara, let's go for a walk," Alrion said. He walked over and offered her his hand. Lara's heart skipped a beat and she held on tight.

What's going on?

In all the time they had been travelling together, not once had Alrion taken her aside. Her mind raced, wondering what might be the cause of it. But the realist in her shot down any fanciful thoughts.

Alrion just has no clue. He'll just want to grill you about Alyx.

They walked in silence across the snow, heading towards a building Lara had not yet explored. Alrion opened the door and motioned for her to enter. She stepped inside and looked around. It was a sparse, empty room but had what looked like a large pool in the middle.

"This is where we did our training. It's nice and quiet here," he said.

"Don't worry, I'll find Alyx," Lara blurted out. She didn't want him to be disappointed in her again.

"I know. This is not about Alyx, forget her for a minute." Alrion paused and look to be gathering his thoughts.

"This has been a really tough time. Being infected and on the run, fearing each day if we would be attacked and feeling like I couldn't even defend myself. I haven't exactly been the easiest person to be around during all that."

"I don't blame you. But you got through it."

"I did, well we all did. Together. But I've learned something through all this. I've got a different perspective now. We can't use destructive things as a crutch, not anymore. I used my anger, my frustration to fuel myself and push forward. But that's their way, that's what the Blight does. And we need to be better than that." Alrion seemed to be building up to a point.

"I understand." Lara didn't know what he was getting at though. It was all very confusing.

"And it's so easy to focus on those emotions, and neglect the other parts. It's not just about what we're doing, it also has to be how we do it. We have to embrace the better way." Alrion shifted uncomfortably and looked around the room.

Why is he philosophising so much? Lara thought. She remained quiet and let him continue speaking.

"It's our connection that helps us succeed. It's love being the opposite to all the hate that they thrive on." Alrion swallowed hard. Lara was starting to get a sense of what he was trying to say.

"I love you," he said abruptly. His face started to turn red, and he looked like he was trying to turn away. But he looked her directly in the eyes. She could see the sincerity of his words.

"I know," she said, almost laughing. He started to say something else but she just leaned in and kissed him. It was lovely and warm and felt so right after so long. She withdrew, and looked at him. He looked equal parts happy, and surprised, and relieved.

"I love you too. You're stuck with me now."

"I could think of worse things," Alrion gave her a smile. It was a real smile, one that she hadn't seen for a long time. That warmed her heart. His old self was coming back, from before being infected.

"You had me worried for a while there with Alyx." Lara gave him a pointed look and Alrion looked sheepish.

"I'm sorry about that. It was just respect and admiration. And I wanted to treat her like a human being. All that talk of being a weapon and a tool, that wasn't right."

"I thought that might be the case. But we worked that all out."

"You ... talked about me?" Alrion looked surprised.

"Of course we did. I care about her too, so don't be surprised about that. We'll find her. We just need to figure out a way to do that."

"It's of absolute importance. I can't move forward until we do. She's the one person I swore I would cure, and I won't be able to focus on what I need to do until she's found and cured."

"So, everything else is on hold?"

"Things can still continue to happen. But my entire focus from now on will be learning how I can find and save her. The quest is on hold." Alrion had a fierce determination to him. Lara loved that; that he cared so much. But it was also worrying.

"Are you sure that's the right thing? I'll support you, but it's a big thing to put everything else on hold."

"I'm sure. I can't be the hope people need, if I can't even save one person."

"Then I guess we need to step up our game." Lara shook her head. Things were different but also the same. But there was a gentle relief in her heart. She felt like she knew how he felt, but she didn't know if he realised it. Or if she had been mistaken. But his words today had lifted a great weight off her, one that was heavier than she had realised.

36

SPARK OF TRUTH

Alrion stepped through a hallway, the sounds of his footsteps echoing strangely around the space. He looked around and had a sudden realisation.

"I'm in a dream. One of those dreams." He stepped through the doorway and saw his grandfather sitting at a desk, writing away.

"Here we are again," Alrion said. He pulled up a chair and sat next to his grandfather.

"Here we are. You are nearing the end of your quest."

"How do you know?"

"Because you have completed the three trials. Don't forget, I'm just a part of you that is interpreting your knowledge and your memory."

"I realise that. Each time you show me something. Or I'm showing myself something. What is it this time?"

"Very well." Granthion stood slowly and walked over to a heavy stone doorway. He opened it slowly and it revealed a scene behind. Alrion walked over and looked closely.

A much younger Granthion held an orb of light in front of him as he walked through a dark cavern. The walls were worn down, as if by the wind and rain. Which seemed odd for what seemed like a deep cave. There was the occasional stalactite, but otherwise the cave was unadorned.

The young wizard walked forward without fear or hesitation. He trekked further and further down, like he knew what he was looking for. Finally, he reached the end of the cave. It was a wall. The cave just ended abruptly.

Granthion slowed and approached the wall carefully. He held up his light and gasped. Alrion could see why.

The wall wasn't like the rest of the cavern. It looked like it was oozing and fluid. It pulsed and moved with a strange rhythm. It was alive.

"Is this really it?" Granthion said. He peered closer at the surface. He stepped back and took in the whole of the wall.

"This can't be it," Granthion muttered. He walked around the small space inspecting all of the walls. But he returned all the same to the strange oozing wall. He brought the light closer and closer. The wall seemed to react to it, shrinking away from the light ever so slightly. Granthion reached out with his other hand, slowly and tentatively. Closer. Closer. Finally, his hand touched the wall. For an instant nothing happened. Then the wall came alive, swallowing his hand. Granthion yanked it back in horror, thick black tendrils of oozing substance clinging to his fingers. He couldn't shake them off.

A stream of fire erupted from his hand, encasing the black goo, and burning it. The flames leapt onto the wall itself. But once they transferred they fizzled out instantly.

"What have I done?" Granthion said. He hurled more and more spells at the oozing wall, and struggled harder to free his hand. Eventually he managed to yank it back, the black substance that had been on him retracting back into the wall. But it had left a mark. Black streaks lined his hand.

The vision quickly collapsed and all that was left was blackness. Alrion closed the door and turned back to the now seated Granthion.

"That was you! Where was that?"

"That was the source of the Blight."

"You found it? And you touched it?"

"Yes, I became infected. And I always suspected that it had greater repercussions than just that." Granthion looked back down at the book before him. Alrion thought through the statement.

"What do you mean?" Alrion said. Granthion looked up again.

"In the time since that moment, there have been two rather major turning points in the existence of the Blight. The widespread creation of Shades. And the turning of the four generals." Granthion returned to his book.

"Oh no. That explains your obsession. You sought out and found the source of the Blight. But not only were you infected, you think that it somehow grew and changed because of its contact with you?"

"That is correct."

"That explains so much." Alrion was stunned. His mind was buzzing with all the potential of that revelation.

"That ruined your life."

"I have to assume so, looking at the other information available. Although, a great many things were achieved because of that."

"I wish I could stay here and talk to you. Why can't I do that?"

"Because your mind is not open or strong enough to join too much information together at once. There are protections in place."

"How do I overcome that?"

"I cannot tell you."

"Because you don't know, or you won't?"

"Who takes care of the Pool of Knowledge?" Granthion said. Alrion paused then answered.

"Nominated guardians. They also drink from the pool."

"And would these guardians know how to expertly access the available knowledge?"

"They should."

"And what happens when they drink from the pool?"

"Their knowledge is added to the rest. So, I must have the knowledge myself. You're just having fun with me, aren't you?"

"You're asking the wrong person." Granthion smiled.

"Fine, I get it. I can't rush this. Surely you can give me something else." Alrion was desperate. He needed to know more. This revelation by itself opened up too many questions. Which was probably why he wasn't being shown more. Granthion looked thoughtful, and finally spoke.

"The crystal amulet that you wear. You should figure out what's inside." Granthion smiled once more, then vanished. The room itself started to break up and Alrion was swallowed by blackness.

Alrion awoke with a start, thrashing his arms around. He realised he was in bed, and it was still dark. But that was just because nobody had lit any lamps, he couldn't tell what time of day it was. As his eyes adjusted he looked over at everyone else. His parents were asleep, as was Lara. He couldn't sleep again, so he crept out of bed, pulled on a coat and boots, and left the quarters.

The first light was breaking across the mountain, the bright rays and pink sky looked stunning. Alrion realised how much natural beauty he was surrounded by. He felt like he understood why his grandmother had lived here for so long. It wasn't just access to the source of Soul power. It was the beauty, quiet, and isolation. Something that made sense to him now.

Without a direction he wandered, but found himself standing before the great hall. Temporary doors had been built from wood and placed there without any decoration. He pushed one aside and stepped inside the room. There were a few candles lit, and the minimal glow from the water fountain helped illuminate the throne. Marla was sitting there.

"What brings you here so early?" she said. Her voice carried through the hall.

"I couldn't sleep, and found myself here."

"It must be for a reason." Marla seemed to stare at him as he approached.

"Are you their leader now?"

"I am not the eldest, but I feel as though I was meant to be her successor. I will gather all the Mystics and we will vote. Together we will reach a decision."

"You have my vote, if that counts." Alrion stopped just in front of the fountain of water. He peered into it, wondering how his grandmother had used it to see visions. The slight glow of the water reminded him of something.

He pulled out his crystal amulet and looked at it. It was the same as always, a thin black tendril stuck within it. He remembered the final words from his dream. There was something to discover.

"I've never seen a Soul crystal like that." Marla walked over to get a better look. Alrion removed it carefully and handed it to her. She turned it over in her hands, inspecting it. Alrion saw her eyes flash as she used her Soul power.

"As expected. And there's a strand of Blight in there too. This is incredible. Where did you get this?"

"My grandfather made it. Every wizard gets one as part of the initiation ritual."

"A wizard made this? That's unbelievable. To think that a wizard could manipulate Soul power." Marla handed the crystal back, and Alrion put it back over his head.

"It's strange, but I noticed that before when I was fighting. The Spark seemed to attract the Soul power and drag it along. I'm guessing that is why it worked."

"I still haven't learned how to put Soul power into vessels like that. It is a difficult and restricted skill. The eldest never taught it to me."

"But did she have it written down?" Vincent said as he approached. Alrion hadn't even heard his father enter the room.

"Possibly. Why?"

"She told me that Alrion and I must learn as much as we can. There's a manual of some kind in her quarters."

"The forbidden tome. Very few of us were even told of its existence, but I never thought it would be so accessible. I assumed it would have been hidden away somewhere else." Marla looked shocked.

"What safer place than under her watchful eye?" Vincent said.

"Very true. Well, we must honour her wishes."

"If you're to lead, you must lead from the front. You must learn with us," Alrion said.

"Of course, you're right. It's time I stopped fearing the unknown. The eldest spent so much time instilling in us the dangers of other techniques."

"She must have known that she would not be around to guide you in them," Vincent said. Marla grew very still and quiet.

"I must learn everything there is about storing Soul power in objects. It's the key somehow." Alrion started peering into the water fountain.

"I'm sure everything we need will be in that book. The eldest was always prepared."

"Good. I have a few ideas already, but I need to think them over."

"Such as?" Vincent gave Alrion a suspicious look.

"Why ruin the surprise now? Let me figure it out more, then I can show you instead of just telling you."

"Fair enough. We'll just have to wear protective clothing." Vincent laughed and even Marla smiled a little. Alrion looked at his father, thinking of the key revelation he received from his dream. He considered asking the question, but thought better of it. For now, there were more important things to focus on.

"I need to go for a walk. Can we all look at the book together later today?"

"Of course. I will coordinate with your father," Marla said.

"Thank you." Alrion turned and started walking away. He realised that he still hadn't achieve the whole purpose of his initial walk. He had to think through what he had learned in his dream.

Each time, he had been shown his objective. First it was the vault of silence, then it was his grandmother, and the power of Soul. This time it was a little different.

But what if it's not?

If he took the information on as presented, then he needed to find the source of the Blight and cure it from there. As his grandfather had so foolishly tried many years ago.

He also knew that wizard spells would not work. And since the dream had showed him his grandfather, he had to suspect something else as well.

"My grandfather sacrificed himself to cure Avaria. What will this do to me curing the whole world? Especially if I'm doing it at the source of the Blight?" The thought sent cold shivers down Alrion's spine. He felt his stomach churning at the idea of it all.

Whatever the situation is, you need to expect that it will end in sacrifice. It's worth it, isn't it? Alrion thought carefully. His life was still so young, and he had so much more to do. But he couldn't live on knowing that he had a chance to stop the Blight and he had not taken it. What had happened to Alyx was tearing him up. He had no choice.

Plan for a better way, but know that if it comes to it, you can do this.

"You have that look on your face," Lara said. Alrion looked up in surprise.

"What do you mean?"

"I haven't seen that look since you last had one of those dreams. Do you know how to end this?"

"I only know the location. You're not going to like it."

"Where?" Lara's face was a picture of concern.

"The source of the Blight." Alrion watched her face go ashen.

For her sake, be strong, he thought and put on a brave face. Lara said nothing, and when Alrion started off again she joined him. It was a difficult path ahead, and for now at least, it was a relief to know that he would not need to walk it alone.

SOUL OF
LIGHT

Book Four of The Hidden Wizard

Vaughan W. Smith

For Hugo

PROLOGUE

Alyx was lost in a haze of grey and black mist. Her diminishing eyesight had gone to an extreme she never thought possible. She felt her body moving and doing things, but she had no idea how it was happening.

There were flashes of images. She saw the missing Tracker. Alive then dead. She felt somehow involved in that, but it was such a strange and distant memory. Like it was in a previous life. Or something not yet done.

What's happening to me? she thought. The more she tried to wrestle some control back, the more pain she felt and the more she drifted away. Something terrible had happened, but she wasn't sure what it was.

Suddenly, she felt drawn to something. The landscape started to clear, and she recognised the terrain. She had somehow travelled a long way from the scene of the battle. The last thing she remembered properly.

There was a figure standing before her. She had trouble making out any features. But she could tell from the silhouette that he was armed. A sword and shield, and possibly armour as well.

"Well, well, well. What have we here?" the figure said. It sounded like a man. But it was not a normal voice. There was something wrong with it. Alyx tried to speak, but nothing happened. Just silence.

"Perhaps that was cruel of me, pausing. I know you can't respond. In fact, the only reason you can even hear my words is that I am allowing it. So, I guess that does make me cruel. Not that it would be a surprise to anyone." The man paused again. Alyx wanted to scream something, but she couldn't move or do anything else. She was just aware of him and his voice.

"You're not who I came for. It was that meddlesome wizard. He had outlived his usefulness, but I'm not one to let that stop me. I would have enjoyed turning him to some lesser purpose. But you, you're a better prize." The man walked closer and reached out. Alyx had to assume he was touching her head, but she felt nothing.

"We have never met, so I should introduce myself. My name is Darvin. I go by other names, but that will do for now. I've been so preoccupied that I never thought to look for you. And had you not been infected, I probably wouldn't have found you. But that fool Wraith did one good thing for me in the end. Yes, this is too perfect." The man stepped back and looked her over.

"When you killed my brother, it was a dagger through my heart. That's how I felt it. The sharp, sudden loss. The unexpected nature of it is what hurt me so badly. I thought he was invincible, undefeatable. But he made a crucial error. He underestimated you. I won't make that same mistake."

Alyx, even in her haze, had started to piece things together. No doubt her mental faculties were available to her on his whim, which made it worse. But she knew who he was now. And it scared her.

"I felt that. The tremor of fear. Good, you know me. You should be afraid." Darvin started pacing around.

"I've had this feeling within me for some time now, and I didn't know what it was. It was a burning desire for revenge, to hurt you for what you did to us. But I hadn't identified it and acknowledged it. But now it's all rushing out. And I have the answer. I know what will fill the void I've been feeling." Darvin stopped right in front of her. She had trouble making out his features. But she couldn't miss the wicked smile.

"You are a Shade now, which is nice, but not enough. I won't underestimate you. You have a strong will, and maybe you would find a way out. No, I've got something special in store for you. I can bring you into the fold. I can transform you into one of us, and you can sit at our table." Darvin paused, watching her. Alyx had no idea what he was getting at, but it sounded bad.

"If only you could respond. Oh well, in time. But I won't keep you in suspense any longer. To right the wrongs that you did to us, you can serve us. You can fill the gaping hole in our number. You will become the Skull Queen and serve in place of the one you so cruelly stole from us." Darvin clapped his hands, the excitement so obvious.

Alyx understood the words and felt complete and utter horror.

"Nooooo!" she screamed. Some part of it must have gotten through because Darvin took a step back.

"Interesting. I didn't expect that. Never mind, come with me. We have a lot of preparations to make." Darvin turned and left, and Alyx felt herself moving with him.

I can't let this happen, she thought, steeling her resolve. But the fog was coming back, and she was soon lost within it.

1

THE POWER OF SOUL

Alrion sat back, and let the ideas collect and form together.

"I know we've only read a little, but it's been enough for me to puzzle something out," he said. Vincent and Marla looked at him with interest.

"Are you going to keep us in suspense?" Vincent said after a while.

"I've figured out how my grandfather cured Avaria." Alrion looked around, and both his father and Marla looked shocked. He enjoyed that for a moment.

"Go on then," Vincent said.

"He needed two things: access to the Blight and access to Soul Power. Neither of which he had."

"I understand the need for the Soul Power. Why did he need access to the Blight? You were cured yourself when you cured Wraith," Vincent said.

"Yes, but I found a way to insert the Soul Power into Wraith's body. He was right in front of me. I didn't need any special connection to target him."

"I see. But my father managed to create a net so large it covered the entire country of Avaria." Vincent nodded along.

"Therefore, he needed those two things. How did a wizard do that, when he had access to neither?" Marla said.

"Because he mastered the skill of transferring them into vessels. One for Soul Power, one for Blight. The crystal I wear has both. It's proof that he could do it."

"That's good. But how does that help you?" Vincent looked sceptical.

"There's no way I can source and store enough Soul Power to cure everyone of the Blight. It won't help me there. I'm mostly just glad that I've puzzled out how he did it. Considering his limitations, he did such incredible things."

"He really did." Vincent let out a deep sigh. Alrion could sense the regret in his father. He decided to quickly move on.

"Anyway, I'm starting to think of other applications."

"Such as?" Marla said.

"If I can put Soul Power into a vessel. And if the right amount of Soul Power inserted into a body can drive out the Blight. Then what's stopping me from creating something that someone else can use to cure the Blight?" Alrion looked over at his father and Marla. They had confused looks. But he saw them thinking it over, and the realisation showing.

"You're absolutely right. Why did my father never try that?" Vincent said.

"He would have had a finite amount of Soul Power. He never returned here to get more, so he must have been using it sparingly, knowing that he needed it," Marla said. Vincent nodded with understanding.

"It's all theoretical right now. But I know I can get this to work. Those generals of the Blight won't see any of this coming. It's time for the tide to change. We're going on the offensive now." Alrion saw doubt in their faces.

But he believed it, and soon they would too. In the back of his mind, there was the nagging doubt about how he would end this war and cure the Blight. But he silenced it. There was time to figure that out. For now, he had to trust in himself and those who were on the journey with him. They had defied the odds repeatedly. What was one more impossible task?

If this works, I don't need to be there to cure Alyx.

Lara crested the snowy hill and paused to catch her breath. She looked over at Celes and saw the older woman breathing heavily.

No need to put on appearances then, Lara thought. She let down her guard and showed how exhausted she was. They had spent enough time together that she no longer felt like she had to prove herself. Celes caught her breath enough to laugh.

"Good to see that you tire as well. I thought it was only me."

"I'm not really the hiking type. I think I've done a lifetime these last few weeks." Lara surveyed the landscape. There was enough greenery poking out from the layers of snow that it felt alive, and not completely whitewashed. The sweeping hills and rocky mountains in the distance were awe inspiring.

I should try to appreciate this while we're still here. I wish I could get Alrion out to see it.

"Ready to push on?" Celes looked like she needed another minute.

"I need another two minutes." Lara watched Celes's reaction and saw the woman's face relax noticeably.

No need to be rude.

"Do you think this mysterious trader will turn up today?" Lara looked at Celes, curious.

"I hope so, we've got no other leads. We have so completely canvassed this whole area." Celes sighed. "We need to be moving, not making camp."

"If we bring him something, he'll move. But not before. He's obsessed with this project of his."

"The Soul Orbs?" Celes brushed the snow off a nearby rock and sat. She cleared a spot next to her. Lara sat next to her, trying to ignore the cold. A chill ran down her spine.

"Yes. He won't talk about anything else. Well, except news of Alyx of course."

"He's always been stubborn, even as a child. Once he gets his mind set on something, he won't budge. But I don't see why he's so fixated on this. If he wants to save her, shouldn't we be out doing more than just looking?" Celes stared out into the distance, deep in thought.

"I've been thinking about that too. I think I know the answer." Lara noticed that she suddenly had Celes's full attention.

"And?"

"He doesn't want to be in that situation again. Where he has to choose."

"Choose?"

"He chose to cure Branthor, and he could do nothing for Alyx in the moment." Lara could see the scene playing out again in front of her. The desperation on Alrion's face. The defeat in the face of his amazing victory. She pushed the images away.

"And if he develops this Soul Orb, he can cure someone while still retaining his Soul Power?" Celes clarified.

"If it works, then yes. I think that's what this is about."

"You're right. He's grown so much, but he hasn't changed. Not one bit."

"Isn't that great though?"

"Oh, it is. Despite all this, he's still my boy. I still see him that way. It's not really fair to anyone, but that's how it is. I have to keep reminding myself that he's saving the world." Celes rose awkwardly.

"I'm not made for this intense cold. Let's keep moving."

"The sooner we get to this outpost the better." Lara blew warm air into her hands and took off after Celes.

The hike didn't take that much longer. Soon, they saw the top of a wooden shack rising out of the snow. It was nestled amongst tall fir trees and looked like the landscape had grown around it. A small plume of smoke wafted out of a small chimney.

"That's our place." Lara pointed to the shack.

"Good. I hope this trader is legitimate. How do you want to do the interrogation?"

"Interrogation?" Lara stopped suddenly.

"Perhaps that was too strong a word. But we need to figure out what he knows, and I don't have the patience for some ego-driven idiot."

"I'm curious what you would consider normal?" Lara felt a sudden pang of fear. Maybe she didn't know Celes at all.

"Oh, don't give me that look, I'm not like that. I meant more along the lines of 'the cudgel and the honey'."

"Oh, I see. In that case, why don't you choose? I'll follow your lead."

"I'll be honey, you be the cudgel."

"Sounds like fun." Lara winked and Celes returned it. Lara upped the pace and took the lead before heading into the shack.

A wave of warmth rippled out as soon as she pushed open the heavy wooden door.

Finally! Lara lingered for a moment in the doorway, then remembered Celes. She quickly shuffled inside, held the door and closed it quickly. There was a raging fire which explained the warmth. Otherwise, the shack was very simply furnished. There were a few chairs and couches, and one writing desk in the corner. Two men occupied the room. One silver-haired gentleman in adventurer's gear sat at the desk, and another man lounged in front of the fire. He was younger and dressed like a well-to-do merchant. He was reclining in the chair and playing with a silver ring.

He's not dressed for the elements at all. I don't trust him already.

The man at the desk nodded towards the hearth, and Celes approached first. She took a seat directly opposite the merchant. Lara pulled up a chair next to her. The merchant paid them no attention.

"Excuse me, I was led to believe that you have some information of the recent Blight attacks." Celes's voice sounded sweeter than usual. Lara almost laughed. The merchant looked up.

"Oh yes, good of you to finally join me. I was promised coins." He held his hand out.

"Certainly." Celes handed over a small bulging sack. "My name is Celes. And you are?"

"Gunthram." He pocketed the coins without delay and started to resume his previous position.

"And the information?" Celes maintained her polite voice. Gunthram looked annoyed.

"Yes, yes I can confirm the attacks. I was there at one. Ghastly business." He turned his attention to the hearth.

"We're quite interested in hearing more. What was unusual about these attacks?" Celes tried again.

"I'd rather not say." Gunthram started spinning his ring idly. Celes nodded at Lara. The young thief stood quickly and snatched the ring from Gunthram.

"Well, I never!" He started to rise. Lara shoved him back down, making a show of inspecting his ring.

"Nice ring, if a little plain. Does this have some special significance?" She looked him directly in the eyes. Gunthram gulped but did a good job at hiding it.

"No, not really. Just a trinket I picked up."

"You won't mind if I keep it then." Lara pocketed the ring. Gunthram's face grew red. Celes reached out and held his hand tenderly. She looked back at Lara.

"No need to be rude, Gunthram has been through a lot. Clearly, the attack was quite traumatic."

Gunthram seemed to relax and nodded. But he kept his eyes on Lara.

"Why don't you share some more details, I apologise for my associate. She's really quite hasty. I tell her every day, but she just doesn't listen!" Celes was almost using a motherly tone. Lara had to stifle a laugh.

"Very well. I, well I'm. It's just... it wasn't normal." Gunthram seemed quite preoccupied. He started fidgeting. Celes nudged Lara and she returned the ring. He took it without looking and resumed twirling it around.

"The truth is, I can't believe what I saw. There was a creature unlike any I've seen before. She was jet black, dressed in a simple black uniform adorned with silver. But she wielded a giant great sword and her face." Gunthram stopped speaking. He grew pale, and a haunted look came over his face.

"Go on. Please." Celes encouraged him.

"It was like you could see her skull. It was horrific. The few that stood up to her, she was like a whirlwind of death. There seemed to be another standing back and laughing. I ran." Gunthram sank into the chair. He closed his eyes.

"That's quite a story. We're so appreciative of the information. I know that must have been hard for you."

"I see that face in my dreams. I try to pretend it never happened."

"Why did you come here? Why admit you saw it?" Lara softened her voice slightly but still challenged him. Gunthram looked up, fear in his eyes.

"I lost everything. I bragged about my survival in taverns to get the odd drink, and conversation. I felt that I was somehow moving past the whole thing. Then I was offered the odd coin for more details on the story from concerned travellers hoping to avoid trouble. I thought I could keep going and get enough money to travel back to Avaria, without truly reliving it. But no. As many times as I kept it back, it wouldn't stay back." Gunthram slumped into the chair. He focused on the hearth, the flame dancing around and chewing on another log. Celes pulled out another sack of coins and pressed it into his hands.

"What did they call it?" she said softly. Gunthram's lips quivered.

"The Skull Queen." Lara stifled a gasp and looked over at Celes. She nodded, and they turned to leave.

"What are you going to do?" Gunthram said, apprehension in his voice.

"We're going to cure her of the Blight." Lara shoved the door open and rushed out into the freezing cold.

2

DIFFERENT PATHS

Alrion held the crystal delicately and examined it from all angles. From normal inspection, it looked quite average. You could not discern anything special about it. But by accessing his Soul Power, he could see the surging of Soul within the crystal. Not a lot, but definitely there. A knock on the door interrupted him, and he placed the crystal down on the table next to him.

Vincent walked in, nodding to Alrion. He eased himself down in the chair next to Alrion.

"How's it going with this?" Vincent pointed to the crystal.

"See for yourself." Alrion handed it over and watched his father's reaction. Vincent turned the crystal over and seemed to see something. He handed it back.

"It looks successful. What does this mean for your plan?"

"It's a major win. I just need to settle on the right vessel and the right amount of Soul Power." Alrion turned the crystal over once more, before setting it down.

"Provided that it works as intended?"

"Yes, I will need to test it on a Blighter initially. But the applications are vast once I get going."

"Is that your plan? To become a craftsman creating tools to fight the Blight?" Alrion was caught off guard by his father's question.

"What are you talking about?"

"You've been holed up here for weeks, tinkering away while the world moves on." Vincent looked Alrion directly in the eyes. The challenge was obvious.

"It was a good use of my time, while the search for Alyx continued."

"We both know this is not critical to saving her, or your quest. You're just buying time. You're stalling." Vincent paused, watching.

"It's, not like that." Alrion almost stammered the words out.

It's true, isn't it? You're hiding here.

"I'm doing the best I can. It's been relentless getting here." As he spoke the words, Alrion realised how bad an excuse it sounded.

"I know that, nobody's judging you. You've overcome incredible hurdles to get this far, moved mountains. But this is not the kind of situation where you can just put things on pause." Alrion picked up on the sense of urgency from his father.

What's driving this? Maybe it's time to find out.

"I never properly explained to you my last dream." Alrion watched his father's reaction. His face changed quickly, to one of curiosity. The hard edge fell away.

"Go on."

"I saw a vision of the source of the Blight. And my grandfather." A look of recognition passed over Vincent's face in an instant, but Alrion was watching. He noticed.

"Really?" Vincent spoke evenly, keeping his composure.

He's feigning ignorance. But he knows.

"But you already know what I'm about to say. Because you've always known." Alrion's voice raised slightly in volume.

"I'm not quite sure what you are referring to, son. Just tell me."

"He touched the source of the Blight, and it changed. He caused the problems that we now face. That's why he was so hell-bent on solving the problem of the Blight. It was guilt. And you knew about it. All this time. There's no way you didn't." Alrion was on a roll now. The emotions of the past few weeks, the discovery that he had kept to himself, all combined into a single moment.

"That had to be why the two of you were so estranged. He wanted you to take on his legacy, but you couldn't. And you ran away. Now that I'm here, and I'm doing it, you're here to push me forward again. To make sure your father's unfinished business is done." Alrion was shouting now.

Where did that come from?

He saw his father shrink back. Vincent lost that sense of assurance and confidence. He looked pained.

"Alrion, I." Vincent paused. "I understand how you feel. You're right. I did know about my father's part in this. It was what drove us apart. I am sorry that I kept it from you."

"Why didn't you tell me? Even now?"

"I didn't want to put that burden on you. It's a heavy toll, and you had enough to contend with." Vincent reached out, but Alrion shrank away.

"When were you going to tell me?"

"At the end, once we were done. It would have been a nice close to this whole chapter. We could both put it behind us."

Alrion didn't know what to say. He could hear the sincerity in his father's words.

But another lie?

"I... there's no words right now. Don't worry, I'm not abandoning my quest. I'm just trying to prepare something to be one step ahead. I'm sick of having to make bad choices."

"Which one are you hoping to avoid?"

"Having to choose who to cure." Alrion's voice was soft and trailed away. Vincent stepped forward and enveloped his son in a tight hug. Alrion didn't return it initially but then gave in.

"This does not make things right. You better not be hiding anything else from me?"

"That's it. How many more skeletons can I have in the closet?" Vincent laughed. Alrion was about to respond when he noticed the door opening. Lara and Celes entered the room.

"Oh good, you're both here. There's something we need to tell you," Lara said. Alrion could see from the look on her face that it was bad news.

Something about Alyx. Oh no.

"Do we need to get Marla?" Vincent said.

"No, not yet. We found word of Alyx, and we're pretty sure it's a real lead." Lara looked over at Celes, who nodded.

"And?" Alrion said.

"And it's worse than we expected. She's become something else."

"Something else?" Alrion saw Lara look down briefly before meeting his gaze.

"She's become the Skull Queen."

"What?" Alrion looked from Lara to his mother. Both wore serious and apologetic looks. Even his father looked shocked and saddened.

"I don't understand. She was turning into a Shade. What's this?"

"The enemy must have found a way to transform her further. It's quite cruel really, considering her past." Vincent shook his head.

"She killed the Skull King. I can't believe this. I knew I should have been out looking. Instead, I've been wasting time with these toys." Alrion threw the crystal to the floor. It clattered with a loud noise but didn't break. Lara stepped over and picked up the crystal, examining it.

"Does this work?" She handed it to Celes.

"It should do. But I need to test it. I don't know how much is needed and if the effect will be the same." Alrion started pacing.

"Alright, we need to get moving. No more waiting around. Where were the sightings?"

"Some smaller towns at the foot of the mountains. They must be moving towards bigger settlements."

"Do we have maps? Let's figure out where we need to get to. Maybe we can predict their destination and cut them off."

"I know where some are, give me a minute." Lara left immediately.

"Alrion, I'm not sure we should be pursuing this right now," Vincent spoke gently.

"Did you just say that? After we just had that conversation?"

"It's your quest, and you've worked on your tools, your extra options. You can continue to refine those on the road ahead. But you need to learn the spell you need and the place to cast it."

"Listen to your father, Alrion. We are here to support you, but you need to keep moving forward. On the task at hand. You can't save everyone?" Celes reached out and held Alrion's hand. After a moment, he pulled away.

"Alyx is not just anyone. She sacrificed so much, and now the worst has happened to her. It was bad enough her running around as a Shade. But now she's been transformed into her worst nightmare. That should make it more important to save her, not less."

"You can save her by saving everyone. I know how important she is, and what she did. But isn't saving the world more important?"

"You don't understand. I can't save the world if I can't save her first." Alrion slumped down into a chair.

How could I let this happen?

Vincent put a hand on Alrion's shoulder. Alrion felt the warmth and reassurance. He looked up and saw his father smiling.

"You need to do the right thing for yourself, this is your quest. I only want to provide you with some perspective. I've been around a while, I have learnt a thing or two." Vincent winked.

"So you think," Celes said, laughing. Vincent feigned injury and turned back to Alrion.

"All jokes aside, I've just had a realisation. We are your support team, I shouldn't forget that. And I understand that keeping things from you has made it difficult. So, here's my suggestion." Vincent paused and drew in a deep breath.

"Your mother and I will go hunt down clues for the location of the source of the Blight. You can pursue and save Alyx. We can meet up later and go together to end this quest." Alrion nodded, taking the words in. It wasn't the first time they had split up to achieve different things. He looked over at his mother. Celes nodded her approval. But he still noticed her giving his father a questioning look.

So, it wasn't planned. I'm sure he'll get in trouble for that, splitting us up again.

"It's a good plan. If you perfect your Soul Orb, then either one of us could cure Alyx. And once we have her back, we will be much stronger." Lara spoke slowly but seemed to be gathering in enthusiasm with each word.

"But how can we even coordinate ourselves? Where will your search take you?" Alrion said to Vincent. The blacksmith rubbed his chin in thought.

"I was just thinking, that while we don't know where the source of the Blight is, we do know where it is near." Vincent paused.

"Where?" Alrion said.

Don't tell me you've been hiding more!

"Remember the story of the four generals of the Blight?"

"Yes, of course."

"Where did those generals come from?"

"Valrytir." Lara gasped after speaking. Alrion looked over at her, shocked.

"It makes sense, doesn't it?" Vincent raised the question. Alrion didn't know what to think.

"Are you sure?"

"Well, it doesn't really matter if I'm right. They successfully reached the source of the Blight from there, so it's as good a place as any to stage our final approach. They are well-versed in fighting the Blight and have the world's largest and most sophisticated armed force."

"He's right, if you're looking for raw firepower, that's the place to go," Lara said.

"You've been there before, haven't you?" Celes said to Vincent. He nodded.

"Many years ago, before we met. I'm not in a rush to return, but I think it's the right place for us to go."

"This is all very sudden." Alrion sighed. But he thought about what his father had said.

I do need to move forward, I can't delay it any longer.

"I guess this is it. We shall investigate appearances of the Skull Queen. Then we will look for a lead concerning the source of the Blight. If we don't find one, we can meet at Valrytir. Does that sound right?"

"Exactly. Your mother is quite skilled at information gathering. I'm sure she will have this solved within the week." Vincent winked at Celes.

"Right, don't set any reasonable expectations." Celes laughed.

"I think it's the best path, considering the circumstances." Lara's voice was quiet. Alrion could sense some hesitation in her, despite her agreeing to the plan.

"Is everything alright, Lara? Is there something about the plan?" Alrion thought a moment, it was more than that. "About Valrytir?"

"I was born there, but I've not been back in a long time. It will be... strange."

Don't pry, there's some sort of history there.

"That's fine, I'll do whatever I can to make it easier. But first, we need to save Alyx." Alrion looked around the room. Everyone acknowledged him. His father with a tight nod, his mother with a warm smile. Lara gave him an apprehensive smile.

"We will make preparations and leave." Vincent guided Celes towards the door. She stopped and stepped back to Alrion.

"Take care, son. We shall see you soon. Don't forget, that we're so proud of you." Celes pulled his head over and lightly kissed the top of it. Alrion fought down embarrassment.

"Send my regards to Alyx." Vincent opened the door and, after Celes left, followed her.

"I guess it's just us again," Lara said.

"So it is. Just like old times."

"Maybe we can skip the whole 'take on a field of Blighters and almost die in the process' though this time?"

"I'll consider it." Alrion gave her a grin, then his mind started working through the consequences of his decision. But he was still firm.

Alyx, we're coming.

3

AN IMPOSSIBLE CHOICE

Alrion hugged Marla and stepped back.

"Are you sure you have everything you need?" Marla gestured to the storeroom again. Alrion let his eyes wander over the shelves and mentally catalogued everything.

"Yes, any more would weigh us down. And the crystals you gave me to experiment with the Soul Orbs are reusable. We are ready."

"Thank you for your help. Do we know when we will return?" Lara said, looking at Alrion. He shrugged.

"I don't expect to return until it's over. But I will come back and see you. I'm not going to follow in my father's footsteps." Alrion sighed, but Marla laughed.

"Good, we look forward to seeing you back here. You are a part of us, so you belong here. But I understand if you decide to spend your life somewhere a little warmer."

"You do have a tendency to get snowed in." Lara gave an exaggerated shiver.

"Well, thank you again. I will try and send word if possible." Alrion paused, thinking it over.

"Yes, if you leave word with any Mystics you come across, we will get the message. Good luck and look after each other." Marla waved, and Alrion pushed the door open, waiting for Lara to exit.

A blustery wind assaulted them immediately.

"Not looking forward to the initial hike one bit." Lara kicked at some snow and pushed forward. Alrion noticed small clusters of Mystics out and about. They all seemed to slow and stop, watching them leave.

"Do you think they're glad to be rid of us?" Alrion said.

"In a way, yes. We brought so much death and destruction with us. Even if it wasn't our fault."

"True. That's why I'll set things right. This won't happen again. I'll make sure of it."

"And I'll watch your back while you do it." Lara pivoted around and walked behind Alrion, fending off phantom adversaries.

"Maybe save that for later?" Alrion laughed. But he appreciated Lara trying to lighten the mood. The news of the Skull Queen had sent him reeling. He thought that he was prepared to help Alyx, but now he was not so sure. There was a niggling doubt that maybe he would be unable to help her.

First things first—I need to find her.

The path outside the Mystic's home was foreign. Alrion hadn't paid much attention on the way, he had been preoccupied. While staying with the Mystics, he hadn't strayed beyond his accommodation at all, leaving the job of combing the countryside to his mother and Lara.

"You must be an expert in this area now," Alrion said.

"By necessity. We spent more than enough time traipsing around, looking for hidden paths and alternate tracks. It will come in handy now."

"I hope so."

"I can take us the most direct path out of here. But where are we heading to?"

"Do you know where that lead came from? Where the Skull Queen was last sighted?"

"A small town really. Called Londarth."

"Londarth it is. I'm not naive enough to believe that she will still be there, but we can find a trail."

"There's always a trail."

"There wasn't one here. How did we lose her?" Alrion practically mumbled the words. Lara stopped and grabbed him by the arm.

"You have to stop beating yourself up. Sometimes you can't do it all. We'll make it right." Lara looked directly into his eyes. Alrion could see the same pain that he felt. It was reassuring.

"Good." Alrion strode forward, "let's get a move on."

"Try and keep up." Lara darted forward, picking an odd path between the large stones littered along the path. Alrion almost lost sight of her.

Here we go. He started to really move, and the exercise awakened him in a way that was surprising. It was invigorating.

I've been too static. This is good. It was time to just lose himself in the journey for a little while.

～

Hours passed, and Lara finally slowed.

"You really do know these lands now. I didn't think it was possible to cut a path through here that wouldn't require us to take a break." Alrion heaved in a deep breath. He could augment his physical endurance somewhat with the Soul Power, but it had nothing on actual training. The more he learned, the more he realised that it wasn't a shortcut. It was more of an augmentation. He couldn't create fitness. But he could create speed and strength in short bursts.

"Trust me, it became pretty boring heading out time and time again. We needed to find ways to make it more interesting. And cut the duration. There's a limit to how much you can explore in a day." Lara drew in measured breaths. It seemed like she had used this as a rest place before.

"I need to figure out a way to travel faster with magic."

"And take away another thing I can still beat you at?" Lara grinned. Alrion was thinking of a witty retort when he noticed something suddenly hurtling towards them. He reached out by instinct, sending a wave of force. The object stopped immediately and hovered in the air. Alrion stepped over to investigate. It was a jet-black arrow.

"Good reaction." Lara had a dagger in hand and was staring into the distance.

Alrion activated his Soul Power and examined the arrow. He could see the taint of the Blight on it. He could even see traces in the air, where the arrow had displaced it.

This is interesting. He followed the signs, tracking the arrow's point of origin. A flat rock in the distance. There was a man standing on it, but at this distance was only a silhouette.

"There. Let's go ask him a few questions." Alrion grabbed the arrow out of the air. He could feel the Blight within it. A familiar and unsettling feeling.

Don't worry you are past that.

Alrion approached carefully, Lara by his side. She stalked along, sweeping left and right looking for threats. Alrion maintained his focus on the figure ahead of them. The man remained still, looking in their direction.

Details began to emerge. Alrion could see the bow and quiver clearly now, as dark as the arrow. The man was wearing a black hood over his face, with a black leather jerkin. His legs though, they were something else. They were black and wiry, and the stone beneath him seemed to ooze blackness. Alrion conjured a fireball and held it in front of him as he moved closer.

"Ahoy there. Don't shoot the messenger!" The man's voice was almost normal, but there was a strange accent to it that sounded off. He quickly raised his hands and backed away a little.

"Don't trust him, keep alert." Lara started to circle around to approach the man from behind.

"You shot first," Alrion said.

"Just to get your attention. I didn't want to make the wrong impression."

"Too late," Lara said. She was almost within striking distance. However, the man seemed unfazed by her.

"Trust me, it would have been a lot worse had I done this." The man seemed to become a blur and ran rings around them before settling down in the same spot. It was almost too fast for Alrion to react. But rather than loose the fireball, he had held on to avoid friendly fire.

"See? I'm rather fast."

"And you leave a trail." Lara pointed to the ground. A black tar coated the ground in a circle around them, showing his path. It quickly dried up and started to flake away.

"What are you?" Alrion said. He had encountered nothing like this at all. Not even the Trackers were like this.

"I prefer who. Fermur, pleased to meet your acquaintance. You may have heard of me?"

"You're one of the generals of the Blight."

"Alrion, wasn't it?"

"How did you find me? Why are you here?" Alrion created a second fireball. Fermur backed away more, but then noticed how close Lara was.

"Easy now, as I said, don't shoot the messenger. That's all I am. I have a message for you." Fermur seemed a little apprehensive.

He's probably heard of what I can do. Alrion let both fireballs dissipate into nothing. They were a distraction and were probably too slow to deal with this thing anyway.

"Pass on your message then."

"With great delight. I have a message for you from our fearless leader, Darvin. He sends his regards." Fermur paused, watching Alrion.

"And?"

"And he would like to inform you of two events. First, his new comrade the Skull Queen will be leading an assault on a town nearby called Carth."

Alyx. We've found you.

"Why should we trust anything you say?" Lara inched closer, with her dagger still poised to strike.

"I am honour bound to relay only truth. I am a messenger after all. Never liked fighting, not really. It was a benefit of my transformation then, that I could have a legitimate reason to avoid it. Do you want to hear the second part of the message?" Fermur looked at Alrion. He nodded. Fermur beamed a smile.

"Excellent! Now, the second event of note is that Darvin himself will be leading a separate assault on the city of Hurdenor. He provides you an opportunity to confront him as the hero you are." Fermur stopped again and assumed a waiting pose.

"That's it?" Alrion said. *What are they playing at?*

"Yes, that is all. Were you expecting something else?" Fermur grinned like he was expecting the reaction. Alrion looked to Lara. She shrugged her shoulders lightly and kept her focus on Fermur.

"What do you think he's trying to tell us?" Alrion said. The grin faded from Fermur, and he took on a confused look. He leaned back and pulled out an arrow. But rather than preparing it to fire, he rubbed it between his fingers, deep in thought.

"You know, nobody ever asked my opinion. They either tried to kill me or chase me away."

"You seem quite intelligent to me. I would like to hear what you think." Alrion could see Fermur coming around. The general put the arrow back in his quiver.

"Very well, that's not against the rules. I think that he is taunting you. He wants you to choose between going after your friend and saving a city."

"Why?"

"You are his adversary. He wants to know how you think, also, I believe, to cause you pain. That is his way. But as I said..."

"Yes, you're just a messenger. We get it." Lara didn't hide the frustration in her voice.

"You do listen. Fantastic. I must be away then, message delivered after all." Fermur started to whir and move away. But Alrion was ready.

You're not leaving. Alrion sent out a wave of force and wound it around Fermur. It prevented him from moving from the spot.

"Curious." Fermur looked around his feet while straining to run.

I have to try. Alrion started releasing his Soul Power, using his magic as a conduit. He activated his enhanced vision, watching the Soul Power travelling along hidden waves. It started to wrap around and permeate Fermur.

"Oh no, that's cheating." Fermur quickly drew and fired multiple arrows at Lara. She dived down and Alrion quickly refocused his wave of force. Two arrows hit the ground and two others were diverted away by Alrion's spell. In that instant, Fermur was gone, the only sign the trail of black ooze. It seemed to be drying up and flaking away faster than before.

"I'm fine." Lara stood and Alrion ran over. He helped her up.

"No, really I'm fine." Lara turned and looked over the slowly disappearing trail behind Fermur.

"Do we want to follow him? It might be possible."

"No, he's probably going to return to Darvin. Our focus needs to be Alyx." Alrion noticed surprise in Lara's face.

"You've already decided?"

"I can't move on otherwise, no matter the cost. If we don't act now, we will lose her again." Alrion saw doubt in Lara's face before she looked away.

"You don't agree, do you?"

"I thought you were about saving everyone. Maybe there's a way we can?"

"Not this time. Please, support me on this." Alrion looked into her eyes. She held his gaze.

"Always. Let's go save our friend." Lara gave him a hug. The warmth was reassuring. But it was like he could feel it weighing on her.

I won't do this again. I promise.

4

INVESTIGATION DIVERTED

Vincent paused and looked around. The sweeping hills and clear sky were breathtaking. The contrast of the bright green leaves with the remnants of the snow made the surroundings much more colourful than he had expected.

"Beautiful country around here." Vincent brushed some snow off a knee-height rock and eased himself down.

"You really should have tried visiting sometime." Celes gave him a wry smile.

"I know, I know."

"What do you think we will find out here? Lara and I found so little." Celes leaned against a tree and brushed some snow off her shoulder.

"As thorough as you were, your search was constrained by how far you could go and easily return to the Mystics. There's a lot more going on around here, the news about Alyx is just one thing." Vincent sighed. Alrion had taken the news harder than expected.

He's so blind to anything else right now.

"He's been tasked with the impossible. And you haven't made it easy for him."

Here it is. I've been waiting for this conversation.

"Our family history? I was protecting him!"

"You may have started by protecting him, but you ended up protecting yourself." Celes pointed at his chest with a finger and he felt real pain. She was right.

"I know. I hope he understands. The weight of something like that, it's crushing. I didn't want to put it on him, nor did I want to have to deal with the fact that

I had kept it silent." Vincent paused and shook his head, "that's always the way, isn't it?"

"What is?"

"Secrets come out at the worst times."

"Always. I think it's a golden rule. Makes life interesting though." Celes chuckled, and Vincent showed a tiny smile.

"So, was there a plan here? Or did you just want to run away from our son?"

She's on fire today.

"Definitely a real plan. I wanted to get you to a bigger city, so you could get to the bottom of what's happening around here. I think any major Blight activity will turn into a lead towards the Source. It's inevitable."

"And I suppose that it's a complete coincidence that the big city around here will be the only place with decent blacksmiths?"

"Of course. If we need to do some investigation at the smithy's, then, of course, I will reluctantly accept the responsibility." Vincent grinned at Celes.

"You are having way too much fun." He pointed at her in a mock accusatory way.

"I know. But I feel like we're finally free again after twenty years of just living a different life. Not a bad one, but different. And it's the last one."

"The last one?"

"This quest, journey, adventure—whatever we are calling it. It's the last one, I can feel it. So, I'm enjoying it for what it is when I can."

"I can't argue with that." Vincent rose and shook off the weariness. He needed to be active and strong.

"Let's push on and find civilisation."

Vincent put down the mug of ale and settled into the warmth. The little tavern was packed full of people, which was a nice change from the lonely wilderness. He gave Celes's hand an affectionate squeeze.

"Feeling more comfortable now?" She smiled.

"I hadn't realised how remote that area is. This feels better. We're still on the fringe, but there are people and activity."

"Shhh." Celes nudged her head towards a nearby conversation. Vincent nodded and tried to pick out the voices.

"I'm telling you, I saw them. Headed towards Hurdenor. A whole horde of Blighters. But they're using the forests to hide their movement," an old man said. He was nursing an ale and, as he spoke, flecks of spit flew across the table. His friends laughed him off.

"Gurt, you old dog. You've been on the piss again. You wouldn't spot a horde of Blighters if they were in here with us!"

"I swear, I hadn't even been drinking. But now, now I need to forget all about it." Gurt downed the rest of his drink and wiped his mouth. One of the men at the table jumped up to return to the bar.

"Good man, Frand. You know I'm telling the truth." Frand turned back.

"Not really, I just want to hear what kind of ridiculous story you'll be telling us next!" The rest of the table burst into laughter and Gurt grumbled with annoyance. Vincent leaned over.

"Sorry, friend, I couldn't help but overhear. Which forest was it?"

"Finally, someone with some sense! It's just over to the east. Easy to avoid, it's not the way you'd normally travel. Although I'd avoid Hurdenor just in case. They couldn't have been heading anywhere else."

"I wouldn't want to risk that, not after hearing your story." Vincent fished out a coin and flicked it onto the table in front of Gurt, "for your trouble." Gurt quickly pocketed the coin.

"Thanks." He looked about to say something else, but Frand returned with his drink. Vincent looked over at Celes.

"I know that look."

"Good, we can skip the conversation where I convince you to follow me into the woods." Vincent finished off his ale and slammed the mug down.

"You know, you're lucky that I love you." Celes rose carefully and threaded her way between the bodies and tables and found the door. Vincent followed close and paused before he left, relishing the heat.

The cold chill was worse than he expected. Night had fallen, and a stiff breeze brought the temperature down even more. Vincent nodded towards the edge of town, and Celes followed close.

"Do you really believe there's an attack brewing?"

"I believe enough to go tramp through the cold and drag you with me."

"Good. This is one of those situations where I would rather you were wrong and had dragged me out here for no reason."

"Likewise. I can't explain it, but it just feels like something is brewing. I can't ignore this." Vincent found a path between two houses, that headed into the trees. He noticed a lantern by the side of the path and bent down to pick it up.

"Looks like we're not the first to venture down here. Can you light it?" Vincent handed it to his wife. Celes retrieved something from her cloak and knelt on the ground. Within moments, she had a flame going and handed the lantern back to Vincent.

"After you." Vincent accepted the light and walked ahead. He noticed Celes walking closely behind him on the narrow path.

"Do you think we are being followed?" Vincent didn't stop to wait for a response and kept walking. The path was easy enough to follow but didn't seem to be much in use.

"No, all clear."

"That's a relief. I'm so hasty sometimes, this whole thing could have been a setup."

"That's why I'm here, to keep you out of trouble. Speaking of which, what have you been up to these last weeks?"

"What do you mean?"

"While I've been out in the countryside, you never ventured out. What have you been up to?"

"Keeping an eye on Alrion mostly and making sure he had what he needed. At other times, practising with the Soul Power."

"You just couldn't help yourself, could you?" Celes laughed.

"What do you mean?"

"First chance to do something that I think of as magic, you're all over it!"

"Hardly. I did it to be responsible and not shirk away from my duty. It should be helpful in our quest." Vincent expected a quip back, but there was silence. He continued to forge through the forest, pausing occasionally to look for signs of activity. There were none.

"What can you do? With the Soul Power?"

"I'm still figuring that out. But I seem able to heal myself and enhance my body. Gain extra speed or strength, push it beyond its normal limits."

"That sounds useful. I assume there's some sort of limits to how much you can use it?"

"Of course, once it runs out, I need time to recover. Stop a moment." Vincent thought he could hear something. He handed the lantern to Celes and motioned for her to stay put. She nodded. Vincent enhanced his vision and was able to see in the dark. He crept forward, straining his ears for confirmation of what he had heard. Nothing yet. Then, a quiet rustling.

Vincent stalked forward, using care to glide through the forest. Stealth wasn't his strength, but he knew enough to avoid twigs on the ground and errant branches. The rustling became louder, spurring him on. He reached a tree and clambered in, bracing himself on the lowest branches. Vincent stifled a gasp.

Before him marched an army of Blighters. With care and minimal noise, they were slowly advancing through the forest. Each one looked intensely focused and in control.

What is this? The tip was good, he needed to warn Celes. Vincent spun quickly and almost lost his grip. He paused, feeling his heart pounding. After a few deep breaths, he lowered himself down and ran back as quietly as he could.

"What's wrong?" Celes hissed as he approached. Vincent slowed.

"Blighters. A whole army."

"What?" Celes's voice was raised, and she quickly covered her mouth.

"I've never seen anything like it. They're marching slowly and quietly, like well-trained soldiers. This is not good."

"This is terrible. You were right to investigate this." Celes looked out into the darkness and shook her head.

"I'd rather be wrong."

"How far ahead did you think this through? Are we going there now?"

"Yes, we must. I wish I could warn them…"

"But they'll never believe you, even if you could get there in time," Celes said, finishing the thought.

"Let's get a horse and try and get ahead of this. We can figure out a plan on the way."

Not long after, Vincent stepped back out of the inn, following an old and bemused farmer holding a lantern out in front of him.

"You young'uns and your urgent tasks. I was once like that. A long time ago. Always rushing around."

I'm not a young'un!

Vincent was about to object but Celes put her hand on his arm. He grumbled to himself and swallowed the retort.

"We appreciate you helping us out on such short notice," Celes said.

"Oh, don't you worry, I'm being amply compensated." The farmer chuckled and started whistling. It only took a few minutes to reach the stables. The farmer used his lantern to light another just inside the entrance.

"Now, I know you're in a big rush, but I can't spare my best stallion. You can take Brenda over there." The farmer pointed to a medium-sized mare, staring out at them with a vacant expression. Vincent handed over a small sack of gold. The farmer weighed it up, peeked inside, then pocketed the sack.

"I trust you can sort the rest out. Good night, and good luck." The farmer waved and left the stables.

Vincent had the horse out and saddled within minutes. Despite first impressions, Brenda seemed responsive and energetic. He helped Celes jump onto the back.

"Now the fun begins." Vincent guided the horse out onto the main path and gently nudged her into a canter.

"We are on the way to warn a city that won't believe us about a horde of Blighters that are going to attack. But look at you, you're still having fun." Celes grabbed him and held on tight.

"I did say this was the last journey. But we're not at the end yet."

I hope Alrion finds a way here too. These people are going to need all the help they can get.

5

TRACKING THE QUEEN

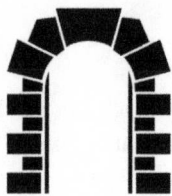

L ara ambled up the hill, keeping slightly ahead of Alrion. She paused to take in the view. A cluster of houses nestled together amongst the woods. Snow was lighter here, and the trees more densely packed together. She watched Alrion make the last few steps. There was a heaviness to him.

His decision is weighing on him. It was the opposite to what he had done before. When the stakes were high, he used his power to cure Wraith and restore Branthor. It was the greater of the possibilities. But doing so had lost them Alyx. Now he was ignoring an opportunity to confront the leader of the Blight and potentially save a city in the process.

Is it guilt that he let her go before?

"You look deep in thought," Alrion said with what looked like a forced smile.

"As do you."

"There's much to think about." Lara watched his expression darken, but he hid it quickly.

The weight of the world on his shoulders.

"Let's go find the inn down there, I'm sure they have something approximating one, and warm up. Then I have an experiment I want you to help me with." Lara watched Alrion's face. It lit up with genuine excitement and interest. Her heart jumped a little, she loved that about him. His eager curiosity and how genuine he was.

"I'm intrigued."

"Good, hold that feeling." Lara crested the hill and headed down to the buildings below.

The town, if you could call it that, was named Plort. Lara didn't even bother asking about the origins of the name. But she did confirm their bearings and destination. She found Alrion tucking into some spiced chicken and potato. The warmth and the food were returning some of his usual behaviour.

"Where's my food?"

"Coming, I ordered you something special." Alrion winked.

I don't even care what he ordered, it's worth that spark in him.

"You'll be pleased to hear we are just a day's hike from Carth. We can rest here tonight, hike all day tomorrow, and we will arrive late in the day. Then we can see what's happening there."

"Shouldn't we go tonight?" Alrion had a questioning look.

"No. We won't hike all day on no sleep when we think we're going into a battle."

"But maybe we'll be too late?"

"It doesn't matter if we get there before or after the battle, it just matters that she's there. You've made that quite clear." Lara let her frustration out a bit.

"It does matter, we shouldn't put lives at risk unnecessarily."

"We've already done that by coming here instead of confronting Darvin." Lara took a deep breath. "Look, you've made that choice already. Now we need to make sure that you achieve the objective. There's no point to this if you can't save Alyx." Lara watched his face, wondering if she had been too direct. He looked pained.

"You're right. Whatever we need to do to ensure we get the job done." Alrion returned to his food, reluctantly picking at it. Lara's food arrived. It was a plate of steamed vegetables.

"Looking after my weight, are you?" Lara gave him an angry look, and Alrion looked shocked. He almost spat his food out.

"No, no. Not at all. I was just getting you something healthy. You were complaining about too much meat." He suddenly stopped. "Hang on, you're smiling now."

"Got you."

"That wasn't fair."

"You becoming despondent wasn't fair. I think sometimes you need to remind yourself of what you are."

"And that is?" Alrion looked her in the eye. Lara leaned close and whispered.

"The greatest wizard of our time, wielding the power to cleanse the Blight. Also, you have the attention of the most beautiful and graceful thief of all time." Lara leaned back, satisfied. Alrion had a grin on his face.

"I thought you weren't a thief? More of a collector of things?"

"That's not as catchy."

"You're right again." Alrion sighed.

"Right again?"

"About me. I'm sorry, I do lose sight of things sometimes. I thought that when I was..." Alrion looked around at the crowd, "cured, everything would be fine and easy. But it's not. Because now I need to find a way to do something my grandfather couldn't."

"And you will." Lara forced some steamed broccoli into her mouth and kept smiling.

"See! I knew you'd enjoy the vegetables." Lara couldn't tell if he was being serious or not.

Later that evening, they settled into the guest room. Two low beds, and nothing else. But Lara was satisfied, it was somewhere to rest before the long hike ahead of them.

"You mentioned an experiment?" Alrion said. He looked at Lara with curious eyes.

"Yes, I've been thinking about your Soul Power. What did you say it could do again? Other than of course drive out the Blight."

"It seems to amplify your body. Healing, improving performance. Somehow the Mystics can use it to help heal others too, but I'm still not completely sure about that." Alrion looked confused by the question.

He's really so focused in one direction.

"And you managed to cure Wraith of the Blight by using your magic as a way to infuse him with Soul Power?"

"Essentially, yes."

"And finally, you are developing a way of containing Soul Power within a vessel for the purpose of making someone else capable of using Soul Power?"

"Yes, exactly that." Alrion's face turned into a frown. "I don't see where this is going?"

"Oh, Alrion. You are so single-minded. All about the Blight." Lara crossed the room until she was right in front of him. She was practically breathing on his face.

"Ever thought that I could use that Soul Power?" Alrion's reaction was priceless. He gaped at her like a fish out of water.

"How?"

"If you could inject a Shade with your Soul Power, then why not another person?" Lara watched Alrion's reaction. He withdrew from her, sitting down on the bed behind him. He was staring into space, concentrating.

"Why did I never think of that?" Alrion looked up at her.

"That's why you have me, for doing the thinking that you'll never get around to." She cracked a smile and he returned an even bigger one.

"Try it now. Without that orb, just give me your Soul Power."

"I'm not sure."

"How did you do it to Wraith? Or even Fermur? You were doing something to him, right?"

"Well, I touched him with my magic, which was like a conduit to apply Soul Power."

"Then do the same to me." Lara put her arms out like she was welcoming him into a hug.

"Alright. Sure." Alrion concentrated, and Lara slowly rose above the floor, floating in the air.

"This is quite interesting." Lara tried walking, but it didn't work.

"You want to move? Let's figure that out later. For now, I think I have a way to transfer to you." Alrion scrunched his face up in concentration. Then his eyes flashed and seemed to reflect the light differently.

Lara was about to ask him how he was going when she felt it. A strange warmth creeping up her body. It started in her feet and kept on rising.

"I think it's working."

"You can feel that? I'm not sure how much to do."

"Keep going." Lara concentrated on the sensation. It was quite strange, but somehow comforting. Her hand tingled, as the Soul Power passed through it.

Time for a test.

Lara drew her dagger and quickly cut her palm. She pushed away the initial pain and clenched her fist.

"What are you doing?" Alrion cried with surprise.

"A test. See what this Soul Power can do." Lara saw him nod absently, then continue to focus on what he was doing. She didn't feel any different. She tried focusing on her hand, urging the warmth to go there and fix it. Nothing seemed to happen. She tried again and again, labouring the point. Finally, she gave up and opened her hand. The cut was healed.

"It worked!" Lara stared at her palm amazed. Alrion strode over and examined it.

"Hmm, good. Let me borrow that." He took the dagger from her hand and sliced his own hand the same way.

"Huh?"

"Comparing," Alrion grunted. He was concentrating.

"What are you thinking?"

"I think the Soul Power is less efficient in your body. It looked like you consumed a great deal to heal that wound." Alrion looked back at Lara, examining her. She felt a little uncomfortable.

"What are you seeing?"

"I can see the Soul Power within you. There's still some left. It seems to be staying around."

"That's good, right?" She could still feel the warmth when she concentrated, but it was less enveloping, less intense.

"If it can persist a long time, that could be very useful." Alrion looked lost in thought.

"Well, well, well. Guess I was right, wasn't I?" Lara laughed.

"You really were. This is a whole new way of thinking that I never explored."

"It wasn't in that big book you were reading?"

"Not much. The Mystics were quite concerned with keeping their practices secret and to themselves. With good reason. But either they didn't document much of this, or never experimented much." Alrion looked Lara in the eyes, "thank you for suggesting this. We need to really see how far we can take it."

"I agree, but tomorrow on the journey over. The first experiment can see if the Soul Power is still present in the morning."

"Agreed." Alrion started preparing to turn in.

I can't believe that worked. It's like everything just changed dramatically.

Alrion awoke first. Within moments, he remembered their experiment from the night before and enhanced his vision. He couldn't see the Soul Power clearly.

"Lara."

"What?" She sat up immediately, looking around.

"It's daylight. And I need to check your Soul Power. Can you stand?"

"Good morning to you too," Lara muttered. She stood and let the blanket fall away. Alrion could see remnants of Soul Power within her, but not as much as the night before.

"The good news is that there seems to be some left over. But it has diminished."

"Why do you think that is?"

"Do you feel any different?" Alrion couldn't see anything different about her. Lara looked down and went through a quick routine working her individual muscles.

"Everything seems normal, I had a good night's sleep?"

"I can only guess the Soul Power found an outlet within you, but it doesn't seem to have done much."

"That's fine, how much did you use last night?"

"I think around half? I wasn't really paying attention. It could be less, I don't have a full gauge of my strength yet. I was also supplementing it while at the Mystics."

"We can figure that out as we go. And since we have a long hike ahead of us, best we get prepared."

"Absolutely." Alrion started packing his things. The discovery about Soul Power was exciting, and a good distraction. But his mind had quickly turned back to thinking of Alyx. Within the day they would find her. And he would have to face her. Face what she had become. All because of him.

You had no choice, you needed to stop Wraith. The words made logical sense, but it still gnawed at him. He still didn't feel confident that he was even doing the right thing now, targeting Alyx above all else. But at least he knew that a part of him would finally rest. A burden would be lifted, and he could focus more on his quest.

It's almost done. I just need to be strong enough to save her.

6

LOOMING BATTLE

The city walls of Hurdenor loomed above them in the early sunlight. The city was just waking, preparing for a new day.

They have no idea what's coming.

"I think we're here in time, no signs of panic or a battle yet."

"They can't be far away. What do we do?" Celes said.

"We can't say anything to the gate guards, they'll turn us away. Call us crazy and troublemakers."

"How can they mount a defence without the guards at the ready?"

"They can't. We need to find someone with authority who might listen." *Easier said than done.*

Vincent eased his horse down to a light trot. As he approached the guards, one let out a loud yawn without even bothering to cover it.

"You lot are up early. State your business."

"I'm a blacksmith looking for work. Do you know where I can find the smithies in town?"

"I'm not your tour guide. The market district is well signposted." The guard waved them through, his companion now yawning as well.

"That bodes well," Celes said.

"Indeed. Let's go take a look at the smithies and see what we can find."

"I hope you have a plan." Celes sounded doubtful, and she poked him in the back.

"A glimmer of one. We need to start with what we know." Vincent spotted a tattered sign pointing to the Market District and guided the horse to the right. There weren't many people out and about. Vincent pressed on, trying to make good time without going into a full-on gallop. There was no need to raise alarm, just yet.

Here we go. As he suspected, the smithies were all up and working. Vincent could feel the heat from the forges. He slowed and glanced at the different establishments.

"What are you looking for?"

"High-end armour or weapons. The kind favoured by the captain of the guard."

"Oh, I see where you're going with this." He thought he could hear some surprise and admiration in her voice.

"It's a long shot, but worth a try." Vincent brought the horse to a stop. They were outside a shop called *The Haughty Helm*. Vincent jumped down and helped his wife dismount more gracefully. After tying up the horse, he opened the heavy door and ushered her inside.

The shop was richly furnished, and a wide array of armaments hung on the walls. Some smaller items were arrayed on tables, mostly knives, daggers, and small armour pieces. Vincent spotted a bored man sitting up the back. He awoke with surprise, almost falling off his chair.

"Never had a customer this early. Old Henry always insists I man the shop at first light, but usually, I'm catching a few extra winks of sleep. Oh, how we will enjoy this!" the man said. He seemed genuinely intrigued.

"I certainly hope so. Could we talk to him? I'm a blacksmith myself and have something of importance to discuss."

"He didn't mention he was expecting anyone, but why not. Come through here." The man lifted a panel in the bench and gestured towards a door set in the back of the shop. Vincent and Celes entered and followed closely behind him.

Vincent drew in a breath as they entered the workshop. It was much bigger than he expected. The only person present was an older man with wiry hair and a short, slim frame which made his arms look enormous. He was sitting on a stool staring at a sheet of paper.

"Henry, I've got some guests for you." Henry looked up, assessing them both.

"Very well, get back to the shop, Jones." Henry watched Jones head off then looked back at Vincent and Celes.

"I don't recognise you. Travellers?"

"Yes, my name is Vincent, and this is my wife Celes."

"Henry, as you may have gathered." Henry stopped abruptly and just waited.

"You must be wondering why we have dropped in on you so early and unannounced," Vincent said.

"Still wondering."

"Of course, sorry. It's just that we need help and I thought that a fellow blacksmith could be of service."

"Again, I'm still wondering."

"There's an army of Blighters headed towards the city," Celes blurted out. Vincent looked at her, shocked.

"Well, when were you going to get to the point?"

"I like her." Henry grinned, "if what you are saying is true, why come to me? Why not go to the guard?"

"There's no time, they will be here within hours."

"And we think the guard will send us away and think we're crazy," Celes said.

"What proof do you have?"

"None other than my statement. The truth will be quite obvious when they attack." Vincent hoped that he was swaying Henry. But the old blacksmith didn't seem too keen on helping.

"You're completely mad. But what if you're right?" Henry muttered. He started pacing around the room.

"I can't vouch for you, I'm sorry. Even if they believe me, it's too late to do anything. And if you're wrong, I have nothing to fall back on. You've literally walked in here off the street." Henry looked at Vincent like he was challenging Vincent to dispute his words.

"You're absolutely correct."

"But we have to do something. If you're not helping us, we'll find someone else." Celes started to walk off.

"I didn't say I wouldn't help." Henry looked thoughtful. "You're a real blacksmith, right?"

"Yes. Do you need me to prove it?"

"No, we're out of time. I'll supply your materials and you can fortify the entrance to the market district. If you're a maniac, all I lose is some materials which can be reclaimed if need be. But if you're right, then I was prudent to take measures. How does that sound?"

"Done, we'll take it!" Celes spun around and ran up to Henry, grabbing his hand and shaking it. Henry looked at her with surprise.

"She's always full of surprises." Vincent shrugged at Henry.

"You can use anything from that corner." Henry pointed to a far part of the workshop with stacks of lumber and different types and sizes of metal. "I'll open up the side door, so you can get out without using the shop." Henry stalked off.

"Let's get to work." Celes started off towards the materials.

"What's gotten in to you?" Vincent said as he trailed after her.

"You blacksmiths are stuck at slow speed. We need to get something happening before this city is slaughtered."

"I can't argue with that." Vincent picked up the pace and rushed ahead of his wife.

∾

Vincent paused and brushed the sweat away from his face. He ignored the curious looks of passers-by, often stopping to watch him work. Celes handed him another sheet of steel and he lay it across the stakes he had dug into the ground.

"We're running out of time, you can rest later." Celes slapped him on the back.

"Any sign of Alrion?" Vincent said in between hammer swings.

"Nothing. I'll go have another look." Celes took off and Vincent paused again to draw in his breath.

I hope this is not for nothing.

With a final swing, he stepped back to survey his work. A rough fence had been constructed, leaving only a small gap for traffic to pass through. A guard strolled up.

"You, there. Who authorised this work?"

"Old Henry. There's been word of an incoming attack, and he thought it prudent to shore up defences. Here I am, creating a way of funnelling enemies into a smaller space."

"This is not going to work. Why now?" The guard muttered something and slapped the steel sheet in annoyance.

"Don't ask me, I'm just the help. I was instructed to get something up for now, then we can look at how to integrate it better for continued use."

"This is ridiculous. I'm going to have words." The guard strode off, heading towards the smithies. Vincent watched him go.

Sorry, Henry, I needed to buy some time.

Vincent noticed Celes run back through the makeshift doorway.

"Prepare yourself, it's time."

I know that look. This is no game.

Vincent put down his hammer and retrieved his sword. His muscles ached, but there was nothing else he could do. He calmed himself and searched inside for his Soul Power. He directed some to the muscles that ached the most. A wave of calm swept over him, and the complaining was dulled.

That will do. I should save something for the battle ahead.

"Is there somewhere else we can fight?" he said.

"There are some good places just past the main gate. We should ideally start there and fall back here."

"So be it." Vincent drew his sword and led the way. Celes followed close behind.

Alrion, where are you?

Vincent heard them first. The snarls and cries, the sounds of metal on metal,

metal on flesh. Guards poured into the gates, reinforcing the fallen. But there was no end to the Blighters. Each time one fell another eagerly stepped in. The guards were holding well but tiring. Vincent looked around and spotted a guard with a red sash over his shoulder.

Captain.

"Wait here a moment." Vincent gestured to Celes and she nodded. He then jogged forward to talk to the captain.

"Excuse me, Captain."

"Fall back, use the shelters." The captain didn't even turn to look.

"We have reinforced the entrance to the Trade District. There're some walls in place to stem the tide of Blighters. They won't last forever, but they should make a difference." Vincent waited for a response, but the captain was silent.

"Judging the fight, you will have to retreat within minutes. This is an opportunity to regroup and buy some time."

"Buy time for what?" The captain turned, and his expression was grim.

"A miracle."

"Start praying." The captain turned back to the fight and walked towards the active fighting. Vincent retreated, finding Celes.

"What did he say?"

"Start praying. I think he heard me though and will fall back to the Trade District."

"We can't win this, can we?" Celes whispered.

"You're right as usual. Maybe you can find us a way out?"

"You're dreaming. Find a way out of this city we've never seen that is being assaulted by a horde of Blighters?"

"Yes." Vincent gave his wife a smile.

"Sometimes I wonder how you ever survived without me." Celes shook her head, but Vincent noticed a small smile. But it was quickly gone, replaced with a worried look.

She's right to worry. This city is doomed.

Vincent gestured to a few guards lingering on the fringes. They gave him confused looks and turned back to watching the battle.

"OVER HERE. NOW!" Vincent shouted in his best commanding voice. The confused guards almost jumped and cautiously approached.

"There's no place for watchers here, we need every man. Come with me and fortify this choke point." Vincent didn't wait for acknowledgement, he just stalked off towards the makeshift walls he had constructed. As he walked, he listened out and heard the crunch of footsteps behind him.

Good, something has survived from their training. He showed them where to stand, putting the two nervous ones behind the wall.

"You two are to clean up any that get through. Understand?" The two guards nodded. One nervously adjusted his gauntlet. Their armour was mostly chain, with a few plates on the arms and legs. It looked like it had never seen real battle.

Either they're new, or there's not really a Blight presence here normally. Either way, they're not equipped for this.

Vincent heard shouts and turned quickly to observe. The guards were breaking rank. The captain shouted furiously at them, whipping some back into a formation. But the gates were lost. Vincent saw the captain leading the retreat, drawing the enemy towards the Trade District.

Here's where it gets interesting. If you're going to show up, boy, now's the time. But Vincent had the distinct feeling that they were alone in this fight.

7

FIGHT FOR A FRIEND

The Town of Carth lay before them, nestled amongst some rolling hills. Alrion looked for signs of distress but couldn't see any.

"Did we make it in time?" Alrion looked to Lara. She had a good instinct for these things.

"Maybe." Lara wrinkled her nose.

There's something she's not telling me.

"We better get in there then, maybe we can get the advantage." Alrion started to walk off but noticed Lara was standing still.

"What's wrong?"

"We don't know what we are walking into. How are you feeling? We have just hiked for most of the day."

Tired.

"Pretty refreshed, all things considered."

"Have you been using Soul Power to maintain your strength?" Lara pointed at him with an accusatory finger.

"Some."

"See, you need to be aware of that. She's not going to play fair."

"I know. Because she's probably not really there."

"Good. Remember that. Because when you see her..."

"It's going to be difficult." Alrion sighed and tried to steel himself.

You must save her, no matter what.

"Do you have any of those Soul Orbs?"

"I have one that's filled. Why?"

"Give it to me." Lara held out her hand.

"But, it's untested."

"Doesn't matter. Hopefully, we don't need it. But if it works, it works." Lara beckoned again for him to hand her the Orb. Alrion reached inside his robe and removed it. He activated his enhanced vision again for a moment to verify its contents.

"Still there." Alrion started to hand it over and stopped. "Just be careful with this." He handed it over and Lara deftly hid it away.

"After you." She pointed at the road ahead. Alrion nodded and started walking.

This is really happening. Time to set things right.

Carth wasn't particularly big. In many ways, it reminded him of home. A few trades, a few homes. But the streets were empty.

"It's too quiet. Could you tell from back there?"

"I had an inkling. But we don't know what it means."

"True." Alrion kept walking. He peered around houses as he went but didn't see any people. Or signs of fighting. He stopped suddenly. In the middle of the road was a deep hole and displaced earth all around.

"What happened here?" Alrion knelt to inspect the ground. There were traces of a black sludge. He looked them over with enhanced vision.

"Traces of Blight." Alrion stood and looked at Lara. Her eyes were on the distance.

"Must be something up ahead. There have been no other signs of a struggle. Keep your guard up."

"Don't worry about that." The truth was, Alrion couldn't be more on edge. He continued, looking more closely for any signs of what might have happened. But the town seemed quiet and undamaged. Left just as it should have been. The road curved around behind the town.

"Whatever it is, it'll be back there." Lara pointed to where the road went out of sight.

"I hope we're not too late." Alrion's pulse quickened, his heart pumping faster and faster.

You can do this. This will save your friend. Just get the job done.

Alrion walked faster. He needed this to be over already. Lara kept pace, her dagger out. The sounds of their footsteps crunching louder than expected, the still air seemingly amplifying any sound.

"Well, there's the townsfolk." Lara pointed. Alrion could see them all. There was a clearing behind the town, and all the people were bunched together. They murmured softly but were otherwise quiet and still. Alrion could see the reason why. Before them stood a creature, one that inspired terror. His first instinct was to look away, but he forced himself to face it.

The creature had Alyx's frame, although its skin was black and seemed more muscular. It wore a modified black tunic, with light armour on the arms and legs. But its face was unadorned. It was black except for the exposed bones of the skull. And the piercing white eyes. He understood finally.

"The Skull Queen," Alrion whispered.

"I can't believe what they have done," Lara said softly. The Skull Queen reached behind and retrieved a massive black great sword. It was jet black and the edge seemed to ooze with something.

"That's no ordinary blade. It seems to be somehow infused with the Blight."

"This is not good. This is not good." Lara shifted her stance. She seemed to be weighing up her options.

"We just need to engage and get it done. I doubt she's as fast as Fermur, we should end this quickly." Alrion took a deep breath and prepared.

It's time at last. Don't hesitate. Go.

Alrion drew up his Spark, preparing a spell. The Skull Queen instantly turned and hefted the giant sword. She started to swing towards the mass of people.

"No!" Alrion screamed. He threw out a wave of force to try to knock the Skull Queen aside. But the strike was unusually quick. Instead of carving through the people, a trail of black collected into a cloud and sunk down over them.

"What was that?" Lara said. Her mouth hung open. The Skull Queen stepped aside to show her handiwork. The gathered people started to cough and choke as the black substance infused them.

"This could get really ugly." Lara fidgeted, spinning her dagger. She looked between the Skull Queen and the transforming people.

"No. No. No." Alrion muttered. "Not again." Something was building within him. Frustration. Fury. Pain.

"Don't forget that Alyx is in there somewhere." Lara put a hand on Alrion's shoulder, but he shrugged her off.

"Don't involve them in this!" Alrion shouted. He gathered everything he had. Spark and Soul Power. And he ran straight at the Skull Queen. He saw a wicked smile form on her face, and she held up the great sword in a ready position.

"Here we go," Lara said quietly and ran alongside him. She threw out some daggers aimed at the Skull Queen's head. The creature didn't move, and they bounced harmlessly off.

Alrion's focus grew smaller and smaller. He was only barely aware of Lara's attack. Something was happening, and he wasn't getting in the way. He was acting on instinct. A part of him thought that maybe he was losing himself, that he should regain control. But he didn't want to. He had to let this happen.

Alrion continued, travelling faster and faster. Only he didn't stop and confront the Skull Queen. He headed straight for the middle of the townsfolk. He was amongst the writhing and screaming as they were forcefully transformed into something else. Alrion stopped quite suddenly. And he gave in to the feeling, he let go of the force that had been building up.

It was like an explosion of force and Soul Power. It felt like the time he had attacked Ashra in desperation, but instead of the deadly white-hot power that removed everything from existence, it was like the Soul Power was used as the medium. He lost all sense of time, surrounded by a haze of white gold.

Slowly, his vision returned and he surveyed the scene. All the townsfolk were knocked down and looked unconscious. The ground was clear of dust, and the strange black cloud had been dispelled. Realising his own lack of awareness, he quickly turned to look at the Skull Queen. She was crouched down, glaring at him. Something appeared different.

"The sword. The black edge is gone." Lara crouched down next to Alrion.

"Good."

"Are you alright? What was that?" Lara looked worried. But he couldn't find the words to explain.

"I can't say, it was something else. I think it worked."

"It must have." Lara rose and focused on the Skull Queen.

"She looks relatively unharmed. Do you have any Soul Power left?"

"Not really." He felt a pang of despair. He had squandered his best chance at restoring Alyx. Even though he had done the right thing.

It's like I can't save her. Why?

"Don't worry, that's why I'm here." Lara was turning the Soul Orb over in her hands.

"It might not have enough power."

"We'll have to take that chance. But we only get one shot." Lara's gaze focused even more. She was planning something.

"I'll follow your lead." Alrion stood and dusted himself off. His Spark was still available, and his Soul Power would recover in time. At least the towns-people were out of the picture. It was just them.

The Skull Queen swung her sword and readied herself. She looked from Alrion to Lara. Waiting.

I need to be careful. I need to restrain her, but not kill her. Then we can try the cure.

"Let's try and shut down her mobility," Lara said.

"Sure. You distract, and I'll try and lock her down." Alrion watched Lara run off and he approached with caution.

How much of you is in there?

Lara ran straight at the Skull Queen, and the creature prepared to engage. At the last minute Lara changed direction, trying to flank. The Skull Queen turned also, doing a short swipe to keep Lara away. Alrion seized the opportunity, manipulating the earth to swallow up and encase the Skull Queen's feet. She didn't react initially, just looked down after it was done.

"I hope it holds." Lara stayed out of range of the giant sword. After a few moments, the Skull Queen casually moved her legs and the ground broke away. Like she was dusting off sand.

"Try again." Lara darted off, trying to circle around the Skull Queen. She ducked in quickly and tried a slash with her dagger. It glanced off a piece of armour, but Lara managed to retreat safely.

"She's quite fast, but still needs time to manoeuvre the giant blade. I have some options."

"Hopefully, you won't need them." Alrion started to prepare another spell. He sent a wave of force at the Skull Queen, trying to wrap her up completely. She swung her great sword, the movement seemingly cutting through the waves of force and rendering them useless.

What? That's not possible.

Taking advantage of their surprise, the Skull Queen launched a sweeping attack at Lara. The young thief only narrowly dodged away and quickly retreated.

"Too close. Your spell failed?" Lara said in between breaths.

"She somehow cut it down. I need to keep trying." Alrion went back to basics. He launched a small fireball, aiming for the Skull Queen's head. This time she batted it away like it was nothing. Lara had to dodge the fireball, and it exploded into the ground nearby.

"Her sword, it's magical somehow."

"I can see that," Alrion muttered. He tried again. Drawing upon even more Spark, he raised a cage of fire around the Skull Queen, ensuring the flames rose to twice her height. She used her sword like a giant fan, blowing away a section of the flames and stepping through unharmed.

Is she grinning? This is so frustrating.

He needed something else. Ranged attacks were not working. But he had to conserve what little Soul Power he had. It took a long time to regenerate.

Desperate times. Alrion drew his sword. The diamond on the pommel shone brightly in response to the Skull Queen.

"Alrion, no. That's too dangerous. She's an elite fighter." Lara started to retreat further, approaching him.

"There's no other way. I can protect myself." Alrion gripped the sword tightly, then remembered Alyx's training. He forced himself to relax, although it didn't quite hold. But at least he had the right idea.

"It's me you want!" Alrion yelled. He strode forward in a defensive stance, closing the gap. He stared her in the eyes. Those pure white eyes on a ghastly face. He tried to picture Alyx within.

There's no way a bit of Soul Power can fix this.

The Skull Queen closed in. Alrion stepped forward, launching into the most common sword routine they had practised.

Remember. Remember, Alyx.

The Skull Queen parried easily, anticipating each strike. Alrion kept pushing, going faster and faster. A strange unearthly laugh came from her. Despite his upping the intensity, she wasn't even slightly challenged. As he prepared the final strike he stopped suddenly and dropped his sword. The Skull Queen had already begun to swing to counter him. However, the strike extended further out putting her slightly off-balance but sending the great sword hurtling at Alrion's chest.

"No!" Lara screamed. Alrion could sense her running in. Two knives bounced harmlessly off the Skull Queen. As the blade came in, Alrion used the remaining Soul Power he had to infuse into his hands. He caught the blade with his hands and threw it towards the ground.

The swing in momentum threw the Skull Queen off balance, and the sword clattered away as she lurched forward. Alrion threw himself forward, tackling her, and they both fell to the ground. He found himself on top of her, staring into her ghastly face. Lara joined them immediately, helping to pin the Skull Queen to the ground.

"You're crazy," Lara whispered.

"Yes." Alrion could say nothing else. He just stared into the eyes of his friend.

8

THE FALL OF HURDENOR

The initial rally was heartening. The captain and the remaining guards defended the makeshift gate that Vincent had constructed. And initially, it worked. But Vincent could see a looming problem.

Now that they're in the gates, they can reinforce much faster and swarm us. Where's the relief?

Vincent sliced through a Blighter's arm and kicked it to the ground. He turned quickly to look for his wife.

No sign yet. Hopefully, she's found something.

Vincent returned to the fight. He was slowly draining his Soul Power, trying to keep his body from tiring too quickly. It was unfortunate that he had exerted himself so much in the frantic rush to build some fortifications. And they were paying dividends. But he was tiring way too quickly.

How are we going to win this? Where's Alrion?

The battle raged on. Vincent pushed forward to the front line. His Runesteel was working wonders, quickly and efficiently slicing through Blighters. But he was just one man, and he was not a young man. Despite his level of activity and proficiency, the blade could have done more in the hands of an elite fighter. Vincent was not that man, although he accounted well for himself.

The assault slowed, and the Blighters started to hold back.

"Hold!' the captain shouted. Vincent nodded at him. The man knew when to keep the men in line. The guards waited, a strange silence falling over them. The Blighters parted, and a man walked out. He was dressed in black armour, with white trim along most of the edges. He had a sword and shield strapped to his back.

"I wondered who I would find here. I so wanted to meet Alrion, but I knew that the bait was just too tempting." The man spoke loudly, to no one in particular. The guards murmured amongst themselves.

"Blacksmith, show yourself. I would speak with you." The guards looked amongst each other, then noticed Vincent. Vincent checked again for Celes, but there was no sign.

Play along for now.

Vincent sheathed his sword and slowly picked his way through the defenders until he was alone in front of the Blight horde. The man regarded him.

"I don't believe we have formally met. I'm Darvin. I..."

"I know what you are." Vincent interrupted him.

"Good, that makes things easier. Your name is... Vincent?"

"Yes."

"Well, not your true name. But, you see, I can play along with everyone."

"I appreciate that."

What is he playing at?

"You are probably wondering where your son is. He's with the Skull Queen right now. I gave him a choice, you see. Come here and save a city or go there and save one person."

"I see."

"Not very good at arithmetic, is he?" Darvin laughed.

"There are different ways to save people."

"How interesting. I'm so glad that you came, this was going to be quite a bore otherwise." Darvin started pacing around. Vincent watched him with caution, hand on his sword hilt.

"That's a nice blade you have there. But it's not enough." Darvin paused his pacing and regarded Vincent. A cruel smile came across his face.

"Ah, I have it. I am going to give you a choice as well." Darvin chuckled. Vincent tightened his grip on the sword.

Where is Celes?

"Everyone, pay attention. If this man here accepts a one-on-one fight with me and wins, I will spare this city. If he runs away, or if he loses, then you all die." Darvin watched the crowd. Murmurs ran through the guards. The captain walked over to Vincent.

"Are you going to accept?"

"Likely. Although I have no chance."

"We have no chance of winning this battle. Any chance is better than that." Vincent nodded.

"I am sorry this falls to you, although you seem to have some connection to this. Perhaps you can perform a miracle this day." The captain clapped Vincent on the shoulder and started to walk away.

"The name's Douglas by the way. We should call you Vincent?"

"Yes."

"Good luck, Vincent."

"Thanks." Vincent looked again for a sign of his wife but found nothing.

I'll try and drag this out as long as possible.

"I accept your challenge. What are the terms?"

"We duel, and the loser loses."

"To the death?"

"I'll see how I feel about that." Darvin laughed and started to arm himself.

I need to be careful, he could do anything. I don't even know what his real strength is.

Vincent unsheathed his sword and took a ready stance. He felt within himself for his Soul Power. There was very little remaining.

I need to save it. Use it for an advantage.

Darvin was ready, his shield strapped to one arm and his sword in the other. He banged the shield with the sword, and the dread shield reverberated through the space.

"Let's see what you can bring." Darvin started advancing. Vincent took a deep breath.

Here we go.

Vincent struck first, stepping into a sequence of blows, alternating low and high. Darvin led with his shield, blocking the strikes easily. The Runesteel bounced harmlessly off. Darvin then parried the final attack and lashed out with his shield. Vincent noticed just in time, tumbling to the side and quickly scrambling back onto his feet.

"You are resourceful. But as you can see, your weapon does nothing. I can withstand your blows all day." Darvin advanced again, looming in front of Vincent. The general was of average height, but he had a huge presence.

Just focus on the basics.

Vincent stepped back and waited. Darvin became inpatient and launched into an attack of his own. He led with his sword, opening with a criss-cross pattern of slashes that forced Vincent to parry, dodge, and retreat. Darvin grew bolder, launching another series that interspersed his shield seemingly at random. The clangs of sword on sword, sword on shield rang out through the space. Vincent was holding his own but couldn't press Darvin. The general's defences seemed impenetrable.

I need to create an opening. But even if I do, how would it work?

Vincent felt within for his Soul Power. It sat there, waiting. He could try to use it for a burst of speed or strength. But neither seemed like enough. There had to be more he could do.

Purely by instinct, Vincent started channelling the Soul Power into his hand.

But then further. He tried to force it into his sword. He could sense the resistance. Then it started to give way.

It's working.

It was a slow progress, but it seemed to be holding. Darvin hadn't seemed to notice, and as the blows continued Vincent didn't notice any difference in the clashes between blade and shield.

It's almost like I need to have more, or I need to activate it.

Vincent dashed back and found more space. He continued the slow infusing of the weapon.

"I'm getting bored, Vincent. You started with a bit of fire, but now you're just playing for time. I won't put up with that. Let's get this really going." Darvin charged forward.

I need to be ready.

Vincent waited cautiously, gauging the right time. With every shield block, he did his best to notice the way the shield had been constructed. Gradually, he built up a mental map of the shield's formation and potential weak spots.

It's clearly special, but it was still built. I can do some good here.

Vincent let the last of the Soul Power go. He was ready. Launching a flurry of blows, he took Darvin by surprise. Again, and again Vincent moved forward, seeking the advantage. At the end of each strike, he pivoted and found another angle. Vincent could sense the frustration in his opponent and built on it. More and more he pushed. Finally, the blacksmith had a good opening.

This is my only chance.

Vincent wound up a powerful strike. Darvin shifted back and held up his shield to absorb the blow. Vincent adjusted his arm slightly, aiming for a spot where he thought the shield was weakest. At the same time, he unleashed whatever Soul Power he had been saving. The blade glowed white hot, the light and heat streaking off in a fiery blaze. Vincent heard gasps from the crowd as the blade fell, biting into the shield.

Darvin stumbled back, swearing. Vincent stumbled, having put everything into that blow. He looked up to see his handiwork. There was a great big crack through the dark shield. It wasn't broken, but it was weakened.

I've laid the foundation. That's all I can do.

A cheer rose up from the guards. But they didn't realise, not yet, that this wasn't the start of a comeback. That was Vincent's best and only shot.

"Nice trick, blacksmith. But the shield still held." Darvin practically snarled the words. His eyes were alight with a fiery anger that wasn't present before.

Should I feel proud or distinctly afraid now?

"You may feel like you've won, but all you've done is annoy me. The real fight starts now." Darvin rushed forward with incredible speed. Vincent watched the sword closely, teasing out the real strike amongst all the movements.

There! He picked it up and went to parry. Even with perfect timing and execution, he was knocked back by the pure force and intensity of the strike. The noise from the onlookers suddenly dropped. It was clear how the rest of the fight was going to go.

I can't fall here. There's too much at stake.

Vincent rose from a crouch. He felt weaker, his strength was fading.

Not now. Not now. With weariness, he forced himself into a ready stance.

"We both know you're done for. Now you've shown them all the true power of the Blight. I wonder how I'll finish you off?" Darvin gave Vincent an evil grin.

"You're wrong. I broke your unbreakable shield. I am not the one to take you down, but I've shown it's possible. Word will spread, don't you worry."

"Fear will spread when they hear of what I've done to you!" With each word, Darvin's voice escalated until he was shouting.

"Not on my watch, creature!" Celes shouted, drawing his attention. He didn't spot the thing she had hurled until the last second. The vial shattered at Darvin's feet, a mini explosion staggering him and the ensuing smoke screening the battlefield.

"Now!" Celes shouted. Vincent turned and ran. There was no honour in dying here, as much as it pained him to leave these people.

"I don't like this," he said.

"Be thankful that you're alive to not like it." Celes led him back through the makeshift fortifications, deeper into the Trade District.

"But what of them?"

"They've already started evacuating, you bought them some time. Now it's time for you to leave." Celes tightened her grip on his hand.

"I'm not arguing." Vincent tried to shake his hand free, but Celes just tightened her grip.

"And I'm not letting go. There's a tunnel we can use to escape the city." Celes dragged him into a shop and rushed towards the back. There was a rug pushed to the side, and a square trap down in the floor.

"Open her up." Celes pointed. Vincent dropped down and heaved the trapdoor up. He could see a set of stairs descending into darkness. Some rather bad smells wafted up as well.

"Quick. Go." Celes almost shoved him into the hatch. Vincent started climbing down, then stopped.

"Hey, what about you? Don't worry about hiding this."

"I've got a guy lined up for that. Just keep going so I can join you."

Vincent continued climbing and noted with relief that his wife was joining him. As they reached the bottom, there was enough light to see their surroundings. It was an old and disused tunnel. Murky and wet.

"Grab that torch and let's get moving. You really riled that monster up."

"He asked for it. Do you think he'll follow us down here?" Vincent said as he retrieved the torch. He started walking quickly down the tunnel.

"Absolutely. He wants to make an example of you, that much is clear."

"Hasn't he already done that?" Vincent picked up the pace.

"No, you have a way with people. And monsters." Celes let out a small chuckle.

"I really wish that wasn't the case." Vincent felt conflicted running from the fight. But he knew he couldn't win. And it was reassuring that Celes had helped the townsfolk evacuate.

Alrion, I hope you're safe. What are you doing?

9

FALL OF THE SKULL QUEEN

The Skull Queen hissed at him and struggled to throw him off. But Alrion held on, and Lara's weight helped pin her down.

"This is not going to last long."

"I know. We have to try." Lara grunted and shifted her weight again.

"Hand me the Soul Orb." Alrion held out his hand. Lara fished it out and handed it over. The Skull Queen shifted suddenly, knocking the orb to the ground. It clattered away out of reach.

"I'll get it." Lara scrambled off to retrieve the orb. The Skull Queen capitalised, shaking Alrion off. He quickly rose, keeping close. The Skull Queen looked cautiously between the two, eyeing off her blade. She needed to go through Lara to get there.

"There's no time. I'll make a distraction, you try to finish it." Alrion started advancing at the Skull Queen.

Without her sword, my Spark is more useful.

Alrion decided to be cautious. He threw a wave of force at one leg, trying to upset her balance. The Skull Queen noticed the magic but mostly shrugged it off.

Let's try some fire.

Alrion let loose a series of small fireballs, aimed at her chest. The creature let some impact, the flames licking at her armour and burning out. She swatted two away.

Keep your eyes on me.

Alrion tried something else. He needed something with more power, that wasn't so easily dealt with. He combined wind and fire, and something else. The combination was instinctive, drawing from his desire for a new form. Lightning arced from his hand, surprising the Skull Queen. She roared in pain, and crouched down, trying to shield herself. But there was nothing to be done.

"This won't last long," Alrion shouted. He could see her testing her strength, fighting against the lightning. He saw Lara sneaking up behind the Skull Queen, the Soul Orb in her hands.

"You need to find a way to insert it. On my mark." Alrion didn't know how the lightning would affect Lara. He waited until she was in position. The Skull Queen was writhing around more, looking like she could break free. Alrion increased the intensity briefly, then let go.

"Now!" he shouted. Lara dashed in, leading with her dagger. She made a small slit in the Skull Queen's back and rammed the Soul Orb in. The Skull Queen's back seemed to start to repair the wound and integrated the Soul Orb. She stopped thrashing and, for a moment, everything was still.

Is it working?

The Skull Queen started to shudder and glow. She screamed out in pain. Light flared within her, pulsing from location to location. Lara ran over to Alrion's side.

"Something's happening."

"I hope it's enough." Alrion checked within and found that he only had the slightest amount of Soul Power.

Please work.

The Skull Queen seemed to be changing, but the process was slowing down.

"It's not complete." Alrion started to quickly think what else he could do.

"What will happen?" Lara looked anxiously from the Skull Queen to Alrion. The wizard closed his eyes and reached out. He embraced the Skull Queen and she grew calm. He withdrew and placed a hand on her chest.

"This is the last." Alrion transferred the last of his Soul Power. He suddenly felt weak and dropped to his knees.

"Alrion!" Lara rushed over and helped him up.

"It's not good to fully deplete it, but I'm fine. Look to her." Alrion pointed. The Skull Queen was lying down now and seemed to be restful. Suddenly, a flare of light exploded out and black particles started to float away like a mist. Once it cleared, Alyx lay on the ground.

"It worked!" Lara stepped over to check Alyx. "She's breathing."

"Good." Alrion slumped back and allowed himself a moment to rest. The townsfolk were stirring too. One by one they woke and looked around in confusion.

"I'll stay with her; can you go help them?" Alrion gestured to the crowd of people. Lara nodded and took off.

"Everything is fine now, the Skull Queen has been defeated," Lara shouted. A few weak cheers rose from the crowd.

"Return to your homes and rest," Lara continued. After a short pause, the first people started leaving.

"Lara!" Alrion said. He had noticed Alyx moving. The weapon master opened her eyes, then squinted immediately.

"So bright." She looked at Alrion and Lara.

"You saved me. I... I can't explain the nature of it. I can't thank you enough."

"I got you into this, so I can't explain how relieved I am that you're back." Alrion looked over at Lara, and she was smiling too. Alyx sat up with a little help.

"I hate this armour, but it's better than nothing. I can't remember so many things, it's like a fog." Alyx stared out into the distance.

"That's fine, information is the last thing I'm worried about."

"Wait," Alyx said, an urgency to her tone. "There's something else." Lara looked at Alrion and he shrugged.

"There's a strike force coming. To mop up regardless of the result of our encounter. We have to get away." Alyx tried to get up, and Alrion assisted her. He then transferred her to Lara.

"Get Alyx somewhere safe and prepare to travel. I'll deal with the strike force."

"But you're exhausted!" Lara gave him a sceptical look.

"That's fine, I have plenty of Spark left. I didn't save Alyx and the townsfolk to just let the Blight come back and reclaim them." Alrion watched Alyx to see her reaction. She gave a weak nod.

"Use the pass behind the town, they'll come that way." Alyx indicated the direction with a slight head movement. Alrion gazed over, recognising the path.

"Thanks. I'll take care of this, you take care of our exit." Alrion lingered a moment, then strode forward. He wanted to appear more confident than he was.

Theoretically, I'm fine, I just need to push through.

Despite trying otherwise, he had saved the people again. And almost lost the chance of saving Alyx. But he had succeeded, if barely. He tried not to think about the city that he had abandoned.

I need to be realistic. I couldn't focus myself knowing that Alyx was out there.

Now he needed to protect what he had achieved. He had sacrificed to save both Alyx and the townsfolk. But Darvin wouldn't let that stand. Of course, he had sent more forces.

You're a wizard, and you've learned a lot. Show them.

Alrion stopped and surveyed the scene. He could see the Blighters coming down through the pass. The relatively narrow path hid their numbers, but they stretched so far that Alrion knew the force was big.

What can I do from here?

He considered creating a landslide but dismissed the idea. He couldn't control it enough, and there could be real danger for the town. But he did have another thing to try. Alrion gathered his Spark and created an intensive wave of fire. He sent it down the path, using waves of force to hem the fire in and keep it on the path.

It's working!

Now that it was on its way, he worked on increasing the speed. There was no point if the Blighters had too much opportunity to avoid it. The fire sped along, following the track of the path. Alrion found that with minimal effort he could keep steering it. But soon enough, he would not be able to see where to direct it.

The Blighters were caught off guard. Those at the front turned to run or jump off the path. However, the bulk that Alrion could see were in a narrow section between rocks and had nowhere to go. The fire slammed through them, charring and incinerating as it went.

I need more.

Alrion gathered more Spark and tried working it as he did before. He imagined a dark cloud forming above the track, then sent down bolt after bolt of lightning. Chunks of earth and Blighters exploded from the ground as each bolt struck, wreaking havoc on the Blighters. Since most of them were trapped by the surroundings or other Blighters, they had nowhere to go.

One last try.

Alrion gathered the rest of his Spark and altered the landscape. A large section of the path opened, dropping the Blighters within. By guessing the nearby landscape, he sculpted the path such that it became a steep incline leading into the newly created pit. He could barely see but did notice Blighters falling in. After a few moments, he closed the ground up, burying all the Blighters in the area, alive or dead. There was suddenly silence and no movement.

Alrion collapsed down onto his knees. He drew in some deep breaths.

You pushed too far again.

He forced himself to look up. If there was another wave of Blighters, he would be in trouble. But there were no signs of any other Blighters.

I got them all, or the rest left.

Unsatisfied, he stood. The act did not leave him feeling as he expected. He expected to be triumphant, turning away a host of Blighters. But he just felt sick. So much death on his hands, even if it was justified. He turned and stumbled away, one step at a time.

That's why I'm doing this quest. The needless death and destruction can stop.

He pushed forward, looking for Lara and Alyx.

~

Lara saw Alrion approaching and her heart leapt.

He's fine.

He did look exhausted and stumbled. But he was there, and alive, and there was no horde of Blighters to be seen. She looked over at Alyx and noticed the same relieved expression. Not much time had passed, but they had managed to secure horses. The townsfolk had been bewildered, but thankful.

"It's done," Alrion said with weariness. His shoulders seemed to slump even more.

"You did great." Lara ran forward and gave him a hug. He almost fell into her. "The townsfolk offer their heartful thanks. We have horses and directions to somewhere to rest." Alrion looked over at the horses.

"Only two?"

"We didn't want you being too comfortable. Besides, don't you remember our approach to the Mystics?" Alyx forced a laugh and drew a small smile from Alrion.

"Very well. Who am I riding with?"

"Me. You're in poor shape, and Alyx isn't great either."

"But I'm well enough to keep myself on a horse."

"No complaints here."

"I suggest we leave then." Lara ensured that their bags were secured to the horse and helped Alrion up. She joined him and took the reins, in minutes, they were on their way.

Lara looked around and saw the faces of people staring from their windows.

"They're terrified of us," Alrion said.

"They just don't understand."

"They are right to be, Lara. I destroyed that Blighter force from afar. It wasn't pretty, but it was effective. And horrible."

"It had to be done. I'm sorry you had to do that." Lara reached back and found his hand, giving it a quick squeeze.

"I know. But it shouldn't be like this. I thought being a wizard would be about helping people."

"It is."

"There's too much destruction. I don't want that to be my journey."

"This is good."

"What do you mean?"

"Remember when we arrived at Brangtur?"

"I do. I was a little reckless," Alrion said quietly. Lara imagined a sheepish expression on his face.

"You were downright deranged. And almost pushed too far."

"I wasn't in a good place."

"I know, which is why I'm saying this is good. You're maturing."

"As long as I don't mature so much that I can't get the job done." Alrion went quiet, and Lara didn't know what to say back. She sought out Alyx, and the weapon master caught her gaze and nodded slightly.

Alyx will know what to say.

Lara focused on the path. It was mostly dirt, with the occasional signpost to show another path. It looked like once upon a time there had been small stones littering the path, but they were all displaced now. Finally, she started to see their destination.

A tiny cottage appeared out of the surroundings. It had a large porch and some grass around it. But otherwise, it was just plonked in the middle of nowhere, surrounded by trees and shrubs.

"What's this place?" Alrion said.

"A retreat. They don't use it often and said we could rest here before moving on."

"That's nice of them," Alrion said. But his tone meant something else.

"Yes, it was nice of them. Don't judge them too harshly."

"I know, I know." Alrion sighed and leaned against her. It felt good to have him close again.

I can't carry that burden that you do, but I can help. You just need to let me.

10

BACKTRACKING

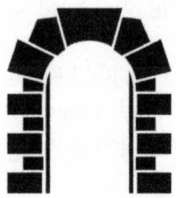

V incent observed the town before him. The cluster of houses huddled together seemed tiny and the main street looked too quiet. Not at all like he remembered.

"You were right, there is a town here." Celes couldn't hide the surprise from her voice.

"Well, it's been a while, so I wasn't completely confident. Things do change. But something is off down there." Vincent grabbed the pommel of his sword. As soon as he noticed, he forced himself to let it go.

"I feel it too. Let's go investigate." Celes led the way, tramping ahead.

I'd rather not uncover another disaster.

The main street was deserted. Vincent saw people occasionally peering at them through a window, but otherwise, the townsfolk stayed out of sight.

"I wonder what happened here?" Celes whispered. Vincent wondered too. And he understood why she had whispered. It felt like they were disturbing something, encroaching on the townsfolk.

"That looks like an inn, surely they will talk to us." Celes pointed and charged off. Vincent quickened his pace and followed close behind. The inn was titled Ample Ale and looked incredibly small.

Just a watering hole, no need for accommodation in a town like this.

Celes pushed open the door and Vincent held the door, looking inside. The inn was almost empty, with a bored portly bartender leaning back against a cabinet at one end of the bar. Vincent stepped inside and let the door close behind him. The bartender looked up and seemed to debate moving. He did finally haul himself up and leaned over the bar instead, one hand resting on his head amongst his thick curly black hair.

"Visitors? What brings you here?"

"We're just passing through. What happened here?" Celes said. The bartender paused, searching for words.

"A bad thing. Folks don't really understand it." The bartender looked from Celes to Vincent.

We need to gain his trust.

"We know all about that. We just fled Hurdenor. The city fell to the Blight." Vincent opted to speak simply and see how the bartender reacted. The man spat on the floor and cursed.

"We fared better." The bartender shook his head. "Those animals!"

"They really are. I'm Celes and this is Vincent. And you are?"

"Bruce. Sorry, you've come at a bad time. We had an attack here too. But no one can really understand it."

"Seeing as where we just came from, maybe we can make some sense of it?" Celes gave Bruce a reassuring smile. He perked up a little.

"Perhaps. At least you won't think me crazy."

"Not at all. We've seen some crazy things lately, there's no judgement here." Celes looked to Vincent and he nodded.

"It was the strangest thing. This evil creature turned up brandishing a giant sword. I think it was a woman, originally. All dressed in black and its face. Oh my god, its face." The bartender poured himself a brandy and threw it down in one go, wiping his mouth and shivering.

"What about its face?" Celes said.

"You could see its skull, it was unholy, let me tell you. They spoke of it as the Skull Queen."

Alrion.

"They? Who are you referring to?" Celes said. She closed the gap between her and Bruce and peered into his eyes.

"Uh, you know. The travellers. A man and a woman." Bruce looked away and licked his lips.

"Was the man by any chance a wizard?" Vincent kept his voice calm and friendly. Bruce seemed to flinch at the word wizard, but then seemed to calm down.

"Aye, that's a good way of putting it. The two of them freed us from some sort of spell that the creature cast over us. It was like some strange black fog." Bruce looked like he was going to keep talking but suddenly stopped.

"Please relax. We believe you. We think we know the two people you mentioned. We were travelling together until recently." Celes placed her hand on the bartender's arm. His breathing slowed, and he seemed less anxious.

"Terrible business. We're just waiting around to see what else happens."

Celes drew a gold coin and pressed it into his hand. Bruce adeptly whisked the coin away and began to speak again. This time he seemed a little bolder.

"This, you won't believe. The woman returned to the town with another woman. And the man joined them later. People were whispering that the other woman used to be that creature, but I don't believe it."

"I do. Go on, please." Celes flashed Bruce a warm smile.

"We told them of a house they could stay in, away from town. That seemed to satisfy them, and they left immediately."

"On foot?" Vincent said.

"Oh no, they bought horses." Bruce looked from Vincent to Celes, and back again.

He's waiting for something.

"There's something else, isn't there?" Celes said. Bruce stared into the distance for a time, before refocusing on them.

"Just more stories. Some folk said they saw some strange lights coming from the track out back. But everybody's too scared to go investigate."

"That's a completely normal reaction. Why don't we go take a look?" Celes said to Vincent.

"We should. We'll return shortly." Vincent turned to leave, but the bartender grabbed his arm.

"You have to tell us it's safe again. Not for me, you know. For the others." The look in his eye betrayed his true emotions.

"It's safe again. If there's anything to concern you, I'll deal with it." Vincent looked Bruce in the eyes and he nodded. He visibly relaxed and settled back against the bar.

"Happy travels." Bruce waved. Celes smiled and waved but Vincent turned and started walking.

"He was helpful," Celes said.

"To a degree." Vincent opened the door and held it open for his wife. She brushed his shoulder gently and left the inn. More eyes followed them as they walked through the town.

"The people are petrified."

"I can understand why. It sounded horrific. The Skull Queen?" Celes shivered.

"Now I know why Alrion didn't come to our aid. He had to be here."

"Do you think he even knew about the other attack?" Celes said. Vincent stopped walking and thought about it.

"He might have. Darvin was being quite strange. I wouldn't put it past him doing something like that." Vincent resumed his walking, faster now. It had been a long time since his last visit, but the town itself hadn't really changed. Just his perception of it. The path behind Carth was much as he remembered it. But as they progressed, he began to see evidence of a battle.

"Something's not right with the path. Look ahead." Vincent pointed into the distance.

"You're right, the path looks disturbed. And not in a normal way for the passage of time." Celes went forward. Vincent let her run ahead, curious about what she would discover.

"It doesn't make sense. We need to go a bit further and see for sure." Celes didn't even wait for Vincent, she just took off again and disappeared around a corner. Vincent took his time approaching. He had an idea of what had happened.

Alrion, what did you do here?

Vincent found his wife standing at the end of the path. It looked like it should have continued but the ground was completely different. The earth had been broken or disturbed and there was only the occasional sign of there ever being a path. The ground wasn't flat anymore, it was uneven and had frequent marks or holes.

"If you look up there it looks like there are some remains. Likely Blighters." Celes took off again and Vincent followed closely behind.

I don't like the look of this.

Celes was standing over a black leg sticking out of the ground.

"This Blighter looks like it has been buried."

"Not by hand." Vincent looked over the scene. Magic was definitely at play here.

"You think?"

"Alrion. This is his handiwork. I wonder how many he dealt with." Vincent could see scorch marks on the nearby hills and the aftermath of explosions on the ground.

'This is huge. It was probably a whole force of Blighters. Our son did this?" Celes whispered.

"He did. And he saved Alyx. He's growing beyond our influence now." Vincent turned and started to walk back.

"What do we do now? Should we go after him?" Celes ran ahead and stopped in front of Vincent, blocking his path.

"No. We need to let him go."

"And what? Continue this search for the source of the Blight? Based solely on a vague lead? There are real people dying around us."

"No, I've been thinking about that. The aggressive nature of our enemy changes things. Alrion doesn't have as long as he thinks." Vincent sighed. He stepped past his wife and kept walking.

"Where are you going? He needs us more than ever. Whatever he did here, it's not good. He must be hurting. And finally getting his friend back? That's huge!" Celes kept getting louder until she was almost shouting. She grabbed Vincent's arm and stopped him.

"He needs to walk this path alone. The best thing we can do is find the information he needs."

"And take him the information?" Celes's voice was quieter.

"Yes. We should give him the space he needs but come in with the location of the Blight in case he does not discover it himself."

"And what if he does? We'll be left behind." Celes crossed her arms in front of her.

"It's a risk. But it's reduced if we go to a place guaranteed to have the answer."

"Guaranteed?" Celes gave him a sceptical look.

"Guaranteed. We need to go back to go forwards."

"That doesn't sound quick to me."

"Trust me, once Alrion gets his head straight he will come to the same conclusion. Only we'll get there first." Vincent showed a tiny smile.

Yes, this will work. We can be one step ahead of him.

"You seem quite pleased with yourself."

"I think we can pull this off. And I'm also looking forward to your reaction."

"My reaction to where you want to take us?"

"Yes. You ready?" Vincent saw Celes narrow her eyes and stare at him.

"Just get it over with."

"Paperton." Vincent said the word quickly and waited for a response. Celes started to speak, then stopped.

"I see you're speechless."

"That's a long way."

"We can pass through Brangtur. Take care of some unfinished business."

"Oh, you're good." Celes paused, thinking. "I wouldn't mind settling the score with that rat Wilhelm. The fun opportunity aside, what happens when we get ourselves to Paperton. Are you suggesting we drink from the Pool of Knowledge?"

"Possibly. Or we work with someone there who already has. Either way, we get the information. It's the only place that we know for sure has it."

"It seems like a reasonable plan. I have to admit, I found the idea of Paperton and the Pool of Knowledge fascinating when Alrion told me about it."

"No guarantee they will let us see it. They're probably a little jumpy since the last incident there."

"I'll take my chances. If you think this is the best way I can help my son, then I'm in."

"This way then." Vincent pointed to a trail and they started hiking.

I hope I'm doing the right thing.

11

A CURIOUS PROPOSAL

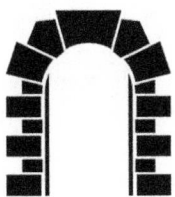

Alrion handed Alyx a cup of water and she accepted it graciously. After a long drink, she set it down with care and cleared her throat.

"Better?" Lara said.

"Yes. I'm starting to feel more human." Alyx visibly shivered.

"We're just glad to have you back." Alrion gave her a reassuring smile.

"I am glad to be back, I thought I was lost forever. In a way I already was. My consciousness and awareness shifted back and forth. I was a passenger more than anything." Alyx stopped talking and looked uncomfortable.

"I can't possibly understand how that felt, but I understand what the Blight can do. And feeling like you're losing yourself. I won't let it happen again."

"We won't," Lara added. Alyx pondered for a moment before replying.

"As painful as that was, you should let it happen if it needs to. The quest is more important than any of us."

"Don't worry, I won't allow that situation to happen again." Alrion was firmer in his voice, and that seemed to stop the line of conversation. A stillness sat over the group.

"So where to next?" Lara said. Alrion sighed and leaned back in his chair.

"Now that we've saved Alyx, we need to find the source of the Blight and I need to finalise the spell required. I can finally stop all this." Alrion started to speak again but quickly stopped. He jumped up from the chair and ran outside. Lara and Alyx scrambled to follow.

Alrion saw the flames leaping through the air. He immediately swept them away with a wave of force then looked beyond, seeing the wizard. Without waiting, he sent more waves of force at the wizard, hoping to destabilise him without causing damage.

The hooded wizard just made a minor gesture with his arm and the waves of force fell away. He approached slowly, and the flames in the air winked out.

"Just announcing myself. I come in peace." The wizard pushed back his hood.

"Branthor!"

"That's my name. Well, now that I'm back to myself. I see you fixed your friend too." Branthor gestured at Alyx and smiled.

"What are you doing here? How did you find me?"

"Wizards have ways, as you know. First, I had to escape the immediate danger and I did. Lucky for me, Darvin went after your friend there and had his fun with her. But now that I'm recovered, it's time for a little payback. And you came to mind."

"I saved you. I stopped the Blight from corrupting you further." Alrion raised his voice, showing his frustration.

"I know, which is why you're the perfect partner to assist with my revenge. I'm after Rindale."

"Rindale? The other general?" Alrion looked at Alyx.

"I don't remember seeing him."

"He was behind your transformation." Branthor pointed at Alyx. "And mine. He's the architect behind all the developments of the Blight."

"What do you mean exactly?"

"He's the one behind the evolution of the Blight. The new variants coming out. Destroy him, and you cut off the Blight's advantage." Branthor spat on the ground.

"I can see why it benefits us. But why you?" Lara said.

"He was instrumental in using the Blight to control me. But more than that." Branthor trailed off. A brief look of pain flashed across his face as he remembered something.

"Rindale was the one that captured your father and was the reason my wife was infected. He needs to be stopped for good." Branthor clenched his fist, and his posture straightened. He looked ready to fight.

"That's all great, but why should we trust you? You've been working against us every step of the way." Lara looked to Alrion and he nodded.

"Have I really? Yes, I wanted to stop you and control you. But I stayed my hand. Even in my grotesque form, I still fought you fairly and gave you a chance. I tried to recruit you rather than kill you. And you freed me from their influence."

"If you're so powerful, why not just do this yourself."

"I can't risk failure. And I want this over quickly. The Blight are drawn to you, I will find them faster this way. They can't escape us working together."

"You're welcome." Branthor turned to Alrion. "No offence, but you have a lot to learn still."

"No offence taken." Alrion bristled at Branthor's manner, but he couldn't fault what the wizard had said. He did need to do better, and he had lots to learn.

"Ride with me," Lara said. She climbed onto one of the horses and leaned forward, making room for Alrion. He joined her and looked over at Alyx. She seemed comfortable with Branthor riding behind.

"It's not that far, don't worry. We can resolve this awkward travel arrangement shortly." Branthor made himself comfortable and closed his eyes.

He's just infuriating, the way he behaves. Strides in here like he knows better than everyone. But I need him, at least for now. I need to learn what I can. There's wisdom in there, despite his flaws and his corruption.

"Take this trail," Branthor said, pointing. Alyx took the lead, and Lara and Alrion fell in close behind. Alrion closed his eyes and thought about what he needed to do. He could at least try to use the travel time for something useful.

He carefully leaned over and rifled through the saddle bag, retrieving a glass flask with a cork stopper.

"What are you doing back there?"

"I'm doing an experiment."

"For what? You're not going to explode us, are you?" Lara laughed. Alrion could tell it was a bit forced, but he appreciated the effort. These were strange times, and a little laughter couldn't hurt.

"No promises. I'm going to see if I can store my Soul Power in an ordinary flask."

"Really? So, I can drink it?"

"That's the plan." Alrion smiled. Lara let out a genuine laugh that went right through him, warming his soul.

I'm on the right path now. It's not what I expected, but it's the way forward.

12

UNCERTAIN STEPS

Lara slowed the horse, signalling the rest to be quiet. She heard sounds ahead. Alyx drew close and leaned in.

"I heard something ahead," Lara whispered.

"Do you want to investigate?" Alyx said. Lara nodded and carefully dismounted. She turned to look at Alrion and he gave her a slight nod too. Lara glanced at Branthor out of the corner of her eyes, but he seemed to be still and disinterested.

I don't know what to make of him.

Lara crept forward, veering off the path and finding a way through the shrubs and trees that lined the road. She hoped that it was nothing, but her intuition was eerily accurate. As she progressed, sounds wafted over. Definitely conversation.

Lara realised that she was quite close but couldn't see without revealing herself. Her view of the path was blocked by a dense collection of shrubs and leafy plants. She glanced at the surroundings and saw a promising tree. The lower branches were accessible and sturdy.

Here goes.

Lara clambered up, almost slipping as she reached for the first branch. She grabbed it securely, bracing herself as her feet looked for somewhere to rest. She found small knobs on the trunk that would suffice and rested for a moment. Next, she hauled herself up and perched in the crook between the branch and the tree trunk. She could see more now, but it was just vague shapes. The view was obscured by the leaves of the tree.

Probably for the best.

Lara found another branch to try to ease along, trying not to make any sudden movements. Any suspicious movement from the tree would draw attention, and she didn't know what was before her.

I bet it's the Blight. With my luck, probably a Shade or worse.

Lara gingerly shimmied along the branch until she had a better view. Leaning the right way, she could just peer through the foliage and see what was below her. Finally settled, she allowed herself to concentrate on the dialogue.

"This is definitely the right town," a male voice said. There was a strange rasp to it that grated and made Lara's skin crawl.

"You don't seem sure," another voice replied. It was deeper but had the same rasping quality. Lara couldn't decide which voice was worse.

"I don't see you confirming anything, you should know as well as me."

"We could ask?"

"And look foolish? Never. I don't want to be an example like Wraith."

Something about them seemed familiar, although she could barely see with the fading light. A flame burst into being, flickering next to one of the men. In the light, she could see more details.

A Shade Wizard! Now it all makes sense.

Lara carefully retreated, being extra careful to not make any noise. One twig snapping could out her completely. She was not equipped to really deal with a Shade Wizard, let alone two.

We need to agree on a plan. At least I'll go report this.

Lara reached the trunk and skirted down a little faster than she had hoped. Her feet scraped against the tree and there was a loud crunch as she reached the ground. She heard movement nearby and cries of surprise.

No time now. Move!

Lara kept quiet, but sped through the brush, weaving between trees. She could sense fires being lit behind her but dared not look back.

Push on, let them be distracted looking for you.

As Lara put distance between them, she allowed herself to be a little noisier and increased her speed. It was paramount to alert everyone. She arrived suddenly and quickly stopped, allowing a moment to catch her breath. It seemed as though everyone was already alert.

"We sensed trouble. Wizards or worse?" Alrion said.

"Two Shade Wizards. I didn't notice anyone else."

"See? I told you."

"Nothing is confirmed yet, but it's a good lead. What do we want to do?" Alrion looked around at the group.

"I say kill them, they're an abomination and could get very dangerous. The less the better."

"I could cure one at least," Alrion offered.

"We could see that one for information too," Lara added. Alrion looked to Alyx for an opinion.

"Either way we need to kill one or both. I have no particular preference."

"Let's advance then and try to separate them. That way we have a chance at capturing one."

"You're the boss," Branthor said with sarcasm. He hurried away without waiting for anyone else.

"Lead the way," Alrion muttered under his breath. He took off at a fast pace, Lara and Alyx by his side.

"They were on the path but noticed me leaving and started torching the nearby area."

"That's fine, it will make them easier to find."

"Not in that smoke," Alyx said. With the sun setting, there was much less light. And the smoke from the ongoing fires was hanging over the whole area. It looked like the Shade Wizards had let the fires continue burning.

"What are they doing?" Alrion said. He shook his head.

"Smoking me out?" Lara shrugged. She remembered Branthor and looked ahead. "The wizard is gone."

"What's he going to do?" Alrion sighed. He suddenly perked up and changed direction.

"This way." Alrion pointed and drew his sword.

Why is he doing that? He's more powerful than the sword. Lara noticed that the diamond was glowing blue, as expected.

Lara kept pace with Alrion and saw a white-hot glow explode from the distance. She increased her speed, sprinting as fast as possible. After a brief delay, Alrion caught up to her.

He must be using his Soul Power. The smoke was beginning to disperse, and Lara observed what looked like a wizard. She slowed and approached carefully, Alrion taking the lead.

"It's just me," Branthor shouted. The smoke quickly disappeared, and the scene became clear. Before Branthor was a small crater.

"What did you do?" Alrion shouted. He roughly shoved his sword back into its scabbard.

"They were too dangerous, I had to react." Branthor shrugged. Lara saw a mischievous smile cross his face.

"That's a forbidden spell." Alrion was outraged.

"For good reason. But it suited my purposes here. They have ceased to exist, and there are no remains either. It covers our tracks."

"Won't it be obvious when they've completely vanished that a wizard was behind it?" Alrion paced over and knelt, looking at the crater. He dug fingers through the dirt.

"At worst, they will expect me. This is not how you fight them, so they'll be off guard."

"Seems like an extreme response." Lara didn't like how carelessly Branthor had employed such a spell. She still remembered vividly when Alrion had used it back in the desert. He had come so close to destroying them all.

"I have a little more control than this one." Branthor chuckled. "Magical control, I should say."

"What do you believe in now?" Alrion said.

"Revenge. Didn't I say that?" Branthor's voice was hard and he turned from them to view the road.

"Charming." Lara noticed movement and turned to look. Alyx emerged from the brush on the opposite side of the path.

"No other enemies in the area."

"Thanks for looking out for us," Alrion said. He looked a bit embarrassed.

"I have no weapon, it was the best use of my skills."

She still looks dangerous.

Alrion started to fumble with his clothes and removed his sword belt.

"Take this." He offered the sword to Alyx. She stepped back and put her hands up.

"No, that is your blade. You need it."

"It's holding me back. You can borrow it for a while." Alrion threw the sword onto the ground. Alyx glanced at him, then turned her gaze onto Lara. She nodded and smiled, trying to encourage the weapon master. Alyx gave a short bow and retrieved the sword. She strapped it around her waist then drew the blade. After a quick circular motion, she expertly sheathed it.

"As you wish." She turned to observe the path ahead.

Alrion strode over to Branthor and roughly pulled him around so that the wizard was facing him.

"If we're going to work together, I can't have you going off on your own." Alrion glared at Branthor, and the master wizard's eyes glinted with delight.

"Oh, how interesting. And what then am I supposed to do?"

"Agree a plan and stick to it. Clearly, we've encountered worse than two Shade Wizards and survived. We do this my way, or we don't do it at all."

"Oh, is that a threat?" Branthor arched an eyebrow and observed Alrion. "Are you really that willing to let my information go?"

"I can find a way without you, if need be. But I can't continue if I can't trust you to behave in a way that's acceptable to me." Alrion stood taller and stared intently into Branthor's eyes.

"Fine, you can dictate terms. I will, however, offer my expert opinion on whatever plans you come up with." Branthor stuck out his hand. Alrion grabbed it and shook firmly. After a brief pause, he turned and addressed the group.

"Well, that's done. We have at least some confirmation of Branthor's informa-

712   VAUGHAN W. SMITH

tion. Let's go investigate the town." Alyx kept staring out into the distance but nodded. Lara stepped closer to Alrion and leaned in.

"Well done. I'm proud of you, standing up to him." Alrion blushed but quickly hid it. He turned to face Branthor.

"Do you have anything to add?" Alrion started walking and didn't wait to hear the answer. Branthor paused then followed. He still retained an amused look on his face.

I still don't understand him. Maybe he's just broken now?

They walked in silence, observing the town as it rose before them. A nearby path converged with theirs, and a constant but slow stream of people filtered along, heading for the town gates. Puffs of smoke rose up giving an idea of the size, and Lara could already see quite a few tiled roofs and a few bigger structures stretching taller than the rest. Branthor finally spoke.

"While I suspect Rindale is based here, I don't think it's his home. I believe he has some lab somewhere else, where he conducts his... work." Branthor spat audibly onto the path. The gesture drew the horrified looks of a few travellers.

"This is where you think the Shade Wizards come from?" Alrion said.

"I think they are perhaps trained here, but they are not made here. I haven't quite figured out the connection. But there's always a presence."

"We will have to be careful. Perhaps they can detect us as well as we can detect them?"

"I doubt that. As you are aware, the Blight connection adds an element of noise. That would be quite distracting. I think we have an edge there. Well, I do. I suspect you haven't quite honed that skill yet." Branthor looked at Alrion, clearly to gauge his reaction. Alrion looked a little annoyed, but he quickly hid it.

"I've not yet seen the need, but it's something I can work on. How do you suggest I do that?" Alrion spoke slowly and purposefully.

He's really maturing. He's not as defensive now.

Branthor seemed surprised at the response. He didn't reply immediately.

"We can look at that later, it's not critical to discuss right now. Obviously, I have agreed to defer to your judgement, but I suggest we focus on locating the base of operations for the Shade Wizards and see if we can track them to Rindale." Alrion looked to Lara.

"What do you think?"

"Well," Lara said before pausing. She thought carefully about her response. "Given the information we currently have, I think that's the most prudent course. If Branthor can pinpoint a location, I can infiltrate and follow them."

"I can live with that. Just don't get spotted next time," Branthor said. "We can't have them turn you into a monster too. We've all had a turn." Branthor laughed and pointed at Alyx, Alrion, and himself.

I couldn't think of anything worse. Lara shivered and pressed forward.

13

BRANGTUR REVISITED

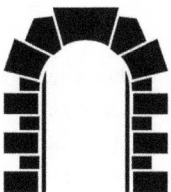

V incent pulled his horse up short and took in the sight. Brangtur was not nearly as impressive when viewed from the minor service entrance, but his mind filled in the blanks.

"This is where it all started." Celes slowed her horse and brought it alongside her husband's. Vincent gazed at his wife and recognised the nostalgic look on her face.

"Our great adventure together. We have Wilhelm to thank, after all." Vincent chuckled and Celes broke into a delighted laugh.

"We'll have to give him an appropriate thank you present." Celes winked.

"What did you have in mind?"

"I'm thinking it through. Let me work out some of the knots then I'll talk you through it."

"As you wish." Vincent nudged his horse forward, knowing that his wife wouldn't share any details until she was ready. But he could already guess at a few options. Celes wouldn't settle for anything less than would pull the rug out from under Wilhelm. He was far too comfortable in his position and enjoyed lording it over everyone.

"Is there anything you need to do here?" Celes said. Vincent took in a deep breath and looked around.

"Nothing I can think of." Workers bustled around in the early morning, none of them paying any attention to travellers entering via the service entrance. They knew better than to ask questions. Anyone coming in and avoiding the main entry had good reason and usually the authorisation to do so. Something Vincent himself had learned many years ago.

They rode in silence. Vincent kept an eye on any approaching guards, but none seemed interested in him or his wife. Celes seemed to be in her own world, and Vincent had to frequently remind her to make space between townsfolk that she didn't seem to notice. Yet somehow, she seemed to be pressing ahead with purpose, as they were clearly heading towards the entertainment district. Celes suddenly stopped and looked up.

"Good, I'm ready. Let's get a meal and I can fill you in."

"Sure. Anywhere in particular?"

"Hmm." Celes stared into the distance, concentrating on something else.

"The Lucky Lance."

"That old place?"

"It's a classic. Don't you remember the significance?" Celes's eyes flashed with humour but also something dangerous.

"Ah yes, I could never forget that. It's where you plied me with drink to agree to help you with your fool's errand." Vincent grinned.

"Exactly. It worked last time, it'll work again." Celes winked and led the way. Vincent sighed and followed close behind. Within a matter of minutes, the Lucky Lance was before them. It seemed to be the busiest inn around, and the clamour of drinks and music seemed to be cheerier and more genuine than the others.

The energy in the room was almost overpowering as Vincent pushed the doors open. Two musicians were frantically playing, one on a stringed instrument and the other on a giant flute. The patrons were loving it, some clinking their tankards together, others dancing on the tables.

"Business is booming." Celes tapped Vincent on the shoulder and pointed to a table.

"Your usual?" Vincent said. Celes didn't even respond, just waved him on. Vincent chuckled and wove his way through the crowd. He couldn't remember the place being so busy.

"What can I get ya?" the bartender said, leaning close to try to hear Vincent over the noise.

"Two chicken plates and two ales." The bartender started to walk away, but Vincent reached out and grabbed the man's arm.

"Sorry, but what's going on here? I don't remember this place being so busy."

"I've no idea, but it has to be related to that vagrant we had here. Business really picked up after that."

"Vagrant?"

"Yes, he was an odd fellow and did the rounds begging for drinks. One person tried to run him out, but it ended rather poorly, so we all suffered the rag-riddled man. But one day, a young couple came in and drank the vagrant under the table. He left with them and never returned. The story spread, and I guess the rest is history."

"What a remarkable story." Vincent handed the bartender the coins and struggled back through the crowd.

"That took a while." Celes was still observing the room and didn't look at Vincent.

"It's incredibly busy. Bartender said that things took off after a young couple drank a vagrant under the table and convinced him to leave with them."

"Of all the places for them to find Certan. I suppose it is the Lucky Lance after all. We'll have to tell them about how famous they became."

"I hope it doesn't encourage him to drink more." Vincent laughed.

"Have you met that girl before? I'd wager she helped him more than you'd expect." Celes relaxed into the chair finally.

"You've settled on a plan then?"

"Yes. It's really quite brilliant." Celes paused, looking over Vincent's shoulder.

"And now we can discuss it." Celes accepted an ale and held it up waiting for Vincent. They clinked glasses, and each took a deep drink.

"Hopefully this time you won't need as much encouragement."

"Really? I'd hoped to top Alrion's record." Vincent smiled and Celes shook her head.

"It is so nostalgic here. Ah. Well, onto the plan. Do you remember the Silver Sceptre?"

"From Valrytir? The one owned by the Regent General?"

"Yes. The very same one that I swapped out and smuggled all the way here."

"Where is it now?"

"It's in Wilhem's collection. I was double-crossed by a supposed friend who was paid off by Wilhelm."

"You want to steal it back?"

"Even better. I want to get caught stealing it."

"Again? Are we that old now that we can't do things properly?" Vincent burst into laughter. Celes retained her smile and waited for him to finish.

"Not only is there a bounty on that Sceptre, but the Regent General has an outstanding extradition order on whoever stole it."

"If you can convince them he stole it and has been hoarding it all this time..."

"Then the guards have no choice but to ship him out to Valrytir, away from all his precious goods. Many of which will be under suspicion." Celes had a wicked grin on her face and took a sip of her ale.

"That works for me. But won't you still be arrested for thieving? He can still out you as the Shadow Fox."

"That's my problem, don't you worry about it." Celes flashed a smile, but it didn't help. Vincent was still worried. He grunted and shook his head.

"Relax. Drink your ale." Vincent took another deep drink. He suddenly felt suspicious.

"You haven't mentioned me. What part do I need to play?"

"Oh, yours is so easy. Just visit some of your old blacksmith friends so they know you're back in town."

"Word will spread, you know. Is that what you want? Wilhelm has spies everywhere, and now he knows what to look for."

"It's no fun if he doesn't know it's coming. He will be up all night wondering what I'm going to take next. Oh, this is good, you can't imagine how much I've missed it." Celes was practically glowing.

"I'm glad to be of assistance." Vincent finished his ale quickly.

"I best make some appearances then?"

"Please. I'd prefer we strike tonight, and I want Wilhelm to have time to prep the guards."

"As you wish." Vincent leaned in and gave Celes a quick kiss before heading back into the crowd. He gently forced his way through until he was outside.

The shadows were growing longer, signalling the end of the day. They had decided to leave the horses at the inn for the time being. Vincent needed to move with real pace to the Blacksmith district if he was going to plant some information in time. As he strode, Vincent thought about his old contacts, some of which he had seen on his most recent visit. One, in particular, sprung to mind. Vincent chuckled to himself.

I bet that old codger will run straight to Wilhelm himself!

Vincent picked up the pace so that he could arrive in time.

The Blacksmith district was still full of life. Many craftsmen were still working away, some had pre-emptively lit lanterns to ensure consistent light over the transition to night. Vincent almost stopped a dozen times to observe what was being crafted, but each time dragged himself away.

You have a job to do. Your former life is on hold.

He gave wide berth to a few of his favourite places, knowing that the smiths there were loyal and friendly. He needed the opposite.

There we go.

Vincent stepped inside *The Jewelled Marvel*. The owner, and skilled gold-smith and silversmith, Benton, was still inside. He was tall and thin and wore his work apron, with small glasses hanging off the top. Rather than working on anything new though, he was swanning through the shopfront observing customers and offering advice. Although he unashamedly was scrutinising all his wares to make sure nobody was thinking of stealing. His eyes widened when he saw Vincent and he hurried over.

"Vincent! Why it's been a while. And you left under such strained circum-stances."

"Benton! Great to see you. Yes, being chased out of the city by the guard is thankfully a rare occurrence. I see business is good."

"Always, I work hard to keep this running. What brings you back here?"

Benton ran a hand through his curly, greying hair and quickly ran his eyes over the customers and his goods.

"Just passing through, don't have time to sort out that whole misunderstanding with the guard. My wife has some unfinished business, so I thought I would attend to my own business." Benton quickly turned back and gave Vincent his full attention.

"Which is?"

"Well, I wanted to get her something as a memento. Since we probably won't be back for a while. Women love jewellery, and I know we've had our disagreements, but you're the best. I can't argue with that." Vincent gave a forced smile and Benton broke out with a wide grin.

"My friend, you are right there. You have come to the right place. What did you need? I have rings, amulets, bracelets, pendants, you name it. All at a special price for you." Benton started off, beckoning for Vincent to follow. The goldsmith pointed out different pieces, clearly highlighting the expensive ones.

He wants to make a lot of money off me today. I better oblige him.

"I want something that she can wear on her neck," Vincent said. Benton paused and scratched his forehead.

"Yes, I have the perfect thing." He performed yet another look around the cramped room and didn't seem satisfied. Ducking behind a door he yelled something and a timid apprentice in an apron shuffled out into the store.

"Go on, make yourself useful." Benton gave the apprentice a light shove and the apprentice started walking the aisles.

"So hard to get good help. Ah, here we are." Benton held up a thin gold necklace with a stunning stone set in the bottom. It was pure white with veins of blue throughout.

"A beautiful and rare piece, and a perfect companion to the Pure Diamond, don't you think?" Benton gave Vincent a knowing look. Vincent laughed and winked at Benton.

"I don't know what you're talking about. But I do like the look of it." Vincent retrieved a pouch of gold coins and opened it to look inside.

"How much am I in for?" Benton snatched the pouch and looked inside. He then closed the pouch and tucked it into his clothes behind the apron.

"The whole lot, and that's a discount. I expect you'll want a pouch for this?"

"Please." Benton huffed about and found a purple velvet pouch, carefully dropping the pendant inside.

"Give my regards to your wife. Will I have the pleasure of seeing her wear the piece?"

"I doubt it, I think we will need to leave shortly. But I promise I'll come visit next time we are here."

"I look forward to it. Have a pleasant evening." Benton didn't even wait for a reply and strode off to talk to a customer. He waved the apprentice away, who seemed all too glad to be escaping to the back of the store.

I could see his mind ticking over. I'm sure he thinks that he can get paid tipping off Wilhelm, and maybe even recover what he just sold me. What a piece of work. At least, though, I've set things in motion. Now to find Celes and make sure she's ready for this. It's not going to be easy.

Vincent rushed out of the store and walked with purpose.

14

THE MESSENGER

A lyx kept her hand on the sword hilt as they entered the town.

"Welcome to Twingley," Branthor said with a grandiose gesture. The town was relatively busy but quite small. It was overshadowed by a large structure behind.

"Looks like a fortress back there," Alyx said.

"That seems to be where the Shade Wizards are too. Not surprising when you think about it. There's nowhere to hide in this town otherwise." Branthor sighed and curled his lip in disgust. He kicked at some small rocks on the dusty path.

"Let's enquire at the local inn." Lara pointed out the largest building in their vicinity and took the lead. Alrion nodded and followed along. Alyx waited for them all and surveyed the area before bringing up the rear.

I'm not sure who to trust.

"The Sprained Spear," Lara announced. She shared a laugh with Alrion, but Branthor wasn't paying attention.

"You two sit and be quiet, I'll go ask for information. Care to join me, Alyx?"

"Sure." Alyx looked over the room and joined Lara. There didn't seem to be anyone dangerous, so it seemed fine to leave Alrion alone. Lara didn't need as much protection, she had good instincts.

"I'm not sure you need my help," Alyx said as they approached the bar.

"Probably not but having a sword around sure does keep people polite." Lara glanced back at Alrion. Alyx followed her gaze and saw the two wizards sitting as far from each other as possible and facing different directions.

"I also want them to get used to each other. For now, at least." Lara turned back to the bar.

"I would not be so understanding. But perhaps my way was not the best."

"It must be quite a burden, holding onto that feeling of revenge for so long."

"After a while, it becomes part of you." Alyx shuddered. She inadvertently started to remember her time as the Skull Queen. It seemed that any such feeling easily brought on that experience. She needed to be careful. As crazy as it sounded, it felt like she could be drawn back at any time.

"Four ales, and a moment of your time," Lara said to the innkeeper. This time it was a middle-aged woman with curly black hair. She had it tied back with a scarf and was in constant motion. She nodded and poured the ales expertly, bringing them over immediately.

"I'm not the chit-chat type." The innkeeper held out her hand. Lara dropped in five coins.

"Then I won't keep you. I just want to know what the deal is with that giant fort back there." Lara looked over the innkeeper's shoulder. The woman pocketed all the coins.

"Not much to say really. Back in the day, this town was a staging area for the Valrytir army. They used to camp out in that fort and do manoeuvres. Run small campaigns. Said this was a strategic location due to its proximity to certain routes. I was quite young at the time, so I don't know the whole history." The innkeeper walked away a few paces and started cleaning some glasses.

"What about now? Doesn't look deserted."

"Some rich recluse moved in. Has a lot of visitors but there doesn't seem to be a large staff there. We get more customers here, more traffic through the town." The innkeeper hesitated but stopped talking and returned to her work.

"Sounds like there's more to the story." Lara tossed over another coin. The innkeeper pocketed it without any acknowledgement and kept working.

"Just rumours. Some say they're practising dark magic up there. There's often strange lights and sounds. There are folk that stop by here that don't seem right. They don't talk, just keep their faces covered and pay well. So, we don't ask questions." The innkeeper strode away to the far end of the bar and busied herself with something else.

"That's about it. Help me back." Lara picked up two mugs and Alyx grabbed the others. They returned to the table, and it was still quiet.

"I thought you hated this stuff," Alrion said.

"It was easier to buy more. We learned a bit about that fortress."

"The information checks out. As soon as she started talking, I remembered there being something out here. But I never came here myself." Alyx took a sip of the ale.

"Good to know. Essentially, it used to be a Valrytir outpost but now there's an eccentric recluse living there and rumours of dark magic." Lara looked over at Branthor.

"Yes, well we already knew that. You could have asked about access routes." Branthor sighed.

"And take the fun out of it? Alyx and I can scout. In fact, why don't we do it now. You two wizards can sit here and talk wizardly stuff." Alyx gulped down half her ale and stood quickly.

"But don't you need help?" Alrion said. He looked quite uncomfortable. Branthor leaned back and started drinking his ale.

"Do you think there's anything Alyx and I can't handle out in the open?" Lara gave Alrion a pointed look and Alyx started to draw the Runesteel sword.

"Let them go, rest and recover while you have the time," Branthor said. Alrion nodded and leaned back.

"Have fun, let me know what you find."

"Of course. Don't go anywhere," Lara teased. She took the lead and Alyx followed her out.

"More bonding time?" Alyx said.

"Doesn't hurt. Also, I trust them to watch each other. I'd rather we determine what options there are, without having to worry about either of them jumping in head first."

"I agree with that." Alyx liked Lara's caution. It was something she had lived by for so long. Even with her considerable abilities, she had also acted alone. You needed to maximise your chances and tip the scales in your favour. Otherwise, you were dead. Or worse. Alyx shuddered again.

The one time you let loose and gave in, you were infected. You can't do that again.

"Not the talkative type, are you?"

"I have a lot on my mind."

"Since we're alone, maybe you can talk freely. One comment of yours has been bugging me for a while." Lara stopped walking and looked straight at Alyx.

"Yes?"

"You said I looked familiar, but you would discuss it with me later."

"Yes, of course. I recognise you, and I know your father. Alrion doesn't know, does he?"

"No, I haven't said anything. It's not relevant anyway." Lara turned away.

"I'm no expert in these matters, but surely he needs to know if you two are to continue to be together."

"In time."

"I think it is inevitable that the truth will come out on this journey, sooner or later."

Lara turned back and faced Alyx. "I know." Lara bit her lip. "It's fine, I'll deal with that later. Please don't say anything."

"As you wish." Alyx pointed to the road ahead and Lara started walking once more.

There was only one path out of the town that headed towards the fortress, and they followed it without discussion. Alyx let Lara lead, interested to see the thief's approach. There wasn't much to look at on the path, only the odd tree and plant. Mostly it was just slightly yellowing grass. Halfway to the fortress Lara suddenly stopped.

"Look over here." She paced towards something on the edge of the path and Alyx hurried over. There was some sort of black residue on the ground, flaking away. Something about it seemed familiar to Alyx, but the more she grasped at it, the more it escaped her.

"Looks important. Do you know what it is?" Alyx said.

"Yes, I've seen this before. Recently. It's a trail that's left by Fermur, the Messenger."

"Oh. That explains why it looks familiar. I must have interacted with him... before."

"You must have. We met him recently." Lara saw Alyx's expression. "Wait, we don't necessarily need to kill him. He was interesting and seemed more neutral than you would expect. Like he's forced to do their bidding."

"Isn't that just something he's put on to confuse you? They don't exactly play fair."

"I'm just saying to not be too hasty about how we deal with him. But we must hurry, this trail won't remain for long. He must be close by." Lara pointed to the area she had first flagged, and the black flakes were almost gone.

I could get my revenge right now. Darvin was so angered by the loss of the Skull King, I could make him hurt by destroying his messenger.

"I'll do my best, let's follow the trail." Alyx started to jog and matched Lara's pace. The trail was getting more defined the more they followed it.

"We must be getting a lot closer. He's super-fast if he wants to be, I suspect he's leading us somewhere intentionally." Lara didn't slow, however.

"Do you think it's a trap?"

"Possibly. Just be prepared." Lara removed a dagger from her jacket and maintained her pace. Alyx let her hand hover above the sword pommel.

Surely Runesteel can end these things.

She caught Lara glancing at her, but Alyx didn't try to hide her emotion.

She should know what I am capable of.

The trail veered off the path, taking them away from the fortress. They pushed through bushes, crossed rocks, and ended up amongst a dense copse of trees flanked by rock and hill.

"There's no escape here," Alyx said.

"For him too? Let's slow down." Lara dropped down to a walking pace and Alyx did the same. They emerged into a clearing, and Fermur was sitting on a giant rock, waiting. Alyx was instantly repulsed and drew her sword. She felt Lara's hand on her arm and allowed herself to be temporarily restrained.

"You took your time. I had to write you an entire invitation and drop breadcrumbs. I felt like I was in a fairy tale." Fermur laughed and grinned at them both.

"Why are you here? Why bring us here?"

"Why, I have news, of course. Updates. So nice to see you again, Skull Queen. Although something dreadful seems to have happened. You look mighty pale. And what's with all that colour in your face?" Fermur laughed even harder, and almost toppled backwards.

"Monster, just tell us what you want and be gone before I permanently house this sword within your chest," Alyx growled. The fact that he was so fast was probably the only reason she had remained still. If she made a move he would be gone, and their chance would be lost.

"Oh, I'd love to converse with you two, it'd be quite enlightening. But, sadly, I invited your friends to join us and I really can't disappoint them."

"Alrion and Branthor are on their way here?" Lara said.

"Of course, it would be very rude otherwise. Oh, and here they are." Fermur pointed behind them. Alyx turned and saw Alrion and Branthor rush into the clearing.

"There it is. Oh, and Lara and Alyx too," Alrion said. Branthor looked ready to start fighting.

"Good, good, you're all here and now I can deliver my message."

"Just die," Branthor said. He made a move but Alrion stepped in front and the two glared at each other.

"Eventually, of course. But if I did so before telling you of the secret entrance to Rindale's fortress wouldn't that be a terrible waste?" Fermur batted his eyelashes, or at least what seemed to approximate them. Branthor appeared to stand down, and Alrion relaxed a little.

"Why? Are you betraying your own?"

"Hardly, I do as I am told. But I am here to tell you there are two ways into that fortress. And Rindale is within."

"Go on." Branthor gestured for Fermur to get on with it.

"As always, I am here to give you choices. Do you charge in through the front door, appeal to Rindale's ego and topple him when he thinks he has the upper hand? Or do you take the secret passage behind me, and appear when he least expects it?"

"That sounds obvious," Lara said.

"Oh, you think so? You must be smarter than me. So glad that you're so confident."

"Why are you like this? Like a person?" Alyx said. She didn't bother to hide the distaste from her tone.

"Oh, that's so nice of you. Darvin fought for us, to keep our personalities. Of course, a lot changed. But we evolved, rather than become something else. It keeps things interesting, doesn't it?"

"Why is your master giving us this information? We'll just make good use of it and continue to defeat him and his supporters. It doesn't make any sense." Alrion stepped in front of the rest, addressing Fermur directly. He didn't seem to be that wary of the strange creature. Alyx stepped forward to within reach of Alrion.

"Now, I can hardly speak for my master, but perhaps I'll offer some words of wisdom to one who speaks so plainly. Do you think that your Soul, the special power within you, is omnipotent and infallible?" Fermur peered into Alrion as if appraising it himself. Alrion thought for a few moments before replying.

"No, it's just a tool."

"So is the Blight. Now, considering that you can use your tool to overwhelm and remove the Blight, don't you think that the opposite is also possible?"

"Perhaps."

"Don't you think it interesting that we've never really tried to kill you outright, instead we," Fermur looked at Branthor," and our agents have been trying to bring you to our side?"

"That's because I was vulnerable before."

"True, true. But do you think you won't be vulnerable when you arrive at the source of the Blight, where its true power is gathered all in one place?" Fermur cocked his head and looked at Alrion. The wizard gasped and stepped back.

"You don't think we know what you are up to? Grow up, young wizard."

"You can't scare me away," Alrion said, regaining his composure.

"Not trying to, not my job. Alas, it seems I have said too much. I do take this messenger thing far too seriously. Or maybe not seriously enough, since I invariably say more than the message. Well, for now, one more thing." Fermur paused as if to speak, and suddenly he became a black blur and disappeared into the large hill behind.

"Impossible creature," Alyx cursed and sheathed her sword. Branthor put his hand on Alrion's shoulder.

"I hope you know what you're doing, kid." Alrion shrugged it off and stared into the space where Fermur had disappeared.

Next time he won't get away.

15

JUSTICE OF THIEVES

C eles stood before the tiny door, almost imperceptible in the twilight. It looked rarely used, which suited her just fine. She fished a dull key out of her pocket and turned it over in her hands.

Will it still work?

This was her ace in the hole, one of the things that she had convinced Vincent to make for her all those years ago. But she had never used it. Not on the ill-fated Pure Diamond heist, nor the more recent and ultimately successful attempt. She had been saving it for this moment. Because once Wilhelm knew she had this sort of access, she would never get another shot.

Darkness had not yet set in but would soon. She was sure Vincent had succeeded. He knew the right people to talk to, and just being seen might have been enough. With any luck, she could make the right moves before Wilhelm had a chance to prepare.

When has luck been on your side? Really?

It did seem like she had more than her fair share of terrible luck. But she still had her freedom, and that was something. One more heist would be fine. Then she would retire for good.

Celes carefully inserted the key and turned it slowly. At first, there was no movement. Gradually she increased the force until the lock roughly clicked and the door jumped open slightly. Peering around she could see nobody looking and slipped inside.

The room was completely dark and silent. Celes let her eyes adjust and took it in.

Yes, just as expected.

It was a dusty and rarely used storage room. By itself, completely boring and unworthy of attention. But it was right next to another room of considerable interest. Celes padded through the room, taking care not to disturb anything. She expected this area of the mansion to be quieter but still didn't want to take any unnecessary risks. With each step, she moved further in, and her heart started to thump faster and faster. There was no denying it. She had dreamed of this opportunity for years.

At the far end of the room was a long corridor. Celes crept up to the edge and peeked out. There was nobody around. The room directly opposite called to her, and the door was left ajar.

Shouldn't it be locked?

After another glance, Celes stalked across and pressed up against the door. She quietened her breathing and strained to hear a noise. Nothing. She slowly pushed the door open, hearing a jarring squeak from the hinges. Wincing, she kept going, trying to keep the noise to a minimum. In a few moments, it was over, and she was inside.

Finally, after all these years.

The room was packed full of wooden crates, each stuffed with paper. Way too much paper. Impossible to look at with the available light. Celes took in the rest of the room, focusing on the walls. She noticed a few lanterns and moved closer to one to investigate. It was an oil lantern, and with a few adjustments, it was lit.

Oh, it would be a joy to accidentally knock over this lantern. But then I'd waste this opportunity. Ah well.

Celes sighed and refocused on her task. She picked up the nearest box and started rifling through.

Not even close, although they do seem to be of similar age. Keep looking.

She systematically worked her way around the room, increasing her speed as she went. Her plan only worked if she found what she needed. Suddenly she paused, feeling unsafe. She listened carefully and heard footsteps. Scrambling as quietly as possible, she doused the lantern and hid behind the door. The footsteps kept approaching at a steady pace. They stopped right at the doorway.

Celes held her breath, running different options through her head, should she be discovered. The presence lingered, waiting.

"Must be my imagination. He never uses this room anymore anyway. We should just torch it and be done with it," a male voice muttered. The footsteps continued once again. Celes kept listening until she couldn't hear them anymore.

The guard wants to torch this place? Lucky I'm not doing their job for them.

Celes waited as long as she could tolerate, then relit the lamp. Time was running out. If she didn't appear in the expected place, they would start to suspect something else was up. And she couldn't afford for that to happen.

Finally, she was done. Celes looked up and swore under her breath. She had searched the entire room and come up empty.

What's Plan B?

Celes stared at the door she had entered through and was considering what to do next when something caught her eye. A rough box, smaller than the rest. It was shoved up against the door and she hadn't noticed it when entering.

No way.

Celes ran over and rifled through the box. One of the papers stood out and she snatched it from the box and looked over it carefully.

Yes! I have it!

She folded the note and pocketed it, heading over to the lantern to extinguish it once again.

Why couldn't that have been the first box I opened? Oh right, because that would be too easy!

Celes shook her head then stopped in her tracks. She needed to get back into the right frame of mind, else she'd make a mistake.

Just hold it together a little longer.

She eased herself into the corridor and headed deeper into the mansion. After a few turns, she found herself in familiar spaces. None of which held any guards.

I suppose that's to be expected if they want to catch me red-handed.

Going by that logic, she needed to just head directly for her prize and the way would be clear. But it was too risky, and she needed to play the part even if they were making it easier. She took a circuitous route, checking for guards and thankfully noticing a few. Even if they were in odd places.

At least the place isn't completely deserted.

Celes slowly descended until she reached the lower level housing the secret vault.

Maybe not so secret now.

There were two guards posted outside, but the vault was open.

Maybe Wilhelm himself is inside?

Either way, she needed a way in, without causing too much of a fuss. It was time for something tried and tested. Celes removed a tiny smooth stone from her boot and tossed it across the room. It skidded and rattled, drawing the attention of the two guards.

"Movement over there, go check it out." One of the guards rolled his eyes and stomped off to investigate the noise. The other watched him go with a grin. Celes crept up behind him and grabbed the guard in a hold. The guard tried to call out, but the thief was too precise and too fast. She smothered any noise from his throat and soon he was collapsing to the floor. She dragged him into the shadows nearby and darted into the vault before the other guard noticed her.

The vault was much larger than she expected. Lanterns were lit along the walls, showing the array of riches. Celes almost gasped as she recognised the many artefacts.

"I thought I was a big-shot, but compared to this I was just dabbling," she whispered. Celes pushed the line of thought away and focused back on the task. The sound of the vault door slamming shut made her jump, and she looked around to see if she had been spotted.

"Come forth, Shadow Fox, I know you're hiding there," Wilhelm said. Celes composed herself and strode forward with feigned confidence. Something about the situation didn't feel right. Wilhelm stood at the end of the vault, holding the Silver Sceptre. To his right was another man that Celes didn't recognise.

"Ah, there you are. Right on cue. I'd like to introduce you to a good friend of mine, Magistrate Ronder." The magistrate nodded.

"Is he here to arrest you finally?"

"Quite the opposite. When Wilhelm told me he could give me the Shadow Fox, why I was willing to do quite a deal." Ronder chuckled and started advancing.

"You don't remember me, do you? I wasn't always a Magistrate. I used to work in the town guard. I was assigned to every single crime you committed. I failed in my duty, and today I can finally make things right."

"But Wilhelm is a bigger crook than I ever was! Look at this place!" Celes gestured at the many riches lining the walls.

"What can I say? Except that I caught the Shadow Fox red-handed, trying to steal from a local icon. That's all that needs to be said. Everything else here is irrelevant."

"But that Silver Sceptre, that's a matter of national security. Valrytir could start a war over that thing if they find out you have it!"

"Oh, they don't care anymore. It's been over twenty years! And they won't find out anyway." Ronder wore a wide grin and Wilhelm burst into laughter.

"I won't let you get away with this."

"I already have." Ronder joined Wilhelm in his laughter.

This is bad, they've caught me in the trap intended for them. Vincent better have remembered the original plan.

"Well, laugh it up. While you still can. Because my coming here was the easy option for you. And now we're going to invoke something a lot more painful."

"We? And how do you suppose you do that while you're in my custody?" Ronder sprayed spittle as he talked and ended it with a little laugh. He was quite pleased with himself. His face, however, suddenly changed when a large crash sounded at the entrance of the vault. A large section of the vault door fell in and Vincent stood before it, his Runesteel sword gleaming in the lantern light.

"We, as in me and the guy with the Runesteel sword. That's my cue." Celes turned and ran, after taking a moment to remember the looks on Wilhelm's and Ronder's faces.

"Impeccable timing," Celes said as she neared Vincent.

"Of course. Things not go to plan?"

"I'll explain later. My optimism got the better of me." Celes turned to the bewildered men and shouted, "when your world comes crashing down, just remember the Shadow Fox made it so!" Vincent stepped back and ushered Celes out. She ran through the vault entrance and Vincent sheathed his sword. The two of them quickly ascended the nearby stairs.

"I assume there's some sort of backup plan?"

"Of course. I assume you're still chummy with Mason?"

"Sure. If by chummy you mean I've not seen him in twenty years, severely disappointed him when I abandoned Valrytir and actively avoided him in Brangtur. Then yes, extremely so."

"Good, since we'll be dropping in tonight." Celes grinned and Vincent groaned. They faced no opposition leaving the mansion, the few guards that spotted them weren't sure how to react and did nothing.

Within minutes they had arrived at a large stately house. A single guard was posted outside the large gate.

"No visitors. Make an appointment in the morning." The guard yawned and waved them away. Vincent drew his sword. The guard stiffened and put his hand on his sword.

"Show him this. He will ask to see us immediately." Vincent handed the guard the sword. He looked it up and down, sceptical. But he eventually nodded, unlocked the gate and disappeared inside.

"I had a thing too," Celes said.

"This requires less explanation. You can talk to yours once we're inside."

"Such a show-off." Celes smirked at Vincent. He gave her a wry smile. True to form, the guard returned within a few minutes and wordlessly waved them in.

The house was beautifully but starkly furnished. The few pieces inside were a dark wood, immaculately finished but simple in design. A white-haired mountain of a man stood behind the dining table, examining Vincent's Runesteel sword.

"I'd recognise this work anywhere. Quite a surprise, considering how we parted ways. You said you'd never make another weapon. What are you playing at, Vincent?" Mason spoke without looking up, his deep voice echoing around the large room.

"My wife has some business with you, I only enabled the conversation," Mason grunted and looked at Celes.

"Out with it then. Vincent has already wasted enough of my time."

"I sincerely doubt that." Celes removed a piece of paper from her pocket and offered it to Mason.

"What's this? An inventory receipt?"

"Yes, for the Silver Sceptre. Note the date. Wouldn't you like to recover that?" Celes watched Mason's reaction. He looked up sharply.

"I can't ignore such an opportunity. Who has this?"

"Wilhelm. You're familiar with him, I suspect?"

"Of course. And you've seen the item?"

"Tonight, in fact. I had hoped to steal it back as a sign of good faith. But it seems the local magistrate Ronder is also in on this." Celes watched Mason's face harden.

"Valrytir will not stand for such treatment. We are supposed to be allies and friends."

"Then I suggest you move at once. They might get spooked and start moving things out. You may even find more national treasures, he's been collecting for a while." Celes watched with delight as Mason started pacing the room. He stopped suddenly and addressed them both.

"Thank you for this information. This should be enough to get me back home. I've done my best to... enjoy this posting, but I grow weary of it. If this plays out, you've redeemed yourself, Vincent." Mason held out the Runesteel sword and Vincent accepted the blade, sheathing it.

"But you shouldn't tease me with such weapons. That is a cruelty." Mason shook his head.

"My apologies, but time was against us and I needed your attention. As you see, this is not a matter that can wait."

"Indeed. Off with you, I have work to do."

"Thank you, and good night." Celes and Vincent turned to leave. Before they could walk out, Mason called out.

"Send my regards to the Shadow Fox."

16

OUTMANOEUVRED

Alrion walked over and sat down on the rock Fermur had been on. He carefully avoided the black residue and stared at the wall where Fermur had disappeared.

"From this close, you can see the entrance. That's quite clever." Alrion reached out and his hand touched no resistance.

"Well, the secret tunnel entrance checks out, if we believe that it goes into the fortress," Lara said.

"His information was good last time, it led us to Alyx. For whatever reason, he's been telling the truth."

What Fermur said is concerning. Are they just leading me on because they think I'll convert to their side?

"What did he say last time?" Branthor walked forward and glanced at Alrion then Lara.

"He told us about two options. One was the location of Alyx, another was a town that would be attacked," Alrion began.

"And both options were real. We chose to save Alyx."

"I see. Well, I'm not one to discount a chance to catch Rindale. There's four of us here, why not split up? We can follow both approaches." Branthor pointed to the group and let the question hang.

"That's not a bad idea. We meet where Rindale is, and there will be no escape." Lara looked thoughtful.

"It does reduce the risk of selecting the wrong option. If we set the groups accordingly it should be relatively safe." Alyx nodded along as she spoke.

"Time is crucial; therefore, I won't belabour the discussion. One wizard with each group then? Who should I take?" Alrion looked to Lara.

"Take Alyx. I'll go with Branthor."

"Are all fine with that?" Alrion gave each person a chance to respond, but Alyx and Branthor just nodded.

"I'll go up the guts. I'll draw their attention and Lara can sneak in behind me and avoid detection. It will put Rindale at ease, in a manner of speaking. He will feel like he knows my approach and skills," Branthor said.

"I actually think that could work," Lara said.

"Fine, we will explore the tunnel and find a way to meet you. Just remember, if you get there first, we need Rindale alive. He's too valuable to just slaughter." Alrion glared at Branthor. "No excuses, you can restrain yourself."

"That's fine, once he's secured, I have no qualms holding back. Just as long as you hold up your end of the bargain and deliver him to me."

"Fine." Alrion stood up off the rock and stepped towards the secret entrance. He could feel a cool breeze tickling his skin.

I still don't feel like I can trust Branthor. Hopefully, Lara can keep him in check.

Alrion felt a touch on his shoulder

"Take care and take your time. There might be traps." Lara leaned in and gave him a quick hug.

"Thanks, you too. Don't let him riot too much."

"Of course. I have a few tricks if I need them." Lara gave him a wicked smile.

"See you on the other side." Branthor started walking off and Lara rushed off to join him.

"Let's go investigate this tunnel." Alrion started to move but felt Alyx holding him back.

"Me first. You can provide light." Alyx stepped inside and Alrion shrugged and joined her. He created a ball of light and hung it above them. He adjusted the size and glow to illuminate them and a short distance ahead.

"Let me know if you need more, but I assumed we didn't want to create too much of a beacon."

"This is fine." Alyx walked on. Alrion looked around at the tunnel. It seemed to be a natural formation. At least originally. The ground was well worn from footsteps.

"What a strange tunnel, it doesn't look man-made," Alrion said.

"Perhaps the fortress was built in that location for this reason. It had a dedicated exit."

"Perhaps." Alrion walked a bit further but felt something strange from Alyx. It had been bugging him the whole time.

"Alyx, how much do you remember of your time with them?"

"Very little. I was like a passenger encased in fog. Occasionally I could grasp glimpses of what was happening."

"But you remember Fermur?"

"Not clearly. But he is familiar? Does that make sense?" Alyx walked faster and Alrion almost stumbled on an errant rock trying to keep up.

"Then why does he make you so angry? We could all see it." Alrion paid more attention to the path as he waited for a response. There was silence for a long time.

"It's not so much that creature, although he is repulsive. It is what he means. And he is one of their leaders, even if he's used for errands."

"Shouldn't you pity him then? Knowing what it's like to be used?"

"I should but I cannot. I'm sorry, that's all I have to say." Alyx went quiet and Alrion decided not to pursue it.

I'm not sure what to make of them. What if that had happened to me? How would I want to be treated?

The cavern began to change and have more human elements. Wooden planks to smooth out certain sections of the ground where there were dips or holes. A few handrails here and there. Soon enough, there were supporting structures and frames to no doubt maintain the stability of the tunnel.

"This isn't just a secret passage. This looks well-trafficked," Alrion said.

"I agree. It just depends on how frequently it is used, and by whom. If we're lucky, Rindale has not told many about it."

"True." Alrion decided not to talk too much, in case they drew attention. After a few more turns they encountered a large wooden door with metal handles.

"This must be where it connects to the fortress." Alrion reached out, but Alyx pushed his hand away.

"Wait. Let me." Alyx gently touched the door, feeling it all over. She suddenly opened a tiny panel and Alrion heard a metallic click.

"It should be open now." Alyx gently pulled the door and it opened with a creak. There were torches lit inside, showing a stone hallway and steps leading up.

"Here we are. Did you know about that?" Alrion said.

"No, I just had a feeling." Alyx entered the fortress, holding the door for Alrion. He let it close gently behind him.

"And here we go." Alrion followed Alyx's lead as they crept through the bowels of the fortress. It was cold and felt damp.

"I doubt it's as easy to drop in on Rindale as Fermur said," Alrion muttered.

"Of course not. But as Lara pointed out, the information is good. Let's just hope we can capitalise on it." Alyx drew the Runesteel blade and stalked forward. They continued along a corridor, Alrion noting nothing of interest along the walls. Finally, they came to an intersection with two options: left or right.

"We have a fifty-fifty chance of picking the right option," Alyx said.

"Wait a moment. Let me think." Alrion remembered what Branthor had said about sending wizards. There was a chance that he could do it as well. Surely the presence of any wizards would be a sign of Rindale's location.

Alrion closed his eyes and imagined his Spark. He held onto the feeling then went searching for something like it. He sensed something out there but couldn't quite figure it out.

"I'm at a loss. Any ideas?" Before Alyx could speak, a large boom sounded in the distance and seemed to send shockwaves through the fortress. The ceiling rattled, and flakes of stone fell from the ceiling.

"That definitely came from that direction." Alyx pointed to the left tunnel.

"Agreed. I hope that's not Branthor."

"I admit I don't know the man that well, but he doesn't seem known for his tact."

"No, and he seems to be worse after being cured." Alrion shook his head slowly and followed Alyx. The tunnel they had selected was the same as the main corridor. All built in stone and with regular torches, but nothing else of interest. They continued at the same pace, looking for signs of life or the enemy. Finally, they came to another intersection.

"Do you want to wait for more signals?" Alyx said.

"No, we need to press on. I'm feeling quite nervous about this." Alrion looked left, then right. Nothing was visibly different.

"Let's go right." Alrion pointed and Alyx started off. She didn't even question his direction.

I hope I picked right. I don't even know what I based that on.

Sounds started to echo through to them. Voices, banging, and other general commotion. Each time a new sound came through they paused, but there was no immediate danger and no way to tell where exactly the sound had come from.

"I suspect we should just press on."

"Agreed. Let's see where this takes us." Alrion continued, the slow progress was agonising. He kept imagining what Branthor was doing, and none of it was good.

Please be safe, Lara.

"Here's something." Alyx stopped and let Alrion take it in. Ahead was a large metal door. It looked incredibly strong and thick. Before it, on each side of the corridor, looked like smaller doors leading to rooms.

"Good. Let's explore the smaller rooms then investigate the big door. Maybe it'll lead to Rindale?"

"Not with our luck, but I won't discount it." Alyx took off with a bit more speed and Alrion stayed close behind. Once they reached the rooms, Alrion waited behind and Alyx crept into each one, checking for enemies.

"Nothing but boring supplies. Maybe these tunnels are for deliveries after all?"

"Perhaps. But that door is something." Alrion walked up and examined it at close range. There was a keyhole in the middle, but otherwise, it was quite solid. It seemed even sturdier than he imagined.

"We need a way inside."

"True. But first, we need a way to see what's on the other side," Alyx said.

"I'll see what I can do." Alrion leaned close to the keyhole and had a look inside. It was pitch-black and there seemed to be something restricting the light from the other side. But if he concentrated, he thought he could hear something.

Think. You've amplified your voice before, maybe you can do something here.

Alrion gathered his Spark and imagined creating a wedge of force that he could stuff into the keyhole that would amplify the sounds coming through. He finished the visualisation and finalised the spell. At first, nothing, then a few whispers.

"Did you do something?" Alyx said.

"I think so, but it needs more work." Alrion tried increasing the volume of the spell. Nothing happened. He injected more and more Spark into it. Words started to come through.

"It's up to you, Branthor, what will you do?" a male voice said.

"Recognise that?" Alrion said.

"Not sure, maybe?"

"I won't let you get away," Branthor said. The anger in his voice was obvious.

"We need to get in there before he does something rash." Alrion stepped back and looked at the door.

Are there any weak points?

"I doubt we can get through this with any subtlety unless you can lockpick?" Alyx paced around the door, examining it.

"I could maybe destroy the surrounds or cut a hole in the door. Hmm."

"You can't escape me!" Branthor shouted.

"Time's running out." Alyx stood back and braced herself.

No choice now, we need to get in there.

Alrion built up his Spark and created a fire spell. He shot rays of extreme heat around the edges of the door, burning right through. He outlined the shape of the door and, once he had finished, the weight of the door, now free from the hinges and stonework, fell in with a crash. Smoke and rubble went everywhere. As soon as it was possible Alyx darted in and Alrion followed. They clambered over the remains of the door into the massive room beyond.

There seemed to be a lot more rubble than expected. Looking around the room, Alrion saw Branthor and Lara emerge unscathed.

"There you are," Lara said. She had a strange expression that Alrion couldn't quite pick.

"You imbecile, you ruined everything," Branthor roared.

"Where is he?"

"Who knows? He escaped through a Wizard Gate and you DESTROYED IT!" Branthor waved his arms in frustration and stormed off.

"A Wizard Gate? We heard they were getting away, so I had to act. Branthor sounded like he was going to kill the lot of them!"

"He was actually playing along. He wanted them to escape so we could follow them to their real base," Lara said quietly. Alrion looked from her to Branthor.

Oh no. I have ruined things. Rindale escaped because of me.

"I'm sorry, I had no idea."

"Amateur! I followed your rules, I could have wiped him out."

"How was I supposed to know that a Wizard Gate was here, let alone what one is!"

"If you had paid attention, you would have felt it. You sensed enough to find your way." Branthor threw his hands up in despair and a nearby fallen chunk of stone disintegrated.

"So, we got good information. But it was incomplete. Dangerously so," Alrion said. He tried to make out what from the rubble was this supposed Wizard Gate.

"What else should we expect?" Lara said. Alrion looked to Alyx. She had sheathed her sword but was looking at Branthor warily.

"You acted on instinct, which is usually better than not acting. Tough luck on this one. There's a lesson to be had."

Alrion knew she was right. But in the moment, he couldn't think of it that way. Branthor's insults were hurting too much. Mostly because they had a lot of truth in them.

17

A FAMILIAR FACE

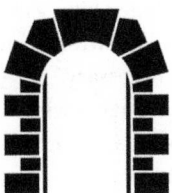

C eles pulled the horse up, surveying the land before her. Beyond the rolling hills, she saw the spires of an odd little city.

"Is that Paperton down there?"

"The very same. We're not far now, although we should take our time on the descent."

"When were you here last?"

"A long time ago. I had to skip it when Alrion journeyed there. Had I known the dangers he would face, I would have chosen differently." Vincent looked dismayed as he recalled. He was acting a lot more thoughtful lately and reflecting a lot. Even at times being nostalgic.

"You know, I've been thinking. We didn't need to pass through Brangtur. In fact, given our recent history, it was actually a risk to do so."

"We've got a pretty good record of not being detained there. Low risk, don't you think?" Vincent gave her a quick grin.

"But not without risk. You did that purposefully. Why?'

"An incentive to make this long journey worthwhile, remember?"

"No, that's not it. I'll get the answer, you may as well just tell me." Celes gave Vincent her best direct glare. He actually laughed but quickly recovered.

"I wanted to tie up some loose ends and have a little adventure with you. Everything has been about Alrion and his quest, I thought it would be nice to do something for us on the way." Vincent stared out towards Paperton.

He does look very thoughtful. What's going on?

"But why now?" Vincent started to speak but paused. He began after a little while.

"We don't know how this quest will end. We've all been in incredible danger at one time or another. Things are not going to get easier. We lost Falric on the path to Paperton. There's a chance that we're not all going to journey home at the end."

"That's rather defeatist of you, isn't it? We always scrape through!" Celes was alarmed by the tone.

He's always optimistic and supportive. There's definitely something going on. And he's all reflective too and tying up loose ends.

"What aren't you telling me? Is there more to this that you aren't saying?" Celes crossed her arms and challenged him. Vincent sighed.

"It's just a feeling. Hopefully, I'm wrong, but what we did back there was completely right and completely necessary."

"That's at least something I can agree with. Let's just hurry up, I can get the truth out of you later." Celes spurred her horse on and took the lead. Vincent quickly caught up and matched her speed.

Just a feeling? We'll see about that.

The ride to Paperton was swift and easy. The paths were well-maintained, and even the route down to the town was enjoyable, even if they did need to occasionally pull the horses up to be safe. Celes's first impression of the town was that it looked like a mess of papers with ants crawling all over.

"Such a literal name," she muttered.

"It's perfect, isn't it? Hasn't changed at all." Vincent was smiling.

"I didn't take you for a scholar."

"Oh, I'm not, but they do have a wealth of knowledge here on blacksmithing. It's amazing."

"Of course they do." Celes laughed at her husband and he shrugged. As they reached the town, they saw quite a few people out and about. But none really paid them any attention.

"I expected scholars to be more sedate. And inquisitive." Celes looked at the people with wonder.

"They're all incredibly busy. Or busy looking like they are busy. They don't need to know about us yet."

"Very different. Do you know how to get to the Pool of Knowledge?"

"Alrion explained how he accessed it, but we won't fare well just trying to sneak in. We better announce ourselves and follow the proper channels. I think there's an administrative office around here somewhere." Vincent took the lead and Celes was happy to let him navigate through the completely haphazard assortment of buildings.

"Let's try in here." Vincent held the door open and Celes stepped inside. It was a relatively small building with a large desk in the entry and an old couple sat behind the desk. Both wore thick glasses and were inspecting stacks of paper.

"Excuse me," Vincent said. There was no response. He repeated himself, "Excuse me."

"We need to visit your Pool of Knowledge," Celes said. The old woman looked up and adjusted her glasses. She stared at Celes for a full two seconds before bursting into laughter.

"Oh, that's a good one. Did you hear that, Earl?"

"Hear what, Mona?"

"These people want to visit the Pool of Knowledge!"

"Ha! Fairy tales!" Earl didn't even look up but did bury himself deeper in the paperwork.

"I'm happy to fill out the required paperwork. But I don't really have time for games, my son is a wizard and was here recently and drank from the Pool. He needs help accessing critical information." Vincent waited after he spoke. Celes watched the older couple carefully and noticed them discreetly pass a look between them.

"Earl, do you have someone who can set these people straight?" Mona said. Earl sighed.

"Fine, I'll interrupt my work again." Earl rose slowly, stepped around the desk carefully and marched out of the building.

"We really don't want to cause any trouble, but we're here on quite an urgent need."

"Sure, sure. Just wait on those chairs." Mona pointed to two wooden chairs, well-worn without any cushions. Vincent and Celes sat down and waited.

A while later Earl returned, with a much younger man. He was short in stature and quiet and looked at Vincent and Celes thoughtfully.

Now, he looks like a scholar.

"Nice to meet you. My name is Caleb and I'm here to assist with your enquiry."

"Hi, Caleb. I am here on behalf of my son Alrion. He's a wizard who visited you recently," Vincent said.

"Is that so?"

"Yes. He spoke highly of the citizens of Paperton and their sacred duty of protecting the Pool of Knowledge. However, we need your help. Perhaps you can direct us to someone who can confirm the information I have just provided."

"Is there anything more you can say, to assist?"

"Well, Alrion was sent here by his mentor, Falric, a master wizard. Unfortunately, Falric passed away. But Alrion used Falric's spellbook as proof of his claims."

"Do you also have the spellbook with you?"

"No. I do not."

"Were you also acquainted with this wizard, Falric?"

"Yes, we travelled together but were separated before Alrion arrived at Paperton." Vincent waited for another question, but there was nothing. Caleb closed his eyes and appeared to be thinking.

"When can we talk to someone who can help us?" Celes said, exasperated.

"I apologise, but I must fulfil my duty and ask the appropriate questions. This process assists us both. Without it, I cannot verify your story and introduce you to the right person to further your query."

"Very well," Celes grumbled.

"However, I have heard enough to continue your application. Please follow me." Caleb gestured to the door and immediately left. Celes looked at her husband, who just shrugged, and held open the door for her. Caleb was waiting for them outside. He began walking at once.

"It won't take long, please keep up." Caleb walked at a brisk pace, weaving through the wandering scholars on the streets. They seemed to be heading to a rather large building at one end of the town.

"I think that's the main hall," Vincent said.

"Makes sense. Does that sound like the right place to be going?"

"Definitely." Vincent looked optimistic so Celes decided to keep her hopes up.

Maybe this next person can help us break through all the bureaucracy.

"This is the main hall. Visitors are not normally allowed within, but you seem quite sure of your story." Caleb pushed open the giant doors and kept walking, not waiting for them. Vincent and Celes rushed through and kept pace with the shorter scholar.

"Quite a grand hall." Celes looked up at the ceiling and took in the immense size. They were heading towards a large stage at the back. However, rather than step up to the stage, they turned and entered an old wooden door to the side.

"Please step inside." Caleb waited next to the door but did not enter. Vincent entered first, then Celes. Inside was a small chamber with a scholar in robes behind a desk. He looked up at them.

"Who brought you?" he said.

"Caleb," Vincent replied. The scholar nodded.

"Go on through." He waved them over to a passage in the back of the room. Vincent went first and Celes whispered her thanks as they passed by the scholar. After a short walk, they entered a much larger room. Bookcases lined the shelves, each one stuffed with books in every possible orientation. A ladder was propped up against one bookshelf. In the centre of the room, an old man with a brown robe sat writing. The hood was up, obscuring his face. He kept writing, not acknowledging their presence. After they stood for a few moments, the man put his quill down and looked up.

"Not going to say hello?" he said. Celes gasped and ran up.

"Falric? You're alive!"

Falric gave her a wry smile. He looked over at Vincent.

"Good to see you both. Welcome to Paperton."

"It's good to see you too. A lovely surprise. But you better start explaining what you are doing here." Vincent didn't look impressed after the initial shock.

18

CHANGE IN APPROACH

Alrion looked around the room, his mind reeling with what had just happened. He tried to think of what to do next, and his mind was blank. Lara gave him a reassuring smile, but he knew that it was just for support. She knew that he had blown it too. Branthor finished his rant and wandered back. He had a strange grin on his face.

"Alrion, Alrion, Alrion. What are we going to do now?"

"I don't know. That's what you expected, right?"

"Of course, we just lost our lead. But it was the one they gave us. Always trouble that. I think something else is required." Branthor eyed off Lara and Alyx.

"You two can search this fortress for any clues. I doubt Rindale left anything, he's a careful operator. But we need to know. Alrion and I need to do some creative planning. What do you say?" Branthor waited for a response.

That's not a bad idea. Maybe I should listen to what he has to say. We can't keep ignoring each other and trying to work separately.

"Sure, let's try that. Please meet us back at the inn with your findings."

"We'll leave no stone unturned." Lara led Alyx to the opposite end of the room.

"Shall we take the secret tunnel? I'd love to see it."

"If you must." Alrion started picking his way over the rubble and they started down the tunnel to return to town.

"Nice work with the door, by the way, that was very clean." Branthor noted the cuts in the stonework as they entered the tunnel.

"You didn't seem so impressed a few minutes ago."

"I was caught up in the moment. I expected more awareness, but your precision was good. Credit where credit is due."

"Sure. Thanks." Alrion continued walking, after giving Branthor an odd look. *I can't figure this guy out. He's all over the place.*

"Not much to this tunnel, is there?" Branthor said as they progressed.

"No, the only thing to note is over there." Alrion pointed to the storage rooms and Branthor quickly checked them out.

"Ah, secret supply tunnel. Nice one. Nothing more needs to be said."

"Fair enough. I'm amazed it didn't collapse while I was in it."

"And why would that be?"

"Whatever you did rocked the entire place. Stone was falling from the ceiling." Alrion looked at Branthor and the wizard was grinning.

"Pretty amazing, yes? And note the tunnel did not collapse. I didn't even disrupt the Wizard Gate."

"Are they quite sensitive?"

"Not really, but I wasn't sure exactly where it was." Alrion stopped walking.

"You didn't know where it was, but you berated me for not knowing about it?"

"Precisely. You didn't detect it, you were practically on top of it. There's quite a difference." Branthor resumed walking and Alrion sighed.

"You have much to learn." Alrion shook his head and kept walking.

The trip back to town was uneventful, but Alrion was curious where Branthor was heading. It wasn't too surprising when they ended up back at the inn.

"We've done this, haven't we?" Alrion said.

"No, that was the prelude. The warmup. This is the main event. Take a seat." Branthor didn't specify where, he just sped over to the innkeeper. Alrion picked a table in the corner. The plump seat was damaged and sagging, but the location was good. It provided a wide view of the rest of the inn. He saw Branthor negotiating with the innkeeper. Whatever it was about, the innkeeper seemed quite dissatisfied. Finally, Branthor produced a rather hefty sack of coins and the innkeeper relented. Branthor ran back with excitement, brandishing a nondescript brown bottle.

"Ah, we are in luck. Managed to score the innkeeper's special reserve. This stuff will put hair on your chest, and other places I imagine."

"I sincerely doubt that."

"I can put a spell on the bottle?" Branthor winked.

"Just open it." Branthor stood and fetched a few glasses from the bar and returned, pouring two thumb-widths in both glasses.

"First glass, down the hatch. We can sip the rest."

"This is going to help us. Two wizards getting drunk?"

"You'll thank me later." Branthor lifted his glass and waited for Alrion. The young wizard raised his, they clinked glasses and quickly downed the contents.

Alrion's throat burned away into nothing, leaving him wondering if he'd even manage to swallow anything ever again. The pain eventually subsided, leaving a warm glow.

"That was ridiculous!" Alrion barely squeezed the words out, his voice hoarse and a coughing fit followed soon after. Branthor laughed and slapped Alrion on the back.

"Good on you for not lessening the impact."

"I'm not going to give you the satisfaction of commenting on that."

"Very well." Branthor chuckled, and Alrion could tell that the wizard had probably done something to reduce the effect of the alcohol.

"Why don't you start with your ideas," Alrion said carefully, trying to avoid another coughing fit. Branthor refilled both glasses to the same point. He pointed to the glasses and they both had a sip. It still burned terribly, but not as bad.

"We'll get to that. But first, I think we need to understand each other a bit more. That will improve our cooperation."

"Yeah, you can explain how you did all that evil stuff and can look at yourself in the mirror."

"I see the special reserve is already working. Happy to discuss my own short-comings, but right after you answer this: why do you need information from me on the location of the source of the Blight?" Branthor had an intensely serious look on his face which surprised Alrion.

"Why? Because that's where I need to go. You know that."

"Ah-hah, yes now we're getting to it. Yes, I know the location. I know the purpose, the general workings of the spell too. Because I drank from the Pool of Knowledge. As did you. Why don't you know?" Branthor kept his gaze fixated on Alrion. The younger wizard looked away and took another sip of the drink.

"That detail has not been revealed to me yet."

"Obviously. I learned a bit about how the Pool works, from those guardians. Mostly they threw it in my face as reasons why I would fail, but it was useful all the same. The short explanation is that your mind brings out the information when you need it."

"Are you saying I don't need it?"

"Well, you reached the Pool. You completed that Vault of Silence trial and pulled a big ol' trick afterwards. And you cured me. That sounds like you should be ready. Why aren't you?" Branthor downed the rest of his drink and poured another. Alrion was floored.

What is he getting at? Does he know why?

"I don't know why. You tell me."

"Oh, I think you do. I can only guess. Why can't you complete your quest? Why, Alrion?"

"I don't know why. Lucky you can tell me what I need to know."

"No, not this time. We have a deal, so I will eventually. But you don't need me. Why? Why? Why? Why can't you see it!"

"Because I'm not good enough. I'm not ready," Alrion blurted out, louder than he expected. He looked around the room sheepishly. Nobody seemed to notice.

"And why is that? You managed to beat me without any real training. You have all that knowledge in your head. Why not?" Branthor kept pushing. Alrion was tired and frustrated.

"Because I keep failing people. Falric was killed, by you no less. Alyx was infected then turned. And transformed into the Skull Queen. My grandmother sacrificed herself to save me. I sacrificed a whole town to save Alyx. The list goes on." Alrion slumped down in the chair and sipped the drink again. It was empty and Branthor refilled it. He leaned back finally, looking satisfied.

"You're taking it all too personally." Branthor took a deep swig of his drink. "And don't get hung up on Falric. That old paper-pusher went down far too easily. I wasn't even trying!"

"That's not helping."

"Listen, kid. I'm not your mentor, not cut out for it. At least Falric seemed to be good at that. But it doesn't take a genius to see what's going on here. You need to sort this out, or you'll fail. Because I can tell you the location, but if you don't correct this..."

"Then I'll never figure out the rest of the spell?"

"Precisely. And take it from me, you're going to want to know the full details before you step in there." Branthor leaned back and closed his eyes, deep in thought.

"That's all you're going to say?"

"Yes. Perhaps we should move on to discussing our plans for Rindale?"

"What about you, though? Why are you the way you are? You don't get to change topic so easily."

"What's there to say? Sometimes people get broken one too many times. Now I just want to get my revenge on those who have wronged me."

"Rindale?"

"Yes, he's my main target. There were others responsible, but of lesser importance." Branthor finished his drink once again and refilled it.

"Like who?"

"Your family."

"My family?" Alrion drained his glass and Branthor quickly added more from the bottle.

"Your grandfather, your father to a lesser extent. More recently you've been a thorn in my side. Your mother, well she seems alright actually." Branthor laughed.

"You're twisted."

"I told you, didn't I?" Branthor sighed. "Today is not a day for my darkness." Branthor slammed down the drink in his glass and lounged back, his eyes closed.

"The plans then. We need another way to track down Rindale, one that we trust."

"I doubt we can track the Shade Wizards again," Branthor added.

"Maybe not, I'm not sure if they caught on to that as an approach. But if they were training them here, we may have less luck." Alrion took a sip of his drink.

"Do we know anybody that can get to Rindale." Branthor kept his eyes closed.

"Not really. We know Fermur, but he's not quite in the trustworthy camp." Branthor sat up and opened his eyes.

"Yes, but he could be persuaded to speak something that we can trust in a relative sense, yes?"

"If we had no other options."

"Do we have other options?" Branthor stared at Alrion.

"None come to mind."

"Then we should see what your companions think." Branthor made himself comfortable, leaning back in the seat and assuming a sleeping position.

"You're going to nap?"

"Why not? You can keep drinking if you want." Branthor pushed the bottle closer to Alrion and closed his eyes. Within moments, Alrion could hear him snoring.

"I'll never understand him," Alrion muttered under his breath. He tried to think of alternative options while waiting for his friends.

Hours later, Alyx and Lara stumbled into the inn, weary. They sat down roughly next to the wizards.

"Any luck?" Alrion said.

"No. We combed that place, and it was picked clean. I think Rindale was ready and waiting." Lara looked to Alyx who shook her head.

"I agree. It was a fool's errand. But we eliminated the possibility."

"Alrion had a bright idea," Branthor added. He didn't change position, but he did open his eyes.

"Which is?" Lara said, prompting Alrion to speak. But Branthor jumped in.

"Fermur. He's the only one that seems to know of Rindale's movements. We just need to figure out a way to get information from him that is complete and trustworthy."

"No easy task," Lara said.

"And we need to figure out where he is. I'm not sure stumbling around until we find the trail he left for us is the most prudent option." Alyx was looking over at the bar as she spoke.

"Hold that thought." Branthor jumped out of his chair and rushed over to the bar. He returned swiftly with two new glasses. Placing them before Lara and Alyx he filled them to the same level he had been doing previously. Lara smelled the liquid.

"You've been drinking this? How bad is it?"

"I thought I would lose my ability to speak," Alrion said. Lara laughed.

"You better not drink it, he promoted it as putting hair on your chest." Alrion laughed and Lara smirked, taking a swig. She made a pained face and Alrion could watch her forcing it down. Alyx threw it down like water and looked bored.

"Great, great! Good teamwork, all," Branthor said. "In the interests of team-work, I thought it helpful to mention that I can track Fermur's location." Alrion stared at Branthor.

"How?"

"When we met earlier, I imbued a speck of dust with a unique signature from my Spark and attached it to his leg in a way that will not come off." Bran-thor poured himself another glass and took a sip.

"You started tracking Fermur but didn't think it worth mentioning until now?" Alrion said, anger building in his voice.

"It's not as simple as that, and I didn't want to jump to conclusions. Besides, we just did some valuable bonding."

"You're impossible!"

"Truly. But, as I said, I am a master wizard who has visited the Pool of Knowl-edge." Branthor shrugged.

"All that aside, it means we have a lead on Rindale and a way to find him. We just need to figure out how to get what we need from Fermur," Lara said. Alyx grunted, and Alrion didn't like the expression on her face.

This could get ugly.

19

CAPTURING THE WIND

A lrion waited for silence before speaking.

"I think the most important question, to begin with, is: where is Fermur now?"

"That will take some pinpointing," Branthor said. Alrion kept his gaze on the older wizard.

"You'll need to give us something to both back up your claim and begin our planning," Lara said.

"Very well." Branthor closed his eyes. His breathing slowed, and he looked deep in concentration. After a few minutes, his eyes snapped open.

"There's another town not too far away. He seems to be circling it but not staying put. My guess is that he's waiting for something and is staying out of sight." Branthor gave Lara a smirk.

"Town have a name?" Alrion said.

"Not sure, but I can see how to get there."

"Good enough to start with. We need a way to deal with his speed once we get there." Lara started drumming her fingers on the table.

"Alyx, I remember you being good with a whip. Does that extend to ropes and other similar items?" Branthor asked.

"Yes, of course."

"That's our best bet of restraining him. I don't believe he's that strong, if we can get enough steel chain around him, he won't get away."

"I can handle that, provided he is stationary or moving at a walking pace," Alyx said.

"Maybe we can just ask him nicely?" Lara chuckled.

"I might be able to catch him with a force spell," Alrion mused.

"That's too obvious, but a good idea." Branthor poured himself another drink and slowly drained it.

"You know, I wonder if you can pull a similar trick like you did back at the desert temple. You trapped me quite handily."

"Yes, you never saw that coming. I'm not sure though."

"Why not?"

"At the time I had just cleared the trial, and I think the location of the temple somehow amplified the effects."

"We don't need something of the same magnitude. Just enough to disrupt that speedster." Branthor looked to Alyx and Lara for support.

"If you can do something on a smaller scale, that will help."

"Maybe focus more on slowing him down rather than trapping him?" Alyx added.

"Happy to try, but we need a proper test. We can't waste the next opportunity." Alrion finished his drink and blocked Branthor from adding more.

"A test!" Branthor stood immediately, his chair falling behind him. He scooped up the bottle of alcohol and tucked it into his robe.

"No time like right now," Alrion muttered. He stood a little shakily and eagerly accepted a steady hand from Alyx.

"You have a sobering up spell?" Lara said to Branthor.

"No, that would ruin my fun. Follow me." Branthor left the inn and strode away with confidence. The light was fading but he didn't seem bothered. They walked down the path a little until Branthor led them into a clearing.

"This will do." With a wave of his arm, four big balls of light appeared and ascended into the corners of the clearing, bathing the area in bright light.

"How is this supposed to work?" Alrion said.

"I'll create a projectile of the appropriate speed. Alyx here will…" Branthor stopped suddenly. "Alyx will go back to town and find a suitable steel chain then return." Alyx sighed and left.

"You will practise slowing down the projectile. Once that is working, Alyx will practise catching it with the steel chain."

"How should I slow it down then?"

"Use your Will or whatever you call it. I'll leave the mechanics up to you."

"And what about me?" Lara said.

"You can tell us what we're doing wrong."

"Happy to." Lara winked at Alrion. He nodded and thought about the test.

I need to alter reality so that the projectile moves slower. But it will be quite hard to focus on it. Maybe I can alter the properties of the area it is going to move through, and that might work better.

"I have an idea of how this will work, but let's start with something small."

Alrion looked around for a small stone. Branthor clicked his fingers and a stone floated in front of Alrion.

"Was that absolutely necessary?"

"Yes. Now tell me where to send it." Alrion walked into the middle of the clearing. He picked up a stick and drew a large circle in the dirt. He stepped over beside the circle.

"Send it through here. You may want to catch it on the other side, regardless of what I manage to do to it."

"Sure. Let me know when you are ready."

"Wait. Before you do it, show me how fast you think it should be," Lara said to Branthor. He sent the rock flying across the space and it stopped just past the circle Alrion had drawn.

"It's not fast enough. Try again." Lara pointed back to the starting position. Branthor sent the stone flying again, so fast it was barely visible.

"Too fast, slow it down a bit." The stone floated back to the start position and flew again. Slower, but still barely perceptible.

"That's it. Alrion, do you agree?"

"Looks about right to me." Alrion wondered how he was going to slow it down so much. But then he remembered it was just a small stone. He started to prepare his mind. He created the visualisation, that the space within the circle was different. The air was thicker and slowed everything down.

"Go now." The stone flashed by as before.

"Nothing happened," Lara said. Alrion nodded. He needed to focus more.

Remember, you aren't thinking about it, you're adjusting reality. Remaking it as you need.

"Again." The stone flew but something happened. It seemed to alter its trajectory slightly and slow down. But it was still incredibly fast.

"Something happened there. What were you doing?" Lara said.

"I made the air thicker and slower."

"I don't think you should mess with the air. What if we're breathing it?"

"Good advice there," Branthor added. Alrion pondered that.

"You're right. I don't think I need that detail anyway. Let's try again." Alrion held his hand up to make them wait. He concentrated on changing the reality within the circle, so that everything moved slower. Much much slower. Then he clicked his fingers and knew that it was so. He let his hand down and nodded to Branthor. The projectile flew with incredible speed and, amazingly, once it passed into the circle it moved in slow motion. As soon as it exited the circle it sped up quickly until Branthor stopped it.

"Now that, that can work." Branthor sounded impressed and a little surprised. Lara beamed up a smile.

"That's incredible."

"I have surprised myself a little, to be honest." Alrion wiped away a bead of sweat on his brow. Even though he wasn't expending as much direct concentration, the effort was taking its toll.

"This will be tricky to maintain for long."

"Luckily I'm back with the steel chain." Alyx had the chain coiled around one arm, with a length trailing down and almost touching the ground. She expertly flicked the chain around, doing circles and other movements so fast that the chain was a blur.

"Try it in the circle." Lara pointed. Alyx walked over without pausing her display of skill. She flicked the chain across the circle boundary and part of the chain moved very fast, whilst the other part moved very slow.

"This is hard to judge." Alyx moved within the circle. As soon as she did, she also moved in slow motion. She immediately left the circle. Alrion dropped to his knees and was short of breath.

"That was quite an experience. What you did is great, but we can't be within that space."

"Agreed." Alrion paused and tried to catch his breath. "Influencing you was a huge burden. We need to be smart about this. I'll struggle with Fermur, for sure."

"Don't worry we can trial it more tonight."

"And I can start using human-sized rocks." Branthor actually sounded excited.

One thing's for sure, I'm going to sleep well after this.

Alrion awoke with a terrible headache. Cradling his head, he looked around the room and barely recognised it. Lara was leaning against the wall next to the doorway and turned to look at him.

"You're up. How are you feeling?"

"Terrible." Alrion remained seated, he didn't trust himself just yet.

"Branthor expected this. Said you've probably never worked that hard in your life."

"He would say that." Alrion forced himself up and he was steadier than expected. He tried focusing some Soul Power and directing it into his head. Maybe that would help.

"Grab some bread on the way and join us outside. We need to head out immediately." Lara darted out of the room and Alrion started moving too. Each step felt like his head was pounding with the same rhythm, but he kept his momentum. Slowly but surely, he did feel better, and once he emerged downstairs into the inn, he felt relatively normal. Grabbing a bread with seeds on top that looked like there was cheese inside, he moved swiftly through the empty room and emerged into the sunlight.

"Good morning. Just." Branthor acknowledged Alrion with a slight nod and mounted his horse. Lara and Alyx were already mounted. Alrion saw what was to be his horse, and took his time getting on. Luckily, his body seemed fine and he eased into the saddle. Retrieving the bread he had selected, he took a big bite.

Wow, I'm really hungry.

"We need to get a move on, our quarry hasn't moved but he's fast and may take flight at any time." Branthor spurred his horse on and took off.

"I see you've been busy," Alrion said to Lara.

"Your recovery was critical for the success of the plan, so we did what we could to expedite things once you were ready. Approved?"

"Yes, this is quite delicious." Alrion quickly polished off the rest of the bread.

"Did you even chew that?"

"Probably. Do you think this will work?" Alrion gave Lara a long glance.

"Probably. Now let's keep moving, we can discuss tactics when we're closer."

"No problem." Alrion focused on the ride and let his thoughts wander. But he didn't let them dwell on the encounter ahead.

Within a few hours, they could see the town.

"There she is, the quaint little town of Quagmire." Branthor showed off the town with a flourish of his hands.

"Sounds delightful," Lara said.

"It's quite apt, isn't it? The name?" Branthor responded with a chuckle.

"Let's hope so," Alyx grunted.

"Where's Fermur?" Alrion went straight to the point.

"Hold on." Branthor closed his eyes again. Alrion thought about probing Branthor on the spell some more but opted to do it at another time. Within moments, the master wizard snapped his eyes open.

"There's a field at the edge of the town. Fermur is sitting in the middle."

"Doesn't like surprises, does he?" Lara said.

"No, I suppose he likes to use his speed. If anyone approaches, he's got ample time to flee, often before they've even spotted him." Branthor stroked his chin.

"We have to bank on the fact that he wants to talk to us and feels safe. I can't be effective at long distance," Alrion said.

"Then let's make ourselves known. If we don't hide our approach he may feel more in control." Alyx drew her sword and started moving forward. The rest followed. They skirted the edge of the town, battling through shrubs and plants until they found a serviceable path. They continued in silence.

Alrion ran through the plan over and over in his mind. It was a good plan, and they had practised it well. But he still wasn't sure if he could pull it off.

Don't overthink it. Just stick to the plan.

Soon enough Alyx emerged into a clearing. The grass was low like it had been recently cut. In the middle of the clearing stood Fermur, arms crossed. He was motionless and stared at them.

"So far so good," Lara said.

"Just keep going." Alrion moved just behind Alyx and matched her pace. He wanted to be as close as possible. Closer and closer they went, and Fermur was still motionless. Finally, he unfolded his arms and spoke.

"I see you've tracked me down. I hear things didn't go quite to plan."

"You gave us bad information," Alrion said. He continued to advance. They weren't far now from the range he had been practising.

"It wasn't good or bad, it was just information. As I was instructed. You made the most of it, approaching on two fronts. A shame then that you missed your opportunity."

"Maybe you can give us another." Alrion kept approaching, passing Alyx. Fermur started to back away. As soon as Alrion stopped, so did Fermur.

"We can speak from here if it makes you more comfortable." Alrion sized up the distance. It was further than he liked. Not terrible, but not guaranteed. Alyx sheathed her sword and put her hands behind her back. Fermur relaxed a little. Alrion watched Alyx prepare her hands, ready to pull out the steel chain when required. Lara and Branthor fanned out, not going any closer but forming a wider line.

"It does. After your last disaster, I don't feel entirely safe."

"Yet you let us approach," Alrion said.

"So that we may talk further. I suppose you want more information? A precise location for Rindale?" Fermur laughed.

"Yes. Very much so." Alrion started preparing his visualisation. He kept his eyes open, which seemed harder. But he didn't want to tip off Fermur. Lara glanced at him and Fermur twitched. He seemed ready to flee at the slightest hint of danger.

"Would you kindly tell us what we need to know?" Alrion said. Fermur smirked and prepared a response. Alrion closed his eyes and finished his visualisation. He started to apply the speed adjustment with his Will. Without a circle, and at a further distance, it was more difficult to get the right area and the right power. So, he threw everything into it.

Fermur must have felt something was off because he started to run. He looked startled as he ran slowly but sped up faster and faster. Alrion felt a strong resistance blocking him. He took in a deep breath and disregarded it. There was no opposition to his Will. Even so, he felt tiny cracks forming in the strength of his resolve.

Alyx was running in but she was too far away. She wasn't going to make it in time. Rocky formations grew out of the ground and started to wrap themselves around Fermur. He knocked them away forcefully, but they did manage to delay him. Alyx was there and hurled out the steel chain. Fermur slowly turned to see what it was and missed another piece of stone that had risen and blocked his path. He stopped momentarily, and the steel chain connected, wrapping itself around the general. The stone formations disintegrated into dust and slowly fell to the ground. But they obscured the whole scene.

With a gasp, Alrion let go of his modification and turned on his Soul vision. He could see Fermur still there.

"Go confirm," Alrion rasped and fell to the ground, drawing in more and more rapid breaths. He could see his team rushing over to the scene.

20

A WIZARD'S TALE

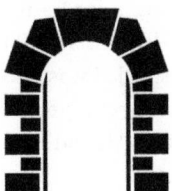

Falric motioned for Caleb to fetch chairs and leaned back in his chair.

"You have every right to say that. I will tell you my story." Falric paused and waited. Caleb fetched two chairs from an adjoining room and presented them to Vincent and Celes.

"And you?" Vincent said.

"No need. Please make yourselves comfortable." Caleb stepped to the side of the room and stood near the door. Vincent waited for Celes to sit then he joined her. Falric looked at Celes, then Vincent.

"I imagine much has happened. But first I will tell you a story." Falric drew in a deep breath, sighed and began.

"I awoke suddenly on that morning, sensing something was wrong. I was able to detect a wizard nearby, which was quite alarming. For two reasons. The first is that the wizard had never announced himself before. The second is that there seemed something familiar." Falric coughed and looked around at the table. Caleb disappeared and returned quickly with a glass of water. Falric gulped it down and seemed more content.

"Right, yes so I detected this other wizard and resolved to confront him immediately. We were so near our goal I couldn't risk anything else happening. It didn't take long for me to find him, he was waiting patiently. He laughed and challenged me for facing him alone, and it was then I realised what was so familiar. It was Branthor." Falric looked up at their reactions and seeing none kept talking.

"I was completely shocked, and I couldn't understand what had gone wrong. Branthor was not forthcoming either. He just began a battle. He seemed to be toying with me, holding back. He was always better at battling, and he knew it too. I played his game, matching his attacks and thinking of a way out." Falric reached for the glass and took a small sip.

"It was around this point that I noticed young Alrion. He had found us, and I worried terribly about his safety. I made a split-second decision right there, to try to protect him from Branthor. I waved him away and let Branthor's next spell take me down. Luckily, it was big enough to do the job admirably. I did help it along though."

"What do you mean?" Celes said.

"I have a few tricks of my own. I used a tiny spell of equal parts Will and Spark to burrow myself further down than should have occurred naturally. By controlling my own burial, so to speak, I was also able to provide myself a way to breathe. Small pockets of air, connecting to the surface. The spell was small enough that Branthor didn't notice. He did hang around I believe to check if I would emerge, but he finally left."

"And then?"

"Of course, I waited for some time. I felt a presence and noticed magic above my position. I initially panicked and thought that Branthor was back, rooting around for me. I dug myself deeper still and waited patiently. However, I believe it was actually Alrion looking for me."

"Why didn't you reveal yourself then?" Vincent said, not hiding his anger.

"I was weakened and had dug myself a lot further down than expected. I did not have enough power to spring myself quickly and safely, nor to communicate. I had to slowly and carefully extract myself. The whole effort took days, I barely survived."

"Alrion was gravely injured in his encounter with Branthor. Surely you could have still made it to see him?" Vincent said.

"Yes, I could have. I approached Paperton with caution, unsure of what I would find. My enquiries led to the discovery that Alrion had survived in his quest and that the enemy wizard was nowhere to be found. I resolved then to let Alrion continue, knowing that he would meet you in Brangtur. I decided to wait for him to leave, then begin my stay in Paperton." Falric stopped talking and waited for a response.

"Why did you not attempt to join him? I know nothing of wizard training, but Alrion's had barely begun." Celes sounded annoyed too. Vincent sat back and let Falric answer.

"He had accessed the Pool of Knowledge. He had proved himself and he had a way to further his training. I thought that it would be best to let Alrion continue his growth and his journey, and I could learn the secrets of the Pool of Knowledge."

"You left him alone, so you could do more research?" Vincent's voice grew in volume with every word.

"Branthor bested me too easily. I am well-travelled, but the knowledge is old and out of date. Alrion had found a new companion and had you to join him. It was a risk worth taking." Falric paused but started again. "And I knew that if he had a roadblock in his journey he would return. And I would be ready to help him in whatever he needed. Imagine my surprise to see you both here instead."

"I expected more from you. I didn't expect you to abandon him when things became difficult," Celes said.

"And what of the Wizard Academy? Surely you're needed there?" Vincent said.

"There are protocols that I have already established. Things will go on as they should. I spent my life building up the Academy. You can fault me on many things, but not that."

"I'm still not happy with this. I went along with everything, I supported your approach the whole way. Surely you could have guided him from the shadows, supported him in other ways?" Vincent studied Falric's reaction. The wizard did look a little guilty, embarrassed. He turned away before returning his gaze.

"I took the easy option and justified it to myself. Luckily for me, it worked out. I would have to live with it if something happened. But I believe all is well?"

"He's alive, and he's accomplished quite a lot. He can cure the Blight now." Vincent felt annoyed by the pride and joy in Falric's features.

He started this, but I feel like he betrayed us.

"Then he's so close. What is his goal now?" Falric said.

"He needs to determine the source of the Blight to complete the final spell I believe," Vincent said.

"Which is why we are here," Celes added. Falric looked confused.

"If he's come as far as you say, he should have the information already. It's a crucial part of the spell. And if he needs it, why is he not here with you?"

"I suspected he would be here or would be soon. He had other matters to attend to."

"I see." Falric rubbed his chin. "Something has gone wrong. The mechanics of the Pool of Knowledge are infinitely complex, but the concepts are simple and reliable. What he needs should have been revealed to him already."

"Then your training has been incomplete," Vincent said. Falric nodded.

"Perhaps. Well, I must say I doubt that he will find what he needs without coming here, based on what you have said. I am glad that we will be reunited."

"We could take the information to him?" Celes said. Falric shook his head.

"Telling him details is not the answer. He needs to understand it all, together."

"Then come with us. You can help him," Vincent said.

"No, this is not a matter we can just wave away. Alrion needs to continue the journey to learn the answers he seeks. There are no shortcuts. That's a primary rule." Falric closed his eyes and looked deep in thought.

"Take me to the Pool then. I'll learn what needs to be done and assist." Vincent stood and stared at Falric defiantly. Falric cowered back quickly but regained his composure.

"I'm afraid that won't be possible. Caleb?"

"Yes, as Falric said. The Pool has been closed off and no further access is allowed."

"Surely we can discuss..."

"And only a wizard can properly incorporate and use the information that Alrion seeks," Falric said. Celes placed her hand on Vincent's and he sat back down.

"We just want to help our son. Surely we can do something?" Celes said.

"You can start by telling me everything that has happened. I may have some ideas on how to help Alrion once I know the full details."

"You should find yourself a chair," Vincent said to Caleb.

~

Vincent sighed and looked over at Celes.

"That's it all, isn't it?"

"Yes, now you know everything, Falric." Celes picked at a leftover scrap of bread. Caleb had disappeared and brought food on two different occasions while they spoke.

"There's one thing I can't figure out. This wizard who has been helping Alrion. It doesn't make sense," Falric said.

"What doesn't make sense?" Celes said.

"You need to come into contact with that magical notebook to send messages. It should be obvious, then, who you have come into contact with." Falric paused, deep in thought.

"Those messages started after the Pool of Knowledge, correct?"

"To the best of my knowledge. We haven't really spoken at length about it," Vincent said.

"There's a Wizard Store near here. Because of its location, it has some additional security. All wizards who visit must provide a name which is recorded in a book. We may find some clues there." Falric eased himself out of the chair and straightened out.

"Right, let's go then." Falric started walking off.

"Is this really the most important thing we could be doing?" Vincent jumped out of his chair and almost knocked it over.

"Yes, this is at the heart of it all. Caleb, you can join us."

"It would be an honour." Caleb gave a short bow. Vincent pulled him aside.

"Look, even if I can't get access you need to explain more about the Pool, so I can help my son."

"Of course. That is within my power and I will happily so do."

"Good. Thanks." Vincent rushed to catch up with Falric and Celes.

They emerged into the night air, the slight chill surprising Vincent. Falric walked with an almost fevered pace. He led them through buildings until they came to a run-down shed.

"This is it?" Celes said.

"Of course. Hiding in plain sight." Falric walked up to the door and knocked three times. After a bell sounded, he said, "Falric." After a few moments, the door unlocked and Falric opened it.

"Let's go." Falric ushered them in and close the door. The Wizard Store was quite small. There was a corner with clothing and travelling supplies. But the rest was filled with books.

"Seems fitting," Vincent said.

"What's that?" Falric asked.

"The store here in the scholar's town is full of books."

"These are the recordings of those who have studied or experienced the Pool of Knowledge."

"Good to know." Vincent started browsing the shelves. Falric walked to a bench set in to one of the walls and unlocked something underneath. He pulled out a dusty book.

"Come over and look at this." Vincent closed the book he had opened and walked over. Celes was already there hovering over Falric's shoulder.

"Now, see here is the entry that we just created." Falric pointed to a space in the book. The word 'Falric' was written in script with the date.

"That's quite impressive!" Celes slapped Falric lightly on the back.

"I'm afraid this was Granthion's doing. I know enough to maintain it, but the exact way it was created escapes me. I suppose with sufficient study I could recreate it, but never felt the need." Falric started paging through the book.

"Obviously, all the recent entries are me. Here, it should be around this time." Falric ran his fingers over the page.

"This one is me. And above it are..."

"Branthor. And Aydan?" Celes said with surprise.

"Branthor didn't even try to hide his identity. Not that it would be easy, and I suppose he had already dealt with me."

"And the other name? Is it familiar?" Vincent said.

"It's an odd one. It's in the old language. Nobody uses it now, except scholars. Or wizards."

"What's it mean?" Celes asked.

"Lost One," Caleb said. Celes spun quickly to face the scholar.

"I learned the language as part of my training. I'm no wizard, Falric can attest to that." Caleb held his hands up and chuckled.

"This may just be the clue we need," Falric pondered.

"Do you believe it's a real name?" Vincent said.

"It needs to be. Well, actually not explicitly." Falric paused and gathered his thoughts. "It needs to be a name that the person believes is true. I suppose an alias could fit if it was used for a long time."

"And it has to be a wizard?" Celes asked.

"Yes, absolutely. No way around that. Aydan it is then. Now we need to find the man behind the name." Falric walked away from the book. Vincent leaned over and observed the script himself, then he closed the book.

"Any other mysteries in here we should be aware of?" he said. Falric didn't hear, he was already poring through another book.

"Maybe we can find something here ourselves," Celes whispered in Vincent's ear. He nodded and strode over to select another book.

21

THE RIGHT WAY

Branthor closed the door, the creaking sound annoying him. He surveyed the room and gave a satisfied nod.

This will do. The kid actually pulled it off.

Fermur was seated on a wooden chair in the middle of the room. He was chained up and immobile and quiet.

"Are you sure I can't fully encase him in stone? We only need his head," Branthor said. Alrion glared at him.

"This is sufficient. He knows that he's in our custody." Alrion made eye contact with Fermur and the general nodded weakly. Lara hovered nearby, checking the strength of the restraints.

"Fine, fine. Now, I got us this opportunity. What are we doing with it?" Branthor started pacing the room.

"We achieved this, and we're going to ask Fermur some questions." Alrion dragged over another wooden chair and sat in front of Fermur.

"We're not monsters," Alrion glanced over at Branthor, "well, most of us aren't. Please cooperate and tell us what we need to know. Where is Rindale?"

"I can't tell you," Fermur almost whispered. His voice had lost its confidence and strength.

"Can't or won't?" Branthor added.

"I cannot betray them. It is impossible."

"Would you? If it were possible?" Alrion leaned in.

"I'm not sure. It's not the answer you want, but it's the truth." Fermur shuffled against the chains, clearly uncomfortable.

"He's too conditioned. We can't trust what he says." Branthor grew irritated and sent a pile of dust flying under the door.

"We have to try. What was the point of capturing him anyway?" Lara walked up to Branthor.

"There was always a chance he would talk. But if not, he's leverage. They will want him back. Or we could just remove him now, save everyone the trouble." Branthor grinned. He knew it wouldn't win them over, but he enjoyed their annoyance and disgust too much. Although, he did notice a serious look from the weapons master.

She's on my side. She's experienced it as I have. There can be no middle ground, no quarter. Since she understands, this may go well.

"Absolutely not. We need to figure out a way to get the information safely. I'm not like them, or you." Alrion pointed a finger at Branthor.

"As you wish. I'm just pointing out the inevitable conclusion to this affair." Branthor walked back and leaned against the wall.

Time will bring them around. They won't get anything from that creature.

"We need to think about how to release him from whatever restriction is holding his tongue." Alrion stood quickly and moved the chair away.

"You could cure him, wouldn't that do it?" Lara said.

"Possibly. Alyx, do you remember much of what you experienced before you were cured?"

"Not much. What little I do remember, I think was because they allowed me more consciousness."

"True." Alrion turned to Fermur. "Didn't you say that when you were transformed you were allowed to keep your personality?"

"Yes."

"That would suggest that he's conscious of his thoughts and actions and would more likely retain them. Don't you remember everything?" Alrion turned to Branthor.

"Don't compare me to that!" Branthor dismissed Fermur with a hand gesture.

"Alyx?"

"I can't offer anything concrete supporting this course of action. It may work, it may not." Alyx spoke with no emotion, her voice flat.

"You would treat this monster with humanity? He's no longer human." Branthor spat on the ground. Fermur remained still, his head bowed. Alrion walked up to Branthor and looked him in the eye.

Kid's got some steel in him. Good.

"I don't think there's anything you can say that can sway me from this. He will be removed as a tool of the Blight, and he may offer the information we need. But he is not a tool to be used. That makes us the same as them." Alrion kept a steady gaze on Branthor.

"It's your show." Branthor backed away a little. "I'm just offering the voice of reason. Just because you return him from being a monster, doesn't mean it's permanent. There's every chance he will get recaptured and reconverted."

"A risk worth taking. It's the right thing, and soon enough everyone will be cured." Alrion glared at Branthor. The older wizard chuckled.

"Be my guest." Branthor gave them space and observed. Alrion walked up to Fermur slowly.

"Is there anything I should know before we try this?"

"Does it really work?"

"Ask them. They're living proof." Alrion pointed to Alyx and Branthor.

"That one's still quite mad, I think you made a mistake." Fermur pointed to Branthor and Alrion laughed. Fermur had managed a wry grin.

"No, I think unfortunately that's just how he is."

"You're welcome!" Branthor shouted out. He hung back and let the young wizard work.

It will be interesting to observe this process.

Alrion closed his eyes and went still. Branthor monitored the wizard, watching and waiting. He noticed Alrion gathering his Spark. He was forming it into some sort of spell. But it was a nothing spell, not special in any way.

Maybe you do need those Mystics to make it work.

Fermur went rigid suddenly. He strained against the chains. Branthor readied a spell, just in case he needed to subdue the general. A warm light began to envelop Fermur, and soon he was obscured by it completely. Branthor heard the chains drop to the ground. He readied himself. Alrion dropped to his knees, panting. Lara rushed to his aid and Alyx went over to investigate what had happened.

Fermur lay on the ground, motionless. Black flakes drifted off him and dissolved in the air. There was more colour to his face, and he seemed more human.

Branthor felt a cold shiver run through him. Knowing it was possible, having it happen to him was one thing. Seeing it happen was another.

Maybe he can do this? No, saving one at a time is manageable. What he must accomplish is impossible. Don't get fooled.

Branthor wandered over, clapping.

"Good show! I'm no expert, but I think it worked."

"He appears to be breathing normally. The Blight markings are gone." Alyx examined Fermur.

"He needs to rest then?" Branthor said.

"Yes, Alyx needed time. Maybe he needs more." Alrion looked around the shed. Branthor saw what the wizard needed.

"There's enough here to work with." Branthor created the visualisation in his head, then summoned his Spark to complete the spell. An earthen bed sprung up through the wooden floor. With another quick spell, some rough cloth and straw flew over to the bed, acting as a makeshift blanket.

Alrion picked up Fermur under the arms, Lara helping him with the feet.

"I could have done that. So could you, much easier," Branthor commented.

"Didn't feel right." Alrion lowered Fermur down. "I need to rest now. Try to keep him alive if you don't mind."

"Sure, boss." Branthor chuckled. "I'm going to go for a walk, that way I won't accidentally do anything." Branthor channelled some Spark to fling the door open and sauntered out.

Once outside Branthor continued walking. He didn't aim for anywhere in particular. He found himself standing beneath a tree. He formed himself a stone chair and sat down.

What is this feeling?

He scoured his body for any signs of the Blight, but there were none. The boy's cure had worked, even though he kept doubting it. He let himself enter a meditative state and floated for a while, his mind not latching onto anything in particular. Suddenly he sat up.

There. There it is.

It was like a wound festering within him. His pain. His desire for vengeance. Even the thought of Rindale's name brought up waves of anger and anguish.

I can't be normal again, can I?

He couldn't continue the journey with Alrion. He was torn between wanting to be there, and not wanting to. He believed that there was a chance, however slim, that Alrion would succeed. But there were consequences for that too. Better not to be there. One way or another it would end with Rindale.

Branthor detected movement back at the shed and rose slowly. He let the chair collapse back into dirt and dust. With purposeful strides, he made his way back to meet them.

Your journey will end soon. His will go on.

The thought was oddly comforting. Branthor even smiled when he opened the door.

Inside, he saw Fermur sitting up and sipping some water. His eyes darted around the room feverishly. He looked like a spooked animal ready to bolt.

"He's awake. Does he understand you?" Branthor said. Fermur almost jumped at the sound of Branthor's voice.

"I think so. He seems better by the minute, although he's quite nervous as you probably noticed." Alrion remained crouched near Fermur, and Lara was feeding him the cup of water. Alyx hung back, but she had a hand on her sword. Branthor strode forward, pushing Alrion aside. He hauled Fermur to his feet and held the man's head in both his hands.

"Where's Rindale? Do you know where he is?" Branthor was loud and forceful. Fermur looked terrified, staring directly at the older wizard. Fermur managed a tiny nod.

"Is that a yes? Where is he?" Branthor continued, although he noticed Alrion had risen and was looming nearby. "I'm not hurting him, he needs to be focused."

"Rindale," Fermur said quietly. He nodded again.

"Can you tell us where to find him?" Branthor spoke a little softer but retained his tight grip. Fermur started to speak but stopped. He looked distraught. He started waving his hands.

"He's trying to tell you something," Lara said.

"I think he wants to show you," Alyx added. Branthor removed his hands and stepped back.

"Will you show me the way to Rindale?" he said. Fermur nodded feverishly. Branthor nodded and turned away, looking to the door.

"Good. I will destroy him and prevent him from doing any more experiments. I'll save the world, in my own way. No more vile creatures will haunt us." Branthor clenched his fist. He knew all too well that he was part of that category. But his words were still true.

"There's no guarantee that there isn't more like him. Or that they won't convert him again. Isn't that what you said?" Alrion remarked. Branthor wheeled around to face Alrion, not bothering to hide his anger.

"When I'm done with him, there will be nothing anyone can do to bring him back or use him further. It ends with him." Branthor stormed outside before his rage completely unleashed itself.

22

THE SCHOLAR'S PATH

Vincent closed the book and stood. He stretched, relieving the stiffness from sitting for such a long time. Celes and Falric seemed quite content and comfortable, glued to their books.

"Is this really productive?" he said.

"The pursuit of knowledge is always productive." Falric closed his book and turned to Vincent. "Just, sometimes you don't need that knowledge right away."

"I need to keep moving. Do we have somewhere you can point us to?"

"Like the source of the Blight?" Falric said.

"Sure, that'll do." Vincent headed towards the day as if he were leaving immediately.

"No point being there without Alrion. You also can't ignore Aydan, that other wizard. Whatever his game is, he's interfering. I fear that if we don't do something, he may cause problems at the end."

"You think he's waiting for Alrion to do the spell?"

"Why else would a wizard help, hover, yet refuse to make himself known? He has an agenda and until we know what it is, it is a huge risk to allow Alrion to complete his quest." Falric looked quite concerned.

"Sounds like a bit of a wild goose chase to me. If this wizard is really up to something, then we just need to prepare and head him off when he arrives. What do you think?" Vincent looked to his wife.

"I'm more inclined to find and confront this wizard sooner rather than later. Then we can focus on ensuring Alrion has what he needs."

"Your wife is quite wise." Falric smiled and Celes batted her eyelashes at Vincent.

"I see that I'm outnumbered. Where do we go from here then?" Vincent sighed.

"You'll need help to continue following the trail." Falric rose and started pacing around the room.

"Trail?" Celes said.

"Well, you'd want to investigate other Wizard Stores. They will paint a picture of his movements, and you may find other clues."

"The trail might not lead anywhere. What if he only visited this one?" Celes said.

"If this wizard is interested in Alrion's quest, then he would definitely have visited the Wizard Store at Valrytir." Falric stopped pacing.

"Why is that?"

"It's at the heart of this. And near Alrion's destination."

"Ah-hah!" Vincent pointed at Falric. "That's what I needed to know."

"Oh, but it's not the final destination. And I haven't told you where the Wizard Store is."

"You're going to guide us then? That's a good plan." Celes looked like she was working through some ideas.

"No, I cannot. I must wait here for Alrion. Plus, I can further my knowledge at the same time."

"Can't Caleb do that? Help Alrion retrieve the knowledge he needs?" Vincent looked over at the scholar.

"It is true that I may be able to help Alrion," Caleb began to explain.

"But as he's not a wizard he can't learn all the details that Alrion needs. He will likely want another wizard to talk it through," Falric said.

"If you're staying here, how do we visit Wizard Stores?" Celes said.

"Excellent question. For that, we will need to return to my quarters." Falric paused for a moment then strode off to the door. Vincent gave Celes a questioning look and she shrugged.

"Let's see what he has," she said softly. Vincent nodded, and they followed Falric out of the room.

Falric led them back to Paperton, and they retraced their steps to the room where they had found him. He asked them to wait a moment and started looking through a dusty wooden chest.

"Ah-hah!" Falric dusted something off with his robe then presented it to Celes.

"What's this?" Celes turned the object around in her hands. It was a metallic disc with some inscriptions on it.

"It's a Wizard's Marker. One that I made. It's infused with my Spark and can be used to open Wizard Stores."

"How do we use it?" Vincent said.

"Instead of knocking with your hand, use that. If the door doesn't open, then state your name. The door will do the rest." Falric grinned, looking quite pleased with himself.

"This solves our problem then." Celes looked to Vincent.

"True, we just need to know the location of the Wizard Store we are supposed to visit."

"Yes, yes. I should write that down for you." Falric sat down at his desk, pulling out a sheet of parchment and a pen. He wrote copious notes and even scrawled a small drawing.

"This will make sense once you reach Valrytir." Falric handed the paper to Celes who studied it.

"Are you sure about that?" Celes handed it to Vincent.

"Trust me, you'll find what you need. I can't explain it better without making it usable by anyone. It's imperative that we keep this location secret." Falric gave Celes a serious look. Vincent handed her back the page.

"I think we can work with this. We need to trust Falric."

"You want to trust him now? You didn't seem too happy with his behaviour earlier?" Celes gave Vincent a pointed look. The blacksmith raised his hands in a surrender gesture.

"We're at his mercy on this. As much as I don't agree with some of his decisions, his knowledge about Wizards and related matters can't be argued with. If we're on this path, then we can trust his information." Falric gave them a satisfied smile.

"I suppose you're right on that. This better work." Celes shook the medallion at Falric.

"Go try it now, I'll wait here." Falric pulled out a book and started reading it immediately.

"After you." Vincent gestured to the door. Celes sighed and started walking. They kept a quick pace through the town.

"I just feel like we're missing something. I can't explain it," Celes said.

"I know what you mean. I think Falric knows something but he's not telling us. He wants us to discover it ourselves." Celes stopped abruptly.

"You're right. That's it. It makes sense now." Celes shook her head. "Now I know what you mean about wizards. You just feel like they're manipulating you."

"For your own good, they'll say." Vincent chuckled.

"Maybe so. But I have to agree with it. We need to deal with this wizard that is shadowing Alrion. It'll be catastrophic if we don't. I'm not going to interfere with his quest, but I am going to make sure nobody else can."

"That I can agree with. Let's test out this trinket." Vincent started walking and Celes rushed ahead.

They arrived at the dusty shed quickly. Celes retrieved the medallion from her jacket and knocked it on the door three times. Nothing happened. Vincent nudged her and pointed to her mouth.

"Celes," she said. The door opened a crack, and Celes smiled at Vincent. She pushed the door open and entered the room.

"Let's check out the ledger," Vincent said. Celes headed straight for it and flipped it open. It didn't take long to find the right page.

"Here it is." Celes pointed to the newly added entry.

"There's your name. Oh, and it says, 'on behalf of Falric'. Very clever." Vincent chuckled.

"Yes, I can see why Falric was so pleased with this. I'm glad it works." Celes looked around, "do you think we can find something of use in here before we go?"

"Perhaps. You start looking around, I have a hunch I'd like to investigate." Vincent returned to the book and flipped through the pages. He was looking at all the entries. Apart from the recent activity, there was very little. Soon it became years between entries. Finally, he stopped flipping pages and tapped on the page with his index finger.

"Celes, come look at this." Vincent waited for her to join him and stepped back.

"Aydan. He's been here before? When?"

"It looks like it's almost twenty years. A long time."

"How interesting. So, that would suggest that he is older."

"Indeed. That helps narrow it down, doesn't it?" Vincent looked at Celes and she smiled.

"Fine, yes you're not too bad an investigator yourself. That was a very helpful discovery." Celes looked back to the room. "What else could we find here?"

"I'm not sure, but let's see what kind of information is here. We might find something to help Alrion." Vincent started on the nearest bookshelf, his wife started at the opposite corner of the room.

Vincent noticed that the tomes seemed to be organised by wizard. The volumes corresponding to the same author were all clustered together. Many didn't involve dates, but with a bit of reading between the lines, you could spot something which aged the information. By sampling from different books, he started to notice a trend.

"They're grouped by author, but also chronologically." Vincent stepped back and mentally traced the timeline through the shelves.

"What are you looking for?"

"Books by my father."

"I see. Where do you think they will be?"

"That corner most likely." Vincent pointed then joined Celes. They looked through the books, carefully looking for information about the authors and the contents.

"So much of this is unreadable," Celes sighed.

"Yes, it must be about spells. But surely there is other information too." Vincent pulled out a book and recognised the handwriting. He excitedly turned through the pages.

"Look at this." Vincent offered the book to his wife. Celes took the book and examined it.

"I can read this. Who wrote this? I don't see any signatures."

"My father, I recognise the handwriting."

"Wow, this is quite a find. Maybe we will learn something from this. Do you think we can take it with us? It looks quite dense." Celes flipped through the book and sampled different pages.

"Why don't you try, you have the medallion."

"Good idea." Celes closed the book and strode over to the door. She opened the door, paused then walked outside. Vincent rushed over to the ledger and flipped to the most recent page.

A treatise on the Pool of Knowledge and information transfer, by Granthion. Borrowed by Celes on behalf of Falric.

"So far so good." Vincent closed the book and left the room, joining his wife.

"Looks like it worked?" she said as he approached.

"Yes, I even saw a line in the ledger. Falric will know that we have taken it."

"Fine by me."

"Likewise. Why don't we call it a day then? We have a long journey ahead of us." Vincent started off towards Falric's lodgings and Celes kept pace.

"I'm excited. It feels like we have something we can help with." Celes was positively beaming.

"Me too. It's a good feeling." Vincent put his arm around his wife and they kept walking.

23

THE ANCIENT TRIAL

C ertan struck out his palm, feeling the force of the strike then holding his position. After a few moments, he relaxed and bowed. The monk opposite him bowed too and quickly retreated.

"They'll trust you more if you actually hit them," Graem said.

"It's a matter of respect. I am restraining myself."

"It looks like disrespect, you assume that they can't take a hit." Graem shook his head and started leaving the room. The rest had already left, and the giant stone room seemed unnaturally still. Certan rushed off to catch up with his fellow monk.

"I feel like I brought destruction here," Certan said.

"That creature? It would find its way here eventually anyway. You brought the wizard, that was helpful. And he did marvellously. Helped me out too."

"You as well?"

"Yes, he cleared out some Blighters trying to scale the walls. In return, I led him down to the Vault of Silence."

"Have you done the trial?" Upon Certan's words, Graem stopped dead still and turned around.

"That's not something you can ask a fellow monk. It's not respectful."

"It's a simple question."

"No, not really. Perhaps I have not reached that level of seniority, and as I am your senior that questions my ability. Perhaps I tried and failed and carry that wound with me. Or perhaps I have succeeded, yet you haven't recognised my mastery despite my success. Which of those options seems respectful to you?" Graem gave Certan a stern look.

"I'm sorry, I hadn't thought it through like that. Perhaps I've been away too long."

"No, you're just clutching at anything because you have no purpose." Graem started walking. "Although, now I bet you're wondering whether I've actually done the trial in the Vault of Silence."

"I think I've worked it out."

"And your answer?"

"Will not be revealed." Certan grinned and Graem laughed out loud.

"Now you're thinking like a monk. There's hope for you yet." Graem stopped suddenly. He looked back at Certan with curiosity. Certan joined Graem, wondering what had given the monk pause.

An elder monk stood before them. They almost never left the Vault of Silence, even now that the extensive repair work on the temple had turned everyone's routines upside down.

"Certan, you have not accepted our summons," the elder monk said in a low monotonous voice.

"Summons? There's been no summons."

"Directly? No, we don't work like that. But you have been shown the signs, you've had the Trial mentioned to you. Even by this one." The elder pointed to Graem.

"Perhaps you're right."

"Perhaps?"

"Yes, you're right."

"Why have you ignored us?"

"I don't know." Certan looked at Graem, the monk was staring at Certan with no emotion.

"Don't look at him for help, tell us the truth." The elder's voice had a tinge of annoyance in it.

"I don't deserve to take the Trial. I failed the order once and acted poorly. Even by attempting to redeem myself I brought ruin and death to this sacred place. It is enough that you suffer my presence so that I might earn my place among you." Certan bowed deep. The elder stood perfectly still, not reacting. After a long pause, he spoke.

"Are you done?"

"Speaking?

"Yes."

"I am done."

"Good. Follow me now." The elder dismissed Graem with a gesture and turned the corner. Certan followed closely behind.

What's going on? Is he taking me to the trial? I'm not prepared. This is not the right time.

Certan recognised the route they were taking. All the monks knew the way, even though many would never be asked to join the elders in that place. With each step, he felt a pit in his stomach. Fighting evil, dying if need be, did not concern him. He had already thrown his life away when he turned to drinking. But this, this was terrifying. His life would be examined by the monks, and if he was to do the trial, then that would be something else.

Every whispered tale of horror concerning the trial flooded back to Certan's memory. He was more anxious by the moment, the intense shame of his behaviour when he had been banished came back even stronger.

"Enter." The elder stood by the door and ushered Certan in. He entered the room and saw the three other elders all sitting. The last elder took his place with them.

"Why do you approach us, Certan," one elder said.

"Because you summoned me."

"Why did we summon you?"

"To do the trial and enter the Vault of Silence."

"You are not ready," another elder said. Certan was taken aback by the comment. He thought about it for a moment.

"You're right, I should come back another time."

"Refusal of the trial is the same as failure. Only, with failure, you are sometimes given another chance."

"Why summon me if I'm not ready and I cannot refuse without forfeiting my chance forever?"

"You should be asking yourself that. Why have you forced us to act this way?" Certan felt like he had been given a gut punch. He felt faint.

I'm set up to fail. They're punishing me for what I've done.

"The Vault of Silence is the catalyst that removes doubt. You will move forward, stronger, or you will be broken. It is the next step that you must take."

"Why? I've done everything I can to keep my place here. Can I stay if I pass the trial?"

"No," another elder shouted, his voice ringing through the space.

"I don't understand."

"Your place is not here. Your place is with him."

Alrion.

"The wizard?"

"You should never have left his side. He has suffered much but continues to gain in strength. Yet, he cannot succeed alone."

"There are others to support him. Let me prove myself here first."

"Pass the trial. Go aid your friend. Only then will you be worthy of a place here."

"There is always a choice. But if you wish to remain a monk, then you must accept our price," another elder said. In unison, they bowed their heads.

Maybe I made a mistake, and Alrion is in more trouble. I thought I could fix my situation. This feels so rushed, but perhaps it's as it should be.

"Very well. I accept your terms." Certan stood forward with confidence. There was nothing to lose. If he refused, everything was lost anyway. He had gone down that road, and it had ruined him. It was time to stand up, whatever the cost. Certan saw a doorway opening in the distance, white and shimmering. He walked towards it, slowly but carefully. He tried as much as he could to peer in, but he couldn't see anything.

Here goes.

Certan stepped into the light and in a flash, he was somewhere else. It looked like a bar. Wooden floors with a thick wooden bar, with only one table and chair. The walls were lined with shelves, and each shelf was crammed full of alcohol.

No, no, no.

Certan spun around, taking the room in. He could smell it, the intoxicating mix of vapours that hung in the air. He thought he might get drunk from the smell itself.

This is just a test. I can do this.

Certan strode over to the nearest shelf and grabbed a bottle. He opened it, looking inside. Certan dropped the bottle in shock and it smashed soundlessly on the floor, the contents oozing out. The smell was stronger now.

They're not empty or fake. It feels real.

Certan realised something was wrong though. He kicked the biggest piece of the bottle to the corner. The bottle spun and ricocheted off the table legs on its way over. All without making a sound.

The Vault of Silence? It's not all for dramatic effect.

There was definitely no exit, just bottles upon bottles of different drinks. Spirits, wines, ale, it was all there.

I will clear these from the way.

Certan started at one part of the room and methodically broke every shelf and bottle as he worked around the perimeter.

The exit will be hidden here somewhere. I need to withstand the lure and pain of the alcohol to get out.

Certan kept himself focused on the task, not letting himself notice the alcohol being scattered everywhere. After a time though, he started to tire.

Why am I tired so fast?

The monk stopped and stepped back to observe the room. The shelf before him was reforming before his eyes. He looked back, and every shelf had completely restored itself.

How many times have I already cleared these same bottles?

An answer lay on the ground. The bottles were slowly disappearing, but the alcohol was not. The more he broke bottles, the more the floor was soaked through with alcohol. Much of it was pooling as well.

I'll eventually drown myself.

Certan laughed. He had never imagined drowning himself this way.

I can't destroy the alcohol, and I can't drink it. How do I get out?

Noticing his elevated heart rate and breathing, he walked to the nearby chair and sat. He calmed himself and closed his eyes. Once he felt composed, he opened his eyes and saw an open bottle and a chunky glass full of a brown liquid. He resisted the urge to swat it away, and carefully carried the drink to the bar and set it down. After returning to the table, Certan sat down on the table instead, cross-legged.

No more creation of alcohol here now that I'm covering the space.

He closed his eyes and kept his mind clear, as much as possible until sleep came.

~

Certan opened his eyes, for a moment forgetting where he was. But the vast amounts of alcohol quickly reminded him. He felt incredibly thirsty and started to reach for a bottle instinctively.

Is the room smaller than before?

Certan noticed several bottles of what had to be flammable liquids floating in front of him. He knocked them away, the bottles crashing and contributing to a pool of liquid. Something looked strange about it. Certan quickly rose and climbed off the table, walking over to inspect the puddle.

It looks quite deep, surprisingly so. He plunged a hand in and couldn't feel the floor. Leaning in further and further, he finally reached something. But he wasn't sure what it was.

I could dive in.

He instantly rejected the idea. But then, he couldn't shake it.

This is a trial of Will. Perhaps I need to immerse myself in that which I cannot control.

Certan took a deep breath. This test was never meant to be easy. He released the breath and drew in one even bigger. Then he dove headfirst into the strange puddle. After the initial shock, it felt like swimming. It only took a few strong strokes to get down to where the strange surface was. He couldn't see properly but did manage to feel around. It was definitely some sort of doorway. He searched frantically for some sort of handle or latch. But there was nothing. Certan clawed at the door, looking for a way to open it. But it didn't budge. His breath was running out, so he turned and leapt back out of the puddle.

He stood on the edge, drawing in deep breaths and ignoring the potent alcohol running down his face and clothes. He absolutely stank of alcohol.

This isn't working. I immersed myself and it wasn't enough.

Certan looked around the room. He was missing something. He sank down and closed his eyes, meditating once more. The answer would come to him in time, he was sure of that.

~

Certan awoke quickly, feeling disoriented. He had fallen asleep without realising. The room was exactly as he remembered it. Only there was a wood chip floating slowly over the strange puddle of alcohol. It triggered a memory.

I demonstrated Will to Alrion and Lara this way. The fundamentals of Will.

Certan remembered the lesson. How Lara had been so good at effortlessly hovering the chip of wood. Certan did the same here, this time making the wood float a long way above the puddle.

I've been foolish. I have not seen what was right in front of me.

Certan stood and looked around once more. He picked a section of wall and reimagined the room with the door in that location. But not just imagined, he remade it the way he wished. Certan closed his eyes and opened them again. The door had moved. But it still had no way of opening. He walked forward with confidence and placed his hand on the door. It opened inwards, bathing him in a white light. With a smile, Certan stepped through the door.

He found himself back in the same chamber. The elders looked at him and nodded.

"You have passed the trial. You have proven yourself as a master of Will."

"Thank you for the opportunity."

"Do you know what you must do?"

"I do." Certan gave them all a deep bow.

"Do you know where to go?"

"No, but I can find out."

"No need. Head to Valrytir." The elder gave Certan a wry smile.

"I will. When we meet next, the world will be free from the Blight."

"Good, that is the right time for you to return." The elder closed his eyes and Certan knew he was dismissed. He turned and left.

Thank you again. Your faith in me has been unwavering, and I will not let you down. Alrion, I am coming. We will finish the journey we started.

24

PLANNING THE ASSAULT

Alrion looked at the landscape before him. The ground slowly descended into a deep valley. The grass thinning and becoming dirt. And within looked like a rounded stone fortress. Unlike anything he had ever seen.

"You're sure this is the place?" Alrion said. Fermur nodded.

"It makes sense. This will be Rindale's tomb." Branthor clenched his right fist.

"It looks really old. I don't think he built this, it would have been here before," Lara said.

"Agreed. This will be a very difficult place to attack. It will be heavily fortified." Alyx folded her arms and shook her head while she took it in.

"Sentries will spot us coming from a mile away. Have you guys got a spell for that?"

"Invisibility I can do. It's hard to maintain for the whole group, however. Much easier to do on myself," Branthor muttered.

"He can scout then if we trust him." Lara looked to Alrion. He shook his head.

"It's not a matter of trust. We all need to be there. Rindale can't get away again." Alrion turned to Fermur. "Is there something you can tell us, to give us an edge?"

"Hmm," Fermur muttered. He still seemed to have trouble speaking.

"We will protect you. Nobody will transform you again."

"There... is a path." Fermur strained, the words sounding quite difficult to utter.

"And that will get us inside?" Lara said.

"Avoid most traps." Fermur looked relieved that the words came out.

"Sounds like a good idea to me. Any objections?" Lara looked around the ground. Nobody said anything.

"Then…" Lara started to say but was cut off by Branthor.

"Are you completely stupid? He did this to us last time. That didn't end well, did it?"

"It's different. He's cured now, and Rindale isn't expecting us," Alrion said.

"Not expecting us? Are you that naive? Fermur hasn't checked in and actually isn't infected anymore. Isn't it obvious where we will be going next?" Branthor looked quite agitated.

"We're not going to let him get away again." Alrion turned to Fermur. "Can you draw us a map of some kind?"

"Yes." Fermur nodded as well. Lara searched through her jacket for some paper. Branthor formed a table and chairs out of the ground. Tufts of grass littered the table top.

"Be my guest." Branthor pulled up a chair for Fermur. The reformed man looked at Branthor warily but did sit down. Lara handed him a sheet of paper and a rough pencil. Fermur started sketching.

"This is a much better idea. We can plan how we attack the fortress." Alyx was looking over Fermur's shoulder.

"Fine. But you need to let me verify some of the details. I don't want to blindly trust what he says." Branthor glared at Alrion.

"That's prudent. And you have the invisibility spell too. But you must promise that you won't enter the fortress without us there."

"You trust my word?"

"You can swear an oath."

"On what?"

"Rindale's life." Branthor burst out laughing.

"You better not let me down."

"He has nowhere else to retreat to. It ends here." Alrion looked at the group and they all nodded.

"I think he's almost finished," Alyx said. Moments later, Fermur leaned back and pushed the paper across the table. Alrion picked it up and Lara looked over his shoulder.

"The scale looks consistent. This must be the path he was referring to." Lara pointed to a winding path that joined about halfway through the building.

"What are these crosses?" Alrion asked.

"Traps," Fermur said.

"Oh, I see. Yes, the path does seem to enter the building past the main traps. Is this meant to be Rindale's chamber?" Lara pointed out a spot on the map. Fermur nodded.

"His chamber is in the middle of all the traps."

"Can you enter through the front?" Alrion said. Fermur nodded again.

"Sounds to me like we should just take the most efficient entrance if we have to encounter traps anyway," Branthor said. Alrion wasn't sure. There had to be some reason that Fermur mentioned the other path.

"How did you visit Rindale if he was surrounded by traps?" Alrion said. Fermur scrunched up his face a little as he thought.

"Disable. Some."

"There! See, if we go this way, we might be able to disable enough traps to get through safely." Alrion glanced at Branthor.

"Fine. I'll go and investigate. If Fermur's access point and information checks out, we can move forward with that plan." Branthor closed his eyes and concentrated for a few moments. Alrion studied him intently, wondering what he was doing. He noticed the surge of Spark, but it didn't feel like a huge amount. Suddenly, Branthor was gone.

"That's how a real wizard operates," Branthor said. He was still invisible.

"Very impressive, see you soon," Alrion said. He heard Branthor's feet crunching on the ground as he walked away.

"We can hear you!" Lara shouted after him. But she looked shaken. Alrion drew in close.

"Are you alright?" Lara turned quickly and smiled at him.

"Yes, I just found that invisibility a bit shocking is all. Would be quite useful in my line of work, provided you don't tramp around like a bear."

"I can imagine so. I'll figure out a way to make you invisible if you'd like?"

"As long as you can turn me back." Lara winked.

"Maybe I should practice on something else first." Alrion chuckled and received another smile from Lara. Alyx was just staring off into the distance.

"Are you concerned about him?" Alrion said.

"He is like me, only worse. His rage is so barely contained, something will give way soon."

"How did you contain it?" Lara said.

"I channelled my anger into my training, my deadliness. All in preparation for my revenge. Lucky for me, I was occupied enough by my growth and development. And the fighting was a good outlet."

"But for him it's different?" Alrion said.

"Yes, he's already a master wizard. Has been for a while. And the Blight... it changes you. Amplifies the worst. You would understand." Alyx glanced at Alrion and he gave her a slight nod.

"One way or another, his rage will consume him. Hopefully, we meet Rindale before that happens."

"Or else?" Lara whispered.

"He'll destroy himself and everything else. Him first." Alyx pointed to Fermur. The man gulped and cowered.

"It won't get to that. We'll deal with this now. Then everyone can move on."

"You can't save everyone." Alyx shook her head and looked out in the distance once more. Alrion let the conversation die. Lara pulled him aside.

"You do realise that Branthor will eliminate Rindale. By the most destructive means necessary."

"I do."

"Are you fine with that?"

"No. I'll try to get a better outcome."

"If Rindale doesn't perish, Branthor will go crazy. You even made a deal with him."

"I know, let's just see how things go." Alrion's voice faltered slightly. Lara gave him a disapproving look.

"Sometimes you need to make the hard choice. Rindale has already had his chance. Your grandfather cured him, remember?"

"So we think. Look, I know I should be harder about this. But I know what it's like to have this transformation. I've seen what it does to people, what it did to Branthor. Rindale is a real person, just like us. Look at Fermur, he's a broken shell. That's what we need to protect, that's the reason I'm doing this." Alrion sighed.

"I don't disagree, but I'm warning you. This is going to get ugly."

"It always was. Branthor is too far gone. We just need to do our best with the situation we have before us."

"Of course. As always, I've got your back." Lara smiled and winked, then her face changed completely. A serious look came over her.

"Hey, there's something I need to mention. I've been thinking about it for a while."

"Oh alright. What is it?" Alrion didn't have a good feeling. To see Lara's face change so suddenly, it couldn't be good.

"Don't leave me out," Branthor said. Alrion spun and he couldn't see the wizard.

"Oh, you're back. How long have you been here?" he said.

"Not long. Just enough to hear mention of how crazy I am." Branthor didn't sound annoyed. He appeared suddenly right next to them.

"Good, then we're all going into this with open eyes. What did you learn?"

"The information checks out. The path is as described and allows easy access into the compound. I didn't venture further because I didn't want to set off any traps." Branthor sounded annoyed at that.

"Thank you for following the plan. Do you spot many guards?" Lara said.

"None. It was suspiciously quiet."

"He's inviting us in, you think?" Alrion commented.

"He must be. We should be prepared for anything."

"We are. Alyx, come closer so we can discuss the finer details." Lara waved Alyx over. She strode over and left Fermur sitting against a nearby tree.

Hours passed, and twilight was falling. The plan had been discussed and agreed, and Alrion was itching to go.

"Now is the time." Lara started to walk down the path and the rest followed. Alyx escorted Fermur, and Branthor and Alrion stayed close to Lara. As expected, they found no sentries or guards on their descent. The fortress itself was eerily quiet, and dark. Alrion distributed tiny lights for each person to see better as darkness fell. They walked in silence, their boots crunching along the dusty and sometimes stone littered path. Frequent stops were required to ensure Fermur was well, he seemed to have minimal energy and had barely eaten or drunk anything since he was cured.

The fortress loomed above them. As they approached, it looked like it had been carved out of a mountain. Years and painstaking labour would have been used to sculpt it to its present shape, and the enduring years smoothing it out even more.

They took a fork in the path, and they wound through the territory and around the edge of the fortress. Alrion spotted their destination, a side gate. It was an obvious fixture in an otherwise bland and featureless wall.

"Something is not right with that," Alrion said. He couldn't quite make out all the details, but he could tell.

"It's open! That's the problem." Lara stopped and turned to Branthor. "Did you leave it open?"

"I'm crazy, not dumb. I closed it properly and quietly," Branthor replied.

"Then either someone is really careless, or it's an even more obvious invitation." Lara looked annoyed. Alyx stood still, her arms folded. Lara turned to Fermur.

"Is this normal? Is this gate normally locked?"

"Always."

"Great. Just great." Lara stared at the gate again.

"Should we just proceed? If they're expecting us, it's better to convince them we are still coming. Rindale may flee again if he gets nervous." Alrion didn't like the idea of walking into a trap, but he liked the idea of Rindale getting away again even less.

"It's quite foolish, playing to Rindale's tune. He has everything stacked in his favour." Branthor was looking elsewhere on the fortress, no doubt assessing another way in.

"That's ideal. He will get complacent and make a mistake. We can capitalise on that." Alrion took a step forward. Lara grabbed his arm.

"Are you sure about this?" She looked nervously over at Branthor.

"Let's spring the traps. Branthor, you're about to have some fun." Alrion looked at the master wizard. He laughed and rubbed his hands.

"Good, I was beginning to think we were going to talk all day."

I just hope I can keep everyone safe. Ugly doesn't even begin to cover this.

25

SPLIT FOCUS

F alric regarded Celes warmly.

"You two take care, and good luck on your search."

"You take care as well. You sure you won't miss this book?" Celes felt the outline of the book through her bag.

"No, not at all. I think I've practically memorised it. Besides, I'm sure Vincent will appreciate having something from his father."

"I will."

"There, see. Glad you found it." Falric looked away, his mind preoccupied with something.

"I just had a thought. I know you are in a rush and all to get to the location of the Wizard Store near Valrytir. But I thought there was something else worth mentioning."

"What is it?" Vincent had a cautious and almost annoyed tone to his voice. Celes almost laughed.

He's so suspicious of Falric, it's adorable.

"There are some ruins near here. An outpost that used to be a staging area for wizards. Granthion established it, but it's been abandoned for a while. It's not from here, and since you're on a trail that's quite old, maybe there's something there?"

"It's worth considering." Vincent looked to Celes.

"The place isn't destroyed, right?" Celes asked.

"No, no, no. The Wizard Store is protected. Not sure what's left inside, but it'll be safe to enter. I think there's a Wizard Gate there too as well, but that's of no consequence since you can't use it. And I wouldn't even know where it went." Falric trailed off.

"How do we find this place?" Vincent said.

"When you leave town, follow the path north and look for a dirt track. It will lead you to some old ruins above the town. Good spot, it's a real shame."

"What exactly happened?"

"I think it was Blight attacks. Due to the sensitivity of the location, it was decided to not reinforce too heavily in case the Blight took an interest in it and started to poke around nearby. As far as I can tell that all worked because there's been no activity since."

"Great. Fancy a stroll?" Celes said to Vincent.

"Certainly, I thought you'd never ask."

"Off you go then. I'll tell Alrion hello from you both," Falric said with a chuckle.

"And tell him we will see him soon. When he's ready," Celes added. They finished their goodbyes with Falric and Caleb and left the building.

"I'll miss him," Celes said.

"Miss him? The wizard? He was gone and presumed dead, and now he's back. I don't think it's possible to miss him in these circumstances." Vincent grinned at her.

"True. Very logical." Celes smiled back. They hiked up the path out of town without much chatter. Celes was deep in thought and enjoyed the quiet.

How will we ever find this wizard? The trail is over twenty years old. And until recently nobody even thought to look for him.

Celes sighed deeply and kept walking. Vincent glanced at her but said nothing. Soon they had finished the long winding climb and were on the main path.

"Now the hunt begins. Keep an eye out for this dirt path," Celes said.

"Sure. Maybe I'll spot it first."

"In your dreams." Celes pushed further ahead.

I'm glad he's cracking jokes, like the old days. This whole thing feels so aimless. But I've had slimmer leads than this before, we need to follow it along and see what comes up.

Celes kept looking for the dirt track, conscious of not wanting to miss it. She also wanted to beat her husband and find it first. It was silly and meaningless, but it also focused her. There was value in that. For the most part, the path was lined with dense shrubs. But that's where the danger lay. The path could be overgrown and easily passed over.

Vincent started to slow.

"Shouldn't we be spotting this path soon? I feel like we've already come so far already."

"Probably. I'm worried that the path will be overgrown and hard to spot."

Celes focused less on the surroundings, and more on the path itself. All she needed to see was evidence of a dirt track beginning. The rest would come after that. Celes looked past where Vincent was standing and saw something interesting. She jogged over, pushing past her husband. There was definitely something.

"There's potential here." Celes could see that the edge of the path was unusually dirty and dusty. She forced back the bushes and could see something different starting.

"Vincent, over here, help me with this." Vincent walked over and placed a hand on her shoulder.

"Stand back please." Vincent had his scabbard angling forward, ready to remove his sword.

"Certainly." Celes stepped back to give him room. Vincent drew his sword in a smooth motion, slicing through the main bush. He followed it up with three more precise strikes then cleaned his sword on his cloak. He kicked one of the fallen shrubs out of the way and grunted.

"I think you're on to something."

"Not going to clear away your mess?"

"I wouldn't want to detract from your find." Vincent winked at her. Celes groaned.

"Always with an excuse." She rushed over and dug the fallen greenery out of the space. Vincent had hacked away just enough to reveal a dirt track. It looked old, and largely worn away.

"I think that's it. Congratulations!" Vincent bowed.

"You should have known better than to challenge me, I'm the best at finding things."

"Oh I know, I just thought that this would be faster." Vincent grinned at her. Celes smacked him playfully on the shoulder and started striding down the path.

"At least we know it's completely abandoned. This path was well hidden," Vincent said as they walked.

"You were worried about it being inhabited?"

"The Blight are always a concern. You weren't worried?"

"No, I have you to deal with them." Celes changed her tone and talked more seriously. "I really didn't think about it. Am I losing my edge?"

"No, I just think you're more balanced than you were. Logically, there was no reason to worry about this place being infested with the Blight. It's certainly seen better days though." Vincent pointed ahead. Celes followed his gesture and saw the ruins. A tall tower sat at the back, with a few buildings in various states of disrepair littered around the space. A tall stone wall extended around one half of the site and had crumbled away from the other. Only littered stones remained.

"Which building do you think holds the Wizard Store?" Celes said.

"Likely the tower. Wizards love them for some reason."

"Is it because they think they're above everyone else?" Celes quipped.

"Couldn't have said it better myself." Vincent chuckled. "Well, to be fair I don't actually know the reason. Maybe it has something to do with how their powers work. Maybe they need to see their targets."

"Maybe. Let's start with the tower then." Celes started off again, Vincent keeping pace with her. Nature had started to overgrow a lot of the stonework, giving it an ancient look.

"I think some of this damage was deliberate," Vincent said, pointing to a charred wall.

"By the Wizards or something else?"

"Not sure. I don't know who else can wield fire on this scale." Vincent paused to examine the wall further. Celes pressed on.

"This tower looks in good condition, considering." It seemed to be resistant to the worst of the decay and overgrowth. It almost looked like the tower had taken on the look to blend in.

Don't think such ridiculous things, it's not alive.

Celes stopped in front of the door. It was large and wooden and appeared to be intact.

"Time to give your medallion a spin?" Vincent said.

"Of course." Celes removed the medallion and rapped it on the door two times. Nothing happened. Vincent nudged her with his elbow.

"Celes," she said. There was silence, then suddenly the door creaked open.

"It still works. And it needed my name as well."

"Must be the additional security around here. Maybe there's something of value inside," Vincent said. He pushed the door open and waited for Celes to enter.

The room inside was almost pitch-black. Celes felt around the walls and found a metal bracket with a lantern. With a little effort, they were able to light it. Celes held up the lantern and looked over the room.

It was similar in structure to the last Wizard Store they had visited, but it was in complete disarray. Books were everywhere, shelves knocked over, and there were some broken chairs and other furniture.

"This place looks, I would say ransacked, but the books appear to be here still." Celes stepped around a pile of books and investigated the room.

"Very odd. Let's find the ledger." Vincent navigated around to the bench, looking inside. He retrieved a dusty book and placed it on the counter.

"Let's see who last visited." Vincent opened the book and Celes joined him, looking over his shoulder. She accidentally knocked over a pile of books on her way.

"Don't worry, they've survived worse," Vincent said without looking up. He was carefully flicking through the pages.

"There's us." Celes pointed to an entry.

"Exactly. The previous one is..."

"Branthor." Celes looked at Vincent. Her husband shrugged.

"That's not surprising. Maybe he came here after his transformation began? That might explain the redecorating." Vincent cast his eyes over the room again.

"That seems plausible. Let's see who else visited." Celes pulled the book closer and scanned through the entries herself. There were a few names she didn't recognise, in addition to Falric.

"Nothing noteworthy in recent times. Let's go back and see if our mystery wizard paid this place a visit." Celes flipped through the pages, taking care to review the entries.

"Ah-hah!" Celes pointed to a place in the book.

"You found him?"

"Aydan. Not long after he signed into the last place." Celes looked at Vincent with a triumphant smile.

"Looks like your trail is here. I wonder if there's anything to suggest where he went next." Vincent leaned back slightly and appeared deep in thought.

"Hang on. There's an asterisk next to the entry," Celes said. Vincent looked up sharply.

"Oh, that's different. I wonder what that means?" He refocused on the book. Celes looked at the page, there was nothing else to explain it.

"Why don't you try the beginning of the book, maybe there's a guide or explanation of the notation?" Vincent said.

"Of course!" Celes quickly flipped to the first page and skim read the contents.

"How to read this ledger," she said as she read. She used her finger to trace the words until she found what she wanted.

"To make an entry as having additional commentary, use an asterisk. Add your note in the Observations journal," Celes quoted.

"Falric never mentioned that," Vincent muttered.

"No, he didn't. Maybe he doesn't know?" Celes rifled around through the nooks under the bench and pulled out several books.

"This is it." Celes slammed the book down on the counter, unable to contain her excitement.

"Maybe don't destroy the book in the process," Vincent said. Celes ignored him and opened the book and started reading. There were quite a few comments throughout. Each one had a date and a name associated with it. But no details of the person who recorded the comment.

"It's just a matter of finding the right one," Celes said. Suddenly she found it. Without any delay, she started reading out the entry.

"Suspicious visitor today. I scanned the log to see his reported name and was surprised to notice that it was the old language. Wizards are never given these as a name, which further cemented my suspicions. Gareth thinks I am being overly cautious, but there is something not quite right with this one. He does not come across as having much Spark at all, yet he can read from any tome in our library. When questioned about his purpose, he just deflects any questions and responds with as little as possible." Celes paused and looked up at Vincent.

"This is our wizard. Maybe there's something about where he's going."

"Maybe. Keep reading." Vincent looked as hooked as Celes felt. She didn't think it possible, but her excitement increased even more.

This trail is still here, you just need to know where to look. And we've got it!

"In case he returns he has long dark hair and average build. Green eyes and above average height. Whilst I was unable to ascertain his next destination, I did overhear him muttering something about the desert. I am going to send messages to my colleagues in other Wizard Stores along that route to see if they can learn anything. It may be nothing, but I have a strange feeling and I can't ignore it." Celes stopped reading.

"This sounds right. It would make sense for this wizard to be interested in the desert, and the Vault of Silence. He had no trouble following Alrion's journey. Maybe he already did something like it before?" Celes couldn't quite read Vincent's face. It was a mix of confusion and concern.

"Perhaps. It's a good lead. I doubt we will find much else of value here." Vincent waded into the mess of books, picking through some at random.

"Didn't Falric mention a Wizard Gate here as well? What's that?" Celes said.

"I'm not too familiar. But they're supposed to be a means of travelling around."

"And you didn't think to mention these before?"

"I'm no wizard! I don't know how they work, or if they still work. You should be grilling Falric instead!" Vincent sounded annoyed.

"Oh, that's fair enough. Let's try to find it." Celes looked at Vincent to see what he thought. He frowned.

"I don't quite understand why, since we can't use it."

"But maybe Alrion can?" Celes could see Vincent thinking it over.

"I suppose we can look. I can't find anything else here, and we can at least verify if it's been obviously broken or not."

"Great. Let's go." Celes turned and started towards the door. Vincent sighed and followed closely behind.

They emerged into the ruins, Celes looking around.

"I wonder where that Wizard Gate is? Do you think it's big?"

"I assume so." Vincent looked over the rest of the buildings. "None of these look in as good condition as the tower we just entered. Maybe it's here somewhere?" Celes nodded and started circling the tower. Nothing jumped out at first, but after stopping and staring at the rear she noticed something.

"Look here." Celes stepped forward and touched the surface. There was a very faint outline of a door etched into the stonework. The charring of the stone and other dirt and debris made it almost invisible.

"If that's a door, try your medallion again." Vincent walked up until he was shoulder to shoulder with Celes and peered at the prospective door too. Celes retrieved the medallion and rapped it against the door outline. Light started to shine around the outline of the door, and the wall started to rumble and move. The stonework swung inwards, revealing a staircase.

"Onward and upward!" Celes said.

"As you wish." Vincent waited for her to start ascending before he followed. The stairs were incredibly narrow and quite dusty. But all things considered, they were in good condition.

"No lanterns in here," Celes commented.

"I suppose they didn't need them, what with being wizards and all."

"Seems plausible. Doesn't make this climb any easier." Celes pushed on, taking care to ensure each step she found solid ground before continuing. As they progressed the darkness started to lighten slightly. Even though there were no windows.

I wonder what's up here? Maybe it's causing the light?

Celes let her mind search for answers while she continued to climb. Soon the light became more obvious, and she could tell it was a pale blue glow.

"Something glowing up here," she said.

"Good. Let's see what it is." Vincent sounded close behind. Celes rounded another corner and stopped dead. Vincent almost fell into her.

"Look at that." Celes stepped into the room, mesmerised by the sight. A stone archway sat in the middle of the room, blue light illuminating its edges.

"I'd say it's still working." Celes approached slowly, Vincent joining her.

"What can you tell me about them?" she asked.

"Not much. Obviously, it looks like it is active. Maybe even used recently?"

"Where does it go?"

"Your guess is as good as mine. I think they can be single or multiple destination. But I don't think you can just go wherever you want."

"Predefined options then?"

"That's what I'm thinking. My father never used one with me, so I don't have that experience to pass on." Vincent looked deep in thought. Celes walked closer, examining the stone structure.

"It looks like there are two distinct destinations. Don't you think?" She pointed to some markings, one at each end of the arch supports.

"Yes, it looks like there's an East and West option."

"Didn't that note say that Aydan was heading to the desert? That's East."

"Yes, you're right. Do you think he used this?"

"Why wouldn't you? If I was a wizard I certainly wouldn't walk around if I had access to this." Celes leaned forward, staring into the blank space filling the arch. She touched the stonework describing the East option and it suddenly started glowing.

"Look! I've selected a path."

"This is not a good idea. We don't know where it goes, and if it goes into the desert that's a big risk. Valrytir is the opposite direction." Vincent looked concerned. He took a step backwards.

"What if..." Celes whispered. She withdrew the wizard medallion and dangled it in front of the gate.

"What are you doing?" Vincent said.

"I'm seeing what we have to work with." Celes slowly swung the medallion toward the gate.

"You're really sure about this?" Vincent said.

"If it works, we need to do it. This is the only way I can help Alrion right now." Celes stepped closer. She gripped the medallion tightly and thrust it into the gate.

"Why do you think that's going to work?" Vincent said.

"Clearly this thing is already active, it just needs a trigger. If it worked for the regular door, why not this as well?" Celes looked back at Vincent and winked. He sighed.

The Wizard Gate suddenly roared into life. Blistering heat issued out of the gate, and a shimmering image stabilised in front of them. It looked like a desert scene.

"I don't believe it." Celes almost dropped the medallion.

"I'm in shock." Vincent looked back at Celes with a curious expression.

"Maybe I should be a wizard." Celes chuckled. "How long will this stay open?"

"I don't know, not long. If you go through, I can't follow. One of us needs to be at Valrytir when Alrion gets there."

"We can find another one of these surely, don't be silly." Celes held out a hand for her husband.

"I can't. There's too much at stake. Alrion could use this gate to shortcut much closer to Valrytir and we'll miss him entirely."

He's right. What do I do?"

Celes looked from Vincent to the shimmering image. It was a big risk, stepping into the unknown. She wasn't really equipped for a proper desert journey. But this opportunity was too good to pass up. She knew she could solve this puzzle, follow the trail, and find the answer. She would reveal the identity of the mysterious wizard. And find a way to reach Alrion in time.

"I just feel it in my bones, I have to go."

"I know. If anyone can solve this, it's you. I need to be there for Alrion, just in case. And if I get to Valrytir first I'll check out the Wizard Store there."

"But you don't have the medallion!"

"I'm sure I can find a wizard." Vincent walked forward and gave Celes a quick kiss.

"Go, follow the trail. I'll make sure he waits for you at Valrytir."

"You better!" Celes smiled and stepped through the gate, her whole world being enveloped in an intense white heat.

26

RECKONING

Alrion approached the door with caution. It looked safe, but he didn't trust it.

"Can someone take a peek inside?"

"Done." Branthor disappeared and his footsteps showed him walking away. Within a minute he was visible again before them.

"Nothing to report. We'll need to rely on some inside information." Branthor looked at Fermur and sneered. Fermur bowed his head and looked down.

"Then let's at least enter and assess the situation." Alrion stepped inside and looked around. They found themselves in a large open room, barely furnished. There was only a round table with a few chairs in the corner. The stone floor was otherwise left bare.

"There's only one way through. Fermur, how far until the traps?" Lara said. Fermur held up two fingers.

"Two rooms? Fine, let's visit the next one." Lara went first, and the rest followed. Alrion glanced at Branthor, trying to assess the wizard's temperament. He seemed to be quietly muttering something, but otherwise focused.

Just hold it together.

The next room was much the same, only there was a statue in the middle. It was cast from a smooth black stone and showed a single figure holding a vial in one hand and a dagger in the other.

"That's Rindale," Branthor said, spitting on the ground before the statue.

"How nice," Lara muttered.

"What kind of traps? Can you tell us anything?" Alrion said to Fermur. The man tried to speak but nothing came out. He sighed and looked down.

"Great. Just great." Branthor strode forward and peered through the next doorway.

"Lara and Alyx will assess then we will come up with a strategy," Alrion said. Branthor lingered for a moment more, then stepped aside. Lara and Alyx walked up to the doorway.

"This room is pretty obvious." Lara pointed. Alrion saw a single path heading through the room. On each side was a sizable drop into pitch-black.

"I think the lack of a handrail is hardly a trap," Alrion said.

"Look at the sides of the room." Alyx pointed. Alrion stepped closer and focused. He saw small tube-like devices all around the room, all at the same height.

"What are they?"

"I bet they fire something horrible when you walk on the path." Lara looked to Alyx. She nodded in agreement.

"How did you get through all those times?" Alrion said to Fermur. He shrugged.

"This is not exactly difficult." Branthor strode ahead and raised stone walls either side of the path. He then broke off a pebble and flung it along the ground. The traps triggered, sending wave after wave of arrows from each wall. They bounced harmlessly off the stone walls and fell into the gap.

"See?" Branthor started to walk along the path. It seemed safe. Alrion waved the others along and walked last, looking out. He couldn't see anything else and Lara seemed satisfied, if still quite cautious.

"Now I understand why you want to do it this way. The traps are childlike." Branthor sneered. After his next step, a clicking sound happened, then a deep rumbling.

"What was that?" Lara said. Alyx pointed to the far door.

"Look!" Alyx started running towards it. A strange metallic substance was sliding down and closing the door. Branthor chuckled and threw waves of force at it. Nothing happened. The spells slid right off.

"Now we're in trouble. Run!" Alrion shouted. Branthor stood motionless, trying different spells. Alyx drew her sword and sliced away a big chunk of stone.

"Use this," she shouted to Alrion. He understood immediately, and propelled the stone under the door, slowing the descent of the metal. But the stone began to tremble.

"We're out of time. Get through the door!" Alrion ran forward with Alyx right beside him. Lara had dragged Fermur ahead and pushed him through the gap first.

"Watch him," Alrion said to Lara. She ducked through next.

"You next." Alyx pointed to the gap. Alrion created a wave of force and whisked Alyx through, despite her protests.

"Branthor, there's no time. Come with us." Alrion held out a hand and beckoned for Branthor to join them.

"C'mon, you can just reinforce the stone and come," Alrion shouted. Branthor stood motionless.

"No, I will not crawl through and abide these traps. I will not suffer the indignity and make that creature feel any delight at my expense. No, I will go back and do what I wanted to do the first time. I will destroy his home and him with it." Branthor turned to leave.

"No, don't be foolish. We can do this together!" Alrion shouted.

"Time's up." Alyx dragged him back. Within seconds the stone crumbled, and the door was sealed.

"Well, that was interesting," Lara said.

"Yes, looks like we can't brute force our way through these traps."

"I meant Branthor storming off by himself. So he can destroy the place." Lara did not look impressed.

"If there are traps here using magic-resistant materials, there will be there too. We might beat him there." Alrion stood and took in the next room. There was a small platform just past where they were standing, then the rest of the space was full of water. The door was not visible.

"Oh great, a water feature." Lara sighed.

"I can understand how Fermur could traverse this, I'm just wondering where the door is," Alrion said.

"I'm wondering why Fermur bothered to enter this way. Either he had a key to deactivate them, or the other route is rather inconvenient."

"It would have to be quite inconvenient to be worse than this." Lara shook her head. Alrion chuckled.

"Let's hope so, for Branthor's sake." Alrion walked to the water's edge. "I wonder what I can see." Alrion enabled his enhanced vision and peered into the water. He could make out shapes below the surface, they looked to be metallic and seemed suspicious. He could see the door just below the surface, at the other end of the room.

"The door is where it should be, just low enough to be in the water."

"Do you think we need to drain the water?" Lara said.

"Or do we somehow move the door?" Alyx added.

"I don't know. Have a look, see if there's anything to interact with." Alrion let his eyes wander over the walls, there was no detail whatsoever.

"Have a look up there." Lara pointed to the ceiling. Alrion could see something sticking out of the ceiling. It looked like a hook of some kind.

"Do we have rope? We could perhaps swing across?" Alyx said.

"I have some, but I'm not confident it's long enough. And how would we get it there?"

"I can help with that." Alrion smiled and winked. Lara retrieved the rope and handed it to Alrion.

"Oh yes, this won't be long enough at all."

"Sorry, I wasn't exactly planning for this. I can't carry a whole store with me."

"No, don't worry I'm glad we have something." Alrion felt the rope in his hands. It wasn't too heavy, but it would be problematic if it fell into the water. He prepared a visualisation, that there was a powerful layer of air covering the surface of the water and would stop things from falling in. He channelled some Spark and set the spell.

"Lara, could you please let me know how cold the water is?"

"Sure." Lara bent down and reached for the water with her hand.

"Hang on, something's wrong."

"What is it?" Alrion feigned worry.

"I can't touch the water, something is stopping me." She looked up to Alrion. He started chuckling.

"Good, it's working."

"That was not funny!" Lara shot him a dirty look but Alrion laughed even more.

"Sorry, I just needed someone to test it. And I thought we could use a laugh."

"You thought you could use a laugh, actually."

"I found it amusing." Alyx had a small smile, which quickly disappeared.

"Careful, you'll be a full-blown Branthor if you don't watch yourself!" Lara smirked and laughed at Alrion's reaction. He couldn't stop the look of horror on his face.

"Anyway, let's give this a go." Alrion threw the rope into the air then tried to catch it with waves of force. He didn't quite get it, and the rope wobbled and fell back to the ground. Thankfully, it bounced and rested on the layer of air. Alrion shuddered slightly.

"What's wrong?" Lara said.

"Maintaining the air while there's an object trying to break through is quite taxing. I don't want to overdo that." Alrion took in a deep breath. Then he used a wave of force to encircle and grip the rope, ensuring it couldn't fall through.

"That's better." He slowly raised the rope until it was level with the large hook.

"Now's the tricky bit." Alrion slowly adjusted the rope until it was above the hook. He gently lowered it, until it was hanging evenly over the hook. He released his spell and waited.

The rope kept moving, sliding around the hook. But it settled down and was still.

"Great work!" Lara slapped him on the back.

"Now we can test it. It's not long enough to reach, but can you pull the hook down with the rope?" Alyx said. Alrion nodded and concentrated once more. He

VAUGHAN W. SMITH

used waves of force to grab the ends of the rope and pull it down. The hook started to move with a groan and a rumbling. Alrion started to release the spell.

"Hold it!" Alyx shouted. Alrion scrambled to keep a hold of the spell and maintain the force on the rope. The rumbling continued until the doorway rose above the water.

"Great work. It looks like there's just enough of a platform across there to stand and open the door. We just need to get across." Lara looked up at the hanging rope.

"I don't think we can use that to swing across."

"If Alrion has created a surface above the water, surely we can just walk across?" Alyx looked at Lara, and the two of them looked to Alrion.

"We can try. It will just be difficult." Alrion sat down near the water, cross-legged. He needed to concentrate very carefully.

"Try to put one foot's weight on," he said. Lara walked over and carefully placed a foot down. As she increased her pressure, Alrion felt a pressure building within his head.

"So far so good, try the other foot." Alrion waited, and he could tell immediately when she had started, because he felt the pressure inside building again, even more.

The Spark component of this spell is minimal. I'm doing this the hard way. I need to remember the Vault of Silence.

Alrion tapped into his Soul Power and circulated it around his body. It seemed to calm him, knowing that he had another source of power, while his mind was under intense pressure. Then he focused, remembering the lessons of the past. The way he had escaped the Vault, and the way that Certan had taught them about the power of Will.

It's just like the trap you set for Fermur. Set a change and make it part of your beliefs.

Alrion adjusted his mindset. It was like trying to make a puzzle piece fit. But when it suddenly did, the pressure in his mind became background noise.

"I'm stable now. Go on. One at a time." Alrion could tell that Lara was walking, but he tried not to focus on it. Instead, he found a piece of the wall that he could examine in detail. In the back of his mind, he was aware of Lara's walking, but he didn't overthink it. Soon, he felt a wave of relief and turned around to look. Lara was standing on the small platform at the other end.

"Go, Fermur." Alrion pointed to Lara. Fermur hesitated, looking over at Lara, and back at Alyx.

"Go on." Alyx nudged him forward and Fermur stepped out carefully. After testing that he seemed supported, he shuffled forward awkwardly. The strange and uneven gait did prove a distraction for Alrion, but he adjusted things so that it was normal. Before long, he was across too. The small platform was quite crowded with the two of them standing on it.

"Feel free to open the door if you need to," Alrion said.

"We'll wait as long as possible," Lara shouted. Alrion nodded and gestured for Alyx to begin walking. She did so carefully and cautiously, her sword drawn the entire time. Alrion felt a little weariness from maintaining his Will but otherwise felt fine.

This is working well. It should be fine to cross myself.

Alyx could barely squeeze onto the platform as well.

"Open the door, it's fine now. Otherwise, I won't have room to cross over." Alrion stood and watched. Lara tried the door, and thankfully it opened inward.

"Looks clear!"

"I'll make a start." Alrion began to walk across when he heard something behind him. A piece of wall was opening, and something was coming out. It was a Shade.

Time to move!

Alrion didn't trust his ability to maintain his Will-created platform and fight at the same time. He rushed across as fast as he could, trying not to think about the fact that it was carrying him. The Shade had realised that it could chase and was hurtling along.

"Quick, get over here." Alyx held out a hand for Alrion. He felt like the Shade was moments away, and his back twitched. He reached out and grabbed Alyx's hand, letting his Will transformation fall away. Before he was whisked into the next room Alrion heard the satisfying sound of a large splash.

27

SUCCESSION

Alrion surveyed the scene before him. His mind struggled to take it all in. The room was largely destroyed, with large stones wedged into all the walls and ceiling. A giant flaming hole showed where Branthor had entered the room. The bodies of Shades littered the ground, some even looking like Shade Wizards. In the centre of the room, Branthor and Rindale stood, arms locked together, stuck in an epic struggle.

"Stay back!" Branthor shouted. Alrion looked to Lara and Alyx. They were just transfixed on the scene before them. Fermur was cowering in the corner. Alrion took one step closer and tried to analyse what was happening.

Rindale had a long dagger with a jet-black blade pressed up against Branthor's throat. Branthor had one hand protecting himself, and another pressed up against Rindale. Rindale was covering that hand. It seemed like a stalemate.

"I can sense the hatred in you, wizard. Why do you detest me so?" Rindale spoke like he was mocking Branthor.

"You took everything from me, you monster!"

"Oh, I really doubt that. All I did was inadvertently infect your beloved. You should be blaming the boy's family for what happened."

"That was incidental, you caused it!" Branthor bellowed.

"Granthion tasked you with following his son. Andar got himself caught and fled at the first opportunity. And Granthion withheld from you his spell to cure the Blight." Rindale gave Branthor a wicked smile. "I'm almost innocent in this. All I did was pursue a man. You just got in the way."

"But it didn't stop there, did it? You had to transform me into an abomination!" Branthor pushed back with intensity and Rindale almost lost his balance. But he regained his cool and his twisted smile returned.

"You called me, what was I to do? You would have died. I gave you power and a way to get your revenge on the boy."

"No, you twisted my mind so that I was working for you."

"It was in both our interests, surely you can forgive that?" Rindale laughed. Alrion started to move forward but Lara held him back.

"Don't step in prematurely. Branthor is on edge, he might kill us all." The horror in Lara's voice convinced Alrion to hold back.

"You should spare a thought for me. I was cured by Granthion's spell and had to rebuild my life. It was a long and difficult road, with many missteps. For years I was considered an invalid."

"I have no sympathy for you, vile thing. You should have taken that opportunity to start afresh."

"Oh, but I tried. I really did. I found respectable work, even though it was below my capacity. I withheld all my darker tendencies. For a time." Rindale focused on Branthor with an intense look and pressed harder.

"And then you decided to just return to evil?"

"No. That was when Darvin found me. There's no escaping, you see. Eventually, we'll find you. Or sometimes you come to us." Rindale turned and winked at Fermur. The broken man sobbed.

"Never again, I won't let you do this. Your work ends now."

"My best work is already complete, you're too late." Rindale laughed. "There's no win here. You can't even get revenge, because I know exactly how your spells work, wizard." Rindale's voice was harsh.

"I'll do what it takes to eliminate you forever," Branthor muttered. He looked feverish.

"You cannot succeed. The instant this blade touches you, you'll be infected once more. A tool of my bidding." Rindale laughed. Branthor looked furious like he was going to explode. Alrion took a step forward. He shook away Lara's hand.

"I can end this. Both of you stand down."

"I caution you against interfering, young one. You'll get your turn eventually." Rindale turned slightly to stare at Alrion, then turned back to Branthor. "I see your father in you, Alrion."

"I don't care. Branthor, prepare yourself. I'm going to restrain Rindale." Alrion took another step forward. Branthor looked livid.

"You. Will. Not. Take. This. From. Me." Branthor struggled, then appeared to just give up. Rindale smiled as the dagger started to move forward. But it diverted from Branthor's neck, plunging into the wizard's chest. As Rindale was celebrating, a bright white light formed on Branthor's fingertips.

"Don't!" Alrion shouted. But it was too late. In seconds the white light became overwhelming and an explosion rocked the room. Alrion threw up a wave of force to act as a shield but was still knocked down. He quickly stood up again, unsteady on his feet. The power of the shockwave was incredible. The whole room looked turned upside down. It was even more broken and dispersed than before.

Alrion checked on Lara, and she was fine. Alyx had shielded her, and Alrion's barrier had done the rest. Fermur was still cowering in the corner and had started whimpering.

They're fine, but where's Rindale?

Alrion activated his enhanced vision and searched the room. He could find no trace of the Blight General. He did locate Branthor, under some rubble in the corner of the room. But he looked in bad shape. And infected too.

Alrion strode over and knocked the rocks away with a force spell.

"Branthor!" Alrion rushed across now that Branthor was visible.

"It's done. Not a trace of that creature exists." Branthor's voice was hoarse and quiet, and he coughed soon after.

"Just stay still, I'll heal you." Alrion started to prepare his Spark. Branthor grabbed his wrist.

"Don't! I'm done. Please, let me go." Branthor looked up at Alrion, pleading.

"You don't need to be." Alrion looked at Branthor, assessing his wounds. "You'll turn into one of them anyway if I leave you."

"No, I'll die first. This is a critical wound." Branthor tapped his chest, then closed his eyes.

"But..."

"If it's about my promise, then I'm sorry I changed my mind." Branthor took a deep ragged breath and continued. "I was going to tell you the location, but I won't now. That would play into their hands."

"But, why?"

"You're not ready. If you were, you'd know. Maybe you're ready now, I can't say for sure. But there's only one place you can find out."

"Where?" Alrion knelt next to Branthor.

"Paperton." Branthor managed a pained laugh.

"What do you mean?"

"There they can assess you, explain how to unlock the information. There's more to know than just the location. You can't undertake the journey without knowing."

"Thank you, Branthor. There's good in you, there's part of you that can be saved. Let me help you!" Branthor shook his head.

"No, you mustn't. This is momentary clarity, now that my revenge is done. The rage, the anger, and the shame. It consumed me. But this is enough. You must let me rest." Branthor closed his eyes. His breathing slowed. He opened his eyes once more.

"Good luck, Alrion. May you overcome your fate." Branthor smiled and closed his eyes. He took one last deep ragged breath and sagged. The life drained from him. Alrion leaned back, feeling the depth of the loss.

I should have saved him. Why? Why did I let him go?

He felt Lara's arm around him, pulling him up. She guided him over to the rest.

"That was meant to be. He did us a great service." Alyx bowed.

"I don't know what to do now. I could have saved him."

"You already did." Lara gave him a hug. Alrion wiped away a tear.

"That could have been any of us."

"It very nearly was. What did he tell you?" Alyx said.

"He refused to reveal the location of the source of the Blight. He said that it was a mistake to tell me, that it would lead to my undoing if I went now."

"Really?" Lara sounded confused.

"Yes. He explained that I should return to Paperton, to the scholars. There will be experts there to guide me through what I need to know, and that I can't complete this journey without the right knowledge."

"He was dangerous and unhinged, but he was a master wizard. It doesn't sound like he withheld the information in spite." Alyx sounded thoughtful. Alrion turned around to look for Fermur. The man was gone.

"Where did he get to?" Alrion sighed.

"Don't worry, we'll look for him," Lara said.

"I don't know what to do now. I'm just exhausted." Alrion let Lara lead him over to a place he could sit. Alrion glanced over at Branthor's body.

"Well, I need to help him before we go anywhere."

"Of course we will. His journey has ended, and he needs a proper farewell." Alyx bowed again in Branthor's direction.

"I didn't like the guy, but he achieved a great thing today. I know it wasn't how you wanted this to end, but this is a great win against the Blight." Lara gave Alrion a slight smile.

"But then why does it feel like this?"

"Because everything comes with a price." Alyx's face was hard, her expression impossible to read. Alrion dragged himself up.

"Let's attend to Branthor before I go collapse somewhere." He started to walk back through the rubble, Alyx and Lara flanking him on both sides.

How many must die before this quest is through?

28

THE HIDDEN GATE

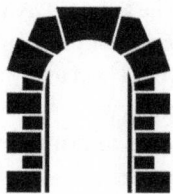

A lyx rushed back into the room. She didn't like being separated from them, even though she had found no other enemies in the fortress. Seeing Alrion and Lara was a relief, and she sheathed her sword and walked slower.

"You're back. Anything to report?" Alrion said. He was standing over Branthor's body. They had cleared the area around where he had fallen.

"There seems to be a lot of equipment around the place, it all seems like it's quite dangerous. I couldn't find anybody at all, let alone Fermur."

"I think we need to be alright with the idea that he's gone. Hopefully, with Rindale eliminated, Fermur will be left alone."

"I hope so." Alrion stood still and bowed his head slightly. Alyx walked over and joined them.

"I've figured out what to do here," Alrion said. He turned and looked at both Lara and Alyx. "I will destroy Branthor's body and destroy this place. It should never be used again, and it will send a signal to Darvin."

"I suppose, especially if there doesn't seem to be anyone left. And that would take care of the equipment that Alyx mentioned." Lara still sounded a bit hesitant though.

"Don't worry, we won't be inside at that point. Have you explored the annex?" Alrion said to Alyx.

"Annex?"

"There's another building connected to this one. I can feel it."

"No, I haven't noticed anything. It might be on the other side of the building?" Alyx looked to Lara who shrugged.

"I certainly didn't notice anything else on this side either."

"There's something else here. I almost missed it, but the more I think about it, the more I'm sure. Maybe it's wizard related, I can't say."

"Well, let's investigate before we go," Alyx said. Alrion nodded and turned again to Branthor. He motioned for Lara and Alyx to come closer.

"Farewell, Branthor. You lived a hard life, tormented by the Blight and the loss of your wife. I forgive you for all that you did and thank you for your advice and help. I hope that you have reached a place of peace." Alrion paused, silent. After a few moments, he spoke again. "I don't know the appropriate way to bury a wizard, but I also know that you won't want your body to be taken by the wrong people. And we don't want this evil dagger to remain. Therefore, I will take steps to protect you in death." Alrion motioned for Lara and Alyx to stand back. He remained exactly in the same spot, however, and raised one hand.

Bright light started to accumulate on Alrion's hand, just like Branthor had done. However, Alyx also noticed a bit of a golden tinge to the light. The brightness was mesmerising, and she kept staring into it. Suddenly she realised what she was doing and came to her senses. She grabbed Lara by the arm and dragged her away. When they reached the other end of the room, white flashed everywhere, temporarily blinding Alyx. Her vision slowly returned, and she saw Alrion was still standing in the same place.

"At least he hasn't blown himself up," Lara muttered. She dusted herself off and started walking. Alyx joined her. As they neared Alrion they saw a deep chasm in the ground. It was impossibly smooth like it had been carved out of the ground and cleaned.

"Do I even want to know what happened here?"

"I used a modified light bomb. There's no trace of Branthor or that cursed weapon left."

"I see. You're not going to make that a regular thing you do, are you?" The nervousness in Lara's voice was obvious. Alrion turned to look at her and took on a sheepish grin.

"No, I won't put you in danger unnecessarily. I also don't approve of the destructive power. It's too... final. You're bound to destroy too much, and there's no going back."

"Which was the idea. As long as you can control it and use it sparingly, we will be fine." Alyx gave Alrion a respectful nod, which he returned.

"Absolutely." Alrion's face returned to stony sadness. He shook his head and started walking off toward the hole in the wall that Branthor had made.

"Where's this extra building you mentioned?" Lara said.

"We may need to go outside to find it. But keep your eyes open as we walk through. There may be a path from in here." Alrion walked through without comment, but Alyx was stunned by the destruction on display. The room was ripped apart, and scores of Blighters were scattered all over the room.

"No wonder we can't find anything left alive," Lara whispered.

"I'll never fully understand him. For all that he hated us, he never did this," Alrion said.

"There was a part of him that still remembered how to be human. It's just it became quieter and quieter as time went on." Alyx could sympathise. She had been on a similar path to vengeance. It was not as satisfying as it should have been.

Better that he died, he could not handle the life afterwards.

They passed through another room of horrors until they came upon the main gate. It was mangled and bent like it was a child's toy that had been stepped on. Lara let out a small gasp.

"This is what we are capable of, but choose not to do," Alrion said.

"I can see why you don't." Lara rushed forward and didn't look back. Outside the fortress was quiet and peaceful. There were no sounds of wildlife, and there was only grass and a path. Alrion led the way, following the path around the exterior of the fortress. Around halfway down the length of the building, he paused.

"I can feel something. It's in this direction." Alrion turned left and stepped onto the grass. He continued forward like he was following an invisible path.

"I don't see anything." Lara stopped periodically and peered into the distance. Alyx couldn't make out anything. Just flat countryside and grass, with the occasional rock, shrub, or tree.

"Here," Alrion said. He stuck his hand out, reaching for something. Lara bent down and picked up a tiny stone. She hurled it into the distance. It sailed through the air, and suddenly made a 'tink' sound and bounced off something.

"Well, I'll be," Lara said.

"I'm not imagining it," Alrion said.

"I never suggested that." Lara turned and looked at Alyx

"Clearly, there's something there." Alyx moved forward until she was next to Alrion. She reached out with her hand and felt around. There was something cool and smooth there, but invisible. She used her hand to feel around and get an idea of what it was.

"It's made of stones, smooth stones." Alyx pulled her hand back.

"I'm not really familiar with this kind of magic." Alrion placed his hand on the invisible surface and closed his eyes. He looked to be deep in concentration. His breathing slowed, and he seemed almost asleep. Suddenly his eyes shot open, and he pulled his hand back. Where his hand had been, a transformation was taking place. The invisible was becoming visible, like a wave of light was illuminating it all. Within moments, a stone building with a metallic wooden door stood before them.

"Wow," Lara whispered.

"I wonder if Branthor knew about this," Alrion said. He pushed on the door and it opened slowly. Alrion created a ball of light which floated above him, then he entered the building. Lara rushed after him and Alyx turned to look behind. She could spot no enemies.

Hopefully, we didn't trigger any traps or alarms.

Alyx drew her sword and followed them inside. The room was quite bare, with stone on the floor and all the walls. The only item of note was a carpet in the middle of the room. Lara rushed forward and inspected the carpet.

"As expected." She quickly pulled it aside and revealed a trapdoor.

"Good. Let's keep moving." Alrion started forward and helped Lara haul the trapdoor open. There was a ladder inside, and no way to see what else was below.

"I'm going first." Alyx squeezed in between the others, sheathed her sword and started climbing down before they could protest. The ball of light drifted down until it hovered above Alyx's right shoulder.

"Be careful," Alrion said.

"I can handle a ladder," Alyx said drily. Given that the area was so well-hidden, she didn't expect too much else in the way of security. Nothing the wizards had done before to their spaces was dangerous, to her knowledge. Once she reached the bottom, she sensed a source of light. She turned and took a look. It was faint, but there was a blue glow emanating from the distance.

"There's something down here. Safe to proceed." Alyx stepped aside and made room for the others to descend.

Maybe this is one of those Wizard Gates. It must be functioning too. I wonder if Alrion can operate it?

Lara descended first, then Alrion.

"I think that's a Wizard Gate. Let's investigate." Alrion took off at pace, and Alyx rushed ahead of him. There was nothing else in the long room and no other sources of illumination. As they neared the source of the light, Alyx could see the structure properly. It was definitely some sort of gate. Two stone columns with an arch over the top, glowing blue.

"So that's what they look like when they aren't destroyed," Lara said, nudging Alrion. He chuckled.

"Yes, yes I deserved that. This is really interesting though." Alrion stepped forward and studied the gate up close. Alyx joined him, looking at the symbols.

"Maybe you need to press something?" she said. One symbol stood out for her. It looked familiar. She pressed on the stonework and the symbol suddenly glowed. Alyx stepped back quickly, looking for other activity. Nothing else changed.

"I think you did something. But the gate isn't open yet." Alrion peered closer into the space and examined the remaining symbols. Lara circled around and looked at the gate from the back.

"There's nothing back here, I think the gate acts as some sort of special door-way. When it's working."

"That would make sense. I encountered something similar at the Vault of Silence. Different of course, but similar in idea." Alrion walked around the gate, observing it from different angles and finally stopped in front of it once more.

"Hmm, I wonder..." Alrion reached out, his hand glowing. The gate flashed then roared into life. Blue and white light arced around the room, then settled down. The view was obscured, but there was definitely some other location at the other end of the gate.

That's Valrytir!

The scene was blurred but unmistakable if you were familiar with the city. It was a location on the fringes, one she had visited often as part of her training. Alyx shuddered with the realisation. This gate could take them a tremendous distance. She glanced over at Lara who seemed to be having the same realisa-tion. She must have also recognised the location. Alrion, however, was transfixed by the sight.

"Wow, it works. I wonder where it goes?" He looked to Lara, who shrugged.

"It's too hard to tell from this side. It could be quite dangerous," Alyx said.

"Right, we should think carefully about this," Lara said. Alrion turned back to the gate.

"We'll only know by going. Hmm, there's something strange about this." Alrion looked puzzled. Lara and Alyx exchanged glances.

"What do we do?" Lara mouthed to Alyx.

"I'll go," Alyx mouthed back and pointed from herself to the gate. Lara nodded.

"Here's an idea. Why doesn't Alyx step through first. She can assess the other location for safety, then we can follow?" Lara said. Alrion whipped around, looking at her curiously.

"It sounds logical but, if it works, you'd have no way of coming back. Alyx?"

"It's a good plan, and honestly it's the only option if we're intent on trying out this gate. If I'm separated, then I can easily continue ahead on my own and meet up with you later. Lara, of course, could do the same, but you two have shared a lot more of this journey together and should remain so."

"Absolutely, just what I was thinking. Remember, our best lead right now is to return to the Pool of Knowledge. The chances that this gate goes there are practically zero!"

"That's true. Maybe none of us should go through?" Alrion said. Lara shrugged.

"No, I don't agree. We need to assess the viability of these gates. If they work as intended, they will be crucial to enable us to travel longer distances safely." Alyx looked at Alrion, he looked conflicted.

If I can get to Valrytir sooner, I can prepare them for what is coming. It's the best plan. These two don't need me right now.

Alyx had made her decision. She looked at Lara, and the thief gave her a slight nod.

"Don't do anything I wouldn't do," Alyx said. She pushed past Alrion and dove into the gate. As it swallowed her up, she turned just in time to see the look of surprise on Alrion's face.

I hope this works. Oh well, better me than anyone else.

Alyx closed her eyes and let the gate transport her.

29

THE LOGICAL MESSAGE

In a flash, the gate closed and Alyx was gone. Alrion reached out too slow like he could just pull her back.

"She's gone," Lara said. Alrion ran his hands over the gate. It still glowed blue as it had before, but it seemed dormant.

"I don't get it, I activated it before. What's going on?" Alrion muttered. He located the symbol that Alyx had pressed and tried it again. Nothing happened.

"Maybe it needs time before it can work again?" Lara offered.

"It doesn't seem like that's how it should work." Alrion hit the gate in frustration. It sat still, motionless.

Alyx is gone. How do I get her back?

Alrion let Lara pace around the room, looking for anything that might be useful. He knew there was nothing else, but he wasn't always right. He had been wrong about this. Or had he?

I sensed something was off. Maybe it was rigged for only a single activation?

"Do you know where it went?" Alrion said. Lara hesitated before answering.

"Can't say for sure. It felt like it was a long way away, from what I could gather." Lara disappeared off to keep searching the space.

"It did feel like a different climate. I can't believe it, she's gone, and I have no idea where she is!"

"You know," Lara said, approaching Alrion, "I know it just happened, but let's think logically about it. Is this really the worst thing that could happen? Alyx is most likely alive and well, and she's armed with her deadly survival skills and a sword that can cut through anything." Lara looked directly into Alrion's eyes. "I think she's going to be just fine."

"I know, of course, she is. I just feel responsible for transporting her to the middle of nowhere!"

"It might be a very nice place. And you didn't transport her, she transported herself. You can't take complete responsibility."

"Perhaps." Alrion pondered the thought and kept poking around the gate. He remembered the moment it had activated. The gate had just responded to his Spark, he hadn't really needed to do anything special. That suggested that it would work independently of him having to power it. With that in mind, he activated his enhanced vision and examined the gate. As expected, the gate was infused with Spark.

This should just work. I don't understand what's going on. Maybe it's been altered somehow.

"Any insights?" Lara said.

"No. It should be working. I can only guess that there's some sort of limitation on it."

"What do you want to do?"

"I can't leave Alyx without at least trying everything. Let's make sure there's nothing else we can do here and figure out the next move."

"Sounds good to me. Should we explore the grounds?"

"Yes. Let's go for a walk." Alrion led the way back to the ladder and they climbed up to the entry room. They left the building and Alrion turned back to look.

"It's invisible again."

"Good. We know where it is, and nobody else should notice it." Lara looked out at the fortress and surrounding area.

"I don't see anything obvious, should we just do a lap of the building?"

"Yes. I'm confident there's nothing else in there that we need to be looking at." Alrion started walking and Lara kept pace with him. As they walked, he let his mind wander, considering the Wizard Gate and what had happened. No matter what path he went down, he kept coming back to the fact that it had to have been altered somehow.

Their exploration of the fortress grounds revealed nothing. There was nothing of note in the nearby area, just grass and some basic stone fencing.

"Nothing here." Lara took another look and returned her gaze to Alrion.

"Agreed. Do you want to take another look inside the fortress?"

"No, there's no need. I'm not interested in Rindale's ghastly experiments."

"Good. Then I can make sure they're never repeated." Alrion picked out a spot a bit further away and started walking over. Once he reached the spot, he turned and sat down on the ground. He patted the grass next to him.

"Sit here, please." Alrion waited for Lara to sit and closed his eyes.

"I'm going to set things right."

"Sure."

"Please stay here." Alrion focused his attention on the building. He pictured the building in his mind, creating a visualisation. This would need to be a complex combination spell.

First, he prepared the ground. He prepared the fact that the ground would open up, swallowing up the entire fortress. Like when he had entombed Wraith in the desert. But the earth would need a kick. He added some Spark to the mix and let it go. Exactly as pictured the ground opened, inviting the fortress inside. The massive structure dropped suddenly. But Alrion wasn't done yet.

He twisted the centre of gravity around, making the centre of the fortress attract all the area around it. The fortress began to compact itself into a much smaller space, the materials grinding away into dust as they did so. Finally, before that process was completed, he created a giant ball of intense fire and hurled it into the gap, sealing the ground over the top.

"I think that will do it." Alrion relaxed and lay back.

"I think so." Lara lay down next to him. "You don't think you overdid it at all?"

"I didn't want the place to be there anymore, but I didn't want to destroy the whole area."

"I was right. You are delusional. I'm getting flashbacks to when we took on an army of Blighters by ourselves." Lara chuckled.

"Some things never change I guess." Alrion cut the laughter. "You know, I was trying to do something Branthor would approve of."

"You don't owe him anything."

"I know. He did some terrible things, but I understand. It could easily have been me in that situation."

"Oh, that's true. But he still had a choice. Don't forget." Lara jumped up. Alrion hesitated and Lara offered him a hand. He sighed and accepted, letting her pull him up.

"We can't sit around here all day. Are we going to go back to the Pool of Knowledge?"

"I'm not sure. Let's go try the gate one last time."

"Fine by me." Lara led the way back and waited patiently once they reached the spot. Alrion unlocked the building once more, and they slowly descended the ladder and approached the Wizard Gate. It looked exactly the same.

"Time to try your luck." Lara stood aside and waited. Alrion stepped forward and pressed on the symbol that Alyx had used. Nothing happened.

"Still might work." He activated his Spark and reached into the gate. Again nothing.

"Something is not quite right. It won't work until we figure out what's different."

"Then we need some advice." Lara looked thoughtful. "Hang on, we have someone to consult for advice."

"Who?"

"That mysterious notebook you carry around. It hasn't steered you wrong yet."

"The messages haven't exactly been controversial. But yes, I haven't looked in there recently." Alrion retrieved the notebook and flipped through the pages. Everything looked the same, all was familiar. Suddenly he noticed another entry.

You're missing a vital piece of the puzzle. Return to Paperton and fill in the gaps. Then you will understand the true nature of your quest.

"Oh, now that's interesting." Alrion handed the notebook to Lara.

"That's quite clear in intention. Wow, it does sound like we need to go back." Lara started to hand back the notebook but stopped suddenly.

"You don't think Branthor was that wizard? Do you?"

"No, why would you say that?" Alrion took the notebook back and studied the handwriting. It didn't seem familiar. Not that he could recall Branthor's handwriting.

"Didn't Branthor just give you that exact same advice?"

"Yes, but that's not conclusive by itself." Alrion flipped back and looked at the other entries.

"When was the first one? Wasn't it after the Pool of Knowledge?"

"Yes, I'm sure of it."

"That was after your encounter with Branthor. And wasn't he at the Academy when you joined?"

"Yes, he was."

"So, couldn't he have somehow interacted with that notebook before? Maybe that's how he was tracking you!" Lara looked at Alrion with amazement.

"Hang on, don't get carried away." Alrion read the messages again. "It doesn't sound like Branthor. And for most of this, he was Wraith, he wouldn't have been able to write like this. Like a normal wizard." Alrion shook his head. It couldn't be Branthor.

"He would have said something. At least at the end."

"Not necessarily. He admitted that he decided not to tell you the location of the source of the Blight, remember? He might have decided to withhold other information too, in your best interests." Lara looked convinced.

"I'm not so sure. Let's just see what happens. We'll know soon enough at any rate."

"How's that?" Lara said.

"If there's another message, then it's not Branthor."

"Yes, but that doesn't mean it was never him." Lara gave him a challenging look.

"You don't have to win every conversation you know." Alrion chuckled.

"I'm just saying, it's a good theory don't discount it."

"Fine, I won't discount it." Alrion started walking back to the ladder. They ascended to the hidden building then emerged outside. Alrion headed towards the main path. Lara kept pace with him, occasionally looking behind.

"Alyx is not going to appear behind us," Alrion said.

"Not checking for her." Lara looked again. "Something about this place doesn't feel right, even after you removed that fortress."

"It's fine, we'll be gone soon enough." Alrion stumbled but managed to regain his footing.

"Are you alright?" Lara rushed over, ready to help him up.

"Yes, just a bit tired. Perhaps I overdid it a tad."

"Wow, that's unusual. It's never happened before." Lara gave him an unimpressed look. "Go sit against that tree over there." Alrion listened dutifully and rested against the tree. A gentle breeze blew past, making him feel relaxed.

"I don't suppose you know the way back to Paperton?" he said. Lara settled down next to Alrion.

"Not exactly. But I'm pretty confident if we follow this path past the fortress, we'll come to a relatively big town soon enough."

"That suits me. We can resupply and plan our trip back."

"Does it feel strange? Heading back there?"

"A little. It feels like I'm backtracking, almost retreating. But I can't think of it like that. It's important."

"The wizards seem to think so. And Branthor had all that knowledge too. I wonder what he wasn't sharing with you?"

"I wonder that too. He definitely knew a lot more than he was willing to share."

"That other wizard seems to know too. If that last message was anything to go by."

"Yes, you're right. Maybe he's visited the Pool of Knowledge too? Maybe we can find out something when we return."

"I hope so, I love a good mystery." Lara leaned over and rested her head on Alrion's shoulder. It was a good weight to have.

30

ON THE TRAIL

The intense bright heat of the gate was replaced by the dry oppressive heat of the desert. Celes stepped out of the Wizard Gate and into some barely shaded ruins.

At least it worked. Can I use it to get back?

Celes looked back at the gate and it seemed like the one she had passed through.

Looks promising. Let's see if I can find myself a clue.

Celes wandered around the location. It was reminiscent of an old temple of some kind, constructed from stone. But it was terribly worn down by the elements. She had no idea how the paltry structure shielding the Wizard Gate was still standing.

"Any clues here are long gone. What a bust," Celes whispered. The wind picked up, as if in answer. Celes stepped into the minimal shade and gave herself a moment to think.

The wizard came this way, years ago. What was he looking for in the desert? It can't be whatever was just here because it's already gone. Maybe there's something nearby.

Celes carefully sipped some water and evaluated her situation. She could afford to search the nearby area for anything of value. But she was not equipped for a proper trip across the desert.

That gate better work, that's for sure.

Celes followed what looked like used to be a path. There was nothing immediately outside, or much of anything to look at. Just sand dunes and the remnants of a path. But something didn't seem quite right.

I need to follow this a bit, I feel it in my gut.

She tried not to think about how foolish this was and set off. The walk was easier than she expected, even though the harsh desert wind and extreme heat made it uncomfortable. Somehow, though, her hunch had borne out. She could see what looked like an oasis up ahead.

I could really use a drink, here's hoping I'm not hallucinating.

Celes pressed ahead with as much pace as she could manage. The sun's rays seemed even more intense, and her throat was parched. But she didn't dare drink the last of her water. She just needed to go a bit further and reach the oasis.

And, like that, she was there. It was a small stone-fenced area, with some shade and water in the middle. Even the sight of water made her feel better. She stumbled forward, eager to drink. Just as she was within reach the water disappeared. Instead, there was a dry hole that she tumbled into. As she picked herself up, she saw a dark shape leaning over her then blackness.

Celes awoke in a cooler place, amongst pillows. She darted to her feet and assessed her surroundings. She was in a small dwelling that was sparsely but comfortably furnished. A jug of water was set before her and a glass. She inspected the water and smelled it, checking for any known additives. It seemed clean. She poured a glass and drank it down fast.

"You're a cautious one. Good instincts." A man with a sand-coloured robe approached and sat on a cushion at the far end of the room. Close enough to enable easy conversation, but not too close. His hair was a mix of grey and black and his green eyes studied her closely.

"I have you to thank for my accommodation?"

"And the mirage. Perhaps the two cancel each other out." The man chuckled, his thick beard drawing her attention. He pushed it down and waited for her response.

"You're a wizard then?"

"Yes. The name's Ashra, although some call me the desert wizard." Ashra stood and bowed with a flourish.

"Celes. You lure a lot of travellers in with that mirage?"

"Not that many. You came from an interesting direction, and you aren't really prepared for a desert journey."

"Yes, it's a bit of a long story. But suffice to say, I'm here and I likely need your assistance. Since you're a wizard and all."

"Intriguing. And what is it you're after in this rather inhospitable place?"

"I'm following a wizard, well his trail. It brought me here. Perhaps you will know what he was after?" Celes studied Ashra's features. He definitely knew something.

"This wizard has a name?"

"Not a real one, just an alias. Aydan."

"I see. And who set you on this path, Celes?"

"A master wizard named Falric." Celes noticed surprise in the man's features.

"I know him, from a long time ago. I'm sorry to say, last I heard..."

"His death was feigned. He's very much alive." Celes tossed the medallion to Ashra and enjoyed the shocked expression on his face.

"He gave you this?" Ashra asked, turning over the medallion. He then handed it back.

"Yes, to get me into Wizard Stores. That's how I've been tracking this wizard, Aydan. Although the trail is old, over twenty years."

"Falric, that old scholar. I didn't know he had it in him, giving us all such a great scare." Ashra paused and pointed at Celes. "There's something familiar about you, what's your connection to Falric?"

"He took my son away to become a wizard." Ashra burst out laughing.

"Now, this is something. Your son is named Alrion, correct?"

"Yes."

"I know him well, we crossed paths when he came through here. His father too. A very difficult time for them. How is Alrion now?"

"Alrion is well, he cured himself of his affliction. Vincent is also well, we were travelling together until recently."

"When you stepped through the Wizard Gate?" Ashra wasn't dancing around the topic any longer, it must have been obvious where Celes had come from. There was no point in denying it.

"Yes. We've had to take different paths for a time. I'm following the trail of Aydan, and Vincent is pressing forward to prepare for Alrion."

"I see. What does your husband think of your hunt for this mysterious wizard?" Ashra gave her a curious look.

"He's supportive. He agrees that it's important to get to the bottom of who is meddling with Alrion's quest before it's too late. And that I'm the one best suited to find him."

"I see. Vincent is quite wise then?" Ashra chuckled.

"Well, he knows when he needs to let me have my way. Besides, I am uniquely qualified to track this wizard down."

"I can see that. How can I be of help?"

"You've already done enough." Celes pointed to the room around her, and the water. "Although, if you can think of a reason why a wizard would travel here twenty years ago, I'm all ears." Celes watched Ashra's face. He nodded and closed his eyes, deep in thought.

"The temple of the monks is quite a trek, I doubt it was that. There is something near here that might be of interest."

"What is it?" Celes leaned forward, desperate to find out.

"Another Wizard Gate. It's special in that it's only one way."

"So, you need to come here to use it?"

"Precisely."

"Where does it go?"

"A small town, rather unremarkable I believe." Ashra had a glint in his eye.

"You're hiding something, aren't you?"

"What? Me?" Ashra laughed. "Honestly, there's no major mystery in that place that I am aware of. But not many know of this gate. It's a good way to travel without drawing attention. Perhaps it was just a step in your mystery wizard's trip." Ashra poured himself a glass of water and drank deeply. Celes let the information brew in her mind.

Is this all there is to it? The wizard came here to throw people off the trail?

"Wouldn't anyone who could take the gate to get here, be aware of the other gate nearby?"

"I can count on one hand the number of people who have come through that gate in the last twenty years." Ashra chuckled.

"Were you here when this wizard passed through?"

"Twenty years ago? It's unlikely. It was around that time that I first came to the desert. I think it's more likely that this wizard passed through before then."

"I see." Celes wanted more to go on, but this was a good option. She wouldn't need to spend much time in the desert, and with any luck, the next trip in the gate would get her closer to Valrytir so she wouldn't be too far behind Vincent.

"And you're sure there's nothing else here for this mysterious wizard?"

"Honestly, no. I think your best option is to follow that gate and see if you can pick up the trail. Where's Vincent heading?"

"He's going to Valrytir. We're going to meet at a Wizard Store near the city. Falric said that it's a key location for the end of Alrion's quest."

"Ah, that's interesting." Ashra closed his eyes, deep in thought. "I believe the source of the Blight is around there somewhere, which makes sense. This next gate will definitely take you closer, or at least negate this rather large detour you've just made." Ashra grinned at her. Celes gave him a quick smile in response. The wizard stood and stretched.

"It's time we got moving. I feel a storm coming in, and you won't want to get stuck in it."

"Sure, I see no reason to hang around. Especially in such an inhospitable place." Celes paused and looked around. "Excluding your home of course." Ashra laughed without restraint.

"You probably think me crazy for coming out here and living in these conditions."

"Not really, I know what people are like." Celes gave him a grin and he returned it with a conspiratorial look.

"Ah, a fellow enlightened one." Ashra walked over to a ladder and directed Celes up. She climbed up and waited for him. Through the sparse windows, she could see the wind beginning to whip up.

"I feel like we may not have as much time as you thought."

"Don't you worry, I'm a wizard, remember? We're good for some things." Ashra strode outside and waited for Celes to join him. The heat and the dryness seemed a little less intense. She didn't notice the wind as much as she expected either. Before she could say something, Ashra spoke.

"You're probably noticing that I'm shielding you from the extremities of the weather."

"I was just about to say something."

"I know. Just remember that I can do more if we need it." Ashra said no more and Celes kept as close as she could. Whatever he was doing, it made the desert much more bearable and she didn't want to miss out.

They walked along a sand dune, following no discernible path. Ashra adjusted their course a few times, and within an hour he stopped abruptly.

"We're here."

"I don't see anything." Celes looked over the whole landscape and could see nothing.

"You just need to know where to look." Ashra brushed away some sand, revealing a metal ring attached to a square.

"Is that a trapdoor?"

"You tell me." Ashra stood back and let Celes inspect it. She yanked the door open and noticed a ladder going down.

"Ladies first." Ashra didn't make eye contact, he seemed preoccupied with something else. Celes clambered onto the ladder and carefully descended. It was almost pitch-black, even after her eyes adjusted to the gloom. Once Ashra climbed in and closed the hatch it became completely dark.

"My apologies, light is on the way." Ten little lights floated down and attached themselves to different parts of the structure. Celes could now see that they were in a tunnel leading to something.

"We've not far to go." Ashra climbed down quickly and joined Celes at the bottom. He started to walk and Celes followed along.

"Do you know why wizards have such bad reputations?" Ashra said.

"Because you meddle?" Celes said, hoping to get a laugh out of him. But Ashra stopped and looked serious.

"Oh, that is just a matter of perspective. But you're close. The reason that people dislike us, is that we tell them what they need to hear, not what they want to hear." Ashra started off again, letting the comment linger.

"What's so bad about that?"

"It's a matter of perspective. Because the wizard may have a different one, he sees what he does as completely reasonable. Even helpful. But the person interacting with the wizard only sees the wizard as being obtuse and unhelpful. And they get frustrated."

"Well, you're all individuals. Why not just change the way you behave?"

"It's funny that. There's a common thread through us, and not even Granthion can lay claim to it. Maybe there's something we gain through our Spark? Regardless, no matter how they are brought up, all wizards gravitate to this same behaviour. To serve the greater good and longer-term benefit." Ashra stopped to inspect something on the wall, it looked like a tiny carving. But Celes couldn't make out anything interesting about it.

"Branthor didn't seem like he was doing that. Was he an exception?"

"Again, it's all a matter of perspective. He believed himself to be serving a greater long-term goal and sacrificing everything else to get there. Quite extreme, but classic wizard behaviour." Ashra turned a corner and stopped completely.

"Ah, here we are. Looks like it still works." Ashra looked at Celes, to see her reaction. The gate was almost identical to the one she had travelled through. She walked closely and examined it. She could feel Ashra's eyes on her, watching her carefully. She shrugged the sensation off and looked at the markings.

"As far as I can tell there's only one destination."

"Very good. Now show me how you activated the last one." Ashra stood back, continuing to study her. Celes almost felt self-conscious. She retrieved the medallion and thrust it into the opening of the gate. Nothing happened. She left her hand there for a few seconds and tried again.

"No such luck?" Ashra said. He gave her the strangest look like he was testing something.

"Hmm, it was delayed but it worked last time." Celes turned and saw Ashra was standing right there. He held out his hand, and she gave him the medallion. He turned it over again and handed it back.

"Very curious. I hadn't expected it to work, and this has proven me right. I think you lucked out at the last gate. That or whatever happened to this medallion was a one-time deal."

"In that case, I feel incredibly lucky to have your assistance." Celes started to imagine what it would have been like to be stuck in the desert. She gulped.

"Not your wisest move, but it paid off." Ashra reached out and the gate activated, the light taking Celes by surprise and temporarily blinding her. The gate shimmered and showed a different scene this time, but it was quite dark and hard to make out.

"This is where we part ways." Ashra held out his hand, and Celes shook it. Ashra held on to her arm.

"Before you go, I feel I must come clean with you. This wizard you are searching for..." Ashra paused, watching her. Celes stared at him, waiting for his next words.

"I've met him. I know who he is." The shock ran through her like a bolt of lightning.

"Tell me!" Celes shouted. Her ferocity surprised them both. Ashra quickly changed his expression into a friendly smile.

"Think on all that I've said so far. I've told you what you need to know, not what you want to know." Ashra's smile had a hint of sadness and he pushed her back, Celes tumbling into the gate before she could respond.

31

THE SCENIC ROUTE

Alrion tossed a saddlebag onto the horse and hiked up himself. He took a moment to steady himself and look for Lara. She was ready to go and nudged her horse forward the second she noticed Alrion was mounted.

"Keen to go?" Alrion said as he caught up.

"Desperate. I just found this whole town to be sucking the life out of me." Lara cracked the reins, speeding up the horse further. Alrion knew what she was talking about.

Everything they had done since arriving at the town had been slow and drawn out. Finding somewhere to stay, finding supplies, finding horses. Each activity had been like pulling teeth. Everyone had been polite, but unhelpful.

"Good riddance, Beetham," Alrion muttered. He matched Lara's pace and soon they had passed through the town surrounds and were onto the main path.

"How long is the ride?" Alrion said.

"A few days I think, it's not too bad. Hard days though."

"Well, we have nothing better to do. I'd rather not draw this out, the sooner we can return the more comfortable I'll feel."

"Because it's holding you back?"

"Yes. Now that the whole situation with Branthor is resolved, and Alyx is cured, there's nothing left on my list. I can't afford any more distractions."

Alyx, now you've gone and disappeared again. At least this time you can protect yourself.

"It does seem like we need to move things forward. Darvin is getting more and more aggressive."

"He's got nobody left now." Lara turned sharply to look at Alrion, and he could see the realisation dawn on her.

"Alyx had already killed the Skull King, and when Darvin turned her you cured her."

"I cured Fermur."

"Rindale was just obliterated by Branthor, who you also cured."

"That doesn't leave anyone else, does it?" Alrion smiled at Lara. She nodded, a satisfied look on her face. The expression changed quickly.

"I'm still concerned by Rindale's last statement. That we were too late to stop his work."

"Well, he may have achieved something, but whatever it was, nobody else can continue the work. I'm happy with that."

"True." Lara slowed down and came to a complete stop.

"What's the problem?" Alrion said.

"There's a fork in the road."

"Don't we just consult the map?" Alrion watched Lara's face. She seemed quite puzzled by something.

"This fork isn't on the map. It's probably nothing, but it does raise doubts."

"But one of the ways is? We can just follow that?"

"Of course, the way I planned is still there." Lara looked down the alternate path. Alrion followed her gaze. He could see why she was confused. This wasn't a rough-and-ready dirt track. It was an established road. It looked like until recently it had been well-maintained. Alrion rode his horse over, to take a closer look.

The road wound into the distance, he couldn't see where it led. There seemed to be more vegetation, and it appeared to be less wild, and more curated.

"There's something odd about this. I get the feeling that this way was the better-maintained way. The main road is the one that was neglected, at least until recently."

"I had the same feeling, which is why it's so strange. But, maybe it's just a local residence and therefore no map required."

"You're probably right." Alrion stared into the distance. He felt something. It was almost imperceptible. The more he concentrated, the more he felt it. It was like a pull.

"We need to investigate." The words surprised Alrion as much as Lara.

"Why is that? I thought we were in a hurry?"

"We are. But there's something there. We need to check it out. Maybe it's nothing and I apologise for the detour. But, if it's something..."

"I get it. Well, it's your quest. We can take the scenic route on occasion." Lara sighed and started riding. Alrion pushed forward, taking the lead. Lara seemed content to trail behind, periodically looking behind.

The countryside was vibrant with lots of colourful flowers and an exotic mix of different trees and plants. However, Alrion couldn't spot a lot of animal life.

"Looks nice but seems rather quiet." Alrion looked to Lara to see her reaction.

"You're right. I'd expect an environment like this to have a lot more animals or at least evidence of them."

"Maybe there's something here." Alrion smiled and kept riding. As he turned the corner he stopped suddenly. Peeking over the tree line he could see what looked like a castle or manor house.

"Now look at this!" Alrion pointed.

"Luxury home, as expected. This could still be nothing. And it would explain the unmapped road."

"Still doesn't mean that it's nothing." Alrion took off again, curious to see what was there. As he rode, he noticed movement in the tree line in the distance. It was minimal but noticeable.

"Did you see that?" he said.

"I did. There's something there, and it's probably not friendly. Let's hide the horses and approach on foot."

"Agreed." Alrion found a spot just off the path with enough space for the horses. They tied up the horses and approached the path.

"I think we'll need a few things." Alrion tracked back and retrieved his bag from the saddle. Lara did the same.

"You're right, if things don't go well, we won't have an opportunity to come back."

"Let's see what's going on." Alrion started walking off and Lara held his arm.

"Wait, let me go ahead." Lara took the lead, staying near the side of the path and taking cover as she went. After a minute of this careful approach, she remained hidden and waved Alrion over.

"Take a look over there." Lara pointed out a spot between two tree branches. It took Alrion a few moments, but he saw what she had pointed out.

"Blighter."

"Exactly. Likely a lot more where it came from. We haven't been spotted yet, we could just go back the way we came." Lara watched Alrion, gauging his reaction. He could see that she wanted to return and not invite another Blight encounter.

I understand her thinking, but something is not quite right. I need to investigate this properly.

"My gut says we need to properly investigate. At least figure out why they are here, in the middle of nowhere."

"I thought we were back on track, prioritising the quest?"

"We are. These Blighters are here for a reason, and we're going to find out why. I'm sure it's strongly linked to my quest." Alrion grinned and noticed a quick smile from Lara that was gone as soon as he noticed it.

"In that case, let me go ahead. I'll assess how we approach. If you notice a commotion, come in and bring your spells."

"Absolutely." Alrion nodded and watched Lara leave. She kept to the path a little longer, then completely entered the trees. Alrion lost sight of her, and instead focused on the Blighter they had spotted. That would be his sign.

Nothing happened for a while. Alrion kept looking for Lara and saw nothing.

No commotion, but no sign of her either. Do I need to do something? I'm going to investigate, I can't stay here any longer.

Alrion stepped forward and noticed something. He scanned the distance and realised what it was. The Blighter was gone.

She's there. I'll see if I can approach without being seen.

Alrion continued along the path, looking for the way that Lara had entered via the trees. He found a tiny way through the thick trunks and decided to follow it. Now that he was on the way, he had a relatively simple trail to follow. There was only really one path through the trees from the direction that Lara had taken. Soon he spotted a single Blighter corpse.

More than we expected, at least out here. No wonder she took so long. I don't like dealing with Blighters now that I know that they can be saved. But I can't avoid them until I'm ready to do the spell. And I sure can't cure them one at a time.

Alrion steeled his resolve and kept following the trail. He found another road, this one leading off the main one and heading to the main gates. The gates were open.

"Time to go in. I'll find Lara," Alrion whispered. He continued to stalk quietly, not wanting to sound the alarm. There was a good chance that Lara had already taken out any patrols, but he didn't want to take a chance there were more lingering.

As he passed through the gates, Alrion noticed Lara crouching behind a small outpost building. She noticed him and waved him over furiously. Alrion rushed over, not looking behind him.

"Why are you here?" Lara hissed at him.

"You were taking too long. I understand why, now."

"I had it under control." Lara's attention was diverted by a crash. The main doors of the keep swung open and a Shade strode outside. It was flanked by a host of Blighters.

"Still have it under control?" Alrion said. Lara flashed her Runesteel dagger.

"Absolutely." As Lara looked on, more came through the doors.

"Shade Wizards," Alrion said.

"Only two."

"Still nasty."

"Isn't this where you channel your overpowered ego and take them all out?" Lara smiled at him.

"Ouch, I'd like to think I've grown a little." Alrion acted hurt. "I'll humbly take them all out." He walked out immediately.

"What are you doing?" Lara whispered after him.

"I'm trying something," Alrion replied. Within moments he had their attention.

"Who's in charge here?" Alrion said. He was met with some confused looks. One of the Shade Wizards eventually stepped forward.

"I'm in command, I'm the highest ranked here."

"I'd like to explore this keep. Would you so kindly vacate the premises?" Alrion smiled broadly. The Shade Wizard sneered.

"I've heard of you. Almost one of us, but you were too good for it."

"You should watch your words. Otherwise, I'll cure you."

"Never!" The Shade Wizard started gathering his Spark and hurled a large fireball at Alrion. He held out his hand and the fireball seemed to be drawn into it and fizzle into nothing.

"What?" the Shade Wizard shouted.

"You're going to have to do better than that." Alrion could feel the absorbed heat and Spark in his hand. He was a bit surprised that it worked. It was a mixture of ideas and memories from all the jumble in his brain. He could use his Will to break down the spell into harmless components. Lucky for him, the spell was so familiar that it worked fine. But it only just worked. Not that he had to let them know.

Wanting to keep the advantage, Alrion added to the Spark and fire essence in his hand and compressed it into an ultra-hot spear of fire. He shot it out at the Shade up the front. The shade collapsed to the ground immediately, black dust starting to flake away.

"What did you do?" Lara whispered.

"I burned away its heart. The transformation is reversing now. Unfortunately, the person inside is also gone." Alrion spoke loud enough so the Shade Wizards could hear as well. They looked at each other and nodded, before taking off in opposite directions to attack Alrion.

"Do you mind taking one of them out?" Alrion said.

"It would be my pleasure." Lara remained in the shadows but started to stalk away. Alrion focused his attention on the other one.

They saw how I dealt with a long-range attack, they're likely to come in close. I can take advantage of that.

Alrion approached the Shade Wizard that was closing in. The enemy smiled and, as soon as he was in range, thrust his hands out, a wave of fire spewing forth. He laughed as it happened.

"Seen it before," Alrion said. "And I had no Spark at the time." Alrion threw up a shield of earth and the flames died away harmlessly. He pulled up another piece of earth, toppling the Shade Wizard to the ground. As the wizard rose, Alrion stepped forward and grabbed the Shade Wizard with one hand.

"It's over." Alrion sent a pulse of force through the wizard. He almost channelled his Soul Power into the strike, feeding more and more into the enemy wizard. As it was happening, he remembered what Branthor had said about the cure. There had to be a better way.

Alrion imagined his Soul Power entering the enemy's body, and gently travelling through the body's own pathways. It found every site of Blight infection and gently overcame it, breaking down the Blight and purging it. Once he had finished, he opened his eyes and watched the Shade Wizard collapse to the ground. The sight was enough to distract the other Shade Wizard, long enough for Lara to plunge the Runesteel dagger into its heart.

With all the leaders dispatched, the Blighters broke ranks and fled. Alrion thought about finishing them off but Lara stayed his hand.

"Individually, they aren't a problem for those around here. Maybe they'll keep under the radar long enough for you to cure them."

"Are you sure?"

"In this situation, it just feels unnecessary. Let's get this one inside." Lara gestured to the unconscious man at Alrion's feet. He enveloped the wizard in a mesh of force and gently lifted him off the ground. Next Alrion turned to the body of the dispatched Shade and Shade Wizard and incinerated them. Only dust remained.

"Let's see what all the fuss was about." Alrion started towards the gates and Lara followed, checking to see if there were any more enemies to worry about. Inside, the keep was like a stately home. Lush furnishings and plush carpet with polished wood and lots of fancy rugs. They found a bedroom on the main floor and Alrion placed the wizard on the bed.

"Do you think he'll be normal again?"

"I hope so, otherwise this cure is going to be a bit of a bust when everyone is touched by it."

"Branthor seemed relatively fine."

"He did. With any luck, this one will mostly regain himself." Alrion took one last look at the sleeping wizard and left the room.

"Up or down?" Lara said.

"Down. We seem to have more luck in the dungeons." Lara nodded and headed towards the stairs down. They reached a stone storeroom with a giant lock on the door.

"Perhaps you would like the honours?" Alrion pointed to the lock. Lara sidled over and pulled out some tools, tinkering with the lock for a few moments. It clicked open and she tossed the lock to Alrion.

"Impressive."

"Thanks." Lara winked and pulled the door open. There were a few empty wooden crates and more stairs down.

"This looks promising." Alrion started down and Lara stayed close behind. He found a torch hanging on the wall and kindled his Spark, lighting it with a tiny flame.

"This is more fun," Alrion said, pointing to the flaming torch.

"Absolutely. Not that I don't appreciate your magic lights."

"They're a bit too perfect." Alrion pressed on, waving the torch slowly in front of him to illuminate the passageway. It was plain stonework with no furnishings. Eventually, he noticed another source of light and extinguished the torch. A faint blue glow was visible in the distance.

"If you were a betting woman..." Alrion said.

"Then I'd bet that's another Wizard Gate."

"Let's see if you're right." Alrion upped the pace, his excitement bubbling over.

I knew there was something here. I don't think they were using this either, just guarding it. It must lead somewhere good. I'll definitely go through this one.

As expected, the closer they walked, the more it looked like a Wizard Gate. Until Alrion confirmed it.

"I've another shot it would seem."

"Do I get to go through this one?" Lara laughed.

"Not without me. I'm not splitting my team up on opposite ends of the world." Alrion moved in closer and examined the symbols marked on the gate.

32

UNEXPECTED RETURN

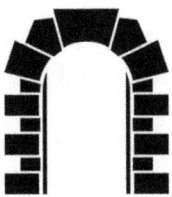

T he blazing heat and light subsided and Alyx found herself in a luxurious garden setting. The Wizard Gate was integrated into the stonework and Alyx had never noticed it before. But she knew this garden well. She spent so much time here.

Back in Valrytir. In the Specialist Training camp, no less.

It looked to be early evening and the garden was empty. Not that it ever attracted many people. Few had access, and of those who could come, they weren't the type to appreciate gardens. Initially, Alyx hadn't either. But it was a place she could train without unwanted eyes on her, so the garden had become a regular haunt during her time here.

Alyx didn't dally and started rushing out. She thought about the path she would need to take, and how to best avoid bumping into anyone. That was an awkward conversation she would rather not have.

The layout of the building seemed the same, not that she expected any changes. It hadn't been that long, really. She knew the new recruits would likely be in the mess hall, so she entered the large wooden building near their quarters, hoping the area would be deserted.

The polished floors and trophies along the walls brought back a lot of memories. Mostly good memories. A few painful ones. But she pushed them all aside, this was not a time for reminiscing. Now that she was back, she needed to find a quiet space to plan her time. Alrion would be coming here at some point, and he would need support in the city. Lara's influence would be quite useful, but it wouldn't hurt trying to line up more before they arrived. If she knew one thing about the Blight, it was that nobody took them on single-handedly and got away with it. Although she had almost done it.

At too great a cost. Then I was foolish enough to get infected after the fact.

Alyx made it through the building with speed and exited the giant doors. She was out on the path, heading towards the entry gate when she heard a voice.

"Alyx!" She kept walking, pretending she didn't hear.

Hopefully, she thinks she has the wrong person.

"Alyx, I know it's you!" The voice was accompanied by running footsteps. Alyx sighed and turned around.

"Mary?" The woman had not changed a bit. Still a ridiculous height and long blonde hair. Of course, it was tied up, and her uniform stole away a lot of her femininity.

"I don't believe it. You're here of all places?" Mary looked incredulous.

"I was in town, so wanted to sneak a look. It hasn't changed."

"You were in town? I thought you'd never come back. And stories of your exploits have gone around."

"What exactly?" Alyx asked, nervously.

How much do they know?

"The Skull King? I thought you were just having me on, I didn't realise you were serious. It's unbelievable!"

"I trained my whole life for it." Alyx looked away, trying to find a reason to leave. Mary must have sensed something.

"Look, I don't know why you're back. But come have a drink with me. I can't let you go without hearing your story." Mary's eyes had that look in them. Alyx knew it too well.

"Fine, lead the way. I know I have no choice."

"That's the spirit. And you can tell me where you got that sword too, and what happened to your one."

"This is just on loan." Alyx tapped the hilt with her hand.

"And your old sword?"

"Do you want that drink or not?" Alyx gave her a wry smile and Mary chuckled.

"Can't help myself. Can you blame me? That sword was bigger than you were!"

"I understand completely."

"I just can't believe you're here." Mary led her through the streets to a familiar place, *The Hard Stuff*.

"Did you expect anything else?"

"Not really, I just hadn't thought this far ahead." Alyx followed Mary inside. Mary directed her to a table, and she went up to the bar.

Alyx looked around at the clientele. Luckily, she didn't recognise anyone. But it would happen in due course. This was the preferred bar for all the specialist units. Mary returned with two cups and set them down carefully.

"So, spill. What happened exactly, on the day that you left?"

"We went on a skirmish. Small team. Was supposed to be reconnaissance, but we thought we could take out the scouting party."

"You and who else?"

"Just Adam."

"Oh, I see." Mary grabbed one cup and pushed the other towards Alyx. She drank deeply then set it down.

"It was a trap. The scouts were actually Tainted ones, and they had swarms of Blighters hidden a short distance away. We took two down but were then completely surrounded." Alyx had another drink.

"Did they offer terms?"

"No, they wanted to infect us and hold us until we were almost turning then send us back."

"Urgh. Horrible."

"Exactly. I... I didn't do justice to my name that day."

"What did you do?" Mary leaned forward, concern in her eyes.

"I became enraged, and just started attacking. I dragged Adam along with me. I created enough of an opening for us to make a break for it. But I didn't take it."

"You kept fighting?"

"Yes. I wanted to punish them for trying to trick us. It was a foolish move. Adam chose to stay too, and he got mauled. In the end, I had to do the same thing anyway. I created another opportunity and hauled him out of there. But it was too late."

"The infection had taken hold?"

"Exactly." Alyx drained the rest of her drink. She leaned back and closed her eyes. She could still see his expression. It wasn't anger or hate. That would have been fine. It was sadness at letting her down. That they would be separated. She drove the vision from her mind.

"And the commander went ballistic?"

"You better believe it. Did you know Adam was the general's son?"

"No. Really?"

"Yes. It was done in secret, to ensure he received proper training and didn't get treated differently to the rest. I knew, but most didn't."

"Is that why you left?"

"No. Looking back, I think I just felt like I had failed and couldn't stay any longer. And I don't think it was helping me anymore, I was only staying for his sake at that point."

"I'm so sorry."

"Yeah, well, can't change it now. Just try to make different mistakes." Alyx looked into her empty cup. Mary jumped up and charged over to the bar. She returned soon with two more cups.

"And what of your revenge? The Skull King?" Mary's eyes were alight with curiosity.

"I can't go into the full story. But I'll tell you this much." Alyx paused and took another sip of the new cup.

"I worked my way through his twisted arena bouts. Finally, as the champion, he needed to grant me a boon."

"Did you ask him to stab himself?" Mary laughed.

"That would have been a waste, he'd only regenerate."

"Oh, I see. What a monster."

"Yes, he was a piece of work. I challenged him to a duel to the death. He accepted quickly and laughed."

"And you fought him alone?"

"Alone and in front of a crowd, in the arena. He knew all about my family sword and thought that he had protected himself. But there was a secret he didn't know about."

"Which was?"

"Still a secret." Alyx paused and had another sip of her drink.

"That's no fun."

"I suppose not. At any rate, I won the day. But my sword was destroyed, I left it behind. And fled."

"But you won? Why did you flee?"

"Just because I won, didn't mean I was safe. The shock of what happened gave me an opportunity. But there were plenty of folks who used the Skull King's dominance for their own ends. I had a target on me. The best thing I could do was disappear."

"Wow. Even after all that, you still kept wandering."

"For a time."

"Well, now I have something to share that you won't believe." Mary gave her a secretive smile and slowly sipped on her drink.

"I'm waiting."

"It's about your sword."

"Yes?" Alyx stared at Mary

What is she talking about?

"We retrieved the pieces, they're being held here in Valrytir in an exhibit!"

"What?" Alyx almost shouted. She composed herself. "It doesn't matter, it can't be reforged. The technique required magic and nobody living knows how to do it."

"Not necessarily. But it is true that right now we can do nothing with it. For now, it's just a symbol of your triumph." Mary stared at Alyx. "But now we have you."

"I'm not back for that. I have a new mission." Alyx saw she had Mary's interest.

"Oh, now I have to hear about this."

"I'll need your help." Alyx hadn't thought this through, but it was obvious. Alrion would need military support when he arrived. Mary was the best way to start that conversation.

"You'll need my help?"

"Yes. We're going to need a rather large force."

"To do what?"

"Good question. Crush the Blight? Take down Darvin?" Mary burst into laughter.

"You don't aim small, do you? You don't think we haven't been trying?"

"You haven't had anything worth risking it all for."

"Oh, haven't we? And what have you got that changes everything?" Mary had a strange look on her face. It sounded like she was dismissing Alyx. But her expression, it was different. She was looking for hope. Looking for that spark that they didn't have. And Alyx had it. She had the missing piece.

"I have a wizard that can cure the Blight."

"Nonsense." Mary dismissed her with a hand gesture.

"I've seen it firsthand. He cured himself, and he even cured me." Alyx could see she had Mary's attention.

"I don't believe it."

"He'll be here soon enough, and you'll know then." Alyx leaned back and finished her drink. She had done what she could. Planting the seed would do for now. At least for Mary. She would act differently when Alrion arrived. Then she would claim prior knowledge and pretend like she was pulling everything together. This could still work.

"You think you can just waltz in and drop that information and disappear?" Mary looked annoyed.

"If that's what it takes." Alyx smiled.

"No, it's going to take more than that." Mary finished her drink and stood. She stood over Alyx. "If you want my help, you need to rejoin the unit."

"I have different priorities now."

"You did before as well. I can see your reluctance. It's alright, I'll sweeten the deal. You can duel me for a place in the unit. If you win, I'll take you in and help you build support for your wizard friend. If you lose, you can slink away and return when you're ready to fight."

"Why are you doing this? Helping me is in your interests. The Blight will be done. Ended."

"So, you say. It's not even about that. You abandoned us. You fled and didn't even say goodbye. You need to prove yourself again. If you can't beat me, then you don't want this enough. And that's not going to work for anyone." Mary stormed out of the inn. Alyx chased after her.

"Just like that?"

"Just like that. Follow me back to the training ground, or don't. It's your choice." Mary didn't utter another word.

I didn't realise she was so upset. I thought they understood. But I was wrong. If this is what it takes, so be it. I can beat her. I won't let Alrion down.

Alyx tried to remember how Mary fought, but she couldn't remember anything in particular. They didn't spar much, and Alyx was often on assignment with other squad members. They had mainly bonded because there were precious few women, and it had been because of Mary's insistence. Alyx had been so single-minded, she hadn't really tended to that friendship at all. And this was the price.

As they walked through the main building, people started to notice. Whispers followed them, and people started to trail along as well. Once they reached the training ground, there was quite a following. All wearing the uniform of the elite, the black and brown padded vests with armoured plating on their forearms and legs. Mary walked into the centre of the training ground and waited. The murmurs reduced to nothing. A lone man ran out with a sword, handing it over and rushing back into the crowd. Mary looked up and addressed the crowd.

"We are joined tonight by an old comrade. She was highly respected, a core member of the unit. But she abandoned us in a time of need, to fulfil her own quest. She's returned, not to serve, but to ask for more. For that reason, she needs to prove herself. Right here, right now." Mary clenched her right hand into a fist and whoops sounded all around the training ground.

Looks like I'm quite popular here.

"Alyx here figures herself quite the accomplished warrior. Which is why she has agreed to duel three of us at once." Mary smiled and waved over two other fighters. One was male, and the other was female. They looked like they were twins.

Oh no. Not them.

Alyx recognised them. The terrible twins. An impossible pair, they harried any force with amazing precision, each one instinctively guessing what the other was thinking, leading to manoeuvres that were impossible to see coming. Mary could just sit back and let those two wear her down or create an opening. Then Mary could swoop in and finish it off. It wouldn't even take long. Alyx closed her eyes and focused.

You can do this. You destroyed the Skull King. You survived being infected, you survived being cured. You made it all the way here. Alrion is depending on you. It's time to win them over, it's time to show them why you're the best.

Alyx opened her eyes and drew her sword. A quiet murmur rippled through the crowd as the Runesteel glinted in the light.

"Begin!" Mary pointed with her sword and the twins moved in, their swords whirling in confusing patterns as they approached.

Divide and conquer.

Alyx targeted the male twin, named Shane. She went all-out attack, forcing him into a defensive stance. His sister, Sherry, tried to flank, but Alyx had pressed so hard that Shane was constantly retreating. That gave Alyx a little breathing room. Not for long.

Mary moved in, poking dangerously and interrupting Alyx's assault. This gave both Shane and Sherry ample opportunity to close in. Now it was Alyx retreating, blocking and parrying the multiple sword strikes coming from different directions and heights.

I can't keep this up forever.

Alyx knocked a few attacks back harder than necessary, to force the attackers to pause momentarily. The effort worked and made a strange sound.

What's that about?

Alyx dashed backwards to give herself some space. She was reaching the limit of the training ground. Mary approached from the front with a wicked grin. Shane and Sherry approached from the other sides. As Sherry whirled her sword around Alyx noticed something.

There's a nick on the blade.

Then she remembered. I'm wielding Runesteel. These must be ordinary swords. I can end this fight quickly. Alyx changed her stance, inviting attacks by lowering her guard. She needed to parry quickly and bide her time. But she was running out of space and she was beginning to tire. Fighting three high-intensity sword wielders at once was a huge drain. Suddenly she saw an opening, a slightly sloppy strike from Shane. Rather than parry, Alyx let it slide by and aimed for the sword. She swung with all her might, and the blades connected with a crash. But the Runesteel won out, and after the initial resistance, the other blade snapped apart, the metal dropping to the ground. Shane stepped back, perplexed. There was a murmur of wonder running through the crowd. Alyx took the advantage and turned her focus to Sherry. She hastily parried the strikes, trying to minimise the risk of Alyx also breaking her blade.

Alyx swung high, then kicked a leg out, dropping Sherry to her knees. Alyx quickly recovered and swung her sword down, forcing Sherry to raise hers to defend herself. With the high position and momentum, Alyx sliced through Sherry's blade. She didn't even pause and stepped to the side to continue her movement. She advanced on Mary immediately.

"Nice trick, but it won't work on my blade." Mary laughed. But Alyx could see the frustration behind her eyes.

"Now, we are back to what should have been the contest." Alyx was still tiring, but she felt a wave of renewed energy now that the twins were out of the fight. Thankfully, they accepted their defeat honourably and retreated to the sidelines.

Alyx slowed her attacks and paused. Mary stood at the ready, watching warily.

"It's time to finish this." Alyx steeled herself and prepared to attack. Mary raised her sword, waiting.

Just one opponent and she's human. Should be easy.

Alyx closed her eyes for an instant, drawing upon all her energy and focus. She became one with her weapon and charged it with all her will. She and the weapon were a force of skill and power. Like one they glided forward, nothing was an impediment. Each block, parry, or strike from Mary was just another step towards the next attack. Mary kept up well, but the constant fluidity and single-purpose of Alyx's attack could not be turned back. Bit by bit, Mary retreated, and she started making mistakes. Strikes glanced off her armoured forearms, which caused further mistakes. Finally, Alyx pushed even harder, with a final flurry of attacks. Her final attack was so strong that Mary's weapon was knocked from her hands and she cried out, dropping to her knees.

"Yield." Alyx pointed her weapon at Mary's neck.

"I yield. You won." Alyx sheathed the sword and started walking away.

33

A LIFETIME AGO

A lrion stepped back.

"Looks like this one can do multiple destinations."

"Try it?" Lara said. Alrion pressed one of the symbols. It lit up in a faint blue light and the gate itself roared to life. A flash of light and heat then a shimmering picture hung before them.

"That was easy." Lara stepped forward and stared at it. Alrion held onto her shoulder.

"Don't fall in by mistake."

"Of course not." Lara chuckled and continued inspecting the scene before them.

"It's not clear where this is, looks awfully dark."

"Let's check the other one." Alrion pressed another symbol and there was another flash, the scene changing again. This looked to be somewhere in the mountains.

"There's not really mountains near Paperton are there?"

"I wouldn't say so. We're probably better off with the dark one."

"Provided it isn't a trap."

"I'm sure the two of us are pretty safe. Besides, only wizards can use these."

"Don't forget that we just took two Shade Wizards." Alrion looked at the different symbols. He couldn't read what they were supposed to say. He looked to Lara.

"I'm just saying, we know that one of these is definitely the wrong direction. What harm can it be trying the other?"

"I can't argue with that." Alrion pressed the button and the light flashed again, the scene changing back to the dark one.

"Ready?"

"Absolutely." Alrion stepped forward, bringing Lara with him. He felt an intense light and heat go over him. Suddenly he was somewhere else. It was a dark room, constructed of stone. He created an orb of light and attached it to the roof.

"It's a bit cooler here, definitely not a desert but not mountains either."

"There are no windows in here. Are those stairs over there?" Alrion pointed to the end of the room.

"Yes. Let's investigate." Lara walked ahead and Alrion took his time, trying to work out where they were. But it became clear that they needed more to work with. The stairs were narrow and cramped and were slow to descend. Alrion floated the orb of light ahead of them, illuminating the stairs. Finally, they reached the bottom, and it was a simple entry area with a door.

"It's so enclosed, I have no idea where we are. Did we come down from a height, or did we descend deeper into the ground?" Lara said.

"I have no idea. But it doesn't feel like we are underground." Alrion placed a hand on the door and it activated, opening instantly.

"Curious." Alrion noticed light stream in as the doors opened.

"Good, I wasn't looking forward to being underground again." Lara stepped outside immediately. Alrion followed her and looked around. They were in a small settlement, which looked ravaged by fire and other damage. The building they had been in was a tower, which looked like it had survived better than the rest.

"That must be a wizard tower. Which means there might be other things here of interest." Alrion started walking around the tower, seeing what else was there. He noticed another large door, made of wood, on the opposite end of the tower.

"Let's take a look." Alrion stood before the door and Lara joined him. She tried to open the door, but nothing happened. Alrion placed a hand on the door. He felt something resonate within. But the door didn't open.

"Is it a magical door?" Lara said.

"I believe so. It must be a Wizard Store. In the past, I used a knock to open it. This one seems different."

"Maybe it needs your name?"

"I doubt that." Alrion stared at the door. "Alrion," he said finally. The door unlocked and started to open.

"Maybe I should be a wizard?" Lara said with a laugh.

"I think so, you're more qualified." Alrion stepped inside and took it in. The room was rather dishevelled. He created another few orbs of light and floated them into the space, attaching at different parts of the ceiling.

"Looks kind of trashed." Lara walked inside, stepping around the debris. Alrion picked up a few books and looked at them.

"Nothing interesting here, just general wizard tomes." He kept picking his way through, trying random books.

"This looks like something official." Lara was standing before a desk of some kind, tucked into the corner. Alrion walked over to join her.

"There's some sort of ledger here on the counter." Lara started flipping through.

"What's inside?"

"I think it's the name of visitors." Lara skimmed over the contents, trying to find the last page.

"There's my name!" Lara looked at him with excitement.

"You're right. Hang on, what's this?" Alrion pointed to the next name.

"Celes? Your mother was here?"

"Recently. What's she doing here? In a Wizard Store?" Alrion stepped back. It didn't make sense.

"Didn't your parents say they were going to Paperton to track down information for you? Maybe this is part of their journey."

"Maybe we're closer to Paperton than we realise. Can you open up that map?" Lara retrieved the map from her bag and opened it up.

"I can't tell from here, we don't know what this place is called. And they sure don't have Wizard Stores and Wizard Gates marked on it."

"Maybe something else in here has the name." Alrion looked around the room. He grabbed a book at random and looked in the covers, and the first and last pages.

"Here's something. 'Property of Arnthorn Wizard Store. Please return after you are finished.'"

"Let me check the map, surely that's the name of this area." Lara pored over the map and stuck her finger on a spot.

"This is it. Barely registers, but it's here. You're in luck." Lara looked up and smiled.

"Yes?"

"We're so near Paperton. We could get there by tonight."

"Wow, that's great. Pity we had to leave the horses behind." Alrion sighed.

"I know. I'm starting to think we should just stop getting them. Unless..." Lara trailed off.

"Unless what?"

"Do you think that horses could go through a Wizard Gate?" Alrion laughed.

"I'd like to see you get one up those stairs."

"Don't tempt me." Lara winked and folded the map. She stashed it back into her jacket.

"Let's be off then." Alrion closed the ledger and carefully stepped over to the door. He held it open for Lara and they both left the building.

The rest of the area looked more damaged.

"Something bad happened here, that's for sure."

"At least that tower survived. It really saved us," Lara said.

"I know, I feel like we've traipsed all over the world. It was nice that we found a little shortcut on the way here. Especially when it feels like we are back-tracking."

"It's not backtracking, it's returning. You are coming back with more skills, experience, and knowledge." Lara smiled.

"That's a good way of looking at it." Alrion returned the smile and looked past the burnt and ruined buildings. There was a small trail outside and they started to follow it.

"This should link up to a main road, which we can follow all the way to Paperton."

"Excellent." Alrion lost himself in his thoughts and followed along. As Lara predicted they found the main road and kept walking. After a while, Alrion piped up.

"I wonder how Caleb is going?"

"It really hasn't been that long, but it feels like an age has passed. I keep picturing him old and wizened, but I know that's ridiculous."

"I know what you mean. Maybe he will have grown a beard?" Alrion chuckled and Lara joined in.

"He's a good man, hopefully, he can help you."

"I'm sure he can. Both Branthor and the mysterious wizard think so." Alrion sighed.

"One thing at a time. We'll figure out who's behind the scenes. But first, let's act on what we can. You need to learn as much as you can, so you know how to complete the quest. This whole thing won't end until you can perform that spell."

"I know. We've done a lot of good already. But we need to reverse everything. Darvin will keep building otherwise, or someone else will rise up to replace him. The Blight is so resilient."

"It is. But so are we." Lara leaned in and gave him a kiss on the cheek, then sped off. Alrion laughed.

"Where are you going?"

"Just follow me!" Lara kept running, aiming at something in the distance. Suddenly, she stopped. Alrion slowed down and stopped alongside her.

"Now look at that." Lara pointed at the scene beyond. Alrion drew in a breath. They could see all the way into the valley, looking down at Paperton. It was dusk now, and tufts of smoke and a few lights could be seen coming from the odd-shaped buildings.

"There it is, just the same. Do you remember when we first came?" Alrion said.

"Yes. We had a horse then." Lara laughed. "But seriously, it was quite intense. We were racing against time. Falric had just passed. It wasn't a good time."

"It wasn't." Alrion remained quiet for a moment. "But we're in a better place now. Eventually." Lara pulled him close, so their heads were side by side and they could watch Paperton breathe. Alrion felt calm.

"It's time, let's go." They separated and started the descent down into Paperton.

∼

After a long and winding walk, they arrived at the entry to the town. Most of the scholars had taken shelter within their homes and the streets were empty.

"Where do we start?" Lara said.

"Let's try the main hall. It worked last time."

"Sure." Lara started off towards the large building. The lights were on, which was promising. Alrion remembered when he had charged in and disrupted the whole meeting. It was all done on instinct, with a little prompting from Lara. But they had achieved the impossible. They convinced the scholars and he gained access to the Pool. Things should be easier now.

I bet they're not.

Alrion chuckled to himself.

"What's so funny?"

"Oh, nothing. I just thought that even though things should be easier this time, they probably won't be."

"Don't be like that. Think positive. We're going to get the best possible outcome!" Lara poked him in the side with her index finger and smirked at him. It worked, he couldn't possibly carry on that pessimistic line of thinking. Continuing, they soon reached the giant doors of the main hall. Alrion reached out to push open the doors when they started to open of their own accord. A short bald man was leaving at the same time. He stopped, surprised. Then he wore a broad grin.

"Alrion! Lara! Wow, this is a surprise." Caleb looked thrilled.

"Caleb, you haven't changed a bit." Alrion reached out and shook the scholar's hand.

"We thought maybe you would have a beard or something," Lara said. Caleb laughed.

"Not for lack of trying. Come in, come in." Caleb turned around and ushered them into the main building. It was empty, as expected. But Alrion could still remember when it had been full. He chuckled to himself as he remembered his antics on that day.

"Have you spoken to your parents?" Caleb said.

"Not for a while. Are they here?"

"Oh, no. They were here, but they left. They did say you might be coming, but I didn't know whether to expect you or not. I must say, this is a happy reunion!"

"It is. I'm curious, did they leave because they got what they were after?"

"I don't know how to answer that one, but I don't think so. It's something we should discuss further." Caleb led them through the hall and over to a small door at the back.

"How have you been? Studying hard?" Lara asked.

"Oh yes. I have been working closely with my mentor to master my ability to manage the knowledge from the Pool, and coach others in its use. There is a great deal we can share."

"Great, that's why I'm here. When can I start?" Alrion held the door open for Lara and entered last. They were walking down a narrow corridor and ended up at a desk, with a man sitting there.

"More visitors?" he said.

"Yes, they're with me." Caleb turned to Alrion. "We can start as soon as you want, but I need to introduce my mentor to you. We will be working closely together." Caleb beamed another big smile.

Wow, he must really like this mentor. I guess that's good, it may speed things up if he's good at what he does.

"Off you go, you know the drill." The man waved them away, and Caleb led them through another door. A short walk later they found themselves in another chamber. An old man sat at a desk at the rear, wearily turning the pages in a hefty book. As he looked up Alrion stood dead in his tracks.

"No way. You died. I tried to save you."

"I appreciated the effort. But I wasn't going to let myself go that easily." Falric smiled a little sheepishly.

"Falric!" Lara ran over and hugged him.

"Have we met?" Falric said with a laugh. Lara stepped back and looked at him curiously.

"I don't think you ever met me. But I've been with you all for a while."

"Since Carford," Alrion said with a wry grin.

"Yes, Vincent mentioned you. There is a lot we must discuss."

"I agree." Alrion couldn't quite share Lara's enthusiasm at finding Falric. Yes, he felt an overwhelming sense of relief. And happiness that his mentor was alive. But it was also accompanied by a sense of emptiness, of abandonment.

Why did he stay here and say nothing? Or is he that mysterious wizard, trying to help me in other ways?

Alrion walked over to talk to the master wizard at length.

34

DIVING IN

"Come take a seat, so that I might tell you a tale." Falric gestured to the empty seats. Caleb brought them closer to the desk and waited at the edge of the room. Once Alrion and Lara were seated he began again.

"Alrion, your father had almost the same reaction." Falric sighed and shook his head. "I feel like this is just a repeat of that scene."

"What explanation did you tell him?"

"The truth. At heart, I'm a scholar, not a warrior. I made a pretty good administrator as well, and researcher too. This place was my home, so when things played out the way that they did, it made sense for me to stay here."

"What do you mean played out the way they did?"

"I confronted Branthor. Once he was close, I knew it was him, although I didn't understand why. When you saw us, I couldn't risk you being dragged into the conflict. I hoped that by succumbing to him, that he would be satisfied and move on."

"Then why didn't you just rejoin me straight away?"

"I overdid things. My own ruse, whilst protecting me, helped hinder my escape. It was quite an effort to emerge from that rubble. You know better than anyone. I sensed your efforts on the surface."

"I've never felt more powerless. It has followed me ever since." Falric bowed his head when he heard the words.

"I am deeply sorry for that. I never wanted you to feel that. You should never feel responsible for an old wizard like me, I can take care of myself. I'm accountable for my actions and decisions, nobody else is." Falric paused and coughed. "I see now the impact it had on you. More than I foresaw. Which is my oversight."

"I am at least glad you're alive."

"Oh, I know that. I know that. I also expected that you would return, for one reason or another. Because you would need to seek clarification here before moving forward."

"Why would you think that?"

"The Pool works in mysterious ways, but there's a strong theme of protection within it. It hides knowledge from you that you aren't ready to know. It's mostly a practical measure, to protect the mind from being overwhelmed. But the more we study it, we believe it to be more nuanced than that." Falric looked to Caleb. He nodded.

"Especially when it comes to wizards. The knowledge of spells can be catastrophic. There seem to be additional protections in place."

"Such as?" Alrion asked.

"You know how a spellbook will have blank pages until you have the skill and capability to handle the spell?"

"Yes."

"Similar to that. Knowledge pertaining to spells within the Pool will be hidden from you until you are ready to receive it."

"You're talking about the final spell. The one to cure the Blight for good?"

"Yes. I know just about all there is to know about it. But even for me, it didn't all come at once."

"But it's not something you'll tell me, is it?" Alrion looked Falric directly in the eyes. He looked surprised.

"Oh, yes you are quite correct. Why did you say that?"

"Branthor said the same thing to me. That he knew what lay ahead, and he couldn't share it either. That there was something missing if I didn't yet have the knowledge." Falric closed his eyes and looked to be deep in thought.

"You've worked wonders, young man. You didn't just cure Branthor, you saved him. That is the advice I would have expected from him, from the old Branthor." Falric looked like a weight had been lifted from him.

I didn't think about it, but he must have been carrying the weight of Branthor's fate too. Although, he mustn't know how it ended.

"I'm sorry to say that Branthor has passed."

"What? How?" Falric sat upright, keenly attentive.

"He destroyed Rindale but took a fatal blow. I wanted to save him..."

"But he asked you not to?" Falric sighed and closed his eyes again. Alrion saw a single tear escape them.

"He really is at peace then." The master wizard gave them a weak smile, and he looked older than he ever had before. "Thank you for sharing that, and for treating him with such humanity. He walked the wrong path, but it was some-thing easy to do and hard to turn back."

"I know," Alrion said quietly.

"Well, I guess you're keen to get on with things. But before we do, it's appropriate that I briefly mention what your parents are doing."

"Sure."

"We discussed the idea that a wizard has been sending you messages via the notebook you took from the academy."

"Go on." Alrion wondered if Falric was going to be making a revelation.

"It's not me."

"Oh, I thought that it might be since you're alive."

"Although that's a good theory since I'm confident that the wizard must have handled the notebook to be writing in it!"

"Really?" Alrion burst out. That narrowed down the list of people substantially.

"Don't get too carried away," Lara said.

"Why not?"

"Didn't you lose that notebook for a time?" Lara looked at him sceptically.

"Yes, you're right. I recovered it from one of those Trackers. But I was getting messages long before that."

"Let's not get hung up on that detail, for now, there are many ways that a wizard could access your personal belongings, especially if they've been trailing you." Falric gave Alrion and Lara serious looks. He seemed intent on getting back to the topic he had introduced.

"Sure. Please continue."

"I will. We determined that a wizard named Aydan accessed the Wizard Store in Paperton. That is likely an alias, and there's good reason to suspect it is the identity of the wizard that is watching you from afar."

"Aydan. That's his name. Or at least what he calls himself."

"Can't say that I've ever heard of it," Lara said.

"It's in the old language. It means 'Lost One'."

"Interesting. What's this got to do with my parents?"

"We jointly decided that the best way for them to help with your quest was to determine the identity of this individual. So that there were no surprises when you were ready to perform the final spell."

"Is that because you can't tell them things about my quest?"

"Primarily, yes. Although your mother was quite concerned about the risk of this wizard interfering more directly."

"That's why we saw her name in a nearby Wizard Store," Lara said.

"Oh, you found that one?"

"We came in through that Wizard Gate," Alrion said. Falric looked surprised.

"I'm surprised that it's still working. They aren't used much anymore, too prone to failure."

"I've discovered that also." Alrion instantly thought about Alyx, trapped somewhere far away.

"Where are Vincent and Celes off to?" Lara said.

"They're following an old trail. Aydan first passed through here around twenty years ago. They believe that there's more chance of unlocking a clue to his identity in the past."

"That's a good idea. Do you know where they were heading?"

"I know where they will end up." Falric paused for a moment, looking from Alrion to Lara. "They will end up in Valrytir." Lara let out a short gasp but quickly hid it. Alrion still noticed.

"Why Valrytir?" she said.

"The conclusion of Alrion's quest is nearby, and there's also a notable Wizard Store there."

"All roads lead to Valrytir. It all ends there." Alrion's voice was more solemn than he expected. Falric gave him an odd look.

"In a sense, not necessarily a literal one. Right, now that I've brought you up to date, I think we need to address your training. Caleb?" Falric beckoned for the scholar to come over. He strode over immediately.

"Caleb will be your primary instructor in this. I will provide additional instruction and advice from a wizard's perspective."

"How long will this take?"

"As long as it needs. You are the decider of that." Caleb bowed to Alrion.

"You talk like a wizard," Alrion laughed. Falric chuckled too.

"He's right though. A good deal of this is up to you."

"I get it. Can we start?"

"Absolutely. Come with me." Caleb walked back to the doorway and waited for Alrion.

"Here we go. Don't let Falric off too easy on the questions." Alrion winked at Lara and joined Caleb. In moments, they were walking back through the building.

"Are we going back to the Pool?"

"Oh no, there's no need for that. I don't think it's recommended either. What we're going to do is visit the immersion room."

"That sounds interesting." Alrion tried to picture what it looked like but wasn't sure. He kept imagining something like the Vault of Silence but figured it had to be different. Caleb brought them back to the main hall, but he led Alrion to another door, almost hidden around the other side of the stage.

"We're almost at the entrance," Alrion commented.

"Almost, but not quite." Caleb stood before the door and waited. "Please enter." Alrion pushed the door open and walked inside. There was a tiny window in the ceiling letting in the sun's rays, otherwise, the room was quite dim. It looked like a pool in the middle. The walls were all painted white.

"What is this room?"

"This is a tool to help your mind relax and detach from the everyday. You will see a chest over there, that's for your clothes."

"Really?" Alrion looked back at Caleb.

"You would not be comfortable with them weighing you down. We also recommend you scrub yourself down over there." Caleb pointed to a bucket and stool at one end of the room.

"Are you going to stay in here?"

"Oh no, we have thought of that. There is an adjoining room that I can use to talk you through what you need to do. Your privacy will be respected."

"Sure. I guess I better get started."

"Please. I will await your signal." Caleb left the room, closing the door softly behind him. Once the door closed the space seemed extremely quiet.

"It's worth a try," Alrion muttered to himself. He removed all his clothing and dutifully used the bucket and brush to scrub down. He rinsed himself as best as he could and approached the water. It was nicely warmed somehow and felt comfortable. He stepped in and found himself standing at the bottom, the water up to his neck.

"Lay back," a voice said from somewhere else. Alrion looked around and couldn't find the source.

"Lay back, you will float." Alrion realised that it must be Caleb, and he tried leaning back. With careful manoeuvring he was able to lie on his back, floating in the water. He was fully submerged except for his head.

"Good, close your eyes and start to picture the Pool of Knowledge." Alrion closed his eyes and thought back to that day. He had been terribly injured by Branthor and had stumbled over to the Pool. While drinking, he had tumbled into it and blacked out.

I don't think you get more immersed than that.

He kept waiting for Caleb's voice again, but there was nothing. Just quiet. He started to lose track of time, and where he was. His limbs too were almost indistinguishable.

"Imagine that you are diving into the Pool of Knowledge. All that you need is there, right at the bottom. You are diving deeper and deeper." Alrion tried to follow along, and imagine the story that Caleb was speaking.

"What does the Knowledge look like?"

"A chest. But it's locked," Alrion said. He could see the chest now. It was made of wood and reinforced with steel. A large keyhole adorned the front. He knew he couldn't force it open.

"Where's the key?" Caleb's voice said. Alrion searched all around, there was no key. He banged his hand on the chest in frustration. The pain coursed through him, way more intense than expected.

"You must find the key." Alrion held his hands up in annoyance. There seemed to be markings on them. He searched his arms and found more markings.

The key is on me somewhere.

Alrion kept searching, checking his shoulders, legs, and head. Finally, he saw it. The key was emblazoned on his chest. He tried touching it and the heat almost burned him.

Ouch. How do I get it?

He tried again, reaching out. This time he kept his hand on the key, embracing the heat. He let it pass through him. The pain lessened. Dark thoughts started to bombard him. Fear. Doubt. Regret. Anxiety. Rather than resist, he let them pass through as well. He didn't need those, they could go. Suddenly he had the key in his hand. Without any hesitation, he thrust it into the chest and turned sharply.

35

CLOSING IN

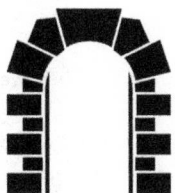

C eles stumbled to regain her footing and looked around. She looked
like she was in a cellar, with some light leaking in from nearby. The
gate itself was almost invisible.

That snake Ashra, he played me. Bloody wizards.

Ashra was right about the gate though, it didn't look like it was working at
all. The space felt oppressive, and she didn't want to return to the desert, so she
ignored the gate and cautiously walked towards the stairs. They were cut from
stone and headed up to somewhere well-lit.

Might as well see where I am.

She took each stair one at a time and listened carefully. It seemed quiet
above her, although she did hear the occasional sound of footsteps. As she
reached the end of the staircase, she noticed a shadow up ahead.

"Hello?" Celes said.

"Please show yourself," an older male voice said. It sounded strong, but also
a bit apprehensive. Celes approached slowly with her hands up, trying to look
non-threatening.

"Can I ask who you are?" the man said. He looked like a retired farmer, his
grey hair belying his age and his simple work clothes looked faded and worn.

"My name is Celes. It sounds rather incredible, but I just walked through a
Wizard Gate."

"Yes, that's the one. Clearly, you're no wizard though." The man eyed her
suspiciously.

"No, a wizard activated it for me. I had no idea it opened up in your cellar?"
Celes paused, offering the man a chance to introduce himself.

"I'm Lyle, and this is my home. I'm no wizard either." Lyle looked her up and down. "You seem harmless enough, come over and have some tea and you can tell me why you ended up here." Lyle beckoned for her to follow and walked off. Celes cautiously followed, looking around the home. It seemed quite nicely built, but old. It seemed a bit too grand for a farmer's home.

"You're probably wondering why I live here?" Lyle said as he walked into the kitchen. There was a black pot simmering over the stove. Whatever was in there smelled wonderful.

"I was. Not everyone has a Wizard Gate in their basement." Celes smiled and Lyle chuckled.

"No, they do not. Take a seat, please." Lyle sat down at a tiny rectangular table and offered Celes the other chair. They were wooden and old but looked sturdy.

"This place has been in my family for a while. The going story is that a long time ago a wizard lived here. He built this home because he loved the area and constructed that Wizard Gate so that he could return here from his travels."

"I see. Do you have a lot of visitors popping in?"

"No, it's incredibly rare. It's been years since I had anyone. Easy to tell too, that thing goes off like a firecracker. You can't miss it."

"Good to know. So, you can count the number of people you've seen come through here?"

"Absolutely. You're the first that's not a wizard." Lyle gave her a curious look and stood, checking the bubbling pot. He seemed content and pulled out two bowls from a nearby drawer and carefully ladled steaming liquid into both. He gently placed them down on the table and laid down spoons and a rough but clean cloth serviette.

"Now's the part when you tell your story." Lyle carefully spooned some stew into his mouth. Celes looked at hers and decided it was too hot.

"It's a long story, but I suppose I can describe it like this. A strange wizard is following my son around and sending him messages. All we have to go on is a name, so I'm following his trail to try to unearth his identity."

"Oh, now that's interesting." Lyle had another spoon of food. Celes decided to try it. It wasn't as hot as it looked, and the food was delicious. More spices than she expected.

"This is lovely. Quite an unexpected flavour."

"Thank you. It's a local dish, makes use of our produce. The blend of spices is not normally used, so visitors really get a kick out of it." Lyle took another spoon.

"Where is here anyway?"

"Stonebridge. We're in a tiny little town in the hills outside Valrytir."

"Wow, I never heard of this place."

"Not many have. The name comes from the stone bridge connecting this town to Valrytir. Some say it was the only way in back in the day. Who knows?" Lyle shrugged and had some more stew. Celes kept eating and looked down into the bowl. She had almost finished.

"Lyle, I have to thank you for the meal, and the hospitality. I don't want to intrude on you any longer than necessary. But before I go, is there anything you could tell me?"

"About your mystery man?"

"Or the area. Is there anything special here?"

"Other than the gate? I don't think so." Lyle scratched his head and looked thoughtful.

"Now that you mention it, there is something." Lyle leaned forward, a conspiratorial look on his face.

"It would have been around twenty years ago, a man passed through that gate. I don't remember the name he gave, but it could be the one you are looking for."

"That's great. Can you describe him at all?"

"He was young. Tall with dark hair. Intense looking eyes. Seemed a little bit troubled, you know?"

"Sure. Did he do anything special while he was here?"

"He did ask about the place. Seemed like he knew something. He asked me to take him into the cellar."

"Where the gate is?"

"Yeah, there's a trapdoor there and another room underneath. To be honest, I was surprised that he knew about it." Lyle paused and finished his stew, pushing the bowl away.

"What was down there?"

"Some old trunks, nothing of value that I could see. But then it was the strangest thing."

"What's that?"

"He asked me to hang back, so I retreated back to the room with the gate. I waited and waited. But he just up and vanished. I couldn't see where he went. And he never came back." Lyle sat back in his chair and looked at Celes.

"That's an interesting story." She wondered if this man was trustworthy. On the surface, he looked like he was, but at the same time, the whole story sounded sketchy. And a good way to get a woman trapped in a cellar.

Do I take the bait and investigate, or do I just leave?

Despite asking the question, Celes knew what she would do. It was the same impulse that led her to stepping into that Wizard Gate and landing in the desert. She stood quickly.

"Lyle, if you don't mind, I'd like to see the space that you are talking about."

"Really?" Lyle gave her a confused look. "There's nothing there."

"Something doesn't add up. I know he was a wizard, but my gut is telling me he did something down there. He didn't just vanish."

"Well, if you insist, I can take you there. Certainly gone through myself many a time and found nothing." Lyle stood up and walked around the table, making his way out of the room. Celes was sure he was telling the truth, but she had to investigate. She followed him back to the room with the Wizard Gate. He grabbed a lantern off the wall and ran it back to the kitchen to light it. He returned quickly, lighting the room.

"See over there?" Lyle pointed to the corner of the room. It was barely noticeable, but Celes did see a metal trapdoor.

"That's quite subtle." Celes walked over and investigated. It wasn't locked. As it swung open, she could see a ladder leading down. She couldn't see what was below.

"I'd appreciate it if you..." Celes turned and addressed Lyle but she was cut off. He roughly shoved her, and she stumbled into the hole. She managed to grab one of the ladder rungs with one hand and quickly steadied herself with the other hand. She reached up to climb and saw the trapdoor closing above her. She kept climbing and shoved the trapdoor as hard as she could.

You idiot, how could you let him do that.

Celes banged the trapdoor.

"Don't be foolish, let me out this instant!" Celes kept banging. After a few moments, she paused and listened.

"I'm sorry. I had to promise him."

"Who?"

"He called himself Darvin. Said I had to hold any who came through the gate. It was the only way to save myself."

"He won't know! Just let me out!"

"I'm sorry, I can't take that chance. I really wish it didn't have to be this way." Celes heard something sliding into place. She banged against the trapdoor again and it still wouldn't budge.

I can't believe this just happened. Think, Celes, think.

Celes took a deep breath and climbed down the ladder. It was pitch-black, and she could see nothing.

He hid his intentions well, and I walked right into it. But I know he wasn't lying about this room. I know for sure. Maybe, just maybe, Aydan found a way out of here that Lyle never did.

Celes didn't have a choice. Or anything else to do. So, she stepped onto the ground and felt around for a wall. She found it easily, solid stone. With a little effort, she found she could reach the ceiling as well.

Time to start the search.

Celes felt her way along the wall, taking care to press the entire surface and feel for anything different. So far, nothing. Just more of the same stone. After a while, she kicked something solid and swore. Regaining her composure, she bent down and felt around. The object felt like a chest. It was definitely closed. She found the latch and opened the chest.

Please don't regret this.

She stuck her hand into the chest slowly, feeling around. It seemed empty. She did find what seemed like a scrap of cloth in one corner.

Nothing. Keep going.

Celes stood and navigated her way around the chest, continuing her search. She came across two more chests in the same fashion. And again, after a careful probe each was empty. One had a scrap of paper, but she had no way of looking at it.

So far, you've verified Lyle's story about the contents of this room. Now assuming the wizard could go invisible, he may have just given Lyle the slip. However, he had knowledge of this place. Maybe he knew of something that Lyle didn't. A secret passage created by the original wizard. You have to keep looking.

Celes pressed on, following the rest of the walls. Eventually, she had traversed the whole room and found nothing. She sank down and sighed.

Nothing on the walls. Maybe this is a fool's errand.

Celes suddenly had an idea.

The floor!

She started to crawl along, feeling around with her hands. The stone felt the same as the walls, albeit a bit more worn down. She kept exploring, keeping up the disciplined search. She couldn't afford to miss anything. Systematically she scoured the room, working her way along the floor. Finally, she noticed something. It felt like a depression in the floor. Small and circular. She tried pressing it with her hand, but nothing happened. As much as she felt around it there didn't seem to be any switches or toggles. But it did remind her of something.

The wizard medallion.

It was a long shot, but she had nothing to lose. Celes grabbed the medallion from her clothing and pressed it into the floor. She heard a strange hum and a click, then something moved. Celes scrambled back, trying to see what was happening. A rumbling sound continued, then eased off. Surveying the room, Celes couldn't see anything different. She carefully approached the area and probed with her hands. Something was there. A set of stairs going down. She carefully negotiated her way down backwards, letting her feet find the next step while she clung to the stairs. It was quite a way down. Once she reached the room her feet stepped onto a metal plate of some kind. It made a clunking sound then the stairs started to move. Celes jerked back and found a wall to lean on.

I did it! And now the way is closed. I'm safe, for now. If you can call alone in a pitch-black tunnel safe.

Celes laughed softly and started to make her way.

36

REVELATION

The chest burst open with light, disorientating Alrion. When he regained his senses, he was in a library. Sitting at a desk, scribbling away, was Granthion.

This is just like that dream I had.

Alrion walked up to his grandfather.

"Hello," he said hesitantly. Granthion motioned for Alrion to sit but didn't look over. Alrion pulled up a wooden chair and sat, leaning on the heavy table. After a few moments, Granthion looked up.

"Ah, you're back. Good to see you."

"I suppose I passed that? I'm worthy of the knowledge?"

"I'm not here to judge you." Granthion leaned back and chuckled. "You see I..." he began to speak again but Alrion cut him off.

"Yes, I know. You're a part of my mind, generated as a representation to help personalise this information I have inside me."

"Good, you're a quick study. Well, maybe not quick, more that you seem to retain knowledge well."

"I can see why my father found you difficult."

"Oh yes. He found it testing, and well it wasn't easy for me too. But he'll never truly understand that. Just think..." Granthion trailed off. He seemed to be waiting for a prompt.

"Just think?"

"I was going to say something, but I can't tell you yet. Not my fault." Granthion looked at Alrion disapprovingly. Alrion sighed.

"Of course. Can I at least see the spell now?" Granthion tapped the spellbook and it slid across the table. Alrion stopped it with his hand and started reading.

"Curing the Blight," he read out loud. This time the rest of the text was readable. With his heart pounding, he read on.

That's hardly a revelation. More basic information.

Alrion looked up. Granthion was sitting patiently, waiting.

"This is pretty basic so far. Why was this information held back?"

"I'm not sure. Maybe you weren't ready for even that? Maybe there are subtle hints within the background information that are too crucial to expose?" Granthion shrugged. Alrion turned back to the tome. He kept reading.

Here we go. Some juicy details.

He read about the location. It was described in detail, although he couldn't make sense of the directions. But the directions did start with Valrytir.

"Good, it is near Valrytir." Alrion looked over but Granthion didn't respond in any way. He turned back to reading. There was a section about how the Soul Power needed to flow through to the Source of the Blight. That made sense. More details that weren't particularly exciting. He knew there was something more to this, separate to all these incidental details. Suddenly, he spotted it. Alrion reeled back, almost falling from his chair.

"No. No, this can't be. Why would you do this?" Alrion stood, pointing at Granthion. The wizard looked saddened.

"I'm sorry, I don't make the rules."

"That's not fair. Why should it be like that?"

"There is a balance to all things. Do you believe the power of the Light is all-consuming and all-powerful?"

"Yes."

"It's not. Your will and purpose propel it forward. But it does not make you untouchable."

"I'm not asking to be untouchable."

"It sure sounds like you are. You want to withdraw the power of the Blight from the world, stuff it back where it came from, and suffer no consequences?"

"Yes. Isn't this journey sacrifice enough?"

"No, far from it. The journey you are on is a privilege. The opportunity you have is a privilege. The cost is fair."

"My life? That's not fair. Not after everything." Alrion sunk back down into the chair. Now he understood why he had been kept in the dark. He understood why he had been shown that vision of Granthion touching the wall of darkness. It wasn't about his family history, it was a preview of what Alrion would be dealing with. A sign of the true nature of his quest, and what it would require. Alrion slammed his fist down on the table, the spellbook closing in response.

"That's a normal response, I suppose," Granthion said. He looked sympathetic, but also slightly detached.

"Is this what you were like?"

"I can only assume so since my knowledge and memories have been contributed to the Pool."

"Don't you care?"

"Very much so. In fact, you could say I cared too much. Why else would I sacrifice myself to save my son with an incomplete spell?"

"You knew it would kill you?"

"Of course. Even though it wasn't the proper spell, more a cheat, the principles were the same. The reversal of so much Blight, it has to go somewhere. Better death than the alternative. You've seen it." Granthion gave Alrion a serious look and he felt chills. He remembered the process happening within him, he could vividly recall what it had done to Branthor and Alyx.

"So, I'm to just push forward and give myself up?"

"No, don't give yourself up. Give of yourself. It's a winning trade. One life for thousands. You'll do more good than anyone who ever lived. You'll set things right."

"But I'm so young. Why me?"

"You were looking for a purpose, were you not? Unsatisfied with your life. And here you are, with the most important and fulfilling purpose of us all. Is that not enough?"

"I just need time. And you're far too logical and reasonable. That's not fair either."

"True. But I'm also not real. I'm just an image in your mind, taking the form and manner of a great wizard and drawing upon the knowledge of those smarter and wiser than us all." Granthion grinned and Alrion shook his head. It was too much, and while a small part of him thought it made sense, but he couldn't let himself go.

"I can't deal with this now. I just need to move forward and see what my options are."

"Charging ahead and hoping for a different outcome? That's definitely going to work." Granthion stood and turned, examining the bookshelf that was behind him. Alrion stood and wandered over, curious.

"Is there anything useful over here?"

"Oh no, nothing. I was just waiting around for you to leave."

"Great. You've been a great help." Alrion turned to go, but a hand held him back. Granthion stared into his eyes.

"Don't forget, you're not alone in this." The intensity in Granthion's stare was unnerving and Alrion pulled away. He took a few steps away from the scene before he stumbled into another pool of light.

∽

Alrion opened his eyes, seeing the dark chamber slowly rise around him. He was still floating on the water, but no voices could be heard, just silence. He started to speak, but it felt wrong disturbing the stillness. With some effort, Alrion swam over to the edge and dragged himself out. His limbs felt loose and useless. With great difficulty, he managed to dry off and dress himself. He all but stumbled out of the chamber. Caleb rushed over, concern all over his face.

"You were gone a long time. You should not have risen without help. Your limbs will be sluggish and limp. You could have drowned!"

"Nope, a different fate awaits me." Alrion let the scholar help support him. They walked slowly back, with no further words exchanged, to the room where Falric was working. The master wizard noticed them come in but didn't look up, he kept working. Only once Alrion was seated did Falric address him.

"You look like a man who has seen a ghost."

"I have, in a fashion."

"Did you get the answers you were looking for?"

"Yes, but not what I was looking for," Alrion said bitterly. Lara rushed in.

"What did I miss?"

"I have learned the location of the source of the Blight, and also what must be done."

"That's great. Isn't it?" Lara said, trailing off. She looked between Alrion and Falric.

"There is a price involved. My life." Alrion directed his attention at Lara. She gasped and looked concerned. She pulled over a chair and sat near him.

"Surely that's just one possibility."

"You tell her." Alrion looked to Falric.

"Whilst we shouldn't discount the idea, the facts don't look good." Falric shook his head slowly.

"What do you mean? What are we talking about here?" Lara said with alarm.

"Alrion will interact with the source of the Blight. And in order to strip it from the entire world, he must be the conduit for it. The entire power of the Blight will flow through Alrion back to the source."

"Which will destroy my body, and likely my soul, in the process. Great, huh?"

"We don't know that for sure."

"Look at what happened to my grandfather. If he couldn't avoid it curing a country, how can I avoid it curing the entire world?"

"That's still not a foregone conclusion. You're different from your grandfather!"

"I appreciate your optimism, and I won't discount it." Alrion sighed. "But we need to accept the fact that this quest will likely destroy me if I succeed." Alrion watched Lara's face. She looked from Falric to Caleb, and neither gave her any reassurance.

"There's always a way. No need to be glum about it." Lara beamed a smile around at them all and got none in return.

"Let's focus on what we can do. You said you knew the location of the source of the Blight? Can you describe where it is?"

"Hmm, it was described to me, but I don't know the area well. But I suspect I could point it out on a map. Do you have one?" Alrion said to Caleb.

"Oh no, sorry. Valrytir are very precious about their maps. Detailed maps are kept close to their chest. Perhaps for reasons such as this. At any rate, we only have very high-level charts showing different regions and major routes into the country."

"I have one." Lara rummaged through her jacket and retrieved a neatly folded thick piece of paper. She unfolded it onto the desk in front of them. Caleb walked over and investigated it.

"This is amazing. Where did you get it?"

"I have my sources." Lara winked at Caleb and guided the map closer to Alrion. "Do you think you could point out the location?"

"Let me see." Alrion absorbed the details of the map, looking at the different roads and landmarks. Without realising he started to move his hand to the right spot. He hesitated.

"Is this a bad idea showing everyone?" he said to Falric.

"That's a good question. I believe those in this room can know, but I wouldn't show others. The fewer people who know, the better."

"You already know anyway." Alrion let his hand navigate the map, pointing to a spot. Lara gasped.

"I know where that is. It's not far from the city at all!"

"That's a bit unnerving, but there we go. I think the best course of action is to start our journey."

"How do you intend on getting there?"

"Are you offering your assistance?" Lara said.

"No, no. I've done my share of adventure and performed rather dismally. I was going to suggest the Wizard Gates."

"Go on."

"There's a special gate combination that gets you close to Valrytir. Not many know of it."

"And it's nearby?" Alrion said.

"Yes, it's in a tower not far from here."

"We came back through that one." Lara looked puzzled.

"Indeed, one thing to remember is that Wizard Gates aren't necessarily the same in both directions. Sometimes you cannot travel back to where you came from."

"I see. Is there anything else we should know? There's been one occasion where I was unable to activate the gate again."

"That sounds like a restriction of some kind. Quite rare, but then again, we don't have all the answers. I was going to say that the passage of time is inconsistent within the gate. You will not travel instantaneously."

"What do you mean?" Lara said.

"It will feel like only a few moments between when you stepped into the gate, and when you arrive. But it's longer than that. Each gate is different, and the areas you travel to make a difference. At any rate, I just wanted to alert you."

"It's not the same as actually walking, is it?" Alrion didn't feel like these gates were all that reliable. No wonder he hadn't heard about them prior.

"Oh of course not. But you might lose a day in some cases. Just something to keep in mind."

"Thanks. And that combination you mentioned?"

"Take the desert option." Falric looked at Alrion. "Then you'll need to search out the next gate. Are you confident enough to do that?"

"I have managed before."

"Good, I assumed so because you managed to find and use a gate already." Falric stood and walked over to Alrion. He leaned back against the desk and took Alrion's hands in his own.

"Lad, this is too much for one person to bear. But I cannot help you with this. As far as the spell goes you are on your own. I can't say exactly what will happen, but you need to be prepared for the worst. Otherwise..." Falric looked away.

"Otherwise what?"

"Otherwise the worst will happen. Alrion will fail, and he will be consumed by the Blight. Transformed into something terrible." Falric sighed, and his hands trembled.

"There can be no hesitation. No doubts. Travel now, yes. But don't rush in before you are ready. There's only one chance, and the consequences are dire."

"Great pep talk." Lara shook her head.

"Listen, I know that I've failed you. I haven't been the support you've needed, you've had to go elsewhere. But it's made you stronger, and you have people to watch over you. You can do this, but don't walk in there if you have doubts. It's better not to. We can make do, there are other options." Falric rose and stepped over to join Caleb.

"This is goodbye then," Alrion said, a little more stiffly than he intended. He stood with some effort and ambled over to Falric, hugging the wizard and almost toppling him over. He did the same with Caleb.

"It's been an honour to serve you. We will await your return. I know you'll find a way." Caleb smiled and bowed.

"Well, that's one of us." Alrion turned and left the room, Lara by his side.

37

THE FELLOWSHIP REBUILDS

Alyx adjusted her uniform again.

I can't believe I'm wearing this.

She had avoided it as long as possible, but there were no excuses left. If she wanted to join, she had to look the part. The black and brown did help her blend in, and the padding and design were good for fighting in. The armoured plates were more of a hindrance than anything else, but she could use them as required too. Mary walked into the room, looking Alyx up and down.

"Good, it was about time. I was beginning to think you had forgotten how to get dressed."

"I did." Alyx laughed but Mary did not. She did almost smile though.

"You certainly didn't forget how to fight. So, have you considered when you are going to talk to the commander about your request?"

"Soon, but not yet. I want to time it just before the wizard gets here."

"You might want to do it sooner rather than later."

"Why?"

"Go talk to the scouts." Mary waved and left the room.

She couldn't tell me herself, could she? Probably still hurting from losing the unfair duel.

Alyx left the room promptly, striding down the corridor quickly. Thankfully, they hadn't given her any active duties, just the usual training. She hadn't been assigned to a squad either.

Maybe she is protecting me?

It was all odd, but Alyx didn't want to question too hard when it suited her just fine. The scout's office was at the front of the building. It had two rooms, one of which was more a reception area, and a back room. That's where all the scout reports were filed and compared. A small group pored over all the reports and tried to draw out larger trends or things of interest.

Alyx entered the reception area and nodded slightly to the staff manning the desk. The two men saluted and went back to their duties. She continued to the back room, marvelling at the rapid pace of activity.

They do never stop.

At the back of the room, she spotted Baker.

He'll be my best bet.

Alyx weaved through the many desks and scouts rushing around. Nobody paid her any attention, which was how she liked it. Baker was running his hands through his thinning hair, reading some paperwork.

"Baker, it's been a while." Alyx stopped right in front of his desk and waited. He continued reading.

"Nice to see you, Alyx. I heard all about your big return. Sweet of you to pay us a visit."

"How are things back here? Busy as usual?"

"Probably busier. Is that why you're here?"

"I can't be here just to see you?"

"You never did before, so why start now?" Baker's eyes were still on the paperwork. But Alyx could tell she had his full attention.

"Always quick off the mark, I'll give you that. Mary said that your team had something significant."

"Oh, I wouldn't say that, not yet. But it's building towards such a statement." Baker put down the papers and looked at Alyx for the first time. His blue eyes looked tired.

"Tell me a story." Alyx walked around and moved the stack of paperwork in the chair next to Baker, placing them on an empty space on his desk. She eased herself down into the chair and made herself comfortable.

"You aren't going until you get what you want, are you?"

"Of course not." Alyx smiled.

"As you wish, I needed a break anyway."

"What's the big news? In a single sentence."

"The Blight are massing," Baker whispered. He rummaged through his papers and seized a thick wad. He unfolded it, showing Alyx a map of Valrytir. There were tiny markings all over it.

"See, each mark is a sighting of Blight activity. It's never been this busy. But they're being smart too. We're not seeing huge masses of Blighters. But when you add them all up, there's a massive force building. And it's getting bigger every day." Baker leaned back, looking conspiratorial.

"They're planning something."

"I can see that. It's not unexpected, but I had hoped we had more time." Alyx could see Baker's eyes light up. He was hungry for more information.

"Sorry, I can't add anything right now. You'll find out soon enough. But I think it's time I talked to the commander. Have you briefed him on this?"

"Of course!" Baker jerked and nearly fell out of his chair. "As per usual he said to sit on it. Nothing to do until they start mobilising and we have cause to expect an attack."

"Oh, I don't expect you'll see an attack. More of a defence." Alyx smiled. She enjoyed watching Baker trying to piece things together.

"Now that's an interesting scenario. I can look again with that in mind. Reinforcement to protect some sort of goal." Baker started digging through his papers again.

"Before I go, where can I find the commander?"

"This time of day? He's taking a walk in the gardens. Best time to catch him."

"Excellent. I think I'll do just that." Alyx waved but Baker didn't notice. He was buried in paperwork once more.

I wonder if he'll turn up anything else.

Alyx's stomach started to churn. She wasn't afraid of the commander, far from it. But knowing what she had done would make it a difficult and awkward conversation. And she needed to ask him for something too. But there was no choice. She had to press on.

Willing to die by the sword, but hesitant to talk to a superior officer. Doesn't make sense.

Alyx dismissed the thought and charged through the hallways, heading towards the garden. She needed to not dwell on such thoughts and get to it. The sooner she confront the commander, the better.

There were more and more soldiers out in the gardens training. More than when she had taken advantage. It was a good sign, but surprising. Alyx stopped and looked over the scene. If she was the commander, she'd focus on the secluded patch near the back. It would be the best place for a quiet interlude before going back to the heavy burden of leadership.

As she wound her way through the gardens Alyx saw fewer and fewer soldiers and recruits until she found the garden she sought. It was leafier than she remembered, the tall trees bigger and more plants were in between. The whole area felt cooler and more at peace. She naturally slowed her pace and tried to enjoy the walk. There was no point wasting such a nice spot, and she figured that the commander would get quite annoyed if she burst in and destroyed the sense of calm.

She found him seated on a stone bench in the middle of the garden. Small hedges were to each side of him, and he leaned back, looking into the distance. He looked exactly the same as she remembered, the short-cropped grey hair and the tidy moustache. His eyes were hard, the brown irises looking like volcanic rocks. His uniform was almost the same as hers, save for a few decorative elements on his shoulder. He had pioneered this style of uniform and armour and led by example. It gave him more credibility amongst the troops.

"Commander Brady." Alyx gave him a small bow and stood ready.

"Alyx. So, the rumours are true, you have returned. And you're in uniform. This is a surprise."

"It's been a turbulent time. I hope you've been well."

"A turbulent time indeed. Yes, I've been as well as can be expected. Luckily, there's been nothing out of the ordinary to test us. Until recently."

"You mean the new massing of Blighters?"

"You heard about that? News travels far too quickly." Brady shook his head softly.

"I don't think it's travelled that far, but I do still have my contacts."

"Of course you do. I won't dredge up the past, but I just want to ask. Was it worth it?"

"Yes. But the cost may have been too high."

"I expected as much. Don't worry, I'm not as sentimental as Mary. I knew you'd leave suddenly one day, though the situation did surprise me." Brady paused for a moment, collecting his thoughts. "I could see that you wouldn't stay with us above your personal mission. Though I had hoped you would come back." Brady looked her directly in the eyes.

"Are you really back?"

"Honestly, sir, I don't know. I have a job to do, and after that…"

"Tell me about this job. Is it as extreme as your last one?"

"Possibly. I'm assisting a wizard, who will be here soon."

"For what purpose?" Brady shifted his posture, leaning forward.

"To cure the Blight." Brady let out a barking laugh.

"That's preposterous. You've been taken in on another suicide mission."

"No, it's not like that. I've seen him do it. I've seen him clear the Blight from people. He even saved me." Alyx watched Brady's reaction. He was hard to read, but she could tell he was shocked. He knew Alyx didn't lie.

"This is rather sensational news."

"It's why the Blight are massing. They know he will be coming, and they are preparing their defences. We'll need to meet them head-on, to bear the brunt of the attack so that the wizard can make it to the source of the Blight."

"Stop right there." Brady held out his hand and spoke with annoyance. "I will not commit any of my men or women on such a fool's errand. It was flights of fancy like this that created the generals of the Blight. I will not sacrifice my personnel on another disastrous venture." Brady stood abruptly.

"I know you've been through a lot, but I expected more from you."

"You'll see that I'm right. I'm only here to prepare you." Alyx met his gaze without faltering.

"Is this uniform a joke to you?"

"No, although, right now, it's a means to an end."

"So be it." Brady started to walk away but stopped before he passed her. He turned and addressed her.

"Is this because of what happened to that young man? Do you feel responsible?"

"I am responsible. But this is not because of that."

"You are on the bench. Let Mary know when you're available for active duty." Brady stiffened his back and marched off. Alyx watched him go wordlessly. Once he turned the corner, she let herself relax. She let out a deep sigh.

Still not good with people. And I didn't communicate the situation that well.

Alyx started to walk back. It wasn't the time to beat herself up. She had achieved her aim, planting the seed with the commander. He was quite astute and would start to put things together. Hopefully, when Alrion and Lara arrived he'd be more inclined to support them.

Alyx wandered back through the gardens, ignoring the soldiers training. She didn't want to spot anyone that she'd have to stop and talk to. She just wanted to walk and let her mind wander. As she reached the street, she stopped suddenly.

Who is that?

She spotted a monk walking around. He stuck out like a sore thumb, but it seemed like he was looking for something. Unsuccessfully.

What an oddity.

Alyx dismissed the thought and kept walking. But within moments the monk ran up to her.

"Excuse me," he said.

"Yes?" Alyx said. The monk had a worldliness about him that suggested he hadn't been just confined to a temple or monastery. And he was on alert and active, like a soldier. She could feel his presence. Relaxed, but ready to pounce at a moment's notice.

"Where did you get that sword?" The monk pointed at the blade. Sheathed at her waist, the diamond on the pommel was quite prominent.

"A friend of mine let me borrow it. Why?"

"A wizard?" the monk said.

"Maybe."

"That's Alrion's sword, I was there when his father presented it to him. Is he well? Is he with you?"

"That's correct. How do you know him?"

"I'm Certan. I'm the monk that travelled with Alrion and guided him to our temple." Certan held out his hand. "And you are?"

"Alyx." She shook his hand, noting his strength. "I met Alrion after that, and we travelled together for a while. He gave me his sword for a time. I do remember him mentioning a monk, it's good to meet you."

"This is quite fortuitous. I came here to find Alrion, but I have no idea where he is. Is he here?"

"Not yet, although he's on his way. Did you arrange to meet him here?"

"No, the elders directed me here. They said he needed my help at Valrytir. I've journeyed quite a way to be here."

"Interesting. That's why I'm here as well. Do you drink? No?" Alyx was surprised by Certan's strong reaction. He shook his head and looked annoyed.

"No matter, let's go for a walk. We can share a few stories."

"Don't leave me out," a voice said from behind. Alyx whirled quickly to see who it was.

No way.

Vincent stood there on the street, smiling. He was dressed in a travelling cloak and had the companion Runesteel sword strapped on his back.

"I think we all have a lot to discuss. Alyx, I'm delighted to have you restored back to full health." Vincent winked. "And I'm glad that you two have met. It's good to have you both here." Vincent started to approach, Alyx still shocked at seeing him.

38

REFORGING THE LEGEND

"How did you get here?" Alyx said. Vincent gave her a mysterious smile.

"I should ask you the same question, I'm sure you've had quite the journey. Weren't you with Alrion? That's his sword."

"I was. Alrion gave me this temporarily to use. We were with Branthor for a time as well, as crazy as that sounds." Alyx noticed Vincent's features change, a look of concern crossing them.

"He was completely focused on destroying Rindale. He finally succeeded but at the cost of his life."

"I'm sorry to hear that. Let's go somewhere we can talk. You too, Certan." Vincent started walking away and gestured for them to follow. Alyx looked at Certan, who shrugged and started following. Vincent led them through the city into the trades district. They passed several blacksmith workshops before he stopped in front of one.

"Balzar's Blades. This place is an institution," Vincent said.

"I know this place, it's impossible to get a weapon from here." Alyx wasn't joking either. This blacksmith was for the elite of the elite.

"I go way back with the owner. Follow me." Vincent entered the shop, Alyx and Certan keeping close. The shopfront was lavishly decorated. Gleaming weaponry of all types hung on the walls. The main floor was clear save for a nicely finished wood underfoot and a counter down the end for the staff to use. Vincent waved, and they waved back. He stopped midway down the room, opening a door and ushering them through. They entered a plain room with some benches and notebooks.

"This is just a planning room, it's not being used right now. Take a seat."

Vincent pointed to a bench with a few stools around it in the far corner. He waited until Alyx and Certan were seated, then he eased down into a stool.

"I have something to discuss, but first let's hear your updates. Certan?"

"Well, after you all left, I stayed to help rebuild the temple and heal those who could be saved. A surprising number recovered fully, although we lost so many."

"I'm sorry for the loss, the bravery of your order was astonishing. And I'm sorry I couldn't get there sooner."

"You did what you could. I was content with doing the hard work, trying to build myself a place there, but the elders had other ideas." Certan chuckled softly to himself, shaking his head.

"They asked you to leave?" Alyx said.

"In a fashion. They said that I had unfinished business. I was to complete the trial within the Vault of Silence then travel to Valrytir to support Alrion in completing his quest."

"Congratulations!" Vincent stood up and offered Certan his hand. They shook firmly.

"Can you fill me in?" Alyx said.

"It's a special trial designed to test a person's Will. It is the pinnacle of achievement for a monk and designates mastery over one's self and the world."

"Alrion completed the trial as well," Vincent added.

"I see. Can outsiders be admitted?" Alyx was very interested in this trial. She had heard stories of how the monks could fight, and what they could do. Things that would be incredibly useful for her to know.

"I suppose, yes, that is how I was first introduced. But you'd have to undergo the full training. I'm not sure if they accept students who don't plan to stay with the monks."

"Perhaps I'll travel after all this is done and see for myself."

"I'd be delighted to take you." Certan bowed.

"We're very lucky to have you joining us. Alrion is going to need all the help he can get," Vincent said.

"I can't agree more. The forces that the Blight are massing here in Valrytir, it's unheard of." Alyx noticed that she had Vincent's undivided attention.

"What did you say?"

"The scouts have been tracking Blight sightings. They are massing within Valrytir. They're sticking to smaller groups, but we've picked up on what they are doing. I'm not sure we've ever faced a force this big."

"Perhaps the elders had some insights," Certan mused.

"We're all here for a reason, we each have a role to play. Alrion can't face that alone." Vincent looked determined.

"The three of us are a good start. We're worth far more than our number," Certan said.

"I couldn't agree more. I think I have a way to improve our odds too." Vincent rose and took a few steps towards another door. "Come and see."

"I'm intrigued." Alyx stood and followed along, waiting for Certan to catch up. Vincent led them through to another room. It was an active workshop. At the far end of the room, blacksmiths were hammering or working metal in different stages of completion.

"I'll never get tired of that sound. It's so welcoming," Vincent said. An older man was overseeing the work, thick glasses sitting atop his grey hair. He was well-built and looked strong despite his age. He noticed their presence and approached quickly.

"Vincent! When I received your letter, I couldn't believe it. But here you are, in the flesh." The man encircled Vincent in a huge hug. Vincent returned the gesture. They parted, and the man slapped Vincent hard on the back.

"Who do you have with you?"

"This is Certan. He's a monk from the order of a thousand eyes. He travelled all the way here from the desert." The man nodded.

"This is Alyx. She is a weapons master that made a name for herself here, before going on to taking down the Skull King single-handedly."

"Oh," the man said, his eyes alive with interest.

"This here is Balzar himself. We worked together many years ago." Vincent and Balzar exchanged a smile. Balzar started to shake his head.

"This one couldn't stay put! Just when he was starting to get good, he ran out on me!"

"Sorry, I was young and impulsive."

"Oh, you think you've changed now. Has he?" Balzar laughed.

"Not that I've seen," Alyx joked. Certan refrained from saying anything. Balzar let out a few additional peals of laughter then composed himself.

"Right, well, Vincent, I was able to satisfy your request. Come with me," Balzar started off, weaving through the various workbenches. He brought them to a heavily fortified metal door. He produced a key and unlocked it, heaving the door open. Alyx marvelled at the size of it, the door was as thick as a man. Balzar charged ahead, stopping midway through the room.

Alyx stopped dead still. Everywhere she looked hung legendary weapons. Ones she had heard about as a child, or when she was training. The Foe Lance, the Sparkling Blade, and even the Haunted Hammer.

"What is this place?"

"This is my collection of legendary weapons. A few of them I had the privilege of making myself, but the vast majority I've sourced from across the land. Vincent here asked about a particular item. I thought it was lost, but once I made enquiries it wasn't as difficult as I imagined." Balzar waited patiently and Alyx approached, curious. As she reached the table, she let out a gasp. It was a giant sword, broken into three pieces.

"This is…"

"The sword that slew the Skull King. The sword passed down by your family."

"Andrylir," Alyx said with reverence. "Why are you showing me this?"

"I asked Balzar to retrieve it for a purpose. I'm going to reforge it." Vincent looked Alyx directly in the eyes. She could see the fire and passion in his look. She felt overwhelmed.

"Is that even possible? It was enchanted."

"I won't be able to restore the power it used to have, but I don't think that it's appropriate anymore. You need a weapon you can use, correct?"

"Yes." Alyx reached out and glided her hand along one of the pieces. The feel of the metal was familiar, reassuring. It was like a part of her. She had carried it her entire life. She remembered suddenly what it had been like, and the emptiness became apparent.

"I need this," she whispered.

"You will have it, I swear."

"Is there anything I can do to help?" Certan said.

"No, not with this. I will consult with Balzar and do the work myself."

"I will then focus myself on helping Alyx with her task."

"Just let me know when you would like to start, Vincent. I'll reserve whatever equipment you require," Balzar said.

"Later today, I have something else to finish first."

"As you wish. I look forward to working with you again." Balzar smiled and directed them out of the vault. After they had all left, he locked the door once more. He was called by a member of his staff and quickly left to address the issue.

"What task is on your list?" Alyx said. She wasn't just keen for him to start, she was curious about what Vincent had planned.

"I need to get the armed forces mobilised for when Alrion arrives. With all that talk of the Blight massing, we're going to need a few extra hands."

"I've already done that. Why do you think I'm in uniform?"

"Don't worry, I think together we can crack this. Who did you speak with?"

"Brady, commander of the special elite unit. He was quite dismissive."

"Take us there again. Please." Vincent looked determined.

"Sure." Alyx started off leading them back.

～

They arrived back at the building quickly. Alyx knew that Brady would no longer be wandering the gardens.

"Let's try his office, I'll show you the way." Alyx entered the building, weaving her way through the corridors.

"This is much bigger than I expected. How many are in this special elite unit?" Certan said.

"I think the name is a bit misleading. Although the soldiers here are specially trained, it's more a distinction from the main forces. There are a few thousand in total, although not all are stationed here at once."

"Still, very impressive. And this commander is the one in charge of them all? What about the main army?"

"Yes, he's the leader. The general runs the entirety of the armed forces, general and special unit, but Brady has a lot of influence. We need his support first."

"Then let's get it." Certan smiled. Alyx sighed.

I was just with him before, he won't change his mind so easily.

Before long they were outside the office. The door was closed.

"Here we are. He's probably busy, are you still keen?" Alyx said.

"Absolutely." Vincent opened the door and strode in. Brady was sitting at his oversized desk, deep in conversation with a man not in military uniform. Brady looked up, annoyance on his face and his moustache skewed on an angle. Just as he was about to speak his expression changed to complete surprise.

"Vincent?" Brady said. He rose immediately.

"It's been a long time, a lifetime. I'm surprised you still recognise me." Vincent laughed. Brady looked to his guest.

"I'm sorry, Marlin, let's finish this off tomorrow. Same time?"

"Of course." Marlin nodded to Brady, acknowledged the rest of them and quickly left the room.

How does Vincent know Brady? He never said anything about being a soldier.

"We always wondered what happened to you." Brady looked to Alyx and Certan.

"How do you know Alyx? And is that a monk?"

"We ran into Alyx at an opportune time, while surrounded by Blighters. She's been an invaluable ally on our travels. Certan, likewise, has proven himself an able fighter and reliable companion." Vincent took a seat, and Brady sat down as well. Alyx and Certan stood at the back of the room.

"I'm a family man now. Busy blacksmithing, before I made this trip. I'm helping my son out."

"I thought you were against making weapons." Brady pointed to the Runesteel blade.

"An exception had to be made. I crafted only a few for people that I trust. Alyx is currently wielding the one I made for my son, Alrion."

"Alrion, nice name. He must be grown up by now. Where is he?"

"He's on his way here, but I'm not sure when he'll arrive. I wanted to see you before then, on official business."

"Official business?" Brady looked at Vincent with suspicion. "Does your son want to be a soldier?"

"I doubt it, although he's keen on learning how to wield a sword properly. Alyx has been extremely helpful in that regard. No, I want to talk to you about your assistance in tackling the Blight." Vincent's expression lost the smile and became quite stern. Alyx watched Brady shift his focus from Vincent to her.

"Is that what this is about? Alyx has already talked to me." Brady leaned back in his chair, unimpressed.

"My son is a wizard, Brady. This is real."

"What?"

"Yes, my father was Granthion."

"Hang on, really?" Brady looked completely thrown.

"You never told him?" Alyx said incredulously.

"It's not something I advertised, I was trying to live my own life. But, as it turns out, you can't get away from your past."

"This story about the Blight is true? Your son is a wizard who can cure the Blight?"

"Yes, I've witnessed it myself. So has Alyx."

"It's true. Did you hear the reports of the Skull Queen?"

"Of course. We were preparing ourselves in case we were targeted. Some were discussing options for going after her. Suddenly though, she disappeared."

"That was me. They infected me and transformed me into that thing, as payback for what I had done."

"What? No, it can't be."

"The Skull Queen wielded a great sword. I destroyed the Skull King. It's not a coincidence. But Alrion cured me."

"It's fantastical, but it's true. Alyx has mentioned reports of the Blight massing. It's for one purpose. They know Alrion is coming and they mean to block his passage. This is our chance to end this cycle." Vincent spoke with real passion, and Alyx could see Brady starting to be swayed.

These two must have had some sort of bond back in the day.

"I trust you, Vincent, even though you abandoned us. It seems like that's a bit of a trend in this room." Brady glanced at Alyx. "But I can't promise you support without some proof. Have Alrion demonstrate his power to cure the Blight when he arrives, and I'll declare my forces and recommend that the general do the same."

"Thank you, that's all I can ask." Vincent started to rise, but Brady motioned for him to sit.

"You can't drop this on me and leave. Stay and let's catch up."

"Sure, that's only fair. I bet you have a lot of great stories to share." Vincent turned to Alyx.

"I'll come find you when it's ready. In the meantime, why don't you two go acquaint yourselves."

"Sure. Let's go, Certan." Alyx was about to say goodbye to Brady but he was fixated on Vincent already.

I can't believe that just happened.

Alyx walked out, trying to make sense of it all.

39

THE MAKING OF A WIZARD

The boy entered the cave, the dark consuming him. He pushed forward, knowing each step intimately. Following the twisting of the path, the light behind him soon faded and he kindled his Spark, creating an orb of light and floated it ahead of him. Quietly, his steps resounded within the cave, and he observed the interesting formations on the walls.

There were multiple ridges and geometric constructions that looked unnatural. But at the same time, they didn't appear to be made by human hands or tools.

I'll have to ask him about that.

But the boy shook his head immediately. That would not do. He knew the answer he would get. None at all. He continued to progress through the cave, the depth of his exploration no longer causing concern. But deep within he could still remember the terror he had initially. There was something wrong about venturing that deep into the bowels of the earth.

In no time he had arrived. He could see his father standing and waiting. No matter what expression was on his face, the wizard always had fierce piercing eyes.

"You're late."

"Sorry." The boy knew not to use any excuses. They just made his father angrier.

"We've discussed this. Punctuality is paramount."

As is everything else.

"Have you selected a name?"

"Yes." This was actually a task he found interesting. He had pored through all the old tomes, looking at old names and the old language.

"And?"

"Aydan." He tried to say it with confidence, but it still felt strange. The wizard laughed.

"How poetic, *Lost One*. Is that how you really feel?"

"Yes. I'm kept away from everyone. I feel so alone. I don't understand." Aydan sighed.

"I've explained it to you countless times. I have powerful enemies, and they would do terrible things to you knowing you were a wizard. This is for the best, for both of us."

"Can't you just teach me to defend myself?"

"I can and will. But today I will teach you something much more important." The wizard closed his eyes. Aydan closed his eyes also, waiting. He felt something, like a prodding at him. But it wasn't a physical sensation. It was more like a magical nudge. The more the feeling continued, the more he tested it. Suddenly he understood, it felt like his Spark. But not, at the same time.

"Is that your Spark?" he said.

"Yes. Wizards can sense each other's power. Sometimes from great distances, if the wizard is particularly skilful. I was amplifying that sensation, hitting you over the head with it so you could feel it properly."

"I did. I couldn't tell it was you though. Only because we were here alone."

"That's true. But with practice, you could learn to recognise mine and distinguish it from others."

"That could be useful. For finding you."

"Yes, but that's not the purpose of what we are doing today." The wizard stepped forward.

"Today, I am going to teach you how to hide your Spark."

"Hide it?"

"Yes. You need to be completely invisible. Indistinguishable from a normal boy."

"Why is that important?"

"I cannot protect you all the time. If you are hidden in plain sight, then that is the best protection I can provide. It will deflect attention away from you. I expect great things of your potential, and if they even suspected what I think is possible..." The wizard looked away, staring out into the distance. He didn't even try to hide the concern on his face. He rarely showed it.

Maybe he's trying to worry me?

"My enemy will stop at nothing. They will never rest, never lay down their fight." The wizard stepped closer, putting a hand gingerly on his son's shoulder. Aydan almost jumped and looked up at his father.

"One day you will understand when you have a son of your own. But for now, you have to trust that I'm doing the right thing." The wizard cleared his throat and stepped away again, putting his hands behind his back.

"Now onto the lesson. I need you to focus and feel the Spark within you." He paused and watched Aydan closely.

"Good. Now, this is a visualisation exercise. It's remarkably simple, but as far as I can tell nobody else has achieved it. They never even thought it necessary. But this, this will save your life." The wizard waited until Aydan nodded then he continued.

"You need to take your Spark and wrap a metal box around it. A box so thick and heavy that the flame of your Spark doesn't even heat the box a tiny bit. A box so tight it suffocates the air from your fire. Imagine that you can touch the outside of the box and it feels completely cool." The wizard paced around the room, observing Aydan from different angles.

"More. Your Spark is a core of flame, but it is being stifled by the box. It's going back to a smouldering ember, waiting for ignition." The wizard poked Aydan in the back.

"Good. But you're trying too hard. It needs to be effortless, something you can slip on and off. You need to create a mental state of the box and, once placed, maintain it automatically."

Aydan let out a deep breath and bent over, panting.

"Was it working?" he said between breaths.

"Almost perfectly. You have a talent for this. But you need to go to the next level. You need to create a reality that supports this state. As you can see, it requires too much concentration. Do you know why?"

"Because I'm thinking about it so much?"

"Yes, you're trying to actively maintain an abnormal state of being. Instead, you need to declare a new state of being and simply activate it. Do you see the difference?"

"Maybe." Aydan shifted his feet and looked at the ground. The wizard sighed and started pacing again. He stooped down and picked up a rock, striding over to Aydan. He opened the boy's hand and placed the rock onto his palm.

"Where is the rock?" the wizard said.

"It's on my hand."

"Close your eyes." The wizard watched Aydan comply. Then he added, "now, where is the rock?"

"It's still in my hand."

"How do you know?"

"Because I can feel it."

"And if I made you stand here for an hour until your arm and hand became numb. Would you still wonder where the rock was?" The wizard loomed over Aydan. He thought carefully before answering.

"No, because I had no reason to think it had moved. I could always just look if I wanted to confirm that."

"Good. Now, you know." The wizard stepped away and put his hands behind his back once again. Aydan closed his hand around the rock.

"I think I see what you're saying. I can create the change, like holding the rock then my mind will think it's still there until I change it. Or I can peek to double check."

"Close enough. That's your new instruction. You are to practice until it becomes second nature."

"For how long?" Aydan could feel his stomach starting to protest. Some of these magic lessons had gone on for entire days.

"As long as it takes. It's the best way to immerse yourself. The next time you leave this cave, I want to be confident that you'll have mastery over this. You must be invisible." The wizard locked his gaze onto Aydan's eyes, making him want to look away.

No, not this time. Aydan stared defiantly back.

"Fine, I can do this. But you need to explain why you're so paranoid. I've seen what you can do, you're a powerful wizard." The wizard stepped back and leaned against a nearby wall. The energy seemed to drain from him.

"Boy, I'm playing with things I should not be. Things that will change the world. I can't have that knowledge lost forever. I have a plan to ensure that it is not. But I also do not want to endanger you. I believe you will have a part to play in this too."

He's not concerned about me. He's more concerned about what I can do for him.

Aydan's cheeks felt hot. He flung the rock at the wizard as hard as he could. Instinctively he used force to propel the rock even faster.

"I'm not your tool." The rock stopped suddenly, inches from the wizard's face. The rock started to crumble, turning into dust. The wizard's face softened.

"Son, what I feel like I need to do is of paramount importance. And I'm hard on you, I know. But please, believe me, it is all for your own wellbeing. I could not live with you coming to harm above myself." The wizard smiled weakly, momentarily breaking up the bleak expression he always wore.

I have to trust him for now. Maybe after I master this, he will relax a bit. This can't go on forever.

Aydan returned to the lesson, stopping and starting the suppression of his Spark. He had to make the transition effortless, otherwise, he would never achieve the level of perfection his father demanded.

40

STARTLING DISCOVERY

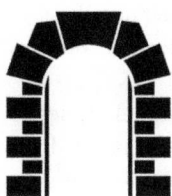

C eles rushed down the tunnel as quickly as she could without stumbling. She kept a hand on the walls, making sure she was heading in the same direction and using it as a way to stay balanced.

Wherever this ends up, I'll be happy to be away from there.

She didn't blame the farmer, in that situation anyone would act the same. But it showed that the Blight was more advanced than anyone realised. They were proactively trying to gain the advantage and close off routes.

I hope Alrion finds a safe way in.

It made her quest for the mysterious wizard more important. If he truly was an ally, then they needed his help directly, rather than from the shadows. And if he was truly a danger, better that he be confronted and dealt with now before the end of the quest.

Alrion needs a way to do the spell safely.

Time became hard to judge as she pushed forward in the tunnel. She tried looking back once or twice but there was no sign of any pursuit and she didn't hear the tell-tale rumbling. Finally, she started to see glimmers of light in the distance.

I hope that's an exit.

Celes kept up the pace, spurred on by the possibility of escaping the tunnel. As she approached, she noticed what looked like a stone staircase leading up. She rushed ahead as fast as she could handle and surged up the stairs. As she ascended, she could see signs of a room up ahead. But she couldn't quite make out any details.

Celes reached the top of the stairs and stepped out into the room. It was all stone, with a single torch lit and hanging on the wall. There seemed to be old supplies in the room, going by the crates, sacks, and other storage she saw. There was a wooden door slightly open at one end. Celes walked towards it, carefully peeking through the door. Beyond was another room, organised like a store-room. Or a library. There was a robed man reading a book at one end. Celes slipped through the door and assessed the situation.

This looks like a Wizard Store. Is that man a wizard? He must be.

"Hello," Celes said. The man looked up, surprise and alarm on his face. He closed the book immediately.

"Who are you? How did you get here?"

"I'm Celes. Is this a Wizard Store? In Valrytir?"

"Yes, it is. How did you get in?"

"Through an underground tunnel." Celes pointed to the back room she had entered through. The wizard looked puzzled.

"I've looked through there, it's a long tunnel with a dead end. There's no way out."

"That's good to know. But you should know that there's a way in!"

"How curious. I've never had anyone come through there. By the way, my name is Magnus, I'm the assigned wizard representative for Valrytir." Magnus bowed. "What business do you have here? Did you just stumble through? I'm quite curious what leads here."

"It's a house in Stonebridge, that used to be a wizard residence."

"Ah, yes I know the one."

"I entered the house via the Wizard Gate, and then discovered the under-ground tunnel. Quite fortuitously, it would seem, as the owner of the house had tried to lock me in."

"Really? For what reason?"

"Seems like he's been coerced by a representative of the Blight. He was to detain any who came through the Wizard Gate." Celes walked closer so she could converse from a more comfortable distance.

"How odd. I think I need to pay this man a visit."

"I think that's wise. But before then, perhaps you can help me."

"I will do what I can. After you describe how you used the Wizard Gate." Magnus gave her a stern look.

"Another wizard activated it for me. His name is Ashra."

"The desert wizard? He's still alive?"

"Very much so. He was quite helpful. I'm actually on the trail of a wizard."

"Go on." Magnus looked intrigued.

"He has the alias of Aydan, and the trail leads here. But it's an old one, prob-ably twenty years old."

"You're looking for this wizard, but you're following a trail from twenty years ago?"

"Exactly. I'm trying to find out his real identity. I believe there's a clue hidden in the past." Celes looked at Magnus and gave a small shrug. He started to rub his chin, thinking.

"How odd. Well, I've been stationed here for at least twenty years. Chances are, I met him long ago. The name does not mean anything to me off the top of my head."

"Do you keep notes here in your ledger? He's appeared in other Wizard Store ledgers, so maybe there's some information here?" Celes hoped that Magnus would be helpful. This was the first time she'd encountered someone else in a Wizard Store that she didn't know.

"That's a fair request. Let me dig it out." Magnus walked into the corner and searched through a small cabinet. He withdrew a dusty book and placed it on a table for Celes to review.

She flicked through the pages, examining the contents.

"There's no entry logs?"

"No, since this store is usually occupied there was no need. There should be a notes section though."

"Let me see." Celes flipped through the book, sampling different sections to see what was there. She skipped a few that seemed to be inventories of things then discovered a note section. Not all the entries had a date, but enough did so she could figure out the chronology.

"Now we're close." Celes tapped a page dated just over twenty years ago. She started looking more carefully. It could be a mention of his name or something suspicious that would trigger her interest. And there it was.

"He was here. The wizard at the time recorded where he was staying, The Innhospitable Inn."

"That place is an institution, I can't believe it's still standing. It's near here if you'd like to investigate."

"I may as well." Celes closed the book.

"Aydan, you say? I'll keep an eye out for any references."

"Thanks, Magnus, that's a great help." Celes headed for the main door.

"Good luck," Magnus called out. Celes waved and left.

She found herself on a main street, almost knocked over by a rushing pedestrian. Looking back at the Wizard Store, it was almost invisible. The building was run-down and blended in with the scenery completely. She studied it and the surrounding buildings well just to make sure she could find it again.

Off we go.

It didn't take long to find the Inn. It was a large establishment with the named painted on the wooden exterior and had lots of people milling around outside. Celes navigated her way inside and was surprised to see it was nicely decorated. In an older style, but well-done. Tasteful furniture and clean floors. She made her way over to the bar and looked at the bartender. The woman had to be in her fifties with her long grey hair tied back and was expertly wiping down the bar and collecting empty glasses.

"Hey, love, what can I get for you?"

"A minute of your time, to indulge my curiosity." Celes smiled and watched for the bartender's reaction.

"It's fairly quiet so I'll hear you out, so long as you buy a drink after."

"Deal, I happen to be on the hunt to track down an old friend of mine. I know that he stayed here a long time ago, and I just wondered if there are any clues as to where he went next. I can't find any trace of him here."

"How long ago?"

"Twenty years or so." The bartender laughed.

"That's some hunt you're on."

"It's important, so if I can dig up anything that would be much appreciated. Do you have any records from back then?"

"Hmm." The bartender had a think. "Jones keeps ledgers of all those staying. Let me see." She started rifling through a drawer under the bar.

"No, that's too new. Nope. Oh, this is probably about right." The bartender emerged holding a rectangular leather-bound book.

"May I take a look...?"

"Christie. And yes, of course, you can. It's ancient history, knock yourself out." Christie chuckled and walked off to serve a customer.

Celes eagerly opened the ledger and flipped through. The system was quite easy to read, it was simply names and dates of check-in and dates of checkout. There seemed to be some additional markings next to some names, presumably to reference something.

This I can work with. Knowing more precise dates might help track down something more concrete elsewhere.

Celes carefully pored through the pages, starting close to where she expected an entry and working backwards. There were so many names, and she was starting to expect that there wouldn't be anything. But there it was.

Aydan! So, you did come here, and now I know when. What's this though?

Celes noticed the letter 'j' circled at the end of the entry. She looked up for Christie, waiting for the bartender to be free.

"Christie, I have a quick question before I get that drink."

"Sure. Did you find something."

"Yes, my friend definitely stayed here. What's this at the end of the entry? It's some sort of code." Celes spun the book around and pointed out the spot to Christie. She examined it for a moment.

"Well, I'll be. Lucky for you we still use that system of notes."

"What does it mean?"

"It stands for junk. It's our way of saying that the guest left stuff behind. We usually keep it for a while, in case they come back. As long as it's not decomposing or something." Celes' heart rate just about doubled. She tried to gather herself.

"Would it be silly of me to think that maybe you still have that stuff?" Christie laughed.

"You know, there's a chance if it was just shoved in a corner. There are things here that I have no idea where they came from."

"Make it two drinks and a hefty tip. If it's at all possible I have to see. This could be incredible." Celes could see Christie weighing things up.

"I am a bit curious to see if we still have that stuff. C'mon, let's be quick about it." Christie waved her over and walked to the end of the room and into a corridor. She rushed down to the last door, opening it with a key from her belt.

"This is long-term storage, I think it's mostly guest related. If we kept that box, it'll be here." Christie paused for a moment. "Good luck, I'll see you back at the bar. Please don't make a mess here, it'll just cause trouble for me."

"Absolutely, I promise it'll be like I was never here."

"Good." Christie left promptly and Celes surveyed the room.

So many boxes. Better get started.

She began by examining those closest to the door, she wanted to avoid another situation where the thing she needed was near the entry and she looked there last. After checking a few boxes, she noticed a definite trend. A lot of boxes had a big 'J' on top and tacked on somewhere else on the lid was a piece of paper with a name. Unfortunately, there were no dates. And none bore the name she needed.

I need to look for dusty boxes, probably up the back.

Celes had a good look and determined that there was a cluster of older boxes in the far-right corner. She carefully picked her way through, making sure she didn't disturb any shaky towers of boxes. It didn't take long to look over the boxes. It definitely wasn't the ones on top.

Here we go.

Celes systematically moved boxes around carefully to examine the ones on the bottom of the stacks, or near the bottom if they were particularly high. It all came down to the last box in the corner.

Please, please be this one.

"Aydan, I've got you," Celes whispered as she read the label. She set the box aside, pushing down the sudden urge to rifle through it.

The box has been here this long, I can wait a few moments before opening it. She focused on setting the room back to what it was, then carefully opened the lid. It was mostly empty. She found a few gems of different types, and some slips of paper. They looked to be receipts, but it wasn't clear what was purchased. One, however, stood out. It was a receipt from the Valrytir Restricted Library. It was confirmation of a restricted loan book titled *The History of The Blight*.

This looks interesting. If it's a restricted library, there's probably some records there too. I can feel it, this is a good lead.

Celes emptied the contents of the box into her satchel and returned to the bar.

"Hey, any luck?" Christie said.

"Yes, thank you. I couldn't believe it, but there you go. Just a few papers and some gems, but so interesting."

"Wow, that's quite lucky. Glad to be of help. What'll I get you?"

"Two shots of your best spirit, and some more information." Celes sat down at the bar. She watched Christie select a bottle and start pouring out shots.

"What else were you after?"

"The Valrytir Restricted Library. Is it nearby?"

"Oh, yes that's at the end of the main street." Christie picked up both glasses and set them down before Celes.

"Is it restricted access?" Celes retrieved some coins from her pocket, holding them in her closed hand.

"I don't believe so, just more security." Christie was eyeing off Celes's hand. Celes dipped her hand in again and grabbed a few extra coins. She pressed them into Christie's hand.

"Thanks again for your help." Celes threw the shot down, letting the burning sensation pass through her. She stood quickly.

"The other one is for you. Take care." Celes waved and walked off.

"Thanks, and good luck," Christie said. Celes quickly left the inn and started down the street.

Much more hospitable than they let on.

Celes could feel the case closing in. She was practically running down the street. It wasn't hard to find the library, it was a large stone building with an impressive dome on top. She rushed up the stairs and into the massive foyer.

The stillness of the room was a stark contrast to the hustle and bustle outside. People moved slowly and with purpose, and even the staff were quiet with whatever they were doing. Celes located a reception desk and walked over.

"Hello, I'd like your help with something."

"Good day. How can we assist you?" The librarian looked somewhat disinterested and moved her brown wavy hair off her face. Celes judged the woman was only in her early twenties.

"A friend of mine borrowed a book from here years ago. He wants to read it again, and I'd like to borrow it as well."

"What's the book?"

"The History of the Blight." Celes handed over the borrowing receipt.

"It's available. You can find it in the stacks." The librarian handed the slip back.

"Good. But, before I get it, I just need to double check. I need to make sure it's the same exact one."

"We only have one with that exact title, although there are similar books." The librarian seemed annoyed.

"If I could just look at the list of people who borrowed it, then I can make sure."

"I'm not sure I should do that."

"It's nothing, I'll just glance at the list. I'll see my friend's name and I'll be confident when I take it back that it'll be exactly the one that he wants. I'd only be looking at the names from a long time ago, nobody cares about the fact that they borrowed a book twenty years ago." Celes smiled and watched the librarian's reaction. She seemed to be coming around, despite being uncomfortable.

"You can look at the list while I'm here." The librarian turned and walked over to another section, rifling through different books. She returned within a few minutes with an old-looking book.

"This is the borrowing ledger. Let me see the slip again." The librarian checked the slip and carefully looked through the ledger.

"I've identified the appropriate entry, as expected. Take a look." The librarian spun the ledger around and guided Celes on where to look. Celes could feel her heart pounding. She read the name and suppressed a gasp. It wasn't Aydan. It was a real name.

"Thank you so much, you've been incredibly helpful. That's the exact confirmation I needed. You were so professional as well, I respect your devotion to the library."

"Why, thank you. I hope your friend enjoys the book as much as he did the last time." The librarian smiled and Celes thanked her again while she left. She made a show of walking over to where the library books were kept, but once the librarian was distracted, she left the building.

I actually did it! I've got you now.

Celes couldn't believe that she had solved it. Everything was coming together at last.

41

THE WAY TO VALRYTIR

The Wizard Gate shimmered in front of them, revealing a hot dusty scene.

"Here we go." Alrion grabbed Lara's hand and stepped through the gate. The strange sensation that was starting to become familiar washed over them, light and heat and blankness.

The heat was all he expected.

"This is definitely the desert," Lara said. "I hope you have an idea of where this next gate is?"

"I do, but I also have a theory." Alrion started walking through the old temple surrounding them. It was largely destroyed, random pillars slowly eroding away, providing little to no shelter.

"What's the theory?" Lara said as they walked. Soon the temple was behind them, and a barely noticeable path stretched out ahead.

"It needs a bit more time to test. Hopefully, I'm not wrong, or this is going to be a really unpleasant journey."

"I agree with you on that point." Lara stopped and pulled out a small flask of water. She offered it to Alrion first then had a sip. They walked on without conversation, the dry heat and oppressive sun was too much. Alrion was content with just walking forward. He knew there were ways to reduce the effect of the heat, but he was happy just moving forward. Not grappling with the environment and just moving through it.

Eventually, he noticed what looked like an oasis.

"Ah-hah!" Alrion said, pointing.

"There's something familiar about that," Lara mused. As they walked closer, Alrion noticed a figure standing there.

"Ashra?" Alrion said.

"The very same. Welcome back, Alrion." Ashra smiled and waved them over.

"I knew you had to be located close to the Wizard Gate here," Alrion said.

"Lucky for you, even luckier for your mother."

"You saw her?"

"Yes, I helped her on her way. A most interesting hunt, looking for a wizard by following an old trail."

"Was she well?"

"Yes, perfectly well, although she would have struggled in the desert had I not found her. She wasn't properly equipped for it."

"Where did you take her? Another gate?"

"Of course. Come inside and we can talk more." Ashra led them into the house and down into the coolest space. He served water and Alrion drained a few cups.

"How is everything going? Are you ready to complete your quest?"

"Did she tell you Falric was alive?"

"Yes, that was a good surprise. Although I admit I half-expected something like that. It seemed odd that he fell so quickly and easily."

"I'm doing pretty well, I just need to complete my travel to Valrytir." Alrion poured himself another cup of water.

"He's lying of course. We had to track back to the Pool of Knowledge because Alrion couldn't pull the location of the Blight from his accumulated knowledge."

"Hang on," Alrion started but Lara cut him off again.

"And when he finally found that out, he also found out that completing the spell will kill him." Lara stared at Alrion defiantly.

"Why?" he said, not even bothering to hide his annoyance.

"Ashra can help you. He's probably the wisest wizard you've met yet, and he trained you so much in the little time you were here. He's more practical than Falric."

"Practical? Because he lives in the desert?"

"Please, be still. Calm yourselves." Ashra got their attention then focused on Lara. "Thank you for being so blunt. I suspected something serious was up, and I appreciate the opportunity to discuss it." He then turned to Alrion. "You should thank her for saying what you could not. It is not a sign of weakness to ask for help."

"I'll be honest, I'm not sure what you can do to help."

"You've got it all figured out then?" Ashra smiled and gave Alrion a funny look.

"No, but I can figure it out then."

"That worked well for you before didn't it, when we duelled?" Ashra started with his gaze on Alrion, but then shifted it to Lara. She shivered noticeably.

"Lara doesn't have fond memories of that."

"Well, he did obliterate the area. Lucky you saved us."

"What's that got to do with this?"

"You weren't prepared and acted on instinct. And you lost control. Had I not intervened, it would have been tragic. Are you going to leave the fate of the world to chance?"

"No. I've come a long way. I've passed all the trials, I've cured myself and others of the Blight. And I've learned the details of the final spell and where to perform it."

"And you're confident then? No doubt whatsoever?"

"Of course not."

"Then you're not ready! Nobody is taking away from your considerable achievements. I can see the depths of your knowledge, perseverance, and willpower. But as you have no doubt noticed, having those abilities is not all that is required."

Ashra is making too much sense. In a way, it's a relief, but it doesn't make me any less annoyed. Why am I so affected by what he's saying?

"You're right, as much as it pains me to hear it. I'm not confident. I don't know how I'm going to avoid death. That doubt, you've just increased it."

"Good."

"What?" Lara said.

"He's in the right place. Mentally, and physically." Ashra gave them a mysterious smile.

"What are you planning?"

"One more lesson. Are you game?"

"Yes." Alrion nodded.

"Good. Let's go at once. Afterwards, I'll take you to the next gate." Ashra stood and immediately headed off. They followed him out of the house and back into the desert. Alrion suspected they were heading back to the same place where they had duelled before.

"Before we reach Valrytir, there's something you should know." Lara looked quite apprehensive.

"What is it?" Alrion stopped suddenly, looking at her with concern.

What has she been hiding?

"Um..." Lara stumbled over her words, "well, you're going to need military support. There's no way you'll be able to walk up to the source of the Blight without an army behind you."

"I hadn't really considered that. Can I count on them?"

"Not for sure. They're quite adept at fighting the Blight and are geared up and have the numbers to do so. But they'll be quite reluctant."

"Hmm, I suppose that's something I can think about. Do you have any special insights?" Alrion watched Lara's reaction. She still looked uncomfortable about something. And this revelation about the military didn't seem quite like it was what she meant to discuss.

"Not really. Not anymore, I've been away for a while."

"Right. Well, do let me know if you remember something." Alrion noticed Lara's face relax a bit when the conversation wound down.

I'll have to ask her about it later when I get an opportunity. Something about Valrytir is troubling her, maybe it's in her past.

Alrion hurried to catch up to Ashra. Soon enough they emerged into the arena. Despite the shifting sands, Alrion could still tell what he had done here. He felt a shiver go down his spine.

"Lara, please go wait up where you did before. You can observe and report back after the duel."

"Sure. Good luck." Lara gave Alrion a quick peck and jogged off to find safety. Alrion watched until he could see her reach the right area. Then he gave his attention back to Ashra.

"What's this going to involve?" Alrion said.

"Where's the fun in that? Just know that I'm going to test you. I want to see how far you've come." Ashra looked mischievous. Suddenly, he dropped the expression and became quite focused. Alrion started to notice darkness covering the area.

Another illusion.

Within a minute, the entire area was dark, with minimal light shining through. A swirl of dark sand surrounded Ashra. When the sand subsided, Alrion couldn't really see anything. But he did notice movement. He activated his enhanced vision, and then he could see.

Ashra wasn't there anymore. Instead, it was a dark humanoid shape. Alrion expected to see the tell-tale signs of Ashra's Spark, but it was hidden or invisible. The shape didn't look or move like a Shade, it felt like something else. Alrion prepared a fireball and shot it over. Black tendrils shot out from the shape and grabbed the fireball, squeezing it into nothing.

Now that's strange. What is he playing at?

Alrion decided to up the ante. He built up his Spark then unleashed waves of fire, followed by a seismic fissure, splitting the earth on a path to intercept. The black figure spawned more and more black tendrils. Simultaneously they swept away the fire and stopped the earth spell. Before Alrion could start another, the black shape suddenly multiplied. There were now four of them, and they all started to advance on Alrion.

He spun quickly, throwing waves of force at each one. Bit by bit he increased the Spark imbued into each one. But even these new figures had the same ability to knock away Alrion's spells. He reached for his sword and remembered he didn't have it. He had loaned it to Alyx.

I can't underestimate these.

But he already had. Something grabbed him from behind. Alrion turned his head to look back and saw one of the shapes behind him. It had grabbed him and was now spawning more tendrils to wrap around him.

There were five. *How did I get cornered so easily?*

Alrion struggled and struggled. But the hold on him became tighter and tighter. He noticed the other shapes advancing. They would be on him soon. He lashed out with waves of force, but they just cancelled out when they reached the black shapes. He forced fire into his arms, hoping to shake the figure off him. But the fire just dissipated as soon as it touched a black tendril.

Alrion started to panic. He was being smothered, and soon he would be completely enveloped. He thought about using the light bomb again but remembered how poorly he had done before, employing it in desperation. Images of Branthor using it flashed through his mind, but he didn't have the patience and presence to carefully control it, and his arms were not free to try to target it precisely.

What do I do? I can't be helpless.

The shapes were almost on him now. He saw one of them oozing a black substance.

Not again. Never again!

Alrion felt the Spark swelling in him. He was panicking. He felt the composition of the spell. It was a light bomb. He felt powerless to stop it. But he needed to. He needed to soften it somehow, to hold it in.

And then he felt his Soul Power. He knew that could help. Purely by instinct, he started to let it out, he let it infuse and mix with the Spark that was becoming a light bomb. He imagined a sphere surrounding him. It would suck all the dark shapes in like a magnet, and it would also contain the light bomb. His Soul would act as a container, keeping the force within a tight radius. He completed the visualisation and had a microsecond of peace and calm before he let it loose.

As he planned, the black shapes were drawn closer in. He was smothered completely. But it was by his choice. They were prevented from moving, and the altered light bomb exploded. Its effects were restricted to that small sphere he had set out, so the excess power and light shot up straight into the air like a beacon.

The darkness was dispelled instantly in a flash of white. Alrion looked around. The ground was cleared near him, but the rest of the arena was untouched. He saw Ashra standing off in the distance. He started approaching immediately.

"How did you find that?" Ashra said.

"Intense. How did you do that?"

"Trade secret, sorry." Ashra chuckled softly. "You really surprised me there. What's with you and light bombs?"

"I don't know. I guess deep down I know that they can wipe anything away."

"That they can." Ashra stopped in front of Alrion and put his hands on the young wizard's shoulders. He stared into Alrion's eyes. "Well now, do you feel any different?"

"Yes." Alrion searched his feelings. "I feel less burdened, a little more resilient."

"Good. You have the right instincts, but you need to be more aware, and more in control. Do you agree?"

"Yes, I know. I felt the panic there. But it was good to find a way out. That was horrible, by the way. Where did you come up with that?"

"I've listened to a few good stories in my day, thought you might appreciate it." Ashra grinned.

"You could say that." Alrion turned when he heard footsteps. It was Lara.

"I couldn't really see much, until that burst of light. Was that you, Alrion?"

"Yes. I think I passed?" He looked at Ashra. The wizard nodded.

"Good. Did it help?"

"Yes, it did. I must admit though, I didn't expect that."

"What did he do this time? Another illusion?"

"He outdid himself. Black figures with long dark tendrils advancing on me and smothering me." Alrion saw Lara recoil. "My reaction exactly."

"Ashra, you have a wicked imagination."

"Thank you for the compliment." Ashra bowed then walked past them. "We better get moving, you don't want to get stuck out here."

"Agreed." Alrion started walking, Lara by his side. Images from the recent confrontation kept bubbling up but he pushed them away. There was something terrifying about it that he didn't understand. For another time.

They found their way back onto another trail. It was slow going along the path, up and down dunes. Suddenly Ashra stopped and waited for them to catch up. Once they had, he reached down and pulled up a trapdoor.

"Wow, that's sneaky," Lara said.

"One day I'll forget how to get back here," Ashra said. He gestured at the ladder down. "After you."

Alrion climbed first, creating some orbs of light to dispel the complete darkness. They were in some sort of stone underground structure. Ashra closed the hatch and climbed down, before leading the way. They passed through nondescript passages until Ashra slowed, inspecting a wall.

"This way." He led them around a corner and there stood a Wizard Gate, glowing and at the ready.

"This is where we part ways. This gate only goes to one location. It's a small town that will get you close to Valrytir."

"Thank you." Alrion held out his hand and shook Ashra's.

"It was a pleasure. I look forward to your success."

"Thanks again," Lara said. Alrion reached out and activated the gate. It flashed and shimmered into existence, showing a dark scene beyond.

"Any last words of advice?" Alrion said.

"Say hello to your mother when you find her. Also, be careful. I suspect you'll meet that mysterious wizard that's been following you around once your quest is done." Ashra wasn't giving anything away with his expression. Before Alrion could ask a follow-up question he found himself tumbling into the gate.

Alrion found himself in darkness. Only the light of the gate was illuminating the area. Luckily, Lara was with him.

"That Ashra, can't help himself," Alrion said.

"He's just trying to help you. And look, we definitely made it here. Wherever here is." Lara started to explore, so Alrion created more orbs of light and attached them to the walls. He noticed stairs leading up to somewhere else, somewhere where there was light. As he approached the stairs, he noticed two shapes waiting up the top. They started to descend, one of them was carrying a torch.

Lara gasped before Alrion could see them. But he soon saw why. The one carrying the torch looked like an old farmer, the other was clearly a Shade. They seemed to be working together.

"Well, well, well. More through the gate," the farmer said. He licked his lips and looked nervously over at the Shade. The creature didn't notice, it was fixated on Alrion.

"I think we can work with this," Alrion said to Lara. He then turned his attention back to the farmer. "Before we start, I'd like to hear about a woman who passed through here recently." Alrion noticed the farmer's eyes widen.

Time to get to the bottom of this.

42

THE PRODIGAL DAUGHTER

Alrion emerged into the room, full of curiosity. It looked oddly familiar, the stacks of books and the small selection of equipment in the corner. Once he spotted a wizard, he knew where he was.

"This is a Wizard Store," Alrion announced. The wizard flinched, a look of annoyance passing over his features.

"Another one? Is that becoming a thoroughfare now?" the wizard grumbled.

"A woman passed through here recently?"

"Yes, are you related to her?" The wizard looked suspicious.

"It's his mother," Lara said. The wizard looked like he remembered something.

"Oh yes, she was on the trail of another wizard. She found a lead for a local inn, and I haven't seen her back."

"Glad to hear she passed through here. My name is Alrion, and you are?"

"Magnus. I'm the caretaker here and representative for Valrytir."

"Great to meet you. I may need to call on your help." Alrion gave him a small bow.

"Of course, anything for a fellow wizard." Magnus inclined his head slightly to acknowledge Alrion and went about his business.

"Let's go find this general that needs convincing." Alrion noticed Lara's features pale a little. Even though she seemed onboard with his plan, she seemed quite nervous about the whole thing. He started off towards the door, just as he was about to open it, he heard Magnus again.

"Sorry to be a bother, but what is that?" Magnus pointed to the large wooden box floating behind Alrion.

"Oh, it's just a magic trick for the general."

"High General Wynston? Commander of all the forces of Valrytir?"

"I believe that's the one." Alrion grinned.

"He's not one for magic, son. Or tricks. Or anything not rooted in reality. I don't know where you got your information." Magnus sighed.

"Don't worry, he'll love this one." Alrion smiled and opened the door. Lara left soon after, and the box floated out after them.

Alrion took a moment to revel in the scene. Valrytir was a huge city. There were clearly different districts and styles of buildings. But everywhere was busy. What drew his attention most was the large keep at the rear of the city. It gleamed white and sandy, the two types of stone used in its construction.

"I take it we head into the keep?"

"We should, but perhaps it would be wise to make one stop beforehand."

"Such as?"

"There's an elite unit of special troops in their own base within the city. Winning over their commander would help your cause."

"If you think it's worth the stop, I'll do it. But he or she would need to come along with us, I'm not wasting this on anyone less than the general."

"Fine, hopefully, we can convince him."

"Lead the way." Alrion waited for Lara to head off. He kept close but continued to marvel at the sights and keep tabs on his box. He was getting some attention for it, but clearly, the population weren't that surprised by wizards and they went back to their business.

After a brisk walk, they were in another district. It seemed more sedate and reserved than the one they had been in. A bit more polished as well. Lara confidently led him through the streets until they reached a large building. It looked almost like a school. He saw a lot of people his age going in and out in special uniforms. It reminded him of the academy.

That was a lifetime ago, and such a brief stay. Could I go back there?

Alrion's train of thought was interrupted.

"Alrion!" a voice shouted. He looked over and saw Alyx waving and running over.

"Alyx! You made it!" He couldn't believe it. Alyx was already here! And she was wearing the same uniform as those training.

"Lara, good to see you too," Alyx said.

"I see you signed up." Lara was sizing up Alyx's outfit.

"I used to be a member, it made sense given that we need their help."

"How'd you get here?" Alrion said.

"That gate went straight here. I've been trying to prepare things as well as I could." Alyx paused and lowered her voice. "Did you get what you needed?"

"Yes, I did." Alrion didn't add any extra detail and he maintained a straight face. He could see Lara giving him an odd look but ignored it.

"Has Lara filled you in on Valrytir?" Alyx said.

"Barely. But she did suggest quite rightly that we would need military assistance to approach the source of the Blight, and that the general would need some pretty strong evidence of our mission." Alrion noticed Alyx give Lara a questioning look, but it passed quickly. Alyx went on.

"As it so happens, I've started the campaign for you. Brady, the commander of the special unit, has agreed to voice his support, as long as you can demonstrate evidence of your need."

"That's amazing!" Lara said, genuine surprise on her face.

"We had a stroke of luck. Vincent and Brady know each other from a long time ago, that tipped the scales in our favour."

"My father is here? Already?"

"Yes. He's working on a special project. And Certan is here too?"

"What?" Alrion couldn't believe it. What were the odds of everyone being here?

"Your team is coming together when you need us the most. It's how it should be."

"Have you seen my mother?"

"No, can't say I have. Vincent didn't mention anything either. Is she here?"

"Yes, but maybe she hasn't been lucky enough to run into you all yet." Alrion took a deep breath. "Alright, well we can't just stand around in the street. I need to go see the general. Do you think you can get your commander to come along?"

"Absolutely, just let me get him. And I'll send a runner for Vincent as well." Alyx jogged back over to the large building.

"It's really happening." Alrion sighed. He was so relieved that his friends were there to support him. But part of him had hoped he would have more time to get things ready before he moved ahead. It looked like he wouldn't have much time at all.

The more time you wait, the more the enemy can prepare as well. Maybe this is for the best.

"Are you sure you want to do this now?" Lara said. She looked anxious again.

"I don't really see another option. How long are we going to lug this box around?" he said.

"I suppose you're right." A look of resignation passed over her face. Alyx didn't take long to return. She had Certan with her, and a man with grey hair and a moustache. Clearly the commander.

"So, you're the wizard I keep hearing about?" the commander said. He held out his hand and Alrion shook it.

"That's me. Alrion, nice to meet you."

"Brady. And likewise. I'm very curious about what you can do."

"All in good time. Let's go see the general."

"I'm sure he's keen to see what you can do as well." Brady chuckled. "I'll follow your lead," he said to Alyx. She nodded and took two steps away, before stopping and returning.

"It's time you had this back." Alyx unbuckled the Runesteel sword and handed it back to Alrion. He hesitated before accepting.

"Are you sure?"

"Yes, it has served me well, but now you need it back. Don't worry, I have other options."

"If you insist, I won't say no. I can see the value in having it back." Alrion adjusted the belt and slung it over his shoulder. Alyx started off again, leading them through the city towards the keep.

"Certan, I'm so surprised to see you here."

"It's great to see you," Lara added.

"Thank you. My heart is warmed to see you restored. I must apologise to you for not helping you more. I realise now that you needed my help more than the temple did. It's a mistake I won't repeat again."

"Don't worry, I had enough help and you had an opportunity to reclaim your life. What brought you back here?" Alrion let his attention lapse momentarily, taking in a giant gate that they were going through. They were passing through a much more fortified area of the city, the keep had to be close.

"The elders insisted. They said it was a job unfinished. I cannot return until you are successful with your quest. I'm afraid you're stuck with me." Certan smiled and Alrion returned it.

"That's a fate I can live with."

"One other thing." Certan paused and made sure he had Alrion's full attention. "I passed the Vault of Silence."

"Wow, that's amazing. We'll have to compare notes a bit later." Alrion could see Certan's eyes light up.

It's a simple thing but having someone to talk to about it will be quite novel. I wonder how much our experiences differed?

Alrion returned his attention to the environment. They were drawing near the keep now. Alrion could see the giant stone entryway. It was guarded by two very heavily armoured soldiers. One had his visor up and was conversing with people going in and out. The other just stood perfectly still, waiting for something.

"Papers," the guard said as they approached.

"We don't have papers," Alyx said. She pointed at Brady.

"Commander Brady, of the special forces unit. We need an urgent audience with the high general."

"Absolutely not," the guard said. "Only people with pre-approved business with authorised paperwork are getting in today." The guard folded his arms to reinforce what he was saying. Alrion was about to say something when Lara strode to the front. She looked the guard up and down.

"Francis, cut the act and let us in." Lara glared at him, and his face drained of blood. He looked completely white.

"Certainly, please make yourselves at home." Francis made a quick bow and walked over to the other guard, giving them plenty of space.

"What was that?" Alrion said to Lara.

"We go way back." Lara led the way, walking into the door. Alrion followed, ensuring the box stayed close.

"Uh, I'm going to have to look inside that box," Francis said. Alrion stopped and let the box rest on the ground. Lara walked up to Francis.

"Are you sure?"

"Yes." Francis licked his lips. "Sorry."

"Be my guest." Lara gave him a wicked grin, and Francis walked over to the box.

"I wouldn't open it all the way," Lara advised. Francis pried the lid open and raised it just enough to look inside. He suddenly let the lid drop closed and stepped away.

"Uh... alright. Go on." Francis spoke in a broken fashion and joined the other guard.

"You heard the man." Lara took off, and Alrion followed closely behind.

This is all very strange. The gate guard is scared of Lara? And we're meeting the general in the keep? Wouldn't it make more sense to be in a military building?

Alrion wasn't that familiar with Valrytir and pushed his concerns aside. This was a meeting they needed to get. They entered a large reception area, with a main hallway leading into another great room with big doors. A finely dressed man stood in front of the door, his dark hair slicked back. He smiled as Lara approached.

"Welcome back, milady."

"Thank you, Rogers. Kindly open the doors please," Lara said. Rogers nodded and threw open the giant doors. Alrion's mouth gaped open. It looked like a throne room. It was long and narrow, with various nobles clustered on the sides, discussing things amongst themselves. At the back of the room, an older man sat on a giant silver throne, looking bored. A couple were retreating from the throne. Rogers ran ahead.

"The Lady Lara attends with retinue," Rogers announced. There was a silence that passed through the crowd. Alrion drew close to Lara.

"What's going on?" he whispered.

"Later. Trust me." Lara strode forward with confidence. She walked halfway up the carpet leading to the throne, paused and bowed.

"I am here to present myself and my companions to his highness, Regent of Valrytir."

"No need to be so formal, my daughter." The man stood and walked slowly over to her.

Daughter! Isn't he the king? Or acting king?

Alrion was stunned. He looked at his companions. Alyx didn't seem surprised, Certan was his usual reserved self. Alrion heard footsteps behind them. He noticed his father rushing in.

"Apologies for my lateness." Vincent gave a bow at the entrance to the room then joined them. The Regent was conversing quietly with Lara.

"My daughter says that you have business here with Valrytir. As a thank you for ensuring her safe return, I will hear your business."

"Thank you, Your Highness." Alrion hoped he wasn't making a fool of himself. He had never addressed a king before.

"Please, I prefer my name, Wynston. Or if you must, use my regular title: High General."

"As you wish, High General." Alrion collected himself and started to speak again. "My name is Alrion and I'm a wizard. I've come a long way to be here, and my quest is almost at an end. Your daughter has been instrumental in helping us reach this point."

"And your quest is?"

"Cleansing the Blight." Alrion saw Wynston raise an eyebrow.

"That's quite a quest. Is it a real quest? Or a fanciful waste of time?" Wynston looked at Lara.

"It's real. Alrion can demonstrate so."

"Ha! The only way he could do that is cure the Blight in front of my eyes. Who are these other people?"

"All these people can vouch for the importance and legitimacy of this quest. This is Alyx, a formidable fighter. She is best known for destroying the Skull King." Alrion hoped that Wynston was impressed. But his face darkened considerably.

"I am quite aware of ALL her exploits. Who else?"

"This is Certan, a master monk that hails from the desert temple. And this is my father, Vincent. He is a master blacksmith, one who can work with Runesteel." That point captured Wynston's attention.

"Interesting. I'm quite familiar with Brady. Tell me, Commander, what's your link to this quest?"

"It's only very recently come to my attention, High General. Alyx brought the matter to my attention, and I knew Vincent as well, who added legitimacy to it. I was not aware your daughter was involved until just now."

"Very well." Wynston nodded and looked them all over. "What is the nature of this quest? Why have you come here?"

"My quest is to cleanse the Blight at the source. As you are likely aware, the source is not far from Valrytir." Alrion was about to continue speaking but he was cut off.

"Hearsay. I will not have you spreading such rumours!" Wynston bellowed. Alrion wanted to argue, but Lara touched his arm and shook her head. Alrion adjusted his approach.

"Nevertheless, I need to pass through to reach my destination."

"And scout reports show extremely large numbers of Blight massing just outside Valrytir," Alyx added.

"Brady?"

"That is true, High General. They avoided our detection initially because each Blight sighting is quite small, under our threshold. However, the scouts started to notice so they adapted their reporting to include all sightings. Now we're getting a real sense of the number." Brady finished speaking and waited for further questions. Wynston sighed and started to rub his chin.

"Let's assume that your quest is legitimate, and you need our assistance to reach your destination, due to the numbers of the Blight. I need something else, other than your word to commit so many lives to such an undertaking."

"Absolutely, High General. That is why I have organised a demonstration." Alrion stepped to the side and gestured for his companions to do the same. He brought the giant box into the middle of the carpet.

"Please, keep your distance." Alrion ensured everyone was a safe distance away, and he pried the lid off the box. Next, he reached into the box. There was a scream, and a dark shape climbed out. It was a Shade. Terrified screams rang through the room. The high general drew his sword instantly, as did his retinue. Alrion quickly wrapped up the Shade in waves of force, pinning it in place. The Shade was strong, but Alrion's Will was stronger. As much as it struggled, the Shade was unable to move.

"Is everyone satisfied that we have a Shade here?" Alrion looked around the room. No one said anything.

"I am satisfied. But keeping a Shade at bay, whilst impressive, is no mere demonstration, young wizard." The high general sheathed his sword and waited.

"Nor should it be. I am merely showing you that the Shade is real, but I do not wish to endanger anyone during the demonstration. Be prepared for what happens next." Alrion walked closer to the Shade. He stepped up until he was incredibly close.

"I am going to release you from your prison," Alrion said softly. The Shade shrieked again, but Alrion ignored it. He wrapped his hand in a force spell, at the same time mixing in his Soul Power. Reaching forward he placed his hand on the Shade's chest. Using his Spark as the conduit, he poured his Soul Power into the Shade. Activating his enhanced vision, Alrion took note of the key points of concentration of the Blight and took care in directing his Soul Power to wash them away. He kept Branthor's words in his mind, trying to minimise the damage to the person within.

As he worked, the room was silent, watching. Alrion wasn't sure how much of what he was doing was visible by an observer. But he was too caught up in what was happening to worry too much about that. Suddenly, he had finished the job, the last Blight retreating from the Shade. The chain reaction began.

After a quick burst of light, the Shade started to fall. Alrion adjusted his force spell to let the creature down slowly. The black exterior of the Shade started to flake away, turning to dust and disintegrating. Alrion watched the whole process with his enhanced vision on. He could see the body rebuilding, replacing what had been lost. Soon there were no more traces of the Blight. Just a man remained, his breathing shallow and weak.

"Bring a stretcher," Alrion said. The high general nodded to an aide, who rushed off. Within moments two guards returned bearing a stretcher. They set it down gently near Alrion. He thanked them and gently lifted the former Shade, using his force spells to bear the brunt of the weight. He gently lowered the man onto the stretcher.

"Lift him up and let those who need to see for themselves look." Alrion watched as the guards lifted the stretcher cautiously, trying not to look within.

The high general strode over. He stared into the stretcher, and reached in, feeling the man's hand.

"It's warm, he's alive."

"Of course. How do you think the Blight survives? It needs us."

"What of the man within?" The high general looked up at Alrion.

"That's a good question, I haven't gotten to the bottom of it. Some have had a full recovery, others I'm not so sure about. I think it depends on a lot of factors. With luck, he can lead a normal life again."

"Brady, come look." The high general stepped back and waited for the commander to view the man.

"I'm convinced, even though I can't believe it. It seems like it should be impossible." Brady looked at Alrion, an incredulous expression on his face.

"You should keep the man here, and care for him. You can review his progress, and hopefully, he can speak to you once he's recovered. There is probably a lot we can learn for the future."

"Alrion," the high general said as he crossed the last few steps between them. "You swear you can do this for the whole world?"

"I swear. It's why I need to get to the source. I can't exactly cleanse the world one person at a time."

"Of course." The high general closed his eyes, deep in thought. He stayed that way for minutes. Finally, he opened them once more.

"I've made my decision. Whatever you need, we will provide. Today is an auspicious day. It is the start of the end of the Blight." The high general held out a hand. Alrion held out his and they shook on it. The deal was done. Alrion beamed confidence. Inside, he was a wreck.

This is really happening. There's no turning back. I have to find a way to make this work. I don't want to create a world of peace that I can't also enjoy.

43

A HEAVY BURDEN

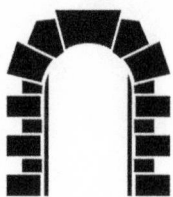

Alrion felt a hand on his shoulder and instantly awoke. It was Lara, leaning over him. She looked worried.

"Good morning. You looked restless. Did you sleep?"

"Good morning. I must have, I don't remember anything." Alrion looked around the room, remembering where he was. It was a spare apartment that his father had arranged for them. He'd arrived late at night, and it looked different in the morning sun. Alrion tried to shake off the sleepiness.

"We need to hurry. We've been summoned by the high general. There's something urgent to discuss."

"You mean your father?" Alrion glanced at Lara long enough to see her embarrassed look then sat up in the bed.

"I know, I should have told you."

"You're practically royalty, Your Highness." Alrion made a mock bow in the bed, before getting up. "Now I know why you never really talked about your family."

"It was difficult. It all happened so close together. My brother dying, the king being killed, my father being called up to the keep."

"That's why you left? All of that?" Alrion rose and started getting ready.

"Yes. It completely exacerbated my father's behaviour. He's always been so traditional, not letting me get involved like my brother. I had to read my books and do my lessons. But Leon was the son. He had the weapons training and the opportunities. And he was good, he became a squad commander in the elite unit that Brady commands. Lucky for me, he taught me quite a bit. Mostly in secret. My father didn't approve."

"You said your brother was a victim of the Blight. What happened?"

"There was a huge battle, my brother held off a whole legion of Blight, leading his men to an honourable death. Those who managed to send a message for help brought reinforcements that crushed the Blight. But they were too late to save him."

"I'm so sorry. But I'm glad that he went out doing something important." Alrion was ready, and he held the door open for Lara.

"Me too." Lara sighed, walking out the door. "Now that I'm back, I feel a bit foolish for just running away. But if I hadn't, well the world wouldn't be on the brink of being cleansed by the Blight."

"I suppose so." Alrion gave her a weak smile. They started walking towards the keep, Alrion noticed that there weren't a lot of people around.

"You're so lucky I decided to pickpocket you."

"I really am." Alrion believed it too. She had been the one constant on a journey that had surprises around every corner.

I suppose it was only natural that she had a secret too. I'll cut her a break, for now, I can see why she'd want to be clear of all this. But I don't know if I can act the same around her.

"What do you think this urgent message is?" Alrion said, changing the topic.

"Not sure. Maybe we have more information about when to make a move? I think the army will take time to mobilise."

"Time is a tricky thing. The more we prepare, the stronger the Blight gets. The more they concentrate their forces. But if we go too early, we blow the whole thing."

"Exactly. But that's what all those army men are for, they live for this."

"What do you live for?"

"I would have said liberating treasures. But now it's different." Lara gave him a mysterious smile.

"And that would be?"

"Something to be shared another time. Oh look, here we are." Lara pointed to the gates outside the keep.

"So we are." Alrion walked through, keeping an eye on the guards. They didn't make eye contact with Lara or Alrion, they just kept out of the way. It didn't take long to return to the throne room. Alrion noticed that everyone else was already there. His father looked like he hadn't slept at all.

In the middle of the room was a strange looking man. He was half height and had thick black hair. He turned to face them as Alrion arrived. The features of the man caused Alrion to gasp. The man looked like a Blighter, only with proper clothing on.

"Now I can give my message," the man rasped. He looked directly into Alrion's eyes.

"I know you are coming, Alrion. I know where you need to be. Only, I'm not going to make it easy for you. If you meet me directly, I'll face you honourably. We can settle this little disagreement like gentlemen. And it's your best chance to destroy me yourself. But if you try to sneak off, well I'll turn my army on Valrytir. We'll crush it and destroy every little piece. And we won't stop there, we'll keep on going until the whole world is under our control."

Alrion pondered the message for a moment.

"What you're saying is that I need to face you and your army now? Or you'll descend upon Valrytir and beyond?"

"Yes. No more hiding. No more tricks."

"And what if I don't agree?"

"There's this and more." The man finished speaking and his stomach started to rapidly expand.

"Everyone, get back!" Alyx shouted. The room almost cleared instantly. Suddenly, the Blight-touched man exploded, and a toxic black gas started to billow throughout the room.

That looks bad.

Alrion activated his enhanced vision and saw what he expected. The gas was strands of the Blight, seeking to infect people. Alrion shuddered and started to deal with the situation.

First, he created waves of force to box the smoke in, moving it into a smaller area. Then he had an idea. He visualised an empty glass orb in the middle of the room. And to top it off, the orb attracted the smoke. It couldn't help but get sucked in. Once Alrion added some Spark to the mix, it started to work. The smoke swirled around like it was resisting. Then it rapidly flowed, being drawn into a single space. Once it was done, there was a dense sphere of something floating in the middle of the room.

Alrion approached it carefully. It looked the same in terms of it being tainted by the Blight. He reached out and touched it with his hand. He felt the slick, disgusting taint immediately. To start with, he created a flame and set the orb alight. Next, Alrion touched the flame with his hand and pushed Soul Power into the spell. It looked like it was working.

The flame burned with a golden colour and soon died out. There was nothing else left.

"I think that's it," Alrion said. He looked around the room. Nobody who was left had moved since the gas explosion. The high general was flanked by Magnus, both of whom had stayed but were a good distance away. Alrion's companions were all there but had retreated to positions behind him. They cautiously approached again.

"That was fantastic," Lara said.

"We knew you could handle it." Certan clapped Alrion on the shoulder as he returned. Vincent gave Alrion a satisfied nod and returned to his former position.

"That was quite dramatic. I think the creature made its point," the high general said.

"They're constantly surprising," Alrion said.

"Well, let's not beat around the bush. Either you're an amazing charlatan, or we have a big problem on our hands."

"Charlatan? How could you even think that for a minute?" Alrion was annoyed. The high general was a bit taken aback but launched into his response.

"You show up with a Shade that gets miraculously cured, now another Blight figure threatens everyone and blows up. Sounds like a good way to get us committed, and if you were an agent of the Blight it would all be easy for you to arrange. I'm just saying that this all looks rather convenient for you?"

"This isn't convenient in the slightest. And you know what? I almost understand you doubting me since I did just come out of nowhere. But your own daughter? And Alyx, a soldier that served in your own army?" Alrion watched the high general's anger bubble over.

"I'm actually being quite accommodating, really. My daughter ran off when things became too difficult, hardly a reliable person. And Alyx? She's the reason my son died. Wasted on a trifling skirmish. Again, hardly someone I want to rely on." Wynston pointed at Alyx and practically shouted the last part. Lara gasped and countered.

"What are you talking about? Are you mad?" Lara said.

"Go on, ask her." The high general was fuming. Lara looked to Alyx.

"It's true. The man I fell in love with, the one that was killed during our scouting mission. He was your brother, Leon. I thought you knew." Alyx spoke softly and looked away from Lara.

"But you said he died in a great battle? He died saving others?" Lara started approaching her father.

"I said that to protect you. But in truth, the scouting mission did save lives."

"You made me feel even more worthless than I was, by saying he died for a great cause? And then you turned around and said the exact opposite to her?" Alyx said to the high general. He didn't look concerned.

"I don't answer to you." He looked over at Lara. "Or you either." Lara shook her head muttering under her breath.

"What will it be, High General? Are we moving forward or not?" Alrion was sick of the discussion and hated how his friends were being treated.

If only we didn't need these forces. But we can't walk into that alone, it'd be suicide.

"I don't see that I have a choice. Our forces will be ready to march at first light. But you, little wizard, need to be up front and centre."

"Fine, I'll be there." Alrion left in disgust. He could hear his friends leaving too.

"You can see why I didn't want to stick around," Lara said. Alyx closed in and pulled Lara aside.

"I'm so sorry. When we spoke about my past, I spared the detail so that I would not bring up old wounds. I had no idea that you didn't know."

"I don't blame you, I blame him. It's too much to sort through right now. Let's just go ahead with what we need to do." Lara started walking again.

"Let's figure out what we are doing." Alrion led them back to his temporary quarters. They needed to be clear about what was happening.

"If you don't mind, I'll find you later? I need to finish that project." Vincent was apologetic and started walking off before they could respond.

"That's fine," Alrion said to nobody in particular. He walked the path deep in thought, not looking up. Soon enough they were in the little apartment. There wasn't even anywhere to sit, so they all stood in a circle to discuss their plans.

"Here we are, my companions. You have stood by me on this journey and saved me. None of you has any connection to me, except that you chose to help. I owe you all my life."

And I'll be paying that price most likely.

"Before we begin this final planning, I just want to thank you all. Truly. It's been a long road and I wouldn't be here without you." Alrion smiled and received smiles and acknowledgements from them all.

"Now, on to business. Will the high general be riding with the army?" Alrion looked to Lara and Alyx.

"I expect so, but not up front. Maybe at the rear. Lara?"

"Agreed. He will be present but at the back."

"It's amusing then, that he wants me at the head." Alrion chuckled.

"To reinforce the Blight that you're there, no doubt," Alyx added.

"That's fine, it's not a danger to me. We can deal with the army, and then I can proceed to the source."

"Who should go with you?" Lara said.

"Nobody." Alrion noticed some surprised looks. "You can't help me in there, and it would be an additional complication. I shouldn't need backup, that's the benefit of taking out their forces."

"True, but shouldn't we at least guard the entrance?" Alyx said.

"That is the minimum I would do," Certan said.

"Let's assess on the day, but my preference is to have nobody there if we can help it."

I can't let them interfere. Certan and Alyx don't even know that I may die. Should I tell them?

Alrion looked at the expressions on the faces of his friends.

I shouldn't have even told Lara. I'll hold off for now and see how I feel tomorrow.

"I have preparations to make, so I'll meet you all early tomorrow morning for the ride out. I'm going to be extremely focused, so please just leave me be."

"What about offering you good luck?" Certan said.

"Maybe do it now, instead." Alrion cringed as Certan came in and gave him a big hug. But he felt reassured and was then surprised by Alyx then Lara coming in.

"You can try as you might, but I'll never leave you," Lara whispered into his ear. Alrion smiled.

"Alright, thanks, everyone. You know how to best prepare, I won't pretend to advise you on that. But, Certan, please stay behind for a moment. I have a special assignment for you."

Alyx and Lara said goodbye and left the room. Certan approached his face a mixture of curiosity and surprise.

This should work, but it's a bit of a gamble.

44

END OF THE INVESTIGATION

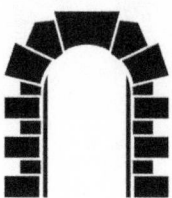

Celes wandered through the district, looking for Vincent. She knew he'd be working on something, which is why she had left him alone. But with her new discovery, it was time to finally look him up.

There's just too many blacksmiths and related trades around here. This could take a while.

Suddenly, she spotted him leaving a shop.

"Vincent," Celes said as she ran over. He beamed a wide smile and gave her a warm hug and kiss.

"Well, aren't you a sight! You must have had an amazing adventure."

"I sure have."

"I hope you weren't in the desert too long. That's where it sent you, right?"

"Absolutely. Lucky for me I ran into that wizard, Ashra." She watched Vincent's reaction. He smiled and nodded.

"He's a good one. Has his own ideas about how to do things, but always does the best for people."

"Best in his own opinion." Celes laughed and Vincent joined in.

"Come on, I've borrowed a small residence and I was about to eat. You can tell me about the rest of your investigation." Vincent led her through the hustle and bustle into a side alley then into a tiny little dwelling at the end. It consisted of a bedroom, and just outside it two chairs and a table. There was some bread, cheese, and fruit laid out on the table.

"Did you prepare this?" Celes said.

"No, I've been working. Thankfully, they organised this for me." Vincent pulled out a chair for Celes and she sat down graciously. He joined her and offered her the food. She started picking at the fruit.

"That Ashra, let me tell you. He's a real trickster. He told me he knew the identity of the wizard, right before pushing me through the next Wizard Gate." Celes shook her head at the memory.

He was right to tell me that much, as infuriating as it was.

"That does not surprise me one bit. I've heard so many stories. So, another Wizard Gate. Where did that take you?"

"A basement of a house in Stonebridge." Vincent looked surprised.

"That's quite unusual but convenient."

"Yes, Ashra thought that perhaps the wizard had taken that route for speed and to keep away from established routes, not that there were any particular things to find on the way."

"It's a good theory. What sort of house holds a Wizard Gate?"

"An old wizard's home. Only there's a farmer living there now. Polite fellow, he even gave me dinner."

"Oh, that's a nice surprise." Vincent smiled.

"Oh, the surprise wasn't nice. He locked me in the basement and went to fetch some sort of Blight assistance." Vincent paused mid chewing and stared at her.

"Lucky for me, there was a secret tunnel that sealed behind me." Celes grabbed a hunk of bread and started chewing. It was surprisingly tasty. Maybe she was just hungry.

"Had I known this would happen, I would have insisted we travel together. I still would have made it here, and you would have had help."

"How were we to know? And I think in a way it was good. I had to rely on myself again. I succeeded, you know."

"Succeeded?"

"Yes, I found out the identity of the mysterious wizard."

"Really?" Vincent looked surprised, and a bit anxious.

"Yes. Lucky for me the secret tunnel linked up with the Wizard Store. By reading the log and conversing with a helpful wizard called Magnus, I was able to track the mysterious wizard to a local inn."

"That's a good lead. How'd you identify him from that?"

"It wasn't the inn itself. But the inn did have a box of his belongings. And in those belongings was..."

"A signed confession?" Vincent offered.

"No, even better. A library receipt."

"A library receipt?"

"Yes. And when I tracked that down, I found the original borrowing ledger. It turns out that book was a restricted loan."

"What was the book?"

"History of the Blight."

"Makes sense." Vincent reached for the fruit now. "How did that solve the puzzle?"

"As it turns out, our mysterious wizard signed his real name for the book." Vincent froze and stared at her.

"He signed his real name?"

"Yes. Can you believe it? I caught him with a twenty-year-old trail. Using a library receipt!" Celes was beaming. Finally, she could share her elation at the find. Vincent looked deep in thought.

"Hmm yes, he would have needed a real identity, not an alias, to borrow a restricted book. And you found the receipt in his belongings, identified by the alias." He looked up at her. "I knew you were a genius. This is phenomenal!"

"It is, isn't it."

"I knew you'd do it. Who else could return on such a long shot?" Vincent smiled at her, and she felt warm inside.

"Alrion needs to know." Celes watched Vincent's face become more serious.

"I agree. I'll tell him at the right time. Things are progressing."

"What do you mean?"

"Darvin has issued an ultimatum—Alrion must meet him face-to-face or he will bring his army to Valrytir and beyond."

"And what did Alrion decide?"

"He had no choice. The high general is mobilising the army at first light, with Alrion at the head."

"I see. We will protect him."

"I must protect him." Vincent stared at her with intensity.

"From an entire army?"

"There's always a way, you should know that. I must go with him and keep him safe. Until he sees it through. Only I can do it."

"If you insist. I can still help." Celes didn't like where this conversation seemed to be going.

"Of course you can, you can support his other companions in their fight. I'll be the one to follow him into the unknown and protect him while he performs the spell. That is the way it must be." Vincent had a sad expression.

"Well, look at us, then. Working together as a family. I never expected it." Celes smiled, hoping to break Vincent out of the mood he was in.

"You're right. It reminds me of the Blind Tiger heist."

"Yes, that was amazing."

Such a clever reference, there are so many parallels with our current situation. Only...

"Wait." Celes studied Vincent's expression. And she thought about the story he had referenced and his last few comments. "You're not coming back, are you?" Celes stared in horror and watched him nod his head.

"I don't expect to, save a miracle."

"But why! This doesn't make any sense." Celes started shaking her head subconsciously.

"I can't get into the details. And maybe I'm wrong, but I don't think so."

"There has to be another way. Surely." Celes searched Vincent's face for some sign of hope. He seemed resigned.

"Darling, what would you do to save our son? What would you give?" Vincent looked up at her.

"Anything."

"As will I." Vincent rose and fetched something from his belongings. He handed it to Celes. It was a few leather-bound books.

"I've catalogued everything I've learned in here. If I don't make it back, there will be answers within. Just promise me you won't read it yet." Vincent held her hand. She stood slowly and embraced him.

"You've been planning this for a while, haven't you?" she whispered.

"Yes. Just in case. I fear the worst."

"I refuse to say goodbye."

"What then?"

"I'll think about it. I have until morning." Celes hugged him tighter, a tear sliding down her cheek.

This can't be it. We must find a way.

THE MAIN ASSAULT

Alyx had a restless sleep. It was filled with images of the Skull King, and Darvin. Right at the end, to make matters worse, she experienced what she thought were memories of the brief period that she was the Skull Queen.

Alyx awoke in a sweat, her hands shaking. She steadied them and looked up. It was almost first light. She was in a single room, a luxury for a soldier. Mary had organised it, an uncharacteristically nice move. Alyx wasn't ready to bunk with other soldiers yet.

She quickly dressed and left the room, not fussed about eating. There would be snacks later if she wanted. To her surprise, there was a well-dressed messenger waiting outside her room. Upon seeing her he became quite animated.

"Good morning, Lady Alyx. I have been dispatched to bring you immediately to Master Balzar." The messenger gave her a deep bow and waited for her response.

"Sure, lead the way." Alyx started walking and had to increase her pace to keep up with the messenger. He wasn't joking around.

This must have something to do with the sword. At least, I hope it does. There's no more time.

Alyx had become accustomed to having Alrion's Runesteel sword, and her lack of a weapon right now felt wrong. She was still incredibly deadly without it, but it was still something to be fixed.

The messenger led her expertly through the city, taking some side roads and shortcuts she didn't know about. Before long they had reached Balzar's workshop. As before, she was led into the back area and down to the large vault. Balzar was standing outside, arms crossed. He beamed her a smile as soon as he saw her.

"This is an auspicious day. Welcome again, to my humble store." Balzar bowed.

This is hardly humble, but I'll let him have his pomp and ceremony.

"Thank you for the invitation and being ready so early in the morning. I need to be out as soon as possible."

"Of course, we've all heard. Lucky for you, Vincent worked some magic." Balzar paused, "figuratively speaking of course. But you'd be forgiven for thinking otherwise." Balzar opened the massive door and eased it open. He disappeared inside, and Alyx followed him in. She found him standing next to a table. He was sporting a huge grin and Alyx could see why. She ran over to the table.

"Andrylir," Alyx whispered under her breath. The sword was gleaming and looked strong. She ran her fingers along the blade feeling it. There were no hints of the previous fragments, it was completely restored.

"Go on, pick it up," Balzar urged. Alyx carefully reached for the sword, remembering its weight. She used two hands, lifting it carefully. She almost dropped it and looked at Balzar sharply.

"Don't look at me, it's all Vincent's work." Balzar held his hands up. "I couldn't believe it either."

"How could it be lighter? It doesn't make any sense?"

"Vincent did say something to me about the blade. He said it won't be the same as it once was but, in some way, he's made it better. Something about Soul Power?" Balzar looked confused.

"I know what he means. I wonder..." Alyx looked around the vault.

"Woah there, I know that look. If you're after something to try it on, I'll set you up outside, not in here." Balzar looked concerned, his eyes tracked hers almost manically.

"Don't worry, I was just seeing what else was here of comparable strength. A more mundane test is fine." Alyx let Balzar lead her out and excuse himself. Within a minute, he had two assistants hauling in a large piece of stone.

"Not sure what we're doing with this. Feel free to test your blade." Balzar's apprentices looked shocked at the suggestion, but they stayed and stared at Alyx.

This is a risk, knowing that I could damage the blade. But I need to know how strong it is, and how sharp.

Alyx hefted the sword and swung diagonally at the stone. It was almost effortless. The sword passed through the stone like it was water, and she felt something as it passed through. A warmth came through the blade.

"Excellent!" Balzar was clapping enthusiastically. His apprentices just stared with their mouths open. Balzar rushed over and inspected the stone.

"Incredibly clean cut, look at this, boys." He called them over and they ran their hands over the stone.

"Do you have something I can use to strap this?" Alyx said.

"Certainly. I had a colleague whip something up. It's not flashy, but it'll work well." Balzar disappeared again and returned with a leather strap system. He helped Alyx put it on, then she was able to almost clip the sword in. After a few more adjustments she could relatively easily remove the sword and return it.

"This works. I cannot thank you enough for what you have done."

"I was merely the facilitator. Give Vincent your thanks, and mine, when you see him."

"I will." Alyx finished her goodbyes and rushed out of the workshop. She needed to get to the rendezvous point before Alrion left with the main force.

Alyx found Lara at the city gates. Just beyond, the forces were massing.

"Am I too late?" Alyx said.

"No, we're just about to move." Lara was peering into the distance.

"Where are the others?"

"Alrion is out there already, I can see him mounted. Certan, I'm not sure. Maybe his special assignment is taking longer. I haven't seen Vincent either."

"Vincent had a special assignment also," Celes said, approaching them both.

"Celes!" Lara ran over and hugged her. Celes smiled.

"You're looking well. You too, Alyx."

"Thank you." Alyx bowed.

"And I can see you're equipped well. At least my husband hasn't been slacking off." Alyx drew Andrylir and let Lara and Celes examine it.

"This sure beats my Runesteel dagger." Lara looked impressed.

"Phenomenal work, I'll have to compliment Vincent." Celes looked out into the distance. "I think they're starting to head out?"

"You're right. Why don't we get started then?" Lara looked at them each in turn. Alyx and Celes both nodded.

"We should push through to catch up to Alrion." Alyx didn't wait for agreement, she started moving out. She could sense the others just behind her. Alyx could recognise the different sections of the army. Even though they were on the move, it was relatively easy to slip between them with their smaller group focused on moving faster. Within half an hour they had reached the front. Alrion was riding out front alone, on a horse. However, he still stayed relatively close to the main force.

I wonder what he's thinking? He looks like he's deep in thought. Almost meditating.

That made sense, he needed to prepare himself for the coming conflict. Although something looked different. Alyx couldn't quite pick it. Until suddenly she realised.

"He doesn't have his Runesteel sword."

"Oh, you're right. That's odd, isn't it?" Lara said. She paused for a moment before continuing. "I didn't see it back at the apartment."

"Do you think he left it somewhere else on purpose?" Celes said.

"Perhaps. Maybe Certan is taking it somewhere for him?"

"It's not cause for concern, his power greatly outweighs what he can do with the sword." Alyx didn't want to upset the others, she was just surprised. He had seemed genuinely relieved to have the sword back, despite freely giving it to her.

After a short while, Alrion stopped completely still. He didn't say anything, just remained on the horse. Alyx could see why.

The Blight forces were visible now. They had massed into a seething horde that stretched as far as the eye could see.

"The Blight are here. They weren't messing around, I did not expect them to march this far," Alyx said.

"Just as well we mobilised quickly. As much as the city is designed to withstand a siege, it would be devastating to the population."

"I'm no soldier, but do you think we can handle such a large number?" Celes looked at them both.

"Normally, I would say no, but we have Alrion up front. He can decimate their forces before we even engage." Lara turned to Alyx. "Do you agree?"

"Yes, that's an accurate assessment." Alyx was about to speak more when she saw movement from the Blight. There was something rippling through them. Suddenly Darvin burst from the front lines, storming forward. He stopped when he was near Alrion.

"Thank you for heeding my call," Darvin shouted, addressing the army at large. He focused his attention on Alrion. Lara started creeping forward, and Alyx and Celes joined her.

"It's time we put aside this misunderstanding and allow each other to peacefully coexist," Darvin said. Alyx looked to Lara.

"What's he on about?"

"I'm not sure."

"I've encountered him before. He's not one for peace, but he is one for manipulation. Don't trust a word he says." Celes shook her head, glaring at the Blight General.

"No response, young wizard? Nothing to say for yourself?" Darvin started approaching. He drew his sword and shield.

"Perhaps I should beat it out of you?" Darvin laughed and started running forward. Alrion skilfully leapt off the horse, holding his footing. He stepped forward, his eyes focused on Darvin. The Blight General leaned in with a giant swing. Instead of fighting back, Alrion merely stepped to the side. Darvin continued by slamming his shield at Alrion. The young wizard held out a palm and blocked the strike. A ripple seemed to roll through Alrion.

"That's odd, I didn't realise he could enhance his body like that," Alyx said.

"I haven't seen that either. I know he can enhance himself with the Soul Power, but he's never really demonstrated it." Lara looked concerned. Celes crept further, looking like she had noticed something.

"I need a closer look," she said, creeping forward again. Darvin attacked, again and again, Alrion just dodged and blocked where required. The movements were simple but skilful and completely efficient.

I've never seen him move so well.

"We have a problem. I'm sure of it now." Celes turned back and looked at Lara and Alyx.

"What's wrong?"

"I don't think that's the real Darvin. Vincent cracked his shield when they fought. Now there's no sign of it."

"Couldn't he have just fixed it?"

"A shield like that? I don't think you can. Vincent did something strange to it, drawing on his Soul Power." Celes looked like she was thinking it through. "I bet it's not him and that's a lookalike shield. If I'm right, Alyx should slice right through it."

"I'm up for that. For some reason, Alrion isn't fighting back either." Alyx strode forward, preparing to draw her blade. Again, Darvin was pressing the attack, and again Alrion was dodging around. He didn't make a single offensive move.

"Time for me to show you how it's done." Alyx drew her sword and launched into a wide arcing strike. Alrion retreated, and Darvin threw up his shield. Just as Celes had predicted Alyx sliced through without issue.

It felt even less resistance than the stone. This is not the same.

"You're not Darvin, are you?" Alyx said. Darvin laughed.

"Of course I'm Darvin, my dear. I remember all about you. It's just, well how do I put this, I'm not the original." Darvin threw her a cackling laugh and retreated into the mass of Blight.

"Good work, Alyx," Celes said as she approached. She was about to speak again when Alrion dropped to his knees. He was in intense concentration.

"Let it go, Certan." Alyx watched as Alrion's features flickered and disappeared. Certan was there, kneeling before them.

"What?" Celes said. Lara too looked shocked. Certan rose, taking a deep breath.

"I apologise for the subterfuge, it was at Alrion's request. He did not expect Darvin to fight fair, so he thought he shouldn't either. I guess he was right."

"If Darvin isn't here, then he must be waiting for Alrion. With his entire strength and who knows what else." Lara looked panicked. Alyx felt the feeling too. It was a dread realisation in the pit of her stomach.

Alrion is alone behind enemy lines, and the enemy commander is likely preparing an ambush.

"He needs backup, but we're in even more trouble here now that we don't have him to help thin them out." Alyx was in two minds about where to go. But Lara had no such hesitation.

"I'm not a front-line fighter, please do your best here." Lara dashed away at speed, threading her way through friendly forces. Alyx looked to the enemy.

I can do a lot of good here, but I feel like Alrion needs me.

Just as she felt herself leaning towards joining Lara, she saw a shape emerging from the crowd.

It can't be.

The creature was wearing exactly the same twisted grin. It was like no time had passed at all.

"The Skull King is mine," Alyx said as she began to advance.

46

A FALSE BATTLE

Alrion stumbled through the undergrowth, not seeing one of the tree roots. It was so hard concentrating on his spell, and he was so tired. All night he had worked with Certan to perfect the illusion spell in a way that Certan could maintain it. Now he was keeping himself invisible and masking as much noise as possible.

But he was weary. The effort was taking its toll, slowly but surely.

Maybe I'm far enough away from the armies to relax a bit.

Alrion leaned against a tree trunk, taking a moment to catch his breath. He decided to push on a little further. He could rest soon once he saw the cave. Once he entered, that would be it.

I hope the plan worked. If Darvin thinks I took the bait, I might be able to get in and finish the spell before he can intervene. If I'm incredibly lucky.

It was a lot to ask for, but it was worth a shot. He almost tripped again and swore.

Time to let the invisibility go. It's not worth it anymore.

Alrion let the spell go, feeling a huge weight lifting from his shoulders. There were a few ways to create and maintain an invisibility spell. He had chosen one with a strong Will component. He didn't want to burn too much of his Spark too soon.

Noises of the conflict reached him from afar, but he tried not to think too much about it. That battle was important, but not what he had come here for. His battle would be entirely different. Alrion saw a clearing ahead and charged towards it. Maybe he was closer than he realised.

The cave looked exactly as he expected. A rather ordinary looking entrance flanked by rough rocks. The grass didn't grow on it, the ground above was dry and lifeless, and the rest of the stone was free from any greenery. But there was a feature he had not anticipated. Darvin was standing in front of the entrance.

"Come out, Alrion, no need to be shy." Darvin grinned and beckoned into the distance. Alrion stepped out of the trees into the clearing.

"This is a surprise and not a welcome one." Alrion looked Darvin in the eyes.

"I would say almost the same thing. All reports were that you were heading up the attack force. But you see, I wasn't worried about that. I wanted to make sure if you made your way here, we could have a little conversation. And here we are." Darvin stepped a few paces closer then stopped.

"I have other business to attend to. What do you want?" Alrion made himself sound wearied and disinterested, which was quite easy to draw upon. He was weary of games, and Darvin no doubt had another.

"Your business is my business if you don't mind. You know, my orders are to let you through. Collectively, we think that you'll help us, not hinder us. But I'm not so trusting. There's no way I'm letting you in there until you become infected." Darvin drew his sword and shield and took up a ready stance.

"I see. In this situation, it's not in my interests to kill you when I can save you. But I'll do whatever I need to in order to get inside and fulfil my quest. It's best you step aside now. Wait it out, and you'll be free from these burdens in no time."

"That's a matter of perspective. In my eyes, the burdens will be brought by you!" Darvin took another step forward.

"It's a fight then?" Alrion drew his Runesteel sword. He glanced at the diamond and it was shining brightly.

Maybe I can wear him down without using too much Spark. I don't want to be in a position where I can't perform the spell.

Alrion started a standard form, warming himself up. Darvin seemed to know it well, he moved at the same pace and anticipated each strike, blocking or parrying with ease. Alrion did notice that Darvin's shield seemed especially strong. He expected his Runesteel to do more to it than it did. If Darvin wasn't so able with the sword, Alrion would have believed that Darvin just relied on the shield.

After a few exchanges, Alrion realised that Darvin was just too good. Even as Alrion got faster and more involved, Darvin just upped the tempo and was always one step ahead.

I'm not a sword fighter, how can I beat him this way? I can't ignore my talents.

Alrion dismissed the option of using his Soul Power. He needed to conserve it as much as possible. There was no knowing how much he would need to perform the spell. That left his Spark. He was a wizard, after all, he'd have to win this fight like one.

Alrion stepped back and sheathed his sword.

"Giving up already? We've barely started!"

"I know where this is going. At my best, I couldn't really trouble you with the sword, not for more than an instant."

"Very wise, you have good instincts." Darvin sized Alrion up. "What are you going to do now?"

"This." Alrion focused his Spark into a quick release fireball that hurtled towards Darvin. He held up his shield and the spell fizzled into nothing. Darvin laughed.

"Did your encounter with the Skull Queen teach you nothing? You thought you could just waltz in here and blow me away?" Darvin's laughter turned into cackling. Alrion was furious.

He's getting under your skin. Just think carefully.

Alrion could see that the direct spell was dispelled by the shield. He did remember that the Skull Queen had done something similar with that sword she had wielded.

Direct attacks won't work. But other things will. And my Will should still be effective.

Before Alrion could plan another attack, Darvin was on the move. He launched into a flurry of strikes, weaving his shield into the attack pattern. Alrion used his Runesteel sword to block and parry, but he was losing ground quickly. And the exertion on his already tired body was worrying. He stumbled back, and Darvin used that as inspiration for another string of attacks.

Alrion acted on instinct. He raised a chunk of earth, upsetting Darvin's footing and using the distraction to roll away. He drew in deep breaths, taking the time to recover.

"So now you're thinking like a wizard. About time." Darvin grinned.

Is he enjoying this? Probably. He's been consistent in that. Taunting and such the whole way through. Maybe I can unsettle him, maybe that will turn the tide.

Alrion had a few glimmers of a plan, but it hadn't quite formed. In the meantime, he had to keep Darvin busy.

"I can't target you with my spells, but I can have some fun myself." Alrion sent multiple waves of rippling earth at Darvin, all from different directions. The Blight General stepped aside, dodging some and using his shield to deflect the rest. He looked inconvenienced, but not concerned about the attack.

At least his shield didn't completely negate the attacks. I can work with this.

Unfortunately, Alrion couldn't use the approach he had done with the Skull Queen. He had no backup and he needed to conserve his Soul Power. But there had to be a way he could wear down Darvin using his magic.

Before Darvin could start up a new attack, Alrion was already preparing his next. He lifted chunks of stone out of the ground and hurled them at Darvin.

"You'll have to do better than that." Darvin sneered at Alrion then spun around, slicing two of the large stones and battering another away with his shield. Alrion wasn't using too much Spark, but it was adding up and he wasn't really damaging Darvin at all.

I need something better. Can I use my Will to influence the environment more?

Alrion had an idea, but it was going to be hard to do. He took in a deep breath and steeled himself. He started building up his spark and preparing a visualisation. Darvin started approaching.

"Why are we fighting like this, Alrion. Surely you know what you're up against." Darvin kept approaching, his shield and sword in a relaxed position by his sides. "Why are you so insistent on completing this quest? The Blight can be a tool for your use. Join us and influence us from within. Together we can make the world a better place."

"No. I've already had a taste of that, and it sickens me." Alrion kept his concentration. Darvin came closer still. Time was running out. Alrion reached down and slapped the ground with his hand. It wasn't necessarily required, but it was an easy focal point for him. At that moment, he enacted a change in the area's gravity. Darvin started to stoop slightly and moved a lot slower. He started to raise his arms. Outside the area of influence, Alrion was building stone spears from the ground. More and more and more. Soon he had ten, twenty, fifty spears. Each honed to a razor point.

Consider this my thanks and acknowledgement of you, Branthor. Alrion lifted them all into the air, all aimed directly at Darvin. The Blight General was still lifting his shield and sword to protect himself. Alrion sent his stone spikes in, and at the last moment changed the space around him. Suddenly, everything moved incredibly quickly. It didn't last long, but it was enough to have an enormous impact.

Almost instantaneously the array of spikes appeared next to Darvin, on a collision course. There was no way he could block or strike them all. But then he did something unexpected. He tapped his shield and it expanded its size. Much faster than Alrion could track. And as the spikes impacted, Alrion heard a giant clang sound, like an ominous bell.

Once the dust settled, Alrion saw that Darvin was not there. Instead, his shield was spread out like a small dome.

"Are you under that?" Alrion said, incredulously.

"Of course. Did you think I would let you hit me with all that?" Darvin's voice echoed from within the shield dome, sounding harsher and more unusual than ever before. Alrion looked around, seeing the broken bits of stone spikes all over the ground.

"I'll break through eventually; your shield isn't perfect. Look, it even has a crack in it." Alrion noticed the crack and his hope increased. But the more he looked at it, the stranger it appeared. It had to be older than just now, and it didn't look like his stone spears had done the damage. It was too clean.

"Yes, but not by your hand. I can last long enough to bring more pain to you, mark my words."

"Fine, I'll just walk by you." Alrion stopped walking but he heard Darvin's laughter and stopped.

"Be my guest. When you least expect it, I'll be there, interrupting your plans and forcing you to our side." Darvin kept laughing.

I didn't expect this. He obviously did. He had this stalemate as a fall-back.

"This is what you get for sneaking off without me," a voice said from behind. Alrion whirled around. It was Lara. She did not look impressed.

It's good to see her.

"Impeccable timing. I have a cowardly Blight General to deal with." Alrion pointed at the shield.

"I know, I've been watching this fight. You had us fooled for a while, I didn't expect that. Nice trick with Certan." Lara glared at him, but he could see some small amount of surprise and respect in there.

"It was necessary. Unfortunately, Darvin had plans too."

"He sure did. Certan was fighting another Darvin before I headed over."

"Another one?" Alrion glanced back at the shield. Nothing had changed.

"Yes, it didn't elaborate. But we figured out it was not the original." Lara walked past Alrion and pointed at the crack in the shield. "And I know how that shield was damaged."

"How?"

"Your father used some sort of strike that used Soul Power. Have a think about it." Lara looked at Alrion then at his sword. Then she pointed at the crack. He nodded.

She's not speaking additional detail out loud.

"That's all well and good, but I can't waste Soul Power on this. I don't know how I could break that shield." Alrion said the words for Darvin's benefit, but quietly drew his sword.

If my father could enhance his blade with Soul Power, I can too. He tried pushing some through his hand into the blade. It felt strange, but it began to work.

"I can likely only create the opening, you need to complete the job," Alrion whispered to Lara. She nodded.

"Maybe you have some sort of potion that will damage the shield?" Alrion said to Lara. She winked at him and started rummaging through her things, retrieving her Runesteel dagger and holding it ready.

"Oh, perhaps. Let me look." Alrion smiled back at her and focused on his sword. He could spare a bit of Soul Power, enough to work on that crack that was already there.

"Take your time, I don't think he can actually bring any help here." Alrion advanced slowly, nodding at Lara. She followed too. He hoped that their conversation would distract Darvin, or at least invite him to focus on communicating with others. Once they were close, Alrion made himself stable.

Here goes.

Alrion focused the Soul Power in his blade towards the tip, and it seemed to collect more there. Next, he leaned back and thrust forward as hard as possible. The Runesteel impacted with the shield with a great crash but didn't bounce off. It found space within the crack and started to press further. Lara stood at the ready. As the shield started to give way, it started transforming.

Oh no, he's changing his stance. I'll probably miss completely.

Darvin rose as his shield reverted to its normal size. The transformation threw Alrion's strike off, and he lost his balance. Darvin started cackling. He dropped his sword and withdrew a black dagger with a thick inky substance dripping off the blade. As he prepared to attack Alrion, he suddenly dropped to his knees.

Lara stepped back, admiring her handiwork. She had circled around Darvin and thrust the Runesteel dagger into the creature's heart, from behind.

"This cannot be," Darvin muttered, before falling face down into the ground. He started transforming once again, a black dust flaking into the air. His body was returning to what it once was, before the Blight.

"I'm sorry that I couldn't save you," Alrion said.

47

A LONELY PATH

L ara drew Alrion aside, and they walked away from both the cave entrance and Darvin's body. She sat him down on some rocks in a nearby glade. They hadn't spoken at all since the fight.

"What were you thinking? You could have died back there!" Lara shouted at him, pounding his chest with her fists. Alrion let her.

"I'm sorry, it's my journey to take. Nobody else can do this for me."

"What was your plan? I saw what he did to your spells. He wasn't afraid of you at all. What would you have done if I hadn't shown up?"

"If I couldn't wear him down enough? I'd try to cure him."

"Wouldn't that weaken you for a long time?"

"Yes. But it would have worked if I needed it." Alrion looked away. He couldn't argue with her, she was right. But there was another reason he had snuck away. A more painful one.

"I'm just glad I found you in time."

"Have you used what I gave you?"

"Not yet." Lara retrieved the two small glass vials. They almost looked empty. Alrion activated his Soul Power and saw the power within them.

"Still looks good. That will help you in a pinch."

"I'm going with you." Lara gestured back towards the cave.

"You can't. Nobody can."

"I think you just proved that you can't be left alone." Lara looked annoyed. But she stopped glaring at him and looked worried instead. "There's too much at risk. Can't you trust me?"

"Of course, I trust you. I don't trust myself." Alrion looked past her, towards the cave.

"What do you mean?" Lara sat closer, holding his hand in hers. He didn't look at her, not yet.

"I need to be alone in there. If I have you with me, maybe they can use that against me."

"That's not a good enough reason, it's worth the risk." Lara reached over and turned his head, so he was looking at her.

She's right. She must suspect something else is wrong.

"Fair enough. Let me put it this way." Alrion sighed and collected his thoughts. "If I must sacrifice myself for this, I need to be at peace with that. And having you there will make it much harder to do. I'll probably cling to my life and make a bad choice. I need to keep my focus and do what is required." He let himself look into her eyes. She had tears in there.

"The world is not your responsibility. There's always another way." He could see the sadness behind her eyes, he knew the extent of what the Blight had meant for her and her family. It was not easy for her to say those words.

"I don't want to die. I don't want to be sacrificed for everyone else. But if that makes all this go away, I'll do it. You said there was another of Darvin, the Blight will keep reinventing itself until it wins. I have to stop it here." Alrion felt his resolve harden a bit more.

Maybe I'll get taken by this process, but it would protect Lara and everyone else. That's worth it, isn't it?

He saw Lara wiping away her tears. He gave her a hug and felt her warmth seeping into him. He put everything aside for a minute and basked in it. Alrion then pulled away, standing up.

"I need to keep going. I'm sorry."

"What if I..." Lara said, but Alrion raised a hand.

"You can't enter the cave, that's final. But you can help everyone else. Isn't that worth doing? We don't know how my actions here will affect the battle being fought elsewhere." Alrion saw Lara thinking it over. She looked like she was coming around.

"I don't like this, but I can see you won't be swayed. I'll search the area out here for more forces or traps, then I'll rejoin the others." Lara gave him a weak smile. Alrion walked in close and leaned in. He kissed her deeply and gave her a hug. She held him tightly for a long time. Eventually, she pulled away.

"You better come back, or I'll be forced to find a way to drag you into the light. And you won't enjoy that!"

"Doesn't sound like it." Alrion forced a chuckle. They started walking back to the glade where they had fought Darvin. His body had completely returned to a human one. Alrion forced himself to look for a moment.

"Good luck," Lara said. Alrion reached into his pocket and retrieved a small bag. He threw it to her.

"What's this?"

"It's the ring you stole from me."

"Why are you giving it back?" Lara had a confused look.

"You can hold it for me."

"I will. Although, it's not as fun if you just give it to me."

"Sorry about that. Thank you." Alrion turned and started walking to the cave entrance. He turned back just before he reached it, and saw that Lara was still standing there, waiting. He gave her a short wave then entered the darkness.

The cave was pitch-black. Alrion created an orb of light and had it hover just above him. Now that he could see better, the cave was completely featureless. It was just dark and boring. He walked on, listening for any signs of life. Nothing was there, save for the echoes of his footsteps. As he walked, he felt like he was going down. But the cave seemed to be getting lighter. Soon he started to see rays of light, then areas of the cave bathed in natural light. He pushed forward, curious.

Alrion emerged into an impossible space. It felt like he was outdoors. Lush trees and shrubs grew thickly around the path, and he could see glimpses of blue sky through the tree coverage.

Where am I?

This was not what he had expected. He was supposed to be heading to the source of the Blight. Darkness and decay are what he expected.

Did I go to the wrong place?

Alrion looked behind him. The cave tunnel he had travelled down was still there. It didn't look like a trick.

Time to march forward, see where I end up.

Alrion slowly progressed through the dense forest. It was eerily quiet. After a time, he picked why it seemed so odd. There were no signs of life. No animals at all. And there wasn't any wind either. Everything seemed so static.

Maybe there's a reason this is here.

Alrion could see something up ahead. It looked like a big rock formation. He made his way over, carefully. The light and life, as still as it was, felt refreshing. He soon found himself before a large lake. The water was light blue, and it almost glowed. Alrion knelt and ran his hand through the water. It tingled.

Is that Soul Power?

Alrion activated his enhanced vision and looked at the lake. It was definitely infused with Soul Power. He cupped his hands and tried drinking some. It was refreshing and energising.

This doesn't make any sense. But I may as well use it.

Alrion took a moment to drink and rest. But he didn't completely relax. There was still something strange about this environment. And he couldn't waste too much time. He stood and looked for a way around the lake. There didn't seem to be one.

Let's just try.

He started to wade through, instantly sinking down to his waist. It was slow going, but he managed to progress. Step by step he progressed through the lake. He didn't trust himself swimming and pressed forward. Slowly but surely, he made his way across. He expected it to get dark, but the light and environment remained unchanged.

As he reached the other shore, he noticed a small opening in the rock formation. It was another tunnel. Alrion climbed out of the water and used a bit of his Spark to dry his clothes.

Now, let's see where this goes.

Alrion started off, creating another orb of light to see. He noticed a change instantly. There was a strange architecture in this new tunnel or cave structure. It looked like there were places where it was narrow and other places where it expanded. There was almost an odd geometry in the walls. Regular shapes such as rectangles and squares were formed out of the rock.

It doesn't make sense.

Alrion pressed on. One section was pitch-black, another bathed in light. He lost track of where he was, and where he was going. Onward and onward he walked, no signs of any other life.

Then he saw it. It began with an uneasy sensation running down his spine. Something he felt before he noticed it. He almost didn't see it. But in the distance, in a darker section, he saw something that was blacker than black. A mass of living shadow.

"The source," Alrion whispered. Even from this distance, he recognised it from his dreams. His destination was so close. He steeled himself and took a step towards his destiny.

48

DARKNESS IN NUMBERS

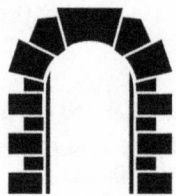

Certan watched the Skull King emerge from the opposing army. He turned and witnessed Alyx's reaction. It looked like a mix of fear and rage. She was trembling.

"I don't want you to interfere." Alyx was fixated on the Skull King. She started to advance.

"As you wish. Is it another copy?"

"It has to be, but I don't care." Alyx kept advancing. The Skull King was laughing, an evil sound that made Certan's skin crawl.

If Alyx has bested this creature before, she should do so again. I doubt it is as strong as before. But she will need backup.

Certan noticed that a retinue of creatures followed the Skull King out. Not only that, but the Blight forces were losing their tight formations. At any moment, they could break out into open warfare.

"I don't like this. Chaos is about to be unleashed."

"I suggest you do what you do best," Celes said, joining him. She had a dagger in one hand and a vial of orange liquid in the other.

"I will." Certan removed a vial of his own. It looked empty, but he knew it wasn't. It was a gift from Alrion. Certan opened the vial and poured it over his hand. He felt the Soul Power wash over him like a warm glow, and it enveloped his hand, using that as a way into his body. He let the sensation settle and prepared his approach.

Certan counted two Shades and a Shade Wizard supporting the Skull King. Alyx would struggle with that combination. But he could do something about it.

"Try not to engage too soon, save your firepower for when they break loose." Certan saw Celes's acknowledgement and he instantly ran off to assist Alyx.

The Weapon Master had drawn her sword and began a duel with the Skull King. However, the creatures following the Skull King around had started flanking, looking for an opportunity to interfere.

"Not on my watch, foul creatures!" Certan shouted. They looked over at him, surprised. Certan composed himself for a moment, winding himself up. Then he shot out at surprising speed.

This power works fantastically.

Certan practically appeared in front of the Shade. He used a single punch to breach the creature's heart and watched it drop instantly, a shocked expression on its face. The other Shade began to fight back but Certan swept its leg out with his, causing it to stumble. Using that moment of weakness, he performed the same attack, killing it instantly.

The Shade Wizard was not to be caught the same way. It started throwing fireballs at Certan at close range. He rolled away, using his speed to create some distance between them. Wizard fire was hard to judge, and it could burn him quite badly if he miscalculated or the Shade Wizard was more powerful than expected.

The Skull King looked over, distracted by Certan's attack. Alyx used the moment to gain an advantage, forcing the Skull King back and getting a strike on the creature's arm. It howled with pain and rage then regrouped, attacking Alyx with twice the ferocity.

She can handle this. I need to shut down the Shade Wizard quickly.

Certan wheeled around, looking to close the distance quickly. The Shade Wizard was throwing fireballs, and waves of force. Certan saw the attacks coming and shifted his heading and stance to avoid them with minimal loss of momentum. The Shade Wizard started to panic and created a wall of fire.

Be faster.

Certan focused himself even further and pushed through the fire. He felt a searing pain for an instant but passed through. The Shade Wizard was stunned and struggled to throw more spells. But Certan was close enough. He knocked the Shade Wizard down with an open palm then broke its neck. With utmost precision, he destroyed its heart before it could recover.

Looking up, Certan could see that while he was fighting, the main Blight force had entered the fray. The battle lines were now muddled, with Valrytir soldiers and Blight fighting everywhere he could look. The Blight had overwhelming numbers. He heard an explosion over his shoulder and saw Celes throwing some of her vials. Clumps of Blighters were knocked away or retreated while on fire.

It's not enough. We need to create an advantage.

Certan considered joining Alyx's fight, as she would add considerable might to the general fight. But he decided not to, it wasn't arranged and could put her in danger if he upset the balance. Certan scanned the crowd and noticed something unusual in the distance.

"Celes, what's that?" Certan pointed.

"That's another Blight General I'd say. My guess would be Rindale?"

"Rindale. The architect of their creatures?"

"Yes, the very same."

"He might be behind these copies of the generals."

"Very astute." Celes threw a flurry of daggers over Certan's shoulder. Two Blighters dropped to the ground.

"Let's change the course of this fight." Certan didn't wait for Celes to reply. He launched himself into the Blight lines. He could feel the Soul Power draining, but he continued to use it. He focused his body completely, wasting no motion at all. He glided forward, each movement advancing him and becoming an attack. He stepped forward and kicked a Blighter over, tripping another. He elbowed another, slamming it into two more and used the collapsing heap as a springboard to launch himself into another cluster of Blighters. He landed on one and quickly rose into a spinning kick that cleared the area and killed some Blighters instantly. Others backed away immediately. Certan heard a blood-curdling cry and looked back anxiously.

Alyx was throwing herself at the Skull King, her blade gliding through the air as though it were a leaf. He was managing to block the strikes, but he was being pushed back. Any Blighters that were close were just cut down in the process. Certan thought he saw something golden on the blade, but an instant later it was gone.

"Eyes on the prize, monk." Celes pointed to Rindale. He was trying to sneak away. Certan took in a deep breath and composed himself once more.

It's too inefficient fighting the whole army. I need to be smarter.

The master monk planned his course, prepared his muscles and steeled his will. Then he launched himself into the air. He cleared a group of Blighters and landed on another. He picked up a nearby Blighter and charged forward, using the Blighter as a shield to bludgeon away anything in his path. As fast as Rindale retreated, he was held up by the sheer number of bodies surrounding him. Before long Certan had caught up. He threw the Blighter he was holding, clipping Rindale's leg just enough to make him stumble.

"I'm not so weak, monk." Rindale stood quickly and readied himself. Certan walked up slowly, not trying to attack. Rindale watched him suspiciously. Once Certan was right in front of Rindale, he held out his hand.

"What is this?"

"There is no honour in this chase, this fight. I will spare you if you come back with me."

"Come back where?"

"Back to beyond the intense fighting. I believe you have valuable information." Certan watched Rindale's reaction. The creature was intrigued. He flicked his eyes left and right, clearly evaluating his chances of getting away.

"I'm not so easy to kill, just so you know."

"I know." Certan left his hand outstretched. Rindale reached for it. As his hand closed around Certan's, the monk noticed a strange black nail. He felt it soon after.

"Ha! You're mine now." Rindale cackled. Certan was not impressed. He grabbed Rindale by the wrists and hauled him away. No matter how Rindale struggled, Certan's grip did not waver. He methodically strode back through the battlefield. The Blighters all stayed out of his way, terrified. Once they had reached a safer spot, Certan put Rindale down on the ground.

"You haven't won, you're infected."

"Am I?" Certan showed Rindale his hand. There was no wound.

"Impossible! I injected you with the Blight."

"Try again." Certan left his hand out. Rindale snatched at it and tried again. But his nail could not pierce Certan's skin. The black liquid oozed away with no effect.

"This cannot be."

"Perhaps the original Rindale could have done the job, but you're not him. What are you?"

"A shadow of my former greatness, I'm afraid," Rindale muttered.

"How did you do it?"

"You wouldn't understand." Rindale shook his head.

"I'm sure you can explain in a way we'll understand," Celes said. She approached, twirling one of her daggers.

"It was a contingency plan to keep control of the Blight. I managed to preserve the look, personality, and power of each of us. But none of the host bodies could manifest them with the right strength. We're all weaker. Lesser." Rindale shook his head.

"How many are there?"

"Just one of each. It takes time." Rindale looked around. He pointed at the Skull King. "He was a great success."

"How so?" Certan asked for curiosity's sake, but he could see what Rindale meant. Even though Alyx was fighting the creature furiously and with incredible speed and accuracy, the Skull King was not letting up or tiring.

"Darvin pushed me to find a way. The Skull King was the first of us to fall, he was missed the most. After much experimentation, I managed to succeed. Great power, at great cost."

"What was the cost?" Celes said.

"Many lives. And his personality. It's a mere shadow of him. Fine for this, but not what any of us wanted." Rindale sounded disappointed, and perhaps even sad.

"Keep questioning him. I need to stop this." Certan walked off, towards Alyx. He dispatched any lone Blighters in his path, his attention fixated on the fight. The more Alyx pushed, the further they went into enemy territory.

She will tire and be overwhelmed eventually. She needs to cool her head.

Certan jogged over and drew in close.

"Alyx, this creature is not him. It's just a monster with his appearance and attributes."

"No, this grin. It haunted me for years!" She increased her intensity again. There were nicks and breaks on the Skull King's blade, but he seemed to be fine.

"Rindale himself admitted that it's just a shadow, but an incredibly strong one. You need to fight smarter." Certan shadowed her movements, trying to figure out how to get through to her. But he could see it now. She was in a blind rage. The Skull King's reappearance had tapped into something else. He knew what he had to do.

Certan watched carefully, then he made his move. Alyx had a fantastic opening and she lurched forward with a massive overhead strike. Certan dashed in, one hand catching her blade, and another stopping the Skull King's. He could feel both weapons surging ahead, trying to eat through his hands. But he steeled his will and held firm.

"Alyx, listen to me." Certan could see her blindly pushing on. "Alyx, you can't defeat him like this." Alyx barely noticed him. She just pushed harder with her sword.

Nothing else to do then.

Certan let go of each sword but guided their path as soon as they jumped free. Both swords were thrust into the ground. Certan shoved them even further, to ensure they were hard to dislodge. As Alyx struggled to free her sword, Certan tapped into the minimal Soul Power left in his body. It felt so close to his own life force. He mixed the two and prepared a special technique. He turned and faced the giant tower of evil, the Skull King. It wasn't even trying to reach its sword, it was reaching towards Certan. He ducked under its hands and moved in close. He placed both palms on the creature's chest and let loose a blast of pure energy. He stumbled back with the effort, but the Skull King fared much worse.

A large hole was created in the creature's chest, and it toppled to the ground. Instantly, the body started to flake away. Certan turned and regarded Alyx. The rage seemed to have subsided. She tugged at her sword and managed to free it. She looked up at Certan.

"I owe you my life. I'm sorry, I lost myself."

"We all have, at one time or another. There's no time for that now, let's turn the tide of this fight." Certan pointed to a large cluster of Blighters heading towards where he had left Celes and Rindale. Alyx nodded and they jogged along, carving a path through the mass of Blighters. Certan looked back to gauge the rest of the battle's progress. It was hard to see, but he thought it was evenly matched.

Hopefully, we can change the momentum now.

"They're after Rindale, there's no time!" Celes shouted. Certan launched into a sprint. He noticed Alyx by his side.

"Follow my lead." Certan didn't even bother to look at Alyx's response. He knew she would follow. Certan aimed at the middle of the pack. He wasn't focused on killing them, he was more focused on knocking them down and keeping them occupied. After he had their attention, they changed their focus to try to swarm him. But then Alyx swooped in.

With large arcing slices she decimated them with ease. With their attention divided, they had no way of avoiding her blade. Any that tried to run, found Certan knocking them back into the path of Alyx's blade. Within minutes, the group had been dispatched.

Certan drew in more deep breaths. His stamina was running out. He looked over and saw Celes questioning Rindale. She looked concerned. He rushed over as fast as he could.

"You look concerned. What happened?"

"That push happened because Rindale started to spill. I hope Lara found Alrion."

"Why, what is it?"

"Not only did the real Darvin go to intercept him, but there's another surprise lying in wait. Something dark and horrible." Celes didn't bother hiding the dismay on her face. Certan understood the feeling completely. He looked up at the battlefield.

"We need to trust in their strength, there's too much to be done here." Certan stood and started his return to the fighting.

Be safe, Alrion, and may wisdom guide your path.

49

STRUGGLE

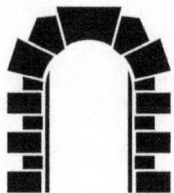

Alrion moved forward, one step at a time. He didn't want to make a wrong move. There was something incredibly unsettling about the darkness beyond. He couldn't make out any details, perhaps that is what made it worse.

Definitely in the right place.

He couldn't see anything past the mass of black. It seemed like it sucked the light out of anywhere nearby, it was that dark. Quiet too. Completely silent, save for his footsteps. They echoed around on the rocky floor. He decided to create an orb of light and send it over to get a better look at what he was heading towards.

The orb floated over towards the darkness. The closer it moved, it seemed as though something was pulling the light from it. Alrion waited and watched. Soon enough the orb was dimmer.

That's strange. I better investigate.

Alrion's mind started imagining some crazy scenarios and dreamed up some ridiculous monsters. But he pushed that aside.

I've seen this before, it's just a wall or gateway or something like that. I don't need to build it up more than it needs.

As he approached, he cast another orb of light and floated it over near the first. The extra light helped a little, although it began to fare the same as the other one. But he did catch sight of something.

There was movement. That shouldn't be happening. He took a few more cautious steps. He sensed movement again and turned sharply. Nothing was happening, but he knew there was something.

"Show yourself," Alrion said, his voice stronger than expected. He didn't hear any response or notice any motion. He stepped forward again. Suddenly there was movement. From multiple directions. Alrion sent out a wave of fire and watched it alight several things at once. But he couldn't get a sense of what they were. He activated his Soul vision and gasped.

They were black sinewy tendrils of darkness, full of the Blight. They looked as though they were somehow made from the Blight itself. They snaked through the air, shrugging off the flames which soon died out.

I can't believe it. This is what Ashra sent at me!

Alrion was stunned. His body went numb.

Don't freeze up! Fight them!

He channelled his Spark into another fire attack. He knew it wouldn't do much, but he needed to keep moving. The tendrils were accelerating now, and he couldn't count how many there were.

Did I fight them the right way last time? Isn't that a waste of Soul Power?

Alrion tried waves of force, trying to batter them around so they tangled one another. It did work a little, but the tendrils seemed to coordinate perfectly, never quite coming into contact with each other. He pulled at a rock jutting out of the wall, and wrenched it free with a force spell, throwing it towards the biggest mass of tendrils. One was knocked about a little, but the rest expertly dodged away.

They started to converge now and sped towards him in a tight clump.

Maybe I can get them with a more intense heat.

Alrion gathered his Spark and created a beam of condensed flame. It shot out at incredible speed and blazed across the space. The collection of tendrils fanned out, then came at him from different angles. Alrion knelt and worked the earth beneath him. It formed a protective barrier that they all smashed against. But they were strong, and the barrier wouldn't hold for that long.

Maybe there's no choice?

Alrion took a moment to compose himself. It was difficult with the vast number of creatures banging against his defensive wall. But he knew that he had a few moments.

Think through the spell and try it.

Even though he had succeeded in Ashra's trial, it wasn't a very targeted spell. It had been a lot safer to use, but he hadn't exactly wielded it with precision. This situation, however, required more finesse. He didn't want to bring the whole place down on him. Alrion started to gather his Spark and create the basis of a light bomb. But as before, he fed in Soul Power. This seemed to somehow contain the energy a little. The two powers were in equilibrium in a glowing sphere. He pushed it out against his wall. The sphere passed through the wall, burning it away like it wasn't there. It must have hit one of the tendrils because he heard a sizzling and wailing sound.

At least it works. Alrion sensed that the bomb was still intact, so he sent a pulse of Spark into it. This upset the balance and the light bomb exploded. After a flash of white Alrion opened his eyes. His defensive barrier was gone, and there was a small piece of floor removed. There seemed to be fewer tendrils than before, but still a lot. And they were completely spread out now.

Well, that worked. A little too well. Even that small size and the Soul Power didn't make it that safe. Maybe I can use it as a tool, rather than an explosion.

The spell had taken out one of them by merely making contact. Alrion created another and dubbed it a Soul Bomb. It floated in the air before him. It shone so brightly, he could barely look at it. The tendrils of black seemed to avoid it as well. Just as he started to feel like he had a handle on the situation, he felt something wrapping around his right leg. He looked down and saw a tendril had snuck up on him. As he turned, it wrapped around tighter, causing him to drop to his knees. Alrion used a wave of force to tug at the Soul Bomb, bringing it around to his leg. With a quick adjustment of its trajectory, it burned through the black tendril, turning it to ash.

That's better.

Only Alrion saw that his leg was quite damaged by the attack. It was quite weak and he almost stumbled when getting up.

They're not trying to infect me, they're trying to weaken me. And it's apparently quite easy to do.

Alrion directed some Soul Power to the injured leg and lamented yet another drain on it. He didn't have an unlimited amount. More tendrils had circled around and were going for his legs. Alrion drew his sword and took a swipe. They expertly dodged and came in close. Alrion pulled his Soul Bomb closer and managed to clip one before the other flew away.

I wonder if this would work.

Alrion used his hand to channel Soul Power into his sword again. This time he found a way to manipulate it so there was a bigger area of coverage. It extended beyond the blade's edge. When the next three tendrils attacked, Alrion carefully aimed his sword to look like he was just missing. The tendrils did not dodge but were knocked down by the Soul Power attached to his blade. While they were incapacitated, he swung his Soul Bomb down, burning them away.

That was more effective.

Alrion took a few steps back, surveying the scene. There were still more enemies, but they were more cautious now that he had defeated quite a few. But it was taking a toll on him. He decided to end it quickly. He sheathed his sword and let the Soul Bomb dissipate. He closed his eyes and waited.

He could hear them howl as they flew in. They seemed to delight at the opportunity. He wanted to run, to defiantly fight back. But it would be too draining. This would be better. He drew all his Soul Power into a small spot, condensing it. He was thinking about the barrier that his grandmother had done. Only, he wasn't going to overcharge it. This would be something else.

He felt them attacking now. First his legs, then his arms. Then his torso, and even his head. They had completely wrapped around him. A wave of panic ran through him. He was being smothered.

Control the situation.

Alrion pushed his Soul Power out as a barrier, just far enough to encompass all the tendrils of black attached to him. They shrieked in agony as it passed over them. But it did nothing more. However, he then used his Spark to build a light bomb. He mixed in a tiny bit of Soul Power, then triggered an explosion. A flash of white, a bang, then nothing.

Alrion pulled himself up off the ground. There was a ringing in his ears and he could barely see. His eyes had to readjust to the darkness. It took a long time. Or there was more darkness, which was just as likely. He couldn't see or sense any more of those things. His body was battered and sore. He had some Spark left, and some Soul Power, but nowhere near as much as he would have liked.

Nothing ever works out as you'd like.

Alrion found his sword and sheathed it. The darkness beyond was still there, only it didn't seem quite so dark.

Maybe those creatures had made it appear darker. He took a deep breath and pushed on. He created a tiny orb of light to help, but it did little to penetrate the darkness. Tentatively he kept walking. The geometry on the walls was here too, and there were some wild shapes that seemed impossible. But they weren't why he was here. Soon enough he saw what he expected.

A wall of darkness, in slow but constant motion. At the same time, it looked like it was oozing yet also a void of nothing. He saw in his mind the image of his grandfather touching it. He could understand why. It defied logic. There was an irresistible urge to just take it in your hand and see if you could make sense of it. Alrion forced his hands to stay in his pockets. He didn't want to be too rash.

Some of the elements of the spell came to the front of his mind. He would need to interact directly with the wall to enable the spell to work. As he considered the best way to do that, he noticed something odd. The wall itself was changing. Forming something. A head. No, more than that. An entire body stepped out of the wall, made of the same substance and connected to the wall by millions of tiny strands.

"Welcome, Alrion, we've been waiting for you." The creature of black spoke to him.

"What are you?"

"I'm the Blight. The manifestation of consciousness behind all those connected to me. We have much in common."

"I very much doubt that." Alrion didn't know what to think. He hadn't expected this. Nothing mentioned this.

"We are both born of Granthion." The thing smiled and Alrion shuddered.

"I don't understand."

"The great wizard Granthion caused all this, as you know. Our sentience is thanks to him. His power awakened the ability in us to act. And so we have. Developing our own people, our own ways. Strengthening our bond. And yet, here you are. Trying to take that all away from us."

"You have no right to those gifts when you only have them by destroying human lives."

"Destroying? No, we enhance them. Do you not believe that?"

"Of course not. I've experienced the terror myself."

"You were just afraid and rejected the bond. In time, you would accept and find joy from it. Ours is just a different way." The creature held out a hand. Alrion stepped back.

"What are you doing?"

"It doesn't matter what you want to do, you need to interact with us anyway. Hold my hand, so that we may understand each other better." The creature held out its hand. Alrion looked at it warily.

This doesn't feel right. What do I do?

Alrion stepped back again and channelled his Soul Power into his hand as a precaution. The creature of the Blight did not move, perhaps it was restrained to the source. He debated in his mind on how to move forward. He doubted he could even interact with the source without touching the creature. Just as Alrion reached a decision he heard footsteps. He turned to see who was approaching.

50

THE MISSING PIECE

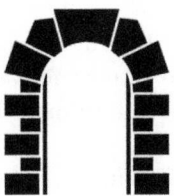

Alrion saw a figure in the distance, approaching. It looked like a man in a hood. A wizard.

It's him!

Alrion turned completely and ignored the creature of the Blight. He started walking away. The wizard kept approaching.

"Announce yourself. Who are you?" Alrion said.

"You know me as Aydan. We've been conversing for a while now." The wizard kept approaching at a steady rate. His voice sounded strange, like it had been altered.

"So, you're the one that's been following me around everywhere. And sending me messages in that book. Finally, you show yourself." Alrion was annoyed.

Now this wizard shows up, at the critical time. A time when I can't use help from anyone else. A time when this wizard would just be a hindrance.

"I came at the appropriate time. I apologise for all the subterfuge, I needed to keep my identity secret."

"I could have used your help before. Now, it's pointless. Even five minutes ago would have been helpful. What comes next is just for me, as you should know."

"I am sorry, I was supposed to be here. I thought you had returned to the battle, but I made a mistake. That delayed me getting here." The wizard had approached Alrion and was standing right before him. His face was still hidden by his hood.

"Now you're here, you could at least show me who you are."

"Yes, you should know." The wizard spoke without the voice masking. Alrion gasped.

"No, it can't be. That's impossible."

"It's not impossible. You and everyone else just accepted a false truth." Alrion stepped forward and thrust back the hood. He was staring into his father's eyes.

"I still don't believe it. Prove it."

"As you wish. We are safe for a time." Vincent held out his hand and a small flame appeared above it. Alrion shook his head, not impressed. The flame grew larger then morphed into three different-sized flame spheres, all rotating at different speeds.

"Must I go on?" Vincent said. He let the flames dissipate.

"I don't understand. Why do all this? You've spent your entire life lying to me, lying to everyone." Alrion's voice sank. This was not the revelation he expected, or even wanted.

"It was my father's idea. At first, he was scared of me being targeted by the Blight. And then he wanted me kept secret to keep his progress on a cure secret."

"What do you mean cure? You?"

"You know I can use Soul Power. My father knew that too. He intended on us curing the Blight together, as father and son."

"But he died saving you?"

"Yes, because I left him alone. Then I was captured by Rindale and infected. My father knew he would lose his chance at saving the world from the Blight, but he could save me instead. That was his gift to the world." Vincent wore a sad smile. Alrion thought about it, he let the thought sink in.

I know what it's like to have that weight on your shoulders. Has he carried it all this time?

Alrion stepped back.

"I can't believe you lied to me again. Is there anything else you haven't told me?"

"No, nothing important. I left some papers with your mother, that will explain more than we can discuss here."

"Does she know? Weren't the two of you investigating the mysterious wizard?"

"We were. We parted ways so that your mother could continue the investigation. She found me out, as I had hoped."

"But why not just tell her?"

"It is easier to come to the understanding yourself, rather than being told." Vincent paused, thinking before he continued. "Also, there is a great danger in this information becoming widely known. I was genuinely interested to see if there was any evidence that she could find to tie me to that identity."

"And was there?"

"Yes. But now it is safe with us." Vincent looked past Alrion, to the darkness beyond. "You've seen it?"

"By it, do you mean the wall or the human-like figure?"

"The human one. Whatever you do, don't hold its hand." Alrion looked over at the creature, and back at his father.

"What do you mean?"

"It's the wrong connection to make. You'll be compromised too quickly, and unable to complete the spell."

"What do you suggest I do instead?"

"Something else. Together with me. As my father intended." Vincent smiled again, this time it was warm.

"Together? You keep saying that. There was no mention of two wizards in what I read."

"The information from the Pool of Knowledge is quite selective. As you know, it tells you what you need to know, not what you want to know. It's like a wizard in that respect." Vincent chuckled. "It was always designed for two. One as a conduit for the Light, one as a conduit for the Darkness. Guess which one dies."

"Knowing as much as you do, having lived this for your whole life. Are you willing to just resign to that fate? Why must death be a part of this spell?" Alrion challenged his father, daring him to keep up that line of thinking. Vincent looked thoughtful.

"Well, my son, I suppose we should keep an open mind. When my father designed this, he was imagining one wizard with Soul Power, not two. Perhaps there is a way." Vincent gave Alrion a slight shrug.

"I'll take that, it's something I can work with. I've done enough impossible things already, that this can just be another one."

"Very well, I won't argue the point. You've certainly grown into a resourceful man and a wonderful wizard. As I always knew you could be."

"Yet you kept trying to get me to be a blacksmith?"

"It's a good life, you should try it. And remember, there's a lot of overlap between what I taught you like the keys to blacksmithing and being a wizard." Vincent looked distracted.

"Is something wrong?" Alrion looked around himself, trying to see what was happening.

"We can't delay any longer. We need to do what we came to do." Vincent held out a hand to gesture Alrion forward, and they walked side by side towards the darkness. The creature tilted its head, regarding them.

"Two wizards from Granthion, how odd. I did not expect this."

"It's not going to go down as you expect." Alrion clenched his right fist then relaxed it.

"Whatever you think you are planning, you cannot avoid the inevitable. Your family's history of sacrifice will be continued." The creature spoke solemnly, but its eyes seemed to tell a different story. They appeared to be mirthful, almost laughing. Alrion stepped forward, but Vincent held him back.

"Don't take the bait. The Blight is masterful at manipulation. We can engage on our own terms. Observe." Vincent stepped forward and the Blight creature extended its hand again. Vincent stepped around it, and the creature couldn't follow. Before Alrion could say anything, Vincent had thrust his hand into the darkness beyond.

51

SOUL OF LIGHT

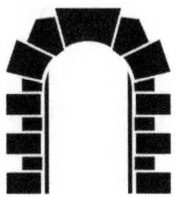

Vincent felt himself immersed in the other world, that of the Blight. It was overwhelming. But he didn't let himself be taken in completely.

"Alrion, quickly now. Follow my lead and hold my hand." Vincent couldn't see clearly back into the space he had been, but he sensed the movement. A shining light weaved around the space then grasped Vincent's hand. He instantly recognised his son.

"Well done, let's navigate this together." Vincent pulled Alrion with him, and the two were thrust into a dark void. After a few moments of disorientation, Vincent found himself in a different space altogether. Alrion thankfully was by his side. As they surveyed the strange stark horizon, they noticed a pool of darker substance to one end.

"Did you read about this?" Alrion said. He looked out in wonder over the strange place they were in. Vincent shook his head.

"No, I think this is new territory. Nobody has been here before. Let's investigate the black mass over there." Vincent led the way, his son staying close.

We can do this. Maybe he's right about finding a better way.

As they neared the black mass, Vincent had a good idea of what it was. He stopped before and turned to Alrion.

"I think this is quite clear."

"Yes. That's the essence of the Blight. It's that substance they use to turn people really quickly." Alrion looked disgusted. Vincent looked out over the expanse. He couldn't see where it ended.

"There's nothing else here."

"Not quite," a voice said behind them. Vincent whirled around quickly. A black figure was standing there, watching them. It had to be the same one that had confronted them outside.

"It was clever of you to infiltrate our space. But you still won't succeed." The figure moved in a bit closer.

"We may need to take our chances." Vincent looked at Alrion. He was staring intently at something in the distance.

"Agreed." Alrion dove into the blackness, surprising Vincent. He didn't hesitate and joined his son. They were engulfed in the thick black liquid, which was like tar. It was very hard to move through and seemed to pulse with a regular beat of energy. It felt alive. Vincent wanted to say something, but he couldn't. He dragged Alrion back up to the surface and they managed to get their heads above the inky substance.

"This is not good. But I see an opportunity further ahead." Alrion didn't wait for confirmation, he surged forward.

He's got good instincts. Let's see where this takes us.

Vincent followed along, turning occasionally to see if the figure was following them. It was. Soon enough though, Vincent saw what Alrion was hinting at. There was a platform in the middle of the Blight. It was simple stone and had a tiny altar upon it, also made of stone. Atop the altar sat a strange orb.

"That's the ticket." Alrion powered ahead and reached the platform first. He bent over the orb but didn't do anything. Vincent sped up and reached the platform as well. The black figure was still advancing, hovering over the black substance.

"Look in here. What do you see?" Alrion said, peering within. Vincent looked and gasped. It looked like people. Images of faces flashed by fast.

"This must be the link to all those who are infected. What do you think?"

"This is it, this is how we can help them all."

"I doubt you have enough Soul Power for all that. You're going to need help." Vincent looked around. He knew there had to be something else. There was a tugging on his mind, reminding him of an extra element that they would need. He walked around the platform staring out, then he saw it. A glimmer of white amongst the sea of black. He instantly knew what it was.

"Alrion, I know what we must do. Look out there and tell me what you see." Vincent directed Alrion's gaze. After a few moments, he almost jumped.

"There's something down there. Soul Power?"

"Precisely. It's all coming together now. You need to reach it and drag it back here. We can use that to cure all those people."

"It's pretty deep, I'll be drowned in that stuff. Unless." Alrion concentrated and focused on the deep sea of Blight. Vincent watched with curiosity. Nothing was happening.

"This isn't right. Try using your Spark on the Blight there." Alrion kept staring at the spot he had been focused on. Vincent gathered his Spark and tried using a wave of force to part the Blight, making a path. The flows were absorbed by the black mass. He tried again and looked closer. It was more like the Blight was drawing in the spell. Vincent tried flames, and it was the same result.

"Still trying those old tricks?" The figure of Blight was close now, but it didn't move onto the platform.

"We get it, old spells don't work in your place." Alrion didn't bother turning to look at the creature. It burst into horrific laughter. The sound was like loud gongs being banged right near their ears.

"You don't get it at all. Why do you think we made Shade Wizards, but not Shade Mystics?" The figure regarded them with curiosity. Alrion looked thoughtful.

"It was easier for you, no Soul Power."

"Close, but you're so far away from the truth. Why do you think your first experience of your Spark was triggered by feelings of frustration and anger?" Alrion turned and looked at the creature, shocked. Vincent was starting to put it together.

"We don't just target wizards for no good reason. Your grandfather wasn't involved for no good reason. Everything needs an equal and opposite force. Soul Power fuels the Mystics, the Blight Source powers your Spark." The figure leaned its head back and cackled, delighting in the revelation.

"That's why our spells are ineffective. That's why I needed to use Spark as a method for transmitting Soul Power." Alrion was nodding along.

"Don't be fooled by this creature. It speaks the truth, but it omits what it wants. There is a greater truth here." Vincent approached Alrion and put his hand on his son's shoulder.

"The source and origin of your gift do not reflect on you, nor what you can do with it. Take away the utility of that knowledge. Your Spark cannot be a weapon against them here, at the source. We must use the other tools that we have." Vincent gave Alrion a reassuring smile. He nodded one more time.

"Soul Power it is. Let's go get some more." Alrion concentrated for a moment, and Vincent did the same. Soul Power, when channelled correctly, should keep the Blight at bay, for a time. Alrion climbed down, the Blight parting just enough to avoid touching him. Vincent followed then grabbed his son's hand.

"Let's be quick about it. Support each other and we can make the trip."

"We just need to make it there, no need to conserve for the way back." Alrion set off, slowly drifting through the space. The Blight parted for Alrion's path and stayed back. Vincent tried reducing the amount of Soul Power he was emitting, and it worked.

Good, we may need some extra down the road.

It was slow going, and hard to gain glimpses of where they were headed. But they kept going and reoriented themselves when required. Finally, they reached something.

Before them was a stone circle, floating amidst all the Blight. It was glowing with Soul Power.

"Doesn't look like much, does it?" Alrion examined it. Vincent could see the Blight starting to encroach. He forced some Soul Power into Alrion, causing the Blight to shrink back. Alrion touched the circle.

"There's Soul Power in here, but I don't know how to open it." Alrion felt all over the circle, looking for something. Vincent could see the Blight massing behind them. It was in motion, trying to find an opening.

"Try using Soul Power to open it." Vincent turned back to watch the Blight. It seemed to be forming into a denser material.

It's trying to compensate for our barrier and will likely overwhelm us soon.

Vincent looked over at Alrion. He seemed to be making progress.

"It's working, but it's taking a lot of Soul Power. I think it's a kind of lock."

"Keep going, I'll pass you as much as you need." Vincent found it easier now, to flood Alrion with the Soul Power.

"Almost there." Alrion was completely focused on the Soul Power. He didn't notice the danger looming around them. The Blight started its move. Part of Vincent's barrier failed. He could feel it beginning to wrap around his leg.

"Alrion, we're almost out of time." Vincent pushed out the last of his Soul Power then drew more from his life force. A dangerous, and potentially deadly move.

I just need to hold out a minute longer.

He could feel the strain on his body, on his life. He would burn out soon. Suddenly, a flash of light emanated from Alrion.

"I did it. This is incredible, Dad. It's the source of the Soul Power. They're connected!"

"Draw it out, we're out of time." Vincent felt the Blight consuming more and more of him. He turned to look at his son. Alrion was glowing brighter. The Blight was shrinking back. Alrion turned and looked at Vincent, noticing for the first time what was happening.

"Not on my watch." Alrion held out a hand and blasted all the Blight from the area. He then placed his hand on his father's back, returning Soul Power. Vincent could feel his body recovering from the Blight. But he still felt weak from burning his own life force.

"It's my turn to protect you," Alrion said. Glowing like a being of light, with an incredible aura, Alrion led the way. As he progressed, the Blight shrank away. Vincent looked behind them. There was a thick visible cord of Soul Power linking Alrion back to the source. The other source.

Vincent looked upon his son in awe.

He's come into his own. To have that much Soul Power flowing through him requires tremendous strength of Will and control, it's incredible.

The return trip to the stone platform was faster. Vincent didn't even feel the passage of time. It was like a strange dream experience. Alrion reached the platform first and pulled Vincent up onto it. The figure of Blight looked upon them in horror.

"What have you done?"

"I've brought light to the darkness." Alrion disregarded the creature after he spoke. But it continued.

"How dare you? This is my domain. I built this. You have no right to come in here and do this!" The Blight creature was furious. It looked like it was trying to bully Alrion into doing something. But he ignored it.

"So be it. You've underestimated the Blight once again." The Blight figure closed its eyes and concentrated. Vincent sensed movement and looked over at where they had come from. The gigantic black mass of Blight sludge was on the move. But it wasn't targeting them.

The avatar of the Blight was absorbing it all. It looked to be growing darker and stronger. As it strengthened it became less and less affected by the light that Alrion was producing. Finally, it let out a satisfied sigh.

"Your power is not stronger than mine. You have the entirety of your source at your disposal. As do I." The figure finally stepped onto the platform. It was oozing the black sludge, and its eyes were like black pits of eternity.

"I'm not afraid of you. But you're afraid of me." Alrion stared at the creature defiantly.

"You're not strong enough to hurt me."

"Maybe not. But together we're strong enough to do this." Alrion held out his hand and Vincent grabbed it. Together they put their hands on the strange orb on the pedestal. Vincent could feel all the Souls of those who were trapped by the Blight.

"Now!" Alrion started drawing the Soul Power through the source and funnelling it into the orb. Vincent could feel the torrent, it was frightening how fast and powerful it was. He couldn't match it, but he could help. He reached out with his Soul Power and touched Alrion's chest. Their Souls bonded, and their collective glow more than doubled.

"This is as it should be." Alrion smiled.

"Yes, my son." Vincent smiled back. As the orb was overflowing with Soul Power, they could start to sense the effect it was having on people. They had used the Blight's system of control and connection against it, hijacking the link and using it to cure people.

The Blight avatar wailed and shrieked. It seemed to lessen in darkness, strength, and stature.

"You feed off them, don't you? How much of this is borrowed power?" Alrion said, surprise on his face.

"A mere drop in the ocean." The creature sneered at Alrion and tried to press forward. Vincent stepped in front of the orb.

"Don't even think about it." Vincent watched the creature pause, and he held his ground. Between staring off with the creature of Blight and being a party to the Soul Power curing, Vincent had no sense of how long everything was taking. But after a time, Alrion sighed and looked at him.

"Dad, there's only one soul left." Alrion looked to the avatar of the Blight.

"That thing? It has a Soul?"

"Of course I do. I'm more like you than you realise."

"I think it has a fragment of Granthion's soul. And built upon that."

"Really?" Vincent walked back to the orb and placed his hand on it. He could sense the last soul, and what Alrion had said.

It's true. Unbelievable.

"You've stopped because you can't do this through the orb, can you?" Vincent looked at his son. Alrion nodded. He pointed behind them.

"See?" Vincent turned to look at what Alrion had been pointing out. It was a similar stone circle, but it was filled with endless darkness.

"You've sealed the Blight from all those people back into the source?"

"Yes. But that thing can't go back for some reason." Alrion pointed at the creature.

"I understand now. It's why my father wanted to be a part of this." Vincent walked forward to the Blight avatar. It was giving him a curious look.

"In the name of my father, I return you to where you belong." Vincent reached out and grabbed the Blight Avatar. It laughed and readily accepted his touch, leaking a black substance into him. Vincent held strong though and kept pulling at the avatar. It started to lose its form, and as it melted it was sucked into Vincent

"No! What are you doing?"

"I'm incorporating it into my Soul. It's the only way I can destroy it, from within me."

"But what will it do to you?" Alrion looked distraught.

"I can't say for sure. My Soul will survive, but my body might not handle this concentration of Blight." Vincent stepped into the avatar's body and sped up the process. He could feel the creature rebelling within him. But at the same time, he could sense the part of his father that had created it.

I hope you'll forgive me.

52

THE BREAKING OF A WIZARD

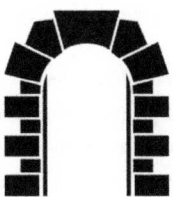

A ydan stepped into the forest. He had never been here before, and it was a break from routine. Something must have changed,
Father has been so occupied lately. Maybe he's had a breakthrough.

It had been long enough. Aydan was a boy no longer. Yet he still suffered the same restrictions. The same need for complete secrecy. He walked amongst his father and the other wizards, and none of them had a clue. He had perfected the skill of hiding in plain sight, but it was eating him away inside.

Maybe we're at a turning point. Maybe I can finally emerge from the shadows.

Aydan continued through the forest, moving towards the meeting point. Once he arrived there was no doubt. There was a small glade that was a lot more open, but it was still masked well with tree cover.

At least it's not a cave.

Within moments he heard footsteps behind him.

"Punctuality is a virtue. Glad to see you've finally embraced it."

"Nice to see you too."

"I'll overlook that comment, today is an auspicious day. Today, we kick off a new endeavour." Father looked excited and energised. That was a good sign. He led Aydan to the middle of the glade, then removed a lantern.

"I've made a bit of a breakthrough, and I need you to verify it for me."

"What's that? It looks like an ordinary lantern."

"I can assure you it is not." The wizard turned the lantern around then handed it to Aydan.

"What's it for?"

"It's particularly sensitive to a wizard's Spark. Try it." The wizard gestured to

Aydan. He looked the lantern over, wondering how it worked. He started gathering his Spark and nothing happened. He looked over at the wizard.

"Not that sensitive. Just apply a little." Aydan nodded and applied the tiniest amount of Spark to the lantern. It roared to life, a medium-sized flame dancing within it. Aydan stared at the flame.

"That's quite sophisticated. What's it for?"

"I'm thinking of using it as a test for new wizards. What do you think?"

"It should work, it's quite sensitive. If a wizard can't light it, they may not fare well with training." Aydan thought the conclusion was quite obvious.

"Exactly my thinking." The wizard held out his hand and Aydan returned the lantern.

Why has he got me testing such obvious things?

"That was just the warmup. I've got something much more interesting next." The wizard reached into his robe and removed a white stone. Aydan received the stone, turning it over in his hand. It didn't take long to see the black streak through it.

"I haven't seen anything like this before."

"Take a close look, tell me what you think." The wizard studied him, waiting.

So, it's another test. Let's see.

Aydan peered into the black substance. It didn't look natural, but it also didn't look painted on or separate to the stone. It was somehow part of the whole piece. The more he stared, the more he started to get entranced by the blackness. He imagined it pulsating and beating like it had a heartbeat. He started to become terrified by it and started to reach for his Spark.

What is happening to me?

He felt an uncomfortably warm feeling inside, and a rush of heat. And then, out of nowhere, a gigantic white flame spewed from the stone, rushing into the air and lighting some of the tree cover. The wizard quickly doused the flames. Aydan was in shock.

What just happened?

"Fantastic!" The wizard was looking up at the area that the flames had burned, then turned his attention to Aydan. "Better than I expected."

"That was a bit surprising." Aydan wanted to say frightening, but he didn't want to admit that.

"The reaction was a little stronger than I expected but good. This we can work with."

"What does that mean?"

"It means you can cure the Blight. Well, in theory. More testing is required. But no matter how I approach it, I can't do what you can do."

"Cure the Blight? That's not possible." Aydan stared in disbelief.

"It shouldn't be, at least the way that I'm thinking, but somehow it is." The wizard started pacing, talking to himself.

"This is what you've been working on all these years? Some trippy test for a fairy tale?" Aydan was just getting started. He'd lived a double life from childhood, suppressing who he was, all for this?

"This is no fairy tale. I've done many successful experiments, small scale mind you, using the stored Soul Power I have available. The results are consistent. Applying enough Soul Power to a person infected by the Blight should cure them."

"What is this Soul Power? I'm a wizard, I have Spark."

"Oh, but you have both. Soul Power is a gift from your mother. Perhaps it's time to make a trip to see her." The wizard resumed his pacing.

"I thought you lost contact with her, and it was all too difficult to talk about."

"It is difficult to talk about. And she lives at the end of the world, she may as well be lost." The wizard spoke carefully. Aydan could not believe what he was hearing.

"Let me get this straight. You know exactly where my mother is and haven't bothered to contact her. Only now, when it's convenient for you, you're thinking of going to see her?'

"Don't be silly. Where do you think I received the orbs charged with Soul Power? We've been corresponding for some time. It's slow and strictly business, but she knows and supports what I'm doing, even though we have our differences."

"This just gets better and better." Aydan threw his hands up in frustration. "You've kept me in the dark about everything. I'm not a child anymore."

"Easy, son, I was just protecting you. There are burdens you don't need to bear."

"I feel like I've been bearing them anyway. Why have you spent both our lives on this fool's errand?" Aydan glared at his father defiantly.

"It's better you don't know. Let's just leave it at that."

"I refuse to do any more until I know the truth. Either include me or admit that you're just using me as a tool, and I'll be gone for good." Aydan's heart was racing. He wasn't sure where this had sprung up from, and it surprised even him. But he meant it." The wizard sighed and walked in closer.

"Son, this is not an easy thing to discuss. But you deserve to hear it. Many years ago, on my travels, I was researching the power of Spark, and looking for sources of it. I must admit I was jealous of the Mystics, they were able to build around a source of great power, and I had visions for what wizards could do with that same sort of organisation. My research brought me to something strange." The wizard had a faraway look in his eyes, then he continued.

"Something didn't feel right, but I couldn't put my finger on it. So, I investigated. And I found myself standing before it. The source of the Blight. There was no question." The wizard started to shake his head. "My curiosity drove me forward. Why had my search brought me there?" The wizard looked pained.

"What did you do?" Aydan almost whispered.

"All I did was touch the wall with my hand. But my contact changed it, irreversibly. In that instant, the fate of the world was altered."

"What happened?"

"My touch created a being of intellect. I saw it form before my very eyes. And it spoke. It spoke of the wonder of creation, of the opportunities that now awaited it. But the creature was very new, very immature. I knew it would take time to grow, take time to realise its own aspirations. But it was the beginning of everything."

"Everything? Like what?"

"The Blight was a force of nature. Unpleasant, but random and contained. But I gave it the means to act independently. It started to organise, it created enough trouble that Valrytir sent the four generals. They were turned to the Blight's cause and have started to wreak true havoc. Who knows what will happen if we let this continue!" The wizard looked weary. Truly, the burden was weighing him down. And he didn't look eased by sharing it with Aydan.

"You really are responsible for all this. All the terror, and the Blight activity." Aydan was amazed. It hadn't seemed possible, but now. Now he knew. He understood.

"Yes. I cannot allow my legacy to be one of darkness. I must right my wrong. Together, we must solve this." The wizard held out his hand. Aydan shied away.

"This is too much. I've gone from being hidden and ignored, to being required for your redemption. I can see your pain, your sense of responsibility. But I'm not the answer. I've lived enough of my life under your thumb, trying to compensate for your mistake."

"Don't you dare walk away from me. I've given you everything. You will save our family and save the world."

"In secret still? I thought it could be different. But I see now nothing will change. True, I know the reasons why. But you'll still keep me hidden away. I'll still have to pretend to everyone that I'm not what I truly am. All to protect you and your plans. I've had enough." Aydan turned to walk away.

"Andar. Stop. Please. Let's talk about this." Granthion grabbed his hand and stopped him from going. Andar turned and shook off his father's hand.

"Calling me by my true name won't make a difference. You took everything from me. I have no relationship with my mother, I cannot be my true self with anyone. I can't do it anymore. I need to start living for myself." Andar walked away, forcing his legs to move before he lost the willpower to follow through.

I can't keep going like this. I need to try living for myself. He will find a way to do what he must, he always does.

Andar kept walking through the forest, trying not to think about what had just happened.

53

LEGACY

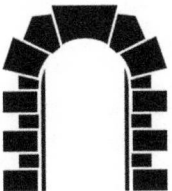

Alrion opened his eyes and peered into the gloom. It looked like they were back in the cave. He found his Spark and manage to create a weak orb of light and attach it to the wall. The effort almost made him pass out.

Why am I so exhausted?

The memories of what happened flooded back. Particularly the torrent of Soul Power that had flowed through him. That probably did something.

Father!

Alrion looked around for his father. He almost missed him. Vincent was lying on the ground, and his skin was incredibly pale. Alrion ignored his pain and rushed over, gently lifting his father up into a sitting position against the nearest wall. Alrion collapsed next to his father, the effort sapping the last of his strength.

"Dad, you're still with us."

"For now. I fear the worst." Vincent weakly pointed at his leg. Alrion could see a glimpse of his father's foot, and the skin was pure black.

"You can fight this. We won." Alrion frantically searched his body for any semblance of power or magic. He found nothing.

"I don't think we can, not now. But you're right, we did win. That creature is gone. Look at the wall." Vincent leaned back and closed his eyes. Alrion looked over at the dark wall of Blight. It seemed almost inert now, it didn't have the same vitality and motion that it did before. And there certainly wasn't a figure in black addressing them.

"We did it. I can't believe it." But Alrion couldn't revel in the moment. He could see that his father was dying.

"Alrion, what will be, will be. We must accept our fate."

"Surely there's something I can do."

"Yes, there is." Vincent paused, a pained look on his face. "Listen closely." Vincent drew in a few sharp breaths. Alrion held his father's hand.

"Son, now's the time to discuss what happens next. My body is failing, I will be gone soon. But not lost. I will live on in you, and your mother. Your memories, and the feat we achieved here today, that will give me eternal life."

"But you won't be here."

"Not in the same way, but just trust me. Also, I need you to promise me something."

"Yes, what is it?" Alrion leaned in closer.

"Don't tell anyone about me being a wizard. This is your quest and your achievement."

"Your story deserves to be told!"

"No, it does not. I can be the supportive blacksmith that followed his son to the end of the world. That's good enough for me. There's no need to confuse things now." Vincent coughed, a ragged sound that pained Alrion just to hear it. After a few moments, he settled down.

"Now, I left your mother with some writing that explains a lot. Some you will already know. But it may help fill in the blanks and understand me better. I'm sorry for hiding so much from you. In that way, I was too much like my father."

"Dad, it's alright. I know you were trying to do the best for everyone." Vincent shook his head.

"No, I was a coward. And angry. And I ran away from my responsibility. And yes, my father was not an easy man to work with, but he was brilliant, and he gave me impeccable training. And I still couldn't step up. So, I lived a whole new life. I changed my name and pretended my old life didn't exist. But you can't just close the door on your past, as we have discovered." Vincent opened his eyes and stared directly at Alrion.

"But you, my son, you achieved all this with minimal training and minimal information. You used your instincts, you took chances, and you trusted people. You succeeded where I could not. I am so proud of you, and I know your grandfather is as well. You are the true hero, and it was my pleasure to be here to witness you." Vincent cried, the tear turning black as it ran down his face.

"Dad, I had the best preparation. You taught me everything I needed and gave me the desire to be better. You're my hero." Alrion could feel his father's life slipping away. His pulse was weak and fleeting.

"What do I do now? I need your advice." Alrion wanted to ask his father so much, but there was no time.

"Alrion, I can't possibly tell you that. But I can get you started." Vincent closed his eyes. "Go back to our home and investigate my workshop. I've left something there for you. It will show you the way." Vincent's face tensed. He gripped Alrion's hand hard.

"Dad?"

"Goodbye Alrion. Be free and find your own path." Vincent sighed and relaxed. His body started to disintegrate and turn into a fine black dust which floated away. And within a few mere moments, there was nothing left of him. Alrion couldn't hold the tears back, and he lost track of time. Until everything became black.

54

AFTERMATH

Alrion felt an overwhelming warmth. He opened his eyes and saw a figure standing over him.

"Dad, you came back?" As his vision improved, he saw the dark shape next to him was someone else.

"It's me, Lara. Are you alright?" Lara sounded incredibly worried.

Maybe I'm in worse shape than I realise.

"Mostly. Don't touch the black stuff."

"I figured that. Can you stand?" Lara bent down and put her arm around him. With her help, he managed to get himself to a standing position, albeit hunched and leaning on her.

"I lost my dad." Alrion sobbed into her shoulder. He couldn't help it, he didn't even intend to say that.

"I'm sorry, Alrion. Let's get you out of here, then we can figure this all out." Together they took a step forward. It wasn't as hard as Alrion thought it would be. His body felt numb and worn out. But at least it was moving. They struggled wordlessly through the cave, Alrion not knowing what to say, or having the energy to mutter any words. After an age, they came to the strange lake, the one infused with Soul Power.

"Stop." Alrion eased himself down near the water's edge. He leaned in and cupped water in his hands, drinking it carefully. The hydration was nice, but the Soul Power burned as it flowed through his body.

"This water has Soul Power in it."

"I thought there was something odd about it."

"I'm all burnt out, so let's try to keep this quick." Alrion knew he wasn't fully explaining what had happened, but he couldn't say any more. He was just too tired. Lara seemed to understand though.

"We'll be quick through the water, don't worry." Lara took the lead, letting Alrion travel in her wake. The lake did seem to have a restorative effect, even though his body couldn't handle the Soul Power. The burning feeling came and went, and when they emerged at the other end Alrion dropped to the ground and lay on his back.

"I feel like I've just run for a week straight." He tried to slow his breathing, bit by bit. His body was not really paying attention. It was doing whatever it wanted.

"I'm not going to pester you with questions, but... did it work?"

"Yes," Alrion rasped. Lara nodded and didn't ask any follow-up questions. Alrion closed his eyes and rested a little. After a few moments Lara woke him, and they were off again.

Once they finally reached the exit, Alrion stumbled. His body wouldn't go any further.

"Don't worry, I've got a horse." Lara smiled.

"Have you got rope? I doubt I can hold on."

"Usually do. We'll organise something." Lara busied herself then helped Alrion up into the saddle. He swayed immediately, but she seemed ready for it and, before he knew it, he was tied to something.

"Rest if you can, it's a bit of a ride." Lara nudged the horse off and Alrion closed his eyes immediately, losing track of anything else.

Alrion awoke with a start and sat up immediately. He was in a clean bed, in a room he didn't recognise. Lara looked up sleepily.

"You're awake!" She smiled and rose from the chair she was slumped in and walked over. She peered into his eyes and examined his face.

"You look better. More alive. How do you feel?"

"Like everything in me has been squeezed out and nothing is left."

"We'll have to do something about that." Lara looked out at the door, deep in thought. She looked back to Alrion. "Can you handle a few guests?"

"Sure." Alrion wasn't sure, but he couldn't say no. He was pretty sure his mum was waiting outside. Lara walked over to the door and opened it, saying something to someone.

True to form, Celes entered the room first. Certan and Alyx were close behind.

"My son, I'm so relieved you're alright. Celes rushed to his side and almost crushed him in a hug. Her eyes were full of tears.

"I'm sorry but..."

"I know, there's no need to go into it now."

"Alright." Alrion had a panicked thought and looked over at the group. "It worked, didn't it?" They all nodded. Certan stepped forward.

"It was a sight to see, Alrion. I'm not sure if you caught sight of the Blight army, but it was huge. Despite intense fighting and having some successes, they were still ridiculously strong. I didn't think we could turn the tide. But when it started happening, wow. It was incredible!"

"What did it look like?"

"It looked like rays of golden light raining from the heavens. One for each creature. They were enveloped in the light and fell to the ground. The darkness was driven from them and dispersed into nothing." Alyx spoke with such wonder like she still couldn't believe it.

"It's true, Alrion. It's a day that nobody will ever forget." Celes gave his hand a squeeze and she stepped back to join the others.

"I'm glad. Please, can I have some water? Then I will tell you the tale of what I encountered." Alrion was eager to tell the tale, and to be free of telling it.

Alrion spoke at length of his experience but took care to leave out any parts that referenced his father. Only at the end did he mention how Vincent had shielded him from the Blight while he completed the spell, and how that had enabled him to be successful. He noticed many sad looks at that part, and he exchanged a knowing glance with his mother.

She will need more details when we can talk privately.

"What of that mysterious wizard? Was he a problem?" Lara said. Alrion sighed. He had forgotten about that thread, especially since both he and his mother knew the truth of that.

"He did make an appearance and was helpful. I can't say more about it right now."

"I see. It's not a problem anymore?"

"No." Lara looked relieved, and the others seemed content with that. Once Alrion had finished the tale, the rest of the talk came quickly.

"I'm so sorry I left you there. Even though you asked me to. Only when I reached the others did I realise that Darvin had left other horrors for you to encounter. I should have been there." Lara looked pained. Alrion held his hand out and enclosed hers.

"It was as it should have been. You already helped me immensely with Darvin."

"He was a tricky one, that's for sure."

"I have a question for you all: what became of those who were cured? Are they lost?" Alrion was a little apprehensive at what the answer might be. He knew there was a chance they had all died, and all he had done was reduce their suffering.

"Many seem to have survived. The copied Blight Generals, however, were a different story." Lara looked to the others. Alrion spotted many awkward expressions.

"I don't know much about that."

"I know the most, I questioned the other Rindale," Celes explained. "He was unable to replicate the Blight transformation in a simple way, so those copies were made using multiple people. I'm afraid they had no chance to return, and there's also no chance for the original person to return from that creation."

"I see." Alrion thought over what his mother had just said. "What you're saying is that any generals of the Blight that died are gone forever."

"That's right. It's a small price to pay, isn't it?"

"On the scale of what we did, yes." Alrion resumed his thinking. He almost forgot they were all there.

"You're all probably wondering what's next?" Alrion looked and saw nods from his friends. "I have an idea, I just want to fully form it first. Could you all return tomorrow?"

"That's fine," Celes said, speaking for the rest. They took this as a cue to leave, but Alrion held on to Lara.

"Can you stay for a moment?"

"Of course." She waved to the rest then pulled up a chair next to Alrion.

"What did you want to talk about?"

"I'm going to ask everyone tomorrow, but I need to know now about you. What are you going to do now? You're home at last." Alrion watched Lara's face and saw a pained expression on it.

"My father is going to try to keep me here. Something about lineage." Lara shook her head.

"Is that what you want?"

"No. You've seen what he's like? They can find someone else. I'm sure there are other members of the royal family that can be substituted."

"As long as you're sure. I'd like you to come with me."

"Where to?" Lara looked extremely curious. He had her full attention.

"I'm not quite sure yet. Wherever the wind blows us?"

"Sounds good to me. I've travelled the world by myself, without a purpose. There's a reason I latched on to you and your quest." Lara laughed. "But now I'm not sure what to do next. I'd like to find out, with you." Lara suddenly reached into her pocket and pulled out a soft pouch. "This seems like a good time to return your ring." She handed it to Alrion. He opened the pouch and took out the ring, examining it. He chuckled to himself.

"My father said this would keep me safe. I know why, now." Alrion noticed Lara's face go pale.

"What is it?" he said nervously.

"There's something I never told you. About that mysterious wizard?"

"I'm listening."

"He met me several times. In fact, he was the one that suggested that I stick with you, and work with you directly." Lara looked down. Alrion was shocked. He didn't expect it. But the more he thought about it, the more it made sense.

"Well, that's a surprise, but it's all coming together now. A wizard with the appropriate knowledge can track that ring." Alrion was amused at Lara's surprise. "Now I understand why the mysterious wizard was delayed reaching me. He was tracking the ring, and you."

"Oh, really. Was that a problem?"

"No, not at all." Alrion handed the ring back. "Will you take the ring? I can promise that it will keep you safe." He smiled.

"Not that you'll get a chance to use it, I'm not going to leave your side ever again." Lara winked at him. Alrion let out a small chuckle.

"And don't worry about working with that mysterious wizard. There's something you'll need to know if we're going everywhere together." Alrion leaned in and whispered into Lara's ear. Her eyes widened, and she gasped.

"No way! I can't believe it!"

"It's true. I find it hard to say out loud, but yes it was my father. But he asked for secrecy. That is not the legacy he wishes to leave. Can I trust you on that?"

"Absolutely, I'm a vault. You didn't even need to ask."

"I know, I just wanted to be clear, for his sake." Alrion sank back into the bed. "I think I'm going to drift off again. Let's talk a bit later."

"I look forward to it." Lara gave him a quick kiss and left the room, closing the door behind her. Alrion drifted off into a dreamless sleep.

The next morning his companions were all gathered once more. Alrion was better recovered, fully dressed and sitting on his bed. He awkwardly stood when they were all gathered, to address them properly.

"First, I need to thank you all again. We really did achieve the impossible, and we've set the world on the right course." Alrion smiled and took in all the smiles in the room. "I know you all have plans, I just have one more request for you all." Alrion paused before continuing. "I want you all to accompany me to the Wizard Academy. There's a special announcement I'd like you all to be part of."

"It would be an honour," Certan said.

"For me as well," Alyx added.

"I already told you I'm following you to the ends of the world." Lara winked at him.

"I never saw the place before, I would enjoy the opportunity to come," Celes said.

"Great, I'm glad that it's settled. I'll see if there are any ways to speed up our journey." Alrion thought about consulting Magnus for more details concerning local Wizard Gates.

This feels right. I'm excited at what might happen next.

55

A NEW ERA

L ara was excited by the Wizard Academy. She had seen it from a distance
but hadn't dared sneak in when she was following Alrion. The main
building looked like a miniature castle, with an impressive tower rising
behind it. A small welcoming party waited out the front. She recognised Falric.
He waved them over.

"Great to see you all. Congratulations." Falric embraced Alrion and wept
tears of joy. Lara couldn't help smiling.

"I'm just glad we could lure you back here, even if only for a limited time."
Alrion stepped back and gave Falric a broad smile.

"I owe you this much. And I must admit I'm intrigued by what you are
planning."

"You'll find out the same time as everyone else. I'm assuming since you
stepped down, I can do what I want."

"Well, you are Granthion's heir, you've earned your place. The wizards are all
assembled."

"Let's not keep them waiting then." Alrion and Falric took off. Lara sped up
to stay close. The trip here had been an interesting one. Fast, yet slow at the
same time. Travel between places was very fast, as Alrion extensively used
Wizard Gates. Yet he often stopped at odd places and talked to different people.
It was all very secretive, he didn't involve them in any of it. Whenever Lara
probed too much, he told her 'don't ruin my surprise'. Lara had even compared
notes with the others, and nobody had much to add. Not even Celes.

But it was good to be here, and once Lara walked out into the courtyard the sight took her breath away. The outside of the courtyard was lined with wizards in white robes. The tower stood tall behind. Alrion walked out with confidence. Lara slowed and stopped, wondering what her part in all this was. Alrion seemed to notice the slackened pace of his companions, as he stopped and looked back.

"Come on you lot, you can't hide in the back." Alrion grinned and started off again. Lara exchanged glances with Celes and shrugged.

I suppose we just follow along.

Once they reached the centre of the courtyard, Alrion stopped. He pointed to a spot nearby.

"Please stand there, if you don't mind." He watched them all take their position, then he conferred quietly with Falric.

"It is time," Falric announced. He used his normal voice but must have enhanced it with magic. It reverberated around the space effortlessly. The wizards quietened down, and soon silence reigned over the Wizard Academy.

"We come together today at the request of Alrion. As you should remember, we recently welcomed Alrion into our number. He was charged with a special task, one that seemed incomprehensible. The quest to cleanse the Blight." Falric paused and let that last sentence sit upon the audience.

"Against all odds, he succeeded. His only request was a special audience with you all, and to play his part in the future of the Academy. Please all give Alrion a hero's welcome." Falric started clapping and the wizards joined in. Most of them were restrained, but a few were quite enthusiastic. Once the clapping died down, Alrion stepped forward.

"Thank you, Falric. The last time we were all here, Falric stepped down as your leader. He adopted a new role, to guide me through the trials and my own training on this incredible journey. Falric's task then took on a new dimension, assisting with research into the Pool of Knowledge, so that we could most effectively glean its secrets and apply its knowledge to the problem of the Blight." Alrion looked out at the wizards, watching their reaction. After a few moments, he started again.

"Falric's reign quite rightly came to an end, as he was ready to move on to his next challenges. His successor, Branthor, was also a pivotal part of my quest. Unfortunately, he was lost to us, losing his life in trade for that of the General of the Blight, Rindale." Alrion paused and let the commotion swell up then die down again. He started pacing around the area.

"This leaves us with a void of leadership. I have learned an incredible amount in a short time and have much to share with you all. But I'm not the right person to lead the Academy. But I did find the right person." Alrion held out a hand like he was presenting someone. But there was nobody there. Suddenly there was a bang, and the silhouette of a man appeared out of nowhere, obscured by smoke. Slowly the smoke cleared. Lara stared, her heart thumping faster and faster.

Who is it? It's Ashra!

A strange silence settled over the crowd. Alrion walked over and embraced Ashra, ending with a handshake. He stepped back and addressed the crowd again.

"Many of you won't recognise this wizard, but you have all heard of him. Your new leader is none other than the legendary desert wizard, Ashra." As Alrion finished his proclamation, a series of fireworks exploded in the sky above. Ashra bowed with a flourish. He cleared his throat and offered a few words.

"Meeting and helping Alrion on his quest activated a part of me that I thought was lost. I had been a hermit for so long, an outcast of my own doing. I didn't think that I'd miss the world of men, or the simple act of sharing another's hopes and dreams. But I was wrong. It is with great pride and honour that I take up this post. I vow to personally help each and every one of you take the steps you need to become wizards of great strength and character." Ashra turned to Falric. "Thank you for this opportunity, I will do my best to continue your legacy." Ashra then bowed. Falric returned the bow.

"Now I believe Alrion has an announcement." Falric stepped back and beckoned Alrion to step forward. He did a little nervously. But then something changed, he adjusted his posture and projected confidence.

That's the way. Whatever this is, just own it.

"To say I've just been on an incredible journey, would be an understatement. And by myself, I would have failed. Several times over. But I had this group of people to help." Alrion used his arm in a sweeping gesture to represent his group of companions.

"You've already met Falric and Ashra. They were my mentors and guides in my development as a wizard." Alrion acknowledged them both then turned back to face his companions.

"Before I address my companions, I must speak of one that cannot be here." Alrion took a deep breath.

Be strong. You can do this.

"I speak of course about my father, Vincent. He was a master blacksmith and a former soldier. He supported me every step of my quest, created legendary weapons to support myself and my companions, and followed me into the abyss itself. He sacrificed himself so that I may live, and for that, he has my eternal thanks." Alrion kept his eyes closed and looked deep in thought. He slowly opened them and looked over at his companions again.

"First, I must speak of Lara. Treasure Hunter, Scout, and an expert climber." Alrion looked at her and chuckled. Lara blushed as she remembered her exploits climbing over that gigantic wall.

"Lara was the first companion to join my quest, and the most important. She came at a time when I needed help the most and was there through every major trial. She was the person I didn't know I needed." Alrion gave her a smile and she flashed him one back.

"Next, we encountered Certan, the monk. He was facing demons of his own devising, which is why we were fortunate enough to find him. But Certan proved himself to be a loyal and key member of our team. He led us to the sacred temple in the middle of the desert and helped fight off hordes of Blight forces. He mastered himself, bested the Vault of Silence, and became a master monk in his own right. And he still came to my aid." Alrion bowed to Certan. "You taught me a lot about Will and mindset, lessons I will never forget." Alrion turned next to Alyx.

"Alyx is likely the best fighter in the whole world. Not only is she a weapon master, but she single-handedly took down the Skull King. Alyx intervened when we were going to be overrun by a massive Blight attack and risked herself for no good reason. She suffered dearly for her assistance to us but rose above it and continued to help us when good sense would have been to run away. Thank you for showing me how to fight and being a rock-solid ally when we needed you the most." Alrion bowed to Alyx. Finally, he turned to Celes.

"Last, but not least, we have Celes. She happens to be my mother, but her contribution was much more than that. In another life, Celes was a master thief and treasure hunter in her own right, and she not only tracked us all down and helped expose Blight conspiracies, but she also revived a twenty-year-old trail to unmask the Hidden Wizard." Alrion paused and watched the crowd. Confused murmurs ran through the group. Lara was alarmed.

What's he doing? Surely, he's not going to reveal anything?

"The last companion that you don't see here is known as the Hidden Wizard. He helped us from the shadows, fighting battles we weren't aware of, and ensuring that we as a group could continue to advance in our quest. He asked for nothing, save that his identity is kept secret. To thank him, I have a special announcement." Alrion closed his eyes and concentrated. Suddenly a pillar of light appeared in front of him and shot up into the sky, exploding into a shower of golden sparks that dissipated above the crowd.

"Today, I am announcing the formation of a new organisation. I am calling it the Order of the Hidden Wizard. As a tribute to that wizard's mission, this organisation is dedicated to watching and preventing the spread of the Blight. The world has been cleansed, but without a watchful eye, it could easily slip again." Discussion started immediately, the square filling with the sounds of multiple conversations. Lara looked at Alrion, confused.

"Is that it?" she said. Alrion smiled at her.

"No, there's more." Alrion held up his hand and the commotion slowly died down.

"That's not all. There's little point creating an organisation, but not empowering it. So, I am therefore opening all the Wizard Stores to members of the Order of the Hidden Wizard. For the first time, we will openly share our secrets and resources. And, once I figure out a way, I'm also going to open access to Wizard Gates." The commotion was a lot louder now.

"You've certainly got this lot talking," Lara said. Alrion laughed.

"I think it's what my grandfather would have wanted. Open cooperation against the Blight, preventing another disaster. It's the only way to protect the world." Alrion looked over to Falric, and the master wizard smiled and nodded. Ashra, too, seemed to agree. Alrion walked over to his companions.

"I hope you are all fine with this?"

"Of course we are." Alyx spoke up but looked at the others and nobody raised a complaint.

"Good. I'll work with Falric and Ashra to figure out how to provide you with the entry tokens you need for Wizard Stores, and the locations of each. But for now, where will you go?" Alrion looked to Certan first.

"No surprises here, I will return to the temple. My service is promised there. But I will take a meandering path. I wish to see for myself the fruits of our labours. I want to see the new world we have created together." Certan stepped forward and offered Alrion his hand. They shook and Certan stepped back.

"I'm going to visit my hometown. It's been a long time. After that, who knows. I think I'll spend some time in Valrytir. I owe them that much. If I run out on them again..." Alyx smiled sheepishly. Alrion walked over and gave her a big hug.

"I'm sorry again for everything we put you through."

"Don't apologise, I was party to it all. I made all my choices, and I stand by them."

"I was going to go home. It's been a long trip, and I don't know what I'll do next. At the least, I'll spend some time with what Vincent left me." Celes sighed. Lara could see the tears welling up, but they were being held back.

"Do you mind if we join you? I'd like to go visit as well. And maybe I can look through the papers too."

"Of course, I would be delighted." Celes looked at Lara then back at Alrion. "And you're bringing a girl home? I'm not sure if I approve." Celes winked and laughed.

"You better win her over," Alrion whispered to Lara loud enough for everyone to hear. They all laughed. Falric and Ashra walked over to join them.

"Enjoy a break. You've done enough for a lifetime. When you're ready for something else, we can work out all these things you promised." Falric slapped Ashra on the shoulder. "Or should I say, Ashra will work them all out. I have urgent business to attend to." Falric waved goodbye and wandered off.

"I've never seen anyone run so fast to paperwork," Lara said.

"Exactly. I fear I have maybe committed to too much." Ashra grinned. He wished them well, and the companions all walked to the main gate together.

"You know where to find me." Certan waved.

"Me too. Don't be a stranger." Alyx waved as well. With that, the two rode off on horses supplied by the Academy. Alrion and Celes wanted to walk.

I don't think they're in a rush to get home. Especially with him gone.

56

THE RETURN

T hey made the wise decision of borrowing horses at Carford. As much as Alrion had enjoyed the walk and the change of pace, he was now eager to get home. It felt like an age since he had ridden out with his father and Falric.

One of them I thought had died, the other one now has.

"This is new territory for me, I never travelled this far," Lara said.

"I felt the same way, long ago. I'm not quite sure why Vincent insisted on us living here. It was quite an adjustment, coming from the big cities. But we built a nice life here. It was a different pace, and a different focus." Celes looked around as she spoke. Alrion recognised the terrain quite well. They would be back in Hamley soon.

"Is that it?" Lara said, pointing. Alrion peered into the distance.

"That's it. That's where I lived my entire life until recently." Alrion realised just how small the town was. It looked like nothing from a distance, and as they approached, he realised that unlike other places, it didn't really expand into something else. What you saw at long range, was it.

"Cute sign," Lara commented as they rode by. They were entering the town proper now.

It's like I never left.

The usual hustle and bustle of the small town continued. Men and women travelled from place to place, visiting artisans and buying or delivering goods. The familiar smells of the carpenter and leatherworker wafted over before he spotted the buildings. The noise and smells from the blacksmith were noticeably absent. He couldn't remember a time when the shop hadn't been open.

He noticed a few townsfolk regard them, but nobody said anything.

"Why aren't they greeting us?" Alrion said to his mother.

"You and your father left in a hurry, and then I left. There's been no word, and we're returning without him. They don't know what to think, let alone say. Don't worry, that'll change. They just need a few days to get used to having us around again."

"I suppose that's fine." Alrion turned to Lara, "It's not much, but this is home."

"I have a good feeling about it. Don't worry about a few people you haven't seen in a while." Lara gave him a reassuring smile.

I wasn't sure what she would think, but I'm glad she's giving it a shot. Even if we don't stay a while, this will always be home.

Soon Alrion pulled up before his home. It looked exactly the same. The white paint was a little more faded, as was the red door. But it was minimal. They dismounted and tied up their horses, and Celes approached the door, unlocking it.

"We're home," she announced as she walked through the front door. Alrion noticed a musty smell from the house being closed, but otherwise, it was unchanged.

"Don't worry, I wasn't sure when I was returning so I prepared the house appropriately. The only downside is that there's no food." Celes disappeared into the rear of the house, and Alrion sat on the couch, inviting Lara to sit with him.

"It was here that Falric announced I was a wizard. A lifetime ago."

"Your father was quite surprised. Although now I'm not sure what to believe." Celes started to keep talking, but she abruptly stopped.

"Don't worry, I told Lara. She needed to know."

"Well, yes that's fine." Celes gathered her thoughts and began to talk again. "He must have known you were a wizard, perhaps he was surprised at Falric appearing to take you away."

"I think so. Have you had a chance to read through much of what he gave you?"

"Not really. I've been waiting. Now that we're home, it makes more sense." Celes started to cry and turned away. Alrion was about to rise to comfort her when she quickly turned around, hiding it. Celes sat on the nearest chair.

"You discovered it was him, didn't you? In your investigation?" Lara said.

"Oh yes, it was quite a shock. I suspect he intended it that way."

"He did tell me that it was the best way to make you believe it. And, he wanted to find if there was any evidence tying him to that persona." Alrion watched his mother. She shook her head and chuckled.

"I suspect he didn't know how to tell me. It's quite a secret to keep all those years." Celes looked far away, lost in some sort of memory. She abruptly addressed them again.

"When I confronted him with the information, he didn't even formally acknowledge it. Even though we both knew. It was like he didn't want to say it out loud. But he did reference a story about the Blind Tiger heist. That said a lot."

"I'm not familiar with that story," Lara said.

"It's an interesting one. Well, perhaps it's worth sharing." Celes eased back into the chair and made herself comfortable. "It all started with a thief, who was part of a larger group. His name was Michael. He was tasked with stealing a pristine jewel, known as the Coded Citrine."

"I've heard of that!" Lara said, excited.

"What is it?" Alrion asked.

"It's an orange gem inscribed with tiny characters. We're not quite sure what it's for, but it looks incredible. Anyway, it was held in a special vault, and only one man knew the precise method to open the vault. And he never did it in the presence of anyone else. This group had investigated every angle, and they had no way of breaking it out."

"How did Michael play into it?" Lara said.

"Well, he proposed a plan whereas he was introduced to them as a blind man. But a specialist servant, one who could assist with tasks in a way that was capable, but also discreet. The thieves weren't convinced by the feasibility of the plan, but they let him try it. Michael found a way into their service. He was an advisor as well as an organiser. They tested his blindness in every way they could conceive, and he passed."

"Wow, so he found a way to convince them he was blind, even though he could see."

"Precisely. Although in many respects, he needed to almost be blind, to continue his cover. As he gained their trust, he became enamoured with the family's niece, who had come to stay at the estate. Over time, they developed a relationship and married. And had a daughter."

"Over what period? What happened to the thieves?"

"Years. The thieves were split apart by a rather terrible heist gone wrong, and Michael believed that he could just abandon his mission and live out the new life he had made for himself." Celes paused and shifted in her seat. Alrion was about to ask another question but she continued.

"You're probably wondering what went wrong? Well, one day he was confronted by two men. The leader of the thief group, and the man who had assigned the task to Michael. They had remembered about him and had come to collect what they were owed. When Michael refused to help them, they took his daughter hostage."

"What happened?" Alrion asked.

"He was forced to help them. He had seen the way to open the vault and helped them get the jewel. But he confronted them both and died in the process."

"But what of his daughter? And the jewel?" Lara said.

"The head thief fell in the tussle, but the other man got away with the jewel. The daughter, thankfully, was left in the middle of nowhere by the gang and found her way home. She was fine but traumatised by the whole ordeal. The family, however, did not discover Michael's treachery. They assumed that he had been coerced by the thieves and died honourably."

"How did you get involved?" Lara said.

"I overheard the thief that got away bragging at an inn. His name was Morgan, by the way. It didn't take much to convince Vincent to help me. I can see now that he obviously identified with Michael."

"What did you do?" Alrion said.

"It wasn't hard to liberate the jewel. We just followed Morgan home. Vincent kept watch while I located and stole the gem. Morgan was so out of it we had no trouble."

"And the gem? What of it?"

"Vincent wanted to return it to the original family, but we didn't get around to it right away. It was some distance to travel. Over time, we just ended up keeping it. I think it's stowed away here somewhere." Celes finished the story, and the energy seemed to leak out of her. She slumped back in the chair.

"So that's how I figured out that he wasn't coming back. And he was right. Of course, he was right."

"I thought we had a chance to do it, and both survive. But I think deep down he knew what would be required. Maybe that's why he couldn't work up to it until Falric involved me."

"Maybe that's true." Celes stood up and walked into another room.

"Are you alright?" Lara said. She looked really concerned.

"I'm alright, it's just weird being here. I keep expecting him to walk in the door, returning from the workshop." Alrion paused, remembering something. "If you don't mind giving me a moment, there's something I need to do." Alrion stood abruptly.

"Of course, I'll be here." Lara gave his hand a squeeze and let it go.

"Thanks." Alrion strode over to the door and left immediately.

He left something for me at the workshop. I need to see what it is. It must be important if he didn't include it with what he left for Mum.

Alrion saw people he recognised in his peripheral vision. He ignored them and kept walking. Strangely, though, they didn't pay him any attention either.

Maybe they don't recognise me?

For now, it was one less distraction. Alrion stopped before the workshop and fished around for the key. He found it and unlocked the door. He slowly swung it open, surveying the shop.

It looked exactly as they had left it.

Dad knew we wouldn't be coming back. That's why he was so adamant about finishing everything.

Alrion walked through the workshop, running his hand over some of the counters. Everything was packed away, nothing was left out.

He left something for me. Where would it be?

Alrion stopped and looked over the room. Perhaps he had left something, but it had always been there. If that was the case, it had to be in a safe location.

Where was he always working?

Alrion walked over to the bench that his father always worked at. Without fail. In fact, he always ensured Alrion used another bench.

It must be here.

Alrion slowly pushed the workbench away, sliding it into an open space nearby. There was a rough, threadbare mat underneath it.

That's curious, why put a mat under a workbench?

Alrion pulled the mat aside and noticed a trapdoor. He gingerly pried the top off, sliding the cover off. There was a ladder leading into a dark area.

Now, this is promising.

Alrion stood and walked to the front door, locking it from the inside. He couldn't afford to be interrupted. Returning to the open trapdoor, Alrion peered inside. He could see a ladder leading down. He created an orb of light and sent it down before starting to climb.

This is oddly reminiscent of that place in Stonebridge.

He climbed down carefully and took stock of where he was. It was a tiny stone cellar. Completely empty save for one thing.

There's a Wizard Gate under the workshop!

Alrion couldn't believe it. All this time he had lived and worked here, never knowing that a portal to another place was just sitting here. He rushed over, curious to see it. The gate looked like any other. He impatiently examined the pillars and saw only one symbol. He activated it, curious to see where it went. The gate roared to life, the blinding flash subsiding quickly. Alrion could see what looked like a room, but there wasn't a lot of other details he could glean from it.

Is it wise to take this? I have no idea where it goes, or how I could get back.

Alrion paused before the open gate. He thought carefully. If this was a place his father used, it had to have a return function. Because his father never went on strange unexplained trips. He was always around.

He asked me to find something here, I must try.

Alrion stepped through the gate, unsure of where he would end up.

❧

Alrion stepped into a study. It was made from stone, the walls filled with shelves and books. A single window lit the room. But what caught Alrion's attention was the desk in the middle. He recognised that desk.

It's Granthion's desk. From the dreams.

Alrion rushed over, spotting something on the desk. He touched it reverently.

"Granthion's spellbook," he whispered. His father had had access to this the whole time. Alrion stepped back, curious about where he was. He walked through the room, seeing no entrances or exits. Just the Wizard Gate, and the window. He wandered over to the window, peering out. It looked like Avaria. There was a rather large hill that dominated the view.

You don't suppose.

Alrion let the thought mull over. Was that hill the place his grandfather had cast the spell over Avaria? He walked back to the desk, looking at the spellbook.

I have so many questions now. I wish I could talk to someone about it.

But Granthion and his father were gone. Alrion started leafing through the spellbook. He could read all the words. Mostly they were mundane spells, but he had a realisation.

Now I can find more spells that I need and consciously learn them. This will be amazing!

He set the book down and turned to leave. As exciting as it was, he needed to go back and make sure everything was fine at home. He would have plenty of time to come back and forth, as his father had.

57

DREAMING

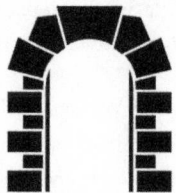

Alrion was dreaming. The realisation was sudden, but also confusing. He was in the same room that he had discovered that day. His grandfather's desk prominently sitting in the middle.

Is the Pool of Knowledge trying to tell me something else?

Alrion saw a wizard looking out the window. He started to approach, and the wizard turned to face him.

"Dad?" Alrion said, not sure if he believed it.

"Hello, Alrion. How are you doing?" Vincent smiled. Alrion had to suppress the urge to run up and hug his father.

"Oh, I get it. You're not really there, you are a manifestation of my mind trying to help me realise some crucial knowledge from the Pool." Alrion sighed.

"I take offence to that, I made considerable effort to get here." Vincent shook his head and chuckled.

"What do you mean? You died. Unless..."

"No, I'm pretty sure I really died. But I did arrange to have a conversation with you, so I'm glad we are here talking."

"That doesn't seem possible. Say something that nobody else would know?"

"Let's see here. Your mother knows I'm the mysterious wizard that's been following you around all this time. Does that work?" Vincent smiled. Alrion felt himself grinning. He couldn't help it.

"So, it is you!" Alrion ran over and hugged his father. It did feel like him too. The pain at losing him suddenly arced up and Alrion had to fight back tears.

"I'm so sorry, Alrion, to be so secretive and then disappear from your life. It all worked out, didn't it?"

"Yes, we did it. The Blight is back to what it was, and the world is cured. Many people have awoken, although there are also many who didn't survive the transition back." Alrion tried not to think about those.

"Good, good. I'm glad it wasn't in vain. Who is running the academy now?"

"Ashra. Falric came back to help initiate him but won't stay long."

"Hah!" Vincent laughed. "I suggested to Ashra that he should do that. Glad to hear he's there."

"I suggested it too, I guess great minds do think alike."

"I think we just don't want to be responsible for a group of wizards." Vincent grinned.

"I think you're right." Alrion sighed. "How does this work? How long are you here?"

"I'm not entirely sure. I think it's a one-off short-term type arrangement. To be honest, it was very much luck on my side. I wasn't sure it was going to work."

"What did you do?"

"Remember when we were in the thick of it? Saving the world? Well, I grafted a piece of my soul onto you while we were linked. And here we are." Vincent shrugged.

"You didn't know what would happen?"

"Not at all, but I had suspicions. It was all a bit desperate really, but it worked. So I'll claim it. Anyway, I want to hear what you're doing now. Did you follow my instructions?"

"Yes, I found this place." Alrion gestured at the room they were standing in. "And I found Granthion's spellbook."

"Amazing! Hopefully, you'll get more out of it than I did."

"What do you mean?"

"Well, since I never advanced my study of Soul Power, a lot of it was unavailable to me until recently. And I didn't exactly have time to sit down with it. But you do."

"Yes, I have nothing but time at the moment."

"It's good, enjoy it for the rest of us." Vincent paused, then his eyes brightened. "You know, Alrion, this is the part where I'm supposed to wish you a long and prosperous life and tell you to follow your heart and discover your true path." Vincent watched Alrion, gauging his reaction.

"That would be a nice thing to say. But instead?"

"Instead, I'm going to ask a tiny favour." Vincent walked over to the desk and opened up Granthion's spellbook. "It's not even a favour, it's just a recommendation. When you do have time to look at the spellbook, I suggest this one. It looks quite interesting." Vincent tapped the page and stood back. Alrion walked over and carefully leant over, looking at the page.

Resurrection Spell

"You know, I think I could find time to look at something like that." Alrion looked up, but his father was gone. Nowhere to be seen.

"You have impeccable timing." Alrion laughed to himself. But his father was right. The spell did look quite interesting. And he needed a new challenge. As the dream started to fade, Alrion smiled and started planning his next move.

WANT MORE FROM THE HIDDEN WIZARD?

While this story is complete, I am working on other stories in the world of **The Hidden Wizard.** If you are interested in reading more please check out the below page on my website:

http://vaughanwsmith.com/finished-the-hidden-wizard/

ABOUT THE AUTHOR

Vaughan W. Smith is a fiction writer from Sydney, Australia, who explores big life questions through story. His favourite genres are Fantasy, Mystery, Science Fiction and Thrillers.

www.vaughanwsmith.com

CPSIA information can be obtained
at www.ICGtesting.com
Printed in the USA
BVHW080018301119
565169BV00001B/16/P